THE MYSTERY QUARTET

A Collection of Crime Fiction

NICK SWEET

Copyright (C) 2024 Nick Sweet

Layout design and Copyright (C) 2024 by Next Chapter

Published 2024 by Next Chapter

This book is a work of fiction. Names, characters, places, and incidents are the product of the author's imagination or are used fictitiously. Any resemblance to actual events, locales, or persons, living or dead, is purely coincidental.

All rights reserved. No part of this book may be reproduced or transmitted in any form or by any means, electronic or mechanical, including photocopying, recording, or by any information storage and retrieval system, without the author's permission.

BAD IN BARDINO

CHAPTER 1

I was woken up by the sound of my mobile ringing. My head hurt and felt like it was about the size of a watermelon. I supposed that I might have had one or two too many the night before, as I sat up and grabbed the phone. 'Hello?'

'Is that Arthur Blakey, the private investigator?' a feminine voice asked.

'It is indeed.'

'Oh Mr. Blakey, I've heard that you are an expert when it comes to finding people, is that right?' Whoever she was, she spoke English with a foreign accent. Germanic, I should have said.

'Only when I manage to do it.'

'Do what?'

'Find them.'

'This is no laughing matter, Mr. Blakey.' She didn't seem to go for my line in humour. A lot of people don't, not that it's ever bothered me much.

'Never said it was.'

She went quiet for a moment and as I waited to hear what she was going to say next I could picture her in my mind's eye, or thought I could. I reckoned she was a pretty brunette. They often are, when I picture them. Not brunette necessarily, I don't mean, but pretty. I don't know why, but they just seem to come out that way. I suppose you could say I'm an optimist by nature. Maybe you have to be if you're going to last very long in my line of work. You get to see a lot of nasty stuff working as a private investigator, and you can't let it get to you. They should put having the ability to forget and bounce back from things in the job description.

Anyway, as I was saying, I pictured her as a pretty brunette, but kind of prim and proper in an old fashioned sort of way; and right now, I imagined how her brow might look as it furrowed in a cross expression. Then she said, 'Could you find somebody for me?'

'I could certainly try.'

'I should be most grateful if you would.'

I found her old-world tone of voice faintly amusing, or I would have done if my head hadn't been giving me so much grief. It must have been that last drink that did it, the last one or two, anyway. It or they were responsible for setting up the little arrangement the inside of my head currently appeared to be failing to enjoy with a rhythm section that featured some young skinhead thug on the drums. 'I shouldn't be too grateful,' I said. 'I don't come cheap.'

'How much?'

'Three hundred euros a day plus expenses,' I said. 'And another thousand if I find whoever it is I'll be looking for, half of which I get upfront.'

'And what if you don't find her?'

'You get the five hundred back.'

'I see...well that sounds reasonable,' she said. 'So you'll find her for me, then?'

'Find *who*?'

'My sister Gisela, Mr. Blakey... She's disappeared, you see.'

'I'd need a last name.'

'It's Schwartz.'

'And you are?'

'Inge,' she replied. 'Inge Schwartz.'

'Where are you now?'

'I'm in the street outside your office...the door is locked.'

'Yes, I've been called away,' I said. 'If you could come back in about an hour, I'll see you then.'

'Why so long?'

'There's a man I've been chasing and I've just caught up with him, only he's armed with a gun and—'

'Oh dear...do you want me to call the police?'

'No, I can handle it.'

'But it sounds as though this man is dangerous.'

'I can deal with him,' I said. Besides, I might have added, some of the cops in Bardino don't like me much, and I don't like them any better. But I decided to keep this last thought to myself. And anyway, I was only kidding her about chasing a man with a gun. Not that I don't chase armed men around a lot, because I do; only I wasn't doing so right then. What I was doing was sitting up in bed, having just woken up. 'Okay, well if you'd like to call round to my office in about an hour, I'll see you then,' I told her and hung up.

I looked at my watch. It had just turned half-past ten, which is late for some people to be lying in bed, perhaps, but par for the course for me when I'm not working. I'd just successfully solved a tricky murder investigation and made myself enough to last me for the next couple of months, so I was in no desperate hurry to find new clients. Of course if a suitable case came my way, then so much the better; but if it didn't, there was nothing to prevent me from sleeping late and enjoying a little time taking it easy.

I put my mobile back down on the bedside cabinet and scratched my head as I wondered what the sisters of nice Germanic girls were doing coming to places like Bardino and forgetting to call or write home. I was still wondering about this as I got dressed, then left the flat and headed for my office, which was just a few minutes' walk away, over on Calle Veracruz. I went in through the narrow doorway, which is squeezed in between a shop that sells watches on one side and a ladies' shoe shop on the other, then climbed the stairs. I took out my key and opened the door with the frosted glass window, bearing the legend ARTHUR BLAKEY, PRIVATE INVESTIGATOR, then entered. The solid oak desk was in that state of ordered perfection normally only achieved by the unemployed, and behind it the venetian blinds were partially drawn, so that the room was striped with shadow. There were two upright chairs on this side of the desk, and my more comfortable swivel number was on the other side. I went and sat in my chair and swiveled around on it a little as I waited for Inge Schwartz to show.

CHAPTER 2

The very moment I opened the door to her, I realized I was all wrong about Inge Schwartz: she was no pretty brunette, not at all. She was a blonde, for a start.

'Perhaps you'd like to come in?' I said.

'Perhaps I would.'

I closed the door behind her and tried hard not to look her up and down too many times. I failed miserably in this, though, because she was a stunner. What's more, she knew it. She was honey blonde hair, neatly bobbed by an adept hand, tawny skin, china-blue eyes, red-painted bee-stung mouth, and bone structure that would have made Rodin throw away his chisel. She was slender in all the right places and less slender—in fact not slender *at all*—in all the right places, too, and she came wrapped in a fuchsia-coloured linen dress that she wore with a cream jacket of the same material and black court shoes.

She shrugged off her jacket and handed it to me like I was the doorman at some posh joint. The garment smelt of her perfume - Chanel No 5, if I wasn't mistaken. She said, 'I've brought some things for you.' She opened her handbag, a neat little Kelly number, took out an A3-sized manila envelope and handed it to me.

I took a look inside. There was a wad of money in it, as well as a photograph and a piece of paper. I took out the wad of money and riffled it. Then I counted it quickly and slipped it into the breast pocket of my jacket. Next I took out the photograph and had a look at it. It was a photograph of a girl of about eighteen or so. 'She looks a little like a younger version of you,' I said.

'We aren't sisters for nothing, Mr. Blakey.'

For a brief moment I was almost tempted to tell her she could dispense with the Mister business and just call me 'Art', short for 'Arthur', like everyone else I knew; but then I came to my senses and said instead, 'When was this photo taken?'

'Two or three years ago...it's the only one of her I could find.'

'How old is your sister now?'

'Twenty-one.'

I looked at the photograph. Her sister sure was a beautiful-looking girl. I took out the sheet of paper and examined it. It had been torn from a letter-writing pad, and so it shouldn't have surprised me, I don't suppose, to find that a letter had been written on it. What did surprise me, though, was the nature of the letter itself. I'm no graphologist, but the large spidery scrawl seemed decidedly childish to me, more like what a thirteen-year-old might produce than the sort of thing you'd expect from an adult, even a young one; and I noticed that none of the i's were dotted, which might suggest an absence of feelings of self-worth in the writer. Then there was the subject matter of the letter. It read like a young girl writing home from summer camp, where she was in the busy flurry of her first affair, and not at all like the letter of a young woman who had come to Bardino to live and then perhaps taken a wrong turning in her life and dropped out of contact. In short, there was an innocence bordering on outright childishness about the writing that struck me as a little odd, given that the date at the top of the page was June of this year.

'Please take a seat,' I said, and Miss Schwartz duly parked herself on one of the two upright chairs. She crossed her legs neatly at the knee, smoothed her dress down, and her foot kept time with some imaginary music that may or may not have been playing through her mind. From the expression on her face, though, music seemed to be the last thing she was concerned about.

'Is this letter the last you've heard from her?' I said as I sat in my padded swivel number.

She nodded and bit down on her lower lip, and for a terrible moment it looked like she might be about to break down in tears. Even while this was taking place, however, I continued to wonder whether I should believe what I was witnessing. Whether I could safely assume, in other words, that what I was seeing, or being permitted to watch, was in fact 'for real'.

I took a deep breath, puffed out my cheeks like a blowfish, and turned my attention back to the letter. Having taken note of the local address at the top of the page, I asked Miss Schwartz if she had called round to the place to see if her sister was still living there. She replied in the affirmative, shutting her eyes, as if she were being weighed down by heavy emotions. The person who was currently residing there, she explained, had told her that Gisela took off somewhere a couple of weeks ago. Where she'd gone and why, the man didn't know. Neither had he known when she was likely to return. All he'd been able to tell her was that she'd packed in her job and skipped town.

I figured that I would make the address, which was nearby as it happened, in the Bocanazo, my first port of call. Then I asked Miss Schwartz if she and Gisela had been brought up together and by the same parents; and if so, then where were they from? 'Yes,' was the answer to my first question, and 'Hamburg in Germany' her reply to the one that followed. I'd never been to the city and, beyond its geographical location, knew next to nothing about the place.

'So you will take the case?'

'I've taken your money, haven't I?'

'Do you think you can find my sister for me, Mr. Blakey?'

'Most probably...but what if she doesn't want to be found?'

'What on earth do you mean by that?'

'Imagine she's fallen in love with some lucky young brute and shacked up with him, but she doesn't want Daddy to find out.'

'Daddy passed away last year, sadly.'

'Well Mummy, then.'

'She died three years ago.'

'I'm sorry.'

'Don't be.'

'Do you have any other siblings?'

She shook her head and sighed, then took a delicate chew on her lower lip. 'It's not like her, to fail to write or call like this.'

'Did you have an argument with Gisela?'

'No.'

'How would you describe your relationship?'

'We were rather different.'

'Only you looked the same.'

'Similar, but not the same,' she corrected me.

That was true: while the girl in the photograph resembled the woman I was talking to, and indeed was clearly something of a stunner in her own right, her looks lacked the classical purity of those of her older sister. 'You didn't get along, then?'

'I never said that.'

'No, but you didn't say much.'

'I've always been the sensible one, Mr. Blakey, and Gisela just seemed to do exactly as she pleased.'

'So you resented her?'

'Stop putting words in my mouth,' she said. 'Anyway, it hardly matters how she and I got along, does it, if all I want is for you to find her?'

'It might matter a lot,' I replied, 'if you had an argument and she's decided not to talk to you anymore.'

'I can assure you that's not the case.'

'Is it possible you don't think it's the case but Gisela might?'

'No, but even if it was like that then I'd still want you to find her for me, just to know that she's all right.'

I took out my Parker and began to roll it between my fingers. 'What was Gisela doing in Bardino?'

'She was never the same after mother and father died.' Her brow furled like a coiled caterpillar. 'She was very close to them, you see.'

'Only to be expected, isn't it?' I said.

'Yes, but I mean...' She broke off, gripping her Kelly bag as if she thought somebody might be about to run off with it.

'I can see that you're upset, Mrs. Schwartz.'

'It's Miss.'

'Pardon me, *Miss* Schwartz,' I said. 'Can I get you a glass of water?'

She brushed my offer aside with a curt shake of the head.

'Something a little stronger then?'

'It's still morning,' she said, and regarded me with the sort of expression the headmistress of an expensive finishing school might reserve for the young man who has had the temerity to sneak into the girls' dormitory at night.

'You were saying how Gisela was very close to her parents...'

'Yes, she became depressed for a time after they died. Then once she'd snapped out of it, she came to Bardino with the intention of getting a job.'

'What sort of job?'

She shrugged. 'Waitressing or working in a hotel, something like that, I think.'

'Did she ever find any work?'

'I don't think so...not that she told me about, anyway.'

'Did she have much money?'

'She would have had some.'

'How much is some?'

'Well I'm not sure exactly,' she said. 'But what's all this got to do with anything, anyway? I want you to find my sister, not write a book about her.'

'I realize that.' I smiled, but you shouldn't read anything into that, because my smile is cheaper than chewing gum. Inge Schwartz blushed and looked away. I wondered if her blush was for real, or if it was all part of her act. I wondered which was cheaper, her blush or my smile, then said, 'But the more you can tell me about Gisela's lifestyle and situation, the easier it will make the job of finding her.'

'Well I've told you everything there is to tell.' She got to her feet as if she'd been ejected from the chair by a spring. 'I don't want to sit here taking up your time, Mr. Blakey, when you should be out there trying to find Gisela.'

She stopped when she got to the door and shot me an accusatory glance over her shoulder. 'You will let me know as soon as you find her, won't you?'

'I really don't know how you expect me to do that,' I said, 'if you haven't given me a number to call or an address where I can contact you.'

'Oh yes, how silly of me...you'd better have my mobile number.' She told me the number and I gave the Parker some work to do.

'And where are you staying right now?'

'In the hotel Las Palmeras.'

'Do you have a room number, or have you taken over the entire hotel?'

'Number four hundred and twenty three,' she said. 'And there's no need to be so snotty, is there?' She fixed me with her angry head-mistress expression for a moment. 'Call me as soon as you know anything.'

'It will be my pleasure.'

Her eyes, which were as cold and beautiful as coral, raked me over as though she were considering whether to give me some kind of parting shot, but then she must have thought better of it because she opened the door and went out, leaving nothing but the subtle waft of Chanel No.5 and a thousand and one questions behind her.

CHAPTER 3

I found the Porsche where I'd left it earlier and drove over to the Bocanazo, then parked round the back of the large sports complex there and walked to the block of flats where Gisela Schwartz had been living. It was four storeys tall and certainly nothing to write home about, which I figured might very well explain why the Schwartz girl had stopped doing just that. The block, like all the others, was designed so that it stood at forty-five degrees to the street; the walls were painted white and each flat had its own small balcony.

It was fairly quiet in the *barrio* right now, but that was only to be expected at this hour. Things could often have a way of livening up here after dark, though. I asked myself what was a girl from a nice German family doing living in a dump like this, as I entered the block.

I heard all sorts of noises as I climbed the stairs: a woman screamed at her child, who then must have picked up a smack because the next moment the child began to bawl. A man was yelling in some form of Arabic; and somewhere else, another man was yelling in what might have been Russian. As well as the shouting, there was a fair amount of cooking going on, so that I felt as though I were taking a lightning-fast tour through a number of nightmare holiday destinations.

The address I had for Gisela Schwartz was flat 4D, up on the top floor. I rang the buzzer and nobody came to open up, so I went back down and found my Porsche, then drove round to the front of the block and pulled up and waited behind the wheel. There was only the one way in and out of the building, and I was watching it, so I was bound to see her if and when she showed.

I waited for two hours, by which time the September sun was working up a temperature. A glance at my Swatch told me it was coming up to two in the afternoon, which is lunchtime in this part of the world. I might be an athletic kind of guy with the kind of build that makes me look good in the slim fitting summer suits I favour, but I do like to eat even so, and my belly was cranking out an overture on the theme of hunger. I went and parked myself at one of the several vacant tables, from which I had a perfect view of the only entrance to the block across the way, and asked for a *bocadillo* with *jamon serrano*, a dish of olives and a cold bottle of Cruzcampo. The waiter nodded and said '*Muy bien*' or 'very good'; then I took the photograph from my pocket and held it up. 'You recognize this girl?' I asked him.

He looked at the photo, then took it from me and studied it. 'Looks like the girl lives in the block over there.' He pointed with a stubby digit. 'Only she's younger here, in the photograph, no?'

'The photograph was taken two or three years ago.'

'Yeah, that's her.'

'You know anything about her?'

'Told me she's German,' he said. 'Sure speaks good, though.'

'Talks like one of the locals, does she?'

He shook his head. 'No, she speaks educated, not like us down here.' I'd often had cause to remark how quick the locals can be to denigrate themselves for the abuses they visit on the Spanish tongue.

'Is she still living in the block there across the street?'

'I imagine so.'

'When did you last see her?'

'Couple of weeks ago.' He shrugged. 'Maybe more.'

'Know anything else about her?'

'Can't say I do, no.'

'But she comes in here?'

'For breakfast sometimes, yeah.' He shot me a sharp sideways glance. 'Why all the questions anyway, if you don't mind me asking?' he said. 'You a cop or something?'

'Just a friend.' I smiled and pocketed the photograph.

The merest suggestion of a twinkle came into the man's eyes, though the rest of his face continued to hang down like washing left out in the rain, and he said, 'She's quite a looker.' Then he turned and went inside the café, to see to my order.

It was a beautiful day and the sun's rays were busy giving the Bocanazo a regular toasting. I wiped a bead of sweat from my nose as I sat and watched the entrance to the block across the street.

The man came back and placed my beer and the ham roll down in front of me. He looked at me. 'She in some kinda trouble?' he asked, his brown eyes narrowing in a suspicious expression.

'No, not that I know of...I'm just looking for her.'

'You're a friend of hers, you said?'

'That's right.'

The man looked like he wasn't sure whether or not to believe me, so I gave him my brightest and most honest Eton smile, and he nodded, still not seeming entirely convinced. I suppose he saw a slim, stylish-looking Englishman, with a caramel tan dressed in an expensive linen suit, and must've wondered what a guy like me was doing come here and asking him all these questions. 'You've forgotten to bring me my olives,' I said.

The man went back inside, then returned moments later with the olives in a small dish. I tasted my beer then had a nibble on an olive, before I started in on the ham roll. I kept my eyes on the entrance to the block across the street as I ate. The cured ham tasted pretty good and the bread was fresh.

At that moment a navy-blue Mercedes came purring round the corner and pulled up outside the block, just along from where I'd parked. Now if you're sitting on the terrace of a café further down in the *pueblo*, then seeing a Merc go by might not seem to be any big deal. But the Bocanazo isn't further down in the *pueblo*, and they don't get that class of automobile up this way very often, to the best of my knowledge. Or if they do, then it's only because the car is on its way somewhere else, to the seafront, or some place where people who aren't broke live. But here was this Merc pulling up right across the street from where I was sitting, just a little way down from my Porsche.

Interesting, I thought, bringing out my iPhone and taking a photo of the driver as he climbed out of his car. I left a five-euro note under my plate and set off. I took a photo of the registration plate of the

Merc and another of the car itself, before I followed the man into the block of flats and began to climb the stone steps.

Not wanting to tread on the man's heels, I slowed down and let him get to the top before I began to climb the final flight. I took my time going up and, as I approached the landing, I saw that the man was ringing the bell I'd tried earlier. And he wasn't having any more luck than I'd had, which didn't surprise me. Now I had to invent a pretext for being on the top floor, so I took my wallet out and dropped it in such a way that the contents fell all over the place. That gave me an excuse to hunker down on my haunches and gather up my credit cards and file them all away in my wallet. As I was doing that, the man I was following gave up ringing the bell, and I got a good look at him as he turned. He was five ten, of lean build, short brown hair that he'd greased down and combed back, pale complexion, black pinstriped suit, white shirt and black lace-up shoes. His clothes smelt of money and the good tailoring that comes with it. In order words, the guy looked all wrong for the Bocanazo.

Perhaps he's Gisela Schwartz's boyfriend, I thought. Although he must be pushing forty, so the word hardly seemed to fit. Lover, then. But I was only guessing, of course.

I wondered briefly if I should stop him and ask what his business was with Gisela Schwartz; but I rejected the idea no sooner than it had occurred to me. I gave the man a little slack before I followed him back down the stairs, and he was climbing in behind the wheel of his Merc by the time I got back down to the street.

I ran back to my Porsche, climbed in and set off in pursuit. My task was made easier by the fact that he drove at a leisurely speed up out of the Bocanazo; but then he stepped on it a little, as he headed out of town and up into the hills. It was easy enough to follow him at a discreet distance, without giving the game away at first, but then it got more difficult as the traffic thinned out. And before I could work out whether or not he knew he was being tailed, he drove off the road and headed for an isolated farmhouse.

I drove on past and pulled over in a little copse of trees and killed the engine. Down below the coastline was spread out. It all looked harmless enough down there from this distance. The sort of place made for families to come and enjoy a relaxing holiday. Spend some time on the beach and get a tan. Well, it was that all right, only it was a whole lot of other things, too. They don't call it the Costa del Crime for nothing.

I climbed out of the Porsche, locked it with a swish of the remote, and headed through the pine trees; then the land sloped up towards the farmhouse, where the man I was following must have gone. I spotted his Merc. He'd driven along a dust path for about three hundred metres and pulled to a halt in a little forecourt, and I watched him get out of the car and go into the house. He didn't look around, so I figured he couldn't have seen me.

It was hot and I could feel sweat running down my back as I walked over the dry land towards the house. It didn't seem to be much of a place from the outside. Just a sort of caramel-painted rectangular-shaped box, with two large windows either side of the front door, both covered with black iron bars, and a pitched roof with red tiles. The place had a fair bit of garden, and was fenced off from the dry stony land I was walking on. I went over to the fence and peered in at the property, before I walked along, crouching as I did so, towards the entrance to the driveway where the Merc had entered.

Still crouching, I hurried over to the back of the house, and stepped onto the stone ledge that went round the building. I peered in through the back window but didn't see anything of interest, so I tiptoed along the ledge, then stopped by the side of the next window I came to and stood with my front pressed against the wall and listened. Birds were busy chirruping and a car was driving along the road, then I heard a voice. It was a deep masculine voice but I couldn't make out what it was saying. I peeped in through the window and saw the man I'd been following in profile. He had a telephone pressed to his ear.

Just then, something hard hit me on the back of the head.

CHAPTER 4

When I came round, I was lying on the floor and my head hurt. I reached back and felt the big lump I had there. As I did so, I wondered where I was and who had hit me. Whoever it was, they were long gone. Above me there was a high white-painted ceiling with thick wooden beams going across it, and the tiled floor was as hard as a bastard. Then I saw a man sitting on a Laura Ashley-type sofa. The man wasn't looking very chirpy. In fact, he was looking very dead. That wasn't surprising because he'd been shot in the forehead and there was blood everywhere.

I got up and went through the dead man's pockets. I found his wallet and in it was his ID card or *carné de identidad*. I took a close look at it. Juan Ribera was the man's name. I took out notebook and pen and jotted down the man's name and NIE number. There was nothing else of any interest in the man's wallet, so I put it back where I'd found it.

Seeing the telephone in the corner of the room, I called the local police. 'There's a Juan Ribera sitting on the sofa in his living room,' I told the man who'd picked up.

The officer said, 'That's nice for him. Anything we can help him with? Perhaps he'd like some champagne sent over along with a few choice *pinchos*.'

'I doubt he'd be in a state to appreciate it,' I replied. 'But the coroner might when he arrives.'

'I see...in that case, perhaps you'd like to tell me where we can find him?'

I gave the man directions, and he asked who I was. Some people do ask such naïve questions, I find, don't you? I hung up and left the house. Before I got back to my car, I heard the police sirens. Whoever it was that had hit me must have called them. No doubt he planned on framing me for the murder. As it turned out, I'd come round before the cops showed. I figured it must be my lucky day and so I'd better make the best of it.

I hid in a ditch down by the road, and watched the police drive up then climb out of their cars and go into the house. Then I hurried the rest of the way back to my Porsche, climbed in and set off as discreetly as I could.

I drove back to Bardino and parked outside of Las Palmas, the big hotel in the middle of the *pueblo* overlooking the seafront. Upon entering, my senses were immediately stirred by the pressed and starched air of the interior. I made my way over to the reception desk. The man behind it was busy doing something on a computer. Fiddling his income tax, most probably, like any self-respecting Bardinado. If you want to get past a person in Bardino without their noticing you, act like you want to ask them a question or get them to do something. It's a manner I've perfected over the years. Any Bardinado worth his salt can spot it a mile away and, realizing that you want him to perform a duty of some kind, he will instantly begin to act as if you were invisible. Thereby having achieved my aim and conferred on myself a cloak of invisibility, I took the elevator up, then made my way along the carpeted corridor to room 423.

I knocked on the door but there was no sign of life inside, so I took out the lock picks I carry with me wherever I go and made short work of getting the door open. I entered on tiptoe, just in case the occupant was sleeping or in the shower—and saw immediately that there was nobody in the bedroom. I took a quick look in the bathroom, to ascertain that I had the place to myself, before I rummaged through the drawers in one of the bedside cabinets. I found the passport of one

Mark Wellington, an ugly pug-faced guy with a sleepy look in his eyes. I went through the drawers in the cabinet on the other side of the bed. There was no passport for any Inge Schwartz. Nothing, in fact, to suggest a woman was staying in the room. A boxing magazine lay on the bed, and there was a faint odour of cigar smoke.

So Inge Schwartz fed me a line in baloney, I thought, and ground my teeth. There'd been something about the woman I hadn't liked right from the first moment I set eyes on her, mixed in with all the stuff about her there was to like. Things that I had to confess, to myself at least, were legion. Question now was, what was the woman's game? And who was she playing it with?

Apart from me, that's to say.

I went out onto the balcony and looked down at the beach. It being the middle of September, the season had more or less finished, but there were people on the beach down below. Not as many as you'd find in July and August, but the sand was seeing some action. Give it another month or so, and the temperature would drop and the tourists would stop coming. The kind of people I was interested in came here all the year round, though, which I guess was bad news for the town; but it provided me with a way to earn enough to eat and drink and do a few other things.

I left the room, took the elevator down and went back to the flat in the Bocanazo. Nobody came to the door when I knocked, so I took out my lock picks and went to work. The door opened directly into the living room, which was a medium-sized affair with a low ceiling. The floor was covered with the sort of linoleum that pretends to be tiles and there was an old cherry-red moquette sofa directly to my right, against the wall. Over by the window, a matching easy chair had been squeezed in between the sofa and the French doors that gave on to the tiny balcony. The flock wallpaper was a sickly, mawkish burgundy, and an old television set was sitting on a sideboard that faced the sofa. Though old, the furniture looked like it would collapse long before it got to become antique; and even if by some miracle of science or fortune it were to last that long, no future antiquarian would ever want to come near it with someone else's barge pole. There was a smell of stale beer and au de cologne in the air, and old copies of *Pronto* and *Elle* were splayed out on a cheap glass-topped coffee table.

I held my .38 out in front of me, just in case there was going to be some action, as I veered to my left along the short narrow hallway. There were four doors leading off it. The door immediately to my right was ajar, and I gave it a gentle nudge. I found myself looking in at a small bathroom. A shower with a curtain rail and a toilet were squeezed in next to each other on the far wall. I pulled the curtain back, to assure myself there was nobody in the shower. There wasn't.

Just then I heard what sounded like a key in the front door, so I turned and let myself into the room across the hallway and found myself in a bedroom. It was a girl's room all right. The bedspread was pink for a start, which I figured was a bit of a giveaway. And there were heart-shaped mirrors with fuchsia-coloured frames. Right now, though, I was more concerned with the fact that I had company. I hid behind the door and, peering through the crack, saw a man dressed in jeans and a red T-shirt. He was about five-eleven, and slim all over except for about the gut. He had blond hair and didn't look Spanish.

Figuring it was time to introduce myself I stepped out from behind the door, and shuffled along the short hallway, keeping my .38 pointed at the man.

He looked at me without appearing to see me at first, and then he saw the .38. 'Hey,' he said, 'what the fuck is this?'

'Who are you?' I asked him.

'Funny question to ask a man when you've broken into his flat.'

'It would be if this really was your flat, only I know that it isn't.' I didn't really *know* this, but I'd figured it was perhaps time to hazard an inspired guess and see where it took me, if anywhere.

'Huh?'

'I'm looking for the girl who lives here, Gisela Schwartz.'

'Why'd you expect me to know where she is?'

'Because you're in her flat.'

'She said she was going away for a time, and asked if I wanted to stay here while she was gone and keep an eye on the place.' His Spanish seemed fluent enough if freighted with a heavy accent. I'd have said he was German or something along those lines. Perhaps he was related to the Schwartz sisters. 'Who are you anyway,' he said, 'her ex or something?'

'No.' I took out my badge and tossed it at him. He caught it and looked at it.

'A private dick.'

'You can read. I'm impressed.'

'One who thinks he's clever.'

'Cleverness is a relative concept,' I observed. 'But let's just say that I'm the one holding the gun.'

'Which makes you right, does it?'

'You'd better believe it, buddy,' I said. 'You still haven't told me your name.'

'It's Kurt.'

'What's your surname? And don't tell me it's Cobain.'

'Heinlich,' he said. 'Look, just take what you want and go, okay?'

'What's your relationship with her?' I asked him.

'You could call me a friend.'

'That what she calls you?'

'Sure hope so,' he said. 'She's let me stay in her flat anyway, so what do you think?'

'I don't think anything.'

'I don't like to have to say it, but it kinda shows.'

'You in the habit of throwing wise cracks around when you're standing in front of a man with a gun?'

'I don't make a habit of it,' he replied. 'But then, guys don't make a habit of breaking into flats I'm staying in and questioning me at gunpoint.'

'I'm very pleased for you.'

'If you were that pleased you might consider lowering your peashooter.'

'Already considered it,' I told him. 'Didn't figure it as a sensible option.'

'It might be a healthier one.'

'For you or me?'

'Both of us.'

'Can't say I follow your logic.'

'The thing might go off,' he said.

'That's what it's made to do.'

'The guy who made it wasn't thinking about the consequences.'

'Sure he was,' I objected. 'He was thinking of how much money he'd be able to make from selling it.'

'Like I say,' the man said, 'he didn't think the consequences through. And neither are you.'

'What consequences would these be, pal?'
'You wouldn't want to kill me.'
'Why wouldn't I?'
'Why would you?'
'You tell me, pal. You're the one with all the ideas.'

CHAPTER 5

Of course I had no intention of killing anybody, but even so it was interesting to hear the guy talk and try and work out what he was thinking. Besides, allowing him to blab gave me a little time to consider the situation.

He said, 'You'd do some serious time, for one thing.'

'If they caught me.' I was following the logic of the conversation, no more nor less. Just seeing where it would lead. He was the one who'd brought up the subject of my wanting to kill him, after all. And if he was so keen to insist on finding reasons to be afraid of me, then I couldn't see why I should tell him any different.

'Sure they would,' he said. 'Besides, you don't even know who I am.'

'Yes I do, you're a friend of Gisela Schwartz.'

'That's no reason to kill me, is it?'

'I didn't say it was,' I said. 'Neither did I say I wanted to kill you, but I will if I need to. Now make yourself comfortable.'

He sat on the moquette sofa, but I wouldn't have said he looked at ease on it. Mind you, it didn't look like the kind of sofa anybody would ever be able to get very comfortable on. Then again, it isn't always easy to make yourself feel at home when a stranger's pointing a gun at you.

He dropped his hand onto the cushion to his side.

'Put your hands on your knees, where I can see them.'

'Any reason you wanna see my hands?'

'Maybe I like to look at them.'

'You just like hands in general,' he said, 'or my hands in particular?'

'Quit the wise guy talk and do as I say.'

He did as I said.

'There,' I said, 'I knew you could do it if you tried.'

'Now what?'

'I'm going to ask some questions and you're going to give me answers.'

'I had a feeling you were gonna say something corny like that.'

'I want to know what Gisela Schwartz has got herself mixed up in.'

'I had no idea she'd got herself mixed up in anything.' He shrugged and looked at me with the kind of expression schoolteachers must be used to seeing on the faces of kids who don't follow a word they're talking about. I wondered if this guy was really as ignorant as he pretended, or if he had reasons of his own for playing the class dunce.

'No,' I sneered, 'you're the sort of guy who doesn't know anything, right?'

'I wouldn't go that far.'

'Now you're starting to test my patience,' I said, 'and I wouldn't do that if I were you, seeing as I'm the one who's holding the peashooter. So why don't you quit the clever talk and have another try.'

'Look, if I knew where she was I'd tell you.'

'What was Gisela Schwartz doing in Bardino?'

'She worked at a bar down on the seafront. *Georgie's* is the name of the place.'

'Until when?'

'She packed it in a coupla weeks back.'

'Why?'

He shrugged. 'Gisela's not one to tell people everything about what she does. She's kinda private and proud, y'know?'

'So how's she been supporting herself since then?'

'I guess she has some money saved up, but I mean it's really none of my business.'

'How long have you known her?'

'We first met three or four months ago. We dated and slept together a few times, nothing serious you understand.'

'You know anything about her sister or her family?'

'Nope, nothing at all.' He shook his head. 'She's from Germany, I know that much.'

'Where in Germany?'

'Hamburg... I'm from Munich, which is nowhere near where she's from, but even so our both being German's something we have in common.'

'So what's she into—selling drugs, is it, or what?' I knew I was clutching at straws, but there was nothing else to hand for me to clutch at.

'Gisela's not that kind of girl,' he said.

'So what kind of girl is she?'

'She's nice, beautiful, funny...and law-abiding.'

'That's quite a character reference.'

He shrugged. 'Also happens to be true.' He sighed and said, 'Listen, I don't know what you think she's done, but whatever it is I'm sure you must have your wires crossed somewhere. I was you, I'd leave the girl alone.'

'Thanks for the advice. I'll remember not to take it sometime.'

He frowned. 'Thought you'd say something like that.'

'The name Juan Ribera mean anything to you?'

'No...why, should it?'

'What about Mark Wellington?'

He shook his head. 'Now if you'd said the *Duke of* Wellington it might've been different.'

At that moment I heard a noise from behind me. Whoever it was, they must have come from one of the two rooms I didn't have time to check. Before I could turn, whoever was there said, 'Don't move unless you wanna hole in the back of your head.'

I figured I'd better not move.

'Now drop the gun.'

I dropped it.

As I did so, the German reached under the cushion on the sofa and brought out a gun. He was pretty fast but not fast enough, because he took a shot to the head before he could fire. The force of the bullet threw him back against the sofa, so that he lay there with his arms and legs splayed, dead fish eyes looking up at the ceiling. As this happened, I reached down for my gun. But just as I straightened up and was about to turn, something hard hit me on the side of the head and that was the last thing I knew—for a while, anyway...

CHAPTER 6

When I came round, it didn't take me long to realize that I was in the middle of a crime scene. There were uniforms, plainclothes officers and members of the *Policía Científico* team all over the place. The latter were dressed in weird outfits that made them look like astronauts.

Somebody helped me to my feet and said, 'Hey, we got a live one' over his shoulder.

I shook my head and looked into the man's face. He was mid-thirties, wavy short black hair, tanned face, five-nine or ten, slim, dressed in jeans, trainers and a pale-blue shirt that he wore open at the collar. I knew him. His name was Salvador Cobos, and we kind of got along. By which I mean that he tolerated me a little more than some of his colleagues, because I think he knew I was basically an honest guy and that I wanted the same thing he wanted, which was to catch the bad guys, even if I did get in his hair from time to time.

A look of curiosity came into his eyes, bringing the faintest suggestion of a smile along with it. 'Boy, you're lucky you didn't go to the same place as your buddy on the sofa.'

'I know,' I said, 'it doesn't look like much of a sofa, does it?'

'Still making with the wisecracks, huh?' He shook his head. 'You find yourself in the middle of a scene like this and you act like it's a joke?'

I shrugged and said, 'Guess I'm just the sort who always likes to see the jar as being half full instead of half empty.'

'I guess you are at that.' He looked me up and down like he'd just seen me for the first time. 'So perhaps you wouldn't mind telling me what happened here?'

'Still trying to work it out myself.'

'Tell you what,' Cobos said, 'why don't we take you down to the *Jefatura* and give you a push in the right direction?'

'Is there really any need for that, Sal?'

'I think there is, Arthur, yes.' He frowned and appeared to give the matter some further consideration for a moment, before he added: 'I think there most certainly is.'

So they took me down to the station, over by the mosque there, and led me into the Serious Incident room. I was given a black plastic chair to sit on, and Salvador Cobos sat the other side of the gunmetal-grey desk. There were pictures of offenders who were wanted by the police on the wall directly behind Cobos's head. The white walls were bare otherwise. I looked at some of the mug shots and thought what an ugly bunch they were.

'Okay, Arthur,' Salvador Cobos said, 'we can do this the hard way or we can do it the easy way.'

My Spanish is reasonably good, by which I mean that I can understand what the locals mean most of the time, certainly when they're speaking formally. And when they're not, I can usually get the gist. I looked at Sal and weighed the situation up. I only needed a moment to do this, because it was obvious that I didn't have a leg to stand on. 'Look,' I replied, 'why don't I tell you what I can, Sal, and save us both a lot of hassle?'

'I'm listening.'

'There's something going down, but I'm not sure what it is,' I said. 'I was given this address, the one you found me at...a source told me a friend of hers was living there, only she seemed to have disappeared.'

Salvador Cobos lit up a cigarette, took a drag and exhaled out of the corner of his mouth. He screwed up his eyes so that he peered at me out of tiny crevices in a face that was dried sandstone. He offered me the pack, perhaps because he wanted me to share in his suffering. I shook my head. 'I kicked the habit,' I said. 'Get to live longer that way, so they tell me.'

'Interesting logic,' he said.

'Stuff fucks up your lungs, Sal. There's no two ways about it.'

'Since when did they start saying that putting yourself in situations where you're likely to get shot's good for your health?'

'That's different.'

'How come?'

'It's work. I do what I have to do. If I get shot, so be it.' I dug out a smile from somewhere. 'It's happened to me before.'

'You got lucky.'

'Maybe I'll get lucky if it happens again.'

'Maybe you will,' he said. 'Then again, maybe you won't.'

I shrugged. 'I'll take my chances.'

Salvador Cobos shook the caterpillar of ash that had formed on the end of his cigarette into the plastic cup he was using for an ashtray. 'Who gave you the address?'

'My client,' I said.

'Your client got a name?'

'Sure has, only I can't give it to you.'

'*Won't* you mean.'

'You know the way it is, Sal.' I gave him the benefit of my breeziest smile. 'I've got my job to do and you've got yours. If I can help you any way without making it impossible for me to do my work then I will. If not, then...well, that's where I draw the line.'

He sighed. 'Strikes me this line of yours is likely to get you in trouble with the law more often than not.'

'The law is an ass, Sal, you know that.'

'And the man who takes it too seriously's an even bigger one, right?'

'You said it.'

'You're not helping me, Arthur,' Sal Cobos said. 'And that means you're not helping yourself.'

'Like I just told you, I'll help you all I can.'

'Okay, so who's the guy who was shot?'

'He told me his name was Kurt Heinlich.'

'That sounds German.'

'From Munich, or so he told me.'
'You believe him?'
'How should I know?'
'How did you end up in the flat?'
'I let myself in.'
'With a key?'
'No.'
'How then?'
'Without a key.'
'I guessed that much,' Sal Cobos said. 'It's called breaking and entering.'
'Bit harsh.'
'What's harsh about it?'
'I only went there to visit someone who was out,' I said. 'If she'd been home then she might have let me in.'
Sal Cobos took a last pained drag before he killed the cigarette in his makeshift ashtray. 'I'd say you had a pretty weird relationship with the truth, Arthur.'
'Truth is a relative concept,' I said. 'Hadn't you heard?'
'You been reading that Albert Einstein guy again, Art? You wanna be careful, he'll play with your mind, fuck you up big time.'
'How'd you work that out?'
'He only works with theoretical particles that are so small they hardly exist. In fact, for our purposes we can say they *don't* exist.'
'That's impossible.'
'But you know what I mean,' he said. 'We're both in the business of chasing criminals, who are not invisible.'
'That's open to question,' I replied. 'Some of the best criminals stay invisible practically forever.'
'Now you're getting clever on me again, Art.'
'You're the one who brought up Einstein, Sal.'
He sighed. 'I dunno why,' he said, 'but whenever I talk to you it always ends up getting complicated.' He frowned. 'I mean why can't anything ever be simple and straight down the line with you, Arthur, huh?'
'I'm giving it to you simple and straight down the line, Sal... I just told you the guy's name and where he's from.'
'We already know that, Art, and his name wasn't Kurt Heinrich—'

'Hein*lich*,' I corrected him.

'Or Heinlich, either, and he wasn't from Munich.'

'That's news to me.'

Sal Cobos looked me in the eye like he was trying to work out whether I was on the level. I looked right back at him, as levelly as I could.

CHAPTER 7

Sal strummed his fingers on the desk and said, 'How did you come by the idea his name was Kurt Heinlich and he was from Munich?'

'He said so himself, like I already told you.'

'When was this?'

'After I entered the flat.'

'You ever see or talk to this guy before?'

'No.'

Cobos gave me another of his straight looks. It was as he were trying to see into my mind. 'Are you on the level, Art?'

'I've no reason not to want to help you on this,' I said. 'Only thing I can't tell you's the name of my client.'

'What's the relationship of your client to the German?'

'Again, I'd help you if I could,' I replied, 'but I really don't know the answer to that yet.' I threw up my hands. 'Sounds like you know more than I do, Sal.' There was a first time for everything, I supposed.

'How did you end up on the floor?'

'Somebody hit me from behind.'

'Who hit you?'

'Didn't see who it was,' I said. 'If I had I'd've stopped him from hitting me.'

Sal Cobos ran a hand through his black hair, which was tinged with grey at the temple. 'Sounds like you've really got yourself mixed up in something this time, Arthur.'

'Sounds like I have.'

We looked at each other some more in silence.

He sighed in a way that let me know just how weary he was with my little act. 'What about Juan Ribera?' he said. 'Run through how you ended up at his place for me again.'

'I was watching the flat in the Bocanazo when a Merc shows, and this guy gets out and enters the block I'm watching. Well, Mercs aren't so common in the Bocanazo, as I expect you know, so I went in after the guy.'

'And?'

'He knocks on the door to the flat I've been told to keep an eye on.'

'You see him do this?'

'That's right,' I said. 'Okay, look I'll give you the full rundown, but then you've got to play fair with me, right?'

Sal nodded. 'Okay.'

'Nobody's home, or if they are they're not opening up, so he goes away and I follow him in my car to a farmhouse up in the hills.'

'Who shot him?'

'Not sure.'

'Somebody hit you again?'

I nodded. 'I was peeping in through the window at him...he was on the phone to somebody, and then something hard hits me on the back of the head... When I come round, I'm lying on the floor inside the house. I sit up and there's the guy I'd been following on the sofa, and he's not looking very alive.'

'So what do you do then?'

'I go through his pockets, find his ID card and learn from it his name's Juan Ribera, then call you guys before I make my exit and drive back over to the Bocanazo.'

'Where you pick the lock to invite yourself into the flat, only to get yourself into another pickle.'

'That's it,' I said. 'Anyway, I've told you everything I can, so what about telling me who the German was and what he and Juan Ribera were up to?'

'We're not sure what they were up to yet, Art, but we do know that they were both involved with organized crime. Ribera was working with a bunch of guys who were mostly Serbs. As for the German, his name was Joaquim Gross and he was with a group of Germans who've been making their presence felt more and more in the criminal underworld of late.'

'It sure sounds like I've got myself in the middle of something.'

'Mm.' Sal Cobos didn't look impressed. 'I oughta lock you up in a cell and forget where I put the key.'

'But you don't want to do that.'

'Don't I?'

'No.'

'What makes you so sure about that?'

'I'm your bait, for one thing,' I said. 'You sling me out into the sea on your hook and things start to happen, right?'

'That sure is true, but it's always things that *shouldn't* happen. Dead bodies have a nasty habit of collecting around you.'

'Exactly...that means I'm close to something.'

'Close to what...?'

'I don't know yet,' I said. 'But neither do you. We both want to find out, though, and so there's a sense in which we're playing for the same team.'

'I wouldn't go that far.'

Neither would I, but I didn't want to tell Cobos that. 'We both want to catch the bad guys, and you know that so long as I'm out there dangling in the water the bad guys are likely to come out of hiding. You're not quite sure why, but that doesn't really matter at this stage.'

'Okay, but whatever team it is you think you're playing for, Art,' Sal Cobos said, 'you'd better shape up and stop scoring own goals, or you'll find yourself sitting on the bench.'

'I've had a run of bad luck lately, Sal.'

'So you'd better start getting some good luck, and quick, Arthur, if you know what's good for you.'

'I'll go and consult my astrologer.'

'Still with the wisecracks, huh?' Cobos shook his head. 'Don't you ever let up?'

'I guess not.' I stood up. 'So I take it I'm free to go, then?'

'For the time being,' he said. 'Go and enjoy your freedom while it lasts, because I have a funny feeling it's not going to be for very long.'

'Been looking in your crystal ball again, Sal?'

'Yeah, only they call it a computer nowadays... I've been checking on the stuff that's accumulated in your file over these past few years, ever since you came down here and started up as a dick, and I have to tell you it makes for some pretty sorry reading.'

'You ought to take a leaf out of my book and read a couple of pages of Jane Austen every night in bed before you sleep,' I said. 'Be likely to have a much more calming effect on your nerves.'

'Jane *who*...?'

I gave him a sort of wave-cum-salute as I went out the door.

CHAPTER 8

I'd barely eaten all day and it was coming up to six in the evening, so I went into a bar on Calle Veracruz and took a seat near the window. The waiter came over and I told him I'd have an *ensalada mixta* and the *rabo de toro*, or mixed salad and bull's tail, and I'd have a carafe of Rioja to help it down.

My head was hurting from where I'd been hit, and I was aching from where I'd fallen, and my belly was noisy with hunger, but I began to feel better as I ate. When I'd finished my meal, I had the waiter bring me a *café con leche* with a glass of brandy.

I tasted the coffee and then I tipped the *cognac* into it and stirred to make what the Spanish call a '*carajillo*'. I had just sipped it when my mobile began to ring.

'How are things going?' a female voice asked. It was Inge Schwartz.
'Oh so-so.'
'Have you managed to find my sister yet?'
'No, but I did nearly get killed a couple of times. Where are you?'
'I'm at the hotel.'
I said, 'I'll meet you in my office in an hour's time.'
'Oh I really don't think that's convenient right now.'
'If you want me to continue to try to find your sister you'll be there,' I told her and hung up.

I settled the bill then left the restaurant and walked along to my office. I went over to the window, pulled one of the slats in the venetian blind open a little and gazed down at the street. The sun had gone down by now and the traffic was passing in a steady stream, the cars all with their headlights on. Then I saw her making her way along the pavement. I saw, too, the way the men she passed would stop and stare; not that she seemed to notice. She moved with a sure-footed rhythm, and then, as she entered the building, I heard her heels as she made her way up the steps. Then I saw the door handle turn and Little Miss Butter Wouldn't Melt breezed into the room. 'So glad you could make it,' I said. 'I missed you earlier.'

'Oh?'

'I paid you a visit at your hotel.' I studied her face to see how she'd respond to what I'd just said, but she didn't so much as bat an eyelid so far as I could tell. 'Yes,' I said, 'I went up to your room. It was four-two-three, wasn't it?'

'What?'

'Your room number?'

'Oh, yes.'

'Well I went up but you didn't let me in.'

She shrugged. 'I must've gone out.'

'I didn't say I didn't *go* in,' I said. 'Just that you weren't there to open the door for me.' Her brows bunched and her right one formed a beautiful arch that was almost like a question mark lying on its side. 'Because I did...'

'You did...?'

'Yes.'

'You did what...?'

'Enter your room.'

She took a step towards me and dropped her Kelly bag onto my desk. 'You entered my room?'

'Yes, but you weren't in it.'

'Well that was rather naughty of you, wasn't it, Mister Blakey?'

'I'm apt to do rather naughty things from time to time, Miss Schwartz... I even ate two chocolate sundaes on Saturday.'

'You'll get fat if you're not careful.'

'I worked out afterwards.'

She moved a little closer, so that we were almost touching, then she gave me the old up-from-under look so that her right eyelash cut across her eye. She had the most beautiful blue eyes, and the effect of the eyelash cutting across it made it all the more stunning. She sighed and said, 'Alone?'

'What?'

'Did you work out alone, Mister Blakey?'

'That's kind of a personal question, isn't it?'

'What if it is?' she said. 'Don't you ever get up close and personal with anyone?'

'I have been known to,' I said, 'but I can't see that it's really any business of yours, Miss Schwartz.'

'But I'm your client, Mister Blakey.' She moved closer to me so that her red lips, so full and succulent, were within kissing range and something inside my head did a pirouette. All I'd have to do is lean forward half an inch and–bingo. I held myself still and stiff, only not in the sense you mean, and then I felt my head spin again. It's funny what the proximity of such beauty can do to a man. So much beauty, I thought, gazing on her as an art connoisseur might pore over the Mona Lisa; so much of it, and all of it far too close to home.

'Precisely, Miss Schwartz,' I said. 'You're my client.'

'And do you mean to say that my being so doesn't buy me certain... certain privileges, Mister Blakey?'

'You're being so *what*, Miss Schwartz?'

'My being your client, I mean?'

'Sure it does,' I said.

'What might the privileges I can expect to enjoy as your client be?'

'Complete confidentiality and discretion,' I said, 'and whatever the job is, you can be sure that I always give it my best shot.'

'That's reassuring, I must say... And what special qualifications and experience have you got that make you the man for the job?'

'I've got a badge which says I've the right to work as a private eye,' I said.

'And are you experienced?'

'Yes, very.'

'Would you like to tell me about how you resolved some of your hardest cases?'

I kissed her on the mouth and she didn't do anything to give me the impression she minded it.

CHAPTER 9

'Look, Inge,' I said, 'you can stop bullshitting me, okay?'
'I didn't think that's what I was doing.'
'What's the word you use in German, then?' I asked. 'Whatever it is, you weren't in the room at Las Palmas because somebody else was staying in it.'

She smiled so that the corners of her eyes wrinkled up. 'Oh well,' she said, 'you can't expect a girl to tell you everything straight off when she's only just met you, now can you?'

'I expect my clients to play straight with me, Inge, so I can play straight with them.'

'Are you always this hard on your women after you ravish them?' she asked.

'I figured we kinda ravished each other, Inge.'

'Whatever.' She shrugged. 'There's no need to come on so tough, though, is there?'

'There wouldn't be,' I said, 'if I didn't get the feeling I was being taken for a mug.'

She sighed. 'And to think I took you for a romantic.'

'Look, Inge, you're gorgeous, and that's another thing you know very well. What's more, you play on it. So don't take me for an utter fool, okay?'

'I really don't know what you're trying to say.'

'You waft all that beauty and sex appeal you've got around and hypnotize people with it...and you've worked it on me, so I should know, because I'm as big a sucker as anyone when it comes to that sort of thing and I'm the first to admit it.'

'Gee, that was almost sweet and romantic, coming from you. Should I feel as if I'd been complimented?'

'Yes and no.' I leered at her. 'The simple fact is, Inge, that I don't trust you. I could fall for your tricks, and maybe I already have fallen for them, but that doesn't stop me from seeing through it all.'

'Seeing through what, Arthur?'

'You're not being straight with me,' I said. 'In fact, I seriously doubt if you've ever been straight with any man in all your life.'

'That's a rotten thing to say.'

'Maybe it is,' I conceded. 'Only I'm not some kid playing at cops and robbers but a professional private investigator, and I can't have some blonde bombshell walk in here and stomp all over me like I was a piece of carpet. Are we understood?'

'Yes and no,' she said.

'What do you mean by that?'

'I've no idea what makes you think I'm not being straight with you.'

'You act as if butter wouldn't melt in your mouth, Inge, but you're as worldly as a banknote.'

'I'm not sure I like your tone.'

'You weren't meant to,' I replied. 'Because I don't like working for clients who lie to me about where they're staying, and who seduce me in my office afterwards when I question them about it.'

'I thought you were the one that seduced me?'

I shrugged. 'That's just a matter of semantics.'

She sighed. 'Do you mean that you didn't like being seduced?'

'I loved it and you know it, so you can quit the Little Miss Sweet And Innocent act.'

'I don't just give myself to any man like that, Arthur.'

'Maybe you don't,' I said. 'But you do when you want something badly enough.'

'Hasn't it occurred to you that it could've been you that I wanted, Arthur?'

'I'm afraid I'm neither young nor stupid nor vain enough to believe that coming from you, Inge.'

'But why not, Arthur? Don't you believe in love at first sight?'

'Maybe I do,' I said. 'But if so then there's a little voice in my head that tells me I'd be a fool to in your case.'

She dropped her head and made a wonderful job of looking truly hurt. 'You think I'm no better than a common tramp, don't you?'

'That was a beautiful performance,' I said, 'but you really don't need to waste all that effort and talent on somebody like little old me, you know. After all, you have hired me to work for you.'

She slapped me across the face. 'How dare you talk to me like that.'

I felt the blood all rushing to my cheek, where I'd been struck. It was wonderful.

'I'm sorry I hit you.'

'No you're not.'

'Okay, I'm not because you deserved it.'

I smiled. 'There's a real tigress in there under that phony sweet exterior, isn't there?'

She slapped me again, even harder if anything.

'There,' she said. 'That's what you get for talking to me like that.'

I took her in my arms and kissed her on the mouth, and this time she tried to push me away a little at first. I pulled her back close to me and looked her in the eye. She smelled like heaven on a nice summer's day, and her eyes were little blue and black lakes that contained galleons full of untold treasure. She was everything I'd ever wanted and everything I knew was bad for me, all wrapped up in one impossibly attractive package.

'Why do you want to make love to me so much, Arthur, is what I don't understand,' she sighed, 'seeing as you clearly despise me.'

'I despise you and I love you,' I told her honestly. 'You're everything bad and everything good.' I kissed her.

And kept on kissing her for quite some while; then she slipped out of my arms and opened the door. 'I'll call you tomorrow,' she said, and then she was gone.

And I still hadn't even got her to tell me where she was really staying.

CHAPTER 10

I wondered for the umpteenth time what it was that Inge Schwartz's sister could have got herself involved in. I blew out my chops like a tired blowfish, then reached into the drawer at the side of my desk and poured myself another large one. I'd just taken a sip of it when the telephone rang. I reached out and picked it up. 'Hello?'

'I hope you're not still angry with me.'

'Look Inge, I need to know what it is your sister has got herself into.'

'But that's what I thought I'm paying you to find out, Arthur.'

'So you're pretty sure she's into something, then?'

'I really don't know,' she said. 'But I'm getting more and more worried all the time.'

'If you were so worried why didn't you go to the police straightaway, before coming to me?'

'I did, but they didn't take it seriously...they seemed to think young women stop writing home all the time, and that it's no big deal. I tried telling them Gisela's not that sort, but they didn't want to know.'

'Two men have already been killed, Inge, and all because of whatever it is your sister's involved in.' I was finding it easier to talk to her on the phone, easier to get my thoughts together, now that I didn't have the solid magic of her beauty there in the room to have to deal with.

'Oh but that surely can't be.'

'I'm afraid it surely can,' I said. 'The names Juan Ribera and Joaquim Gross mean anything to you?'

'No, I can't say they do.'

Somehow I figured she wouldn't have told me if they did.

'Should they?' she asked.

'All I know for sure is that they were both mixed up in the underworld somehow.'

'You mean they were gangsters?'

'That's a fairly grand way of putting it,' I said. 'These two guys were bit-part players, the types that get sent out to do the dirty work. Sure, Ribera drove a Merc and liked to dress like he was big shot. But my hunch is it was all show. He was the sort to spend most of what he had on making himself look the part. My point is, he looked like he was somebody but he wasn't. But he was working for somebody else who was.'

'Was what?'

'Somebody.'

'But what do you make of it all, Arthur?'

'My guess is, Gisela either stepped on the toes of the wrong person, or she had something that they wanted.'

'Something valuable, you mean?'

'Gangsters don't normally do cheap, Inge. It's not their way. It's part of what makes them gangsters.'

'But Bardino seems like such a quiet sleepy little *pueblo* by the sea,' she said. 'Just another holiday resort.'

'It's all that and an awful lot more. And when I say awful, I mean *awful*. They don't call it the Costa del Crime for nothing.'

'Oh poor Gisela...what you're saying is starting to make me more worried than ever.'

'I don't want to frighten you for the hell of it, Inge,' I said. 'But you hired me to find out the truth, and so you may as well know something about the lay of the land down in this part of the world.'

She didn't say anything, and I sat there listening to her breathing down the line at me. A part of me wanted to rush over to wherever the hell she was and fold her in my arms and protect her from all the bad people in the world, and another part of me wondered if she weren't one of the bad people herself. She said, 'So now what are you going to do?'

'I'll take a little stroll down to *Georgie's* later, the bar Gisela was working in, and see if I can turn anything up.'

She said, 'I'm grateful for everything you're doing to help me.'

'No need for that, just so long as you pay me.'

'I don't think you like me a great deal, do you, Arthur?'

'You want to go fishing,' I said, 'go get yourself a rod and take it down to the beach.'

'What on earth do you mean by that?'

'I'll talk to you tomorrow.' I hung up.

I finished what was left in my glass, then locked the office and took a stroll down to the seafront. It was dark by now and there was a pleasant breeze blowing up, and I could smell the sea as I walked along and hear the rise and fall of the surf.

Georgie's was doing a good trade when I got there. It was a cocktail bar with bamboo tables and chairs outside. Couples were sitting whispering sweet nothings to each other and sipping their drinks, and the place seemed like an advertisement for the good life. For life as a sort of enlargement on the general theme of sun, sea and romance that was what Bardino tried to sell itself as. I walked up a few steps and entered the bar, which was dark with subdued lighting and low-key music. I dropped my elbow on the wooden counter and turned and looked at the couples out on the terrace.

CHAPTER 11

The barmaid came over, an attractive girl with fine ash-blonde hair that came down to her shoulders and nice eyes. She was wearing jeans that she must have shoehorned herself into and a white top that didn't do go out of its way to hide her ample cleavage. I told her to give me a Scotch with a glass of iced water on the side.

When the drink came, I handed her a ten-euro note then took a sip of my whisky. It tasted pretty good. I find that Scotch usually does. The barmaid came back with my change, and I took out the photograph Inge Schwartz had given me of her sister and held it up. 'This is Gisela Schwartz,' I said. 'I was told she worked here.'

The girl nodded. 'She doesn't anymore.'

'Any idea why she left or where she went?'

She shrugged and her cleavage shrugged along with her. 'The girl at the table over there might know,' she said. 'She was friendly with her.'

There were a few couples sitting at tables. 'Which girl? Can you point her out for me?'

'The pretty brunette in the corner sitting with the man in the suit.'

I looked over and saw the girl she meant. I recognized the man she was sitting with, too. His name was Vicente Caportorio and he was a player in Bardino's criminal underworld. 'Thanks,' I said. 'What's the girl's name?'

'Rosa.'

I asked the girl if she'd like a drink. 'Sure,' she said. 'Mine's a Bacardi and coke.' She gave me a sideways look. 'You a cop, right?'

'How did you guess?'

She turned and fixed herself a drink, then came back with my change on a little dish. There wasn't much of it so I left it there.

I sipped my Scotch and looked over at the girl in the corner, whose name I now knew was Rosa, and the man she was with, whose name was Vicente Caportorio. Or Vince, as everybody called him. The man looked like a gangster if anyone ever did. He was wearing a blue shark's tooth suit that looked like it was bespoke, along with a light blue shirt and a burgundy tie. He had a deep tan the colour of roasted peanuts, and his jet-black hair was swept back and gelled down. His face was lean and looked like it had been fashioned with a chisel, but it was the eyes that you noticed. They were alive with the glare of a hungry animal. As for the girl, she was gorgeous in a Penthouse-magazine sort of way.

I took my drink and went over to their table, then stood there for a moment and waited for them to look up and notice me. They didn't seem to want to. They were deep in conversation, and they looked like whatever they were talking about must be pretty interesting. The man, Vince, was drinking Scotch on the rocks and the girl what must be a gin and tonic or vodka. I had the impression they were making a point of not noticing me. Well, you don't get to earn a living in my business if you're the sort who gets upset when people are rude. I sipped my Scotch and carried on standing there, until Vince finally looked up at me. 'The fuck do you want?' he said in a gruff voice.

'Just a friendly word with your lady friend here, if you don't mind. I won't take up much of your time.'

'And what if I do mind?'

I took out the photo of Gisela Schwartz minus two or three years and held it out for the girl to look at. 'You knew her, I believe?'

The girl glanced at it and looked away. Vince did the same. Their faces were a pair of closed books: the sort that you wouldn't want to read.

'Name's Gisela Schwartz,' I said. 'I'm told she used to work here.'

The girl shrugged. 'So?'

'I'm looking for her.'

'You a cop?' Vince wanted to know.

'Kind of,' I said and took out my card.

Vince glanced at it and sneered.

I looked at the girl. 'I've been told you were friendly with her, Rosa?'

'You been told wrong, amigo,' Vince answered for the girl.

I put the photograph away, along with my card.

'Okay,' Vince said, 'you've said your piece so now you can beat it.'

'Maybe I don't like your manners.'

'Maybe you ain't supposed to like 'em,' he said. 'Maybe your problem is you're a little slow on the uptake, chum, *me entiende?* A little slow to get the message, *sabes?*'

'Oh I get the message all right, *chum*,' I told him. 'I just don't wanna hear it.'

A nasty smile spread across the man's face, only his eyes weren't smiling. They had murder in them. 'Maybe you wanna come and talk to me outside.'

I said, 'Anyone ever tell you that you use the word *maybe* too much, Vince?'

That set him thinking, or trying to. 'Who told you my name's Vince?'

He smiled again. 'Ah, I know,' he said. 'I saw you talking to the bitch behind the bar.'

'Wasn't her,' I told him. 'Listen,' I said, 'if you think you're so big and tough then sure I'll come outside and talk to you. But let's leave girls out of it, shall we? Only sissies hit girls.'

That must have touched a nerve somewhere, because he sprang up off the banquette like he was a jack-in-the box and there was a spring affixed to the seat of his trousers. Unfortunately for him, though, the table was in his way, so that he had to move round it before he could get to me. That gave me time to skip down off the step that rose to the booth the pair were sitting in, and as he came at me I moved to the side and tripped him. He fell and I grabbed him and spun him around. His arm flailed, sending flying a tray full of drinks that a passing waiter had been carrying. I heard the crash the glasses made as they shattered on the floor. I got him in a sort of bear hug only from behind, with one arm round his neck. He swung his elbow back and got me in the ribs. I'd been hoping he would be all talk, the way some of these types can be. But this guy was a lump of granite with arms and legs attached. I groaned as I felt my ribs crack and must have let go of him for a moment, because the next thing I knew he'd spun round and was facing me. He threw a punch that I saw coming, but only as it was about to break my windpipe. I ducked and got it in the jaw. I reeled back and felt something hard hit my spine about half way up. I realized I'd hit the counter, and I looked up just in time to see him coming at me again. He was a solid rhino made of stone, only he was a hell of a lot uglier than any rhino I'd ever seen and much more violent. The man was one big ball of rage and hate. But maybe that was his weakness. Because he came charging at me just like a rhino, the way a man does when he has no plan of attack. He just wanted to tear me apart, and that was all he had on his mind. I could sense this, the way you can sense things about your opponent when you're in a fight. The man was all violence and no finesse, and as he came lunging at me I feinted and skipped to the side. Then I hooked one of his feet out from under him, and I was able to use the man's own weight and momentum to send him crashing into the counter. Before he could turn I hit him in the kidneys, then I kicked his other foot out from under him and he went reeling backwards, but managed to reach out and break his fall by grabbing onto the table that the girl he was with, Miss Penthouse, was still sitting at. He regained his balance then glared at me, with his head low. He reminded me of a bull, the way it looks before it's about to charge. And I didn't have a cape handy. Or a sword, for that matter.

Then big trouble struck in the form of something hard on the back of my head.

When I came round I was in the back of a car. I had huge lumps of muscle on either side of me, so there was no way I could move or try anything brave. 'What the fuck is this?' I said.

'You'll find out,' Vince replied from the passenger seat in front.

His mutts had obviously shown just at the wrong time, and I presumed they must have carried me out through the back entrance of the bar where they'd have had the car waiting. My only chance was that some onlooker might have thought to make a note of the reg and phoned it in. But it was a long shot at best. Besides, I thought, the registration plate's almost certainly a false one. What these guys did, they stole different cars and swapped the plates round to make it difficult to trace them. If a cop car didn't appear on our tail before we got to wherever it was I was being taken, then I knew I was up the nameless creak and paddles would be in short supply.

I'd like to be able to say that I was too busy thinking of ways to escape to be frightened, but that wouldn't be true. I was afraid all right.

Looking out through the window, I saw that we were now driving up into the hills. 'Look,' I said, 'the fight was between me and you, Vince, so what's the big deal getting your mates involved?'

'You wanna know what's good for you,' Vince replied over his shoulder, 'you'll shut the fuck up.'

'I don't get it. I just wanted to ask your girlfriend a couple of questions and so you abduct me. What is this?'

'I said shut the fuck up.'

I figured there was no point in trying to goad or shame the man into letting me go, because that tactic just wasn't going to work. So I took his advice and gave my chin a rest.

CHAPTER 12

We headed on up into the hills, then we turned off the road up a dirt track. The car jumped and bobbled along worse than ever for the best part of a mile and then it pulled up. I was pulled off the back seat by one of the bears that had been guarding me, and found that we had come to a big farmhouse. A warm breeze was blowing, bringing with it the pungent scent of *dama de la noche*, a smell I'd always liked until now. The two bears took an arm each and walked me over the shingle forecourt. Vince rang the bell and somebody came and opened the door.

No sign of the cavalry, I thought. Never is when you need 'em. Forget what you see in the old cowboy flicks.

They took me through the house and out back. I found myself in a big indoor swimming pool, with pitch lighting and no windows. Vince aimed a wink over in my direction and said, 'Not bad, is it?' He made a noise that was somewhere between a snarl and a chuckle. 'And they say crime don't pay.' He jerked his head back, then looked from side to side like he'd just come to this place for the first time and was amazed by what he saw. 'Well I dunno about you, but the evidence on show seems to point to the contrary, wouldn't you say?'

I didn't say anything.

'Cat got your tongue, has it?'

'What do you want from me?' I asked.

'Who are you working for?'

'I can't tell you that.'

'That's the wrong answer,' he said.

'I never divulge the identity of my client to anyone.'

He made a face like he was pretending to be disappointed. 'I'm afraid that was the wrong answer again.'

He turned to the two bears that'd escorted me in here. 'You know what to do, lads,' he said.

The next thing I knew, one of them disappeared through a door in the far wall and a small crane came down from the ceiling, unfolding itself as it did so. The two men held me as Vince tied a rope around my ankles, and then I found myself being hoisted up out of the air. Then I was swinging in an arc as the crane moved, and when I came to rest I was dangling over the pool.

I heard Vince say, 'Thing you gotta understand is, time's money. And I don't have time nor money to waste on scum like you.'

Then he said, 'Take him down,' and I found myself being lowered into the water.

I took a deep breath before my head went under, and held it for as long as I could. When my breath was all gone, I began to thrash around and just when I was about to pass out I felt myself being lifted back up. I panted and writhed like a fish out of water, as I tried to get some breath back into my lungs.

Vince said, 'You having fun?'

I was still trying to catch my breath and so found myself unable to speak.

'So how about telling me who your client is?'

Finding I was finally beginning to be able to breathe normally once more, I considered how to respond. I didn't fancy the idea of pretending to be a fish again, because I'd already learned how bad at it I was; so I said, 'It's Gisela Schwartz's father.'

'Where's he hanging out?'

'He didn't say.'

'Boy, you really must like the water, huh?'

'No, honestly he didn't...he called from somewhere in Badajoz. Said his daughter'd stopped writing home and he wanted me to check on her and make sure she was okay.'

Vince said, 'So you reckoned I had something to do with all this mess and came looking for me, that it?'

'No, I hadn't even begun to think about you or connect you with it in any way.'

'You're lying.'

I shook my head. 'Fact is, your name hadn't cropped up. I went to *Georgie's* because I was told that Gisela worked there and then I saw Rosie, whom I'd learned was friendly with her, so I tried to talk to her. You just happened to be there with her.'

'Nice try,' he said.

'But it's the truth...anyway you've got no reason to kill me, Vince.'

'What makes you think I need you to tell me what I got a reason to do?'

'Look,' I said, 'I take the point. You wanted to teach me a lesson. Fine. But you don't need my blood on your hands. Where's that gonna get you?'

'Where it's gonna get me's that there'd be one less punk like you running around dirtying the pavements in my town.'

'Look, Vince–'

'You say *look* to me once more'n I'll kill you right here and now, you got that?'

'Okay.' It's surprising how sensitive some of these tough guys can be about words, grammar, semantics, stuff like that. 'But think about it, a lot of people saw us fighting.'

'A lot of people see what I tell 'em to see, and they don't see what I tell 'em not to.'

'Maybe so,' I said, 'but not everyone, Vince. There's always one who talks...and Sal Cobos, the Inspector Jefe del Homicidios in Bardino, happens to be a close friend of mine. He gets to hear I've left the scene, he's gonna come knocking on your door.'

'Like I got to worry about punks like Sal Cobos.'

'Thing about men like Sal,' I said, 'he's got a lot of buddies.'

'So do I got a lotta people.'

'Not as many as Sal's got...he's got the whole of the police force. We're talking thousands of men, Vince. You don't need all that heat.' In reality of course what I'd just said was a gross exaggeration, given how stretched police resources were; but concerns as to the veracity or otherwise of what I had to say were the least of my worries.

'Anybody ever tell you that you talk too much?'

'Lots of people.'

The half-amused look had left Vince's face by now. 'I've had enough of all this talk.' He nodded to the other two men and said, 'Put a mask on him and introduce him to Estrella.'

Somebody must have pulled a lever or something somewhere, because I found myself swirling through the air again. When I came to a stop, there was no longer water but the tiled flooring that ran along the side of the pool beneath me. Then somebody slipped an oxygen mask over my face, and something was being attached to my back.

The goon who was busy with the straps said, 'Boy, you really gonna enjoy what you got comin',' and chuckled.

I didn't like the sound of this.

I figured I wasn't supposed to like it, either.

I wondered who in hell Estrella was supposed to be.

Whoever she was, I didn't want to meet her.

But I knew I was going to, whether I wanted to or not.

CHAPTER 13

My dear departed father always had the right idea. 'Go into banking, my son,' he told me. 'Avoid working with your hands or doing physical work of any kind,' he always said. 'And avoid making or creating anything of any sort, too, while you're about it. If you want to earn money then you need to work with money,' was another of his tenets. They were like commandments; only he never set them out in stone. He just kept repeating them over and over again. It was all sound advice. Why had I never listened to him? Probably because he was my father, and guys like me never listen to their fathers. Not even when their fathers give them good sound advice. *Especially* when their fathers give them good sound advice. If my dad had given me a copy of *Thus Spake Zarathustra* and told me to travel the world and seek ancient wisdom in its forgotten corners, I would probably have run all the way to Savile Row and bought myself the best pinstripe I could find, or had myself measured up for said garment, and then seen about trying to make a career for myself in the Square Mile. Go figure.

But why was I thinking about all this now? you may wonder. Well, it's funny all the stuff that can pop into your head when you're dangling on the end of a rope and wondering if the time has come for the finale, and a particularly gruesome and anything but grand one at that. Just then, I found myself moving through the air again, and when I stopped

I could see water beneath me once more. So it looked as though I was headed for another ducking. I wondered why they'd fitted me with an oxygen mask this time. What was going on? And who was this Estrella? Or more to the point, *what* was she?

I had the feeling that Vince had something nasty in mind. He didn't strike me as the sort of guy who'd ever have any *nice* ideas, after all. Maybe this is going to be it for me, I thought. Maybe this is going to be the end. Well if it was then there didn't seem to be anything I could do about it.

This time when I went under the water, I had oxygen to breathe. Which might sound like good news so far as it went, only it didn't go very far if you catch my drift. You see, looking through the window in my mask, I was able to see that the wall that ran around the edge of the pool was made of thick glass. And there was an enormous and particularly vicious-looking shark on the other side of the partition. And it wasn't just any old sort of enormous and vicious-looking shark, either, but a great white. In order words, the worst sort.

Then my blood froze as a gate in the partition slid open, and I knew it was only a matter of time before the shark came through the opening and joined me in the pool.

So this is Estrella, I thought.

That bastard Vince wanted to send me on a blind date with a great white shark.

CHAPTER 14

I had an affair—no that's too serious a word—an *adventure*, shall we say, with an Estrella once. She'd been no beauty, but she was a nice enough sort of kid. Nothing like *this* Estrella at all.

I just hoped that it would be fast when it happened, and that I wouldn't know too much about it.

Time dragged like a bastard and a bitch combined. I mean you can imagine. Or maybe you can't. Maybe you don't even want to try. I can't say I blame you.

After a while of this, I started to think maybe the shark wasn't interested in me. Maybe it wasn't going to bother to come through the gap in the partition. Maybe it wasn't a very sociable shark. Maybe it was the shy type. Maybe it had already eaten its dinner. Maybe any damn thing, just so long as it stayed where it was. Just so long as *I* didn't end up as its dinner.

Then she made her appearance. She looked almost casual at first, like she wasn't in any particular hurry to come over and check me out. Then she turned and eyeballed me. Estrella. Which means *star* in Spanish. Now there's nothing quite like being eyeball to eyeball with a great white shark, I can tell you. Especially when you're unarmed and dangling underwater from a piece of rope.

Then she made her move and started to come towards me. Now I'd found myself in some tight squeezes before. They went with the job, you might say. But this one was as bad as any I could remember. Not only that, but I was convinced this squeeze was going to be my last, and just when I feared I was about to become Estrella's dinner, I found myself being hoisted up out of the water at quite a rate of knots. Estrella was within sniffing distance before I left the water, and she jumped up and took a snap at me with her enormous jaws - and only just missed.

I went swirling through the air again, until I was no longer hanging over the water in the pool but the tiles that ran along its edge. Vince and his two stooges seemed to have found the little scene rather entertaining, because they were laughing fit to bust.

Vince said, 'Have fun in there with Estrella, did you?'

'I'm afraid she's not my type...rather too toothy.'

'No, well one man's meat, I guess...although it's not what you think of Estrella that's important, but what *she* thinks of *you*. Whether she finds you to her taste, if you catch my drift.'

The two mutts laughed like Vince was some genius comedian. I reckoned it was easy to come across like a wiseguy when you were in his position. He should try coming out with the comic lines when he finds himself in the situation I was in. 'So anyway,' Vince said, 'you were saying...'

'Was I?'

'About your client, I mean.'

'What about him?'

'It was the dad of this girl's gone missing, you say?'

'Yeah.'

'You do realize you're going to spend some more time with Estrella if I don't believe you?'

'I rather gathered as much.'

'You rather gathered as much, didya?'

'Yeah.'

'What made you gather so much?'

'Look,' I said, 'I have no idea why you're getting so worked up all about nothing. And I've no idea why you got so tough back in the bar either and wanted to fight, just because I wanted to ask your girlfriend a few questions about a girl who seems to have gone missing. And I've no idea why you're torturing me with a shark now.'

'And that's your final story, is it?'

'It happens to be the truth,' I said. 'Unless you'd prefer it if I made up a lot of lies.'

Vince looked at me and there was a twinkle of amusement in his eye 'You know, punk,' he said, 'it's lucky that you came to see me like this because you're just the person I needed to talk to.' He chuckled. 'It's like you were brought to me by Providence, you know that?'

I didn't have the faintest idea what in hell's name he was talking about, so I kept mum and listened to what he was going to say next, figuring he might explain himself a little better.

'I've been hearing about the Rembrandt the sister has and I figured it was time I looked into it a little...and now here you are to tell me.'

'Tell you what?'

'Where she's keeping the Rembrandt, of course, you dumb punk. I gotta spell it out for you?'

'What Rembrandt?' I said. 'I don't know anything about any Rembrandt.'

'Well I guess it's just not your lucky day in that case.'

'If you're gonna kill me,' I said, 'then can't you just shoot me in the head like any other gangster? I mean what's all this shit with the shark?'

Vince looked at me stony-faced, and I had the feeling that he was trying to make up his mind what to do with me. He lifted his chin and moved it around a little, so that the chords in his throat showed. Then he ran a hand through his short black hair. I noticed that he was wearing cufflinks with the figure of a miniature shark mounted on them. The man seemed to have sharks on the brain. 'Look,' he said, 'I know you're lying, okay? I know your client's the girl's sister, so you can quit bullshitting me.'

'It's Gisela's father.'

'The old man's dead,' Vince snapped. 'Now I'm going to say this once and only once. Where's the Rembrandt?'

'This is the first I've heard anything about any Rembrandt.'

'Okay,' he said to the two mutts, 'get him down from there'n drive him some place.'

'Then what, boss?'

I didn't hear Vince's reply, because the next thing I knew I hit the ground and passed out.

CHAPTER 15

When I came round, I was in the boot of a car. The road must've been rocky, because I was being shaken about like a lone pea in a can that was being rattled by a playful gorilla. I wondered where I was being taken, and what would happen when we got there. My wrists were tied behind my back and they were hurting like a bastard.

A little earlier, back when I was in the pool with Estrella, I would have settled for a bullet in the head rather than ending up in the shark's belly. But it's funny how quickly a man's ideas on such matters can change. I worked out a theory on that once. Forgotten most of it now. But it had something to do with circumstances. That was it. The relationship between circumstances and a person's attitude. Change the one and you could find the other changing with it. Some philosopher me. Anyway, taking a bullet in the head no longer seemed like such an attractive option.

The car pulled up and I heard doors opening and being slammed shut. Footsteps over dry land. Then a key in the lock on the boot. The lid opened, and the two mutts were standing there looking down at me. Bastards thought they were somebody, because I had my hands tied. They got me up out of the boot, and I found myself looking down over the edge of a ravine. I could just make out the bottom by the light of the moon. It was a long way down. I figured I'd better try and make a run for it. Only that was easier said than done, with my hands tied behind my back and the mutts holding me by the arms.

The bigger of the two mutts took out a gun. So this was going to be the end. At least that was what they had in mind. But I had a different script up my sleeve. I'd been in tight squeezes before and wriggled out of them, I told myself, so why couldn't I do it again this time? Granted this latest squeeze was pretty tight, but some of the others had been, too, and I'd managed to live to tell the tale. I thought about trying to kick the gun out of the mutt's hand with a karate kick, but he was just out of range. So I took a step towards him. Seeing me do this, he told me to stay put or he'd shoot.

'The fuck you wanna shoot me for?'

'That's none of your business.'

'That's a new one,' I said. 'Since when hasn't it been a man's business if another man shoots him?'

'Never.'

'I don't follow you.'

'You ain't supposed to.'

The second mutt took his gun out, which I took to be a bad sign. My plan to kick the gun out of the hand of the mutt who was aiming at me, and then take my chances with the pair of them went up in smoke on the instant. Not that it had ever been much of a plan. Truth is, I wouldn't have stood a chance. Even I could see that, now that I'd had a moment or two to reflect on it; and I'm a natural born optimist.

The second mutt was aiming at me now, too. 'The fuck're we standing here talking to the bastard for? Let's do him.'

Just then, a car came round the corner in the road, and the beams of its headlights raked us over. The two mutts lowered their guns. They didn't want a witness after all.

It's now or never, I thought, and I turned and went over the side of the ravine. Next thing I know, the world's going ass over tit, if you will excuse the expression, and I'm going down the ravine at a rate of knots. I heard a shot being fired, then a second one, but they both missed. Then I hit something hard and stayed where I was. The impact of the crash took the wind out of me for a moment, and I heard myself let out a groan. It took me a few moments to get my breath, then I looked back up the ravine. I'd fallen a fair old way, and had hit the trunk of an olive tree.

I could see the two mutts up above, peering down over the edge. With any luck, they'd get back in their car and leave.

'You see the bastard?' said one.

'Na...too dark.'

'I can see a lot of the way down and there ain't no sign of 'im, so he must've gone right to the bottom.'

'Guess so...think we should go'n check?'

'No need. I'm sure I got him when I fired.'

'Think I did, too,' the second mutt said. 'But even so, maybe we oughta go'n make sure.'

'Fuck it,' the other mutt said. 'I bought this suit new last week. Last thing I want's to go on a fuckin' climbin' expedition and ruin it.'

'Fucking steep, too.'

'You ain't fucking kiddin' me. Cost me best part of four hundred euros.'

'No, down there, I mean.'

'Oh, yeah.'

'We could fall ourselves if we was to try'n go down there, I meant.'

'Specially in the dark.'

'So we're gonna leave him, then?'

'Fucker's dead, ain't he?'

'I guess he must be.'

"Course he's fucking dead. If you got him with your shot and I got him too then the bastard's gotta be, right?'

'I guess so.'

'Can you stop giving me that you guess so shit, Arturo?'

'What you talkin' about, Juan?'

'You talkin' like you ain't sure.'

'I just wanna be thorough, tha's all. No need to get fuckin' pissy, is there?'

'I understand you wanna be thorough, Arturo, but fuck it, the man's dead, ain't he?'

The mutt called Arturo didn't muster an answer.

'Well fucking ain't he?'

'I guess he is, Juan. Yeah.'

'There you go again, see.'

'See what...?'

'Givin' me that fuckin' *you guess* so shit. What are you saying,

Arturo? Are you saying you wanna go down there'n look for the bastard?'

Arturo didn't say anything.

'Well are you...?'

'I dunno, Juan.'

'Well it's about fuckin' time you did know, Arturo... Now what's it gonna fuckin' be? Either we go down there or we don't. Which is it?'

'You already said you don't wanna go down there.'

'I didn't say that exactly.'

'What did you say then?'

'I said the bastard's dead, ain't he? And you agreed with me. Or d'you wanna go down there?'

'No.'

'Why not?'

'Why not what, Juan?'

'Why don't you wanna go down there?'

'Wouldn't wanna have you ruin your new suit, Juan.'

'Fuck my suit, Arturo. Forget I ever mentioned it, you got that?'

'I've forgotten it, Juan.'

'Now d'you wanna go down there, yes or no?'

'I guess not, Juan.'

'You guess not, or you're sure not?'

'Fuck it, he's dead, ain't he? I mean he's gotta be, right?'

'I think so.'

'Let's get the fuck outa here.'

CHAPTER 16

Moments later I heard the doors of the car slamming shut, first one then the other. The engine started up with a mechanical purr, and I saw the raking beams of the headlights and heard the wheels biting on the dry rubble up above as the car turned around. Then I heard it set off.

So they were gone. I breathed a sigh of relief and figured it was safe for me to move. My chest felt like it had been in a meat-grinder when I set about disentangling myself from the olive tree that had broken my fall, and it was with some difficulty that I managed to get up onto my knees.

I needed to free my hands, so I knelt with my back to the olive tree and began to rub the rope against the bark. It took me a while but I eventually cut through it. Now I had the use of my hands back, I was in a position to plan how I was going to get out of the spot I was in.

The ravine was too steep for me to be able to climb back up it, and the drop down to the bottom was no better. But a little way below me a natural shelf had formed in the limestone. I eased myself down onto it, and began to walk along. It was dark by now and so I moved slowly, taking care about where I placed my feet. I could see well enough where I was about to step, thanks to the light from the stars, although I had little idea of what lay more than ten or fifteen metres ahead of me. I considered using the torch in my iPhone, but decided against the idea. Perhaps the two mutts hadn't gone very far. What if they'd doubled back, in order to look for me? Or maybe they'd only pretended to drive away, in the hope that I would do something that would enable them to spot me. Like turn on my torch, for instance.

Just then, a car went by up on the road, the beams of its headlights raking through the darkness and temporarily lighting up parts of the ravine before me. Up ahead I could see a bend in the road, so I made my way towards it.

When I rounded the corner, the gradient became even steeper so that I found myself shuffling along a narrow shelf in what was otherwise practically a sheer drop down to the bottom. I've never liked heights, and I could feel the hairs standing up on the back of my neck. Easy, kid, I thought. Slip up here and you can say goodbye to your enemies forever.

I stopped and wondered about whether to turn back. Then another car went past up on the road, and I was able to make out, in the beams of its headlights, the rough contours of the land ahead of me. Some fifty metres or so further along, the gradient changed into a much gentler slope down to the bottom. If I could make it along that far then maybe I'd be able to walk through the ravine and it would lead out somewhere. I reckoned it was worth a try, anyway.

So I pressed on, and as I did so I began to feel rather more hopeful so far as my chances of getting back to safety were concerned; that is, I did until the ledge I'd been walking along all but disappeared. Fortunately, I just managed to see where it narrowed in time: another step and I would have found myself walking on thin air—all the way to the bottom of the ravine. I took a deep breath as I stood there on the last bit of the ledge.

I got down on my knees then reached out a hand and felt the ground ahead of me. Where it continued, the shelf could have been no more than ten centimeters wide. It was far too narrow to walk along. My being unable to see ahead in the darkness further complicated matters. I thought of the torch in my mobile and figured it was safe to use it now. The two mutts would hardly have stayed up on the road this long, on the off chance that I might reveal myself, would they? No, they were too stupid for that, I thought.

When I shone it on the ground ahead of me, I could see in the light of the torch the way the narrow ledge continued, before it broadened out again; and then the sheer drop softened into a gentle slope. If I could only make it along that narrow shelf for another twenty metres then I'd be able to work my way down to the bottom without any risk. But the shelf where it continued was too narrow for me to walk along it. The only way of passing it would be to shuffle along sideways, clinging on to any cracks and crevices in the rock face with my fingertips as I did so. It was an operation that called for an experienced climber; and I suspected that no such climber would attempt the crossing without a safety harness. Only a madman would consider it otherwise, I felt sure. The ledge was so narrow and the rock face at this point was a sheer cliff face. Now it may be fair to say that I've been known to have my reckless moments and, as any private investigator is only too well aware, the job comes with certain risks attached, but I was no climber. In fact, as I may already have mentioned, I do not like heights.

Just then, as I tried to weigh the situation up, I heard voices up above and I turned the torch off. 'So where's the fucking body, then?' said a voice that I recognized: it was Vince, the gangster who had entertained me at his country house a short time ago.

CHAPTER 17

'He went down just here somewhere,' said one of the mutts.
By now I had climbed to my feet and pressed myself against the rock face, in the hope of making myself invisible to those above. I just hoped that they hadn't seen the light from my torch.

'Where exac'ly?'

'Just down there it was,' said the mutt. 'We shot him, too, like I was saying, both of us. Ain't no way he coulda survived, Boss. Is there Juan?'

'Na,' said the second mutt. 'No fuckin way, Boss. Man's a goner.'

There was the answer to the question I'd just asked myself: no, they clearly hadn't seen the light from the torch.

'What I don't like,' Vince said, 'is that you ain't really sure, are you, either of you? It just ain't professional, the way you carry on like this... First you shoulda shot the man *then* you throw 'im over the edge, right? Then there's none of this guessin' lark, is there? I mean, there's no need for it, then, if you do it right, is there?'

'No, but we did it right, Boss,' said the first mutt—who must be the bigger one, I thought. The one in the new suit. 'That right, Arturo?'

'Tha's right, Juan.'

So the first one—Fatty in the suit—was Juan, I thought. Juan and Arturo.

'I don't believe this,' Vince said and he shat in the milk.

'Believe what, Boss?'

'You two...must think I'm fucking stupid the pair a you. That what it is, Juan? Think old Vince's gone soft up top, do ya?'

'No, Boss, nothin' like that. Not at all.'

'What about you, Arturo? Thinkin' you can get together with Juan and pull me by the hair is it, or what?'

'No, Vince, course not.'

'What it fucking sounds like to me, I have to say.'

'But he's dead, Boss.'

'Listen to me,' Vince said. 'I'm running things, okay?'

'I know that Vince.'

'Don't call me Vince. It's 'Boss' to you.'

'Sorry, Boss...but what I was gonna say is, the bastard's dead.'

'Already heard you say that, Arturo, and I didn't like it any better the first time you said it.'

Juan said, 'So now what, then?'

'I'll tell you what,' Vince said. 'You two're gonna go down there'n get him and bring him to me.'

'But he's dead.'

'So bring 'im to me like that then.'

'You want the body?'

'I want the body.'

'But it's a sheer drop down there, Boss.'

'Shoulda thought of that before, shouldn't you?'

The one who was called Juan said, 'Can't see fuck all down there in the dark's the problem, i'n'it?'

'Let's shed a little light on the problem, then. Juan. Here's the car keys. Open her up and shine the lights over the side here.'

'Right, Boss.'

Figuring that they would spot me once the headlights came on, I bit the bullet and stepped onto the ledge. It was so narrow that my heels were hanging over the side. Fortune did favour me with a number of handily placed nooks and crannies in the rock face, though, and I was able to prevent myself from falling backwards to my death by gripping onto them with my fingertips. My heart was beating like a lunatic, but there was no time to think: I had to cross the ledge and start to make my getaway before they saw me. To remain where I was just wasn't an option.

I began to shuffle my way across the narrow shelf of rock, and I had managed to get about half way when my right foot slipped and I would surely have fallen to my death had it not been for the strength of my fingers, which gripped the holds I had found in the rock with great tenacity. And as I did so, I was able to find my footing once more. Just then, the car's headlights came on, the long raking beams lighting up a section of the ravine just a few metres to my left.

'The fuck is he, then?' I heard Vince say. 'I can't see the bastard, can you?'

'No, Boss. Maybe he's further over that way.'

Vince shat in the milk again and said, 'Shoulda let the shark eat him.'

'What I thought you was gonna do, Boss.'

'Considered it, only then I thought they can catch you like that,' Vince replied. 'Happened to someone I know. Opened up the belly of his pet croc, didn't they, and there was the evidence lying inside. Better to get rid of it altogether, I thought.'

I felt certain that they would spot me any moment. And once they saw me, there'd be nothing to prevent them from being able to pick me off. I would be an easy target for them, a sitting duck. I had to get across the ledge.

I slid my right foot along a few inches, then freed my left hand and gripped a hold that I had already found in the rock moments earlier. Sweat was pouring down my neck and back, even though the night air was little more than mildly warm. As I moved my right hand I accidentally dislodged a small stone that went skittering down the cliff face. Then I heard a voice—Vince's—say, 'What was that?'

'What?'

'I heard something.' Vince said. Then he called out: 'Move the car so the lights are shining over here.'

The engine let out a growl, and then I heard the tires bite into the gritty surface of the roadside. I feared that the headlights were going to pick me out any moment, and that I was about to get to play pigeon in a pigeon shoot. Then as the lights came raking over the area near to where I was, I saw a big whole or cavern in the rock face just above me. Using the holds that I found in the limestone, I climbed up to the cavern and crawled into it. The next moment the car's headlights came raking over the ledge I had just left. I had just managed to climb up in time. A second later and it would have been too late. I would have been a dead man. But luck had been with me. I was safe—for the time being, anyway.

The roof of the cavern was too low for me to be able to stand, so I crawled along on my hands and knees. Maybe it will lead out somewhere, I thought. Wishful thinking, perhaps; but nothing ventured, nothing gained. I took out my iPhone and turned on the torch so I could see ahead of me. But even with the light from the torch it was still difficult to see whether the tunnel led anywhere, and I figured the only way to find out was to keep on moving.

After I had been crawling in this way for some while the tunnel came to an end, and I found myself looking down over a sort of underground pond, which must have been five or six metres in diameter. On the other side, I could see another tunnel that led upwards. Maybe it would lead up to the road, I thought. At any rate, it was worth taking a look.

Leaving the torch on, I tossed my iPhone through the air and heard it hit rock. Fortunately it hadn't been broken by the impact and, since I had thrown it so that it would be facing me when it landed, I was able to see the water down below. I jumped down into it, and discovered as I did so that it was way too deep to stand in, so I swam the short distance over to the far side; then I dragged myself up onto the bank. I retrieved my iPhone and then began to make my way along the tunnel.

I hadn't gone far before I heard a noise and looked down, shining my torch in time to see a tiny lizard go skittering across my path. I was soaking wet and dog tired, and two or three of my ribs were almost certainly broken, but I was driven on by my will to live and by the desire to get even with Vince and his two mutts. If I were to drop now then they would have won, and I told myself once more that I would see myself in hell before I allowed that to happen.

The tunnel sloped upwards, and this gave me cause to hope that I was heading back towards the road or somewhere near it. I walked about a hundred metres or so, and then my heart did a somersault in my chest as I found myself looking up at the crescent moon. I turned my torch off and pocketed my iPhone; then it was just a case of climbing a wall of rock before I dragged myself out onto what turned out to be a grassy knoll. This last feat of gymnastics proved agonizing, given the state of my ribs; but I was greatly relieved to find myself back on terra firma. And turning my head, I found myself looking down on a parked Mercedes.

Realizing that this must be the car Vince and his two mutts had come here in, I feared for a moment that they might spot me. But fortune favoured me once again, because there was no sign of the three men. Then I heard voices, and realized that they were looking for me down below and that they'd left the headlights of the Mercedes on to help them in their search.

Crouching and moving cautiously at first, I dashed down to the road. From there, I could see that Vince and his mutts had gone along to the part of the ravine where the gradient was gentle enough to make it safe to walk to the bottom, and they were descending the incline.

Figuring they were best left to continue their futile search alone I set off towards the Merc, and I heard the engine running well before I reached the vehicle. The fat man had obviously left it running when he'd turned the lights on, in order to avoid running the battery down. That being so, I figured the key must be still in the ignition, in which case the door couldn't be locked. I tried it and it opened, so I climbed in behind the wheel. Thanks, buddy, I thought, and turned the key in the ignition. The engine growled nicely. I slipped her in gear then brought up the clutch and I was away.

The three mutts down below must have known what had happened straightaway, of course, as soon as the headlights stopped shining over the area of the ravine they were in the process of descending. But it would take them a few minutes to get back up to the road; and when they got there, they'd find themselves short of a car. 'Hard luck fellas,' I said aloud, as I put my foot down.

CHAPTER 18

When I got back to Bardino I dumped the Merc by the train station. A glance at my Swatch told me it was ten past three a.m. It had been quite a night. My ribs were hurting like a bastard as I set off for my flat on foot and I was soaked to the skin, but I was still alive and that was the important thing.

The street was quiet and my footsteps echoed as I approached the door to the building; then, as I took the key out of my pocket and slipped it in the lock, I saw in the glass door the reflection of a car pulling up at the curb behind me.

I kept a close eye on the reflection of the car as I turned the key, then I went inside. Perhaps I'm being a little paranoid, I thought, but I'd already been taken for a mug once that night, and I wasn't in any hurry to be caught out again. So, figuring it was better to be safe than sorry, I crossed the tiled lobby and, instead of going up the stairs to my flat, I left the building by the back entrance. Then I doubled back and, peering round the corner, I saw the car still there only now the driver was getting out. I watched him go over to the front entrance to the building. If Vince had sent him—he would only have needed to call one of his boys on his mobile, after all—then he would try and pick the lock, I figured. But he didn't. Instead he studied the names on the console at the side of the door, then he pushed a buzzer. I waited to see what happened. Nothing did. Either the person he was calling on wasn't in, or they weren't in a mood to talk. Few people would be at this late hour. Maybe the man's wife has locked him out, I thought. Only I didn't recognize his face, and I'd seen enough of it in profile by now, courtesy of the light from the streetlamps, for me to do so if he lived in the building. So perhaps the man was calling on his girlfriend, then, I thought. Whoever it was, the other party wasn't interested. It hadn't failed to occur to me that the other party might well be yours truly.

Moving quickly but taking care to be as quiet as possible, I set off and came up behind the man. I wasn't carrying and there was always the chance he might be—in fact, he certainly would be if it was Vince that had sent him over—so I figured it would only be sensible to take every precaution. I gave him the old stiff finger in the back and said, 'Better not move, pal. It's loaded.'

'Don't shoot,' he said, sounding terrified.

'Tell you what, pal, we're gonna play a little game. You tell me who sent you over here and who you've come to see and why, and if it sounds kosher you get to carry on breathing. How's that sound?'

'I'm a journalist,' he said. 'I work for *La Vanguardia*.'

'Likely story.' I knew the newspaper he claimed to be working for had its offices in Figarillo and served the region of Catalonia. That was the best part of a ten-hour drive away.

'No, it's true, honestly...but what's with the gun?'

'What's your name and who are you calling on?'

'Javier Fontana's the name, and I've come here to speak to a man by the name of Arthur Blakey. Works as a private investigator.'

'Funny time to be calling on him.'

'It's kinda important.'

I hooked a foot round the man's ankle and shoved him in the back. He tripped, so that he fell against the glass door, using his hands to break his fall. As he did so, I kicked his other foot out from under him and he bit the concrete. I didn't want to take any chances about him getting up again, so I kicked him in the jaw. And scored with a knockout.

That gave me the chance to go through the pockets of the light grey suit he was wearing. I didn't find a gun, but I did find the man's press card. So he really was a journalist. And his name really was Javier Fontana. Seems it's not only my line of work that comes with certain risks attached, I thought, as I slapped the guy about the chops to try and bring him round.

Then his eyes opened. 'Where am I?' he wanted to know.

'You've taken a trip down south, pal,' I told him. 'You're in sunny Bardino.'

'Oh yeah...' That seemed to register with him. 'And who are you?'

'Name's Arthur Blakey—Art to my friends.'

'Rings a bell.' He felt his jaw where I'd kicked it. 'Ouch.'

'In a little pain, huh?'

'Feel like I've been trampled by a giant rhino,' he moaned. 'Think my jaw might be broken.'

'You took quite a tumble, mister.'

'What happened, exactly?'

'You slipped.'

'No, I didn't.' It was coming back to him now all right, and his eyes flashed with anger. 'You held a gun in my back and then you hit me.'

'Sorry, didn't mean to.'

'How can you attack someone by mistake?'

'Thought you were someone else.'

'But I told you who I was.'

'Sure you did,' I said. 'Only I didn't believe you.'

'Kinda suspicious, aren't you?'

'You would be if you'd been in my shoes a little earlier.'

I could see I'd got his interest now. 'Why, what happened to you?' he asked.

'More a question of what *didn't* happen.'

'Okay, what didn't happen, then?'

'I didn't get fed to a shark in some mutt's swimming pool by a whisker,' I said. 'And I didn't get shot in the head and then have my dead body thrown down a ravine, either. Just missed out on all that by the skin of my teeth.' I considered the statement I'd just made and then decided I ought to qualify it a little. 'Actually I only missed out on the first two of the pleasures I just described.'

'Huh?'

'I took a tumble down a ravine,' I explained, 'only I just managed to avoid getting shot first.'

'I still don't follow.'

'Never mind, it's a long story,' I said. 'Let's just say I had my suspicions that someone who doesn't like me sent you here.'

'This would be the guy who didn't feed you to the shark in his swimming pool, I take it?'

'It would.'

'And would it also be the guy who nearly shot you and threw your dead body over a ravine?'

'That was the two goons he has working for him,' I said. 'But you get the picture... I can see you learn fast. You should go to night school. No saying how far a bright young man like you might go.'

'Who's the guy who wants you dead?'

'One Vicente Caportorio,' I said. 'If you've never heard of him he's a gangster with something of a rep down in this part of the world, and it's a rep he's earned by being a thoroughly vicious savage.'

'I get the picture.' He winced and touched his jaw where it hurt.

'Sorry I hit you so hard.'

'I guess you had a reason.' There was a thoughtful expression on the man's face as he turned his head and looked at me. 'So what did you do to get up this Vince guy's nose?'

'I tried to ask his girlfriend a few questions.'

'Obviously not a man who thinks it's good to talk.'

'You have a nice line in humour, my friend,' I said. 'Carry on like that and you might end up as a private investigator.'

'Since when did private investigators need to have a nice line in humour?'

'Didn't you ever read those Philip Marlowe novels?'

'Never got into Chandler, I'm afraid,' he said. 'Faulkner's more my bag.'

'It's gone three in the morning and here we are talking literature,' I said. 'How about I invite you in for a coffee?'

'Sounds like an improvement on a blow to the back of the head.'

I opened the door and pressed the timer delay light switch, then made my way up the stairs. I kept my eyes peeled while I was about it, just in case, but I didn't run into anybody on the way up who was waiting to give me a nasty reception. And a quick check round the flat, once we'd got in, didn't reveal any of Vince's mutts, either.

'Nobody waiting in the bathroom or behind the bedroom door with a gun, then?' Fortuna said. 'That's a relief.'

'Sure is,' I said, 'although it's always possible they just haven't shown yet.' I went over and double-bolted the front door. 'Things are looking up,' I said. 'Now if only I wasn't out of coffee...' I looked at the hack and saw that he was still feeling jaw on his head where I'd hit him. 'It was coffee you said you wanted, right?'

'Only if you haven't got anything better.'

'What's your idea of better?'

'Scotch, if you have any.'

'You're right,' I said, 'Scotch would definitely be better.' It usually is, I find. 'Won't be a minute.' I went into the bedroom and found some clean underwear and a tracksuit and changed into them, before I returned to the living room and began to search for the Scotch. I found the bottle in the drinks cabinet over by the wall, but to my dismay it was empty. I was still feeling bad about having roughed the man up, and wanted to make amends by giving him the drink he'd asked for. Then I remembered I'd gone to buy some more and left the fresh bottles in the larder. 'Hang on a second,' I said.

When I returned with the bottle and two tumblers, moments later, I saw that my guest had fallen asleep on the sofa. I wondered for a moment whether I should wake him and tell him I had his Scotch, but then figured it would probably be best to leave the man in peace and let him stop the night where he was. It was the least I could do after the way I'd roughed him up earlier. So I set the tumblers down on the table, along with the bottle, and poured myself a stiff one, then I slumped into the easy chair and took pecks at the Scottish treasure while I watched Fontana get his beauty sleep. If he could write half as well as he could snore then I reckoned he ought to be up for a Pulitzer. I knocked back what was left in my glass and got up to give myself a refill. I was feeling a little sorry for myself and tetchy and like Scotch might just have the answer to my problems. I'd been in this sort of mood before many a time, and somewhere there were the empty bottles to prove it.

I struggled up out of the chair, with all the inelegance of a man who's been dangled on a rope as shark bait and thrown down a ravine; a man whose ribs were probably broken and who should really go to see a doctor about it. I figured the doc could wait until the morning. I went into the bedroom and worked off my shoes. They were lace ups and so I had to sit on the bed to do it, and it proved to be a tricky task. Shoeless, I lost the rest of my things and climbed gingerly between the sheets. It was agony lying on my right side, so I figured I'd better turn over. I did it in the end, but it was painful and felt like one of those operations that involve cantilevers and cranes and lots of cables. Okay, maybe I'm exaggerating a little. Maybe I like to exaggerate a little, but I'd had a tough night.

I fell asleep immediately and dreamed that I was escorting somebody down a street. Then a car pulled up and I realized that the two men in it were about to start shooting at me. I hid behind a parked car, but fell on my side and fired only for water to come out. Damn it if it's not a bloody water pistol I'm holding, I thought, and realized on the instant that I was done for. Only somehow the water pistol changed, in the mysterious way such things can come about in dreams, into a proper gun. I fired twice and got the two thugs who were after me.

Then I woke up.

CHAPTER 19

The sun was peeking through the gap in the curtains, and I realized that I was aching like a bastard all over. Then I recalled the events of the night before and figured it was no wonder my body had known happier awakenings.

A glance at my Swatch told me it was coming up to ten in the morning. Time to get up. I didn't much fancy the idea, so I bribed myself with the thought of coffee and a croissant. It was only as I stepped into the living room, en route to the kitchen, that I recalled I'd had a guest staying the night and, wondering if he'd left yet, I looked over to see if he was on the sofa. He was.

And he wasn't about to leave in quite a while.

Not until somebody carried his body out, anyway.

I went over to take a look at him. Just to check my eyes hadn't deceived me.

They hadn't.

He'd been strangled. His eyes were staring up at me with a terrible fixity, and he had turned a decidedly unhealthy shade of pale. I say 'he', but of course it was just a body now. The man who'd once been Javier Fontana had long left it behind.

I laid the back of my hand against the forehead. It was still warm, so the murder couldn't have taken place very long ago. Fortunately there was no blood anywhere, as you would expect, given the nature of the murder.

Whoever had done it couldn't have made much noise coming in, I thought, and he must have attacked Fontana when he was asleep, because I didn't hear a thing.

I went over to the door, to check the lock. It was still bolted. So how did the killer get in? I wondered. Then I saw that the barred iron door that gave onto the balcony was open. Had I not locked it the night before? I couldn't remember doing so. But then, I couldn't remember having opened it, either. And I normally always locked it before going out.

Maybe Fontana opened it in the night, I thought. But why would he do that? I went out onto the balcony and took a look around. A mug had been left on the tiled floor by the side of the lounger. I looked and saw that there was still some tea in it, cold now, of course. On the small table, a packet of Chesterfields had been left along with a silver lighter. The lighter wasn't mine and I don't smoke Chesterfields. Fontana must have woken up and felt restless, so he'd gone out onto the balcony for a cup of tea and a smoke. Then I supposed he'd gone back inside, to take another crack at getting off to sleep and left the door open. And whoever killed him must have climbed up from the garden onto the balcony. It wasn't that far up. The willow tree that conveniently covered my bedroom window, so that I could go around naked with the curtains open if I wanted to of a morning without the neighbours seeing me, would have helped the killer. He could have climbed the tree and then jumped from the branch that was nearest to my balcony. I'd been meaning to tell the man who tended the garden to cut the tree down a little, too, because I suspected it of being a haven for mosquitoes.

I wondered what to do next, and considered calling up Sal Cobos and telling him what had happened. The idea bounced around the walls of my cranium for all of a second or two, before I rejected it. I might know Sal Cobos and chew the cud with him from time to time, but I didn't want to overvalue the stock I had with the man. Not that he's a bad sort or anything. In fact, Sal's a pretty decent all round individual as cops go, but that doesn't mean he isn't still a cop, and I'm sometimes liable to forget that. And sometimes I'd do well *not* to forget that. And I reckoned this was one of those times.

I turned the matter over in my head some more for another minute or so. As I was doing this, it occurred to me that the cops might be on their way here any time now. Because it was a sure bet whoever killed Fontana called the murder in. It seemed to be the way things were working round here just lately.

I had to get rid of the body. But how? It was easier said than done, after all. Was I going to leave the building in broad daylight carrying Fontana's body in a fireman's lift? Somebody would be sure to see me.

Thoughts were buzzing about like a nest of mosquitoes in my head, and I was trying to make sense of them. No, I couldn't just go down in the lift with the body over my shoulder. So what should I do? I realized that I'd better come up with some ideas fast, before the cops showed. But my mind was a blank. Come on, man, I chided myself; you're supposed to be expert at this sort of thing: making dead bodies disappear and then catching the killer, without the cops being any the wiser. I cursed myself and then I cursed Inge Schwartz. Then it came to me right out of the blue, what I had to do.

I left the flat and used the spare key Mrs. Hopkins had given me to let myself in next door. Mrs. Hopkins is a very nice old English lady who lives alone, has done ever since her husband Michael passed away some six years ago. I had been in the habit of calling in on her from time to time, just to check she was all right and to ask if there was anything she wanted or if there were any odd jobs that might need doing. That explains why she'd given me a spare key. Whenever I went to the supermarket I'd usually buy some groceries for her and I'd use the key to let myself in, if she was out or sleeping when I called, and leave the things I bought in her kitchen. Today was different, though. I hadn't done any shopping for her, and I was hoping she was either sleeping late or out.

I opened the door to her bedroom and heard her snoring away. Then I found the wheelchair that her son used to take her out, when he came over from England. If I were quick then she wouldn't even notice it was gone, I thought, and I left with the wheelchair and returned to my own flat. I found a couple of baseball caps and two pairs of shades, then lifted the body and dropped it into the wheelchair. I slipped the hat and shades onto the dead man, then I put my own on, before I positioned the body so that he was sitting up.

Next I went through the dead man's pockets and found his driving license. I figured his car must be parked nearby. It was just a case of finding it. I considered leaving the body here, and going out in search of Fontana's vehicle. It was a navy-blue Seat Ibiza that he drove. Hardly an uncommon car in this part of the world. But I had the reg, so it shouldn't take me too long to find. Fontana must have parked nearby, after all. Yes, I'll do that, I decided, and had just opened the front door when I heard a police siren.

Realizing there was no time to waste, I dashed back inside and wheeled the body out, then hurried to the lift. I pushed the button and had to wait for the lift to come down. The sirens were getting louder. My heart was pumping hard and loud in my ears. The lift was here. I opened the door and wheeled the body in. It was quite a squeeze, but I managed to get in with him. Then I took it down to the ground floor. A little bell chimed as the lift came to rest. I pushed the door open then wheeled the body out. The police sirens came to a sudden halt, and I realized the squad cars were outside the building. I headed out through the back exit.

A uniform came dashing over, having just emerged from a squad car. 'Morning, sir,' the man said breathlessly. 'Do you live in this block?'

'I do indeed.'

'Did you hear anything unusual earlier or in the night?'

'No, I can't say I did,' I said. 'Why, has something happened?'

'It's all right, sir. Nothing to worry about.'

The man went on into the building through the back entrance, leaving me to go on my way. I was sure he wouldn't recognize me later on. He'd have looked at me and seen a guy in shades and a baseball cap pushing another guy in a wheelchair. That's all he'd be able to tell his superiors, assuming he thought it worth mentioning that he'd spoken to a man as he was leaving the building. I felt confident that I was in the clear as I set off for my car, which I'd left parked up one of the side streets that lead from the *rotunda* or small circular island that the block was built upon, having abandoned my original plan which was to take the dead man's vehicle

Having found my Porsche, I opened the doors then took a quick look around to make sure the coast was clear. It was, so I lifted the body into the back and sat it up. The head fell backwards and, realizing that it looked odd that way and might attract the attention of other motorists, I pulled the body down so that it was slumped in the chair. That's better, I thought. Looks like he's asleep.

I folded the wheelchair and put it in the boot. I looked up the street. There were no coppers in sight. Makes sense, I thought. They're all busy looking for a body back at my place.

When they don't find it, they'll probably think it a little odd, I thought. Then they *will* find it, only later and somewhere else...which they'll no doubt think is even odder.

CHAPTER 20

I headed up into the mountains, pulled over by the roadside somewhere beyond Mirjarvo and dumped the body down a ravine. Then I headed back to Bardino. I travelled by the more rustic or scenic route. The roads were narrow and there was a fantastic view from this height down over the coast and out to sea. Not that I was in any mood to be enjoying sea views right then.

Back in the *pueblo*, I parked in the exact same spot I'd left my car in earlier, then headed down to the Café Sevilla on Calle Zaragoza. I had the Colombian waitress, Marta, serve me with orange juice, with coffee in a glass and a toasted roll with tomato and garlic mix in a dish. I scooped the tomato onto the toasted roll with a spoon, then spread it with a knife and poured olive oil on it, in the local style. I read *El Bardinado* while I ate my breakfast. There was nothing about Fontana, my dead journalist friend. Well there wouldn't be yet. It was still too early. I'd have to wait until the evening edition, or else for tomorrow's papers for that. There was an account of the fight I'd had with the charming Vince the night before. The journalist could not be sure as to the cause of the fight. Vince had been sitting with a lady friend, talking peacefully, until yours truly had shown, it said. Then I must have said something or other that Vince took exception too, and the fight broke out. Friends of Vince had got involved, and I was last seen being bundled into a blue BMW. The reg was not known. The said car had set off at speed, so that onlookers had needed to jump out of the road sharpish to avoid being hit. Nobody had any idea where the car was headed. I had not been seen since.

Who was littering my path with corpses and why? I asked myself.

I had no idea. All I knew for sure was that people had suddenly formed a habit of falling dead wherever I was, or wherever I was about to go. I'd been walking on razor blades ever since Inge Schwartz came waltzing into my office that day trailing a breeze of perfume and a storm of sex appeal with her that Strauss would have sold his right hand and the rights to *The Blue Danube* to get to grips with. But she couldn't be trying to set me up, could she? What would she get out of that? What would be the point of it?

It didn't seem to make any sense. My mobile started to buzz and purr. I reached into my jacket pocket and took it out. 'Hello?'

'It's me.' She sounded anxious. 'I need to see you.'

'What's happened?'

'I can't talk over the phone.' Call me Mystic Meg if you like, but somehow I'd just known she was going to say that.

'In that case, I'll see you in my office in ten minutes.'

'No, I think someone may be following me.'

'Where, then?'

'In the lobby of the hotel Las Palmeras.'

'Okay, I'm on my way.'

We hung up.

CHAPTER 21

It was only a short distance, so I decided to go there on foot. I walked up to the corner, took a right down to the main road and crossed over. As I did so, I began to get the feeling I was being followed. I headed up the main road, then stopped for a moment and looked in a shop window. I was looking to see the reflection of the mutt that was following me. There. He stopped a little way behind me and looked in a window. Nice one. I entered the shop, which turned out to be one of these all-purpose Chinese stores. I took a tour of the place and checked out the quantity of pots and pans and notepads and diaries and all the other cheap junk in the shop, then came back out and there was the guy who was following me waiting just along the pavement. He was trying hard to look casual. So hard that casual was the last thing he looked. Just to devil the guy, I set off back the way I'd come and then turned the corner to see if he was coming after me. He was. I entered a newsagent's and bought a copy of *El Bardinado*, just for something to do. Then I headed on down to the seafront. As I walked, I took out my mobile and called Inge. 'I'm being followed,' I told her.

'Who by?'

'Dunno yet, but I'm curious to find out,' I said. 'Guy looks like a cop to me.'

'Be careful.'

'You almost sound concerned about me.'

'You are working for me, after all.'

'It's kind of reassuring to know your interest is purely economic. Keeps things simpler that way.' If anything could ever be simple where the likes of this woman was concerned.

'Stop fooling around with me,' she told me off, and I have to confess that a part of me loved it. 'I've got something important to discuss with you.'

'Yes, well I'm on my way, but I may be a little late,' I said. 'That's why I'm calling.'

'You need to shake him off, you mean?'

'Exactly.'

'Make sure you do,' she said.

Then hung up.

I went up to the curb then glanced over my shoulder as I crossed the road, to see if I was still being shadowed. I was. So I cut into the arcade there, at the side of the shoe shop, then ran to my right, past people sitting on the terrace of a café, then took a left and hid round the corner. Peering round the wall, I saw the man come past the café. He was looking from side to side, clearly worried that he'd lost me. I hurried along the narrow road that crossed the arcade, and concealed myself behind the next corner.

Trouble was, I could no longer see if the man was coming after me. Then I noticed that the clothes shop nearby had doors either side of the corner. I entered the shop, sure in the knowledge my shadow couldn't have seen me, then made a show of looking at some T-shirts. I had my chin down, in case the guy happened to glance in through the window, but I was able to keep an eye out for him at the same time.

Perhaps he went the other way, I thought.

But no, there he was.

I let him go past the window, then left the shop through the other door, so I was now behind him. He was short black hair, about five-ten, but stocky, dressed in jeans, white Adidas trainers and a blue sleeveless shirt. That's what I could tell just from looking at the guy. But I was a lot more interested in what I *couldn't* tell that way. Who had sent him, for instance?

There was another cafe up on the next corner, and I figured the tables outside it might come in handy for what I had in mind. I drew level with the man just as we reached the café and shoved him sideways, and he fell over a chair and brought a table down on top of him. As he tried to get up, his face full of fury, I stamped on his hand. He cried out and tried to push himself up on the other side. This time I kicked his wrist. He cried out again.

By now the waiter had come out wanting to know what was going on. When he saw that I was stopping the guy who'd been shadowing me from getting up, he threatened to call the police. 'Go ahead,' I said. Then the owner of the place came out. I know the man. Not well, but I stop by for a drink in his café from time to time, and whenever I do we'll chew the cud about this and that. He's a Londoner, married to a Spanish woman, Rita. Likes to talk to me about the old days, when he used to run a bar in Soho. He looked at me. 'Arthur,' he said. 'The fuck's going on here?'

'What I'd like to know, Steve,' I said. 'This guy seems to think he's my shadow...been following me everywhere I go.'

'Has he now?' Steve, a balding man in his late thirties, beer belly, tats, looked at me like he understood the situation I was in and was on my side. 'Want me to call the cops?'

'I am a fucking cop, you idiots,' said the shadow.

Steve looked at the man, then he looked at me. I looked at the shadow. 'Some ID might come in handy,' I said.

'I could show it to you, if you'll only stop kicking me.'

'Easy does it,' I told him, and took out my gun.

'You got a license to carry that thing?'

'You bet.'

'You'd better put it away,' he said. 'I've already told you I'm a cop.'

'And I heard you, but I haven't seen any evidence yet.'

He reached into his trousers and brought out a leather pouch, opened it and held it up. I wrested it from the man's hand and took a good look. 'Very nice,' I said.

'So can you stop the fun and games and let me get up now?'

'Sure.' I put my gun away, and helped the man to his feet. But no sooner was he up than he punched me in the gut. The blow took me by surprise. Not only that, but it hurt. I doubled up and must have grunted with the pain. As I did so, I felt something hit me again and I went flying backwards over a table.

It must have been a pretty good punch, because when I came round

I was being helped into the back of a squad car. 'You saw it all, Steve,' I shouted over my shoulder.

'Too fucking right I did, Arthur.'

'I'll need you to come to the station,' I shouted. 'That way they'll have to let me out.'

That was all I had time to say, because the bastard who'd knocked me out pushed me into the back of the car. 'What the fuck is this?' I wanted to know.

'You'll find out,' the beefy bastard said.

'You can't arrest me. I haven't done anything wrong.'

'You assaulted me, for a start. Then you threatened me with a loaded gun. You could be looking at going away for a nice little stretch, amigo.'

'You were following me,' I protested.

'Just doing my job.'

'But there was no way I could've known you were a cop...And I helped you to your feet, once you showed me your ID.'

'That's your story,' Plod replied. 'And anyway, I'm a police officer and you...' He flashed me a nasty wink. 'Well you're not.'

'What were you following me for, anyway?'

'You're a suspect in a murder case,' he said. 'Hadn't you heard? In three murder cases, in fact. Rumour has it dead bodies have a thing for you, seem to like to follow you about. Not so much love as *death* at first sight.'

'I'm a private investigator,' I replied. 'Somebody obviously doesn't like the heat I'm putting on them and wants to cause trouble for me. Hadn't that occurred to you, *agente?*'

'Seems like this person who wants to cause trouble for you's succeeding, *amigo.*'

Very funny, I thought.

'Look,' I tried once more, 'I'm on the same side as you are...'

'I'm a policeman and you're a wannabe...take my advice and study for your *oposiciones,* you want to be a proper cop.'

Seeing that I was getting nowhere, I figured the best thing to do was shut up. So I did.

The cuffs were tight and hurt like a bastard, but I wasn't about to complain. I didn't want to give the two men the satisfaction of telling me it was my own stupid fault for getting myself arrested. Because I knew that's what they'd say. It's probably their favourite line.

CHAPTER 22

The cell they put me in had blood and shit on the walls. The décor was nothing particularly new or *avante garde* where I was concerned: I'd seen it before more times than I cared to recall. Even so it was less than pleasant. The pillow was filthy, and there was nothing to read or look at. Nothing to do but pace the small cell, or lie back on the bed and think. I couldn't even look into the corridor, as the two sets of thick bars were designed so as to make it impossible to see through them to either side.

I'd been in a cell like this before, of course, and so it wasn't really such a big deal. But it was irritating all the same, and I felt frustrated and impotent, powerless. Which I suppose is how I was meant to be feeling, because that's the whole point of putting somebody in a cell.

I was in there for the best part of the day, and then my lawyer, Carmen Gordano, finally showed. Carmen is tall, slim and kind of elegant in a quietly terrifying sort of way; but far more important so far as I'm concerned, she's sharp as a whip. Once I'd explained to her what had happened, she arranged for us to go up and have an interview with Sal Cobos. Sal had mellowed a little since the last time I'd spoken to him but not so much that he wasn't prepared to stick up for his colleague. 'I dunno what you expect, Arthur,' he said. 'You punched a police officer and then proceeded to kick him and stamp on his hands, so as to make it impossible for him to get up... Then you brought out a gun and threatened him with it.'

'He was following me,' I said. 'And I have witnesses who can vouch for the fact that I helped him up once he'd shown me his ID. Then he punched me twice, and knocked me out with the second one.'

'You're getting soft, Arthur.' Sal grinned. 'Whatever's happening to you? I remember the days when you used to be able to take a punch.'

'I object to the way you're addressing my client, Inspector Jefe,' Carmen said. 'He isn't some punch bag that your officers can use for boxing practice. He's a victim of assault by a police officer, and you're treating it as a joke which makes it worse.' She played her part so well that you could almost feel the gravity of the situation weighing you down. 'Quite frankly, I'm shocked to find that this is what you and your force have come to,' she went on. 'I'd like to know what the Minister in charge of this sort of thing would make of it.'

Cobos's eyes nearly left their sockets at the mention of the Minister. Good old Carmen, I could have placed a hand either side of her head and planted a smacker of a kiss on her lips at that point. I do like a strong woman. Particularly when she's my lawyer and I'm in a mess that she's trying to get me out of.

'I'm sorry,' Cobos said. 'It's just that Arthur and I go way back.'

'That doesn't give you the right to treat him with the sort of familiarity you'd ascribe to a doormat.' Carmen's outrage was on the point of going viral. 'That's the kind of logic men use to justify themselves when they launch physical attacks upon their wives.' While I'm not totally sure that I enjoyed playing the role of the abused 'wife' in this cozy little scenario that Carmen was working up, I had to give her full marks for theatricality and verbal wizardry. She was a true master of her trade: a bullshitter *par excellence*.

CHAPTER 23

I listened starry-eyed as my heroine of the hour, my cavalry and my Zorro said, 'My client has witnesses who can vouch for the fact that he was attacked, and I really must insist that he be released immediately.'

Sal Cobos held up his hand. 'Okay, okay,' he said. 'Maybe the officer played a little unfair, but nobody likes to get punched and kicked.' Cobos sat back in his padded swivel chair, frowned, tented his fingers. I sensed that he was all out of ideas and merely trying to recover from the whirlwind of words he'd just been subjected to, courtesy of Carmen, and that he was merely pretending to ponder the situation. I could almost have felt sorry for the man, if I'd been so inclined. But I didn't and wasn't.

'So I take it I'm free to go, Sal, right?' I said.

'For now,' he said.

I got up and made to leave, along with Carmen.

'Oh and Arthur,' he called to me, as I got to the door. 'Try not to let any more dead bodies show up around you, will you? It's getting more than a little difficult for me to call the dogs off.'

I tried to think of *something* to say in response; something that would give me the last word and cut Sal dead, but nothing sprang to mind. I was tired and my mind was a blank. So I just turned and went on my way.

I retrieved my things—my mobile, keys, wallet—and signed for them; then, on the way out, Carmen asked me if I wanted to press charges. 'What for?' I asked her.

'Assault, unlawful arrest, abuse of police power, and whatever else we can cook up...'

I laughed.

'What's so funny?' she asked me.

'I'm a private investigator.'

'So?'

'A dick can't take the cops to court.'

'If he's got witnesses he can.'

'They'd soon find a way to put me out of business.'

'But if you've really got a solid witness, as you say you have, you'd win.'

'You don't understand,' I said. 'Cops are sore losers. It gets to go with the cop mentality. Besides there are lots of them, and there's only one of me. If I won my battle in court, I'd soon find myself in a never-ending war with only one loser—yours truly... No, it would only screw things up for me all the more.'

'You're your own worst enemy, do you know that?'

'I should do by now.'

'What does that mean?' Carmen asked.

'I lost count years ago of how many people have told me that same thing.'

'The people who told you it were right, Arthur,' she replied. 'They were trying to get you to look out for your own interests.'

'Look, Carmen,' I said, 'you're a great lawyer but–'

'You don't want me to do my job.'

'You've already done it...you got me out of the cell, and that's all I wanted.'

I kissed her on either cheek and thanked her again, and then I went out.

CHAPTER 24

There was a warm balmy breeze blowing up, and it felt good to be out in the open air and free to enjoy the rest of the evening after having spent the best part of the day banged up.

I walked along for a bit, then crossed over and zigzagged my way down to Tahiti, a bar I sometimes use on the seafront. I found myself a vacant table, sat at it, and listened to the boom of the Mediterranean and smelt the salt sea air. I studied the drinks menu and considered trying a Mind-blowing Orgasm, but the conservative in me won the day and I went for a Manhattan instead. It went down well – so well, I had the pretty Spanish waitress bring me another, and I had just sipped it when my mobile began to ring. I took it out. Surprise, surprise, I thought, when I saw who was calling. 'What's up this time?'

'I need to speak to you,' she said.

'Well I don't recall trying to stop you.'

'There's no need to take that tone with me.'

'What tone would that be?'

'There you go again,' she said. 'It's like you want to poke fun at me.'

'Well the feeling's mutual, I'm sure.'

'And what exactly does that mean?'

'You have been leading me on something of a wild goose chase of late, I seem to recall.'

'Look,' she said, 'I'm paying you to work for me...or I thought I was.'

'Oh you've paid me all right. But not enough for what I've had to go through to earn it. I've been required to allow myself to be framed for three murders, and I've been dangled head first into a swimming pool inhabited by a hungry great white shark. I've been shot at and accused of murder by the local police and thrown in a cell... Now the way I see it, Inge, I think we could say you've been getting your money's worth, don't you?'

She hung up. As I figured she would. Her type always does. But then she called me back again a minute later. As her type also always does.

'The matter, I said, your temper get the better of you?'

'I just don't know how you can seem so nice at times and then be so abominably rude, like you were just then.'

'If some of the things I've been through happened to you, Inge, then I'm sure you'd be a little rude, too.'

'Okay,' she said, 'maybe you've a right to be a little angry... But everything has its limits.'

'You're too right it does Inge, and right now one of the things that's reached its particular limit is my patience.' I hung up, just for the sheer pleasure of being the one to do it.

She called me back immediately.

'What?'

'How dare you hang up on me?'

'You hung up on me first,' I said.

'Do you always act like this with women?'

'Act like what?'

'Do whatever the woman does?'

'No, only sometimes. Why—where's the problem in that, anyway? Men and women are equal nowadays, haven't you heard?'

'We're equal, but that doesn't make us the same,' she said. 'If I put my lipstick on, does it mean you're going to put some on, too?'

I laughed and said, 'As we were saying a moment ago, Inge, everything has its limits.'

'I need to talk to you.'

'So go ahead and talk.'

'Not over the phone,' she said.

'And what's this about a Rembrandt?'

'What?'

'One Vicente Caportorio seems to be under the impression you own one, and he wants it.'

'Where are you?'

'Do you?'

'Yes, but I'll explain about that when we meet up. Where are you?'

I told her.

'Don't go anywhere. I'll be there as soon as I can.'

So I stayed put and waited. I finished my Manhattan and ordered another while I did so. I was halfway through it when she showed.

She was wearing a peach-coloured dress that showed off her figure to perfection. The slender waist and full bust. Boy oh boy. But that wasn't all. She walked with the easy rhythm of a cat and she had about her the slightly haughty air that is common to beautiful women. It's hard to say what it is exactly. Something about the way she held her head so erect, on the long slender stalk she had for a her neck. *You can look but don't think you can touch* was the general gist of the message she gave out. 'Take a seat,' I said.

She looked as though she were unsure as to whether she ought to, but then she parked herself on the plastic chair. She fixed me with a serious look, her eyes two blue gems, cold but beautiful. 'You're sure we're not being watched?'

'Not to the best of my knowledge.'

She looked at the glass I'd just held to my lips and said, 'How many of those have you had?'

'Is that any of your business?'

'I can't see why I shouldn't be able to take an interest in whether or not you're sober, seeing as I'm paying your fee.'

'I'm sober enough.'

'You would say that.'

'I'm the one who's doing the work, right?'

She battened her eyelids and gave me a school-teacherish look. 'If you say so,' she said.

'I say so.'

'Okay,' she said, 'there's no need to raise your voice.'

'What's all this about a Rembrandt?' I asked her in a quieter voice.

'It's true,' she said. 'I inherited one.'

'What do you know about this guy Vince Caportorio?'

'Who?'

'He's a gangster.'

'I can assure you that I've never mixed with types like that.'

'Well he knows who you are, and what's more he knows you own a Rembrandt and he sounds as though he's very interested in finding out where you're keeping it.'

'I'm in rather a frightening situation right now.' She brushed a few stray strands of hair out of her eyes. 'I feel as though you're the only person I can depend on, Arthur.' She gave me the old up-from-under look. She'd probably practiced it on a thousand and one other guys before she'd got to me, but somehow that didn't matter. 'I can depend on you, can't I?'

'Of course.'

'You can be rather sweet at times,' she said. 'When you want to be.'

Something turned over in my chest again, and I knew I had to fight against it.

She took a quick glance around, as if she half expected that she were being watched. Which she was, of course, but only in the way that a girl who looks the way she looked can never go anywhere without being watched.

'How about you finish your drink and pay,' she said, 'and we take a little hike along the seafront.'

'Sure.'

I knocked back what was left in my glass and signaled to the waitress and paid my bill. Then we got up and set off.

CHAPTER 25

We crossed over, and walked along by the wall that separates pavement from beach. She walked quickly, with her chin up and I could hear the heels of her court shoes beating out a fierce tattoo as we moved along. She was frowning, too, I noticed, like something was eating at her.

'Has something happened?' I asked.

'You could say that.'

'Well are you going to tell me?'

'Let's go somewhere a little quieter.'

We walked right to the end and crossed the modern bridge they've built there that goes over the canal. There were children down below in the water riding with their parents in little paddleboats shaped like swans and ducks. To the side of the canal there was an outdoor café, and further up there was a small play area with a roundabout and swings. We crossed the bridge and went past the old castle, which had recently been restored so as to serve as a tourist attraction, and it wasn't until we'd passed the new hotel, with its domes and minarets all done in the Arabic style, that she led me down onto the beach. It was almost deserted at this hour, although I could see a young couple sitting down by the water's edge.

'I think we're alone now,' I said, 'so if you've got something to tell me I think you'd better hurry up and get it off your chest.'

'I don't know what to do, Arthur.' Her voice sounded brittle, like it was about to break into a shriek.

'Do about what?'

'They've got her.'

'Who has?'

'If I knew the answer to that I'd tell you.'

'You mean you've got evidence that Gisela's been abducted?'

She nodded and then the next moment she threw herself on me, and I held her close and smelt her jasminey scent. Maybe she was full of lies and was taking me for a fool, but even so I felt at that moment like I was prepared to go to the ends of the earth for her. I would be her St. George and do battle with the dragon, if that's what she wanted. 'Do you always offer your clients this kind of service, Arthur?' she sighed.

'Not usually,' I whispered in her ear.

'So what's different about me, then?'

'You're not my usual kind of client.'

'How come?'

'You're more gorgeous than the rest of them.'

'Is that all it is?'

I didn't know and I didn't care. I gazed deep into her eyes, that were black in the reflection of the moon, and then I kissed her on the mouth. She didn't seem to be bored or show any signs of wanting me to stop, so I just carried on. When we finally came up for air, I realized that it wasn't just the sound of the sea and the stars and the balmy breeze and her jasmine scent that had got to me—although I'm sure all of those things provided a helping hand—but there was more to it, a lot more. I was hooked on her, whether I liked it or not. And if I were honest with myself, then I'd have to admit that right now I liked it. I liked it a lot. Why, I'd even stopped calling myself a fool, which was a really bad sign, I know. But there you are. I'm not the first guy to fall for a gorgeous girl, and I sure as hell won't be the last. If I was an idiot, then I was no more of one than a long list of other guys. Of course I had this thing about wanting to appear tough. It was part of the image of the job, I suppose. And a part of me couldn't see how my slavering over Little Miss Butter Wouldn't Melt like a puppy that has just got its mitts on its first bone fitted in with the tough guy role I was playing. Although it wasn't as simple as that, either; because I'm no weed. I mean, I don't like to boast, but I really *am* a pretty tough sort of guy. It's just that I've got my weak spots, I guess. And Little Miss Butter Wouldn't Melt here had found them all.

I made an effort to pull myself together. 'You were telling me about Gisela,' I said.

'Yes,' she sighed.

'But you don't know who's taken her?'

'No.'

'Somebody's been in contact with you, though?'

She nodded and buried her face in my lapel. I felt her body judder and heard her sobs. 'She's been kidnapped.'

CHAPTER 26

I wondered if Vince Caportorio might be behind this recent development. Right now, he was my star suspect on a list of one.
'It's okay,' I said. 'I'll get her back for you.'
She lifted her head and looked at me. 'Will you really, Arthur?'
'Yes.'
'Promise me.'
'Cross my heart and hope to die,' I said.
'Oh Arthur,' she sighed. 'I'm so lucky to have found you.'

I wasn't sure what to say to that. In fact, I wasn't at all sure that I could make good on my promise. How could I be, after all? But she needed reassurance, and nothing good ever comes from acting as though you lack confidence.

She gave me her up-from-under look again. 'I can trust you, Arthur, can't I?' she said. 'I'm mean, you're not just spinning me a line, to make me feel better, right?'

'No, of course not.' I was going to get her sister Gisela back if it was the last thing I did, even though I had no idea how I was going to do it. 'I need you to tell me everything you know.'

She dried her eyes with the backs of her hands. 'I'm sorry if I've appeared to be a little...emotional.'

What was I meant to say in response to that? Was I supposed to forgive her for bringing me to this lonely part of the beach and throwing herself on my neck, and then letting me kiss her the way I had?

'You must think I'm a perfect fool,' she said, looking away in the direction of the breaking waves.

'Why do you say that?'

'I've behaved like one and we both know it, so there's no need for you to deny it, Arthur.' There was something rather quaint about the way she said my name. Although I suppose Arthur is a pretty old-fashioned sounding moniker. If you shorten it to Art it can sound kind of with-it and funky. But Arthur is old school. It's black-and-white movies and high tea with scones. It sounds rather prim and faintly ridiculous, I've often thought.

She gave me the benefit of her up-from-under look again. 'Well don't rush to my defense, will you?' she said. 'Just because I say you don't have to deny it when I say I've behaved like a perfect fool doesn't mean you have to take me at my word.'

I laughed.

'My sister has been kidnapped and you think it's funny?'

'How about we give the amateur dramatics a rest, Inge, and you tell me what you know?'

She slapped my cheek. It stung a little.

'I hope that made you feel better?' I said.

'It did. But only a little.'

'You're a feisty little thing under that glossy exterior.'

'You make me sound like a magazine.'

I thought she looked like she ought to be *in* a magazine, but I wasn't in a mood to tell her that after being slapped. 'So are you going to tell me what exactly the kidnapper said to you?'

'He wants something from me.'

'They usually do.'

'You needn't sound so cool and callous about it.'

'Sorry, that wasn't my intention,' I said. 'What is it that he wants?'

'A painting.'

I was having to drag the information out of her, sentence by sentence. 'It wouldn't be a Rembrandt by any chance?'

'You got it in one.'

'Do you know who the kidnapper is?'

'No.'

'It's Vince Caportorio,' I said. 'It's got to be.'

'Who's he?'

'He's a local gangster,' I said. 'I asked you earlier if you knew of him. He's the guy who wanted to feed me to a shark and sent his two mutts to kill me and dispose of my body.'

'Whether you're right or wrong about the kidnapper's identity doesn't really help us much.' She shrugged. 'I mean he's got Gisela, and so I have to give him what he wants or he's going to kill her.'

I figured she probably had a point. 'Has he told you where and when he wants the painting delivered?'

'No, only that he's going to call me again tomorrow, and when he does he's going to tell me then. But he did say I'm to have the painting with me, ready to be delivered to him an hour after he calls.'

'And do you have it with you?'

'I have it where I can get it by tomorrow, yes.'

CHAPTER 27

I looked at her again. I'd never met anyone quite like her. Not anyone who was as beautiful as her, to begin with. Or anyone who could muster up a Rembrandt, or have one handy, waiting in the wings in case of an emergency. Rembrandts are fairly rare and expensive articles, after all. This all struck me as being ridiculously outlandish, like something out of a book or film. Then again, Inge herself was like something out of a book or film - and not just any book or film, either, but an outlandish one. You only had to take one look at her to see that. 'You didn't tell me that you owned a Rembrandt,' I said.

'You never asked, Arthur... Besides, so what if I do? What's that got to do with anything?'

'Quite a lot, by the sound of things.'

'It does *now*,' she said. 'But it didn't when I first came to you... I mean, I didn't know Gisela had been kidnapped then, did I?'

'What Rembrandt is it, anyway?'

'It's a self-portrait.' When she lifted her chin and looked at me there was a pitiful expression in her eyes. 'You will help me, Arthur, won't you?'

'Of course... But what do you want me to do?' I asked her. 'Do you want me to hand over the Rembrandt to the kidnapper?'

'I don't see that we have much choice, do you?'

'No, I guess not,' I said. 'But how is it that you've got a Rembrandt in your possession?'

'It's been in the family for several generations.'

'If you're from a rich family,' I said, 'then what was your sister doing living in the Bocanazo and working in a bar on the seafront?'

'Who knows?' She wiped her nose and shrugged. 'She was trying to find herself, I suppose.'

'Why'd she come to Bardino of all places to do that, do you think?'

'Why shouldn't she come here?' she replied. 'It doesn't always have to be India that people go to, to discover their inner self, you know. Not everyone's John Lennon.'

'But even so, Bardino is the last place most people would come.'

'Well it doesn't seem so bad to me.'

'Maybe that's because you haven't been here long enough to get a good look at what goes on.'

'Everyone who lives here can't be a rotter, surely, can they?'

'Can't they?' I grinned. 'You could have fooled me.'

'Well you live here, Arthur.'

'Don't I just.'

'And you're not a rotter, are you?'

'I figure that would be a matter of opinion.'

'I certainly don't think you are, anyway,' she said and gave me the old dove-eyed look that was supposed to melt your heart. This girl knew her way around a man's mind the way a grandmaster knows his way around a chessboard. I could almost feel her fiddling with my pieces.

We both fell silent a moment, then Inge ran her hand over my lapel. 'So you will do it?' she asked.

'Make the exchange, you mean?'

She nodded.

I realized that there were only really two answers to this question: yes or no. While our thoughts and feelings can be subject to an infinity of shades of grey, to invoke the old cliché, the world of the private dick has a distinctly Manichean flavour: one elects either to act or not to do so. I was either in on this one or I wasn't. And if I wasn't then I figured I was *out*, so far as Inge Schwartz would be concerned, which is to say I'd be off the case. Now as you have probably gathered by now, I had a whole bucket-load of doubts and questions floating around in my head where Inge was concerned, but I was more than a little gone on her and so the bucket had sort of gone out the window. Besides, I wanted to follow the investigation to its natural conclusion. Right now, I was half way to nowhere and I didn't like the feeling it gave me. The fact that I could use the money was the very least of it. So there was really only one answer I was ever going to give to Inge's question. 'Sure,' I said. 'First you'll have to give me the Rembrandt, though, and tell me where to take it and when.'

'I'll let you know, don't worry. But I'll need you to be ready to drop everything at the drop of a hat.'

'No problem.'

'Thanks. You know you can be very good and nice when you want to be, Arthur.'

I felt like a little kid who's just been praised by the Sunday school teacher he has a secret crush on.

'I'm tired,' she said. 'I'm going to go and get some sleep now. Tomorrow's going to be a busy day.'

'Call me as soon as the kidnapper's contacted you.'

'Okay.'

She set off over the sand, and I watched her move in silhouette from the light of the moon, a cutout figure carrying my heart in her hands. What's that line from the poem where the guy urges his ladylove to tread carefully because it's his dreams she's walking on?

I don't know how long I stood there, but she was well out of sight before I went home and turned in for the night.

CHAPTER 28

I was woken up the following morning by the sound of my mobile ringing. I dug it out of my pocket and saw if it was who I thought it was. Then wondered what she wanted as I said, '*Hola*, sweetness.'

'Arthur, you've got to help me,' she said, sounding all breathy with excitement, as if she'd been running. 'I'm being followed.'

'Where are you?'

'I'm sitting outside a café on Calle Soroya... I wondered what the man who's following me would do, if I came and sat at a table.'

'What did he do?'

'He's sitting at a table not far away.'

'Maybe he likes the cut of your jib.'

'My jib...?'

'Well your skirt, then...'

'He doesn't look like a tailor to me.'

'You know what I meant.'

'I know what you meant, Arthur,' she said. 'But I wish you'd stop being so facetious. It's as if you like to poke fun at me all the time.' Maybe I do, I thought. But seeing as I'd been putting my life on the line for the lady ever since I'd agreed to work for her, I felt I had the right at least to engage in a little light banter. 'I'm being serious,

Arthur,' she said. 'Now are you going to help me? Or are you just in a mood to carry on making fun of me and laughing at my expense?'

I told her that I was being serious. 'You're not an unattractive little package, after all,' I went on. 'I mean, the idea may not have crossed your mind, what with how sweet and innocent you are and everything, Inge, but there could be men out there who'd take a certain pleasure from looking at you.'

'He's doing more than just looking at me, Arthur. He's *following* me, like I just told you.' She sounded nervous, too: her voice had an edgy brittle quality to it, like a violin whose strings are too taut. 'I'm convinced he's been sent by the kidnapper,' she said. 'Maybe the man's plan is to intercept me once I've gone to pick up the Rembrandt, then they won't even have to hand Gisela over, will they?'

'It's not the way kidnappers normally work.'

'I wouldn't know about that.'

'Just try to stay calm.'

'I'm trying to, Arthur. But I'm frightened.'

'Okay,' I said. 'Stay where you are and I'll come over and meet you.'

'Are you sure that's wise?' she said. 'Once this man sees you he'll know what you look like, won't he?'

'So?'

'How are you going to be able to help me, then?'

'So what do you want me to do exactly?'

'I was thinking it might be wiser if you were to go and pick up the Rembrandt for me, Arthur,' she said. 'Would you do that for me?'

'I guess so, if you'd care to tell me where it is.'

'I can trust you not to run off with it, though, Arthur, can't I?'

I laughed at that one.

'What's so funny?'

'If I were going to disappear with it, then I'd hardly tell you, now would I?'

'No, I don't suppose you would.'

We both went quiet a moment. I figured she must trust me all right and I wondered why. I mean okay, I was a private dick and I was supposed to be working for her, sure; but if I were to disappear with this Rembrandt of hers then the chances were, if I played my cards right and knew how to fence it properly, I'd never have to work again. Inge interrupted my train of thought, saying, 'I suppose it was a silly question, you're right, Arthur. But I'm nervous and frightened. I've never been in a situation like this before, and I don't know who to trust.'

'Well I'm afraid I can't really help you there, sweetness,' I replied. 'I mean you're either going to have to trust yours truly or you're well and truly screwed.'

'It would appear that way.'

'You don't sound too happy about it.'

'Would you be?'

'I really don't know how to reply to that question, Inge—except to say that I didn't get my licence to practice as a private investigator by stealing from my clients.'

'No, I'm sure you didn't, Arthur,' she said. 'But I'm equally sure that it's not every day that you have a client who asks you to pick up an original Rembrandt for her. You could run off and sell it, then you'd never have to work again.'

So she'd finally got round to considering this possibility, I thought. But of course she had. What kind of a fool did she take me for? 'Gee, you're right,' I said. 'You know, I'd never thought of that, but now you're starting to give me ideas...'

'Now you're mocking me again.'

'Sorry, but it's the line I tend to take with people who insult me.'

'But I didn't insult you, did I?'

'No...not unless calling somebody a liar and a thief passes for paying them a compliment nowadays... Although, given where we are, maybe it does.'

'What on earth are you talking about, Arthur?'

'Don't you read the newspapers over here?'

'What?'

'They're practically all at it.'

'All at what?'

'Never mind,' I said. 'So do you want me to help you, or don't you?'

'Yes, I do.'

'You mean you've made up your mind?'

'Yes, I think I have.'

'You think you have, or you have?'

'I have.'

'That was quick,' I said. 'Don't tell me, you remembered looking into my honest baby blues and knew that I was the man for the job, right?'

'Something like that, Arthur.'

'Good, well in that case, perhaps you'd like to stop taking me for a chump, seeing as I'm supposed to be working for you.'

'What do you mean by that?'

'I mean that you can cut the sweet and innocent act, Inge, because it just doesn't wash with me. It didn't wash the first time you tried it on me and it's been working a little less every time since then.'

'I really don't know where you've got your manners from,' she bit back at me; 'but quite frankly I don't think I've ever been spoken to in such a rude fashion in all my life.'

'You can blame the teachers at my old alma mater, Eton.'

'I've heard of that school,' she replied. 'Isn't it supposed to be one of the better ones?'

'So they say,' I said. 'Anyway, are we going to waste time talking about my schooldays or are you going to tell me where I've got to go?'

She went quiet for a moment, as if she needed time to consider whether or not she could trust me; or maybe she'd simply taken a moment out to powder her nose. Then she said, 'Have you got pen and paper handy?'

'Sure. Fire away.'

She gave me a set of directions and instructions that she'd clearly thought out in advance. Then she said, 'And make sure nobody follows you there, okay?'

'Don't worry. I've got a lot of experience at this sort of thing.'

CHAPTER 29

I was to go to the Hotel Belmondo on Calle Ronda, and pick up a key that she'd left in reception.

It was just a five-minute walk, and turned out to be a three-star establishment with flags hanging over the entrance. The flags seemed to confer an air of diplomacy on the place that had little to do with the ordinary running of a hotel, so far as I could make out. The man in the reception–skinny, mid-forties and wearing a purplish waistcoat with a white shirt, bowtie and not much hair on top–was reading a newspaper, and he looked up at me with a sort of studied suspicion for a moment. Then he put the newspaper down and asked me if I wanted a room. I shook my head and told him that a Señorita Schwartz had sent me over. She had left a key for me to pick up. The man nodded. Yes, he'd been expecting me. He turned and reached up to take a small manila envelope from one of the cubbyholes that covered the wall. 'Here you are, sir.'

I opened the envelope and, sure enough, there was a key inside. I thanked the man and went out in search of a taxi. It didn't take me too long to find one, and I skipped in the back and told the driver to take me over to the Bocanazo. As the cab pulled away, I looked through the back window, to see if we were being followed. We weren't. Minutes later, we pulled up outside of the building I'd been told to go to. I paid the fare, then got out and took a look around, just to check there was nobody on my tail. There didn't seem to be. Just to make extra sure, I decided to take a turn round the block before I entered the building. It was the next block along from the one I'd come to before that time, in search of Gisela Schwartz, and it was built upon the same design. There was no elevator, so I climbed the stairs.

Many of the residents were Moroccans or else from Eastern Europe: economic migrants who'd come here to try and better their lot but hadn't succeeded in doing so to any great degree so far. At any rate, it was a strange place for the daughter of a rich man to choose to come and live. And an even stranger place to hide a Rembrandt. Or maybe it wasn't so strange, I thought. Maybe Inge had figured that a rundown block in the Bocanazo was the last place anyone would look. Of course her sister Gisela had been living in the next block, but Inge assured me that nobody who knew Gisela knew about this second flat. It was a two-bedroom number, she said, and she'd only started to rent it a few days ago. Whether she lived in the place, or had just rented it for a short period in order to have somewhere to store the Rembrandt, I wasn't sure. We didn't go into details on the phone. She had been nervous and keen for me to go and pick up the painting as soon as possible.

I found the door and slipped the key into the lock. It fit. I turned it and pushed, and the door opened. So far, so good.

I had my gun in my hand as I entered the flat, and I held it up in front of me as I took a look around. I remembered what had happened the last time I'd come to the Bocanazo, and I didn't want to be caught out the same way again. I moved with the slow, deliberate, light-footed caution of a big cat as I went through the flat.

The door opened directly into the living room, and there was nobody in it. There was a sofa upholstered in caramel-coloured imitation leather, and there was a hard chair over by the window. In front of the sofa there was a coffee table, which looked like it was made of deal. There was an empty ashtray on it. The television faced the sofa, and there was one of those consul cabinets behind it. The cabinet was affixed to the wall, and took up most of it. There were a number of little knickknacks on it of the sort you can pick up for a song in the markets or the local Chinese shops.

The place smelt of dust, and seemed like it hadn't been lived in for quite a time. Maybe Inge Schwartz wasn't planning on living here after all, I thought, recalling now that she'd told me she only rented the place out 'a few days ago'. Had she rented it for the sole purpose of hiding the Rembrandt here? In many ways it might be the last place anyone would look for a priceless painting.

The flat was built on the same design as the one my client's sister had rented, in the next block along. There was a kitchen, off to the left. I kicked the door open and crouched with my feet placed well apart, and holding my gun out with both hands, ready to fire if I needed to. I didn't. There was nobody in the kitchen. It was a rather basic and gloomy oblong-shaped affair, with sky-blue painted walls. The fridge was humming away noisily.

I turned slowly to my right, and moved up the small hallway that ran off the living room. There were four doors on it, two of them closed and the other two were ajar. I kicked the one immediately to my right all the way open, and looked in at what was the bathroom. There was nobody in it. I did the same with the other doors, and checked there was nobody standing behind them, waiting to hit me with something or point a gun at me. There wasn't. I checked in the wardrobes, just to make sure, and under the bed. I wouldn't say I was paranoid, but after what happened the last time I came to this part of town I certainly reckoned it was wise to err on the side of caution.

Having satisfied myself that I was alone in the place, I went back over to the television, in the living room. On top of it there were two control units, one for the DVD player and the other for the television. I turned both television and DVD on, then I looked under the sofa and found the DVD that Inge had told me would be there. I took it out of its case and fed it into the DVD player, then pushed *Play*. The screen was full of snow for a few moments, and then Inge's face appeared. 'If you're watching this, then it's because you'll have been sent here by me. In which case, you'll be wanting to know where it is. Listen carefully.'

CHAPTER 30

I did more than listen. I wrote down the directions that she gave. Then I took the DVD out, slipped it back into its case and returned it to its place under the sofa. I turned the television and DVD off, too, figuring I might as well leave everything as I'd found it. Then I left the Bocanazo and walked back over to the block where I lived. It was only a few minutes' on foot, even though it was light years away in terms of the economic and social status of its residents and the quality of the houses and flats they lived in. I found my Porsche, climbed in and set off on the road out of Bardino. It wasn't long before I was heading up into the mountains for the village of Magro. I'd heard of the place, but had never been there. It was a forty-five minute drive along narrow, twisting mountain roads, and it wasn't the sort of place you'd want to come back from late at night after a few drinks. Make a slip and you could easily find yourself shooting off over the edge of a cliff. Goodnight, Irene. Go take the long sleep nobody wakes up from, why don'tcha?

If you had the guts to look out of the side window and the time to appreciate such things, then I'm sure the landscape was spectacular in its own dry and rugged kind of way. High up over the mountains in the distance, I could see what from the size of its wingspan must be an eagle wheel-arching its way over the landscape.

I drove with the windows down, and the sun seemed to get hotter and meaner the further inland I went. Then I got a glimpse of the village, just beyond the hill in front of me. It turned out to be a tiny affair: just a matter of a few streets converging on a main square with a church and a couple of bars and restaurants. I pulled over, then got out of the Porsche and stretched. So this is Magro, I thought. The sun bounced off the white walls of the houses and other buildings, and I found myself screwing my eyes up in a squint behind my Ray Bans. At a first glance, the village looked like an unusual location for a woman like Inge Schwartz to spend her time.

I was after number 11. It was on the main street, she said. I found the house and put the key in the door. It fit. I turned it. The door opened. So far, so good. I entered the house warily. The place smelt of dust, and you could tell it hadn't been lived in for quite a while. The curtains were drawn and so it was dark, or at least relatively so, and the contrast after the brightness of the sunlit street outside blinded me temporarily. So I stood there by the door, with my gun up, ready for anything. Anything didn't happen. In fact nothing did, which may or may not be the same thing. As my eyes gradually adjusted to the light, or comparative lack of it, I saw that I was standing in a large living room. There was a tiled floor, with a leather three-piece suite and a television and video over in the corner. The walls had all been painted white, and by and large they seemed to have stayed that way. There was a large stone fireplace and, in the recesses either side of it, floor to ceiling pinewood shelves had been fitted. The shelves were empty but for a few paperbacks.

The door in the wall off to the left was ajar. I gave it a nudge with my toe. It moved. I found myself looking in at the kitchen. Tiled floor, pinewood worktops, new-looking cooker, fridge, washing machine. Nobody in there. I opened the door to the next room, which had a large double bed in it. The bed had a metal frame with a big imitation-porcelain bauble at each corner. It had been made up and was covered with a quilt done in a floral pattern. It didn't look like it had been slept in for quite a while.

I went in and checked out the *en suite* bathroom. It was fairly big and was equipped with a shower, toilet, sink and bathtub. Nobody in there, either. I went over to the fireplace, which looked as though it had never been used, got down on my haunches and reached an arm in, as I'd been directed. Sure enough, there was a little lever in there, right at the back. It was hidden out of sight, so that you'd never find it unless you were told it was there. I yanked it, and the shelves to my left moved away from the wall. There was a little recess area with a safe in it, just as Inge had said there would be.

I played with the nob on the front, twisting it this way and that, so as to feed in the combination she'd given me, and sure enough it opened.

CHAPTER 31

I reached in and took it out, taking care to pick it up by the frame. It was covered with sackcloth, which I carefully removed, and then I found myself looking at a portrait of Rembrandt as an old man. He looked tired in the painting, beleaguered, weighed down by the quantity of junk the world had thrown at him. It was all there in the eyes. They were full of a knowing sadness, almost as though they pitied you, the viewer. They were eyes that had seen a lot of the world - too much of it, perhaps.

I heard voices outside the window. I took my gun back out of its holster, and I stood there pointing it at the door, waiting. But then the voices became less distinct, as their owners must, I presumed, have passed on up the street. I reminded myself that I was standing in a house that was situated on the main street in the village, a fact that I'd forgotten for a moment, so caught up was I with the painting I was holding in my hand and my own thoughts. It was only to be expected that people would pass up and down past the window there, but the curtains were drawn and so nobody could see in.

I told myself not to be so jumpy and put the Rembrandt back in the sackcloth, then went and peeped through the curtains out at the street. It all looked quiet enough out there, so I left the house and made my way the short distance back to my Porsche. I opened the boot and put the Rembrandt in there, then I climbed in behind the wheel and set off back the way I'd come. I hadn't gone far before my mobile began to ring. I took my right hand off the wheel and reached into my jacket. '*Hola?*'

'Where are you?'

It was Inge and she sounded anxious, uptight.

'I've just picked it up,' I said. 'Now I'm driving back to you. I left the village just a few minutes ago.'

'Good.'

'Are you still being tailed?'

'Yes.'

'Same guy?'

'He's on the corner opposite.'

'Where are you now?'

'At the hotel,' she said. 'He followed me back here. It makes me nervous, the thought of him out there.'

'And it's always the same guy that's been following you, is it?'

'Yes,' she replied. 'You don't think he could be the kidnapper?'

'No, that would be too easy. I mean, the man who's got Gisela would have to be stupid to work that way...he must have this guy working for him.' I suspected the kidnapper was Vince Caportorio and the man on Inge's tail was one of the gangster's mutts. 'Has he called you again?'

'I was going to tell you,' she said. 'He called a few minutes ago.'

'And?'

'He wants to make the exchange this evening at nine o'clock.'

'Where?'

'He's going to call me again at eight and tell me,' she said. 'I told him about you and said you'd be coming with me. He agreed to that, but said if he gets the slightest whiff of a cop the deal's off and we'll never see Gisela again.'

'Did you tell him who I am?'

'No, I just said that you're a friend of the family.'

'Good,' I said. 'Well I don't have a problem with forgetting to call in the cops if you don't.'

'I'd never be able to look myself in the mirror again if we did and the kidnapper found out and killed my sister.'

'How did you get him to agree to allow you to take me along?'

'I told him I can't drive and that I'd be too frightened to go through with a thing like that on my own in any case.'

'What did he have to say to that?'

'He said he'd kill Gisela if I didn't go along with what he said, and I said I was sure he'd kill us both if I were to go there on my own.'

'Nice negotiating style you have, Inge.'

'I wasn't aware I was negotiating anything,' she replied. 'I simply told him the truth. I don't trust the man, and for all I know he could be planning on killing me too.'

'And if I go with you then he could just be planning on making it three.'

'I suppose that's a possibility, Arthur, yes.'

I chuckled despite myself. 'You don't sound as though you're overly concerned by the prospect.'

'I'd certainly feel a lot safer if you came with me.'

'You sound like you have faith in me.'

'Right now you're the only person I can turn to,' she said. 'Besides, I'm sure you're used to this sort of thing and will know how to get us all through it if anyone can.'

'You've gone quiet, Arthur,' she said, her voice gone all husky and full of honey and smoke.

'I was thinking.'

'What were you thinking about?'

'Lots of things.'

'Was I one of those things?'

'You were lots of them, babe.'

CHAPTER 32

She let out a sort of snort that I figured must pass for a laugh in her language. 'Take the Rembrandt home with you,' she said, 'and wait for my call.'

'You're sure they don't know where I live?'

'How could they?'

'All right.'

'You don't sound very convinced, Arthur. Don't you trust me?'

I let that one go sailing by. 'You've gone quiet on me again, Arthur.'

'I said all right, didn't I?'

'There's no need to be like that.'

'I'm not being like anything.'

'So you'll go home and wait for my call, with the Rembrandt, then?'

'I said all right.'

'All I want is to get Gisela back,' she said.

'Well you should have her back before the day's over.'

'Let's hope so. I'm so anxious and worried for her right now I can hardly stand it.'

'Worrying about her won't get you anywhere.'

'I know you're right, Arthur, but I just can't help it.'

We both went quiet again.

'I can trust in you, Arthur, can't I?'

'What's the matter?' I said. 'You think I'm going to run off to Brazil with your precious Rembrandt?'

'No, but–'

'But what?'

'Some people would.'

'Yeah, well some people might do a lot of things, but I'm not them.'

'I don't think you are, Arthur, either,' she said. 'I didn't think you were the first time I set eyes on you. I just had this feeling about you, right away, you know?'

'What sort of feeling was that?'

'Oh, that you were nice and honest and straight down the line.' She paused a moment and then went on: 'You've got that nice old-fashioned way about you that some Englishmen have. I spotted that about you right away.'

'You sound as though you like the English, Inge.'

'I've always had a soft spot for them, if I'm honest,' she confessed. 'There's something wonderfully sincere and...well, straight about them.'

'Straight?' I replied. 'That's a good word.'

'I'm using it in the old-fashioned sense of course.'

'It's funny,' I said, 'but I'd always got the impression you Germans didn't like us Brits very much.'

'What on earth gave you that idea, Arthur?'

'Oh I don't know, just the little matter of those two wars you waged against us, I suppose.'

'You shouldn't let that sort of thing mislead you.'

'No?'

'That was just politics, after all.'

CHAPTER 33

'You almost make it sound like you had me down for the kind of guy a girl wouldn't mind taking home for tea,' I said.
'That's exactly what I meant, Arthur.'
'You mean you're going to invite me to meet Mutter?'
'She's dead, unfortunately.'
'I'm sorry.'
'Don't be...you didn't kill her, after all.'

I wished I'd never brought up the idea of having her take me to meet her mother in the first place. It had been a stupid thing to say. Some charmer I was turning out to be, I thought.

She said, 'I'd be happy to invite you to tea, though, when this is all over.'
'With scones and cream and fresh strawberries?'
'I know just the place.'
I laughed.
'What's so funny?'
'Nothing.'
'Well something must be.'
'This is hardly the place to enjoy high tea,' I said.
'No, but you can get it if you know where to go.'
'Like most things, I suppose,' I said. 'Why, you can even find a Rembrandt here, if you look hard enough. And I should know.'

She didn't say anything.

'How did you get it, anyway?' I asked.

'I thought I told you.'

'Perhaps you wouldn't mind running it by me again?'

'I inherited it from my father.'

'And he's dead, too, I take it?'

'Yes.'

'So how did Papa come by a Rembrandt?'

'I suppose he must've bought it.'

'You suppose?'

'I never asked him.'

'There can't be that many of them floating around in this part of the world, I shouldn't've thought.'

'I really wouldn't know.'

'You're sure it's an original Rembrandt and not a fake?'

'Of course.'

'What makes you so sure?'

'Father had it checked by experts.'

'So the kidnappers must've found out that you'd inherited it.'

'I guess so.'

We both went quiet again. In the distance, away to my right, I could see an eagle circling high up in the sky. I wondered if it was the same one I'd seen earlier, on my way up here. It must be on the lookout for prey.

Just then, I saw a huge boulder come bounding down the rock face. It was heading straight into my path. I jerked the wheel hard to the left to try to avoid hitting it, and that's the last thing I remember before my car crashed into the roadside.

At least I had the good sense to steer away from the edge, because if I'd steered the other way I'd have been a goner. And so would the Rembrandt.

CHAPTER 34

It took me a few seconds to work out where I was when I opened my eyes. Then I realized I was at home, and in my own bed. But how had I got here? I was confused. The last thing I could recall, I was driving my car. It was hot and my shirt was wet with sweat. Away in the distance, an eagle was wheeling through the sky, high up, lording it over all below like some ancient country squire of the skies. I was on the phone, talking. To Inge. Yes, that's it. I was talking to Inge. I had to make a real effort to try to think in a logical fashion. I told myself that I wasn't in my car any more. I was in bed. In my own bed, at home. Yes, I'd already established that. Had I been drunk? No. I'd been driving and I was perfectly *compos mentis*. But what about after that? What happened after I stopped talking to Inge on my mobile? Ah yes. The rock fell into my path. Yes. I'd crashed. Yes. Not that I remembered the crash itself. That was all a blank. Just the rock falling. I recalled seeing it coming down the cliff face. Recalled the feeling I had when I saw it. Recalled thinking, Oh my God, it's going to hit me. Recalled steering hard to the left. That was lucky. If I'd gone the other way, I'd have gone over the edge. I must have crashed into something. I think I may still have been suffering with concussion, because I couldn't remember a thing after that. I moved my toes, just to check they were all in place. They were. I bent my knee. That was still there, too. And it bent okay. As for the other knee, it hurt, which must mean that it was still there, too. I figured I must have hurt it in the crash. It moved, though, when I asked it to, although it did need a little coaxing. I wriggled my fingers. Everything seemed to be in place. So far, so good. But how did I get in bed, then? And how come I wasn't in a hospital? Somebody must have brought me home. And seeing as I didn't have any clothes on, except for my pants, I figured somebody must have undressed me and put me in bed. Who, though? I had no idea. I must have been knocked out in the crash, because everything after that was a blank.

I heard voices. There were people in the flat. Who? I wondered. I swung a leg over the side of the bed. That doesn't sound like a particularly difficult operation to perform, but it all depends on the circumstances, and on this occasion it cost me some, I can tell you. Next I swung my other leg over. That one proved to be easier to move. Now all I had to do was stand up. I heard the voices again. Who the hell was out there? The people who brought me here, I supposed. They'd be ambulance men, then, maybe a nurse or a doctor. But why had they brought me home instead of taking me to a hospital? Or had I been in a hospital and forgotten I'd been there?

I figured I'd better go and investigate, see who it was that was out there. I pushed myself up off the mattress and just hoped that my body obeyed the commands I was giving it. It did, by and large. Enough to get me up on my feet, anyway. I was feeling kind of lightheaded and weak, but I was standing. Looking down, I realized that I was naked apart from my underpants. What the hell, I thought, and took a step. It felt a little like walking on the moon. Not that I've ever been up there and given it a go, but if I ever do get the chance to go there for a holiday then I reckon walking on it would feel pretty much like I was feeling right then.

Just then, the door opened. My oh my. Who should it be but my old friend Salvador Cobos. Only he hadn't been so friendly to me of late. 'What are you doing here?' I said.

Sal threw me a look that was about as warm as a wet mackerel. 'I was about to ask you the same thing, Arthur.'

'It may have escaped your attention, Sal, but it's my bedroom we're in.'

'It hasn't escaped my attention, Arthur. I'm pretty observant that way.'

'Glad to hear it,' I said. 'It speaks volumes for your powers of observation. I just thought I'd mention it in case.'

He looked me up and down. 'Might be an idea if you were to put some clothes on.'

'It might,' I agreed.

Looking around the room, I saw that my clothes had been left in the chair over in the corner. I did my moonwalk over to said chair, and I can tell you that I didn't resemble Michael Jackson the slightest bit while I was about it.

'You're looking a little out of it, Arthur.'

'That's not so bad.'

'What do you mean by that?'

'If I only look a *little bit* out of it, I mean...because I feel *one helluva lot* out of it.'

'I was using understatement.'

'Irony, you mean?'

'If you'd like to call it that.'

'I thought irony was my line.'

'Must be catching,' Sal said.

'Clearly is.' I was having a fight with a pair of socks. They were only a dinky little pair of black things, but they were giving me no end of trouble. I was trying to get them acquainted with my toes and they were having none of it. I had the feeling we could go on like this all day, my recalcitrant socks, my toes and me.

'Like watching a game of chess,' Sal Cobos observed.

'What is?'

'Never mind,' he said. 'Perhaps it might help if you were to sit on the bed while you do that.'

'Perhaps it might,' I agreed.

I sat on the bed and had another go.

'You want some help?'

'That would be cheating,' I said.

He gave me a straight look. 'You been drinking, Arthur?'

'Nope.'

'What, then?'

'I was in a car crash,' I explained, 'and now I'm trying to play chess with a pair of socks ... If I can only move my rook to pawn four then it should free my little toe up with any luck.'

'Very funny.'

'You started it.'

'Perhaps you won't find it so funny if I tell you that you're under arrest.'

'Me?'

'Nobody else but us in this room, Arthur.'

'Since when's it been illegal to play chess with a pair of socks?'

'I'm not arresting you for that.'

'What, then?'

'Try and think back, Arthur.'

'Already tried that.'

'Try harder.'

I had another go, then shook my head. 'I already told you,' I said. 'I crashed the car and that's all I remember.'

'Was the girl in the car with you at the time?'

'What girl?'

'Come on, Arthur, don't try and get cute with me.'

'I'm not trying to do anything except put my socks on, Sal.'

'You're always trying to get cute, Arthur. It's the way you are.' Sal Cobos sighed. 'Think you're a cut above, don't you?'

'Do I?'

'Course you do,' he said, rolling the product of his excavations between forefinger and thumb. 'Think you're too good to wear a uniform, that it? See yourself as that English detective, no doubt. Sherlock Homes, do you?'

'Holmes,' I corrected him.

'*Eso es*.' He nodded. 'That's what I said. Sherlock Homes.'

CHAPTER 35

'What's Sherlock Holmes got to do with anything?'
'The lone genius who solves the case single handed, but not before he's tied the local gendarmerie up in knots along the way.'
'The gendarmerie are French,' I said, 'and Sherlock Holmes was English.'
'Same difference.' He shrugged. 'Gendarmerie. Policia. Polizei. Police. All means the same.'
'They call them bobbies in English.'
'If I ever want EFL lessons, Arthur, I'll be sure to drop you a line.'
I turned my attention back to my recalcitrant toes.
'Isn't it about time you grew up, Arthur?'
'Isn't it about time you got to the point, Sal?'
'I'm getting there.'
'What's that you were saying about a girl?'
'Yes, the girl...Was she in the car when you crashed, Arthur?'
'No, she wasn't.'
'So you picked her up afterwards, then?'
'Maybe she picked me up.'
'You mean she was flirting with you, is that what you're saying?' he said. 'Do you mean to say that you knew this girl from before, Arthur?'
'What girl would this be, Sal?'

'The one that you said flirted with you.'

'I never said any girl flirted with me.'

'But you just said it.'

'No, it was you that said it, Sal. I was just trying to follow your train of thought, and finding it a little tricky to do so, I must admit.'

'It's not going to do you any good, Arthur, getting clever like this.'

'Since when's it been an offence to be clever in this part of the world?'

'Look,' he said, 'your goose is cooked, so you might as well play ball now. It's the only thing to do in a situation like yours. What do you say?'

'What situation would that be, Sal? Are we talking about my not being able to get my socks on, and you watching me not being able to do it?'

'We're talking about the girl you killed, Arthur.'

'The girl, I *what*...?'

'You heard.'

'I didn't kill anybody.'

'Where did you pick her up, Arthur?'

'What girl are you talking about?'

'You said you knew her from beforehand, right?'

'No, wrong.'

'So how come she was flirting with you, then? Where did you meet her?'

'Where did I meet who?'

'The girl, you idiot. Are you drunk or something?'

'I think I may be a little concussed.'

'That figures.'

'After the accident,' I said.

'So you killed her before and put her in the car, is that it?'

'You keep talking to me about this girl, Sal,' I said, 'but I don't know who you mean.'

'Oh I think you do, Arthur.'

'What girl are you talking about?'

'The one you killed.'

'Which girl am I supposed to have killed?'

'The one who's lying on the carpet in the front room.'

'In the front room...?'

'That's right,' Cobos said. 'At least she was in there the last time I looked, just before I came in here. And she sure didn't look like she was about to go anywhere. Been murdered. Strangled, to be precise. And in my experience, Arthur, girls who've been strangled don't generally get up off the floor and leave a place. I mean, I know you might think I'm a dumb cop and all, but even I know that much.'

I could hear the words that Salvador Cobos was saying, but I was having difficulty making any sense of them. This girl, he said, where did I pick her up? Maybe she was flirting with me. Had I known her from before? This girl who was lying on the carpet?

Wait a moment. On *the carpet, did he say? Yes, on the carpet? On my carpet? None other. In the front room,* he'd said. The carpet. The one with the floral pattern. Only he didn't say that about the floral pattern. That's me thinking. That's me, trying to make sense. *Strangled.* He'd said she'd been strangled. Girls who've been strangled aren't in the habit of getting up and walking out of a place, he said. Well he was right there. It was starting to come to me. I was starting to piece it together, what he'd been saying. Starting to take the words and see how he'd connected them up. But they couldn't mean what I thought they meant. No. Sal Cobos couldn't have said what I thought he'd said. I was concussed. It was after the crash. The rock came down the cliff face, you know. Oh yes. I steered hard to the left. Good choice, that. Right was no good. Steer right and I'd have been a goner. Good night, Irene. Don't call me, and I won't call you. On the carpet, he'd said. The strangled girl. He couldn't mean that. No. He couldn't have said that. He said I was trying to play a game of chess with my socks. That was funny. He was being ironic. Not his usual style. He was learning from me. My pinky was the rook, the next toe was my knight, the middle one was the bishop; the next was the queen, then the king. Or did I say that about playing chess? So where did the sock come into it? And what about the girl? And who strangled her? And what was she doing on my carpet, in my front room? There was something about my front room lately. That journalist guy had wound up dead in there, too. On the sofa. Fontana. Somebody Fontana. Javier. Worked for *La Vanguarda.* Came all the way down here from Figarillo, to talk to me. How was it that people seemed to end up dying around me?

Just then, the sock slipped all the way up my foot. Check mate, I thought. Wait a moment, I thought. What was that about a girl again? Did I dream all that, or was it for real?

I looked at Sal Cobos, just to check he was really Sal Cobos and not just a Sal Cobos I was dreaming about. He was the real Sal Cobos, all right.

I said, 'What's been going on, Sal?'

He cocked a grey-flecked brow, and looked at me like he was trying to make out whether or not I was for real; then he said, 'That's what I need you to tell me, Arthur.'

CHAPTER 36

So they took me down to the Jefatura and threw me in a cell. It was nothing new to me, but even so I didn't feel good about being in there. Who does? The walls were stained with blood and excrement, as were the mattress and blanket.

I banged on the bars of my cell and invoked my right to speak to my lawyer in raucous terms and tones. The guard on duty outside employed similarly raucous terms and tones to tell me to shut the fuck up. So much for my human rights, I shouted back. The guard came over and peered in at me through the bars of my cell. He told me they didn't 'do' human rights here. I wanted comfort and luxury, I could go check out the Hilton. Except I couldn't right now because I was banged up. Very funny. But of course we did, I replied. Bardino was in Europe, after all. The guard begged to differ. I suggested he go take a look at a map. He suggested I go take a flying fuck at my mattress.

But in fairness it wasn't too long before the door opened and my lawyer, Carmen Gordano, was shown in. Truth is, I heard her coming. You can always hear Carmen coming. It's part of her style. Carmen has always struck me as something of a cross between Uma Thurman and Cruella Deville. I mean, she's tall and she's got these cheekbones and shoulders and legs. Today she was wearing a grey shark's tooth jacket with a matching skirt and a silk shirt and she looked uncompromisingly, indeed almost violently professional, which is to say just the way you'd want your lawyer to look if you were in trouble.

She looked at me like she'd already decided she was going to hit me and was trying to make up her mind whether to go for my glass chin or my even glassier balls. Carmen always looks at me like this when I'm in trouble. It's her way. Then she cracks this grin that she has. It's her way of letting me know that she's going to forgive me just this one more time. Never mind that she's already started charging me an hourly rate that is criminally exorbitant, right from the time she was called, and the clock is ticking. I do mind this, of course. Who wouldn't? But I know better than to let it show. I cracked a smile. It wasn't much of a smile, but it was the best I could muster in the circumstances. 'Glad you could make it, Carmen,' I said.

'I gotta get you out,' she replied, 'if it's only for the laughs. You're too cute to be locked up inside, have your ass pronged by some primate.'

'I'm so glad you appreciate my ass, Carmen.'

'So what've you been up to this time?'

'It's a long story.'

'I'm listening.'

I ran it by her, cutting the story down to the bone.

'You really *are* getting to be a magnet for corpses, Arthur,' she said after she'd heard me out. 'What's got into you lately?'

'Ask not what I'm doing following corpses, but what the corpses are doing following me.'

'Have you got into voodoo or something?'

'My ex reckoned I was capable of working magic in the sack,' I said, 'but that's about as far as it goes.'

'Uh-uh,' Carmen nodded. 'That why she left you?'

I grinned and figured I'd better take the Fifth on that one, even though I wasn't a Yank.

'You know either of the two birds that got dead in your flat?'

'Nope. Never seen them before.'

'Mm...well if you want me to get you out of this one then you're expecting a miracle, you do know that?'

'What I've got you as my lawyer for, Carmen.'

'Yeah,' she said, 'well it's going to cost you. Miracles don't come cheap, you know.'

I shrugged and she had me sit down with her and go through everything that had happened, or as much as I could remember. When I'd finished telling her, she gave me a straight look and asked me if I really expected her to believe the story I'd just told her. I said that I did. 'It's the truth, after all,' I said.

She continued to look at me, long and hard. 'The truth, huh?'

'I'm being framed by someone.'

'Tell me a little more about the client you're working for.'

I told her that my client had hired me to find her sister, who'd gone missing; but I didn't reveal her identity. Carmen asked me to name her. I shook my head. 'Oh come on, Arthur. Your ass is on the line here.'

'You know me, Carmen. It's the way I work.'

'Carry on the way you're going and you won't be working much longer.'

'I've told you everything that I can,' I said. 'Besides, what does it matter who my client is? Her identity's not relevant... I mean I'm not in here because of her.'

'So it's a girl, then.'

'I never said that.'

'You said it was a *her*, and most hers are female in my experience.'

'You just haven't been around as much as I thought, Carmen.'

'You mean it's a shemale you're working for, a lady boy, or what...?'

'No, I was just joking.'

'This is no time to joke, Arthur, if you value your ass.'

'I value it.'

'Yes, but how much do you value it?'

'Okay,' I said, 'why don't you take what I've given you and see how far you can get with it?'

'You haven't give me much.'

'I've told you everything I know.'

'Two people have wound up dead in your living room, Arthur, in the past few days, and you're saying you don't know anything about it.'

'That's right.'

'You're bullshitting.'

'I'm telling you the truth, Carmen.'

'You wouldn't know the truth, Arthur, if it snuck up and bit you where it hurts.'

'It's already bitten me there,' I said. 'And I've got the marks to prove it.'

Carmen took a deep breath, battened her eyelids and breathed a little fire down her nostrils. 'What about this gangster character?'

'What about him?'

'He hung you in a pool with a shark in it, you said?'

'That's right.'

'What's he got against you?'

'I told you, I got in a fight with him.'

'Even so, I mean that's an extreme reaction, isn't it?'

'The man's an extreme character,' I said. 'I mean he's a psycho. The sort of guy just smiling at him could get you killed.'

'Sure sounds it.' She took a moment to reflect. 'Do you think he could be behind this?'

'It's possible, I guess.'

'Have you got any proof that this guy abducted you?'

'It was in the newspaper.'

'So people saw you fighting him, and then saw you being driven away in his car?'

'Yeah.'

'Well that's something,' she said. 'But we need to connect this Sharky character to the two bodies.'

I nodded. The man in the next cell had begun to yell his head off. He was saying something about his being a gypsy and not being able to stand it being locked up. Should've thought of that when you stole the car, the officer on guard outside shouted back at him. The gypsy wanted to know how else he was going to support his heroin habit. The guard told him he should have considered all this before he started using. I had the feeling those two sweethearts were capable of going on in that way all through the evening, just like some married couples I know.

Carmen produced a pack of Camels from her Gucci handbag and lit up. She drew on it like it meant something to her. '*Por cojones*, Arthur,' she said. 'How did you manage to fuck up like this?'

I shrugged and said, 'I didn't do anything to make it happen.'

'Seems to me that there're two possible causes of all this.'

'Which are?'

'Either somebody hates you real bad and's out to get you.'

'Or?'

'You're bullshitting.'

'And I'm not bullshitting,' I said. 'I already told you that.'

'That's right. You did.'

She didn't seem like she was totally convinced.

'You do believe me, right?'

'I guess so.'

'I've never lied to you in the past, Carmen.'

'There's always a first time for everything, Arthur.'

'Well this ain't it.'

'Okay,' she said. 'I'll do my best for you, but I can't promise anything.'

It sounded pretty bad. But then, it *was* pretty bad. In fact, it was worse than that.

The door to the cell opened and two guards came in. One of them had a belly, the other didn't. The one with the belly said it was time for me to go up to the Interview room, so Carmen dropped her cigarette and stamped it out, then we went up with the guards.

CHAPTER 37

Sal Cobos was sitting at the desk waiting for us when we entered the Interview room. He was wearing a grey suit, a white shirt, the top two buttons of which he'd left undone, and the kind of expression you might have expected to find on the mug of someone like Al Capone while he was planning the St Valentine's Day Massacre. 'Glad you could make it, Arthur,' he said. 'Why don't you come in and make yourself comfortable.'

Carmen and I sat on the two upright chairs that had been set out for us. They didn't make us feel at all comfortable; but then, I got the impression they weren't there for that purpose. Carmen fixed Sal Cobos with a feisty look and said, 'My client could do without being ridiculed, Inspector Jefe.'

'Just being friendly and trying to put him at his ease,' Cobos said. 'Anyway, your client and I know each other, don't we, Arthur?'

'That's no excuse. I refuse to allow you to intimidate my client.'

'Intimidating Arthur was the last thing on my mind, I can assure you. Besides, Arthur's not the kinda guy it's easy to intimidate.'

'You're making unfair assumptions about my client.'

'Okay, okay.' Cobos showed her a clean pair of palms. 'Let's just cut to the chase, shall we?'

'By all means.'

Cobos pushed a button to set the tape rolling. He said the date into the mic, then gave the names of all present and said where we were. 'Fact is,' he said, 'as you and your lawyer will recall from the last time we convened here to discuss recent events in your life, we had a call to say we could expect to find a journalist by the name of Javier Fontana at your place, Arthur.'

'And you didn't find him there.'

'No, we didn't...but he did show up dead the same day.'

'Sorry to hear about that.'

'Sure you are, Arthur.'

Carmen Gordano said, 'The fact that somebody's called you up to say a body can be found at my client's residence cannot be used against him, as the body wasn't found there.'

'No, that's true...but another body was, wasn't it, Arthur?'

'If you say so, Sal.'

'I do say so, Arthur. And the reason I say so is that the body *was found there*. A woman by the name of Gisela Schwartz. Strangled to death. What have you got to say about that, Arthur?'

I kept mum.

'Maybe I'm a little deaf, but I didn't quite catch what you said.'

'I don't make anything of it.'

'The girl was lying dead on your sofa when we arrived.'

Carmen Gordano said, 'What made you think you would find her there?'

'We had a tip off.'

'Thereby hangs a tale,' I said.

'What does that mean?'

'What you think it means.'

'I don't think it means anything.'

'Sure you do, Sal. You just want to act like you aren't thinking it.'

'Since when you been working as a shrink, Arthur?'

'I haven't.'

'So can we cut the amateur psychiatry bullshit?'

'It isn't bullshit.'

Carmen Gordano said, 'My client was merely quoting Shakespeare.'

'Was he now?'

'The English poet and playwright.'

'I know who Shakespeare is... Now can you please stop trying to sidetrack me?'

Carmen said, 'I object to the accusation that you have just made against my client.'

'Do you now?'

'I most certainly do. My client is cooperating with you, or at least he is trying to, despite your persistent attempts to intimidate and bully him.'

Sal Cobos took a deep breath. 'With all due respect, I'm trying to get at the truth.'

'So am I,' I said. 'I think you already know that, Sal. I want to catch the bad guys, too, and I've got a long history of catching them.'

'So?'

'So you know as well as I do that I've not killed anyone, so what's with all this bullshit?'

'I'm afraid I don't know any such thing, Arthur.'

'If you don't know it then you ought to.'

Sal Cobos leaned back in his chair and tented his fingers on his belly. His eyes narrowed to slits and his lips disappeared. 'All I know for sure, Arthur,' he said, 'is the facts. And the facts are that Gisela Schwartz got dead in your place. And I also strongly suspect that Javier Fontano called into your place to breathe his last, too.'

'What you've just said about this Fontana guy is pure supposition,' I replied. 'It's fiction, in fact. In so far as the girl is concerned, I wouldn't mind betting she got dead someplace else first and was then carried to my place and dumped there while I was unconscious.'

'You got anything to back up that assertion with?'

'The person or persons who tipped you off killed her, Sal. That's why they called you—to frame me. It's so obvious a child could see it.'

Inspector Jefe Salvador Cobos balled his fists and sprang up from his chair. 'You've got some balls to be talking to me like that, Arthur Blakey.'

Carmen said, 'I really must object to the violent, intimidating and distinctly inappropriate and unprofessional tone you are using in this interview, Inspector Jefe.'

'Listen to the two of you,' Cobos said. 'I can end this interview now and charge Arthur with murder in the first degree if that's the way you want it. And I can do it if it's not the way you want it, too. I'm only trying to give Arthur here the chance to play ball.'

'But my client *is* playing ball, Inspector Jefe,' Carmen replied, in tones you could have cut your steak with. 'With all due respect, Inspector, it's *you* who isn't.'

'What he means,' I said, 'is that he wants me to confess to the murder. That's what he'd call *playing ball*.'

'To both murders,' Cobos corrected me.

'But my client is hardly about to confess to a crime or crimes that he didn't commit,' Carmen snapped.

'It'll go easier on him if he does, and you both know it.'

'I didn't do it, Sal.'

'I know.' He shook his head and let out a sigh that also let us know just how

fed up with me he was. 'You didn't do it and you don't know nothing, Arthur, is that it?'

'That's it.'

'It's way too late to be taking that line with me,' he said. 'I mean, I want to help you here, don't you understand?'

I said, 'I thought you said you were after the truth?'

'I am.'

'In that case I've told you everything I know.'

'There's something you're not telling me,' Cobos objected. 'Either you killed the two victims or you're covering for someone. Whichever it is, you're going down if you don't open up and tell me what you know. I need you to give me something, and whatever it is it'd better be good because this is your last chance, Arthur.'

At that moment, the door opened and a plainclothes officer—five-ten, lean, short brown hair, black jeans and short-sleeved white shirt—entered the room. Without looking at me or Carmen Gordano, he came over to the table and whispered something in Sal Cobos's ear. Sal nodded slowly when he heard what the guy had to say, and he bit his lip and frowned. It looked like whatever it was he'd just heard had given him plenty to think about. And he didn't seem to be enjoying the process, either, judging from his expression. His eyes peered out at me through their curtained lids with a smoky ferocity. If he could have sentenced me to a stint of spontaneous combustion there and then, I'd have been nothing more than so much smoke and dust.

'Is that all?' I asked.

'Yes, it is.'

I'd hardly been expecting to hear him say that. 'You mean that I can go?'

'Yes, you're free to leave.'

I stayed where I was, as if gummed to my chair.

Cobos said, 'Didn't you hear what I just said? You're free to go.'

'What's it all about?' I asked.

Carmen was on her feet. 'Come on, Arthur,' she said. 'Let's get out of this place. You heard what the man said. You can buy me a glass of Chablis someplace.'

I was too curious to leave my chair right away, or to take my eyes off Inspector Jefe Sal Cobos. 'But what did that man say to you when he came in a moment ago, Sal?'

'It really is ironic, do you know that?' He mustered a sour grin. 'You go to all these lengths to keep your client's identity a secret, even allowing yourself to be banged up and face being charged with murder, and then she just comes waltzing in here and spills the beans.'

'Who does?'

'Why your client, of course—Inge Schwartz.'

'What did she say?'

'She said that you're not the man who killed her sister, for a start.'

'That was nice of her.'

'You think she was only saying it because she likes you?'

'No.'

'Because if she was lying then you can tell me, Arthur.'

'No, she was telling you the truth, Sal.'

'But you sounded surprised.'

I shrugged. 'Just because a thing's true, it doesn't mean you can't sometimes be surprised when you hear that someone's told it like it is.'

'You don't exactly sound as though you trust your client, Arthur.'

'I didn't say that.'

'Just a cynic by nature, that it?'

'What else did she tell you?'

'That she employed you to look for her sister who'd been kidnapped, and that you'd been hit on the head. She reckoned the kidnapper or kidnappers must've killed her sister someplace else first, then broken into your flat and put her on the sofa there. She says you were with her all evening, and seeing as we know that the time of death was last evening it seems like you're probably in the clear for the time being.'

'For the *time being*?'

'That's right,' Cobos said. 'The woman could be lying, so you're still a suspect, but I've decided not to arrest yet.'

'Did my client tell you who kidnapped her sister?'

Sal Cobos shook his head. 'Said she didn't know...that's why she employed you, right?–to try'n find out.'

'That's right.'

'But you didn't find out, did you, Arthur?'

'No, I didn't, Sal.'

'Mm...well either that makes you a liar or a private dick who failed to get his man.'

'It makes me the latter.'

'Which ain't good, Arthur.'

'No, good it sure isn't, Sal, but it's better than being a liar.'

'I'd agree with you there.'

I got up and made for the door. Carmen followed me. Just as we were about to go out, Sal said, 'Arthur, if you ever find out who did kidnap Gisela Schwartz you will tell me, right?'

'You're the first person I'll call, Sal,' I said, and with that Carmen and I left the Jefatura.

It was good to be out in the street again. It was hot and sunny still, despite the fact that it was coming up to 9 p.m., and I was a free man once more. Things could have been a lot worse. I turned to Carmen and said, 'Seems like I got lucky.'

'Seems like you did, Arthur.'

CHAPTER 38

As I walked something kept gnawing at my conscience. I felt like I'd screwed up and owed Inge big time. Not only had I lost her priceless Rembrandt original but I'd also failed to find her sister Gisela—until the poor girl had shown up dead on my sofa of all places. Then Inge had taken pity on me and got me out of jail, after everything I'd done—or failed to do, rather.

I figured the least I could do was return the fee I'd charged her. I called her number several times, but she didn't pick up. I figured she must be angry with me all right. Not that I could blame her.

Having reached the building where I live, I went in and started up the stairs. I was so tired by now that my feet felt like lumps of lead. I reached into my pocket and brought out the door key as I headed along the landing, and I'd just put it into the lock when I heard something—or some*body*—move behind me. I turned and found myself looking at Inge Schwartz.

'It's you,' I said.

'Who did you expect, the Boston Strangler?'

'Not exactly...he's been dead for years.' She took a step towards me. 'Look, I wanted to give you back the fee I charged you.'

'That's very gallant of you,' she said. 'Maybe somebody ought to tell you that nobody returns fees they've earned nowadays. That sort of thing went out with Philip Marlowe.'

'Inge, I screwed up big time and I feel bad about it.'

'Don't bust your balls crying over spilt milk, mister.'

'Was that all your sister was to you–spilt milk?'

'I loved Gisela, but now she's gone. And beating yourself up about it's not going to bring her back.' She let out a heavy sigh. 'Besides, you didn't kill her, even if you're talking like you think you did. On the contrary, you did everything you could to try to find her.'

'Then there's your Rembrandt.'

'Yeah, well I wanted to talk to you about that. Maybe if you'd like to invite me in?'

'Sure,' I said. 'Be my guest.' I turned and opened the door, then held it for her before I followed her into the flat.

'Make yourself comfortable.'

'I'm not in that kind of mood, Arthur.' She stood very close to me there just inside the doorway, next to the coat stand, and the irises of her eyes were blue as the sea. 'I think you're honest, Arthur, and that's a quality I value in a man.' Her voice was throaty and husky, full of smoke and honey.

'If you're trying to massage my wounded male ego then you needn't bother.'

'Do you expect me to say sorry to you, after everything that's happened, Arthur?'

'No.'

'What then?'

'Oh I don't know.' I could smell her jasmine scent and it was playing jazzy scales up and down my spinal cord. I took her in my arms and kissed her on the mouth. When I finally came up for air, she buried her face in my lapel and began to sob. I ran my hand through her hair and said, 'Inge...' That was all I could manage. She straightened up and dabbed at the corners of her eyes with a small handkerchief she'd produced from her pocket, then she said, 'I need you to find the man who killed my sister.'

'I'm not sure I can do that.'

'But you can at least try, can't you?'

'Okay,' I said. 'I'll give it my best shot.' I reckoned it was the least I could do.

'And if you happen to turn up the Rembrandt while you're at it then I'll pay you well for your trouble.'

143

'I'll only charge you my usual fee plus expenses.'

'But I insist on offering you a little commission, Arthur.'

'I can't take it. If I do find the Rembrandt then I'll only be getting back what I lost, is the way I see it.'

'You didn't lose it exactly, though—rocks fell into your path. You might have been killed.'

'You paid me to deliver the Rembrandt over as ransom, and I failed to do.'

'But has it occurred to you that the kidnapper didn't want you to deliver it?' she replied. 'I mean, it had to be him who took it.'

'That possibility had occurred to me, yes.'

'The way I see it, Arthur, it's more than just a possibility.'

'Maybe you're right,' I said. 'And if you are then the kidnapper never had any intention of handing Gisela over alive.'

'Exactly.'

'What I'm wondering is how he found out where I was.'

'I have no idea, Arthur. You're the detective, you tell me.' Inge reached into the rose-coloured jacket she was wearing and brought out her purse, opened it and took out a wad of fifties. 'Here,' she said, 'this should keep you going.'

I took the clump of money and looked at it. I had no idea how much was there, but it was certainly a tidy sum and much more than I felt I had earned. 'Keep it,' I said.

'No, I want you to have it, Arthur. You're a pro, right?'

'I like to think so.'

'So act like one,' she said. 'And you can start by putting the money I just gave you into your wallet. I don't like to work with amateurs. They give me the willies.'

I did as she said. As I was putting my wallet away, she made for the door. 'I'll be in touch,' she said, 'and good luck.' With that, she opened the door and went out.

So I was back on the case. Not that I'd ever really left it.

CHAPTER 39

Right now I had about as much juice left in me as a bunch of dried out grapes, and I felt like all my pips had been surgically extracted. I found the bottle of Scotch and poured myself a large one, then sat in the easy chair and did some hard thinking about the case. I wondered how the kidnapper had found out who and where I was.

Of course Inge had told him she would be bringing me along to swap the Rembrandt for her sister, Gisela, but she hadn't mentioned my name. She'd just said that I was a friend of the family. Obviously the kidnapper hadn't bought her story and had done a little digging around of his own. Whoever he was, the guy was clearly one step ahead of Inge and me.

I took a drive down to the morgue and spoke to Pedro Morante, the doctor who'd performed the autopsy. Morante's medium height and build and was wearing green chinos with yachting loafers and a short-sleeved shirt. He's in his mid-forties and has a calm and methodical manner. I treated him to breakfast in the local café, and he told me what he knew about Gisela Schwartz and the manner of her death. He began by telling me she'd been a fine specimen of womanhood, and what a shame it was when a beautiful young girl like that gets killed. Then he told me that Gisela Schwartz had died as a result of asphyxiation due to strangulation. Forensics had not found any foreign prints or DNA of any kind on the body. He realized that the body had been found on the sofa at my place, but there was nothing to suggest I had killed her—beyond the circumstantial evidence inherent in the fact he'd just described. I was pleased to note this, but assured him I'd never had any reason to fear the contrary might be the case, given that I had not in fact killed the woman. I had been hired to try to find the girl, I explained. Well I'd sure done that, Morante said. That I had, I agreed, although sadly I'd arrived on the scene a little too late. Ideally I should like to have found her *before* she was killed. Ideally that would indeed have been a better outcome all round, the doctor agreed. He was very calm and methodical in his speech, as he was in his manner of eating and drinking. Watching him bite into his ham roll, I half expected him to take it apart first and give its constituent parts a thorough inspection. He didn't, though. He merely chewed and gazed across the bar as if he were rather sad and bored by the way the day was turning out.

I finished my beer and paid the bill before I thanked Morante for his help and took my leave of him. I wondered what my next move ought to be as I walked back to my car. I still hadn't come up with an answer by the time I'd started up the ignition, so I just cruised around the streets of Bardino for a time and hoped that something would occur to me. The sun went down while I was driving and the lights came on, and I began to wonder about Vince Caportorio and what he got up to when he wasn't feeding people to his pet shark. Perhaps he was behind all this. He was bad and mean enough for the job. Not only that, but he'd expressed a definite interest in ascertaining the whereabouts of the Rembrandt the last time our paths had crossed, so he had to be a prime candidate. In fact, right now he was the *only* candidate on my list.

I went and parked across the street from his bar and kept watch on the place, figuring he'd probably show sooner or later. I wasn't quite sure what I was going to do when he did, but I figured I'd think of something. I usually do.

I'd been waiting there for the best part of an hour when who else but Sal Cobos showed. He tapped on the window and when I buzzed it down he said, 'I thought I'd find you here, Arthur.' He sighed to add a little dramatic effect to what he had to say and went on: 'Anyone else, anyone with a head on their shoulders that's to say, would have enough sense to leave Vince Caportorio and his people well alone. But not you.'

'I suppose I just didn't get the proper kind of schooling.'

'That's not what I heard about you,' he replied. 'I was told you come from money.'

'I wouldn't go that far.'

'The rumour is the school you went to's about the poshest there is.'

I grinned at him and he asked what was so funny. 'I didn't figure you for the type to be impressed by that sort of thing.'

'I'm not, Arthur,' he said, 'and you can wipe that silly smile off your face.'

'I'm a happy sort of a guy, Sal.'

'You won't be for very long, if Vince and his mutts have another chance with you.'

'That's between me and Vince.'

'Yes, I suppose it is,' he agreed. 'But you might like to know that Vince is planning on spending a quiet night in with his ladylove.'

'What makes you so sure of that?'

'We've got men outside keeping an eye on his place, and he had his driver go and pick his girlfriend up earlier and take her to his. He only does that when he's not going out anywhere.'

I considered what Cobos had just told me for a short while; then I looked at him and said, 'How's the investigation into Gisela Schwartz's death going?'

'We've got a few interesting leads, Arthur.' He peered at me like I was something under a microscope. 'Thing is, most of them seem to lead to you.'

I figured this was my opportunity to come back with some witty riposte, but for once I was lost for words. Finally I said, 'I think you know that I didn't kill the girl or the reporter or those other two, Ribera and Gross, Sal.'

'I think what I always think where you're concerned, Arthur.'

'What's that?'

'You're not telling everything you know,' he said. 'And the stuff you're telling's not worth knowing.'

I glanced at my wristwatch. I was tired and Vince was having a night in, so there didn't seem to be much point in hanging around outside of his place. 'Oh well, Sal, I'd love to be able to sit and talk like this all evening,' I replied. 'But I've been working hard lately and sleep's been short on supply, so I think I'll call it a day.'

Sal said, 'Take care nobody breaks into your place and dies on your sofa while you're asleep tonight, Arthur.'

CHAPTER 40

I dreamed that night that I was swimming in the sea. The tide was going out and I was heading back to the beach, and it was hard going. Then I spotted a fin sticking up out of the water, and my heart started to pound away in my chest. Maybe it's a dolphin, I thought, but I knew it was a shark. Then it began to come towards me. All I could see was the fin moving through the water very quickly. I figured my only chance was to try and punch it on the nose. Then I woke up with a start. I wondered where I was for a moment, and then, when I realized I was at home, I breathed a sigh of relief. I told myself I was a fool for dreaming about having a shark come after me, because everyone knew you didn't get sharks in the Med.

I was feeling clammy and thirsty, so I got up and went out into the kitchen, where I poured the tap and let it run a little. Then I filled a pint mug and drank it all down in one, before I went back to bed. But I lay there tossing and turning for what seemed like ages. My mind was too full of the case to let me sleep. How did the kidnapper know I had the Rembrandt when I went and retrieved it from the house in the village for Inge? Hadn't I taken great care to ensure that I wasn't being followed?

The same question kept going round in my mind, and I kept coming up with zilch for an answer. Then I figured it might be worth taking a drive back to the spot where I'd been when I last had the

Rembrandt. I could remember the rocks coming down the mountainside into my path, and that was it. Everything was a blur after that. But maybe if I went back there, it might help me to recall what happened. It was a long shot, but right now all I had was long shots or no shots at all. And the former were better than the latter.

I looked at my wristwatch: 6.30 a.m. If I left now then it would be light by the time I'd got there. So I had a quick breakfast of toast with olive oil and coffee, then went and found my Porsche. It wasn't long before I'd left Bardino behind me and was climbing up into the mountains. I drove with the windows down, and the scent of the scorched land wafted in as I went along. Then I found myself looking down over the *pueblo* from above. It was like a jewel laid out on a bed of satin, and beyond was the large vast darkness of the Mediterranean.

I reckoned I could remember how to get to the village all right, so I gave my GPS a rest and drove from memory in the hope that it might help me to recall the day I'd gone there. And sure enough all sorts of memories began to come back to me as I drove. I remembered going into the house and finding the Rembrandt. I remembered leaving the house with it, and thinking everything was cool. Certainly I hadn't thought I was being followed. By now the sun had come up, but it was still quite cool, although I was sure it would be hot later in the morning. A road sign told me that I was just some eight kilometers from Magro. I was eager to get there, for some reason, even though I had no reason to be confident that I'd turn up anything worth a bean once I did. But that's the way I am. I tend to work on instinct a lot of the time. Sometimes my instincts are right and sometimes they're wrong, but I'd be nowhere at all without them. It's not the sort of stuff they teach them in the police academies nowadays, I know, but that's never bothered me. I thought of Inge Schwartz, and how beautiful she was. And how good holding her in my arms and kissing her the night before had made me feel. I realized that I'd been thinking about her in that way quite a bit of late. But what guy wouldn't get to thinking that way about a girl like her, if he knew her? I was only human, after all.

Then I came to the spot where I'd had the accident. If 'accident' is the right word, I thought. Because I still wasn't sure about that. It was what I'd come here to try and find out.

I pulled over and got out of the car. To my right, there was a small metal barrier where the road curved, and I found myself looking down on the ravine that lay in wait for the hapless driver. The barrier, which only stretched some four or five metres, had clearly taken a few knocks, which was hardly surprising because it was a sharp corner. Turning away and looking back up the road, I recalled driving along here. I recalled how hot it had been. Recalled seeing the rocks falling from the cliff face to my left, and then jerking the wheel to avoid crashing into the barrier and possibly through it and going on down to what would have been certain death in the ravine below. After that it was all a blank.

I crossed the road and a great stone boulder that jutted out of the rock face caught my attention. There seemed to be something familiar about it, and I concluded that it might well have been the last thing I'd seen before I crashed. Somebody must have been waiting for me on the side of the road, I thought. But I couldn't recall having seen anyone.

Or there was another possible explanation, which was that the person or persons who'd taken the Rembrandt hadn't been waiting for me at all, but rather had come to my aid in the first instance. Presuming that was what had happened, they could have set about trying to help me and then decided to rob me when they saw that I had a Rembrandt in my car. It was certainly true that times were hard over here right now, and nowhere was the pinch being felt more than in this part of the country, in the small mountain villages, where work was so scarce as to appear to be out of fashion. If this theory was correct, then whoever it was that found me might have seen me as easy pickings. Somebody from the city who drove a flash car and possessed all the things they wanted but had no way of acquiring. Could that have been what happened? I wondered.

It was possible, I supposed. Somehow I didn't fancy this idea, though. It seemed too haphazard, too much of a coincidence. And I've always hated coincidences. I've seen too many of them over the years that just haven't added up. Coincidences that ultimately turned out to be anything but; seemingly chance occurrences that long hours of toil finally led me to conclude were in fact part of a carefully conceived plan engendered by some ingenious criminal. And as if I'd needed any more confirmation where this theory of mine on coincidences was concerned, I only had to reflect on the habit of following me about that dead bodies seemed to have acquired lately.

I looked up above, half expecting to see a huge boulder come crashing down the slope towards me. But there was no sign of any loose rocks being about to fall upon me, or into my path, today. The question was, whether the rocks that caused me to crash had fallen, or whether they were given a helping hand.

I followed the road on round the corner. From there it climbed back on itself, and I walked on up until I was able to look down upon my car where I'd left it by the roadside. If someone had been waiting for me to come back along the road, ready to ambush me by hurtling rocks down the cliff face into my path, then this would have been the perfect spot for it. I pushed at a few of the boulders that were jutting out of the cliff face. They refused to move an inch, and I was sure an elephant couldn't have caused them to budge. Perhaps they brought some rocks with them in the back of a car or truck and offloaded them into my path, when they saw me coming along the road, I thought. Was that possible? Sure it was.

But presuming somebody had been up here waiting to ambush me, I was still no closer to discovering the person's identity.

The sun had definitely clocked on for work by now, and I was feeling its effects. From now on the day would just get hotter and hotter, and it would stay hot until sundown. It must be easy being a weatherman in this region. If only my own job were half as straightforward. I was angry and frustrated, because somebody had taken me for a fool. And whoever that somebody was, they had my client's Rembrandt and were no doubt looking to sell it. I reckoned that might not be such an easy thing to do, though, in these parts. The list of potential buyers would be severely limited by a number of factors, the way I saw it. For a start, few people had the kind of money the thief would want to sell it for. And presuming people did have that kind of money, then they were likely to be put off by the thought that they'd be buying stolen property. Popular myths with regard to art thefts being carried out to order for criminal billionaires were very often just that. And you couldn't very well go hawking a stolen Rembrandt around town.

These thoughts bucked me up a little, so that I began to feel that I might be down but I was not yet out. I wandered along the road, looking down over the ravine as I did so. I was on the lookout for something, only I didn't have any real idea as to what that something might be. So much of detective work is going through the motions, doing the things that you know you're supposed to do, and looking in the places you know you're supposed to look, and feeling all the while you're about it that you're most probably wasting your time; but you do it even so. You do it because you have to do something. You do it because you never know. Because just when you think you're never going to find something, you can sometimes chance upon a vital piece of evidence or information. I'd been here a thousand and one times before. Not here, up on this particular road and looking down over this particular ravine, I don't mean, but working on a case where I was all out of leads and found myself searching places without really knowing what I was looking for. I was feeling frustrated and bored and angry, all at the same time, if that's possible—which it must be. I kept thinking about poor old Rembrandt, and how he'd got mixed up in all this, all these years after his death.

Then I spotted something down there, lying on a shelf of rock, on the very verge of the ravine. I hunkered down to take a closer look, careful as I did so not to overbalance and take a tumble, because if I did that then it would be the last tumble I ever took. It was a book of matches. I picked it up and looked at it. The book was empty, which no doubt helped to explain what it was doing here. There was a black unicorn on the cover set against a red background. I flipped it over and saw that the name of a bar was printed on the back: BAR LOPEZ. The address was written in small print below: 297 Avenido Diego Farol, Figarillo.

Neither the name of the bar nor the address meant anything to me. I don't know Figarillo very well. I'd spent a weekend there once, and could remember a few street names and certain images but that was all. How much can anyone ever hope to see in a single weekend, anyway? And it had been a few years ago that I'd gone there.

I dropped the empty book of matches into the plastic bag, then tied the end and put it in my jacket pocket. Then I straightened up, and went back to walking up and down the roadside, on the prowl for anything that might have been discarded there. Any innocent little articles, which might or might not turn out to be every bit as innocent and innocuous as they looked.

But there were none, so I headed back down the slope and round the corner to where I'd left my car.

CHAPTER 41

Before heading back to Bardino, I figured it might be an idea to check out the village of Magro a little.

I parked on the main street and climbed out and took a wander, until I came to a bar and went inside. It was a dark cavern of a place, so that I had a job to see anything upon first entering and had reached the tin-covered bar by the time my eyes had adjusted. The bar was empty save for a group of three old boys at the other end of the counter. It was hardly the sort of place you'd associate with a Rembrandt. Not even a stolen one.

The barman–a man in his fifties, standing at around 165 and with short black hair, a ruddy complexion and a round belly–came over and asked what he could get me. I said I'd have a Cruzcampo. When it came it was nice and cold, so that there were beads of moisture on the side of the bottle. I took a swig. It was just what the doctor ordered.

'Nice *pueblo* you've got here,' I said to the barman.

He smiled. 'Yes, I like it well enough.'

'It always this quiet?'

'Pretty much...not a lot happens here.'

I took another sip of my beer.

'You come to live here or just visiting?'

'Just passing through,' I said. 'A friend of mine has a place here.'

'Oh?'

'Inge Schwartz,' I said.

'I know her.' The man nodded. 'Pretty girl.'

'Yes, *muy guapa*.'

'I haven't seen her here for a long time,' the man said. 'Is she still living with Jaime?'

Jaime? Who was he? I wondered.

'I'm not sure if they were married or not.' The man squinted as though he were making an effort to remember. 'The house they used to stay in when they were here belongs to Jaime's cousin. They would come for a week or two and then you wouldn't see them for a while.'

I had another swig of my *cerveza*.

'They used to like to go skiing in the Sierra Nevada, I seem to recall.' The man gave me a curious up-from-under look. 'So what brings you to these parts, then?' he asked. 'Not come in the hope of finding Inge here, have you?'

'As a matter of fact,' I said, 'I was here yesterday and something unusual happened to me.' I studied the man's face closely, to see how he reacted. Whether he looked surprised or like he knew what I was about to say. But his expression didn't appear to change at all. Either he had no idea who I was or why I was here, or he was the greatest loss to the cinema or the Secret Intelligence services since Mata Hari lit out. 'I was driving along the road out of the village, you know.' There was only the one passable road, and you had to drive up the mountain a little way and back on yourself before it curled round and began to slope down. 'Anyway, I was just approaching the corner up there when a number of rocks came bounding down from the cliff face into my path. I jerked the steering wheel hard to the left, which was all I could do, and that's the last thing I recall... Perhaps you heard about it?'

'Yes, I heard something about it.' His ruddy face creased in a jovial drinker's grin. 'Still, you managed to survive it all right, I see.'

I nodded slowly, still observing him closely. 'Guess I got lucky,' I said.

'I should say you did...could've went the other way'n gone flying down the ravine.' He smiled. 'You'd done that'n you'd have been a goner.'

'Yes.' I carried on watching him, trying to make up my mind whether or not his comments were meant in all innocence. 'So what did you hear about it, then?'

'Just that someone'd crashed up there, like you said.'

'Nothing more?'

'I heard that nobody was seriously hurt.'

'What else?'

'Nothing else.'

'You sure about that?'

The jovial smile left the man's face as fast as a drunkard being expelled from a pub at closing time, and a confused sort of frown took its place. 'Not sure I follow your meaning,' he said.

'I just wondered if you heard anything else about it?'

'No...well I already told you I didn't.' He flashed me his suspicious up-from-under look again. 'Why, what was it that happened that I didn't get to hear about, then?'

'I crashed into a stone boulder on the roadside up there,' I said, 'and lost consciousness. Then when I came round, sometime later, I found that I'd been robbed.'

'No.'

'*Si*,' I said.

'What did they take? Nothing valuable, I hope?'

'A painting.'

'Oh, that's not so bad, then... I thought for a moment you was gonna say they took your bank cards, or something like that.'

'No, they left my wallet intact.'

'You were lucky in more ways than one, then,' the man said.

'Not really.'

'How come?'

'The painting was worth an awful lot of money.'

'Oh, is that so?' His eyes lit up. 'Not by some famous artist, was it?'

'It was a Rembrandt.'

He whistled softly. 'Even I've heard of him.'

I noticed a number of photographs on the wall near to where I was standing, and I turned to take a look at them. 'These photos of the villagers, are they, I take it?'

'That's right...everyone who lives in the village should be in at least one of them somewhere.'

'What about Inge?'

'Yes, she should be in there, if you look.'

I ran my eyes over the rows of smiling faces, hopping from one photograph to another, until I spotted her. She stood out like some gorgeous butterfly caught up in a crowd of moths. 'The blond chap standing next to her would be Jaime, I suppose?' I said.

The man came out from behind the bar, putting his glasses on and slipping the temple arms over his ears as he looked at the photographs.

I went up close to the photograph and pointed.

'Oh, yes, that's him.'

I brought out my iPhone and took a couple of photographs of the figure in the photograph. Then I blew them up and took a good look at the face. He was the sort of handsome bastard you'd expect to have a girl like Inge on his arm if anyone was going to. Needless to say I hated him at first sight. Arrogance and confidence seemed to stream from his very pores, the way sweat runs off a pig. His blond hair was cut short at the sides and swept across in one of those kiss curls that I'd always found desperately cheesy, but which I imagine girls must love. He was tall and slim and dressed in jeans and a navy-blue Lacoste T-shirt. His mouth was slightly parted in a surly grin, revealing white teeth. Here was a man, I thought, who'd never been made to struggle for anything. A man for whom doors would have been opened before he even bothered to knock on them. Well, I for one should have liked to slam a few in his face. I turned my head to look at the barman and said, 'Do you know if anyone in the village comes from Figarillo, or if any of the villagers have been up there recently?'

He shrugged. 'Can't say I do,' he said. 'Although now that you mention it, Inge herself was from Figarillo originally, I think.'

I left a couple of coins on the counter. 'Nice talking to you,' I said, and then I turned and made for the door.

'Any time,' the man called after me.

CHAPTER 42

I went back to my car and wondered what my next move ought to be. As I was wondering, I began to ponder upon the book of matches I'd found up on the road. I'd just started the engine up and set off, when somebody popped up from the floor under the back seat. Whoever it was held a gun to the back of my head. 'Long time no see,' he said.

Moving my eyes only, I looked in the mirror to see who it was. And recognized the big man in the suit who worked for Vince Caportorio. 'What are you doing here?'

'My boss wants to see you.'

'I don't want to see him.'

'That's not very nice.'

'He's not a very nice guy.'

'He likes you a lot.'

'Does he always try to kill the people he likes?'

'He didn't try to kill you,' the fat guy said. 'I did.' I could see him grinning at me in the mirror. 'Now I want you to reach into your pocket real slow and take your gun out. Any fast movements and I'll shoot, understand?'

'Shoot me and I'll crash.'

'I'll take my chances on that,' he said. 'I want you to hold the gun by the barrel and hand it back to me, okay?'

I did as I'd been told. Then I said, 'So how come you didn't kill me that time, huh?'

'Never mind, Arthur, you know what they say about if at first you don't succeed and all that jazz.'

'Can't you come up with anything more original than that?' I said. 'That line must been six centuries old.'

'The old ones are always the best, don't you know that?'

'Do you apply that rule to everything in life?'

'Pretty much.'

'You mean you like your women old, too?'

'That supposed to be funny, Arthur?'

'I dunno, you tell me.'

'I don't think it's funny, but I think you do,' he said. 'Think you're cute, don't you?'

'If you say so.'

'Why don't you shut the fuck up and drive.'

'That's what I was just about to do,' I said.

'Yeah, only we ain't going where you was about to go.'

'So where are we going?'

'I already told you—Vince wantsa see you.'

'So where's that?'

'Just keep driving and I'll tell you where.'

The sun was turning the screw by now and my shirt was as wet as a rainy Sunday in Shrewsbury, which is pretty damn wet. I drove up to the next corner and, as I rounded it, so memories of my last date with Vince flitted through my mind. How could I ever forget it? Vince's hospitality was certainly of the sort that leaves an indelible mark on the memory. Most hosts don't dip you in the family pool by way of introducing you to their pet shark, after all. I guess dinner parties would go out of fashion pretty quickly if they did. I never did get to rub cheeks with the toothy Estrella, but it had been a close call. Now if there was ever a girl to whom the term 'man eater' truly applied then it was her. To rub cheeks with her was to lose your head, literally.

It's funny the way a man can get to thinking when he's scared. I figured my time was up unless I could shake off the bruiser on the back seat; but I didn't see how I might do that, given that he had a gun pointed at my head.

I drove in silence for quite some time, and then the coastline came into view. 'I know I'm a nice and friendly kinda guy,' I said, 'but I really don't see why someone like Vince should go to such lengths to seek out my company.'

'Vince wants to see a guy, he sees him.'

'But what's it all about? I mean I never did get to find out during my first visit.'

'You could try asking him, see what he says.'

'Maybe I will,' I said.

When I turned the next corner, I found my path blocked by a large black van. 'Stop here and get out.'

I considered my options for a fraction of a second, until I felt the muzzle of the mutt's gun against the back of my skull and figured I'd better do as he said. When we got out of the car, the back of the van opened. And there was Vince grinning at me. 'Get in,' he said.

Vince Caportorio looked at me. I couldn't see his eyes because he was wearing shades, but I figured I wasn't missing much. 'Where's the Rembrandt?' he said.

'I thought you had it.'

'Still trying to bullshit me, huh?' He shook his head. 'Listen, you haven't told me what you did with it by the time we get home, I'm going to let Estrella have you this time. Poor thing hasn't eaten for a coupla days. Starved her just for you.'

'Very thoughtful of you.'

'She'll appreciate you all the more.'

'Look,' I said, 'I'm telling you the truth.'

CHAPTER 43

Vince took off his shades, blew on the lenses, then took out a rag and began to wipe them. 'You ain't so stupid that you don't know you're gonna talk one way or the other,' he said. 'So you may as well make it easy on yourself.'

'Okay,' I said, 'I'll tell you everything.'

'Make it short and sweet, 'cause patience ain't my strong point.'

'She sent me up to her house in Magro, to retrieve the Rembrandt. She had it stashed away there in a secret place.'

'Why'd she want to send you to pick it up?' Vince was looking at me now, a frown on his face like I'd got his interest.

'I was working for her...I thought you knew. Her sister Gisela'd been kidnapped—by you, I assume—and she wanted me to go and get the Rembrandt.'

'You might've run off with it.'

'I might've done if I was a crook, but I'm not.'

I saw the corners of Vince's mouth turn up, like he found the idea of my not running off with the Rembrandt, or even wanting to, vaguely amusing.

'Anyway, I'm sure you know the rest.'

'Tell me anyway.'

'I was ambushed by you or your mutts after I left the village.'

'Ambushed?' He seemed surprised. 'News to me.'

'You mean it was you that did it?'

He shook his head. 'Tell me about it.'

'Coming down the mountain,' I said. 'Some rocks came tumbling down into my path and nearly killed me. I swerved to avoid them and crashed into a rock jutting out of the cliff face at the side of the road. I lost consciousness and when I came round the Rembrandt was gone.'

'So who took it?'

'No idea,' I said. 'I mean, I figured it must be you or the guys you've got working for you.'

'What made you jump to that conclusion?'

'I remembered from the time I was at your house that you seemed to be very keen to get your hands on the painting.'

'I was,' he said, 'and still am.'

'You mean it really wasn't you that took it?'

'No.'

'Was it you that kidnapped Gisela?'

'Think I'll take the Fifth on that one.'

'So why did you kill her?'

'I didn't.' He grinned. 'You did.'

'Very funny...but why kill her and then dump the body in my living room?'

'Don't ask me, I dunno the way these criminals operate.' He stifled a theatrical yawn. 'Suppose you can follow the logic, though, can't you?'

'What logic?'

'Imagine you was the kidnapper,' he said. 'You set a deadline. The person you've taken's gonna get it if the ransom ain't delivered by whenever it is...then the person you're dealing with fails to deliver, so the sister that's been kidnapped has to go.'

'Okay, but why dump the body on my sofa?'

'Frame you, old chap, I suppose.' He chuckled. 'Thought you might turn out to be of some use to me, even if you weren't to your client.'

'What about Juan Ribera and Joaquim Gross?'

'The fuck're they?'

'The two gangsters that got it in the neck.'

'If I was a bettin' man,' Vince said, 'then judging from what you just told me, I shouldn't be surprised if they was a coupla wannabes trying to poke their nose in where it wasn't wanted. Rembrandt's a very popular artist, so I've heard.'

'And it sounds as though he's every bit as much of a hit with the criminal underground as he is with the art lovers and critics.'

'I shouldn't doubt it, seeing how much money's on the end of it.'

I ran a hand over my face as I considered what I'd just learned. 'So who took the Rembrandt, then?'

'That's the question. Not to be or not to fucking be, but where's the fuckin' Rembrandt?'

'There must've been someone else who knew about it.'

'Unless you're feeding me porkies.'

Vince Caportorio was close enough for me to be able to smell his sweat and stink, and the thought that the man was going to get away scot-free made me sick. Then I remembered Javier Fontana and said, 'Did you kill the hack that got dead on my sofa, too, Vince?'

'If I were you, Arthur, I'd do something about that sofa of yours.'

'Yeah? What would you do about it?'

'I'd start by throwing it out.'

'How come?'

'Just hearing you say about those two young people that got dead on it,' he said. 'You ask me, that don't sound too good.'

'It wasn't the sofa that killed them.'

'I dunno.'

'What don't you know about, Vince?'

'I wouldn't have a sofa like that in my home, that's for sure.'

'You got a shark there.'

'She's different.'

'She's *that* all right.'

'Sofa like that sounds to me like it got the voodoo or something.'

'Have you got African blood, Vince?'

'No, I ain't.'

'But I thought voodoo's what the Africans believe in, isn't it?'

'What the fuck,' he said. 'All's I'm sayin's that I would get that sofa checked out. Or better still, I'd throw it out.' He appeared to consider what he'd just said and shrugged. 'Little late now, though, I suppose, seeing as where you're going.'

I looked at Vince and he looked at me. I thought he was a no-good ugly bastard, and from the expression on his mug it was safe to assume he felt similar sentiments where I was concerned. 'What with all this talk about my sofa,' I said, 'you still haven't answered my question.'

'Question's that?'

'Why you killed the hack.'

'Hacks can be a nuisance, I find.'

'Hacks in general, do you mean? Or are you talking about the one particular hack?'

Vince shrugged. 'The fuck makes you so curious?'

'It's my job, remember?'

'You're gonna die anyway.'

'We're all headed that way, Vince. Haven't you heard?'

'Yeah, but you're gonna head there a lot sooner'n most.'

I didn't like the sound of that, but I tried not to let it show. 'His name was Javier Fontana.'

'Who was?'

'The hack.'

'You still talking about him?'

'Came all the way down from Figarillo.'

'Nice for him.'

'Not so nice, I should've said, all things considered.'

'Already told you, hacks are a nuisance. They're like flies on a joint of meat. Who needs them?'

Just then, we slowed down, and moments later the van came to a halt. The driver got out and came and opened the doors at the back, and the mutt with the peashooter told me to get out first. I did as I was told, and any thoughts I might have had of making a move were cancelled out when I saw the gun that the guy who'd been driving was pointing at me. It was a Walther PKK. A small piece, but the punch it packed if you got it angry was more than big enough to put a hole in a man.

The mutt poked me in the back with his pen and I moved like a line of prose. A shaky line of prose that was sweating and shaking with fear. 'We're going into the house,' he said.

If ever there was a reluctant guest, then I was that man as I trudged forward towards the large white farmhouse. I just kept telling myself that I had to make my move, but there was no way I could do so with the mutt there behind me, jabbing his pen in my back.

The house was quite a place, but I was in no mood to appreciate the superior architecture and swanky interior. All I could think about was how many people had died under the man's roof, and whether I was going to be an addition to that number. I found myself being shoved through the house and out back to where the pool was. By now my guts were turning over. It's one thing to get killed, but to end up being eaten alive by a hungry shark is something else. And what made it worse was knowing that it was going to happen in advance. No words can express it, so I won't even bother to go there. I tried to make a run for it, but I'd left it too late and there was nowhere for me to go. Vince had his mutts hold me down, and then they trussed me up like the Christmas turkey, the way they had on my previous visit, and the next thing I know I'm being hoisted out over the pool. They lower me down and my nose is full of the smell of the chlorine in the water, and I can hear Vince chuckling away to himself like he finds all of this just so fucking amusing.

Looking below, I could see the shark circling. She was a big beast and I just hoped that it would be over quickly. It hurt like hell to think that Vince was going to get away with all this. Then I got to thinking what a lot of stupid oafs the local cops were, to have allowed Vince to get away with so much killing for so long. And to think he was here living in this palace he had for a home, like some latter day king. All this flashed through my mind as I watched the shark circling beneath the water.

Then I felt myself being lowered until my head was just a couple of inches from the surface of the water. Out of the corner of my eye I could see the shark's fin moving up the other end of the pool, some thirty metres or so away. I saw the beast turn as it got to the far end, and then start to make its way back towards me. It wouldn't take her long now, only a matter of seconds...

Just then, I heard someone shouting, then a gunshot rang out. The fin was cutting through the surface of the water like an electronic saw through butter. The creature moved with an oily sleekness. It was an efficient underwater killer. A beast that seemed to my mind to do little other than kill and eat, and then procreate. I'd never had much time for sharks. To my way of thinking they're mean, cold-hearted killers, just like Vince. And what I was going through now wasn't likely to change my mind on that score.

CHAPTER 44

I heard more gunfire. Something was going on in the house, although quite what it was I couldn't begin to imagine. I heard Vince barking at his mutts. At least he wasn't laughing anymore. But what was going on? I wondered, as the shark passed right underneath me, and I watched it go on up to the other end of the pool. It was checking me out, I thought. Now it knew I was here, so next time it would probably make its move.

I heard more gunfire, then something or somebody fell into the pool with a splash. Craning my neck, I saw the shark's fin as the beast glided through the water. Then I heard screams, and saw the shark's head come up out of the water. It had a man's legs in its mouth. The water was red with blood. Somebody had clearly come a cropper. I wondered who. And what was all the shouting and gunfire about?

I saw the shark's fin moving through the water towards me once more. It was some fifteen metres away from me now, and I knew that I was soon going to end up like the guy who'd just been chewed in half. Then just as the shark was about to get me, I felt myself being hoisted up through the air. What was going on? I wondered.

Moments later, I was lowered onto the tiles at the side of the pool, and three men were untying me. I recognized one of them. It was Inspector Jefe Salvador Cobos. 'Sal,' I said, 'it's you of all people.'

'None other.' He grinned. 'Seems like you had a lucky escape, Arthur.'

I was giddy when they stood me up, so that they had to hold me to prevent me from falling. All that hanging upside hadn't done much to improve my directional sense, and I wouldn't have known which way was north from a bunch of bananas. But Sal had his men help me through the house out to one of the squad cars parked out front. A policewoman came over and offered me a cup of coffee. I took it and drank. It tasted like sawdust. But even drinking bad coffee beats getting eaten by a shark, so I wasn't about to complain.

'You look kinda the worse for wear,' the officer said.

'I always get like this after I've had a workout,' I told her.

She nodded like she knew what I meant, but then she gave me this sly look like she couldn't quite make me out.

Within the hour Sal Cobos and I were talking over a drink in Marco's, a little place off the seafront in Bardino. Sal seemed to have his nice hat on. He'd just bought me a large Scotch, anyway. We were sitting at the wooden counter, and the television was on up on the wall. Some film with Al Pacino. The barmaid was busy washing glasses.

Sal grinned and said, 'Seems like it's your lucky day, Arthur.'

'I guess.'

'We hadn't arrived I dread to think what would've happened to you.' He sipped his Ballantines. 'You'd've ended up like that other guy, worked for Vince. Shark severed his legs from his trunk.'

'How did that happen?'

'He fell into the pool in the fighting that took place, after we arrived on the scene.'

'Fell or was pushed?'

'His own stupid fault.' Sal shrugged. 'Some of my officers are tough, but none of them would've wanted to see what happened to that man happen to anyone.'

Something occurred to me. 'I thought you said Vince was planning on having a quiet night in with his ladylove?'

Sal grinned. 'Guess he must've changed his mind.'

I nodded and took a sip of my Scotch, figuring there really wasn't much to be said about the matter. I'd nearly been killed, but I got lucky. That was it. Sal didn't seem to feel quite the same way about it, though. 'You must feel pretty shook up about it still, I should think,' he said. 'Nearly getting eaten alive like you did.'

I shrugged. 'It's over now.'

'So it hasn't made you have second thoughts about what you do for a living?'

'Are you kidding me?'

'No, I'm being serious, Arthur. You've just been through a harrowing experience that would affect any man.'

'It was harrowing when it happened,' I told him. 'But it's not harrowing anymore.'

'How come?'

'I didn't get eaten, did I?'

Sal laughed. 'Simple as that, huh?'

'Simple as that.'

He laughed again. I couldn't see the joke. 'You must have some balls,' he said, 'that's all I can say.'

'Not really. I was scared while it happened. But that was then, and now is now. It's over and I'm okay.'

He nodded thoughtfully. 'So what was it all about, Arthur?'

'You tell me, Sal.'

'I was hoping you might be a little more forthcoming,' he said. 'After all, we did come and rescue you.'

'That's true...how did you know I'd be there, anyway?'

'We followed you.' Sal took a Camel from the pack on the wooden counter, put it between his lips and lit it. 'I knew you'd be getting up to something.' He squinted, rubbed at his eyes as grey ribbons of smoke billowed from him. 'You're a mysterious man, Arthur. I mean just take the way people seem to've developed the nasty habit of getting dead around you.' He smiled. 'So we wanted to keep tabs on you and see what you were getting up to... And we still want to find out.'

I figured I owed Sal something, all things considered. 'Okay,' I said. 'I was ambushed coming out of Magro yesterday. When I came round, a certain article I'd gone to pick up for my client had gone.'

'Care to shed a little more light on the nature of the article that went missing?'

'It was a Rembrandt original.'

Sal Cobos made an O with his lips and whistled. 'So somebody was expecting you, you're saying?'

'Must've been.'

Sal nodded, took a drag on his Camel. 'Wait a minute,' he said, 'this all happened up in Magro, you say?'

'That's right.'

'You mean that Inge Schwartz had a Rembrandt original stashed away there?'

'In a house in the village.'

'So what's happened to it?'

'Wish I knew.' I shrugged.

'Mm.' Sal Cobos tasted his Scotch. 'So where does Vince Cap come into all this?'

'I went back to Magro, like I said, to try and work out what happened when I was robbed, and see if I could perhaps remember anything or talk to somebody who saw something.'

'Did you?'

'I talked to the man who runs the bar in the village.'

'He see anything?'

'No.'

'So then what?'

'I'm driving home and one of Vince's mutts pops up from below the back seat.'

'Takes you to see Vince and he wants to know where the Rembrandt is or he's gonna feed you to his shark.'

'That's it.'

'I know because we were watching you from further up the mountain, and we tailed you once you got into the van.' Cobos gave his nose a thoughtful scratch. 'So Inge Schwartz has asked you to retrieve her Rembrandt for her?'

'Correct.'

Sal looked at me. 'Any idea where it is?'

'Nope.' I sipped my Scotch. 'That's why I went back to Magro, but I was just clutching at straws.'

'So now what are you going to do?'

'Keep looking, I guess.'

'But where?'

'Where'd somebody go if they had a Rembrandt to sell?'

'Good question, Arthur.' He ground what was left of his cigarette to death in the ashtray. 'Can't imagine it would be easy to sell one around these parts.'

'Unless it was stolen to order.'

'I doubt that very much. People I've spoken to who know about these things tell me that rumours of that sort of thing happening are all just that—rumours. I mean just think about it, Arthur. Imagine you're some rich guy. Would you really want to shell out a few million to men you probably can't trust for what amounts to stolen property?'

'Maybe you're right,' I said. 'But they must think they're going to sell it somewhere.'

'Could just've been an opportunist. Somebody who gets to hear that you've gone to Magro for the Rembrandt and spots his chance.'

'But I didn't tell anybody why I was going there.'

'So what do you reckon, then—any ideas?'

'No, not really.' I finished my drink, then slid off my stool. 'Better be off now, Sal,' I said. 'Been nice to catch up, and thanks for the Scotch.'

'Stay and have another one.'

'I need to go and pick up my car.' I smiled. 'Wouldn't want me to be driving under the influence, now would you?'

As I reached the door, Sal Cobos called to me and I turned. 'What?'

'Take my advice and stay clear of water for a while.'

CHAPTER 45

When I got home I checked the place out before entering, just to make sure nobody was about to spring out on me, because I'd had enough surprises for one day. The place was empty, though, and everything was cool. There were no bodies on the sofa, dead or otherwise—or anywhere else in the flat for that matter.

I was feeling tired, so I took a long hot bath and then I went to bed and slept right through till the middle of the following morning. I'm normally one of these types who find it hard to drop off, but it's surprising what having been scared out of your wits will do for your capacity to sleep. Not that it was a particularly peaceful night for me, because I had a nightmare about being in a swimming pool with a shark.

After I'd showered, I logged onto my laptop and booked myself onto the next flight to Figarillo. It had just turned 2 p.m. when the plane touched down. I hurried through Passport Controls and passed out through the electronic doors, then took a taxi into the centre of the town, where I booked myself into a room in a shabby two star hotel. Then I went out and found an Avis outlet, where I rented a Lexus, and I took a drive over to Calle Diego Farol and pulled up outside of a place called Bar López. There were a few people sitting at plastic tables on the pavement, enjoying the sunshine. I sat there for a long time, watching the front of the bar, and nothing much seemed to be going on. Then I started to get the feeling I was being watched. I wasn't totally sure, but the guy sitting in the Seat Ibiza that was parked across the street had sure been there a long time.

I figured it might be an idea to run a little test, just to see if the man was watching me. So I started the engine up and set off. And sure enough, the guy tailed me. He was trying not to make it too obvious, because there were two cars between mine and his, but he was there in my mirror all right. Now as a man who spends a fair amount of his time searching for and watching and following others, it rather sticks in my craw when people think they can tail *me*. I suppose that's just human nature for you. Anyway, I decided to have a little fun with the guy. So I took a left, then started zigzagging my way through the streets, and sure enough the Seat Ibiza came after me.

I pulled over outside of a hotel and, seeing my shadow pull over some forty metres behind me, I climbed out of my Porsche and crossed the road, locking the doors with the remote without looking back. I entered the hotel—the Don Carlos, I think it was called. It was a big and fairly classy place—the sort of establishment you wouldn't normally find me dead in on account of the prices they charge; but this was different. I crossed the lobby. There had to be a back way out of a place this big, I thought. It was just a case of finding it, which I did easily enough. Then having left the hotel, I went up to the corner and found myself looking across at my shadow. He was sitting behind the wheel of his Seat Ibiza, watching the entrance I'd gone in through like a jealous husband spying on his wife. I took out my shades and put them on, then set off across the road. I walked quickly, and was at the man's side before he'd noticed my approach.

'*Buenas tardes*,' I said in his ear, and the guy almost jumped out of his seat.

CHAPTER 46

His brown eyes were flashing alarm signals as he turned to look at me. '*Buenas tardes.*'

I looked at him closely as I tried to work out whether I knew his face from somewhere. Late twenties, maybe early thirties, on the skinny side, thinning brown hair, brown eyes—his face sure didn't ring any bells with me. So why was the guy following me? Perhaps he was a fellow private eye, or else a plainclothes cop, who'd been hired to tail me. But somehow he just didn't look the type. Too pale and nervous.

'Sorry,' he said, 'but I don't think we've met.'

'No, I don't believe we have.' I grinned at him. 'But it looks to me like you're pretty keen to change that.'

His mouth opened, but no words came out.

'Who are you and why have you been tailing me?'

'Sorry,' he said, seeming to relax a little now that he realized he'd been rumbled. 'I'm a reporter.'

I brought out my gun and pointed it at his temple. 'Got some ID you can show me?'

'Sure, but there's no need for the gun.'

'I'll be the judge of that,' I said. 'And it had better be your ID you bring out of your jacket or your brains are gonna make a mess of your nice new upholstery.'

'I'm not carrying a weapon.'

'Easy does it.'

'Okay.' He reached inside his jacket and brought out his wallet. 'Here.'

'You open it for me.'

'Sure.'

He held it out so that I could see it. I read from the man's card that his name was Miguel Pasqual and that he was a staff reporter for *La Vanguardia*.

'Okay,' I said, 'you can put it away and move over.'

'What?'

'Onto the passenger seat. It's time you and I had a little talk.'

He did as he was told, and I put my gun away, then opened the door and climbed in behind the wheel. 'I won't bother to waste time introducing myself,' I said, 'because you obviously know already who I am. But I think you owe me an explanation.'

'Javier Fontana, the reporter who was killed, was a colleague and a good friend of mine,' he said. 'He was investigating a story that took him down to Bardino, and somehow he ended up dead in your flat.'

'On my sofa, to be precise.'

'Which is why I've been following you.'

'You thought I had something to do with your friend's death?'

'Did you?'

'No, I'm a private detective.'

'That doesn't tell me much.'

'Somebody was trying to frame me for his and other murders.'

'I understand that you're working for Inge Schwartz?'

'Who told you that?' I asked. 'And how did you know I was in Figarillo?'

'I didn't,' he replied. 'I came here for the same reason you did.'

'What makes you think you know why I'm here?'

'I noticed you were keeping an eye on the same things I am, so I got curious about you.' He shrugged. 'I called a friend and gave him your reg number and asked him to check you out.'

'But hacks don't normally tail guys like me around.'

'They do if they want a story badly enough.'

I figured the guy was probably on the level.

'Look,' Pasqual said, 'I've got some information about your client that might be of use to you, but I can't see why I should level with you if you don't want to play straight with me.'

'What information's this?'

'So she is your client,' he said.

I looked at Pasqual and he looked right back at me. He might have had a scrawny build, but he had a determined, ballsy look about him. I said, 'Why do you ask me questions you already know the answer to?'

'Do you trust her?'

'Why do you ask that?'

'Just answer yes or no.'

'I wouldn't be working for her if I didn't.'

Pasqual chuckled and I asked him what was so funny. 'I guess she must've got under your skin, huh?' he said. 'Hardly surprising, because she sure is a babe...the sort can wrap any man round her garter string whenever she feels like it.'

'Don't sound as if you like her very much.'

'I don't know her personally.'

'So why're you so keen to give her a bad press?'

'I'm out to get at the truth,' he said. 'That's the bottom line for me.'

'Sounds like we're both travelling on the same train.'

He looked at me like he was trying to read me. 'How much do you know about her?'

I shrugged. 'She employed me to find her sister.'

'And she ended up dead on your hands, too, right?'

I nodded and blew out my cheeks as I remembered the sight of Gisela Schwartz's body lying there on my sofa. Her eyes staring up at me as I went in and looked at her. The feeling of shock I experienced. 'I found her all right,' I said. 'Only it was too late.'

'So who killed her?'

'Guy who kidnapped her.'

'And who was that?'

I looked at him. 'You're doing a pretty good job of milking me, kid,' I said. 'What about a little *quid pro quo* here?'

'What do you want to know?'

'You were going to let me in on some information you had on my client.'

'Sure,' he said. 'Her father, you know about him?'

'No. Should I?'

'It might interest you to know that he was a rich art dealer,' Miguel Pasqual said. He reached into the pocket of the leather jacket he was wearing, brought out a pack of Marlboros. 'Want one?'

'No, thanks.'

'Been trying to give up, but haven't got very far with it.' He took out a cigarette and lodged it between his lips, then brought out a Zippo and lit it. I watched him take a long drag.

'Look like you needed that.'

'I did,' he said.

'Only one way to do it,' I said, 'and that's to make a clean break.'

'You talk like it's easy.'

'Talking about it is easy. It's doing it that's the tough part.'

'Like anything, I guess...difference between talking the talk and walking the walk.'

'You got it.'

I sat in silence for a moment and watched him smoke. 'Your client spent some time at school in Germany as a kid, so she speaks the lingo and can pass herself off as a Kraut easily enough. But she's actually from Figarillo, and her real name's Barbara Borrell. Her father made his money back in the days of the regime,' he resumed. 'Sold stuff on the black market. You name it, he could get it for you's what they used to say about him, so I understand. He becomes friendly with General Franco, which doesn't do his business interests any harm whatsoever-quite the reverse in fact, as I'm sure you'll understand. Rumour is he'd get basic foodstuffs on the cheap by using his connections, back in the days when Franco was doing his best to screw up the economy, and then he'd sell whatever it was for several times what he paid out. It was the next best thing to having a license to print money for a guy like him, lacking in scruples as he was. Cut a story short, it's not long before he's stinking rich. But he's keen to get respectable, so he invests his money in art treasures. I guess he probably figured that being an art collector had a certain ring to it, a certain cachet that might perfume over the stink of where his millions actually came from. Whatever. Fast forward a few decades and he leaves his entire art collection to a state museum.'

'What about his daughters?'

'Didn't leave them a single penny—or painting.'

'Bet they were happy about that.'

'Deliriously so, I'm sure.' Pasqual took a last drag on his cigarette before he crash-landed it into the ashtray. 'The girls contested it, of course, and the collection was frozen as a result.'

'Because of the court case?'

'Exactly. The art works were all held at the family mansion, which was locked up, and the understanding was that they were to be kept there until the case had been concluded. But then, surprise, surprise, a few of the paintings, among them the pick of the bunch as it turns out, go walkies and nobody seems to have any idea where they are. The most famous work in the entire collection is a certain Rembrandt. It's a small work, but of great value and it's gone missing.'

'Sounds like it must be the one that the kidnapper was asking for as ransom,' I said.

'Did she hand it over to him?'

'No. She asked me to do it, but I was ambushed on the way.'

'So now she's asked you to get it back?'

'That's right.'

'What made you come here of all places?'

I told him about the book of matches I'd found and where I'd come by it. 'I put two and two together,' I said. 'Javier Fontana was killed after he came from this city to investigate a story that involved my client.'

'So you reckoned all roads must lead to Figarillo, and to this café in particular?'

'You tell me,' I said. 'What exactly was it that brought you here?'

'Place has got a rep in certain quarters as being the place to come if you want to make contacts in the art world,' he replied. 'Rumour has it you can buy all manner of stuff in there that's not on the menu, if you get my meaning.'

'Call in for a cappuccino and find yourself being talked into buying a stolen Canaletto?'

'Exactly. Or order a panini and the waiter thinks you're using the word as a proper noun and gives you a list of titles with the corresponding dimensions.'

'I never knew there was a painter called Panini.'

'You learn something every day.' Pasqual grinned. 'Best known perhaps for his view of the interior of the Pantheon.'

'Sounds like an interesting menu they do over there,' I said. 'I wonder if a certain stolen Rembrandt might not be the order of the day.'

'I can see our thoughts are starting to converge.'

'I think it's high time I took a little wander over there.'

'Worked up an appetite, have you?'

'Sitting around here watching people eat's hungry work.'

'You bet it is,' Pasqual said. 'I'll stay here a while, and perhaps you'd like to keep me updated on how you get on. I mean, we could work as a team on this.'

'Okay, so long as you don't print anything until I've got to the bottom of it. If you do, our marriage is over.'

'Wouldn't dream of it.'

'Wish me luck,' I said, and climbed out of the car.

CHAPTER 47

It was a long rectangular-shaped joint, with round wooden tables big enough for two, or three at a pinch. I sat by the window and reached that day's *El Pais* down from the rack that was on the wall just behind me. Not that I was in a mood to read the news, but it gave me something to do, as well as something to hide behind if it became necessary for me to do so.

I heard the waiter's shoes clunking over the polished wooden boards as he approached my table. He said '*Buenos dias*', a skinny guy in a white shirt and bow tie. I bade him good morning in return, and he handed me a card menu and asked if I was ready to order. I said I'd have a croissant and coffee. The man said,'*Muy bien*,'then turned and went off. When he returned with my order, minutes later, he smiled and asked me if I was here on holiday. 'That's right,' I told him. 'Just taking a few days out.'

He scratched at his handlebar tash and said, 'Figarillo's a beautiful city and there's plenty to see and do here.'

'So I gather.' I smiled. 'I'm particularly interested in checking out the city's galleries.'

'You take an interest in art, *señor*?'

'Sure do.'

'Who is your favourite artist?'

'There are so many,' I said.

'But if you had to pick one?'

'It would have to be Rembrandt.' I watched him closely as I said this, but didn't observe any noticeable change in his expression or manner. I decided to push the matter to its natural conclusion and see where it took me. 'Fact of the matter is,' I said, 'I've heard there's one on sale over here and I'm interested in making an offer.'

'A Rembrandt, *señor*?'

'Yes.'

'For sale?'

'So I've heard.'

'How interesting,' he said. 'Where did you come by this information?'

'I have friends who take an interest in the international art market, and they keep me updated on what's going on.'

'How fortunate for you.'

'I guess so.' I smiled. 'Don't tell me that you're an art lover, too?'

'I certainly am.'

'In that case, I don't suppose you'd be able to help me?'

'Help you, *señor*?'

'Find out about this Rembrandt that's for sale?'

'Which Rembrandt would this be?'

I told him the name of the work.

'I can certainly keep an ear out for you, *señor*.'

'I'd be very grateful if you would,' I said. 'And there'd be some money in it for you, of course.'

The man ditched his false smile and Vaseline charm. 'If you come back here tomorrow around the same time, I'll see if I can manage to turn something up for you.'

'I appreciate it.' I took out a fifty-euro note. 'Keep the change,' I said, 'as a little token of gratitude.'

'*Gracias*.'

It didn't take me long to make my breakfast of *café con leche* and croissant disappear, then I got up and went out. The hack, Miguel Pasqual, was still waiting in his car across the street.

I went over and climbed in beside him.

'How did it go?'

'Just put out some feelers,' I said. 'Man told me to come back tomorrow, same time same place, and he might have something for me.'

'That sounds promising.'

'Maybe, maybe not.' I smiled. 'Just thought I'd tell you now, so you'll know where to come and won't need to keep following me everywhere I go until then.'

'I appreciate it.' He killed his cigarette. 'I get the feeling this could be the start of a beautiful friendship.'

'If you don't want it all to end it tears, just make sure you keep your promise and don't print anything until it's all over.'

'I already gave you my word.'

'That's right, you did.' I climbed back out of the car, then leaned over and said, 'Till tomorrow,' before I slammed the door.

I figured that I ought to check my new buddy out, just to make sure he was the hack he claimed to be. So no sooner had I climbed in behind the wheel of my Porsche than I took out my iPhone, then I drove up to the car Pasqual was parked in, and as I drew level I came to a stop and called to him. 'Hey, Miguel,' I said.

He turned and looked at me. 'What?'

'Don't be late tomorrow.' I held my iPhone up as I spoke, and pushed the button to take a photograph of him. Then I drove off. The next time I had to stop for a red light, I ran a Google search to find the number for the head office of *La Vanguardia*, the newspaper. The light changed to green just as I got the number up, and I made the call with my left hand while I used my right to steer. A woman picked up and said, '*La Vanguardia*, head office,' and I asked her if a Miguel Pasqual worked for the newspaper. Then when the woman replied in the affirmative, I asked if I could speak to him. 'I'm afraid he's out of the office at the moment,' she said. 'Is there anybody else that might be able to help you?'

'Could I come in and talk to someone?'

'What's it concerning?'

'The journalist who was killed, Javier Fontana.'

'Oh...are you a policeman?'

'Yes,' I lied.

The woman asked me to wait while she got someone else to talk to me. The line went dead for a short while, then a man came on. 'Jorge Roig speaking,' he said.

I told him that I was investigating the death of Javier Fontana, and asked if I could come in and talk to him or one of his colleagues who knew anything about the story that Fontana had been working on. 'But I've already spoken to you people,' Roig said.

'Truth is, I'm a private investigator.'

'So why don't you go and ask the police what they know?'

'They can be a little cagey with private investigators,' I said. 'Seem to resent the competition.'

'Well I'm sorry to hear that, Mr. uh—'

'Blakey. Arthur Blakey.'

'Yes, I'm sorry to hear that, as I say, Mr. Blakey, but quite frankly I've already spent a lot of time talking to the cops and precious little seems to have come of it.'

'But you want to see whoever killed your colleague brought to justice, right?'

'Of course I do...we all do. But there doesn't seem to be any sign of that happening.'

'Look,' I said, 'before you hang up, perhaps I ought to tell you that it was me Javier Fontana came to see before he was killed.'

'Oh...well what did he want to see you about?'

'That's just it, you see I'm not sure,' I said. 'He was killed before I got to talk to him... Now I'm trying to find the man's killer so he can be brought to justice.'

'Who are you working for?'

'A private client.'

'Mind telling me who this client of yours is?'

'I'm afraid I can't tell you that.'

'Sounds to me like you want me to help you, and the first time I ask you a question you refuse to answer it.'

'No private investigator worth his salt would,' I told him. 'It goes with the job...same with journalists and their sources sometimes, isn't it?'

'Guess so.' He coughed down the line. 'So are you saying you actually spoke to Javier Fontana?'

'Yes,' I said. 'Look, I can tell you about this, if you'll agree to meet me.'

'Okay, if you can come over at three this afternoon,' he said. 'Ask for me at the switchboard, and I'll come down and meet you. I'll try and find out as much as I can about it by then.'

'Thanks. Until later, then.'

We hung up. It was just coming up to 2 a.m., so I drove over to the newspaper's offices and parked, then I got out and found a café. I sat at a vacant table outside, and had the waiter bring me a newspaper and a glass of *cerveza*, and I used up an hour or so poring over the news. Then I paid the bill and headed into the office building across the street, went over to the reception desk, and asked to speak to Jorge Roig.

The girl on reception called Roig, to tell him I'd come to see him, and he came down almost straightaway. A stocky man in his forties, dressed in a grey pinstripe number, he looked like he'd just crawled out from under a pile of assignments. 'I was just going to the cafe,' he said, 'so we can talk over a drink.'

'Sure.'

I followed his stocky frame out through the glass doors, and we walked up to the next corner and entered a little place just along on the left. Jorge Roig ran a hand over his mouth and black chinstrap beard and blinked his eyes a couple of times. 'So you wanted to speak to me about Javier Fontana,' he said.

'That's right.'

'I haven't been able to talk to anyone about it since you called.' He puffed out his cheeks and blinked again. 'One of those days, I'm afraid. Most days are, come to think of it.'

'Busy?'

'And some.' He scratched his nose. 'Javier was a good man and a good reporter,' he said. 'If I can help you in any way then I will.'

The waitress came over. A slim brunette in her thirties, she smiled at the journalist and asked him how he was keeping. 'Can't complain, Carmen. What about you?'

'Oh I'm not so bad.'

'Your mother okay?'

'Not so good.'

The girl began to tell Jorge Roig about her mother's ailments, and the journalist listened with apparent sympathy. 'Oh well,' he said, 'I hope she gets better.'

The waitress offered up a sad smile, full of resignation, then she asked us what she could get us. '*Café con leche* for me,' Jorge Roig said.

'And I'll have one, too.'

The waitress turned and disappeared.

'Look,' I said, 'I've just been talking to a Miguel Pasqual, who tells me he's a reporter for *La Vanguardia*.'

'That's right.'

I got the photo I'd taken of him up on my iPhone and held it out, so Roig could see it. 'Mind telling me,' I said, 'if this is him?'

'Nope, that's not him.'

'You totally sure about that?'

'Positive,' Jorge Roig said. 'I know Miguel Pasqual. He's a colleague of mine—and that's not him.'

'Thanks.'

'You sound surprised,' he said. 'But what's all this about?'

'Seems like somebody's been pretending to be your colleague, that's all.'

'But why'd they do that?'

'To trick me into trusting him, I guess.' And into leading him to the Rembrandt, I thought. Although I saw no reason why I should share everything I knew with this journalist whom I'd only just met. He'd only write it up in his newspaper. And if he did that then he'd let whoever the guy was that was pretending to be Pasqual know he'd been rumbled. That wasn't what I wanted. I preferred to let the guy think I'd bought what he told me.

Jorge Roig frowned, ran a chubby hand through his short black hair. 'Shouldn't be surprised if it was some freelance trying to rustle up a story,' he said. 'We've had that in the past.'

'Oh...?'

'Sure have.' He nodded. 'Guys pretending to be working for our paper, so they can have better access to information they need to work up a story... Then they have the balls to try and sell us the stuff they write.'

'I'm glad I've spoken to you,' I said. 'Now I'll know better than to give the guy the time of day.'

'Tell him to go take a hike in a latrine.'

Just then, the waitress appeared with our coffees. She placed them down on the table in front of us then disappeared again.

'About Javier Fontana,' I said. 'What exactly was he onto?'

Jorge Roig sighed, sat back in his chair. 'All I know is that he was investigating a lead he'd had...it was something to do with the Borrell family... Don't know if you've heard about them?'

I shook my head, sipped my coffee.

'Old Borrell was a rich art collector. Died last year and left his entire collection to a local state-owned gallery.'

'Didn't he have any kids?'

'Two daughters, if my memory serves me right.'

This sounded familiar, I thought. And said, 'Bet they were chuffed about that.'

'Oh, I bet.' He looked at me over the rim of his cup. 'The daughters disputed it and the house and art collection were held under a court order. But then the best pieces in the collection went missing.'

'So where are they?'

'That's anybody's guess...but Javier Fontana reckoned it was a sure bet the sisters had taken them.'

'So what was he doing down in Bardino, then?'

Roig's mouth rose in a lopsided grin. 'Look, Mister Blake,' he said.

'Blakey,' I corrected him.

'Sorry, Mr. Blakey... I don't know if you think I was born yesterday, but if so then maybe I ought to disabuse you.'

'No need to use the long words with me,' I told him. 'I'm just a private dick. Not one of your intellectual sorts.'

He zipped his lips together and gave me a look like I was a pile of numbers waiting to be added up. 'If Javier Fontana went down to Bardino, then it would have been because one or both of the sisters were down there,' he said. 'And you know that better than I do, Mr. Blakey, so can we cut the bullshit now?'

I looked at him and didn't say anything.

'If Javier wanted to speak to you,' Roig said, 'it must've been because you're working for one or other, or both of the Borrell sisters.'

'I'm afraid client confidentiality is everything in my line of work, Mr. Roig. It's a bit like the Hippocratic oath where doctors are concerned, I suppose, only more so.'

'I know, you already told me that.'

I shrugged. 'All I want is to get at the truth.'

'In that case we're both after the same thing, Mr. Blakey.' He took another sip of his coffee. 'Perhaps we could work together on this, favour each other with a little *quid pro quo...?*'

'Sure,' I said. 'Only problem is, I've already told you everything I know.' Much more to the point, I had the impression that Roig had told me everything he knew, and I didn't want him to rush to print. 'Listen, if you can hold fire on what we've talked about then I'd appreciate it.'

He shrugged. 'It's hardly worth printing, in itself. I mean there's the basis for a story there, and it could be a big one... But there are still far too many unknowns for me to want to rush to print.'

This was music to my ears. 'Okay,' I said, 'I'll tell you what. I'll give you the story as an exclusive, once I've got to the bottom of it, just so long as you promise to hold fire until it's over and tell me anything that you happen to turn up.'

'It's a deal.' I reached across the table and shook his hand. Then I took out a five-euro note and dropped it onto the table. 'That's for the coffees,' I said, and got up and went out.

CHAPTER 48

I walked back to the car and drove to my hotel, found a place to park and went in and lay on the bed. So this Miguel Pascual character was no hack, I thought. Question was, who he was working for?

Whoever it was, they were after the Rembrandt. There could be no question about that. And they reckoned I'd be dumb enough to lead them to it. Well I wasn't as dumb as they reckoned.

Maybe it was Vince that sent the guy, I thought. Or Vicente Caportorio, to give the man his full name. Whoever he was, the would-be scribe was actually a mutt and he was sniffing where he shouldn't. Question was, what I was going to do about him.

I wondered about this for a while, and I was still wondering about it a little later when I was in the shower that was just along the hallway. The shower was about the only thing in the hotel that wasn't old and looking like it was about to fall apart, and the water came out nice and hot.

Dried, I went and dressed back in my room. Then I went out for a stroll through the narrow streets of the *Barrio Gogol*. Place had its own kind of atmosphere, I thought. All those old buildings with the louvered shutters. After a while, I found a place to eat. I had a plate of *lentejas* for the first course, followed by steak and chips. A cheap bottle of *tinto* came with the meal. The steak was thin as a miser's wallet and the wine was rougher than a thug's manners, but I was hungry and thirsty so I drank and ate it all anyway. And as I did so, I thought about the case. I thought about what had happened up till now, and what was likely to happen tomorrow. I planned out a course of action in my mind.

I showed at the Bar López at 2 p.m. the following afternoon, and sat at the same table I'd sat at the day before. The waiter came over and said, '*Buenos tardes*,' and I bade him good afternoon in return. 'It's quite a city you've got here,' I said.

'I expect you've been enjoying the many art treasures that Figarillo has to offer, *señor*.' His handlebar moustache rose in what I supposed must be a grin, but it didn't extend up as far as his eyes, which were watchful, I noticed.

'You're too right I have.' I smiled back at the man. 'Although I'd be enjoying myself a lot more if I could only purchase a certain Rembrandt that I've heard is currently on the market.'

The man nodded and lost his smile as he looked about him, to make sure nobody was within earshot. 'I have some news for you about that,' he said. 'If you'd like to come back here at five o'clock, I'll be able to set up a meeting with a man I know.'

'Does this man own the Rembrandt?'

'He is working for the owner, I believe.'

'Like an agent, you mean?'

'Something like that.'

'Okay.' I tried to think of a suitable location for what I had in mind. Of course, not knowing the city all that well didn't help. 'You know of any multi-storey car parks that are not too far away?'

The man smoothed down his tash as an aid to thought. 'There's one not all that far from here.'

'Can you print the name of the street it's on here for me?'

'Of course.'

He wrote on his pad, then tore the page off and gave it to me. I looked at what he'd written. The name of the street didn't mean anything to me. I folded the piece of paper and slipped it into my trouser pocket. 'I'll be back at five, then.' With that, I went back out without having eaten or drunk anything. I spotted the guy who was pretending to be a newspaper hack. He was sitting behind the wheel of his Seat Ibiza across the street.

He turned his head at that moment and seemed to notice me. I raised a hand in a sort of lazy salute, then I headed over to his car and climbed into the passenger seat. He looked at me and said, 'How's the shopping going?'

'Waiter's just given me an address to go to,' I said. 'Come along for the ride, if you want.'

'Sure. I appreciate it. I'll drive if you like.'

'Okay.'

'Where is it?'

I reached into my trouser pocket and brought out the piece of paper with the address of the multi-story car park written on it. 'Here,' I said and handed it to him.

He looked at it, then he looked at me. 'The waiter just give you this?'

'That's right.'

He screwed up his eyes as he scrutinized the paper. Then he nodded. 'Top of a multi-story car park,' he said. 'Bit of a strange place to go meet an art dealer, I should've thought.'

I shrugged. 'He said we're to meet the owner's agent first.'

'Maybe he'll take us to the other guy, is that it?'

'I dunno. I mean, I know as much as you do.'

'Waiter just wrote this down and gave it to you, and he didn't say anything else?'

'That's it.'

'Mm.'

'Well are you in on this or not?' I said. 'It's your call. I mean, you don't have to come if you don't want to.'

'No, I'm in on it, sure I am.'

'So let's get going, then.'

We set off through the busy city streets and the man seemed to know where we were headed so I left him to it. Minutes later, we arrived at the multi-storey car park. 'It's on the top floor,' I said.

'Private a place as any, I suppose.'

'Guess so.'

We entered the car park and climbed to the top. There were plenty of free parking spaces and he glided the Seat Ibiza into one of the empty bays. As he turned off the engine, I brought out my gun.

'What is this?' he said.

'You tell me.'

'I thought we were partners.' He looked genuinely upset and surprised. The guy was quite an acting talent gone to waste.

'What I thought, too,' I said. 'Till I found out you're not really a reporter at all.' I gave him my icepick smile. 'You see, I went to the offices of *La Vanguardia* and checked you out.'

He ditched the surprised and upset look.

'Who are you working for?' I said. 'Is it Vicente Caportorio?'

'Who?'

'Don't fuck with me, okay, because I'm just not in the mood.'

'I'm working alone.'

'Got your eyes on the Rembrandt, huh?'

'No, I'm a freelance reporter.'

It was always possible that he was telling the truth, but I couldn't take a chance on that. It would be too risky. 'I gave you the chance to play straight with me,' I said. 'Shame you didn't take it.'

'Look, I'm sorry I lied to you,' he said. 'But the truth is, a lot of people don't take you seriously if you tell them you're a freelance.'

'Get out of the car. And easy does it.'

I kept the gun pointed at him as I climbed out on my side. Or I tried to. But I was unsighted for a moment, as you always are in such circumstances, with the body of the car blocking your line of vision, and the mutt took the opportunity to bolt for it. He was skinny as a whippet and almost as fast as one, and he'd nearly reached the door to the stairwell by the time I spotted him. 'Hey, come back here,' I said. 'I need to talk to you.'

He glanced over his shoulder at me, then opened the door and went through it. I gave chase, but he'd already gone down two flights by the time I got to the door. I went after him, but he was nowhere to be seen by the time I got down to the street.

I'd handled the situation badly and could have kicked myself.

CHAPTER 49

I returned to the Bar López for my appointment there at 5 p.m., and checked to see if there was any sign of the would-be hack or his Seat before I sat down. There wasn't, so far as I could see.

The waiter with the handlebar tash came over. '*Buenas tardes,*' he said. 'The man you have come to see is inside. If you'd like to come with me, I'll take you to him.'

'Sure.' I got up and followed the waiter into the café, our footsteps sounding as they struck the polished boards. The waiter led me through the long rectangular bar and past the horseshoe-shaped wooden counter. There were several tables right at the back, all of them empty save the one in the corner, and the waiter stopped at it. The man who was sitting there put his newspaper down and looked at us.

The waiter said, 'This is the *señor* who wanted to talk to you.'

The man nodded, then looked at me. 'Please take a seat.'

I parked myself on one of the upright wooden chairs and waited for the man to speak. He threw a look at the waiter, who got the message and took off, leaving us alone.

'I have been told that you have a taste for art treasures, *Señor* uh–'

'Ruiz,' I lied. 'Yes, that's so...'

'And you expressed an interest in buying a certain Rembrandt, I am told?'

'Indeed.'

The man continued to look at me, and he nodded almost imperceptibly as he did so, as if he were agreeing with some comment that had been whispered in his ear by an infinitesimally small elf in a voice so quiet as to be all but silent. He had shortish blond hair and blue eyes and was wearing newish jeans with a black Polo shirt and a camel-coloured suede jacket. He was a handsome son of a bitch, the sort you'd imagine the ladies would go for, and his face was vaguely familiar to me from somewhere. 'Who wouldn't want such a work on his wall?' he said. 'The question is of course, how much you want it.' He continued to look at me as if he were trying to weigh me up. 'Or to put it in slightly cruder terms, *Señor* Ruiz, how much you are willing or able to pay for it.'

'How much is the asking price?'

'Four million euros.'

'That's a lot of money.'

'The work we are talking about is a lot of painting, *Señor* Ruiz...it is a Rembrandt, after all.'

I acted as though I was trying to weigh the matter up in my mind for a moment, and then I said, 'Okay, four million it is.'

'You have the money?'

'I can get it, yes.'

'By when?'

'Tomorrow morning.'

'In that case, perhaps we should arrange a time and place where we can affect the sale and purchase of the painting.'

'The sooner the better, so far as I'm concerned.'

'Shall we say one p.m. tomorrow, then?'

'Fine with me.'

'Good...so if you'd like to give me your mobile number, I'll call you in the morning to tell you know where to come.'

'Sure.' I told him the number.

He called at just before twelve the following morning, and told me where to go and meet him. The address turned out to be a rundown block in one of the poorer parts of city. The flat was on the top floor. I went in through the front door and found myself in a dark and grimy lobby. I looked for the lift but there wasn't one, so I made for the stairs. When I got to the top, I found the door to the flat and pushed the buzzer. Somebody buzzed me in and, without saying a word, a big, shaven headed man frisked me, to checked that I wasn't armed. Finding that I wasn't, he said 'Follow me,' and led me along a dark hallway. He stopped outside a door and knocked once then entered, before he turned and beckoned me to follow.

Upon entering the room, I found myself looking at the man I'd spoken to in the Bar López the day before. He said hello and gave me a smile that was about as genuine as the Ray Bans they sell in the Chinese bazaars. He was wearing jeans with trainers and a navy Polo shirt today, and I'd worked out by now who he was and where I'd seen his face before.

'I'm so glad you could come, *Señor* Ruiz,' he said. Then he turned and went over to the fireplace and slid the Van Gogh lithograph that hung there to the side, to reveal a safe, and started moving the dial this way and that. He clearly knew the combination by heart, and opened the safe without bothering to listen for the clicks. Then he reached inside and brought out a small rectangular-shaped portrait. 'The Rembrandt that I believe you were interested in,' he said.

I examined the painting for a few moments, then I asked him how he had acquired the work. 'I inherited it,' he said, and I could almost have believed him were it not for the fact that I knew the painting had been stolen.

At that moment, the door opened and Inge Schwartz walked into the room. Or perhaps I should call her Barbara Borrell, seeing as that was her real name. She was holding a gun. '*Hola*, Arthur,' she said. 'I would introduce you both, but I see that you have already become acquainted.'

'But what are you doing here, Inge?' the man who was called Jaime asked. 'And what's with the gun?'

'Just a precaution,' she said. 'After you gave me the slip that last time, I figured I might need it.' She fixed him with a look that would have sunk a ship. 'I let myself in,' she said. 'I do hope you don't mind.'

'Where's Bruno?' I assumed he was referring to the hired muscle.

'He's working for me now,' she said. 'I made him an offer he found impossible to resist.'

'But this is all a big mistake,' Jaime said. 'I didn't mean to give you the slip. It's just that I've been rather busy just recently.'

'Oh I know you have. You've been rather busy stealing my Rembrandt and trying to sell it. Then once you'd done that you were planning on disappearing forever.'

'It's not yours but your father's and he left it to the state, so I don't see what you're getting on your high horse about.'

Inge shook her head in disgust and looked at me. 'It was Jaime here who waylaid you on the road outside of Magro, Arthur.'

'I rather guessed as much,' I said. 'So you set up the kidnapping of your sister with Jaime from the beginning, then he double-crossed you, is that it?'

'You're not as dumb as you look, Arthur.' She looked tearful all of a sudden. 'It wasn't meant to be like that,' she went on. 'Gisela wasn't supposed to get hurt. She was in on it with us, you see. Jaime had made contact with a couple of low life types who were supposed to carry out a false kidnapping for an agreed fee.'

'Are you saying he'd found a couple of goons who were going to pretend to kidnap Gisela and then let her go?'

'For a fee, yes, that's right.' She sighed. 'But that gangster Vince found out,' she went out. 'It was him or his henchmen who killed the two.'

'They killed Joaquim Gross and Juan Ribera, you mean?'

'Correct.'

'And I suppose it was Gross who provided you with the false German passports?'

She nodded. 'Then Vince kidnapped Gisela for real.'

'And that's when Jaime decided to go solo and ambush me and make off with the ransom, leaving Gisela with no hope, is that it?'

Inge's eyes were full of deadly poison and hatred. 'Exactly,' she said. 'Jaime killed her just as surely as that bastard Vince did.'

'So then you asked me to find the person who killed her and get your Rembrandt back, and you figured that you'd just follow me and see if I led you to Jaime.'

'I'm sorry that I used you in that way, Arthur,' she said. 'But you see, you were the only person I could really trust.'

I realized that I still loved her, despite everything. I told myself that I was a fool and that she'd been using me from the start. She'd taken me for a prize chump and I knew it; but somehow it didn't really seem to matter anymore. 'So now what?' I asked her.

'Jaime has to pay for his mistake.'

'You don't mean you're going to kill me, Barbara?' Jaime said.

'Murder's not your style, Inge,' I said. 'Or perhaps I mean Barbara.'

'It never was,' she agreed. 'But people change—and somebody has to make him pay for what he's done.'

'They'll lock you up and throw away the key,' Jaime said.

'Right now I really don't care all that much what happens to me.'

I cared. I cared a whole lot, even though I didn't think it would exactly have been politic to tell her as much. It was hardly the time or the place, after all.

I turned my head and looked at the man Inge/Barbara had come here to kill. I had of course recognized him from the first moment I set eyes on him in the flesh, as the man holding my client's hand in the photograph up on the wall in the bar I'd gone to in Magro that time. I remembered being insanely jealous of him when I'd seen him and Inge/Barbara together, looking so happy and in love. Well, so much for their great love. Jaime had cheated the two girls. Perhaps he was planning to have Inge/Barbara bumped off as well, so that he could make off with the Rembrandt and sell it someplace then keep the money all for himself.

A part of me was stunned to think that a man, any man, could give up the love of a woman like Inge Schwartz/Barbara Borrell for money, no matter how much of the stuff. Or for a Rembrandt, no matter how much it was worth. I just didn't know what to make of it. But then, I thought, there really was nothing as strange as people.

At that moment a voice said, 'Drop the piece,' and I turned my head abruptly. It was the man that had frisked me on the way in. He was holding a gun. Inge had reckoned she'd won him over to her side with the promise of a big payoff, but the man clearly had other ideas.

I tried to think of something to say to him. Something that might help persuade him that it wasn't such a good idea to shoot us both. No ideas sprang to mind.

Then the door opened and the guy who was passing himself off as Miguel Pasqual entered the room. Seeing Bruno turn to see who it was, I took a step towards him and kicked the gun out of his hand. Bruno jumped on my back as I moved to pick it up. He was a strong bastard, as you might expect, given that he was the hired muscle, and I was having a hard job getting him off me, but then a voice told him to quit the monkeying around and, to my surprise, he did so.

I turned and my heart sank once more as I saw the man who was passing himself off as Miguel Pasqual standing there with the gun in his hand. 'Get against the wall the three of you,' he said, and Bruno, Jaime and Inge/Barbara did as they were told.

He flashed me a sideways glance. 'Lucky for you I showed up in time, Arthur.'

'Don't tell me,' I said, 'it was Vince Caportorio who sent you here, right?'

He laughed. 'Trouble with you is, you don't ever trust anyone.'

'Who, then?'

'I was telling you the truth when I said I was a reporter after a story,' he said. 'The only part I lied about was when I said I was on the staff at *La Vanguardia*, because I'm actually a freelance.' He grinned. 'I purloined a press card that'd belonged to a Miguel Pasqual, a reporter with the newspaper, and have been operating under his name ever since. When I send stories out, I write them under my own name of course. I just use the alias to gain access to places and people. My real name's Javier Moreno.' He shrugged. 'I knew I had to follow you around if I was to have any hope of getting a story out of the whole business.'

I nodded slowly as I struggled to take it all in. Too many things had happened in too short a space of time, and my mind and senses were reeling. I looked over at Inge/Barbara and my heart went out to her. Okay, she hadn't exactly turned out to be as pure as the driven snow, but I'd never bought that act of hers anyway. It sounded like she'd only meant to find a way of reclaiming her lost inheritance, which wasn't really such a terrible thing to do after all. Or so it seemed to me at that moment, as I took out my mobile and called the police. Vince Caportorio and Jaime were the real villains of the piece, I told myself, as I listened to the ringtone.

Or was my readiness to believe Inge/Barbara's story only another sign of just how hopelessly in love with her I was, and what a fool I had become? I was still wondering about this, when the desk sergeant picked up and asked how she could help.

FLOWERS AT MIDNIGHT

PART I

CHAPTER 1

Bella smiled. "Taste okay, darling?"

"I'm sure you could find worse stuff on the wine shelf at Waitrose," Alex replied.

Bella had been trying to persuade Sir Alex to drink her urine ever since they first slept together ten days ago, and he'd finally agreed to play ball. The best part was that she'd secretly used the spy camera in her wristwatch to photograph him guzzling it down.

Sir Alex said, "I have to be at the House in a couple of hours."

She threw him a coquettish glance over her shoulder and saw the greedy lust sparkle in the old goat's eyes. Sir Alex was an extremely rich man with a wife of around his own age who probably loved him, but that wasn't enough for the wrinkled bastard. She turned and smiled at him. "Can I do anything else for you?"

"A cup of tea would be nice, darling."

Bella patted her bobbed black hair into place, and as she pouted into the mirror to check that her cherry lipstick was on right, she saw Sir Alex ogling her ass. She lifted her white cotton dress from the hook on the back of the door and slipped it on. The dress clung to her wet buttocks, their rounded contours shifting like miniature seismic plates as she padded softly to the kitchen.

Sir Alex followed in a black silk bathrobe, his greying hair still wet from the shower. He shuffled up and took her in his arms. He smelt disgusting when he kissed her, and Bella almost gagged. The next thing she knew, he was lifting her onto the worktop, and he entered her for the second time that day. She dug her nails into his back as he fucked her hard.

The knowledge that her boyfriend, Martin, would kill her if he knew what she was doing only heightened her excitement.

Sir Alex cannoned into orgasm, and Bella came with him. Then she slipped down off the edge of the worktop. "I say," she giggled, "we *are* feeling hot today."

"It's hard not to feel that way when I look at you." Sir Alex took a deep breath and smiled as he let it out.

"You only want me for one thing, Alex." Bella balanced this accusation with a coquettish smile.

"I love your pussy, darling, it's true," he confessed. "But that's only because I love *you*, Gina."

Gina was the name Bella was using.

"A case of love me, love my pussy, is it?"

"Precisely."

"But is that the man or the politician talking?"

"How can you possibly say such a thing? I'm only Machiavellian when I'm in the House, darling. Never with you."

"What's that supposed to mean?"

"Machiavelli was an Italian political philosopher. He wrote a book called *The Prince*, which is all about how to succeed in politics."

"Don't tell me. He says you need to bullshit a lot, right?"

"Something like that, yes, as it happens."

"Did he like to drink women's pee-pee, too?"

"You'd have to ask him—only that might prove a tad difficult."

"How come?"

"He died in 1527."

CHAPTER 2

Martin Butler developed Bella's film and printed the photographs the following morning down in his darkroom at the Chelsea Centre. Having satisfied himself that they'd come out okay, he went out and called Mrs. Big from a phone box on King's Road. He stood there in his stonewashed jeans and leather jacket, thrumming his fingers on the window as he listened to the ringtone.

"Hello?"

"It's me. I've got the photographs."

"And they came out as clearly and as I wanted, did they?"

"They came out perfectly."

"Good. In that case, I need you to bring them to me. Be on the embankment by Putney Bridge, on the northwest side, at eleven sharp tomorrow morning."

"Sure."

"I'll need the camera and the chip you used in it, too, of course. Bring it all in an A4 manila envelope. An associate of mine will be there to meet you."

"Why won't you be there?"

"I'll be nearby. You will need to wait a minute or two while my man brings me the package so I can check it. Then so long as everything's in order, he'll come straight back and pay you."

"How long's all this gonna take?"

"Couple of minutes, tops."

"But how will I recognize this associate of yours?"

"You won't. He'll recognize you."

"And how do I know you're gonna pay me once your guy leaves with the camera and the photographs?"

"Listen, if people who work for me do a good job, then I pay them —that way I can always use them again. You understand me?"

"Sure."

"Good. Don't be late."

They hung up and Martin drove back to the flat in Cambridge Gardens off Portobello Road.

Bella was sitting up in bed reading a magazine when he walked in. She was wearing one of his old shirts and nothing else and looked utterly ravishing. "All right, Bel?" He winked at her and worked his arms out of his leather jacket, dropping it over the back of an upright chair.

"What happened?" She put her magazine down and looked at him.

"I've spoken to the lady."

"Mrs. Big?"

Martin sat on the side of the bed, took his brown leather loafers off and swung his legs up. "We're gonna make the exchange tomorrow morning at eleven." He turned and caressed Bella's cheek, which was very white and wonderfully smooth to the touch. "You look'n smell terrific, babe."

"What about the photos, Mart?"

"What about them?"

"You're sure they came out okay? I mean, you can see that it's definitely *him* in them, can you?"

"Old David fuckin' Bailey couldn't 've made the guy come out any clearer, Bel, I'm telling you. No worries."

"Let me have a look at them, then."

"They aren't here. I've got them stashed away in a safe place along with the camera."

"Can you see my face in them, too?"

"Course you can't. D' you think I'm stupid or something?"

"I was only asking."

"Fuck me, Bel." Martin shook his head like he couldn't believe she could ask him such a dumb question.

"But what if he comes into the Revuebar looking for me, Mart?"

"Who?"

"Alex fucking Boulton, our politician friend. Who d'you *think* I meant?"

"But he doesn't know you work there."

"He might be able to find out, though... I mean, he must have all sorts of contacts, a man in his position."

"Now you're starting to get paranoid. Anyway, even if he did find out you work at the Revuebar, he's not gonna try'n come after you, is he?"

"How do you know he won't?"

"The man's a fucking *politician*, not some bloody lunatic."

"You just love the danger of it, don't you?"

"We need the money, Bel. Besides, we need to move out of this place. That mad hubby of yours 'll be out to kill us both if he knows I'm shacked up here with you."

"But Joey's banged up in nick."

"He won't be in there forever."

❋

Mona Chapman drove through South London and pulled up outside of a particularly dilapidated squat on Brixton Hill.

After climbing out of the car, she walked and hammered on the door. A lad with his hair in dreadlocks came and opened up. "I've come to see Al," Mona said.

"Ain't no Al lives here, man." The lad went to shut the door in Mona's face, but she used her foot to stop him.

"I'm an old friend of his. Tell him I've got some good news."

The lad eyed Mona up and down suspiciously for a moment, but then he told her to wait and disappeared inside the house.

Moments later, Al came to the door. An extremely pale and skinny man of medium height, he was dressed in dirty jeans and a dirtier T-shirt. "Oh, Mo, it's you. This's a surprise. How're tricks?"

"I don't do that kind of thing anymore."

He laughed. "You always did have a sense of humour."

"I've got a job for you."

"You mean you're bringing me a commission?"

"Not exactly. There's money in it, though."

"What do I have to do, Mo?"

"I'll explain on the way. Come on, let's go."

"Hang on a sec." Al disappeared for a moment, then when he came back he was wearing an old pilot's jacket.

"Aren't you going to brush your hair?"

"This is the way I wear it."

"I've seen tangled spaghetti that looked less of a mess."

Mona pushed the button on the fob in her hand, the locks on her Volvo opened with a clunk, and they both climbed in. "Good solid set of wheels you got here," Al said, patting the seat.

"You know me. I never did buy into the starving artist bit, not even when we were at the Slade."

"You look good, Mo."

Mona flashed him a sideways glance. "You look like shit, Al. Whatever *happened* to you?"

"Right now, I need a fix and I'm broke."

"Just think of me as your fairy godmother."

"You mean you've got some smack for me?"

"No, but I can help you get some."

"I like the sound of this. What's the catch?"

"The usual *quid pro quo*, Al."

"Quid *what*?"

"You scratch my back…"

"What kind of back-scratching are we talking about?"

"How much does a wrap of heroin cost nowadays?"

"Twenty quid."

"Well, you do something very simple for me, and in return I will give you twenty quid to score a wrap. How does that sound?"

"Will you drive me there, too, to save me the fare?"

"Think I can probably stretch to that."

"Okay, so what's this very simple something you're talking about?"

"You go and meet a man."

"What man?"

"You don't need to know."

"Must be someone dangerous. Who is it, General fuckin' Gaddafi?"

"No, he's dead. Don't you read the papers?"

"So who is it, then?"

"Nobody you need to worry about. The guy's completely harmless."

"What's keeping *you* from meeting him, then?"

"He's my ex, and I know he'd only start pleading with me to go back with him. You know the score."

"You were always more into girls back in the days when we were at the Slade."

"Still am."

"But this ex you're talking about's a *bloke*, you said, right?"

"He was a mistake's what he was."

"The Mr. Wrong who confirmed for you that you were right to want to be with girls all along, you mean?"

"Something like that."

"All right. First we go and score some smack, though, yeah?"

"No, we get the heroin after. Didn't they ever teach you at school that you have to do your work first and then you get to play?"

"I didn't go to that kind of school."

❄

They drove over Putney Bridge, took a left, and Mona found a place to park. Then she reached into the glove compartment, brought out a pair of binoculars and looked through them. She saw traffic moving over the bridge in a steady stream, passengers walking along the footpath, and a red bus. The sky was dull grey as was the river. Blocks of flats and offices ran along the far bank.

Mona shifted the binoculars to the left and saw a man out walking his dog along the embankment. She moved them again, only too far, and found herself looking at the high towers of the city's financial district in the distance. She adjusted the angle slightly once more, and spotted Bella Armando's photographer boyfriend, Martin Butler. He was standing on the embankment by the start of the bridge and had a large manila envelope under his arm.

Mona turned to Al. "He's over there—look." She handed him the binoculars, trying to keep them pointed at the same angle. "Shortish, brown hair, wearing faded jeans, scuffed brown loafers... a brown leather jacket over a T-shirt that has ABERCROMBIE written across it."

"Yeah, I got him."

"Just ask him to give you the large envelope he's got for me and bring it straight over. And don't open it or anything on the way. Think you can manage that?"

"And then we go'n score some heroin, right?"

"Sure, once I've checked that he's handed over what I asked for. Then, presuming he has, you'll have to go back and give him something from me."

"And what if the guy fails to cough up what you wanted—I still get my twenty quid plus the ride to Brixton, right?"

"Of course. I just meant you wouldn't have to go back and give him anything, in that case. Oh, and one more thing... don't get into conversation with him."

"Why, is he likely to want to talk?"

"No, but if he tries to, just cut him off, okay?"

"Right."

"Good, so get to it."

Mona watched Al through her binoculars as he went over to Martin Butler and took the envelope from Butler's outstretched hand. "Good lad, no talking, that's it," she said aloud, as she watched Al turn and start to make his way back.

As soon as he got back to the car, Mona stuck her hand out the window and snatched the manila envelope from him. She slid one of the photographs out, taking care to hold it up so that Al couldn't see what she was looking at. Then her head spun with excitement as she looked at a photograph of Sir Alex Boulton. In the photo, the MP was lying in a bathtub with his mouth open while a woman whose face was off-camera pissed into it. Mona was experiencing the sort of "buzz" a person gets when they know they are close to making a great deal of money at a stroke.

Mona handed Al the envelope with the money in it. "Now give him this."

She watched Al through the binoculars once more as he went and handed Martin Butler his fee. The moment he got back into the passenger seat, he told her he needed his fix.

Mona couldn't get over what a *mess* the guy had become.

CHAPTER 3

The thought that she now had the photographs in her possession added a certain rosy glow to Mona's mood as she sat fondling her beloved Winifred. They were in the Revuebar, watching the show, and Mona was feeling *gooood*. She reckoned she understood now what her brother Donny meant when he talked about the feeling of elation that comes from perpetrating a crime and getting away with it.

The best bit was how she'd got those two stupid innocents, Bella Armando and her wannabe photographer of a boyfriend, Martin Butler, to do all the legwork. She'd given them a measly ten grand for their trouble, but what they didn't know was that she was going to be raking in a couple of hundred grand for herself.

What made it even better was the fact that Mona was a "friend" of Bella's... only the poor girl and her boyfriend didn't know that it was her they'd been working for. Those two pathetic amateurs had *no fucking idea*. They just didn't have any class. Credit where it was due, though, Mona thought, as she watched Bella Armando strut her stuff up on the stage. The girl did have one hell of a cute butt, even if she didn't have much in her head.

After the show, Mona and Winifred walked from the Revuebar down to Le Caprice, the restaurant near Covent Garden, where Winifred had arranged to meet her husband John and dine with Sir Alex Boulton and his wife Prunella.

"Well thanks for a lovely time, Mo."

"The pleasure was all mine, Win."

"I can assure you that's not true." Winifred narrowed her eyes and gave Mona a certain look, then the two women brushed cheeks.

"Oh, you're such a hot little minx," Mona murmured.

Winifred chuckled before she turned and went into the restaurant.

Mona peered through the window and saw Winifred and John. And across the table from them were Sir Alex Boulton and Prunella. Sir Alex was a multimillionaire, and he was widely tipped to win the coming leadership race and go on to lead the Labour Party to victory over the Tories at the next election.

And Mona wished him every success, because she planned to rise with him...

She took out her mobile, dialled the man's number, and saw him reach into his jacket pocket.

"Hello?"

"Sir Alex?"

"Yes, who am I speaking to?"

"You don't know me, but I have something that you will want."

"I'm sorry, but I'm about to eat. Who are you? How did you get this number?"

"I'm talking about some photos of you and that nice young girlfriend of yours."

"Photos?" the MP squealed. "What *photos*?"

"She's come out very well in them... and so have you as a matter of fact."

"Who the devil *are* you?"

Through the window, Mona saw the MP frown as he rose from the table with his mobile pressed to his ear. She headed off up the street, saying, "That's for me to know and you not to, I'm afraid."

"Look, what is it that you want?"

"I'm sure you can work that one out without my help. You do me a little favour and I'll do you one."

"How much is your idea of a little favour?"

"Two hundred grand in used notes, of course. I'm afraid I can't take a cheque—against company policy."

"Now wait a minute. Where on earth do you think I'm going to get that kind of money?"

"Oh, I'm sure you'll think of something. You're a very wealthy man, Sir Alex."

"What gave you that idea?"

"Oh, come on... it's common knowledge, and has been ever since you first made it to into the *Sunday Times*' Rich List. What number were you last year... thirty-seven, I believe?"

"You realize that you could find yourself doing some serious time in prison for this sort of thing, do you?"

"What... for having a hobby? I don't think so, old chap. I like taking photos. If you like to pose for them and then purchase them, that's your affair."

"I never did anything of the sort and you know it."

"You're lying in the bathtub in one of them and the girl's standing over you. Let me see now, what is it that she's doing? Oh, I *say*, she's takin' a piss... right in your mouth. That's going to look really good in the newspapers and on the internet, I'm sure you'll agree. Just think what it'll do for your image, not to mention your marriage. You'll have to say goodbye to the idea of ever becoming prime minister. But then, you don't need the likes of me to tell you that."

"All right, listen! I'll do as you say, but I'll need some time to get the money together."

"You have twenty-four hours. When I call tomorrow, it'll be to arrange the exchange. If you don't have the money, I'm selling these photos to the newspapers."

Mona hung up.

❋

Sir Alex Boulton had excused himself soon after he finished eating earlier at Le Caprice, then he took his wife Prunella home and paid a call on his elder brother Charles at his flat in Pimlico.

Charles was a great reader, and the oak coffee table was cluttered with newspapers and periodicals, while the shelves in the alcoves either side of the fireplace were crammed with a thousand and one different titles. There were historical volumes, political memoirs and various weighty tomes on finance and economics, as well as a number of spy novels and investigative books on the SAS, MI5 and MI6, three organizations that Charles had worked for in the past.

"The blackmailer wants two hundred thousand in cash for Christ's sake." Sir Alex took a long gulp of the stiff gin and tonic Charles had fixed for him. "She says I've got twenty-four hours to free up the cash."

"*She?*"

"Yes, it's a woman."

Charles, who was dressed in a checked shirt, brown corduroys and matching suede shoes, let out a sigh of exasperation. "Does Prunella suspect anything?"

"Not a thing."

Charles ran a hand through his fine grey hair. "You're quite sure of that?"

"Absolutely."

"So, what are you going to do?"

"That's what I'm trying to make up my mind about." Alex Boulton rose from his chair and began to pace the room with his big hands clasped together behind his back. He was in a state of panic and really had no idea as to how to proceed. All he knew for sure was that he was angry as hell—angry and frightened.

He turned to face his brother, who was sitting on the sofa with his legs crossed at the ankle. "What would *you* do, Charles?"

"Well, I think that I'd call on some old friends of mine from my days with MI5 and MI6 and have them use their tracking devices to locate where the bitch was calling from. Then, we could have a helicopter go after her and squad cars on a radio link. We'd have her picked up in no time."

"Yes, but then it would be all over the newspapers, the very thing that I'm trying to avoid."

"I suppose it would be difficult to guarantee keeping the affair secret if we were to go down that road, yes."

"So what do you suggest, then?"

"Strikes me, Alex. You've either got to pay up or tell the blackmailer to go to hell and face the music."

"Yes, well I know *that*."

"What's likely to happen if you tell the blackmailer where to get off?"

"She says she'll send the pictures to the press."

"Well obviously, yes, but *then* what?" Charles frowned. "I mean, let's start with Prunella—how's she likely to react to all this if she finds out?"

"She'd probably file for a divorce." Sir Alex Boulton loosened his burgundy tie and undid the top button on his striped shirt.

"That would cost you over half of everything you own," Charles reasoned. "And then there are the children to be considered. If you're lucky, you might end up getting to see them at weekends. You'd have to resign from politics, of course, just as I had to." In Charles's case, the advent of one of his gay affairs becoming public knowledge, thanks to the good offices of the press, had put an end to both his marriage and his political career in one fell swoop.

"Thanks for trying to cheer me up."

"What do you want me to do, Alex? Tell you to go home to your wife and forget about it and the whole sorry mess'll just go away? What's that going to solve? You've got yourself into a tricky situation here, and it's no good trying to deny it."

"You're right, of course. It's just that I keep turning the whole business over in my head, and... well, I really don't know what to do for the best."

"What do your instincts tell you to do?"

"I'm wondering if I should just hand over the money." Sir Alex Boulton grimaced at the thought and he began to wring his hands. "But a couple of hundred grand's a lot of fucking dosh to have to cough up for a quick bloody fling with some bimbo."

"Yes, I see your point, but the alternative could potentially be infinitely more damaging. Looking at it logically: you stand to lose a couple of hundred grand if you pay the blackmailer, but you could end up losing your entire *lifestyle* if you don't."

"So, you agree that the thing to do's just pay up and have done with it, then?"

"Looked at from that angle, yes." Charles's broad, high forehead creased with worry lines. "Only..." He broke off as if he were frightened to say what was on his mind.

"Only *what*, Charles?"

"Well, damn it, Alex, you're a man of the world... You know as well as I do that blackmailers can have a nasty way of bleeding their victims dry. First of all, it's a couple of hundred thousand, then you get another call a few months later and they want some more money. And it can go on like that indefinitely."

"I wouldn't pay it."

"You'd be right back in the same situation you're in now."

"Not if I tell her I want the photos and any copies, along with the camera and the chip she used, in exchange for the money I'd be paying her."

"And how can you be sure, when you pay her, that the blackmailer won't have more copies she's keeping for a rainy day?"

"If it came to that then I'd do whatever I had to."

"Meaning?"

"I could pay someone to bump her off and save myself a lot of money in the process." Sir Alex paused a moment to ask himself if he really meant what he'd just said. "Of course, I don't want it to come to that."

"Are you saying you know who the blackmailer is, Alex?"

"Presumably, it's the girl herself."

"The one you had the affair with, you mean?"

"Who else *can* it be?"

"But how did she manage to take the photographs without you seeing her do it?"

"She must've used a tiny camera of some kind, I suppose. I don't know - you know, more about that sort of thing than I do."

"She could perhaps've used a spy camera, it's true." Charles scratched his chin. "But going back to what you were suggesting a moment ago, frankly, bumping people off sounds like a very risky game to me. Besides, it just isn't your style, Alex. If you were thinking of going down that road, then perhaps you should let me deal with it."

CHAPTER 4

Mona Chapman parked her Honda up a side street off Fulham Broadway before she put on her blonde wig along with her hat and Ray Bans. Then she checked herself out in the mirror. Why, she wouldn't have recognized herself in this get-up in a million years. I almost look *feminine*, she thought.

She was still feeling antsy, though. So to calm her nerves, she reminded herself that this was the opportunity she'd always been waiting for. She was about to make a couple of hundred grand.

Mona climbed out of the car, then she crossed the road and went into the precinct. She walked up to the end, past shops on either side. Then entered Sainsbury's and headed over to where they had the sandwiches and sushi meals—which was where she'd told the MP to wait for her.

She noticed a man standing there with his back to her. He was middle-aged, tall, and dressed in a smart blue suit. It's *him*, Mona thought, but she wanted to get a closer look at his face to make sure. So she walked down to the end of the aisle, then turned and came back up towards him. She looked at the stuff on the shelves as she came along, like she was just out shopping.

She stopped next to him, picked up a packet of sushi and began to inspect it. Standing there in her hat, blonde wig, and shades, she told herself once more that the MP would never recognize her if he saw her again. This thought gave her comfort, and right now Mona needed all the comfort she could get because she was feeling nervous.

She glanced quickly at the man's face, and he looked back at her. It was *him*, no question. There was no mistaking those intelligent grey eyes. She'd seen them looking out of her TV set, and from the pages of newspapers and magazines, enough to recognize them. She took in the big ears, the large strong nose and the broad mouth that sloped down slightly to one side, the crinkly and perfectly coiffed greying hair.

Mona went back to resuming her inspection of the sushi that was on offer. And still looking at the sushi, she asked the MP, in a low voice that wasn't hers—or didn't sound like it—if he had anything for her.

"That would depend."

"What does that mean?"

"On whether you have anything for me."

"I've got the photos here."

"*All* of them?"

"Yes."

"And the copies and the camera?"

"Yes... have you got the money?"

"What if I haven't, Gina? What if I were just to snatch that manila envelope I can see you've got in your handbag and leave with it? What would you be able to do about it?"

"You wouldn't dare."

"What makes you so sure?"

"Are you seriously thinking about doing something crazy like that *here*, in full view of everyone... not to mention all the security cameras? *Robbing* a woman—because that's what it would be. Your career would be over the moment you did it, and you'd probably be lucky to avoid going to prison."

"You'd be the one to go to prison."

"Not only that, but the photos would go to the newspapers. Because you'd be stopped and searched and they'd be taken off you, once the police had heard what I'd have to say. So you'd be the loser any way you look at it."

Mona's quick and confident dismissal of the scenario Sir Alex had just sketched out appeared to take the wind out of his sails, and he seemed to be about to hand over the package, but when she went to snatch it, his grip was firm.

Sir Alex looked about him, to ensure that there was nobody within earshot. "Okay, now you listen to me," he told her in a voice that was somewhere between a growl and a whisper. "I'm only doing this once. So, if you were planning on coming back for second helpings, then you'd better think again. Because if you do, I promise you'll regret it."

"I hardly think you're in a position to make threats."

"On the contrary, that's exactly the position that I *am* in," he snarled. "I'm handing this over to you now, but that doesn't mean I do this sort of thing lightly. I'm rich, as you have rightly concluded, and therefore it wouldn't be at all difficult to persuade any number of people to do all sorts of things for me, if you follow my drift. I'm not yet desperate enough to take action of that sort at the moment. In fact, I'd prefer just to hand over the sum you've asked for as things stand. But if you are under the impression that this sorry little show of yours is going to enjoy an extended run, then you'd better reconsider. Is that understood?"

"Sure."

Sir Alex released the package and Mona put it in her handbag. Then she turned and made her way out of the supermarket, on through the precinct and into the street. The Broadway was buzzing with people and traffic, as usual, and rain had just begun to fall out of the uniformly grey sky.

She crossed the road and hurried back to her Honda, climbed in and locked the doors. Adrenaline fizzed through her veins as she tore the package open, safe in the knowledge that nobody could see what she was doing through the tinted windows.

She quickly checked the different bundles of banknotes, until she'd satisfied herself that they were all made up of fifties and all of the same size. Then she counted one of the bundles.

There were two hundred notes in it, which came to £10,000.

Next, she counted the number of bundles and found there were twenty of them...

The bastard's coughed up, all right, Mona said to herself.

She was now a woman with two-hundred grand to her name.

❉

Mona drove over to Hammersmith and parked. Then she took off the hat and the wig before she got out of the car and went into her bank.

She told the man behind the counter she wanted to take a look in the security box she had in her name. She had to wait a couple of minutes, then a man came and led her down to the vault. She deposited all but one of the bundles of bank notes there, figuring £10,000 ought to keep her going for a while.

After that, she went home and hid her spending money under the floorboards. Then she smoked a joint and danced around her tiny kitchen to the sound of Radio Head. She felt *gooood*.

It was like fate, she thought, the way the opportunity had presented itself to her. It all started when she'd had a one-night stand with a girl called Margot Peterson, whom she met at a swingers party the week before she first bedded Win. It turned out that this Margot was a shrink who'd boasted to her, while they were in bed, of having some rich and important patients. Mona asked her who these important clients were and whether they had any kinky secrets, and Margot just grinned and said that was privileged information and strictly between her and her patients. But then when Margot went to take a shower, Mona noticed that she'd left her briefcase open. So she went through it and happened to come across a file on one Sir Alex Boulton. Well, Mona had never been all that interested in politics, but even she knew who *he* was. The man was often on the telly, for a start. Not only that, but Win—who was still just a mate she'd have pawned her favourite vibrator to fuck at that time—happened to tell her the day before about how the man was a close friend of her husband's. Mona's curiosity was aroused, and to cut a long story short, she ended up reading part of the transcription of a session in which the MP talked to Margot about his sexual fantasies...

MARGOT: And why do you think that might be so?
ALEX BOULTON: I really have no idea... which I suppose is why I'm here... I mean, that's your job... to explain it to me. To explain *me* to myself, as it were.
MARGOT: Have you ever tasted urine?
ALEX BOULTON: No, never... I already told you.
MARGOT: It's interesting...

ALEX BOULTON: There are times when I am really quite appalled at myself, I can assure you... a mature, married man such as I am... and a father, too, of course.

MARGOT: Aren't you being just a little hard on yourself?

ALEX BOULTON: *Am* I? I really don't know... I mean, it does strike me as being a pretty ridiculous and appalling thing for a decent, respectable man in my position to be fantasizing about—wouldn't you agree?

MARGOT: Oh, I don't know... people fantasize about all kinds of unusual things... even people who are respectable.

ALEX BOULTON: Well you should know, I suppose...

A short pause.

ALEX BOULTON: So am I to understand that my fantasies are not so very unusual, then?

MARGOT: They are of what, broadly speaking, we can call a deviant nature... but it's not at all unusual for perfectly normal people to have such fantasies, is what I'm saying... I'm interested in why you should feel so bad about having them... Why do you think that might be?

ALEX BOULTON: Because of a sense of shame, that's quite obvious.

A short pause.

ALEX BOULTON: I mean, it's scarcely the sort of thing one would want to own up to, is it?

A short pause.

MARGOT: Have you ever mentioned any of this to your wife?

ALEX BOULTON: Good heavens, no!

MARGOT: How do you think she would respond if you were to do so?

ALEX BOULTON: I should think she would be perfectly horrified... and quite rightly, too...

A short pause.

MARGOT: And what if you were to become involved in a relationship with a woman who was amenable to such ideas?

ALEX BOULTON: A woman who allowed me to...

MARGOT: ... To drink her urine, yes.

ALEX BOULTON: Oh, that would never happen.

MARGOT: Why shouldn't it?

ALEX BOULTON: I should never suggest the idea in the first place.

A short pause.

ALEX BOULTON: I mean, it's not something I should ever talk about outside these four walls...

MARGOT: What if the woman were to be the one to suggest the idea?

ALEX BOULTON: What kind of woman would ever suggest such a thing?

MARGOT: It's not impossible... Anyway, just supposing it happened... in that eventuality would you be tempted to go ahead and act out your fantasy?

ALEX BOULTON: But that would never happen.

MARGOT: But *if* it did?

ALEX BOULTON: Speaking hypothetically, you mean...?

MARGOT: Yes.

ALEX BOULTON: Now there's a question...

A short pause.

MARGOT: I can take that as a *yes*, then...

When she got to that point, Mona heard Margot coming out of the bathroom, and she quickly slipped the file back into the briefcase, just as she'd found it.

Her mind started working overtime after that, and it wasn't long before she hatched her plan to make herself some serious money fast. All she needed was a sexy and attractive girl who'd be up for what she had in mind, and a photographer... And then she thought of Bella Armando, the girl who danced at the Revuebar. She'd befriended Bella after first meeting her and her boyfriend at a house party in Hackney several months back. Bella was the kind of sexy piece any guy would go for, Mona thought. And it so happened that her boyfriend, Martin, was trying to make a career for himself as a photographer while he worked the door at the Revuebar. He wasn't getting much luck, though. She also recalled how Bella had told her that she and Martin both had credit card debts that were starting to "go quantum," which meant they could surely use a little extra money. Why look any further?

So she called the number Bella had given her, and when Martin

Butler picked up she put on a funny voice and ran her proposition by him. She asked him, in a nutshell, how he and Bella fancied making themselves some easy money. Like all of the best ideas, it was beautifully simple.

And what was more important, it had *worked*.

※

But while Mona was busy congratulating herself, Martin wasn't feeling so happy with things. Okay, he and Bella had made ten grand from the stunt they'd pulled. It was better than nothing, sure. But it was hardly enough for them to be able to change their lifestyle, and *that* was precisely what Martin was so desperate to do. He wanted them to be able to get out of London and start afresh someplace where it was hot and sunny. Spain would be just the ticket.

First, though, they needed to get a stake up together—enough for them to be able to move into a small place down on the Costa somewhere. Maybe they would be able to find themselves a nice little bar to run, down in that part of the world. That would be pretty cool.

It would sure beat the hell out of working at the Revuebar six nights a week, anyway. What Martin hated most about the place was the way the punters ogled Bella when she stripped.

Martin loved Bella and he wanted her all for himself. Sometimes, though, he found himself wondering whether he could trust her to be faithful. And it hadn't failed to occur to him that she probably wasn't telling him the whole story when she said *all* she'd done with the MP was piss in the guy's mouth.

She'd fucked him. Martin was practically *sure* of it.

Highly toxic images of the MP and Bella *going at it* began to play themselves out in his imagination.

He came to the conclusion that the man owed him.

The man owed him *big time*.

It also occurred to Martin that Mrs. Big must have taken the man for a lot more money than she'd paid him and Bella. And he began to feel like they'd been used... like he and Bella had done all the legwork while Mrs. Big reaped the lion's share of the reward. It was like they'd been fucked over both ways, first by the MP and then by Mrs. Big.

Martin began to wonder who Mrs. Big was, and he tried to picture what she was like. He didn't have anything beyond the sound of her voice over the telephone to go on, though, so it was a pretty hopeless task.

His thoughts turned to the MP once more.

He started to work up a plan that involved him and Bella getting their own back on the man, and coming by the stake they needed in order to make a fresh start in life.

What they were going to do, he decided, was blackmail their politician friend themselves and cut out Mrs. Big. He'd kept hold of a couple of real nice shots of Bel making pee-pee into the MP's mush, and Mrs. Big didn't know he had them. He could threaten the guy with those. Tell him to cough up the dosh or the pictures go to the newspapers.

Finding the MP's telephone number wouldn't be a problem, because it would be on Bella's mobile after he'd called her. She'd kept that mobile solely for talking to the MP. That had been Mrs. Big's idea. The beauty of it was that they knew the MP's number but he didn't know theirs. All the MP had to go on was the number of a mobile that Mrs. Big had either stolen, or had stolen for her. A burner phone Bella received through the post.

Martin reckoned they could do it. And he began to wonder how much they should take the guy for.

He found the mobile at the bottom of Bella's handbag, tapped a couple of keys, and got the man's number up. Then he pressed the *call* tab.

The man picked up and Martin told him why he was calling.

"Look, I already told you I'd only pay once," the MP said. "I warned you not to try this again."

"Now you listen to me," Martin said. "Number one, you're in no position to go issuing threats to anybody and number two..."

But the MP had already hung up.

CHAPTER 5

"What are you grinning at, Mo?" Winifred asked.

"You," Mona said.

"What about me?"

"I was just thinking how much I'd like to eat you alive."

They were dining at the Ivy, and Mona was feeling on top of the world.

"Oh, Mo, look at the prices," Winifred cooed when she saw the menu. "Perhaps we should go somewhere else a little more within our budget."

"I told you *I'm* the one who's paying this evening, so you needn't concern yourself with the cost."

"But you can't afford these prices. I've eaten here before several times, but it's always been John or someone that's paid. I never realized just how expensive it is."

"What you have to understand is, *you're worth it*, Win."

"It's not a question of that."

"What's is it a question of, then?"

"Look, I know you want to be romantic, and that's awfully sweet of you, but you're on the *dole*, darling."

Mona offered up a smug smile, as her thoughts turned to the MP's two-hundred grand that were now sitting safely in *her* bank box. Then she told Winifred that it was up to *her* how she chose to spend *her* money.

"But I don't want to be responsible for putting you in a position where you won't be able to make the rent, or leave you broke halfway through the month."

"Win, darling, you worry too much."

"I know you, Mo... you're generous to a fault, but—"

Just then, the waiter came over. Mona ordered fresh salmon for herself, and Winifred went for the paella.

❄

The following morning, Mona went over to Wormwood Scrubs to visit her brother, Donny, otherwise known as The Dog.

They sat either side of a table in a room full of other prisoners who were being visited by their wives and girlfriends or family members. Donny was a big mountain of a man with the face of a Rottweiler that has been in a car crash.

"How you doing, Donny?"

"All right, Mo. Can't complain too much. It's nice to see you, gel. How are ya?"

"I'm all right, Donny. It's *you* that I'm worried about. How have you been doing?"

"I been doin' a lot a thinkin', Mo."

"Oh? And what's been on your mind?"

Mona reached across the table, to squeeze Donny's hand, but the guard coughed loudly and she quickly moved back. Then the guard came over and warned her that he would terminate her visit if he saw her try anything like that again.

Donny waited for the man to move away. Then he said in a voice that was little more than a whisper, "I been hearin' that Joey B's gonna get out tomorrow."

"No."

"That's what I been hearin', Mo."

"But how can that be?"

"Rumour is he done a deal."

"What kind of a deal?"

"The way the story goes, the filth didn't have nothin' on me and

Ricky Red after we done the bank robbery... not until they got their hands on that cunt Joey, that is. Then they told 'imp he was lookin' at doin' ten years, but if he gave 'em all the stuff on us, two they'd cut it down to three."

"But Joey wouldn't do a thing like that to you two, would he, Donny? I mean you're his mates."

"Not any fuckin' more we ain't."

❆

That afternoon, Martin took out Bella's mobile again and dialled the MP's number. He listened to the ringtone for a short while, then he heard the man say, "Hello?" in that posh accent of his.

"It's me."

"Oh, you again."

"No need to sound so pleased."

"How do you *expect* me to sound?"

"I'm just offering to do you a service, is the way I look at it."

"And how have you managed to arrive at that rather outlandish idea?"

"Simple," Martin said. "I'm the man who's gonna keep your name out of the newspapers. All you gotta do is pay me my fee for services rendered."

"What's your relationship to the woman?"

"*What* woman?"

"The one I paid last time."

"I don't know about any woman you paid. I'm on my own in this."

"And what about the girl, Gina? She's your girlfriend, I suppose, is that right?"

"That's enough with the questions," Martin said. "Now, I'll tell you this. You either pay me a hundred grand or the pictures go to the press, you got that?"

"What guarantee do I have that you won't come back for more money in future?"

"You'll just have to trust me."

"Give me one good reason why I should do that."

"You don't have any other option."

"But that's just where you're wrong, old chap, because you see, I could go to the police, or I could take matters into my own hands."

"Meaning just *what*, exactly?"

"I know a lot of people who'd be only too happy to make you and that pretty girlfriend of yours disappear, and they'd charge me a damn sight less than a hundred grand to make it happen."

"We both know you wouldn't want to go down that road, though, Alex."

"Why wouldn't I?"

"Because you're a gentleman, and gentlemen just don't do that sort of thing."

"Excuse me for saying so, old chap, but I really must say that I think you're being frightfully naïve."

They both went quiet for a moment.

"Okay," Martin broke the silence, "well, there's your guarantee, then."

"Meaning?"

"You'll pay me the fee I'm asking for this once, because you know it's worthwhile to pay it. And because you don't want to get involved in having me bumped off. Murder just wouldn't be your style, when all's said and done. But you also know that I won't be stupid enough to try and squeeze you for more in the future, because if I do, then I know what I can expect the next time around."

"When I paid the woman, I told her I'd only pay her once and I meant it."

"I already told you, I've no idea who this woman you're talking about is."

"You're lying."

They both went quiet again.

Then Martin said, "So what's it to be, then?"

"Okay, I'll pay you the money, but I'll say the same thing to you as I said to the woman. Come back for more—whether it's you that calls, or whoever it is—and you know what you can expect. And I *mean* it."

"I'm glad to see that we both understand each other," Martin said. "You've got twenty-four hours to get the money up together."

He hung up.

Martin called the MP again the next day, as he said he would.

"You got the money?"

"No, not yet, but I'll have it by tomorrow."

"That's not good enough. I told you I wanted you to get it today."

"Have you ever tried being discreet about taking a hundred grand out of an account, old chap?"

Martin didn't say anything.

"No, I didn't think so," the MP answered his own question. "To begin with, I need to do it so that my wife doesn't suspect anything. I could do without having her asking me questions I might find hard to answer. That entails a certain amount of juggling things around. Just try and put yourself in my shoes for a moment. Most of my money is all tied up in long-term savings accounts and bonds, shares, pension funds, property and what have you. People just don't leave large quantities of cash sitting idly in a bank, you know, unless they want to find themselves out of pocket."

"You're bullshitting me."

"No, I'm not. Listen, I want this to go smoothly the same as you do."

"Okay, I'll call you again the same time tomorrow, then. But this is your last chance. Because I'm warning you, if you haven't got the money tomorrow when I call, the photos go to the press."

"And if you try and sell them, you'll end up in prison, because I shall go to the police and tell them everything."

"You wouldn't dare."

"Try me."

"Anyway," Martin said, "even if you did go to the police, they'd never catch me if I sell the photos anonymously."

"Do you really think the newspapers would print photographs that they'd received from an anonymous source?"

Wouldn't they? It was a good question.

But it wasn't one that Martin was in a mood to be considering right now.

"Like I said, tomorrow's your last chance. You let me down and the photos go to the press. End of story. I'll be in touch."

Martin hung up.

❋

"What's the score?" Bella asked Martin as soon as he got back.

"The guy's saying he can't get the money till tomorrow."

"D' you think he's just playing for time?"

"Could well be."

Bella nodded thoughtfully. "So what happens now? Are we gonna go to work this evening, or aren't we?"

"I think it's best to carry on as normal, Bel, right up until we've got the money and're ready to blow."

Bella thought that made sense. Besides, having something to do would help take her mind off things.

CHAPTER 6

Charles picked up the two tumblers that he'd poured and went over to his brother, Alex, who had been pacing the room like a caged tiger for the past few minutes. "Get that down you," he said.

Sir Alex Boulton wrested the tumbler from his brother's hand. "Right now, I'd like to grab the little shit who's blackmailing me, whoever he is, and wring his bloody neck."

"Spoken like a true man of action, dear boy. And those sentiments are quite understandable in the circumstances, I am sure. But you have to try to keep a cool head, that's the important thing here. It's all about striking the right note with the blackmailer, so that you get him to negotiate with you. You've got to make him realize that he's not going to get everything his own way, and that you'll only be pushed so far and no further. Make him understand that there are going to be consequences for him if he is foolhardy enough to go beyond what you have agreed to."

"Yes, well that's what I tried to do. I mean, you heard what I said to the man when I spoke to him on the telephone."

"And you did rather well, old chap. Anyone would think you'd been trained by British Intelligence, the way I was."

Sir Alex Boulton looked his brother in the eye. "You know I'm terribly grateful for the way you're helping me get through all this. I'm not sure that I'd have been able to do it alone."

"What are brothers for?" Charles shrugged. "The important thing is that you've now managed to put your own stamp on the situation. Instead of it being *his* show, it's now a two-way process, a *dialogue*, whether he likes it or not." Charles ran a hand through his layered grey hair and nibbled at his Scotch. "At all times, you need to make him realize that you are also a *player* in this... that way his *demands* cease to be such and become *requests*."

"I get the picture, Charles. But *now* what should I do?"

"I think I'm going to do a little digging around."

"Digging around for *what*?"

"Well, we know that the girl you were involved with must be part of it," Charles reasoned. "What is her name again... Jean, was it?"

"Gina... at least that's what she told me."

"Yes, well this girl's obviously complicit and working in tandem with the man who's been in phone contact, I should say, wouldn't you?"

"It seems highly probable."

❄

When Martin got back to the flat, there was no sign of Bella anywhere, so he went into the bedroom to see if she was sleeping.

She wasn't.

But then the light went on. Martin turned abruptly and saw a man he didn't recognize standing in the doorway.

"Seemed like you was havin' trouble seein' what you was up to," the man said. "So, I thought I'd better shed a little light on the matter." He was a huge mountain of a guy stuffed into a navy-blue tracksuit, with a shaved stone boulder for a head, two rocks for hands and a lump of chipped granite for a face.

Martin wondered who on earth the man could be. Was he a burglar? If so, then he seemed to have a rather unusual way of going about things. No, he must be Bella's husband, Joey B. Bella had assured Martin that Joey B wasn't due to be let out of prison for another couple of years at the earliest, but even so Martin had worried from time to time about what might happen if the man were to get out early. Well, it seemed like he was about to find out.

Martin did his best to muster a smile. "We've never met, Joey," he said, "but I've heard a lot about you."

"First thing is, my name ain't Joey."

"But I thought…"

"Look at me."

Martin had been looking at him all the while.

"Do I seem like the kinda person'd give a rabbit's fuck what you think or don't think?"

The man brought out a gun.

If Martin hadn't been so afraid, the fact that this mountain of a man should reckon he needed a weapon, with just the two of them here like this, might have struck him as a curious form a flattery.

"That was a question, case you didn't notice. I'm waitin' for an answer."

"N-n-no," Martin stammered.

"The fuck'd you say you was again, anyway—the Scarlet fuckin" Pimpernel, is it, or what?"

"I'm Martin… Who are you?"

"They call me The Dog. I bark'n people jump."

It sounded like a funny name for a guy to have, but Martin wasn't about to argue the point. "I'm afraid I'm going to have to ask you to leave."

"I ain't goin' *no* place—and you ain't neither."

"Look, what's all this about?"

"We'll save the explanations for later." The Dog jerked the hand he held the gun in. Then he turned the light back off and marched Martin out of the bedroom, along the narrow hallway, and into the living room.

Newspapers, magazines, and articles of clothing of various kinds lay where they'd been dropped, in the chairs and on the carpet. "Right," The Dog snarled. "Now you just sit there'n shut the fuck up till Joey shows, you wanna live through this. You follow my drift?"

"I'm afraid we're going to be waiting an awful long time."

"What d'you mean by that?"

"Joey's in prison. He's still got a lot of time to serve."

"That's where you're wrong, 'cause the B man just got out."

"Are you *sure* about that?"

"Never been surer of anythin' in my whole life."

"But how *can* he have, if he hasn't served all of his sentence?"

"What I 'eard, the man did a deal."

"What kind of a deal?"

"One that involved rattin' on his friends."

"So that's why you're here."

"That's why *I'm* here, but what about *you?* The fuck you doin' in Joey B's flat?"

"I've been living here."

"What, moved in with the man's missis, did ya?"

"We were just about to move out, as it happens."

"Somethin' tells me you shoulda moved a little sooner."

Something told Martin the man had a point.

"What makes you think Joey'll be comin' here now?"

"It's the man's home, right?" The Dog said. "And home's the place where people go sooner or later, when they get out of nick."

Martin reckoned the man had a point there, too.

"So now what?"

"You always axe a lotta dumb fuckin' questions?"

Martin didn't say anything.

"I could always just shoot you now," The Dog said, like he was thinking aloud.

"There's no need for that."

"That's for me to decide."

Martin figured he'd better just shut up and do as The Dog said. So they sat there for what felt like ages, neither of them saying a word. And then, when they finally heard someone opening the door, The Dog put a finger to his lips. At the same time he aimed his blue-steel Model 27 Smith & Wesson at Martin's face. The gun had a four-inch barrel, and Martin knew that if The Dog were to pull the trigger then the bullet would take his head with it.

They heard the sound of the key turning in the lock. Then the door slamming shut... footsteps out in the hallway. And then a man Martin presumed must be Joey B walked into the room.

Joey B had the air of a man who thinks he's alone in his own home until he saw The Dog standing over by the wall with a big smile that wasn't really a smile at all. Joey blinked a couple of times, like he couldn't believe his eyes. "Well I'll be blowed," he said. "If it ain't The Dogman himself."

"You a fuckin mole or somethin', Joey? You like livin' in the dark?"

Joey reached out and flicked a switch, and when the light came on, Martin was able to get a better look at him. The man stood at around six-four, his greased black hair was swept back over his head, and he had shoulders the way Jayne Mansfield had breasts. He was wearing newish Diesel jeans, a blue Lacoste polo shirt, and a black leather jacket. His shoes looked like they were Italian, probably Gucci's. The guy dressed in a certain style, and Martin figured some women would probably find his swarthy looks attractive, in a gangsterish kind of way. That must have been what Bella saw in him.

Joey was looking at The Dog. "Long time no see, man."

"Thought I'd come'n pay you a visit."

"Who's your friend?"

"He ain't nobody."

"Nice for 'im... well, it's good to see you anyway, Dog. I appreciate it, you droppin' in like this... Get you a drink?"

"Not now."

Joey made what Martin reckoned was a pretty decent stab at a smile, all things considered. "So, what've you been up to?"

"Lotta thinkin."

"You always was a deep one, Dog."

"Not much else a man can do when he's cooped up like I was."

"No, I guess not."

"No thanks to *you*, Joey."

"The fuck you sayin?" I went down the same as you did, Dog."

"That's right, you did... only you got out in three."

"Yeah, well I just got out today, as it happens. Seems like you managed to get out all right, too, though, huh?"

"Yeah, but only 'cause I ixcaped... I didn't do no *deal* or nothin like you did."

"What're you on about, Dog? Keep talkin' in that canine fuckin' language a yours'n there ain't no way I'm gonna be able to understand you, man."

"I always thought we was mates, Joey."

"You're too fuckin' right we are, Dog. So what's with the fuckin' peashooter?"

"Fuckin' obvious, i'n it?"

"Well no, it ain't to me, Dog."

"Fuckin' peashooter's for shootin' fuckin' peas wi', i'n it? Any kid knows that."

"No need to take the piss, Dog."

"Well, ain't there now, Joey? Ain't there *really*? Well that *is* a bit of a turn up, I must say 'cause I thought that was what you'd been kinda specializin' in these past few years."

"What the fuck was it give you that idea?"

"Just the way you been actin'... the stunts you been pullin', you know."

"What stunts is that you're talkin" about?"

"I'll do the questions."

"No need to start comin' on like a fuckin' pit bull with me, Dog."

"I don't need you to tell me how I gotta start comin' on with you, neither."

"C'mon, Dog, *fuck me*. It's your old mate, Joey B you're talkin' to. The fuck's the matter with you, man? Somebody hit you on the head when you was inside or somethin', did they?"

"No, nothin like that, Joey."

"So what the fuck is it, then?"

"What's the matter with me is that I heard you been talkin'."

"Talkin', Dog?"

"Yeah, that's right."

"Talkin' to *who*, Dog?"

"To some old friends of yours."

"Which old friends of mine might they be, Dog?"

"Your friends in blue."

"Whoever told you that wants his fuckin' head read."

"That ain't the way I heard it, Joey."

"I dunno what the fuck you're on about, Dog. I mean, fuck me, just take a look at you. You come round here'n accuse me of a thousand and one different kindsa bullshit, all because some asshole who needs his fuckin' head read's fed you a pack a fuckin' fairy stories. I mean, I just can't fuckin' *believe* this."

"What is it you can't believe, Joey?"

"*This*, Dog, this fuckin' bullshit you're laying on me. This is fuckin' *unreal*, Dog. I mean, you just wanna stop and listen to yourself a moment, I tell ya... I mean, what the fuck's happened to you, anyway? I mean, *hel-lo*? Dog? Is anybody *in there*? Or has somebody come along 'n nicked your old brain and left you with another one that don't fuckin' work too good? I mean *fuck me*."

"I hear you talkin', Joey."

"Do you, Dog? Well at least you ain't deaf, anyway, which is somethin' I suppose."

"I hear you makin' with a lotta words, anyway, but the fing is, it's practically what you might call *common knowledge* round my way that you been keepin' bad company."

"You must live in a funny area, Dog, 'cause anyone who knows me knows I don't talk. End of story. You know what they say, if you can't do the time, don't commit the fuckin' crime. When I was inside, I didn't talk to nobody, Dog. I always been one to keep my nose clean, me."

The Dog took a couple of steps forward and held his gun against Joey's forehead. "I take exception to havin' people insult where I live, Joey. You should know that of all people, seeing as you was born'n bred there, the same as me."

Joey swallowed hard and said, "I was only sayin', Dog.—"

"How 'bout sayin' where my fuckin' money is?"

CHAPTER 7

"*What* fuckin' money?"

"You owe me'n you know it, so you can stop shittin' me."

"I ain't shittin' nobody. Fuck it, Dog, you don't know how much it pains me, man, to see you distrustin' me like this."

"It don't cause you nowhere near as much pain as *I* will if I don't get my fuckin' money."

"You must know the cops took it all. Man, you barkin' up the wrong tree if you think I got it."

The Dog kicked Joey hard in the nuts, and he collapsed in a squealing mess on the floor. The Dog picked him up and punched him in the gut, and as Joey fell backwards, he punched him in the face this time. There was a loud cracking noise and blood started to stream from Joey's face as he slid down the wall. Then The Dog dragged him out of the living room and into the bathroom.

Finding himself alone in the living room, Martin reckoned it was time to make himself scarce.

He hadn't made it as far as the front door before he was struck on the back of the head by what felt like a block of cement. He lost consciousness and hit the carpet.

When he came to a short time later, Martin was lying on the bathroom floor and he could hear someone screaming. It took him a moment or two to work out where he was and how he'd got there. He got to his feet just in time to see The Dog shoving Joey's head into the bathtub and holding it underwater.

Martin tried to intervene, but The Dog stopped him in his tracks with a hard punch to the gut. He followed up with a punch to the jaw that sent Martin crashing back down onto the tiles.

The Dog turned his attention back to Joey. "Hey, Braincell," he snarled. "You gonna tell me what you did with my money or you wanna die in a lotta pain instead? Choice is yours."

Joey tried to say something but found that he couldn't.

"Can't hear you, man. Speak the fuck up."

"O-kay," Joey finally managed to croak out.

"So come on, then, where the fuck is it?"

"In a bank."

"*Which* fuckin' bank?"

When Joey looked like he was having second thoughts about telling, The Dog grabbed him by the throat. "Fancy playin" some more water polo, with your fat fuckin' head for the ball or the puck, or whatever the fuck it is they use, do ya.?" Joey shook his head and The Dog loosened his grip a little. "Okay, so we"ll try again—*where's the fuckin' bank?*"

"Over in Geneva."

"You're gonna have to tell me more'n that." The Dog held his gun against Joey's crotch. "Now this's your last fuckin' chance—either you tell me or you can say goodbye to where you keep your brains."

Joey told The Dog the name of the bank.

"And the address'n the number of the account?"

Joey told him.

"Got anythin' can prove to me you ain't lyin'?"

"In the safe... in the next room."

"Let's go'n open it, then—you go first and your girlfriend can go in the middle. And remember my gun'll be pointin" at your backs all the way."

Joey struggled to his feet and led them into the bedroom. He flicked the light switch before he hopped onto the bed. Then he pulled the painting of the lion back from the wall and started turning the dial on the safe this way and that. He moved it without even bothering to listen for clicks.

Martin could see that the man knew the combination by heart, as he watched him move the dial. He continued to watch, as Joey opened the door and reached inside the safe. Then he spun around with a gun in his hand and shot The Dog right between the eyes.

The force of the bullet threw The Dog back against the wardrobe, and his blood spurted over the magnolia-painted walls and beige shag pile. All this happened without the shot making much noise, because there was a silencer on the gun. If any of the neighbours heard it, they wouldn't have given it a second thought.

Joey went and stood over The Dog. He fired a second shot into the man's head at point-blank range, just to make sure he wasn't ever going to get up again.

"The Dogman didn't even have a chance to bark," Joey chuckled.

❄

Joey had Martin take the rug up off the floor and wrap The Dog in it. Then they carried the bundle out and put it in the boot of Martin's old Ford Fiesta. Joey held his end with one hand and kept his other hand on the gun he had hidden in his pocket. The gun was a Glock 9 mm, and having seen what it could do, Martin didn't want to give Joey any reason to use it again.

"You're gonna drive." Joey opened the passenger door. "Get your ass over behind the wheel."

Martin did as he was told, and Joey climbed into the passenger seat. "You do know how to drive, I take it?"

Martin was just about to start the engine up, when his mobile began to ring.

"Give it to me."

Martin took his mobile out of his pocket. Joey snatched it and turned it off. "The fuck're you waitin' for, Christmas? C'mon, let's eat some tarmac."

"You still haven't told me where we're going."

❄

They drove all the way up through North London and out into the open countryside with Joey giving directions. Then they carried on for another twenty minutes or so before Joey told Martin to take a left. They went down what turned out to be a long muddy lane until they came to a tumbledown old farmhouse hidden away behind some trees.

"Now, stop and get out."

Joey kept his gun aimed at Martin as he stepped onto the shingled forecourt.

Joey fished a key from the pocket of his trousers with his free hand and tossed it for Martin to catch. "Open up the garage."

Turning the key in the lock, Martin figured he needed to make a move before it was too late. It was impossible to try anything right now, though, with Joey jabbing him in the back with his Glock.

Joey told Martin to grab the spade from over by the wall, and Martin did as he was told. Then Joey marched him round the back of the house. The garden at the back was enclosed by a hedge that was high enough to prevent strangers from prying. Anyway, even if Martin had been able to peer over it, all he'd have seen was a meadow that stretched as far as some woods. You could scream your head off and there wouldn't be anybody around to hear.

Joey pointed to a spot on the lawn. "Now, start diggin'."

Martin dug for what seemed like hours. How long it was exactly he had no idea, but he sure built up a sweat. He decided he would hit Joey with the spade the first chance he got. It was just a question of getting close enough to the man and catching him off guard.

When he had dug down about five feet, Joey told Martin to stop. Then Joey had him get the body out of the back of the car, drag it round, and dump it in the grave.

It was heavy work, but Martin finally managed it.

Joey looked down at The Dog's corpse. "So long, my old canine friend. . . ain't nobody gonna come lookin' for you here." He turned to Martin. "Or you for that matter."

"Hey, now wait a moment. There's no point in killing *me*."

Joey aimed the gun at Martin's chest. "No point in lettin' you live, neither. Besides, you already seen far too much bad shit goin' on."

He looked as though he was about to fire—but at that moment there was a loud bang that sounded like a gunshot. Both men turned towards the hedge, where the noise had come from.

A second shot rang out and Joey threw himself down into the grave, onto The Dog's corpse. Martin dived in on top of him, and the two men began to wrestle.

Martin managed to bang Joey's head against a piece of stone that protruded from the soil, and knocked him out. Then he grabbed the gun and held it against Joey's head. All he had to do was pull the trigger, and he'd be rid of the man forever. But Martin couldn't do it.

He stuck his head up out of the grave and fired a shot into the hedge and was surprised to find that nobody fired back. He fired another shot.

Still no response.

Maybe whoever it was that fired had gone.

But why would the guy just disappear like that? Martin figured whoever it was must be after Joey, and maybe when the guy saw Joey fall into the grave, he figured he must have killed him... in which case, the gunman would have reckoned his work was done and scarpered.

So, Martin climbed up out of the grave and made a dash for his car. He kept low and zigzagged as he ran to make himself a more difficult target, the way he'd seen them do it in the movies, then he opened the door and jumped in. He turned the key in the ignition, slipped her into gear, and gave it some serious pedal.

CHAPTER 8

Martin had a quick look about the cafe—they were in Costa on North End Road, in Fulham— to make sure nobody was sitting within earshot, He was pleasantly surprised to find himself in a place where nothing dangerous was going on. Nobody was fighting or holding anyone's head underwater, and the froth that the girl a couple of tables along had on her lips was from her cappuccino, and not a sign she was foaming at the mouth because some deadly poison or other had been slipped into her drink. Okay, so Frothy Lips might be accepting something that was being passed to her under the table right now by the dude she was with. Something wrapped in silver foil, which could be heroin or crack, or maybe it was just blow. But, hey, that's just normal everyday life in London. The dealer wasn't about to pull out a gun, or open a safe in the wall where he had one hidden. Not *here* and now he wasn't, anyway. Maybe the guy was saving all kinds of fancy tricks involving flying acrobatics with swords for later on, but right now he seemed as cool as a Cornetto. Everyone else in the café looked pretty cool. There were even a couple of middle-aged ladies who looked as though they'd come here to do nothing more exciting than rest their legs and bitch about their husbands over a little liquid refreshment. One of them even had a pretty neat tattoo of a dragon on her arm. So much normality felt kinda freaky to Martin after what he'd just been through. He took a deep breath and let it out slowly. Then he turned to Bella and said, "You'll never guess what happened to me earlier."

"I know all about it."

"What, you don't mean...?"

"Just as I pulled up outside the flat, Joey showed and went in, so I decided to wait in the car. Then you both came out and drove off together. I'd been to the farmhouse before, so I figured that must be where you were headed. It was me that shot at Joey from behind the bushes."

"*Wow*. You saved my life, Bel. But why didn't you say it was you?"

"I was about to, Mart, but you were too busy shooting at me. Then you ran and got in your car and were gone."

"Where'd you get the gun from?"

Bella sipped her latte. "It was left in the bedroom."

"So you went into the flat?"

Bella nodded. "To get my mobile. I'd left it charging in the bedroom."

"What did you do with the gun afterwards?"

"I threw it down the old well at the farmhouse."

"But has it got your fingerprints on it?"

"I wore gloves."

"Good thinking."

"I'd gone into the flat with the idea of calling the police, to tell them Joey'd abducted you. Then when I saw the blood everywhere in the bedroom, I put two and two together and figured that the big thing you'd carried out in the rug must've been a corpse. I also figured your fingerprints would be all over everything, Mart, so I changed my mind about calling the cops."

"A wise move. There's no saying whether they'd have believed us." Martin felt the lump on the back of his head, which was still sore from where The Dog had hit him.

"So then I called you, but you didn't answer."

"Joey was holding a gun against my balls at the time... one false move'n I'd have been a soprano."

Martin saw Bella's eyes twinkle through the tarantula curtain she had for eyelashes, and he took her hand in his. Then he began to look worried. "Don't reckon Joey'll go to the cops'n try to frame me, do you?"

Bella shook her head. "Joey wouldn't trust a cop any further than he can spit. I should know, 'cause I was married to him."

"He did a deal with them once, don't forget."

"Only because he had no other alternative."

"I just hope you're right."

Bella squeezed Martin's hand. "Suzanne's offered to put us up at her place for a while until we get somewhere else to move into."

"What... the Suzanne that dances at the Revuebar?"

Bella nodded.

"Right nice of her." Martin finished off what was left of his latte.

"Yeah, Suzanne's great." Bella glanced at her watch. "Her place is near here, so we could call in on the way to work if we go now, unless you'd like us to take the night off, Mart, after everything you've been through."

"We'd only have George and Roger chewing our asses off. Besides, going to work might help us take our minds off it all. We already agreed we'd work right up until the day we blow, remember?"

So Bella called Suzanne on her mobile to tell her they were coming, then they stepped out onto the chaos that was North End Road and began to work their way through the crowd of shoppers. Then they turned off into the quieter backstreets and walked to Suzanne's place nearby on Halford Road.

As Bella pushed the bell, Martin said, "I hope we're not gonna have to share a room with Suzanne's dancing partner."

"Who?"

"Y'know, Patrick, her rubber python," as the door opened, and a smiling Suzanne welcomed them in.

❄

Later, at work, Martin entered the theatre, and stopped at the top of the small flight of steps in time to see a giant wedding cake come up from under the stage. Then the sides of the cake fell outwards to reveal a fruity young brunette, whose name Martin knew was Rita, in full bridal gear—not that she looked very excited at the prospect of tying the knot. She shrugged her dress off, then shed stockings, panties and bra, like a snake shedding its old skin in a speeded-up film. The audience got little more than a momentary glimpse of her birthday best before she skipped behind the closing curtains to a roiling chorus of testosterone-generated cheers and applause. Then Bella came on, dressed as *Carmen* from Bizet's opera.

Martin hated the thought of all those dirty lechers out there getting off on the sight of what should have been for his eyes only. He left the theatre and went back downstairs. As he passed through the foyer, he called to Bill Rivers in the box office to tell him he was going for his break.

"Okay," Bill called back, "I'll tell Roger when I see 'im."

Martin went out through the heavy glass doors into Walker's Court, walked down to the corner where the touts were standing on the lookout for business, and crossed Brewer Street. He continued on down Rupert Street past doorways from which busty girls brandished their wares, took a right into the street that runs along the back of the theatres, crossed again at the end, and entered the Lyric. There was a good crowd in, and Martin shouldered his way up to the bar and bought himself a pint of London Pride.

He had just lifted the glass to his lips when who should he see along the other end of the bar but Joey B. Martin did a double take to check he wasn't imagining things and saw Joey's cold, arrogant eyes looking straight into his. Then Joey started to shove his way through huddles of drinkers to try and get to him.

Martin figured he had a choice to make here—stay and face Joey or run. He decided he'd better make himself scarce. And if you were going to run, then there was only one way to do it—as fast as you could.

He couldn't go out the way he'd come in, because Joey would cut him off. Instead, he began to make his way over towards the back exit. He went through the door and ran up two flights of stairs to the gents', then entered one of the cubicles, climbed onto the cistern, and smashed the window.

It was a tight fit, but he just managed to squeeze himself out, and he found himself on a tiny ledge. There was another ledge directly below, and Martin set about climbing down. He had just stepped onto the lower ledge when he saw Joey coming through the window after him. Martin gripped onto a drainpipe with his hands and began to work his way down the wall.

Martin felt himself losing his grip halfway down, so he jumped and landed on the concrete below in what turned out to be a car park. A man in a suit was taking a leak against the wall, and Martin noticed that he'd left the door of his Merc open—and hey, the keys were still in it. Martin ran over and jumped in behind the wheel, then started the engine up and slipped her into gear. He saw the owner of the Merc and Joey B. both coming after him in the mirror as he set off.

He hammered it down to the ground floor, the wheels of the Merc screeching out rubbery soprano notes as he took the corners. He considered driving through the barrier for a moment, but saw the attendant sitting there in his little cabin and thought better of it. So he slowed to a halt and held out a ten-pound note, and waited for the barrier to lift. Then he set off again with a great screeching of rubber before the attendant had time to hand back his change.

Driving to the corner, he turned into Brewer Street and continued a little way before he pulled over. He climbed out of the car and ran the short distance back to the Revuebar.

The foyer was now empty of customers, and the sound of Rhianna's voice drifted down from the theatre upstairs. Martin parked himself on a stool at the minibar and ran a shaky hand through his fine brown hair.

"Fuck's up with you?" Bill Rivers said. "Look like you've seen a fuckin' ghost."

CHAPTER 9

Just before the second show started, who should walk in through the door but Joey B, his shoulders looking very broad in the leather jacket he was wearing.

"What are you doing here?" Martin said, figuring that he'd run away from the man once too often.

"Just thought I'd pop in'n check out the action." Joey attracted the barman's attention. "Make it a Peroni."

"No action to check out in this place," Martin told him. "All happens someplace else. My advice would be to go back out the door and either take a right or a left."

Joey handed over a twenty-pound note, took his change, picked up his bottle, and poured. He made a show of watching the beer going down the side of the glass, the way a man might watch a beautiful woman peeling down her panties.

Martin told himself Joey wasn't going to try anything violent—not here, in front of all these people. The man might be *stupid,* but he wasn't fucking *crazy*.

Joey fixed Martin with those cold, reptilian eyes of his. "Fuck was up with you down in the Lyric? Was gonna buy you a beer, but you looked like you was shittin' yourself, old son."

"The fuck d'you want?"

Joey's eye's flashed a riff on the theme of mock-surprise. His eyebrows were two thin lines, and they were surrounded with lots of tiny interlacing scars. A crossword in evil that crisscrossed its way right across the man's forehead. Between his eyebrows a ledge of bone jutted out that the man probably used for delivering Glaswegian kisses. With four-star service. "The matter? Can't a man come'n see his own wife perform in a theatre without he gotta answer a lotta dickhead questions silly fuckers like you come'n axe him?"

"Bella doesn't want you here."

"Who says she don't?"

"*I* do."

Joey made a show of looking Martin up and down. "I'll need to 'ear that from Bella herself."

"She doesn't want to see you."

"I need any advice from you 'bout how to run my marriage, I'll axe for it... meantime, you can go back to your counselin' service'n shoot yourself at your desk."

Martin was getting sick of being on the back foot all the time with Joey. "Taking a risk in coming here, aren't you?"

Joey gave him a deadpan look. "Fuck is that suppose to mean?"

"After what happened."

"After *what* happened? You always talk in code like this?"

"Cops might be rather interested to learn of The Dog's whereabouts," Martin whispered.

"Never been an animal lover meself."

"I was to tell them what I know, you could soon find yourself going away again—and for a long time."

Joey moved closer to Martin, so that they were practically rubbing noses. "Look, shithead," he growled. "You ain't in no position to go blabbin' to no one."

"That's what you think."

"It's what I *know*. I go away on a vacation, then you go away with me for the same time'r longer. Your prints'n DNA are all over The Dog. They're all over my flat, too. So you better try wipin' the egg off that ugly mug a yours. Much more likely you'd be the one to get banged up'n I'd walk."

"I didn't have a motive."

"What they all say." Joey swigged his Peroni. "And another thing: you better stop sniffin' round my wife if you don't wanna end up like

The Dog." He belched, then said, "be seein' you around," and went out.

Martin went over to the glass entrance doors and watched Joey making his way down Walker's Court, the man's rep going before him. The touts on the corner all paying their respects with smiles and waves, a flattering comment or two.

Martin and Bella were walking along Brewer Street in the early hours, on their way back to Martin's car, when Joey popped up in front of them seemingly out of nowhere.

"Hello, Bella darlin... been a long time."

"Heh, listen," Martin told him. "I already told you she doesn't wanna talk to you."

"I'll be the judge of that."

It was dark and there weren't many people about. Besides, the only people you'd be likely to find here at this time of night, Bella thought, would be types you'd rather not come across. She was feeling nervous about what might happen as the two men squared up to one another on the pavement. It seemed like they were going to fight. If they did, she reckoned Joey would win, because he was taller and bigger about the shoulders than Martin, and he was one hell of a lot meaner.

No sooner had this thought passed through Bella's mind than Joey grabbed Martin by the lapels and pushed him against the wall. Bella put her hand on Joey's arm. "Look, the last thing I want right now is for you two to start fighting over me."

Joey didn't seem to be in a listening mood, which shouldn't have come as any great surprise to Bella. He'd never listened to a word she said back in the days when they were together. Given the way he'd always ignored her, Bella wondered why Joey should even be bothered about what she got up to. Or who she was getting up to it with. But of course none of this was about *her*, she well knew. It was about *him*, just as everything that ever happened in Joey's world was about *him* and that big fat fucking ego of his.

Bella reached into her handbag and brought out her mobile. "Listen, I'm calling the police if you don't stop this."

Joey turned his head to look at her. "All I want is to talk. You're still my fuckin' wife, Bel, case you'd forgotten."

"It's over between us, Joey."

"Nice a you to let me know."

"It was over ages ago."

"Coulda tried talkin' to me about it."

Bella didn't say anything.

"Fuckin' loyalty for you... man goes inside'n his missis picks up with some other bloke faster'n shit can leave a shovel. Doesn't even have the common fuckin' decency to come'n visit 'er husband when he's in nick, and tell 'im the way it is. Surely any guy'd deserve at least *that* much."

"Okay it's true, Joey, you're right. Maybe I should've told you, but I was frightened to."

"Why?"

"You're a violent man, Joey."

"When did I ever lay a finger on you, Bella, hey? Tell me that."

He never did, it was true. He may have done all sorts of terrible things to *other* people, but never to her. Maybe she'd just been lucky.

"You can't ever say I treated you badly 'cause I never."

"No, you just ignored me once we were married."

"I've always been a busy man ... never use to complain about the nice things I bought you with the money I made."

"Look, Joey, it's over between us. There's nothing else to say. Okay, maybe I should've told you, but I was frightened of what you might do. Maybe I was wrong to be so frightened, but I was. So anyway, now you know. I'm sorry."

"So, you wanna divorce?"

"Yes."

"That case, you're gonna have to axe me."

"Okay, I'm asking you."

"Go on, then. Say it."

"I want a divorce."

"That's not axin', it's tellin'."

"What's the difference?"

"I don't fuckin' *believe* this." Joey shook his head in disgust. "You can't be *serious*. I mean, you can't really be leavin' me for this wanker 'ere." The thought of it was clearly too much for his enormous ego to take. "I oughtta fuckin' tear the pair a ya to shreds."

Joey turned on his heel and stormed off down Brewer Street. And as Martin watched the man go, he wondered if that was the last they'd see of him.

Somehow that seemed to be too much to hope for.

❄

Martin didn't say anything as he drove home. He felt stupid, like he'd been humiliated in front of Bella by Joey B. back there. Joey'd grabbed him by the collar and held him against the wall for fuck's sake, and Bella'd had to threaten to call the cops to stop the man from giving him a good kicking. Some doorman.

These thoughts worked themselves up in Martin's brain into a devilish cocktail of shame and impotent rage. He couldn't think about anything else, and fantasized about giving Joey B. a good kicking. He feared the man, but he also feared himself and what he might be capable of doing. Because Joey wasn't the sort of man you could just get into a fight with and then afterwards that would be the end of it. No, at the very least he'd really hurt you if he won. Probably kill you, if he got the chance. Which meant, Martin realized, that you either had to stay away from him, or if you wanted to mix it with the guy, then you had to be prepared to go *all the way*. The stakes were high. Just about as high as you could get, he thought. All these nasty ideas worked their way into Martin's bloodstream as he drove through the dark streets.

When they got back to Suzanne's place, Martin and Bella turned in for the night without speaking. They lay apart on opposite sides of the bed.

It was as if something were lying between them. Or *someone*.

That someone was Joey B.

❄

Martin woke up the following day and looked over at Bella as she lay huddled up in the fetal position on her side of the bed. Then he remembered what had happened the night before, and he got up and took a shower. Afterwards, he put on his terry cloth bathrobe and went down to the kitchen. No sign of Suzanne being up and about, so he fixed coffee and toast with jam and butter just for himself and Bella. Then he took it all back up to their room.

"Rise'n shine, Bel."

Bella stretched her arms and began to rub her eyes.

"You sleep okay?" Martin figuring the way to play it was just to act like last night was no big deal. Last night? Hey, what was it that happened again? Perhaps you could refresh my memory?

Only it *had* been a big deal. For him, anyway.

Bella yawned, then sat up in the bed, so that her pretty pink jugs jiggled pertly. "Ah, you've made me my breakfast... very thoughtful of you, Mart."

"Hey, I'm a thoughtful kinda guy." Martin put everything down on the bedside table before he climbed back in bed and passed Bella her mug of coffee. Then he set the plate, which was loaded with toast, down on the counterpane between them.

Bella looked at him and noticed that he seemed to be avoiding her gaze. She figured he might have brought her breakfast in bed to try and pretend he wasn't in a bad mood when really he was. "Still upset about last night, Mart, aren't you?"

"What d'you mean, Bel?"

"Oh, for fuck's sake, Mart. How long are you planning on keeping up this stupid routine? Look, Joey's a fucking animal—don't say I didn't warn you about him. But that's *his* problem ... I mean, it doesn't have to affect *us,* does it?"

Martin didn't know how to tell her what was going on in his mind. How could you explain to the woman you loved that her ex had made you feel *small?*

Bella began to caress his arm and shoulder. "Joey's fucking Joey is all I'm trying to say, Mart, don't you see? I mean, the man's a total head case... besides, he's history for me. End of story."

Martin chewed on his toast and didn't say anything.

"Look," Bella tried again, "I won't think any the less of you if you're frightened of Joey. Am I getting through to you?"

Martin didn't want to be talking about this. Not now. Not *ever,* in fact.

"What I'm trying to say, Mart, is that I'm not comparing you to him. Or if I am, then you're the one that's always gonna come out on top. Because it's a competition Joey can never win."

"Why don't you have your coffee and toast before it gets cold?"

Bella rolled her eyes. "You guys're all the same. You seem to think us women all want some kinda macho man who's tough'n dangerous. But what I'm trying to get you to see, is that's the very fucking reason that I can't stand the sight of Joey—*because the man's fucking dangerous* . . . whereas you aren't. I mean, you're a nice, decent guy and I know I can trust you. Joey would sell his own mother. Do you think a woman like me wants a man like *that?*"

"You did once, obviously—otherwise you'd never've married the guy."

"Yeah, well everyone can make a mistake, Martin. I was young and stupid, and I was also high as a kite on drugs most of the time back in those days. I seemed to lose any idea of who I was or what I wanted out of life. It's hard for me to explain or talk about it now. But anyway, what I'm trying to say is that you've got to see Joey and my involvement with him against that background. And you've got to understand that I never, *ever*, want to go back to that. I'd die before I ever slept with Joey again or went back to being the person I was when I was with him."

She went back to caressing his arm. "Mart?"

"What?"

"Am I getting through to you? I mean, are you even *listening* to me?"

Martin looked into her eyes for the first time since the night before. "And it's that simple, is it?

"You're too damn right it is ... for me, anyway."

If only that were true, Martin thought.

CHAPTER 10

The moment she saw it, Bella ran backstage and found George, the choreographer, a skinny guy with an Afro wearing a roll-necked sweater. "There's a wanker in the fourth row. Sticks out like a pig in a synagogue."

George's poppy eyes flashed as the music stopped and the audience began to applaud. "Bella, you're *on*, quick," he said. "Don't worry about Woody Woodpecker. I'll make sure he's seen to."

Bella strutted onstage and threw the audience her most arrogant *fuck-you* look. Then the Bizet started up, and she went into her routine, twirling her hands in the air and holding her chin up as she spun round. She tried not to look at the wanker, and told herself that the audience loved her. She was *Carmen*, the Spanish gypsy girl. But who was that other man in the sixth or seventh row, and why was he pointing a rolled-up newspaper at her?

At that instant, a loud bang sounded, and Bella was aware of a sharp pain right before she passed out.

❈

"The fuck was that noise from upstairs?" Bill Rivers burst out.

Martin Butler dashed across the foyer and went running up the stairs. "The fuck're you doing?" Roger Sewell called after him, but Martin didn't stop to reply.

"Hope it wasn't what it sounded like," Steve piped up from behind the minibar.

"Go'n check the backstage door's locked, Bill. Quick about it!" Roger Sewell yelled. "And tell Gary not to let anybody leave."

Bill dashed outside and set off down Walker's Court. Like a mountain of pink jelly trying to run, Roger Sewell thought, watching Bill's fifty-four-year-old legs trying to cope with all that blubber. Roger knew that so long as the backstage door was locked, then no one could leave the building unless he let them out. But what in the name of buggery was that noise? That's what he wanted to know. Was it really what it *sounded* like?

He was still wondering about this when Bill returned, shortly afterwards, panting for breath after his exertions. "Gary Ross is mannin" the backstage door. I told 'im you said not to let anyone out."

Seeing a constable going by, through the glass doors, Bill dashed back out and called to him. The constable, a tall skinny young guy, turned abruptly and asked what was up. "Think we got some serious trouble upstairs, Officer," Bill gasped, and the constable followed him back inside. The foyer was beginning to fill now, as panic-stricken customers spilt down the carpeted stairway in droves.

A man shouted, "C'mon, we all wanna go," and the crowd surged towards the glass exit doors.

"Stop pushing," the young constable yelled back. "No one's leaving this place until CID have arrived. Now if you can all just calm yourselves down a little, please." He took out his walkie-talkie and called for backup. Then he asked Bill Rivers if anyone had left the premises yet through the front exit. Bill shook his head, no, then set about locking the doors in a hurry.

Roger Sewell came over, a skinny man with receding hair and a smile that was about as genuine as the Rolex on a Soho spiv. "Evening, Officer. I'm the general manager."

The constable took his hat off. "There any other exits from the building?"

"Only the backstage door. I sent someone, soon as I heard the noise, to make sure it was manned. There's an exit onto the roof, too, but there's two officers up there already."

"Just make sure nobody leaves."

❄

Martin managed to fight his way through the throng, then he ran along the aisle, jumped onto the stage, and threw himself on his knees. "Bel. . . you all right?"

No answer.

She was bleeding. "Fuck, she's been *shot*." That would explain the noise.

Looking around for help, Martin saw some of the dancers who'd come onto the stage.

"Somebody call an ambulance for fuck's sake."

A voice said, "I'm calling for one."

"Get the police, too." Martin ran his hand through Bella's hair, gave her cheek a couple of slaps. "C'mon, Bel, don't hold out on me."

He could feel her blood, warm against his skin. Fear fizzed through his veins.

"Bel..."

Fuck. Who'd do this to a girl like Bella? Martin wondered as he fought back tears.

He thought of two people.

Looking around the theatre, he saw people screaming and fighting to get to the exit. They were driven by the thought, no doubt, that a crazy gunman was on the loose.

Martin had his own ideas.

No sign of Joey B. or Sir Alex in the audience, though.

He heard a girl's voice say, "Ambulance is on its way. Cops, too."

❄

Some fifteen minutes later, Detective Chief Inspector Preston appeared on the scene—thirty-eight, black hair, tash, olive skin, and a snappy suit. Preston dashed down the aisle and up the stage steps, asking Roger Sewell over his shoulder about what had happened. Then, looking down at the girl sprawled before him, he said, "Who is she?"

"Bella Armando," Sewell replied. "One of the dancers here."

"Name sounds Italian or Spanish."

"Think she has Italian blood, but was born over here. Somewhere out in the sticks, I think."

"That's right," piped up a man in a black jacket and bow tie.

"And you are, sir?"

"Martin Butler. I'm Bella's partner."

"What? Her dance partner, you mean?"

"No, we live together."

"Oh. Did you see what happened?"

"No... but I just hope to God she's gonna be all right."

"Weren't you in the audience at the time, then, sir?"

"No, I was down in the foyer, but I ran up here soon as I heard the noise. I'm the doorman here."

One of the paramedics looked up at Preston. "Been shot... not sure if the bullet entered her chest but it got her in the arm for sure."

The two paramedics lifted Bella onto a stretcher, then they left with her, and Martin followed them. On their way out of the theatre, they passed Preston's number two, Detective Sergeant Johnson – thirty-two, short blond hair, grey suit from Top Man, and slightly out of breath as he hurried along the aisle and up the stage steps. He made eye contact with the Inspector Jefe and said, 'Any sign of the weapon, guv?'

Preston shook his head. 'I've checked the CCTV system...someone switched it off before the gun was fired."

Preston turned to Roger Sewell. "Who'd have been in a position to do that?"

"No idea, Inspector. Don't look at me."

"Must've been somebody who had a key."

"Not necessarily. We don't normally lock the room. I last checked it 'bout an hour ago and it was workin' okay then."

Preston gave his tash a tweak, then turned back to DS Johnson. "Need to find out what we can about the girl who's been shot, Dave ... name's Bella Armando."

Johnson took out his mobile, punched in a number, and went off with the phone pressed against his ear. Preston followed him out of the theatre shortly afterwards, and he found the foyer in a state of chaos when he got there. "Fuck *me*," he muttered as he saw that DS Johnson had become involved in a scuffle over by the entrance.

Preston pushed his way through the crowd over towards where the fracas had erupted. He saw that the man he'd spoken to earlier up in the theatre, Martin Butler, was in the middle of it. Just then, one of the uniforms got Butler in a pretty tasty headlock.

"Nice one, Officer," Preston complimented the uniform, a stocky young guy with bulging muscles.

"Guy won't listen to reason, guv."

"Let me go, you fuckin' asshole," Martin Butler growled.

A second uniform quickly pulled Butler's hands behind his back and slipped on the plastic restraints. Then the officer pushed him through a crowd of people over to the box office.

"Ouch ... those cuffs hurt like hell ... Take the fuckin' things off me."

The first uniform put his hand against the back of Butler's head and rammed his face into the Formica counter.

Preston put his mouth down by Butler's ear and said, "in a hurry to get somewhere, are we?"

"Yeah. I wanna go to the hospital with Bella."

Preston gestured to the two uniforms, and they backed off. Someone shouted, "police brutality!" Then another voice yelled: "fucking pigs never miss a chance to bully people!"

DCI Preston turned to find himself facing a number of people holding up their mobiles to film him. All he bloody well needed.

"Shit, these things're stopping my circulation. Can't you loosen them?"

"No way to do that without slicing them off, once they're on, I'm afraid, Mr. Butler."

"Do that, then..."

"How do I know you wouldn't try'n hit me or burst out of here again?" Besides, Preston wasn't carrying a knife.

"Look, I just wanna go to the hospital for fuck's sake."

Somebody shouted, "bullying bastards!" Then another cry of "pigs!" rang out.

Preston turned to find he was boxed in. "Make way, please," he called out. But the crowd reacted by pushing him back against the box office counter. "I said 'Make way!' I'm a police officer and I'm coming through."

Someone shouted, "we *know* who you are."

"Oink! oink!"

Derisive laughter.

Preston looked at the two uniforms. "I'm taking this man with me."

They formed a triangle, the two uniforms at the front and with Martin Butler behind them, with Preston bringing up the rear. Then they forced their way back through the crowd over towards the doors. It was only a few yards in actual distance, but getting there proved tough work. Preston felt somebody shove him in the back and turned to lash out only to find himself confronted with ranks of people holding their mobiles aloft, recording him. He snarled and turned away, angry and a little unnerved. But he managed to get through to the entrance where DS Johnson and several uniforms were embroiled in an ongoing pushing and shoving match with some of the people in the front row.

"Let us go," someone shouted. "We haven't done anything wrong."

"We paid good money to come here'n be treated like criminals," shouted another.

"We're being held here under false pretences. This ain't Guantanamo fuckin' Bay."

Preston turned to face the crowd. "Look," he shouted. "I can understand that you are frustrated, and we're going to let you all go as soon as we can ... but you need to help us by calming down."

More pushing. "Oink! Oink!"

"Fuck me, guv," DS Johnson gasped. "I get the feeling things could really kick off here any moment."

It was the people at the back who were doing most of the pushing, while the ones at the front, many of whom looked as though they didn't want to cause any problems, were bearing the brunt of his colleagues' wrath. Preston was starting to worry about the public relations angle. He could see himself showing up on the news tonight, if there wasn't a bigger story, to feed the media machine.

He took out his walkie-talkie and called for more backup as two men, both dressed in jeans and casual jackets, came running down the stairs. One of them shouted, "police, let us through," and they began pushing their way through the crowded foyer towards the exit.

DCI Preston blocked their path and flashed his ID. Then he asked to see theirs, not recognizing either of the men. The taller of the two held his ID up just long enough for Preston to see it. "Suspect's gonna escape," the man said, "if you don't get out the fucking way."

Preston stepped aside and the man went to go out. "Doors are fuckin' locked ... Quick ... somebody open it. Who's got the key?" Preston gave his permission with a nod of the head, and a uniform opened one of the doors.

With that, the two plainclothes officers dashed out. Preston went out after them, closely followed by Johnson, the Detective Sergeant overtaking Preston, as they turned the corner. The taller of the two officers Preston didn't recognize—six-two, dark brown hair—shouted, "there he is," and Preston saw he was pointing at a guy in a baseball cap who was running hell for leather along Brewer Street fifteen or twenty yards up ahead.

Preston was having trouble keeping up on account of his dodgy knee, and he got to the next corner some five yards behind the slower of the two plainclothes men, with DS Johnson up ahead. Then, as he ran up Wardour Street, Preston saw the suspect throw a bag through the open window of a red Lexus that took off at speed.

The suspect then crossed the street and was about to enter a bar when the faster of the two plainclothes men took him down with a fine flying tackle that would have earned the cheers of the crowd at Twickenham. The suspect hit the concrete hard, but still managed to turn and begin to wrestle with the plainclothes man, yelling, "get off me, you fuckin' pig!" He was an ugly guy with a pale weasel face and a bum-fluff goatee.

DS Johnson helped hold the suspect down while the other officer slipped on the plastic restraints. "Ouch, those bastards hurt! Fuck's goin' on here?" the suspect complained. "Bastards're cuttin' into my wrists."

At that moment, Preston drew up. "Won't find the gun on him," he gasped.

The two plainclothes men looked at Preston, and the stocky one with the shaved head said, "who said anything about a *gun?*"

But Preston was already calling in the reg on the red Lexus—or the part of it he remembered—the vehicle well out of sight by now. "That's right," he was saying into his walkie-talkie, 'we've got the suspect, but he was able to pass the gun to an accomplice waiting in a red Lexus last seen less than a minute ago moving along Wardour Street at speed in the direction of Oxford Street. I need that car stopped."

Preston pocketed his walkie-talkie, and saw that the two plainclothes officers were both looking at him in a funny way.

"What's up?"

The taller of the two plainclothes officers, a slim man with short blond hair, said, "What suspect are you after?" (

"What...?"

"This guy's a heroin dealer."

"What the fuck..."

"We've been watching him for the past week from the roof of the Revuebar with a telescopic camera."

"You mean you guys are Narc squad?"

"That's right ... the fuck were you thinking?"

"*Shit.*"

"Aren't you guys aware there's been a shooting at the Revuebar?" DS Johnson cut in.

"You taking the piss?" said the one with the shiny billiard ball for a head.

"No, far from it. When you said you were after the suspect, we thought you meant the guy who'd shot the girl in the show, didn't we, guv?" Johnson turned to have Preston confirm what he'd just said, only to find Preston was no longer there. "Guv?" Then he saw Preston running back along Wardour Street, said, "I gotta go," and set off in pursuit. Best way out of an embarrassing situation. And he caught up with Preston as he turned the corner.

"Guv?"

Preston stopped and turned. "Talk about a wild bloody goose chase."

Johnson shrugged. "It's just one of those things ... nobody's fault."

They hurried back along Brewer Street, past Madame Jo-Jo's and the backstage door of the Revue. They passed the touts on the corner and went to enter the Revuebar, only the door had been locked again. Preston knocked on the glass, and one of the uniforms opened up and let them in.

Their arrival inspired another round of pushing and shoving from the crowd, which apparently had been relatively calm in their absence. Chaos again. "Fuck me," Preston muttered under his breath.

Still no sign of any backup.

The minutes dragged until twenty-five men in riot gear showed. Johnson flashed Preston a toothy grin. "Cavalry's arrived."

Fucking media are gonna love this, Preston thought. He told the uniforms to open one of the doors and start searching people and letting them out one at a time. "Ask if they saw anything, and if not, just take their address and a phone number."

Preston led Martin Butler outside and off down Walker's Court, the touts on the corner all smiling and jeering.

"Where're we going?"

"Thought you wanted to see your girlfriend?"

"Can't you take these cuffs off me?"

"Could always charge you with assaulting a police officer and put you in a cell for the night."

"That copper assaulted *me*."

Preston stopped by his old Ford Escort. "Get in."

CHAPTER 11

They hammered it over to Paddington Hospital, and when they got, there Preston wasted no time finding the doctor who was responsible for taking care of Bella.

"She gonna make it okay?" Martin asked him.

"Yes, I'm sure she's going to be all right." The doctor, a tall slim Indian man in his late thirties, paused to adjust his metal-framed spectacles. "But she's still in serious condition."

Preston showed him his ID and explained that he needed to see her, and the doctor shook his head. "Bella isn't in any state to receive visitors. She needs rest. She's been shot—I'm not sure if you're aware of that. Maybe I'll be able to let you go in and see her tomorrow if things go well."

"But I only need a couple of minutes with her. Just to ask if she saw the person who shot her... Every minute is vital at this stage in an investigation of this sort."

"Okay, well let's give it a couple of hours or so and we'll see how she is then... but I can't promise anything. I have my job to do as well, Inspector, and my first concern is the patient's welfare. I'm afraid that's the best I can do for you."

The doctor walked off, and Preston puffed out his cheeks. Then he turned to the armed guard and told him to keep his eyes open. "Never know, the gunman might come here to try'n finish the job."

Preston's belly started making nasty music, which was hardly surprising because he hadn't eaten since breakfast. So they went and found a Macdonald's, and Preston treated himself to a couple Big Macs with fries, lashings of ketchup, and a large Coke.

Martin said. "That's a real pig's supper you've got there, Inspector."

"Pass for biting wit where you come from, does it?"

"Sorry, I couldn't resist that one."

Preston shrugged. "I'm hungry, and just in case you hadn't noticed, Jamie Oliver's not around to fix me up with a healthy option."

Preston got himself a latte afterwards, stirred in three sugars. He took a sip, one eye on the TV screen up on the wall, where Sky News was showing. "Any idea who might've wanted to kill Bella?"

"Nope," Martin lied.

"So where were you when she was shot?"

"Already told you."

"Try telling me again."

"I was down in the foyer."

"You hear the gunshot?"

"We all did."

"You mean you were with other people when you heard it?"

Martin nodded.

"Can you give me some names?"

"Bill Rivers, the box office manager. Steve behind the minibar, and Roger Sewell, the general manager... You can ask them if you like."

"I will."

"What? You don't think *I* shot Bella, do you?"

"All I know for sure is that you claim to be her boyfriend."

"Doesn't make me a homicidal maniac, does it?"

"Never said it did."

"Why all the questions, then?"

"Just routine." Preston looked him in the eye. "Dunno why, Martin, but I get the feeling there might be something you're not telling me." Preston sipped his latte, glanced up at the TV screen, and *shit*... he found himself looking at the foyer of the Revuebar... now Martin Butler's face was being rammed against the box office counter. Preston saw himself turn and lash out. Now he was trying to force his way through the crowd, with the two uniforms and Butler in the middle...

Preston turning and lashing out again, not actually making contact with anyone, but looking wild, potentially violent.

Every detective's worst PR nightmare, right there, unfolding before his very eyes for all the world to see.

"That you I see on the telly, Inspector?"

Preston turned quickly, and found himself looking at a tall guy, with three-day stubble on a long Italian-looking face. The man was wearing jeans with a leather jacket; his collar-length black hair was greased back, and the top two buttons on his silk shirt were undone, revealing a silver chain and a patch of hairy chest. "And you are?"

"Name's Joseph Belagio."

"Your face is familiar from somewhere, but I can't place you."

"Only thinkin', Inspector, you look a bit like an older version of Ray Liotta up there on the telly. Y'know, the guy in *Goodfellas*, Martin Scorcese's classic gangster film."

Preston knew the film. And so he also knew that the character Liotta plays in it ends up having to flush a load of cocaine down the toilet before he gets chased in his car by a police helicopter.

"Pretty natty suit for a copper, if I might say so. Italian?"

"Did you have anything particular you wanted to talk to me about, Mr. Belagio?"

"Just wondered if you might be in this neck of the woods for the same reason as me?"

"Which is...?"

"Come to see Bella... she's been shot."

"Why don't you just fuck off out of here," Martin Butler burst out. "I already told you, Bella doesn't want anything to do with you."

"You two gentlemen appear to know each other," Preston observed.

"Excuse me, Inspector, but your friend 'ere doesn't seem to have any manners. Doesn't he realize that Bella's my *wife*?"

"She's with me now."

"Did you see what happened at the Revuebar, Mr. Belagio?"

"No, I wasn't there, but I heard about it on the telly'n came straight here."

"Why don't you go right back to where you came from?" Martin cut in.

"I can see why you had to put the restraints on 'im, Inspector... looks like a rough customer. Let you in to see Bella, did they?"

Preston shook his head. "Too early... but the doctor did say she's going to pull through okay."

"Well that sounds promising, anyway. Give 'er my love, if you get in to see her before I do."

"Sure."

"Thanks, I appreciate it."

Belagio turned and left, and Preston watched him go, trying to remember where he'd seen the man before. He continued to wonder as he finished his latte. Then he went back to the hospital with Martin Butler, and when they found the doctor they'd spoken to earlier, Preston asked him if he could go in and see Bella, yet.

The doctor looked at Preston like he was trying to make up his mind.

"I only want a couple of minutes with her, that's all."

"Me, too," Martin cut in. "I'm her boyfriend."

The doctor didn't even look at Martin. "Okay ... but I'm going to hold you to your word, Inspector—two minutes is all you get."

Preston and Martin Butler followed the doctor into the room. Bella was lying on her back in bed with her arms down by her sides. Her eyes were open, but she looked tired and was hooked to a spider's web of wires and tubes.

Martin went over and kissed her on the cheek. "Hi, Bel. You okay, darling?"

Bella made a stab at a smile.

"Move away from her now, please," the doctor said, and Martin straightened up.

"Why the cuffs?" Bella asked in a voice that didn't sound like hers.

"They tried to stop me coming here to see you."

Preston held out his ID and introduced himself. "I just want to know if you saw the person who shot you, miss?"

"I only caught a glimpse of him... it all happened so fast."

"Could you describe the person for me?"

"He was white."

"Height?"

"Difficult to say."

"Would you recognize the man if you see him again?"

"Don't think so... no... I didn't really get a look at his face. I just saw this figure standing there out the corner of my eye, and noticed that he was holding a rolled-up newspaper... pointing it at me..."

"Hair?"

"Yes."

"But the *colour*, I mean."

"Black or brown, I think. I'm not sure."

"That's enough, Inspector," the doctor cut in.

Preston puffed out his cheeks, realizing it was useless.

"Take care, Bel," Martin said, "and remember that I love you."

Bella made another stab at a smile, and the three men left the room.

Preston looked at Martin Butler and saw that he had tears in his eyes. "Come with me."

"Where we going?"

"To get a knife."

"What?"

"To cut your restraints off."

"Oh yeah."

Preston drove home in the early hours if the morning and climbed into bed only to find that he couldn't sleep because all kinds of thoughts were bouncing around in his head. So he got up and poured himself a large one. Not a good sign, he realized, needing to drink to be able to get to sleep, but he told himself it was just a bad period he was going through. With any luck, he'd soon break out of it and everything would be all right. Then he had to smile at his own thoughts, despite himself, because when were things ever fucking all right? He'd be out of a job if they were.

It was getting on for half-past three when he finally got to sleep. He woke up with the alarm feeling like he'd eaten a chunk of the carpet for supper. He started to feel a little more human in the shower, and was wide awake and ready for action by the time he'd got his suit on. He stopped off for a light breakfast of coffee and a croissant in the café on the corner, then drove to the station.

When he entered his office, Preston found his desk loaded with files and papers, just the way he'd left it, the mug shots of the same wanted criminals on the notice board on the wall. DS Johnson was already there, working at his desk, which was next to Preston's. "Just gonna get myself a coffee, guv. Get you one?"

"Go on, then."

Preston sat in his chair and started writing up the report on the events of the evening before. It was dull, but necessary work, and he was in the middle of it when Johnson came back in with the coffees.

"What's new, Dave—apart from the fact that the coffee tastes like shit?"

Johnson chuckled and said, "zilch so far."

"What about the Revuebar back exit?"

"Gary Ross says he manned it soon as he heard the noise."

"See you've been busy, Dave."

"As ever, guv." Johnson ran his hand through his short, blond hair. "So, what's our next move?"

"I want you to go'n get the box office manager, Bill Rivers, and bring him here."

"Not a suspect, is he?"

Preston shook his head. "Just got a few questions to ask him concerning seating arrangements and matters to do with the way they run the box office at the Revuebar."

CHAPTER 12

Sir Alex Boulton pocketed his mobile and came out of the bathroom.

"Who was it that called you, Alex?"

"Oh, nobody important, Pru dear, just some civil servant."

"You don't normally lock yourself in the bathroom to talk on the phone."

The MP looked at his wife, and he had a sudden urge to come clean and tell her everything. It's now or never, he thought. I could put an end to all of this once and for all.

Of course there was the thought that she might choose to file for divorce and take him for half of everything he had. But there was more to it than that, because the fact was that he still loved her very much. This truth hit home now, the way such fundamental truths often do—with a quite unexpected force. Prunella's looks might be fading, but he loved her just as much as ever, if not more.

And for the first time it struck him that love really did reach below the surface. Love was an invisible force that grew within you, without your even realizing it, and after a while you began to take it for granted, until one day you found yourself in a corner and it hit you right between the eyes.

No, there was no way he was about to tell Prunella that he'd had an affair. It would break her heart. He would just have to deal with the situation so as to make sure she didn't find out.

He put on his pinstripe jacket, then went over and kissed her on the side of the neck. "I'm going to have lunch with Charles, darling. Shouldn't be late, but I'll call you if I'm going to be."

"Okay. Do give him my regards, won't you."

"Yes, of course. Have a nice afternoon, dear."

Sir Alex went out and climbed into his Mercedes, then set off for Charles's place in Pimlico. It was a nice day, and the streets looked pleasant, bathed as they were in the amber rays of the early April sun, but Sir Alex was in no mood to enjoy such things. His heart was heavy, and he just wanted his troubles to be over and done with.

※

"So what's going on now, then?"

Sir Alex sighed and said, "He wants the money this afternoon, Charles."

They were sitting at a corner table in Goya's, the Spanish restaurant near Charles's place, in Pimlico. Charles got the attention of the waiter and told him they were ready to order. They would both have *gazpacho* and a prawn salad to start, and *paella* for the main course. "And give us a decent bottle of *Rioja*, would you?"

Charles's blue eyes lingered on the young Spanish waiter's lean and athletic figure with a sort of wistful longing, as the man made his way across the restaurant. Then, with what seemed to be a great effort, he turned back to his brother. "So what have you told him?"

"I think it's time just to pay the man and get this over with, Charles —and the sooner the better, so far as I'm concerned."

"Have you got the money he's asking for ready?"

Sir Alex nodded.

"And are you going to pay him all of it?"

"Yes."

Charles frowned.

"Why... don't you think I should?"

"What about if you were only to give him *some* of it?"

Sir Alex thrummed his long fingers nervously on the tablecloth. "Wouldn't that just risk complicating things unnecessarily?"

The young waiter returned with the bottle of Rioja. He popped the cork and poured a little for Charles to try. "Mm, that"ll do nicely," Charles purred, and the waiter put the bottle down and left.

"Don't forget the first golden rule in these situations, Alex—which is never to give in too easily." Charles picked up the bottle and filled both their glasses. "Always try and make the person you're dealing with negotiate—that's what I was taught during my time with the SAS and MI5. Make the enemy realize it's a two-way process and that there can be consequences *for him*, as well."

Sir Alex tasted his wine. "It's all very well saying that, Charles, but this is my *life* we're talking about. I can't afford to screw up here. If I do then... well, I don't even want to *think* about it."

"And that's just what the blackmailer's going to be banking on."

"What is?"

"That you're going to be so frightened and panicky about the whole business you won't be able to think straight. But you need to take into account the fact that he's going to be nervous, too."

"Not half as nervous as I am."

"What makes you so sure?"

"If he were then he wouldn't try and blackmail me in the first place, would he? That's obvious."

Charles scratched at his nose, which was lined with broken red veins. "You're thinking like a rich man again, Alex."

"That's because I *am* a rich man. How am I *supposed* to think?"

"Try and put yourself in the other man's shoes for a moment."

"He's probably a psycho living on some grotty council estate."

"If I were you, I wouldn't ever use that line in one of your speeches in the House. You talk as if you think council estates are a breeding ground for criminals, old chap."

"Dammit, Charles, this is *serious*."

"You've got to get a grip and keep your sense of perspective. You're only assuming that the man's a psycho."

"Well, he's got to be, hasn't he?"

"Maybe he's just short of money and wants to make some fast—and blackmailing you strikes him as a relatively easy option."

The waiter came over with the first course. Charles thanked the man with his eyes in a way that seemed to express an appreciation of more than just the food and the service, before he tasted his *gazpacho*.

"This is rather all right, I must say." He dabbed his lips with a napkin. "If you're just gonna roll over for this guy, then what's to stop him coming back again for more until he bleeds you dry?"

Sir Alex speared a large prawn with his fork. "So what would you do?"

"I'd at least try and make the bastard sweat a little for his money."

❉

"Hello?"

"It's me."

"Oh."

"You got the cash up together, I hope."

"Yes."

"Okay, listen. I want the money in a padded A4 manila envelope, and put the envelope in a white plastic bag ... Take it to the northwest side of Putney Bridge. Go down the steps on the Bishop's Park side— you know where I mean?"

"Yes."

"When you get to the bottom of the steps, walk along the footpath to your right and go'n sit on the third bench you come to. You got that? The *third* bench."

"Okay, but when?"

"Be there at four this afternoon. That gives you over an hour. Don't be late."

"Will you be sitting there?"

"No, but I'll be watching your every move. So don't try anythin' stupid like tipping off the cops, because if you do that I'll know and the deal will be off. That clear?"

"Yes, it's clear."

"If there's someone sitting on the third bench, then go and sit on the next bench that hasn't got anyone sitting on it... Wait exactly two minutes, okay? Two minutes. Then check no one's watching and drop the bag with the money in the rubbish bin that's next to the bench. Then stand waiting by the bin for precisely two more minutes. This is important... you've got to time yourself."

"Two minutes from the time I've dumped the parcel," the MP

repeated. "What if a tramp or someone comes and tries to make off with the parcel?"

"Won't happen, but if it does, take the parcel back and tell 'em to butt out."

"Okay, then what?"

"When the two minutes are up, you walk up the steps to Putney Bridge Approach'n continue walking in a northerly direction, up to where the road becomes Fulham High Street. You know where I mean?"

"Yes."

"That's important. If you try'n double back into the park, or anything fancy like that, I'll know it. And remember, if I smell the faintest whiff of a cop, then the deal's off and the photos'll go straight to the newspapers."

"Yes, but I'm not handing over any money until I've got the photos and the camera."

"The photos and the camera will be posted to you."

Sir Alex remembered the advice Charles had given him and said, "that's not good enough, I'm afraid. I need the photos and the camera before I hand over the money, otherwise it's no deal."

"You're in no position to be calling the shots here."

"I've told you the way I'm prepared to do this. I'll only go along with your demands if you'll meet some of mine as well. Now either you get me the photos and the camera beforehand or the deal's off."

"Maybe you ought to remind yourself just how much you stand to lose here."

"Yes, well that cuts both ways. I'd be looking at divorce and the end of my career if you go to the press, but if it goes pear-shaped for you, then you'd be looking at a fairly lengthy prison sentence. But you already know all that. Now what's it to be?"

"You've got some front, talking to me about prison sentences, mister."

"Listen, I want all this to go as smoothly as you do, but what you need to realize is that it's a two-way process."

Martin had already hung up.

❈

Sir Alex began to panic and he cursed himself for being stupid enough to listen to his brother's advice. Now the blackmailer will go to the press with the pictures, he thought, and I'm done for. *My whole life is about to be torn apart.*

He slammed his fist down on the coffee table.

"What happened?" Charles asked.

"Bastard hung up."

They were in Charles's flat in Pimlico, having walked there after they left Goya's.

"You need to get your nerves under control, Alex."

"And just how do you expect me to do that?" Sir Alex's said. "So much for trying to force the man to compromise."

"Behaving like this isn't going to get you anywhere." Charles had lost count of the number of times he'd got his younger brother out of a hole down through the years, but Alex had never got into a scrape of this order before.

"If he goes to the papers, then I'm ruined."

"But he won't, Alex. He won't."

"What makes you so sure?"

"He's trying to frighten you. And *succeeding* by the look of it."

"Wouldn't *you* be afraid if you were in my shoes?"

"You forget, Alex, that I've been in a similar situation to the one you now find yourself in, so I know a thing or two about what it is you're going through."

"Yes, and look what happened to you, Charles. You were forced to say goodbye to your career *and* your marriage."

"I can't remember who it was that said beyond a certain point all risks are equal, but he was right."

"But it's Prunella and the children I'm thinking of."

Charles's forehead creased like a sheet of corrugated iron. "If you want to protect your family, then you've got to be prepared to fight for them."

He got up from his chair and went over to the drinks cabinet, found the whisky bottle and poured two large ones. "Here, get this down you."

Sir Alex took a swig of his Scotch and felt it burn his throat as it went down.

Charles picked up the remote control unit and turned the TV on.

He surfed through the channels until he found Sky News, and they caught the end of a report on what a mess the Tories were making of the economy that would have cheered both men up at any other time. Then the newsreader said, "*And the woman who was shot onstage whilst in the middle of her act at the Revuebar, in Soho, has now been identified as Bella Armando.*"

"That's *her!*" Sir Alex blurted out as a photograph of Bella's face appeared on the screen.

"My *word...*"

The two brothers listened with bated breath as the newsreader said, "*Ms. Armando was shot in the arm and ambulance men arrived quickly on the scene, to find her lying unconscious onstage. She was then taken to Paddington Hospital, where she is said to be making good progress. Ms. Armando is expected to make a full and speedy recovery.*"

CHAPTER 13

"The fuck is this?" Bill Rivers said. "Don't fink I tried to shoot the gel, do ya?"

"Not at all, sir. We were just hoping you might be able to help us with our enquiries."

"I'll certainly be 'appy to do anyfing I can, Inspector. I'd like to see the bastard that shot Bella get caught as much as anyone."

"That's good to know, Mr. Rivers. Please take a seat."

Bill Rivers was a rotund, balding man in his mid-fifties with a chalky pallor and dark, bulging bags like plums under his eyes. He parked himself in the plastic chair, coughed up a lump of tarmac, and spat it into his handkerchief.

Preston looked across the table at Rivers. "Are you prepared to testify in court that no one left the building through the front exit of the Revuebar after the police were called?"

"I am, Chief Inspector." Rivers picked his nose as he gazed over Preston's head at the mug shots of wanted criminals on the notice board.

"How many people would have left the premises after the start of the show?"

"Might of been ten or fifteen, but I'm only guessin'."

"But you're the box office manager, aren't you?" Preston thrummed his fingers on the metal desk. "Don't you keep a note of how many people leave the building before the show's finished, so you'll know if a seat's vacant and can be resold?"

"No, it don't work like that. The doors are closed shortly after the start of each show, and we don't sell no tickets for the show in progress after that. Only stands to reason, don't it? I mean, we can't go havin' any old Tom, Dick or Harry and his friggin' dog traipsin' in and out of the theatre while the show's goin' on, now can we?

"So you see, it's not my job to worry about whether or not the punters decide they wanna leave the theatre, or even the buildin', before the end of the show 'cause the tickets ain't never resold. You with me?"

Preston tented his fingers and puffed out his cheeks. "But surely you can tell me the number of tickets you sold for the show during which Bella Armando was shot?"

"We sold a hundred 'n' forty-three tickets—I made a point of rememberin' the number, 'cause I thought you might ask. The tickets are numbered, but only so I can do the books along with the general manager. I mean to say, the numbers on the tickets don't designate a seat number nor nothin' like that, so the punters can all just go and sit wherever they fancy."

Preston tweaked his tash. "There were only a hundred and twenty-nine punters in the building by the time I got there, which means fourteen people must've left some time after the show began."

"Sounds like good arithmetic to me."

"And one of those fourteen must have fired the gun, then managed to get out of the building before I arrived along with the rest of my colleagues."

"Impossible, Inspector. We made sure the doors was all locked soon as we heard the gun go off."

"But the place was in a state of pandemonium. Maybe the gunman could've slipped through unnoticed, in the middle of all that chaos."

"No *way*. Someone would've bin sure to've seen 'im."

"Couldn't the killer have left through the backstage door before Gary Ross went to man it?"

"Okay, so the door was left unguarded for what—a minute?—or two minutes max?—'cause it couldn't've been any longer, right?"

Preston nodded.

"But what you gotta remember, Inspector, is that the gunman was sittin' in one of the seats in the theatre when he fired the shot, presumably, right? In which case, if what you're sayin' now was actually to've 'appened, he'd've had to've fought his way onto the stage, in full view of everyone, and then crossed it without no one noticing 'im.

"Then he'd've had to've gone along a narrow corridor, past the dressin' rooms, where he'd've been sure to've been spotted by someone or other—I mean, the place would've been *packed* for fuck's sake, if you'll pardon my French. Then he'd've had to go down the stairway and out the door, and he'd have had to've done all that in the short time it took Gary Ross to get to the back exit.

"All hell'd broken loose in the theatre by then's what you gotta remember, Inspector, like you said yourself. It must've been difficult to move *at all* up there—let alone to move *that* fast."

Preston reckoned what Bill Rivers had just said made sense.

❄

The door opened and the nurse came in. "You've got a visitor, Bella."

"Who is it?"

"Lady by the name of Mona, says she's a friend of yours. Do you feel up to seeing her?"

"Sure."

The nurse went out, and moments later Mona Chapman entered the room. She was looking as unashamedly butch as ever, in her dungarees and baseball boots, and she was carrying a bunch of roses. "I brought you these, Bel."

"Oh, you *shouldn't* have." Bella held the roses to her nose and breathed in their rich scent, before she put them down on the bedside cabinet. "They're beautiful, Mona. Thank you so much."

"Can't stop long, Bel. I just wanted to make sure you were okay."

"I'm doing fine. The doctor tells me I should be able to go home soon."

"Oh that's such a relief. I was so *worried* about you."

"How did you find out about what happened?"

"I was in the audience at the time with Win. Not only that, it's all been on the news and in the papers. You've become a sort of minor celebrity, Bel."

Bella could think of better ways to win her five minutes of fame.

"Police got any leads, yet?"

"Not sure, Mo."

"Don't reckon it was that horrible husband of yours, do you?"

Bella shook her head. "It's not Joey's style."

Mona plumped herself down in the chair at the side of the bed.

"I read he struck some kinda deal with the cops to get out early."

"Where did you read that?"

"In yesterday's *Evening Standard*, and it said in the article about how these other two—that he robbed the bank with—have recently got out of prison as well, only they escaped. You don't think it could've been one of those two men who shot you, Bel?"

"Why would they've wanted to shoot *me*?"

"As a way of getting at Joey, I suppose. Who knows the way these guys think?"

"But I'm not even living with Joey any more..."

"Yeah, but the person who tried to kill you mightn't have known that. Just an idea that occurred to me, anyway." Mona shrugged, "'cause these other two men that've escaped from prison'll both be after your Joey for the money he got away with, I expect, don't you?"

"He's not *my* Joey any more."

"Sorry, just a slip of the tongue. But I was thinking, you want to be careful when you get out of this place, because they might go to your flat lookin' for him."

"We've already moved out, Mo."

"Oh, have you?"

"A friend's putting us up for the time being at her flat in Fulham just until we find somewhere."

"Whereabouts in Fulham's that, then?"

"Racton Road."

"One of the girls in the show, is it?"

"Yeah, Suzanne..."

"Suzanne's the one that dances with the rubber python, isn't she?"

Bella nodded. "Don't tell anyone, though, Mo, because it's a secret."

"Does Joey know where you've moved to?"

"No, and I don't want him to find out, either."

"Why, what would he do, then, do you think, if he knew where you are?"

"Who knows? Joey's a violent man, Mo. He's jealous, too, and he still doesn't want to accept the fact that I've left him."

"I understand, Bel. You know I won't tell anyone." Mona smiled as though she'd been talking about something as mundane as a new recipe for making paella. "Well, I'm so glad you're okay. That's the important thing."

"Yeah, it could've turned out so much worse."

"Thank God it didn't. Anyway, I just thought I'd pop in to bring you some flowers and wish you a speedy recovery." Mona leaned over and kissed Bella on the cheek. "Must dash."

On her way out of the hospital, Mona happened to bump into Joey B, who was pacing up and down by the entrance sucking on a cigarette, his eyes full of thunder.

"Well look who it ain't," Joey said. "You keepin' all right, Mona?"

"Can't complain, Joey."

"How's your brother Donny doin'?"

"Haven't seen him in a while."

"Last I heard he was out."

"Yeah, well he's keeping a low profile I expect."

"Must be it."

"What brings you here, then, Joey?"

"Come to see Bella. What about you?"

"Me, too. I'm glad to see she's looking much better."

"Is she?"

"Why, haven't you been in to see her yet?"

Joey shook his head. "They won't allow me in."

"Didn't you two split up?"

"Yeah, well I need to talk to 'er about that."

"Still love her, do you, Joey?"

"Woman's my *wife*, Mo, and where I come from that means somethin'. Y'know what I'm sayin'?"

"Of course. Well, I hope you two work things out."

"She's with some wanker of a doorman, a *nobody*. Ain't my fault I got banged up, is it?"

"I wish I could do something to help, Joey."

"You could always try'n find out where she's livin' at the moment."

"She told me she's staying with one of the other girls in the show at her flat in Racton Road, in Fulham."

"Very much so. Especially as in the photos I'm lying before her in the shower and she's pissing into my mouth. You can see quite clearly that it's me." Sir Alex choked back a sob. "Look really good in the Sunday papers, wouldn't it?"

"Mm... well, I can certainly see why you'd be feeling stressed. What are you going to do about it?"

"No alternative but to pay the man off. I've already paid a woman off once, and this time it's a man. I've told him I'm not prepared to do it again, and I've also made certain demands of my own."

"So you've entered into negotiations with the blackmailer, then, in a sense, and told him the terms you'll play by."

"It was my brother Charles's idea. He was trained by the SAS and MI5."

"Good advice, I'd say."

"You think so?"

"Seems you've stopped the blackmailer from having it all his own way, at least."

"That's what Charles says. I only wish I could believe it."

"Tell me what it was like..."

"With the girl, you mean?"

"Yes."

"Wonderful ... in simple terms, I acted out my little erotic fantasy and then I gave her a good fucking, twice."

"Well done, Alex."

"That's not the way I feel about it now."

"No, but you weren't to know the girl was going to film you. You mustn't blame yourself."

Sir Alex began to sob.

"That's it, Alex, let it all out ... all that emotion that's built up inside of you."

He cried like a baby for several minutes, and when he finally stopped, Margot said, "How did you feel afterwards?"

"After having sex with the girl, you mean? Oh, fine, as far as it went, until I realized I was being blackmailed."

"If you ask me, this all stems from your inveterate need to punish yourself, Alex."

"My *what?*"

"Why else would you want to drink a woman's urine?"

"That's simple. I want to drink it because it turns me on."

"Of course, but the question you need to ask yourself, is *why* it excites you..."

"That's what I'm coming here to find out."

"Has it ever occurred to you that this obsession might lie in your desire to punish yourself? After all, there's nothing inherently erotic about a woman's urine. It's filthy stuff, and drinking it could make you sick."

"Okay, so I need to punish myself..."

"The next question you need to ask is why you hate yourself."

"But I *don't*."

"You're avoiding the question."

"I see myself as being a pretty decent fellow, all in all, really."

"What are you most ashamed of?"

"Well, I've already told you about all of that."

"No, I'm not talking about your sexual obsessions now, but your day to day life. What's the thing that you most despise about yourself?"

"Nothing comes readily to mind."

"Well let that be your homework."

Sir Alex got up off the couch and stretched his arms before he made for the door. "Until next time, then ..."

"Yes, I shall need to see you again this week."

❄

Joey B had just parked across the street from the place in Racton Road, when a man pulled over on the other side of the street in a white Ferrari.

Joey watched the driver of the Ferrari get out and run up the front steps of the building that Bella was now calling home. The man had a full head of grey hair, and he was wearing an expensive-looking charcoal-grey suit with a light-blue shirt that was open at the collar. The guy might live in the downstairs flat. Or else he could be this girl Suzanne's boyfriend.

Joey got out of his BMW, crossed the road, and followed the man up the steps. He got to the top of them just in time to see the man push the buzzer next to Suzanne Cookson's name on the console.

Joey considered going away and coming back later, but then he heard the man say he'd come to read the gas meter.

Now that seemed a bit odd.

It was odd enough to make Joey change his mind about leaving, and he followed the man into the building. Joey knocked on the door to the downstairs flat, just to be doing something, so the man didn't think he was spying on him.

Nobody came to the door, so Joey made a show of knocking a couple of times more, to give the man he was following time to climb the stairs as far as the landing. Then Joey went after him, but he took the precaution of stopping well before he got to the top of the stairs so that he was out of sight. He heard the man knock on the door to the upstairs flat.

Maybe the man was a detective.

But detectives didn't normally tell people they'd come to read the gas meter when they called round.

So who *was* this guy, and what did he want?

❆

Martin had been wondering how he should play things with the MP when the intercom buzzer sounded.

"Hello, is the owner there?"

"No, Suzanne's out, I'm afraid. Can I take a message?"

"I've come to read the gas meter. All I've got to do is look at the meter and make a note of the number on it. It won't take two tics."

"All right, come on up, then."

Martin buzzed the man into the building, and less than a minute later the doorbell rang. He went to see who it was, and found himself looking at a man of fifty or so, dressed in a classy suit. "I was expecting the man who reads the gas meter."

"Well I wouldn't know about that, but I've got a message for you. Perhaps you'd better invite me in."

Something about this didn't feel right. "Sorry, who did you say you are again?"

"I didn't, but I'm the brother of Sir Alex Boulton." Charles saw Martin's expression change. "Like I said, you'd better invite me in."

"And just why would I want to do that?"

"I can think of two good reasons."

"Which are...?"

"The first is, I'm holding a gun in my pocket and it's pointing right at your heart."

Martin stood aside and opened the door a foot or so wider.

"Huh-huh ... First, you open the door all the way."

Martin did as the man said.

"That's it, now take six paces backwards."

Martin did as he was told again, and Charles entered the flat and shut the door behind him. Then he took the gun out of his pocket and said, "This doesn't have to be violent and messy."

"What do you want?"

"I think the question you should be asking is more along the lines of what do *you* want?"

Martin kept mum.

"Okay, this is the deal. My brother has decided to humour you and play along with your little game—up to a point. But first, you have to listen to me, understood, Martin?"

"How do you know my name?"

"I know a lot about you, Martin. You'd be surprised."

"Such as ...?"

"I know that you were living with your girlfriend, Bella Armando, over in Joseph Belagio's flat, in the Ladbroke Grove area, until Belagio was let out of prison sooner than you expected. I also know that this place belongs to Suzanne Cookson, one of the dancers in the show at the Revuebar, who's agreed to let you and Bella come and stay here for a while. You work as doorman at the Revuebar, in Soho, where Bella dances ... you're small potatoes."

"So it was *you* that shot Bella."

"I also get the sense that you have never tried to blackmail anyone—or become involved in a serious crime of any sort—before, and that right now you are shitting bricks."

He was right, too.

"Now I've got a proposition I'd like to make to you, Martin. But before I tell you what it is, I just want to get things clear from the start. You see, if I wanted to I could have you and that little tart of a girlfriend of yours killed in the blink of an eye.

"I was in the SAS, and I can assure you that I'm well capable of doing it myself if the mood took me. Or I could call on anyone from a list of people as long as your arm, who would all do that sort of thing for me at the drop of a hat.

"As well as the SAS, I've also worked for M15 and M16. I could have it done so that it looked like an accident. There wouldn't be any consequences for me at all."

"Why is it that I get the feeling you're trying to frighten me?"

"I don't need to frighten little people like you, Martin. I'm an important man with lots of friends in high places, and you're nobody. I can make people like you disappear, and I'm not boasting when I say that. Simply stating a fact. It's not the sort of fact that you're ever likely to read in newspapers, but that doesn't make it any less true."

"So why don't you, then? Why come here and give me this speech instead?"

"Because although I don't like your shoddy little game, and although I think you and that girlfriend of yours are scum, I still have certain principles. Now I wouldn't expect someone like you to understand this, but I really would prefer not to have to kill you and Bella, or have you rubbed out by someone else, unless I find it absolutely necessary to do so.

"You see, I've normally only made people disappear in the service of the realm. That's to say, I've only killed people who have been spying for our enemies—doing things that are serious enough to warrant their being disposed of. You, young man, are simply a little piece of scum who hasn't got much"—Charles paused to look around the room—"a piece of scum who finds himself on his uppers, as is most painfully apparent, and who fancies that he can see a quick way to make some easy money.

"And so the situation is simple. To prove that we're not devoid of compassion, my brother and I are willing to give you fifty thousand pounds, in return for all of the photographs and the camera, and then we're all going to forget this whole sorry business ever happened."

"That's only half the amount I asked for."

"I'm sure that it's more than double what you've ever earned in a single year, too, and it's fifty thousand pounds more than you deserve. Now I'm offering you a choice here, Martin, and if I were you, I'd consider your next move very carefully.

"You can either take our extremely generous *gift,* and hand all of the photos and the camera over to me, and we'll call it quits. Or ..." Charles broke off. "Well, I think you know what will happen to you and your girlfriend if you don't let it rest."

Martin didn't really have to think very long or hard about the choice he was being asked to make. "Okay. It's a deal. But first I want to see the money."

❋

From his position out of sight but within earshot on the stairs, Joey B heard the man who'd turned up in the Ferrari say he was carrying a gun, and then heard him invite himself into the upstairs flat. At that point, Joey decided to go and make a note of the registration number on the man's car so he could check it out later.

Once he'd done that, Joey climbed in behind the wheel of his BMW and wondered what his next move should be. He was still wondering about this, minutes later, when the man in the charcoal-grey suit came back out of the building and set off in his Ferrari.

Joey was curious, so he followed him. He tailed the Ferrari all the way across town and right out as far as Epping Forest. Then the man drove off the road into a clearing in the woods and pulled up.

Joey brought his BMW to a stop and watched the man get out of his Ferrari. Joey wondering what the fuck the guy was up to and not liking the feel of any of this.

The man turned and looked at Joey. He was holding a gun.

Joey started the engine up and pegged it.

"It was a piece of cake," Charles told Sir Alex later on, at his flat in Pimlico. "First I consulted one of my foot soldiers, and told him about the girl who's currently in Paddington Hospital. He went and did a little snooping around for me, asked a few people the right questions. Then he called me back with an address where I would be able to find the blackmailer, along with some interesting background info. After that, it was just a question of getting a gun and going over there with the money—or half of it."

"You mean you only gave the blackmailer fifty grand and not the hundred thousand he was asking for?"

"That's right."

"And did he give you everything?"

Charles opened the briefcase that was on the coffee table. "Here it all is. The chip's inside the camera."

"Well done, Charles. And what did he say when you told him you were only giving him half the amount?"

"Didn't say anything, because he realized he was bloody lucky to get that much, and I told him why in no uncertain terms."

"Do you think this is the end of it, Charles?"

"You can rest assured of that."

"But what makes you so confident?"

"You should've seen the look on the man's face when I told him what I'd do to him and that pretty girlfriend of his if either of them ever bother you again. I could have given him ten thousand and he would've been happy, or five. I could've given him *nothing*, and he would still have been relieved. In fact, I'm beginning to wonder why on earth I gave the man a penny. Wouldn't have done if it was me he'd been blackmailing. But I know how worried you've been, and so I thought it was worth it to guarantee your peace of mind. After all, it's not as though you'll miss it." Charles tasted his whisky. "I'll promise you this, though, Alex, if that useless little piece of shit ever bothers you again, it'll be the last thing he and that tart of his ever do. And I mean that."

"But Charles ... you're speaking like some thug."

"I'm speaking like a man who has your best interests at heart, Alex. I'm damned if I'm going to sit by and watch little shits like that jeopardize your future."

CHAPTER 15

Martin was trying to work out how he should feel about what happened. Okay, he was fifty grand to the good, which was fine so far as it went, but the MP's brother had treated him like he was a *wanker*.

So had Joey.

Not only that, but he was convinced that it was either Joey B, Sir Alex Boulton or his brother who'd shot Bella. *What kind of a man just sits back and lets people take potshots at the girl he loves?* Martin asked himself.

He told himself that he had to *do* something about it.

So he went into a telephone box and dialled Sir Alex Boulton's number. When the man picked up, Martin told him he'd better watch out.

"I think my brother told you never to call me again like this, if you want to stay out of trouble."

"If you or your brother *ever* go anywhere near my girlfriend again, I'll fucking well kill you both," Martin said. "Do you understand?"

Then he hung up.

❄

Martin went to the hospital, and Bella was in the middle of eating her dinner when he entered her room.

"You really must be making fast progress, Bel, if you can manage to keep down the food they give you here."

"Yeah, I'm pretty good, considering."

Martin took Bella's hand in his and gave it a tender squeeze. "I can't tell you how much I—"

Just then, the door opened and DCI Preston walked in.

"Evening," he greeted them both. "You're making excellent progress, I hear, Ms. Armando."

Martin said, "You again."

"Don't sound so happy to see me, Mr. Butler."

"I wanted to be alone with Bella..."

"And I want to catch the person who tried to kill her, so we should be on the same side."

"Any closer to making an arrest?"

"We're working on the case around the clock, and I have every confidence that we'll turn something up sooner or later. In the meantime, it would help me a great deal, Bella, if you could talk me through what happened in the minutes leading up to the moment when you were shot."

❄

Martin bumped into Joey B on his way out of the hospital.

"Bella doin' okay, is she?"

"Yeah, she is as a matter of fact," Martin said. "She doesn't want to see you, though."

"Still singin' the same tune, are we?"

"Don't you ever know when you're not wanted?"

Joey said, "You're hanging round with toffs now, I see."

"What?"

"An ex-MP, no less."

"The fuck are you talking about?"

"Charles Boulton, brother to Sir Alex—as if you needed me to tell you... like the man's Ferrari, I must say."

"Never heard of the guy."

"He's gay, so I hear."

"Nice for him."

"Had to resign from his job as an MP when he was outed by the media. Big scandal at the time... remember readin' about it."

"I don't see what any of this has got to do with me."

"What... havin' trouble makin' ends meet, so you're earnin' a little extra money as a rent boy, are you, Martin?"

"Bella always told me you were mad, but I never thought you were this far gone."

"Or's it somethin' else?"

"You're psychotic."

"Like a little *blackmail*, perhaps?"

"You wanna get your head read, mate."

"Nice little earner blackmail can be, I'm sure."

"Was it you that shot Bella?"

"Don't be stupid. I love Bella. She's my *wife*, don't forget. Why would I wanna harm her?"

"Maybe because she doesn't love you."

"No, it's *you* I'm gonna harm, Martin."

"Why don't you just fuck off out the way before I smash your ugly face in for you."

"Wouldn't try'n do that, if I was you, 'cause there's a gun in my pocket and it's pointin' right at your heart, old son." Joey prodded him with the barrel, and Martin felt a cold icy worm start to work its way down his spine. "C'mon, you'n me need to talk."

"I'm not going anywhere with you."

"I only wanna have a little chat in the car."

"I've already said everything I got to say to you."

"Yeah, but *I* haven't. Now let's go."

They walked over to Joey's BMW. "Get into the passenger seat and then move over behind the wheel."

Martin did as he was told. Then Joey quickly took his gun out, safe in the knowledge that the tinted windows shielded him from view, before he climbed into the passenger seat. He took the key out of his pocket and put it in the ignition. "C'mon, let's go."

"I'm not driving to that farmhouse again, so you may as well shoot me here if you're gonna do it."

"I ain't gonna shoot ya ... the fuck gave you that idea? I just wanna talk to ya, like I said."

"You wanna talk, so *talk*, then."

"You got more balls than I thought. I respect that in a man. Maybe we ain't so different after all."

"Oh, we're different all right. I don't go around killing people, for a start."

"You could, though, if you was pushed to it."

"We gonna sit here and make small talk, or what, Joey?"

"No harm in that, is there?"

"Not especially, but if it's true that all you wanna do's talk to me, then you could try putting your gun away. You might find that it aids the flow of the conversation."

"You ain't in a position to tell me what to do."

"I'm *not* telling you what to do."

"What're you doin', then?"

"I'm just *asking* you to put the fuckin' gun away."

"Okay, well since you're axing me nicely then that's different."

And to Martin's surprise, Joey put the gun back in his pocket.

"That better?"

"Much."

Martin turned and met the man's gaze. "Right, well I'm going now, Joey, so if you wanna shoot me in the back, then you'd better do it."

Martin got out of the car and set off at a brisk pace across the car park, half expecting to be taken down by a bullet with every step. But he made it to the entrance of the hospital without being shot. When he turned to look, he saw that Joey's car had gone.

❄

Murderous desires coursed through Joey's veins as he drove back to his flat in Ladbroke Grove. "I just don't fuckin' believe all that 'appened," he said aloud. "The cunt pulled my fuckin' bluff, and I let the bastard get away with it. I must be goin' fuckin' soft or somethin'."

As soon as he got in, Joey filled a tumbler with Scotch and knocked it back in one go. Then he punched the wall a few times and smashed up an old chair. He needed to do something to let out all of the rage that was inside him.

The intercom sounded, and he ignored it to begin with. But whoever it was kept at it, so he went and picked up.

"Hello?"

"Mr. Belagio?"

"That's me. What d'ya want?"

"Detective Chief Inspector Preston here. I wonder if we could talk?"

"What about?"

"Well I'm sure it won't have escaped your attention that your wife Bella's lying in hospital after having been shot."

"I know that, Inspector, and *you* know I know it. It's bad enough as it is, so I can do without the sarcasm."

"That wasn't my intention, Mr. Belagio. I just wondered if I could ask you a few questions?"

"Hang on a mo and I'll come down."

❄

Half an hour later, Preston was interviewing Joey down at the station.

"Just seems a bit of a coincidence, Mr. Belagio, that your wife should've been shot so soon after you got out of prison."

Joey shrugged his broad, heavy shoulders. "*Coincidence* is the word, Inspector. I love Bella. Why'd I want to hurt her?"

"Perhaps because she's left you for another man."

"No reason to want a kill someone, is it?"

"It might be, for some men."

"Not for me. Besides, I wasn't even there at the time. Didn't hear about it till I saw it on the News later. Then I rushed straight to the hospital'n they wouldn't let me in to see her. I seem to remember seein' you in MacDonald's, I think it was, Inspector."

Preston nodded. "So where were you at the time of the shooting, Mr. Belagio?"

"Catchin" up with some ol' mates a mine in the Elgin, near to my flat, on Ladbroke Grove."

"Anyone there that might be able to corroborate what you've just said?"

"Plenty a people."

"We need names."

"Jim, the proprietor, for one. I was chattin' with 'im, and Jed Dixon and Duane Forrest was both there."

Preston turned to DS Johnson. "Perhaps you'd like to go and check that out, Dave?"

"Right you are, guv," Johnson said, and he went out.

❄

Sir Alex returned for another session with Margot Peterson the following afternoon.

"How are you feeling today, Alex?"

"Rather better, as a matter of fact."

"So what's happened to put you in this better frame of mind?"

"I've paid off the blackmailer, and I'm hoping that's the end of the whole wretched business."

"Must be a weight off your shoulders, I should imagine, but we still need to address the issues we were discussing last time, Alex. Just because your blackmailer's disappeared from the scene doesn't mean that your other problems have all been solved, too."

"No, well I can live with the idea that I have a penchant for drinking women's urine, but the thought of having photos of me *in flagrante delicto* spread across the Sunday newspapers, is a different matter."

"I don't think it's quite as simple as that."

"What are you getting at?"

"You need to consider the impulse that got you into the situation in the first place."

"Meaning?"

"I can see you've forgotten to do your homework, Alex, you naughty chap."

"Perhaps you'd better remind me of what it was." Sir Alex had been too taken up with his own worries to remember what Margot had been talking to him about during their last session.

"The question I gave you to ponder on, was why you hate yourself so much."

"But I've already told you that I *don't*."

"I'd have to say that all the evidence points to the contrary."

"I'm afraid I don't really follow you."

"Let me recap, Alex. Your desire to have women urinate in your mouth has its roots in your hatred of yourself. It's this self-hatred that landed you in a situation where you were open to being blackmailed."

"But it was getting caught in the act, surely."

"One and the same thing, Alex. You are punishing yourself by making yourself vulnerable to all sorts of situations."

"You can't seriously be suggesting that I *wanted* to get myself blackmailed."

"On one level, yes, although you're not conscious of it, of course. We're talking about the subconscious here, after all, and the subconscious is, by very definition, that of which we remain *subconscious*."

"And you're saying I'm likely to get myself in more situations of this sort unless I deal with the root cause?"

"Exactly, and having a microwave mentality on this thing isn't going to help."

"Having a *what*?"

"What I mean is, the way you're going about things is like trying to patch up a burst aorta with a sticking plaster. You need to stop trying to wrap everything up in five minutes, and be prepared to put in some serious work on this problem over a period of time."

"I see. Well there is one thing that might be worth considering."

"I'm listening..."

"I am a rather wealthy man, as you are probably aware."

"Go on."

"Well, I do sometimes feel uncomfortable about the fact that most of the wealth I've inherited comes from the family business, which..."

"Yes?"

"What I mean is, certain aspects of the family business sometimes trouble me."

"Which aspects would they be, Alex?"

"To cut a long story short, the family owns a number of factories in India. I was never really aware of the lines along which these factories were run until my father died last year."

"That presumably was when you inherited them, was it?"

"Quite."

"And?"

"Up until then I'd never really enquired into things. I left matters to my father, while he was still well enough to run things, and to my brother Charles, and simply assumed that everything was aboveboard. At that time, I still considered myself to be the son of a very decent family. What I'm trying to say, I suppose, is that I always felt as though I *deserved* the privileges I'd enjoyed. It was as if I felt that I and my family were special in some way... almost as if we were *better* than other people—those who didn't enjoy such privileges, I mean. And then, as I say, Father died, and so I felt it incumbent upon me to go to India to see how the factories were run first hand."

"And what did you see when you went there?"

"Let us say that things were not as I'd expected... in fact, they were not *at all* as I'd expected."

"Are we talking *sweatshops* here, Alex?"

"Not to put too fine a point on it, yes, we are."

❉

A couple of hours later, Preston's mobile began to belch out its jazz riff.

"What've you got, Dave?"

"The proprietor of the Elgin, Jim Watts, has corroborated what Joey Belagio said, guv. He says Joey was sitting at the bar drinking from around seven to sometime after ten the evening Bella Armando was shot."

"Has this Jim Watts got any form?"

"None at all, guv."

"Okay, thanks, Dave, I'll catch you later."

CHAPTER 16

"So we've got the whole place to ourselves, Win."

"Yes, John's away working in his constituency."

"So there'll be room in that big double bed of yours for me tonight."

"I don't think we should, Mo—not in the same bed."

"What d'you mean, Win?"

"Not until I've told John the way it is between us."

"But you were going to tell him, you said."

"I know."

"So why didn't you?"

"John's been under a lot of pressure with his work, lately," Winifred said. "I've been waiting for the right moment to break it to him."

"Not wimping out on me, Win, are you?"

"Of course not, Mo. How could you even think that? I'll tell him when he comes back, on Monday."

"Promise?"

"Cross my heart and hope to die."

"Hardly make much difference, would it, though, if he's gonna find out Monday anyway?" Mona put her glass down on the small end table, and placed her hand on Winifred's fleshy thigh. "You're so special to me."

"I bet you say that to all the girls."

Maybe she had in the past, but she'd never meant it before the way she did now. "Don't laugh at me, Win."

"I'm not, Mo."

"You shouldn't laugh at somebody because they love you. It's cruel."

"That's the thing about John."

"What?"

"I'm sure that he still loves me."

"But I thought you said you suspected him of cheating on you."

"I do, but even so."

"You're not making much sense, Win."

"He loves me in his own way, Mo."

Mona moved her hand further up Winifred's thigh and felt the slithery silk of her knickers. "I'm madly in love with you, Win."

"Me, too, with you, Mo."

"So what're we doing wasting time sitting here talking about John, then?"

"It's just that I still care about him, in a funny sort of way, even though it's all over between us."

"You want to end the marriage without hurting his feelings, you mean?"

"In a nutshell, yes."

'Impossible to do. If he still loves you as you say he does." Mona slipped her hand inside Winifred's knickers and began to finger her labia, felt them moisten nicely. "Lights have changed, I see."

"Uh?"

"Green for go, by the feel of things, Win."

"You're talking double Dutch, Mo."

"*You*, darling... you're possibly *dripping* for it." Mona worked Winifred's skirt up, undid the pink bows on either hip, and pulled away the silky material to reveal her hairy treasure trove. "Where's Steely Dan?" Meaning Winifred's favourite dildo.

"Look in my Kelly bag."

Mona reached over to the end table, and began to root around inside Winifred's handbag. "The fuck's this?" she said, holding up a Home Pregnancy Test Kit.

"What does it look like?"

"You're still fucking him." Mona's face was a portrait of pain and misery, and Winifred realized the seriousness of her mistake.

"It was only a couple of times, Mo."
"But you promised me the sex was over between you and him."
"Well it was."
"So why'd you need *this*, then?"
"These things aren't as simple as you think, Mo."
"The fuck does that mean?"
"It's not so easy to stay married to a man and never have sex with him, even when it's over between you."
"Sounds like it's not really over at all."
"I just told you it was only a couple of times, Mo, and I was drunk."
"That's no excuse." Mona made a fist and was about to punch Winifred in the face, but she stopped. "No," she said. "You want me to hit you, so you could make me share your guilt. Well I'm not playing that game."

Mona ran out of the house, feeling like her heart was breaking.

❉

She went to *George's*, the lesbian bar on Wardour Street, and knocked back four large whiskies, one after another. She was still crying when a familiar face came over and sat next to her at the bar.
"Remember me?"
"Hi... it's Martina, right?"
"Margot, but it was a nice try."
Mona dabbed at her eyes with her hanky.
"What are you drinking, Mona?"
"Black Bush."
Margot Peterson got the attention of the cute black chick behind the bar. "Two large Black Bushes, sweetie."
"Any time you like, darling." The barmaid gave her a certain look, before she saw to the drinks.
Margot looked at Mona. "Woman trouble?"
"How did you guess?"
"Been there myself and got the T-shirt to prove it."
"I've got it bad, Margie."
"Margot."
The barmaid placed the Black Bushes down on the counter, and she caressed Margot's palm and winked as she returned her change.

Margot sipped her whisky and eyed Mona over the rim of the glass. "Why don't you get that down you and come back to my place?"

❄

Back at Margot's, Mona threw up into the sink before she crashed out in bed. Then woke up in Margot's arms some time in the middle of the night.

"What's the matter ... can't you sleep?"

"Just been lying here watching you," Margot murmured.

"Not feeling tired, or what?"

"Isn't that."

"What, then?"

"Horny as hell."

"Don't let me stop you doing anything."

Margot traced a route with her lips, down through the mountains, over the flat plain, and into the mushy marshes that were home to her. Her hot pink tongue played Marco Polo, and Mona lay back and thought not of England, but Winifred.

And came twice, thinking of her.

❄

Afterwards, Margot fell fast asleep and Mona was the one who began to feel restless. She remembered how the last time she'd spent the night with Margot, she found the file on Sir Alex Boulton that enabled her to blackmail the man. She wondered if she might be able to go through Margot's files again this time, see if she could turn up anything else that was interesting.

With this in mind, Mona got up out of bed, and started looking for Margot's briefcase.

No sign of it anywhere.

But then Mona went downstairs, and found Margot's laptop on the table in the front room, and it had been left on.

She opened what appeared to be an index, scrolled down and found the name ALEX BOULTON, then opened the file and began to read all about how Sir Alex was making heaps of money from sweatshops in India.

❄

Mona spent the following three days and nights fucking, fighting, and drinking. It was the only way she knew to go about dealing with the pain she was feeling inside.

On the third night, she was sitting on a stool at the bar in *George's* when a girl strolled in who looked like she'd just stepped out of a dream. Mona was so hot for her, she even found herself forgetting about Win for a while. So she picked her tongue up off the floor and sidled over to the girl with the idea of making a little small talk.

The girl, who had a great mane of silky blonde hair, a fabulous figure, and the most beautiful blue eyes, said her name was Jo. Mona came on to her big time, paid her a million compliments, invited her back to hers, got the brush-off. Then tried a different approach. "Okay, well just because we're not gonna be having hot sex tonight it doesn't mean we can't be friends, right?"

Jo smiled.

"Get you a drink?"

"Sure, mine's a Screaming Multiple Orgasm."

Mona got the attention of the black chick behind the bar and told her they'd have "two Multiple Screamers", before she turned back to the dream girl. "What do you do for a living, Jo?"

"I'm an investigative journalist."

"Oh, that's interesting, and who do you write for?"

"*The Guardian.*"

"Funny I should meet you here like this, Jo, because I've just come across a piece of information that might be of interest to you."

"What's it about?"

"Concerns a certain *very* high-profile MP who's been making lots of money out of sweatshops in India."

"Interesting... got a name?"

"Yes."

"Fancy telling me what it is?"

"Might do... if you wanna come back to mine."

Jo smiled. "That's bribery."

Mona smiled back at her and said, "you're too right it is."

PART II

CHAPTER 17

"You'll never guess what I heard, Rick."

Ricky grabbed a handful of silicone implant and told his English teacher, Janine—or Jan as everyone called her—that he didn't do guessing.

They were in Ricky's cell in Wandsworth, and Ricky was feeling like he was in a mood to make the most of his English lesson. He ran his other hand up Jan's thigh and felt the bit where her stockings ended and the spidery strings of her suspenders began. "I wanna know somefink, I find it out."

The way things were working out, Jan was learning more from Ricky than he was learning from her. A slim redhead with more piercings than an old dartboard, dressed in a red skirt and a white T-shirt, she gasped as she felt first one then two of Ricky's stubby fingers go up inside her. Ricky was a crude, violent man with about as much class as brunch in a greasy spoon, but that was what attracted her to him. "I can see that you aren't one to fuck about, Rick."

"Whoever told you that? I always been one to fuck about *when*ever I want with *who*ever I want... just that I ain't never been one to fuck about while I was doing it."

"Not sayin' you're gonna be unfaithful to me when you get out, Rick, are you?"

"No, I ain't sayin' that, Jan."

"So what *are* you saying, then?"

"Changed me ways 'specially for you, gel, i'n' it."

"Have you really, Rick?"

"Course I have, gel."

"You're not just saying that 'cause of the lack of competition?" After all, with him being banged up like he was, he didn't really have anyone else on tap but her.

"Love of me life, you are, Jan."

"Am I, Rick?"

"You know you are, Jan." Ricky chuckled.

"What's so funny?"

"Just thinkin' if they'd had teachers like you back at the school I went to, then I might never've ended up in 'ere."

"Might've gone straight, y'mean?"

"Never know, do you?"

"Don't think so, Rick, somehow, it just isn't you."

Ricky worked his dick out of his trousers with his free hand, and Janine went down on him.

"That's it, gel." He grabbed a fistful of her hair.

Janine worked on him for a little while until he exploded into her mouth, then she sank back onto her haunches and tried to swallow. But it was a heavy cargo for her to manage all on her own, so she got to her feet and went to kiss Ricky on the mouth in the hope that he might help her out.

"Fuck ya doin', you dirty bitch?"

"What's the matter, Rick—it's *yours*." Seeing that she wasn't going to get any help, Janine gulped it all back somehow, gagging a little as she did so.

"Fuckin' disgustin' stuff, you axe me."

"Don't wanna knock it, Rick. It's what makes the world go round."

Ricky remembered something. "What was that you was saying earlier... about you *heard* somethin'?"

"Oh yeah... about that guy Joey B."

"What about 'im?"

"Rumour is that he's out."

"*Can't* fuckin' be."

Janine started packing away the books she'd brought for the lesson. "Well I've got it on good authority that he is, Rick."

"Who the fuck told ya?"

"Johnny Zimbabwe. He said to tell you he saw him in The Dog in the Manger only the other day."

"But Joey B got the same sentence I got."

"Something sounds fishy there then, Rick."

"Do me a favour, willya?"

"Anything you want."

"Can you go'n axe Jack, just to double-check on that for me?"

"What, Jack Chick, d'you mean?"

Ricky nodded. "Jack'll know if Joey's out or not. Jack's got eyes in the back of his ass."

"Okay, I'll go and see him." Janine glanced at her wristwatch. "I'd better be off."

"All right, but make sure you come again tomorrow, won't you?"

Janine finally succeeded in kissing Ricky on the mouth, and as she pulled away, she told him that she wouldn't miss it for the world. Then she turned and left his cell.

❄

When Janine came back in the next day, to give Ricky his "English lesson," she confirmed all his worst fears where Joey B was concerned, and he looked like he was going to kill someone. Janine figured it might be an idea to try to distract him with thoughts of other matters, so she pulled up her dress and let him see her lacy black panties.

"The matter, Rick, don't you want to fuck me today? I got these knickers from Agent Provocateur 'specially for you 'cause I thought you'd like them."

Ricky looked at Janine without seeing her, his eyes mad with rage. "He must a done a deal."

"What?"

"I said he must a done a fuckin' deal … to get out, I mean."

"What … Joey B?"

"Well it ain't the fuckin' Pope I'm talkin' about."

"Okay, *sor-ry*. You don't have to bite my head off."

"No, not *your* head, Jan. It's Joey fuckin' B's head I'm after, and I want it on a fuckin' wooden stake." Ricky ran his hand over his pate, scratched the shiny bald flesh that was the site of a fairly recent hair-evacuation job. "I gotta get out."

"What d'you mean like escape?"

"That's exac'ly what I mean. I got to before Joey B spends all the fuckin' money we got away with."

"But how're you gonna do it?"

Ricky said, "You're gonna help me." Then he pushed her over the back of the chair and took her from behind.

❇

Ricky lifted some weights for half an hour in the gym that afternoon. Then afterwards, he was tensing the muscles in his arms and watching the tattooed serpents on them expand and constrict as he took a shower, when Vic Braine came in and stood under the faucet next to his.

Vic was thirty-five and he was three years into a ten-year sentence for armed robbery. He stood at around five-ten, weighed around 175 pounds and had a big tattoo of a dragon across his shoulders. He caught Ricky's eye as he was soaping his belly and asked him if he knew that Joey B was out.

"What's it to you?"

"Just wonderin' if you knew." Vic wiped the soap from his eyes. "'cause I'd be worried if I was you, Rick."

"Worried about what?"

"How d'you know Joey ain't gonna be spendin' all the money you got away with on that bank job?"

"Don't remember axin' your advice."

"No, well, I was only sayin' it to be helpful, Rick. I mean, we gotta look out for each other in 'ere, i'n' it."

"I don't need nobody to look out for me." Ricky grabbed his towel and went out, thinking to himself if cunts like Vic Braine knew what Joey was up to then half of fucking London must know it as well.

It was enough to piss a man off big time. If Joey B tried to take any of his money then he'd cut the man's head off. Give it to Johnny fuckin' Zimbabwe to go on holiday with.

❇

When Janine came in the following morning, Ricky told her he had a *plan*.

"What am I gonna have to do, Rick?"

"Not much. Just deliver a paintin' to a man, that's all."

"So tell me the rest of it, then."

Ricky ran his plan by her.

Then that afternoon, Vic Braine came up to Ricky in the weights room and asked him if he'd thought about breaking out, now that Joey B was at large.

"Who said anythin' about that?"

"Nobody, Rick ... just wonderin', that's all."

Ricky punched Vic in the gut and he doubled up. Then Ricky brought his knee up and got Vic a nice one on the nose, sending blood gushing everywhere. Whenever Ricky got the scent of blood he was like a shark, and he rabbit-punched Vic and Vic went down. Then Ricky picked up a dumbbell, and he was about to smash Vic's head to a pulp with it when it occurred to him that he really didn't need all the hassle. Not *now* of all times, just when he wanted to be keeping a low profile and escape.

So he dropped the dumbbell on Vic's chest, then hunkered down on his haunches. "Didn't nobody never teach you it's a good idea to mind your own business sometimes, Vic?"

"No, I don't suppose they could of, Rick."

"What's that mark you got on your cheek there?"

"Scar from a knife."

"Looks like you wanna be careful not to be goin' round upsettin' people, Vicky, old son ... else you might get another scar on the other side to go with it, or somethin' worse could 'appen. Something *much* worse. You followin' my drift?"

"Yeah, I hear where you're comin' from."

"You can consider yourself fortunate this time, Vic." Ricky gave him a slap on the cheek.

"Thanks, Rick ... very good of you, I must say."

Ricky straightened up as a guard came in.

"What's going on here?" the screw wanted to know.

"Nothin', Mr. Bright. Old Vic here just 'ad a bit of a giddy turn."

"Oh, is that so?"

"Yes, that's right, Mr. Bright," Vic piped up, "and Rick was bein good enough to try'n make sure I was all right."

"He's a regular medical man, I see."

"Least I could do," Ricky said, deadpan.

Then marched back to his cell.

❄

Ricky sidled up to Dave Turner, the screw, in the prison yard the following morning, as he stood on the touchline watching a game of football between two teams of inmates. At fifty-three, the screw was getting a little old for the job, had a reputation with the inmates for being something of a soft touch.

"Look at old Donny there," Ricky chuckled. "Thinks he's Vinnie fuckin' Jones."

"Don't tell him that or he'll start getting ideas."

"Like football, do you, Mr. Turner?"

The screw nodded. "I often go to watch Fulham play."

"Really?" Ricky shifted his weight from one foot to the other. "I'm surprised about that 'cause I always 'ad you down as a real man of culture." He pronounced it *kultcha*.

"Yes, well I do take an interest in paintings, if that's what you mean."

The ball came in Ricky's direction, and he caught it and tossed it back. "Fact is, I've got a Rothko in my possession that I'm sure you'd be interested in seein'."

"I'm sure some of the detectives down at the Yard would be interested in seeing it, too."

"No need to get like that, Mr. Turner. I was speakin' strictly off the record."

The screw turned and fixed Ricky with a serious look. He was a tall man, with a pale complexion, thinning brown hair that was graying at the temple and grey fish eyes. "Why are you telling me all this now, Ricky?"

"Only passin' the time of day, Mr. Turner. It's not easy to find someone in this place that you can enjoy a cultured conversation with."

The screw kept looking into Ricky's eyes. "What are you after?"

"Who said I was after anythin', Mr. Turner?"

"I *know* you, Ricky."

"I'm not sure if I find what you're tryin' to insinuate very flatterin', Mr. Turner, if you don't mind my sayin' so."

"I wasn't *trying* to insinuate anything. I was *insinuating* it."

Ricky turned away and pretended to show an interest in the game of football.

"Look," the screw muttered. "Why don't you just drop the social niceties and say what's on your mind?"

"Nothin' really, except that it's a shame I'm not in a position to show you the Rothko I own, 'cause I think a man like you would of appreciated havin' a chance to see it. That's all."

"And this would be an original Rothko that we're talking about, is it? I mean, it's not a copy of some kind?"

"No need to insult my intelligence, Mr. Turner." Ricky looked the screw in the eye. "Know a lot about Rothko, do you?"

"Not all that much, to tell you the truth, although I did go to see an exhibition of his work up at the National Gallery some while ago."

"Good, was it?"

"Didn't really know quite what to make of it at first, to be honest," the screw said. "There was a room full of his paintings and ... well, they weren't of anything, so far as I could tell. I mean, they were just *colours* —different shades of purple, mauve. Hello, what's going on here? I thought. But then I stopped in the room and just looked at the paintings ... no, it wasn't even that. It was more as if I breathed in the atmosphere, and then the strangest thing happened. It might sound funny to you, hearing me say this, but I began to feel things: emotions, you know? I mean it affected me in some way that I couldn't begin to put into words, just standing there in that room."

"There speaks a true man of culture, Mr. Turner."

"If I was that, Ricky, then I wouldn't be working in this place for a living."

"That's where I would beg to differ 'cause the way I see it, a man can be cultured no matter what walk of life he's from. Why, I was only readin' recently about one of the top Mafia bosses, and 'ow he liked to look at paintings and read Shakespeare'n that Italian geezer."

"Dante?"

"That's the one, I think, yeah. 'ad a real appreciation of culture, 'e did, this Mafia boss. Didn't stop him from bein' a first-class villain, though, of course."

"You wouldn't be trying to suggest that I'd have anything in common with a man like that, I hope"

"Wasn't tryin' to suggest anythin' of the sort, Mr. Turner."

"Glad to hear it, Ricky."

The screw turned back to watch the game. "I must say that I should be interested in taking a look at your Rothko, though, one day, when you're on the outside."

"Could be arranged, Mr. Turner."

Ricky looked into the screw's eyes to see if the message was understood.

It was understood all right.

"When did you have in mind?"

"Call round and see it sometime next week, if you'd like, Mr. Turner," Ricky said. "Fact, I was thinkin' maybe you'd like to look after it for me for a while."

The screw's grey fish eyes flashed.

"And why would I want to do a thing like that?"

"I'd make sure you was 'andsomely remunerated for your trouble, of course."

"How long would you want me to look after it?"

"Just for a few days, till I get out of this place, you know."

"You mean you'd buy the painting back off me, is that it?"

"If you'd like to think of it that way, Mr. Turner."

"How much do you reckon a painting like that would be worth?"

"Dunno what it would get at auction, but I'd be prepared to give you a million for it, cash. No questions asked, of course."

"Got that kind of money lying around someplace, have you, Ricky?"

"Ain't been robbin' banks for fun all these years, if you don't mind me sayin' so, Mr. Turner."

CHAPTER 18

Ricky Red called Robbie Banks, a trusted soldier on the outside, and had him go pick up the Rothko from where it was stored and take it over to Dave Turner's place. Then the following day, the screw smuggled Ricky into the back of the laundry van and the driver drove out through the front gates of the prison, taking Ricky with him.

Janine was sitting behind the wheel of her Porsche, round the corner, and she had the engine running ready when the laundry van pulled up. Ricky jumped out the back, climbed into the passenger seat beside her, and she set off, giving it some pedal.

"We made it," she purred.

"Looks that way, don't it?" Ricky smiled, revealing his silver teeth at the front.

They drove to a cottage belonging to Ricky's lawyer, down past Weybridge in the Surrey countryside, where they were going to hide out. And as soon as they got there, Janine cracked one of the bottles of champagne that she had on ice. Ricky drank most of the bottle while she undressed, and then he splashed the rest of it over her and started licking it off her naked flesh.

When he got tired of doing that, Ricky pushed Janine over the table and fucked her from behind hard and rough, the way he did everything. The wooden table banged against the wall as he thrust into her, and Janine cried out in a mixture of pleasure and pain.

After that Ricky got creative, and he fucked Janine against the kitchen sink and over the back of the sofa. Then they took a bath together.

"What you thinking about, Rick?"

"'bout that asshole Joey B."

"What kind of a deal d'you reckon he did?"

Ricky gave his stubbly chin a thoughtful scratch. "One that involved rattin' on me'n The Dog."

"Oh, I was gonna tell you about The Dog. Fat George told me he's escaped, too."

"Has he now?"

"So what're you gonna do about Joey?"

"You don't wanna know, Jan, trust me."

"You're not gonna *kill* him, are you?"

"That'll be the least of the man's problems, once I catch up with 'im."

❄

That evening, Ricky went over to pay a call on Dave Turner at the screw's council flat, which was situated in a block near Fulham Broadway.

Ricky rang the bell, and the screw opened up and led him through to the living room. There was a synthetic sofa and an easy chair made of the same material, and the television was on over in the corner of the room.

"Fuck me, Ricky, you're taking a risk coming here like this. The cop shop's just over on Fulham Road. Anyone sees you'n you'll be nicked, and sent right back to where you came from."

Ricky shrugged. "Me whole life's been one big risk."

"Get you a drink?"

Ricky shook his head. "Got the Rothko 'ere?"

"It's in the back room."

"Go'n get it, then."

"You got the money?"

"Right 'ere." Ricky tapped his briefcase and put it down on the floor.

"Okay, hang on a sec."

The screw left the room and came back in with the painting.

"Here it is, Rick. Now how about my million quid?"

Ricky picked up his briefcase and opened it. But instead of laying it on the table and showing Dave Turner the money, he brought out a .38 Smith and Wesson. There was a silencer affixed to the barrel.

"Hey, what's going on? Play fucking fair, Rick."

Ricky shot Dave Turner right through the heart, and watched the screw's face freeze as he fell to the floor.

Then he went over and put another bullet into the man's skull, just to make sure.

❋

Ricky drove back to the cottage in Surrey, where Janine was keeping herself amused by playing darts.

"Get the painting, Rick?"

"You bet."

"How much d'you pay the man?"

"Don't really think I'd part with my hard-earned cash that easy, do you?"

"What d'you do, then?"

"Shot the bastard. What d'you think?"

"Fuck me, Rick, you shouldn't of done that."

"Who says I shouldn't?"

"The cops'll really be after you now."

"They was after me before ... they've always been after me."

Janine didn't look like she was convinced by Ricky's debonair logic.

"Wanna see the paintin'?"

"If you wanna show it to me."

Ricky took it out of the cylindrical container he'd brought it home in, and unfurled it on the pinewood table.

"What d'ya think?"

"Looks like a pile of shit to me, if you really wanna know."

"Yeah, but what you gotta realize, Jan, is that it's a fuckin' *expensive* pile a shit."

. . .

"What do you make of it, guv?"

Preston glanced around the room. The wallpaper was yellowing in places, the floral carpet had stains on it, and the knickknacks on the fireplace looked cheap and tatty. "I'm not convinced it was a break-in, are you?"

"Makes you say that?"

"Victim was a screw at Wandsworth prison, Dave. He was hardly loaded. I mean just *look* at this place. Who's gonna break in here looking for money or valuables that are worth killing a man for?"

"What else do we know about the vic, guv?"

"Fifty-three years of age, born and bred in Fulham, worked as a screw for the past thirty years or so. He worked at Brixton first, then moved to Wandsworth and had been there for the past nine years. Lived alone and had recently split up with his long-term girlfriend."

"Any enemies that we know of?"

"Only a few thousand."

"Guv...?"

"Like I said, the man was a *screw*."

"I see where you're coming from, but in my experience convicts don't normally take their revenge on screws that've given them a rough time by killing them after they get out."

"Never use to, anyway."

"Why d'you think that's what happened here, guv?"

"Who knows?"

"If so, then the killer's gotta to be a bloody nutter."

"Unless there's more to it, which is what we've got to find out."

❄

Preston knocked off at just after midnight, and drove over to the Spearmint Rhino in Hammersmith.

The guy who worked the door said hello, asked him how business was going. "Line of work I'm in, Jim, I'm always busy," Preston replied with a smile, and headed over to the bar, where he found himself a stool to sit on. In his blue jeans, checked shirt and brown leather jacket, Preston didn't look especially like a cop—but he knew a number of people who hung out in the Spearmint, as well as in some of the pubs nearby, and they all knew what he did to earn a living.

Carole, the busty brunette who worked the bar, gave him a big smile. "Hello, Bob. The usual, is it?"

Preston nodded, and Carole poured him a large Scotch and placed it down in front of him. Feeling his dodgy knee playing up, Preston gave it a rub, then took a look around. The place was about half full, and a tall, slim, black woman was strutting her stuff to the sound of Whitney Houston's *I Wanna Dance With Somebody*. The woman moved with the sensual arrogance of a panther as she rapped herself around the pole, then she turned head over tail and her legs opened like a pair of scissors.

"Your Billy keeping well?"

Carole nodded, and came and leaned on the counter by where Preston was sitting. "He's strictly on the straight and narrow now, Bob. Being away from me'n the kids for so long, that last stretch he went in for, nearly done him in."

"Know what they say—*if you can't do the time don't commit the crime*."

"Yeah, well exac'ly. That's what it comes down to in the end, Bob. He's gone all political lately, though, my Billy has ... become obsessed with these bankers and the huge bonuses they get. Seems to reckon they're the ones should all be banged up in prison. Rob a few grand, he says, and they put you away for ten years, rob ten million, and they pat you on the back and offer you share options'n a nice golden handshake."

Preston nibbled at his Scotch. "Billy always did take an interest in banks, I seem to recall."

Carole went off to serve another customer, then she noticed that Preston's glass was empty and came back to pour him a refill. When he went to pay her, she waved his money away. "This one's on the house, Bob."

The black girl finished dancing and the next girl came on. The girl couldn't have been more than twenty-four, and she danced like her body was doing all this stuff, but her mind was elsewhere. Like she was just doing it for the money and wishing she could do something better. Preston could understand that. Some of these girls danced like they loved all the attention they got. Preston reckoned girls who were like that must be lacking something. This girl seemed different, though.

Not so full of herself. She danced her way through a couple of numbers then went backstage.

She reappeared, minutes later, wearing a blue dress that stopped an inch or so short of the knee, and came and stood at the bar just along from Preston. Guys were leering at her and making comments, but she acted like she didn't notice.

She turned and looked at Preston and he smiled. She smiled back.

Preston kept looking at her, and she took a few steps closer to him. Then she put her hand on the vacant stool next to him and said, "This taken?"

"No, why don't you join me?"

"Okay, since you put it like that." The girl parked herself on the stool.

"Hi, I'm Bob."

She smiled again and showed Preston a nice set of teeth. "Hi, Bob. I'm Sally."

"Get you a drink?"

"Thanks."

Preston gestured to Carole behind the bar, and Sally told her she'd have a vodka and orange, then she turned back to Preston. Her skin was pale and smooth, and she had nice brown eyes. Not only that, but Preston liked her manner. He sensed that she might be somebody he could talk to. Preston hadn't talked with a woman in a quite a while. Not *really* talked.

"I've seen you in here before, Bob."

"I come in from time to time."

"You married?"

He shook his head. "Divorced."

"Oh, I'm sorry to hear that."

"What? You mean you'd prefer me if I were married?"

She laughed. "No ... I meant I was sorry that you'd ... well, you know what I meant."

"Sure, I was just kidding. You've got nice eyes when you smile, Sally."

"Thanks."

"Expect all the guys tell you that, right?"

"No, they don't as a matter of fact."

"I'm sure you're just being modest."

"No, really. I mean, they pay me compliments ... only it isn't usually my *eyes* that they tell me look nice."

"Well, don't misunderstand me, I mean the rest of you is just fine, too. It's just that I happened to notice your eyes first."

"You're a pretty funny guy, Bob, you know that?"

Neither of them said anything for a moment or two, then Sally asked Preston what he did for a living and he told her.

"Must be really exciting."

"Most people run a mile when they find out what I do."

"Not me. I really admire policemen. I mean, where'd the rest of us be without you guys, right?"

"In an even bigger mess than we are right now, if you ask me."

"Exactly what I think."

Preston chewed on his Scotch, enjoyed the little nip it gave him. "You enjoy dancing here, Sally?"

She shrugged. "There's things I'd sooner be doing with my life."

Preston had thought as much. He'd read it in her body language, and he appreciated her honesty. "Like what?"

"Dunno really. I guess that's the problem. D' you like your work, Bob?"

Preston nodded. "It feels *real* to me somehow, I guess that's the thing, know what I mean?"

"Yeah, I think I do."

Preston realized that he was having a good time here. But a little voice somewhere in the back of his head told him this girl was much too young for him.

"Like another drink, Sally?"

She glanced at her wristwatch. "It's almost closing time here. Why don't we go somewhere else?"

"Sure, where did you have in mind?"

"Which would you prefer, Bob—your place or mine?"

Preston smiled, trying not to look surprised. "It's your call."

"Where do you live?"

"Little place on Westbourne Park Road."

"Your place, then. It's closer."

Then when Preston told her his Ford Escort was parked just round the corner, Sally said he'd better call for a taxi because he was way over the limit.

Preston had never been one to allow minor details of that sort to prevent him from driving home in the past, but he figured he'd better play along to avoid giving Sally a bad impression. So they took a cab, and when they got to his flat, he cracked a couple of beers and drank them sitting on the bed watching *Irma La Douce* on DVD.

The film was an old favourite of Preston's, and he roared with laughter, the way he always did, when they got to the scene where Jack Lemmon's nice-guy character fights with the pimp. The pimp was big and mean, but Jack Lemmon's nice guy ended up knocking him out, more by luck than anything else.

Stuff like that could only ever happen in the movies.

CHAPTER 19

The following morning, Preston woke up to find that Sally was already lying there awake, and he made love to her. The sex was pretty good, but not great. They were both a little nervous and clumsy with each other, as was only to be expected seeing as it was their first time together.

Afterwards they went to the café on the corner of the street. Preston had the waiter bring them coffee and croissants, and he kept looking at Sally all the while and thinking how gorgeous she was. She was much too young for him, of course, but if that was true, then why did he feel so *good* when he was with her?

Sally ran a hand through her long blonde hair and eyed him over the rim of her cup. "You're a nice guy, Bob."

"Try telling my ex-wife that. She could probably write a book on why I'm *not* nice."

"You give her any reason to make her feel that way?"

"Thousands, if you listen to her."

"I was asking *you*."

Preston shrugged. "I'm a copper."

"So?"

"Isn't that enough?"

"I already told you that I respect policemen for what they do."

"You're in the minority."

"So it was the job that ruined your marriage, you're saying?"

"Certainly didn't help any."

"I thought that was just a cliché."

"Huh?"

"That you see in films and books, I mean. You know, about cops not being able to combine the job with a happy home life."

"Sadly, it's all too true in most cases."

"So not everything that you see on the big silver screen is bullshit after all, then?"

"No, just most of it."

Sally chewed on her croissant. "You're different from most of the guys I get to meet."

"How come?"

"Most guys just wanna get into my pants."

"That figures."

"Meaning what?"

"You're a sexy-looking girl, Sally. The way you strut your stuff at the Spearmint, it's hardly surprising, is it?"

"But I get the feeling you're not like that." She sipped her coffee. "If I had to sum it up, I'd say it was intimacy that you're looking for."

To change the subject away from himself, Preston said, "One thing I've always wanted to ask, is what you girls think about when you're pole dancing."

"Ask the girls'n they'll all tell you there's only one thing we think about when we're on that pole, and that's making damn sure we don't fall off the fucking thing."

❄

Preston dropped Sally off at her flat in Tulse Hill before he drove over to Wandsworth prison, where he spoke to some of the colleagues and superiors of Dave Turner, the screw who had been murdered.

He didn't discover much that was new about the man, but he did learn a few other things. Like the fact that one Ricky Red—or Richard Redmond, to use the man's proper name—had recently escaped from the prison.

Not only that, but the girl who used to go in to give Ricky English lessons had slipped off the radar, too. So the feeling was that she must have helped him escape.

Preston reckoned Dave Turned probably played a part in it as well.

He drove back to the station, where he got a finger-printing expert on the phone and asked him to check if any of the prints found at the crime scene matched those of a guy by the name of Richard Redmond—or Ricky Red as he was known in the criminal underworld.

"Are this guy's prints on record?" the man on the other end of the line asked.

"You bet they are. He just escaped from Wandsworth."

❅

The fingerprint expert called back early in the afternoon to say they had found a couple of latents that matched those of Ricky Red.

"Nice one." Preston hung up and punched the air.

DS Johnson came in and asked what all the excitement was about, and Preston told him.

"Now all we've got to do is find this Ricky Red character, then, guv. Any ideas where he might be?"

"Well I do know that he's from Stepney Green."

"Wouldn't have gone back there, though, would he?"

"Won't know unless we go and look, will we?"

DCI Preston and DS Johnson paid a call on Jack Greening, a snitch who lived in a council flat in a block in Stepney Green, in the heart of London's East End.

Preston knocked on the door. Greening opened it and peered out at him. The snitch was a skinny man with nervous eyes and nicotine-stained teeth. "Hello, Bob. What do you want?"

Preston brushed past him into the small hallway without waiting to be invited in, and went on through to the living room, with Johnson following close behind. The room was small and cluttered with cheap furniture, and a dank and musty smell hung in the air.

"Wish you wouldn't call round on me like this," Jack Greening said. "Neighbours might start gettin' suspicious."

"Who's gonna know we're cops? Anyone asks, just tell 'em we're mates of yours, Jack."

"Your friend in the pinstripes here's far too smart to be any mate a mine."

Preston flashed Johnson a grin. "You heard that, Detective Sergeant. Jack here says you're too well dressed."

The snitch said, "What do you want, anyway?"

"Information on a man by the name of Richard Redmond, otherwise known as Ricky Red."

"Recently escaped from Wandsworth, so I hear."

"That's the man."

"How much is it worth?"

"Depends on the quality of the stuff you give us." Preston winnowed out three ten-pound notes from his wallet, and the snitch put out his hand. "Huh-huh. First you talk and then we'll see."

"Ricky Red robbed a bank with two other guys a few years back."

"What two other guys?"

"Bloke they call The Dog was one of 'em. Donald Chapman's his real name."

"And the other man?"

"Joey B."

"As in Belagio?"

"That's the geezer."

"Sounds as though you know him, guv," DS Johnson cut in.

"I've come across him." Preston gave his tash a thoughtful little tweak. "What else?"

"Got away with about three million, I think it was, only all three of 'em got caught and went down. Then Joey B did a deal and got out early . . . snitched on his two associates to get his sentence reduced, the way I heard it."

"What else?"

"Ain't given me any money yet."

"You haven't given me much to earn any yet, either."

"What I've just told you's gotta be worth somethin'."

"Don't get greedy on me, Jack. I could've found out what you've just given me from anybody at the bar down the local boozer. Now what else have you got?"

"The Dog's recently got out a the kennel as well."

"You mean he did a deal, or did he escape?"

"Escaped ... way I heard it, Ricky Red and The Dog was both gettin' worried Joey B might start spendin' all the money they got from the bank job."

"But wouldn't Joey B've been forced to tell where the money was stashed in return for getting an early release?" Preston wondered aloud.

"Ain't what I heard, but I should of thought you'd be in a position to know more about that, Bob." Greening looked at the banknotes in Preston's hand.

"Don't stop, Jack," Preston said. "What you were saying was just starting to get interesting."

"All three of 'em are hard men. Violent, you know? Ricky's married to Gloria who works behind the bar at the Green Dragon, over on Mile End Road. Belagio's wife picked up with another geezer soon as he got banged up. She's the girl was in the news ... got shot while she was dancin' onstage at the Revuebar, strip joint in Soho."

"Know who shot her and why?"

The snitch shook his head. "Ain't heard nothin' 'bout that. No one seems to know nothin'."

"Any ideas where Ricky Red or the canine fellow're likely to be hiding out?"

"None at all."

Preston made to leave.

"What about my money, Inspector?"

Preston gave the snitch one of the ten-pound notes he was holding, and pocketed the other two.

"I gave you some good info there, Bob. Gotta be worth more'n a measly tenner."

"It was fairly useful, Jack, I suppose, but it wasn't *that* good."

"Oh, and there's one more thing I heard ... The Dog's sister Mona's a dyke and her girlfriend's married to the MP, John Harris. Mona also likes to go to the Revuebar from time to time, and she's friendly with Belagio's misses, the girl that got shot."

Preston made a mental note of what the snitch had told him. Then he gave the man another tenner. "Not sure that you really earned it, Jack, but I'm feeling generous."

❋

Next Preston and Johnson called round to the council flat, nearby in Bethnal Green, where Ricky Red's mother lived.

Once Preston had introduced himself, Mrs. Redmond, a gray-haired woman in a shapeless dress, told him to go and get fucked. Then she tried to slam the door in his face, but Preston was too quick for her.

"May as well invite us in, Mrs. Redmond. Otherwise we'll only go and get a warrant."

"Ought to be ashamed a yourselves, comin' and harassin' an innocent woman my age."

"Isn't you that we're interested in, Mrs. Redmond, but your Ricky."

"My Ricky's always been a good boy."

"Are you going to let us in or have you got something to hide?"

"What do you want?"

"Only a quick word, coupla questions, and we'll be out of your hair."

"Oh all right, then." The woman opened the door and stood aside, and Preston and Johnson entered the flat.

"I won't offer you tea or coffee."

"Very kind of you," Preston said.

"Don't mention it. Now perhaps you wouldn't mind stoppin' wasting my time and tellin' me what it is you want."

"Ricky's escaped."

"Has he now. Well, all the best of luck to him's what I say."

"You wouldn't've seen or heard from him?"

"No I haven't, but if I had, then you can rest assured you'd be the last people I'd tell."

"Sensible thing would be for Ricky to give himself up."

"Says who?"

"Be better for him in the long run, Mrs. Redmond," Johnson said. "That way he might not end up having to serve all of his sentence, whereas if he stays on the run he'll have to do the full ten years, maybe more."

"Yeah, well you're gonna have to catch 'im first, aren't you?"

Preston gestured to Johnson and they made for the door.

❄

Preston felt his stomach make with a few bars of Charlie Mingus' version of *Moanin'*, so he drove down to Mile End Road and sent Johnson out for a couple of kebabs, and they ate them in the car.

"What I call good healthy nosh, guv, I must say."

"Do I detect a note of irony in your tone, Detective Sergeant?"

"Just think of all the *calories* in one of these things, though."

"Since when have you been a picky eater, Dave?"

"It's Sarah, guv. She's been teaching me all about the importance of having a healthy diet."

"Has she now."

"You are what you eat, Sarah says."

"Careful you don't wake up one morning to find you've turned into a Caesar salad."

"Apparently kebabs are one of the fattiest things going."

"Way with everything that I like, though, Dave."

"Sarah's got me eating lots of salads and vegetables at home."

"Like eating that stuff, do you?"

"Not really, to be honest."

Marriage for you, Preston thought.

After they'd finished their kebabs, Preston drove over to the Green Dragon, and he and Johnson went inside and installed themselves on stools at the bar. The pub was a magnet for criminals and spivs, and Preston recognized a few faces.

He caught the barmaid's attention and said, "Two pints of Pride, love."

She nodded and set about pouring the drinks.

"You wouldn't be Gloria by any chance?" Preston asked her, when she placed the beers on the bar.

"I might be ... who's asking?" She was a middle-aged peroxide blonde with silicone-enhanced boobs, a figure that was going south and a face that was held together by make-up.

Preston told her his name, flashed his ID.

"What do you want?"

"Rumour has it that you're Ricky Red's missis."

"What if I was?"

"*Was* or *are*?"

"What's it to you?"

"You do know that he's escaped, I take it?"

"I heard a rumour."

"So he must've come and seen you, I presume?"

"No, he hasn't as a matter of fact."

"Bit off, isn't it?"

"What...?"

"Him neglecting to come and see you like that?"

"Probably thought it'd be the first place you people would look."

Preston took a swig of his pint. "Sure he isn't playing you false, Gloria?"

"Ricky wouldn't do that to me."

"Not what I heard."

"Maybe you need to get your ears checked, then."

"Nothing wrong with my hearing, Gloria."

She looked at him like she was wondering whether to take him seriously or not.

"What I heard is that Ricky's shacked up with the girl who used to give him English lessons while he was in the nick."

"Who was it told you that?"

"It's what you might call common knowledge in certain circles down Wandsworth way. The girl's slipped right off the radar ever since the day Ricky escaped."

"Maybe she's off sick."

"Already checked. Turns out she didn't call in, and her flatmates haven't seen any sign of her."

"You're full of shit."

"Ask around if you don't believe me."

"I don't need to. I know I can trust my Ricky."

Preston shrugged, then he got off his stool and made for the door, and DS Johnson hurried after him.

"Oy," Gloria called after them, "you ain't paid."

Preston and Johnson went out without looking back.

It was raining heavily now, and the two men rushed round the corner to where Preston had parked and climbed into the car.

"Practically saw her claws come out when you told her about the girl that helped Ricky escape, guv."

"Think I touched a nerve there all right, Dave."

Preston turned the key in the ignition and set off along Mile End Road.

"How's your love life lately, guv?"

"Pretty interesting, as a matter of fact."

"What? Got a new girlfriend, have you?"

"Think so."

"What do you mean you *think* so?"

"I've only just met her."

They were driving through the financial district now, past tall, nondescript office blocks. Buildings that seemed to have no soul.

"But you're dating her, are you?"

"I think I could be."

"You mean you're going to ask her out and you reckon she likes you, is that it?"

"We've slept together."

"You're a fast worker, I can see that, guv. What does she do for a living—not a copper, is she?"

"Working as a pole dancer at the moment, but I don't think she has any plans to make a lifelong career of it."

"I see. So you're shagging a pole dancer, then, guv. Good for you."

"It's not like that."

"Not like *what*?"

"It's not just about sex."

"So what do you do with her when you take her back to yours, then—play Scrabble?"

"Mind your own business, Dave."

"Just curious, guv." Johnson looked like he was trying to prevent himself from laughing.

"Don't recall asking you what you get up to with your missis when you have a quiet night in, Dave."

"Feel free to go ahead and ask if you like, guv."

"Okay, so what do you get up to, then?"

"Since you ask, we play Scrabble."

"Do you really?"

"Certainly do, guv. And when we've finished, we get down to some pretty serious shagging."

CHAPTER 20

Preston drove back to the station, entered his office, and called up a Detective Chief Inspector Mike Newton. He quickly introduced himself and then explained he was interested in finding out more information about three men who had pulled a bank three years ago—Joey Belagio, Ricky Red and a guy everyone called The Dog.

"Yeah, I remember the case," Mike Newton said. "I was head of the team that caught those guys. But what's your interest?"

"Ricky Red has recently escaped from Wandsworth, and one of the screws at the prison's been found murdered."

"And you think it might be Ricky Red that killed him?"

"Screw was murdered in his flat with a shot to the heart, and Ricky Red's prints were all over the crime scene." Preston said. "Rumour is Joey Belagio did a deal to get his sentence reduced. Any truth in it?"

"Yes, that's correct."

"And what about the money from the bank job?"

"Belagio insisted that Ricky Red had hidden it somewhere."

"And what did Ricky Red have to say about that?"

"Refused to talk to us."

"So you reduced Belagio's sentence down to three years, even though he didn't lead you to the money?"

"We only had enough to convict Belagio at first. So we told him we'd reduce his sentence if he could give us sufficient incriminating evidence to enable us to convict the other two men, and he did just that."

"And what happened to the money?"

"We still don't know."

"Sounds to me like Belagio did pretty well out of the deal."

"It was a pretty good deal for both sides, to be honest, and Belagio did still have to serve three years of his sentence, remember. Okay, it's not as long as it should've been, but it's better than nothing. As for Ricky Red and The Dog, they were looking at getting off scot-free, but instead they were both banged up for ten years."

"And now they're all out, so Belagio's going to have to be watching over his shoulder for the rest of his life."

"That's his affair. You know what they say about living by the sword."

❄

Preston had arranged to take his son, Callum, to see Fulham play Arsenal at Craven Cottage that evening, and he pulled up just after six outside the council house in East Putney that he used to call home. His ex-wife, Anne, gave him a cold *fuck-you* kind of leer when she came to the door, then made him wait out on the doorstep while she got Callum ready.

Preston soon felt the rain beginning to soak into his clothes, so he went and sat in his car. He had to wait just over eleven minutes before Callum came to the door. Preston knew because he counted the time on his wristwatch. He felt sure that Anne was only doing this to assert her power over him. It was as if she was saying, "Tough luck, Callum's living with me and you only get to see him when *I* say so. If I want to keep you waiting out in the rain, I can."

Preston had been feeling relatively well-disposed towards his ex-wife on the way over here. Just because they'd stopped loving each other, he'd been thinking, there was no reason why they shouldn't still be able to work together as parents. He'd been in a mood to try and see if they couldn't put the past behind them. But now, with this latest trick that Anne had pulled, Preston's feelings of tolerance and respect were all flushed out of him by a flood of bile.

It wouldn't do to let his son see the way he was feeling, though. So Preston tried to control his bitter mood, when Callum, a skinny lad with short blond hair, came and hopped into the passenger seat.

"Hi, Dad."

"Hello, soldier."

They kissed each other on the cheek, and then Callum told Preston that his mother wanted him to be home before ten o'clock.

Preston started the car up and drove over to McDonald's, on Putney High Street. The place was full of other fans that had stopped off to eat before going to the game. Preston bought a couple of Happy Meals, and Callum told him little stories about what he'd been getting up to with his friends as they ate.

When they'd finished eating, they went to see the game. Fulham played pretty well in the first half, and they took the lead just before halftime. But then Arsenal came back strongly in the second half, and they scored twice in the last twenty minutes to secure all three points.

On the way home, Callum seemed really upset that Fulham had lost, and Preston tried to make light of it and cheer him up.

Callum looked at his wristwatch. "It's nearly five minutes to ten, Dad."

"So?"

"Mummy said I've got to be back by ten."

"Oh yes, so she did. *Shit!*"

"And Mummy says you shouldn't swear, Dad."

"Sorry, Callum."

"That's okay."

"You won't tell her, will you?"

"No, of course not."

"That's a good lad."

"But Mummy says you aren't to ask me to keep secrets from her, Dad."

"Well just a few little ones will be okay, won't they?"

"Yes, I suppose so."

Preston put his foot down and raced through the backstreets.

"Dad, aren't you driving too fast?"

"Probably, but let's keep it between us, shall we?"

"What?"

"I mean don't tell Mummy, okay?"

"Okay."

They pulled up outside the house in Putney at eight minutes past the hour. Preston had done his best to get the lad back in good time. If Anne wanted to make a big deal of it then let her.

He held Callum's hand as they stood on the doorstep, waiting for Anne to open up.

When she did, she looked furious.

A feeling of tenderness welled up in Preston's heart as he kissed his son goodbye.

Anne stood aside to let Callum go in. Then she looked at her watch. "You're late," she said, and slammed the door in Preston's face before he even had a chance to explain or apologize.

"It's only eight fucking minutes," he grumbled to himself, as he went back to his car.

❄

After that, Preston was in a highly emotional state, and he felt like he needed company and a drink. So he drove over to the Spearmint, got himself a large Scotch and drank half of it sitting on a stool at the bar.

The Scotch went a little way towards calming him down, and he'd just got himself a second one when he turned and saw that Sally was onstage. He'd been so taken up with his own thoughts that he hadn't noticed her come on.

Right at that moment, she was busy thrusting her headlights in the face of some guy in the front row.

Preston's heart sank, and he told himself that he should have known better than even to think about taking someone like her seriously. What else could he expect from a girl who took her clothes off for a living, after all?

He knocked back the rest of his drink and went out.

❄

Ricky Red was in bed with Janine hours later, when he thought he heard a noise. So he took his .38 out from under the pillow and went to investigate.

Someone was in the house. Ricky could sense it.

He crept out of the bedroom and thought he saw a shape move out in the kitchen, so he crept over behind the kitchen door and waited. Then when whoever it was came into the room, Ricky whacked him hard on the back of the head and the guy went down.

Ricky flicked the light switch and pointed his gun at the intruder, who was dressed all in black.

"The fuck are you, Will fuckin' Smith or someone?"

"Very funny."

"Ain't gonna be laughin' by the time I've finished with you."

"Go fuck yourself."

Just then, Janine entered the room dressed in a bathrobe. Ricky looked at her and said, "Recognize this cunt from anywhere, Jan?"

She came over and took a closer look at the guy's mug. "Nope."

"You sure?"

"Positive."

Ricky had the man kneel on the floor and put his hands behind his head. Then he held the barrel of his .38 against the back of the man's neck. "Now I'm gonna give you once last chance to tell me who sent you. Otherwise I'm gonna pull the trigger and blow your fuckin' head off, do you understand?"

"It was Gloria."

"Don't fuck with me."

"I'm not. She just wanted me to kill the girl, not you, Rick."

"Why'd she want you to do that?"

"Fuck do I know?" the man sobbed. "I ain't paid to know stuff like that. Maybe the bitch is jealous."

"How d'you know where to find me?"

"Gloria told me you'd be here."

"Let me tell you somethin'," Rick said. "I don't allow anyone to call my Gloria a bitch."

Then he pulled the trigger and blew the back of the man's head off.

CHAPTER 21

The plastic cup was burning Preston's fingers as he carried it into his office, and he quickly put it down on his desk.

Detective Sergeant Johnson looked up from the report he was in the middle of writing. "Morning, guv."

"What's new, Dave?"

"Body's turned up in some bushes just this side of Brighton, guv ... so badly burnt his own mother wouldn't have recognized him. Fortunately, though, pathologists were able to match the vic's teeth to existing dental records belonging to one Vinnie "The Hit" Morrison."

"Name rings a bell."

"Thought to have been living in Hove, and was known to be a hired killer, hence the nickname."

Preston nodded. "I wonder if this Vinnie Morrison's death might not have something to do with Ricky Red and his two friends, Dave?"

"Just what I've been asking myself."

❋

Martin left Suzanne's place and was walking to his car, when someone prodded him in the back.

"Feel that? It's a gun. Piss me off'n I'll blow a hole in you big as a football. You understand...?"

Martin recognized Joey B's voice.

"Was it you that shot Bella?"

"Now why would I do that?"

"I dunno... jealousy maybe."

"Just open the car'n get in behind the wheel."

Martin did as he was told, and Joey B climbed into the passenger seat.

"Now what?" Martin asked him.

"You're gonna drive me to the farmhouse."

"Why?"

"Don't ask questions, just drive ... unless you wanna die right here."

"We've done all this before, Joey. I refused to drive to the farmhouse the last time, and I'm not doing it now. You're not gonna shoot me in the middle of a street in Fulham like this, are you? Come on, you're not *that* crazy."

"Maybe he ain't, but I sure as fuck am," piped up a voice from behind them.

Joey turned round, and there was Ricky Red. He was holding a gun and had it pointed at Joey.

"Rick ... the fuck're you doin' here?"

"Thought I'd pay you a visit, Joey. Ain't you pleased to see me?"

"Sure, but how come you was lyin' in the back of this guy's car?"

"Your car, ain't it?"

"No, whatever gave you that idea?"

"I traced it to your missis."

"I bought it for her, Rick, back before I went inside, but she lets this piece a shit drive it." Joey forced a cobra grin. "Nice to see you, Rick, anyway. How you doin'?"

"Not so bad, Joey ... been worse, you know."

"Yeah, well, you're out at least, I see."

"That I am."

"Gotta be good news."

"Some people might not agree, Joey."

"Nice weapon you got there, Rick."

"Yours looks pretty tasty, too. A Glock, is it?"

"Yeah."

"Drop it in me hand a mo'n let us have a feel."

Realizing that he had no alternative, Joey dropped the gun into Ricky's spare hand. Ricky gripped it and pointed it at the back of Martin's head. "Hefts well," he said.

"Do, don't it, Rick. What's yours, a Beretta, ain't it?"

"Tha's right."

"Thought it was. Same gun as the Twins always used to carry, i'n' it. Rather you didn't point it my way, though, Rick."

"I can see why you might feel that way, but it's just that I've got a little bone to pick with you."

"Bone might that be, Rick?" Joey looked confused.

"Rumour goin' round that you snitched on me an' The Dog. Even the bloke they got writin' in the Evenin' fuckin' Standard's sayin' as much in print for everyone to read."

"You don't wanna believe what you read."

"I'll make my own mind up about what I believe."

"What d'you want from me, Rick?"

"Just to talk, Joey, tha's all."

"Talkin's fine. I can do talkin'. What you want a talk about?"

"Just the little matter a the money from the bank job ... remember it, do ya?"

"Yeah, I remember it."

"Good, 'cause the way you been behavin' lately I was startin' to wonder if Uncle Alzheimer'd paid you an early visit."

"Nothin' wrong with me that way."

"Glad to hear it 'cause I want my money, and I want it now."

"I ain't got it, Rick."

"I don't like that answer you're givin' me, Joey."

"Sorry, but there ain't much I can do about it."

"I'll tell you what I'm gonna do. I'm gonna start countin' and if I ain't got an answer that I wanna hear by the time I get to three then I'm gonna shoot you in the head. You understand me?"

"Yeah, I understand you, Rick."

"*Two*."

"It's in Geneva."

"Whereabouts?"

"Bank of Malta. If you don't believe me, I can take you back to my place'n show you the documentation to prove it."

"Okay, we can go there in a bit. Just tell me the account number first."

"Dunno the fuckin' account number off the top of me head, do I, Rick. Come on, man, play fair. Ain't easy to remember that many numbers, is it? The fuck d'you think I am, Alvin fuckin' Einstein'r somebody? I mean, fuck me, Rick, there's no need to come on like Ray fuckin' Winstone, is there?"

"Ray fuckin' *who* did you say...?"

"Winstone, Ray fuckin' Winstone, Rick."

"What... the actor, y'mean?"

"Yeah."

"Who sez I'm comin' on like Ray fuckin' Winstone?"

"Well you are, Rick, ain'tcha?"

"What's wrong with Ray fuckin' Winstone, anyway?"

"Ain't nothin' wrong with the man, Rick."

"He was in that film where they're all over sittin' round the pool in Spain, i'n' it... end up buryin' that Mahatma fuckin' Ghandi character. Ben what's his fuckin' face ... Kingsley, that's it. Ben Kingsley buried him underneath the fuckin' swimmin' pool."

"Yeah, good film that, Rick."

"It was, but what we fuckin' doin', sittin' 'ere talkin' like a pair of fuckin' film buffs? Your mate gonna start the fuckin' engine up, or what?"

"Yeah, but where we goin'?"

"You know the answer to that, Joey."

"Do I, Rick?"

"Course you fuckin' well do. I want my *money*. Many times do I 'ave to tell you?"

❅

When they pulled up outside of the farmhouse, Ricky took the car keys and pocketed them. Then he had Joey and Martin stand in front of him in a line, before he marched them inside like an evil shepherd with a terrified flock of two.

There was a musty smell in the place and it was dark, so Ricky told Joey to make with some lights and he'd better not try anything clever while he was about it.

Joey pushed a couple of switches, as they passed through the parquet hallway, and on through to the living room at the back of the house. Joey headed straight for the mahogany drinks cabinet, saying, "JD all right?"

Ricky said, "Sure." Then he told Martin to sit on the sofa, before he went and sat in the leather chair to the side of the fireplace.

He kept his gun pointed at Joey all the time, watched him pour the drinks to make certain they both came from the same bottle. "Put mine down on the end table 'ere."

Joey did as he was told.

"Take a load off, old son." Ricky pointed with his gun to the chair the other side of the open fireplace.

Joey sat down, and Ricky watched him sip his drink before he tasted his own.

"Good stuff this."

"Yeah." Ricky raised his glass. "Your 'elf."

"'Elf, Rick."

"Sinatra's drink, weren't it."

"Was it?"

Ricky nodded. "Always used to drink JD, 'e did."

"Never knew that."

"Had connections, too, Rick, what I heard."

"Went ape with that geezer what wrote *The Godfather*, di'n't 'e?"

"Did he, Rick?"

"Saw the geezer in some posh restaurant'n gave him a right fuckin' dressin' down in front of everyone."

"How was that, then, Rick?"

"After the guy wrote about him in 'is fuckin' book, weren't it. Don't you remember the singer in *The Godfather* who couldn't get the part he wanted in some film. Then the director, or the fuckin' producer or whoever the fuck 'e is, wakes up in bed with this fuckin 'orse's head lyin' next to 'im, don't 'e... fuckin' blood everywhere."

"So Sinatra gets the part..."

"You're too right he fuckin' does."

"But hang on a mo, Rick, I don't remember Frank Sinatra bein' in *The Godfather*."

"No, that was *From Here to Eternity*, you plonker."

"*From Here to Eternity*, yeah, I know it. That's the one, Sinatra takes a real beatin' from the screw in the lockup, i'n' it. Right ugly fuckin' bastard."

'Ernest fuckin' Borgnine, yeah..."

"Shame about it was in black and fuckin' white, though."

Ricky shrugged, put his drink down. "Can't have it all, Joey, can you? That would be *greedy*." He gave Joey a certain look. "Speakin' of which, you was gonna tell me where you got the money."

"Yeah, well I already told you that, Rick."

"But like the account number and you was gonna show me the documentation and everyfin', right?"

"Oh yeah, course, Rick, course." Joey went to get up.

"No rush, Joey. Stay and finish your drink first."

"Sure."

Joey sat back down.

Ricky took his tumbler from the end table, lifted it to his lips, and downed the contents in a single gulp. Joey followed suit.

"Now, about that little business matter we need to get sorted."

"I got the paperwork in the safe, Rick. You know, with the account number'n all that written down."

"That's good. So there ain't no problem, then?"

"No, none at all."

"So where's the bank exac'ly?"

"Geneva, Rick, like I told you."

"And my money's all over there, waitin' for me in this account in Geneva you're sayin' about, is it?"

"'Course it is, Rick. That's what I been tryin' to say to you. Everythin's *cool*."

"Hearin' you say that is most reassurin', Joey."

"Oughtta know'd better than to doubt me."

"Never said I doubted you. What on earth ever give you that idea?"

"Way you was talkin'."

"Fuck you on about?"

"You know, the way you was givin' it the Ray fuckin' Winstone and all that, like I was sayin' to ya."

"Just my style, i'n' it."

"Glad to hear it, Rick. So I'll just go'n open the safe up, then."

"Yeah. Before you do, though, I was wonderin'... ain't seen The Dog about lately, 'ave you?"

"No. Why, *should* I have, Rick?"

"He's out. You do know that?"

"Heard a rumour."

"More than a fuckin' rumour, Joey, it's a impirical fuckin' fact. Our canine friend's bolted from the kennel."

"'bout time, too, I'd say. Good on 'im."

"So he ain't come sniffin' round your neck of the woods, then?"

"No, I sure ain't seen 'im."

"Oh, well that's a little funny, I must say."

"How d'you mean, *funny?*"

"Well, not funny ha-fuckin'-ha funny ... more like peculiar fuckin' funny, you know."

"What's fuckin' peculiar about it, Rick?"

"Comin' 'ere to this place of yours, Joey, I felt like I could almost *smell* The Dog's presence, if you know what I mean."

"Well I ain't seen 'im, Rick, I just told you."

Ricky looked Joey in the eye, and Joey knew how important it was not to look away or appear nervous.

They stayed like that for what seemed like an eternity, then Ricky grinned and hiked his shoulders. "Oh well, The Dog'll come sniffin' around sometime, I'm sure."

"Be good to see the man."

"Sure would. Only goes without sayin', don't it? After all, we always been mates, the three of us, well as partners, right? And where I come from, that *means* summin'."

"Means summin' where I come from, too, Rick."

"I should fuckin' well hope it did and all, Joey, seein' as we both come from the same fuckin' place."

"Exac'ly."

Ricky got up out of his chair. "Right, so where's the fuckin' safe?"

"Next room."

"After you, then."

Ricky marched Joey and Martin into the bedroom. Then Joey pulled the picture of the lion away from the wall and opened the safe.

He whirled around with a gun in his hand, but Ricky was ready for him. He shot Joey right between the eyes before he could pull the trigger.

Joey fell down onto the bed face first. Then Ricky went over to look in the safe. As he reached inside, Martin crept up behind him and brought the heavy glass ashtray he was carrying down as hard as he could on the back of his head.

Ricky went down.

He didn't look like he was about to get up for a while.

Martin took the documents that were in the safe and pegged it.

CHAPTER 22

Preston's mobile began to make with a jazz riff.

"Hello."

"Hi, Bob, it's me. I'm at the Spearmint ... don't suppose you'd fancy coming over and getting me?"

Preston didn't even stop to think. "Sure, I'm on my way."

When he picked her up, Sally said she was hungry. Preston felt as though he could eat, too, so he stopped off on the way back and bought a couple of Indian takeaway meals. They ate them at the small deal table in his room.

"How was your day, Sal?"

"Same old routine."

Looking at Sally now, Preston realized once again how young and fresh and attractive she was. She was intelligent, too, and nice, and she seemed to care about him. So where was the problem?

Okay, they might be an unlikely-looking couple, but that didn't necessarily mean the relationship couldn't work.

"Jeez, this curry is hot." Preston got up. "I'm gonna have a beer. You like one?"

Sally nodded, and Preston fetched a couple of cans of Stella from the fridge.

"I've been meaning to ask you, Bob. What was it that made you want to be a cop?"

"What is this, talk-to-the-psychiatrist time?"

"No, I just thought it would be good if we could talk more—about ourselves, I mean, and get to know each other better."

"You want to know about my past?"

"Sure."

Preston cracked open his can. "Well, I was brought up in Fulham, and had what you might call an unusual upbringing in many ways."

"You've got some foreign blood in you, right?"

"Mum was Spanish."

Sally swigged her beer. "First time I saw you I thought you were a little like that actor in *Goodfellas* ..."

"What ... not Joey Pesci?"

"No, *stupid*. He's about a yard too short and doesn't look anything like you *at all*. No, the tall one."

Preston laughed. "One that gets chased by the helicopter at the end?"

"That's the guy."

"Ray Liotta. Yeah, other people 've said that. I suppose it's a compliment. Only seeing that he was one of the gangsters in *Goodfellas*, I've never quite known how to take it."

"Ray Liotta himself isn't a gangster, though. He's a talented actor."

"Yeah, maybe that's the way I should look at it."

"So tell me some more about this unusual upbringing of yours."

"Well, I was an only child and my father was a successful lawyer in the City. He had kinda left-wing views, despite the fact that he was an ex-Harrow boy himself, so he sent me to Holland Park."

"That's a comp, right?"

"Yeah, but there was a real social mix." Preston paused to swig his beer. "You had the sons and daughters of well-off left-wingers, and others were from more ordinary backgrounds. Then there were some kids who came from outright rough families."

"You get bullied?"

"No more than the average kid. I was beaten up a few times by older boys in my first couple of years, but then I got bigger and soon learned how to take care of myself."

"Doesn't sound all that unusual, Bob."

"No, well, my father was gay."

"*Was?*"

"He's dead."

"Oh, I'm sorry. Don't let's talk about it, if you don't want."

"No, it's okay."

"You mean he was bisexual, right?"

"Way mother tells it, he was gay, period."

"But if he was your *father?*"

"You mean he must've done it with my mum, so how could he be gay, is that it?"

Sally shrugged and swigged her beer to put out the fire that had started to rage in her mouth.

"He told her that he could only manage to perform with her by trying to imagine she was a man."

"That must've made her feel real good. So I suppose she divorced him, did she?"

Preston nodded.

"But why did he marry her in the first place?"

"His father was a bigot and a homophobe, so Dad tried to repress his true feelings ... didn't manage to confront and accept himself as he truly was until he was pushing thirty, which was well after I appeared on the scene."

"What kind of relationship did you have with him?"

"Great, for as long as it lasted."

"How did he die?"

"He was murdered."

"Shit. I think I'm beginning to see what made you want to become a cop. They catch the killer?"

Preston shook his head. "Mum was so screwed up by the whole business she got addicted to cocaine and sleeping pills. Then one night she OD'd and never woke up."

"Oh Bob, I'm so sorry. When I said I wanted to hear about your past, I didn't know ..."

"It's all right."

They held hands across the table.

"And what about you?" Preston asked her.

"My dad ran off with a younger woman, left Mum to cope with me and my brother and younger sister. We lived in a council flat in Bethnal Green. I think Mum must've had it really hard."

"You turned out okay, though."

"Sometimes I wonder."

"Hey, don't put yourself down."

"Well I'm not exactly proud of what I do for a living, Bob."

"No reason you should be ashamed of it, either, is there?"

"I try not to think about it most of the time."

"So why do it, then, if you don't enjoy it?"

"It's the only thing I can do that'll earn me enough to pay the bills."

"What would you like to do, if you could do anything?"

"I'd like to have my own restaurant."

"What kinda place would it be?"

"Classy, you know, the kinda place you'd get really up market types in there ... employ a good French chef."

"And you'd run it all?"

"Yeah. I'd be there to make sure the staff are doing everything properly and to welcome the customers. Of course, I'd be responsible for all the décor and the menu and everything, too."

"You have music in there?"

"No piped music. Maybe a little jazz trio."

"Sounds good. I can't wait to go there."

Sally laughed. "It's just a fantasy of mine."

"But you can make it happen, Sal."

When they had finished eating, Sally helped Preston tidy up and then they went to bed.

Preston ran his hands over her firm breasts and down over her flat belly. Her skin was smooth as silk and he was bursting with desire for her as they kissed and caressed each other, but he had a tender feeling, too. Only it was like the feelings of tenderness and the excited feeling were all part of the same thing.

He gazed into her eyes and said, "You do realize I'm almost old enough to be your Dad."

What Sally did next made it clear to Preston that she didn't care how old he was.

And then they tore each other's clothes off.

Afterwards, Preston lay there with his head on the pillow, wondering if this was love. He turned to Sally and said, "Wow, that was really something."

"Do you love me, Bob?"

The very question Preston had just asked himself.

Was this love?

They scarcely knew each other, and yet if this wasn't love then how come he was feeling so wonderfully happy and alive?

Preston was amazed at the changes that were taking place inside him. Only an hour or so ago, he'd been wondering whether they were right for one another.

"Bob?"

"Yeah?"

"*Do* you?"

"Course I do."

"Tell me, then, Bob."

"What?"

"Tell me you love me."

"I love you," Preston said.

And the funny thing was, he reckoned he did, too.

PART III

CHAPTER 23

Bella Armando was sitting up in bed the next day, reading *Cosmopolitan*, when there was a knock at the door and Preston walked into the room. He said hello and asked Bella how she was feeling. She told him she felt fine. "Even so, the doctor's said I've got to stay here another day, just to be on the safe side," she said. "I really can't see what all the fuss is about."

"Another day in this place won't kill you." Preston pulled up a chair and sat on it. "I'm afraid I have to tell you some bad news, miss ... your husband has been killed."

"You mean Joey?"

"Joey Belagio, yes. I am correct in thinking that you were still married to him?"

Bella breathed a huge sigh of relief.

"Forgive me, but you don't appear to be all that upset by the news ..."

"I was frightened for a moment that you might've meant Martin," Bella said. "But who killed Joey? What happened?"

❄

Ricky Red called Gloria and asked her how she was keeping.

"Not so bad, Rick," she said. "How about you?"

"I'm good, Glor."

"I heard you was out, that right?"

"Yeah. How'd you find out?"

"I heard a rumour, so I called your lawyer. He me told me you'd holed up at his place."

"Hey, watch what you say on the phone, Glor, willya."

Gloria said, "Nice a you to think to come'n pay me a visit, Rick, I must say."

"Haven't been able to, Glor."

"Been tied up, have you?"

"Too many people would recognize me if I go back to the old haunts. I might be crazy but I ain't that stupid."

"Could've called, though, Rick."

"Fuck d'you think I'm doin' now, then, Glor?"

"I heard you was shacked up with some bitch that was teaching you in the nick."

"Who told you that?"

"Do me a favour, Ricky, and tell me the truth, will you?"

"I needed to use her to break out. There was no other way a doin' it, Glor."

"Ain't the way I heard it."

"What have you 'eard, then?"

"That you two was really close."

"Okay, I've fucked her a few times, if that's what you're gettin' at. So what? A man like me has his needs. But you ought to know that don't mean nothin' where you and me are concerned, Glor."

"I hear you talkin', but how can I tell whether or not I should believe you?"

"Listen, Glor, all I want is for you'n me to be able to get back together. You gotta believe that. I can hardly wait to have you in me arms again."

"And what about the teacher bitch?"

"I'll get rid of her when the time's right."

"And when will that be?"

"When I don't have no more use for 'er."

"What, you mean when you've got bored of fuckin' her?"

"No, don't be daft, Glor. I got plans."

"What kind of plans?"

"Plans for you and me."

"What's this all about, then?"

"We're going to Rio, gel."

"I can't afford to go on holiday, Ricky. I got a job a work to do."

"No, not on holiday, ya daft cow ... for *ever*, I'm talkin' about."

"You mean you want me to go and live with you in Rio?"

"Got it in one, Glor."

"On *what?*"

"I'm loaded, gel."

"That ain't what I heard."

"You heard wrong, then— only don't tell no one."

"You better not be tellin' me porkies."

"Ain't no pork in what I'm tellin' you, Glor," Ricky said. "Look, I need you to do a small favour for me."

"I wondered when you was gonna get round to that."

"It's for *us,* Glor, for the future we're gonna have together livin' in the sun."

"What have I gotta do?"

"I wanna sell a paintin' and I need you to set up a meetin' with a buyer."

"What do you need me to do it for?"

"'Cause it's too much of a risk for me to go'n meet the people I need to speak to. It's what the cops'll be expectin' me to do. Or else people might see me and start to talk."

"Why don't you just call 'em?"

"I've tried, Glor, but I can't get hold a the bloke who arranges stuff like that... must a changed his number. Ronnie Warner the guy's name is. Dunno if you've heard me talkin' 'bout 'im?"

"Name rings a bell."

"Anyway, I want you to go'n see Ronnie for me'n tell 'im I need for 'im to find a buyer for the Rothko."

"For the *what*...?"

"That's the name of the painter."

"Oh, right, I see. But ain't that takin' a bit of a risk, though, Rick?"

"How'd ya mean?"

"Well, if word gets round you got a paintin' to flog, then how d'you know it ain't gonna be a coupla plainclothes pigs that turn up on your doorstep?"

"No, Ronnie's kosher, Glor... man knows what he's doin'. Only deals with certain kindsa clients, if you take my meanin'. Anyway, he always used to hang out in the Star on Bethnal Green Road. Go in there'n ask around, Glor, see if you can get a hold of the man for me."

"Do me best for ya, Rick."

"Atta gel."

"Just so you remember you owe me one."

"Anythin' you want any time, Glor."

"Just one thing. Don't forget that the bitch goes."

"Like I said, Glor. Just as soon as I ain't got no more use for her."

"I already ran out a uses for her a long time ago."

"Sounds like you don't like the gel."

"I don't."

"Ain't even set eyes on her yet."

"Precisely. Just wait till I do."

Ricky chuckled. "I'm savin' a bullet for her, Glor, don't you worry."

"No, you don't. She's *mine*, Rick."

❄

The following afternoon a Roller pulled up outside on the shingled forecourt. The doors opened and two men got out. They were both wearing shades and sharp suits. One was tall and big about the shoulders and the other was a short, fat guy, and they looked like they were Arabs.

Ricky went out to meet the two men. "Found the place okay, I see," he said.

The fat one nodded. "Where's the Rothko?"

"Come with me."

Ricky led them into the house and through to the living room, where he had the Rothko hanging in a frame on the wall.

The little fat man inspected the painting while the bigger guy, who Ricky had figured for the muscle, stood back with his hands at his sides. The muscle looked like he was ready for trouble, if there was going to be any. Not like he was expecting it exactly, though. As for the little fat guy, he'd taken out a magnifying glass and was now using it to examine the painting.

The man spent a good ten minutes looking at the painting in this manner. Then he turned and looked at Ricky.

"It is very exciting, to come face to face with a Rothko original that everyone thinks has disappeared off the face of the planet." The man smiled, although Ricky couldn't see his eyes behind the shades he was wearing. "May I enquire as to how you came by it?"

"That's my business."

"Yes, quite." The man chuckled. "And my associate has told me that you are looking to sell it for a million pounds, is that correct?"

Ricky nodded. "You wanna pay me the money in cash, then you can walk away with it now."

"It's a deal."

"First I need to see the money."

"My assistant here will just go and get it from the car." The man gestured to the muscle with a jerk of the head, and the muscle left the room.

Ricky watched the muscle through the window as he crossed the shingled forecourt. Watched him open the door of the Roller and reach inside for a briefcase. Then saw him shut the door, turn and head back to the house. The guy walking with a loping gait, his big shoulders hunched up.

Ricky figured the guy was probably packing.

When the man came back into the room, Ricky asked him to put the briefcase on the table and open it. The man did as Ricky asked, and Ricky felt the adrenaline rushing through his veins as he found himself looking at a million beauties.

He checked the bundles were all made up of fifty-pound notes, and then he counted the number of bundles. The money was all there.

"Okay," he told the little guy, "the painting's yours."

Janine entered the room just then, as the muscle went to take the Rothko down from the wall. Ricky took out his .38 and shot the man in the back.

The man went down and stayed there.

The little guy was quick to take out his gun. He aimed it at Ricky, and was just about to pull the trigger before Ricky could turn. But Janine beat him to it, and shot him in the back of the head.

Ricky looked at her and said, "Well done, Jan."

"Is he dead?"

"Sure is. You're a good shot."

Janine looked stunned.

"The matter?"

"I haven't ever killed anyone before."

"First time for everythin', gel."

Just then, Ricky's mobile began to ring and he took it out and snapped it open. Then heard Gloria say, "Okay for me to let myself in now, Rick?"

Ricky said "Yeah" and snapped the phone shut.

"Who was that, Rick?" Janine asked him.

"Dunno."

"What d'you mean, you dunno?"

"I mean I *dunno*. What d'you *think* I fuckin' mean?"

"You said *yeah* to whoever it was like you were answering a question."

"Whoever it was hung up."

At that moment, Gloria walked into the room. She was holding a gun and pointing it at Janine.

Janine said, "The fuck are you?"

"I'm the bitch you'll be seein' in your nightmares in hell." Gloria shot her in the chest, and Janine froze and bit the carpet.

Gloria went over and shot her between the eyes, just to make sure. Then she shot her in the mouth and in the belly.

The last two bullets were to pay the bitch back for trying to steal her Ricky.

"Nice work, Glor." Ricky winked at her. "Always said we was two of a kind."

"What we gonna do with the bodies, Rick?"

"Could take 'em in the Roller out there'n dump 'em someplace."

"There's blood and DNA and prints'n shit all over the fuckin' room as well, though."

"That's a point... What if we was to torch the place, then, Glor?"

"Who's it belong to?"

"My lawyer, i'n' it. He'll be able to claim the insurance, anyway. He won't say nothin'. I got so much dirt on the guy they'd lock 'im up and throw away the key if I was to tell."

"Then you're gonna take me over to Rio, like you said, Rick, is that right?"

"Yeah, but I need to get my money first."

"I thought the bloke'd just paid you a million?"

"Yeah, he did, but that was for the paintin', Glor. I'm talkin' about the three million from the bank job."

"But how're you ever gonna be able to find it, Rick, now that Joey B and The Dog have both been rubbed out? I mean, if Joey hid it someplace'n didn't tell no one where he put it, then how's anyone suppose to know where it is?"

"I've got an idea who might know."

"Who's that?"

"Geezer by the name of Martin Butler. He was there at the house when I killed Joey B."

"What... and you let him get away?"

"Bastard surprised me with a blow to the back a the head. When I come round, he was gone."

"Bit sloppy of you, weren't it, Rick?"

"Didn't think the bloke had the balls to do somethin' like that, to be honest ... didn't seem the type."

"You mean you took your eye off 'im?"

Ricky nodded. "Just for a moment when I shot Joey, yeah."

"What makes you so sure this Martin Butler bloke knows where the money is, Rick?"

"What I was tryin' to explain to you, Glor ... he cleaned out the safe at the farmhouse when he knocked me out that time, and Joey used to keep the details of the account in it."

"Okay, so there's just one more job to do, Rick, is that it?"

"That's exac'ly it, gel, and after that it's gonna be the three s's all the way."

"What're they, then, Rick?"

"Sun, sex, and champagne..."

CHAPTER 24

"Look as though something's on your mind, Charles," Sir Alex said. "Want to share it?"

Charles sipped his champagne and eyed his brother over the rim of his glass. They were lunching at Goya's, in Pimlico. "Just had an old friend of mine from MI6 on the phone."

"Oh?"

"Got fingers in lots of pies ... takes a special interest in all matters Indian."

"And?"

"Some journalist's been doing a little snooping around."

"What kind of snooping around are you talking about?"

"Looking into the family business."

"The sweatshops?"

"Yes, well I'd prefer not to use that word to describe them, Alex."

"It's what they *are*, though."

"Dammit, man, you sound as though you're on the journalist's side. Do you *want* to have our entire inheritance come crashing down about our ears?"

"No, of course not."

"It would put an end to your political career like that." Charles clicked his fingers.

Sir Alex frowned, knowing that his brother was right. "Who is this journalist, do you know?"

"Some girl works for *The Guardian*."

"How much has she managed to find out?"

"More than enough to land us in some pretty deep doo-doo."

"Doesn't sound good."

"No, Alex, *good* is definitely not the word I'd use to describe the situation."

"Any way we can distract her?"

"I've already had contacts of mine in India try to bribe her to keep quiet about it."

Sir Alex gave him a questioning look.

"Nothing doing."

"In that case you know what we have to do, Charles."

"What's that?"

"Double the amount you offered her. It's rather an old-fashioned trick, but I'm told it can still be surprisingly effective."

Charles shook his head. "Already tried it. Seems the girl's a hopeless case."

"An *idealist*, you mean?"

"Of the worst sort. You know what these leftie types can be like … only got out of university two or three years ago and thinks she's about to change the world."

"I know the type, Charles, but what are we going to do about it?"

"I don't know, Alex, but we've got to do something and *fast*."

"Can't you be a little more specific?"

Charles looked into his brother's eyes. "Whatever it takes."

CHAPTER 25

After he'd left Goya's, Sir Alex Boulton headed across town for a session with Margot Peterson, at her practice in Harley Street.

"How are we feeling today, Alex?"

"Rather concerned, as a matter of fact."

"Still bothered by your desire to drink women's urine, are you?"

"No, it's not that so much."

"What, then?"

"It seems some journalist has started snooping around in India, asking questions about the family business. Girl by the name of Jo, writes for *The Guardian*, one of these idealistic lefty lesbians, apparently. It seems she can't be bought off. Rather admirable almost—or it would be, if the consequences for yours truly weren't so appalling."

"I see."

"The thing is, Margot, you're the only person outside of the family I've ever talked to about it."

"Well I can assure you that I haven't disclosed any of the information you've told me to any third party, Alex, if that's what you're implying."

"I'd like to believe you, Margot, because I'd come to value these sessions enormously. However, it also occurs to me that you're also the only person I've ever spoken to about the other matter that led to my being blackmailed."

"I have to say, Alex, that I resent what you seem to be implying. I'll have you know that I run my practice to the highest professional standards."

"I'm sure you do, Margot."

"So what are you saying, then?"

"Isn't anyone you live with, or a friend or someone, that might've had access to your computer, or to secret files, is there?"

"I think that's enough for today, Alex."

❄

Margot went over to *George's*, the lesbian bar on Wardour Street, that evening, in search of Mona Chapman.

There was no sign of Mona, so Margot asked around, and one of the girls who worked there gave her a mobile number. "I used to see her now and then, but that was way back," the girl said, "in the days when she was a swinger. Before she was under the thumb." The girl put her fingers in her mouth and pretended to vomit.

Margot pretended to find her funny. "Thanks for the help anyway."

"Any time, sweetheart."

Margot took out her mobile and punched in the number, listened to the ringtone.

"Hello?"

"Mona?"

"Speaking."

"Margot Peterson here. Remember me?"

"Yes, but how did you get my number?"

"Girl at *George's* just gave it to me."

"I can't talk now."

"This is important, Mona."

"I'm *with* someone. I'm afraid I'm gonna have to go."

"Look, will you just stop and listen to me a moment?"

"It's just that I don't screw around any more. The first time with you was before I met my partner, Win, and the second was—"

"A blip?" Margot suggested.

"Kind of, yeah. Win and I had an argument and ... well, it was all a storm in a teacup, really. Anyway, we're back together again now, I'm happy to say."

"All right, but I'm not calling you about that."

"So what is it you want, Margot?"

"Didn't happen to look at my computer when you stopped over at my place those two times, did you?"

"No, of course not. I wouldn't do a thing like that. Why? What's all this about?"

"It's just that some information an important client of mine has shared with me's fallen into the hands of a journalist who's started to pry into his affairs."

"What kind of information are we talking about, Margot?"

"*Private* and *highly sensitive* information. Information that was for my ears only."

"Well, I wouldn't know anything about that, Margot. Quite frankly, I resent what you're trying to imply."

"Yeah, well this could put me out of business."

"Look, Margot, I really have no idea what you're talking about. I don't even know any journalists ... not the sort of people I tend to hang out with."

"Funny you should say that, Mona, because I saw you with the journalist the man's talking about in *George's* one night. In fact, you left with her."

"Must have been someone else."

"No, it was you all right," Margot said. "Girl's name is Jo and she writes for *The Guardian*. She's a real blonde bombshell. All the girls that drink in *George's* are dying to get into her knickers. I pursued her myself on and off for over a year with no luck ... very choosy sort. Has every right to be, of course. Poor girl must get propositioned fifty times every time she takes her lunch break. That's why I noticed when you left with her that night, and I wasn't the only one. Half the girls in *George's* wanted to scratch your eyes out and the other half wanted to marry you after that. Case of *What's Mona got that's so special to make a dream girl like Jo go for her?*"

Margot waited to hear what Mona had to say in response to that, then realized that she'd already hung up.

❄

When he got back to the station, Preston received a call from Mike Patton who worked in the path lab.

"Something new's turned up that I thought might interest you, Bob."

"Shoot."

"House in Surrey, somewhere out past Weybridge, has been torched and there were three victims inside. Investigators on the scene thought it was an accident at first, but when we had the victims' teeth checked against dental records we have on file."

"And...?"

"One of them turned out to be a Janine Palmerson."

"Not the teacher thought to've helped Ricky Red escape?"

"The one and only."

"Thanks for the info, Mike."

They hung up and Preston told himself he'd better find Ricky Red before more corpses piled up.

Problem was, he had no idea where the man might be. Or even where to start looking. He'd tried all the most likely places and hadn't picked up a single whiff of the guy's scent.

❄

Martin went to the hospital to see Bella the following morning, and when he got there he was delighted to find she was wearing her street clothes.

"They've told me it's okay for me to go home now, Mart."

"That's great news, Bel."

They hugged and kissed, and then Martin went and called for a taxi.

When they got back to Suzanne's place, they went into their room and Martin told Bella all about everything that had happened while she'd been in hospital. Then he got out some papers and laid them on the bed.

"What're they, Mart?"

"I took them from the safe at the farmhouse. They're Joey's bank documents."

"You don't mean the money from the bank job?"

"...Is in the account, yeah, that's right."

"How much is in there exac'ly, Mart?"

"Small sum of somewhere in the region of three million quid, minus whatever Joey's already spent since he was released from prison—which can't be that much, I shouldn't have thought, because he's hardly been out any time."

"You thinking what I'm thinking?"

"Almost certainly."

"Why ... what are you thinking?"

"That we'd better get our asses over to Geneva before this Ricky Red character gets there."

"You know what they say about great minds."

"The account's in Joey B's name, though, Bel, so how'll we get the money out?"

"I can show them my passport and marriage certificate to prove I'm Joey's wife."

"That still wouldn't give you access to the account, not unless it was in joint names, which it isn't."

"No, you're right. The only way to pull it off that I can see, is if you pretend to be Joey."

"The people at the bank are gonna want to see a passport, though, or some kind of identification, to prove I'm who I say I am."

"So we get you a passport in the name of Joseph Belagio."

"How'd I be able to arrange that, though, Bel?"

"Claire that dances in the show knows someone who works at the consulate. Pay him ten grand and he'll fix you up with a passport with any name on it you want."

"Who told your friend Claire about this guy?"

"She did a little research of her own. She had to get her Jamaican boyfriend a passport last year so he could stay living with her in London."

"D'you think Claire might wanna introduce us to this friend of hers at the consulate, Bel?"

CHAPTER 26

Sir Alex was running the speech he'd made earlier in the House back through in his mind as he drove. He wondered what the media would make of it, and turned the radio on in the hope of finding out. Fiddled with the tuner with one hand as he steered with the other, until he found himself listening to a recording of the bit where he'd ripped into the Opposition's foreign policy. Sir Alex nodding as he listened, agreeing with himself.

It was raining so hard, he had to turn the windscreen wipers on, and he pulled up at the lights as the announcer on the radio moved on to other matters: *"And reports have just come in that the Guardian journalist, Jo Morrisson, has been found dead in her room at the hotel she was staying in, in a village in the state of Kerala, in India.*

"Hotel staff became concerned after Ms. Morrison failed to emerge from her room for some thirty-six hours. Upon entering her room, they found Ms. Morrison lying dead in her bed, with marks on her arm appearing to indicate that she had been bitten by a snake.

"Local police have issued a statement saying that the journalist is believed to have left her bedroom window open, despite warnings not to do so. Colleagues say that she went to India to investigate a story, but no further information is forthcoming as to what she was doing there.

"Ms. Morrison was twenty-seven, and friends and colleagues say that she was

a highly attractive and extremely popular young woman, as well as being a true professional. She will be sorely missed by many."

Sir Alex's blood turned cold, and he began to feel as though he was about to hyperventilate so he pulled over. Then his mobile began to spew a riff from Handel, and he fished it out of his pocket.

"Hello?"

"Alex, Margot here. I just heard about what happened to Jo Morrison."

"Yes, I heard it a moment ago myself on the radio."

"Is there something you haven't told me?"

"Meaning just *what* exactly?"

"Don't treat me as if I were a child, Alex."

"I didn't have her killed, if that's what you're asking."

"I wish I could believe you."

"Anyway, the girl wasn't murdered. It was a tragic accident."

"Yeah, she left her bedroom window open, right?"

"That's what it just said on the radio."

"Sure, a skilled journalist who knows her way around, and she leaves her window open in an area in India where everyone's warned not to."

"I'm sorry, Margot, I fail to see what you're getting at."

"It was no *accident*, Alex."

"How can you possibly know anything about it? You weren't there, were you?"

"My guess is that some guy put the cobra in the room with her."

"Yes, well these are all matters for the local police to deal with, Margot, and, frankly, neither you nor I have any business talking about it."

"The person who took the snake into her bedroom would've been a friend of the family, Alex, is that right? Or was it a hit man? Either way, it's amazing what you can do with a single phone call, isn't it?"

"I really think you're starting to lose your mind, Margot."

"Oh, that's rich ... make another great news story, Alex, wouldn't it? *Politician's shrink goes crazy."*

"If you only knew how preposterous you're starting to sound."

"Don't bullshit me, Alex, okay?"

He hung up.

And started to wonder.

❄

"Come on in, Alex," Charles said. "What's happened? You look like you're upset about something."

"I need a drink."

Charles headed for the cabinet. "Scotch?"

"Better make it a large one."

"Didn't your speech in the House go down very well?"

"It's not that."

Charles handed him his drink, and Alex took a big gulp, then winced.

"So what is it that's troubling you?"

"Jo Morrison."

"*Who?*"

"Oh come on, Charles, don't treat me as if I were an idiot. The girl who went to India to investigate the family business."

"What about her?"

"She's dead."

"Yes, a tragic accident, from what I hear."

"*Was* it, though?"

"Why are you looking at me like that, Alex?"

"Just look me in the eye, Charles, and tell me you didn't have her killed, will you?"

"Sure. Anything you want, Alex."

"*Do it*, then."

"I didn't have her killed."

"You're lying, aren't you?"

"So what if I am?"

"It's called *murder*, Charles."

"Dammit, Alex, if you will go about the place blabbing your mouth off when there's no need to, then somebody's got to clean up after you."

Sir Alex buried his face in his hands and began to sob.

"You ought to be thanking me, man. I've saved your career ... With a little bit of luck, you'll be the next prime minister ..."

"But we've got that young girl's blood on our hands, Charles. Doesn't that mean *anything* to you?"

"Of course it does, but I'm just going to have to live with it."

"I don't think I can," Sir Alex sobbed.

"You're going to have to. You don't have any choice."

"What you don't seem to realize is that I've always thought of myself as a decent person. All right, I've got my foibles just like anyone else. I want the best spot in the car park and so on, but I've never thought of myself as the sort of man who would condone *murder*. I'm an *Englishman,* educated at Eton, and that means something to me."

"What exactly does it mean to you, then, Alex?"

"It means I'm fundamentally decent and honest, reasonably so, anyway—at least, with my close friends and family, and, well ... *civilized*. I'm not some gangster straight off the boat from some godforsaken place, and I don't stab people in the back. Not *literally*, anyway."

"All this stuff about honesty and decency and being English is all very well, but you're a powerful man, Alex, and you need to understand that."

"What the devil are you driving at, Charles?"

"You don't know the first thing about the nature of power, and yet you want to be the prime minister of England."

"I'll learn as I go along, no doubt."

"That's not what I'm talking about."

"What, then?"

"You say you're not some gangster just off a boat. Well, if you were, then you'd understand what I'm talking about because those people are born knowing things that you'll probably never know, things to do with power. You see, Alex, assuming power is all about taking responsibility. It's about having blood on your hands and living with it at the end of the day.

"Name me one really great leader, of all the ones there've been down through the ages, who hasn't sent thousands or millions to their death, and don't say Ghandi, because he wasn't a proper leader in political terms. Besides, he's the exception that proves the rule."

Sir Alex was speechless.

"See, you can't." Charles adjusted the collar on his silk shirt. "Now while we're on the subject, let me just give you a little sound advice, one brother to another. The next time you feel the urge to go shooting your mouth off about things that are better left unsaid, Alex, *don't*."

"And what about my psychologist, Margot Peterson?"

"You've told her all of it, haven't you...?"

"Yes, but—"

"Do you really think you can trust her to keep her mouth shut, when she's already been selling the secrets you told her?"

"You can't kill her, too, Charles. I simply won't have it."

Charles sipped his Scotch. "I promise that it will be painless and, as with the journalist, it will be made to look like an accident. And let's hope that I never have to call on people to do this sort of thing again, Alex."

❉

Sir Alex went out to his car, took out his mobile and punched in a number.

"Margot here."

"It's me, Alex Boulton."

"If you're calling to try and intimidate me, then you can forget it."

"No, quite to the contrary. I need to see you, now. I have reason to believe your life is in danger, Margot."

"Okay. I'll meet you in the car park behind Waitrose, by Fulham Broadway. When can you get there?"

"Half an hour, maybe twenty minutes."

"See you there."

Margot hung up, and Sir Alex started up the engine of his Merc and headed off through the rain. He drove up Buckingham Palace Road, took a right by Victoria Coach Station and carried on up to Sloane Square. He went all the way along King's Road, and on past the World's End estate, then took a right and followed the road up to Fulham Broadway, and Waitrose was by the roundabout, near the bottom of North End Road.

He drove round the back of the supermarket and into the car park, then took out his mobile and called Margot again to tell her he'd arrived.

"Okay," Margot said. "I'm in the red Volkswagen in the north-western corner, next to a blue Fiat Panda. Come on over."

Sir Alex set off on foot across the car park in the murky light. "I see it, yes," he said into his phone. But Margot had already hung up.

The Volkswagen had tinted windows, making it impossible for Sir Alex to see inside.

Just then, Sir Alex heard a vehicle coming up behind him. He turned, expecting it to slow, but the vehicle—a green Range Rover—speeded up. Sir Alex jumped, only just managing to avoid certain death, and twisted his ankle as he landed.

Moving with some difficulty now, Sir Alex made another attempt to cross the aisle between the rows of parked cars. At that moment, the green Range Rover came hurtling back towards him, from the opposite direction this time. Sir Alex ran for his life. He just made it out of the aisle as the Range Rover went careering past.

Sir Alex hurried the short distance over to the red Volkswagen and tried to open the passenger door.

It was locked.

He banged on the window, but there didn't appear to be anyone inside. Then he heard a loud bang and threw himself onto the pavement.

My God, somebody was shooting at him, but who the devil—then the penny dropped. *It was Margot ... of course.*

No sooner had this thought passed through his mind than he heard another gunshot, followed by the sound of police sirens and skidding tyres. Sir Alex got up onto his knees and peered over the bonnet of the red Volkswagen in time to see the Range Rover leave the car park through the exit.

He hurried back to his Mercedes and jumped in, then started her up and set off.

As he reached the Broadway, he saw a squad car go whizzing past. Then he spotted Margot up ahead. There were two cars between Sir Alex's Mercedes and Margot's Range Rover. She was driving at a sensible speed, no doubt to avoid attracting attention to herself.

He had to catch up with her before Charles or his henchman did. He followed her over the Broadway, carried on past the shopping precinct and Stamford Bridge, then zigzagged his way down to King's Road, keeping her in his sights all the way. There were three cars between him and her now.

But then the cars in front of him pulled up at a crossing, as the lights changed to red. He hit the dash with the flat of the hand, as he was forced to sit and watch Margot beat the lights and take a right into Manresa Road.

The seconds dragged and Sir Alex willed the lights to change.

Then they did, finally, and he was on the move again. He took the next right into Manresa Road, then saw Margot getting out of the Range Rover up ahead.

By the time Sir Alex had pulled over, Margot was running up the steps at the front of one of the elegant Georgian properties that lined the street. Sir Alex jumped out of his Mercedes and dashed after her.

She stopped at the door and took out her key.

"Margot," Sir Alex called to her. "I need to talk to you."

He saw the panic and fear in her face as she glanced over her shoulder and saw him. Then she turned the key in the door and skipped inside.

Sir Alex made it to the top of the steps just as she went to slam the door in his face. He stopped her with his foot and entered the building.

Margot reached into her handbag for her gun, but Sir Alex grabbed her by the wrist and forced her to drop it. Then he put his hand over her mouth to prevent her from screaming, and she sank her teeth into his flesh. When he recoiled in agony, she kicked him on the shin and dashed up the stairs.

Sir Alex cried out in pain, but he quickly recovered and gave chase. He caught up with her on the landing.

Margot turned and aimed a punch at his nose. Sir Alex tried to dodge it but took a glancing blow on the cheek. Then he grabbed hold of Margot's wrist and, seeing that she was about to bite his cheek, he grabbed a fistful of her hair with his free hand and yanked it hard.

She screamed as she fell backwards, and Sir Alex got her on the carpet and pinned her down with his knees. Then he put his hand back over her mouth, holding her in such a way this time that she was unable to bite him.

"Okay, now listen to me, Margot," he gasped. "You've got the wrong end of the stick. I'm trying to help you. Your life is in danger, but not from me. Now I'm going to take my hand away, so no screaming this time, okay? Blink your eyes twice if you promise to do as I say."

Margot blinked twice, and Sir Alex took his hand away.

CHAPTER 27

"People in high places are extremely angry with you, Margot. They think you're the one that's been selling information about me."

"And so they want to rub me out in order to protect you, is that it?"

"I'm afraid so."

"If they're working for you and it's true that you're trying to help me, then why don't you just tell them to butt out?"

"Already tried that, but listening isn't their strong point, I'm afraid."

"But didn't you say that you're their boss?"

Sir Alex nodded. "Certain individuals just seem to be hell-bent on protecting my career. They seem to think I'm the stuff prime ministers are made of, you see."

Sir Alex got up and helped Margot to her feet.

"Now what?"

"We'd better get away from here before the people who're looking for you show."

"And what if I go to the police?"

"That would only make it all the easier for the people who're after you to find you."

Margot took a moment to consider what Sir Alex had just said. "Okay, so what do you suggest?"

"I think you ought to lie low for a little while, until this whole business has blown over."

"But where shall I go?"

"You could always stay at my grace and favour flat. It's not far from here, and nobody would think of looking for you there."

"Okay, so let's go, then."

They went out and got into Sir Alex's Merc, and he headed off back up to the King's Road and drove on through to Belgravia then pulled up outside his flat on Pont Street. "Here we are."

The building was one of those classy Georgian numbers, with a portico and fluted pillars at the front.

Margot frowned. "But are you sure nobody will come here looking for me?"

"Last place they'll look."

"What makes you so sure?"

"You're supposed to represent a threat to me, remember? They think I'm almost as furious with you as they are."

"And *are* you?"

"Well, you did try to kill me earlier ..."

"That was a misunderstanding, Alex."

He smiled wryly and said, "with treatment like that in the private sector, it's no wonder people are so keen to keep the NHS going."

Margot had made up her mind to trust him, so she figured it was a case of in for a penny in for a pound.

They climbed out of the Merc, ran up the front steps and went in through the front entrance.

Sir Alex had the ground-floor flat. The place was tastefully done out, with the best Wilton carpets and mahogany furnishings.

When she saw the sitting room, Margot said, "you politicians do all right, I must say."

"Must be worse places to hide out, I'm sure."

"But how long am I going to have to stay here?"

"That depends ..."

"On what?"

"How long it takes for me to get the people who are out to get you to see reason."

"And just who might *they* be, I wonder?" piped up a familiar voice.

They both turned to see Sir Alex's brother, Charles, standing in the doorway.

"The devil are *you* doing here?"

"I was about to ask you the same question, Alex."

"Well this is *my* flat you know, Charles."

"What about your friend here?"

"She's a guest of mine."

"Is she now?"

"Look, I know what it is you're thinking, Charles—"

"I doubt that, Alex. I doubt it very much indeed."

Margot said, "Who's *he*?"

"Margot, meet my brother, Charles … Charles, Margot."

"A pleasure, I'm sure." Charles smiled, his eyes cold as blue ice.

"I'm leaving," Margot said.

"Oh no you're not." Charles brought out a gun.

"But I thought you said he's your brother, Alex."

"I am, Margot," Charles said. "But unfortunately for you, I'm also the person Sir Alex felt he needed to persuade that you no longer pose a threat to him."

"But I don't, *honestly*. I mean, I never was."

"Yes, well you would say that *now*, wouldn't you?"

"Look, it wasn't me. It was a girl I slept with."

"Charles," Sir Alex said, "you really must stop all this nonsense and put the gun away."

Ignoring his brother, Charles said, "Sounds as though you need to be more careful with your pillow talk, Margot."

"No, it wasn't like that. She must've gone through my files when I was sleeping. It's the only way I can possibly account for it."

"What was this girl's name?"

"Mona."

"Surname?"

"Not sure."

"Something tells me you're not playing straight with me, Margot."

"I only slept with her a couple of times."

"I'm going to start counting. If you haven't told me the woman's surname by the time I get to three, I'm going to shoot you."

"I don't know it, honestly."

"Two."

"It's Chapman, Mona Chapman."

"Where does she live?"

"I don't know anything about her, except that she's going out with a woman called Winifred, who's married to John Harris, the MP, and her brother Donald's just escaped from prison."

"Where did you meet her?"

"In *George's*. It's a lesbian bar on Wardour Street."

"I see. Well that's very interesting, thank you." Charles shot Margot and her face froze in a look of surprise and agony, then she bit the carpet.

"Margot!" Sir Alex rushed over to her. "*Margot.*" He slapped her cheek, felt for a pulse. "*Margot.*"

He heard Charles say, "It's no use, old chap. She's a goner, got her right in the heart."

Sir Alex began to sob.

"Pull yourself together, man."

"You're the one that needs to pull himself together, Charles. You're behaving like a raving lunatic, going around shooting innocent people."

"I did it for *you*, Alex."

"She never did any harm to anybody."

"Except to you, old boy."

"You can't be sure of that."

"I can be sure enough."

"You're out of control."

"Only loose cannon around here is you, Alex. You need to get a grip."

"But we might've paid her off, the way we did that other fellow."

"Couldn't take that risk. It was different this time."

"Why was it?"

"Wasn't just a little smutty gossip concerning your sexual peccadilloes that she was selling, but details of the family business. Have you got any *idea* how much trouble I've had to go to in order to cover up any links between us and the sweatshops, Alex? The money we make from them passes through a veritable labyrinth of different bank accounts, stretching from one side of the world to the other, before it gets to us. It would be practically impossible to trace through the international banking network, which is why we've continued to be safe these past few years.

"It's getting more and difficult all the time, though. They're really tightening up on things a lot, you know. Dammit, man, it's the *family inheritance* we're talking about. What we've been *living on* all our lives, not to mention your political career. Way things are going, you're a racing certainty to become the next prime minister, Alex. You scarcely need me to tell you what the latest opinion polls are saying. Did you really want to stand by and let that woman rob you of your destiny?"

Sir Alex got to his feet and took a swing at Charles, but Charles was ready for him. He ducked and caught hold of Sir Alex's arm, then brought it down and around very quickly. Sir Alex tried to turn to free himself, but Charles tripped him, sending him sprawling onto the carpet.

"You never could get the better of me back when we were boys, Alex," Charles said, "so it's a bit late to start trying again now, especially seeing as I've been trained to kill, whilst you've been trained to do quite different things."

Sir Alex got up and came at his brother again. But Charles parried his punch with his left, before he hit Sir Alex with a sharp right to the solar plexus. Sir Alex went down onto his knees, and this time he stayed there.

"Like I say, you ought to leave the rough stuff to people who know what they're doing."

Sir Alex was gasping for air and quite unable to respond.

Charles helped him up and led him over to a chair. "Put your head down between your knees and take a few deep breaths ... that's it."

While Sir Alex struggled to regain control over his breathing, Charles went over to the drinks cabinet and poured a couple of stiff Scotches. "Here, take a chew on this, old chap."

Both men drank.

"That's it, get it all down."

Sir Alex did as he was told. Then he looked at his brother. "Now what?"

Charles shrugged. "Nothing."

"What do you mean, *nothing*?"

"When you're ready, you're going to smarten yourself up a little and go home to Prunella."

"And just forget any of this ever happened, you mean?"

"Forget any of *what* happened, Alex?"

❄

Charles took Sir Alex outside and saw him off, then he went back into the flat and made a phone call. Within half an hour one of his underlings, a man by the name of Scully—late thirties, tall, broad shoulders, shaven head—showed done up as an undertaker. "Got the hearse outside," he said in his usual no-nonsense manner.

"You mean you want to take her out in a *coffin*?"

Scully nodded.

"But don't you think we'll attract attention that way?"

"Can't see why we should. Most of the neighbours will be at work, I should think," Scully said. "Besides, it beats the hell out of the alternative, which would be to lug her out as she is in broad daylight."

Charles figured Scully had a point. He usually did.

So they put Margot's body into the coffin and carried it out. Then they drove off to an undertaker's place where Scully had arranged to have it incinerated.

Some twenty minutes later, Margot's corpse was a pile of ashes.

"Sorted," Scully said.

"Where would I be without you, old boy?"

"In Wandsworth or Brixton would be my guess."

CHAPTER 28

Charles collected a rare assortment of funny looks as he entered George's and made his way over to the bar.

He parked himself on a stool and asked the barmaid, a tall butch-looking blonde, to pour him a Scotch. "Think you might be in the wrong place, sweetie," the barmaid said.

"What on earth gives you that idea?"

"Take a look around you, mister. It's a bar for girlies, if you get my drift."

"I'm looking for a girl by the name of Mona Chapman. You know her?"

"Why should I tell you, even if I did?"

Charles produced his wallet, took out a banknote and laid it on the counter. "Here's ten good reasons."

The girl took the ten and made it disappear down her ample cleavage. "She used to come in here, but then she stopped."

"How come?"

"She met Mrs. Right, if you believe in that sort of thing. Hopeless case ... totally under the thumb."

"Any idea where I might be able to find her?"

The girl shook her head and said, "you still want that Scotch?"

Charles turned and went out.

No sooner had he climbed in behind the wheel of his Ferrari than he figured a change of tactics might be in order. If this Mona woman was involved with the wife of John Harris, the MP, then maybe the best way to locate her would be to find out Harris's address and tail his wife.

Charles called Scully again and told him what it was that he needed to find out. Then he called into a gay bar on Old Compton Street. He got himself a Scotch and began feeling up a young skinhead at the bar.

The skinhead turned to see who was caressing his butt.

Charles smiled and said, "What does a cute chap like you drink?"

The skinhead said he wouldn't say no to a pint of London Pride, and Charles reckoned he was in, or would have been, had Scully not chosen that moment to call him on his mobile.

"What's going on?"

"Got that bit of information you wanted, Charles. You got pen and paper handy?"

Charles reached into his pocket. "Fire away."

Scully told him the address. "Bad news is," he said, "the man's up north right now, seeing to matters concerning his constituency."

"That's rather convenient, as it turns out."

Charles hung up.

Then he told the skinhead he had to go, and he took the lad's mobile number and arranged to meet him later.

"Ciao for now, darling," he said and went out.

❄

Charles figured he'd try warning this Mona woman off to begin with, and only kill her, or have her killed, if she left him with no alternative but to do so. After all, it would be difficult to make the woman disappear without Alex finding out. If he did, there was no saying how he might respond.

The memory of the scene he and Alex had acted out over at the flat in Pont Street was still fresh in Charles's mind. Affairs had become rather untidy of late, and the last thing he wanted was to add to the mess. Besides, he couldn't be totally sure that this Mona woman was involved, because Margot Peterson could have been lying.

He drove to the address in Putney and pulled up around the corner from the MP's place, so as not to let the man's wife see the reg on his

Ferrari. The house turned out to be rather an elegant Victorian number.

He pushed the bell, and didn't have to wait long before a large-breasted blonde woman with a plummy accent came and opened the door.

"Evening, Mrs. Harris."

"Sorry. Should I know you?"

"No, we haven't met, but—"

"If it's John you want, I'm afraid he's away on constituency matters."

"No, it's you that I wanted to talk to as a matter of fact."

"Oh, and what would that be concerning?"

"Does John know about your girlfriend, Mrs. Harris?"

"Who the hell are you? What do you want?"

"Just a quick word with you, as I said."

"Your face is very familiar," she said. "Where do I know you from?"

"That's not important."

"If you don't leave now, I'm going to call the police."

"Yes, why don't you. I'm sure they'd be extremely interested to know what I could tell them about Mona."

"What on earth are you talking about?"

"I've got a message for Mona, if you wouldn't mind passing it on, that's all," Charles said. "A friendly word of advice, if you'd prefer to think of it in that way. You see, she has come by certain information concerning an MP whose name I won't mention right now, but Mona will know who I mean."

"Why don't you hurry up and get to the point?"

"If Mona thinks she can carry on blackmailing the man I'm talking about, then she'd better think again."

"Are you threatening her?"

"You can take it any way you like, Mrs. Harris, because the fact is that what Mona's been up to is highly illegal. She could end up going away for a very long time indeed, if the police find out about it."

"I see. Have you got anything else to say?"

"No, that's it. Just tell her to be careful. People in high places know what she's been getting up to and they are extremely angry with her. If she stops it now then all will be forgotten, but she's walking on very thin ice and needs to get back on solid ground. Am I making myself clear?"

Winifred said, "perfectly," and slammed the door in Charles's face.

❄

Charles called the young skinhead he had been chatting up earlier and arranged to pick him up on the corner of Wardour Street and Old Compton Street, in a quarter of an hour or so. Then he headed back into town.

He drove past Harrod's, continued on over Hyde Park Corner and along Piccadilly, then cut up into Soho, and there was the skinhead, waiting on the corner. Charles pulled over. "Get in, darling," he called to the lad. "You've been picked."

Charles fondled the lad with his free hand as he drove home. And as soon as they got into the flat, he kicked things off by bouncing the lad off the walls of the sitting room, just to soften him up a little. Then he pushed him over the back of the sofa, and he was just starting to have some real fun, his mobile began to spew its customary Beethoven...

"Fuck off, Ludwig, old boy. Can't you see I'm busy?"

❄

Sir Alex was taking a hot bath, as he often did when he was upset about something. He was horrified, outraged, terrified, and told himself it really was high time that he retired from politics.

He no longer wanted to be part of a system in which power was linked to murder. "I'm no killer," he said aloud, as though someone else were in the bathroom with him.

Sir Alex got out of the tub and dried himself. Then he slipped into his old plaid dressing gown and poured himself a large Scotch. He gobbled it all down quickly, then poured another.

He carried on like that until the bottle was empty.

Prunella found him lying in a comatose state when she got back, after dining with a friend, sometime later. She passed smelling salts under his nose, to try to bring him round, then began slapping him about the face and throwing cold water over him.

When that didn't work, she called Charles and told him the situation. "I think I should call for an ambulance."

"It'll be all over the newspapers, Pru."

"But I'm frightened he might *die*, Charles."

"What's he taken?"

"There's an empty bottle of whisky next to him."

"Have you checked the medicine cabinet, Pru?"

"Yes. Nothing appears to have been taken. Even so, I'm worried. I mean, he's dead to the world."

"Don't do anything, Pru. I'm coming straight over."

Charles arrived some twenty minutes later, to find his brother still out cold.

He hoisted him up out of his chair, and then he and Prunella took an arm each and tried to get him to take a few steps.

At first it was useless and Sir Alex's legs kept giving way. But then Charles took him out to the bathroom and poured some peppermint down his throat. Sir Alex began to vomit and didn't stop until he'd emptied his stomach. He spent a little time in hell, but at the end of it he finally started to feel better and got back the use of his legs.

"But what on earth were you thinking of, Alex?" Prunella sobbed.

"Pru, perhaps it might be better if you let me talk to him on my own," Charles said. "I'll see if I can't get a little more sense out of him."

Prunella gave Charles a look that would have sunk a thousand ships, if looks could do such things. There had always been something vaguely mysterious and esoteric about the relationship the two men shared, and a large part of her resented Charles's intrusion. Then she remembered that she'd been the one to call him. And he had come and saved the day, after all. So she shrugged and went off to the bedroom, where she sat up reading the same page of a novel over and over as she waited for Alex to appear.

Meanwhile, the two brothers were in the kitchen. "The hell were you thinking of, Alex?"

"I'm no killer, Charles."

"So you thought a bottle of Scotch would make it all go away, is that it?"

"I don't know what I thought. I just couldn't face it."

"You've *got* to, Alex."

"I can't. I want out."

"Out of *what*?"

"Politics, for a start."

"What's politics got to do with this?"

"Everything. You said yourself power is evil, or words to that effect."

"Now you listen to me, Alex. I'm sick and tired of running around after you and having to clean up your mess, do you understand me? If I hadn't come here tonight who knows what might've happened?"

"Is this the moment when I'm supposed to thank you, Charles?"

"You might at least show a little gratitude."

"And if I said I wish you hadn't come?"

"You need to pull yourself together, Alex. Your old masters at Eton would be ashamed to hear the way you're talking now."

"Perhaps they'd be prouder of you, if they knew what you've been getting up to ... killing people, or having them bumped off left right and centre."

"You're too damn right they would."

"I don't want to be prime minister, Charles."

"You're talking like a wimp, Alex. This country needs leadership, and if it falls to you to fit the bill then I'm here to make sure you do it."

CHAPTER 29

Preston was on his way to the Revuebar, where he wanted to run over a few questions with people that worked there. As he was walking along Brewer Street, he happened to spot a tout, whose face was familiar to him from somewhere, talking to a large group of Japanese businessmen.

No sooner had Preston noticed him than the tout, who was short and built like a lump of lard, turned and set off with the entire group of Japanese tourists in tow—there must have been at least twenty of them.

Preston's curiosity was aroused, and he followed the tout down Rupert Street then off left into the connecting road that runs along the back of the theatres. The man stopped at the corner to confer with a much taller associate, who appeared to have been waiting there for him.

Seeing this, Preston hid in a shop doorway and waited to see what was going to happen next.

The tall man went over to a silver BMW that was parked at the curb and opened the door. "Let's see then," he said, "how many've we got 'ere?"

"There's about twen'y of 'em I counted," the short fat one said.

"Well, I think two trips'll prob'ly do it, don't you?"

"Can't see why not. Tiny little bastards, ain't they?"

The tall one sniggered, before he turned to the group of Japanese. "C'mon on then, gentlemen, let's be havin' you ... there's plen'y a room in a back. "

"Excruse me," one of the group who could speak some English piped up. "Are you going take us to Revuebar?"

"That's right."

Having been reassured, the man turned and spoke to his compatriots in Japanese. Then they all formed a queue behind him and, one by one, they began to climb into the BMW.

The car was soon full.

"Right that'll prob'ly do then, I reckon," the tall man said. "You can tell the rest of these geezers to hang on here'n not go nowhere, and I'll be back quick as I can."

With that, he got into his BMW, started up the engine and set off.

Seeing that the tout he'd followed was now alone, Preston figured it was time to come out of hiding. So he walked up to the man and said, "I don't suppose you'd be able to help me? I'm looking for a little entertainment this evening, but it's such a long time since I've come down to the West End. Would you be able to recommend somewhere?"

"I do know a club as a matter of fact, sir. It's just a tenner to get in, and for that you get a free glass of champagne'n there's a great floor show." The man pronounced it *flaw* show. "The gels there are really friendly, too, you can take my word for that."

"The girls there are friendly, you say?"

"Just as friendly as you want 'em to be, if you take my meanin'. Fact, if you was to hang on two ticks, I'd take you there meself, sir, only I'm waitin' for my driver to return, so I can't go nowhere until he comes back."

Preston grabbed the fat man's arm and twisted it behind his back. "DCI Preston at your service," he said. "Now how about if me and you go for a little ride?" And with that, he marched the tout up to the corner of the street and hailed a taxi.

When the cab pulled over, Preston bundled the tout into the back. "What the fack is this?" the tout wanted to know.

"Just drive round the block," Preston told the driver, and he held up his ID for the man to see.

"Right you are, guv." The cabby closed the partition window, so that Preston could talk in privacy, then he set off.

Preston turned his attention back to the tout. "I want to talk about the shooting that took place at the Revuebar."

"I dunno anythin' 'bout that."

"C'mon, you must've heard rumours on the streets."

"I heard 'bout a gel got shot, course I fackin' did ... in the news, weren't it?"

"I've got far bigger fish to fry than your sort. All I want from you's a little cooperation. But if you don't wanna play ball then I know plenty of ways to fuck with you so you'll wind up wishing you had. Do I make myself clear?"

"Like I been tellin' ya, I don't know nothin'."

"You stand on the corner of Walker's Court to conduct your affairs every night?"

"So?"

"Cast your mind back to the evening when Bella Armando was shot. I want you to tell me if you saw anyone go in or come out through the backstage door of the Revuebar around that time. You know the door I mean. The one near to the corner there where you normally stand, in Brewer Street."

The tout took a moment to think. Then he said, "Yeah, I did see a geezer come out through that door at around that time, as it 'appens."

"Recognize the man if you saw him again?"

"I see thousands of boat races every day... besides, it was dark, weren't it?"

"Maybe a few nights in the cells might jog your memory."

"You ain't got nothin' on me."

"That's what *you* think."

"C'mon, then, what you gonna arrest me on?"

"Pick a card. Touting, pimping, selling drugs, suspicion of robbery."

"I ain't never sold no drugs in me life, nor pimped neither."

"You will've done by the time I've finished with you."

"Hey, what the fuck is this?"

"My friends all think I'm a nice enough guy, but it's only my enemies that get to see the real me." Preston tapped on the screen, and the cabby slid it back.

"What you doin'?" the tout asked.

"I think a little trip to the station might be in order."

The cabbie said, "Guv?" at the same time as the tout said,

"Okay-okay," changing his tune, "...Was old Johnny Ritz, weren't it?"

The name was familiar to Preston. Johnny Ritz, a trained marksman and expert on weaponry, had been charged with running arms with some associates of his two or three years ago in what was a fairly big and lucrative operation. The case went to trial, but the gang walked after the prosecution had been unable to make the charges stick. "You positive about that?"

"Yeah. I hadn't seen 'im in ages—which is how come I remember it ... 'cause we both said 'ello, you know ..."

"Friend of yours, is he?"

"Use to hang out with 'im years ago before he got big. Too big for his own boots, some people'd say, i'n it."

"How does Johnny Ritz make his money nowadays?"

"Owns a restaurant, so I'm told."

"Where?"

"Islin'ton. Real up market place, so they say, not that I've ever been there meself."

"What's it called?"

"Dunno, but it should be easy enough to find out."

"Was Ritz on his own when you saw him come out?"

The tout nodded.

"Did you see anyone else come out through that same door afterwards?"

"Don't think so. Pretty sure I didn't, in fact."

Figuring he'd learned everything he was about to from the tout, Preston had the cabby pull over. "You can go now," he said. "But don't leave town."

The tout hopped out of the cab, and Preston told the driver to take him to Charing Cross police station. Then he took out his mobile and called DS Johnson's number. When Johnson picked up, Preston, said, 'Listen, Dave, I want you to get hold of a character goes by the name of Johnny Ritz."

"That spelt as in the hotel?"

"You got it. He owns a restaurant over in Islington."

"Know the name of it?"

"No, you'll need to find that out. Call me as soon as you've got the man, then take him in to the station for questioning."

❄

Several hours later, Preston and Johnson were interviewing Johnny Ritz, a tall powerful-looking man with a boxer's nose, in the Incident Room.

Preston leaned over the grey metal desk, so that his face was close to Ritz's. "If you're not mixed up in this somehow, Johnny," he said, "then why don't you just tell us what you know?"

Ritz ran one of his large paws through his ginger hair. "I've had enough of this shit. I ain't sayin' another fuckin' word till I get to speak to my lawyer."

"Fine, have it your way, but in that case, I won't be able to keep the press from getting their hands on the story." Preston flashed the man a smile that wasn't really a smile at all. "Pity because if you'd been in a position to talk to me off the record, Johnny, then things might've been different."

"What d'you mean?"

"I might've been able to pull a string or two to keep the press off your back, presuming you're really as innocent in all this as you say you are. Of course, if you want to go ahead and call your lawyer, then it's all gonna end up going public.

"Media are gonna have a field day when they get hold of this story. An ex-con like you, who says he's going straight, but isn't really. Must be the last thing you'd need, Johnny, I should imagine, now that you're a successful restaurateur."

"That's blackmail."

"It's the situation we have here, Johnny. Now, what's it to be? It's your call."

Johnny Ritz ran a hand through his thinning hair. "Okay, I'll tell you what I know. But then you've gotta let me go, because I didn't have nothin' to do with it, right?"

"Let's hear it."

"Rumour is someone got paid to put the frighteners on the girl that was shot and her boyfriend."

"You mean it was a hired gun?"

Ritz nodded. "Only they wasn't suppose to kill no one's the way I heard it."

"Why'd anybody want to frighten them?"

"No idea." Ritz shrugged his broad shoulders.

"How did you come by this information, Johnny?"

"I can't say."

"Look, you're going to have to tell us a lot more than this. Otherwise how can we tell whether we should believe you or not?"

"It was somebody high up that ordered it."

"How do you know?"

"They approached me first."

"*Who* did?"

"I can't tell you."

"You don't have any choice, Johnny. Not if you want me to keep the press off your back. Besides, we brought you in here as a suspect, and you still haven't said anything to make me think otherwise." Preston cleared his throat. "Just get it off your chest, Johnny, whatever it is."

"It was somebody I'd never seen before."

"What did he look like?"

"Well-dressed guy in a smart suit, posh accent."

"Where did he approach you?"

"At the restaurant."

"This character a regular customer?"

"No, I'd never seen 'im before."

"So what did he say?"

"Just that he was lookin' for somebody to do a job for him."

"A job?"

"What I just said. They wanted to hire somebody to shoot at the girl to shake her and her boyfriend up real good, but not to kill her."

"They'd want a professional for that."

"Exac'ly."

"You were quite a marksman yourself in your day, so I'm told."

"That's all behind me now, Inspector. I've been goin' straight for a long time now, like I keep tellin' you."

"That's right, Johnny, you do keep telling us you're going straight. Only problem is, we just can't think of any reasons why we should believe you." Preston frowned and laced his fingers over his belly. "So what did you say to the man?"

"Told 'im I wasn't interested."

Preston looked Ritz in the eye and Ritz held his gaze.

"Straight up ... I mean, why would I wanna go back to that, now that I've got the restaurant and everythin's going well for me?"

"So then what did the man say?"

"Arsked me if I knew anyone else I could recommend who'd be able to do it."

"And?"

"I told the guy I'd left the old days behind me."

"Then what?"

"He warned me not to tell no one about the conversation I'd had with 'im. Said he was working for MI6. Then he starts on about the Official Secrets Act and he said that bad things happen to people who go blabbin'."

"What did you say to that?"

"I didn't say nothin'."

"Then what happened?"

"Guy just got up'n left."

"You still haven't told us anything that proves you even had any such conversation. For all I know everything you've just said could be one big pack of lies."

"Why would I make all that up?"

"That's easy, Johnny, to save your skin."

"Okay, there's one more thing."

"I'm listening."

"When the shootin" took place at the Revuebar, I was standin' on the back steps, talkin' to Peaches, gel comes on done up in combat gear?"

"Why do they call her Peaches?"

"It ain't for her syrupy voice, I'll tell you that much."

"Got a nice can, has she?" Johnson put in.

"Your mate just 'ere to supply the comic relief, is he, Inspector?"

"Will Peaches corroborate what you've just said?"

"'Course she will... arsk 'er if you don't believe me."

"We will."

"You can arsk that Gary guy who does security, too, 'cause he saw me with 'er. And why don't you arsk for the footage from the CCTV ...?"

"They don't have cameras at the back entrance." Preston turned to Detective Sergeant Johnson. "Go and get hold of this Peaches, Dave, and see if she corroborates his story."

"On my way, guv."

With that, Johnson left the room, and Preston told Ritz he was going to interrupt the interview.

CHAPTER 30

Johnson arrived at the station sometime later with Peaches, and she corroborated Ritz's story.

"So that counts Johnny Ritz out, then."

"Unless Peaches is lying, guv."

"He's got another alibi."

"I missed something...?"

"I spoke to Gary Ross earlier, while you were out looking for Peaches, and he corroborated Ritz's story."

"What I don't really get, guv, is why we're spending so much time investigating the Revuebar shooting?" Johnson said. "I mean, Bella Armando's survived, so shouldn't we go after Ricky Red?"

"If you've got any ideas where we might find him, Dave, because I haven't. Besides, I've got a sneaking feeling that the Revuebar shooting and the other murders are all linked."

"So what's our next move, guv?"

"I think we should talk to Johnny Ritz some more."

❊

"What happened after you stepped out through the backstage door that night, Johnny?"

"I stayed there with Peaches for while. We was both curious to find out what had been goin' on in the theatre."

"See anyone leave the building through the back door after that?"

Ritz shook his head.

"You quite sure about that, Johnny?"

"Only person I saw come out was a copper in uniform."

"When was this exactly?"

"Minute or two after I'd stepped outside."

"This would've been how long after the shooting?"

"Three or four minutes, max."

Johnson said, "We didn't arrive on the scene until ten minutes or so after the shooting, guv."

Preston said, "You're quite sure that it couldn't have been *ten minutes or so* after Gary Ross came to lock the backstage door that you saw the policeman come out that way?"

"No, it was only a minute or so, two minutes, tops, I'd say. I'm sure about that."

Preston looked at DS Johnson. "But there was only one policeman on the premises at that time, Dave," he said. "That was the constable who called in to report the shooting. I spoke to him personally, and he told me he was down in the foyer right up until the time I arrived."

"Something doesn't smell right, guv."

"We need to check it wasn't the constable we spoke to in the foyer that Johnny saw, or another officer from the Met, for that matter."

Preston turned back to Johnny Ritz. "Would you recognize the man if you saw him again?"

"I reckon I would."

"In that case, I'll need you to help an artist produce a sketch of what the man looks like."

"But if MI6 are behind it then you've got no chance, Inspector."

Preston said, "That's for me to worry about."

❉

When Preston was shown the artist's impression, first thing the following morning, it was immediately obvious to him that the face in the drawing didn't look anything like that of the constable who first arrived on the scene. So he had a computer whiz run some checks, and he was sitting at his desk in his office, some twenty minutes later, when the telephone rang. "Hello?"

"Mark Bowling here."

"Hi, Mark, did you find a match?"

"No, I didn't, Inspector. I don't know who the man you're looking for is, but I can definitely assure you that he's not currently serving in the Met."

"You checked for a match with one of the ex-cons on the database?"

"I'm still trawling through it."

"Okay, well keep at it, and get straight back to me if you find anything."

They hung up. Then Preston brought DS Johnson up to speed.

"What are your thoughts on what Johnny Ritz said, guv, about MI6 being behind the shooting?"

"Still too early to say."

Preston's phone began to ring.

"Hello?"

"Me again, Inspector—I've got a match. The man's name is Michael Tomlinson."

"What's his form?"

"Sentenced to ten years for armed robbery back in ninety-six. He got out after seven on a reduced sentence."

"What's he been doing since then?"

"There's nothing on record, apart from what I've just told you, so your guess is as good as mine."

"Got an address for him?"

"The last one we have a record of was back five years ago."

"Let's have it."

After noting it down, Preston said, "Thanks, Mark," and hung up.

"Name Michael Tomlinson mean anything to you, Dave?"

Detective Sergeant Johnson took a moment to think, then he shook his head.

"Me neither."

Preston got up and began to pace the room. "What I don't get, though, is how this Tomlinson guy could've left the Revuebar through the back exit in a policeman's uniform that night, if all of the reports we have from witnesses—Gary Ross, Johnny Ritz and Peaches excepted, of course—tell us there was only one uniform on the premises at the time."

"Practically everyone we spoke to noticed the constable that was down in the foyer, guv, so why didn't they notice this other guy, if there were only the two uniforms in the building?"

Preston stopped his pacing and clapped his hands. "I've got it, Dave."

"Guv?"

"Our man must've gone in to see the show dressed in his street clothes, fired off the shot, and then gone into the toilet and changed into a copper's uniform..."

"But where would he have got the copper's uniform from?"

"Must've had it with him, folded in a holdall or whatever."

"Then he puts his street gear back into the holdall, guv."

"And by that time everyone's rushing down to the lobby in a mad panic, so nobody notices him as he goes the other way, back into the theatre..."

"Which is empty by that time, presumably."

"He simply crosses the stage, goes past the dressing rooms, down the back stairs, and leaves the premises by the rear exit. Gary Ross has gone to guard the door by this time, but when he sees what he takes to be a policeman coming towards him, he just unlocks the door and lets him out and thinks nothing of it."

"What I still can't figure out is why anyone should've wanted to put the frighteners on Bella Armando and her boyfriend. What have they been getting up to, do you reckon?"

"I've no idea just yet, Dave, but if Johnny Ritz's story's true then it must be something pretty serious for them to have got up MI6's noses like they seem to have."

"Are we gonna arrest them, guv?"

"Not until we've got something we can charge them with," Preston said. "And until we do, I'm gonna keep a close eye on them and see if I can find out just what they're up to."

"So what shall I do?"

"I need you to go and find this guy Tomlinson and bring him in."

. . .

When Preston got home that night, he sat on the side of the bed and turned his computer on to check his e-mails.

There was one from his son, Callum, and Preston opened it up:

Dear Dad,

Steve took me and Mum to Stamford Bridge to see this evening's game. Chelsea won 3-0 and they were brilliant. I wish you could have come so we could have watched it together. Then when I tell you about it you'd know what I mean. Steve's a Chelsea fan. I told him that I've always been a Fulham fan, but I had to admit that Chelsea are a better team. Frank Lampard played really well, and he scored a brilliant goal from a free kick. Drogba got the other two.

I hope you're keeping well, Dad.

Love you lots,

Callum

XXX

The thought of his son, Callum, being taken to see a match by his ex-wife Anne's new boyfriend did nothing to improve the way Preston was feeling.

Worse still, it seemed Anne's new bloke was threatening to try and make a Chelsea fan out of the lad.

Preston poured himself a large Scotch and knocked it back in a single gulp.

Then poured another.

"And since when did Anne ever take an interest in *football?*" he addressed the empty room.

During the fifteen years they had been together, Preston could only ever recall Anne complaining about how football was a game in which twenty-two 'stupid blokes' chased a bit of leather about a field.

Just then, Preston's mobile sounded and he snapped it open.

"Hello?"

"Hi, Bob, it's me."

"Sally. Where are you?"

"I just got off work. Fancy coming over and getting me?"

"I'm on my way."

So Preston spruced himself up a little and drove to Hammersmith. When he pulled up outside the Spearmint, he saw Sally standing in the entrance to try and keep out of the rain that had just started to fall. She was talking to one of the other dancers and didn't see him at first. In her slim-fitting denims and matching jacket, her blonde hair done up in pigtails, Preston reckoned she looked good enough to eat.

He opened the side window and called to her, and she came hurrying over and climbed into the passenger seat. She smelt of some perfume he couldn't put a name to and rain, as they kissed hello.

Preston started the engine up and set off. Sally told him about her day as he drove back to his flat.

When they got in, Preston poured a Scotch for himself and a glass of white Rioja for Sally. She followed him over to the kitchenette and wrested the glass from his hand. But instead of taking a sip, she put it down on the worktop. Then she threw her arms round his neck.

Their tongues entwined as they kissed, and Preston had just begun to caress her breast when his mobile burst into life again. So he stopped what he was doing and fished it out of his pocket.

"Hello, guv. I hope I haven't interrupted anything?"

"This a social call, Dave, or have you got something to say to me?"

"I've just spoken to Michael Tomlinson's mother."

"And.?"

"Said all she knows is he left the country in a hurry."

"Well that's just great."

CHAPTER 31

The following day, Martin went into town to see about buying a couple of guns. He began by talking to one of the spivs that haunted the streets of Soho, a fat guy in baggy jeans and a plaid jacket who said he would arrange a meeting with a dealer for him. "Come back 'ere in 'alf an hour," the man said. The guy had awful teeth and worse breath, but he sounded like he knew how to help Martin get what he wanted.

When Martin returned, the spiv led him into the car park behind the Lyric pub.

"Where is this guy?"

"He's up on the top, waiting."

So they climbed the steps, all the way up to the top story.

When they got there, a big man with spiky brown hair got out of a silver Merc and came over to them. The man was wearing a sharp blue suit, shades and a Cuban cigar. He picked his nose, flicked away a piece of snot, and looked Martin in the eye. "I hear you're interested in makin' a purchase."

"That's right."

The man turned to his associate, who was sitting on the bonnet of the Merc. "Diff, you keep an eye out."

"Okay, Trev."

The man led Martin round the back of the Merc and opened the boot. He pulled back the sheet of tarpaulin that was in there to reveal an arsenal of weaponry. "Take a butcher's."

"Mind if I pick a few up?"

"Go ahead."

Martin took a pair of leather gloves from his pocket and slipped them on, then he began to heft some of the guns. There was one in particular that he liked the feel of. The dealer noticed this and said, "That's a AMT Hardballer Longslide ... gun Arnie used in the Terminator films. Barrel's a hundred'n seventy-seven point eight millimeters."

"Feels pretty good," Martin said. "I need one for a woman, too."

The man picked up one of the smaller weapons. "Can't do no better than the Colt 45 Single Action... classic ladies' gun, otherwise known as the Model P Peacemaker."

Martin hefted the weapon and reckoned it was light enough for Bella to be able to use it okay. "How much for these two?"

He haggled with the man for a few minutes, and when they arrived at a price they could agree on Martin paid him. Then he put the weapons into the sports bag he'd brought with him and went back down to the street.

Next, he made a few more enquiries in order to find himself a pilot. He eventually made contact with a man who said he knew someone who'd fly anybody just about anywhere in his own private aircraft, no questions asked. Martin got the man's number and arranged to meet him a couple of hours later in the Greyhound, at the end of Old Compton Street. The man said, "I'll be standing at the bar and wearing a black leather jacket and a blue baseball cap."

No sooner had Martin entered the pub than he spotted the man. He stood at around six-two and must have been pushing fifty, but he looked like he was in good shape.

Martin went over to him and said, "You the pilot?"

"That's right."

"I need somebody who'd be able to fly me and my girlfriend from Geneva to Barcelona."

"When and what time?"

"Around ten or eleven o'clock tomorrow morning. But I can't be exact about the time, so I'd need you to be there, waiting for my call and ready to appear at short notice. Could you do that?"

"Sure, for the right kinda money."

❄

That evening Martin and Bella flew from Heathrow over to Geneva, and they took a taxi from the airport straight to the Hotel d'Anglaterre.

"Jeez, this is some kinda place," Bella said, as they stood together looking out of the window down over the lake. "Some of those yachts are whoppers."

"Don't sound so surprised about it, Bel. This is where the rich hang out."

Martin called room service and had them bring up a bottle of champagne, with a bowl of fresh strawberries and cream.

"I've always wanted to do this," he said, taking one of the strawberries and holding it up for Bella to take a bite. Then he started to eat the other side of it.

Things soon got messy and they ended up having a long, wet French kiss that tasted of strawberries.

"I love you, Bel," Martin murmured, as he eased her back down onto the bed.

❄

First thing the following morning, Martin called the pilot.

"Hello?"

"I need you to pick us up in half an hour's time. We"ll be in the lobby of the Hotel d'Anglaterre. And listen, if we're not there for any reason just stay and wait for us, okay? Remember to bring the holdall I left with you."

"I'll be there."

They hung up. Then Martin and Bella left the hotel and walked two blocks to the Bank of Malta.

They went in through the revolving door, passed the armed security guard and went up to the inquiry desk. Martin got the attention of the pretty blonde at the counter and asked to see the manager.

The girl said, "I'll just go and get him for you, sir."

They had to wait a few minutes before a middle-aged man in a pinstripe suit, with salt-and-pepper hair, appeared and asked how he could be of assistance.

"I'd like to empty my account," Martin said.

"I see, sir. Well, first may I see some identification, please?"

Martin handed the man the fake passport he'd had made up in Joey Belagio's name. Then he gave him the bank document that had the number of the account written on it.

"Thank you, sir." The man looked at the passport and the other document. "Oh yes, Mr. Belagio, of course. You called to say you would be coming in."

"I thought you might perhaps require some advance notice."

"Indeed. Well everything has been arranged for you. If you wouldn't mind just waiting a moment." The man smiled politely and went off.

Martin watched him pass a number of desks at which people were sitting. Then the man opened a door in the far wall and went into the adjoining room.

Martin's heart was performing feats of gymnastics in his chest. Perhaps the man was calling the police right now.

Martin glanced at Bella. She looked nervous, too.

A long minute passed, and then the man reappeared. His expression didn't seem to have changed any, so far as Martin could tell.

"Just to check that I've understood, sir. You did say you wanted to take *all* of the money in the account with you now. Is that correct?"

"Yes."

"And you said that you would like the money in one-hundred-pound notes, is that right?"

"That's correct."

"Okay, sir, that won't be a problem, but first we'll have to do the necessary paperwork."

"Of course."

The man placed some forms down on the table in front of Martin and asked him to sign in the places he'd marked with a cross. Martin's throat was dry. He tried to swallow and realized that he couldn't. This was the moment of truth. He'd done what amounted to a crash course in forging Joey's signature before coming here, and reckoned he'd got it off pat. . . Well, now he was about to find out if he was right or not. All he had to do was stop his hand from shaking and everything would be fine.

He took out his pen and leaned over the table, then dashed off four perfect forgeries of Joey's signature, one after the other.

"Thank you, sir."

The man picked up the sheets that Martin had just signed and walked off with them. Martin figured he must be going to compare them with the ones of Joey's the bank had on record.

Martin's heart missed a couple more beats as he watched the man make his back way over to them.

"Well everything seems to be in order, sir. So if you would like to come with me. And will Madame be accompanying you?"

"Yes."

Martin and Bella followed the man through to the vault, where the money had all been laid out on the table, ready.

"Perhaps you would like to count it, sir?"

The money was set out in piles of two-hundred £100 notes, totaling £25,000 a stack, and there were a hundred and ten stacks altogether.

Martin and Bella put the money into the large briefcase they'd brought with them. Then they said goodbye and walked out of the bank.

They were £2,750,000 up.

CHAPTER 32

Martin and Bella returned to the lobby of the Hotel d'Anglaterre, where the pilot was waiting for them, as arranged.

The pilot led them out to the car he'd hired, a blue BMW, and Martin gave him an envelope that contained the second installment of his fee. The man counted the money as he sat behind the wheel.

Martin said, "What about the guns?"

"They're in the boot. D'you want them now?"

"It's okay, I'll get them out before we board the plane."

They set off and drove to a quiet spot outside of the city, where the driver had a small private aircraft waiting next to a runway that was used by a private flying club. They got out of the car, and the pilot opened the boot.

Martin took out the guns and gave Bella her Peacemaker. "It's loaded, so be careful with it, Bel," he warned her, before he put the Hardballer in the holster he was wearing under his jacket.

They climbed into the small aircraft, then the pilot started up the engine and they took off and headed for Barcelona, where they planned to deposit the money into an account they'd recently opened in a bank there. Then they'd transfer the money to two accounts in a bank in Jersey, where it would be exempt from tax.

. . .

Hours later, they on a runway that was situated in a quiet field somewhere in the Catalan countryside, and once they'd got off the plane the pilot led them to a silver BMW that was parked nearby. They climbed in and set off for the city.

Martin was with Bella in the back, and he'd gaze into her eyes every now and then and squeeze her hand. They were both feeling nervous still. It was almost as though it had all been too easy, and neither of them could shake off the feeling that people must be coming after them. They didn't want to talk in front of the driver, either. The less he knew about things the better.

When they reached the outskirts of Barcelona, Martin told the driver he wanted him to take them to their bank and he gave the man the address.

The man found the bank easily enough, but it turned out to be closed. A note on the door said that it shut at 1.30 p.m. that day. Martin cursed himself for not having thought to check beforehand.

Once he was back in the car, Bella saw by his manner that something was wrong. "What's up?"

He told her. Then shook his head and said, "Who's ever heard of a bank closing this *early,* Bel?"

The driver said, "Now where do you two want me to take you?"

Martin looked at Bella. "Any ideas ...?"

"Dunno. A hotel, I guess."

"Which hotel have I got to drive to?"

"What's the best one in town?"

"I'm not sure. The Ritz, I should think."

"Sounds good," Bella said. "Don't you reckon, Mart?"

"Sure, why not?"

When they got there, Martin gave the pilot the rest of his fee. Then they checked into the hotel.

Sometime later, Martin and Bella were lying in each other's arms in bed, up in their room, laughing hysterically. It was as though they both needed to find a way of releasing all the nervous tension that had built up inside of them.

Then they stopped laughing and gazed into each other's eyes. "We've done it, Bel," Martin said. "We've really *done it*."

"I know. I still can't quite believe it, Mart."

"Me neither."

"I was bricking it for a while back there, when we were in the bank."

"Me, too."

"But you looked so cool, Mart."

"That's because I *am* so cool."

Bella laughed. "How does it feel to be rich?"

"I don't know yet. *Great,* I guess. What d'you reckon?" Martin would have felt a whole lot better, in truth, if the bank had been open. Then they would have been able to deposit the cash into the account they'd opened before transferring it to the second account in Jersey, as planned.

Somehow the thought of having all that money in the room with them made Martin kinda antsy. Still, they would sort it all out first thing in the morning, just as soon as the bank opened.

"What're we gonna do with all that money, Mart?"

"I dunno. Send it, I guess. But it's not only about buying stuff, is it? I mean, we'll have a lot more time from now on to do stuff."

"What kinda stuff?"

"I dunno—anything we want. I've always wanted to learn to ski, for instance. What about you, Bel?"

"I always wanted to go to the Copacabana. Sit there on the balcony of some hotel, and look out over the sea."

"Well, there's nothing to stop us from doing it."

"I dunno about you, Mart, but I'm feeling awfully horny."

"Maybe it's an aphrodisiac, Bel."

"What is? Getting rich, you mean?"

"Could be, couldn't it?"

"When I'm with you, Mart, I don't need any aphrodisiacs."

Martin kissed her and they began to tear each other's clothes off, and then Martin was in her and they really got into it.

Bella was sitting on top of Martin and riding him like he was a horse, and she threw her head back and cried out as she came. Then she fell forwards and lay on his chest. They were both hot and sweaty and happy.

"Mart, will you promise me one thing?"

"What?"

"Will you promise me that having money won't change you?"

"Course it won't, Bel."

"Promise."

"Okay, I promise."

"And we'll still both be happy and love each other, the way we do now?"

"We'll be a lot happier, because we won't have all the problems we used to have."

"Yeah, but we'll still love each other like now, I mean."

"Course we will. Why's having more money gonna change that?"

"I don't know. I never said I thought it would."

"Sounds like you're thinking it, though."

"No, it's not exac'ly that, Mart."

"What, then?"

"I just think we're gonna have to be careful, is all, and remember who we are and where we came from."

"Ain't no way I'm ever gonna forget that," Martin said.

Bella crossed her fingers behind her back.

"What time is it?" she asked him.

"Just gone five."

"Better set the alarm for early tomorrow, then, 'cause I'm feeling like I could sleep for a week."

❄

Martin reached to his side to push the little button that would silence the ringing sound, and a quick glance at the face of the clock told him it was still only 20:24 hours... which struck him as odd, because he distinctly remembered having set the alarm to go off at 07:30 hours the following morning.

Then he realized that he and Bella weren't alone in the room, because a woman he recognized from somewhere was standing by the side of the bed.

And she was carrying a gun.

He saw that the gun had a silencer attached to the end of it.

The woman said, "I took the trouble of resetting the alarm for you."

"It's *you*," Martin said.

Just then, Bella woke up. "Mona Chapman. What in the fuck are *you* doing here?"

"What does it look like?" Mona picked up the briefcase with the money in it.

Martin said, "How did you get into our room?"

"Little trick I picked up from my brother, Donny."

"But how did you know we'd be here?"

"Before he was killed, Donny told me Joey'd salted away the money from the bank robbery someplace," Mona said. "Then when you were shot, Bel darling, I got to thinking Ricky Red must be after you. I thought at the time that it must've been him that shot you to try and get at Joey, seeing as you were his wife."

"But I've been with Martin for over a year now," Bella said. "Joey's ancient history. I told you all about that."

"I know, but there was no reason Ricky should've known it."

Martin said, "But that still doesn't explain how you knew we were here."

"After Joey was murdered, Ricky Red paid me a visit. He told me about Joey's little trick of keeping a gun in the safe at the farmhouse, but Ricky said he'd been ready for him and he'd fired first. Ricky reckoned that might've been how Joey managed to surprise my brother."

"That was a pretty good guess."

"How would you know?"

"I saw it happen," Martin said. "I was living at Joey's flat with Bella when he was in prison, only what we weren't banking on was Joey B getting an early release like he did. Your brother knew about it, though, and he came to the flat and held me there at gunpoint, on the day Joey was let out.

"He introduced himself as The Dog and made me wait there with him until Joey showed. Then your brother made Joey open the safe, and it all happened just like Ricky said."

"What did Joey do with the body?"

"He forced me to help him carry it out and put it into the boot of my car, then he had me drive to a farmhouse in the countryside someplace. When we got there, he made me dig a grave. He was about to shoot me, too, and bury me along with your brother, once I'd finished digging, only Bella'd got wise to what was going on, and she'd come to the farmhouse. She saved my life by shooting at Joey from the bushes, and I was able to get away."

"Doesn't sound like you to be carrying a gun and shooting at people, Bel."

"You know what they say about desperate situations, Mona."

"Where'd you get the gun?"

"It was your brother's. When I entered the flat and saw it left there, I figured I might need it once I got to the farmhouse, so I took it with me..."

Martin said, "I'm sorry about what happened to your brother, Mona."

"So am I. He was my only brother and he was my hero. I always wanted to be like him, right from the time we were kids."

Bella said, "I still don't get how you found us here."

"Ricky told me about how you surprised him, Martin, after he'd killed Joey, by knocking him on the back of the head."

"So?"

"Ricky also said you took the papers from the safe."

"I wonder why Ricky should've told you all that?"

"He wanted to know if I could help him find you."

"But you had other ideas, is that it?"

"You're too right I did. My brother Donny gave his *life* for the money they got away with, and the way I see it, that means it belongs to me, as his sister, more than it does to anybody."

"The truth is, it doesn't belong to *anybody*, unless it belongs to the bank it was stolen from."

Bella said, "Why don't we do a deal, Mona?"

"You got some nerve. I always did like that about you."

"But if we do a deal, Mo, then that way we're all happy, right?"

"Yeah, but you're forgetting two things, Bella darling."

"What's that?"

"First, you two are lying in bed butt naked."

Bella said, "That's never stopped me from getting what I wanted in the past," at the same time as Martin said,

"And what's the second thing?"

"I'm the one holding the gun."

Mona turned and made for the door.

Seeing that she was about to make off with the money, Martin jumped out of bed and went after her.

Mona turned and fired a shot. It just missed Martin's head, and he hit the deck and scampered under a table.

Then Mona made her exit.

Along with the money.

CHAPTER 33

Preston and Johnson had been hot on the trail of Martin and Bella all the way from London to Geneva, and then on to Barcelona.

And they were outside of the Ritz, in the Seat they'd rented, when someone else that Johnson recognized came out through the front exit.

"Just look who it isn't, guv."

"What? Should I know her?"

"She was in the audience at the Revuebar with her girlfriend when Bella Armando was shot."

"*Was* she now? Can't say I remember her."

"I was the one who interviewed her."

"Well they say it's a small world."

"Yeah, but it's not *that* small, guv."

"Just what I'm thinking, Dave. And I see that she's carrying a briefcase…"

"Wonder what's in it?"

"Somewhere in the region of three million quid would be my guess, minus however much Joey B's already spent." Preston started the engine up as the woman hopped into a taxi.

"Hurry up or we'll lose her."

Preston set off and they followed the taxi as far as the Paseo de

Gracia, where it pulled over. The woman got out and dashed into a café.

Johnson went to get out of the car, but Preston told him to stay put. "What? Aren't we gonna go in and arrest her, guv?"

"And create a scene in the middle of a cafe in Barcelona?"

"If need be. Why—what's wrong with that?"

"We'd have the local police breathing down our necks, and a lot of explaining to do."

"We will have anyway, though, won't we? Unless you're planning on arresting the woman without the local cops finding out?"

"Did I say that, Dave?"

"You didn't say anything, guv. You just gave me that look of yours instead."

"What *look*?"

"You know, the one where you raise your left eyebrow."

"Aren't you reading rather a lot into what I do with my eyebrows?"

"Look—she's just got off her stool. Where's she going now?"

"Probably just going to the loo."

"What if she's going out the back way?"

"Okay, Dave, I'm beginning to think you're right—let's go in and get her."

No sooner had they got out of the car than a taxi came and pulled up outside of the café, and the woman came out through the front door. As she did so, a large lorry came along and blocked her from view. By the time the lorry moved past, the taxi was gone.

"Fuck it, guv, she's disappeared." Johnson turned to look at Preston, and saw that he was running back to the car.

Johnson set off after him.

He got to the car and jumped into the passenger seat as Preston was starting the engine up, and they set off.

"Where did she go, guv?"

"She's in that cab up ahead."

Preston put his foot down, but then he had to brake at a crossing as the lights changed and he lost sight of the taxi. He hit the steering wheel and cursed, as beads of sweat coursed down the back of his neck.

The lights turned green, and Preston set off again and put his foot down. And it wasn't long before he had the taxi back in his sights once more. They traversed Plaza Cataluña and followed the taxi off left, dodging cars on either of side. The taxi took a sharp right at speed, its back wheels skidding as it did so. Preston stayed hot on its tail, zigzagging through the narrow streets, until they came out by the Arc de Triomphe.

The taxi veered off left along Pujades, by the side of the Ciudadella Park, and Preston had to swerve to avoid hitting a young lad on a moped as he turned the corner. He managed to keep the taxi in his sights as it took another sharp left, then followed it through a red light and on, over a bridge. He zigzagged through some more streets until they eventually came out by Gaudi's famous cathedral, La Sagrada Familia, where Preston was forced to stop for some tourists who were crossing the road, and he lost sight of the taxi. Then saw it again, after he'd taken the next corner. And he carried on zigzagging his way through the narrow, winding streets in hot pursuit, until he saw the taxi pull over just up ahead, and the woman got out.

Preston screeched to a halt, and he and Johnson jumped out and chased her over to the entrance to the bullring, which was milling with people. Preston flashed his ID at the man on the gate, and barked out the word "*Polizei*".

The man gave him a blank look, and DS Johnson said, "*Policía inglés.*"

"*Si, si, policía,*" replied the man on the gate, "*pase, pase.*"

Preston and Johnson went in and joined the crowd that was making its way along the concourses. It was impossible to see very far ahead at first. But then when they entered the seating area, they had a better view of what was going on around them.

"There she is look, guv." Johnson pointed some ten or twelve rows behind them.

She was only a matter of thirty feet away, but the next moment she was gone. Preston and Johnson were left chasing their own tails—until Preston happened to catch sight of her leaving the bullring via one of the concourses.

They gave chase but had to keep dodging latecomers who were still making their way to their seats, and they went out through the exit just in time to see the woman climb into another taxi.

Preston and Johnson ran back to their car and jumped in. Preston started up the engine and they set off once more. They followed the taxi over a bridge, and zigzagged through more windy cobbled streets at speed, narrowly missing a woman with a pram at one point.

They passed shops and cafes and lots of elegant old buildings with louvered shutters, none of which they noticed. Then they found themselves driving down the Ramblas, and they followed the taxi off right at the bottom into the *barrio chino*. This was a rundown part of the city, home to a thousand and one dives and brothels, and women were standing around on street corners in skirts that were provocatively short.

Just then, the taxi came to a halt, and the suspect hopped out and dashed into a bar. Preston pulled over, and he and Johnson jumped out of the Seat and ran in after her.

The place was crowded, flamenco music was playing, and the air reeked of marijuana. Preston lost sight of the woman for a moment in the crowd of bodies. Then he saw her again. She was climbing over the bar.

Preston pushed his way through huddles of bodies, and managed to grab hold of the suspect's leg. He pulled her off the counter, down onto the wooden floor, then he got on top of her. She tried to fight him off, but Preston was too strong for her and he pulled her arms behind her back.

"I'm DCI Preston," he said. "You're under arrest."

"*Vete a tomar por el culo!*"

Preston didn't need to know Spanish to realize that the woman had just told him to fuck off. "Show me some ID... identification ... passport."

"In pocket," the woman said in English.

Preston got the woman up on her feet and she handed him her ID card. The name on the card was Marta Sánchez.

※

Martin and Bella threw some clothes on and hammered it down to the lobby after Mona, the moment she left their room with the money.

They stepped out into the street just in time to see her climb into the back of a taxi. "There she is," Martin said, and he and Bella ran to their rented Volkswagen, which was parked just up the street.

They jumped in, and Martin started up the engine. "Where's the taxi?" he said. "Fuck it, we've lost her."

Bella pointed ahead. "It went in that direction."

Martin set off and put his foot down.

Bella said, "Follow that red Seat."

"What red Seat?"

"It's in front of this black car. See it?"

"Yeah ... but what do I want to follow the Seat for?"

"The Seat's following Mona."

"What makes you so sure?"

"I saw it take off after her."

"Who's in it?"

"Can't see," Bella said.

Then when they pulled up at some traffic lights, she said, "There's two men in it ..."

"Not that DCI Preston and his mate, is it, Bel?"

"Could be."

"Yes, it is ... it's *them*."

They followed the Seat down to the Paseo de Gracia and saw it pull over at the curb.

Martin drove on, then passed two more parked cars and pulled over. "Where's Mona?"

"There she is, look ... She's just gone into that café over there." Bella turned to look at Martin. "Now what?"

"We wait."

Minutes later, they saw a woman who was dressed identically to Mona, and of the same build, emerge from the café.

"There she is," Martin said.

"Hang on a minute."

"What?"

"It's not her."

"What d'you mean, it isn't her, Bel? Looks like her to me."

"That's the point."

"Huh?"

"She's *supposed* to look like her, Mart, but it's not her."

"She's a decoy, you mean?"

"Exactly."

"How can you tell?"

"See the way she walks ...?"

"What about it?"

"She walks like a *woman* ..."

"So?"

"Mona walks like a guy."

So Martin and Bella stayed put, and watched the two detectives fall for the stunt Mona had pulled and go careering after the decoy.

"You've gotta hand it to Mona," Bella said. "She sure isn't stupid."

"No, but neither are we."

Minutes later, Mona emerged from the café. Martin got out of the car and went up behind her and said, "Nice to see you again." Then saw the anger and surprise in her eyes when she turned.

"Better not make a scene, Mona, 'cause this time I'm the one who has the gun," he said. "It's right here, in my pocket. I won't use it, just so long as you do as I say. Now if you'd be good enough to give me back my briefcase?"

No sooner had he said this, than Martin noticed a chunky, bald man, dressed in jeans and a leather jacket, coming towards them. At that moment, the man reached into his pocket and brought out a gun.

Mona said, "What took you so long to find me, Ricky?"

"No time to stop and chat, Mo. Just give me the briefcase. Nice'n easy does it."

Mona threw the briefcase at him.

Ricky Red fired. The force of the bullet threw Mona backwards. Her gun fell from her pocket as she hit the pavement, and she reached out and grabbed it.

Meanwhile, Ricky had picked up the briefcase. He turned to shoot Martin, but before he could pull the trigger, Mona fired.

The shot hit Ricky in the chest and he went down.

Ricky jerked a couple of times, like a fish out of water. Then he stopped moving and a glazed expression came into his eyes. Martin reached down and took the briefcase from his hand.

Then he turned and looked at Bella.

She was trying to give Mona the kiss of life.

"C'mon, Bel, let's get away from here before the cops show."

"But Mona needs a doctor."

"Fuck it, Bel, we'll go to prison if they catch us."

"She's a mate of mine, though, Mart, when all's said and done," Bella sobbed. "We can't just leave her here to die."

At that moment, a man who happened to be passing stopped to look at Mona as she lay there.

"Doctor," Bella said to the man. "Call doctor."

"Si," the man said and he took out his mobile.

Martin and Bella made themselves scarce.

❄

Preston and DS Johnson arrived on the scene of the shoot-out sometime later.

"Just look who it isn't," Preston said.

"Don't tell me. It's Ricky Red, guv, right?"

Preston nodded. "I don't think I've ever been more relieved to see a corpse."

"Dead bodies did have a way of piling up whenever he was around."

"There are six or seven murders I had him figured for and probably more we don't know about."

"Would've been a lot more in future, too, guv, if he'd lived, you can be sure of that."

CHAPTER 34

4 *8 hours later.*

"I think a toast might be in order, Bel, don't you?"

"Let's drink to being in love and staying rich."

"Sounds like a good idea," Martin said, and they clinked glasses.

Then they both tasted their champagne.

"So here we are, Bel, the place you said you'd always wanted to come to."

"I feel like we're living the dream, Mart."

They were sitting out on the balcony of their room at the Hilton, in Rio, watching the sun go down into the sea.

To get to Rio, they'd driven down to Algeciras and taken the ferry over to Ceuta. From there, they'd taken a train to Casablanca and flown via Miami. And now they were here, they couldn't see any reason why they shouldn't stay for a while and enjoy themselves.

"Your friend Mona thought she'd outwitted us, but we're a lot cleverer than she was reckoning on." Martin kissed Bella on the lips, but the next moment she pulled away.

"What's the matter, Bel?"

"Nothing."

"I can see you're worried about something … why don't you just tell me what it is?"

"D'you reckon Mona made it all right, Mart?"

"I'm sure she did."

"You're only saying that to make me feel better."

"Well that's just where you're wrong, as it happens." Martin reached down and snatched up the Times from the coffee table, before he began to read from it aloud.

The article he read started by talking about the bank job that was perpetrated three years ago by Joey B, along with The Dog and Ricky Red. It took in the mysterious deaths of Mona's brother and Joey B, as well as that of one of the warders at Wandsworth Prison, the girl who'd gone into Ricky Red's cell to give him "English lessons", and a couple of Arabs (one of whom had been very rich), before it went on to talk about the murder of Ricky Red in a shoot-out in a street in Barcelona. It wound up by reassuring the reader that Mona Chapman was now safe behind bars in Wandsworth Prison, where she was to serve ten years for Ricky's murder.

"At least she survived," Bella said. "I'd have hated it if she'd died."

"Oh she's safe all right."

Safe in prison, he thought.

❇

Preston took Sally out to the local Indian that evening. He kept gazing at her all through the meal and thinking what a lucky man he was, while she tried to get him to explain to her the ins and outs of the case he'd been working on.

When he'd finished telling her about it, Preston had an urge to ask Sally to marry him. But then he thought of the mess he'd made of things the first time around, with Anne, and bit his tongue. Maybe they should just carry on the way they were going for a while, and then he could pop the question sometime later when he'd got over his fear of what marriage might do to them.

After all, it was still early days and there was no reason to rush things.

. . .

Two months later, Wandsworth Prison.

"Will you wait for me, Win?"

"Of course I will, Mo. I was waiting for you all my life up until the time I met you, so what's a few more years?"

"It's gonna be ten years, *ten fucking years*. I really don't know if I can reasonably ask you to wait that long. It doesn't seem right."

"I'd wait for you forever, Mo, if I had to." Winifred reached across the table and their fingertips touched. But then the warder looked over and coughed in a certain way, and they both drew back.

"Anyway, Mo, it won't be ten years, will it, because you'll be able to get it knocked down to five with good behaviour, won't you?

"Good behaviour. That hardly sounds like *me*, now does it, Win?"

They both giggled, but there was a terrible sadness on their faces.

"How's John taken the news that you're divorcing him?"

"Oh, he'll be all right." Winifred dried her eyes. "He was a little upset when I first told him, but I think he's over it now. In fact, I think he's finding consolation in the arms of his secretary."

"Only goes to show that you can't trust them as far as you can throw them."

"Who are you talking about, Mo—politicians, or men in general?"

"Both. They all want to have their cake and eat it."

"Well he's not having *this* particular cake any more, I can assure you of that."

"No, but neither am I, though, Win, and that's all I care about."

"Oh don't get like that, Mo." Winifred began to cry. "I swear you'll break my heart if you carry on in that way."

"All I'm trying to say is that I love you, Win."

"And I love you, too, Mo."

"That's all that really matters in the end, isn't it?"

"Of course it is." Winifred sobbed. "Of course it is."

Le Caprice, Central London: the same day

. . .

"It seems they want you to lead the Party into the next election, Alex."

"I certainly have my supporters, Pru darling, it's true."

"Have you given any thought to who you are going to have in your Cabinet?"

"Well I've already pencilled in my brother Charles as the next Chancellor of the Exchequer."

"It's good to know that we'll have a nice neighbour living next door to us, Alex."

"It's no more than he deserves. It was terrible the way they forced him to resign like that."

"*Medieval* is the word, if you ask me."

Sir Alex sipped his wine, and he looked at his wife over the rim of his glass. "Are you sure it's the right thing to do, though, Pru?"

"If *what* is the right thing to do?"

"What I mean is, do you think I should agree to be the next leader of the Party?"

"But of course, Alex. How can you even *ask* such a thing? This is what you've been working and hoping for all of your life, isn't it?"

"I suppose you're right."

"*Well*, then...?"

"Don't ask me why, dear, but now that the opportunity to lead the Party into the next election actually beckons, somehow it no longer seems so very important to me."

"But you're sure to win the election, Alex—you only have to look at the opinion polls. You'll *be the next prime minister*. Just imagine."

"Yes, now there's a thought."

"You don't sound as excited by the prospect as I thought you would."

"It isn't that, exactly."

"What on earth is it, then?"

"I suppose you could say that I've changed."

"*Changed*, darling ... in what way?"

"I've come to understand what really matters to me."

"What the devil do you mean?"

"I've come to realize you're more important to me than anything, my darling."

"What tosh, Alex."

"No, really, dear. I mean it."

"Do you honestly expect me to believe that if you had to choose between being this country's next prime minister and our marriage, you'd choose our marriage?"

"I suppose that what I'm doing is asking for your opinion, Pru."

"You mean you want me to tell you whether I'm for or against the idea?"

"Something like that."

"On what basis?"

"On the basis of whether it will be good for us and our marriage."

"But we have the country to think of, Alex. We can't just go about our lives like other people, darling. You're a man who is in a position of power and great responsibility."

He gave her hand a tender squeeze. "Pru darling, the whole point of what I'm saying is that we are indeed *just* like any other couple, and as such, we're free to live as we wish to."

"So you mean to say that you won't go for the leadership if I don't want you to?"

"That's exactly what I'm saying, dear."

"That's just about the nicest thing you've ever said to me, Alex, in all these years of marriage."

The MP's lips curved in a shy smile.

"But why the sudden change in your attitude after all these years, may I ask, Alex?"

"As I said, I think it's just a case of my having matured and come to realize what's really important to me in life, Pru—and it's you ... *us* ... and what we have together, my darling."

Prunella wondered if there was something her husband wasn't telling her even as she beamed with pleasure.

She was still wondering when the waiter arrived with the second course.

The End

ONLY THE LONELY

ONLY THE LONELY

Sir George risked a peek at the young man standing under the next faucet along in the shower, and what he saw made him catch his breath.

So *beautiful*, he thought...and hung like a donkey.

Sir George stood there rubbing soap over his bulging belly, telling himself he must behave.

After all, I'm a government minister now, he thought. I can't just do what I want.

Besides, he was a happily married man, too.

Or was *supposed* to be.

Margaret would crucify him if he were to do anything daft.

Not only that but it would break her heart.

The important thing was not to get a stiffy. Sir George was sure the young man next to him was gay, too, but even so there were three other men standing under the faucets on the opposite wall...

Maybe if I wait here until they go, and if the young man stays here, then I'll just play it by ear, he caught himself thinking.

He turned his back to the young man and went back to soaping himself, then turned and risked another peek at the man's manhood, which really was a magnificent piece of work.

As Sir George looked up, he and the young lad made eye contact.

There was a knowing smile in the young man's eyes, and an unspoken communication passed between the two men.

Cheeky young buck, Sir George caught himself thinking.

But he was such a *hunk*, though...

Just then, one of the men on the opposite wall left the shower, and he was quickly followed by one of the other two men...Sir George's heart began to pound in his chest. He was filled with a wild, uncontrollable excitement.

The important thing is not to get a stiffy, he told himself once more.

Not *yet*, anyway...

To think that less than an hour ago, Sir George had earned the applause of many of the bank benchers who were loyal to him in the House, with a stirring speech on the state of the economy.

It irritated him that he had to keep up the pretence of being someone he wasn't all the time. Act the role of loyal husband, when he hadn't touched his wife in ten years...

Right now, he thought, all I want is this young stud standing a few feet away from me, and I'd give anything to have him.

Anything? he wondered.

That was a big word.

But he was sick of all the hypocrisy. His own, as well as that of the nation...and having to play up to the stupid idea they had in mind of what their leaders should be like.

Sick to the back teeth.

Just then, the man in the corner turned off the faucet he'd been under and left the shower room. That left just Sir George and the young hunk he'd taken a fancy to.

Shall I or shan't I? he asked himself.

He figured he'd wait and see if the young man made the first move.

He glanced at the young man as these thoughts passed through his mind, and the lad turned so that he was facing Sir George. They made eye contact again, and if there had been any last vestige of a doubt before, now it was clear that they understood each other.

The lad took a step forward, then reached out his hand and took Sir George's penis in his hand.

Sir George found himself becoming erect in an instant, and the next thing he knew, he was in the young man's arms...

. . .

Melanie's mobile began to ring, and she took it out of her imitation Kelly bag and snapped it open. "Hello, Joanne...what do you want?"

"That's a nice way to talk to the girl you once said you loved."

Melanie said, "That was a long time ago, Jo."

"It was last fucking week."

"Exactly..."

"What's changed, though, Mel?"

"How do you mean?"

"Well if you loved me a week ago, then how is it you don't love me now...?"

"Things are different now."

"How are they...?"

"Well for one thing, you haven't got your tongue five inches up my pussy, and you did when I said I loved you...does that answer your question...?"

"Is that all I am to you, Mel...? Just something to pick up and put down when you fancy?"

"There's plenny a people'd be only too happy for me to use them that way, I'll tell you, Jo...now why don't you stop being such a soppy bitch."

"But I thought we had something together, Mel...something special..."

"We did, Jo...it's called hot sex, and it was exciting as all hell – which this conversation sure ain't."

"You're a cruel bitch, Mel, do you know that...?"

"Take it or leave it, Jo... I never made any secret of the fact that I'm am Amazon goddess..."

"Yeah, but I thought you were *my* Amazon goddess, Mel..."

Melanie could hear the tears in Joanne's voice, and the intensity of her suffering only made Melanie want to hurt her all the more.

"Truth is, I'm in love, Jo."

"Tell me who the bitch is... I want her address... I'll go to her house and fucking well kill her..."

"It isn't a *she* it's a *he*..."

Joanne began to blub down the line.

"Well I never made any secret of the fact that I'm bi, Jo."

The line went dead.

Linda Houseman craned her neck and looked at her psychotherapist, John Emmet, who was a tall, slim man with handsome chiselled features, dressed in an elegant new blue suit. "My life's turned upside down recently, as you know..."

"Ever since your husband's book became a best seller, you mean?"

"Yes...the money's poured in and I should really be having the time of my life, but I'm not..."

"Perhaps you could tell me why you think that is, Linda...?"

"I wish I knew."

"How is your relationship with your husband going?"

"It *isn't* really."

"Tell me about him."

"Oh, he's middle-aged, balding, thickening around the waist..." No dress sense, she might have added but didn't.

And not at all handsome and gorgeous like you, she caught herself thinking.

"But as a person, I mean...?"

"He's working most of the time."

"Perhaps you could tell me a little about your sex life...?"

You sure don't beat about the bush, mister, Linda thought, and said, "What about it?"

The press would have a field day if they could see me now, Sir George Parker thought, as he stood there naked and in the arms of this handsome young hunk he didn't know from Adam.

They were French kissing and the young man was holding Sir George's dick and playing with it. Sir George took the young man's dick in his hand, or some of it, anyway, because it was so big... It's a monstrosity, he thought. But it's so *beautiful*.

The young man pulled away from him and placed his hands on Sir George's shoulders, and Sir George went down on his knees...

. . .

"Our sex life is nothing much to write home about, if I'm honest," Linda Houseman said. "And as I say, it doesn't help that Bob's so obsessed with his work all of the time."

"When was the last time you were...intimate...?"

"Oh, it would've been a few nights ago now."

"Perhaps you'd care to tell me about it...?"

"I'm really not accustomed to talking about this sort of thing."

"Well you need to understand that your reason for coming here is to get at what is going on deep down inside you," Doctor Emmet said. "And that means leaving aside the mask you wear in your day to day social life...leaving aside all the little petty pretences...and talking about the things you would never say to anyone... If you're going to make any progress, then you need to let it all hang out, as it were, and uncover the real you...so that we can see what's really going on in your unconscious mind..."

Wouldn't you like to know, Linda Houseman thought.

The posh vixen type, Melanie thought, as she watched Linda Houseman go out. Slim and elegantly dressed in her linen skirt and matching jacket, nice slim legs with neat ankles, and with her blonde hair done in a pretty cool bob, the woman was, Melanie reckoned, just the sort Emmet would go for.

The bitch had better not go near him, though, she said to herself, because I'd scratch her eyes out.

The door opened again, and John – or Doctor Emmet, to give him his professional title – popped his head out. "Anyone called?"

"Your two o'clock's asked if she can rearrange her session for another time."

"She's just looking for excuses."

"Excuses for what...?"

"Not to come here...she's terrified of facing up to her phobias."

"What shall I tell her?"

"I'll call her myself later."

"You gonna buy me lunch?"

Emmet frowned. "It'll have to be a Chinese."

"Have I sunk that low in your estimation, John?"

"What...?"

"There was a time when you used to take me to classy places in Mayfair."

"That's just for special occasions, Melanie."

"Why is it I get the feeling you're going cold on me?"

***

The young man helped Sir George to his feet, before he gently shoved him against the wall, and the next thing Sir George knew was the agonizing and heart-stopping joy of having the young man enter him.

Sir George groaned and cried with joy as the young man thrust in and out of him, and it wasn't long before Sir George reached a shattering, blissful orgasm, and moments later he felt the young man's sperm shoot up inside him.

***

As Linda Houseman climbed into her Mercedes, her thoughts were full of the session she'd just had with Doctor Emmet.

She felt a little ashamed of herself, talking about her husband the way she had to another man...but she felt as though she'd got a weight off her chest, too.

Talking about her marriage in that way, so honestly and openly, had enabled her to crystallize her thoughts.

Things just can't carry on like this, she said to herself.

She wondered if she and Bob, her husband, were on the slow slide towards a divorce, as she started the engine up and headed off up Harley Street...

***

Joanne Parks stormed into the bathroom and found a packet of twenty paracetamols, and she was about to woof them all down... But then she dropped the packet, and went and got her camera and left the house.

Creativity often came to her at times like this, when she was close to breaking point, or when she'd been thinking of ending it all... She jumped on her Kawasaki and stormed off through the streets of Fulham, then pulled up and got off in the street that runs along the side of Hurlingham Park, and began filming anything that took her fancy.

She saw a sparrow pecking at something on the pavement and filmed it.

A couple of kids who were bunking off school came along, and she filmed them as they went past.

The kids turned and watched her as she did so. Then one of them said, "Oi? What d'you fink yer doin' ya silly bitch? Don't ya know tha's illegal?"

Joanne just kept filming them, and the boy who'd spoken was all for coming and grabbing her camera off her. Or trying to. Not that the prospect worried Joanne too much, what with her being a black belt in Taekwondo, and she was sure she could handle these two. A part of her even welcomed a bit of rough and tumble, given the mood she was in.

After the way Melanie had pissed her off, it might be a good way to let off steam, and sweat out a few negative emotions.

"D'you'ear what I said?" the boy said to her.

From the way he spoke, Melanie could tell the boy must go to one of the local comps.

She just kept filming him as he came towards her.

But then the boy's friend said, "Leave it, Duane...silly bitch ain't worth it."

The boy who wanted trouble, Duane, stopped and looked back at his friend over his shoulder, apparently in two minds. Then a squad car came crawling around the corner, and the boy turned on his heel and made off down the street like nothing had happened.

Melanie kept filming him all the while.

When he got to the corner, the boy stopped and turned once more. And seeing that Melanie was still filming him, he gave her the middle finger.

Melanie stopped filming and played back the little piece of cinema in miniature she had just created.

It was pretty good, she thought. Real, gritty, full of tension and the threat of violence...just like real life.

That was because it *was* real life, of course.

Real life on the streets of London, where the people could often be crude or threatening, and at times outright violent.

You can feel the tension in the air at times just walking down the street in this city, she thought.

Any street.

Even in the posh areas.

Maybe even more so in the posh areas, because they reeked of money – real money...and where there was an excess of money, there was always a hint of violence and treachery and deceit in the air. Something that was hard to define in words, Joanne thought, but you could *feel* it.

"If my work's about anything," she'd told Melanie one time, "it's about the hum of life and energy and violence that you can feel in the air just walking down the street... It's about living in this crazy, bloody wonderful and fucking awful city."

Melanie had just shrugged when she'd said that, and then she told her she was a crazy bitch.

Sir George left the gym and climbed in behind the wheel of his Bentley. He was feeling invigorated but his muscles were aching.

That was quite some workout, he thought, and smiled as he set off up New Cavendish Street.

He glanced in his mirror as he took a right, and saw a red Lexus behind him make the turning, too, but thought nothing of it. He took the next left, and then took a right into Wimpole Street, and found that the Lexus was still right behind him.

Glancing in his mirror again, he saw that there were two men in the Lexus, both of them wearing leather jackets and shades.

Fucking paparazzi, Sir George thought.

"Well, you're too late, my friends," he said, and chuckled. "If only you'd been back there in the shower room, you'd have seen some action...by golly you would."

He turned into the street where he lived, and the Lexus stayed on his tail and went crawling past as Sir George pulled up outside of his house. He waved and grinned at the two men in the Lexus as they went past, still enjoying the private joke he'd been sharing with himself, then killed the engine and climbed out.

To his surprise, the Lexus pulled up a little way down, and the two men got out.

They weren't carrying cameras, either, Sir George noted.

Oh well, they're not going to get a story out of me, if that's what they think, he thought, as he turned and headed up the steps at the front of his Georgian mansion. And he was just about to put the key in the door, when he felt someone's hand on his shoulder. He turned and found himself looking into a hard thuggish face. Some of the riffraff that work for the newspapers nowadays, Sir George thought. Why, it almost beggars belief.

"We need to talk," the man said in a rough Cockney accent.

"Wrong...you mean *you* need to, but *I* don't."

The second man was now coming up the steps.

"I do have one question for you, though," Sir George said. "If you paparazzi chappies are so keen on peering into other people's private lives, why is it you wear shades when it's not even sunny...? You got such a bad conscience you're frightened of people looking into your eyes?"

The man brought out a handgun, and held it in front of his belly. "I don't fink you heard me," the man said. "We need to talk to you."

"What is this...?"

"It's a gun and it's loaded."

"But what do you want...?"

"We can talk in the car."

The man jerked the hand he had the gun in, and Sir George put his keys in his pocket and went back down the steps

Joanne was riding along Wimpole Street, on her way to have it out face to face with Melanie, when she decided to get off her Kawasaki and continue on foot, since the practice in Harley Street was only a short walk away. She figured she'd do a little more filming as she went along, as a prologue to the main event.

The main event being the showdown she was going to have with Melanie, which she also intended to film.

She figured she'd build up a little dramatic tension doing it like this, the way the best directors do...instead of plunging straight into the main scene at the beginning...

So she padlocked her Kawasaki and set about filming anything that took her fancy as she walked along.

She filmed a couple of businessmen as they went by in their smart pinstripes.

She filmed a woman who went by with a frown on her face and muttering under her breath.

And then she saw just the image she was looking for.

It was perfect.

This is *it*, Joanne thought.

This is just *so* what I've been after...

This just sums up what life is like in this city...

And she began to film what she saw.

What she filmed was a man who must have been well into his fifties walking along the pavement flanked by two younger men. What made the image so spectacular was the fact that the older man could have been no more than five foot six, so that he barely came up to the shoulders of the men on either side of him.

And then there was the way they were dressed. The little man was wearing an elegant navy blue suit that looked pure Savile Row, a pink shirt, and black shoes (probably from Church's), while the guys who flanked him were both wearing jeans, Nike trainers, leather jackets and shades. One of the men had his head shaved and the other had his brown hair cut short.

This was...she struggled to think of how to describe it...

It was Danny DeVito, only dressed more like Fred Astaire, meets Vinnie Jones and his brother.

If Vinnie Jones had a brother.

Yeah, Joanne thought, something along those lines...

Classic...

See it in a film and you wouldn't believe it, but here it was, right before her eyes...just one of the many crazy scenes that the streets of London threw at the unsuspecting eye...

This was why London was such a great city to live and create art in.

London's just where everything's at, Joanne thought, as she continued to film the three men, walking behind them now as they headed down the pavement...

They stopped when they got to the red Lexus. "In the back," said the one with the gun, and Sir George tried to make a dash for it.

But the two men blocked his path and bundled him into the back of the car.

"What the fuck is this?" Sir George barked.

"Shut up."

. . .

And Joanne saw everything...

Not only did she see it all, but she'd got it down on film.

They're kidnapping him, she thought.

Her heart was pumping like a lunatic as she continued to film the scene.

Anyone else would have realized the thing to do was stop filming and get away...but Joanne wasn't *anyone else*.

The artist in her overrode the ordinary citizen.

It overrode the nice well brought-up young woman with all of her insecurities...

And then, as she continued to watch through the viewfinder, she saw that one of the kidnappers was looking at her from the back seat of the car...and she knew that it was now time to stop filming and make herself scarce, as the man jumped out of the car and came running up the pavement towards her.

Joanne was shaking like a leaf and filled with adrenaline, as she put her camera back into the pannier. The man was only a few feet from her now, and she was praying that the engine would start up first time, as she turned the key in the ignition.

One more stride and the man would grab her...but the engine fired, and Joanne pulled away and went speeding up the street. As she approached the corner she saw the Lexus coming after her in her mirror, and she zigzagged her way through the back streets with the car right behind her... Then she turned into New Cavendish Street, which was chock-a-block with traffic, and she was able to weave her way through and make her getaway...

Linda Houseman went for her next session with her psychotherapist two days later, and Doctor Emmet kicked off by asking her what she had been up to since he'd last seen her. "I dunno," she said, "the usual, you know."

"Shopping...?"

She glanced sideways at him from where she lay on the couch and grinned. "How did you guess...?"

"Retail therapy is the term, I believe – and with good reason I often think." Doctor Emmet smiled and waited for her to go on.

"I bought myself a pair of Lee jeans...the ones I've got on now, actually, and some Jimmy Choo shoes, and a couple of silk tops from a nice little shop on Bond Street, and then I bought some underwear from Agent Provocateur..." She broke off, telling herself he could make of that what he would.

Doctor Emmet said nothing and silence filled the room, diluted only by the distant rumble of traffic from over on Marylebone Road.

"I like to buy things...is that so abnormal?"

"No, not at all."

"Tell me about the underwear..."

"What about it?"

"It's sexy underwear, I take it?"

"That's the general idea."

"Who are you trying to excite?"

She looked at him, surprised. "Bob, I guess..."

"Did you succeed?"

Cheeky bastard, she thought, and said, "Wouldn't you like to know..."

She wasn't going to tell him about how Bob had tried to make love to her the night before but had been unable to, and how she'd ended up masturbating herself. She knew that he was dying to hear all the juicy details. She could feel those intelligent blue eyes of his boring into her mind, searching for secrets...

It's as if he knows it all anyway, without my telling him, she caught herself thinking.

Then dismissed the idea from her mind as nonsensical.

Linda Houseman was trembling all over as she stepped into the street, and she had no idea why.

She realized that she was feeling angry with her psychotherapist... almost as if she felt he'd got one over on her.

It was a game of cat and mouse they were playing, and she would be damned if she was going to let him win...

Except that she was paying for the pleasure of coming and lying on his couch once a week and talking about herself.

She entered a café and ordered a large latte, then smoked three cigarettes, one after another, while she drank it.

That ruined her plans to pack up.

She'd gone six days without smoking until now.

Six days – and here she was messing it all up.

She felt guilty and full of self-loathing, so she smoked another, just to spite herself.

Then she paid the bill and drove over to New Bond Street, where she figured she'd do a little window shopping, just to get her nerves under control.

She saw a dress she liked, a delightful little pink number.

So she went in and said she'd like to try it on...

And ended up buying it.

For a mere £248.

A bargain at that price, she thought, as she walked back to her car.

The Housemans were both at home that evening. Linda was sitting alone on the sofa reading, while her husband worked on his new book in his study.

Linda found herself reading the same paragraph three times, because her thoughts kept drifting off...

I'm in love with him, she thought.

She set her book aside, her mind full of thoughts of Emmet. She pictured herself in his arms...imagined him kissing her, and then taking her on the couch at his practice... Her passion for her psychotherapist had swept over her like some huge tsunami, carrying everything in its path.

Just then, her husband, Bob, a balding man of forty-five with big sorrowful brown eyes and an expanding waistline, came into the living room. "What's for dinner?"

"There's some pasta in the kitchen."

"I saw it...it's cold."

"D'you want me to heat it up?"

"No...I'll make myself a sandwich."

The phone rang, and Linda made to get up but her husband got it. "Hello?"

No answer.

"Hello?"

He hung up. "Fucking nuisance caller."

Linda wondered if it was John that called.

John...there I go using his first name when I think about him, she thought, even though I've never actually used it in talking to him.

Bob Houseman went out into the kitchen, and came back in minutes later with a tuna sandwich.

"How's your book going?"

"I can't seem to make any headway with it."

Later in bed, he ran his hand down her back and Linda stiffened to his touch.

She figured if she didn't turn to face him, he'd get the message.

He got it all right.

She fell asleep and woke in the night to find him lying on his back next to her, masturbating.

She feigned sleep, as she lay there thinking about John Emmet.

John...

Burning for him...

Joanne had been keeping a low profile ever since she'd filmed the kidnapping. At first she figured she ought to go to the police and show them the film.

But then she figured that might not be such a good idea.

The kidnappers looked like they were pretty serious types...and they'd probably come after her, and maybe they'd kill her, if she testified against them.

On the other hand, she thought, if I do nothing, what'll happen to the man who was kidnapped?

She thought about this for a while and figured the kidnappers must have kidnapped the man for a reason...in which case, they'd contact the man's family and demand a ransom...

Then the family would either pay up or go to the police...

If they paid up, then the man would be set free, hopefully.

And if they went to the police, then it would be up to the men in blue to handle it...

Joanne figured the only sensible option was to do nothing.

Unless she wanted to get herself killed.

As for what to do about Melanie, she figured it might be time to go into one of her long sulks...

"What did your husband say when you told him you want a divorce?" Dr. John Emmet asked Linda Houseman, when she went for her next session.

"He said he'd fight to keep the kids."

"How do you feel about that?"

"How do you *think* I feel?" Linda looked up from the couch. "Listen," she said, "I know you think I'm a no-good bitch, but I love my kids, okay?"

"How much do you love them?"

"That's the sort of love you can't put a price on."

"Meaning there are other kinds of love that you can?"

"Yeah."

Doctor Emmet smiled. "Your honesty when talking of these matter is a good sign."

"Don't get above yourself, mister."

"My patients normally call me Doctor."

"Yeah, well I stopped coming here as a patient long ago, and we both know it."

"I think I explained all about transference, Linda, and the way—"

"Fuck transference and its mother when she's at home."

"Linda, I understand you're upset..."

"Why don't you just cut the bullshit, John, and come over here."

She lifted her bottom off the couch, and worked her black skirt up around her waist. She wasn't wearing panties.

"You know you want it, John, so take a bit of your own advice and stop kidding yourself."

Doctor Emmet buried his face in her matted bush.

"*Fuck me*, John," Linda murmured, and he climbed on top of her.

Then he was in her and lunging away with that great lump of meat he had down there.

This is what I've been missing, Linda thought.

Then she came.

And *boy* did she come. It really was quite a performance. Rather like yodelling, only with the musical edge shorn off...

. . .

Afterwards, the Doc—*John* as she now thought of him—invited Linda for a drink at a bar in Mayfair. The place was all wicker chairs, marble-topped tables and soft lighting. There was a sophisticated crowd in, and the murmur of subdued chatter purred in the air.

Linda eyed Emmet over the rim of her cocktail glass. "Do you seduce all of your female patients, Doc?"

"No...God knows I've had plenty of offers from attractive women in the past, but I've always managed to resist – and please do drop this Doc stuff and call me John..."

"Okay, John..." She put her glass back down on its little mat, and gazed into his eyes. "So why *me*...?"

Emmet hardly knew what the true answer to this question was. The way she'd looked when she worked her skirt up like that...with the sun coming in through the window and those shapely legs of hers, that led up to that big mound of matted black jungle... She'd just made herself available to him in that way, and he'd wanted in.

Boy had he wanted in.

I was like a mad dog back there, he thought.

He couldn't remember ever experiencing a desire so intense.

"Don't tell me," she said. "You're in love with me, right?"

He shrugged. "Maybe I am."

"Wow, you never won any prizes in the romance stakes, I can tell that..."

"I'm not trying to be romantic."

"Tell me something else I don't know."

"Look, something happened...and I hardly know myself what it was..."

She laughed. "We *fucked*, John...it's that simple."

He frowned, ran a hand through his fine brown hair. "It was more than that...you set me on fire."

"*Did*...?"

"*Do*..."

"You mean you want to make something of it?"

"Do you, Linda...?"

She leaned forward, rested her elbows on the marble-topped table, and ran the end of her pink tongue over her painted red lips. "I've been a patient of yours for four months now, and for the past six weeks everything I do, I'm like 'What would John think about that?'"

"So what are we gonna do?"

"I dunno – you're the shrink...you tell me."

Emmet sipped his martini. "You said your husband is having difficulty writing a novel about being kidnapped because he has no direct personal experience of the subject matter, is that right...?"

"So he tells me...although I don't really take much interest in what he says, John... To be honest, I'm sick to the back teeth of him and his fucking writing, and the last thing I feel like doing when I'm with you is talk about him."

"I saw an interesting ad recently..."

"What's all this about?"

He took a magazine clipping from his pocket and handed it to her. "Take a look..."

Having figured that she'd sulked for long enough, Joanne went to pay a call on Melanie at her studio flat in Seagrave Road that evening.

The place was in its usual state of disarray. You could hardly put your foot on the floor without stepping on a pair of Melanie's knickers or tights, and there were books and newspapers left all over the place.

Joanne was in the habit of coming here and tidying up, but this time she resisted the urge to do so.

They were standing by the bed, Melanie in the pencil skirt and white blouse she'd gone to work in, Joanne wearing her usual uniform of dungarees and DMs.

Joanne's face was red and distorted with pain and anger. "Do you *have* to be such a bitch?"

Melanie shrugged. "I can't help the way I am."

"What's that supposed to mean?"

"I'm madly in love with the man, Jo..."

"And I'm madly in love with *you*, Mel, you silly cow."

Joanne put her arms around Melanie's slender waist, then opened the buttons on her blouse, slipped her hand inside and caressed one of Melanie's ripe breasts. Felt her nipple harden nicely as she kissed her on the mouth...then she slipped her tongue into Melanie's mouth, and Melanie gave as good as she got.

They began to tear each other's clothes off, and then they tumbled onto the bed and went into a hot and sticky sixty-nine.

. . .

Afterwards, Joanne said, "Don't tell me you didn't enjoy that because I know better."

"I loved it, Jo...but what does that prove?"

"It proves you love me, you silly bitch."

"No, it doesn't...it just proves you're a sexy cow, Jo, and you know how to push my buttons and make me hot...but it doesn't change anything, don't you see...?"

"You mean you're really in love with this guy?"

Melanie nodded. "I'm a goner, Jo...can't you at least be a little sensitive about it...? I mean, you of all people should understand the way I feel..."

"Is he married?"

"Divorced."

"And does he love you?"

"That's what I'm trying to work out... I think he's just using me..."

"The way you use me, you mean?"

"There's no need to be such a bitch, Jo."

"I'm not...how do you think *I* feel, Mel?"

Melanie dropped her face into her hands and began to sob.

"Don't get like that, Mel."

"How d'you expect me to get, Jo?"

"Why does life have to be such a mess...?"

"What makes it worse is that he's my boss..."

"Has he got other women?"

"That's what I'm wondering about..."

"You mean you haven't found out?"

"How can I?"

"You could always try hiring a private eye."

"You got any idea how much that would cost? I'm in debt enough as it is."

"Why don't you follow him around a little yourself and see what he gets up to...?"

"Like to see me humiliate myself like that, would you?"

Joanne sighed. "Well I could always do it for you, if you like..."

"You'd just make up all sorts of lies about the man, to try'n make me hate him, Jo...I know you."

"If you don't trust me, I could always take my camera and film him for you..."

Melanie sat up and looked at Joanne. "Would you, Jo...?"

"I would if that's what you want."

"That's so kind of you... Do you really love me that much, that you'd do something like that for me and not want anything in return...?"

"Didn't say that exactly..."

"What is it you want, then...?"

Joanne flashed her a naughty grin and lay back on the bed, then she parted her legs and raised her knees. "How about a little quid pro quo, Mel...?"

"You're fucking insatiable's your trouble," Mel said, and then she buried her face in Joanne's bush...

The following day, Linda Houseman asked her husband, Bob, if he fancied spending the weekend at their cottage down in the Cotswolds.

Bob Houseman looked at her with one eye raised and said, "Didn't you say you wanted a divorce?"

"Oh, I dunno what I want."

"Well you sounded pretty sure about it the last time we talked."

"Maybe I was."

"So what's changed?"

"Did I say anything had?"

"But you can't just change your mind every five minutes about something like this, Linda."

"I never said I wanted to change my mind, Bob... I just asked if you'd like to spend the weekend at the cottage..."

"And what if I say yes, I'd like that, and then we go there and end up having a good weekend together...? Would it change anything?"

Linda Houseman shrugged. "Then we'll see, I guess."

"This the way you want us to run our lives, never knowing from one day to the next whether we've got a marriage or not?"

"It isn't a question of what I want or don't want...it's the life we're living right now."

Bob Houseman puffed out his ruddy cheeks, shook his head, and scratched his beer belly.

Linda said, "Do I take it you don't want to go, then?"

"No, I'll go."

"You say it like you don't have any choice. Bob."

"*Do* I...?"

"Sure...you can always say no and tell me you want a divorce."

Yeah, that's true, he thought.

Except he couldn't, because he still loved her.

"I'll go pack a case," he said.

Bob Houseman spent a couple of hours working in the study of the cottage in the Cotswolds the following morning, getting nowhere fast again with the novel he was trying to write. It was getting to him, making him wonder if maybe the success he was now enjoying in terms of sales with his latest book, *Bitter Dawn*, was just a flash in the pan.

He decided to go out and get a little fresh air, take a stroll through the fields at the back of the house. Go on over the stream there and into the woods, maybe, and check out the local flora and fauna.

The sky was grey and overcast, and it started to rain as Bob Houseman crossed the field and, when he reached the little stream, he stopped and looked down at the fast-flowing water. He noticed the way the stones at the bottom had been worn smooth by the water passing over them. Beyond the stream, there was a sloping field which rose to a beech wood, away to the left. To the right, the land ran down to a hedgerow where the road into the local village snaked through the wet greenery.

Just then, Bob Houseman saw two men on the other side of the stream, where the stones in the water formed a natural bridge... The men were both wearing balaclavas under the hoods of their tracksuit tops.

Most odd, Houseman thought, as the men came towards him.

The two men grabbed him by either arm.

"What's going on?"

"Come with us," one of them said in a gruff South London accent. "No need for no one to get 'urt if you just listen'n play ball."

Bob Houseman tried to make a break for it, but the next thing he knew he was being rugby tackled and he hit the ground with a thud. Then one of the men had his knee on Houseman's spine while the other tied his hands behind his back.

They got Bob Houseman to his feet, one either side of him, and marched him across the stream and off towards the woods, where a Range Rover was parked. Then one of them opened the boot, and they bundled Houseman into it and slammed the lid shut.

Houseman began to yell and scream, but it didn't do any good, and then the engine started up and they set off.

They drove for quite some time, before they finally pulled up; then the two men came and got Houseman out of the boot and led him into an old farmhouse.

I'm still in the countryside, he thought, but it must be quite a long way from the Cotswolds.

He had no way of knowing the direction in which they had travelled, of course, and therefore it was impossible for him to hazard an intelligent guess as to where he might now be.

"Best put a blindfold on 'im," one of the men said, "so's he don't cop a butcher's at what we look like when we take the balerclarvers off, i'n' it."

Bob Houseman was lying on a bed in a dark room, wondering why on earth anyone might want to kidnap him.

To think that I was only saying to Linda how difficult I was finding it to write about being kidnapped without having gone through the experience myself, he thought... And then it occurred to him that an alternative explanation might be that this could all be part of some elaborate prank Linda had paid for... He'd read about people who set themselves up in business offering such a service, crazy as it might sound.

Yeah, Bob Houseman thought, perhaps she paid someone to do this so I'll know what it feels like to be kidnapped and be able to write my novel...

Was it really *possible* that Linda could have done something like that...?

Hours passed and then somebody came in with a glass of water and some food.

Houseman said he needed to go to the bathroom, and heard whoever was there say, "Okay." Then the man opened the padlock that kept Houseman chained to the bed frame. "On your feet, then."

Houseman did as he was told, and the man shoved him in the back. "Move."

Bob Houseman had never tried taking a lead with a blindfold on before. "What have you kidnapped me for?" he said over his shoulder.

"Just shut up and try'n aim straight."

"If you were to take the blindfold off so that I could see..."

"If we let you see us we'd have to kill you... Is that what you want?"

"No."

"Didn't think so."

Bob Houseman was zipping himself up. "But listen, I'm not even rich... Are you sure you haven't got me confused with somebody else...? I mean, I still used to think of myself as a struggling author until my latest book was published...and it only came out last year... Okay, it's selling pretty well, but even so..."

"You talk too much."

"All I'm saying is, there's people that are much wealthier than I am you could have picked on."

"Your latest book's sold over six million copies in all formats at the last count, and sales don't show any sign of slowing down... Sounds like a lot of dosh to me."

Bob Houseman supposed the man was right. It *was* a lot of dosh.

He certainly wasn't about to complain, anyway.

Or he wouldn't have done, until this happened...

Meanwhile, over at his practice in Harley Street, Doctor Emmet was running his hands over the sumptuous mounds that were Linda Houseman's breasts. Then he pulled away from her, as if it cost him an effort to do so, and said, "We're going to have to stop seeing each other for a while, Linda."

"Is that really necessary, John?"

"It is if we don't want the police on our backs."

"But I can still come here, right...?"

"Yes, but just for your sessions twice a week..."

"Oh, John."

"It might look suspicious otherwise."

"But there's nobody that knows about us."

"And I want to keep it that way, Linda."

"But what about the future?"

"We already talked about that – or have you forgotten...? We give it a few months until the whole thing has blown over and then we both move away."

"To where, John?"

"It will have to be somewhere far enough away that nobody will connect us with our lives here and what's happened... I was thinking Argentina would be the best bet... Of course, we'll have to learn Spanish...your boys will pick it up in no time, I'm sure...children adapt fast..."

"I've never been to Argentina, John... What's it like?"

"It's pretty much like Spain, in terms of the architecture and everything, only they aren't quite so particular about having people keep to the law...and it's hot, just like your beloved Marbella."

"I've always liked the heat."

"Me, too." He lifted her linen dress and ran his hand up her thigh, felt the skin smooth and waxy to the touch. "A lot of Nazis went over to Argentina after the Second World War and most of them managed to live there peacefully enough until they died, so I figure if they could do it then we ought to be able to..."

"I'm not sure I like being compared with a Nazi, John."

"Sorry, Linda, I didn't mean it like that."

"I'm going to look up British schools in Argentina on Google as soon as I get home."

"That's the last thing you should do... They have ways of checking everything you've looked at..."

"Oh yes, of course... I didn't think of that."

His hand came to rest on the hairy mound between her legs. "I was thinking Buenos Aires might be the place for us." He felt how moist she was, then climbed on top of her.

Linda lifted her knees and said, "Buenos Aires... But do they have good schools there to choose from for the boys?"

"You bet they do...just as good as anywhere in the world."

He entered her and she said, "I'm sure you know what you're doing, John."

. . .

Hours passed and Bob Houseman wondered how long he was going to be kept like this.

He wondered if they were going to kill him in the end.

The man had told him that was why they were keeping him blindfolded – so they wouldn't have to shoot him.

That gave him hope.

Although you could never tell...

He wondered how much they were going to ask Linda to cough up.

The man had a fair idea how many copies of his book, *BITTER DAWN*, had sold, and they'd know roughly how much he'd be getting per copy after deductions...

Linda loved the feel of Emmet inside her. She felt as though she were surrendering herself to him completely...as though she were *his*, to treat as he wished. She had never been in love like this before.

She wanted nothing more than to be able to serve his every whim... and she came as these thoughts passed through her mind.

Moments later, she felt his warm sperm shooting up inside her...

Perhaps Linda's behind all this, Bob Houseman thought.

Perhaps she's paid someone to kidnap me – not as a joke but *for real*.

But why would she do a thing like that?

So she could get rid of him and keep the kids, along with the properties and the millions in the bank – that was obvious.

As Doctor Emmet was zipping himself up, his buzzer sounded and he rushed to answer it. "Hello?"

"Just wondering if it's all right if I go for my lunch now?"

"Why...is it lunchtime already?" He glanced at his wristwatch – a Rolex Linda had given him for his birthday. "Oh yes, I see it's gone one o'clock...Yes, you carry on and go to lunch, Melanie."

He hung up and looked at Linda. "That was my secretary...we ran over time... The last thing we want is for her to catch on that we're involved..."

"Should I leave now, then?"

Emmet shook his head. "You'd better wait until she's gone...you don't look like a woman who's been lying on her back talking about her problems."

Linda Houseman smiled and said, "Well the first part of what you said was right..."

"Huh?"

"I've been lying on my back..."

But was Linda *capable* of doing something like this? Bob Houseman wondered.

Could she really be so evil?

It was true that they hadn't been getting on very well of late, but even so...

Bob Houseman wondered again if he was going to get out of this alive.

He told himself not to think that way. But it was difficult.

He told himself to try and stay positive.

He told himself there was no way Linda could be behind this, and wondered if she would call the cops or decide to keep the cops out of it and just pay the sum they'd ask for as ransom.

He tried to think of someone whose example he could follow.

He thought of the poet, Ezra Pound, when the Italians took him prisoner at the end of the Second World War. It had been baking hot in the daytime and freezing cold at night, and Pound was practically naked in the open cage they kept him in, with no bed sheets or blankets, nothing. Then when his captors finally realized he wasn't the dangerous madman they'd at first taken him for, they told him he could have one little luxury to make his life more bearable, and Pound asked for pencils and paper... Then he saw an ant crossing the floor of his cell, and wrote that famous line about the ant being a centaur in his dragon world...

Good old Ezra Pound...there was a man you could look up to.

Except that he was probably a bit of a nut, and they put him in a lunatic asylum at the end of the war and kept him in there for the next fifteen years, or thereabouts... Besides, he was a raving anti-Semite and a traitor to his country, a man who made anti-American speeches on the radio in Italy during the war...

And I'm neither a raving anti-Semite nor a crazy traitor, Bob Houseman thought.

Nor was Houseman a maverick literary genius, truth be told... He was just a pretty good thriller writer who'd got his lucky break and written a book that had sold.

And now *this*...

"Wherever you go, Linda," Doctor Emmet said, "make sure people see you...you need an alibi, remember."

"That's true."

"Call a friend and invite her to dinner this evening... Go somewhere where the waiters know you, and make a point of talking to them..."

"Okay, John, I will...don't worry."

"We need to be very careful, Linda, because you're going to be a major suspect, simply because you're the man's wife..."

She reached into her handbag and brought out a packet of Marlboros.

"I thought you'd packed up?"

"I *had* – before all this business..."

"You need to stay strong, Linda."

She lit up and nodded through a cloud of smoke. "When am I going to call the police and tell them I'm worried about Bob?"

When Linda Houseman stepped out into Harley Street, Emmet's secretary was there by the door, waiting. "Have you got a minute, Mrs Houseman?"

She was a brunette, early twenties, glasses, pinstripe pencil skirt and matching jacket. Neither especially attractive nor plain, Linda Houseman thought.

"Melanie's the name."

"Hello, Melanie...you took me by surprise for a moment there."

"I was wondering if we could talk...? There's a pub up on the corner... I'll buy you a glass of wine."

"I'm afraid I'm in a hurry... What is it that you wanted to talk to me about?"

"You're seeing John, aren't you?"

"I don't know what you're talking about."

"Yes, you are. You can't fool me."

"Listen, Miss... Melanie... I really think you ought to concern yourself with your job and—"

"He'll use you and then dump you just like he did the others... I should know...he said he was going to marry me..."

Linda Houseman turned on her heel, and hurried back to her car.

All Bob Houseman wanted was to have all this over with so he could get back to his old life, and for him and Linda to iron out the problems they'd been having...except that he wasn't totally sure what the problems they'd been having were.

That is, he knew they argued, but he wasn't always totally sure what it was they were arguing *about*...because sometimes Linda could have a way of coming at you like she was upset about a certain thing you'd done or failed to do, when in reality it was something completely different that was gnawing at her...

Of course his impotence hadn't helped.

I never used to be impotent, he thought, and began to wonder about what had caused him to suffer from this curious malady throughout this past year or so...

It all started around the time that *Bitter Dawn* began selling like there was no tomorrow. Before that, he'd been as virile and up for it, so to speak, as any man he knew...

Maybe it's some kind of subconscious guilt thing, he thought.

Yes, maybe he was feeling guilty about selling so many books.

Maybe he didn't feel worthy of so much attention...

The poet Philip Larkin had a line about his not being one to allow himself to have the money and the girl at the same time...it was about being the sort who needed to suffer.

But that was *masochism*...which wasn't a word that Bob Houseman had ever felt applied to himself.

He certainly didn't want to stay here locked up like this...

. . .

As soon as she got back to her flat in Chelsea, Linda Houseman called John Emmet. "That bitch was waiting for me downstairs, John," she said.

"Who was...?"

"That fucking secretary of yours... She warned me not to trust you...said you're a womanizer..."

"Yes, well she's clearly grown rather bitter... We had a little fling some time ago, but it was practically over before it began...what can I say..."

"She *knows* about us, John."

"She must have been listening at the door."

"She might go to the police."

"Don't worry, Linda... I'll have a serious talk with her tomorrow..."

"But what will that achieve?"

"Listen, Linda, I'm going to take care of this – just trust me, okay?" he said. "And remember to call a friend up and invite her to dinner..."

"Yes, I was just about to."

"And be sure always to use your mobile when you call me from now on...and don't ring me on my landline numbers anymore, because we don't want to raise suspicions..."

"Okay, John...but just tell me you love me."

"You know I do."

"Say it."

"I love you, Linda."

"I love to hear you say it, John."

"I've got to go."

"Okay...ciao."

They hung up, and Linda took out a Marlboro and lit up, then paced the living room as she smoked.

She was a mass of nerves.

Later that evening Linda Houseman was dining with her friend, Janet Fielder, in Bluebird, the restaurant up on King's Road. She was something of a regular there and knew the waiters, and she made a point of talking to them so they'd remember she'd been in, just as John had said.

Janet was a writer herself and she told Linda how she was enjoying *Bitter Dawn*. "If I'm honest, I struggled to get through Bob's other books," she said, "but this one's a real page-turner...it's like he's finally found himself as a writer."

"The funny thing is, he doesn't see it."

"No...?"

"He talks as though it's all a big mystery to him why *Bitter Dawn* is selling so well when the others didn't."

"They say that about some writers...that they can't see their own work with clear eyes." Janet sipped her wine. "I'm so happy for you, though...you must be loving it, living the high life like this at last."

"The flat we have now's certainly a great improvement on our old place."

"I should love to live where you are."

People only see the external things, Linda thought. But she didn't want to tell Janet about how Bob had been impotent with her ever since they'd moved to the new flat. Or about how she'd become involved with John Emmet...

Linda realized that she'd have to leave all her old friends behind her now.

This thought brought with it feelings of anguish, and she picked up her glass and finished what was in it then gave herself a refill.

She told herself that she could face anything, so long as she had Emmet's love...but now they were going to have to stay away from each other for a while – apart from the one-hour sessions she had with him twice a week...

Only now that little bitch of a secretary had found out about them... She must've been spying on us, Linda thought.

John would see to her, though.

Or so he'd said – but what would he do...?

What *could* he do exactly?

Linda reached for her glass and took another swig, as Janet said, "How's Bob getting on with his new one?"

"He says he's struggling with it."

"But writers always say that."

"He never used to complain so much when he started out."

"Maybe that's why the early books weren't as good."

Linda was way past caring about Bob and his writing and whether it was any good or not, but she had to keep pretending. "He's been saying he can't write about being kidnapped because he has no personal experience of it...and so I had an idea to help him get over his block..."

"Oh, and what's this...? I'll tell my students about it the next time I hold a workshop."

"Well, I saw this ad in a magazine..."

When Linda got home that night, she poured herself a large Scotch and lit up a Marlboro then paced the flat, smoking and sipping her drink.

She needed Emmet.

She felt safe when he was near, like nothing could possibly go wrong...which was the opposite of the way she was feeling right now.

She found her mobile and called him. Listened to the ringtone, and then he picked up. "John, I need to see you..."

"But I was just about to go to bed...and besides, we need to stay away from each other for a while, Linda, apart from the sessions twice a week... I told you that – don't you remember?"

"I know but I'm feeling bad... I need to see you...*please*, John..."

The line went quiet for a moment, and then he said, "Okay. but it's too dangerous for me to come to your flat... Someone might see me – it would be stupid to take unnecessary risks... I'll pick you up outside the World's End pub in half an hour."

Bob Houseman was lying on the bed, in the dark room they were keeping him in, wondering whether he'd be able to write about being kidnapped if he did get out of this okay.

The odd thing was, now that he knew exactly what kidnap victims went through, he didn't know if he'd be able to face writing about it.

Maybe he'd be too traumatized even to *think* about it...

He wondered about his wife, Linda. He wished he could talk to her...he wanted to get out of here and patch his marriage up and live happily again with Linda, the way they were before he began to make so much money.

He began to weep, very quietly. He could never remember feeling so sorry for himself. Not even when, as a little boy of ten, he'd been forced to swallow the bitter pill of his beloved father's departure from his life...

My fate is in other people's hands, Bob Houseman thought. There's nothing I can do.

Of course, had he been like the hero in *Bitter Dawn*, Jackson Torrent, then things might have been very different...

But fiction is nothing but lies and fairy tales, Bob Houseman thought.

It's taken me so long to come to terms with that fact and finally accept it... I've lived my life by creating characters who are capable of doing things no man could ever do in real life.

How could anyone escape when they were in a situation like this, after all? he thought. I'm chained to an iron bed frame and blindfolded... My captors are armed, and there's sure to be at least one man on guard at all times on the other side of the door, which is locked...

Even Jackson Torrent couldn't have escaped from this one.

Except that I'd have found a way to get him to do it, he thought. I'd have to, otherwise the readers wouldn't turn the page...

To think that the flat in Chelsea, the expensive boarding school for the boys, the holidays, the whole lifestyle was paid for by the lies he made up and put into his books... It didn't really bear thinking about.

It had just started to rain when Emmet pulled up in his BMW. He reached over and opened the passenger door, and Linda climbed in. They kissed hello, and then Emmet said, "Where shall we go?"

"Someplace quiet where we can talk."

He started up the engine and turned the car around, then set off along King's Road, before he took a right and crossed the Thames. Lights from the riverbank shone in the water, hard as glittering nails.

They drove into a parking area by the entrance to Battersea Park, and Emmet killed the engine. It was dark and there were just a few parked cars about, the nearest of which was some twenty yards away. Impossible to see if anyone was in it.

Linda turned to Emmet, and then she was in his arms and they were kissing. He smelt of expensive cologne and she felt safe. "Oh, John," she whimpered, as she dropped her head onto his shoulder. "I don't think I can get through this without you."

She began to sob, and Emmet straightened up. "You've got to stay strong, Linda...think of *us* and your boys..."

She dabbed at her eyes with her sleeve. "I know it, John...don't listen to me."

Just then, they heard the sound of an engine, and they both turned their heads and saw a motorcycle pull up in front of the car.

"He's pointing something at us," Linda said. "What's he up to...?"

Then Emmet saw what the man was doing, and he opened the car door and jumped out...but the bike was already in motion before he could get to it. He turned and dashed back to the car, jumped in behind the wheel, and started up the engine then set off after the motorcyclist.

He got to the exit that led onto the road just in time to see the motorcycle go through a red light at the corner of the street, and then head onto the bridge.

"But who was it, John...and what were they up to?"

"It's probably some friend of Melanie's, would be my best guess... Whoever it is, they've just taken a photo of us together, and we need to get that camera off them."

Emmet put his foot down and went through the lights at pace, just as they changed to amber. He had to swerve to narrowly miss a car, then headed onto the bridge. There was no sign of the motorcycle at all right now and he began to panic, his heart pumping in his ears...

As he passed over the hump in the middle of the bridge, he saw the motorcycle take a left at the end...but there was a black cab in front of him, and the steady stream of traffic coming the other way prevented him from being able to overtake.

"Come on, for Christ's sake," he said, as he saw the lights change to amber.

Then red.

And the taxi in front of him pulled up.

Emmet pulled out, into the path of a Toyota that was about to turn the corner, and he jerked the wheel and just managed to miss it, then narrowly missed another car as he joined the traffic going westwards. He ignored all the horns of the angry motorists, and put his foot down...but there was no sign of the motorcyclist as he rounded the curve in the road.

"We've lost him," he said.

"He must have turned off."

Emmet took the next right and zigzagged around the back streets at speed, in the hope of coming across the motorcyclist...

But still there was no sign of him.

Bob Houseman was thinking about the day his father left home. Mum was throwing Dad's shirts about the floor and calling him all the names under the sun, he remembered. Telling him to get out and never come back.

"Don't worry," his father had said, "you'll never see my face around here again."

"And what about little Robert?"

His father turned to look at him and said, "Remember that I'll always love you, Robert, and make sure you grow up into the kind of man I'd be proud of..."

"And not into a philanderer like you, you mean, is that it...?"

Robert wondered what a *philanderer* was, as he stood in the doorway, hands in pockets, and watched the scene.

His mother continued to hurl all kinds of insults at his father, who continued to pack his case in a calm manner. Then Dad patted me on the head, Houseman remembered, before he said goodbye and went out.

Never to be seen again.

Bob Houseman didn't want *that* for his kids.

"Please God," he prayed, "let me get out of this alive...if only for the boys."

Joanne took her eyes off the screen for a moment, to flash Melanie a sideways glance. And saw the way her face was distorted with a potent cocktail of anger and heartbreak, as she watched the damning footage of Emmet kissing Linda Houseman in his car... Then the film went all blurry, as the camera angle changed...and then they found themselves watching Emmet and Linda Houseman again...and saw them both turn their heads at the same time, to look out through the windscreen...

"The bitch!" Melanie slammed her fist down on the deal table.

"The *bastard* more like," Joanne said.

"Well, yeah, that as well..."

"Don't like to say I told you so..."

Melanie buried her face in Joanne's shoulder and started to sob like there was no tomorrow.

"What now, John?"

"I'm going to drive you home, and then I need to go and take care of some things, Linda."

"And what am I gonna do?"

"You just sit tight until I call you."

"When will that be?"

"Sometime tomorrow...then you'll have to call the cops."

"And what do I tell them?"

"The truth...well, half of it, anyway..."

"Uh...?"

"You paid for your husband to be kidnapped, but it was just this company that specialize in doing it for a joke... You'll have to show them the ad from the magazine, and then they'll check it out... So far as you're concerned, your husband was just supposed to be getting a simulation of the real thing, and the idea was to give him the feel of what it might be like so he could get over his block and write about it, only now the guys have phoned you up and they say it's for real and they're demanding £3,000,000 as ransom, okay...? But you know all this, Linda...we've discussed it a thousand times..."

She nodded and lit up a cigarette, brought it to her lips with a shaky hand. "You'll need to get them to call me..."

"Who?"

"The kidnappers...so there's a record of the call when the police check."

"Yes, don't worry, I'll take care of that... You don't have to worry about anything."

"I can't help it, John."

"It might even help to convince the cops if you sound worried and upset when you talk to them...even nervous..."

"I won't need to act there."

"Exactly, but that's okay... I mean, they'll be expecting you to be like that..."

"All right...and then what?"

"We sit tight until it all blows over."

"When will that be?"

"We'll be able to talk about it when you come for the sessions twice a week."

"I don't know how I'm gonna cope with just seeing you twice a week, John..."

"It's gonna be hard for me, too, Linda...but we need to be strong."

"Okay."

"So remember to keep your mobile turned on and wait for my call."

"Remind me again about what will happen after I tell the police..."

"I'll get your husband to call you and you'll have the police listening in by then, so I'll have him give you false directions... I'll have him call you 'kidder' and say how the kidnappers can't cook and he's missing your chilli con carne, like I told you...then you can say to the detectives after the call how strange it was that he should call you 'kidder' because he'd never called you that before, and how you'd never made chilli con carne in your life..."

"Yes, I remember it now."

"And let the detectives do some of the work themselves."

"All right... I'll only give them a nudge in the right direction if they need it."

"That's the idea...then they'll believe you're trying to help them and won't suspect anything... Now let's go through it all again, just to make sure you've got it."

As she left Melanie's, Joanne saw Emmet pull up in his BMW across the street, so she hurried over to her motorbike and started up the engine, half expecting him to come after her. But he didn't.

He can't have seen me, she thought.

Or maybe he just hadn't recognized her.

Joanne took out her camera and watched Emmet through the viewfinder, then she filmed him as he ran up the steps at the front of the building.

Emmet pushed the buzzer three times before he heard Melanie's familiar voice say, "Hello? Who's there?"

"It's me...John Emmet... We need to talk, Melanie."

"But it's late."

"This can't wait."

"Okay, hang on a minute."

Melanie came down and opened the door, a pale young brunette in a pink dressing gown.

"Sorry to get you out of bed..."

She looked as though she were undecided as to whether to punch Emmet or kiss him for a moment; but then she shrugged and stepped back to allow him to enter, and he followed her inside and up the stairs to her studio flat on the top floor. The place was in a mess, as it always was unless Joanne came and tidied up.

"So to what do I owe the pleasure...just feeling a little horny, are you, or what?"

"I've had a complaint..."

"What kind of complaint?"

"What's the idea of bothering my patients, Melanie...?"

"If it's Linda Houseman you're talking about, then you and I both know better than to call her a patient, John...*lover* is a more appropriate word."

"And what on earth gives you that preposterous idea?"

"I've heard you in there with her..."

"You mean you've been spying on me?" Emmet's eyes flashed and his hands balled into fists. "Was it you that followed us earlier...?"

"I don't know what you're talking about."

"You followed me down to Battersea Park on a motorbike, didn't you?" He moved towards her.

"Look, John, I don't know what all this is about, someone following you on a motorbike... I just wanted to tell the woman what you're really like, okay?"

"Which is like *what*...?"

"Men like you should come with a warning sign..."

You don't know how true that is, he thought.

"You used me like a toy and then threw me away when you got bored."

"And who are you to say what I can or can't do, Melanie?"

"I'm a woman and I've got *feelings*, John...which is more than I can say for you."

Emmet grabbed her around the throat, and saw the expression of shock and terror in her eyes as he pressed with his thumbs on her windpipe. He was wearing leather gloves, so as not to leave fingerprints.

Melanie kicked out and flailed her arms, and he felt her fists raining down blows on his shoulders as he continued to push.

And push.

Then he felt her begin to go weak, and the fixed expression of death came into her eyes.

He let go of her neck and caught her body, then carried her over to the sofa and laid her out on it.

Time to leave.

He shut the door to the flat quietly behind him and hurried down the stairs, without passing anyone on the way to the front door. So far, so good.

But then when he stepped outside, he looked up to see a figure on a motorcycle pointing a camera at him... It was the man who'd photographed – or filmed – them down in Battersea Park earlier... He ran down the steps, but the motorcyclist revved up and set off, and the vehicle turned the corner before Emmet reached his car.

Emmet opened the door of his BMW with the remote key, jumped in and hammered it up to the corner...but when he got there, the motorcyclist was nowhere to be seen...

That night Bob Houseman dreamed that he was writing about a character who had been kidnapped.

Then he woke up and realized that *he* was the one who'd been kidnapped.

And this was no story.

It occurred to him once more that he might not get out of this alive.

He realized that he wanted to live so much...for the boys, and for his wife, Linda, if only he could patch things up with her.

But not only for them – he wanted to live for himself, too... He wanted to live because he loved life. He loved the smells and the sights and the pleasures of this world, and he wanted to experience them some more before he said goodbye to it all.

After all, I'm only forty-five, he thought. It's one thing to die when you're old...but quite another to do so when you're in your prime.

Then an idea occurred to him that was so utterly simple and obvious that he would have felt silly sharing it with somebody else. And yet it was also one of the profoundest ideas he'd ever had.

The idea wasn't really an idea at all...it was more of an insight...the sudden realization that while other people may be breathing their last breath all over the world, and that not a second passed without somebody dying somewhere, he only had one life...and if he lost it, he would lose everything he'd ever owned or known or felt along with it. He would no longer be Bob Houseman...because Bob Houseman would no longer exist.

Each of us only gets to live one life, he thought, and when it's over, it's over.

And now it's *my* life that's on the line...

Just before noon the following day, Emmet called Linda on her mobile and told her it was time to get the boys in blue involved.

So she dialled the number for Fulham police station and told the desk sergeant who picked up the phone all about how the "little surprise" she'd planned to give her husband, Bob, had gone wrong. "It was just supposed to be a bit of fun," she said. "...You know, a pretend kidnapping...but now the kidnappers are saying it's *for real*, and they're demanding £3,000,000 as ransom..."

Within the hour, Detective Chief Inspector Preston and Detective Sergeant Johnson were at the flat with Linda Houseman, waiting for the kidnappers to call.

Linda winnowed a cigarette from the pack with shaking fingers, lit up and took a nervous drag. Then looked at Preston through the spiralling cloud of smoke.

"What do I say to them when they call?"

"Just keep them talking for as long as you can...and say you want to speak to your husband." Preston, a tanned and rather handsome man, dressed in a leather jacket and jeans, tweaked his black moustache.

"While you're talking, our people will be trying to trace the call from a van that's parked across the street."

"What if they won't let me talk to Bob?"

"Tell them you'll need to talk to him, so you can be certain he's still alive, before you cough up the money."

"What do I say to Bob, then, if they let me talk to him?'

"Just ask him how he's coping, and we've just got to hope that he's clever enough to be able to give us some kind of clue as to where he is."

"That's if he even knows," Linda said.

When Emmet entered the farmhouse, the two kidnappers were there, and they had Bob Houseman tied to the chair. The kidnappers were both wearing track suits and Nike trainers. One of them was a white guy with brown hair and a beer gut, the other an athletic-looking black man.

The white one said, "You come to pay us?"

"That's right...everything go okay?"

"Sure...yer man here will tell you all about it... He still thinks it's for real...we gave him a truly authentic experience he'll never forget... If he can't write that fucking book of his about it now, he never will."

"That's good." Emmet reached into his pocket and brought out not his wallet but a .38 Smith & Wesson handgun.

"Hey," the black guy said, "what the fuck's going on here, man?"

Emmet shot him in the chest. Then he saw the man's eyes get that stunned look in them as he hit the wall, blood splattering everywhere.

The white guy was up out of his chair and reaching for the gun on the table before his partner had hit the floor, but Emmet stopped him with a bullet that hit him in the face and sent him flying backwards into the chair...blood and bits of brains and shit went spurting over the walls and windows.

Shit, what a *mess*...

Emmet turned and looked at Houseman, who was sitting there in the chair in the corner, bound and gagged. "You're going to talk to your wife on the phone, and if you say one word out of place, I'm going to kill you, do you understand?"

Houseman nodded.

"Okay...you're to use the word 'kidder' in referring to her... Say something like, 'Hello, kidder,'–you got that?"

"Yes."

"Good...and you're to tell her that you miss the chilli con carne she cooks, but that you're being fed tolerably well..."

"Okay."

The telephone began to ring and Linda picked up.

"Hello?"

"You got the money up together in cash yet?"

"Yes...but I'll need to speak to Bob first, to know he's okay, before I hand it over."

"Okay...but you'd better not say anything stupid because I'll be listening."

The line went quiet for a moment, and then she heard her husband say, "Linda...?"

"Bob... Oh, my God...are you all right, Bob?"

"Don't worry, Linda, they're treating me okay."

"Oh, that's such a relief."

"Except they don't know how to cook."

"No...?"

Houseman said, "You ought to give them your recipe for chilli con carne, kidder."

The line went quiet a moment, and then she heard Emmet's voice again. "I'll call again tomorrow to give you more details about when we're going to make the exchange...you've got twenty-four hours to get the cash up together, if you haven't already."

He hung up.

"Any good?" Preston said into his smartphone.

"'Fraid not," the sound man replied.

Preston stopped his pacing and puffed out his cheeks. "I need to hear what the man said."

"Sure...here goes."

Preston heard the voice of one of the kidnappers coming down the line at first, followed by the voices of Linda Houseman and her husband.

Houseman was telling his wife he missed her cooking. The man was clearly trying to put a brave face on things, so as not to worry his wife.

Something about a recipe for chilli con carne...

Then the kidnapper came back on the line, to say he'd call again to tell her where and when to make the pickup.

'That it?" Preston said.

"That's all there is."

"Okay, well just stay where you are in case he calls again."

Preston hung up, then he turned to Linda Houseman and said, "No luck."

She took out another Marlboro and lit up.

Preston smoothed his tash down and said, "Your husband told you he's missing your cooking."

"That's right."

"Said he wished you could give the kidnappers your recipe for chilli con carne..."

"Which is a bit odd, I thought," Linda Houseman said, "because I've never cooked chilli con carne in all my life."

She brought her cigarette to her lips, hand shaking. "D'you think he was trying to give us a message?"

"Seems like it... Does it mean anything to you?"

Linda shook her head.

Detective Sergeant, a blond-haired man of thirty-two dressed in a smart pinstripe suit, said, "What are the ingredients you need to make it might be one way to start, guv... And the answer is that it's made with rice, red beans, mincemeat and chilli powder... I should know because I sometimes cook it."

Preston gave his tash a thoughtful tweak. "Is there anything in any of those words, I wonder?"

"You mean, could it be an anagram or something?" Linda Houseman said.

"Could be." Preston took out notebook and pen, and wrote down the words *rice, red beans, mincemeat* and *chilli powder*.

He looked at the letters of the words, in search of some kind of a pattern or clue, and saw nothing.

He tried writing the words down all together, in one continuous line.

Still nothing.

He tore out the piece of paper he'd written on, tossed it onto the marble-topped coffee table and puffed out his cheeks. Then he wrote all the letters of the different words in a big circle, and paced the room as he looked at them.

After a few minutes of this, he looked at Detective Sergeant Johnson and said, "Dammit, I'm just clutching at straws."

Linda Houseman said, "There is one more thing, come to think of it..."

"What's that?"

"Well, it's probably nothing...only I can't remember Bob ever addressing me as *kidder* before..."

"Kidder," Preston said.

"Kidder," Johnson repeated.

"Kidder as in *Kidder*minster... *Kidder*'s the first part of the word, then comes *mince*, which is the main ingredient in chilli con carne... Maybe that's what he was trying to say... What do you reckon?"

"Got to be worth a try, guv."

"What are we waiting for, then?"

They set off for Kidderminster at breakneck speed in Preston's car, and on the way, Preston called HQ to ask for backup. "We'll need a chopper and a team of trained marksmen on this one," he said.

The man on the other end of the line said he'd get a helicopter to where Preston was right away. "I'm in my car somewhere north of the Cotswolds," Preston said, and the man gave him directions so the chopper could land and pick him up.

The helicopter was waiting for Preston as arranged, in a field off the A44, and he climbed out of his Honda and told Johnson to drive it on to Kidderminster. Then Preston climbed aboard the helicopter.

There was a deafening noise and the long grass in the field roundabouts was flattened as they took off, and within seconds they were up in the air and flying in a straight line towards Kidderminster. The fields below were a patchwork of different-coloured squares, and you could see cars edging along the landscape here and there like large insects.

Then the town of Worcester came into view down below and, as they passed over it, Preston could see the river and the cathedral, and the cricket ground.

He got a call from HQ to say that a Range Rover had been reported stolen in the area, and only minutes ago, it had been traced to a farmhouse just south of Kidderminster. "The officer who traced the vehicle has been told not to approach the farmhouse, because we thought you might want to check it out..."

"Do we have any information on the people who live in the farmhouse?"

"It's owned by a family who are believed to be away on holiday in France."

Preston said, "I'll pass you over to the navigator, so he can fix the location."

Minutes later, they were circling over the farmhouse and, as he looked through his binoculars, Preston could see that his colleagues already had the place surrounded.

He saw the cars parked either side of the house, out in the road, and then he saw the two marksmen at the front. The farmhouse backed onto some fields, and he saw there were two marksmen in position there, too.

There was no way the kidnappers could possibly get away if they decided to make a break for it.

Or there wouldn't have been but for the fact that they had the hostage with them.

That complicated things.

Preston had the pilot take the helicopter down and, when they were about fifty feet over the roof of the house, he took out the loudspeaker. "OKAY YOU GUYS IN THERE, WE'VE GOT THE PLACE SURROUNDED, SO YOU'D BETTER COME OUT WITH YOUR HANDS UP...! TRY ANYTHING AND WE'LL SHOOT!"

Preston waited to see if the kidnappers came out.

They didn't.

"I SAID COME OUT WITH YOUR HANDS UP!" Preston shouted into the loudspeaker. "YOU ARE SURROUNDED AND

THERE IS NO WAY YOU CAN GET OUT OF THIS ALIVE, UNLESS YOU SURRENDER!"

Moments later, the front door opened and two men came out with their hands on their heads.

There was no sign of the hostage.

So far, so good, Preston thought.

Unless this is all some kind of trick, he thought, and there's a third guy in the house with a gun trained on the hostage...

Just then, he saw the two men make a dash for the Range Rover. They jumped in, started her up, and headed off down the gravel driveway in an easterly direction.

Preston told the pilot to sweep around the back of the farmhouse, so he could check no one had left that way and made a dash through the fields; and as he scoured the terrain below with the binoculars, he established radio contact with the drivers of the cars that were parked out in the road, fifty yards from the house in either direction. "They're making a bolt for it in the Range Rover," he said. "Don't let them get away."

He had the pilot chase the Range Rover, as he established radio contact with the marksmen who were guarding the exits at the front and back of the house. "Stay awake you guys," he said, "'cause I suspect the men who've made a run for it are acting as decoys and there's a guy still inside the farmhouse holding the hostage at gunpoint...and if I'm right, he may try and make his move any moment."

"Why don't the two of us go in there and nab him?"

Preston turned the marksman's suggestion over in his mind for a moment. "Okay, then, you two men at the back go in, and one of you at the front will have to go and guard the back exit..."

The helicopter was directly above the Range Rover by now, and one of the police cars was some twenty yards behind it. Preston heard gunfire and the next thing he knew, the Range Rover started to swerve all over the road, then it ran up the grassy bank to the left and almost overturned.

One of the men got out of the Range Rover and stood there in the road with his hands on his head.

Preston had the helicopter circle overhead, and he aimed his gun at the man standing in the road. Just then, the police vehicle pulled up and an officer got out. The officer was armed and he pointed his handgun at the man who was standing in the road. Then the driver of the other police car came and pointed his gun at the man behind the wheel of the Range Rover, and told him to get out.

Then he realized that the man was unconscious.

Seeing that the situation was well under control, Preston had the pilot return to the farmhouse and put the helicopter down in the field at the back. Then he went into the house through the kitchen door. He held his gun up in front of him, ready to fire, as he moved through the house.

When he got to the hallway, he heard a noise coming from the room up ahead and off to his left. Preston dashed over to the side of the door and flattened himself against the wall. "Who's in there?"

"It's me, guv," the familiar voice of the marksman he'd spoken to a short while ago called out. "Place is empty."

If the hostage wasn't in the house, then where was he? Preston wondered.

He ran out of the house and down the road, to where the two men were being held. "Where's the hostage?" he asked the one who was in a condition to talk.

The man looked like he didn't understand the question. 'What *hostage?*' he said. "All we did was steal this Range Rover."

The young man then told them about how his parents had taken their car with them on holiday to France, and so he and his mate had helped themselves to a vehicle "just for the week" – because they "were gonna return it, honest" – so they could "get about and have a little fun."

Preston looked at the lad like he'd just popped down from Mars.

"You ever tried being twenty years old'n havin' to live in the middle of the countryside in winter," the young man said, "without a vehicle to get around in?"

Preston realized that he'd just been on a wild goose chase.

And somewhere out there, Bob Houseman was still being held hostage.

Preston received a call from HQ minutes later. Reports had come in that gunfire was heard some while ago coming from a farmhouse outside of the village of Cookley, a few miles north of Kidderminster, and officers had been sent to investigate. "When they got there," the man at HQ said, "they found three dead bodies."

"Identified 'em yet?"

"Not formally, but we think one of them's Bob Houseman."

"Shit."

"We all did our best."

"Yeah," Preston said, "only it just wasn't good enough."

Then he thought of something. "Wait a minute, did you just say this happened outside of a place called *Cookley*...?"

"That's right."

"Of course...that's the clue he was trying to give us... It wasn't Kidderminster but *Cookley*, which is *near* Kidderminster..." Houseman had said the words *kidder* and all that about *cook*ing chilli con carne because he'd been searching for a coded way of saying he was being held at Cookley, which was near Kidderminster... Yes, it made sense, in a crazy and convoluted sort of way...

Especially when you considered the fact that Houseman was a man who had earned his living by working with words.

Preston could have kicked himself, because Bob Houseman had given him all the right information, but he had failed to interpret it correctly. *Shit.*

"So now what do we do, boss?"

There were several other policemen present when Preston arrived on the scene of the murder, and forensics were already going about their work and a photographer was snapping away.

"What a fucking mess, guv," DS Johnson said.

Preston tweaked his tash as he looked at the blood and bits of flesh and mucus splattered over the walls, windows and bookshelves.

Preston decided to go and tell Linda Houseman the bad news personally. It wasn't a duty that he relished the idea of having to perform, but it was one that he knew he might learn something from.

So he drove over to Manresa Road, in Chelsea, and parked outside of the widow's place. It was one of those big white Georgian buildings, once home to the gentry and their servants, before it was converted into expensive luxury flats. Preston ran up the front steps and pushed the buzzer next to the name of Houseman on the consul. The widow came to the door wearing black leggings with a tight white top, which left little of her slim but curvaceous figure to the imagination.

"Oh, it's you." Her attractive brown eyes widened. "Has anything happened?"

"It would be better if we could talk inside."

Linda Houseman took a step back and opened the door to allow Preston to enter, then she led him through to the living room. "Please make yourself at home."

Preston sat on the leather sofa, and rested his elbows on his knees as he waited for the widow to come and sit in the easy chair opposite him.

"So, are you going to tell me what's happened...?"

"We've found your husband, Mrs Houseman... I'm afraid he's been murdered."

The widow turned her face aside as though she'd just been slapped. Preston watched her closely, and as he did so, he tried to make up his mind whether she looked like a woman who'd just found out that her husband had been killed.

He reckoned she did.

Either that or she was a talented actress.

"Where did you find him?"

Preston told her, and watched closely as he did so.

They both went quiet for a moment, then Preston said, "Was your marriage a happy one, Mrs Houseman?"

She looked at Preston. "Why do you ask that...?"

"Just routine... I'm trying to build up a picture of your husband and the life he was leading... The more I can find out about him, the more comprehensive the picture will be...and the better my chances of catching the person or persons who killed him."

"You make it sound like you're directing a bloody film."

"If that's the case, then I must have expressed myself badly, and I apologize..."

They both went quiet again.

Preston took out his notepad and flicked through the pages, pretending to look for something. Then he went back to watching the widow, without saying anything. The silence seemed to fill the room.

"I need a drink," Linda Houseman said.

"Would you like me to pour you one?"

She nodded, then wiped away tears that may or may not have been real with the back of her hand. "There's some Scotch over there." She pointed to a mahogany cabinet in the corner of the room. "Pour one for yourself as well, if you'd like one."

"No, thanks, Mrs Houseman, not when I'm on duty." Preston rose from the sofa. "Would you like anything with it?"

"No."

He poured the drink then carried it over to her, and stood by her chair and watched her sip it. "I could do with a cigarette."

"Sorry, I gave up some time ago."

"There's a packet in my handbag on the table there."

Preston retrieved the handbag and passed it to the widow, and she reached inside and brought out a packet of Marlboro and a lighter and lit up. She inhaled like it pained her to do so, then exhaled two streams of smoke through her nostrils.

She shook her head and wiped her eyes.

"You said you paid some people to kidnap your husband, Mrs Houseman...?'

"It was supposed to be all make-believe, just to help him write his bloody book... But I told you all about that before."

"There were two other men at the house with him."

"Yes, well they would have been the kidnappers."

"But they were killed, too."

"But that's crazy." She took a big swig of her Scotch, then dragged on her cigarette. "You mean Bob and those two men were all together, dead, at this farmhouse when you got there...?"

"Exactly."

"But that doesn't make sense." She got to her feet and went over to the window, and stood there with her back to Preston looking out at the street.

"I'm afraid I need to know where you've been the past twenty-four hours, Mrs Houseman."

"I went shopping this morning – you can ask my butcher," she said without turning around. "... And I went out to dinner with a girlfriend last night at Bluebird, up on King's Road."

"I'll need you to give me the name of the friend you dined with and her contact details."

The widow told him, and he made a note on his pad.

Preston asked her which butcher she used, and made a note of this, too, when she told him.

He saw her shoulders begin to judder.

He got to his feet and said, "I'm very sorry, Mrs Houseman..." Then he made for the door.

Preston called around to the house of Janet Fielder, the woman that Linda Houseman claimed to have dined with the evening before, and she corroborated what the widow had said.

Next, Preston called around to Bluebird, the restaurant on King's Road, just to make double sure. And when he showed the Maitre d' a photograph of Linda Houseman and asked him if she'd been at the restaurant the evening before, the man said, "That's Mrs Houseman... She was here, yes...she comes in a lot."

"Does she ever come in with her husband?"

"Occasionally...but usually she's with women friends."

"What kind of mood was she in last night?"

The man shrugged.

"I mean, was she laughing or did she seem worried...?"

"No, she seemed normal, you know...the same as always..."

Preston thanked the man and drove back to the station and entered his office, where he found Detective Sergeant Johnson hard at work.

"How did things go with the widow, guv?"

"She has various alibis..."

"Reckon she's behind it?"

"She's our only real suspect at this stage, Dave, but we don't have any evidence against her."

Linda Houseman was worrying about Emmet's secretary, Melanie, as she drove over to Harley Street for her "session" the following morning.

But when she entered the surgery there was no sign of the girl, and Emmet came out to greet her. He took her in his arms, in the empty waiting room, and she held him close and buried her face in the lapel of his jacket.

"I just want all this to be over, John," she sobbed.

"Me, too, Linda…"

They went into the room where Emmet listened to his patients, and he led Linda over to the couch and then eased her down onto it. She raised her knees and he pulled her panties down, and then he was in her and they went at it with all the wild abandon of lions.

Afterwards Linda said, "What happened to Melanie?"

"Oh, I dealt with her."

"What does that mean…did you sack her?"

Emmet zipped himself up and said, "I did more than that."

"You don't mean you…" She put her hand to her mouth.

"I had to, Linda…she knew too much about us." Emmet frowned and ran a hand over the back of his neck. "I saw our friend the motorcyclist again – he was filming or photographing me as I left Melanie's."

"Where did you kill her?"

"At her flat."

"And this guy photographed or filmed you straight afterwards, when you came out…?"

"That's right."

"Did you get the camera off him?"

Emmet shook his head. "He got away again."

"You do realize some of these sophisticated cameras record the time and the date when the footage is shot…?"

Emmet hadn't considered this. "So you mean it could serve as evidence once–"

"Once they find the body, exactly…"

Emmet had to get back into Melanie's place and move the body.

Either that, or he had to find the motorcyclist and get the camera off him.

Neither of which would be easy to do. Because he didn't have keys to Melanie's flat, and he had no idea who the motorcyclist was or where he lived…

I need to think clearly, he told himself.

That was a hard thing to do when your heart was racing and you were beginning to panic.

Just then, his mobile began to knock out a riff from Mozart's *Don Giovanni* and he snapped it open. "Hello?"

"I thought you'd dumped Melanie and were involved with Linda Houseman, Doc?" said a female voice he didn't recognize.

"Who is this?"

"We've never met."

"What's the purpose of your call?"

"Melanie told me all about you..."

"All nice things, I hope?"

"Very funny, Doc...she said you're a serial seducer, a regular Don Juan and that you take advantage of your female patients and women who are vulnerable in general."

"Do you make a habit of calling strangers and regaling them with vicious insults and lies...?"

"I figured I'd check you out for myself, when I heard what Melanie had to say..."

"Was it you on the motorcycle?"

"Got it in one, Doc."

"What's the idea of filming me?"

"I was thinking of making a flick about you...call it Doc *Juan*..."

"I don't find that very amusing."

"No, you wouldn't."

"How about if we meet and talk about this?"

"What's there to talk about, Doc? You wanna seduce me, too?"

"I'm much more interested in your career as a film-maker."

"Thought you might be somehow...it's an expensive piece of equipment that I use."

"How much?"

"Two grand."

Meanwhile, Detective Chief Inspector Preston was behind the wheel of his silver Honda, across the street from the widow's place. He'd been about to go and ring her doorbell, but then he changed his mind and decided it might be a better idea to wait and see if she came out and then follow her.

He took out his smartphone and checked his emails. There was one from his son, Calum.

Dear Dad,

I went to see Chelsea play again last night with Mum and Steve. They beat Spurs 2. 0 and were by far the better team. Fernando Torres played well and scored a good goal. I think Chelsea have a good chance of winning the title this year.

I wish you could have been there with us.

Talk to you soon.

Love Calum,

XXX

Reading the email brought a lump to Preston's throat. He loved his son to bits, and hated the idea that his ex-wife Anne's new boyfriend was getting to see a lot more of him than he did.

Not only that, but this bloke, Steve seemed to be trying to turn the lad into a Chelsea fan...

Preston wrote back,

Dear Calum,

Sounds like it was a good game. Shame I couldn't make it...but you know I have too many bad men to catch, and so am very busy.

I think Chelsea are looking pretty good this season, it's true – but don't write off Fulham just yet! They had a great win last week. Did you see it?

I'll talk to you again soon. Got to go now, though, to catch some bad men.

Lots of love,

Dad

XXX

Preston sent the email and, keeping one eye on the door to the building where Linda Houseman lived, he went back into his inbox and checked the rest of his emails.

There was one from his girlfriend, Sally, who was still working as a pole dancer at Secrets, over in Hammersmith, although she was talking of quitting and trying to think of something else she could go into.

Dear Bob,

Didn't see you at the club last night and missed you. I called you on your mobile number but you didn't pick up.

Call in tonight if you can, and we'll get a takeaway and eat it back at yours. If you can't make it, then at least call and tell me what you're up to.

Love Sally,
XXX

Preston reckoned he was lucky to have met a girl like Sally. She seems to love me, even though I'm old enough to be her father, he thought.

And there were days when he reckoned he loved her, too.

Days when he even considered the idea of asking her to marry him.

But there was no point in rushing into things. If he did marry again, he wanted to make sure he didn't balls things up the way he did the first time around.

"For that," Joanne said, "you get the chip and all the footage I took of you..." And the footage of the kidnapping along with it, of course, she thought.

This way, Joanne figured, she'd be able to pass the problem of what to do with the evidence of what she'd witnessed on to the Doc and get paid for doing so. Kill two birds with one stone.

She'd already shown the bits of the film with Emmet on it to Melanie, to convince her of the man's philandering ways, and so the chip had served its purpose anyway in that sense. "It's your call, Doc," she said. "Take it or leave it."

"Why should I be concerned about a bit of footage of me kissing a woman in my car...?"

"Forget it, then...I'll just send it to the woman's husband."

"Okay... Name a time and place."

"Brompton cemetery in one hour."

"Okay."

"You bring the cash with you, otherwise it's no deal."

"Okay, I'll have the cash, but in return I'll also need any copies you've had run off."

"No copies, Doc...it's all on the chip."

"There's no way I can be sure of that."

"Afraid you're just gonna have to take my word for it on that... It's your call."

"Okay...but Brompton cemetery's a big place..."

"Enter at the northern end, from Old Brompton Road, and turn right...go as far as you can, then follow the path that runs along the wall. Got that?"

"Yes."

"I'll be there waiting for you exactly an hour from now... Don't be late."

Linda Houseman left her flat and went and climbed into her Mercedes, and Preston followed her at a discreet distance all the way to Brompton Cemetery, where she parked and got out.

Emmet entered a café over on Baker Street, where he had a ciabatta with Parma ham and sun-dried tomatoes. He washed it down with a glass of freshly squeezed orange juice, then he had a cappuccino and paid the bill.

He glanced at his watch: he had to be over at Brompton Cemetery in half an hour. There was plenty of time.

He walked back to his BMW, which he'd left outside of his practice on Harley Street, climbed in, then put on a CD of Mozart's *Don Giovanni*. He loved *Don Giovanni* – it was his favourite opera – and he hummed along with the arias as he drove through the busy streets of West London.

He had the feeling that things were going to work out just fine.

Emmet pulled up in the little parking area outside the gates on the Old Brompton Road side of the cemetery, then got out of his car, locked it with the remote key, and went in through the arched entrance.

There was a light mild wind blowing, and the sky was uniformly grey. He took a right, once he was inside the cemetery, as he was told, then walked as far as the wall at the end and followed the path down in a southerly direction.

There was no sign of the mystery motorcyclist anywhere.

He continued on down to the bottom, from where he could see the back of Stamford Bridge, the stadium that was home to Chelsea Football Club. Then he turned and saw that a funeral was being held at the other end of the cemetery.

He remembered that Linda had said her husband was to be buried here today, in this very cemetery.

How stupid of me not to think of it, he thought.

But he'd had a lot on his mind.

He wondered if the motorcyclist had chosen to meet him here for this reason...or if it had been mere coincidence.

Linda Houseman stood watching the coffin with her late husband's body in it being lowered into the ground. The vicar said, "Dust to dust, ashes to ashes," and Linda dabbed at her eyes with her handkerchief.

As she was about to leave, Detective Chief Inspector Preston turned up at her side, seemingly out of nowhere. "Hello, Mrs Houseman," he said. "Just thought I'd come to pay my last respects... Your husband was much loved by a great number of people, judging by the turnout."

"Yes, Bob was a good man...he didn't deserve to die as he did."

"I'm sure it's not just the people who've come here today that will miss him, either, but also his many readers."

"Oh yes, of course...he wrote for years without making much money...and now, just when the public seems to have fallen in love with him, he's been taken..." She dabbed at her eyes again and looked away. "But of course it's not his books that I'll miss him for..."

"I'm very sorry, Mrs. Houseman."

Emmet heard the sound of an engine behind him, and he turned and saw somebody on a motorcycle coming along the narrow path.

It's *him*, he thought.

The motorcycle slowed to a crawl and stopped a few feet in front of him, and Emmet was surprised to find that the *him* turned out to be a *her*.

"Glad you could make it, Doc."

"Is that supposed to be funny?"

"You got the money?"

"I'll need to see what you've got for me first."

Emmet walked up to the woman, so that he was standing at her side.

"First you give me the money."

"Where's the chip?"

"I'll give you that, once I've got the money."

"I'll need to see the footage first."

"Look, I'll send you the chip through the post... What do you take me for...? If I'd brought it here with me, what's to stop you taking it and running off and keeping the money?"

"We came here to do a deal."

"Yeah, but you're stronger than I am..."

"Okay, have it your way." Emmet took a look around to make sure the coast was clear. Then, standing with his back to the wall, he held the briefcase up in front of him as if it were a tray. He moved the wheels on the lock until he had the combination, then lifted the lid and reached inside. "Here you are." He picked up the handgun with the silencer attached to it that he had in there and fired through the lid.

Twice.

The first shot got the girl in the belly and the second hit her in the chest. The shots didn't make much noise, thanks to the silencer.

Emmet rushed to catch the girl, and stopped her from falling backwards. Then he supported her head with his shoulder as he shut the briefcase, and took another quick look around to make sure the coast was clear.

It was, so he eased the girl's lifeless body down off the bike and pulled her into the long grass, which was obscured from the path by a little row of bushes.

It would be some time before her body was discovered there.

Now the bike.

He figured he may as well put that in the long grass, too, next to the girl.

He went through the girl's pockets and found her purse. There was a little notebook in it, some spare change, two ten-pound notes, three bank cards and a card for Fulham and Hammersmith libraries... Emmet took the money and slipped it into his pocket.

He took the library card, too, then he dropped the purse next to the body.

Make it look like a mugging, he thought.

He took off the leather gloves he'd been wearing and put them in the briefcase.

Moments later, he was walking back up the path as though nothing had happened, just another Londoner out for a casual stroll...

Emmet climbed in behind the wheel of his BMW, and set off up through Earl's Court. He needed to get the chip that contained the footage of him leaving Melanie's after he'd killed her.

And he had an idea as to how he might get it.

He took a left then a right, and pulled over in a side street off Gloucester Road and entered a phone box.

He called Hammersmith library and said he was calling on behalf of his girlfriend, Joanne, to return a book she'd taken out. "She's got the flu and is too ill to call herself," he said, "so she's asked me to do it."

"Okay, that's fine... Can you give me the full name, please?"

"Parks... Joanne Parks."

"We've got two entries under that name here... Would that be the one at number 4 Alfred Road? Or the one at 296 Harrow Road?"

Emmet hung up and made a note of the two addresses.

Then he called directory enquiries and got the number for the Joanne Parks who lived at 296 Harrow Road, and when he dialled it a woman picked up.

"Hello," Emmet said, "can I speak to a Joanne Parks, please?"

"Speaking."

Emmet hung up.

He'd found out what he needed to know.

He got back in behind the wheel of his BMW and headed over to the address on Alfred Road. He pulled up around the corner, then went and rang the doorbell.

No sign of anybody being at home, but he rang the bell again just to make sure. Then he checked the coast was clear, before he took out the keys he'd taken from the young woman's purse and slipped the one that he'd already decided to try first into the lock. The door opened

481

when he gave the key a turn, and he entered the house and very quietly shut the door behind him.

It only took him a few minutes to find the camera he was looking for. He checked to see if the chip was in it.

It was.

He ran the film, just to check it was the right camera...and watched himself sitting in his BMW with Linda...now they were kissing... Now he saw himself running up the steps at the front of Melanie's place, and ringing the bell...

He put the camera with the chip inside it into his briefcase and went back out the way he'd come in. He held the briefcase with the lid against the leg of his trousers, so that the bullet holes were not visible.

He climbed back into his BMW and set off.

Mission accomplished.

Except that he still needed to get rid of the gun.

So he pulled up near Chelsea Wharf, then took the camera out of the briefcase and put it under the passenger seat. Next, he climbed out of the car and took the bricks that he'd left in a sack in the boot and put them in the briefcase, before he headed over to the riverbank.

He checked that the coast was clear, before he threw the briefcase into the Thames.

The bricks that were inside it would ensure the briefcase sank straight to the bottom of the river and stayed there.

With the gun inside it.

Emmet walked at a brisk pace back to his BMW, climbed back in behind the wheel, and headed off.

He put his favourite CD on and listened to it as he drove.

All of Mozart's operas were wonderful, of course, but there was nothing quite like *Don Giovanni* in Emmet's opinion.

Linda Houseman poured herself a large Scotch and sat drinking it while she watched a DVD of *The Sopranos*.

That is, she looked at the screen while *The Sopranos* was on.

Because she didn't really follow the story.

She was running through recent events in her mind like a film.

She was wondering if everything was going to turn out okay.

. . .

Emmet looked at the red Lexus two cars behind him, and reckoned it had been there in his mirror for quite some time.

Is it following me? he wondered.

His heart began to race. He was a doctor, after all, and wasn't used to this sort of thing.

He might be the sort of cold heartless bastard who could dish out death to some poor girl weaker than himself without a qualm, but he was no fighter.

He told himself to calm down and not jump to any rash conclusions, as he turned off Fulham Road, then took another right, before slowing down.

There was no longer any sign of the red Lexus, so Emmet reached down and took the camera from where he'd left it, under the seat, then grabbed the briefcase and climbed out of the car. He locked it with the remote, as he took a quick look about, and told himself he must have been letting his imagination get the better of him. Unusual for me, he thought, as he opened the gate and walked up to the front door of his house, a three-bedroom number that had cost him just over a million five years ago.

As soon as he was inside, Emmet ran up the stairs and into his bedroom, and he peered down at the street through the thick curtains. A sporting green MG went roaring past...and moments later, a red Lexus turned the corner.

Emmet could hear his heart hammering in his ears as he watched the Lexus come up the street at a slow crawl. "That's it," he said aloud, "just carry on by..."

But the car came to a halt when it drew level with Emmet's parked BMW, then the passenger door opened and a man got out. He was wearing jeans, a leather jacket and shades. The man walked in front of Emmet's BMW and inspected the registration number, then he turned and nodded to the driver of the Lexus, who set about parking in a space on the other side of the street.

Shit, they're onto me, Emmet thought.

He wondered who these people could be.

Were they plainclothes cops?

It was possible...although somehow Emmet had the feeling they weren't. It was something about the look of the man who'd got out of the car.

Emmet's instincts told him he'd better make himself scarce – and fast.

So he ran back down the stairs, carrying the briefcase with the camera and the chip in it. Seeing his bicycle there in the hallway, Emmet wheeled it into the kitchen and on out through the back door. Then he hurried through the small garden, opened the door at the bottom with a key, and stepped out into the narrow dirt lane that ran along the back of the rank of houses. He cycled up to near the end, then got off and peeped around the corner of the wall – and saw a man in sunglasses there, looking along the street in the opposite direction.

Emmet turned around and hammered it down to the other end of the lane, then peered around the wall, and this time the coast was clear so he cycled off. He took the next corner, then went up and joined the Fulham Road and rode up as far as the Broadway. He got off his bike and left it propped against the wall of the pub on the corner, then crossed the road and jumped into the back of the first in the line of taxis that were waiting there.

"Where you wanna go, guv?"

Emmet said, "Take me to Harley Street," and the driver set off. He went around the small roundabout then headed in an easterly direction up the Fulham Road. They passed Stamford Bridge, home to Chelsea FC, and carried on past classy shops on either side, then went through South Kensington and on into central London.

As the taxi turned into Harley Street, Emmet began to have second thoughts about returning to his practice. His original idea had been to go there and hide out for a while. But now it occurred to him that the guys in the red Lexus might have gone there…after all, they knew the reg of his car, so it wouldn't take them too long to work out where he lived and worked.

"I've changed my mind," he told the cabby. "Take me to a hotel."

"Which one, guv?"

"The Hilton will do, up on Hyde Park Corner."

As soon as he'd booked himself into a single room at the Hilton, Emmet set about looking through the stuff that was on the chip in the camera from start to finish.

He watched himself again, coming out of Melanie's place just after he'd killed her...and the time the footage was taken was there, recorded in the memory. Then he watched himself entering Brompton cemetery, again with the time the footage was taken recorded in the memory of the camera.

Pretty damning evidence, Emmet thought.

Then he figured he'd watch the footage from start to finish, so he took it back to the beginning and found himself watching a couple of young lads in the street... One of the lads seemed to take umbrage at the fact that he was being filmed, but then he went on his way, stopping only to turn and stick up his middle finger... Then the background changed, and Emmet fancied he recognized the architecture that was common to the area in which he had his practice... The footage had a random, haphazard quality, almost as if the person who held the camera had filmed anything that happened to take her fancy... Then Emmet found himself watching two large men force another, smaller man into the back of a car... The car was a red Lexus, he noticed on closer inspection...

Emmet pressed the zoom-in button, then froze the film...and realized that he was looking at the two men who had been following him earlier.

That evening, DCI Preston called into Secrets, the place over in Hammersmith where his girlfriend worked. He found himself a stool at the counter and said hello to Carole, the busty barmaid. "What can I get you, Bob?"

"Make it a large one," he said.

"Been that sort of a day, has it?"

Preston smiled, and Carole poured the drink and put it down on the counter in front of him. "How's your Billy keeping?"

"Been busy lately."

"What's he up to, then?"

"Not what you're thinking, Bob..."

"Glad to hear it."

"Been keepin' his nose clean and going down to the Jobcentre every day, and they've set him up with an interview for next week."

"Where's that, then?"

"The branch of Lloyd's just near here."

Preston sipped his Scotch and said, "You sure that's the best place for him, Carole...?"

"I know what you're thinking, Bob, but Billy's promised me he's really going straight this time."

What they all say, Preston thought, and said, "Well let's hope so, luv."

"He knows I'll kill him if he doesn't."

"And that's enough to put most men on the straight and narrow, I'm sure."

"It's not been any sort a life, Bob...never knowing whether he's gonna be banged up again or not...and those were the good times, when he wasn't actually in nick... Then there was the rest of the times...talkin' to him during the visits over a table with a guard watching our every move."

"Prison's not supposed to be a holiday camp, Carole."

"No, I know that, Bob... I mean, don't get me wrong... I'm not complaining, just sayin' what it was like."

"Pretty miserable by the sound of it."

"And the rest."

"Well let's just hope he listens to you and doesn't go back to his old ways."

"He won't, Bob."

Preston hoped Carole was right, for her sake. But he wouldn't have bet on it.

"Changing the subjec', how're you getting on with Sally?"

"We get on like a house on fire."

Carole gave him a straight look. "You wouldn't mess her about, Bob, would you?"

"Course not."

"I know it's none of my business, but that girl's really gone on you..."

Just then, Preston turned and saw who else but Sally walking over towards him. She was a tall, slim blonde, and was wearing a short black dress, high heels and a big smile.

"Hello stranger." She kissed Preston hello, then turned to Carole and said, "Mine's the usual."

"Mine, too." Preston finished what was left of his Scotch and put his glass down on the counter.

"We was only just talkin' about you," Carole said over her shoulder, as she saw to the drinks.

"All nice things, I hope...?"

Preston grinned and said, "She was threatening to have me done in if I don't treat you right."

Carole waved Preston's twenty-pound note away when he went to pay for the drinks. "These are on the house."

Linda Houseman was on her third Scotch as she lay on the sofa, reading the manuscript her late husband Bob had been working on before he died, when the phone began to ring.

She picked it up. "Hello?"

"Hello, Linda. It's Harlan...Bob's agent."

"Oh, hi."

"Sorry if it's a little late to be calling, Linda, but I just wanted to pass on my condolences, because I didn't want to disturb you at the funeral...we were all far too upset."

"Thanks, Harlan."

"You must know the old cliché about the relationship between a writer and his agent often lasting longer than many marriages...well, it wasn't true in your case, of course, but I certainly came to be truly fond of Bob. He was just a great guy..."

"Bob always spoke well of you, too... It's funny that you should have called, because I was only just looking at the manuscript he'd been working on."

"Oh, really...? I tried to ask him about it, but he was always evasive... Many writers are like that – they don't like to talk about the book they're working on...seem to think it might put the voodoo on it or something."

Well he certainly whined about it enough to me, she thought.

"What's all this I hear about you arranging for him to be *kidnapped*, Linda...?"

"Yes, well it was just supposed to be a joke... I paid some people who advertised in a magazine saying they ran a kidnapping service... The idea was to give people the experience of being kidnapped without harming them, and then returning them home safely and all in one piece at the end of it…"

"Sounds pretty weird, if I might say so…"

"Yes, well, Bob was trying to write about a kidnapping in this latest book he was working on, only he couldn't get down to it…said he found it hard writing about something he had no direct experience of…"

"I see…so you paid for this service to help him…"

"Exactly."

"So then what happened?"

"I wish I knew, Harlan…"

"Don't tell me the kidnappers tried to kidnap him for real…?"

"I'm not really sure, to be honest…they were found dead, along with Bob."

"What, the kidnappers…?"

"Yeah…"

"My God…that's weird…"

They both went quiet for a moment, then Harlan said, "Listen, there are some things I'll need to talk to you about, regarding Bob's literary estate… I was wondering if I could buy you lunch sometime, Linda…? They've got a wonderful new chef at the Ritz."

"Okay, then… I'm not doing anything tomorrow."

"You're sure it's not too soon after–"

"To be honest, Harlan, the more I can get out and occupy myself the better…otherwise I'll only sit around feeling like I want to end it all."

They both went quiet again for a moment, then Linda said, "So how about if we say one o'clock at the Ritz…?"

"Sure…oh, and I'd really like to take a look at the new manuscript Bob was working on, if that's all right…?"

"I was reading it, actually."

"That's okay… I'll have some copies run off and get it straight back to you…"

Meanwhile, over at Secrets, Sally got up to go to the toilet when a customer came over and started to hassle her for a date.

"I've already got a boyfriend," Sally told the man.

"How about if we go somewhere nice as soon as you get off?"

"I've already got somewhere nice to go, thanks."

She made to continue on her way, but the man – a bearded guy with more belly than brains – blocked her path.

Seeing what was going on, Preston got up off his stool and hurried over. "Who's your friend, Sally?"

"He's just about to get out of my way, aren't you?"

"You still haven't given me your phone number yet," the man said, acting like Preston wasn't there.

"No, and you're not gonna get it...now are you going to get out of the way?"

"You heard her, pal," Preston said.

"Who's the parrot?"

"I said get out of her way."

"Who the fuck're you?"

"I'm her boyfriend."

The man stepped aside, but then, as Sally went past, he reached out a hand and pinched her on the bottom.

Sally turned and went to slap the man, but he was too quick for her and grabbed her wrist.

Preston got hold of the man's free arm and twisted it behind his back, then rammed the man's face down onto the counter.

Seeing what was going on, Carole said, "Looks like a bit of a rough customer, Bob...you want me to call security?"

"I can deal with this one okay on my own, thanks."

"Get the fuck off me," the man said.

"Not before you buy my girlfriend a drink and apologize to her for your rudeness..."

"Go fuck yourself."

Preston gave the man's arm an extra twist and he cried out in pain.

"Stop it."

Carole said, "Looks like I'd better pour another one for Sally, then."

Preston nodded at her as the security arrived.

"Oh, it's you, Bob," said the bouncer. "Everything okay?"

"Just teaching this chap his manners...he's going to behave himself from now on, aren't you?" Preston twisted the man's arm some more.

"Yeah, all right...you're gonna break my arm."

Preston straightened the man up and eased him backwards onto a stool.

"Now, you're going to pay for the drink," Preston said, "and then you're going to give it to the lady and apologize to her."

The man sat there on the stool, his head down on his chest, trying to get his breath back.

"And you'd better hurry up about it," Preston said. "Unless you want me to twist your arm some more – and next time I'll break it."

The man picked up the vodka and tonic Carole had just placed on the bar and threw it over Sally's dress.

"Fuck you, ya bitch," he said, and he reared up off his stool.

Preston threw a fast right to the man's solar plexus that took the wind out of him, then he hooked his foot around the man's near ankle and pushed him and he went flying onto his back. Then before the man could get up, Preston grabbed the ice bucket and tipped it up onto his head.

Carole grabbed the soda syphon and handed it across the bar to Sally, and she took aim and gave the man a good dousing.

Meanwhile, a second bouncer had appeared on the scene and, seeing what was going on, he said, "Guy didn't want to learn his lesson, Bob, that it?"

Preston looked at the bouncer. "You better kick him out on his ass before I lose my temper…"

The bouncers got the man up off the floor and dragged him out.

Sally squeezed Preston's hand. "Thanks for helping me out, Bob… Boy, I can't believe what a prick that guy was."

"How about we go and grab a takeaway, Sal?"

"So what was Carole saying about me when you were sitting at the bar, Bob?"

"Just what a really nice girl you are."

They were sitting at the deal table in Preston's studio flat in West-bourne Park, eating the Indian takeaway they'd picked up on the way home.

"She say anything else?"

"Just that I'd better take good care of you or she'll break my legs."

"Did she actually *say* that…?"

"Something along those lines." Preston took a swig from his can of Stella Artois. "Carole's got a heart of gold."

"She's been through a lot; from what I've heard."

Preston nodded. "Her husband went inside for a long stretch for trying to rob a bank...and now she tells me he's trying to get a job in one."

"You're kidding me, right?"

"That's what she said."

Sally swallowed a mouthful of her curry. "Boy this is hot."

"You did order a vindaloo..."

"I dunno how you ever get this stuff down."

"Takes practice."

After they'd finished eating, Preston having polished off what Sally left, they lay on the bed and watched Sky News.

Preston's ears perked up when he heard how the MP, Sir George Parker, had been kidnapped and the kidnappers wanted £5,000,000 as ransom. "Another kidnapping," Preston said. "Only a real one this time."

He turned to look at Sally, and saw that she was asleep.

Pole dancing was tiring work.

Preston was woken up by the sound of his smartphone ringing early the following morning, and he snatched it up from the bedside table and snapped it open. "Hello?"

"Body's turned up in Brompton cemetery, Bob."

"Okay, I'll be right there."

He snapped his phone shut and pocketed it.

"What's happened, Bob?" Sally asked him.

He told her as he pulled on his shirt. "I've got to go."

"Well, at least let me get you some breakfast before you leave."

Preston was already over by the door, putting his jacket on. "No time for that..."

"It's my day off, too, and I was planning on spending some quality time with you, Bob."

"Well why don't you stay here and catch up on your beauty sleep – and you can spend the night, too, if you want, of course..."

"Is that you don't mind if I do, or you'd *like* me to, Bob...?"

He looked at her, serious now, and said, "I'd like you to...only thing is, I might not be back until late, so don't wait up... I'll try not to wake you when I come in."

She gave him a certain look. "You know I always love it when you wake me up, Bob..."

He smiled, then turned and went out.

When Preston got to the cemetery, several other police officers were already there, Detective Sergeant Johnson among them, and a forensic and a photographer were also present. The body was lying in some long grass, behind a row of bushes that bordered the path that ran along the western edge of the cemetery, and a motorcycle had been left lying nearby.

The barrier tape that had been used to mark the crime scene stretched beyond the path, right to the wall, and Preston noticed that there was blood on the path. "She must've been dragged from here into the grass, Dave," he said.

Johnson nodded. "Yes, I noticed the blood, guv."

"Looks like she was shot twice..."

The forensic looked up at Preston over his shoulder and said, "That's right...and at very close range."

"When would she've been killed?"

"If I had to hazard a very rough guess, judging by how stiff the body is, I'd say between twelve and twenty hours ago."

Preston tweaked his tash, trying to imagine the scene.

Fuck, he thought, I was here yesterday afternoon at Bob Houseman's funeral. And said, "There's blood on the bike, too."

"Yeah...my guess is, she was shot while sitting on her motorcycle back on the path... The guy drags her into the bushes, then puts the bike next to her and goes on his way..."

Preston noticed a purse that had been thrown down near the body and, seeing him looking at it, Detective Sergeant Johnson said, "Could've just been a simple mugging gone wrong, guv... Guy asks her to hand over her purse, she puts up a struggle, so he shoots her..."

"Or maybe that's what the killer would like us to believe, Dave."

"That's possible, too, guv, of course..."

"Any sign of a struggle?" Preston asked the forensic.

"None at this stage."

"Not an attempted rape, then?"

"We'll have to carry out all the necessary tests, of course, but I should very much doubt it."

Preston turned to Detective Sergeant Johnson and said, "We need to find out everything we can about her..."

"I'll get on it right away, guv."

Just then, there was a crackle of thunder and rain began to fall.

All we need, Preston thought.

Linda Houseman noticed a silver Honda kept appearing in her mirror as she drove over to Harley Street.

She took a detour around the backstreets, then waited for the car to catch up...and when it did, she got a good enough look at the driver in her mirror to be able to see it was DCI Preston.

So he suspects me, she thought.

Well he could suspect her all he wanted, just so long as he didn't have any proof of her involvement.

She headed on over to Harley Street, then parked and went on up to Emmet's surgery, and he was waiting in the doorway for her.

They kissed as soon as he'd shut the door, then she said, "The cop followed me over here."

"You mean you recognized him?"

She nodded. "It was that DCI Preston – the guy I told you about."

"They've got nothing on us now I've got this." Emmet held up the chip.

"Let's make sure we keep it that way, John."

"It's not the cops I'm worried about, but the guys in the red Lexus that've been following me," he said. "They were down in the street the last time I looked."

Linda's eyes widened. "You mean they followed me here, too?"

"No, it's not you they've been following but me."

She went over to the window and peered down at the street. "I can see a red car parked across the road."

"That's it."

"How long's it been there?"

"About half an hour or so."

"Why don't they come up, I wonder, if they're so keen to meet us...?"

"Maybe they reckon too many people would see them."

"You sure they aren't cops?"

"Positive."

"D'you reckon they're dangerous?"

"Probably."

"The copper's still there, too."

"We really are popular these days."

Linda turned and said, "There must be something on the chip those guys don't want anyone to see."

"There's footage of them forcing a man into the back of their car."

"Show me that bit, John."

Emmet put the chip back into the camera, and they watched the two big men forcing the small, well-dressed man into the back of the Lexus. Linda used the zoom facility and scrutinized the face of the man they'd as yet been unable to identify as it grew in size. "I know that face from somewhere..."

"Yes, so do I, come to think of it..."

"He's somebody famous."

"Yes..."

"I've seen that face a lot on the telly, but I just can't put a name to it."

"My God – it's Sir George Parker, the MP..."

"Why yes, of course..."

"But there was something in the news about him being kidnapped, wasn't there?"

"That's right... they're asking for an enormous ransom...five million pounds, I think it was... I saw it on the news this morning."

"Well now we know who's taken him..."

"...Which explains why they're so keen on getting their hands on the chip."

Emmet bit down on his lower lip. "What shall we do with it, then...?"

"I reckon we should get rid of it before these guys get their hands on it, John...because if they do, then we're in big trouble..."

"I think you're right."

"What I don't get, is how these guys know you've got it..."

"My guess is, they must've found out who had taken the footage and where she lived around the same time I did, and then they must've seen me leave the girl's house with the camera—"

"Who was the girl?"

"A friend of Melanie's...Melanie told her about me and you, and they must've worked up a plan to blackmail us between them..."

"Burn the chip and throw it down the toilet, John."

Without thinking any further, Emmet used a lighter to burn the chip and make sure it was destroyed, before he went into the bathroom and threw the charred remains down the pan. Then he pulled the flush.

Linda stood there, watching him do it.

"I've got an idea," she said. "Give me the camera."

"What are you going to do, Linda?"

"I'll give those guys a run for their money."

"But they must be serious criminals, Linda... Are you sure you know what you're doing?"

"Don't worry about me."

Emma followed her to the door.

"Where are you going?"

She turned and kissed Emmet on the mouth, gave his dick a gentle squeeze through the trousers of his blue pinstripe suit and felt it harden nicely. "I'll call you this evening sometime on your mobile, John."

"But don't you want to use the couch?"

She gave him her sexy look and said, "Let's save the fireworks for later."

Then she turned and went out.

Emmet went over to the window and watched Linda leave the building and get into her Mercedes. Then saw the red Lexus, and the cop in his silver Honda, start up and go after her.

What the hell's Linda playing at? he wondered.

Linda Houseman drove up to the corner and zigzagged her way through the streets before she joined the Marylebone Road, where she found herself stuck in traffic that was moving at a slow crawl.

She saw the Lexus two cars behind her, and the cop was right behind it.

The lights changed to red and the line of cars in front of her came to a halt. She checked in her mirror and saw a man get out of the red Lexus and come towards her.

The lights changed to amber just as the man drew level with the passenger door, but the car in front of her still hadn't begun to move. Same story in the lane to her left.

She saw the guy check the handle, and find that it was locked.

What's this character think I'm gonna do, she thought, open the door and say hop in?

Then she saw him reach into the pocket of his leather jacket and bring out a piece of iron tubing...and the next moment, he smashed the side window with it, and the glass fractured in a spider's web. He hit the window again with the piece of iron tubing, and Linda Houseman screamed as shards of glass came flying into the car. She set off without thinking and rammed the car in front of her, which was still stationary, even though the lights had just turned green.

Then Linda saw the man get out of the car in front, an angry look on his face as he came to inspect the damage to the back of his Volkswagen – not that she'd done much to it because she'd only hit the bumper.

The man's expression changed when he saw there was glass everywhere...only Linda Houseman was no longer looking at him, because she was too busy kicking out at the guy who was trying to enter her car... Then she heard a voice say, "Get out of there!"

I pray to God it's that DCI Preston guy, Linda thought.

Then she saw DCI Preston drag the guy back out of the car, and they began to fight there at the side of the road.

The driver of the Volkswagen tried to come to Preston's aid, but the second man, who'd got out of the Lexus by now, hit him with what looked like the handle of a gun. The driver of the Volkswagen hit the tarmac and stayed there. Then the man who'd been driving the Lexus set about helping his mate fight DCI Preston...and while they were going about it, Linda got out of her Merc, then weaved her way through the traffic over to the pavement and ran into a hotel.

"Quick, call the police."

"What's happened, madam?" said the young blonde receptionist.

"Two men just tried to kill me, and now they're beating up a detective who came to my aid out there."

The receptionist picked up the phone and made the call, and Linda stayed where she was until the police arrived in the shape of a number of uniforms.

"What happened, miss?" one of them asked her.

"They were going to kill me."

"Who were?"

"You can ask your colleague...they attacked him, too."

"Which colleague is this, miss?"

"That detective ...DCI Preston."

"Where did this take place?"

"Out in the street... I was sitting in my car, stuck in traffic, and one of them smashed the window."

"Just stay here a moment," the uniform said, and he turned and dashed back outside.

When Linda was finally taken back to her car by a WPC, she found that the camera was no longer on the passenger seat, where she'd left it.

"Do you have any idea who these people were?" the WPC asked her.

Linda shook her head.

"So are you saying that it was a completely unprovoked attack?"

"Unless you'd call sitting in my car waiting for the traffic to start to move provocation..."

She turned and saw DCI Preston sitting over on the pavement with his back against the wall. He was looking dazed and gazing into space.

"I hope the detective who was attacked is all right," she said. "He tried to fight them off but there were two of them..."

"You might say he's stirred but not shaken," the WPC said.

Linda glanced at her wristwatch. "I need to be at the Ritz in half an hour."

"What are you going to do about your car?"

"I'll have to call the garage I use and have someone come and tow it away... I can't drive it like that."

. . .

"I wanted to pass on my sincerest condolences to you, Linda," Harlan said. "Bob was more than just a writer to me...he was a true friend and a wonderful human being... Everyone loved him."

Yes, everyone except for me, Linda thought.

"And why shouldn't they?" Harlan paused to sip his Chablis. "He was such a great guy, after all..."

"Don't, Harlan, please," Linda said. "You'll start me off again." She dabbed at her eyes with her napkin.

"Yes, of course... I'm so sorry, Linda...it's just..." Harlan waved his fork and began to sob his heart out, right there in the middle of the restaurant.

Linda forced a few crocodile tears of her own.

Seeing them like this, the waiter came over and asked if everything was all right.

"Yes, the food's superb," Harlan managed to say through his tears.

"Is there some problem, sir...?"

"No, it's quite all right."

"Can I get you anything?"

The young waiter was clearly at a loss as to what to say or do.

"You could bring me a large Scotch," Harlan said. "Any brand so long as it's a good single malt." He turned to Linda. "I don't know if you'd like one...?"

"Yes, make that two... I'll have mine straight."

"Me, too."

"Of course." The waiter went off and returned in next to no time with the drinks.

Linda and Harlan both knocked them back in one, then Harlan picked up the bottle of Chablis and replenished their glasses. "I can't face the food," he said, "exquisite though it is..."

"Me neither."

Linda was rather put out because she had been enjoying her Dover sole, but she figured she'd better leave it so as not to appear heartless.

Just then, she saw a familiar face coming towards her across the restaurant. Why it's that damned Inspector Preston again, she thought.

. . .

Preston stopped at the table and said, "Hello, Mrs Houseman, I was told I'd be able to find you here."

"Hello, Inspector Boston..."

"It's Preston..."

"Sorry, yes...please allow me to introduce you to Harlan Rokeby... He was Bob's literary agent."

"Still am," Harlan said.

Preston acknowledged the man with a little nod of the head. "There's Mr. Houseman's literary estate still to be managed, no doubt, sir..."

"Yes, quite...and there's also the manuscript Bob was working on up until his death..."

"So there'll be another book from him, then?"

"It's a little early to say... I still haven't had a chance to look at it yet... Linda's brought it with her today... Not that it's been uppermost in our thoughts you understand, Inspector...frankly we're both feeling so upset we've been drowning our sorrows."

Preston turned to Linda Houseman. "About what happened earlier... Have you any idea who those two men that attacked you were?"

"No, none at all."

"What's this about men *attacking* you, Linda?" Harlan cut in.

Preston said, "You mean you'd never seen them before?"

"Never, no."

"But why would they just attack your car like that?"

"I can only presume they were out to get the manuscript."

"The one your husband was working on, you mean?"

Linda Houseman shrugged. "I really have no idea what they were up to, Inspector...but it's the only thing that occurs to me."

"What's all this about?" Harlan said, but neither of them paid him any attention.

"They were pretty rough customers."

"Yes, I gathered as much... I saw you fighting with them, so I took the opportunity to escape and run into a hotel, where I had the receptionist call the police."

"So they took the manuscript, did they?"

"No, I managed to get away with it, thanks to you, Inspector..." She offered Preston a steely smile and said, "You arrived just in the nick of time and saved the day."

Preston frowned. "I'll need to talk to you again, Mrs Houseman."

"Feel free to talk to me in front of Harlan... I'm sure he doesn't mind."

"Not at all." Harlan smiled, but neither of them noticed.

"I believe you have been attending sessions with a doctor in Harley Street quite regularly...?"

"You know that very well, Inspector, so I don't know why you ask... after all, you've followed me over there."

Preston let that one go flying past.

"What's the name of the doctor you go and see?"

"Doctor John Emmet...he's a psychotherapist – but I'm sure you know that, too."

"And in what capacity do you go and see him?"

"I'm not sure I like your tone, Inspector... Are you trying to insinuate something...?"

"I merely asked you a question, Mrs Houseman."

"It's not a crime for a woman to see a psychotherapist, is it?"

"I should jolly well hope not," Harlan said, "otherwise half of my writers would be banged up in prison, not to mention my other friends... I should have to talk to most of my writers across a table with a guard watching our every move."

"If you're going to join us, Inspector," Linda Houseman said, "then do take a seat and place your order."

"I'm working, Mrs Houseman."

"Oh, is that what you call it?"

"Unless of course you'd rather your husband's murder went uninvestigated...?"

"You're putting words in my mouth, Inspector... Why are you so interested in my psychotherapist, anyway?"

"He's an interesting sort of man."

"Shrinks usually are...probably comes with having heard so many people's intimate secrets..."

"His secretary's just been found dead, and that makes him all the more interesting in my book."

"Oh..."

"She was *murdered*..."

"Oh, I say... I'm sure Doctor Emmet will be upset."

"Yes... I had an officer go around to his house in Fulham a short while ago, to tell him the sad news...but he wasn't at home."

"Probably working."

"His practice is closed."

Linda Houseman shrugged. "This is a very sad and distressing business for those close to the person who was killed, I'm sure, but I didn't know the girl and so I really don't quite see what it has to do with me..."

Neither did Preston – yet.

Which explained why he was here.

To ask the widow and watch her response, to see if she made a slip.

"I didn't say it did," he said.

"*Well*, then...?"

"I just wanted to know if there's anything going on that you haven't told me about, Mrs Houseman...?"

"Well there's been plenty going on, by the sound of it, Inspector... but quite how you expect a poor bereaved widow like me to know about it, I fail to understand... Do I look as if I'm some sort of *psychic* to you?"

"Okay Mrs Houseman, well thank you for your time... I'll leave you to finish your meal now, and perhaps we can talk again..."

{.western lang="en-GB"}

Preston's smartphone rang as he was driving along past the theatres on Shaftesbury Avenue, so he picked it up and opened it with the fingers of his right hand, a technique he'd refined with practice. "Hello?"

"It's me, guv...just discovered the name of the girl that was found murdered in Brompton cemetery...it was Joanne Parks."

"Well done, Dave...you talked to her parents yet?"

"No, I was just going to take a drive over there."

"Give me the address and I'll meet you outside the house, and we'll go in and talk to them together."

DS Johnson was standing by his car outside the house when Preston pulled up. The Detective Chief Inspector climbed out and locked the doors of his Honda with the remote as he walked up the pavement. It had just started to spot with rain and the sky was a sad dishwater grey.

"Okay, guv?"

Preston nodded. "Let's go and see what we can find out then, Dave."

They ran up the front steps of the building, which was one of those elegant numbers with a portico and stuccoed facade. Preston rang the bell and a tall slim woman, dressed in a linen skirt and a beige silk top, came and opened the door.

"Hello, sorry to trouble you," Preston said. "Are you Mrs Parks, the mother of Joanne?"

The woman nodded, and Preston introduced himself, holding out his ID for her to see as he did so.

Mrs Parks took the card from his hand and examined it for a moment, before she handed it back. She must have been pushing forty but was still something of a stunner. "You've come to talk about my daughter's murder, I presume?"

Seeing that Preston was momentarily lost for words, she said, "I found out from a reporter who called me up to ask for my reaction to the news…"

"I am very sorry, Mrs Parks."

The rain was getting harder, and Preston hunched his shoulders and looked up at the sky.

"You'd better come in." Mrs Parks took a step backwards, and Preston and Johnson entered the house.

They followed her along the hallway and off into the living room. The ceiling was high and there was a large fireplace with an old oil painting above it on the wall. "Please make yourself at home."

Preston and Johnson both sat on the leather sofa, and they watched Mrs Parks as she came and sat in the chair by the fireplace. Preston leaned his elbows on his knees and gave his tash a tweak or two.

"So how can I help you, gentlemen?"

"We're investigating your daughter's murder, Mrs Parks, as you rightly assumed…and, in order to do our job properly, we need to find out as much as we can about her lifestyle."

"Joanne was a lovely girl, and she would never have harmed anyone…"

"I'm sure that's the case…but it doesn't help me much."

"No…" Mrs Parks's chest rose as she took a deep breath, and she dried her eyes with a small handkerchief. "Well I don't know where to start..."

"I just need to know if she had a job, and how she spent her time... who her friends were...the name of her boyfriend if she had one, that sort of thing."

Mrs Parks took another deep breath and swallowed. "Joanne was a bit of an obsessive type in many ways."

"Oh...?"

"She was a vegan...thought it was wrong to eat meat and anything that comes from an animal... She always used to say humans are the most dangerous and destructive animals on the planet." Mrs Parks dried her eyes again. "She was obsessed with film and photography, too...and was always making little films and taking pictures."

"Could we see her camera, Mrs Parks?"

"We don't have it here... She always kept it with her, so it's probably in the house where she lived...it was almost a part of her...you know, like some sort of prosthetic appendage..."

"But we've been to her house and taken a good look around, and there was no sign of any camera."

Mrs Parks's eyes widened. "That's odd."

"Unless someone stole it, guv," Detective Sergeant Johnson said.

"Do you think that may have been why she was killed, Inspector...?"

Preston flashed Johnson a certain look the Detective Sergeant knew the meaning of only too well. "I'm afraid we have no idea why she was killed yet, Mrs Parks...that's why we're here – in the hope that you can help us build up a picture of what she was like and of her lifestyle..."

"Joanne was gay, and she was in love with a friend of hers who is bisexual..."

"Can you give us this friend's details?"

"Name's Melanie...she lives over in Fulham somewhere and worked as a secretary... The truth is, Inspector, I thoroughly disapproved of the relationship from start to finish..."

"You mean you were unhappy about Joanne's being a lesbian?"

"It wasn't that... I mean, I'd have preferred it if she were straight, for her sake, because I think gay people often lead such complicated lives... But no, David and I both loved Joanne dearly and accepted her for what she was...we didn't have a problem with it in that sense..."

"So it was Melanie you objected to...?"

"Yes...for the way she made Joanne suffer... I mean, Joanne was totally besotted with her...she just wanted to live with Melanie and didn't have eyes for anyone else... But Melanie was only using her as...as an amusement...you know, something to fill in the time while she was waiting for something better to come along... And there was something about a man she worked for... Joanne called me up and told me all about it earlier in the week... I had no idea at the time that it would be the last time I'd ever talk to her..."

"Can you tell me any more about this man you just mentioned...?"

"Melanie had an affair with him, from what I could gather, and he dropped her..."

"And she continued to feel things for him, is that it...?"

"She was using him to taunt Joanne, was my take on the situation... You know, telling her how great it was with this man when they'd been together, and how she could never feel the same way for a girl, that sort of thing..."

"Hearing Melanie say those things must have hurt Joanne a great deal."

"Oh it cut her up terribly." Mrs Parks dried her eyes with the back of her hand. "I used to tell Joanne to leave her and look for someone else..."

"Anyone else in particular?"

"Any nice girl who'd at least treat her with the respect she deserved."

"It all must have been very distressing for you, Mrs Parks."

"I could write a book on the subject of parental distress, Inspector...and my husband David could, too, I'm sure...because we both loved Joanne to bits."

Preston got to his feet. "Thank you very much for speaking to us, Mrs Parks."

She got up out of her chair. "I only wish I could help you more, Inspector."

"You've helped me quite a bit, as it turns out."

"Well I'm really not sure how."

She saw them to the door, and when they stepped outside, they found that it was pouring with rain.

. . .

"Now what, guv?" Johnson said.

"We need to talk to Dr. John Emmet... I shouldn't be at all surprised if he was at the centre of all this somehow."

When Preston and Johnson called around to Emmet's house in Fulham, a young blonde wearing an overall and jeans came to the door. "Hello," she said, "can I help you?"

"Yes, I'd like to speak to Doctor Emmet...is he in?"

"No, I haven't seen him this week."

"I see...and you are, miss...?"

"I come in to clean the house... Would you like me to leave him a message?"

"Perhaps you'd tell him that DCI Preston would like to talk to him."

Preston turned and walked back to his Honda, shoulders hunched against the heavy rain, and Johnson followed him.

They stopped on the pavement by the side of the car, and Johnson said, "Now what, guv?"

"Let's see if he's at his practice in Harley Street."

But when they tried the door to Doctor Emmet's practice, it was locked.

"Surprise surprise." Preston puffed out his cheeks.

"Shrink seems to've disappeared," Johnson said. "Or maybe he's just *shrunk* outa sight..."

"Very funny, Dave."

"What's our next move, guv...?"

"I need to think."

"Reckon a beer might help?"

"Wouldn't do any harm."

They drove over to Baker Street, where they entered the King & Queen and found themselves a couple of spare stools at the bar.

When the barmaid came over, Preston said, "Two pints of best, luv," and the girl, a busty peroxide blonde in her twenties, set about pouring.

Preston took out his smartphone and checked his messages. There was one from Sally saying she hoped to see him later. He wrote back to say he'd probably be very late.

Seeing him tapping away at the keys, Johnson said, "Wossup, guv... sorting out your love life, are you?"

"Something like that, Dave."

The barmaid placed the beers down on the counter, then took the tenner from Preston's outstretched hand.

"How're things going with Sarah, Dave?"

Johnson wrinkled up his mouth. "Could be better."

"Like that, is it?"

"Bit up and down, yeah."

Preston would give the marriage another couple of years, max. Dave was too dedicated a cop to be a successful husband as well. Because the big thing about a marriage was, you couldn't run it as though it was a bit of something on the side. It was either everything or nothing...and if it was everything, then you couldn't be a very good cop. Because the job needed everything you had, too, and then some.

Preston knew because he'd lived it.

And had the divorce to prove it.

Only the lonely can do this job, he thought.

"How are you getting along with your new girlfriend, guv?"

"We're doing just fine."

"She still working as a pole dancer?"

Preston nodded, tasted his beer. "She wants to get out and do something else."

"What's stopping her?"

"Nothing else she could do that pays anywhere near as much."

"So why doesn't she go on a course or something?"

"What I told her... She says she's going to, but she's still trying to make up her mind what she wants to do."

"Some people never do find out..."

"Uh...?"

"What they want to do in life."

"She says she'd like to run a restaurant..."

"Where's the money gonna come from to start it up?"

"Exactly."

"So why doesn't she go into catering and work her way up?"

"Says the pay's crap and you can't work your way up to owning a business...you either own it or you don't."

Johnson shrugged. "How does she feel about pole dancing?"

"Hates it."

"That figures...can't be much fun, having to prance about on a pole for a load of lechers, can it, guv...?"

Emmet was lying on the bed in his room at the Hilton, drinking Scotch and wondering if anyone had been to the house asking for him.

He called the mobile number of the girl he had in to clean the place.

"Hello...?"

"Hi, Gemma – it's John... Is everything okay?"

"Yeah, but the police have been around here...a plainclothes detective with a moustache...he said to tell you he wants to talk to you."

"Did he leave a name?"

"DCI Preston."

"And did he say why he wants to talk with me?"

"No, he just asked if I'd seen you, and I said I hadn't for a few days."

"I see...well thanks for letting me know..."

"No problem." They both went quiet for a moment, and then Gemma said, "I was wondering, when are you going to pay me this week, John?"

"That's what I was calling about," Emmet lied. "I'll put a cheque in the post, okay...?"

"I'd prefer to be paid in cash, John, otherwise the dole people'll be onto me."

"I'm afraid it's the best I can do right now."

They both went quiet again for a moment.

Gemma said, "You haven't popped by to spend any time with me in ages... What's up – gone off me, have you...? Or've you met somebody else...?"

"It's just that I'm rather tied up at the moment."

"You're not in trouble or anything, are you, John...?"

"No, of course not...look I've got to go, okay... Talk to you soon."

He hung up.

. . .

"What's our next move, then, guv?"

"We need to find Doctor John Emmet and talk to him."

"I know that, but where the fuck is he...?"

"Maybe we should start checking hotels."

"There's a heck of a lot of hotels in London, though."

"Sooner you start going through them the better, then, Dave."

Emmet's mobile rang and he saw that it was Linda calling. "Hello, darling...are you okay?"

"As well as can be expected in the circumstances...those bastards in the Lexus caught up with me."

"Where...?"

"I was stuck in traffic on the Marylebone Road..." She told him all about what happened. "Anyway, they took the camera."

"Yes, but they didn't get the chip."

"Which means they'll be back for it... I'm scared, John."

"But it was you who said we should destroy it, Linda."

"What alternative did we have...?"

"What about the cop?"

"What about him?"

"Do you think he's suspects anything?"

"He may do, but he hasn't got any proof... He came to talk to me while I was having lunch with Harlan, Bob's literary agent..."

"What did he say?"

"Asked if I knew why they were following me and what they were after... I told him the only thing I could think of was they must be after the manuscript of the book Bob was working on before he was killed."

"Good...you did well."

"I'm more worried about the two men who've been following me in the Lexus...these people aren't gonna stop until they've got what they want."

"Have you got any relatives you can go and stay with?"

"There's my sister."

"Where does she live?"

"Down in Hove...but what about the boys?"

"Take them with you."

"I need to see you, though, John."

"That's probably not a good idea right now," Emmet said. "Look, Linda, you're right...these people are dangerous and they're gonna try again... Get the boys and go to stay with your sister."

Preston figured it would be a good idea to talk to the widow again, so he took a drive over to Chelsea and pushed the buzzer to her flat.

No answer.

He went and sat in his car outside and waited.

Stayed there for about an hour.

No sign of her.

He called Johnson and asked him if he'd had any luck checking through the hotels.

"Not so far, guv...but I'll call you straightaway if I do... Where are you now?"

Preston told him.

"Don't think the widow's done a runner as well, do you?"

"No reason to assume so, Dave...perhaps she's just popped out to do a little shopping... Could be anywhere."

"That's true, I suppose."

"Talk to you later."

They hung up.

Emmet was in the shower when he thought he heard someone enter the bedroom. He turned the water off, and called out: "Anyone there?"

The door opened and a man walked in. The man was totally bald and he was wearing jeans, trainers and a leather jacket. "Room service," he said.

And then Emmet saw that the man was holding a gun.

"I've come for the camera with the film in it."

"I don't know what on earth you're talking about."

The man took two steps towards Emmet and hit him in the mouth with the handle of his gun. Emmet went flying back against the wall. Stars exploded in his mouth and head as the ceiling began to spin and, before he could reach out for something to hold on to, the man pushed him down into the bathtub.

Emmet cried out as he fell, and the next thing he knew the man was on him. "Who are you?" Emmet said. "What do you want?"

"I already told ya...we want the chip with the footage on it." The man rammed the end of his gun into Emmet's mouth. "And if I don't get it, I'm gonna kill you, d'you understand?"

Emmet blinked his eyes and tried to nod.

The man removed the barrel of the gun from Emmet's mouth and held it against his forehead. "Now...let's try again... Where's the chip?"

"I threw it down the toilet... But what's so important about it?"

"I'm gonna give you one last chance to tell me where it is or I'm going to kill you... *Where* is the chip?"

"Listen to me," Emmet said. "There was stuff on it that I didn't want anybody to see... I have no idea why it's so important to you, but it was important to me because...well, you see, I've been playing the field a little just lately, and there was footage of me with a woman on there who...well, I'm sure you understand..."

"Oh I understand all right... Now where the fuck is it?"

"I already told you... I flushed it down the toilet."

"Why would you do a stupid thing like that?"

"Okay, God's truth, I killed a girl and the girl with the camera was a friend of the girl I killed...and she got me on film leaving the victim's house...so then I had to kill the second girl – the one with the camera... The footage on the chip could've been used as evidence against me, so I threw it down the toilet, as I said, and flushed it away...probably in the Thames somewhere by now."

"And that's your final word, is it?"

"It's God's truth, on my mother's grave."

The man pulled the trigger, and Emmet's skull and brains were sprayed all over the walls.

The man unscrewed the silencer before he dropped it, along with the gun, down the toilet bowl. Then he turned and went out, followed by the man he'd come in with.

When he got into the corridor, the gunman took off the black leather gloves he'd been wearing and slipped them into his pockets.

"We'll take the back stairs," he said. "Less people remember seeing our faces the better."

They didn't see anybody on the way down and went through a door, passing along a carpeted corridor, then crossed the foyer and went back out the front exit without incident.

When Preston entered the office, DS Johnson looked up and said, "That was good timing, guv... I was just about to pick up the phone and call you."

"What's this...?"

"There's a John Emmet staying at the Hilton on Park Lane."

"Let's go."

Preston turned and hurried out to his Honda, with DS Johnson close behind him, and they set off. "By the way," Preston said, as they drove up Fulham Road, "how did you manage to locate him?"

"The cleaning lady we talked to just called in, guv...said two guys had turned up at the house and held her at gunpoint...threatened to kill her if she didn't tell them where Doctor Emmet was staying."

"You mean she *knew*...?"

"No...but she'd spoken to Emmet earlier on the phone and was able to get up the number he'd called from on her mobile, and she gave me the number, too..."

"And you called it and got the Hilton..."

"Let's just hope we get there before the guys who're looking for Emmet, guv."

Preston put his foot down the rest of the way, until he got caught in traffic outside of Harrods. He had the siren going by now, and cars tried to make way for him, and he eventually got through.

Preston pulled up in the forecourt, and they jumped out of his Honda and hurried into the hotel.

The doorman rushed over to tell Preston he would have to move his car, but Preston flashed his ID and said, "Keep an eye on it for me and make sure it doesn't get nicked, there's a good chap." Then he and Johnson went on in through the revolving door.

Johnson glanced around the foyer as they reached the reception desk. "So this is how the other half live, then, guv."

"I don't know about the other half, Dave...it's only your top one per cent can afford to stay here."

"Emmet must be loaded."

"Either that or he reckons he's about to come into a lot of money..."

Just then, the female receptionist came over, and Preston flashed his ID at her.

The girl studied it for a moment, then said, "What can I do for you, Inspector Preston?"

"You have a John Emmet staying here at the hotel, I believe...?"

The girl leaned over the computer screen that was just below the counter, and pushed a few keys. She straightened up and said, "Yes, that's right... Why, is there some kind of security problem we should know about?"

"I'll be in a much better position to answer that question once I've had the opportunity to speak to Mr. Emmet."

"Oh, I see... Shall I call to tell him you're here?"

"No, I would prefer this to be a surprise visit... What number is he staying in?"

"I'm not sure I'm allowed to divulge that kind of information, Inspector...perhaps I'd better go and get the manager... If you can just wait a moment..."

"I'm investigating a murder, miss, and I don't have time to wait... Now can you please tell me the number of the room he's staying in?"

The girl looked unsure of herself for a moment as her eyes met Preston's, but then relented and said, "He's in two-o-six."

"Thank you...and he's not to be warned that we're here... We're going up to see him now... I'll need a key."

The girl handed it over, and Preston and Johnson went up in the elevator and stepped out into the corridor of the second floor. Peace and quiet reigned, but Preston knew that didn't mean a thing.

When they found the door, they both took out their guns, before Preston put the key in the lock. They charged in with their weapons raised...only to find that the room was empty.

Preston noticed that the door to the bathroom was open and he gestured to Johnson with a shake of the head, and they moved with the slow stealth of big cats across the room.

Preston gave the door a push, then burst into the bathroom with his gun raised, ready to fire...and was met with the sight of John Emmet's corpse.

There was a lot of blood everywhere, as well as bits of Emmet's skull and flesh and brains.

Preston blew out his cheeks as he put his gun away.

"Looks like we got here too late, guv."

"You don't say, Dave."

Meanwhile, Linda Houseman was driving down through South London in her Merc. "Where are we going, Mum?" asked her eldest son, Jason, who was a slim boy of twelve with blond hair and a face full of freckles. "We don't normally go home this way."

"We're going on holiday."

"But you didn't tell us…"

"Well I wanted it to be a surprise… I'm taking you down to stay with Aunt Sarah…"

"We need to go and talk to Linda Houseman again, Dave."

"D'you reckon she's behind all this, then?"

"All I know right now is that people who knew her seem to have a funny habit of getting themselves killed…"

"And all around the same time, too, guv…it is a bit of a coincidence, I agree…"

"I've been in this job long enough to know that coincidences of this sort only ever occur in books…"

"Didn't know you read crime novels, guv?"

"I don't."

When they got over to Linda Houseman's place in Chelsea, though, she didn't come to the door.

"I had a funny feeling she might be out," Preston said.

"Don't suppose you've got a funny feeling where she might be, guv…?"

"Sarcasm doesn't become you, Dave."

"Only asking."

"Well she's got two sons to take care of, so the normal thing would be for her to go and pick them up from school and bring them home."

"Could've taken them out to eat somewhere, guv."

"Or she could have gone with them to stay with a relative."

. . .

Linda Houseman was lying in bed that night at her sister Amanda's place in Wilbury Avenue, which backed onto Hove train station, when she heard a noise…and the next moment the door flew open and two men burst in.

It was dark and Linda couldn't see the men very well, but she knew it must be the two who'd been following her.

She sprang up out of the bed, but one of the men grabbed her by the hair and put a gun to her head.

"Look," Linda said, "this must be some kind of mistake… I have no idea who you are or what you want…"

The second man left the room, and Linda figured he must be going after the boys. She tried to scream, but the man who was holding a gun to her head put his hand over her mouth.

"I know all about you," he said. "You and your boyfriend, the shrink, had your husband killed, then your boyfriend killed his secretary because he thought she was getting suspicious…then he killed the girl with the camera… "

The second man came back into the room with the two boys and Amanda. He was holding a gun against little Mark's head.

Amanda said, "Just give them whatever it is they want, Linda."

"I don't have it."

"What do you mean, you don't have it?"

"It's the chip you want, right?"

"Yeah," the man said.

"John took it out and flushed it down the toilet."

Just then, they heard a noise and the next moment a voice said, "This is the police, now drop your weapons and come out."

"I've got a unit of crack marksman out here," Preston said. "You've got two choices – either drop your weapons or die."

Linda Houseman shouted, "Run boys!" and she tried to kick the man who was holding her in the crotch, but he fired a bullet into her head and she fell to the floor, dead.

As that happened, Amanda lunged at the second man. He fired as he fell back against the wall, and the bullet ricocheted about the room without hitting anyone.

Preston and Johnson and the team of marksmen entered the room the moment they heard the first shot, and one of the marksmen shot the second man in the gut. The man dropped his gun and went down

The man who'd killed Linda Houseman fired a second shot and one of the marksmen went down. The man turned and kicked the window-pane out.

It was the only way he could go.

He stepped onto the ledge, but before he could reach for the drain-pipe, little Mark Houseman, the youngest of the two boys, ran over and shoved him in the back, and the man went plunging down and landed face-first in the cement garden.

Preston went over to the window and looked down, to check the man was dead.

No question.

Somebody turned the light on, and Preston went over to the other man, who was now sitting on the floor. The man had his hand on his belly, where he'd been shot. "Right then," Preston said, hunkering down on his haunches. "You'd better tell me what's been going on if you want me to call for an ambulance…"

"Fuck off."

"Fine…have it your way."

"Get me a fuckin ambulance."

"Uh-uh." Preston shook his head. "First you talk, then I make the call…"

"It was us that kidnapped the MP, Sir George Parker."

"Where's he being held?"

The man told him.

The following evening, Preston called into Secrets and plumped himself down on a stool at the bar.

"Usual, Bob?" Carole said.

Preston nodded.

"I see they got that MP that was kidnapped back in one piece, then."

"So they tell me."

Carole put the drink down on the bar, and Preston picked it up and tasted it.

"What I heard, it was you that saved the day."

Preston grinned and said, "You know me, Carole...never was one to boast."

"What I read, you solved too cases in one," she said. "'Cause the kidnappers ended up killing that woman an' her boyfriend, some shrink, who were killers themselves..."

"You could call it poetic justice." Preston took another sip of his Scotch, gave his tash a tweak.

"I do feel sorry for those two young boys, though, Bob...although I suppose they'll be given all the help money can buy."

Preston turned and looked over his shoulder as the music changed, and Sally came onto the stage to start her dance.

"I hope you treat that girl right, Bob," Carole said. "She positively idolizes you..."

"I care a great deal for her, too."

"In that case, I dunno why you don't pop the question and make an honest woman of her."

"Not sure that's what she really wants, Carole."

"Can't know her as well as you think, then... Sally'd jump at the chance to marry you, Bob."

"She'd have to leave this place."

"She hates it anyway...she told me so herself."

Preston knew that was true.

What he wasn't so sure about, was how Sally would adapt to life as a copper's wife.

In fact, he wasn't sure how *any* woman would adapt to life as a copper's wife.

"She's the sort of girl'd make any man happy if he was to treat her right," Carole said. "I could see you two making a go of it, Bob."

It sure is pretty to think so, Preston thought.

SWITCH

PART I

CHAPTER 1

Terry Statham walked over to the canvas that was standing on an easel in the middle of the room and went 'Du-du', just like a little kid, before he pulled away the cloth that was covering it, and Angie found herself looking at Rembrandt's 'Self Portrait at the Age of 63'.

They were in the front room of Terry's flat, which he'd had converted into a studio. Paintings that Terry had done in a variety of different styles were hanging all over the whitewashed walls, but it was the face of the 63-year-old Rembrandt that claimed all of Angie's attention. Having a man like Terry as a father, Angie had been made familiar with the works of the Old Masters from a ridiculously early age, so that even as a small child she knew certain canvases the way many little girls nowadays know their Barbie dolls and Bratz.

'Whaddaya think?' Terry said.

Angie went right up close to the painting to get a better look at the surface texture, then she took a few paces back and the painting came into clearer focus before her. Yeah, that was Rembrandt all right. Her father had managed to capture him right down to the tiniest nuance of expression and gesture – that was presuming.... Angie turned to Terry and said, 'It's a copy, right?'

'You tell me.'

'Well I mean it must be, obviously – except that it looks far too good for that...too *authentic*...' She shook her head, her pretty brown eyes wide with disbelief. 'How'd you manage to make it seem so *real*?'

'I guess I must've improved with age.' Terry ran his hand through his thick silvery-grey hair as he spoke.

'Wait a minute,' Angie said, 'you can't be planning on selling it if the original's still hanging on the wall in the National Gallery, surely?'

Terry just kept grinning at her and didn't say anything, and Angie reckoned she knew what that grin meant. 'Dad, you'll never do it,' she said, 'you'll get caught.'

The following day Terry Statham walked into the National Gallery with an easel, paint and brushes. He set up the easel in front of Rembrandt's 'Self Portrait at the Age of 63' and began to paint an imitation of the masterpiece that was hanging before him, there on the wall. Terry made a point of making the imitation appear very different from the original, and of vastly inferior quality, for the benefit of any onlookers.

Then, at a time when the room was nearly empty, he threw a small cylinder down onto the floor. Smoke came out of the cylinder and Terry cried 'Fire!' and the few people who were in the room ran out.

Brian Silver, the gallery attendant who was acting as lookout, immediately deactivated the gallery's CCTV system and took out the tapes that had been used that day. Then he went and manned the entrance to the room, and began directing people to the exit from the building by a different route.

While Brian was busying himself with preventing anyone from entering the room, Terry and his partner, Kenny Jarrow, set to work. They just looked like two ordinary guys in their forties who were doing something that they did every day.

They lifted Rembrandt's 'Self Portrait at the Age of 63' down off the wall and removed it from its frame. Then they removed the canvas that Terry had been working on that day from the easel, and underneath it was the 'real' forgery that he had already finished some time ago.

They took this 'real' forgery of Terry's and put it in the frame, in place of the original, and hung it on the wall. They put the inferior, amateurish-looking copy, on top of the Rembrandt original, wrapped both the paintings in a piece of lamb's wool, and put them in the case that Terry had brought with him.

Then Kenny went and got the CCTV tapes from Brian Silver, their man on the inside, before he and Kenny and Terry left the gallery separately.

No one stopped Terry as he went out the back exit carrying the Rembrandt original.

'Hello, Jeremy Willoughby speaking.'

'I've got the Rembrandt... When can we make the exchange?'

'Soon—I just need a little more time.'

'Not going cold on me, are you?'

'No, it's nothing like that, I assure you,' Willoughby said. 'I just need a few more days to free up the whole of the fifty million... I should have it all by Saturday morning.'

'I'll call you Saturday morning,' Terry said. 'But listen, you'd better have it by then if you still want the painting.'

Terry hung up.

'So this is it,' Angie said.

'It's not much to write home about, but you said you wanted to see it, so here we are.'

There was a small kitchen area directly in front of you as you entered the flat, the bed was away to the left, under the window, and squeezed in between the kitchen area and the bed was a desk with a computer on it. Either side of the computer the desk was crammed with books and papers.

Angie smiled and Liam took a step forwards, so that they were almost touching. They kissed and Angie felt like she didn't want to stop. She figured she better had, though, because she didn't want to appear too keen on him. They'd only been going out for a week, after all. 'I'm starving,' she said. 'What about you?'

'I could eat.'

'Why don't I make us both something?'

'Sure, if you'd like to.'

So Angie fixed some pasta with tomato for the two of them. And she had just sat down next to Liam, and was about to take her first mouthful, when her mobile began to bleep. She took it out and snapped it open. 'Hello?'

'Hi, Angie, it's me.'

'Hi, Dad... what's up?'

'You seen the News today?'

'No... why?'

'Maybe you should...'

'Da-ad... can you stop talking in code and tell me what you're on about?'

'I don't wanna spoil the surprise, love.'

'What are you talking about, Dad...?'

'Just watch the News, darling... Must dash... Love you.'

Terry hung up.

'What was that all about?' Liam asked her.

'Wish I knew.' Angie picked up the control unit and turned the TV on, then surfed the channels until she found Sky News.

'Not on the telly, is he...?'

'All he said was to watch the News.'

They listened to a report on the economy, and another on the local by-elections, and then the anchor man said, '*Today the chief curator at London's National Gallery has announced that one of the gallery's most valuable and important paintings has been stolen in what appears to have been an elaborate and cunning operation.*

The police say the job must have been carried out by extremely intelligent professionals who possess a great deal of knowledge of the art world.

What is more, it appears that the perpetrators of the crime must be in contact with one of the world's very best art forgers, because in stealing the painting they left a brilliant imitation in its place...

In fact, so brilliant was the forgery that the thieves left hanging on the wall in the National Gallery, in the exact same spot where the original used to hang, that nobody noticed the crime had taken place until one of the thieves called in to inform the gallery's curator of the fact.

And there I was wondering if Dad was just bluffing and maybe looking for a little attention, Angie thought...

She phoned him up on his mobile number.

'Hello?'

'Dad,' she said, 'I hope to God you know what it is you're doing.'
'Don't worry, okay?'
'How am I *not* going to worry?'
'You're just like your mum used to be.'
'Just be careful, Dad, will you, *please*.'
'I'm always careful, babe... It goes with the territory.'
Angie crossed her fingers.
'Take care,' Terry said, 'and I'll be in touch soon, love.' He hung up.

Terry's buzzer rang and he wondered who the fuck it could be, as he went and peeked through the net curtains down at the street.
 'Well I'll be blowed,' he said, when he saw who it was.
 And figured the best thing to do was pretend to be out.
 Just a case of waiting for her to go away...only she didn't...and then he remembered he'd given her a key.
 Then he heard sound of a key turning in the door to the flat...
 'Hello, Naomi darling...well this is a nice surprise, I must say.'
 They hugged, and then she said, 'You didn't call.'
 'Been kinda busy, darlin'... Get you a cup a tea?'
 'A cold lager'd be better.'
 'I'll see if there's one in the fridge.'
 Terry went out to the kitchen, and came back into the living room with two cans of Stella Artois and a couple of glasses.
 He'd picked her up in a club a week ago, and bedded her the same night. Then she took off in the morning and said she'd be back. That was when he'd given her the key... He'd given it to her on an impulse, without really thinking things through, and forgotten all about it.
 Stupid of me, he thought.
 Now that she wasn't a nice girl...only the timing was all wrong.
 Terry put on some Sonny Rollins and they talked for a bit about nothing much, and then they both found themselves sauntering into the bedroom next door.
 Terry had some trouble getting it up at first, so Naomi went down on him. He lay there while she was going to work on him, looking up at the ceiling and thinking.
 He couldn't wait for Saturday to come around. But what if Willoughby were to say it was no go and pull out right at the last

moment? Then he'd have to find another buyer somehow. He'd worry about that if and when it came to it.

Then Terry found himself getting hard, and he rolled Naomi over onto her

back and they began to make love.

It went well.

Afterwards he said, 'You gonna spend the night?'

'You want me to?'

'Course I do.'

What else could he say?

It would have been true, under normal circumstances.

Terry was the first to wake up in the morning, and he lay there, thinking about things and watching Naomi sleep. Then she woke up and had herself a good stretch.

She looked at Terry and said, 'I need a shower, wash all this sweat off me.'

'You know where it is.'

So she got up and left the room, and Terry winnowed a Marlboro from the pack on the bedside table and had himself a post-coital smoke. They were the best kind of fags a man could get, an old mate of his used to say. Terry had always wondered what exactly his mate had meant when he said it... whether he'd really meant that the fags had actually *tasted* better because they came after the sex—like the sex sensitized your taste buds or something... or if he'd just been joking and meant that they were good being post-coital because you must've had a fuck before you got to smoke them....

Terry finished his cigarette, then he started to feel like he needed to take a leak, so he went next door to the bathroom, and to his surprise Naomi wasn't in there. *What the fuck...?*

He hurried back out of the bathroom and into the studio room at the front, which overlooked the street, and there she was standing butt naked in front of the Rembrandt self-portrait.

Shit, I must've forgotten to lock the door, he thought.

But what Terry would have liked to know was what on earth had possessed Naomi to enter this room in the first place, when she had no right to? And then what did she think she was doing going over to the canvas and pulling away the cloth covering that had been masking it?

She looked at him over her shoulder and said, 'You the one pulled off the robbery's been in the news, i'n' it?'

This is all I fuckin need, Terry thought.

So now his secret was out.

Terry knew he had to think of something and act fast, but his head was in a mess.

Naomi said, 'How much you gonna sell it for?'

Terry could see the way her mind was working. 'Who says I'm going to sell it?'

'What else you gonna steal it for?'

CHAPTER 2

Terry drove his Porsche the short distance over to Redcliffe Square and pulled up outside of the building where Angie lived.

He pushed her buzzer and she buzzed him into the building, then came to the door of her flat wearing a rose-coloured bathrobe and looking a little knackered. 'Did I wake you up when I rang earlier, love?' he said. 'Unusual for you to be sleepin' so late...it's gone half-ten —and it was only a few minutes ago when I called you.' He gave her a kiss on the cheek and she turned and led him into the flat.

Angie said, 'I've been taking it easy since I lost my job.'

'Yeah, I was sorry to hear about that, love.'

'What's that you've got there?' Angie pointed at the case he was carrying.

Then the penny dropped.

'Heh, wait a moment,' she said. 'Oh no you don't... You're not bringing that here... It's the painting that you stole, isn't it?'

'I don't have no other choice, love.'

'What's that supposed to mean?'

'Well, it's like this... I had a...well, a visitor, see, love,' Terry said. 'And the silly cow only wanders into me studio when I'm not watchin' her'n takes a butchers at the fuckin paintin', doesn't she...'

'Who was this girl?'

'Like I said, a visitor.'

'A *visitor*,' Angie said. 'What, you mean a girlfriend, was she?'

'Kind of... I only met her last week, but we seemed to hit it off, you know, so I gave her my door key.'

'So if you like her then what are you so worried about...?'

'Well liking the woman's one thing, Ange...but I mean, I hardly know her, really...'

'You know her well enough to give her your door key...'

'Yeah, but that was before I had the Rembrandt stashed in the flat, Ange...'

Angie shook her head like she just couldn't believe what her father was telling her.

'So you wanna dump the painting on me, right?'

'It'll only be for a coupla days.'

'For fuck's sake, Dad, half the cops in London and half the criminals are out looking for that bloody painting, and you want to leave it in my flat.'

'I don't have nowhere else to put it, love, now that the girl I just told you about's seen it,' Terry said. 'Anyway, it ain't like you don't stand to get nothing out a this, Ange...'Cause once I sell it then I'll make sure you're all right... I mean you won't never have to work again, I'll see to that.'

'Like I haven't heard that one before, Dad.'

Angie wished he hadn't had the hare-brained idea of stealing the painting from the National Gallery in the first place. But steal it he had and, loving him as she did, she wasn't about to leave him in the lurch.

It wasn't about money but about blood.

She picked up the case with the painting in it, then carried it into her bedroom and put it under her bed.

'Can't you think of a better place to hide it, love?'

'No, I can't to be honest, Dad...At least if I put it there I know it's not about to get stepped on or have a cup of tea or whatever spilt over it.'

Terry figured that she had a point.

'Thanks, Ange, you're an angel.'

'I just hope you'll hurry up and get rid of the bloody thing before half of London comes banging my door down.'

'Don't worry, love, it'll be sold before you've even noticed you got it.'

I've already noticed, Angie thought.

But it was pointless complaining and making a big deal about it now. Her father was what he was, and she...well, she was his daughter.

'You had lunch yet, Dad?'

He shook his head.

'Well I was just about to make some for myself – you wanna eat some with me?'

'I wouldn't want to put you to any trouble, love.'

Angie had to smile at that.

When Terry got in, he put on a CD of Miles Davis playing live at the Carnegie Hall in 1961, and was digging Miles' playing on *Oleo* when his mobile bleeped. He snapped it open, said hello.

It was Brian Silver, the man on the inside at the National Gallery. Brian wanted to know when he was going to get the rest of his share of the money for deactivating the museum's CCTV system and looking the other way.

'Look, Brian, you'll get your cut just as soon as I've sold the painting...but I can't fuckin give it to you till I've got it, can I?'

'So when you gonna sell it, Tel?'

'Fuck it, Brian mate, what is this...you don't trust me'r sumpthin'?'

'I ain't sayin' that, Tel.'

'No, and I should fuckin well hope not an' all, I mean fuck me...You got your twenty-five grand up front, di'n'tcha?'

'Yeah, I know, Tel.'

'Yeah well tha's twenty-five fuckin grand more than I've seen so far outta this, right...? Now listen, Brian mate, it's important that you don't go gettin' no silly fuckin ideas... I wouldn't try'n sell you down the river on this one, 'cause that'd just be stupid...you with me?'

'Yeah, I'm with you, Tel...but all I wanna know's like how long are we talkin'?'

'I'll get back to you within a few days—how's that suit you?'

'By when exac'ly?'

'By Sunday all right?'

'Okay, Tel, by Sunday you say...Sunday's fine.'

'Be talkin' to you.'

No sooner did Terry hang up than the intercom sounded. Now who the fuck could that be?

'Hello?'

'Tel? It's me, Kenny.'

Oh fuck, Terry thought, and buzzed him in.

Now he was going to have to explain about the girl, Naomi, and how she'd seen the canvas...and how that explained why he'd had to move it over to Angie's.

Kenny wouldn't be impressed.

Terry was watching an old DVD about Picasso that evening, when the intercom sounded.

It was Naomi.

He buzzed her in, and went and stood at the door to his flat to welcome her in.

'You came back sooner this time,' he said.

'Don't sound so surprised.'

How could she stay away, now that she knew he had the Rembrandt?

He figured she liked him, too, though.

Naomi had brought a bottle of cava. Terry opened it, and put on *Sinatra at the Sands*, with the Count Basie band backing him, and they danced to it and drank their cava in between songs.

Then they went to bed and made love.

It was the best way Terry could think of to calm his nerves.

After they'd done it a couple of times, they both fell asleep.

Naomi fried a couple of steaks for lunch the following day.

'You nervous about sumpthin', Tel?' she said, as they sat eating at the kitchen table.

'Na...what've I got to be nervous for?'

'You sure actin' nervous.'

'What you talkin' about?'

'When you gonna sell that paintin'?'

'Soon... Why do you wanna know?'

'Just curious.'

'Not a word to anyone about that, mind, Naomi, okay? And I mean *anyone*...'

'You already told me that, Tel... you think I'm stupid or somethin'?'

'Just so you realize...people will kill for a painting like that.'

'So what happens once you sold it?'

Terry shrugged. 'I'll be rich, I guess...'

They arranged to meet in a room Willoughby had taken at the Ritz, at three on Saturday.

When they got there, Kenny made sure the table was clean and dry, then he and Terry took the Rembrandt from its case, and Willoughby had the expert he'd brought with him, Dawson Kruger, a bald little man in his fifties, do his stuff.

When he had finished his examination of the painting, Kruger looked at Jeremy Willoughby and said, 'It's the original all right.'

'You're absolutely certain of that?'

'I'm a professional, Mr Willoughby... I don't make mistakes.'

Willoughby turned to Terry and said, 'In that case, I would like to proceed with the purchase.'

What Willoughby didn't know, was that Terry had already arranged to pay Kruger five million pounds to say what he'd just said.

'Where's the cash?'

'My son has it...he will be here with it in a couple of minutes... I just need to call him.' Willoughby took out his mobile and made the call

Kenny said, 'You was supposed to bring the money with you.'

'It's on its way... There's no problem...'

They stood waiting in silence, the four of them, for what seemed like ages but was actually only a few minutes, and then there was a knock at the door.

Kenny reached into his jacket pocket and slipped his hand around the handle of his gun, as Willoughby went over and looked out through the peephole. Then Willoughby opened the door and his son came into the room carrying a suitcase.

Willoughby senior opened the suitcase and brought out two briefcases. 'Here,' he said, 'each of these contains twenty-five million pounds, just as you requested.'

'We'll need to check it first,' Terry said.

'Go ahead.'

Terry paid Brian Silver the rest of the £2,000,000 he had coming to him, then he called Angie and told her that he was going to be dropping out of circulation for a little while, so if she didn't hear from him for a few weeks she wasn't to worry. 'But don't try'n call me, love,' he said, 'because I won't be contactable.'

Terry was frightened the police might be able to trace his movements through his mobile phone, so he'd thrown it away.

'So where will you be?'

'It's better if you don't know,' Terry said. 'Trust me.'

'Fuck it, Dad...'

'I'll contact you when I think it's safe to, okay...? 'Bye then, love... And don't worry, okay?'

Brian Silver put most of the £2,000,000 that Terry paid him into an account he'd opened in a bank in Gib. He spread out the rest, putting a little spending money in six different UK bank accounts, figuring that way he wouldn't arouse suspicion.

One thing Terry had told Brian, carry on living normally for a few months, before you pack your job in, so as not to draw attention to yourself, and Brian knew that what Terry said made sense.

But *saying* a thing and *doing* it were two different things, and Brian couldn't resist the temptation to indulge in the odd extravagance here and there. He bought himself a few expensive Italian suits, with shirts and shoes to match. He had his hair done at one of those places where the stars go up the West End, and took to hanging out in pubs on Mile End Road and Whitechapel Road with the kind of girls that wouldn't have pissed on him if he'd caught fire only a few weeks earlier.

Brian's sudden transformation attracted the attention of one or two barmen, and they began to talk, as barmen do...and one of the people who was listening was the East End gangster Frank Nicholson, or Frankie Nic, as he was known to his friends.

Frank put two and two together and began to wonder if he hadn't stumbled upon a way to find out who'd stolen the missing Rembrandt everyone was talking about. So he found out where Brian Silver lived and paid the man a visit at his flat, over in Canary Wharf.

Silver didn't want to talk at first, so Frank doused him with lighter fuel and took out a match...

'Okay-okay,' Silver said, 'I'll tell you, just put the match down.'

'The name...?'

'It was Terry Statham and this other geezer called Kenny.'

'Kenny who?'

'Dunno.'

Frank went to strike the match.

'On my life, I don't fuckin know,' Brian said. 'It was only Terry I ever dealt with, weren't it...? He come to me on his own and axed me if I wanted in... I only saw the other bloke, Kenny, for the first time when they done the job... Only reason I know the geezer's name's 'cause I heard Terry call him it.'

'Where's this Terry Statham live?'

'Over Earl's Court way somewhere, I think... I used to know 'im years ago, back in the days when he used to live around 'ere. Then he moved across town and we lost touch.'

'He got any family?'

'His wife died.'

'Kids...?' Frank started to fool with the match again.

'He's got a daughter named Angie...that's all I know, on my life.'

Frank dropped the box of matches on the floor and walked out.

PART II

CHAPTER 3

Once he'd satisfied himself there was no one about, Frank went up the path and rang the doorbell. His swarthy features, gangsterish face and mean brown eyes didn't exactly go with the green ambulance man's uniform he was wearing. Neither did the big scar that ran across his cheek like a coiled cobra every time he grinned. But then, it wasn't like Frank really worked for the ambulance service. Ask him to take care of someone and he'd bring out a gun.

The place had money written all over it. The geranium bushes were in flower in the small front garden, there was a Venetian blind in the window to prevent people from being able to peer in, and the door was black with a big brass knocker.

Just then, a vehicle drove up and Frank turned to check it out, but as he did so he heard the sound of footsteps coming from inside the house. He turned back again as the door opened and there was the woman standing on the doorstep.

She was a tall, slim brunette, dressed in a bright fuchsia-coloured T-shirt and a pair of Diesel jeans. She squinted at Frank like she was a little short-sighted, then a confused, questioning expression came into her attractive blue eyes...but before she had time to speak, Frank was pushing her inside, and he closed the door behind him with a kick of the heel.

She tried to scream and struggled to get free, but Frank gagged her mouth with his hand. He told her just to relax and she wouldn't get hurt, so she stopped struggling.

'Okay,' he said, 'I'm gonna take my hand off your mouth and you're not gonna scream if you're a sensible girl...'Cause if you do then I'm only gonna have to rough you up a little and put my hand back there again, you understand me...? Blink your eyes twice if you do.'

She did as he'd said to show that she understood, and then Frank took out his gun.

The next moment there was a knock at the door.

Frank moved over by the wall and gestured for the woman to see who it was with a jerk of the head. So she went and opened the door, holding it close to the jamb.

'I need to talk to your husband.'

'I'm afraid he's not home from work yet, Jim.'

'In that case I'll come in and wait for him, if you don't mind.' The caller pushed the door, sending the woman back a pace, and he entered the house. He was a tall, blond muscled man dressed in chinos and a white Fred Perry.

Frank pointed his gun at him and said, 'Welcome to the party.'

'Who the fuck are you?'

'Just shut the fuck up'n get in on the sofa the both a you.' Frank waved the hand he held the gun in.

They did as he said.

Frank went and sat in the easy chair by the side of the stone fireplace, keeping his .45 Biretta pointed at them. He took out his mobile and pushed a couple of keys, using the fingers of his left hand.

The woman said, 'What do you want with us?'

Frank said, 'A little peace and quiet wouldn't do any harm for starters.' Then into his mobile: 'You managed to park yet...? Okay, so hurry the fuck up.' He snapped his mobile shut and pocketed it.

'You still haven't told us who you are,' the woman said.

'You could think of me as a sort a party animal... Do as you're told and you might just get out of this without gettin' bitten.'

They sat in silence for a while, and then the doorbell sounded again. 'Get up, you two,' Frank said.

They did as they were told.

'Now get over by the door.'

As they were crossing the room, the man made a lunge for the gun and knocked it out of Frank's hand, and Frank found himself being forced back against the wall and they began to wrestle.

Then Frank saw the woman make a move for the gun, and he kicked her in the back of the head.

That took care of her.

Frank was starting to gasp for breath now, in between telling the blond man he was gonna roast his nuts if he didn't let go of him.

Then Frank stopped using his mouth to talk with and used it instead to bite the man's arm...and the man cried out in pain and pulled his arm away.

That gave Frank the opportunity he needed to kick him in the groin, and he followed up with a good body punch and an even better punch to the jaw.

The man went down, and his head banged against the stone grate, so that he lost consciousness...then Frank jumped in the air and landed with both feet on his face. The man's head cracked against the stone grate again, harder this time, and Frank kicked him as hard as he could in the head. Then he picked his Biretta up off the floor and shot him in the eye at point-blank range.

There was a silencer on the gun, so it didn't make much noise, but that didn't make the work it did any less ugly. The man's eye was driven back into his head, and some of his blood splashed over the stone fireplace and over the rug...then more of it came out of his mouth and ran down his cheek.

Frank bent down and picked up the casing from the shot he'd fired, and he'd just slipped it into his pocket when he snapped out of the violence induced trance he'd been in and realised that Donny was out there, ringing the doorbell like a lunatic.

Donny, a skinny guy of medium height, was wearing a green ambulance man's uniform, the same as Frank, and he had brought a medical box with him.

Frank saw him looking at the body over by the fireplace and said, 'That cunt's dead.'

'Ain't her old man, is it?'

Frank shook his head. 'Just some stupid fucker that come poking 'is nose in where he had no business to...'

The woman started to come around at that moment, so Donny gagged her before she could start to scream. Then he tied her up so that she couldn't move.

Frank said, 'We'll dump 'im up on the bed?'

'You're thinking that way we'd make it look like the girl – or more likely 'er husband – did it, right...?'

Frank was too busy going through the woman's handbag to bother to listen to Donny had just said. He took out her mobile and slipped it into his pocket, then they lifted the body and carried it up the stairs.

Once they'd dropped it on the bed, Frank drew the curtains. Then he rumpled the bedclothes up a bit, to make it look like the dead man and the woman had been working up a storm between the sheets.

'Come on,' he said. 'Let's go.'

The traffic slowed to a crawl along Bayswater Road, so Frank put the siren on and the vehicles up ahead all made way for him. He drove on like that until he got as far as Lancaster Gate, when he heard the sound of a police siren. Fuck me, don't say the filth are onto us, Frank thought, looking in his mirror now.

The police car that was making all the noise was coming up behind them, so Frank reached into the glove compartment for his Biretta. Then put the gun on the seat, between his legs, so it was there, ready, if he needed to use it.

Now the police car was about to overtake him, so Frank slowed down...then he watched it go past, wondering if he was going to find himself being waved over...

But no, the police car just kept on going, and Frank breathed a sigh of relief.

He cut down through Hyde Park and pulled into the little parking area at the side of the Serpentine. Then he climbed out from behind the wheel and got into the back with Donny and the woman.

'Call your old man,' he said, handing the woman her mobile.

So the woman got up a number and pressed *call*, then Frank grabbed the phone from her and waited for the guy to pick up.

And when he heard him say, 'Hello, Jane?' Frank got down on his haunches and put the mobile phone back in the woman's hand.

'Say hello'n tell 'im you've been kidnapped and nothin' more,' he told her. 'You understand?'

She nodded, then said into the phone, 'Giles, something has happened... Two men came to the house, and...they... They've kidnapped me.'

'...'

'Giles, this is serious and I need you to listen to me.'

'...'

Frank jerked the mobile phone away from her and said into it, 'We got your wife and you're gonna have to clean the safe out and bring us everything that's in there if you ever want to see her again, understand...?'

'Yes, I understand.'

'Oh, and by the way, we left some guy called Jim, big fella with a bigger mouth, lying on the bed at your place, and he was looking pretty dead... So just in case the thought of never seein' your misses again doesn't bother you very much, you might wanna consider that I only got to make an anonymous call to the cops'n tell 'em where to find the body, and you're gonna be their number one murder suspect... You hear what I'm saying?'

'Yes, I hear you.'

Frank said, 'You sound like a sensible kind a guy,' and hung up.

Giles Morgan, a tall well-groomed man in his mid-thirties, undid the collar of his white shirt, loosened his tie, and got to his feet. He felt the room spin and leaned on his desk, to prevent himself from falling.

He couldn't believe this was really happening...

But he knew it was.

He took the jacket of his pinstriped suit from the back of his swivel chair and slipped it on, then glanced at his watch, a Rolex he'd received as a birthday present from his wife, Jane. It was just gone six, which meant most of his staff would have left for home.

He made a tour of the bank, and found that there were only two employees still in the building. Elvira, the young Italian woman who had started working at the bank as a cashier a few weeks ago, was sitting at a desk behind the cash counter, talking to Sally Graham. Morgan smiled over at them and said, 'You two ladies still here?'

Sally, a plump brunette in her early fifties, smiled back. 'We're just conscientious about our work's our trouble, Mr. Morgan.'

'There's no need for that now, Sally—it's Friday evening…Your husbands'll be wondering where you are.'

The two women got their handbags, said goodbye, have a nice weekend, and went on their way. Then Morgan finished his tour of the bank, just to check there was nobody else still in the place.

There wasn't, so he turned the alarm and CCTV systems off.

Then he opened the safe and emptied it out.

There was somewhere in the region of three million in there, in total.

Morgan took the money and packed it into a large briefcase, then he locked the bank up, went out and got into his marine-blue-coloured BMW, and called his wife's mobile number.

The man he'd spoken to last time picked up. 'You cleared out the safe yet?'

'Yes.'

'Okay, now listen to me…'

Giles Morgan turned into Hyde Park and drove over to the small parking area to the side of where the bridge started, then he got out of his car, as he'd been told to, and stood there, holding the briefcase with the money in it.

He saw the doors at the back of the ambulance open, then a man got out and came over towards him. The man was tall and he was wearing an ambulance man's uniform.

The man stopped a few paces in front of Morgan, close enough for him to be able to get a proper look at his face, see the nasty look in his eyes and the scar across his face. Morgan noticed, too, that the man had his hand in his pocket. Maybe he had a gun in there.

The man looked at him and said, 'That the money you got in that briefcase?'

Morgan told him that it was.

'All of it?'

'That's right.'

The man nodded and said, 'Take the briefcase over to the ambulance'n let my friend in the back see what's inside it... All the money's in there then you're both free to go...but just in case you get any ideas, perhaps you ought a know I got a gun in my pocket and it's pointing right at your heart... My accomplice is armed, too.'

So Morgan did like the man said and went over to the guy who was now standing by the ambulance, skinny guy with nasty beady eyes. Morgan looked at him and said, 'Where's my wife?'

'First things first...give me the money.'

Morgan turned and looked back at the man with the scar who'd sent him over here, and saw that the man was now facing him, ready to shoot if he had to.

Or maybe he'll just shoot us both anyway, Morgan thought.

Whatever was going to happen, Morgan realized that he didn't have any alternative but to do as he was told.

So he handed over the briefcase.

The man with the scar came back over and took it from the one with the weasel face. 'Shoot him if he moves,' Scarface said, then he climbed into the back of the ambulance.

A long, terrifying minute passed, and then Scarface re-emerged from the back of the ambulance. Weasel Face looked at him and said, 'Money all there, Frank?'

'Sure is,' Scarface said.

'Now what?'

As Giles Morgan pulled up outside the house in Linver Road, he glanced in his mirror and saw a police car come around the corner behind him.

This is it, he thought, those bastards must have tipped the cops off.

But the police car went on past and came to a halt twenty yards further down, on the other side of the street, and two men in uniform got out.

The Morgans sat in their car and watched the policemen knock on the door to one of the houses.

Jon Samuel's house, Morgan thought. Then he remembered that

Jon had retired and moved to Malta only a few weeks ago, and he'd let the place.

A blonde woman in her twenties came to the door. Morgan saw the woman nod, then she opened the door wide and the two policemen went inside.

'Someone up there likes us,' Morgan said. 'Come on, we've got work to do, Jane.'

They got out of the car and hurried into the house, and Morgan ran on up the stairs and entered the bedroom—and there was Jim Broe's dead body lying on the bed. One of Jim's eyes was missing, and his entire face was a bloody mess.

Morgan ran out to the bathroom and retched into the toilet bowl.

When he came out of the bathroom, his wife was standing there on the landing, and Morgan said, 'We've got to get rid of the body.'

'Don't you think it'd be better if we were to call the police, Giles?'

'And tell them *what* exactly?'

'What if we just told them everything?'

'They'd never believe us... What proof do we have that you were even kidnapped, Jane? Or that we didn't kill Jim...? And what was he doing here in the afternoon anyway?'

'I wish I knew... He just said he needed to talk to you and barged his way in... He seemed like he was angry about something—angry with you, from what I could make out.'

'We've got to take the body somewhere and dump it, Jane.'

'Let's get and do it, then.'

'No, not yet... We'll have to wait until it gets dark...' Morgan thought things over for a moment or two. 'I'll do it, and you stay here and clean all the blood stains up, okay?'

Morgan and his wife each donned rubber gloves and wrapped the body in a sheet of tarpaulin that they found in the loft. And as soon as it was dark, they carried it that way out to Jim's Mercedes, and put it in the boot.

Morgan got in behind the wheel and set off, leaving his wife to clean up, as planned. He drove over to Wandsworth Bridge, crossed the river, then joined the fast road out of London and put his foot down, and it wasn't long before he was driving by green fields on either side.

After he'd been driving for the best part of an hour, he came to the Sussex Downs. Carry on for a few more miles and he'd be in Brighton, but Morgan had other ideas.

He pulled up on a quiet road that ran along the edge of a ravine and killed the engine.

CHAPTER 4

Frank drove the ambulance down past Weybridge and pulled up in a quiet country lane. Then he and Donny changed into their street clothes, before they doused the ambulance with petrol and set it alight, with the uniforms they had been wearing inside it. Then they got into the Porsche Donny had driven down in and headed back to London.

When they got back to Frank's place on Globe Road, Frank gave Donny his share of the stash. 'Count it if you want to.'

Then Donny had finished counting the money, he said, 'I'm short.'

'Oh no you ain't—d'you reckon I can't fuckin count or somethin'?'

Donny put his share down on the battered coffee table, and said for Frank to count it himself if he didn't believe him. But Frank didn't even look at the money. Instead, he kept looking up at Donny and told him to count it again.

So, Donny started putting the money into piles of fifty grand, counting aloud for Frank's benefit now, saying, 'There's one, look...and there's another, that makes two,' and so on.

While Donny counted, Frank kept his hand in the crack between the cushion seats of the sofa, where he'd left his .45 Biretta.

Donny finished counting the money a second time and said, 'See...? I told you there's only a million there...it's half a million short.'

Frank said, 'Somethin' happened to your memory...?'

'Ya fuckin talkin' 'bout?'

Frank came on like he was talking to some small kid who'd disappointed him, as he reminded Donny that *he* was the one who'd killed the guy back at the house. 'Not only that, but I was the *brains* behind the whole fuckin operation.'

'You fuckin talkin' about, the brains behind it... We done it together'n we agreed right from the start it was gonna be straight down the middle.'

Frank said, 'We started out on the assumption that we was both gonna take equal fuckin responsibility for the work that had to be done... But then I ended up havin' to fuckin do everythin'...'

'We done it together, what're you talkin' 'bout?'

'It was me that killed the guy and had the idea to go'n dump him on the bed in the house...'

'So...?'

'I'm sorry to hear you're takin' it like this, Donny.'

'The fuck d'you expect me to take it like...? I thought we was partners.'

'Y'know what they say—don't never mix friendship'n bizniss.'

'I thought that was bizniss an' pleasure.'

'Same fing.'

'Look, Frank, we always been mates, but don't try'n fuck me on this, okay?'

'Nobody's tryin' to fuck no one, Don... Fair's fair, it's just you ain't bein' reasonable's all. I mean *fuck me*... You s'pectin' to let the other guy do all the work and then you want a be able to just come along'n take half the fuckin stash... It don't work like that, old son, I'm afraid.'

'You're just lookin' for an excuse,' Donny said. 'Fink I stupid or somethin, do ya? Fact is, you're gettin' greedy.' He shook his head. 'It ain't gonna work with me, though, Frank.'

Donny reached inside his jacket for his Mauser, but Frank pulled out the Biretta before him. He shot Donny twice, first in the gut, and then, after Donny had slid down the wall onto the floor, he went over and finished him off.

Put his gun to Donny's ear and said goodbye to him for the last time.

. . .

Then Frank put the body into the large freezer he had in the kitchen.

When he got it back out the following morning, it was frozen stiff. Perfect.

Frank went to work with the electric saw.

Giles Morgan pulled up across the street from the bank at the usual time on Monday morning, and waited for his colleagues to start to arrive.

His deputy manager, Neil Thompson, a tall, lean man in his late twenties, was the first to show, at just after eight-thirty. Morgan watched Neil go into the bank, then he waited five minutes before he got out of his car and went in after him.

'But what's going on?' he said, as soon as he saw Neil, who had already picked up the phone to call the police.

'Looks like we've been robbed.'

'How come the alarm's not working, then?'

'It's been deactivated.'

'And the CCTV system...?'

'Not sure.'

Morgan pretended to go and check, and acted all surprised and angry when he found that it had been turned off.

'Hello?' Neil said into the phone. 'Give me the police...Yes, this is an emergency...I'm calling from a bank—there's been a robbery...'

When the police arrived, a short balding man, who introduced himself as Detective Chief Inspector Childs, cautioned Giles Morgan.

Morgan acted appropriately shocked, and DCI Childs told him that, as manager at the bank, he would have to come down to the station to make a statement.

'But I didn't know anything about it...'

'In that case you haven't got anything to worry about, sir.'

Meanwhile, a WPC and a male plainclothes officer called around to the house.

The plainclothes officer held up his ID and said, 'I'm Detective Chief Inspector Preston.'

'What's happened...?'

'There's been an incident at the bank where your husband works...'

'An *incident*...?'

Preston—six-two, Mediterranean complexion, droopy tash—said, 'There's been a robbery...'

'Oh, I see...'

'We need to search your house as a matter of course...given that your husband is the manager at the bank.'

'And if I say no...?'

'We'll just go and get a warrant and come back...'

'But you don't honestly think that my husband—'

'At this stage we don't think anything, Mrs Morgan...but if you've got nothing to hide then it'll look better for you, if it goes to court, if you let us in now.'

She shrugged. 'I suppose you'd better come in, then, if you have to.'

Preston and the WPC took a good look around the house.

They didn't find anything.

The failure of the detective and the WPC to find anything at the house didn't surprise Jane Morgan, because she and her husband had made a bonfire in the garden earlier, and burnt the bedclothes and the rug that had been spotted with Jim Broe's blood. Then they'd washed the bedroom carpet and given the entire place a good clean, and scrubbed the fireplace and all the walls, as well as the stairs and wooden flooring and all the other surfaces, so that everything now smelt of the detergent they had used.

As for the bullet, it had gone straight through poor Jim Broe's head and ricocheted, and they'd found it stuck in the wall when they were cleaning the place up. It was lodged very deep into the stone, so her husband had put plaster into the hole and then painted over it to make sure that it was no longer visible.

When they'd finished looking around, DCI Preston told Mrs Morgan she would have to answer some questions, and they took her with them in their car to the station on Fulham Road.

Upon arrival she was taken to the Major Incident Room, where she was interviewed by DCI Preston and his sidekick, a younger, blond-haired man who introduced himself as DS Johnson.

All through the interview the tape recorder on the table was left running, and Jane Morgan realized that was so the tape could be used as evidence in court. So it was important to be careful about what she said, remember everything and then stick to the same story from here on in.

After the interview had terminated, she was asked to make a written statement.

In her statement she wrote that she didn't know anything about what had happened at the bank—and no, her husband hadn't mentioned anything about stealing any money from the safe, either in his sleep or when he was fully conscious.

As for Morgan, they kept him banged up in a cell for several hours, then they got him out and took him down to the Major Incident Room, where DCI Preston began to question him.

It soon became obvious to Morgan, from the Detective Chief Inspector's line of questioning, that Preston was trying to connect Jim Broe's murder with the robbery. He already seemed to have discovered that Jim's wife, Carla, was a good friend of Morgan's wife, and Morgan would have liked to know how the man had found this out.

He said, 'I never knew Jim Broe or his wife.'

'But your wife has already told us she's a good friend of Mrs Broe.'

'Yes, so she tells me.'

Preston tweaked his tash and looked at Morgan. 'So are you saying that you've never met Carla Broe or her husband Jim?'

'That's exactly what I'm saying.' Morgan had never even told his wife about the affair he'd had with Carla Broe, so he certainly wasn't going to tell about it now, so that the detective could smell a motive and try and pin Carla's husband Jim's murder on him.

'Little bit of a coincidence, though, isn't it, all this happening at the same time?'

'All *what* happening?'

'Three million pounds are robbed from the bank where you work as manager and you don't know a thing about it... Then the husband of one of your wife's best friends is found at the bottom of a ravine after someone blew his brains out... Now are you seriously asking me to believe that these two circumstances aren't linked?'

'Are you seriously trying to imply that they *are* linked, Detective Chief Inspector?'

DCI Preston left Giles Morgan to stew in his own sweat, and gave the order for his clothes and shoes to be seized from his house, packed into polythene bags in the appropriate manner, and sent to the path lab for testing. Then he drove to East Sussex to take a look at the Mercedes that had gone off the road down there with Jim Broe in it.

When he arrived, Preston quickly changed into a one-piece disposable suit and slipped on a pair of nitrile gloves. Then the man who appeared to have appointed himself as Crime Scene Investigator, a DCI Williamson of Sussex Police, asked Preston who he was and what he was doing there.

Preston showed the man his ID and told him that he would be taking over as Investigator to the crime scene. Williamson, who was a tall, thickset man with short brown hair, said, 'This is my patch.'

'So it might be,' Preston said, 'but I've already okay'd everything with your superior, DCS Rollins...so I'd appreciate it if you'd get out of my way and allow me to do my job.'

'I'll have to check out what you've said first.'

'Well get a bloody move on, then...this is a murder investigation, man.'

'Okay, keep your shirt on...just doing my job.'

So Preston had to wait for DCI Williamson to get confirmation from his boss, and then he passed through the two cordons used to preserve the crime scene—the first formed with police barrier tape, and then an inner one formed with cones—and hurried over to the Mercedes. The vehicle was lying on its side, and had sustained a fair amount of damage on its descent from the road up above.

Taking care not to touch the vehicle, Preston peered through the windscreen at the dead body inside, and he saw that there was a lot of blood everywhere.

He would have to get forensics experts to go over the vehicle and the body for FDR, DNA and fingerprints, and have a photographer take the necessary shots, and so it was important that no one should touch or enter the vehicle. To do so would be to risk contaminating any evidence that might be available.

With this in mind, DCI Preston took out his walkie-talkie and got on to Detective Superintendent Chivers, at Fulham Police Station, and told him what he needed.

Detective Superintendent Chivers agreed to get three forensics experts and a photographer there as soon as he could arrange it, and they hung up. Then Preston went back over to DCI Williamson and told him that no one was to interfere with the crime scene.

Next Preston had the area where the Mercedes had left the road cordoned off, as a little annexe to the crime scene. Then he had an officer stand guard, to make sure no one passed the cordon—with the exception of the photographer and the forensics experts, who were all on their way.

Preston's belly rumbled. A bite to eat for lunch and some coffee wouldn't have gone amiss.

Then he remembered that, as Crime Scene Investigator, it was his job to lay on the grub.

Meanwhile, back at the station, the lawyer who was now representing the Morgans was pressing Detective Sergeant Johnson to let his clients go, so Johnson called the Preston on his mobile number and asked him what he should do.

Preston said, 'They've only been in custody for—what is it, since ten o'clock or so this morning...? So we can hold them until that time tomorrow morning before I have to decide whether to seek an extension.'

'Right you are, guv...but I was just wondering what exactly I should be saying to the brief.'

'Just tell him to go fuck himself.'

'Like me to quote you verbatim on that one, guv?'

'Keep the sense of my words, Detective Sergeant, but you can feel free to give them a gloss as you think appropriate.'

Frank threw the chunks of sawn-up flesh that were what remained of Donny into a couple of bin liners and put them in the back of his Mercedes, which he'd left parked outside, down on Globe Road. Then he got in behind the wheel, started her up, and headed off.

It was funny driving along Mile End Road, because it was long and straight and flat as a table, and then at the western end of it you had this great ginormous gherkin.

Stick a couple of pickled onions down there, Frank thought, and we'll be sorted.

Turn the East End into a reg'lar fuckin salad bar.

He drove in an easterly direction, past council estates, ranks of shops and houses, and kept on for quite some time, until he got to Epping Forest. Then when he'd found a nice secluded spot, he turned off the road into the trees.

He had a good look about to make sure he was alone, before he got out of his car, then he took the bin liners and a spade from the boot and started to dig a ditch.

While he was digging, the skies crackled and groaned like a lifer's dick and it began to bucket down...then a gunshot rang out from the trees.

Frank took out his gun and fired back in the direction the shot seemed to have come from. But it was hard, trying to hit a target you couldn't see...and he realized that if anyone was going to get hurt it was probably going to be him.

He fired a second shot, then turned and ran back to his Merc, got in, and gave it some pedal...

Frank took a good hot shower, when he got back to his flat on Globe Road, to wash the stench of bloody murder from his skin.

He wondered who the joker that was firing at him in Epping Forest could have been, as he soaped himself.

Whoever the guy was, Frank had the feeling it wouldn't be too long before he he'd be putting in another appearance.

And next time I'll be ready for him, Frank thought.

He got out of the shower and stood in his living room, drying himself, in all his hairy glory, or lack of it, when the telephone rang. He picked it up and a man's voice he didn't recognize said, 'Have fun out in the woods, did you?'

'Who am I talking to?'

'Never you mind... All you need to know for now is that I'm onto you.'

'What the fuck do you want...? Who are you?'

'You could look on me as your future business partner.'

Frank said, 'You wouldn't want to be no partner a mine, believe me.'

'What, you mean you'd rub me out the same way you did Donny?'

'How do you'—Frank'd been about to say 'know about that?' but he checked himself, figuring whoever this was could be taping what he was saying.

'Go on, Frank, say it...how do I know about what you been up to?' Malicious, mirthless laughter. 'That's for me to know and you not to, old son.'

'What do you want from me?'

'That's quite simple...in a word, I want half.'

'Half a what?'

'The three million.'

'What three fuckin million?'

'Oh come now, Frank.

'Listen, whoever you are, we're gonna have to meet'n talk.'

'That's just what I was about to suggest.'

'Name a time'n a place, then.'

'I'll be in touch.' And the line went dead.

Frank reached for the whisky bottle and poured himself a large one, then slumped back into the easy chair, trying to get his head around the situation he found himself in here.

The phone began to ring again a little later and Frank snatched it from its cradle. 'Okay, so when're we gonna pack in playin' silly buggers like this'n meet face to face?'

'I think that's a great idea.'

'Resma, darlin', it's *you*.'

'Why, who did you think it was, Frank...? Ain't been two-timing me, have you?'

'Now Rezzy, baby, would I go'n do a thing like that?'

'I'm on my way over to your place,' she said.

CHAPTER 5

Frank buzzed Resma into the building, then he went to the door and looked through the peephole, to see if anyone had followed her up the stairs.

He didn't see anyone.

So he opened the door, and looked out, holding his Biretta ready to shoot.

'You alone, Res?'

'Yeah...—why... What's the gun for?'

Frank stood aside and let her in, then he shut the door. 'Anyone follow you here...?'

Resma said, 'That's what I was worried about.'

'What, so you mean someone *did*...?'

'I don't know if he followed me or not, but I was thinking he might of.'

'Thinking *who* might of...?'

'My dad, of course... Why – who did you think I meant?'

'Your *dad*...? What's your old man wanna be followin' you for?'

'I told you about him, don't you remember?'

Frank led her over to the sofa, then when she'd sat down he asked if he could get her a drink. 'All I got is Scotch.'

'Okay, I'll join you in one.'

Frank went over to the drinks cabinet, poured one for Resma and gave himself a refill, then re-crossed the room. And he got a good view of her ample cleavage as she wrested the tumbler from his hand. 'Nice dress, Res.'

'Thanks... I bought it yesterday... I was wondering if red suits me—what d'you reckon...?'

'It suits you all right...what there is of it.'

She gave him a look.

'Like waving a red rag at a bull.'

'You mean you're getting the horn, Frank...?'

Resma reached under his towel and felt him. 'You're loaded and ready to fire...' She pulled the towel away and began to work on him with her hand.

Frank swigged his Scotch. 'What's this about your old man...?'

'I told you about how he wants to marry me off to some bloke I've never even met over in Dhaka, didn't I...?'

'What—an *arranged marriage*, y'mean...?'

Resma licked the tip of his nib. 'He threatened to kill my last boyfriend and serve him up in the curry at the family restaurant.'

'What did he have against him, then?'

'Nothing—he never even met the guy.'

'Not that's what I *call* prejudice,' Frank said. 'But what are you sayin'—that your old man's after me?'

'He will be if he knows what you'n me have been up to, that's for sure.'

'In that case, how about if we take a holiday somewhere nice, and get away from it all for a while, Res...?'

Resma said, 'Just so long as it's not to India or Bangladesh...'

The following morning Giles Morgan was set free. He'd been careful and managed not to leave any DNA or prints at the crime scene, and so DCI Preston didn't have enough hard evidence to press charges.

Besides, Preston had a sneaking feeling that the man was innocent of the crime.

Frank booked a double room in the Stella Maris hotel, overlooking the seafront, in Fuengirola, and as soon as they got there he had room service bring them a bottle of champagne.

'What I like, this is,' Frank said. 'Sittin' in the warm balmy air, drinkin' the bubbly'n list'nin' to the sound a the tide washin' in...'

'You've earned it.'

'You wanna show me somethin' else I've earned, Res...?'

'Anytime you like, Frank.'

'What about right now...?'

Resma slipped the straps of her dress over her shoulders and let it fall to the floor, and she stood there before him on the balcony in her birthday best.

She was nineteen and succulent as Frank's favourite tandoori chicken. He went and picked her up, and carried her over to the bed...

Frank popped out later that night to buy a bottle of Scotch and, as he entered small shop, he had the feeling someone was tailing him... then when he came back out, he saw a man watching him. Skinny guy, early twenties, ginger top in a blue T-shirt, jeans, shades.

Realizing he'd been rumbled, the guy legged it as far as the next corner, then took a right...and Frank went after him, trying not to drop his bottle of Scotch while he was about it.

By the time Frank turned the corner, there was no sign of the guy anywhere.

Frank would have bet anything this guy was the joker'd been taking pot shots at him in Epping Forest, when he'd been burying what was left of Donny...

Guy looked like a punk.

Fact, Frank reckoned that was a good name for him...The Punk.

Yeah, that was what Frank was going to call the little bastard.

Frank was eager to meet him.

He had a hard-on for the guy a yard long.

He wanted to meet him so that he could make him disappear once and for all.

That afternoon, Frank sent Resma out before him to act as a decoy, then he followed her along the promenade minutes later.

It was two p.m. and the Andalusian sun was beating down.

When Frank spotted The Punk, he called Resma on her mobile and told her the score. 'Just keep goin', Res, and lead him off somewhere nice'n quiet, like I told you.'

Frank quickened his pace, but it was as if The Punk knew he was being followed, because be stepped on the gas, the crossed and went up a side street.

Then he entered a hotel.

Frank followed the Punk in, and he saw him step into the elevator.

Frank made for the stairs and ran up to the next flight. Then checked on the elevator and saw that it was still going up, so he ran up another flight.

Still going up.

When he got to the next flight, he saw that the lift had stopped on the sixth floor.

Gotcha.

Frank ran the rest of the way up...and got there just in time to see a door closing along the corridor.

Number 604.

Nice one.

Now I know where you live, mate.

Frank went and knocked on the door to the next room and called out 'room service', and a little old lady came and opened up. Hello, Ma'm, Frank said, he hoped it wouldn't be an inconvenience only he'd been asked to come up and check the plumbing in the bathroom.

The old dear seemed unsure at first but Frank smiled encouragingly, then he took advantage of her indecision and brushed past her into the room. Went out into the bathroom and started turning the taps on and off.

'All looks fine to me,' he said, 'they must a given me the wrong room number—which number's this, love?'

'Six-o-three,' the lady told him.

'That explains it...'cause I was supposed to go next door... Only problem is, the person who's staying in there's left the door locked and the master key has been lost...'

The old lady seemed confused, and looked as though she was going to ask him something. But instead of stopping to answer her queries, Frank went out onto the balcony, climbed up onto the ledge and hopped over onto the balcony to the next room.

Then he tiptoed over up to the French doors, which had been left open, and peered inside.

No sign of the Punk anywhere.

But then he heard the sound of running water...

The Punk was in there taking a shower... Frank took out his gun and tiptoed over the carpet, towards the open bathroom door.

But before he got to it, Frank felt something hard crash into the back of his head.

When Frank came around, he wondered where he was for a moment...and then it all came back to him.

He looked up and saw The Punk.

He was pointing a gun at him.

Shit...

'The fuck are you?'

'Name's Dylan... Dylan Morris.'

'You ain't Donny's brother...?'

'Got it in one.'

'The fuck you doin' here?'

'You always ask questions you already know the answer to, Frank...?'

'You ain't an easy person to communicate with, you know that?'

'Neither are you, Frank...Donny found that out, didn't he...?'

'I ain't seen Donny in a while.'

'Nobody has, Frank...that's because you killed him... Don't tell me you forgot...?'

'You got it all wrong, kid.'

The Punk shook his head. 'You disappoint me, Frank...big man like you trying to wriggle your way out of a situation by tellin' lies... I'd have expected you to admit what you did like a man.'

'What do you want with me?'

'You'll find out...but first we're gonna go down in the elevator'n out through the lobby, and I'm gonna be stuck to the back a your trousers like a piece of chewin' gum all the way... One false move'n you'll get it in the back. You understand me?'

'No offence,' Frank said, 'but you don't strike me as bein' the kinda guy'd ever say anythin'd be difficult to follow.'

'Get the fuck up off the floor, wise guy.'

Frank had no alternative but to let The Punk march him to the elevator, and they took it all the way down to the basement car park.

Then The Punk marched Frank to his Range Rover and, once they climbed in, The Punk tied his hands together.

'The fuck are you gonna take me?'

'You'll find out soon enough.'

Frank didn't like the sound of that.

He didn't like the way The Punk sneered when he spoke to him, either.

He didn't like any of it.

He figured if he just sat here and allowed The Punk to take him wherever it was the guy had in mind, then anything could happen.

He thought some more and came to the conclusion that *anything* was exactly what *would* happen if he didn't stop The Punk from taking him wherever it was they were going.

There was a sharp corner coming up.

As The Punk went to round the bend, Frank raised his leg and managed to hook his foot in the steering wheel, and they went skidding across the road and started to tumble down a rocky slope...and they hit a tree.

Frank banged his head and lost consciousness.

When he came round, minutes later, he turned and saw that The Punk was out cold.

With any luck the bastard might be dead.

Maybe not, though, and Frank knew that he had no time to lose. So he set about freeing himself from the wreckage...then he went and stood with his back against an olive tree and rubbed the rope his hands were tied with against the bark.

It was slow going, but finally he cut through it.

He looked down at his hands, rubbing them together now to bring some feeling back into his fingers, and the thought of what he was going to do to The Punk brought a grin to his face... Only then when he looked up, Frank saw The Punk standing there by the side of the Range Rover, pointing his gun at him.

'Strikes me it just ain't your lucky day, Frank...'

The Punk made Frank walk in front of him over the dry scrubland, under the fierce heat of the afternoon sun. Glance upwards and it would strike you right behind the eyeballs like a punch.

The Punk kept his hand in his jacket pocket, on the gun that he had in there, ready to shoot if Frank tried anything.

Frank wondered where it was The Punk was taking him, but when he asked him, all the guy said was that he'd find out soon enough. Frank didn't like the sound of that. He figured The Punk was going to take him to some farmhouse he must've rented, then he'd tie him up and go to work on him. Try and get him to tell what he'd done with the three million.

If he thinks I'm gonna tell him that then he's gotta be stupid, Frank thought.

But then he began to wonder... He recalled a story he'd once heard about a gang back in the East End of London that had grabbed a member of a rival gang and taken him to a cellar in some pub of theirs, where they'd tortured him. As the story went, the guy was begging his torturers to kill him by the end... Didn't take too much imagination to see how it could happen... They strap you in a chair and then you were well and truly fucked...

The Punk here might not be much to look at, but if Frank allowed the bastard to take him someplace and tie him up then he knew what he could expect—and it wasn't going to be pretty.

Frank knew that he had to make his move before they got to wherever it was they were headed.

It would be better to die out here, under the sun, than in the darkened room of some isolated farmhouse cellar.

They worked their way down a dusty escarpment to a road and, hearing the Diesel noise of a lorry, Frank sensed his chance... He grabbed hold of The Punk's arm, and pushed him into the road just as the lorry came around the bend...and heard The Punk scream out as the lorry went over him.

The guy driving didn't slow down to take a look at the damage.

Frank reckoned it couldn't have happened to anyone nicer...

Giles Morgan's boss sent him home, and told him to have a good rest until the Board had looked into the matter of the missing three million pounds.

Morgan knew that meant they were going to make a decision on whether to get rid of him or not.

And he reckoned the odds were stacked high against him...because okay, he might only have done what as any good husband who loved his wife would have in the situation, but he knew the members of the Board were unlikely to see it that way.

Not that a good many of them weren't husbands themselves...but those guys left their hearts at the door when they went to work.

Not only did the bank's interests always have to come first, but they had to *be seen* to come first.

Morgan was convinced that his career was about to be flushed down the pan, and he was gutted big time.

Not only was he gutted, but he was also angry as hell.

What threw salt into the wound was the thought that the bastard who'd ruined Morgan's life was out there someplace enjoying himself on the three million he'd got away with.

Where was the justice in the world?

No point in getting out your magnifying glass to look for it, because there wasn't any.

Boy, how he'd have liked to meet up with that bastard again.

Or would he...? That's to say, would he *really*?

Morgan pondered this question long and hard...and then he hatched a plan.

To kick things off, he hired a private dick to find out the name of the man who'd kidnapped his wife and where he was hiding out.

The private dick got Morgan to work with an artist to produce a pencil portrait of the man, then went to work...and came back three days later with the news that the kidnapper was a man by the name of Frank Nicholson, otherwise known as Frankie Nic, or just plain Frank... And far from 'hiding out', the man was staying at the Stella Maris hotel in Fuengirola, over on the sunny Costa del Crime.

When Morgan told his wife Jane what he'd found out, she said in that case they'd know never to go to Fuengirola on holiday.

'No,' Morgan said, 'but what about if I were to go there on *business*?'

'What...you don't mean—'

Morgan gave his wife a look she recognized and nodded.

'If you're going, Giles,' she said, 'then so I am...'

. . .

The Morgans flew over to Malaga the following day, and they took a room for the night in a hotel in Marbella. Then the next day they bought a second hand Range Rover and started looking for a place to rent.

They viewed several properties, before they found an isolated old farmhouse up in the hills that was just perfect. So they took it for the summer.

Now all Morgan needed was a gun.

So he went out and bought one.

Just a matter of making a few enquiries at the local brothel... Morgan couldn't get over how easy it was...

The following evening, Morgan and his wife drove down to the seafront and parked outside the Stella Maris hotel.

And they waited.

And waited.

Then Morgan saw him. 'Quick, start the engine up, Jane.'

They watched Frank walk along for a bit, and then saw him turn up a side street and Morgan said, 'Let's go.'

They followed Frank in their Range Rover to a quiet square, and then Morgan told his wife to pull over and got out.

He went up behind Frank and prodded him in the back with his gun. 'Let's go for a ride.'

'The fuck's going on?'

'Get in the back of the Range Rover, unless you want me to kill you right here.'

Frank did as he was told, and Morgan got in after him.

Then they set off for the farmhouse.

The sun had already gone down and it was dark once they got up into the hills. The roads were uneven, and when the Range Rover jolted, as they hit a large bump in the road, Frank made a grab for the gun. The two men began to wrestle each other for it on the back seat... then the gun went off, and the vehicle veered across the road and crashed into a large stone boulder.

Morgan heard the horn blowing...and then he saw his wife slumped over the wheel.

He realized that she was dead.

Something in him broke—perhaps it was his heart...and the next moment Frank had the gun.

He fired, once...twice.

He climbed in the front and put the Range Rover in gear, and he jumped out in time to watch it go crashing off the road and down what was a fairly steep ravine. The Range Rover turned over a couple of times before it hit the bottom.

Frank was sure the Morgans were both dead.

Frank bought a piece of land just outside of Marbella, and then his new mate, Dave, explained to him the way things worked, and he introduced him to a man who was high up in the council.

Frank and the local bigwig came to an amicable arrangement, with a little help from Dave and another local man who was a friend of Dave's.

Frank was to give the bigwig an envelope with a hundred thousand euros in it, and the man would produce the necessary papers bearing his signature, to say that planning permission for the hotel had been granted.

Frank came back the next day with money, and building commenced the day after that.

The men worked quickly, and Frank was happy with the way things were going. He oversaw the project personally, and made sure he knew where his money was going right down to the last penny.

He felt good about the project.

It was the best way of laundering the money he'd made from his recent dealings he could think of.

But then he found that his money—all £3,000,000 of it—was about to run out, and the hotel still didn't have a roof on it.

A few more floors would come in handy as well, Frank thought, because the more rooms the hotel had the more money he'd start raking in once the place was finally up and running.

Frank needed to get some more of the magic paper from somewhere...

PART III

CHAPTER 6

Liam pushed the buzzer on the intercom. 'Hi, Angie, it's me,' he said into it, and heard the clunk sound of the door unlocking.

He entered and walked up to Angie's flat on the top floor.

The door was slightly ajar when he got there, so he went on in without knocking, calling out, 'Angie...?' as he made a beeline for the bathroom. 'I'm just gonna use the loo a mo',' he called over his shoulder, and undid his fly.

Then he felt Angie put something against the back of his head.

'Don't mess around, honey,' he said, 'or I'll miss my aim.'

Then Liam heard a male voice that definitely wasn't Angie's say, 'I'm not messing around and I never miss.'

'Who the fuck are you...?'

'Where's the girl?'

Liam said, 'What *girl*...?'

Liam was back at Islington Green Comprehensive, and he was fighting with his old sparring partner, Spud, in the playground.

Spud was a pretty tough kid, but Liam usually got the better of him in their frequent battles...on this occasion, though, Spud had him down, and he was grinding his knuckles on the back of Liam's head.

Then Liam came to and realized he was lying on the floor in a bathroom somewhere and his head hurt.

He put his hand back there and felt the bump where he remembered being hit, it all coming back to him now.

Then he clambered to his feet and checked himself out in the mirror. At least he was still in one piece and nothing seemed to be broken.

Whoever it was that hit him had been here waiting.

The guy'd had a gun, too.

He figured he'd better see if he was alone in the flat, so he opened the bathroom door and peeped outside.

No sign of anyone...

Then Liam noticed that the front door had been shut. Maybe the guy who'd hit him shut it on his way out... Liam tiptoed into the bedroom, then he went into the living room...

As he'd suspected, he was now alone in the flat. I must have surprised whoever it was, Liam thought, so he knocks me out and leaves.

Just then, he heard voices in the hallway, outside...and the next moment, he heard the door to the flat open and someone came in, so he crept back into the bedroom.

The voices were coming from the hallway at first, but then they moved to the living room.

Without giving the matter a moment's thought, Liam sprang out from the bedroom into the living room and punched the man he saw before him on the chin. The man—middle-aged, ginger hair, posh threads—went down and stayed there.

Liam winced as he stood over him, wondering if he might have broken a bone in his hand.

'What's going on?' said the woman who had come in with the man. She was blonde and in her early thirties, Liam would have said, on the tall side and wearing a navy-blue coloured trouser suit.

'Siddown,' Liam said and the woman made a dash for the door, but he grabbed her by the arm.

She struggled to free herself, then she seemed to realize he was too strong for her and gave up. She looked at Liam, a mixture of fear and rage in her eyes, and asked him who he was and what in hell's name he thought he was doing here. Liam said he'd just been about to ask her the same question.

'If you'd let go of me a moment, I'll tell you.'

He apologized and sat the woman down in a chair, and she told him that she'd come here to view the flat. Liam said, 'Hey, wait a minute my girlfriend Angie's already living here.'

'But the estate agent told me the previous tenant had moved out.'

'If she did then she didn't say anything to me about it.'

Liam had an idea. 'Hang on a sec,' he said, and he got up and went back into the bedroom, then opened the wardrobe...and found that it was empty...so it was true—Angie *had* moved out.

Or had she been abducted...?

Liam didn't like the feel of any of this, and he feared for Angie.

I need to talk to her and make sure she's okay, he was thinking as he re-entered the living room.

Hey, but where'd the blonde go...?

She'd clearly flown.

I probably scared the life out of her, he thought.

At that moment, the man on the floor came to and started looking about him, like he was wondering where in hell's name he was. 'It's okay,' Liam said, and he helped him to his feet. 'Come and take a seat over in this chair... That's it... Let me get you a glass of water.'

'Oh, thank you,' the man said. 'But what on earth happened...? I remember coming in here to show a prospective client the flat, and then—it's all a blank in my memory after that.'

'That crazy bitch must've hit you with something...You ought to be more careful.'

'But who are you might I ask?'

'I live in the flat across the landing,' Liam said. 'I'd just come back from the shop when I heard a noise and saw this woman go dashing out, so I came in to see if I could help... I'm a good friend of Angie's—she's the girl who lives here... But where is Angie?'

'The previous tenant moved out and put it up for let...which explains why I brought someone here to view the property...'

Liam nodded and went to pour the man a glass of water, but then he heard a police siren, and figured the blonde must have called the fuzz.

Time to make himself scarce.

Liam dashed out the door, and had reached the bottom of the first flight of stairs when he heard the voices of police officers on their way up. There was no other way out of the building, and it was too risky to try and pass the cops on the stairs, so he knocked on the door of the girl who lived directly below.

The cops were getting closer, when the girl who lived there opened up. 'Hi, Cassandra... D'you mind if I come in for a chat a mo'?'

'No, of course not, Liam—but what is it...? Is everything all right?'

Liam brushed past her, saying, 'Yes and no,' and he went into the living room and made himself comfortable on the three-piece suite.

He smiled at Cassandra as she came to a halt behind one of the chairs and put her hands on the brown leather. She was tall and slim and somehow there seemed to be something horsey about her, Liam couldn't help thinking. 'You've got it nice in here, Cassandra,' he said, just to have something to say. Although it was true that the high ceiling gave the room a spacious feel, and the furniture was of high quality.

'Can I get you tea or coffee, Liam?'

'Scotch would be nice.'

Cassandra went to the kitchen and came back moments later with a drink in either hand. 'I thought I'd better join you... Bad manners to leave a guest to drink alone.'

She handed Liam his Scotch and sat down next to him on the sofa. 'My excuse, anyway,' she said and smiled.

'You still going with my friend, Quincy...?' Liam had first introduced Cassandra to his neighbour one time when she'd come to him asking if he knew anyone who sold good blow.

'Kind of... I mean, it's casual between us—you know, nothing serious.'

Liam sipped his Scotch and wondered how the cops were getting on with the estate agent in the flat directly above.

Poor bastard's probably wanting to know why I'm taking so long to get him a glass of water, he thought.

The cops shouldn't be up there too long, he supposed, and then he would be able to move on.

'So what's new, Liam?'

'I just came around to visit Angie, only she's not in.'

'But that's strange, because it sounds like someone's up there moving around right now—and whoever's up there was making the most frightful racket earlier on.' 'It certainly wasn't Angie and me that were making all the noise, I can tell you that much... Fact is, she seems to have moved out in a hurry.'

'But she can't have—not just like that. I'm sure she would've come down and said goodbye to her old friend Cass first.'

'She didn't even think to say goodbye to her good old friend Liam, and he has been known to share her bed.'

Cassandra tasted her Scotch. 'You two haven't had a tiff, have you?'

'Nope...not to my knowledge, anyway.'

'So you mean she's just scarpered?'

Liam nodded.

'So where's she gone?'

'I was hoping that you might know, Cassandra.'

'You got any idea who's up there now?'

'An estate agent.'

'In that case, why don't we go up and ask him... He might have her forwarding address.' Cassandra made to get up, but Liam put his hand on her arm to restrain her. 'It might not be a good idea to go up there right now.'

'There's something you're not telling me—what is it?'

'It's a long story.'

'Is Angie in some kind of trouble?'

'That's what I'm trying to work out,' Liam said. 'I've got to find her.'

Liam passed through a doorway that was squeezed in between a smelly Italian restaurant to the one side and an even smellier kebab house to the other, and climbed the stairs. Then when he entered his flat, he heard the sound of the flush being pulled, and he hurried over to the door of the tiny bathroom...then heard a voice he realized was Angie's say, 'Oh, damn,' and he gave the door a gentle push.

'Ah there you are, babes,' Angie said. 'I let myself in and was wondering where you could've got to.'

She squeezed herself out of the tiny bathroom, and the next moment she was in Liam's arms.

'Angie...where the hell have you *been* all this time?'

'It's a long story.'

'For fuck's sake, I've been worried sick about you.'

Liam gazed into her beautiful brown eyes, ran a hand through her mane of thick, silky dark hair. 'You look frightened and you're trembling... What's the matter...?'

'This guy's following me.'

'What guy?'

'His name's Frank...he knows my dad from way back.'

'Where is he?'

'He's sitting in the café across the street, so he can watch the front door of the building and see when I leave.'

'Sounds like I'd better go over'n have a word with this character.'

'That wouldn't be such a good idea—he's probably carrying a gun.'

Liam said in that case it was time they made themselves scarce, and he led her from the room, down the stairs and rang the bell to the ground-floor flat.

Quincy, the black guy who lived downstairs, opened up. 'Happen, man...? You smoked all that weed I sold you yesterday *already*...?'

'No, I need to ask you a favour...'

'What's that?'

'Can we go out through your window...? This is a real emergency...'

'Sure, man...'

Quincy took a step back and opened the door wider, to allow them to enter the room.

'Whassup...? There some dude you forgot to pay...? Or it the cops you runnin' from...?'

'I'll explain everything later.'

Liam hurried over to the window, then pulled up the sash, and he and Angie climbed out into the small cement garden.

He helped Angie over the wall at the back and they dropped down into another garden. They went over a couple more walls in the same way, then over a higher one, before they found themselves in the street—and they hurried to Liam's thirty-six-year-old E-Type Jaguar, where he'd left it parked, and jumped in.

Liam started up the engine and said, 'We gave that ugly bastard the slip all right.'

'Let's get right away from here, before he finds out we've left.'

'Maybe a short break down in Brighton'd be just what we need.'

He'd call in sick, say he had the flu and wouldn't be in for a few days. Then they'd be able to take in some sea air and rest up a little, he thought. Make a little love, drink a few cocktails. Go for a few walks along the seafront and plan their next move.

'That sounds cool.'

Angie put on some Amy Winehouse as they went over Battersea Bridge.

'So what's this all about, Angie?'

'It must have something to do with my dad.'

'How do you mean exactly...?'

'If I tell you a secret, will you promise on your life never to tell anyone...?'

'Sure.'

'Promise.'

'I promise.'

'Did you hear about the Rembrandt that was stolen a few days ago...?'

'The one that was in the news...?'

'That's the one.'

'What about it...?'

'It was my dad and his mate that nicked it...'

'Fuck *me*...'

Liam took a little while to take in what he'd just been told.

And then he began to wonder how he felt about it...

Then he said, 'So you think this bloke's following you to try and get to your father...?'

The Metropole in Brighton was running a special offer, so Liam and Angie booked themselves into a nice room with a balcony that overlooked the sea. Then Liam had room service bring them a bottle of Scotch and *The Times*.

He poured himself a stiff one, then sat down on the bed with it and began to read the story on the front page of his newspaper about the missing Rembrandt.

Angie said she was going to take a shower and disappeared into the bathroom.

When she came out, some twenty minutes later, with a towel wrapped around her, Liam was still reading *The Times*.

Angie went over to the French windows and gazed out. 'I love hotels,' she said. 'Especially nice ones like this where you have a sea view... I think I'd like to spend the rest of my life moving from hotel to hotel, and just go all around the world that way and never stop anyplace for more than about a week at a time.'

Liam said, 'That's the gypsy in you talking.'

'Wouldn't you like that, too, though?'

'I guess so...if I could afford to do it.'

Angie loosened the towel and let it fall to the floor, and stood there naked before him.

She saw Liam's eyes light up, and the next thing she knew he was kissing her passionately...but at that moment her mobile began to ring.

'Hello?'

'Angie? Cassandra here... Listen, I was at the market earlier, reading people's fortunes with my crystal ball—'

'Yes, I've always wanted to get you to read mine, Cass, but somehow we've never got around to it...'

'No, but listen, Angie, what I'm calling for's to tell you this really creepy looking guy with a scar across his face came to my stall and started asking me where you were....'

'Thanks for calling to let me know, Cass.'

'Is it true that you've moved out?'

'Yes, I had to move in a hurry and didn't get the chance to say goodbye.'

'But where are you now?'

Angie told her. 'But keep it under your hat, Cass.'

'Don't worry, mum's the word.'

CHAPTER 7

Cassandra was with Tarquin in a cafe on King's Road, an hour or later, when her mobile began to ring.
'Hello?'
'It's me, Carmen.'
Carmen was the woman Cassandra had in to clean her flat every day.
'What's up?'
'It's just that I thought I should to tell you a man he come calling at the flat earlier.'
'What?'
'He said he was from the BT to checking your phone.'
'Yes...the line wasn't working properly, so I called customer services and asked to have somebody come around to sort it out... I thought I told you?'
Carmen said, 'You did, yes. That's why when he come I let him in... only it was what happen after that I thought it was strange, so I was thinkin' I will phone you to telling you so you will know.'
'What happened?'
'The man he come in and he's doin' somethin' to the phone, and then he left... And after there was the other man who he come in as well.'
'Another man...?'

'From the BT.'

'Oh.'

'He said the first man who come he forget to do somethin', and just he want to check to see if he is doin' it all properly. Otherwise, he said, the phone it might not working.'

'The second man said this?'

'Yes,' Carmen said.

'What did this second man look like?'

'He have the short black hair, the dark skin, and have big scar on his face.'

Something strange was going on, Cassandra thought... First Angie moves out in a hurry and then this guy with the scar turns up at my stall and starts asking after her...then he shows at my flat pretending to be working for the BT... Angie must have got herself involved in something...and there must be a lot of money involved, too.

Cassandra would have liked to be able to talk to Angie and find out what was going on, see if she couldn't maybe cut herself in on whatever it was... But she might never have a chance to talk to Angie again if the man with scar on his face caught up with her.

Cassandra said, 'Was I doin' wrong to letting him in?'

'Yes.'

'I'm sorry, but I—'

'It's okay, it wasn't your fault.'

'But I—'

'This second man...the one with the scar on his cheek...do you think you would recognize him if you saw him again?'

'Yes, I think so.'

'If you ever see that man again, don't let him in, okay?'

'Okay, but who is he?'

'You don't need to worry about that, Carmen...just make sure you don't let him in if he comes again, okay...? Ciao.'

Cassandra hung up and gave her lower lip a bit of grief with those pristine-white incisors of hers as she turned the situation over in her mind. Then Tarquin brought her the mint julep he'd just made, and she took a swig of it.

'Something worrying you, Cass?'

Cassandra didn't look at Tarquin so much as through him. 'Calling

Angie's the very last thing I should have done if it's bugged,' she said as if she were thinking aloud.

'Bugged...? What's *bugged*, Cass?'

'That means Scarface must've been able to listen in to the conversation I had with her earlier... And if he did, then he now knows where she is.'

'What?'

She picked up the phone and dialled Angie's mobile number.

'Hello?'

'It's Cass again. Listen, I think that man with the scar knows where you are... I mean, I have reason to believe he's broken in to my place and bugged the phone, in which case he could well have listened in on the conversation we had a little earlier— when you told me where you are, I mean...'

'Which means he could be—'

'Listening in now, or—'

'Exactly, on his—'

'Way to—'

'It must be an hour ago that we talked—'

'And Brighton to London's doable in an hour or less.'

Angie said, 'I'd better go.'

Angie gave Liam a poke in the back to wake him up. 'C'mon, quick, we've gotta get out of this place.'

'Eh?'

'The guy who's following me knows I'm here.'

'What?'

They both got dressed in double-quick time and then, just when they were ready to go, there was a knock at the door. 'That's probably him now,' Angie whispered.

'You answer it and I'll take him by surprise.'

There was another loud knock.

Liam picked up a flower vase, held it upside down to empty it of water and flowers, then went and concealed himself behind the door and Angie opened it. He heard her say hello, trying not to sound nervous, even though he could see she was... then saw her open the door and stand back for the man to enter...and without even pausing to think, Liam took a step forward and brought the solid flower vase crashing down onto the back of the man's head.

It wasn't until she saw him lying on the floor at his feet, out cold, that Angie realized the man Liam had just hit wasn't who she'd feared it was going to be but one of the staff at the hotel.

The man, who was built like a bear, looked up at Liam and said, 'What the...?' But before he could say another word he passed out.

'I hope I haven't killed him.' Liam began to slap the man about the face to try to bring him round.

'It's no good, he's out cold.'

Angie picked up the phone and called room service, and it wasn't long before a man showed and called through the door. 'Come in,' Angie called back, and the man entered. He was in his forties, had thinning brown hair and was built like a jockey.

'I believe you rang?' he said, and then he saw his colleague lying on the carpet.

Angie said, 'He had an accident.'

The Jockey hunkered down and was about to take his colleague's pulse—but just then someone hit him hard from behind, and he fell unconscious on top of his colleague.

The man who had hit him was Frank Nicholson.

He had a gun in his hand, but was holding it back to front at that moment, having just used it to pistol-whip the man from room service.

Liam lunged at Frank before he had time to turn the gun around in his hand, and managed to push him back against the wall. Then Liam got a hand to Frank's throat, and the two men began to wrestle each other.

Frank pushed Liam away, but then Liam got Frank by the wrist and banged his arm against the wall so that he dropped the gun. Angie made a dash for it, but Frank kicked it, sending it skidding over the carpet and it went under the bed.

Angie went after it again...and she had just got her fingertips to it when the Jockey came around, and he got to his feet and grabbed a fistful of Angie's hair. She lashed out at him with her nails, and he punched her on the chin and knocked her out.

Meanwhile, Liam and Frank were still fighting it out. Liam hit Frank in the face, sending him hurtling against the wall, but then Frank bounced back and kicked Liam between the legs.

Liam doubled up, feeling like he wanted to vomit, and Frank got in a punch to his head. Liam fell backwards, onto the man from room service who was built like a bear, and the Bear came around.

Then Frank got down on his knees and began to try to strangle Liam, but the Bear got a fistful of Frank's nuts, so that Frank stopped what he'd been doing and screamed out in pain. This gave Liam the chance to scramble to his feet, but at that moment the Jockey jumped on his back.

Liam saw Frank kick the Bear in the gut and the Bear got hold of Frank's leg and pulled him down onto the floor, and they began to wrestle.

Just then, Liam felt the Jockey's hands squeezing his throat, and he began to twist around and buck like a wild horse at a rodeo, to try to shake him off...but the little guy kept holding on.

Liam stopped for a breather, and the Jockey started to try and gouge his eyes out. Then Liam had the idea of backing up and ramming the little bastard against the wall, only as he did so, he tripped over the Bear and fell onto his back, with the Jockey under him, and he heard the Jockey cry out in pain.

Liam got up in time to see Frank knock the Bear out, and then Liam and Frank went at each other again and Liam managed to knock him out with a lucky punch. Then he dragged him out to the bathroom and dropped him into the tub.

At that moment Frank came around, and he grabbed onto the sides of the bathtub and tried to pull himself up, but Liam got him with another good right to the jaw, and Frank fell back into the tub with a bang.

Then Liam hit him again, and he heard Frank's head bang against the enamel. That took the fight out of the bastard for long enough for Liam to be able to turn the taps on as far as they would go, drenching Frank's suit.

Frank seemed to get a second wind after a short while, and he kept trying to get up out of the tub. But each time Liam would hit him with a right and send him back down into the tub...and finally Liam caught Frank with a good one on the chin that took the last bit of fight out of him.

Then Liam held Frank's head under water, until his feet began to kick about in the air, like he was some kind of big fish...and when he reckoned Frank had had enough, Liam let him up and allowed him a few breaths of air, before he went back to holding him under again...

After he'd done this a few times, Liam said, 'Okay, now if you want me to stop then you'd better tell me what it is that you want.'

Then someone hit Liam from behind, and he passed out.

It was the Jockey.

He'd hit Liam with Frank's gun, as he explained later...and he now put the gun down and helped Frank up out of the tub. The Jockey clearly having got things all skewed and garbled, the way guys often do when they come in in the middle of a fight and then end up taking a few good blows to the head...

'You okay?' the Jockey asked Frank.

'Yeah, I think I'll live.'

The Jockey went back into the bedroom and picked up the phone, and he was about to dial reception when he heard Frank say, 'Put it down.'

The Jockey turned and saw that Frank was pointing the gun at him.

That was what Liam saw when he came around.

He turned and saw Angie lying nearby. She was rubbing her head and groaning.

Frank went and got Angie up on her feet, then he held her from behind and pointed his gun against the back of her head.

'You,' he said to Liam, 'go an' cuff those two goons to one of the pipes in the bathroom.'

Frank reached into his pocket and brought out a couple of pairs of police issue plastic restraints, and he tossed them onto the carpet.

'Get a move on, unless you want me to shoot the girl.'

Frank stood in the doorway to the bathroom with Angie in front of him, and watched Liam handcuff the men.

'Okay,' he said, when Liam had finished. 'Now turn the taps on in the bath'n get back in here.'

Frank moved away from the doorway, pulling Angie with him, to let Liam come through. 'Shut the door behind you and go'n sit over on the bed.'

Liam did as he was told

'Now listen,' Frank said, 'and listen good, if you wanna see your girl-friend again, understand?'

'Yes.'

'I'm taking her with me now, and you're gonna wait for my call... then you do what I tell you... Just don't tell the cops nothin'...'Cause if you do, I'll know about it... I smell a whiff a fuzz, she gets it.'

'Okay,' Liam said, 'no cops, I promise.'

'They ask why'd I take the girl, you don't know nothin'... and you don't tell them I'm gonna call you, understand...?'

'Okay.'

'What you do, you shut the fuck up, got it?'

'Whatever you say.'

'Sounds like maybe you ain't so stupid after all.' Frank brought out a mobile phone. 'Now you take this'n don't let the cops know you got it, 'cause this's the phone I'm gonna call you on... The cops'll be busy buggin' your home, waitin' for me to call you on your landline, but they don't know you got this... Take it and don't tell no one I gave you it.'

Liam took the mobile and put it in his pocket.

'You play it my way, no one gets hurt, you get your girlfriend back, coupla days later it's all just a bad memory... You wanna try something, get the cops involved, then it ain't no film anymore. The girl gets it and it's for real. You value the girl's life then you be sure you know the difference. You get me?'

'I got you.'

Frank pulled Angie by the arm. 'C'mon,' he said, 'we gotta go.' Then Angie found herself being bustled out of the room and over to the elevator.

Frank pushed the button, the doors opened and they stepped inside. A middle-aged couple got in on the next floor down. The woman looked at them as though she were about to say good afternoon or something, but then she seemed to think better of it. No one got in on the floor after that. Then they missed a floor, and then the doors opened and they stepped out into the lobby. Frank told Angie, in that rough gravelly voice of his, just to keep walking and she did just that.

When they got outside, he jerked her to the right. They walked to where he'd left his Lexus parked. 'You drive,' he said.

Tarquin said, 'Why don't we go for a drive?'

'You and your drives.'

'There's something I'd rather like to show you, Cass.'

'What?'

'It's a surprise.'

Cassandra said, 'You and your surprises... Are you going to tell me what it is, or aren't you?'

'First you must promise never to tell anyone what I'm about to say.'

'Okay,' she said. 'I promise.'

'The fact is, my father is in possession of one of the most valuable paintings in the world.'

'And how did he get it?'

'He bought it—how do you think?'

When the cops arrived on the scene at the Metropole, Liam gave them a carefully edited version of what had taken place.

The officer in charge of the investigation was a tall man in a grey suit with a Mediterranean complexion and a moustache. He showed Liam his ID said, 'I'm Detective Chief Inspector Preston and my colleague here is Detective Sergeant Johnson... Have you got any idea why this man might've taken your girlfriend...?'

'Your guess is as good as mine.'

Preston tweaked his droopy black moustache. 'There's something you're not telling me.'

'If it's money he wants then I haven't got much and nor's Angie.'

'You have something—or your girlfriend does... something that this man wants— and you'd better hurry up and tell me what that thing is, if you ever want to see her again.'

'Why aren't you out there looking for her's what I'd like to know, instead of wasting time sitting here talking to me?'

Detective Sergeant Johnson, a handsome man around the age of thirty dressed in a pinstriped suit, said, 'And where do you suggest we start looking?'

Liam shrugged. 'You're the cops. Isn't it your job to know stuff like that?'

They were driving along a quiet country road, somewhere between London and Brighton, when Frank had Angie turn off up a lane, then he told her to stop and get out.

Angie did as she was told, and Frank marched her around the back of the car and opened up the boot. 'Get in,' he said.

She caught Frank off guard and kneed him in the groin.

Frank groaned in pain and doubled up, and she pushed him so that he fell backwards down into a cowpat, then she made a dash to get back into the car...and was in the driving seat before Frank could get to her.

She turned the key in the ignition, slipped her into gear, and set off across what was a large empty field... Looking about her, she saw that the only way out was the way they'd come in. So she set about turning the car around, and then a hand started tugging at her hair.

It was Frank.

Somehow he'd managed to get up onto the roof, and he kept yanking her hair so that her head was going back and forth like a puppet on a string, and she lost control of the wheel and the car started to zigzag over the field.

Then Angie found she couldn't see anything, because Frank's hand was covering her face. She sank her teeth into his wrist and bit him as hard as she could...and the next moment, there was blood everywhere. It was in her face and eyes, so that she couldn't see anything but red... and then the car hit something and that was the last thing she knew.

Until she came around later, and found that she'd been blindfolded.

Then she realized that Frank had shut her in the boot.

CHAPTER 8

⁂

Tarquin led Cassandra along the parquetted hallway, and stopped outside a panelled door. 'Not a word about this to anyone, mind you, Cass.'

'Mum's the word.'

He unlocked the door to the room and said, 'I give you Rembrandt's Self Portrait at the Age of 63.'

Angie was being kept blindfolded, and with her hands tied in front of her, in a room with no windows. She tried to scream for help at first, but Frank came in and hit her in the mouth. 'It ain't like I'm worried anybody's gonna hear you, 'cause they ain't,' Frank said, 'only it's just I can't stand the noise you make when you do that.'

Angie stopped screaming for help after that.

She could tell it was a city she was in because of the muffled sounds that drifted into the room from outside...the sound of cars going by in the street and sometimes of people calling out.

Planes were going over quite frequently, too.

That told her they must be situated under one of a number of different flight routes.

Angie considered counting aloud to see if she couldn't measure the intervals between each plane going over, figuring that this information might be useful to someone if only she could smuggle it out somehow.

Just then, the door opened and someone came in. 'Who's there?'

Liam spent a sleepless night worrying about Angie, and DCI Preston called him first thing in the morning.

'Just making sure you're up and ready for the kidnapper's call,' Preston said.

'I'm ready...but thanks for the call, anyway.'

'I'm on my way to your place...be there in about ten minutes.'

They hung up, and Liam continued to pace up and down. He was like a cat walking on barbed wire.

Then Preston arrived with a sound man, who hooked up the phone to a recording device.

'I don't know about anybody else,' Preston said, 'but I could do with some coffee.'

'Help yourself.' Liam looked at his watch. There was still another twenty minutes to, until the time the kidnapper said he would call.

The minutes dragged.

Then, finally, the phone began to ring, and Liam picked it up.

'Hello?'

'You wanna see your girlfriend again you better listen to me.'

'I'm listening.'

'I'll call again at nine this evening and tell you what to do.'

Liam said 'Okay, but wait—'

Then the line went dead.

Angie was woken up by the sound of the door opening. 'Hello?' she said. 'Who's there?'

She didn't get a reply to her question, but she could tell it wasn't Frank because whoever it was smelt different...it was the cologne the man was using. Angie didn't know the brand, but it had a strong spicy smell.

There must be two of them, she thought.

'You got any idea how hard it is being shut up like this?' she said when the man failed to respond. 'With the blindfold on, I can't even tell whether it's day or night... I mean what's the point in making me suffer like this? You trying to drive me nuts or something?'

Angie heard whoever it was drop the bucket at the side of the bed, and then the door slammed shut.

Cassandra came out of the gym on Earl's Court Road, walked the short distance up to Quincy's place and pushed his buzzer.

She could smell the spicy cooking from the pizzeria next door as she heard Quincy say who's there, and she said, it's me, Cass. Hang on a mo', he told her, and then he came down and opened up, looking lean and athletic in the yellow tracksuit he had on. He smiled and showed her those perfect white teeth of his, then turned and led her along the shoddy hallway and into his room... And Cassandra launched herself at him the moment they got in there.

Quincy pulled away for a moment and looked at her. 'You hot for ole Quincy, huh?'

Cassandra said, 'Why don't you just shut up and get your kit off?'

Afterwards Quincy sat up in the bed and lit up a joint, then took a good long toke. 'You freak me out.'

'How's that?'

'Girl like you's used to a certain sort a life'n enjoyin' certain privileges, right?'

Cassandra said, 'I make a point of enjoying all the privileges I can at each and every opportunity.'

'What I don't get's just where I fit into the picture... I mean I'm from a diff'rent world, baby...What've we got in common?'

'We both like fucking – and not just that, but we like fucking *each other*.'

'That how you judge people – whether'r not you like to fuck with them?'

'It's one way of doing it.'

'But you're from a posh family, ain'tcha?'

'Yeah...a posh family who don't give me anything.'

Quincy leaned his head back and took another long slow toke. 'So why don't you just marry one of your rich boyfriends'n all your problems'd be solved, right...?'

'I suppose so...if you don't consider my being bored to death a problem.' 'You plannin' on continuin' to take that little crystal ball a yours over to Camden market to make ends meet the rest a your life, that it?'

'I've got a little plan in mind, as a matter of fact—and if you'll only give me some of that joint I might just tell you all about it.'

Quincy passed her the joint and she inhaled on it, then breathed out the smoke through her nostrils. 'My friend's father has a painting on his wall that's virtually priceless.'

'You don't mean that you think we should—'

'Help ourselves to it and sell it then split the money, sure—why not...?'

'Ain't a nice girl like yourself stopped to consider maybe one good reason why not could be 'cause it don't belong to us?'

'But it doesn't belong to the guy who's got it, either...it's stolen property.'

The door opened and someone came in. It wasn't Frank but the other man, the one who wore the strong, spicy smelling cologne. 'I brought you some water,' he said.

Angie reached out and the man took her hand and put it around the glass, then he helped her lift it to her lips. 'Thanks,' she said, when it was all gone. 'If it wasn't for you that other bastard'd leave me here to die of dehydration.'

The man wrested the glass from her hand.

'Listen, it's my time of the month... Can't you at least buy me some Tampax and some clean clothes?'

There was no answer, so Angie said, 'Oh, c'mon, have a heart, will you...? You've got a mother, haven't you...? Maybe you've got a wife or a sister, too... How'd you feel if they were being kept like this...? The blood's soaked right through my jeans.'

She paused and heard the man breathing like he was a little out of breath from climbing the stairs.

She asked him his name.

'What you wanna know my name for?'

'Just tryin' to be polite and friendly, that's all... How on earth did you get hooked up with a bastard like Frank, anyway?'

'He said not to talk.'

'What else did Frank tell you not to do?'

'He said you was likely to wanna get friendly wid me and for me not to let you.'

'When they made Frank, they forgot to give him a heart.'

'This is bizniss,' the man said. 'Nothin' personal. We got a job to do...Your father plays ball'n we let you go, end of story.'

'Strikes me you're just trying to make it rich fast like anyone else,' Angie said. 'Only difference between you and most other people is, you can't be assed to go out and work for it...You know what, I reckon if we were to've met under different circumstances then we could've got on, you and me. You're the kind of guy a girl can talk to...not like Frank.'

'What you gotta und'stan' about Frank is, he wants to get the job done right.'

'Who says you have to treat a girl like an animal to do that...? I mean, is it too much trouble just to pop out to the local store and bring me some pads, some fresh underwear and a coupla cheap dresses, huh?'

'I'll see what I can do, okay?'

'Thanks.'

'I gotta go.'

'Why?' Angie said. 'What's the hurry?'

'It's jus'—'

'I know, you don't have to tell me, it's Frank, isn't it? You're scared of him, aren't you?'

'No, it ain't that.'

'So what are you panicking for, then?'

'Heh, lady, listen, who's says I'm panickin'? Johnny White ain't frightened a nobody.'

'You ought to stand up to him, Johnny.'

'Heh, who tol' you my name was Johnny?'

'You did, just then.'

'Listen, lady—'

Frank said, 'What's goin' on here?' He'd entered the room without either of them hearing him come up the stairs.

'Nothin', Frank,' Johnny said.

'So what you standin' here chinwaggin' for?'

'We wasn't, Frank.'

'The fuck you wasn't... Sounded like a reg'lar heart to heart you two was havin', somethin' right offa fuckin' Trisha.'

'The fuck is Trisha?'

Frank said, 'I thought I told you not to talk to the girl.'

'I told you I weren't talkin' to no one.'

'So what you sayin', it was yourself you was talkin' to?'

'Okay,' Johnny said. 'I talked to the girl for a moment, di'n't I, but what I mean to say is, it weren't like we was havin' a proper confab nor naffin... It's jus' she was tellin' me she's on her monthlies, i'n' it, and she was axin' me if she can't have some clean clothes and some pads'n stuff.'

'What d'you tell her?'

'I said I'd talk to you about it.'

'So what was that she was sayin' 'bout you gotta stand up to me I heard when I was comin' up the stairs?'

'For fuck's sake, Frank... I'm gettin' sick a this.'

'So you're gettin' sick of it, are you?'

'I ain't gonna have you treatin' me like no fuckin kid, Frank. Not you nor no one else.'

'So the bitch is startin' to get her way, just like I thought.'

'Leave her out a this.'

'She's already in it, way you're talkin'.'

'This's between you'n me, Frank.'

'You're too fuckin right it is...We got a job to do here.'

'Tha's right. It's bizness.'

'Tha's right...and there ain't no room for gettin' soft on people when it comes to bizniss, you got that?'

'Who's talkin' 'bout gettin' soft, Frank?'

Time passed and then Frank came into the room again.

'Now listen, sister,' he said, 'we goin' a call your Daddy, okay? He brings us what we're after, we let you go, nice 'n' simple, right? Either of you try any funny stuff'n the deal's no longer so simple... So you wanna get out a this in one piece, you do just as I say, un'stand?'

'Yes.'

'Right, that's good... I hate to be misunderstood.'

Frank snapped open his mobile, then tapped in a number and began to talk to Angie's father, Terry. Listen, I've got your daughter, was the gist of it. You wanna see her again, you'll hand over the Rembrandt you stole from the National Gallery.

To prove that he really had Angie with him, Frank put her on the phone. Hello Dad, she said. Yes, she was okay, and yes, she would try not to worry. She had great faith him. He was her dad after all. Yes, she believed him when he told her he would get her out of this mess.

Angie began to sob and Frank snatched the phone from her. 'Listen,' Terry said, 'we need a little time.'

'What for?'

'We don't have the painting here right now...it's in Italy.'

'You got twenty-four hours to get it...You haven't got it by the next time I call, you never see your daughter again.'

Frank hung up.

CHAPTER 9

Terry called Kenny and told him what had happened.

Kenny said, 'Ain't planning on givin' 'im the Rembrandt, are ya?'

'What we're gonna do, Ken, we're gonna pinch back the fake we sold to Willoughby... So long as we hold on to the original a little longer no one'll know it's a fake. That way we can keep Frank happy and get my Angie back in one piece...Then when she's back safe and sound, we just send the original Rembrandt back to the National Gallery, like we planned, and there's no crime, so no one's ever gonna come looking for us'n everyone's happy... 'cept for Lord Willoughby, and he's too rich to take it personally, anyway.'

'I ain't so sure, Tel... fifty million's a lot of money in anyone's book.'

Terry shrugged and said, 'Well if he takes it personally then he can just go'n fuck himself...'

'And what about the guy that's kidnapped your daughter, once he finds out it's a fake we palmed off on 'im?'

'Don't you worry about Frank,' Terry said. 'I'll take care of him.'

At ten to six, Liam told DCI Preston that he was going out to get some fresh air.

'Just so long as you're back well before nine, in case the guy calls early...'

'Don't worry...you think I'm stupid or something...?'

The kidnapper called Liam on the mobile he'd given him at seven, like he said he would.

'Listen, we've encountered a little hitch. It's nothin' major...but this is gonna take a bit longer than we expected... I'll be in touch.'

Liam said, 'What about...' and was going to say 'Angie' but the kidnapper had already hung up.

Cassandra parked in the woods that abutted Jeremy Willoughby's Surrey mansion at the back, then she and Quincy put on their balaclavas and got out of the car.

They climbed over a wall and dropped down the other side, into the grounds, then made their way over to the house, which was a gorgeous old eighteenth century number.

Quincy punched a hole in one of the latticed windows with his gloved fist, and the next thing he knew the alarm bells started to ring.

'Quick,' Cassandra said, 'go in and turn the switch off.'

'Where is it?'

'Over on the wall, to your right.'

Quincy reached inside and opened the window, then climbed inside the house, leaving Cassandra to clamber in behind him, and he set about looking for the alarm switch.

Then the light came on.

Quincy turned and found himself looking at a man who stood at around five-eight and was dressed all in black. 'Who are you,' Quincy said, 'the Milk Tray Man?'

'I'm more interested in knowing who you are than in answering questions.'

'We're friends of Tarquin's,' Cassandra said.

'Just visitin', heh?'

'That's right.'

'Normally come in through the window wearin' a balaclava, do you?'

'Thought we'd surprise him.'

The man reached into his pocket and brought out a gun.

Cassandra said, 'Where's Tarquin?'

'He ain't here.'

'Why don't we give him a call, then, just to let him know we got here before him...?'

'I got a better idea—why don't you get your asses out a here before you get 'em shot off.'

'But who are you?'

'I'm paid to watch over this place while the owner's away,' the man said. 'Now I'm gonna give you one last chance to leave this place of your own accord.'

'It's okay,' Quincy said, 'we're going,' and he took Cassandra by the arm. 'C'mon, you heard what the man said.'

And with that, they went back out the way they'd come in.

'I'm trying to figure out where we went wrong,' Cassandra said, as they were driving back towards London.

'You axe me, our big mistake...was havin' the stupid idea in the first place.'

'We should've approached it differently.'

'Like how exactly?'

'That's what I've got to work out.'

Later, in bed at Quincy's place, Cassandra said, 'I've been wondering why that guy didn't call the police, and the more I think about it, the odder it seems...'

'Obvious why he didn't, i'n' it?'

'No, it isn't actually... Have I missed something?'

Quincy took a last toke on the joint and passed it to Cassandra. 'Your mate Tarquin's daddy bought the Rembrandt on the black market, right...? So he's not gonna want the cops involved, is he...?'

Cassandra nodded.

Cassandra toked on the joint. 'Even so, you'd think he'd've made us take out balaclavas off... I mean, the guy didn't even seem to be interested in finding out what we look like...'

The following day Cassandra got Tarquin to take her to the family mansion again, and as soon as they arrived there, Tarquin set about fixing them both a mint julep.

Cassandra asked him if his father paid people to guard the house when it was empty, and he shook his head. 'Truth is, Dad asked me if I'd stay here while he's away, to keep an eye on the place... I promised him I would, but I've failed to be as good as my word because I've been spending most of my time up in London with you.'

That's funny, Cassandra thought. So who was the guy with the gun that had been here last night...?

At that moment, the door opened and Quincy walked in wearing shades and a balaclava, as planned. 'Right,' he said, 'hands up, both of you.'

They did as they were told, and then Quincy gave Cassandra a piece of rope and had her tie Tarquin's hands behind his back. Then Quincy tied Cassandra up and told her to lie on the floor.

Tarquin said, 'If it's the safe you're after, it's behind the portrait on the wall there.'

The portrait on the wall being one of Tarquin's great grandfather

'It's the Rembrandt I want.'

'The *what*...?'

Quincy went over to where Cassandra was lying on the floor and held his gun against the back of her head. 'Don't bullshit me, okay, or the girl gets it.'

'All right, I'll show you anything you want, only leave her alone.'

'Show me the Rembrandt'n we'll get along fine—do we understand each other?'

'Follow me.'

Tarquin led Quincy out of the room and along a hallway, then through another room, and they came to a door that was locked. 'The key's in my back pocket.'

Quincy reached in for it, then he put the key in the lock and went to turn it, but— 'Hey,' he said, 'it's not locked,' and he pushed it open.

'That's strange.'

Tarquin stepped into the room...and looked in dumb amazement and horror at the giant empty space on the wall where the painting should have been.

'So where is it?'

'That's what I would like to know...it was right there on the wall.'

'Pull the other one.'

'No, honestly...'

Quincy thought of something.

'I need you to phone the guy you had guardin' this place last night and tell 'im you wanna know where he's hidden the fuckin' Rembrandt.'

'What *guy* are you talking about?'

'Fuckin guy was here...Milk Tray Man.'

'But there wasn't anybody here last night,' Tarquin said. 'The only person who's supposed to be looking after the place at the moment is me... After all, my father bought the Rembrandt in secret, so he didn't figure he'd need to get anyone in to guard the painting, because no one else but him and me knew about it.'

Quincy looked Tarquin in the eye. 'You piss with me'n the girl gets it.'

'I'm telling you the truth...'

I think he damn well is, too, Quincy thought. And then it hit him. 'So tha's what happened,' he said, thinking aloud.

'What?'

'The crafty bastard.'

'*Who...?*'

'He's here pretendin' to be guardin' the place when the bastard's really come here to help 'imself to the Rembrandt... Now that's what I call fuckin classical.'

After Quincy had left, Tarquin managed to work himself free, then he untied Cassandra. 'Thanks,' she said, stretching her arms and wriggling her fingers, to get the blood circulating back into them.

'You okay?'

'I think so... Did he take anything?'

'No... what he came for had already been stolen.'

Cassandra said 'What...not the–'

'Yes, the Rembrandt...'

'What you don't mean it's...'

'Gone, yes...'

'*Shit*...' Cassandra was as stunned as Tarquin. 'So now what?'

'That's what I'm trying to work out, Cass.'

'Aren't you going to call the police?'

'And tell them what? That someone's stolen dad's stolen Rembrandt?'

'You don't mean your dad stole it in the first place?' she said, acting all naive.

'No, he had it stolen for him...'

'Wow, stealing art treasures to order...sounds like quite a business.'

Tarquin ran a hand over his neck. 'Dad's going to fucking kill me.'

'But it wasn't your fault.'

'I was supposed to be keeping an eye on the place for him and I wasn't even here.' Tarquin threw his head back and puffed out his cheeks. 'Fuck it, Cass, what am I going to *do*?'

'You might try and get your painting back.'

'Yes...but *how*?'

That was the fifty-million-pound question.

'It's okay, I got the painting,' Terry said.

Frank said, 'Listen to me.'

'I'm listenin'.'

'You go into the lobby of The Ritz Hotel on Piccadilly at seven-thirty this evenin', and I'll be there waitin'.'

'Then what?'

'My man'll have your daughter nearby,' Frank said. 'We make the exchange – I get to keep the painting and you get your daughter back, end of story. Sound okay to you?'

'Sure.'

'But I'm warnin' you, Terry...one false move—'

'There ain't gonna be no false moves.'

'I'm just tellin' you the way it's gonna be, in case you start gettin' any ideas.'

Terry said, 'I ain't the sort to get any ideas... All I want is to get my Angie back in one piece, but if anythin' happens to her, I'll—'

'The way I see it, you ain't in no position to go makin' threats, Terry.'

'I'm just tellin' you so we both understand each other is all... I only got one daughter and she means the whole fuckin' world to me.'

'Just be there and don't try'n contact no one else beforehand, or call in the fuzz,' Frank said. 'I'll be watchin' you.'

He hung up.

. . .

It occurred to Terry that if his Vera had been alive today then this business with their daughter Angie would have been enough to kill her off all over again. 'Vera, love,' he said aloud, 'if you're up there somewhere looking down on all this, then please don't worry, darlin', because I'm gonna get Angie out of this mess safe and sound, and then I'm gonna take care of the bastard who's kidnapped her.'

Terry had never thought of himself as a violent man... On the contrary, he'd always prided himself on being the sort of criminal who could get what he wanted by other means.

But nobody had ever kidnapped his daughter before.

Frank called Liam on the mobile he'd given him that evening, as arranged. 'You alone?' he said.

'Yeah.'

'Good...so this is what you do. Go to the Slug 'n' Lettuce pub on Fulham Broadway this evenin'... I've arranged it so the girl's father'll be there to meet you. He'll be there some before eight o'clock, and I told 'im you'd be at the bar... Once he arrives he hands the paintin' over to you'n then you leave and get in your car with it'n drive up towards Kensington High Street and wait for my call. Got that?'

'I bought you some stuff.'

'Why thank you, Johnny.'

'It's only bizniss, like I said... No sense in you havin' a hard time for no reason, is there?'

Angie said, 'Do you think you could undo my hands and take the blindfold off? Otherwise, how am I gonna be able to see what it is you've got me?'

'Can't see why not.'

'Ooh, that's better,' she said, once her hands had been untied. Then she took the blindfold off herself.

At first she felt dizzy, as her eyes adjusted to the change...but then the feeling passed and she looked inside the Primark bag Johnny had given her. It said on the receipt that it was Primark's Hammersmith branch.

Angie took the things out of the bag. As well as a packet of tampons, there were two dresses, one pink and the other blue, and then there was a bag containing four pairs of panties.

'I hope I got the size right,' Johnny said, and Angie took a look at him for the first time. He was a stocky man of medium height with tattoos on his forearms, and he was dressed in a blue tracksuit and trainers. He had his hair cut very short, and must have done some boxing in his time, Angie reckoned, judging by the cuts above his eyes and the way his nose had been flattened.

'They're just fine, Johnny... Thanks, you've been very kind.'

He looked at the floor – almost as though he was embarrassed, Angie thought. 'Now, do you think I could go and wash and change a moment?'

'Can't see why not.'

So he led her out to the bathroom. 'Try not to be too long,' he said, and waited outside the door.

Angie stripped off and washed herself, then there was a knock at the door and Johnny told her to hurry up. 'Okay,' she called back, 'I won't be a minute.'

Then Frank bashed the door, breaking the lock, and burst in. 'You think this is,' he said, 'a fuckin beauty parlour?' and grabbed her by the hair.

Angie tried to push him away, but he slapped her hard across the face so that tears sprang to her eyes and she cried out in pain. 'Your sweetheart's on the phone,' he said. 'Wants a know how you're keepin' and if we been feedin' you okay.' #

He yanked her upright and thrust the mobile phone into her hand. 'Here,' he said, 'and don't say nothin' stupid.'

'Hi, Liam,' she said, fighting back the sobs.

'Angie... Are you all right?'

'As well as can be expected.'

'They been mistreating you?'

'No... why, they even got me some clothes from my favourite Primark—'

Frank grabbed the phone from her hand. 'I told you not to try nothin' stupid,' he said and struck her across the face again, even harder this time.

CHAPTER 10

P*rimark*, Liam thought... Her *favourite* one, she'd said... That must be the one in Hammersmith.
So they must be keeping her somewhere in the Hammersmith area.
Liam figured there must be ways of narrowing things down a little more. So he took a taxi over to Hammersmith and got off outside an estate agent's on King Street. But when he rang the bell, the young woman who came and opened the door said, 'Sorry, we closed at five-thirty.'

'I realize that, but I need to find out the addresses of any properties that have been let through the agency in the area recently.'

'I'm afraid I'm not allowed to divulge information of that nature.'

'Listen, my girlfriend's been kidnapped and I have reason to believe she's being held in a house that's been let recently somewhere in Hammersmith.'

'If that really is the case, sir, then it would be a police matter... So my advice to you would be to call them.'

'I already have.'

'We wouldn't have any problem with talking to the police directly, but I'm afraid I'm not authorized to give out the kind of information you're asking for.'

Liam turned and hurried off.

. . .

'Guv...? Dave here.'

'What have you got?'

'Just been following Liam O'Rourke along King Street in Hammersmith.'

'What's he doing over there?'

'Dunno exactly...but we got a call from an estate agent saying she was pestered by a man who met his description, guv...seems like he wanted to find out about houses that've been let in the Hammersmith area recently.'

'Where is he now?'

'On the number 295 bus, and I'm following it down North End Road...just gone by West Kensington Tube station, guv, and am moving slowly in heavy traffic in a southerly direction down towards the Broadway.'

'Stay on his tail and don't lose him...but don't arrest him... We need to find out what he's up to, so cut the guy a little slack.'

Minutes later, Johnson saw Liam get off the back of the bus and enter the Slug 'n' Lettuce, on Fulham Broadway, so the Detective Sergeant pulled over across the street and called DCI Preston back, to ask what he should do.

Preston told him just to stay put while Liam was in the pub, and start following him again if he came out. 'I'm on my way over there,' Preston said. 'We've got a plainclothes officer, man by the name of Ron Summers, already in the place, watching him.'

Every time someone walked in through the door, Liam looked around, expecting it to be Angie's father.

But half an hour passed and there was no sign of him.

Liam was edgy as a rabbit on speed, sitting there tap-tap-tapping his foot and thrumming his fingers on the wooden bar, wondering to himself what was keeping the man.

He waited another twenty minutes and still there was no sign on him.

By now Liam had given up hoping that Angie's father might show, and had begun to wonder what that bastard Frank's game was...

. . .

At seven-twenty, Frankie Nic and Johnny White walked into The Ritz Hotel, the pair of them dressed in smart suits.

Frank took a seat in the lobby and had a waiter bring him *The Times*, then peered over the top of it, never taking his eyes from the entrance for a moment as he waited.

Then Terry Statham walked in. He was wearing jeans, a blue Lacoste Polo shirt and a leather jacket, and was carrying a case of the kind that is used for transporting canvases.

Frank gave Johnny the nod, then he put his newspaper aside, and stood up and went over to Terry.

When they were standing face to face, Terry said, 'Well-well, if it isn't Frankie Nic of all people...'

'Long time no see, Terry...'

'I never thought you'd stoop to kidnapping, Frank...to think we're both from the same patch, too... Enough to give the East End a bad name.'

'Before you say another word, Terry, you should know that my man Johnny's got a gun pointin' at your spinal column.'

Terry turned his head and saw a man he recognized from somewhere standing there with his hand in his jacket pocket.

Frank said, 'Just turn around and walk back out the way you come in and we'll be right behind you... Take it nice'n easy and nobody gets hurt.'

They went out of the hotel like that, with Terry in front and Frank and Johnny right behind him, then Frank led them around the corner to where his red Lexus was parked. Frank said, 'Get in, Terry,' and Johnny opened the rear passenger door.

'Where's my Angie?'

'I said get in.'

'Not until I see my Angie... C'mon, Frank, this is bizniss... A simple trade—we agreed, right...? You get to keep the Rembrandt'n I get my Angie back. The fuck's goin' on here?'

'Just get in the fuckin car'n we'll take you to see Angie now.'

'But that ain't part a the deal...You was supposed to bring her here'n we make the exchange.'

'Well she ain't here.'

'I can see that.'

'So get in.'

Liam got up off his stool to go to the gents' and Ron Summers, the plainclothes man, took out his mobile and called DCI Preston, who was still sitting in his car across the street from the pub.

Preston said, 'What's going on...?'

'Not much.'

'No sign of anyone coming to talk to him?'

'Nope,' Ron Summers said. 'So now what...?'

'You sure there's not a back way out of there?'

'No, this pub's only got two doors, both leading out onto the Broadway.'

'Even so,' Preston said, 'if he's on to you he might try and go through a window or something.'

'I'm sure he's not onto me.'

'Don't underestimate this guy.'

'Okay, I'll go see what he's up to.' Ron Summers pocketed his mobile and made for the gents'...and when he opened the door Liam came out.

Ron Summers wondered for a moment whether to turn on his heel and go back to the bar. No, that wouldn't look so good, he decided, so he went on into the gents', then he took his mobile out and called DCI Preston again. 'I came to see what he was up to, and we crossed on the way.'

'Where are you?'

'In the toilet.'

'And Liam?'

'Gone back to his stool, I presume...but keep an eye on the doors just in case he leaves.'

Johnny started up the engine and they set off along Piccadilly in the Lexus, with Frank sitting in the back next to Terry, holding his gun on him in case he tried anything stupid.

They went over Hyde Park Corner and on through Knightsbridge.

Terry said, 'All I want is to see my Angie.'

'You're Angie's okay, Terry, trust me. We seem like the kinda people to go in for hurtin' women?'

'I even went out'n bought her some clean clothes earlier, Terry,' Johnny said over his shoulder. 'Strictly bizness this is, I told 'er. Nothin' personal to it. Your old man 'ands over the goods'n you go free, end a story.'

Terry said, 'You expect me to thank you or somethin'?'

Frank told Johnny to shut up and keep his eyes on the road.

DCI Preston saw Liam leave the pub, and he watched him walk off in a westerly direction up Fulham Road. Then a bus pulled up at the stop that was just a little way along from the pub, and Liam boarded it.

Preston set off in his car and followed the bus.

When they got to the house in Hammersmith, Johnny frisked Terry, and he found a handgun with a silencer in the inside pocket of his jacket.

'Nice try, Terry,' Frank grinned. 'Right, so first things first...let's see the Rembrandt.'

'Where's my Angie?'

Frank gestured to Johnny with a nod of the head. 'Go get her down here.'

Terry heard footsteps overhead going in one direction, and then when the footsteps headed back the way they'd come it sounded like there were two people up there. Then he heard the footsteps on the stairs.

Frank said, 'You really love your daughter, Terry, don't you?'

Terry looked at him with hatred in his eyes and didn't say anything.

Then the door to the living room opened and Johnny came back in, and he had Angie with him.

Terry hurried over and took her in his arms. 'You all right, love?' He could feel her trembling as she sobbed.

While Terry was untying the rope that bound Angie's hands, Frank and Johnny took the painting from its case and laid it out flat on the table.

'To fink people's willin' to part with fifty million for this,' Johnny said. 'Fuckin' paintin' a some ugly old bastard lookin' miserable and tha's all there is to it, i'n' it, you axe my 'pinion.'

'Nobody is.'

'What?'

Frank bent over the canvas to get a closer look at it. 'It's the original all right,' he said, and he told Johnny to help him roll it up again and put it back in the case.

Just then, Terry went to leave with Angie, but Frank said, 'Where the fuck d'you think you're goin'?'

'Tha's it now, Frank, i'n' it. Deal's done'n dusted, right? Fair's fair.'

Frank fired and the bullet hit Terry in the chest. His face froze and he put his hand to the wound, and then he bit the carpet.

Angie screamed and threw herself on him. 'Dad,' she sobbed. 'Dad...? Don't leave me...' She felt for a pulse in his neck but couldn't find one. Then she felt his wrist.

Nothing doing.

Angie realized that her father was dead, and she screamed 'NO! NO! NO! NO! NO!' at the top of her voice. Then she lifted her head and looked at Frank. 'You didn't have to do that, you worthless bastard.'

'Shut up.'

'My father was a good man and you're scum.'

Frank went over to where Angie was kneeling and kicked her in the face, and she rolled over onto her back and lay there on the carpet, sobbing. Then Frank took out his Biretta and aimed it at her, but Johnny said, 'Don't do it, Frank. Not the gel.'

'What else'm I gonna do...? She's just seen me kill 'er ol' man... Not only that, she's doin' my fuckin head in with all the screamin'.'

Johnny aimed his gun at Frank and said, 'Drop it.'

Frank looked at him, still keeping his gun pointed at Angie.

'Shoot him, Johnny,' Angie said. 'Then you can sell the painting and have the money all to yourself.'

Frank told her to shut up.

'You can't trust him, Johnny. You're a nice guy but he's different... First chance he gets he'll shoot you when your back's turned.'

Frank said, 'I told you to shut up.'

'The only reason he's not killed you yet, Johnny, is 'cause you're still useful to him... But as soon as you no longer are he'll think of a way to make you disappear.'

Frank said, 'Don't listen to her, Johnny.'

He got Angie up off the floor, and held her in front of him with the barrel of his gun against her head.

'Drop it, Johnny, or she gets it.'

Then he pushed Angie, sending her flying towards Johnny, and fired... Johnny fired back, but he missed as Frank ran out the door.

Angie ran over to the window, and watched him get into his Lexus and drive off. Then she heard a groan from behind her, and turned to see Johnny put his hand to his belly, where he had been hit. His shirt was wet from where the blood was running from the wound.

Johnny pointed his gun at her. 'It's you'n me now, kid.'

CHAPTER 11

'Where d'you think you're goin'?' Johnny said, seeing Angie looking as though she were about to leave.

'I'd better go'n get you a doctor.'

'No you don't.' Johnny was lying on his back on the sofa and he had his gun pointed at her.

'But you'll bleed to death.'

'You're stayin' right here wid me.'

'Listen, Johnny, you've gotta trust me... I just want to see you get better. You've been good to me... I know you're not really a bad sort. If it was that other bastard, Frank, I wouldn't've lifted a finger to help.'

'You fink I'm stupid or somethin'? I let you walk out a here I'm a sittin' duck.'

Angie said, 'I wouldn't tell anybody,' and Johnny gave her a look like thousands might believe you.

'So you're just gonna keep me here, are you?'

'Only till I'm recuperated.'

'Then what...you shoot me between the eyes the same as Frank would have, is that it?'

'You know I ain't like that.' Johnny groaned and gritted his teeth against the pain. 'I helped you when you was in trouble'n kept you from gettin' killed by Frank— that true or not?'

Angie nodded.

'So now you gotta return the favour. You help me get out a this little fix I'm in and then you go your way'n I go mine...That fair?'

'So what do you want me to do?'

'You can start by bringing me the phone.'

Angie did as he said and Johnny dialled a number. "Ello?' she heard him say. 'Doc?' Then, 'Listen, I'm 'urt rill bad...took one in the gut... Yeah...I need you 'ere an hour ago.' Johnny told the doctor the address to come to and gave him some directions. 'And make it sharp, Doc, 'fore I conk out...Yeah, don't worry, I'll make sure you're all right.' Johnny hung up and said to Angie, 'Doc's on 'is way... And just in case you was wonderin', him'n me know each other, so don't go gettin' no ideas.'

'Don't worry...you can trust me, Johnny.'

Johnny groaned again and squirmed about a little on the sofa. 'Bring me the whisky bottle, willya? It's over there in the cabinet.'

She went and got the bottle, and gave it to him.

They waited in silence and the minutes dragged. Then there was a knock at the door and Angie said, 'That'll be the doctor. I'll go'n let him in.'

'Not so fast.' Johnny put the bottle down. 'Come here'n 'elp me get up.'

Angie did as she was told.

There was another knock at the door.

'You go first.'

Angie opened the door, and it was the Doc.

She let him in, and he went to work on Johnny.

But it was too late...and Johnny died.

The Doc packed his bag and made himself scarce, and Angie picked up the phone and called the police.

'How has your father taken it, Tarquin?'

'I thought he might kill me at first, Cass, but he calmed down eventually.'

They were sitting at the kitchen table in her flat.

'So now what?'

'We need to try and get the Rembrandt back.'

'But how...?'

'I'll need to hire someone from the criminal underworld to help me.'

'I might be able to help you with that.'

'But you can't possibly know anybody of that sort, Cass...?'

'No...but I know someone who might know someone...'

Cassandra called Quincy later, and told him about Tarquin's plan to try and recover the Rembrandt canvas for his father. 'So I was wondering if you might happen to know anyone who'd be able steal it back for us?'

'A few possible names spring to mind,' Quincy said.

Towards lunchtime, Quincy went to pay a call on a guy called Jed who lived in a flat over a shop on Seven Sisters Road.

Jed came to the door looking like he'd just got out of bed. He was of medium height, and had tattoos and a beer belly. His brown hair was a mess, his skin was unhealthily pale, and you could see the marks where he'd had acne when he was younger.

Quincy grinned at him and said, 'Hey, man, sorry to disturb your beauty sleep.'

'Goin' on, man?'

'I could have some business to put your way, i'n' it.'

They walked down to the Black Swan and made themselves comfortable on stools at the bar, and Quincy told Jed what needed to be done.

When Quincy had finished talking, Jed said, 'So what's in it for me, man?'

'Three grand...you interested?'

'Yeah.'

'Okay,' Quincy said, 'so write this down...'

'I love you so much, Angie.'

'I love you, too... and I was starting to wonder whether I'd ever see you again.'

They were lying in bed at Liam's place, on Earl's Court Road.

'Try and forget about all that,' Liam said. 'You're back here with me now.'

'How can I forget about it when my own father was shot dead right in front of me?' Angie began to sob and Liam gave her a hug.

'You know,' she said, 'I've always hated violence, but I've been having dreams about killing the man who killed Dad... Then I wake up and find myself fantasizing about doing it...'

'Do you think you'd be capable of doing it if you actually had the chance?'

'I don't think, I *know*.'

Liam said, 'Have you ever thought of seeking help?'

'Seeing a shrink, you mean?'

'Just to get you over this thing you're going through... I mean, it's only normal the way you're suffering.'

'I'm not crazy.'

'No, I never said you were.'

'What I am,' she said, 'is mad – and you know what they say –.'

'Don't get mad, get even...'

'Exactly.' Angie sat up in the bed and looked into Liam's eyes. 'I've got an idea that keeps nagging at me and won't go away.'

'Want to tell me about it?'

'It's that we find that bastard Frank and kill him, and get the Rembrandt off him... We could sell it and live happily off the proceeds for the rest of our lives.'

'Sounds like a good idea for a film script.'

'I'm not talking about writing it down in any film script, but doing it for real,' Angie said. 'What do you think?'

Jed went into the Greek place on Goldhawk Road, bought himself a large whisky soda and sat on a stool at the bar, taking occasional sips of his drink and getting the feel of the place.

He struck up a conversation with the barman, a tall guy with two chins and three bellies, and told him that he was interested in talking to anyone who could give him any information on the whereabouts of 'the missing Rembrandt'.

'I'll ask around for you,' the barman said, 'if you want a leave your number.'

That night Jed got a call from a man who said he was in possession of the missing Rembrandt. 'What's your interest in the painting?' the man asked him in a deep, gravelly voice.

Jed said, 'I'm workin' for a man who wants a buy it... Why don't you give me a number he can call you on?'

'Listen,' Jeremy Willoughby said, 'I'm interested in buying the Rembrandt, and I have the money you're asking for...but I'll need to see the canvas first, of course.'

'That can be arranged... Who am I talking to?'

'Jeremy Willoughby...and you are...?'

'Frank.'

'Okay, Frank...where do you have it?'

'You might say tha's privileged info'mation right now... What about if we was to meet in a hotel room...? You bring the money'n I bring the Rembrandt...We're both happy then we do business...'

'Which hotel did you have in mind?'

'Somewhere in London... You choose...perhaps one of the big well-known places...'

'All right,' Jeremy Willoughby said, 'let's say Claridges for the sake of argument.'

'Okay, Claridges it is.'

'I'll need to be able to bring my assistant along to verify that the painting is genuine, otherwise I couldn't possibly consider it.'

'Fine with me.'

'Give me twenty-four hours to arrange everything and then I'll get back to you.'

'I wouldn't take too long,' Frank said, 'or you might lose out to another buyer...'

'Twenty-four hours is all I ask.'

They hung up.

Willoughby was discussing the situation a little later with his son Tarquin. 'What's worrying me,' he said, 'is the thought that the man could be planning on seeing to it that I walk out of there fifty million down and *without* the Rembrandt...'

'Then why not take this chap Jed along with you, and have him sit down in the lobby...? If there's any funny business then he'll be there to put a stop to it.'

'But how would he know what's going on up in the room, if he's waiting down in the lobby?'

'Well, if you feel like that, Father, then perhaps you should insist on having Jed go up to the room, so that he's there at your side whilst you inspect the painting.'

'Yes, I'm rather inclined to feel that may be the best way to proceed.'

'And you're going to have Dawson Kruger on hand again, to check that the painting's genuine, I trust?'

'Of course.'

So Jeremy Willoughby called Frank back and told him the deal was on, on condition that he could bring his 'business associate' along with him to view the canvas.

Frank said, 'As you wish.'

'Right, so all we have to decide on now then is when we do it.'

'I'm ready when you are.'

'How about if we were to meet tomorrow at three p.m., then, at Claridges...? Would that suit you?'

'Suits me fine... If there's any change of plans, call me.'

'You can rest assured of that,' Jeremy Willoughby said. 'I was thinking if my assistant, Jed, were to be there in the lobby to meet you...and then he'll be able to bring you up to my room, where we'll be able to conduct our business... Does that sound all right to you?'

'Sure.'

'Good.'

'Okay,' Frank said. 'Till tomorrow at three, then.'

They hung up.

Cassandra called Angie that evening. 'I'm so sorry about what happened to your father,' she said. 'But it's great to know you got away unscathed...'

'The truth is, Cass, I sometimes think the only thing that could make me feel any better'd be to see the bastard who killed my dad get his.'

'I know how you must feel, Angie...but you don't mean to say you're actually going to try and *kill* him...?'

'I would if I knew where he was.'

Cassandra said, 'Well in that case...'

'What...?'

'Oh, I don't know whether I ought to tell you this...'

'Come on, Cass.'

'Well, I read in *The Times* that your father is thought to have been the person who stole the Rembrandt that went missing...'

'So...?'

'Nothing, really...except that Tarquin said his father's going to meet the man who's now in possession of the canvas at three o'clock tomorrow afternoon in Claridges... And I just wondered if this man could be the one who killed your dad.'

'What's the man's name?'

'Frank.'

'It's him—'

'Don't breathe a word about any of this to a soul, mind, Angie...'

'Mum's the word.'

'Oh, but Angie, you wouldn't be thinking of going there and doing anything stupid, now would you?'

'No, of course not...What's the number of the room he's gonna be in?'

'I dunno, but if you were to park across the street from the entrance to the hotel sometime before three, then you'll probably see him go in.' Cassandra paused a moment, then said, 'Oh, but what am I saying...? You've got *me* at it now, Angie... Listen to the two of us, we're talking like a pair of characters out of *The Godfather*.'

Jeremy Willoughby was sitting with Dawson Kruger in a room on the fourth floor of Claridge's Hotel the following day, nervously thrumming his fingers on the briefcase that was on the mahogany table in front of him.

There was fifty million pounds in used banknotes in the briefcase.

At just after three o'clock, he received a call from Frank on his mobile.

Angie was sitting behind the wheel of her BMW, across the street from the entrance to Claridge's.

She had the gun loaded ready on her lap, hidden out of sight under a newspaper, and the only reason she hadn't shot Frank in the back when she saw him go into the hotel was that she knew he'd come to sell the Rembrandt...which meant when he came out through those doors a little later, he'd be carrying enough money to make her rich...

'Hello, Frank... I'm Jeremy Willoughby.'

The two men shook hands.

'Who are your friends?'

'Sorry...allow me to introduce my assistants, Dawson Kruger and Jed... Dawson, Jed, this is Frank.'

Frank's face showed no expression as he eyed the two men.

'Now if you'll show us the canvas, so that we can satisfy ourselves that it is indeed the Rembrandt original, then I shall be able to let you know whether or not I am in a position to do business with you.'

'First you show me the money.'

'All right.' Willoughby opened the briefcase for him. 'Count it all, if you want to.'

Frank riffled a few wads of notes with his fingers, then he started counting the stacks, calculating in his head as he did so.

'Satisfied?' Willoughby said, when he had finally finished.

Frank nodded.

'Now how about letting me see the Rembrandt?'

Frank took the canvas from of its case and spread it out on the table...but then, as Jeremy Willoughby and Dawson Kruger both leaned over the painting to take a closer look, Frank reached inside his jacket for his Biretta.

Jed saw what he was doing and pulled out his Walther .38.

Frank went to shoot, but Jed fired first and got him right between the eyes and Frank hit the floor and stayed there. The shot didn't make much noise on account of the silencer, so nobody outside the room would have heard it.

Jeremy Willoughby looked down at Frank, then he looked at Jed. 'You've killed him.'

Jed said, 'So I did,' and shot Willoughby in the chest, and watched him hit the deck the same way Frank had.

Dawson Kruger was standing with his hands in the air, the light shining on his bald head, his eyes filled with terror. 'There's no need to shoot me,' he said, 'I'm nothing to do with these two... I was just hired to check that it's the original.'

Jed shot him in the chest, then shot him again in the belly, and Dawson Kruger hit the wall and slid down it.

A man came out of the hotel carrying a briefcase and a second case of the sort used to carry canvases.

The man got into his Roller, which was parked a little way along the street, and a moment later a black man, who must have been lying on the floor in the back, popped up...and Angie saw that the black man was holding a gun against the back of the other man's head.

Then the Roller set off...

Angie waited a little longer for Frank to come out, but then she got to wondering if maybe he might have sent the black guy out instead of him.

Or maybe he'd left the hotel by another exit...

But none of that really seemed to make much sense.

And where did the black guy come into all this? was what Angie would have liked to know.

She sat there chewing things over for a little while, then she took out her mobile and dialled Detective Chief Inspector Preston's number.

CHAPTER 12

Jed was driving along a country road somewhere outside of London, wondering how in hell's name he was going to get out of this mess he was in, when Quincy told him to take a left up a muddy lane.

Jed said, 'What you got in mind?'

'You'n me're goin' for a little walk.'

As he drove along the country lane, Jed was thinking maybe he'd be able to make his move when they got out of the car.

Quincy told him to pull up.

Jed said 'Sure,' and killed the engine. 'For fuck's sake, Quincy, what is this...? I thought we was mates.'

Quincy fired a shot into the back of Jed's head and blood splashed all over the windscreen.

'Hel-*lo*,' Preston said, when he entered the room at Claridges, and saw the three dead bodies.

DS Johnson said, 'What d'you reckon's been going on here, then, guv?'

'Whatever it was, Dave, it's sure made a mess.'

. . .

'Now all we gotta do's sell this piece a shit for fifty million'n then that'll be a hundred million wid the fifty we've already got,' Quincy said. 'Then it's just a question of findin' a nice safe place to store it, like a bank in Switzerland, say, and we can sit back'n think about how we gonna spend the rest of our lives together, just you'n me, Cassie baby.' He chuckled and stroked his little jazzman's goatee. 'We so motherfuckin rich we can even afford to get married now.'

Cassandra said, 'You sure you're the marrying type, Quincy?'

'Now I'm loaded, babe, I gotta act the part, i'n' it.'

They were lying in bed at his place.

She ran her hand down his lean, black body. 'Being rich is such a wonderful aphrodisiac, I find, don't you?'

'Sure is.' Quincy got up out of the bed.

'Where are you going?'

'I got to take a leak.'

'Aren't you going to make me happy again?'

'How much happiness you want all in one day, girl?' Quincy padded out to the bathroom.

When he came back in, Cassandra was sitting up in the bed holding his gun. There was a silencer attached to the end of the barrel. 'Hey, don't go foolin' with my piece, baby,' he said. 'That ain't no toy.'

Cassandra said, 'No, so I gathered,' and she shot him in the chest and saw a surprised expression come into his eyes...then she shot him again as he staggered towards her and fell onto the bed facedown, blood spewing out of his mouth all over the clean counterpane...

'It's me, guv.'

'What's new, Dave?'

'Some interesting developments, as it happens.'

'Let's hear it, then.'

'Ever heard of a Kenny Jarrow?'

'Name rings a bell...why, what's he done?'

'Just been picked up by Interpol in Spain, guv... They arrested him at his villa in Marbella.'

'So...?'

'They found the Rembrandt that went missing recently at this

Kenny Jarrow's villa,' Johnson said. 'He's been talkin' to some of our guys and they've got him to do a deal.'

'And...?'

'This is where it gets interesting, guv, 'cause Kenny Jarrow's spilled the beans on a whole lot of other stuff... To begin with, he's willing to testify that he stole the Rembrandt along with Angie Statham's father, Terry, the man who was already the chief suspect...'

'Then Frankie Nicholson gets to hear about it and decides to kidnap the girl and demand the Rembrandt as ransom.'

'Exac'ly, guv.'

'But instead of trading like they'd agreed, Frank kills Terry and keeps the Rembrandt.'

'Only what Frank didn't bargain on was the fact that it was actually a fake he had... You'll recall that the thieves left a brilliant forgery in place of the original when they nicked it from the National Gallery, guv... They'd already palmed a second forgery off on a multimillionaire by the name of Jeremy Willoughby for fifty millionaire quid, before Frankie Nic got his hands on it.'

'Jeremy Willoughby, father of Tarquin Willoughby, who just happens to be dating Angie Statham's ex-neighbour, Cassandra Whitley.'

'Jarrow went on to say how Terry Statham then decided to steal his forgery back from Jeremy Willoughby, after Frankie Nic and Johnny White kidnapped Angie... Terry must've decided it was better to trade a fake Rembrandt for his daughter than hand over the real thing.'

'On the basis that if an apparently cultured man like Jeremy Willoughby couldn't tell the fake from the original, then the likes of Frankie Nic wouldn't be able to, either...'

'Exac'ly, guv...but Frank shot Terry and his accomplice Johnny White dead, and then he scarpered with the fake Rembrandt... Then Willoughby decides he wants to buy back the fake Rembrandt that's been stolen from his home—which, of course, he's still convinced is the original... He asks around and ends up being put on to Frankie Nic, and they set up the deal at Claridges... But an as yet unidentified third party scuppers the deal by killing Frank and Willoughby, along with a guy by the name of Dawson Kruger, before he scarpers with the forgery and, presumably, also with the money Willoughby'd agreed to pay to get it back.'

'I get the feeling we'll be hearing of the forgery's whereabouts before too long, Dave,' Preston said. 'And as you said, it's a safe bet the person that has the forgery also has the money... They'll probably be keen to sell the fake soon as they can, and to do that they'll need to put word out in certain quarters that they have it...' Preston tweaked his tash, then something occurred to him. 'I was just thinking about that place on Goldhawk Road where stolen art treasures are touted, Dave... Get a good undercover man over to the place straightaway... and tell him to keep his eyes and ears open, and to let us know as soon as he turns up anything.'

'Okay, guv.'

'Oh, and call Interpol, a.s.a.p., and tell them it's essential they keep the discovery of the Rembrandt original over in Spain secret for a little while – just until we've wrapped this case up...'

The following day DCI Preston got a call from Trevor Armstrong, the undercover detective he'd given the job of keeping an eye on what was happening at the place over on Goldhawk Road. 'There was a woman there earlier, guv,' Armstrong said, 'advertising the fact that she had an original Rembrandt to sell, for £50,000,000...'

'Just what I wanted to hear...'

'But that's not all... I've arranged to meet her at the café this evening, at around nine o'clock.'

'Good work, Trevor...'

Preston was outside of the café behind the wheel of his Ford Escort, when the woman arrived on the stroke of nine.

He had men waiting in a white van across the street, ready to listen in when the time came, and Trevor Armstrong had a tiny gadget stuck in his ear that would enable them to send him messages...

At that moment, one of the men in the can called Preston on his walkie-talkie. 'Suspect's just told our man she has the Rembrandt, guv... but he'll have to show her the £50,000,000 asking price before she'll let him see it.'

'Tell him to say he'll have the money up together by tomorrow, and to arrange to meet her...'

'Okay, guv.'

Trevor Armstrong saw the woman sitting alone, over by the wall, the moment he entered Balan's café on Earl's Court Road, the following day, and he went over and sat across the table from her.

She looked him in the eye and said, 'You got the money?'

'Sure have.' He put his briefcase on the table and tapped it. 'It's in here.'

'I'll need to see it.'

'You don't seriously expect me to open it here...?'

'Okay...at the flat, then.'

Armstrong said, 'Ready when you are.'

'Let's go.'

He started to get the feeling this was going to be like taking sweets from a child, the woman striking him as being more than a little naive to be inviting a guy like himself, someone she didn't know from Adam, to go and see the Rembrandt with her, just the two of them... But as soon as they entered the flat, she brought out a gun and said, 'Put the briefcase on the table over there and open it.'

Maybe the woman wasn't quite so naive after all, Trevor Armstrong thought, and he did as she said.

'What kind of an idiot are you?' she said, when she saw that the briefcase was full of old newspapers. 'You deserve to die for this...'

'I would put your gun away if I were you.'

'And why would I want to do a stupid thing like that?'

'Maybe because I'm a cop...'

'You're lying.'

'My ID's in my pocket...'

The next moment, DCI Preston and a team of men burst into the flat. 'Put the gun down, miss,' Preston said.

She thought about it for a moment or two...then she did as Preston said.

PART IV

CHAPTER 13

In court Cassandra gave the best performance you ever saw as the innocent upper-class young woman who wouldn't ever *dream* of breaking the law. She told the judge that she'd only been trying to sell a painting that had chanced to come into her possession...a painting which she took to be a Rembrandt original. As for her being a murderer, well, that was just ridiculous, Cassandra assured everyone... and she chose that moment to break out into a round of sobs which seemed to express the indignation of an honest woman wrongly accused. Her timing was perfect.

The judge set bail at two hundred grand.

Cassandra was outraged. Where was she going to get that kind of money from?

She asked her lawyer, Jon Prowse, what she was supposed to do now, and he advised her to ask her father to come up with the money.

Fat chance of that, Cassandra thought, but she tried it anyway.

And as she'd expected, the old bugger wrote her saying that he'd known for some time that she was a bad apple. He had tried everything within his power to make her see the error of her ways, but she had rebelled against him at every turn. Now it fell to her to face the music and accept the consequences of her actions... And he signed the letter off at the bottom 'with love and affection from your father, as always'.

Cassandra wrote to her brother, Edward, and he came in to visit her, but he was hard up as a result of his gambling debts and so was unable to help.

So she was sent to prison on remand.

Cassandra's cellmate, Ruth, a redhead in her early forties, had been charged with attempted murder after she tried to shoot her husband in the heart but missed and got him in the shoulder. She seemed to like Cassandra, though.

Ruth got in a fight with a big black girl in the shower one day, and the black girl ended up with a split lip and a couple of broken ribs, so Cassandra figured she'd better watch her step. So when Ruth showed her her tattoos, Cassandra said she thought they were cool, even though she hated them.

Then one night Ruth climbed up onto her bunk, and before Cassandra had the chance to ask her what she thought she was doing, Ruth had her hands all over her and was kissing her breasts. Cassandra knew it would have been pointless to try and fight her off, so she just lay back and let Ruth get on with what she was doing.

As she lay there, Cassandra wondered if she would have to think of a way of killing Ruth. It would be easy enough to do, even though Ruth was much stronger than her... Just a question of doing something to her when she was asleep.

Like what, exactly?

Cassandra rolled some ideas around in her mind.

How about pouring petrol over her and then setting her alight...?

Problem with that would be, she might get caught in the fire herself.

No, she'd only have to scream and one of the guards would come and get her out in time. It would just be a question of having to gauge it right, so that Ruth was past saving without waiting so long that she put herself at risk.

Yeah, that might be the best way to do it, Cassandra thought, as she lay there on her back with her legs apart, letting Ruth do as she pleased.

Filthy bitch, Cassandra thought ...But then, she was surprised to discover that some of Ruth's passion began to communicate itself to her, and she found herself swooning with pleasure...and then, the next thing she knew, she was crying out in ecstasy as she juddered into a pretty cool orgasm...

The following day, a big busty blonde smiled at Cassandra over the breakfast table, and Ruth beat seven shades of shit out of her later on in the shower...

Ruth put her arm around Cassandra later, when they were alone in their cell. 'Anyone looks at you Cass,' she said, 'and they know what they can expect.'

'What's so special about me?'

'I love you's what... I'd do anything for you, Cass.'

'Anything...?'

Ruth nodded.

'Like what?'

'I dunno... Anything you can think of... I'd kill for you, if it came to it.'

'I feel really flattered, Ruth... You're so good to me.'

'You're beautiful, Cass...and you got class written all over you.'

'And I always thought women like you hated women like me.'

'Why would you go thinkin' a stupid thing like that?'

'You know...what with me being born with so many advantages and speaking the way I do.'

'Let me let you into a little secret...You're the very thing that women like me dream about...You're what we'd all like to have been but can't, love.'

'Actually it's not so much fun being me, Ruth... Most people take one look at me and, I suppose because of the way I talk and everything, they just assume I've got it made in life...when in fact nothing could be further from the truth.'

'No, well I don't s'pose you'd be in 'ere if you had it made, love, would you...?'

'Exactly... The truth is I'm broke... I mean, when I get out of here I'll have nowhere to go... I'll be homeless.'

'But ain't you got no family you can go to, a gel like you?'

Cassandra wiped her eyes with her sleeve. 'I used to get on well with my mother, but she died,' she said, 'and now there's only my father left and my brother... and my father's cut me out of his will.'

'Worth very much, is he?'

'Something over four hundred million, according to *The Sunday Times*.'

'Fuckin hell... And you mean to say you ain't gonna get none of it?'

'Not a penny.'

'You tried talkin' to the man?'

'It's useless... He even refused to pay my bail.'

'But why...?'

'He said prison would do me good.'

'Ain't very nice of 'im.'

'No, well, he's got some funny ideas...'

'Sounds like it,' Ruth said. 'But maybe if you was to go'n see 'im, once you gets out of this place, he might change his tune... I mean, he might just be sayin' it to try'n get your attention, or to try'n get you to stay out a trouble.'

'No, it's not like that. I've tried everything and nothing works with him... He's dead set against me... That's how I ended up in here in the first place.'

'How'd you mean?'

'I couldn't afford to pay my mortgage,' Cassandra said, 'and I had credit card debts... I asked him to help and he refused.'

'What, despite havin' all that money...?'

'I know, that's what upsets me so much... Because if he was broke then I could understand it... I mean, I wouldn't even have asked him to help me in the first place... But seeing as I know for a fact that he's got at least *four hundred million* to his name...'

Ruth said, 'Maybe we could 'elp each other out, you'n me.'

'How do you mean?'

'What I'm thinkin' is that we could both be out of this place before too long, with a bit of luck, and...well maybe if you was to scratch my back then I could scratch yours.'

'Scratch your back in what way, Ruth?'

'I fink I told you about my old man, di'n't I?'

'Sounds like a right bastard.'

'Yeah, well if I was to go'n finish the job where he's concerned then it'd be difficult for me to get away with it... I mean, I'd almost certainly find meself lookin' at a life sentence... You with me...? Whereas, if you was to go down'n catch 'im unawares an' put a bit of lead in the right place, and I was somewhere else at the time—like in here, say...if you was to get out first, I mean...then there's no way they could charge me with anythin', is there...? And in return, I could sort out fings with your old man, when I get out.'

'You're not saying that you'd *kill* my father?'

'It's what you want, isn't it...? I mean, it ain't like the old bastard's exac'ly actin' like a dad to you, is it?'

'He's dying anyway, as it happens...but my brother stands to inherit everything because of the will.'

'Your brother got a wife'n kids?'

'No, he's gay.'

'Ah, well in that case, as his next of kin you'd be in line to inherit it all, if they both was to cop it.'

'You reckon?'

'Tha's my understandin' of the law... Just fink of all that money you could have, Cass, and the kinda life you could be livin' if only they was both out a the way.'

'But it's my own flesh and blood we're talking about, Ruth.'

'They don't deserve you, though, from what you been sayin' to me about 'em, princess.'

'I guess that is true.'

Ruth's case went to court at the end of May and her lawyer, Joan Davis, dealt the jury a clever line in sexual, psychological and physical abuse. The story she served up was that Ruth had been raped, beaten and verbally abused by her husband, Brian, over a long period of time—practically from the day they'd got married, in fact—and Ruth, the poor lamb who was the innocent victim in all this, finally decided she'd had enough one day, and, in a moment of crazy desperation, she took Brian's gun and shot at him.

The fact that she'd only hit him in the shoulder was proof, Joan Davis argued, that Ruth hadn't meant to kill him. No, all Ruth had tried to do was put a stop to the

beatings he was in the habit of giving her... Not to mention the never-ending torrent of verbal—which is to say psychological and emotional—abuse that he'd heaped on her practically every time he spoke to her.

The prosecution lawyer, James Rice, did his best to tear holes in the defence's story, but it wasn't easy, and the fact that he was prohibited from referring to Ruth's previous run-ins with the law didn't help his case. Neither did Ruth's talent as an actress.

With her hair tied back in a bun, her tattoos hidden well out of sight, and a dab of makeup here and there, Ruth looked like a different woman right from the moment she first stepped into the court-room.

The jury was made up of six men and six women. One of the six men was obviously gay and another was a social worker. A third was a Guardian-reading teacher. As for the judge, he was known on the circuit to be something of a bleeding heart.

Joan Davis reckoned that gave her something to play with.

It turned out she was right and Ruth got off with a suspended sentence.

Summing up, Justice MacKay cited as mitigating factors the 'spontaneity and lack of premeditation' that characterised the offence, along with 'the long history of abuse' that the victim had been subjected to.

So Ruth was free to walk.

The following week, Cassandra's case went to court and she got off, too, as her lawyer had predicted she would.

The two women had lunch together at a pizzeria in Covent Garden to celebrate and plan their next move.

By this time Cassandra's father was looking like he could die any day, according to her brother, Edward, who kept her updated on her father's plight during the regular telephone conversations they were having. And so Cassandra suggested that she should take care of Ruth's husband Brian first, and then, when her father had died, Ruth would see to her brother...

Cassandra stole a Range Rover, put new plates on it, and drove down to Southend. The Range Rover had dark tinted windows, so she was able to park up and sleep in the back without anybody knowing she was there.

The fewer people that saw her, the better, and she figured it would have been risky to stay in a hotel, because the proprietor or someone working there might always remember her face later, if the police started sniffing around.

Cassandra knew from Ruth that this guy Brian supported himself by dealing drugs and drawing state benefits, and he lived in a detached house in a quiet residential street, which was good news... And Cassandra also liked the fact that the man was a drug dealer, because it meant that when she killed him his clients, the people he bought the stuff from, and rival dealers would all be suspects.

The following day Cassandra went and rang the man's bell, and he came to the door and asked her what she wanted. He was wearing a blue string vest and he had ugly tats, a full set of beer belly and moobs, and a scruffy brown beard.

Cassandra said, 'I heard you were in business.'

'You ain't answered my question.'

'I want a coupla wraps of coke.'

'You better come in.'

Cassandra followed him along a dark dingy hallway and off right into the back room. The place smelled of sour milk, stale food and filth. Some rock video was playing on the box over in the corner, and she could see a small scrap of lawn through the window, some crazy paving and a wall at the back.

He said, 'Coupla wraps you said you wanted, was it?' and then when Cassandra nodded, he went out of the room and she heard him climbing the stairs. Cassandra had already ascertained that the man lived alone, and that there was no one else in the house. That made things a lot easier.

She took out her gun and waited for him to come back down.

Right now he was in the room directly overhead. That must be where he kept his supply of cocaine.

The footsteps started to come back the other way, and Cassandra listened as he descended the stairs.

She raised her arm and took aim at the back of the door, ready... then when he came back into the room, she fired and saw the look of shock on his face as he staggered towards her.

Cassandra fired again and he hit the floor.

She went and stood over him, watched him a dance for a moment or two, then put another slug into his head to finish him off.

She took a plastic bag from her pocket and dropped the gun in it with the silencer, then she put it in her handbag and left the house, climbed into the Range Rover and drove down to the seafront.

She walked out to the end of the peer and waited until there was no one about, then threw the gun down into the sea.

There goes the evidence, she thought.

Then she drove back to London, and dumped the Range Rover in a quiet street in Brixton, before she took the bus back to Fulham.

As soon as she got back to the small bedsit on Racton Road that she now called home, Cassandra took off her clothes and dropped them into a bin liner, then she had a hot shower.

After she'd dried herself off, she fixed herself something to eat, then she went down to Fulham Broadway, where she entered a call box and dialled the number Ruth had told her she could always get her on.

Ruth picked up and said hello, and Cassandra said, 'It's me...Everything's been taken care of.'

'Good.'

'How's life over in sunny Spain?'

'Much better now, after that bit of news.'

'Now it's up to you to keep your side of the bargain.'

'When d'you want it done?'

'Not yet,' Cassandra said. 'I'll be in touch.'

From the way Cassandra's brother Edward had been talking on the phone, it sounded as though their father might die any day, but it wasn't until the end of March that the old man finally breathed his last.

Cassandra wept crocodile tears all through the funeral, and she left it for a couple of days before she tried to broach the subject of the awful unfairness of the will with her brother over lunch in a pizzeria on King's Road. Their father had clearly lost his mind by the time he'd written it, she said, because he'd always loved her as a child. But then he'd turned against her, these past few years, and the old man's reduced mental state was the only reason she could find for it.

Edward agreed that their father had 'gone a bit funny' towards the end, and Cassandra said that she was sure their mother would have put a stop to 'the ridiculous state of affairs' had she been alive.

Edward, a short, chubby guy of twenty-two, didn't say anything.

'Look, Eddie,' Cassanda said, 'what I'm trying to say is, surely you're going to play fair and split the inheritance with me...?'

When her brother still didn't say anything, she said, '*Aren't* you...?'

'The way things are I can help you out here and there, Cass—of course I can, I'm your brother,' he said. 'But if you're saying you want half of everything...now that's a different matter... I mean, I'm the one Father left it all to, and so I really think it's only right and proper that we should respect his wishes.'

When she heard Edward say this, Cassandra threw her napkin down and stormed out.

She went to a call box and dialled the number Ruth had given her.

'Hello?'

'Ruth...? It's me,' Cassandra said. 'I'm ready.'

That evening Cassandra flew over to Barcelona and booked herself into a little hotel near Plaza Cataluña. She'd gone there to be out of the UK when her brother was killed.

Now all she needed was someone who would be able to testify later on that she had been here when the murder took place.

Okay, she had flown over here, so she would be able to show the police her flight tickets, if and when the time came, but it would be better to work up a strong alibi or two as well.

And with this idea in mind, she walked into The Ritz, parked herself on a stool at the bar, and figured she'd let her cool porno witch looks do the rest... And sure enough, they soon began to work their spell on a short stocky Spanish guy who tried to chat her up in pidgin English, but she gave him the brush-off. Then an Austrian offered to buy her a drink, but she gave him the same treatment.

Cassandra was holding out for an Englishman, not because she necessarily found Englishmen more interesting or attractive, but because she reckoned someone from her own country would make a better alibi. At least then she'd be able to tell the police where he came from originally and what he did for a living, and so on, and they'd find it easier to trace him—that was her thinking, anyway...

So then when a man came and introduced himself to her as Giles Patterson, in an accent that was as English as Cheddar cheese, Cassandra allowed him to feel like he was seducing her...

And when they had finished their drinks, she went with him up to his room.

Cassandra spent a couple of days with Giles Patterson, going around the city and fucking with him in his room, and then she got the call from Ruth to say that the job was done.

So over dinner that evening at the Siete Puertas restaurant, she told Patterson that she had just received some terrible news and would have to return to England straightaway.

'But why, Cass...? What's happened?'

'It's my brother,' Cassandra sobbed. 'He's died.'

'Oh you poor thing.' Patterson did his best to console her, and even insisted on returning to England with her, so that he could be at her side. It seemed that the poor fool was quite smitten.

'I'll call you when the time's right, Giles...when I've had time to get over what's happened.'

Patterson gave her his business card, and his home address and landline and mobile numbers, and said he hoped it wouldn't be too long before he saw her again...

Before she left the restaurant, Cassandra made a point of tripping over a fully loaded trolley on her way to the ladies' room, so that she sent a barrage of champagne and gateaux flying across the floor. Then when she burst into tears, Giles came over and made a point of explaining to the maitre d' how his friend was distraught because she'd just heard that her brother had died...

And Cassandra could have applauded when Giles said he was going to leave an enormous tip to cover the cost of the champagne and gateaux that had gone to waste.

Perfect, she thought. They're bound to remember us here now, in case the cops think Lover Boy's covering for me when they question him...

CHAPTER 14

Cassandra's lawyer told her the inheritance would definitely be hers, but he warned her that it might be six months or so before she got her hands on it.

The following day, Cassandra flew over to Malaga, and she rented a small villa just outside of Marbella, where she lived quietly until her lawyer called her up to say that she would have to come over to England to sign a few papers and finalize things... The inheritance was now hers.

The following week she put the family mansion in Esher up for sale, and who should come calling that afternoon but Ruth. 'Nice to see you again, Cass,' she said. 'How'd you feel now you got your very own castle?'

'Sure beats hanging out in a prison cell.'

'Well, aren't you gonna invite yer ol' cellmate in?'

Cassandra stood aside to let Ruth enter, then she led her into the enormous room at the back.

Ruth went over to the French windows and looked out at the garden, with its perfectly tended lawn and flower beds.

The place was pure fantasyville.

'I'm surprised to see you're puttin' this place up for sale, Cass... seems just perfect for you.'

'It's too big for me to be living here all on my own,' Cassandra said.

Besides, she'd decided to go and live in Marbella, and she had plans for what she was going to do with the money she'd get from the sale of the mansion.

'How much you lookin' to sell this place for, then?'

Cassandra told her that the asking price was three and a half million and Ruth flashed her a knowing smile that she didn't like the look of.

'Can I get you a drink, Ruth?'

'Wouldn't say no to a cup of tea.' Ruth sat down in the easy chair by the side of the enormous stone fireplace, and Cassandra went into the kitchen, where she picked up the handgun that she had left there when she'd seen Ruth walking up the front path, minutes earlier.

She loaded up a tray and put the gun on it, then covered it with a newspaper, and walked back into the room like that.

She took one hand off the tray when she was about ten feet away from where Ruth was sitting, then slipped her hand under the newspaper and gripped the handle of the gun.

The first shot got Ruth in the belly, and the second got her in the chest. She didn't even know what hit her.

Then there was blood everywhere, and Cassandra set about tidying the place up and thinking about how she was going to dispose of the body.

And she was still wondering about this when the doorbell rang.

Maybe if she ignored it whoever was out there would just buzz off, she thought.

But the bell rang again and then again, and then there was a loud banging, and so there was nothing else to do but go out and see who it was, and get rid of them.

When she opened the door, Cassandra found herself looking at two men in suits she didn't recognize. The taller of the two held something up and said, 'I'm DCI Preston and my colleague is DS Johnson... We'd appreciate it if you'd invite us in, miss, because we'd like to ask you a few questions.'

'I'm afraid I'm very busy at the moment.'

'We won't take up much of your time.'

'Well if you could come back tomorrow then I'd be happy to oblige.'

'I'm afraid working people like us don't have that much time at our disposal, Miss Whitley.' DCI Preston held up a piece of paper with some writing on it. 'We took the trouble of getting a warrant,' he said, and pushed past her into the hallway.

'Make sure she doesn't go anywhere, Detective Sergeant,' Preston said over his shoulder, and DS Johnson grabbed hold of Cassandra's arm.

'Get off me.'

'Let's go on into the house, miss,' Johnson said.

'What for?'

'Just walk in front of me.'

Cassandra figured she didn't have any alternative but to do as he said.

And when she and the Detective Sergeant entered the enormous room at the back of the house, they found DCI Preston contemplating Ruth Boyle's corpse.

Preston turned to Cassandra and said, 'You have been busy, miss.'

'It's all over at last,' Liam said.

'For you it is.' Angie sipped her lager. 'But I don't think it'll ever really end for me.' She said, 'I would've killed that bastard if someone else hadn't done it for me, I swear.'

They were eating in an Italian pizzeria, in a quiet street off Fulham Road

Liam reached across the table and squeezed her hand. 'I believe you would have, as well,' he said. 'But I'm glad you didn't get the chance to, because then you would have been locked up and I would have been sitting here dining alone and worrying about you.'

'But it would've been worth it to know I'd got my revenge on the man who killed my father.'

'Maybe for you it would have been, but what about me?'

'If you really love me, then you ought to want for me what I want.'

'You're putting your finger on a tricky question there.'

Angie sighed and shook her head. 'Going through all that has made me think about things.'

Liam reached into his pocket and kept his hand in there. 'When they were keeping you hostage, I got to thinking about a lot of things, too...'

'And what conclusions did you arrive at?'

'That I love you.'

'That's nice,' Angie smiled. 'Anything else...?'

'Just that you're more important to me than anything in the world.'

'That's even nicer.'

They gazed into each other's eyes in silence for a moment or two, and then Angie said, 'You got anything else you'd like to say to me?'

Liam brought his hand out of his jacket and opened it in front of her. There was a little box in his palm.

'What is it?'

'Open it and see.'

'Not until you tell me what this is all about.'

'Okay,' he said. 'I was just...well, like I was saying, while you were being held hostage I got to doing some thinking...and I promised myself that once I had you back I'd go and see about buying a ring...'

'Now why'd you wanna go and do a thing like that?'

'Can't you guess?'

'I'm afraid my imagination's never been my strong point.'

Liam coughed into his hand. 'What I'm trying to say is...'

'Yeah...?'

'Will you marry me?'

Angie giggled. 'There,' she said, 'it's out... Feel better now?'

'Depends on what you're gonna say next.'

'Uh?'

'Whether you're gonna say yes or no.'

'Oh, the answer's yes, of course.'

Liam reached across the table and kissed her on the mouth.

Then when they pulled apart, he said, 'You'd better try the ring for size.'

THE END

ABOUT THE AUTHOR

Nick's crime novel, The Long Siesta (Grey Cells Press, the crime imprint of Holland House, September, 2015), was praised by a number of top crime authors, including Nicholas Blincoe, Caro Ramsay, Paul Johnston and Howard Linskey. Critic Barry Forshaw also wrote a positive review of the novel in Crime Time and followed up by giving Nick and his book a mention in Brit Noir, a guide to the best contemporary British crime writing and film.

Nick is British, but is currently living with his family in Fuengirola, Spain. Originally from Bristol, he studied at the universities of Cardiff and London, and lived for a long time in the English capital, where he ended up teaching English Literature and English Language in an FE college. He has moved around a fair bit, and has also lived and taught in Saudi Arabia, Abu Dhabi, Brighton, Barcelona, Bilbao and the city of Malaga. His experience of life in different places has helped his writing, and his books are set against a range of backdrops.

❉

To learn more about Nick Sweet and discover more Next Chapter authors, visit our website at www.nextchapter.pub.

The Mystery Quartet
ISBN: 978-4-82419-492-3
Hardcover Edition

Published by
Next Chapter
2-5-6 SANNO
SANNO BRIDGE
143-0023 Ota-Ku, Tokyo
+818035793528

12th June 2024

KEY THEOLOGICAL THINKERS

This fine collection consists of concise interpretations of an unusually large number of significant modern theologians. Indeed, the collection is unique in its capacious attention to Orthodox, Catholic and Protestant theologians alike. The genuinely ecumenical character is rare. All three of the great families of Christian theology (Orthodox, Catholic and Protestant) receive sustained serious attention both independently and interdependently: a welcome harbinger of the ecumenical future for all Christian theology.

David W. Tracy, University of Chicago, USA

The 20th and 21st centuries have been characterized by theologians and philosophers rethinking theology and revitalizing the tradition. This unique anthology presents contributions from leading contemporary theologians – including Rowan Williams, Fergus Kerr, Aidan Nichols, G.R. Evans and Tracey Rowland – who offer portraits of over fifty key theological thinkers in the modern and postmodern eras. Distinguished by its broad ecumenical perspective, this anthology spans arguably one of the most creative periods in the history of Christian theology and includes thinkers from all three Christian traditions: Protestant, Catholic and Orthodox.

Each individual portrait in this anthology includes a biographical introduction, an overview of theological or philosophical writing, presentation of key thoughts, and contextual placing of the thinker within 20th-century religious discourse. Overview articles explore postmodern theology, radical orthodoxy, ecumenical theology, feminist theology, and liberation theology. A final section includes portraits of important thinkers who have influenced Christian thought from other fields, not least from Continental philosophy and literature.

Key theological thinkers include: K. Barth, R. Bultmann, W. Elert, P. Tillich, D. Bonhoeffer, K.E. Løgstrup, R. Prenter, G. Wingren, J. Moltmann, W. Pannenberg, E. Jüngel, H. de Lubac, Y. Congar, K. Rahner, B. Lonergan, H.U. von Balthasar, J. Daniélou, E. Schillebeeckx, K. Wojtyła (John Paul II), J. Ratzinger (Benedict XVI), H. Küng, E.S. Fiorenza, S. Bulgakov, G. Florovsky, N. Afanasiev, V. Lossky, D. Stăniloae, A. Schmemann, M. al-Miskîn, E. Timiadis, J. Zizioulas, A. Farrer, M. Ramsey, H. Chadwick, J. Pelikan, G. Lindbeck, R. Jenson, S. McFague, D. Tracy, S. Hauerwas, S. Coakley, Alistair McGrath, G.K. Chesterton, J. Maritain, E. Stein, C.S. Lewis, N. Frye, P. Ricoeur, T. Merton, C. Yannaras, J.D. Caputo and Jean-Luc Marion

Key Theological Thinkers
From Modern to Postmodern

Edited by

STAALE JOHANNES KRISTIANSEN
The University of Bergen, Norway

SVEIN RISE
NLA University College Bergen, Norway

ASHGATE

© Staale Johannes Kristiansen and Svein Rise 2013

All rights reserved. No part of this publication may be reproduced, stored in a retrieval system or transmitted in any form or by any means, electronic, mechanical, photocopying, recording or otherwise without the prior permission of the publisher.

Staale Johannes Kristiansen and Svein Rise have asserted their right under the Copyright, Designs and Patents Act, 1988, to be identified as the editors of this work.

Published by
Ashgate Publishing Limited
Wey Court East
Union Road
Farnham
Surrey, GU9 7PT
England

Ashgate Publishing Company
110 Cherry Street
Suite 3-1
Burlington, VT 05401-3818
USA

www.ashgate.com

British Library Cataloguing in Publication Data
Key theological thinkers : from modern to postmodern.
  1. Theologians--History--20th century. 2. Christian philosophers--History--20th century. 3. Theology--History--20th century. 4. Religious thought--20th century.
  I. Kristiansen, Staale Johannes, 1971- II. Rise, Svein, 1946-
  230'.0922-dc23

The Library of Congress has cataloged the printed edition as follows:
Key theological thinkers : from modern to postmodern / edited by Staale Johannes Kristiansen and Svein Rise.
     p. cm.
  Includes index.
  ISBN 978-1-4094-3762-8 (hardcover) -- ISBN 978-1-4094-3763-5 (pbk.) -- ISBN 978-1-4094-3764-2 (ebook) 1. Theology--History--20th century. 2. Theologians--History--20th century. I. Kristiansen, Staale Johannes, 1971- II. Rise, Svein, 1946-
  BT28.K46 2013
  270.092'2--dc23

2012026630

ISBN 9781409437628 (hbk)
ISBN 9781409437635 (pbk)
ISBN 9781409437642 (ebk – PDF)
ISBN 9781409474685 (ebk – ePUB)

Printed and bound in Great Britain by MPG PRINTGROUP

OXFORDSHIRE LIBRARY SERVICE	
3302839725	
Askews & Holts	24-Jun-2013
230.0922	£25.00

Contents

List of Contributors	*xi*
Preface	*xv*
Acknowledgements	*xvii*

PART I: INTRODUCTIONS

1   A Century of Theological Creativity:
    Perspectives on the Renewal and Development of the Christian Tradition 3
    Staale Johannes Kristiansen and Svein Rise

2   Protestant Theology in the Twentieth Century   21
    Niels Henrik Gregersen

3   Catholic Theology in the Twentieth Century   37
    Tracey Rowland

4   Orthodox Theology in the Twentieth Century   53
    Aristotle Papanikolaou

PART II: PROTESTANT THEOLOGIANS (CONTINENTAL AND SCANDINAVIAN)

5   Karl Barth   65
    Harald Hegstad

6   Rudolf Bultmann   77
    Svein Aage Christoffersen

7   Werner Elert   89
    Bernt T. Oftestad

8   Paul Tillich   101
    Svein Olaf Thorbjørnsen

9	Dietrich Bonhoeffer *Trygve Wyller*	113
10	Knud Ejler Løgstrup *Svein Aage Christoffersen*	123
11	Regin Prenter *Ådne Njå*	135
12	Gustaf Wingren *Jonny Karlsson*	147
13	Jürgen Moltmann *Idar Kjølsvik*	159
14	Wolfhart Pannenberg *Svein Rise*	173
15	Eberhard Jüngel *Kjetil Hafstad*	187

PART III: CATHOLIC THEOLOGIANS

16	Henri de Lubac *Fergus Kerr*	201
17	Yves Congar *Gabriel Flynn*	213
18	Karl Rahner *Svein Rise*	225
19	Bernard Lonergan *Kirsten Busch Nielsen*	239
20	Hans Urs von Balthasar *Staale Johannes Kristiansen*	249
21	Jean Daniélou *Aidan Nichols*	267

22	Edward Schillebeeckx *Olav Hovdelien*	281
23	John Paul II/Karol Wojtyła *Michael Waldstein*	291
24	Benedict XVI/Joseph Ratzinger *Gösta Hallonsten*	301
25	Hans Küng *Hermann Häring*	315
26	Elisabeth Schüssler Fiorenza *Annelies Moeser*	327

PART IV: ORTHODOX THEOLOGIANS

27	Sergei Bulgakov *Andrew Louth*	341
28	Georges Florovsky *Brandon Gallaher*	353
29	Nicolas Afanasiev *Michael Plekon*	371
30	Vladimir Lossky *Matti Kotiranta*	379
31	Dumitru Stăniloae *Calinic Berger*	393
32	Alexander Schmemann *Sigurd Hareide*	403
33	Matta El-Meskeen *Samuel Rubenson*	415
34	Emilianos Timiadis *Gunnar af Hällström*	427

| 35 | Johannes Zizioulas
Lars Erik Rikheim | 435 |

PART V: BRITISH AND AMERICAN THEOLOGIANS

36	Austin Farrer *Margaret Yee*	451
37	Michael Ramsey *Rowan Williams*	463
38	Henry Chadwick *G.R. Evans*	475
39	Jaroslav Pelikan *Jan Schumacher*	487
40	George Lindbeck *Roland Spjuth*	499
41	Robert W. Jenson *Olli-Pekka Vainio*	509
42	Sallie McFague *Ellen T. Armour*	517
43	David Tracy *Jan-Olav Henriksen*	529
44	Stanley Hauerwas *Arne Rasmusson*	537
45	Sarah Coakley *Linn Marie Tonstad*	547
46	Alister E. McGrath *Olli-Pekka Vainio*	559

PART VI: THEOLOGICAL MOVEMENTS AND DEVELOPMENTS

| 47 | Postmodern Theology
Jayne Svenungsson | 569 |
| 48 | Radical Orthodoxy
Ola Sigurdson | 581 |
| 49 | Feminist Theology
Astri Hauge | 593 |
| 50 | Ecumenical Theology
Peter Lodberg | 607 |
| 51 | Liberation Theology
Sturla J. Stålsett | 617 |
| 52 | Pentecostal Theology
Frank D. Macchia | 631 |

PART VII: THEOLOGY, PHILOSOPHY AND LITERATURE

| 53 | G.K. Chesterton
Torbjørn Holt | 645 |
| 54 | Jacques Maritain
Gregory M. Reichberg | 657 |
| 55 | Edith Stein
Tor Martin Møller | 669 |
| 56 | C.S. Lewis
Oskar Skarsaune | 681 |
| 57 | Northrop Frye
Jan Schumacher | 691 |
| 58 | Paul Ricoeur
René Rosfort | 703 |

| 59 | Thomas Merton
Henning Sandström | 715 |
| 60 | Christos Yannaras
Norman Russell | 725 |
| 61 | John D. Caputo
Neal DeRoo | 735 |
| 62 | Jean-Luc Marion
Jan-Olav Henriksen | 745 |

Index   753

List of Contributors

Ellen T. Armour currently occupies the E. Rhodes and Leona B. Carpenter Chair in Feminist Theology at Vanderbilt Divinity School.

Calinic Berger holds a PhD from the Catholic University of America. He is an Orthodox priest and has taught theology at St. Vladimir's Seminary in Crestwood, New York.

Kirsten Busch Nielsen is Professor of Systematic Theology at the University of Copenhagen.

Svein Aage Christoffersen is Professor of Ethics and Philosophy of Religion at the University of Oslo.

Neal DeRoo is Assistant Professor of Philosophy at Dordt College, USA.

G.R. Evans is Professor Emeritus of Medieval Theology and Intellectual History, University of Cambridge.

Gabriel Flynn is Head of Theological Education at Mater Dei Institute, Dublin City University.

Brandon Gallaher is a British Academy Postdoctoral Fellow in the Faculty of Theology and Religion and at Regent's Park College, University of Oxford.

Niels Henrik Gregersen is Professor of Systematic Theology at the University of Copenhagen.

Gösta Hallonsten is Professor of Systematic Theology at the University of Lund.

Kjetil Hafstad is Professor of Systematic Theology at the University of Oslo.

Sigurd Hareide is Assistant Professor of Religious Studies, University of Nordland.

Astri Hauge is Candidatus theologiae and has been Research Scholar in Feminist Theology at the MF Norwegian School of Theology in Oslo.

Harald Hegstad is Professor of Systematic Theology at the MF Norwegian School of Theology.

Jan-Olav Henriksen is Professor of Systematic Theology and Philosophy of Religion at the MF Norwegian School of Theology in Oslo.

Gunnar af Hällström is Professor of Systematic Theology at Åbo Akademi University.

Hermann Häring is Professor Emeritus of Dogmatics at the University of Nijmegen.

Torbjørn Holt is Rector and Senior Chaplain at The Norwegian Church in London.

Olav Hovdelien, PhD is Associate Professor of Religious Studies, Faculty of Education, Oslo and Akershus University College of Applied Sciences.

Jonny Karlsson is a Doctor of Philosophy, and a priest in the Church of Sweden.

Fergus Kerr is a member of the Dominican Order and Senior Researcher in Theology at the University of Edinburgh.

Idar Kjølsvik is Associate Professor of Religious Studies at Nord-Trøndelag University College.

Matti Kotiranta is Professor of Church History and Vice-Dean of the Faculty of Theology at the University of Eastern Finland, Joensuu.

Staale Johannes Kristiansen is Research fellow in Art History at The University of Bergen. He is also a lecturer in Religious Studies at NLA University College in Bergen.

Peter Lodberg is Professor of Mission Studies and Ecumenism at the University of Aarhus.

Andrew Louth is Professor of Patristic and Byzantine Studies in the department of Theology and Religion, Durham University.

Frank D. Macchia is Professor of Christian Theology at Vanguard University.

Annelies Moeser is a doctoral candidate in Biblical Interpretation (New Testament) at Brite Divinity School.

Tor Martin Møller is First Secretary at the Permanent Mission of Norway to the International Organisations in Vienna.

Aidan Nichols is an English Dominican at Blackfriars in Cambridge and has written widely on various aspects of historical and dogmatic theology.

Ådne Njå is Doctor of Theology from the University of Oslo, and a priest in The Church of Norway.

Bernt T. Oftestad is Professor Emeritus at the MF Norwegian School of Theology in Oslo.

Aristotle Papanikolaou is Associate Professor of Theology and Co-Founding Director of the Orthodox Christian Studies Program at Fordham University.

Michael Plekon is Professor in the Sociology/Anthropology Department and Program in Religion and Culture of Baruch College of the City University of New York and a priest of the Orthodox Church in America (OCA).

Arne Rasmusson is Professor of Systematic Theology at University of Gothenburg, Sweden, and Research Associate in the Theological Faculty, Stellenbosch University, South Africa.

Gregory M. Reichberg is Research Professor at the Peace Research Institute in Oslo.

Lars Erik Rikheim is Canditatus theologiae from the University of Oslo.

Svein Rise is Professor of Systematic Theology at NLA University College in Bergen.

René Rosfort holds a Post-doctoral position at the Department of Systematic Theology at the Faculty of Theology, University of Copenhagen.

Tracey Rowland is Dean of the John Paul II Institute in Melbourne and Adjunct Professor at the Centre for Faith, Ethics and Society at the University of Notre Dame, Sydney.

Samuel Rubenson is Professor of Church History at the University of Lund.

Norman Russell is an independent researcher and the author of *The Doctrine of Deification in the Greek Patristic Tradition* (Oxford University Press 2004).

Jan Schumacher is Associate Professor of Church History at the MF Norwegian School of Theology in Oslo.

Henning Sandström is Associate Professor of Religious Studies at Östfold University College and Lecturer in Theological Ethics at Åbo Akademi University.

Ola Sigurdson is Professor of Systematic Theology and Director of the Centre for Culture and Health at the University of Gothenburg, Sweden.

Oskar Skarsaune is Professor Emeritus of Church History at the MF Norwegian School of Theology in Oslo, and a Member of The Norwegian Academy of Science and Letters and of The Royal Norwegian Society of Sciences and Letters.

Roland Spjuth is Lecturer in Systematic Theology at the Theological College in Örebro and at the Scandinavian Academy of Leadership and Theology.

Sturla J. Stålsett holds a PhD in Theology from the University of Oslo.

Jayne Svenungsson is Associate Professor of Systematic Theology at Uppsala University and holds a position as Senior Lecturer at Stockholm School of Theology, where she teaches systematic theology and philosophy of religion.

Svein Olaf Thorbjørnsen is Professor of Ethics at the MF Norwegian School of Theology in Oslo, Norway.

Linn Marie Tonstad is Assistant Professor of Systematic Theology at Yale Divinity School.

Olli-Pekka Vainio is Adjunct Professor of Ecumenical Theology at the University of Helsinki, and Visiting Research Fellow at The Center for the Study of Religion and Public Life, Kellogg College, University of Oxford.

Michael Waldstein is Seckler Professor of Theology at Ave Maria University in Florida.

Rowan Williams was the Archbishop of Canterbury until 31 December 2012, and thereafter Master of Magdalene College, Cambridge.

Trygve Wyller is Professor of Systematic Theology and Diaconal studies at the University of Oslo.

Margaret Yee is Research Professor at St. Cross College, University of Oxford.

Preface

The twentieth century is a remarkable century in the history of theology, not least because this period is marked by the impressive individual achievements of outstanding theologians, each of whom in his or her way sought to renew theological thinking. The renewal comes from all three of the theological traditions. Within Protestantism, one thinks immediately of Karl Barth's grandiose rethinking of Christian dogmatics, but also of the comprehensive contributions made by theologians such as Paul Tillich, Jürgen Moltmann, Eberhard Jüngel, and Wolfhart Pannenberg. At the same time, the middle of the century and its second half are a "golden age" for Catholic theology, with central figures such as Henri de Lubac, Yves Congar, Karl Rahner, Hans Urs von Balthasar, and Joseph Ratzinger. There is also a tremendous renewal in Orthodoxy from the 1930s onwards. This was linked first and foremost to the Russian exile milieu in Paris, with central names such as Sergei Bulgakov, Georges Florovsky, Vladimir Lossky, and Alexander Schmemann; but the contributions by the Romanian Dumitru Stăniloae and the Greek Johannes Zizioulas are just as remarkable.

This book is an updated and extended version of an anthology published in Scandinavian languages: *Modern Theology: Tradition and Renewal in the Theologians of the 20th Century* (Norwegian Academic Press, 2008). Fifty-six authors have contributed to this new version of the anthology, which first of all presents *portraits* of the foremost theological thinkers of the last century. Each portrait includes a short personal and intellectual biography, an overview of the work, key theological themes and an evaluation of the thinker's influence on modern and postmodern theology. Also included are nine introductory articles on theological traditions and movements.

Compared to similar works on modern theology, the originality of this book lies in its broad ecumenical perspective on the theology of the last century, and not least in the weight placed on Orthodox theological thinkers. We have sought to emphasise all three ecclesial and theological traditions – Protestant, Orthodox and Catholic. This is reflected first in the three introductory chapters on Catholic, Orthodox and Protestant theology in the twentieth century. The next three chapters present portraits of the key theologians from each of these traditions. The chapter on American and British theologians has a natural weight on Protestant (Anglican and Evangelical) theologians. The creative relationship between philosophy and theology, and between literature and theology, finds expression in the last chapters of the book, which include portraits of thinkers such as G.K. Chesterton, C.S. Lewis, and Northrop Frye, as well as Jacques Maritain, Paul Ricoeur, Christos Yannaras, Jean-Luc Marion, and John Caputo.

When we began the editorial work, we did not envisage that this overview would become so extensive, but the size of the anthology is connected with the problem of drawing boundary lines. One editor found it hard to exclude important Lutheran and Protestant theologians, while the other editor had the same problem with the selection of modern Catholic thinkers. At the same time, both editors wanted a broad representation of the most central twentieth-century Orthodox theologians. It was nevertheless necessary to draw a line somewhere, and we were unable to include central theological thinkers such as Emil Brunner, Friedrich Gogarten, and the brothers Reinhold and H. Richard Niebuhr; Marie-Dominique Chenu, Romano Guardini, Louis Bouyer, and Josef Pieper; John Meyendorff, Paul Evdokimov, and Olivier Clément – to mention only a few central names. Nor were we able to include portraits of such influential forerunners of twentieth-century theology as John Henry Newman, Ernst Troeltsch, and Adolph von Harnack.

We have greatly appreciated the collaboration with the many co-authors of the book, and we wish to thank them all for their great courtesy and patience. Work on this book has been a process in which we have learned a great deal, both theologically and editorially.

Many thanks to Tracey Rowland and Peter Lodberg, who both wrote their texts with a deadline of a few weeks. We are grateful to Stephen Donovan, who translated the article on postmodern theology. We are particularly grateful to our co-authors and others who encouraged us and inspired us to continue the work during a critical period in 2010.

We also wish to thank NLA University College (Bergen), MF Norwegian School of Theology (Oslo), and NORLA – Norwegian Literature Abroad, for their economic support.

We express our thanks to Bjørn Hansen and Maria Braadland at Norwegian Academic Press. We are very grateful for all the courtesy on the part of Ashgate Publishing, and especially to Sarah Lloyd, David Shervington and Caroline Spender who have brought the project safely into harbour.

Last but not least, a special thanks to Brian McNeil for translating the Scandinavian contributions, and for his editorial advice.

Staale Johannes Kristiansen and Svein Rise,
Bergen, on the Solemnity of Saint Joseph

Acknowledgements

The editors and publishers are grateful to the copyright holders for permission to use images in the following chapters:

Chapter 5 (image © Karl Barth-Archive).
Chapter 8 (image courtesy of Harvard University Archives, HUP Tillch, Paul (1a) © UTS News Bureau / Werner Wolff, Black Star).
Chapter 18 (image © Walter Schels, Hamburg).
Chapter 20 (image © Archiv Hans Urs von Balthasar, Basel).
Chapter 23 (image © Francois Lochon / Getty Images).
Chapter 28 (image © Andrew Blane). From Andrew Blane *Georges Florovsky: Russian Intellectual and Orthodox Churchman* (Crestwood, N.Y.: St. Vladimir's Seminary Press, 1993).
Chapter 29 (image © Michael Plekon).
Chapter 39 (image © Michael Marsland).
Chapter 42 (image © Sallie McFague).
Chapter 54 (image © Andrew Blane). From Andrew Blane *Georges Florovsky: Russian Intellectual and Orthodox Churchman* (Crestwood, N.Y.: St. Vladimir's Seminary Press, 1993).
Chapter 56 (image © Wolf Suschitzky / Getty Images).
Chapter 58 (image © University of Chicago Divinity School).
Chapter 59 (image used with permission of the Merton Legacy Trust and the Thomas Merton Center at Bellarmine University).
Chapter 62 (image © University of Chicago Divinity School).

***

This translation has been published with the financial support of NORLA.

PART I
Introductions

Chapter 1
A Century of Theological Creativity: Perspectives on the Renewal and Development of the Christian Tradition

Staale Johannes Kristiansen and Svein Rise

The last century was arguably one of the most creative centuries in the history of theology. The most striking examples are the many impressive writings by religious geniuses such as Karl Barth, Dumitru Stăniloae, Karl Rahner, and Hans Urs von Balthasar, but the picture is much more comprehensive. We shall illustrate this by means of fifty-two portraits of religious thinkers from the Christian tradition, from the early twentieth century to the early twenty-first century.

In many of these modern and postmodern thinkers, we find exciting attempts to integrate theology into a larger cultural discourse. The links between theology and forms of expression such as literature, music, and the visual arts are important here, not least in several large-scale endeavours to read theology and philosophy in tandem. This makes it natural to compare the twentieth century with brilliant theological epochs such as the fourth and fifth centuries, or the thirteenth and fourteenth, or the sixteenth centuries; depending to some extent on which theological tradition we are speaking about. The last chapter of the present book reflects the fact that several of the most important contributions to the renewal of Christian theology and of the Christian understanding of reality in the last century come from thinkers outside the circles of school-theology.[1] In the transitions between the theological and the philosophical realms, or between the religious and the literary realms, several postmodern perspectives become more explicit. This is not surprising, given that much postmodern thinking is characterized by a will to overcome modernity's tendency to divide things up into academic segments. Postmodern theological thinkers seek to counter this by means of interdisciplinary approaches to the existential and religious challenges of the present day.

A radical reorientation occurred within all three traditions – Protestant, Catholic and Orthodox – in the decades after the First World War.[2] In many ways, the tragedy of war cleared the ground for the emergence of something new. It dealt a death-blow

---

[1] See especially Part VII of this book.
[2] Parts II, III and IV of the book follow this order – Protestant, Catholic, Orthodox – because of the Scandinavian context in which the first version of this book was published.

to an optimistic faith in development, and opened the door at the same time to an incipient growth of ways of thinking (both religious and secular) that were interested in the existence of the individual rather than in the continuation of the great cultural traditions.[3] The new generation of theologians felt strongly that they were living between two epochs. The question now was what new response theology ought to make to modernity. This question left its mark on the first two generations of the theologians who are represented in this anthology – and continues to leave its mark on contemporary theological discourse.

As the book's subtitle indicates, this collection of portraits covers something of the historical breadth in the theology and the theological thinking of the twentieth century – *From Modern to Postmodern*. Although this book is not primarily a study of the *transition* between modern and postmodern theology, many of the portraits and overview articles seek to show that there is more overlapping and continuity in this process than one might initially think. Already in the first generation of twentieth-century theologians, we find authors who anticipate fundamental insights in postmodern theology. From the period between the Wars onwards, we find more and more thinkers who dynamically combine a positive development of the Enlightenment progress, on the one hand, and a conscious break with what was regarded as the reductionism inherent in the Enlightenment project, on the other hand. Accordingly, several explicitly postmodern theologians have consciously developed insights from the first half of the century, for example, the emphasis on the divine otherness in Karl Barth or linguistic-critical and apophatic-theological insights in writers such as Vladimir Lossky and Hans Urs von Balthasar.[4] It is important to bring out these links, but at the same time, it must be said that we find radical new thinking in postmodern theological thought, a radicality that emerges more clearly from the 1990s onwards. This involves not least a renewed attitude to the mystery in the Christian faith, linked to key concepts in the philosophy of religion such as "gift", "otherness", "the impossible", and "messianity".[5] There is a clearer theological hermeneutical awareness of theology's attitude to "the other", to "the coming of something we did not see coming".[6]

We find already in the 1970s the first beginnings of the theological development that came to be known in the 1980s as "postmodern theology". As Jayne Svenungsson has pointed out, the growth of a postmodern theological thinking during these two decades was marked by a more or less clear opposition between those who wanted to develop further the liberal theological inheritance (the deconstructivist "Death of God" theology pioneered by Mark C. Taylor, and thinkers who offered more

---

[3] See Niels Henrik Gregersen's introduction below.

[4] See, respectively, Graham Ward, *Barth, Derrida and the Language of Theology* (Cambridge, 1988), and Jean-Luc Marion, *The Idol and Distance* (New York, 2001), pp. xxxvi and 139ff.

[5] See John D. Caputo and Michael J. Scalon, "Introduction. Apology for the Impossible: Religion and Postmodernism", in John D. Caputo and Michael J. Scalon (eds.), *God, the Gift and Postmodernism* (Bloomington and Indianapolis, 1999), pp. 1–19.

[6] Ibid., p. 3.

revisionist approaches, such as David Tracy and Sallie McFague) and those who wanted to renew Karl Barth's more traditional theological alternative (Hans Frei and George Lindbeck, and other postliberalists).[7] This more Protestant dichotomy gradually became less prominent in the postmodern discourse in the 1990s – both as a consequence of Tracy's open dialogue with several of the postliberal theologians, and also as a consequence of the significance that other Catholic philosophers of religion such as Jean-Luc Marion and John Caputo took on.[8] Their dialogue with Jacques Derrida and their theological implementations of insights in his more explicitly religious writings played an important role here in the 1990s.[9]

We should note the supra-confessional element in later postmodern discourse. Although one can say that the postmodern element is not so strong in an Orthodox context, a Greek philosopher such as Christos Yannaras contributed, early on, an exciting theological reading of Heidegger in tandem with the church fathers, and later contributed to what he has called "postmodern metaphysics".[10] In recent years, David Bentley Hart has made impressive contributions to a theological evaluation of the relationship between the Western metaphysical tradition and central Christian dogmas, in a lively application of *theological aesthetics*.[11] We find a similar application of holistic theological thinking in an Anglican context. The neo-Barthian movement of *Radical Orthodoxy*, represented by thinkers such as John Milbank, Catherine Pickstock, and Graham Ward, presents a broad critique of modernity, inspired both by Balthasar's theological aesthetics and by Henri de Lubac's critique of modernity's idea of *pura natura*.[12]

Theological Variety and Renewals of the Tradition

It is possible to identify a number of essential common traits in the theological development of the twentieth century, but it is first and foremost the theological *diversity* that typifies that century in comparison to earlier centuries. In other words, we are confronted by a more complex and many-faceted theological landscape. The contributions to both theology and the philosophy of religion point in different directions, *cutting across* the three main ecclesial traditions, but also point at different theological approaches *within* each of the traditions. Historically speaking, the defence

---

[7] See Jayne Svenungsson's article about postmodern theology, below.
[8] Ibid.
[9] See Caputo.
[10] Christos Yannaras, *On the Absence and Unknowability of God: Heidegger and the Areopagite* (London, 2005; first published in 1967 as *The Theology of the Absence and Unknowability of God*); Christos Yannaras, *Postmodern Metaphysics* (Brookline, Mass., 2004). See Norman Russel's article on Yannaras, below.
[11] David Bentley Hart, *The Beauty of the Infinite: The Aesthetics of Christian Truth* (Grand Rapids, 2003).
[12] See Ola Sigurdson's article on *Radical Orthodoxy*, below.

of a *plurality of theological methods* characterizes this period – a gradually increasing awareness that we need a variety of polyvalent approaches to what has been called the *polyphony* in the Christian revelation.[13] The twentieth century has the merit of giving Christian theological thinking a large room for intellectual freedom.

In the midst of the variety, we find interesting connecting lines and shared traits in the theological thinking of the twentieth century, with interesting similarities that cut across the confessional lines. One major driving force in modern theology is the wish to *bring theology up to date* in the contemporary world, to make it relevant both in the form of ecclesial aggiornamento – we find a basis for this motto of Pope John XXIII already several decades earlier, in all three ecclesial and theological traditions – and in the form of a dialogue with contemporary philosophy. The theological aggiornamento entails first and foremost the attempt to give a fresh and new presentation of the Christian truths. At the same time, it points to a process of becoming aware of the church's role in political life, especially in the defence of the individual and of the eternal inviolability of the human person.

From the 1930s onward, we find theological presentations that give an account of the dramatic character of human life, of its fundamental uncertainty, in a way that recalls the insights of existentialist thought. Central names here include Rudolf Bultmann, Jacques Maritain, Karol Wojtyła, Paul Tillich, K.E. Løgstrup, Edward Schillebeeckx, Edith Stein, and Hans Urs von Balthasar. The parallel to existentialist philosophy is connected in part with the encounter several of the modern theologians had with Martin Heidegger and his work, but also to their reading of the same Christian source texts that provided Heidegger with inspiration – especially Meister Eckhart, Thomas Aquinas, and their forerunners in the early Christian mystical tradition.[14] Here we have a key point in the modern attempts to bring Christian theology up to date: the new theological thinking takes the form of *a revitalization of the tradition*.

We find a compressed expression of this in an often-quoted essay published by the Jesuit and patristic scholar Jean Daniélou in 1946, in which he writes about the "Modernist crisis" of the end of the nineteenth and beginning of the twentieth centuries. He regards this crisis as unresolved, because the church and the theologians had not sufficiently grasped the existence of what he calls a "rupture between theology and life".[15] Although Daniélou criticizes the agnosticism of Modernism and the wrong

---

[13] Hans Urs von Balthasar, *The Truth is Symphonic: Aspects of Christian Pluralism* (San Francisco: Ignatius Press, 1988). See also Francis Schüssler Fiorenza, *Systematic Theology: Roman Catholic Perspectives* (Minneapolis: Fortress Press, 2011), pp. 64ff.

[14] John Caputo, *The Mystical Element in Heidegger's Thought* (New York: Fordham University Press, 1986); Fergus Kerr, *After Aquinas: Versions of Thomism* (Malden, Mass.: Blackwell, 2002).

[15] Jean Daniélou, "Les orientations présentes de la pensée religieuse," *Études*, 249 (1946), 6. See also Hans Boersma, *Nouvelle Théologie and Sacramental Ontology: A Return to Mystery* (Oxford, 2009), Introduction, pp. 1–10; Brian Daley, "The *Nouvelle Théologie* and the Patristic Revival: Sources, Symbols and the Science of Theology", *International Journal of Systematic Theology*, 7(4) (October, 2005), 362–82.

paths its exegesis takes, he believes that the condemnation of Modernism by the church leadership cannot be the last word in this matter. Modernism had grasped the distance between theology and people's concrete lives, and had posed a question mark against this. Now, after World War II, according to Daniélou, many instances in contemporary culture are reminding us of the same situation – contemporary voices that make the future "full of promise".[16] Daniélou's essay is programmatic for the rethinking and renewal of Catholic theology in the next decades, a renewal in which he himself took part. He writes that a renewal requires that we do justice to three circumstances that go to the core of the schism between theology and everyday existence.

First of all, theology must "treat God as God, not as an object, but as the Subject *par excellence*".[17] And such a renewal demands a "return to the sources" (*ressourcement*), going back to scripture, the church fathers, and the liturgy, in the attempt to overcome the old schisms between exegesis and theology, and bearing in mind the historical character of theology. Here, Daniélou also points to a renewal of the relationship between theology and spirituality and to the restoration of the liturgical view of the world, in which all things have a sacramental character and where nothing that is human is excluded from theology's field of interest. Secondly, the intended overcoming of the schism between theology and life demands that one enters into dialogue with the contemporary philosophical development – and this means first of all, according to Daniélou, a critical dialogue with Marxism and Existentialism. He refers in particular to Søren Kierkgaard's personal and non-objectifying image of God. Thirdly, theology must give "a response that engages the entire person, an interior light of an action where life unfolds in its entirety".[18] Daniélou emphasizes the importance of the vocation of the laity in marriage and in societal life – for it is only in this way that the universal concern of theology can truly be *incarnated* in the various cultures.

We find parallel rethinkings of the relationship between theology and everyday life in several of the theologians whose portraits are presented below. For example in Paul Tillich's program for a cultural theology, where religion is acknowledged to constitute a deep dimension of culture, and where theology must continuously strive to find new forms – based on the Christian *communio*.[19] We find a different approach to the same concern in Alexander Schmemann's emphasis on a liturgical form of life as the only thing that can open up the church to the world, while at the same time creating an ecclesial "backbone" that resists destructive aspects of secularization.[20]

There are clear parallels in the Orthodox and the Catholic traditions from the 1930s onward with regard to this need for theological renewal through a return *to the sources*. In Paris, we find an Orthodox renewal in the Russian émigré milieu, where Georges Florovsky and Vladimir Lossky were the principal theologians who set the

---

[16] Daniélou, p. 5.
[17] Ibid., p. 7.
[18] Ibid.
[19] See Chapter 2 for Niels Henrik Gregersen's introduction to Protestant theology.
[20] See Chapter 32 for Sigurd Hareide's article on Alexander Schmemann.

tone in what has been called the "neo-patristic school".[21] Both men wanted to regain the special character of Orthodox theology (which they believed had been lost due to Western influence) in the form of a return to the church fathers' writings and to their theological-philosophical concepts. At the same time, Lossky and Florovsky each took part in a positive dialogue with centrally important Western theologians, through their involvement in the ecumenical movement. The parallels between Florovsky's "christological concentration" and Barth's christocentrism can be said to be one of the fruits of the conversations that the two theologians had over many years. In contrast to the dominant theological education at that time, in which the fathers were mediated through isolated propositions and theological manuals from the nineteenth century, Florovsky, Lossky, John Meyendorff, and others pointed their students to the original patristic texts. In Romania, Dumitru Stăniloae criticized the same development in Orthodox theological education. He believed that a theology and a renewal that could combine the church fathers' theology and spirituality would offer the best response to contemporary challenges. Stăniloae created an original theological synthesis in which he combined Byzantine theology and ecumenical insights from contemporary theology with his own personalistic thinking. He translated large amounts of Greek patristic texts in order to make these writings accessible both to clergy and to laity.[22]

In the Catholic context, the patristic renaissance led to an even more dramatic break with the dominant neo-Scholastic (or Baroque) theology that dominated theological and priestly education (see below). Henri de Lubac represented an early break with this dominance, and he led younger theologians such as Jean Daniélou, Hans Urs von Balthasar, and Henri Bouillard during their time as students to the writings of the church fathers. De Lubac, Daniélou, and Claude Mondésert founded *Sources Chrétiennes,* a bilingual collection of patristic texts, in 1942. This was of decisive importance for the patristic renewal in the twentieth century. Up to now, *Sources Chrétiennes* has published more than 500 works of Greek, Latin, and Syriac fathers.

One could say that most of the modern creative theologians of the last century have found inspiration precisely by reading afresh the theological giants from the Church history – depending on the tradition to which they belong. The articles below show the clear connection between modern theologians and Church Fathers like the three Cappadocians and Saint Augustine, and also later theologians like Saint Thomas Aquinas and Saint Gregory Palamas, Martin Luther and Saint Ignatius Loyola. At the same time, a reading of these premodern thinkers shows us that theological renewal and development are not a new phenomenon – and that this renewal occurs in the meeting points with the cultural and philosophical thought of the time.

---

[21] See Chapter 4 for Aristotle Papanikolaou's introduction. See also Brandon Gallaher's chapter on Florovsky and Matti Kotiranta's chapter on Lossky.

[22] See Calinic Berger's article on Dumitru Stăniloae, below. See also Charles Miller, *An Introduction to the Theology of Dumitru Staniloae* (London: T&T Clark, 2000), pp. 16ff.

The Dialogue with Contemporary Culture and the Development of Doctrine

Theologians throughout the whole of the twentieth century were concerned about theology's response to modernity. Using a model borrowed from Hans Frei, David F. Ford classifies five different approaches to this question.[23] He sees a line with five points. The first type of theology is a pure repetition of the tradition, while the other extreme, the fifth form of theology, gives the priority to a secular philosophy or to a secular lifestyle with which Christianity must be in accord, if it is to be relevant. Ford rejects both these extremes in his presentation of modern theology, because the first (as he puts it) is not modern and the last is not Christian. It is the three intermediate positions that are interesting in our present context too. The second of the five forms of theology typically gives priority to the self-understanding of the Christian fellowship, and all understanding of reality must relate to this, since it is based on the motto "faith seeks understanding" (Anselm).[24] Examples among the portraits in the present book are Bonhoeffer, Jüngel, de Lubac, Balthasar, John Paul II, Jenson, Lossky, and Stăniloae. The third type of theology lies on the center of the axis and is a form of correlational theology, where the goal is a more equal dialogue between theology and modernity. The obvious example here is Paul Tillich. The fourth type integrates more strongly modern philosophy and modern concepts in the same dialogue. Ford presents Rudolf Bultmann as a good example, but we believe that his classification of Pannenberg in this fourth group shows the weaknesses in such a model. Ford himself is open to other opinions, and the article on Pannenberg in the present book shows that he probably ought to be read within another of the five types of theology. It is possible that other models offer a more precise approach to the question of theology and modernity than Hans Frei's five-point model. Let us take one example.

There is a parallel to the relationship between *tradition and new thinking* in the idea of *continuity and development* that was so central in the writings of the originally Lutheran theologian Jaroslav Pelikan.[25] The idea of the *development of doctrine* has its primary source in the nineteenth-century theologian John Henry Newman, in *An Essay on the Development of Christian Doctrine*, in which he maintains that Christian doctrine is something organic and alive, that follows the same vital principle as everything that lives in this world – "to live is to change". Pelikan is probably the most important continuator of Newman's understanding of history. As a historian, he always looked for the continuity in the changes, building on Newman's idea that great ideas "change in order to remain the same".

A good illustration of this last insight is Pelikan's account of the church fathers' conscious "contrapuntal reading" of *Genesis* and Plato's *Timaeus*. In the dialogue with Platonism, the church fathers sought to actualize the theology of creation in the Jerusalem creation narrative and to transport it into their own days in such a

---

[23] David F. Ford, "Introduction to Modern Christian Theology", in *The Modern Theologians* (Oxford: Blackwell, 2005), pp. 2–3.
[24] Ibid., p. 2.
[25] See Chapter 57 for Jan Schumacher's discussion of Pelikan.

manner that the main ideas in Genesis (according to the church fathers themselves) did not alter their fundamental theological content.[26] One could say that the fathers establish new expressions for the biblical ideas with the help of Platonic terminology, in order to express the deepest content of these biblical ideas. Thus, they "alter" the ideas (or the expression of the ideas) in order to bring out the deep, immutable truth in them. We find this same kind of contrapuntal reading of scripture, tradition, and philosophy in modern theologians, whether in "reading together" theology with existentialism, phenomenology, or French linguistic philosophy. It is the task of the theologian in every age to actualize and rewrite in order to preserve. It is true that the principle of the development of doctrine appears to open the floodgates to a total relativization of Christian doctrine. This is why Newman presented seven criteria in his essay on *development*, in order to distinguish between an unhealthy and a healthy development.[27] And in his elaboration of the idea of development, the notion of the church plays a decisive role. Correspondingly, Pelikan regards the liturgy as the locus of continuity in Christian theology. One principal idea in Pelikan's discussion of this theme is that continuity and change in the history of Christian doctrine must always be understood in the light of one another. Pelikan sees the important principle that genuinely Christian and Catholic doctrine is "that which is believed in all places, at all times, and by all persons" (Vincent of Lérins) as an impossible idealization of doctrinal continuity, unless it is interpreted in the light of the idea of *the development of doctrine*.[28] Christian doctrine moves forward, lives, and changes, in order to be able to remain (basically) the same at all times.

But is not the idea of a new thinking or development of the tradition insufficiently radical as a categorization of the movements within modern theology? Is there a place here for the elaboration of *something radically new*? Hans Urs von Balthasar writes: "... the form and content in the great theologies always bears witness to the one wonder in new and different ways, and will not construct a neatly arranged unity even in eternity."[29] He has learnt from both Gregory of Nyssa and Origen that scripture, which is the proper object of theology, is always inexhaustible and that language can never grasp unambiguously or systematically the wealth that lies in the divine mystery.[30] A fundamentally apophatic way of thinking about revelation and human language can thus open the path to genuine new discoveries in theology, new discoveries that can be regarded as going more deeply into the mystery or as insights into the revelation that has already been given. The idea of the development of doctrine is taken for granted by all the Catholic theologians in this anthology, provided that it is

---

[26] Jaroslav Pelikan, *What Has Athens To Do With Jerusalem* (Michigan, 1997).

[27] John Henry Newman, *An Essay on the Development of Christian Doctrine* (Notre Dame, Ind., 1845/1989), pp. 169 ff.

[28] Jaroslav Pelikan, *The Melody of Theology: A Philosophical Dictionary* (Cambridge, Mass.: Harvard University Press, 1988), p. 45.

[29] Balthasar, Hans Urs von, *Mein Werk – Durchblicke* (Einsiedeln and Freiburg, 1990), p. 64.

[30] See Chapter 20 on Hans Urs von Balthasar.

accompanied by specific criteria for a genuine development.[31] Balthasar emphasizes that theology is not only meant to preserve. It must also open the human person for his or her continuous movement in towards the truth, taking one deeper into something that can never be understood in itself. At the same time, however, he insists that theology can never get behind that which is concrete – the concrete word of scripture, and the simultaneously historical and mystical realities in Jesus' life and death, his descent among the dead, his resurrection and exaltation. We find a similar emphasis on the concrete in a number of other theologians who are portrayed in this anthology.

Among modern Orthodox theologians, where the negative or apophatic theological attitude is strongest, there is however greater skepticism about the possibilities of new insight into revelation. In a Festschrift for Jaroslav Pelikan (who converted to Orthodoxy in his later years), the Orthodox theologian Andrew Louth denies that the idea of development (of doctrine) is a valid category in Orthodox theology.[32] This does not mean that Louth and other modern Orthodox theologians completely reject the idea of new thinking and development. Georges Florovsky always emphasized positively the importance that the encounter with Hellenistic culture had for the elaboration of Christian theology and thinking. Alexander Schmemann, who always saw the liturgy as the basic source of theology, writes that the liturgy develops because it is organic: it is the organic life of theology.[33] And in his essay on development, Louth emphasizes that although Newman's idea itself is incompatible with Orthodoxy, Orthodoxy has much to learn from the historical thinking that generated this idea. It is also a characteristic of the modern Orthodox theologians who are presented in this anthology that they are open in a wholly new manner to dialogue with thinkers outside their own tradition, because they believe that they have something to learn from this conversation. And it is completely obvious that the same is true in the other direction.

Recurring Themes

One can speak to some extent of theological themes that recur in the theology of the twentieth century, as the reader of the following portraits and overview articles will discover. We find the "rediscovery" of Trinitarian theology by theologians such as Karl Barth, Karl Rahner, Hans Urs von Balthasar, Jürgen Moltmann, Wolfhart Pannenberg, Robert Jenson, and Johannes Zizioulas.[34] Readers who are interested in theological contacts to existential theology can usefully read the articles about Paul

---

[31] See Tracey Rowland's introduction to Catholic theology in Chapter 3.
[32] Louth, Andrew, "Is Development a Valid Category for Orthodox Theology?" in *Orthodoxy and Western Culture. A Collection of Essays Honoring Jaroslav Pelikan on his Eightieth Birthday* (Crestwood, 2005), pp. 45 ff.
[33] See Sigurd Hareide's discussion of Schmemann in Chapter 32.
[34] Stanley J. Grenz, *Rediscovering the Triune God. The Trinity in Contemporary Theology* (Minneapolis: Fortress Press, 2004).

Tillich, Rudolf Bultmann, Vladimir Lossky, Karl Rahner, Hans Urs von Balthasar, Edward Schillebeeckx, Edith Stein, and Jacques Maritain. The articles about Jean-Luc Marion, John Paul II, and Edith Stein touch on the relationship between theology and phenomenology. Many of these thinkers seek to apply the Christian doctrine of the Trinity, the relationship between the Persons in the Trinity, to a theology about the human person. Readers who are particularly interested in the question of the language of theology, in stepping beyond the boundaries of an analytical theological language, and in the link between theology and aesthetic modes of knowledge can usefully read the articles about Christos Yannaras, Northrop Frye, Jean-Luc Marion, Hans Urs von Balthasar, Austin Farrer, Thomas Merton, C.S. Lewis, Paul Ricoeur, David Tracy and John Caputo. For questions about the relationship between theology and philosophy, theology and history, and theology and science, we refer to the articles about such thinkers as Rudolf Bultmann, Werner Elert, Paul Tillich, Wolfhart Pannenberg, Jürgen Moltmann, Henry Chadwick, Henri de Lubac, Jean Daniélou, Joseph Ratzinger, Sergei Bulgakov, Alister McGrath, and Austin Farrer. The renewal of ecclesiology, liturgical theology, and the link between theology and spirituality (theology and the church) is presented above all in the articles about Sarah Coakley, Nicolas Afanasiev, Yves Congar, Henri de Lubac, Johannes Zizioulas, Alexander Schmemann, Karl Rahner, Hans Urs von Balthasar, and Karl Barth.

Modernity and its Aftermath

One interesting example of the polyvalence of the transition from the modern to the postmodern in the theological context is the controversy, mentioned above, that occurred in the Catholic church between 1935 and 1950. The controversy between central neo-Scholastic theologians such as Réginald Garrigou-Lagrange and those whom he dismissed with the negative term *la Nouvelle Théologie* illustrates something of the complexity in the relationship between tradition, renewal, and the task of bringing theology up to date in the theological thinking of the twentieth century.[35] The conservative (neo-Thomist) theologians in Paris and Rome regarded the thought of Daniélou, de Lubac, and Congar as a "new theology", a new variant of Modernism that threatened the immutable character of the truth. But all the indicators point in exactly the opposite direction. In other words, this time too, conservatism represented not the classical and traditional, but rather something that lay just one step back in the past – something old, but not traditional. The backdrop to the controversies was the Modernist crisis from the first years of the century, and the discussion largely concentrated on an adequate interpretation of Thomas Aquinas, who was acknowledged by both parties as probably the greatest thinker in church history. But what did his greatness consist of? The most central of those behind the *nouvelle théologie* knew patristic theology and recognized the historical continuity between the church

---

[35] Réginald Garrigou-Lagrange, "La nouvelle théologie où va-t-elle?", *Angelicum*, 23 (1946), 126–45.

fathers and Thomas Aquinas;[36] they believed that the neo-Scholastics overlooked this continuity because they were influenced by a modern and ahistorical reading of the great medieval doctor of the church. The neo-Scholastic theologians, who dominated the theological education at the seminaries of that period, regarded Aquinas' teaching not only as outstanding, but as the definitive expression of the Catholic faith. The *nouvelle théologie* was aware of Newman's idea of the development of Christian doctrine (see above), and held that the neo-Scholastics' readings of Aquinas overlooked the historical character of the truth, and that it was they who reduced the truth by linking it exclusively to one particular historical expression. Fergus Kerr has pointed out the paradox that the emphasis on Thomist philosophy in the aftermath of Pope Leo XIII's directives, which was meant to protect the church against modern philosophy, did so precisely by applying the rationality of the Enlightenment: "The Enlightenment ideal was to attain timeless, universal and objective conclusions by exercising a unitary and ahistorical form of reasoning."[37] The *nouvelle théologie* breaks radically with this form of rationality through its endeavor to renew the understanding of the dramatic character of revelation (and of the Christ event) that they find in central church fathers such as Origen, Gregory of Nyssa, and Augustine.

Kerr has underlined the role played by the Dominican Marie-Dominique Chenu in this breach with the positivism in Catholic theology at the turn of the nineteenth and twentieth centuries. As we have said, the dispute concerned the correct interpretation of Aquinas, but on a deeper level, it was more properly about the *concept of truth*.[38] Chenu criticized the neo-Scholastics or neo-Thomists[39] for having a metaphysical view of truth where one sought to arrive at the *essence* of things, while overlooking the more dynamic character of revelation, which is full of tensions. Chenu holds that they lay too much emphasis on a Greek approach to reality and to revelation, at the expense of the biblical concept of truth, which is closer to a Jewish or Hebrew way of thinking. The truth of the Bible and of the Gospel "connects directly not with what is but with what comes about, with that of which one has experience".[40] The Neo-Scholastic understanding of truth, like the Greek understanding, leaves out central characteristics in the biblical understanding of truth: "time, the fragility of things, and persons". Chenu writes: "Biblical thought is turned not to essences but

---

[36] Augustine and Ps.-Dionysius the Areopagite are in fact more important for Aquinas' theological vision than Aristotle. See, for example, Marie-Dominique Chenu, *The Scope of the Summa of St. Thomas* (Washington: Thomist Press, 1958; this is the translation in book form of his article "Le Plan de la *Somme théologique* de S. Thomas", *Revue Thomiste*, 45 [1939], 93–107).

[37] Fergus Kerr, *Twentieth-Century Catholic Theologians* (Oxford: Blackwell, 2007), p. 2.

[38] Ibid., 17ff.

[39] There are several neo-Thomist thinkers who cannot simply be called neo-Scholastics. These include Jacques Maritain, who is the subject of Gregory Reichberg's discussion in Chapter 54.

[40] Marie-Dominique Chenu, "Vérité évangélique et métaphysique wolfienne à Vatican II", *Revue des Sciences Philosophiques et Théologiques*, 57 (1973), 637, quoted by Kerr, *Twentieth-Century Catholic Theologians*, 32.

to destinies; it questions itself about the feeblenesses and the promises of life."[41] This is the concept of truth that Chenu wants to rehabilitate. The point around which it revolves is not the question of essence, but of plan and intention; it deals especially with the vulnerability of human existence and with the promises that are given with regard to the goal of human life. Chenu rediscovers this biblical thinking in Saint Thomas, because he reads Aquinas in a historical context, not least in connection with the church fathers who were so important for Aquinas.[42]

There are interesting parallels in Chenu's emphases on the historical character of human life, and on the human person's historical destiny, in the great twentieth-century philosopher Martin Heidegger, who criticizes the same metaphysical tradition from another perspective. Chenu says that the truth in the biblical revelation cannot be reduced to the kind of precise theological proportions that we find in neo-Scholastic positivism. In scripture, God reveals himself both through words and through concrete actions in history. Several decades later, Joseph Ratzinger wrote his professorial dissertation on the same topic (in a study of the theology of history and the understanding of revelation in Bonaventure); he emphasizes the dynamic character of the biblical concept of truth.[43] This dissertation was initially rejected by the neo-Thomist examiner, Michael Schmaus, as a dangerous Modernism that would lead to a subjectivization of the concept of revelation. But at the Second Vatican Council, it was Chenu's, Congar's, de Lubac's, and Ratzinger's view of revelation that won the day as the genuinely Catholic position – something that we see in the document on revelation, *Dei Verbum*.[44]

---

[41] Chenu, ibid., 637–8, quoted from Kerr.

[42] We understand that Chenu is working polemically here, for it goes without saying that both Chenu and the Aquinas whom he presents do not overlook the universal and immovable. What he affirms is that the immovable has moved and has come to meet the contingent and movable world. Here too, Aquinas is inspired by church fathers such as Augustine and Ps.-Dionysius the Areopagite, in their understanding of the relationship between God and the world. See, for example, Vivian Boland, *Ideas in God According to Saint Thomas Aquinas: Sources and Synthesis* (Leiden, 1996).

[43] The version of the professorial dissertation that was ultimately accepted, amounting to one-third of the original text, was published in 1959: Joseph Ratzinger, *Die Geschichtstheologie des Heiligen Bonaventura* (Munich, 1959); English translation: *The Theology of History in St. Bonaventure* (Chicago, 1971).

[44] In the ongoing discourse about the reception of the Council, it is essential to bear in mind the historical controversies from the years before the Council. The conciliar fathers and the conciliar theologians emphasized that, on the deepest level, the truth is a person ("I am the truth", John 14:6), and that this means that we can never *possess* the truth: we must bear witness to it. In this way, they rehabilitated the ancient Christian understanding of truth as historical, incarnational, and Christocentric, and resisted the theological positivism that is entailed in the belief that we can comprehend the truth in linguistic propositions – a positivism that can arguably be found in both conservative and progressive interpretations of the Council texts.

Truth, Gift, The Visual

The discussion of the Christian concept of truth is a recurring theme in the theology of the last century. It has been important for the rethinking of the language of theology, or of an adequate "theological style". The Anglican theologian Rowan Williams has discussed this in several of his writings, not least in his studies of Vladimir Lossky. He emphasizes the tradition of negative theology, which not only contains important distinctions with regard to God's immanence and transcendence, but also reminds us that "both the subject matter and (for lack of a better word) the style of good theology insist upon a radical change of attitude".[45] Williams links this to the gift of self that is inherent in God's Trinitarian life:

> A doctrine like that of the Trinity tells us that the very life of God is a yielding or giving-over into the life of the Other, a "negation" in the sense of refusing to settle for the idea that normative life or personal identity is to be conceived in terms of self-enclosed and self-sufficient units. The negative is associated with the "ek-static", the discovery of identity in self-transcending relation. And accordingly, theology itself has to speak in a mode that encourages us to question ourselves, to deny ourselves, in the sense of denying systems and concepts that are the comfortable possession of individual minds.[46]

We find similarly radical challenges to the language and the approach of theology in Jean-Luc Marion, who develops in an original manner insights from Heidegger, Balthasar, Emmanuel Levinas, and Jacques Derrida. Marion rejects the reductionism that is inherent in an idolizing approach to the divine, to human persons, and to all other phenomena that are not immediately comprehensible. It is the human gaze that makes something either an "idol" or an "icon", according to Marion. The gaze makes idols when it stops short at "the first visible", so that the one who sees receives confirmation of precisely what he or she expected to find in the other. In contradistinction to this, Marion proposes an iconic form of understanding, which is expectant and receptive, which opposes the possessive transformation of the other into an object, and which thus penetrates behind "the first visible".[47]

We should note that visuality and aesthetic categories become very central in this postmodern critique of the modern subject-object thinking. This reflects a shift in recent theological thinking that traces trajectories back to pre-modern emphases on "image" and "symbol" rather than on "word". Marion has written in greater detail about visuality and images in his book *The Crossing of the Visible*, which marks the

---

[45] Rowan Williams, *Wrestling with Angels: Conversations in Modern Theology* (London: SCM Press, 2007), Author's introduction, p. xiii.

[46] Ibid., pp. xiii–xiv.

[47] See primarily Marion, *The Idol and Distance*. See also Jan-Olav Henriksen's chapter on Marion, p. 745.

transition from a theological to a more phenomenological approach in his writings.[48] Christian iconography and the theology of icons play a central role here as a model for our recognition of otherness. The icon's gaze presents itself in a way that opens up for an exchange of gazes between our own gaze and the icon's.[49] The icon characteristically displays a gaze that belongs to a human face ("… it sees more than is seen"). Marion transfers the idea of givenness and of the exchange of gazes to all types of images and all forms of visuality. That which shows itself has first of all given itself; he says that this is his most important theme, indeed his only theme.[50] Marion's concept of "saturated phenomena" includes all types of phenomena, both religious and aesthetic.[51] In Marion's rethinking of subjectivity, it is not the consciousness of the transcendental subject that gives meaning to experience. Rather, the subject is *l'adonné*, the "one who is gifted".

These are only some examples of how the transition from a modern to a postmodern theological thinking can be said to be a gradual transition that has left its traces throughout the last century. Jayne Svenungsson's introductory chapter about "postmodern theology", p. 569, offers a more thorough discussion of the crucial transition at the end of the twentieth century. She shows how postmodern theology attempts to integrate developments in recent philosophy and theory of science. Svenungsson points out that just as postmodern thinking does not entail a delimited philosophical school, so "postmodern theology" is not one single school. Nevertheless, she points to common characteristics in postmodern theology, and especially the attempt to overcome the dualisms in modern thinking. The "hermeneutic character of theology" is proposed in contradistinction to what is seen as a linguistic dualism (whether this is the reference to a pre-linguistic religious experience, or the supposition of an objective revelation). Against modernity's dualism between body and soul, and theory and praxis, postmodern theology emphasizes that religious faith "is something that is lived and shaped by specific human beings in particular contexts". Svenungsson concludes by showing that postmodern theologians, in their attempts to overcome the dichotomies of modernity, seek inspiration in pre-modern theology – above all in the theology of late antiquity and in mediaeval theology's sacramental view of reality.

---

[48] The French original was published in 1996: *La Croisée du Visible* (Presses Universitaires de France); English translation: *The Crossing of the Visible* (Stanford: Stanford University Press, 2004). In the introduction to the book *Étant donné: Essai d'une phénoménologie de la donation* (1997), Marion writes that the transition to a more purely phenomenological perspective means that he can now argue for the *possibility* of a phenomenality that is open for the paradoxes entailed by a revelation. See Jean-Luc Marion, *Being Given: Toward a Phenomenology of Givenness* (Stanford: Stanford University Press, 2002), p. 5.

[49] Marion speaks here of an "exchange of gazes", a "play of gazes": Marion (2004), pp. 20–21.

[50] Jean-Luc Marion, *Being Given*, p. 5.

[51] Thomas M. Alferi, *Kunst als Ernstfall von Wahrnehmung: Kunsttheoretische und religionsdidaktische Studien* (Stuttgart: Ibidem-Verlag, 2002), pp. 89ff.

Ecumenical Outlook

One decisively important element of rethinking that comes into its own in the twentieth century is the growing openness to ecumenical perspectives on theology. Not all those who are portrayed in this book were involved in a direct dialogue with each other, but the articles show that there have been important conversations and debates between several of them, both within and across the various traditions. The nearest we come to a "connecting link" is Karl Barth, since virtually all the theological thinkers in this anthology situate themselves in relation to his work.

Meeting places of a more physical kind were the Russian émigré milieu in Paris, where many of the great Orthodox theologians worked together, in dialogue and debate; and most of the Catholic writers who are presented below met in the 1960s as theological experts at the *Second Vatican Council* in Rome, at which Orthodox and Lutheran observers also took part, such as Alexander Schmemann, Nicolas Afanasiev, Oscar Cullmann, Edmund Schlink and George Lindbeck.

The new perspective in the present anthology, compared with earlier overviews in the same format, is its emphasis on modern Orthodox theology. This is the first time that a presentation of the theology of the last century has given such a broad picture of individual Orthodox theologians. The first three chapters in the book present thirty-one theological thinkers, with a corresponding emphasis on each of the three theological traditions. In addition to the general new reading of modern theologians, this ecumenical perspective is the most original contribution of the present book. This perspective is also reflected in the contributors to the book.

We regard the emphasis on the Orthodox theologians as an important step towards a picture of theological thinking in the twentieth century that is more accurate in ecumenical terms. We also see a fascinating orientation towards the eastern theological tradition in contemporary western theology – influenced especially by the writings of Vladimir Lossky, Alexander Schmemann, John Meyendorff, and Johannes Zizioulas. We have only *begun* to see the influence exercised by the dynamic Orthodox theology of the last century, which will be a rich resource for both the Catholic and the Protestant traditions in the coming decades.

Our hope is that with its emphasis on all three main historical traditions, this anthology can contribute to a deeper ecumenical theological understanding and to a greater theological openness to those insights that are peculiar to each individual tradition.

Bibliography

Alferi, Thomas M., *Kunst als Ernstfall von Wahrnehmung: Kunsttheoretische und religionsdidaktische Studien* (Stuttgart: Ibidem-Verlag, 2002).

Balthasar, Hans Urs von, *Mein Werk – Durchblicke* (Einsiedeln and Freiburg: Johannes Verlag, 1990); English translation: *My Work in Retrospect* (San Francisco: Ignatius Press, 1991).

Balthasar, Hans Urs von, *The Truth is Symphonic: Aspects of Christian Pluralism* (San Francisco: Ignatius Press, 1988).
Boersma, Hans, *Nouvelle Théologie and Sacramental Ontology: A Return to Mystery* (Oxford: Oxford University Press, 2009), Introduction, pp. 1–10.
Boland, Vivian, *Ideas in God according to Saint Thomas Aquinas: Sources and Synthesis* (Leiden: Brill, 1996).
Caputo, John D., *The Mystical Element in Heidegger's Thought* (New York: Fordham University Press 1986).
Caputo, John D. and Scalon, Michael J., "Introduction. Apology for the Impossible: Religion and Postmodernism", in John D. Caputo and Michael J. Scalon (eds), *God, the Gift and Postmodernism* (Bloomington and Indianapolis: Indiana University Press, 1999), pp. 1–19.
Chenu, Marie-Dominique, *The Scope of the Summa of St. Thomas* (Washington: Thomist Press, 1958).
Chenu, Marie-Dominique, "Vérité évangélique et métaphysique wolfienne à Vatican II", *Revue des Sciences Philosophiques et Théologiques*, 57 (1973), 632–40.
Daley, Brian, "The Nouvelle Théologie and the Patristic Revival: Sources, Symbols and the Science of Theology", *International Journal of Systematic Theology*, 7(4) (October 2005), 362–82.
Daniélou, Jean, "Les Orientations présentes de la pensée religieuse", *Études*, 249 (1946), 5–21.
Fiorenza, Francis Schüssler, *Systematic Theology: Roman Catholic Perspectives* (Minneapolis: Fortress Press, 2011).
Ford, David E., "Introduction to Modern Christian Theology", in *The Modern Theologians* (Oxford: Blackwell, 2005), 1–15.
Garrigou-Lagrange, Réginald, "La nouvelle théologie où va-t-elle?", *Angelicum*, 23 (1946), 126–45.
Gregersen, Niels Henrik, "Hjemløshedens teologi", in *Tankens Magt*, 3 (Copenhagen: Lindhardt og Ringhof, 2006).
Grenz, Stanley J., *Rediscovering the Triune God. The Trinity in Contemporary Theology* (Minneapolis: Fortress Press, 2004).
Hart, David Bentley, *The Beauty of the Infinite: The Aesthetics of Christian Truth* (Grand Rapids, Mich.: W.B. Eerdmans, 2003).
Kerr, Fergus, *After Aquinas: Versions of Thomism* (Malden, Mass.: Blackwell, 2002).
Kerr, Fergus, *Twentieth-Century Catholic Theologians* (Oxford: Blackwell, 2007).
Louth, Andrew, "Is Development a Valid Category for Orthodox Theology?" in *Orthodoxy and Western Culture. A Collection of Essays Honoring Jaroslav Pelikan on his Eightieth Birthday* (Crestwood: St. Vladimir's Seminary Press, 2005).
Marion, Jean-Luc, *The Idol and Distance* (New York: Fordham University Press, 2001).
Marion, Jean-Luc, *Being Given: Toward a Phenomenology of Givenness* (Stanford: Stanford University Press, 2002).
Newman, John Henry, *An Essay on the Development of Christian Doctrine* (Notre Dame, Ind.: University of Notre Dame Press, 1845/1989).

Pelikan, Jaroslav, *The Melody of Theology: A Philosophical Dictionary* (Cambridge, Mass.: Harvard University Press, 1988).

Pelikan, Jaroslav, *What has Athens to do with Jerusalem?* (Michigan: University of Michigan Press, 1997).

Ratzinger, Joseph, *Die Geschichtstheologie des Heiligen Bonaventura* (Munich: Schnell und Steiner, 1959; reprinted 1992). English translation: *The Theology of History in St. Bonaventure* (Chicago: Franciscan Herald Press, 1971).

Ward, Graham, Barth, *Derrida and the Language of Theology* (Cambridge: Cambridge University Press, 1988).

Williams, Rowan, *Wrestling with Angels: Conversations in Modern Theology* (London: SCM Press, 2007).

Yannaras, Christos, *On the Absence and Unknowability of God: Heidegger and the Areopagite* (London: T&T Clark, 2005).

Yannaras, Christos, *Postmodern Metaphysics* (Brookline, Mass.: Holy Cross Orthodox Press, 2004).

Chapter 2
Protestant Theology in the Twentieth Century

Niels Henrik Gregersen

"Protestantism" is a collective designation for the part of Christianity that was generated by the Reformation movements of the sixteenth century. As such, Protestantism is regarded as the third main form of Christianity, alongside the Orthodox and the Roman Catholic churches. Nevertheless, the idea of Protestantism is disputed. A split arose in the nineteenth century between a church-oriented Protestantism and a cultural Protestantism, and it has become more and more difficult in the course of the twentieth century to understand Protestant theology simply as a contrast to Catholic theology.

From Early Protestantism to Neo-Protestantism

In its formative period between ca. 1520 and 1560, Reformation theology was developed by means of scriptural exegesis, sermons, catechisms, occasional and polemical writings – and gradually also in a doctrinal form. The writings of Martin Luther (1483–1545) and John Calvin (1509–64) acquired a particularly normative character in this process, and Luther and Calvin have rightly been called *the Magistral Reformers.* Subsequently, in the period from 1560–1700, a number of various scholastic systems of orthodoxy developed, each linked to a confessional church (Lutheran, Calvinist, etc.) and each with its own confessional texts, catechisms, and theological manuals. It goes without saying that it was not natural in this period to use "Protestantism" as a common concept. Lutherans and Calvinists diverged sharply on central questions such as Christology, sacramental doctrine, and the doctrine of predestination.

This did not change until the period that Ernst Troeltsch calls "Neo-Protestantism" in his book *Protestantisches Christentum und Kirche in der Neuzeit* (1906). The development that culminated in New Protestantism began with the Peace of Westphalia in 1648, which ended the Thirty Years War. Thereafter, not only Lutherans, but also Calvinists and Nonconformists were called Protestants. In England, the poet John Milton speaks in his *Eikonoklastes* (1649) of "the Protestant Religion both abroad and home". As a *Dissenter,* he thereby also distanced himself from the established Church of England. It is clear that it was at this period that people began to be aware of the similarities between the Protestant confessions, and this also reflected the political circumstances of the period: they united in the face of common enemies. There soon emerged a political interest in uniting the Protestant world; this was clearest in Germany, where a "Union church" comprising both Lutheran and Calvinist communities was introduced in Prussia in 1817. This gave rise to the idea of a "Protestant church".

No less a figure than the father of New Protestantism, Friedrich Schleiermacher (1768–1834), put himself at the service of this union-theology. In *Der christliche Glaube* (1821/1822, 1831), Lutheranism and Calvinism are placed side by side. Schleiermacher also formulated the idea of Protestantism as a special form of Christianity that differs from the Catholic church through its view of the individual's role in relation to God: "[T]he antithesis between Protestantism and Catholicism may provisionally be conceived thus: the former makes the individual's relation to the church dependent on his [or her] relation to Christ, while the latter contrariwise makes the individual's relation to Christ dependent on his [or her] relation to the Church" (1831, § 24).[1] According to Schleiermacher, Protestantism eliminates the church as a necessary mediator between the believer and God. The church's fellowship is the *result* of the fact that people believe in God through Christ; the church is not the necessary *presupposition* for faith. Schleiermacher thus leaves the door ajar for the possibility that Christianity can grow out beyond the church – for why cannot the individual's relationship to God be realized outside the church?

Neo-Protestantism thus takes on two principal forms, depending on whether the theological identity is linked to an ecclesial consciousness or to a Protestant educational culture. Even in Schleiermacher's days, Protestantism began to be perceived as a form of mentality that in principle can flourish outside the church. Developing ideas of the philosopher G.W.F. Hegel (1770–1831), the theologian F.C. Baur (1792–1860) can speak of a *Protestant principle*: "the autonomy of the subject as opposed to the heteronomy in the Catholic concept of the church."[2] The antithesis is between faith's free self-determination in Protestantism and Catholicism's demand for external obedience. Protestantism is thus perceived as a form of consciousness that operates in the sphere of culture and of consciousness, rather than as a theological position with a specific doctrinal content. Even in the more confessional theology, Protestantism begins to be defined on the basis of brief formulae and principles. This was how Schleiermacher's pupil and successor, August Twesten (1789–1876), applied the concept of Protestantism's two principles: scripture as the *formal principle* and justification by faith alone as the *material principle*.

As a historian, Ernst Troeltsch (1865–1923), whom we have already mentioned, was aware that the Hegelian interpretation of Luther was untenable. He recognized

---

[1] Friedrich Schleiermacher, *Der christliche Glaube nach den Grundsätzen der evangelischen Kirche im Zusammenhange dargestellt* (Berlin: Walter de Gruyter, 1960 [1831]), vol. 1–2, p. 137. English translation after *The Christian Faith*, trans. and ed. H.R. MacIntosh and J.S. Stewart (Edinburgh: T&T Clark, 1989), 102.

[2] F.C. Baur, *Die Epochen der kirchlichen Geschichtsschreibung* (Tübingen, 1952), p. 257, available at www.bibliofile.com/opensource, visited December 22, 2010.

that the Reformation has a Janus face: one face points back to the middle ages, while the other looks ahead and prepares the way for modernity. Troeltsch defines his distinction between Old and New Protestantism on the basis of whether Protestantism presupposes a uniform confessional church or grows out over its own ecclesial form. According to this construction of history, Neo-Protestantism shows that Christianity has detached itself from its historical-ecclesial form. The essence of Protestantism now becomes something that develops en route. One example of this is the *historical-critical method* in biblical research, which made its breakthrough in the course of the nineteenth century. Protestant theology in the nineteenth century can thus be described as a conflict between confessionalism and cultural Protestantism. The Neo-Kantian theologian Albrecht Ritschl (1822–89) formulated the matter as follows: theology is not a circle around a centre, but an ellipse with two focal points, the church and culture.

Dialectical Theology and the Rediscovery of What the Reformers Intended

The early dialectical theology (ca. 1920–33) brought a revolt against the Protestant educational culture. The dialectical theologians included *Karl Barth* (1886–1968), *Friedrich Gogarten* (1887–1967), *Eduard Thurneysen* (1888–1974), and *Emil Brunner* (1889–1966). From ca. 1923, the existential theologian *Rudolf Bultmann* (1884–1976) joined the group. *Paul Tillich* (1886–1965) was on the outskirts of the group. He never felt completely at home in the either/or thinking that was typical of dialectical theology from the outset.

For Barth and the other dialectical theologians, God is *das ganz Andere*, "that which is utterly other". Accordingly, Barth says in the foreword to the second edition of *Der Römerbrief* (1922) that if now he does indeed at last have a theological system, it consists in maintaining everywhere Kierkegaard's infinite qualitative difference between time and eternity: "God is in heaven and you are on earth."[3] Contact is made only where the revelation strikes the human person like a bombshell. But it cannot be held fast: it does not leave the bomb crater. This means that the locus of theology is in the *ruins* of culture. Correspondingly, the time of theology is the *moment*. Revelation touches the human person only in the point where it strikes him. God comes to the human person from the outside, as the event that is always a surprise.

This led to the accusation that liberal theology had put the human being in the center, rather than God. "God means the radical denial and abolition of the human person," declared Bultmann.[4] And so Gogarten could say that the First World War meant the unmasking of cultural Protestantism's illusion about human development. The young dialectical theologians felt that they were positioned "between the times" – beyond the old time, which is past, and ahead of the new time, which will come if

---

[3] Karl Barth, *Der Römerbrief* (Munich: Chr. Kaiser, 1922), p. xiii.

[4] Rudolf Bultmann, *Glauben und Verstehen. Gesammelte Aufsätze* (Tübingen: Mohr-Siebeck, 1933), p. 2.

God wills. They gave their periodical, which was published from 1923 to 1933, the apt name *Zwischen den Zeiten* ("between the times").

It was not for nothing that Paul Tillich called the young dialectical thinkers the "crisis theologians." The religious calm and control in confessional Protestantism no longer existed. Troeltsch's endeavor to base Protestantism on anything other than the word of the Bible and the reality of the church seemed vacuous. The dialectical theologians sensed a theological betrayal behind all this. The American theologian H.R. Niebuhr later described this betrayal as follows: "A God without wrath brought men without sin into a kingdom without judgment through the ministrations of a Christ without a cross."[5]

Dialectical theology was thus a child of the cultural crisis after World War I. But it was also an attempt to return to the agenda of the Reformation: God's Word criticizes the human being who is too much enamored of himself and the church that is all too self-satisfied. They understood themselves as Protestant theologians of the Word of God who concentrated on the revelation in Christ. It is not by chance that the Luther renaissance too occurred in the 1920s and 1930s. The concept of "Protestantism" was now employed only as a historical designation, not as a theological self-description.

The concerns of dialectical theology continued to determine the period up to ca. 1970. After 1933, however, the movement split into a predominantly existentialist-theological direction (Bultmann) and a predominantly ecclesial-dogmatic direction (Barth). Various forms of *Wort-Gottes-Theologie* ("Word of God theology", which is rendered less precisely as "neo-orthodoxy" in Anglo-American books) were developed. One decisive dividing line was the question of how far there existed "general points of contact" for faith, either in the existential experience of the human person (Bultmann), in an already-existing revelation in creation (Althaus and Brunner), or in the dynamic structures of created things (Løgstrup, Wingren, and Prenter). Barth rejected any idea of points of contact in the creation, the human person, or history. Protestant theology has only one center, namely, the revelation in Christ. Tillich, however, developed a methodology of correlation with two focal points: the human person's question and revelation's answer. Barth's ecclesial theology and Tillich's cultural theology thus demonstrate the wide spectrum in Protestant theology in the period from 1945 to 1970.

Karl Barth and the Turning to the Church

Barth's great exegetical discovery in his lectures on the Letter to the Romans was that Paul's expression *pistis theou*, which is normally translated as the human person's faith in God, can be better understood as God's faith in the human person. The human person is not justified by the power of his own faith, but by the power of God's faithfulness vis-à-vis the human person. The theme of the Letter to the Romans is not the ever-shifting viewpoints of the human person, but God's eternal standpoint.

---

[5] H. Richard Niebuhr, *The Kingdom of God in America* (Chicago: Willet Clark, 1937), p. 193.

When Barth speaks in this way, he is following in the footsteps of both Kant and Kierkegaard. Barth has learned from Kant and his Neo-Kantian teachers that God cannot be grasped in the categories of the human understanding. Barth has also learned from Kant that one should always inquire into the conditions that make it possible for something to be known. And this epistemological possibility is God's self-revelation in Christ. Barth has learned from Kierkegaard that the revelation exists only in the momentary point of intersection between time and eternity.

In his dialectical-theological period, Barth formulated this in extremely sharp terms. But it is well known that nothing can be formulated in this extreme manner for long: the continuous dialectic between God's "no" to all that is human and God's "yes" to the human person in Christ gradually threatened to become a vacuous circle. From the mid-1920s, Barth devoted himself to a reconstruction of the theological doctrinal tradition, which he subsequently elaborated in his *magnum opus*, *Die kirchliche Dogmatik*, translated into English as *Church Dogmatics* (hereafter KD/CD), which he began in 1932. Nine thousand pages later, it remained unfinished at his death in 1968. With its massive learning and its theological incisiveness, it stands as the principal theological work of the twentieth century.

Naturally, there has been much discussion of the reasons that led Barth to turn to the church. Was this a discontinuity or a continuity? His contemporaries tended to interpret this as a discontinuity. This thesis could also explain why Bultmann and Barth parted company in 1933, although they took the same line politically in the encounter with Nazism. The idea of a U-turn could also legitimate the view that one could hold fast to the young, "wild" Barth but need not take heed of the older, "dogmatic" Barth. Today, however, there is a stronger tendency to see Barth's development as an organic movement that with an inherent necessity led Barth to develop the positivity of which we have already seen traces in the early crisis-theology. In both cases, the theme is God's faithfulness, not the human person's faith or lack of faith. The decisive point is that God from all eternity has chosen to say "yes" to the human person, despite the human person's continual reservations. The theme of the Gospel is God's great freedom, not the many small freedoms of the human person.

Barth's theological strategy can be compared to an hourglass. He begins with a series of "no's" (corresponding to the narrowing-down of the hourglass). Theology *cannot* build on the religious experiences of the human person, nor can it construct a natural theology that attempts to speak about God on the basis of universally human experiences. In 1934, Barth published the book *Nein!*, in which he totally rejected the natural theology that he saw emerging in his earlier fellow combatant, Emil Brunner. The point in KD is that *everything* in theology must be deduced from God's one self-revelation in Christ (corresponding to the mid-point of the hourglass). But Barth thinks universally on the basis of Christ as the only mid-point and criterion. The decisive thing is God's decision to save *every* human being, not only the Christian or the religiously-minded, but also the godless person. This brings Barth to his christological universalism (corresponding to the lower part of the hourglass).

The background to this universalism is, not least, Barth's epoch-making rehabilitation of Trinitarian doctrine. He posited here a theological norm for

Protestant theology, which won more general acceptance only in the course of the 1960s, in theologians such as Wolfhart Pannenberg, Jürgen Moltmann, Robert Jenson, and Eberhard Jüngel. Barth's claim was that the inner threeness in God can be seen from the revelation in Christ:

1. *God* (the Father) reveals himself.
2. God reveals himself *through himself* (the Holy Spirit).
3. God reveals himself *as himself* (the Son).[6]

The parallel to Hegel's Trinitarian doctrine here is striking:[7] God is the consciousness (the Father) that thinks itself as object (the Son) and realizes itself in the world through the Spirit. But Barth claimed that the doctrine of the Trinity is implicit in the incarnation. It is not in the Zeitgeist, but in Christ that God has revealed himself fully. And here, God has revealed *himself*. We cannot say (as in eastern Orthodoxy) that God remains an ineffable mystery. Nor can we say (as in Thomas Aquinas) that we can draw near to God only through analogical inferences from this world. Nor can we say (as in Luther) that there is a hidden God behind the revealed God. Revelation, in the midst of time, is God's self-disclosure of who God himself is and who he will remain for all eternity.

Once again, we notice the claim about the exclusiveness of revelation. Here too, however, Barth's narrow particularism also contains the strongest conceivable universalism. This is a consequence of the logic of the revelation itself: for *if* the human being Jesus is eternally at home in the eternal life of the Trinity, then humanity too belongs eternally in God. Barth could thus publish a little book in 1956 with the title *Die Menschlichkeit Gottes* (English translation, *The Humanity of God*, 1960). Since God does not want to be self-sufficient, he creates a place for that which is other, namely, the created world. And since God himself is human, he wishes the human person to be his partner.

This had already earlier, between 1936 and 1942, found expression in Barth's radical new interpretation of the doctrine of God's predestination. In Christ, all are chosen for salvation: "In him, God has chosen us" (Eph 1:4). Predestination is God's great "yes" to the human person. At the same time, however, Barth agrees with the tradition that God's will also contains a "no," that is to say, a judgment of the human person's desperate attempts to live on his own, without God. The sinner is to live, but sin is to die. Before all the ages, God has chosen the human person for bliss and life; he has reserved for himself – for the Son – rejection, condemnation, and death.[8]

---

[6] Karl Barth, *Die kirchliche Dogmatik*, I/1 (Munich: Chr. Kaiser and Zurich: EVZ), 1932, p. 312. English translation as *Church Dogmatics*, 1/1, trans. and ed. G.W. Bromiley and T.F. Torrance (Edinburgh: T&T Clark, 1936), p. 296.

[7] Wolfhart Pannenberg, *Problemgeschichte der neueren evangelischen Theologie in Deutschland* (Göttingen: Vandenhoeck & Ruprecht, 1997), pp. 248–60.

[8] Barth, *Kirchliche Dogmatik*, II/2, p. 177; *Church Dogmatics* II/2, pp. 161–62.

In this way, predestination is not a disturbing doctrine about God's hidden pronouncement of judgment, but the Gospel in a nutshell.

The Correlation between Church Theology and Cultural Theology

Let us now look at Tillich's cultural-theological alternative to Barth, since he brings a new tone into Protestant theology. Barth and Bultmann were solidly planted in a German tradition, but Paul Tillich came to have an international career as an American theologian. And while there remained an almost polemical note to Barth's and Bultmann's emphasis on the Bible and preaching, Tillich formulated a cultural theology with a center that can lie everywhere in the world of culture.

Tillich develops a number of elements from the liberal theological tradition. For example, he takes over the idea of the Protestant principle, but in a new interpretation: just as the Old Testament prophets criticized the cult, so too Protestantism criticizes religious symbols. Jesus' cross is unique because it is a self-abolishing symbol. At the same time, however, there is an inherent relationship between the Protestant principle and the Catholic principle, which presupposes the sacramental presence of the holy in time and space. The Protestant appreciation of the distance between God and the world must be balanced by the Catholic appreciation of God as present in existence. Protestantism and Catholicism are not mere opposites; each needs the other.

As early as 1919, Tillich proposed a program for a cultural theology. Its first task is to present an analysis of the religious situation both within and outside the church. Its second task is to draft how religion can find new forms where the old forms have become rigid. Religion thus constitutes the substance or deep dimension of culture, while culture always creates the form of the religious content. Tillich saw contemporary expressionist painting as an example of how the religious content breaks open forms. An *ultimate concern* makes its presence felt in the very heart of the secularity of culture. Like his teacher Troeltsch, Tillich held that a more tradition-oriented theology, with its center in the church's life, must be supplemented by a cultural theology. According to Tillich, however, it would be best if the types of theology could be practiced by one and the same person.

He sees the mistake of traditional theism as the view that God is a separate object "out there" or "up there," whereas God is in the depth, in the very presupposition for human existence. He agrees with F.W.J. Schelling (1775–1854) that God is both ground and abyss. In *The Courage to Be* (1954), Tillich correspondingly interprets faith as a vital energy that must continually be won in a struggle against the fear and doubt that dwell within the human person. Luther asked: "How do I find a merciful God?" But the modern question is: "How do I find a God at all?" Doubt belongs to faith. But faith defies doubt, when it is taken hold of by God as the power in existence, and then overcomes doubt. Faith is not a faith in this or that, but an absolute faith that there *is* meaning and hope, even where one cannot see meaning or hope. The human person must accept being accepted in spite of his unacceptability. This is how Tillich reformulates Luther's doctrine of justification.

Tillich wrote his *Systematic Theology* I-III (hereafter: ST) between 1951 and 1963. Characteristically, he called his work a systematic theology rather than dogmatics or doctrine. The inner coherence in Tillich's thinking is a result of his reformulation of Christianity in a philosophical language. The young Tillich spoke of cultural theology and church theology as two separate tasks, but Tillich now formulates his *correlative methodology*: "Theology formulates the questions implied in human existence, and theology formulates the answers implied in divine self-manifestation under the guidance of the questions implied in human existence."[9] There is a fruitful circle between the questions and the answers, and they can never be separated. One cannot merely say (as Karl Barth did) that God has *genuinely* revealed himself in Christ and that all that is needed is to bring the human person to discover this. God can reveal himself only in such a way that he manifests himself to a human being. Phenomenologically speaking, a revelation is always a revelation of something *to someone.* Here, Tillich is much closer to Bultmann's existential theology, but whereas Bultmann's central interest is in the human person's self-understanding, Tillich is interested in the human person's location in a universe that is larger than just the human person.

This means that Tillich's theology has an ontological orientation from start to finish. God is the power to be in everything and over everything that exists[10] – a formulation that was later adopted by K.E. Løgstrup. God's creative power expresses itself *in* the world, but always in such a way that the power of being extends beyond that which exists, which always and everywhere makes its way towards annihilation. As the source of all that is, God is beyond everything that exists. What we say about God has only a symbolic-metaphorical character, with the exception of the one affirmation that God is Being itself! If we think of God without thinking of existence, we eliminate God. "God" means simply: the one who gives us a share in existence.

Theology under the Shadow of Secularization (1960–80)

Between 1960 and 1980, the "Word of God" theology ceased to be the fundamental paradigm around which there was a consensus. Barth's famous dictum that theology is necessary because one has to preach on Sunday was no longer seen as an adequate description of the tasks of theology in a situation in which religious communication became fluid and took place in many different media. At the same time, the center of gravity in theology moved from German to Anglo-American theology. A more psychological attitude to faith and tradition became general, making less plausible the position held by the Reformers that faith is created in the encounter with God's Word. Faith became first Christianity, then religion, then religiosity, and finally spirituality and a way to cope with existential crises ("religious coping"). Around 1970, it appeared that secularization was in the process of becoming established

---

[9] Paul Tillich, *Systematic Theology* (Chicago: University of Chicago Press, 1952), vol. 1, p. 61.
[10] Tillich, *Systematic Theology*, vol. 1, p. 236.

everywhere, either as a farewell to faith or as a dilution of faith to a mental echo of an ecclesial-religious tradition that had been richer in content. Many regarded the dictum of Dietrich Bonhoeffer (1906–45) that "we are going towards a time without religion" as an accurate analysis of the age.

The theological proposals to encounter the new situation took a variety of forms. At the more desperate end of the spectrum, a number of "death of God" theologies were elaborated in the 1960s. Gabriel Vahanian published *The Death of God* (1961), Harvey Cox *The Secular City* (1965), and Thomas J.J. Altizer *The Gospel of Christian Atheism* (1966). Others attempted to follow up Paul Tillich by reconstructing the idea of God on the basis of an understanding of God as the power of being that sets us free. The Anglican bishop John A.T. Robinson's *Honest to God* (1963) was a bestseller. Others, such as Bultmann's students Ernst Fuchs (1903–83) and Gerhard Ebeling (1912–2001), insisted that the point of Christianity lies in "speech events" that belong to the Gospel without being linked to a metaphysical-religious interpretation of life. Finally, political theologians such as the young Jürgen Moltmann (b. 1926) or Dorothee Sölle (1929–2003) attempted to translate the religious semantics of Christianity into praxis for a new political world order.

Contemporaries tended to see these various directions as incompatible, since despite overlappings, they fought against one another in the manner of distinct schools. From a larger perspective, however, one can see these approaches as varied theological answers to one and the same analysis of the period: namely, that religion had had its day. The underlying theological agenda was therefore to identify how little one actually needed to believe in order to continue be some kind of Christian. In positive terms, we could say that they were attempting to track down the experiences that could make Christianity comprehensible to a secularized epoch. They tried to combine the minimalistic theology with an experiential theology that put words to experiences of transcendence in the midst of daily life.

Where the dialectical theology had claimed that religious experiences were merely expressions of the human person's cultivation of his own self, *experiences* now became the battle-cry that resounded from all sides. In the same spirit, several attempts were made to take up anew the numerous problems that were posed in the tradition of liberal theology. Political theology asks: What is the relationship between faith and society? The discipline of "theology and natural science" asks: What is the relationship between faith and modern science? The psychology of religion and practical theology ask: What is the relationship between Christianity and spirituality? The discipline of "theology of religions" asks: What is the relationship between Christianity and the other religions? Barth had criticized all these "hyphenated theologies," but the neoliberal tendency can be seen as an attempt to recreate points of contact between theology and culture after the collapse of the dialectical theology.[11]

This neoliberal trend played a considerable role not least in Protestant theology, supported by the alliance between secular humanism and Protestant Christianity that

---

[11] Niels Henrik Gregersen, *Teologi og kultur. Protestantismen mellem isolation og assimilation i det 19. og 20. århundrede* (Aarhus: Aarhus University Press, 2001 [1988]).

had developed after World War II. The problem for experiential theology is however that it presupposes the idea that underneath all the culturally determined differences, human beings are homogeneous. Bultmann spoke of the perennial problems of existence, the theologian and philosopher Løgstrup spoke of the "pre-cultural," Paul Tillich of the ultimate concern, and the Catholic Karl Rahner of the supernatural existential. But what if people have experiences of different kinds? Just as the uniform Protestant culture lost terrain, so too the reference to universal experiences lost its immediate plausibility.

Accordingly, the demand that theology should be close to experience led already in the 1980s to a new slogan about the *contextuality* of theology. Theology's dependence on time, place, and perspective was emphasized not least by liberation theology and feminist theology. The watchword now was that theology ought not only to interpret the world, but to change it. This led to increasing questions about the inherent tendency to essentialism in experiential theology. The development within feminist theology can exemplify the problem: whereas women's theology in the 1970s began with a strong appeal to women's special experiences (experiences of giving birth, group experiences, etc.), feminist theology today acknowledges the cultural conditioning of experiences. This anti-essentialism is due to the influence of postmodernism: particular experiences cannot be called "fundamental" or "typical" of women or of men. Black women began to elaborate a *womanism*, Spanish-speaking women a *mujerista* movement, East Asian women a *minjun* theology. Contextual consciousness was winning acceptance within theology.

The Interventions and Ambiguities of American Evangelical Theology

After World War II, conservative groups of "Evangelical Theology" grew up on American soil, first in a reaction to the liberal mainstream Protestantism of their day, and later to the experiences of secularization and diffusion of beliefs. Some of these groups were, and still are, straightforward fundamentalists; membership in the *The Evangelical Theological Society* (founded in 1949) thus requires its members to affirm, "The Bible alone and the Bible in its entirety is the Word of God written, and therefore inerrant in the original autographs."[12] However, many self-designated proponents of "Evangelical theology" (in this US-American sense) today employ much softer hermeneutical approaches to scripture. In reality, evangelical theologians today can be classified in very various groups.

One of the still virulent debates within Evangelicalism can be traced back to the Great Awakenings of the 1730s and 1740s. Some, in the Calvinist tradition, followed the principles of the Synod of Dort (1618–19), later abbreviated into the acronym of TULIP: *T*otal depravity (strong view of original sin), *U*nconditional election (God's election does not depend on human preparations), *L*imited atonement (not all will

---

[12] Quoted from Roger E. Olson, *A–Z of Evangelical Theology* (London: SCM Press, 2005), p. 75.

be saved), *I*rresistible grace (if you get the offer of grace, you cannot refuse), and *P*erseverance of the saints (once saved always saved). Others, in the tradition of the Wesley brothers, followed the view of Jacob Arminius (1560–1609) that God wants to save all human beings, and that God gives all human beings chances of conversion, yet requires a positive response of faith in order for salvation to be realized. These controversies on the relation of divine grace and human personal assent are similar to but not quite identical with the older debate on free will between Martin Luther and Erasmus of Rotterdam (1524–25). For John and Charles Wesley, and those following their version of Evangelicalism, never speak of a human will as independent from God's "prevenient grace." In general it can be said that while most Congregationalists and some Baptists have been on the Reformed side, the Methodists, another part of the Baptists, and all Pentecostals follow the Arminian track.

This debate was re-articulated when Clark Pinnock (1937–2000) formed a group of Evangelical scholars (covering John Sanders and Gregory Boyd) around the idea of "the openness of God," or *Open Theism*. Their basic argument is that God, by creating a world endowed with freedom, gives up a full and predeterminative foreknowledge of future things, in order to elicit a human response of faith: a free and un-coerced response, yet facilitated by divine grace. God thus takes genuine risks in creation by risking a No by human beings to the offering of grace. Even though this view was ruled out as un-Evangelical by the *Evangelical Theological Society* in 2001, its emphasis on human freedom finds many followers in evangelical circles in America, and elsewhere. Proponents of open theism have even established a dialogue with the much more liberal group of process theologians, with which open theism shares the conviction that God is active by persuasion, but not by coercing human beings.[13] However, the long-term impact of open theism is still unclear. Conflicts continue with the Reformed varieties of Evangelical theology, and the risk-view of salvation also speaks against the instincts of contemporary Barthianism. But also seen as a whole, the movement of evangelical theology seems to have exercised only a fairly limited influence on academic theology.

From Neoliberalism to Post-liberalism (1980–2000)

Yet also the attempt by neoliberal theology to speak "from experience to experience" rather than "from faith to faith" (Rom 1:17) remained an intermezzo, although the problem it addressed remains with us. Gradually, the question of the representative character of theology came to be raised, for ultimately, it is not only decisive who writes theology, but also who reads it and makes use of it. Here, Protestant theology was approaching a problem of which Orthodox and Catholic theologians have always been aware: namely, theology's need of a public reception that involves de facto existing churches and communities.

---

[13] John B. Cobb and Clark H. Pinnock (eds), *Searching for an Adequate God. A Dialogue between Process and Free Will Theists* (Grand Rapids, MI: Eerdmans, 2000).

Societal questions brought up this question anew. As early as ca. 1980, it was clear that secularization went hand in hand with a desecularization, even in Europe (which otherwise had been the empirical basis for thesis of a progressive and irreversible secularization). Protestant theology was now confronted with a multireligious situation. For a long time, the Roman Catholic and the Orthodox churches had been on the periphery of the theological consciousness in Protestant Northern Europe and the United States – but no longer. Other religions such as Islam, Hinduism, and Buddhism too became neighbors, thanks to immigration and conversion. This meant that Protestantism lost its hegemonic status as the leading educational culture that had created a synthesis between secular skepticism and cultural Protestantism. Mainstream Protestantism was no longer mainstream culture.

This makes it difficult to argue by means of an appeal to general common sense. The idea of "common sense" must be combined with a "communal sense," that is to say, the appreciation that theology must always be aware of its own perspective when it speaks on behalf of particular cultural or religious fellowships. Theology's ecclesial anchoring thus becomes visible again, no longer as a theological postulate, but as the expression of a particular ecclesial and cultural embedding. It now becomes necessary to take seriously the specific universes of meaning that are represented by different religious groups. In this situation, theology cannot be content to formulate the most minimal Christianity that will repel as few people as possible. The task is to present constructive proposals for an interpretation of Christianity that is able to enter into a constructive dialogue with other religions and with representatives of non-religious worldviews. Religious pluralism makes a comparative theology of religion necessary, while at the same time creating the need for religious clarity.

One example of this is post-liberal theology. This term was already used in the 1960s with reference to Yale professor H. Richard Niebuhr (1894–1962), who together with his brother Reinhold Niebuhr (1892–1971) had formulated a culture-critical "neo-orthodox" theology directed against the contemporary American belief in progress. But it was only in the 1970s that a genuine post-liberal school came into being at Yale. The Lutheran ecumenical scholar George Lindbeck (born 1923) drew attention to post-liberalism in his programmatic book *The Nature of Doctrine* (1984), where he denied that dogmas are to be understood as true affirmations about God as an external reality. The idea of "representing" God is a breach of the prohibition against making images of God. But Lindbeck also rejects liberal theology's idea that dogmas are symbols that merely express what human beings feel when they have experiences of God. Neither the pre-modern "propositional" understanding of dogmas nor modernity's "experiential-expressive" understanding is tenable.

Lindbeck's "post-liberal" solution is that dogmas should rather be understood as *rules* for the understanding of faith and the conduct of life. Dogmas do not *describe* who God is, but *prescribe* how one can draw near to God within the church's fellowship. Faith in God as creator does not entail any knowledge about what happened when God created the world; it guides the faithful in reverence and thankfulness. Faith in Christ as the Son of God does not contain any insight into the relationship between the two natures ("true God and true man"), but means using the stories about Jesus as a model for talking about God and thereby as a paradigm for how we ourselves can become "God's sons and daughters." Faith in God the Holy Spirit does not mean forming opinions about the hidden paths of the Spirit, but knowing where the power of the Holy Spirit can be encountered – in the Word of God, in baptism, and in the Lord's Supper. Inspired by Wittgenstein's theory about language games, Lindbeck calls this post-liberal understanding of dogmas the "cultural-linguistic" interpretation. Dogmas and theological doctrine are meant to guide the church in its use of Christian language in Christian praxis. Christian doctrine as such is not first-order statements about God's being, but second-order statements about the rules one is to follow within a given religious group. At the same time, church doctrine offers paradigmatic examples of how the church's language can in fact sound, when it functions aright.

Up to this point, we can say that Lindbeck understands theology as a normative church theology. On the other hand, he claims that the cultural-linguistic theory, precisely by keeping to the external words and external actions in the church, can in fact describe the church's life in such a way that this can be understood by outsiders. The non-Christian can know what it would mean to be a Christian. A similar method could be applied to Islamic praxis, Hindu praxis, and so on.

Post-liberalism can thus be regarded as a theological response to a situation in which mainstream churches have become minorities. This is why the post-liberals have been accused of being both sectarian and conservative, since they do not have any program for how the churches can develop and for how theology can share constructively in this process. We can however also note that post-liberalism has been able to function as *public theology* in the arenas of public life. Some of the strongest contributions to societal debates have come from circles close to the post-liberals. The Catholic Alasdair MacIntyre (born 1929) and the Methodist Stanley Hauerwas (born 1940) have pointed out separately that morality and values do not have their origin in autonomous, abstract subjects, but in persons who are embedded in moral traditions. It is only through these that one learns what the good life is, and how it could be lived in particular communities. Hauerwas also points out that churches and other faith communities help to form moral persons who are able to take a position on ethical dilemmas. Morality cannot be deduced from abstract principles (as in a Kantian tradition), but has its origin in *stories*. Morality is born in an interplay between small "case-stories" from real life and the great biblical narratives that show what the good life is. The narrative of the Good Samaritan (Luke 10) is one of many examples of how a story can show what the good life is and thus provide inspiration for putting into practice the love of one's neighbor. Against this background, Hauerwas has elaborated a Non-Conformist theological ethic that builds *inter alia* on a pacifist vision.

There is only one short step from this turning of post-liberalism in a new direction to the program for a radical orthodoxy that was elaborated in the 1990s by the English Anglo-Catholic theologian John Milbank (born 1952) and that led to the manifesto *Radical Orthodoxy* (1999). Milbank's claim is that theology cannot be content to reflect on ecclesial praxis (as in Lindbeck). On the contrary, Christianity contains a non-violent ontology that in principle can be reflected upon in every sphere of life.

The movement calls itself "orthodox" because it wants to regain an Augustinian holistic way of thinking about existence. The movement is "radical" both because it wants to return to the roots in the early church and because it makes the case for Christianity as a thoroughgoing confrontation with contemporary culture.

This is because the dominant secular culture is based (according to Milbank) on an ontology that is fundamentally nihilistic, individualistic, and relativistic. The human person is seen as an active being who himself creates his own life. But it is an illusion to think that we merely live in social constructions of existence. In reality, we live on the basis of knowledge, and this comes to us in the form of inspiration. Milbank agrees with Augustine in proposing a theory of illumination: knowledge comes to us in the form of insights, as gifts. But existence itself is also a gift, and the basic Christian idea is that God bestows himself in the gift. The world is woven through and through by God's creative gift, and each one who is given the ability to hand on the gift to others participates in God's life. This ontology of gift is an antithesis to the ontology of struggle that was announced by Marx and Nietzsche and that today functions as a kind of implicit ontology in most academic disciplines. Examples are utilitarianism in economics, the idea of the struggle for power in politics, constructivism in sociology, the idea of contract in legal studies, the idea of rights in ethics, and the theory of selection in biology. Milbank and his colleagues hold that since modernity's unit is the isolated, autonomous subject, its ontology leads almost necessarily to violence. Even psychological models for marriage and love are constructed on a *quid pro quo* idea that presupposes that love's resources are limited. But the Christian ontology claims that existence is a shared project and that less can become more. There is no equilibrium, no shortage of resources in God's existence. It is an excess of existence that continually makes more out of less.

New Alliances

We have seen that after the collapse of the "Word of God" theology ca. 1980, a tension has continued to exist between those theologians who have sought common points of reference with contemporary culture and those who concentrate on clarifying the specific character of Christianity over against other worldviews, whether religious or non-religious. If we now move to leading theologians of Protestant systematic theology in the last decennia, one can observe that this has not been a period for large-scale programs. Yet some exceptions to this rule should be mentioned. The Lutheran theologian Wolfhart Pannenberg (born 1928) has elaborated an overall presentation of the Christian faith in his *Systematische Theologie* I-III (1988–1993). The level of ambition approaches that of Karl Barth's *Kirchliche Dogmatik*, but unlike Barth, Pannenberg draws on philosophy and modern natural science. We should also mention the Lutheran Robert Jenson (born 1930), whose *Systematic Theology* I-II (1997–99) combines a Barthian approach with an emphatic affirmation that the doctrine of the Trinity breaks with an abstract theism. Jenson understands the life of the world as woven together with God's life through Christ, mediated by the church and its sacraments. The perspective of *solus Christus* is here developed into a notion of *totus Christus*, since Christ is never severed from his body, the living church. Others, such as Jürgen Moltmann (born 1926), have chosen to write a series of interconnected monographs on the great themes of theology – from the doctrine of God and creation to ecclesiology and eschatology – on the basis of the presupposition that theology must be formulated as an open system that reflects a contemporary consciousness without forcing theology into a closed, classical form. Jürgen Moltmann may count as probably the single most influential Protestant theologian in the generation after Barth. His work has been read and digested in all parts of global Christianity, and many of his constructive proposals in the doctrine of creation, Christology, and pneumatology have found a wide resonance, both within the academy and in the churches.

When we mention these figures here, this is not only because each of them represents grand-scale attempts to reformulate Christianity for their contemporaries. Pannenberg, Jenson, and Moltmann also show how Protestant theology is no longer formulated in opposition to Roman Catholic or Orthodox theology. This is clearest in Jenson, who founded the *Center for Catholic and Evangelical Theology* with his colleague Carl Braaten in 1991. The view taken here is that Protestant theology, in terms of its own self-understanding, is Catholic (though not Roman Catholic) and that the Protestant interpretation of scripture must be formulated in continuity with the common Christian tradition of the eastern and western churches. Pannenberg also underlines that the Reformers never understood themselves as "Protestants" in the modern sense of the word. They retained their interest in the same problems as the Roman Catholic and the Orthodox traditions. Finally, the Reformed theologian Jürgen Moltmann shows that Protestantism can no longer be identified as an amalgam of Lutheran and Calvinist theology. A number of central problems, such as the theology of the Holy Spirit, were first thematized in the Methodism of the eighteenth century and in the Pentecostalist movements of the twentieth century.

In short, it is difficult to hold onto the picture of Protestantism as a form of Christianity that elaborates its own completely independent tradition in an antithetical relationship to the Orthodox and Roman Catholic traditions. The antitheses remain, but it is precisely in these antitheses that the traditions counterbalance one another.

Bibliography

Barth, Karl, *Der Römerbrief* (Munich: Chr. Kaiser, 1922). English translation: *The Epistle to the Romans*, translated by Edwyn C. Hoskyns (London: Oxford University Press, 1933).

Barth, Karl, *Die Kirchliche Dogmatik*, I/1–IV/4 (Munich: Chr. Kaiser and Zurich: EVZ, 1932–65). English translation: *Church Dogmatics* 1/1–4/4, translated and edited by G.W. Bromiley and T.F. Torrance (Edinburgh: T&T Clark, 1936–69).

Baur, F.C., *Die Epochen der kirchlichen Geschichtsschreibung* (Tübingen, 1952), available at www.bibliofile.com/opensource (accessed December 22, 2010).

Bultmann, Rudolf, *Glauben und Verstehen. Gesammelte Aufsätze* (Tübingen: Mohr-Siebeck, 1933).

Cobb, John B. and Clark H. Pinnock (eds), *Searching for an Adequate God. A Dialogue between Process and Free Will Theists* (Grand Rapids, MI: Eerdmans, 2000).

Gregersen, Niels Henrik, *Teologi og kultur. Protestantismen mellem isolation og assimilation i det 19. og 20. århundrede* (Aarhus: Aarhus University Press, [1988] 2001).

Niebuhr, H. Richard, *The Kingdom of God in America* (Chicago: Willet Clark, 1937).

Olson, Roger E., *A–Z of Evangelical Theology* (London: SCM Press, 2005).

Pannenberg, Wolfhart, *Problemgeschichte der neueren evangelischen Theologie in Deutschland* (Göttingen: Vandenhoeck & Ruprecht, 1997).

Rohls, Jan, *Protestantische Theologie der Neuzeit* I-II (Tübingen: Mohr Siebeck, 1997).

Schleiermacher, Friedrich, *Der christliche Glaube nach den Grundsätzen der evangelischen Kirche im Zusammenhange dargestellt* (1831) (Berlin: Walter de Gruyter 1960), vols 1–2. English translation: *The Christian Faith*, edited by H.R. MacIntosh and J.S. Stewart (Edinburgh: T&T Clark, 1989).

Tillich, Paul, *The Protestant Era* (Chicago: University of Chicago Press, 1957).

Tillich, Paul, *Systematic Theology*, vols 1–3 (Chicago: University of Chicago Press, 1952–63).

Chapter 3
Catholic Theology in the Twentieth Century

Tracey Rowland

The Catholic theological scholarship of the twentieth century is best understood as a development of two different currents in nineteenth-century Catholic thought. On the one hand Catholics of the nineteenth century were contending with the impact of the so-called Age of Enlightenment. This included the promotion of varieties of rationalism which sought to purify intellectual judgements of all attachments to theological beliefs and all movements of the human heart. It also included the rise of liberalism as a political ideology. On the other hand the various Enlightenment projects had themselves been subjected to criticism by the nineteenth-century Romantics. While not denying the significance of the place of reason in human life, the Romantics opposed the tendencies in the Enlightenment legacy to treat the human person as a highly complex machine and to so exalt the universal over the particular that issues like the uniqueness of each human being, their specific personalities and configurations of talents, were of no significance. Above all the Romantics were highly sceptical of the Kantian notion of pure reason. As Hamann expressed the objection, 'reason has a wax nose'. They were however interested in the relationship between reason and tradition, the intellect and the heart, intuition as well as logical deductions (*Vernunft* and *Verstand*), and the themes of individuality and self-development (*Bildung*). While the temper of the Age of Enlightenment was ahistorical, exalting the universal and timeless, the spirit of the Romantics was soaked in historical sensibilities. Since it was the German Romantics who were the most theologically engaged, one finds in German-speaking provinces of the late nineteenth century a network of Catholic theologians addressing Romantic-movement issues. Most prominent of these were those based at the University of Tübingen. The work of the Tübingen scholars also found resonances in the works of the Oxford Anglican-convert John Henry Newman. On the other hand, scholars based at the University of Louvain in Belgium and at the pontifical academies in Rome tended to be focused on what might be called the Enlightenment fronts. Whereas the relationship between history and theology was the central concern of the Romantics, the defence of the reasonableness or truth of Christianity was the central preoccupation of those based in Louvain and Rome. The most prominent schools of twentieth-century Catholic theology can usually be traced back to one of these two orientations.

The Pontificate of Leo XIII and *Aeterni Patris*

Leo XIII's publication of the encyclical *Aeterni Patris* in 1879 had the effect of fostering a renaissance of Thomist scholarship, especially at the University of Louvain and in the Roman pontifical academies and in the American Catholic colleges of higher education. The 'perennial philosophy' of St Thomas was promoted as the antidote to varieties of scepticism, agnosticism and relativism. This project may be characterised as an attempt to answer the Enlightenment charge that the Catholic faith was irrational by the promotion of a hyper-rational neo-scholasticism. Two of its most famous exponents were the Jesuit Louis Cardinal Billot (1846–1931) and the Dominican Reginald Garrigou-Lagrange (1877–1964). Billot was the Professor of Dogmatic Theology at the Gregorian University from 1885 to 1911, while Garrigou-Lagrange held the post of Professor of Dogmatic Theology and Spiritual Theology at the Pontifical University of St Thomas Aquinas (the Angelicum) from 1909 to 1959. The French writer François Mauriac famously dubbed Garrigou-Lagrange 'the Sacred Monster of Thomism'. More recent Catholic authors tend to refer him as the exemplar of a 'Strict Observance Thomism' characterised by the attitude that any patristic thought of any value had been absorbed into Thomism and thus does not merit study on its own terms, that metaphysical system-building is much more important than an analysis of the historical contexts in which theological ideas were forged and that those who want to toy with Romantic movement ideas are crypto 'modernists'.

The term 'Modernism' was used in the encyclical *Pascendi Dominici Gregis* of 1907. In this document, which Billot helped to draft, Pius X condemned a cluster of ideas under the banner of the heresy of 'Modernism'. Although difficult to define precisely, Aidan Nichols has suggested that Modernism was a tendency 'to rely exclusively on historical science so as to determine the theological meaning of biblical and other texts, without acknowledging any rôle for tradition in the hermeneutical process'.[1] The works of Alfred Loisy (1857–1940) and George Tyrell (1861–1909) were treated as prototypical of this heretical orientation. As a caricature one may argue that the Modernists wanted history without tradition and that the Roman proponents of a Strict Observance Thomism wanted tradition without history.

Thomas F. O'Meara OP has summarised the negative aspects of the revival of scholasticism in the century between 1860 and 1960 in the following terms:

> Late nineteenth-century repetitions of medieval thought and baroque scholasticism determined Catholic religious education from catechism to seminary textbook. This restoration was more particularly of philosophy than theology, of Aristotle than Thomas Aquinas, of logic than of Christology. A non-voluntaristic and free theology of grace found in Aquinas was re-formed into a theology of propositional faith, ontology and church authority. A lack of sophistication in method, a questionable

---

[1] Aidan Nichols, *Catholic Thought Since the Enlightenment* (Leominster, 1998), p. 84.

arrangement of disciplines, an absence of history, a moralistic interdiction of other theologies even when based upon Scripture and tradition characterised this theology.[2]

To O'Meara's summary can be added Jean Daniélou's criticism that scholasticism 'located reality in essences rather than in subjects, and by so doing ignored the dramatic world of persons, of universal concretes transcending all essence and only distinguished by their existence'.[3] This was a significant problem since varieties of existentialism and personalism were the dominant philosophical influences on European society after the First World War. These philosophies were focused on what Daniélou called 'the dramatic world of persons'. A Catholic theology that was mute on these issues and which congratulated itself on being 'above history' was not well equipped to address the existential anguish of the generations who endured two world wars, genocide and an economic depression.

Ressourcement Theologians

In 1903, a French philosopher and layman, Maurice Blondel (1861–1949), addressed the history versus doctrine problem. Blondel sought to overcome the dualism by developing a notion of the incarnation of dogma *within* history and he argued that the synthesis of dogma and history lies 'neither in the facts alone, nor in the ideas alone, but in the Tradition which embraces within it the facts of history, the efforts of reason and the accumulated experience of the faithful'.[4] Yves Congar summarised Blondel's approach in the following terms:

> Over against these two opposing caricatures [the hostile to history stance of the Strict Observance Thomists and the historical relativism of the Modernists] Blondel set tradition, in which history and dogmas are united by a live current passing in both directions – from the facts to the dogma, and from faith to the facts. To oppose the data of history and the statements of dogma was to make an unwarranted separation between the two elements of a single reality with an essentially religious nature.[5]

Along with Catholic laymen in French literary circles, above all Charles Péguy and Paul Claudel, Blondel led the way to an expansion of the theological horizons. The inter-war generation of French Jesuit and Dominican clergy based at Fourviére and Le Saulchoir pioneered what became known as the *ressourcement* (back to the

---

[2] Thomas F. O'Meara, *Church and Culture: German Catholic Theology 1860–1914* (Indiana, 1991), p. 50.
[3] Jean Daniélou, 'Les orientations presents de la Pensée religieuse', *Études* 249 (1946), p. 14.
[4] Maurice Blondel, *The Letter on Apologetics & History and Dogma* (Grand Rapids, 1995), p. 257.
[5] Yves Congar, *Tradition and Traditions* (London, 1960–63), pp. 215–16.

sources) project. This took the form of retrieving elements of the neglected patristic heritage with reference to contemporary social problems. The leading names were Marie-Dominique Chenu OP, Yves Congar OP, Jean Daniélou SJ and Henri de Lubac SJ. The work of Erich Przywara SJ (1889–1972) and Romano Guardini (1885–1968) in Germany, though not formally part of the *Sources chrétiennes* translation of patristic and medieval texts project, shared the *ressourcement* property of working beyond the scholastic frameworks. From 1922 to 1941 Erich Przywara was a member of the editorial board of the influential *Stimmen der Zeit*. He wrote numerous essays on contemporary pastoral problems with reference to the great names in European letters. Scholars from St Augustine through to Nietzsche, Bergson, Scheler and Gadamer were evidently on his radar screen. Przywara also fostered the translation of Newman into German and published some significant works on St Augustine. Guardini was similarly at home in the broader world of European thought. Karl Rahner described him as a 'Christian humanist who led Germany's Catholics out of an intellectual and culture ghetto and into the contemporary world', while Joseph Ratzinger spoke of Guardini's 'flair for seizing upon philosophical questions of life and existence of the time between and after the world wars, and illustrating them with literary themes or with great figures of faith'.[6]

In the 1940s the *ressourcement* theologians came under heavy criticism from the proponents of Strict Observance Thomism. In 1946 Reginald Garrigou-Lagrange published a watershed article in the journal *Angelicum*.[7] It was titled 'La nouvelle théologie où va-t-elle?' His charge was that the *ressourcement* theologians were heading into the dangerous territory of Modernism. These alarm bells were echoed in the 1950 encyclical *Humani Generis* which was devoted to the topic of 'new theological opinions threatening to undermine the foundations of Catholic doctrine'. Although the *ressourcement* theologians were never named the encyclical was widely interpreted as referring to their project. In particular there were references to the importance of the doctrinal principle that grace is gratuitous. This was popularly construed as a reference to Henri de Lubac who was critical of the 'two-tier' or 'extrinsicist' account of the nature and grace relationship then being taught in all the seminaries. De Lubac argued that the two-tiered account was a baroque-era (especially Cajetanian and Suárezian) mutation of classical Thomism. In the post-*Humani Generis* theological climate many of the *ressourcement* theologians found themselves marginalised and their research and teaching severely restricted for a decade. Fergus Kerr has written

---

[6] R.A. Krieg, *Romano Guardini: The Precursor to Vatican II* (Indiana, 1997) and V. Cosemius, 'The Condemnation of Modernism and the Survival of Catholic Theology', in Gregory Baum (ed.), *The Twentieth Century: A Theological Overview* (London, 1999), p. 21.

[7] Reginald Garrigou-Lagrange, 'La nouvelle théologie où va-t-elle?', *Angelicum*, 23 (1946), 126–45. For a discussion of the politics of the period see Aidan Nichols, 'Thomism and the Nouvelle Théologie', in *Beyond the Blue Glass: Catholic Essays on Faith and Culture*, vol. 1 (London, 2002), pp. 33–53.

that these debates over the relationship between nature and grace were the bitterest Catholic theological disputes of the twentieth century.[8]

The Second Vatican Council (1962–5)

Notwithstanding their decade in the wilderness, many of the *ressourcement* theologians were invited to attend the Second Vatican Council as '*Periti*' or expert theological advisors to the bishops. Although the *Periti* could not take part in the debates themselves they exercised an enormous influence over those debates through the advice they gave to their bishops and through their work as members of drafting committees for the various documents. *Periti* from Germany, France, Belgium and Holland so heavily influenced the direction of the debates that it became popular to speak of the Council as a moment in ecclesial time when 'the Rhine flowed into the Tiber'. The most prominent *Periti* included: Karl Rahner SJ (1904–84), Hans Küng (1928–), Yves Congar OP (1904–95), Joseph Ratzinger (now Benedict XVI) (1927–), Henri de Lubac SJ (1896–1991) and Jean Daniélou SJ (1905–74). Edward Schillebeeckx (1914–2009) is often cited as a Conciliar *peritus*, though legally he did not enjoy this status. His nomination was rejected by the Holy Office. Nonetheless he was retained by the Dutch bishops as an unofficial advisor and the fact that he was not granted an official status gave him more political space in which to operate. He was not constrained by the confidentiality oaths taken by those who were official *Periti*.[9]

Although the popular press reported the Conciliar debates in terms of divisions between conservatives and progressives, the divisions were never so simplistic. There were in fact at least three significant groups: those wedded to pre-Conciliar scholasticism, in particular to a Suárezian-infused Thomism, those fostering a synthesis of Thomist and Kantian thought, often described as Transcendental Thomism, such as Karl Rahner, and those who followed the decidedly anti-Kantian trajectory of the *ressourcement* theologians, above all, Henri de Lubac. Underpinning these camps there are not only different accounts of the relationship between faith and reason but different accounts of the relationship between nature and grace. Rahner's account of the nature and grace relationship has been characterised as one of naturalising the supernatural, de Lubac's one of supernaturalising the natural, and the Thomists of the Strict Observance wanted to keep nature and grace in separate baskets or 'extrinsically-related'.[10] These three theological clusters ('schools' would be too strong a description) not only represent different interpretations of the Thomist tradition and different judgements about how that tradition may legitimately be developed, but different interpretations of the documents of the Second Vatican Council. The documents themselves bear the hallmarks of the

---

[8] Fergus Kerr, *After Aquinas: Versions of Thomism* (Oxford, 2002), p. 134.
[9] Fergus Kerr, *Twentieth-Century Catholic Theologians: From Neoscholasticism to Nuptial Mysticism* (Oxford, 2007), p. 54.
[10] John Milbank, *Theology and Social Theory: Beyond Secular Reason* (Oxford, 1990), p. 207.

different orientations, and in some cases alternating paragraphs can be identified with the different positions. What were merely general orientations at the Council hardened into different theological camps as the 1960s wore on.

Post-*Humanae Vitae* Fallout

An issue in the air at the time of the Council was that of the moral status of the newly available contraceptive pill. In 1963 John XXIII established a Papal Commission on Population and Birth Control to consider the issue. In 1966 the Commission delivered to Paul VI a majority report (in favour of the pill) and a minority report (against the pill). Although the reports were never officially released, versions were leaked and published by *The Tablet*.[11] This had the effect of creating an expectation that the Church was about to reverse her teaching against contraception as the Church of England had already done in 1930. Contrary to such public expectations, however, in 1968 Paul VI issued his encyclical *Humanae Vitae* which reaffirmed the Church's opposition to the practice of contraception. This encyclical was widely opposed by the Catholic theological establishment and the institution of the papacy itself came under attack. Theologians who opposed the teaching sought to 'read-down' sections of *Humanae Vitae* by reference to foundational principles in moral, sacramental and dogmatic theology, in particular by reference to the notion of the primacy of the individual conscience. In 1970 Hans Küng published his internationally best-selling work *Infallibility: An Inquiry* which was highly critical of papal authority.

One year after the release of *Humanae Vitae* Paul VI approved dramatic changes to the Church's liturgical tradition which had the further effect of exacerbating internal theological divisions. Whereas some Catholics opposed the papacy because of the Church's teachings in the area of sexual morality, others were alienated by the liturgical changes. While Paul VI defended the liturgical changes on the ground that a modern liturgy in plain language was needed for 'modern man' not all Catholics thought of themselves as 'moderns' in the sense of being, culturally-speaking, children of the 1960s.

After the bombshell of *Humanae Vitae* in 1968, and the no less dramatic introduction of the Missal of Paul VI in 1969, in 1970 the former Conciliar *Periti* held a theological conference in Brussels under the auspices of the journal *Concilium*. The journal had been founded in 1965 by a number of Conciliar *Periti* to continue the theological renewal which had begun during the Council. At the conference divisions broke out among the participants to such a degree that it became obvious that there was no consensus among the leading theologians about the interpretations to be given to the Conciliar documents or the future directions of Catholic theology. Although Ratzinger was initially a member of the *Concilium* board he renounced his membership when it became obvious that he did not share the same theological vision as Rahner, Küng, Schillebeeckx and others. In 1972 he co-founded the journal *Communio* with Henri de Lubac

---

[11] See: *The Tablet*, 22 April (1967), 449–54; 29 April (1967), 478–510.

and Hans Urs von Balthasar (1905–88) which sought to offer an alternative reading of the Conciliar documents from that found in the pages of *Concilium*.

Whereas articles in the *Communio* journal fostered an interpretation of the Council according to what Ratzinger called 'a hermeneutic of reform', publications in *Concilium* treated the Council as a dramatic rupture in the Church's theological tradition. At a speech delivered at Cambridge University in 1979 Rahner described the break between pre and post-Conciliar Catholicism as being as great as that which occurred at the Council of Jerusalem in AD 49 when the Apostles reached the conclusion that Christ's revelation was for all of humanity, not merely the Jewish people.[12]

Karl Rahner and Hans Urs von Balthasar

It is generally accepted that Karl Rahner and Hans Urs von Balthasar compete for the title of the most significant Catholic theologian of the twentieth century. Von Balthasar was from a patrician family in Lucerne, the son of a Church architect, the brother of a Superior-General of a Franciscan Order of nuns and the nephew of the Hungarian Bishop-martyr, Baron Vilmos Apor of Győr, to mention just a few of his significant family connections. Henri de Lubac famously described him as the most cultured man in Europe of his time. He joined the Society of Jesus in his youth and was taught by both de Lubac and Przywara. He loved literature and music and found scholasticism boring. He wrote his doctoral dissertation on the subject of the treatment of eschatological issues in German literature and when other seminarians went to play football he would use the time to translate patristic essays or read literature written by lay Catholics. In 1950 he left the Society of Jesus in order to found his own ecclesial movement, the Community of St John. As a result of this departure he was in an ecclesial wilderness during the Conciliar years and used the time to begin work on his magnum opus. It includes the *Glory of the Lord*, a seven-volume work of theological aesthetics, *Theo-Drama*, a five-volume work on the relationship between the human person and God, especially in relation to the Easter mysteries, and *Theo-Logic*, a three-volume work on the relationship of Christology to ontology. In 1974 Balthasar also published *Der antirömische Affekt*, a defence of the Petrine Office, which appeared in English translation as *The Office of Peter and the Structure of the Church*.[13] This work is regarded as the most powerful foil against Küng's anti-papal publications.

Karl Rahner shared with von Balthasar a basic Ignatian spirituality and a belief that pre-Conciliar scholasticism was an inadequate tool for dealing with many contemporary theological problems. However whereas von Balthasar was critical of what became known as the culture of modernity, and in some senses actually anticipated post-modern criticisms of modernity, the theology of Rahner was

---

[12] Karl Rahner, 'Towards a Fundamental Theological Interpretation of Vatican II', *Theological Studies* 40 (1979), pp. 716–28.

[13] Hans Urs von Balthasar, *The Office of Peter and the Structure of the Church* (San Francisco, 2007).

decidedly more positive about modernity. Von Balthasar argued that a fundamental difference between him and Rahner, and one that was largely responsible for Rahner's openness to those aspects of modernity he opposed, was their relationship to Kant. While von Balthasar maintained a stance of opposition to Kant, Rahner appropriated the 'transcendental Thomism' project of Joseph Maréchal (1878–1944) who sought to synthesise elements of Kantian epistemology with the thought of St Thomas.

The 23 volumes of Rahner's *Theological Investigations* and the 15 volumes of von Balthasar's theological reflections with reference to the transcendental properties of beauty, goodness and truth came to be regarded as alternative ways forward for the intellectual life of the Church in the post-Conciliar era. The distance between the two Ignatian theologians is most evident in von Balthasar's 1967 anti-Rahnerian publication *Cordula oder der Ernstfall*, which was subsequently published in English as *The Moment of Christian Witness*.[14] In this book von Balthasar was highly critical of Rahner's notion of the 'anonymous Christian'. In the following paragraph Aidan Nichols offers a summary of von Balthasar's account of problematic Rahnerian ideas:

> In fundamental theology, the belief that a transcendental philosophy can anticipate the distinctive content of Christian revelation; in soteriology, the idea that the life, death and resurrection of Christ are exemplary rather than efficacious in force; in theological ethics the notion that the love of neighbour can be a surrogate for the love of God and Christological confession no longer necessary for Christian existence; in the theology of religions the idea that other faiths are ordinary means of salvation alongside the Christian way; in ecclesiology the idea that the Church becomes simply the explicit articulation of what is equally present (though not implicitly so) wherever the world opens itself to the kingdom; and finally, in the theology of history, the fact that the universal openness of the human spirit to divine transcendence in its supernatural offer of salvation is already deemed to be *Gnadenerfahrung*, 'the experience of grace', even without any further intervention of the redeeming God in the special history of revelation.[15]

Nichols suggests that this list brings together the major orientations of a 'vulgarised Rahnerianism', that is, a list of the popular interpretations of Rahner which were commonly served up to seminarians without much concern for subtleties and caveats. Karl Rahner wrote in such a dense and sometimes convoluted prose style that Rahnerian scholars spend a lot of time explaining what Rahner actually said and what he meant by what he said, and how what he meant was popularly (mis)interpreted by others.

One prominent Rahnerian scholar, Karen Kilby, has suggested that what is at issue between Rahner and von Balthasar 'is not (whatever Balthasar may have thought), a theological objection to a philosophically determined vision, but the coming into

---

[14] Hans Urs von Balthasar, *The Moment of Christian Witness* (San Francisco, 1994).
[15] Aidan Nichols, *Beyond the Blue Glass: Catholic Essays on Faith and Culture: Volume 1* (London, 2002), p. 112.

conflict of two alternative theological visions'.[16] Balthasar, she suggests, is 'concerned to preserve the distinctive relation of Christianity and of the Christian life, to the concrete and particular figure of Christ' while Rahner, on the other hand, 'is determined to think through the full significance of Christ'.[17] Implied here is the idea of thinking through the full significance of Christ with reference to factors *external* to 'the concrete and particular figure of Christ'. This, of course, is not merely a matter of Christology but also a matter of how the notions of revelation and tradition are to be understood.

What is clear, as John Milbank has noted, is that 'the thrust of Rahner's theology is toward a universal humanism, a rapprochement with the Enlightenment and an autonomous secular order' and further, that Rahnerian theology became the point of departure for many of the liberation theologians of the 1970s and 1980s who sought to synthesise aspects of Christian theology with Marxist social theory.[18] Some of the leading names here were: Rahner's student, Johann Baptist Metz (1928–), Juan Luis Segundo (1925–96), Jon Sobrino (1938–), Leonardo Boff (1938–) and Gustavo Gutiérrez (1928–). Most scholars of liberation theology do however emphasise that while Rahner's theology was often their point of departure, they regard his positive appraisal of the Enlightenment and the liberal political theories it engendered, as naïve.

Modernity and Post-Modernity

While the liberation theologians pursued projects of synthesising Christianity with Marxism in predominately third-world countries and the economically chaotic countries of Latin America; in Europe, the United States and the countries of the British Commonwealth, a popular pastoral project was one of 'correlating' Catholic tradition to the trends in contemporary culture and intellectual life. This project was promoted by Edward Schillebeeckx in a series of essays published in the late 1960s at the height of the post-Conciliar enthusiasm for all things *moderne* and it was also associated with the theology of David Tracy (1939–) and Karl Rahner and many others from the *Concilium* circle. As Lieven Boeve and Ben Vedder have noted, Schillebeeckx's theology implied that 'theologians will have to constantly re-evaluate God's presence in the here and now' and that 'tradition is not unchanging; it constantly relates to the spirit of the times'.[19]

Since the 1960s the spirit of the times has moved from the modern to the post-modern and thus contemporary scholars inspired by Schillebeeckx's theological vision are promoting the *re-contextualisation* of the Catholic faith with reference to the

---

[16] Karen Kilby, *Karl Rahner: Theology and Philosophy* (London, 2004), p. 119.
[17] Kilby, *Rahner*, p. 119.
[18] Milbank, *Theology and Social Theory*, p. 207.
[19] Lieven Boeve, Frederiek Depoortere and Stephan van Erp, *Edward Schillebeeckx and Contemporary Theology* (London, 2010), p. x.

culture of post-modernity. In other words, instead of *correlating* the faith to the culture of modernity, the predominately Louvain-based theologians are promoting a strategy of *re-contextualising* the faith with reference to post-modern culture. Central to the re-contextualisation project is Lieven Boeve's premise that those who inherit a tradition are not only its heirs but also its testators, and that tradition develops when there has been a change in context by those who receive it.[20] The use of the testator-beneficiary metaphor was anticipated by the Thomist philosopher Josef Pieper (1904–97) whose works were a seminal influence on the intellectual formation of the young Joseph Ratzinger. Contrary to Boeve's position, however, Pieper argued that the *traditum* is something that in the accomplishment of the process of tradition does *not* grow.[21] Thus, those theologians who follow the Schillebeeckx–Boeve line of thought end up with a concept of Christianity as an 'open narrative', whereas those who follow the Pieper–Ratzinger line of thinking tend to have a more 'restrictive entry' narrative in the sense that while they accept that there can be doctrinal development, any such development has to be an organic development of some element of the original *traditum*, to use Pieper's term. To put this another way, while Ratzinger clearly follows Newman's path with its emphasis on organic development, the proponents of an 'open narrative' see the narrative as open to the spirit of the times, regardless of the origins of the so-called spirit/*Zeitgeist*. The understanding of upper-case T Tradition and its relationship to revelation, scripture and doctrinal development is thus a significant contemporary theological 'hot spot' because the position one takes on these fundamental elements determines how one responds to the culture of post-modernity. To believe that there can be doctrinal development is not the same as believing that Christianity is an 'open narrative'.

Post-modern theology with its celebration of pluralism and difference takes many forms but most post-modern theologians can trace their projects back to issues first raised by Martin Heidegger's *Being and Time* (1927) and then to later themes in continental philosophy, especially in the field of hermeneutics. In the 1930s a number of Catholic theologians were interested in synthesising aspects of classical (predominately Thomistic) metaphysics with elements of Heidegger's existentialism. These included Gustav Siewerth, Max Müller, Johannes B. Lotz and Rahner himself. Rahner remarked that 'Catholic theology can no longer be thought of without Martin Heidegger, because even those who hope to go beyond him and ask questions different from his, nonetheless owe their origin to him'.[22]

Unlike the 1930s generation, however, the leading contemporary Catholic theologians engaged with Heideggerian themes tend to be post-metaphysical. Foremost among these is Jean-Luc Marion, the author of *God without Being* (1991). Marion also draws on the philosophy of Emmanuel Levinas (1905–95) and the

---

[20] Lieven Boeve, *Interrupting Tradition: An Essay on Christian Faith in a Postmodern Context* (Louvain, 2003), p. 24.
[21] Joseph Pieper, *Tradition: Concept and Claim* (Wilmington, 2008), p. 21.
[22] Karl Rahner, cited in Thomas Sheehan, *Karl Rahner the Philosophical Foundations* (Ohio, 1987), p. xi.

mystical theology of Dionysius the Areopagite. As Thomas A Carson explains, 'in the Dionysian appeal to an inconceivable and ineffable "Good beyond Being", Marion locates an extra-metaphysical "God without Being"'.[23] Thus, for Marion the highest name for God is 'not to be found in the metaphysical predication of Being or essence but rather in theological praise of goodness or love'.[24] Central themes in Marion's works are the idol and the icon, love and gift, and 'saturated phenomena' that is, phenomena which 'exceed what the concept can receive, expose and comprehend'.

Other leading names in the territory of post-modern theology include: the Czech theologian, Tomas Halik (1948–) who combines themes in Marion's works with currents in phenomenology, hermeneutics and Jungian psychology; and John D. Caputo (1940–) and Gianni Vattimo (1936–), both proponents of a decidedly non-dogmatic 'weak theology'. Caputo's recent works have focused on an engagement with the ideas of Jacques Derrida and the fashionable continental critiques of St Paul as the founder of universalism, while Vattimo is associated with a positive appropriation of Nietzsche's judgment that all metaphysical frameworks simply represent a play of ideological forces. His most recent work carries the provocative title *Hermeneutic Communism* and is co-authored with Santiago Zabala (1975–), the author of *The Remains of Being: Hermeneutic Ontology after Metaphysics*.

The Wojtyła and Ratzinger Papacies

Returning to the magisterial theological territory, Karol Wojtyła supported the publication of a Polish edition of *Communio* when he was the Cardinal Archbishop of Kraków and after his election to the papacy in 1978 he made Joseph Ratzinger his Prefect for the Congregation of the Doctrine of the Faith and the President of the Pontifical Biblical Commission and the International Theological Commission. He also honoured de Lubac and von Balthasar with red hats, though Balthasar famously did not live to attend the conferral ceremony. As a generalisation one might say that the pontificate of John Paul II was buttressed by a loose coalition of *Communio* theologians and various schools of Thomists, while it was severely criticised and even outrightly opposed on some fronts by theologians who owed their lineage to the *Concilium* circles. Those in this last group continued to regard the Church's teaching against contraception as a mistake and were generally hostile to the papal teachings in the areas of sexuality and the theological significance of gender differences. Magisterial teachings in these areas featured prominently in the early part of the pontificate, especially in the Wednesday audience Catechesis on Human Love, and later in the encyclicals on moral theology, above all in *Veritatis Splendor* (1993). Related to this opposition was the support of many in the *Concilium* circles for the ordination of women. Bioethics and so-called 'gender issues' became the battleground on which

---

[23] Thomas A. Carlson, 'Postmetaphysical Theology', in Kevin J. Vanhoozer (ed.), *The Cambridge Companion to Postmodern Theology* (Cambridge, 2003), p. 58.

[24] Carlson, 'Postmetaphysical Theology', p. 58.

these theological divisions were played out. In 1981 John Paul II founded the first of an international network of John Paul II Pontifical Institutes specifically devoted to the study of these contested areas.

Prominent among the theologians who gave their support to the papal teaching were Cardinal Carlo Caffara, the first President of the Roman session of the John Paul II Institute, his successor Angelo Scola, now the Cardinal Archbishop of Milan, and Cardinal Marc Ouellet, a former professor of the Roman session of the John Paul II Institute who is now the Prefect for the Congregation of Bishops. Angelo Scola was recently described in *The Tablet* as the 'crown prince of Catholicism'. These three *papabile* Cardinals are all proponents of what is called 'Nuptial Mystery theology'. Fergus Kerr has argued that the Nuptial Mystery theology is the dominant school in papally inspired and papally endorsed theology at the turn of the century.[25]

The most significant theological sub-discipline for the 'Nuptial Mystery' theologians is theological anthropology. Much of the project is devoted to relating issues in Trinitarian theology to an understanding of the human person. Central to this anthropology is paragraph 22 of *Gaudium et spes*: 'it is only in the mystery of the Word made flesh that the mystery of man truly becomes clear ... Christ ... the very revelation of the mystery of the Father and of his love, fully reveals man to himself'. Paul McPartlan has observed that this paragraph was the most often quoted of all the paragraphs in the documents of the Second Vatican Council by John Paul II and it appears to have been taken word for word from Henri de Lubac's work *Catholicism*.[26]

Not all contemporary Catholic scholars are in favour of this reading of *Gaudium et spes* or of the theology of de Lubac. Criticisms of de Lubac and of the Wojtyła–Ratzinger reading of *Gaudium et spes* tend to come from two opposite directions. First, there is what might be called the 'liberal criticism' which is ill at ease with the idea that 'Jesus Christ is the concrete universal'. If human beings only understand their humanity to the extent that they know Christ, where does this leave Buddhists, Muslims, Mormons, etc.? On the other hand there is a kind of 'conservative criticism' from neo-neo-Thomist circles where energy has been invested in theo-political projects synthesising the Thomist and Liberal traditions with reference to the notion of 'pure nature'. In a 1969 article on human dignity in *Gaudium et spes* Ratzinger described as a 'fiction' the idea that it is 'possible to construct a rational philosophical picture of man intelligible to all and on which all men of good will can agree, to which can be added the Christian doctrines as a sort of crowning conclusion'.[27] Precisely such a project has however been popular with Catholic scholars in liberal societies, in particular in the United States.

---

[25] Kerr, *Twentieth-Century*.
[26] Paul McPartlan, '*Dominus Iesus* after Ten Years', *Ecumenical Trends*, 39(11) (2010).
[27] Joseph Ratzinger, 'The Dignity of the Human Person', in H. Vorgrimler (ed.), *Commentary on the Documents of Vatican II*, vol. V (New York, 1969), p. 119.

Classical versus Romantic Orthodoxy

The emerging conflict between theologians who follow in the trajectory of de Lubac, von Balthasar and Ratzinger (on the one side) and American neo-neo-Thomists (on the other) has been described by John Milbank as a conflict between a romantic and classical orthodoxy. This conflict can in part be construed as a contemporary variation on the nineteenth-century distinctions between defending the rationality of the Catholic faith with reference to philosophical propositions and doctrinal pronouncements and those interested in an engagement with Romantic-movement issues. Milbank presents the division in the following terms:

> The 'romantics' think that the collapse of a reason linked to the higher *eros* led to the debasement of scholasticism and then to secular modernity. Resistance to the latter had therefore to oppose rationalism and even to insist more upon the role of the 'erotic' – the passions, the imagination, art, *ethos* etc. than had been the case up till and including Aquinas. The exponents of 'classicism' on the other hand (largely located in the United States) trace secularity simply to a poor use of reason and regard the scholastic legacy, mainly in its 'Thomistic' form, as sustaining a true use of reason to this very day ... The conflict between these two parties is therefore one between opposed metanarratives.[28]

In other words, while both the neo-neo-Thomists and the *Communio* scholars aspire to fidelity to magisterial teaching, they each have different readings (metanarratives) of the causes of the post-Conciliar crisis and projects for their resolution. The *Communio* scholars trace the crises to dualisms which came to the fore in the post-Tridentine era and issues which were the unfinished business of the Councils of Trent (1545–63) and Vatican I (1869–70). The neo-neo-Thomists want to defend baroque-era scholasticism and blame the *ressourcement* theologians for the post-Conciliar crisis because they undermined this apparently stable edifice. While some neo-neo-Thomists do concede that the *Communio* theologians have made some valuable contributions to the discipline of theology, they categorise these as mere 'virtuoso performances' which are not easily slotted into a framework for easy digestion by the majority of seminarians for whom the cultural capital of the Balthasar family cannot be presupposed.

Not all contemporary Thomists however fit into the neo-neo category. There are many who are sensitive to the kinds of criticisms made by the Conciliar generation of the seminary education to which they were subjected, of the problems of a philosophical and theological framework which has no room for history, of the significant differences between classical Thomism and baroque-era Thomism and so on. The work of this group can be construed as a Thomistic *ressourcement* project and its most inspirational figure is Servais-Théodore Pinckaers OP (1925–2006), a Belgian Dominican who spent much of his academic career at the Albertinum in Fribourg, Switzerland.

---

[28] John Milbank, 'The New Divide: Classical versus Romantic Orthodoxy', *Modern Theology*, 26(1) (January 2010), pp. 26–38.

Other prominent contemporary figures include Matthew Levering, Augustine Di Noia OP, Serge-Thomas Bonino OP, Thomas Hibbs and Gilles Emery OP.

One final school which deserves to be mentioned in any account of Catholic theology in the twentieth century is that of the Canadian Jesuit, Bernard Lonergan (1904–84). Although he was often labelled a 'transcendental Thomist' along with Rahner, Lonergan did not regard the label as a particularly helpful tag for classifying his work. He did however share with Rahner the common influence of Joseph Maréchal and an interest in the topics of grace and freedom and human cognition. His most significant works were *Insight: A Study of Human Understanding* (1957), *Verbum: Word and Idea in Aquinas* (1967) and *Method in Theology* (1972).

A significant Lonerganian trait is an interest in the empirical sciences, including the fields of mathematics and macro-economics. Lonergan actually came to the study of Thomism via the unusual route of reading an article about geometry in which Aquinas was mentioned.[29] Even his philosophical project is known as the Generalised Empirical Method (GEM). Since Lonergan was especially interested in methodological issues, the most identifying mark of his followers tends to be their devotion to their master's methodology. Many Lonerganians have a strong natural sciences background and, regardless of where they actually stand on specific theological issues such as contraception, occupy the polar end of the *methodological* spectrum from the Balthasarians who tend to have a strong background in the humanities, especially in music and classical literature, and who tend to be much less interested in systematic theology.

Conclusion

In his *Theologische Prinzipienlehre* first published in 1982, Joseph Ratzinger described the 'fundamental crisis of our age' as 'understanding the mediation of history in the realm of ontology'.[30] One could rephrase this and say that the fundamental problem for Catholic theology is dealing with the Romantic movement issue (history) without doing violence to classical theology's favourite realm of ontology (nature and grace). The relationship between nature, grace and history is therefore central to this crisis. Different theological schools represent different accounts of this relationship. Key determinants of where scholars end up are the positions they take on: the nature and grace relationship (do they support Cajetan and Suárez or not?); the position they take on the faith and reason relationship (do they support Kant or not?); the position they take on the cultures of modernity and post-modernity (are these cultures fertile soil for Christianity or not?); the position they take on Heidegger (is there any place for metaphysics or not?, is nature itself entirely historical, or not?); the position they take on the concept of tradition (should the *traditum* develop with reference to the spirit of

---

[29] Kerr, *Twentieth-Century*, p. 109.
[30] Joseph Ratzinger, *Principles of Catholic Theology: Building Stones for a Fundamental Theology* (San Francisco, 1987), p. 160.

the times, or not?) and consequently, whether the Catholic faith is an 'open narrative' or not. Included in this last fault line is the whole territory of the relationship of scripture to tradition, and in particular whether one reads the teachings in scripture as normative for all times, or not. The post-modern theologians have also raised a variety of questions in the territory of linguistic philosophy which impact upon the understanding of how meaning is mediated and the use of doctrinal formulae to this end. At the turn of the twenty-first century Catholic theologians are a long way from resolving this 'fundamental crisis' whose roots were clearly visible in the nineteenth.

Bibliography

Blondel, Maurice, *The Letter on Apologetics & History and Dogma* (Grand Rapids: Eerdmans, 1995).

Boeve, Lieven, *Interrupting Tradition: An Essay on Christian Faith in a Postmodern Context* (Louvain: Eerdmans Publishing Company, 2003).

Boeve, Lieven, Depoortere, Frederiek and van Erp, Stephan, *Edward Schillebeeckx and Contemporary Theology* (London: T&T Clark, 2010).

Congar, Yves, *Tradition and Traditions* (London: Burns and Oates, 1960–63).

Cosemius, V., 'The Condemnation of Modernism and the Survival of Catholic Theology', in Gregory Baum (ed.), *The Twentieth Century: A Theological Overview* (London: Orbis, 1999), pp. 14–27.

Danielou, Jean, 'Les orientations presents de la Pensée religieuse', *Études*, 249 (1946), 1–21.

Flynn, Gabriel and Murray, Paul D., *Ressourcement: A Movement for Renewal in Twentieth-Century Catholic Theology* (Oxford: Oxford University Press, 2012).

Garrigou-Lagrange, Reginald, 'La nouvelle théologie où va-t-elle?', *Angelicum*, 23 (1946), 126–45.

Grumett, David, *De Lubac: A Guide for the Perplexed* (London: T&T Clark, 2007).

Howsare, Rodney A., *Balthasar: A Guide for the Perplexed* (London: T&T Clark, 2009).

Kerr, Fergus, *After Aquinas: Versions of Thomism* (Oxford: Blackwell, 2002).

Kerr, Fergus, *Twentieth-Century Catholic Theologians: From Neo-Scholasticism to Nuptial Mysticism* (Oxford: Blackwell, 2007).

Kilby, Karen, *Karl Rahner: Theology and Philosophy* (London: Routledge, 2004).

Krieg, R.A., *Romano Guardini: The Precursor to Vatican II* (Indiana: University of Notre Dame Press, 1997).

McPartlan, Paul, '*Dominus Iesus* after Ten Years', *Ecumenical Trends*, 39(11) (2010), 161–3.

Milbank, John, 'The New Divide: Classical versus Romantic Orthodoxy', *Modern Theology*, 26(1) (January 2010), 26–38.

Milbank, John, *Theology and Social Theory: Beyond Secular Reason* (Oxford: Blackwell, 1990).

Nichols, Aidan, *Beyond the Blue Glass: Catholic Essays on Faith and Culture: Volume 1* (London: St. Austin Press, 2002).

Nichols, Aidan, *Catholic Thought Since the Enlightenment* (Leominster: Gracewing, 1998).

Nichols, Aidan, 'Thomism and the Nouvelle Théologie', in *Beyond the Blue Glass: Catholic Essays on Faith and Culture*, vol. 1 (London: The Saint Austin Press, 2002), pp. 33–53.

O'Meara, Thomas F., *Church and Culture: German Catholic Theology 1860–1914* (Indiana: University of Notre Dame Press, 1991).

Pieper, Joseph, *Tradition: Concept and Claim* (Wilmington: ISI Books, 2008).

Rahner, Karl, 'Towards a Fundamental Theological Interpretation of Vatican II', *Theological Studies*, 40 (1979), 716–28.

Ratzinger, Joseph, 'The Dignity of the Human Person', in H. Vorgrimler (ed.), *Commentary on the Documents of Vatican II*, vol. V (New York: Herder and Herder, 1969).

Ratzinger, Joseph, *Principles of Catholic Theology: Building Stones for a Fundamental Theology* (San Francisco: Igatius Press, 1987).

Scola, Angelo, *The Nuptial Mystery* (Grand Rapids: Eerdmans, 2005).

Sheehan, Thomas, *Karl Rahner the Philosophical Foundations* (Ohio: Ohio University Press, 1987).

Vanhoozer, Kevin J., *The Cambridge Companion to Postmodern Theology* (Cambridge: Cambridge University Press, 2003).

von Balthasar, Hans Urs, *The Moment of Christian Witness* (San Francisco: Igantius Press, 1994).

von Balthasar, Hans Urs, *The Office of Peter and the Structure of the Church* (San Francisco: Ignatius Press, 2007).

Chapter 4
Orthodox Theology in the Twentieth Century

Aristotle Papanikolaou

In addition to ending the long reign of the Byzantine Empire, the fall of Constantinople in 1453 silenced a long and vibrant intellectual tradition in the Orthodox Christian East, whose last notable theologian was Gregory Palamas (ca. 1296–1359). It took nearly 400 years before a revival occurred in Russia, which is discernible in part with the establishment of the intellectual academies of the Russian Orthodox Church at St Petersburg (1809), Moscow (1814), Kiev (1819), and Kazan (1842). After the fall of the Ottoman Empire, theological faculties were established in traditional Orthodox cities, including Athens (1837), Iaşi (1860), Czernowitz (1875), Bucharest (1884), Belgrade (1920), Sofia (1923), and Thessalonica (1942).

A movement to return to more authentic forms of the Orthodox spiritual and theological traditions began in the late eighteenth century with the Slavonic translation of the *Philokalia* compiled by Nikodemus of the Holy Mountain (1749–1809), which was followed by a series of Russian translations of Eastern patristic texts. The revival of the Orthodox intellectual tradition, however, is also indebted to individual thinkers who were not affiliated with the emerging theological institutions of higher learning in traditional Orthodox countries and who, in fact, were reacting to the theology emerging from these institutions. Although the theological academies throughout the Orthodox world did play an indispensable role in the revival of the Orthodox intellectual tradition, especially in their creative appropriation of the *Philokalia* and in producing translations of patristic texts, they were established on the models of German universities, and much of the theological work produced by the faculties of the theological schools was considered primarily imitative of the Protestant and Catholic scholastic manuals.[1]

Russian Sophiology

Early nineteenth-century Russia saw the emergence of an intellectual tradition that was simultaneously rooted in the Orthodox theological and liturgical tradition and also seeking to engage the modern philosophical currents streaming into Russia,

---

[1] See Christos Yannaras, *Orthodoxy and the West*, trans. Peter Chamberas and Norman Russell (Brookline, MA: Holy Cross Orthodox Press, 2006).

especially German idealism. From this particular trajectory emerged what is referred to as the Russian school.[2] The most well-known and influential intellectual from the Russian school is Vladimir Sergeevich Soloviev (1853–1900), considered to be the father of Russian sophiology. Two ideas were central to Soloviev's thought: the humanity of God (*bogochelovechestvo*), and Sophia. The fact that both concepts remained central to Russian religious philosophy allows Rowan Williams to claim, echoing Whitehead's remark on Plato, that "all subsequent Russian metaphysics is a series of footnotes to Soloviev."[3] The concept of the humanity of God is related to the Orthodox dogmatic principle of the divine–human union in Christ. Soloviev, however, was far from a dogmatician. His philosophy attempts to express this Orthodox principle of the divine–human union in Christ in the categories of German idealism, particularly the philosophy of Friedrich Wilhelm Joseph von Schelling (1775–1854). Although he appropriates the thought of Schelling, Soloviev's philosophy is a unique synthesis of the Orthodox affirmation of divine–human communion and German idealism that attempts to critique the inadequacies of modern philosophies. The humanity of God forms the basis for Soloviev's attempt to conceptualize a God who is both transcendent and immanent to creation. For Soloviev, affirming the humanity of God means that creation is intrinsic, not extrinsic, to the life of God. God relates to creation from all eternity, and creation exists in the life of God insofar as God's life is the reconciliation of all opposites: the material and the spiritual, freedom and necessity, finite and infinite. Creation is a movement of recovery of that original unity that is manifested in the God-man—Christ. Soloviev expresses this particular understanding of the God–world relation with the concept of Sophia and thereby gives birth to the sophiological tradition of the Russian school. God is Sophia, which means that God eternally relates to creation, and creation itself—created Sophia—is a movement of reconciliation toward divine Sophia.

As a result of the particular understanding of God's relation to the world that is implied in Soloviev's sophiology, he had a higher estimation of secular knowledge than the more extreme Orthodox Slavophiles of his time. However, Soloviev was critical of the determinism and meaninglessness of the materialism of modern atheism. His sophiology was a *via media* between extreme ideas and currents of thought prevalent throughout nineteenth-century Russia: rationalism and materialism, freedom and necessity, modern atheism and Orthodox Slavophile nationalism. The identification of the humanity of God with Sophia allowed Soloviev to affirm that all of created reality reflects the divine Sophia and is the movement of created Sophia toward the unity of all in God, which is divine Sophia.

Although the thought of the Russian school bears the stamp of Soloviev's sophiology up until the Revolution of 1917, it would be Sergei Nikolaeivich Bulgakov

[2] The best account of the Russian school is Paul Valliere's *Modern Russian Theology: Bukharev, Soloviev, Bulgakov: Orthodox Theology in a New Key* (Grand Rapids, MI: William B. Eerdmans Publishing Co., 2000).

[3] Rowan Williams, *The Theology of Vladimir Nikolaievich Lossky: An Exposition and Critique* (PhD diss., Oxford University, 1975), p. 209.

(1871–1944) who would advance the most sophisticated theological development of Soloviev's thought. Bulgakov was more conversant than Soloviev with the Eastern patristic tradition, and his sophiology is expressed explicitly in the idiom of the traditional theological dogmas and categories of the Orthodox tradition. Bulgakov was a convert from Marxism to Orthodoxy and was eventually ordained in 1918. After being exiled from Russia, he became the cofounder and first dean of St Sergius Orthodox Theological Institute in Paris in 1925. Bulgakov was active in the ecumenical movement and was one of the most prominent spokespersons of Orthodoxy to the Western world.

The most developed form of Bulgakov's sophiology appears in his dogmatic trilogy, *On Divine Humanity*.[4] Bulgakov follows Soloviev in identifying the humanity of God with Sophia and affirms the core meaning of Soloviev's sophiology—God is always the God for "me," that is, for creation. God's being is not dependent on creation, nor is God exhausted in God's relation to creation; God's being, however, is such that God *is* the God who creates and redeems creation. Bulgakov would affirm the distinction between the world that God relates to from all eternity and the created world, but it is impossible for humans to think of God as not eternally relating to the world.

Unlike Soloviev, Bulgakov's sophiology is more explicitly trinitarian and appropriates the traditional trinitarian language. Sophia is identified with the *ousia*, but as such *ousia* comes to mean much more than that which the persons of the Trinity possess in common. God in God's being exists as the creator and redeemer of the world. *Hypostasis* does not simply indicate that which is particular in the three persons of the Trinity. The divine Sophia does not exist monistically but as Trinity. For Bulgakov, the relations among the persons of the Trinity are best understood in terms of *kenosis*, as a movement of self-giving and self-receiving that has the capacity to overflow and reflect itself in the creation of the world. This kenotic movement is the source of and is reflected in the world, especially in the incarnation and crucifixion of Christ. Anticipating later liberation theology, Bulgakov argued that the crucifixion of Christ reveals the *kenosis* of each of the persons of the Trinity, which includes the co-suffering of the Father with the Son. Always participating in the divine Sophia, the world as created Sophia is moving toward the unity of all in God's life, which is given in and made possible by the *kenosis* of the Son and completed by the Holy Spirit.

The mark of German idealism, particularly the philosophy of Schelling, is evident on Bulgakov's theology, especially in its "deduction of the trinity as the triune absolute subject,"[5] but equally as evident is his embeddedness within the Orthodox patristic and dogmatic tradition. Like Soloviev, Bulgakov's own understanding of the God–world relation allows him to have a more positive estimation of non-theological disciplines. Moreover, Bulgakov identified problems within the patristic tradition,

---

[4] All three volumes have been translated by Boris Jakim and published by William B. Eerdmanns Publishing Co., Grand Rapids, MI: *The Lamb of God* (2008), *The Comforter* (2004), and *The Bride of the Lamb* (2002).
[5] Bulgakov, *The Comforter*, p. 56.

which the resources of German idealism could assist in resolving. The Fathers did not have the last word for Bulgakov, and, as they used the philosophical categories of their time, so must theology today make use of modern philosophy to continue to extract the implications of the divine–human communion in Christ.

The Neo-Patristic School

Sophiology did not survive in any influential form past Bulgakov. Its demise is partly due to the explicit refutation of sophiology by Orthodox thinkers in the Russian diaspora, whose own understanding of Orthodox theology would come to be known as the neo-patristic school. Although this school has roots in the translations of the Eastern patristic texts in Russia, it is most associated with Georges Florovsky (1893–1979) and Vladimir Nikolaeivich Lossky (1903–58). Both Florovsky and Lossky were part of the "Sophia Affair" in 1935—the accusation of Bulgakov's theology as heretical by both the Moscow Patriarchate and what would become known as the Synod of the Russian Orthodox Church Abroad. During the time of the Sophia Affair, Florovsky was professor of patristics at St Sergius and would later serve as dean of St Vladimir's Orthodox Theological Seminary in Crestwood, New York (founded in 1938). Florovsky framed the debate with Russian sophiology in terms of the relation between theology and philosophy. For Florovsky, theology had to be rooted in the language and categories of the Eastern patristic texts. He coined the phrase "neo-patristic synthesis," but such a synthesis must retain the Hellenistic contours of patristic thought. Florovsky argued that any attempt to de-Hellenize the language of the Fathers would only distort their theology and divide the Church.

Lossky was also a part of the Russian émigré community in Paris, but he was never affiliated with St Sergius.[6] For Lossky, much as for Bulgakov, the divine–human union of Christ is the starting point for theological thinking about God. Insofar as this union is one between two opposites, between what is God and what is not God, it is beyond the grasp of human reason, whose capacity for understanding is restricted to created reality. Whereas human reason functions on the basis of the law of non-contradiction, the incarnation demands that theology be antinomic—the affirmation of the non-opposition of opposites. Theology's function is to give expression to the divine–human communion in Christ, which reveals the antinomic God—the God who is radically immanent in Christ and whose very immanence reveals God's radical transcendence. Its purpose is not to attempt to resolve the antinomy through reason but to stretch language so as to speak of the divine–human communion in Christ in such a way that guides one toward true knowledge of God, which is mystical union with God beyond reason. Theology is apophatic, by which Lossky meant two things: that language is inadequate to represent the God beyond all

---

[6] For an overview of Lossky's theology, see my *Being with God: Trinity, Apophaticism, and Divine-Human Communion* (Notre Dame, IN: University of Notre Dame Press, 2006).

representation, and that true knowledge of God consists in experience of God rather than in propositions rooted in human logic.

The affirmation of the God who is beyond being yet radically immanent to creation is the basis for the essence/energies distinction. The (hyper)essence of God refers to God's transcendence, whereas the energies refer to God's immanence and are the means for communion with God. True knowledge of God consists in participation in the energies of God, which are uncreated. The crystallization of the essence/energies distinction can be traced back to Palamas. Lossky, together with Florovsky and John Meyendorff (1926–92), presented the essence/energies distinction as uniquely characteristic of and central to Orthodox theology. Its centrality is affirmed by virtually every twentieth-century Orthodox theologian, including the most famous outside of Russia and Greece, the Romanian Dumitru Staniloae (1903–93), and it is the reason why Orthodox theology today is often referred to as neo-Palamite. The distinction was also used in polemics against neo-scholastic understandings of created grace. For Lossky, the truth of the essence/energies distinction lies in its antinomic character: it expresses the transcendent and immanent God without attempting to resolve the antinomy.

In addition to the essence/energies distinction, there is an additional antinomy that is foundational for theology: God as Trinity. For Lossky, the revelation of God as Trinity is a "primordial fact" given in the incarnation. The goal of theology is not to explain how God is Trinity but to deconceptualize philosophical categories in order to express the antinomy. The patristic categories of *ousia* and *hypostasis* are given in the tradition in order to express what is common and incommunicable in God as Trinity. The trinitarian categories, however, also provide the foundation for an understanding of personhood that is defined as irreducible uniqueness to and freedom from nature. Salvation as the event of mystical union through participation in the divine energies means a realization of true personhood in which the human person is irreducible to the common human nature; thus, the person is unique but also free in transcendence from the limitations of human nature to experience what is other than creation—the God beyond being. For Lossky, this mystical experience of God occurs through union with the deified nature of Christ and through the power of the Holy Spirit. Lossky was also a vehement opponent of the *filioque*, which he interpreted as the natural result of the rationalization of the doctrine of the Trinity.

The debate between the Russian and the neo-patristic schools is often cast in terms of contrasting attitudes toward tradition.[7] The Russian school is portrayed as rooted in, yet going beyond, tradition as it attempts to bring Orthodoxy into an engagement with the modern world through a creative reconstruction of traditional dogmatic formulas; the neo-patristic school is described as wedded to classical dogmatic language and resistant to reinterpretations. This particular way of looking at the debate can be misleading if the narrative does not also include the fact that the Russian school and the neo-patristic school agree on one essential point: the principle of divine–human communion. I would argue that the core of the debate is not about the role of tradition

---

[7] Valliere, *Modern Russian Theology*, pp. 373–403.

within theology but, rather, about the implications of the principle of divine–human communion for conceptualizing the God–world relation.

For Lossky—who contributed a pamphlet to the Sophia Affair, *The Debate on Sophia* (*Spor o Sofii*), which he produced for the Brotherhood of St Photius and which rejected Bulgakov's attempt to unite certain aspects of German idealism to dogmatic theology—the debate with sophiology was not primarily about the relation between theology and philosophy; rather, it was about conceptualizing the transcendent and immanent God. Both Bulgakov and Lossky agreed that divine–human communion is not simply the goal of the Christian life but the very presupposition, the first principle, in all theological thought. The essence/energies distinction, central to Lossky's thought, especially in his critique against neo-scholasticism, also constituted Lossky's response to Bulgakov's sophiology. The attributes of God, such as Sophia, are identified with God's energies, and not with God's essence, since the latter is beyond all being and, thus, unknowable. Lossky also argued that the logic of apophaticism, of affirming the incomprehensibility of God's essence, requires a strict division between *theologia*, or knowing God in Godself, and *oikonomia*, knowing God as God relates salvifically to the world. To think of God as eternally relating to the world, as Bulgakov did, is to transgress this apophatic boundary and to negate the otherness between the world and God that is the very basis for a divine–human communion based on love and freedom. Lossky's fear was that any attempt to justify the principle of divine–human communion philosophically, which is what he saw in neo-scholasticism and Russian sophiology, ultimately forgets that the only justification is the actual experience of union with God.

Bulgakov would not have disagreed with Lossky that the highest form of knowledge of God is *theosis*; however, for Bulgakov, the God who creates so as to bring the created into communion with Godself was the God who is eternally free to create in such a way and, as such, is eternally relating to creation. For Bulgakov, one could not think God without thinking creation and vice versa. This leads to a much less suspicious and more positive appraisal of the role in theology for philosophy and all the non-theological disciplines. Philosophy has its own integrity and reveals truths about being human. Theology does not appropriate those truths to validate the principle of divine–human communion, but it cannot ignore those truths in its never-ending attempt to interpret the realism of divine communion in Jesus Christ.

Despite Bulgakov's and Lossky's differences on the interpretation of the principle of divine–human communion, it is important to see that they were in full agreement that any response to modernity must be rooted in the Orthodox principle of divine–human communion. This consensus makes the labels of "modern" for Bulgakov and "traditionalist" for Lossky inaccurate; both would claim that the traditional Orthodox affirmation of divine–human communion in Christ is non-negotiable and is the basis upon which to assess and to critique modern intellectual currents. Bulgakov and Lossky would have essentially agreed that nothing in modern thought could compel Orthodox theology to abandon its central claim: God has created the world for communion with God, which is effected in the person of Jesus Christ.

The disagreement is over the implications of this claim for the particular questions and challenges faced by the Christian tradition in the modern period.

John Zizioulas

The work of Lossky and Florovsky had a significant influence on a group of young theologians in Greece in the 1960s, most notably Nikos Nissiotis (1925–86), Christos Yannaras (b. 1935), and John Zizioulas (b. 1931). Elements of Lossky's theology, such as apophaticism, the essence/energies distinction, and the theology of personhood, are evident in Yannaras's major work, *Person and Eros* (1970).[8] The most influential of these theologians is Zizioulas, who synthesized the eucharistic theology of Nicolas Afanasiev (1893–1966) and Alexander Schmemann (1921–83) with the theology of personhood of Lossky via Yannaras. Zizioulas was a student of Florovsky when the latter was a professor of Harvard; he also taught dogmatics at the Holy Cross Greek Orthodox School of Theology in Brookline, Massachusetts (founded in 1938), before taking a permanent position at the University of Glasgow.

Zizioulas, like Bulgakov and Lossky, would affirm the principle of divine–human communion as the starting point of all theology, but, unlike Lossky's emphasis on the ascetical, mystical ascent to God, Zizioulas would argue that the experience of God is communal in the event of the eucharist.[9] According to Zizioulas, early Christians experienced the eucharist as the constitution of the community as the eschatological body of Christ by the Holy Spirit. This experience of Christ in the eucharist is the basis for the patristic affirmation of the divinity of Christ and the Spirit and, hence, of the affirmation of God as Trinity. Zizioulas's emphasis of the experience of God in the *hypostasis*, or person, of Christ has several implications. First, it is a noticeable break with the virtual consensus in Orthodox theology on the use of the essence/energies distinction for expressing Orthodox understandings of salvation as the experience of the divine life. Second, it is the foundation for what Zizioulas calls an "ontological revolution," insofar as it reveals God's life as that which itself is constituted in freedom and not necessity. If the eucharist is the experience of God, and, if such an experience is for created reality the freedom from the tragic necessity of death inherent to created existence, then God exists as this freedom from necessity, even the necessity of God's nature, since God gives what God *is*. The freedom of God from the necessity of God's nature is the meaning of the patristic assertion of the monarchy of the Father—the Father "causes" the Son and the Spirit and in so doing constitutes God's life as Trinity through a movement of freedom and love. With the doctrine of the Trinity, for the first time otherness, relation, uniqueness, freedom, and communion become ontologically ultimate. This understanding of divine–human communion in the life of the Trinity through the *hypostasis* of Christ also grounds Zizioulas's theology of personhood.

---

[8] Christos Yannaras, *Person and Eros*, trans. Norman Russell (4th edn, Brookline, MA: Holy Cross Orthodox Press, 2007).

[9] For an overview of Zizioulas's theology, see Papanikolaou, *Being with God*.

Person is an *ecstatic* being—free from the limitations of created nature—and a *hypostatic* being—unique and irreducible to nature. This freedom and irreducibility is only possible in relation to God the Father through Christ by the Holy Spirit because it is only in eternal relations of love that one is constituted as a unique and free being, that is, a person. Zizioulas has maintained the building blocks of Lossky's theology of person, but with an emphasis on relationality and in a decidedly non-apophatic approach. Zizioulas's theology of personhood is the organizing principle for this theology, and it is evident in his theology of ministry, in his ecclesiology, and in his theology of the environment.

In order to understand the place of Orthodox Christianity in the postmodern world, there are at least three aspects from the thought of the post-1960s generation of Greek theologians that are relevant: first, the continuity with the neo-patristic school and the virtual absence of any trace of the Russian school; second, the general audience for this generation of theologians, which is primarily other Christian theologians and traditions; third, the appearance of postmodern concepts and themes, such as difference, otherness, particularity, and desire, without any substantial engagement with some of the icons of postmodern thought, such as Foucault, Derrida, and Kristeva. What emerges in this post-1960s generation is an Orthodox theology with striking affinities with postmodern thought that developed, however, primarily in conversation with other Christian theologies and not with postmodern classics, and which extends the tradition of consensus on the Orthodox principle of divine–human communion—in continuity primarily with the neo-patristic school, while self-consciously rejecting the Russian school.

Issues for the Future

At least three central issues face Orthodox theology in the future. One is the centrality of the essence/energies distinction for expressing the transcendence and immanence of God, as well as the compatibility of this distinction as the language of divine–human communion with the language of the Trinity. Otherwise put, if the language of the Trinity is the language of divine–human communion, as Zizioulas argues, then what does this imply for understanding the essence/energies distinction?

A second issue is the question of the patristic interpretation of *hypostasis* and whether the contemporary Orthodox theology of personhood, which is arguably one of the most distinctive contributions of modern Orthodox theology, is a logical development of patristic thought. This particular understanding of *hypostasis* has been challenged by, among others, John Behr, an Orthodox patristic scholar and Dean of St Vladimir's Orthodox Theological Seminar. It has often been accused of being under the influence of French existentialism.

Finally, the revival of Russian sophiology, especially that of Bulgakov, and its impact on the engagement of Orthodox theology with nontheological currents of thought must be studied. The Russian school was actively engaged in social issues, and its influence is evident in the work of Mother Maria Skobtsova (1891–1944), who died in a German concentration camp for protecting Jews, and of Elizabeth Behr-Sigel (1907–2005), who wrote extensively on gender issues and women's ordination. Engagement in social issues is noticeably absent, however, in the neo-patristic school. The challenge for Orthodox theology is to retrieve what is best in the Russian and neo-patristic schools in order to produce a theology that is simultaneously mystical and political.[10]

Bibliography

Behr, John, *The Nicene Faith* (Crestwood, NY: St. Vladimir's Seminary Press, 2004).
Behr-Sigel, Elizabeth, *The Ministry of Women in the Church* (Redondo Beach, CA: Oakwood Publications, 1991).
Bulgakov, Sergius, *The Lamb of God* (2008); *The Comforter* (2004); *The Bride of the Lamb* (2002) (Grand Rapids, MI: Eerdmans Publishing Company).
Florovsky, Georges, *The Collected Works of Georges Florovsky* (14 vols, Belmont, MA: Nordland; Vaduz: Büchervertriebsanstalt, 1972–89).
Hart, David Bentley, *The Beauty of the Infinite: The Aesthetics of Christian Truth* (Grand Rapids, MI: Eerdmans Publishing Co., 2003).
Lossky, Vladimir, *In the Image and Likeness of God* (1974); *The Mystical Theology of the Eastern Church* (1976); *Orthodox Theology: An Introduction* (1978) (Crestwood, NY: St. Vladimir's Seminary Press).
Meyendorff, John, *A Study of Gregory Palamas* (Crestwood, NY: St. Vladimir's Seminary Press, 1964).
Miller, Charles, *The Gift of the World: An Introduction to the Theology of Dumitru Stăniloae* (Edinburgh: T&T Clark, 2000).
Papanikolaou, Aristotle, *Being with God: Trinity, Apophaticism, and Divine-Human Communion* (Notre Dame, IN: University of Notre Dame Press, 2006).
Schmemann, Alexander, *The Eucharist* (Crestwood, NY: St. Vladimir's Seminary Press, 1988).
Skobtsova, Maria, *Mother Maria Skobtsova: Essential Writings* (Maryknoll, NY: Orbis Books, 2003).
Solovyov, Vladimir, *The Justification of the Good: An Essay on Moral Philosophy* (2nd edn, Grand Rapids, MI: Eerdmans Publishing Co., 2005).
Solovyov, Vladimir, *Lectures on Divine Humanity* (Hudson, NY: Lindisfarne Books, 1995).
Stăniloae, Dumitru *The Experience of God: Orthodox Dogmatic Theology* (3 vols, Brookline, MA: Holy Cross Orthodox Press, 1994–2011).

---

[10] Much of the preceding section also appears in my "Orthodox Theology," in Erwin Fahlbusch, Jan Milič Lochman, John Mbiti, Jaroslav Pelikan, Lukas Vischer (eds); Geoffrey W. Bromiley (English-language ed.); David B. Barnett (statistical ed.), *Encyclopedia of Christianity*, vol. 5 (Grand Rapids, MI: William B. Eerdmans Publishing Co.; Leiden: Brill, 2007), pp. 414–18. I am grateful to the publishers for permission to use material from that entry for this chapter.

Valliere, Paul, *Modern Russian Theology: Bukharev, Soloviev, Bulgakov: Orthodox Theology in a New Key* (Grand Rapids, MI: Eerdmans Publishing Co., 2000).

Williams, Rowan, *The Theology of Vladimir Nikolaievich Lossky: An Exposition and Critique* (PhD diss., Oxford University, 1975).

Yannaras, Christos, *Elements of Faith: An Introduction to Orthodox Theology*, trans. Keith Schram (Edinburgh: T&T Clark, 1991).

Yannaras, Christos, *On the Absence and Unknowability of God: Heidegger and the Areopagite*, trans. Haralambos Ventis (Edinburgh: T&T Clark, 2005).

Yannaras, Christos, *Orthodoxy and the West*, trans. Peter Chamberas and Norman Russell (Brookline, MA: Holy Cross Orthodox Press, 2006).

Yannaras, Christos, *Person and Eros*, trans. Norman Russell (4th edn, Brookline, MA: Holy Cross Orthodox Press, 2007).

Zizioulas, John, *Being as Communion: Studies in Personhood and the Church* (Crestwood, NY: St. Vladimir's Seminary Press, 1985).

Zizioulas, John, *Communion and Otherness: Further Studies in Personhood and the Church* (London: Continuum, 2006).

PART II
Protestant Theologians
(Continental and Scandinavian)

Chapter 5
Karl Barth

Harald Hegstad

It is assuredly no exaggeration to claim that no one more strongly influenced the theology of the twentieth century than the Swiss Karl Barth (1886–1968). A Reformed theologian, he not only left his mark on Protestant theology, but was read and commented on by leading Catholic theologians too. More than anyone else, he came to represent the clash with the neo-Protestant theology of the nineteenth century and with its doctrinal "father," Schleiermacher. He vigorously attacked the neo-Protestant tendency to place the human person and human religiosity at the center of theology. He reacted by calling theology and the church back to what theology is really about, namely, God. In Barth's thinking, God and his revelation in Jesus Christ are the central theme of theological reflection. Another special characteristic of this theology is the close link between theology and the church, which is understood as the real subject of theology.

Barth's theology made an impact not only on academic theology, but also on the church's life in a broad sense, including ecumenical work. He meant a great deal, both during his lifetime and subsequently, not only for those who identified with his theology, but also for those who reacted against it polemically – or who shared some of his concerns, but without agreeing with every aspect of his theology.

Life and Work

Karl Barth was born in Basle, but grew up in Berne, where his father was a professor of theology. He studied theology in Berne, Berlin, Tübingen, and Marburg, and was strongly influenced by Adolf von Harnack and Wilhelm Herrmann, leading representatives of the liberal theology of that time.

After his final examination in 1908, Barth was ordained to the ministry of the Swiss Reformed church, and became pastor of Safenwil near Zurich in 1911. Here, he came to know the problems of the growing working class, and he joined the Social Democratic Party. As he encountered the challenges of the pastoral ministry, Barth experienced the liberal theology that he had brought with him from his student days as increasingly unsatisfactory. It was further discredited in his eyes in 1914, when Barth saw that many of his theological teachers put their names to a manifesto in support of the German war politics. This led Barth to a radical breach with liberal theology – a breach that found its principal expression in his commentary on the Letter to the Romans (1919/1922).

Barth had had no idea of the impact that his theological writings from a Swiss village would have. He himself thought that he was making a few "marginal notes" on the theological situation, without any pretensions to establish a complete alternative to the theology he was criticizing. But Barth's "marginal notes" became a prophetic cry that echoed far and wide. Looking back several years later, he compared himself to a man who is climbing up a church tower and unexpectedly takes hold of the bell-rope instead of the banister; he is startled to hear the great bell beginning to toll out above his head.

Barth attracted notice, and he was appointed to an academic position as professor of Reformed theology at the theological faculty in Göttingen in 1921. This move led to a change in Barth's method of working and his style. Now, he was no longer a man with the task of supplying "marginal notes" to theology. He was himself responsible for formulating a viable alternative. Accordingly, Barth began to study the classical texts of theology, including mediaeval and Reformation works. His use of a classic dogmatic tradition gave a characteristic quality to his later writings.

It was at this period too that Barth joined company with other theologians who were involved in the same kind of confrontation. This took place *inter alia* in the periodical *Zwischen den Zeiten* from 1922 onwards. Barth was a frequent contributor, along with theologians such as Rudolf Bultmann, Eduard Thurneysen, Friedrich Gogarten, and Emil Brunner. This group of young theologians was often spoken of as representatives of "the dialectical theology" or the "Word-of-God theology." But it became clear in 1933, when the periodical was closed because of theological disagreements among its editors, that collective descriptions of this kind glossed over considerable differences and tensions.

In 1925, Barth was appointed to a professorship in Münster. Here, through Catholic colleagues at the university, he came into close contact with Catholic theology for the first time. In 1930, he moved to the chair of systematic theology at the University of Bonn.

After the Nazis took power in 1933, Barth soon became known as a critical voice. He was also involved in the "Confessing Church" and was the principal author of the declaration of the Confessing Synod in Barmen in 1934 (subsequently known as the "Barmen Declaration"). After he refused to declare his loyalty to Hitler, he was dismissed from his position in 1935. He moved to Switzerland, where he was appointed to a professorship in Basle. He remained in this post until he retired in 1962 at the age of 76. He continued his academic work, writing and lecturing, until his death in 1968.

After the War, Barth became involved in the ecumenical movement, for example, in connection with the setting up of the World Council of Churches. In the political sphere, he was reluctant to criticize communism as strongly as he had criticized Nazism, but he criticized NATO and the build-up of Western armaments. In 1966, Barth went to Rome, where he had conversations with Catholic church leaders about the relationship between Catholic and Protestant Christianity.

Barth's theological writings were very extensive. An important presupposition of his enormous productivity was Charlotte von Kirschbaum (1899–1975), his secretary for many years, who was a part of his household from 1929 onwards, together with his wife Nelly and their five children.

Theological Writings

The first book that made Barth truly famous was *Der Römerbrief* (*The Epistle to the Romans*), his commentary on Romans, first published in 1919. A much revised edition came in 1922. Several of his early lectures and articles are collected in *Das Wort Gottes und die Theologie* (1925) (*The Word of God and the Word of Man*) and *Die Theologie und die Kirche* (1928) (*Theology and Church*).

After he became a professor in Germany, Barth began work on a presentation of dogmatics. The first volume of *Die christliche Dogmatik im Entwurf* (*Christian Dogmatics in Outline*) appeared in 1927, entitled: *Die Lehre vom Worte Gottes, Prolegomena* (*Doctrine of the Word of God, Prolegomena*). He was, however, not happy with this project, and instead of writing further volumes, he began afresh, this time under the title: *Die kirchliche Dogmatik* (*Church Dogmatics*, = CD). The first volume was published in 1932, and Barth worked on this project for the rest of his life, without completing it. By the time of his death, the work had grown to 13 part-volumes, running to 9,185 pages!

Posterity certainly regards CD as the most important of Barth's works and also as the most important source for studying his theology. Barth constructs an enormous theological edifice here, which some readers see as a theological cathedral, marked by vigorous intellectual power and a unique ability to find excellent formulations. Barth's presentation is systematic, but he does not intend to create a theological "system" of his own. The various themes come back again and again from new perspectives, where Barth attempts to hold together apparently contradictory concepts in a dialectical unity. Barth is a highly independent and original theological thinker, but at the same time, he incorporates many references to classical and modern theological authors, not least in the many extensive excursuses. An introductory thesis in each paragraph introduces its main content.

In this work, Barth never gives a general philosophical or overall justification for his project. Instead, he goes right to the heart of the matter, to God's revelation in Christ as the true theme of theology. Theology needs no justification apart from this revelation. Another important characteristic is the role played by Trinitarian doctrine in Barth's dogmatics. This work certainly played a central role in the renaissance of Trinitarian thinking that gradually took place among theologians. Another striking characteristic is Barth's refusal to draw a dividing line between dogmatics and ethics. He includes the discussion of ethical topics in his dogmatics.

The work was originally conceived in five main volumes, but Barth was unable to proceed beyond the conclusion of the fourth volume. The main themes are:

- Vol. I (two part-volumes, 1932 and 1937): Die Lehre vom Worte Gottes. Prolegomena zur Kirchlichen Dogmatik (The doctrine of the word of God. Prolegomena to church dogmatics). Here, he discusses the understanding of the "Word of God," Trinitarian doctrine, the incarnation and the outpouring of the Spirit, the understanding of scripture, and the renewal of the church.
- Vol. II (two part-volumes, 1939 and 1942): Die Lehre von Gott (The doctrine of God). Here, he discusses the question of God's reality, the knowledge of God, God's gracious choice, and God's commandments.
- Vol. III (four part-volumes, 1945, 1948, 1947/1950, and 1951): Die Lehre von der Schöpfung (The doctrine of creation). Here, he discusses the understanding of the creation and of that which is created, the relationship between the Creator and what is created, and the Creator's commandments.
- Vol. IV (three part-volumes, 1953, 1955, 1958/1959, and a fragment published in 1967): Die Lehre von der Versöhnung (The doctrine of reconciliation). Here, he discusses Christology: Jesus as Lord, servant, and witness. The concluding fragment deals with the Christian life.
- A final fifth volume was planned, with the title Die Lehre von der Erlösung (The doctrine of redemption). One of the topics it would have discussed was eschatology.

In addition to his voluminous dogmatics, Barth wrote a number of smaller books and articles. In 1931, he published a study of Anselm, *Fides quaerens intellectum* (*Anselm. Fides quaerens intellectum*). Many regard this as a decisively important expression of the new orientation on which CD is based.

In 1934, he published *Nein! Antwort an Emil Brunner* (*No! Answer to Emil Brunner*), a temperamental settling of accounts with what he regarded as natural theology in Brunner. In 1933, he had published *Theologische Existenz heute!* (*Theological Existence To-day!*), a powerful confrontation with the "Deutsche Christen."

Questions of social ethics are taken up in *Evangelium und Gesetz* (*Gospel and Law*) (1935, on the foundations of a political ethics built on the Gospel), *Rechtfertigung und Recht* (*Church and State*) (1938, on the basis of resistance to the state), and *Christengemeinde und Bürgergemeinde* (*The Christian Community and the Civil Community*) (1946, a draft of a christologically based concept of the state). In *Ad Limina Apostolorum* (*Ad Limina*

Apostolorum) (1967), written after Barth's journey to Rome, he takes up questions that had been raised by the Second Vatican Council.

He also attempted to summarize the main points in the Christian faith in smaller books. In 1935, he published *Credo* (Credo), which presents the main points in dogmatics on the basis of the Apostles' Creed. In 1947, he published *Dogmatik im Grundriss* (*Dogmatics in Outline*). In *Einführung in die evangelische Theologie* (*Evangelical Theology*) (1962), he sums up the principal concerns in his theology.

Themes in Barth's Theology

A Theology of Diastasis

Barth's theology appeared at first sight to be an enormous "no" to the attempts in neo-Protestant theology to find the path to God *via* the human dimension, in religious feeling (Schleiermacher) or in the ethical personality (Ritschl/liberal theology). The consequence of a theology of this kind was an anthropocentric understanding of Christianity in which revelation no longer represented something that came to the human person from outside, but was an unfolding and realization of that which was highest and truest in the person himself. Against this theology, Barth maintained the qualitative difference between God and the human person. Where the earlier theology had attempted to establish a synthesis, Barth appears on the scene as the theologian of discontinuity and diastasis.

Barth was most one-sided in his emphasis on the discontinuity in his commentary on Romans. He writes as follows about his own aim, in the foreword to the second edition:

> If I have a system, it is limited to a recognition of what Kierkegaard called the "infinite qualitative distinction" between time and eternity, and to my regarding this as possessing negative as well as positive significance: "God is in heaven and thou art on earth" (p. 10).[1]

Barth maintains precisely this "qualitative distinction" as he resists every attempt to find a positive connection between the divine and the human, between earth and heaven. Nevertheless, the diastasis is not absolute. There *is* a relationship between God and the human person. But Barth does not wish to describe this as a *positive* relationship, since it is *negative*: God is "the negation of this world" (p. 82), "pure negation" (p. 141), "the negation of the negation" (p. 142). God's relationship to the world thus consists in his total *otherness* in relation to it, and in the *judgment* he pronounces on the world.

---

[1] The last sentence is a quotation from Ecclesiastes 5:1. Page references in the text are to the English translations.

The fact that it is at all possible to speak of God also shows that there is, in spite of everything, a relationship between God and the human person. This speaking of God is, however, not primarily the human person's speaking about God, but God's own speaking in revelation. Unlike the neo-Protestant theology, Barth does not understand revelation as something that is communicated through the human religious consciousness, but as something that comes utterly unexpectedly and undeservedly to the human person. When God speaks, this is something that happens *senkrecht von oben*, "it cuts vertically, from above, through every particular human status" (p. 139). In the commentary on Romans, the relationship between God and human beings is discussed primarily in negative categories, but one can see Barth's later writings as an attempt to accept and formulate the possibility of this relationship.

On one point, Barth continually strengthens his emphasis on the autonomy of the knowledge of God in relation to other forms of human knowledge, namely, in its relationship to philosophy. In *Der Römerbrief*, he can appeal to both Plato and Kant, and in *Die christliche Dogmatik im Entwurf*, he draws on existential philosophy. In CD, however, he explicitly renounces every support from philosophy, for fundamental reasons: thanks to its starting point in the Word of God, theological knowledge is absolutely self-sufficient in terms of concepts, categories, and foundation. Such an attitude excludes every attempt to base the truth of revelation in realities that lie outside revelation itself, whether in science or in human experience.

Barth takes his starting point in revelation when he speaks of the connection between the human person and God. Revelation is not some timeless principle; it is an expression of God's free action that enters the human world. If we are able to say something about God, despite the fundamental antithesis between God and the human person, this is because God has spoken into human reality. When God's Word appears in human form in Jesus of Nazareth, this also establishes a genuine connection between the divine and the human realities.

However, Barth's positive exposition of the idea of revelation is made with a certain reservation: although God has entered into human reality, one cannot speak of a direct identity between the divine and the human reality, but only of an *indirect* identity. This is expressed in Barth's view of scripture. He does not agree that the Bible (or parts of it) simply *is* the Word of God. Instead, he affirms that it *becomes* the Word of God whenever the Spirit allows it to appear as a witness to revelation:

> Scripture is holy and the Word of God, because by the Holy Spirit it became and become to the church a witness to divine revelation (CD I/2, 457).

Barth as Theologian of Creation

According to Barth, when theology speaks not only about *God*, but also about the *human person*, it must do so on the premises laid down by revelation and the divine reality. The Word of God is the only source and norm of theology, even when it speaks about human reality. This is thus a typical instance of theology "from above."

This does not mean that Barth remains "up there" in everything he writes, but that he looks at the human reality from the perspective of revelation.

Barth sets out his theology of creation and of human reality above all in the third volume of CD. He admits in the preface to the first part-volume that he has now ventured onto an area where he feels much less familiar and sure than in the areas he has discussed in earlier volumes. Nevertheless, the result was voluminous: four large part-volumes running to 2,735 pages!

Barth's comprehensive discussion of the doctrine of creation does not mean that he now engages in some form of "natural theology" or theology "from below." The doctrine of creation is a part of the theology of revelation, and consists in an exposition of the biblical understanding of the human person and of his or her lifeworld. Accordingly, the relationship to what other disciplines, such as the natural sciences, have to say about this same reality is not a central theme in Barth's presentation. However, this understanding of the relationship between theological knowledge (or faith's knowledge) and other forms of human knowledge does not mean that theology studies a list of topics all of its own. The point of orientation is always the human being in his or her relationship to God, but Barth takes this as the starting point for his endeavor to shed light on human life and the phenomena of human life in great detail. Barth discusses aspects of human life that also interest philosophy and natural science, but he does this on the premises laid down by the theology of revelation. This is exemplified in his treatment of the relationship between soul and body, and of the understanding of time (CD III/2, §§ 46–7).

Since Barth's doctrine of creation is also a part of the theology of revelation, its foundations are to be found in the Bible and the biblical texts. Much of the first part-volume on the theology of creation is quite simply an exposition of Genesis 1–2. And since the theology of creation is the theology of revelation, this also entails that it has a *christological* basis. This is connected primarily with Barth's concept of revelation: God's revelation is not a collage of disparate individual truths, but one thing alone, namely, Jesus Christ. Nor is Barth receptive to the idea of two different forms of revelation, one general-natural and the other special, an idea that is often found in both Protestant and Catholic theology. For Barth, there is only one revelation, one single Word of God, namely, Jesus Christ. Since the theology of creation is the theology of revelation, it takes its starting point in the biblical message about Jesus Christ. Barth believes that all the constitutive elements of faith in the Creator are held together in Jesus.

Instead of beginning in the creation and then approaching the redemption, Barth takes the opposite path. He wishes to start with the redemption, in order to understand and interpret the reality of creation. Faith's knowledge does not presuppose natural knowledge: the opposite is true. Knowledge of the world is derived from faith's knowledge: the world is understood and interpreted in the light of revelation. Whereas Luther and others held that the redemption presupposed the creation, Barth turns this around: the creation presupposes the redemption, the law presupposes the Gospel. This is why he replaces the formula "law and Gospel" with the formula "Gospel and law." According to Barth, the law is not an independent reality alongside the Gospel, but a "form of the Gospel" (CD II/2, 509; see also *Evangelium und Gesetz*).

Barth sees the redemption as the greater, and the creation as the lesser. The creation is "the external ground of the covenant" and the covenant is "the inner ground of the creation." In other words, the covenant is the goal and the intention that the creation is meant to serve, and the goal towards which it is meant to lead (CD III/1, § 41). The key to understanding the work of creation is therefore to see it as a reflection and a model of the redemption. This is an interpretative structure that Barth can apply down the smallest details. For example, he says that the *light* is a sign, a model of the revelation of grace (CD III/1, 118f).

In anthropology too, Christology is the basis and the starting point. As the true human being, Jesus shows us what a human being really is. In his treatment of anthropology in CD III/2, therefore, Barth begins each paragraph with a christological section.

Ethics with a Christological Basis

We find the same pattern of thought in Barth's ethics as in his doctrine of creation. He does not treat ethics separately, but integrates it into dogmatics. There is therefore no "creation ethics" detached from the redemption. On the contrary, what we find here is an ethic with a christological basis and orientation.

Barth's primary concern in CD is ethical problems of a more individual character. He takes up problems of social ethics in other books. In *Rechtfertigung und Recht* (1938) and *Christengemeinde und Bürgergemeinde* (1946), he is chiefly interested in the state and its relationship to the church. Although state and church are understood as two independent and separate entities, it is nevertheless clear that the church, as an expression of the reality of the redemption, is primary and is the starting point for understanding the state. The state and civil society must be understood as a *parable* (*Gleichnis*) of the kingdom of God, which is the object of the church's faith and proclamation.

This means that the concrete ethical norms for life in the state and civil society must be formed on the analogy of what applies in the context of the church and of the kingdom of God. Barth gives examples of what this specifically entails. Since the church is built on justification, the state must be a state under the rule of law. Since the church recognizes Christian freedom, the political and legal freedom of the citizens must also be guaranteed. Since all are equal in faith, there must also be a fundamental equality among the citizens; this excludes every discrimination of persons because of their race or gender. Since the church leads its life in the light of God, all secret politics and secret diplomacy that shun public light must be rejected in civil society too.

Barth's model for justifying ethical norms in the fields of the creation and of life in society on the basis of the doctrine of redemption and of Christology has been very important for ethical thinking in the church and in theology after World War II.

A Lutheran two-regiments thinking that had been used to legitimate a compliant attitude to the National Socialist regime had been largely discredited. Instead, the idea in the Barmer Declaration of Jesus Christ as "God's one Word" was made the point of departure for ethical thinking. We can gauge the influence of Barth's thinking here not least in many statements from ecumenical meetings and conferences in the post-War period, which often argued along the same lines as Barth's model: ethical consequences for life in society were deduced from central points in the Gospel. At the same time, this was a point on which Lutherans put forward the most serious objections to Barth's theology.

God's Divinity and God's Humanity

In his early writings, Barth was chiefly concerned to underline as strongly as possible the difference and the discontinuity between earth and heaven, between the human person and God. In his later writings, he was more concerned to bring the two together and to demonstrate the link between them. In a self-critical retrospect, *Die Menschlichkeit Gottes* (*The Humanity of God*) (1956), he admits that although his emphasis on God's divinity was justified, it was somewhat one-sided. In addition to speaking of God's divinity, in the sense of his otherness and foreignness, it is necessary also to speak of God's *humanity*: in his grace, God turns to the human person in order to have fellowship with him or her.

This, however, does not mean that he returns to the way of speaking about God's humanity that he had once so strongly opposed. For the neo-Protestant theology, thinking about God means thinking about the human person; the doctrine of God came after anthropology. Barth wants to take the opposite path, from God's divinity to his humanity; and this entails a christological starting point. In Jesus, it is not only God's divinity that is revealed, but also his humanity, and thereby the true meaning of humanity. In the encounter with Jesus, we learn what God is and what the human person is. For Barth, the fact that God is human entails a fundamental affirmation of the human person and of all that is human.

It is on this basis that we must also understand the task and the theme of theology. It is not about God in himself, nor about the human person in himself, but about their relationship to each other:

> Since God in His deity is human, this [sc. theological] culture must occupy itself neither with God in Himself nor with man in himself but with the man-encountering God and the God-encountering man and with their dialogue and history, in which their communion takes place and comes to its fulfilment (p. 55).

Karl Barth in the Theology of the Twentieth Century

Barth's influence is not in any way limited to the group of theologians who might be called "Barthians" – a term that Barth himself disliked. In a way that recalls Schleiermacher, Barth's theological work is important because it both sketches a basic framework of understanding while leaving open the possibility for adjustments, supplements, developments, and objections. Indeed, it almost demands these.

Barth was not the only dominant voice in contemporary Protestant theology. He was quick to part company with scholars who had once been his associates. In the 1930s, he broke with Brunner and Gogarten; and in the post-War years, the demythologization program of his former ally Rudolf Bultmann was the most important alternative to Barth's theology.

Eberhard Jüngel is the theologian who has developed Barth's theology in the most autonomous manner. As with Barth, Jüngel's thinking finds its orientation in the word of revelation. At the same time, however, he is concerned to show that faith proves relevant and viable in the encounter with the modern human being and his or her experience of reality.

We find an explicit alternative to Barth's model in Wolfhart Pannenberg. Unlike Barth and Jüngel, he takes his starting point in universal experience and only then approaches the Christian knowledge of God. He wishes in this way to make the link back to the theology of the nineteenth century and to take up problems and challenges that Barth and the dialectical theology had pronounced dead.

Barth's importance is not limited to German-speaking Europe. In the USA, the influence of his theology is often called "neo-orthodoxy." His influence has been felt in more recent years thanks to Hans Frei and other representatives of the so-called Yale school.

Barth's theology has also been important in Scandinavia. There have been few pure "Barthians" (the clearest exception being N.H. Søe), but he has been influential here too, both through the acceptance and through the rejection of his theses. In this context, the most pronounced characteristic of Scandinavian Lutheran theology has been a theology of creation that was very critical towards Barth's theology. Theologians such as Regin Prenter, Gustaf Wingren, and K.E. Løgstrup have emphasized the relative autonomy of the creation in relation to the redemption, and this has made them willing to speak of a natural knowledge of God antecedent to, and relatively independent of, faith's knowledge that is founded in the revelation of Christ. Instead of speaking, like Barth, of one act of God, they have preferred to speak of two acts, in creation and in redemption. And instead of speaking of one revelation, they have preferred to speak of two, the universal revelation and the revelation in Christ. Instead of "Gospel and law," they have preferred to hold fast to the Lutheran "law and Gospel." The case of the Scandinavian engagement with Barth shows that his influence has not only been restricted to his followers, as he has also set the agenda for many of his adversaries.

Bibliography

Primary Literature

Der Römerbrief (Berne: Bäschlin 1919; 2nd ed. Munich: Kaiser, 1922). English translation: *The Epistle to the Romans* (Oxford: Oxford University Press, 1933).

Das Wort Gottes und die Theologie (Munich: Kaiser, 1924). English translation: *The Word of God and the Word of Man* (London: Hodder and Stoughton, 1928).

Die christliche Dogmatik im Entwurf. Vol. 1: Die Lehre vom Worte Gottes, Prolegomena (Munich: Kaiser, 1927).

Die Theologie und die Kirche (Munich: Kaiser, 1928). English translation: *Theology and Church* (London: SCM Press, 1962).

Fides quaerens intellectum (Munich: Kaiser, 1931). English translation: *Anselm. Fides quaerens intellectum.* (Richmond, Va.: John Knox press, 1960).

Die kirchliche Dogmati (Munich: Kaiser and Zurich: Theologischer Verlag) 1932–67. English: *Church Dogmatics* (Edinburgh: Clark, 1936–77).

Theologische Existenz heute! (Munich: Kaiser, 1933). English translation: *Theological Existence To-day!* (London: Hodder & Stoughton, 1933).

Nein! Antwort an Emil Brunner (Munich: Kaiser, 1934). English translation: *No! Answer to Emil Brunner.* In: Brunner, Emil and Barth, Karl: *Natural Theology* (London 1946), pp. 65–128.

Credo (Munich: Kaiser, 1935). English translation: *Credo* (London: Hodder & Stoughton, 1936).

Evangelium und Gesetz (Munich: Kaiser, 1935). English translation: *Gospel and Law.* In: Barth, Karl: *God, Grace and Gospel* (Edinburgh; London: Oliver and Boyd, 1959), pp. 1–27.

Rechtfertigung und Recht (Zollikon: Evangelische Buchhandlung, 1938). English translation: *Church and State* (London: Student Christian Movement Press, 1939).

Christengemeinde und Bürgermeinde (Zollikon-Zurich: Evangelischer Verlag, 1946). English translation: *The Christian Community and the Civil Community.* In: Barth, Karl: *Against the Stream* (London: SCM Press, 1954), pp. 13–50.

Dogmatik im Grundriss (Zollikon-Zurich: Evangelischer Verlag, 1947). English translation: *Dogmatics in Outline* (London: SCM, 1949).

Die Menschlichkeit Gottes (Zollikon-Zurich: Evangelischer Verlag, 1956). English translation: *The Humanity of God* (Richmond, Vi.: John Knox Press, 1968).

Einführung in die evangelische Theologie (Zurich: EVZ-Verlag, 1962). English translation: *Evangelical Theology* (London: Weidenfeld & Nicolson, 1963).

Ad Limina Apostolorum (Zürich: EVZ-Verlag, 1967) English translation: *Ad Limina Apostolorum* (Richmond, Va.: John Knox press, 1968).

Secondary Literature

Busch, Eberhard, *Karl Barth: His Life from Letters and Autobiographical Texts* (Grand Rapids: Eerdmans, 1994).
Busch, Eberhard, *The Great Passion* (Grand Rapids: Eerdmans, 2004).
Hartwell, Herbert, *The Theology of Karl Barth* (London: Duckworth, 1964).
Hunsinger, George, *How to Read Karl Barth* (New York: Oxford University Press, 1991).
Jüngel, Eberhard, *Karl Barth. A Theological Legacy* (Philadelphia: Fortress, 1986).
Mangina, Joseph L., *Karl Barth. Theologian of Christian Witness* (Aldershot: Ashgate, 2004).
Torrance, Thomas F., *Karl Barth, Biblical and Evangelical Theologian* (Edinburgh: T&T Clark, 1990).
Webster, John: *Karl Barth* (London and New York: Continuum, 2000).

Chapter 6
Rudolf Bultmann

Svein Aage Christoffersen

Rudolf Bultmann is one of the most influential twentieth-century New Testament scholars and theologians. He was a pioneer in research into the New Testament and the history of earliest Christianity, in work on the basic theological questions regarding the interpretation of texts and historical understanding, and in the interpretation of the Christian faith today. This article will look primarily at Bultmann's theology and hermeneutics.

Biography

Rudolf Karl Bultmann was born on August 20, 1884 in Oldenburg (Wiefelstede) in northern Germany. His father was a pastor, and Bultmann studied theology first in Tübingen, then in Berlin and Marburg. He took his doctoral degree in Marburg in 1910 with a dissertation on *Der Stil der paulinischen Predigt und die kynisch-stoische Diatribe* (*The Style of the Pauline Preaching and the Cynic-Stoic Diatribe*). In 1912, he took his professorial examination with a dissertation on *Die Exegese des Theodore von Mopsuestia* (*The Exegesis of Theodore of Mopsuestia*) and lectured on the New Testament until 1916, when he became professor in Breslau. It was here that he wrote the book that was to make him all at once one of the leading New Testament scholars of his days and a pioneer of the form-historical method: *Die Geschichte der synoptischen Tradition* (1921 – *History of the Synoptic Tradition*). In 1920, he was appointed to a professorship in Giessen, but he moved already in 1921 to Marburg, where he remained until his retirement in 1951. Bultmann died on July 30, 1976.

One of Bultmann's teachers was Adolf von Harnack, the historian of dogma who was also the most prominent representative of the cultural Protestantism of liberal theology at that time. Bultmann acknowledged Harnack's quality as a historian of dogma, but he did not share his cultural-Protestant theology. Other teachers, such as Herman Gunkel in Old Testament and Adolf Jülicher and Johannes Weiss in New Testament, had undermined the historical basis of cultural Protestantism through their publications in the history of religion and exegesis. This applies not least to Weiss, whose epoch-making book *Die Predigt Jesu vom Reiche Gottes*, 1892 (*The Preaching of Jesus on the Kingdom of God*) had shown that Jesus had expected that the eschatological kingdom of God would come soon, and that his ethic was determined by this expectation. For Bultmann, this meant that the attempt by liberal theology to give history a directly religious significance had collapsed.

Bultmann's teacher in systematic theology, Wilhelm Herrmann, had emphasized that it is not historical research in isolation, but the encounter with Jesus in the preaching of the community that creates faith. Bultmann could not indeed agree with Herrmann that the inner life of Jesus is the ground of faith; but he accepted Herrmann's view of the significance of the community for faith, and he emphasized that the New Testament must be interpreted in such a way that we can see how it can concern us and affect us. He was interested not only in the connection between faith and thought, but also in the connection between thought and life, and hence also in the connection between faith and life.

Around 1920, Bultmann's work was marked principally by the clash with liberal theology, on the basis both of history and of theology. In his book on the synoptic tradition, Bultmann traced this tradition back to its "Sitz im Leben" in the life of the earliest community, and showed that only a very small part of this tradition can shed light on Jesus' life. Bultmann held that an important part of the synoptic tradition does not go back to the earliest Palestinian community, but to the earliest Hellenistic community. In this way, he ended up with a very skeptical attitude to the historical character of the synoptic tradition.

Bultmann's orientation away from liberal theology also found expression in his review of the second edition of Barth's commentary on Romans (1922). He agrees with Barth's attempt to free religion from the psychologizing and historicizing understanding in liberal theology, and with Barth's demand that New Testament exegesis should not be content with giving philological and historical information, but should also arrive at an understanding of what the text is about, or the "matter" of the text, which ultimately is not the human person and his or her religiosity, but God.

Barth's book is regarded as the starting shot for dialectical theology. Together with Barth, Bultmann soon became a leading spokesman for the new theological orientation in the period between the Wars. But although Bultmann and Barth began a personal contact at this time that was to last for several decades and included a voluminous correspondence, their theological relationship was very complicated. Barth always suspected that Bultmann had not completely shaken off the traces of liberal theology. As early as his review of Barth's commentary on Romans, Bultmann formulated an objection that he regarded as momentous in its consequences: if the interpretation of a text is to be concerned with the "matter," it must in principle be possible to criticize the text on the basis of the matter itself. Bultmann writes that he does not find in Barth's commentary this "matter"-criticism of the text on the text's own premises.

Bultmann's clash with liberal theology took its definitive form in "Die liberale Theologie und die jüngste theologische Bewegung" (1924). He begins this essay by observing that the object of theology is God, and that liberal theology has been defective precisely *qua* theology, because it has not been about God, but about the human person. God does not encounter the human person as a confirmation, but as a radical rejection. A theology that wishes to be about God must therefore be "a word about the cross" and thus an offense to the human person. The problem with liberal theology, according to Bultmann, is that it has tried to avoid this offense.

Barth called this article an "Armageddon" – and not without cause. It calls into question the entire foundation and way of thinking of liberal theology. Bultmann believes that the main error of liberal theology is its use of history as the basis for truth. The attempt to attribute absolute significance to historical events that are essentially relative ends in failure; it also involves a form of historical pantheism. At the same time, however, this criticism does not mean that Bultmann is willing to abandon the historical-critical method in theology. In 1921, he took contact privately with Friedrich Gogarten. Bultmann wanted to have him as a professor in Marburg, but first, he needed to be sure that Gogarten would be able and willing to work together with the Marburg theologians, who attached decisive importance to historical-critical research. Bultmann saw this as a central element in theological education, not only in an intellectual sense, but first and foremost as the basis of a critical attitude to contemporary culture and intellectual life.

He did not succeed in brining Gogarten to Marburg, nor did a fresh attempt in 1929 succeed, when the faculty had to appoint a successor to Rudolf Otto as professor of systematic theology. Bultmann rejected most of the names on the list drawn up by the majority in the faculty, including Paul Tillich – since he regarded Tillich not as a genuine theologian or an academic scholar, but as a speculative philosopher of religion with poor knowledge of the dogmatic tradition and an outstandingly good "nose" for the contemporary scene. Instead, Bultmann proposed Gogarten as the first candidate, and Barth as the second. One reason for this ranking was that Barth would tend more strongly to attract students who would accept his every word, whereas Gogarten would train them to work more independently. As things turned out, however, Otto's successor was neither Gogarten nor Barth, but Georg Wünsch.

Bultmann and Gogarten remained in contact for the rest of their lives, and as time went on, Bultmann felt closer to Gogarten than to Barth; but the friendship was put on hold in 1933, when Gogarten joined the National Socialist movement of the "Deutsche Christen," while Bultmann joined the Confessing Church on the other wing. Contact was cautiously re-established in 1940, but it never regained the unreserved exchange of views that had existed in the 1920s.

Another scholar who became a close associate of Bultmann was the philosopher Martin Heidegger, who came to Marburg in 1923 and soon became involved in a wide-ranging exchanging of views with his theological colleague. He took part in Bultmann's seminar on Pauline ethics already in 1923–24. After this, Bultmann attended Heidegger's lectures on the history of the concept of time and on the concept of truth. They held a seminar together in 1927 on Luther's commentary on the Letter to the Galatians. In autumn 1924, they read the Gospel of John together one evening every week. The contact dried up when Heidegger moved to Freiburg in 1928, where he succeeded Edmund Husserl as professor of philosophy.

The encounter with Heidegger was decisively important for the development of Bultmann's hermeneutics. Heidegger gave him a conceptual apparatus that made it possible to speak appropriately of God and of human existence, and Bultmann grasped the importance of pre-understanding for the interpretation of a text.

While Heidegger grew closer to National Socialism in the 1930s, Bultmann went in the opposite direction. He defended the political independence of the church and of university theology, and he did not accept the application of the so-called "Aryan paragraph" to those who held office in the church. This law demanded the removal of all non-Aryan state employees. Through the Confessing Church, Bultmann became involved in the life of the local parish, where he was the chairman of the Marburg Lutheran Community from 1936 onwards.

In the period after the publication of his book about the synoptic tradition in 1921, Bultmann's influence was exercised primarily through lectures and articles in both academic and more general theological periodicals. The exception was his book about Jesus, published in 1926. This differs from other biographies in that it says nothing about Jesus' life, but discusses only his preaching.

A number of Bultmann's articles and shorter studies were collected and published in 1933 under the title *Glauben and Verstehen (Faith and Understanding)*. Three further volumes with the same title followed after the War. The title, *Faith and Understanding*, is programmatic: faith is inseparably linked to the understanding in which faith understands both itself and the object of its belief. Faith is both the understanding of God and the understanding of existence. It is not faith in historical affirmations, but in the Christian message, the *kerygma*.

This theological position is also expressed in Bultmann's monumental commentary on the Gospel of John, published in 1941. In keeping with his historical-critical program, this interpretation builds on a detailed localization of the Gospel of John in its religious milieu and tradition. Bultmann upholds and develops the thesis he had already launched in the 1920s, that the Gospel of John builds on a gnostic, pre-Christian redeemer myth that is given a new and radical interpretation in the encounter with faith in Christ. He also wishes to show that the text we now have was edited by an "ecclesiastical redactor" and thus adapted to a more "orthodox" form of Christianity, with a more traditional eschatology and sacramental doctrine.

After World War II, Bultmann continued this work in a presentation of the theology of the entire New Testament: *Theologie des Neuen Testaments*, 1953, (*Theology of the New Testament*), based on the historical and hermeneutical foundation he had elaborated between the Wars. In this perspective, theology is not something one believes in, but only an explication of the understanding that is established in faith itself. The task for a presentation of the theology in the New Testament is therefore to clarify faith's self-understanding in its relation to the kerygma. This "programmatic declaration" means in practice that Bultmann continues to maintain the "matter"-critical perspective that he had called for in his review of Karl Barth's commentary on Romans.

In this same period, Bultmann's program of demythologization played an important role. He had proposed this in a lecture in 1941 on "Neues Testament und Mythologie. Das Problem der Entmythologisierung der neutestamentlichen Verkündigung" (*The New Testament and Mythology. The Problem of Demythologizing the New Testament Proclamation*). This lecture generated an international debate that has scarcely any parallels before or since. In the "demythologization debate" that raged for several decades and involved Christian laity just as much as academic theologians, Bultmann was both condemned as a heretic who denied the Christian faith and praised as the foremost defender of faith in modern times.

Theology

Faith and History: The Historical Jesus

Bultmann's thinking gravitated from start to finish around the relationship between faith and history. The liberal theology of the nineteenth century sought to employ the historical-critical method to get behind the earliest Christian proclamation of Jesus as Christ, and back to the historical Jesus himself. They not only held that the proclamation of earliest Christianity, its kerygma, and the dogmas which gradually solidified around this, prevented us from seeing the historical Jesus, but also that this kerygma was an obstacle to faith even today. By going back again to the historical Jesus, they wanted to open the door to an encounter with Jesus that could also create faith.

Bultmann rejected this theological concept, for several reasons. First of all, since there is a fundamental uncertainty about the results of historical research, these can never be the basis of a religious certainty in faith. Bultmann demonstrated this fundamental uncertainty through his skeptical attitude to the synoptic tradition as a reliable source of information about Jesus' life. His historical skepticism has been understood to mean that he thought that we know nothing about the historical Jesus, but this is incorrect. Bultmann's books on Jesus and on New Testament theology show that he did in fact believe that we can know rather a lot about the historical Jesus, with an acceptable degree of certainty.

Although Bultmann was primarily interested in Jesus' proclamation, he believed that we can know something not only about this, but also about what Jesus did. We have good reasons to assume that Jesus carried out exorcisms, broke the sabbath commandment and the Jewish prescriptions about purity, spoke polemically against legalist piety, associated with déclassé persons such as tax collectors and prostitutes, and showed consideration for women and children. He was not an ascetic like John the Baptist, but enjoyed food and drank wine. He called people to follow him, and gathered a small group of men and women around himself. There is no doubt that when he preached, he was conscious that God had given him the task of proclaiming the eschatological message about the coming of the kingdom of God, both as a demand and as an invitation.

What we know is one thing; but the significance for faith of what we know is something completely different. Strictly speaking, according to Bultmann, what we know has no significance, at least not in the sense that the believer can build the certainty of his faith upon it. Faith presupposes *that* Jesus lived and that he died on the cross. But faith need not know *how* he lived or what he said and died. Paul shows this perfectly clearly, since Jesus' life and proclamation play no role whatever in the

Letters of Paul or in Paul's preaching. If we follow Paul, this need not play any role for us either. Besides this, we do not know the answer to the decisive question of how Jesus understood his own death. We do not know whether he discerned a meaning in it, or whether he simply caved in.

Bultmann's use of Paul, and to some extent also of John, to demonstrate that faith need not necessarily know anything about the historical Jesus is also expressed in his theology of the New Testament. This does indeed begin with a chapter on the historical Jesus, but Bultmann emphasizes that this is only a presupposition for New Testament theology, not a part of it. He gives the same account of the relationship between Jesus and earliest Christianity in his book *Das Urchristentum im Rahmen der antiken Religionen*, 1949 (*Primitive Christianity in its Contemporary Setting*), where he writes about Jesus' proclamation in the chapter on Judaism, not in the chapter about earliest Christianity. The reason is straightforward: Jesus – the historical Jesus – was not a Christian. If Christian faith means believing in Jesus as Christ, then Jesus is not the subject of faith, but its object.

It is thus impossible to use Jesus himself – the historical Jesus – as a proof that Jesus genuinely was the Christ whom the church proclaims him to be. Every attempt to draw on historical research to supply a proof for faith is in fact totally contrary not only to the specific character of historical research, but also to the essence of faith. One who wishes to attempt by means of historical researches to demonstrate, legitimate, or make probable faith in Jesus as God's decisive (eschatological) act in relation to the world does not know what faith is. This is the second and most important reason why Bultmann implacably resists every attempt to make historical science the basis of faith: a faith that is built on calculations of historical probability is no longer faith.

Philosophy of Religion: God and the Human Person

Faith is faith in God, Bultmann says. But what does it mean to believe in God, and how is it in fact possible to speak about God? Bultmann poses this question in the article "Welchen Sinn hat es, von Gott zu reden?" (1925). This article plays a central role in his attempt in the 1920s to give an account of the relationship between faith and history.

Is talking about God meaningful? No, says Bultmann, if this means talking about God on the same level as other things and situations in this world that we can also talk "about." For God is not a thing, an object, or a person located somewhere in or above this world. God is transcendent, beyond this world, and thus radically different from everything in the world. He is "das ganz Andere" ("that which is wholly other"). But God is also, by definition, the reality that determines everything. This means that we cannot take our distance from him and talk about him from a neutral or untouched position. As the reality that determines everything, God also determines my own self and my life. This means that I cannot speak about God while bracketing myself off, since that would be to deny that God is the reality that determines everything. If I wish to speak about God, I must also speak about myself.

On the other hand, how can I really talk about myself? Does not talking about oneself mean taking up a position outside oneself and looking at oneself as an object on the same level as other objects in this world? Am I not fleeing from my own existence, as soon as I talk about it? In one sense, says Bultmann, this is undeniably what I am doing, if this means that I talk "about" my existence in the same way as I talk about any object in the world. For in that case, I am talking about an object without existential reality. Accordingly, if I wish to talk about God as the reality that determines everything, it is not sufficient that I speak about myself: I must also speak about myself in such a way that I do not place myself outside my own existence or flee from this. Merely to talk incessantly about oneself is no solution to the problem; it makes things worse. Irrespective of how subjective one is, one speaks "about" oneself all the time. One cannot talk one's way out of the problem like this; all one does is to get more deeply entangled in it.

If it is to be possible to speak about God, I must therefore at the same time talk about myself in such a way that my existence never ceases to be my responsibility and my risk. I cannot unload the responsibility for my existence onto others – family, friends, heredity and environment, bad times, or good and bad fortune. Nor can I unload the responsibility onto God. On the contrary, I must speak of God as the one who gives me the responsibility for my own existence, who *invites* me to take on my own existence, with the risk that this entails. Faith is therefore both a free act in which I take on the freedom that I have as a human person and make this freedom my own, and at the same time an act in which I bow in obedience before the God who offers me this freedom in the Christian kerygma. Only thus is it meaningful to talk about God.

But what does such talk look like in practice? It is here that Heidegger comes in. He supplied Bultmann with the concepts that allowed him to speak in a non-objectifying manner of human existence as various *possibilities* of existence. This also made it possible for him to describe the existence of the believer as a possibility of existence.

Bultmann was able to employ Heidegger in his theology in this way because he saw Heidegger as a phenomenologist who made explicit the understanding of human existence that is given with this existence as such. Phenomenology presupposes that the human person has a fundamental openness to his or her own existence, and thereby also has an understanding of what it means to be a human person. This understanding can indeed be hidden or obscured, for example, by dominant ideologies at any given period. Phenomenology is important and necessary precisely because it brings to light this basic understanding. It is not a philosophical system, but a way of uncovering the human person's own mode of existence – and this is described *existentially* as structural possibilities of existence. This does not mean that phenomenology says something *existential* about which possibility of existence a human person ought to choose. The locus of the existential address is preaching.

Thanks to Heidegger's phenomenological approach to human existence, Bultmann also discovered the concept of pre-understanding, which became a key concept in his own hermeneutics. In order to understand a text, we must encounter it with a pre-understanding that can open the text for us. We cannot meet it with a "tabula rasa" or just "take it as it stands," for in that case, we will not be able to understand it at all. Bultmann also calls this pre-understanding "interest." A text must always be read on the basis of a particular interest and with regard to specific questions. We may be interested in using the text to reconstruct a portion of past history, but we can also be interested in understanding history as the human person's living space, so that we inquire into the understanding of human existence that finds expression in the text. The pre-understanding is a consequence of the interest, but it does not anticipate the results of work on the text, since these results can demonstrate the incorrectness of the views we had about the content and meaning of the text before we read it.

Hermeneutics: The Demythologization Program

In the course of the 1920s, Bultmann had discovered the basis of a non-objectifying way of speaking about God and of an appropriate interpretation of theological texts. In 1941, he set out his hermeneutics in a program for the demythologization of the New Testament proclamation. His starting point is that the New Testament picture of the world is mythical. The world is divided into three levels, with the earth in the middle; above it is heaven, and below it is the underworld. The earth is not only the arena for human beings' life and activity, but also the arena for God and his angels and for Satan and his demons. Miracles occur frequently, and the human person is not his own master.

The New Testament proclamation presents the work of salvation in the framework of this mythical picture of the world, and that is the problem – for modern people cannot adopt the mythical picture of the world today. Every attempt to do so would be a form of intellectual dishonesty. Bultmann asserts that we cannot use electric light or the radio, or take modern medicine when we are sick, and believe at the same time in the New Testament's world of spirits and miracles. Nor can we understand ourselves as split and divided in the same way as the people in the New Testament. The modern person understands himself as a unified being who is the author of his own feelings, thoughts, and will.

The myth thus speaks about the divine dimension in a way that is in conflict with modern persons' picture of the world and their self-understanding. But the myth is also in conflict with itself, since it uses this-worldly language to speak about that which lies beyond the world. Above all, however, the myth is in conflict with the New Testament kerygma, which does not seek to speak in an objectifying manner about God and the human person. This is why there are obvious tensions in the New Testament between the mythological form of expression and the non-mythological message.

The solution to this problem is not the elimination of the mythological parts, as liberal theology attempted to do, since the mythology is not one part of the New Testament, but rather a framework of understanding that embraces everything, including the proclamation of Jesus' death and resurrection. Instead, the myth must be interpreted in such a way that the real intention in this proclamation emerges clearly. It is not to be interpreted cosmologically (that is, as the expression of an objective picture of the world), but *anthropologically*, that is, as an expression of the human person's self-understanding in the world. This is why Bultmann can say that the myth, or more precisely, the New Testament proclamation, must be interpreted *existentially*, with regard to the understanding of existence that finds expression in it.

One particularly controversial point in Bultmann's demythologization program concerns his interpretation of Jesus' resurrection. Can the resurrection really be anything other than mythology? It goes without saying that the resurrection is mythology if we interpret it as a confirmatory miracle that is intended to make it safe and free of risk to believe that Jesus died on the cross for us. But the resurrection is not an objective miracle of this kind. On the contrary, says Bultmann, to speak of Jesus' resurrection is to express the significance of the cross. That Jesus is risen means that his death on the cross is God's liberating judgment on the world, in the sense that God thereby also deprives death of its power. The cross and the resurrection are not two separate events, but constitute a unity. To believe in the resurrection is to believe in the cross as God's salvific deed. Accordingly, the appropriate reaction when one encounters the proclamation of Jesus' resurrection is not to conduct historical investigations to establish whether this is true – for historical investigations can never demonstrate this. The appropriate reaction is to accept the cross of Christ as one's own cross, to let oneself be crucified with Christ and thus to live in faith that God, who is not under our control and whom we cannot employ to manipulate life, encounters us as grace and love. The cross means that God pronounces judgment over all our attempts to build our life on what we ourselves can handle and master. One who believes this no longer lives "in accordance with the flesh," but is free!

When Bultmann still wants to talk about God, does this mean that a mythological remnant remains in the demythologization program? He would not agree with this, since the aim is not to eliminate talking about God, but to make it possible to talk about God in an appropriate manner.

Faith and History: The Christ Who is Proclaimed

Bultmann's demythologization program must be seen in the light of the remythologization that had taken place in National Socialism, not least thanks to Alfred Rosenberg, who was put in charge of educating the German people in the National Socialist worldview in 1934. His goal was an Aryan religion formed by and for the German people. There was in fact a place for Jesus in this Aryan religion, but for the historical Jesus – for Rosenberg held that Jesus had been painted over with Jesus concepts after his death, not least by Paul, who had ensured that this world of Jewish ideas had lived on in the Catholic and Lutheran churches. This historical Jesus thought as an Aryan, Paul as a Jew.

In 1936, Bultmann wrote an article about "Jesus und Paulus," which attacks Rosenberg on all fronts. He points out that in terms of the history of scholarship, Rosenberg's distinction between Jesus and Paul has its background in the modernized Jesus of liberal theology, which adapted him to the thoughts and ideas of what was then the modern period. However, research has shown that Jesus was just as much marked by contemporary Jesus ideas and concepts as Paul. Jesus and Paul are two of a kind. We find in Jesus the same mythological understanding of reality, the same view of the human person, and the same concept of God that we find in Paul.

In political terms, the decisive point for Bultmann was of course to emphasize that Jesus was a Jew and that faith in the Pauline sense means that no human being can boast to God on the basis of morality, ethnic origin, social position, or gender. At the same time, the article also shows that demythologization offers a new approach to the question of the relationship between Jesus and Paul. There is a correspondence between the understanding of existence in Jesus' proclamation and in Paul. We must therefore ask why earliest Christianity and Paul could not be content with simply repeating Jesus' proclamation? Why did Jesus who proclaimed have to become the Jesus who was proclaimed – not historically, but substantially? The answer is that Jesus becomes present in the kerygma as God's decisive, eschatological deed. Jesus is thus not only someone who at one point in the past proclaimed the coming salvation, but the one who has already come with this salvation. In the kerygma, that which happened once becomes that which happened once for all. Jesus is risen – in the kerygma.

Influence

Bultmann set the agenda for the theological debate for several decades after the Second World War. His theology also challenged his own pupils to think critically through the questions on which he himself had worked, and they often arrived at different results from Bultmann himself, for example, in the view of the historical Jesus and of theological hermeneutics. But in all his pupils, we find a combination of historical-critical exegesis and theological reflection that is without parallel today.

Bibliography

Primary Literature

Der Stil der paulinischen Predigt und die kynisch-stoische Diatribe (Göttingen: Vandenhoeck & Ruprecht, 1921). (*The Style of the Pauline Preaching and the Cynic-Stoic Diatribe*).
Die Exegese des Theodore von Mopsuestia (Stuttgart: Kohlhammer, 1984). (*The Exegesis of Theodore of Mopsuestia*).
Die Geschichte der synoptischen Tradition (Göttingen: Vandenhoeck & Ruprecht, 1921). English: *History of the Synoptic Tradition* (San Francisco: Harper, 1976).
Jesus (Tübingen: Mohr, 1926). English: *Jesus and the Word* (New York: London, C. Scribner's Sons, 1934).
Glauben und Verstehen. Gesammelte Aufsätze I-IV (Tübingen: Mohr, 1933–65). English: *Faith and Understanding* (Philadelphia: Fortress Press, 1966).

Das Evangelium des Johannes (Göttingen: Vandenhoeck & Ruprecht, 1941). English: *The Gospel of John: A Commentary* (Westminster: John Knox Press, 1971).

"Neues Testament und Mythologie," in *Offenbarung und Heilsgeschehen* (Göttingen: Vandenhoeck & Ruprecht, 1941) English: "New Testament and Mythology," in *Kerygma and Myth*, vol. I (London, 1953).

Das Urchristentum im Rahmen der antiken Religion (Zurich: Artemis, 1949). English: *Primitive Christianity in its Contemporary Setting* (Thames and Hudson, 1956).

Theologie des Neuen Testaments (Tübingen: Mohr, 1953). English: *Theology of the New Testament* (Prentice Hall, 1970).

Marburger Predigten (Tübingen: Mohr, 1956). English: *This World and Beyond* (Lutherworth, 1960).

Jesus Christ and Mythology (London: SCM Press, 1960). English: *Jesus Christ and Mythology* (Prentice Hall, 1997).

Geschichte und Eschatologie (Tübingen: Mohr, 1958). English: *History and Eschatology* (Greenwood Publishers, 1975).

Exegetica (Tübingen: Mohr, 1967). (*Exegetics*).

Die drei Johannesbriefe (Göttingen: Vandenhoeck & Ruprecht, 1967). English: *The Johannine Epistles* (Philadelphia, Fortress Press, 1973).

Der zweite Brief an die Korinther (Göttingen: Vandenhoeck & Ruprecht, 1976). (*Second Corinthians*).

Das verkündigte Wort (Tübingen: Mohr, 1984). (*The Preached Word*).

Existence and Faith (New York, Collection, 1960).

Secondary Literature

Ebeling, Gerhard, *Theologie und Verkündigung. Ein Gespräch mit Rudolf Bultmann* (Tübingen: Mohr, 1962).

Jaspert, Bernd (ed.), *Bibel und Mythos. Fünfzig Jahre nach Rudolf Bultmanns Entmythologisierungsprogramm* (Göttingen: Vandenhoeck & Ruprecht, 1991).

Jaspert, Bernd (ed.), *Rudolf Bultmanns Werk und Wirkung* (Darmstadt: Wissenschaftliche Buchgesellschaft, 1984).

Jones, Gareth, *Bultmann. Towards a Critical Theology* (Cambridge: Polity Press, 1990).

Schmithals, Walter, *Die Theologie Rudolf Bultmanns* (Tübingen: Mohr, 1966).

Chapter 7
Werner Elert

Bernt T. Oftestad

Werner Elert (1885–1954) was one of the most prominent Lutheran theologians in the first half of the twentieth century, during the golden age of the so-called "Luther renaissance" that had begun in the previous century. New scholarly editions of the Reformer's works prompted an increasing number of analyses of his life and theology. Elert was one of the most original, productive, and important representatives of the new Lutheran theology that was generated by the Luther renaissance. He was active as historian and systematic theologian, as researcher and as teacher. Like his contemporary Karl Barth, who had laid the foundations for a new epoch in Protestant theology around 1920, Elert was formed by the cultural crisis at the beginning of the twentieth century. Like the dialectical theologians, he rejected the synthesis between theology and Idealist philosophy that had dominated Protestant theology in the nineteenth century. In his theology and his ecclesiastical attitude, however, he represented a clear and well thought-out alternative to Karl Barth and the dialectical theology. When Hitler came to power in 1933, German Protestantism was divided. Elert was one of those who looked positively on the National Socialists' accession to power.

Biography

Walter Elert was born on August 19, 1885 in Heldrungen in Prussia (in today's Thuringia). He attended grammar school in Hamburg and Husum, and studied from 1906 to 1910 in Breslau, Erlangen, and Leipzig. He had a wide range of interests and worked in theology, philosophy, history, the history of German literature, psychology, and law. He took his doctorate in philosophy in Erlangen and in theology in Breslau. He was ordained in 1912 and worked as a military chaplain on several frontlines during the First World War (1914–18). In 1919, he moved to Breslau and became the director of the Theological Seminary of the Lutheran church in Prussia. In 1923, he became professor of church history at the Friedrich Alexander University in Erlangen. He moved to the chair of systematic theology in the same university in 1932. He was rector of the university in 1926–27 and dean of the theological faculty in 1928–29 and 1935–43. He was a member of the General Synod of the United Evangelical Lutheran Church in Germany (EKDV) and of the theological section of the Lutheran World Federation (established in 1947). He belonged to the commission for the publication of Luther's works (the Weimar edition), which had begun in 1883. He retired in 1953 and died in Erlangen on November 21, 1954.

The Challenge of the Third Reich

The Third Reich was the great challenge to German theologians of Elert's generation, and it had grave consequences for many of them. In political-ideological terms, Elert belonged to a national conservative tradition that emphasized the people and the state; many of his family were officers, and there had always been an Elert in Prussia's wars in the preceding 250 years. This family background and cultural identity explain why it was natural for him to support Hitler's accession to power in 1933 and the National Socialist state. This attitude also agreed with the conservative Lutheran understanding of Christianity that he had learned. From 1933 onwards, the National Socialist racism and hatred of Jews was translated into practical politics. Hitler "cleansed" the German civil service of Jews. Instead of protesting, Elert and his colleague, Professor Paul Althaus, declared in a statement by the theological faculty in Erlangen that those who were ethnically Jewish could no longer hold office in the German Protestant church. This was a consequence of his strict loyalty to the state and of his Protestant ecclesiology. Elert took care not to open himself to the accusation of anti-Semitism: it went without saying that baptized Jews had a right to membership in the Christian church. But as National Socialism intensified its persecution of the Jews, so Elert too became more hostile to them. He supported the laws for the protection of the purity of German blood (the Nuremberg laws). For him, the law of the state was God's law. This was a consequence of his Lutheranism.

Lutheran Rejection of the "Barmen Declaration"

In 1934, the church front against the National Socialist movement within the Protestant churches (the "Deutsche Christen") became better organized. A basic document was drawn up, the "Barmer theologische Erklärung" (The Theological Declaration of Barmen), in which Lutheran and Reformed theologians agreed on a common doctrinal foundation. Elert dissented from this declaration and countered it with the "Ansbacher Ratschlag" (The Advice of Ansbach), a declaration that was supported by his colleague Paul Althaus and several pastors. Elert believed that he was the spokesman of the genuinely Lutheran position. He claimed to recognize in the Barmen declaration Karl Barth's Christocentric understanding of revelation (christomonism) and a lack of emphasis on God's law (antinomism). The Barmen declaration was a deviation from the Lutheran tradition of faith, and no credible Lutheran could support it. In a number of theses, Elert elaborated his alternative theology of the law and God's orderings. Not unexpectedly, the Advice of Ansbach concluded with thanks to God for having given the German people a Führer, a pious and faithful supreme pastor, and a National Socialist state system that would be a "good regiment" for society. In this way, Elert gave the Deutsche Christen some much-needed prestige. But despite strong pressure, and despite his own sympathy with the National Socialist government, he never became a member of the church organization of the Deutsche Christen or of the Nazi Party. Elert's role under the Third Reich is open to discussion. Ideologically speaking, he was not a National Socialist, but he remained faithful to Nazi Germany and to its Führer until the very end of the Second World War in 1945.

Theological History of Ideas and the Lutheran "Morphology"

Elert's first major work was published in 1921. *Der Kampf um das Christentum* (The Struggle about Christianity) was an account, in the context of the history of ideas, of the relationship between German Protestant Christianity and general thinking from Schleiermacher and Hegel down to the beginning of the twentieth century. This indicated the direction his later work would take. He undertook a broad analysis of German philosophy and theology in the nineteenth century against the background of Christianity's loss of hegemony during the Enlightenment. He discussed both the ideological de-Christianization of culture and the various apologetic attempts by theologians to establish the relevance of Christianity in the new cultural circumstances.

A distinction had been drawn in Lutheranism between God's order of creation and his order of grace. Both were from God, but there would never be a complete harmony in this world between these two orders, since the order of creation was always infected by sin. This is the background for Elert's interpretative strategy in 1921. The dialectic between distance and synthesis structured his fundamental view of the relationship between Christianity and intellectual culture. It was especially important to hold fast to the distance between revelation and culture. To be a Christian is completely different from what one is culturally, socially, and ethnically. In the encounter with the challenges of the twentieth century, Elert, like many contemporary theologians, rejected the Christian cultural synthesis. Neither Idealistic speculation nor the transcendental-philosophical religious *a priori* sufficed to ensure the cultural relevance of faith. Such abstract and speculative attempts at a solution failed to do justice to the *historical* character of revelation.

In *Der Kampf um das Christentum*, Elert emphasized that the situation after the First World War was an especial challenge. Under the influence of Oswald Spengler's cultural analysis in *Der Untergang des Abendlandes* (1918/1922) (The Decline of the West), he regarded the zeitgeist as decadent. Culture was in decay, and marked by disintegration. One ought not to attempt to justify the relevance of faith on the premises of this sinking culture, for that would mean that faith too would be affected by the cultural disintegration.

Elert argues that Evangelical Lutheran theology needs an understanding of culture, if it is to meet the demand for relevance. Otherwise, it lapses into Biblicism and/or a revelational positivism. Culture is the embodiment of *freedom*, *clarity*, and *the sublimity of the soul* in relation to its environment. This concept of culture allows one to stand firm against the pressure from contemporary culture. Elert saw Christianity as the truly liberating force, thanks to its unsurpassed cultural excellence. This meant that faith did not need to be legitimated by contemporary culture – for that would supply only "false supports."

The challenge in the 1920s was to demonstrate the relevance of faith and theology. The task was to find the path ahead in a situation of cultural crisis. Elert based his arguments on Schleiermacher's fundamental principle that Christianity becomes culturally relevant when it shows that faith is a special form of consciousness and knowledge. In that case, it is the special Christian experiential knowledge, in the individual Christian and in Christians as a group, that gives faith its cultural relevance. This supplies both distance and closeness vis-à-vis culture. This approach agreed with the conservative experiential theology that had been elaborated in the nineteenth century, especially in Erlangen. Religious revival was to provide theology with its experiential foundation; theology received its contents from the biblical-confessional tradition. The theoretical presuppositions and the framework of theology were found in Schleiermacher's philosophical guarantee of the intellectual right of the religious consciousness in a modern age. Elert had imbibed the Erlangen theology, which was still a living tradition at the beginning of the twentieth century. He adopted and developed F.H.R. Frank's strict systematic account of the subjective experience of faith, as well as Ludvig Ihmel's emphasis on the historical-objective testimony to Christ and God's transcendence. Together with Paul Althaus, Elert represented the Erlanger school in its final stage.

Elert was able to develop in various directions the historical-apologetic work he published in 1921. In 1923, he became professor in the history of dogmas and the creeds. In the following year, he published a short outline of Lutheran doctrine, *Die Lehre des Luthertums* (1924) (The Lutheran Doctrine), and he now concentrated on these dogmatic-confessional subjects. In this short presentation of doctrine, he set out characteristic topics of Lutheran theology such as the struggle with God, reconciliation, and freedom. The key concept in this presentation was not love or grace, but freedom. He underlined the tension between judgment and grace. The order of creation and the order of redemption are at the service of the realization of the true life in the world. The supra-individual orders of creation also include the *fellowship of blood* alongside the legal system and fellowship in work. One decade later, the idea of a fellowship of blood was to become a central topic for Elert.

He published his next large work at the beginning of the 1920s: *Morphologie des Luthertums* I-II (1931/1932) (The Structure of Lutheranism). This is a wide-ranging presentation of Lutheranism both systematically and in the context of the history of ideas and of culture. It remains one of the most important twentieth-century contributions in this field. But Elert also wishes to make a methodological point.

The term "morphology" comes from Goethe and is used in a number of sciences (biology, geology, physics, linguistics), where it generally denotes the study of forms, structures, etc. Elert regarded this kind of approach as fruitful for theology too. This method is much more reflective than the straightforward communication of knowledge about the genesis of the religious confessions, their doctrinal profile, liturgical life, church orders, etc. He goes beyond the strictly ecclesiastical boundaries and seeks to demonstrate the formative power of the Lutheran tradition of faith in culture, society, and politics. He does not restrict himself to the motherland of the Reformation, but includes both Scandinavia and Eastern Europe. This methodology is particularly well suited to the development of the great confessions in the period after the Reformation, as they gradually attained hegemony in religious politics in the various countries and states, and were thus better able to shape the strictly religious life.

Morphologie des Luthertums presents the development of the Lutheran doctrine and church order, but also the pragmatic and ethical approaches of Lutheranism, the understanding of the family and marriage, the Lutheran view of the "popular" dimension ("das Deutschtum"), the state, and the economy. The book covers the period from the Reformation to the nineteenth century. But if a morphology is to bring to light a historical process and not merely a given structure, it must also discover the *force* that lies in the development, and hence the alteration, of the structures. Elert identifies the starting point and "dynamis" of the formative process as the genuinely Lutheran element that was introduced into history by Martin Luther. But when he defines this Lutheran element, he deviates both from neo-Protestantism and from Lutheran orthodoxy. Neo-Protestantism sees the genuinely Lutheran element in "the young Luther"; Lutheran orthodoxy sees it in the formation of the Evangelical-Lutheran confession, which concludes with the Formula of Concord in 1577. Naturally enough, Elert does not locate the dynamic of Lutheranism in the Evangelical-Lutheran confessions of faith; nor does he stop at the young Luther. He finds the exposition of the truly Lutheran or Reformation element in the Reformer's fundamental clash with Humanism in the mid-1520s (*De servo arbitrio*, 1525). Luther's exegesis of Psalm 90 (WA 40/3: 484–94) is also important in this context.

It is in Luther's understanding of God's judgment and grace, in the dialectic between law and Gospel, that Elert finds the theological motif that is the motor in the Lutheran tradition of faith. The human person's terror before God must not be covered over. Elert affirms that every religion begins with terror. It is against this background that Christ, faith, and the Gospel of grace must be understood.

Ethicist and Dogmatic Theologian under National Socialism

Elert faced new academic challenges when he became professor of systematic and historical theology in 1932. In 1940, he published his dogmatic treatise, *Der christliche Glaube* (The Christian Faith) and in 1949, his ethical treatise, *Das christliche Ethos* (The Christian Ethics). These books are systematic presentations of Evangelical-Lutheran faith and doctrine. Elert was not a confessionalistic dogmatic theologian. He seeks to anchor the Lutheran tradition of faith also in pre-Reformation theology, drawing on the extensive knowledge of the history of dogma and theology that he had gradually acquired. His aim as a systematic theologian is to make the Christian faith relevant in the contemporary cultural situation, but without abolishing the distance between Christianity and culture. For such a goal, more is needed than a reflective presentation of the church's doctrine. It is necessary to demonstrate that faith correlates with the existential experience that is characteristic of the age. This was a characteristic goal in liberal Protestantism, but Elert is certainly not a liberal Protestant. He emphasizes much more strongly than is customary in neo-Protestantism the distance and the conflict between revelation and the human person's natural existence. He does not share the optimistic view of religion that is found in neo-Protestantism, nor its concept of God.

In the 1930s, the conflict with the Reformed theologian Karl Barth was the decisive issue for Elert, and this marks his dogmatics and ethics. The fundamental structure in Elert's theology was the classic Lutheran *law and Gospel* – not Karl Barth's *Gospel and law*. His understanding of the law made Elert open to the human person's natural existential experiences, as these are given in a life under the law. On the basis of the dialectic between law and Gospel, Elert also sees a point of contact for the Gospel in the human person's natural existence. While he certainly does not share Barth's rejection of this idea, Elert too sees no positive point of contact. On this question, he diverges radically from both Catholic teaching and liberal Protestantism. It is the human person's existentially tragic situation under the law in the orders of creation and redemption that dialectically constitutes the "point of contact" for the Gospel message. In the theological-phenomenological description of human existence that forms the introduction to his dogmatics, Elert elaborates his "natural" anthropology, which he calls "the human person's self-understanding under the hidden God." The definition of the genuinely Lutheran element in the *Morphologie des Luthertums* is developed here to form the basis of a fundamental theological hermeneutics that can clarify the natural existence of the human person.

There are three principal characteristics of the human person's existential situation: *the questioning attitude,* which certainly does not mean that one abandons the egocentricity ("existence in the midpoint") that directs the person's life; *the ethical attitude,* which unfolds in the interpersonal and the socio-political contexts; and *destiny,* to which the human person's life is subordinate because it inevitably takes the path that leads to death. The development of these anthropological existentials leads to a theological conclusion: in his or her self-understanding, the human person encounters only "the hidden God." This is a God whom one cannot love. One can only fear him – and ultimately, one must hate him.

There is an apparent distinction in *Der christliche Glaube* between the phenomenological-theological illumination of existence that introduces the dogmatics, and the substantial dogmatic presentation of the Christian faith that then follows, where he discusses the traditional themes (the idea of God, reconciliation, justification, the church, the sacraments, eschatology) from a Lutheran perspective. But Elert's presuppositions make the link between the two parts clear. A life "under the hidden God" is a life in the sphere of the Fall and of the law. In the church's kerygma, which has the law and the Gospel as its central content, the human person encounters the revelation that can free him from his insoluble tragedy. God is active in the world, but he cannot be known aright apart from the revelation in Christ. Elert rejected the idea that the revelation in Christ is God's self-revelation. In Christ, God's grace has been "uncovered." This clearly indicated both his distance from the Christocentrism in the dialectical theology and his emphasis on God's transcendence.

In the 1930s, Elert was also involved in the urgent contemporary questions in ethics, especially in political ethics. The positive attitude to Hitler's ascent to power in 1933 and the rejection of the Barmer Declaration in the following year required a theological foundation. For Elert, such a justification must consist in an interpretation of the Lutheran *ethics of ordering*. In the theological tradition, and in Luther himself, God's orderings, above all the family and the authorities, are given in creation. This idea gradually took the systematic form of a Lutheran social teaching such as Elert had presented in his *Morphologie*, centered on faith in God's spiritual and secular orderings in the world, which are exercised on the one hand through the church's administration of the means of grace, and on the other hand through the secular orderings. Characteristically, Elert included the fellowship of the people, something given through "Blut und Boden," in God's "natural" orderings. The fact that we as individuals belong to the fellowship of a people is our destiny as human beings. This is not an ethical theme, properly speaking. The ethical questions are connected to our relationship to the fellowship of the people, for we can let it down and despise it. And since the authorities or the state order my natural existence in the people, an existence that is given with "blood and soil," the state too is a "natural" ordering. It imposes order on society by means of secular laws, demanding obedience to the law under threat of punishment. One's relationship to the state is thus something given by nature. It is conditioned by nature and unavoidably determines one's destiny in exactly the same way as kin and family (parents and children, sibling relationships, etc.). The state acts on behalf of the entire fellowship of the people, in which the individual is only a part. Here, there was in effect no space for a political-ethical critique of the state. In view of the situation in Germany in the 1930s, Elert affirmed that the Germans were bound to the German "Blut und Boden," and were therefore subject to the German state order that was then in force, and to the obedience this demanded. A decisive presupposition for Elert's loyalty to the National Socialist state and for his support of its laws until the very end of the War was also his belief that the de facto existing national state was established by God in the order of creation.

Elert's ethics, published in comprehensive form in *Der christliche Ethos* (1949), was elaborated consistently on the basis of the "real dialectic" between law and Gospel. This gave a *soteriological* character to his teaching about the social and political orderings. The decisive point is his understanding of the significance of the law for salvation, which in turn is reflected in his individual and social ethics.

The law has been seen in various ways within the Lutheran tradition. Already in the sixteenth century, central theologians of the Reformation like Philipp Melanchthon claimed that the law also had a "third use" in addition to the civil use for life in society and the theological use that uncovered and condemned human sin. The law had an ethical-pedagogical use, giving support and guidance to the believer on the path of sanctification. This doctrine also found expression in the Formula of Concord, but it has been a matter of dispute, especially within more recent Lutheranism.

Elert was one of the theologians who vigorously rejected the idea of "the third use of the law." He saw such an idea as incompatible with the genuinely Lutheran element. For Elert, the effect of the law means that it is wholly an ordering unto death, making the human person guilty in relation to God and uncovering his or her desperate situation under God's judgment. The law is the negative presupposition for faith in the Gospel, but it can make no contribution whatsoever to the development of the spiritual life in which the believer shares through the Gospel. Spirit and law must not be joined together. The law is a power of destiny and a power of death in the life of the natural human person, whereas the Gospel brings life and freedom. We must therefore avoid blending law and Gospel together: they must be kept apart. It is only in the soteriological "real dialectic" that they can and should be held together.

A correct knowledge of the law comes "from the outside" through the Christian proclamation, which uncovers sin and guilt in relation to God. But the objective basis of the knowledge of sin is the human person's life in the orderings, which is determined by destiny. In Elert, law and ordering are integrated. Orderings such as people and state are given in creation, and therefore given by God. They are also at the service of the law, and become powers of destiny. In this way, they are also drawn into the soteriological dialectic between law and gospel, and this means that to confess one's sin is to recognize that sin is a destiny that brings guilt. The human person's tragic situation consists in a life in guilt – a life that at the same time is his destiny. As a natural human being, he stands over against a God who is hidden and from whom nothing good can be expected. The church's kerygma about God's salvation in Christ releases the human person from his evil destiny through salvific grace, and imparts a new life.

This doctrine of salvation explains Elert's attitude under the Third Reich. When a dialectic perspective allows the powers of destiny (the fellowship of a people, the state, etc.) to become a presupposition for a purely soteriological understanding of the human person, there is no possibility – on the basis of the law or of the Gospel – to criticize or condemn these powers because of their concrete actions. Nor is there any right to disobedience or revolt. An ethical basis for opposing the state exists only when it *dissolves* itself as a state under the rule of law with power over the fellowship of the people. As a power of destiny, the state must work according to its own legality, which the believer accepts. There is, however, one exception: when it commands one to sin, one must disobey (Acts 5:29).

In his dogmatics, and equally in his ethics, Elert is concerned to draw a distinction between reason and revelation. Everything that is not revealed in the theological sense is subordinate to the reason, that is to say, to life in the orderings created by God under the domain of the natural law. One uses the reason when one develops the necessary guidelines and frameworks for concrete life in society on the basis of the fundamental orderings. But Elert is certainly not a rationalist. When he speaks of the reason, he means something more than the human "faculty of judgment." His understanding of socio-political rationality includes customs and practices, the laws of the state, history, the sense of honor, societal appropriateness, the political will, etc.

Have the church and the believer any kind of ethical mandate in society? In the light of the revelation of salvation, the believer sees the orderings of destiny – "blood and soil" and the state – which are inflamed by sin in the world – as good things that God has given in his fatherly mercy. If the believer is bound to "blood and soil" in this way, the church too is bound to it in a number of ways. But irrespective of external circumstances, the church must be faithful to its mission to proclaim the Gospel in such a way that sinners can become *believing* sinners. It must have freedom to proclaim the condemnation of the law. If the state wishes to force the church to be silent, the church must obey God rather than human beings. But its goal must not be theocracy or ecclesiocracy. Its task is not to rule, but to serve. Elert sums up this point as follows: the state cannot be a theocracy, since it does not rule in *God's name*. Nor can the church be a theocracy, since it does not *rule* in God's name. Elert was profoundly interested in problems of church order. But during the Third Reich, he emphasized that while the old German state-church system had passed away, the national church must be preserved. The Third Reich had brought a renewal of the German people, and this would shape church order too.

Elert's work on the history of doctrine was not limited to the Reformation period and the nineteenth century. Towards the close of his life, he became more interested in the history of dogma and began an intensive study of the early church fathers. He presented Augustine as a teacher for all Christians, and investigated questions about the eucharist and ecclesial fellowship in the early church, as well as patristic Christology. He had a systematically reflective perspective on the history of dogma and theology. The history of *dogma* is genuine history. Its substantial content is expressed "in embryo" in the preaching of the apostles and is developed through the church's tradition, above all thanks to the dogmatic decisions in Trinitarian doctrine and Christology. In this perspective, the Evangelical-Lutheran Reformation was both a full realization and a new development. The dogma about Christ as true God and true man is grasped correctly in the "for me" of the Reformation faith. Inspiration from the early church also helped to expand his Protestant ecclesiology, with its stress on the administration of the Word. In the older Elert, the church's *diakonia* comes into the picture. The fellowship that is created and built up through the means of grace is a fellowship of siblings that is made concrete and realized through diaconal service.

Germany's Defeat in a Theological Light

On June 5, 1945, one month after Germany's defeat, Elert held a lecture in Erlangen in which he interpreted the War and the German collapse as a trial imposed upon by the German people by Christ himself. He had lost two sons on the frontline, one in 1940, the other in 1944. Elert calls Christ a "sharpshooter" whose aim becomes ever more accurate. Elert sees Christ at work in the form of the one who brings a family the news that a father, a son, or a brother has fallen, in the bombs that rained down over

German cities, and in the occupation of a Germany in ruins. In a natural perspective, the War with all its sufferings and the German defeat are brought about by a God who inflicts terror, a God who determines human destiny. For faith, however, these are trials imposed by Christ, and they must be endured in faith.

Elert's attitude to the War not only shows the difficulties faced by political theology when it was confronted with the reality of modern warfare. It also reveals the foundations of his theological position, which he had held as early as the 1920s. God's law is identified with the "natural" processes in the world. God's actions are therefore interpreted on the basis of an irrationalistic view of history in which the hidden God is behind the dynamic of history – a dynamic that consists of struggle and strife. Elert regards the experience of terror as the religious "primal revelation." The Gospel liberates the believer from this "experience of terror," but does not abolish it. The believer is reconciled with it, as a trial sent by God. The sharpshooter is at the service of faith and sanctification. This allows Elert to salvage the unity of the picture of God, but he loses ethical rationality. There is no place here for the classical concept of the natural law.

Elert was a modern theologian, deeply influenced by the first crisis of modernity at the beginning of the twentieth century, when it became clear that the rationality of the Enlightenment was incapable of answering the human person's existential questions. Nor was it able to resolve the cultural crisis that followed the First World War, when the "feeling of life" became tragic. With his emphasis on the person's experience of tragedy, Elert reflects the modern individual culture of experience. But we also notice the readiness of that period to achieve ethical homogenization and the favorable view of a totalitarian state system. He is Lutheran-confessional, but he is equally formed by the neo-Protestantism of the nineteenth century, by late Romanticism, and by the orientation to the "philosophy of life" that marked contemporary German culture. Elert was a German theologian, formed by the German-national tradition, to which he also supplied a basic theological legitimacy.

Bibliography

Primary Literature

Elert, Werner, *Der Kampf um das Christentum. Geschichte der Beziehungen zwischen dem evangelischen Christentum in Deutschland und dem allgemeinen Denken seit Schleiermacher und Hegel* (Munich: C.H. Beck'sche Verlagsbuchhandlung, 1921). (*The Struggle about Christianity*).

Elert, Werner, *Die Lehre des Luthertums im Abriss* (Munich: C.H. Beck'sche Verlagsbuchhandlung, 1924). (*Outline of the Lutheran Doctrine*).

Elert, Werner, *Morphologie des Luthertums. I. Theologie und Weltanschauung des Luthertums hauptsächlich im 16. und 17. Jahrhundert. II. Sozialllehren und Sozialwirkungen des Luthertum* (Munich: C.H. Beck'sche Verlagsbuchhandlung, Oskar Beck, 1931–32). English: *The Structure of Lutheranism* (St. Louis: Concordia Publishing House, 1962).

Elert, Werner, *Bekenntnis, Blut und Boden. Drei theologische Vorträge* (Leipzig: Verlag von Dörffling und Franke, 1934). (*Confession, Blood and Soil*).
Elert, Werner, *Der christliche Glaube. Grundlinien der lutherischen Dogmatik* (Berlin: Furche-Verlag, 1940). (*The Christian Faith*).
Elert, Werner, *Der christliche Ethos. Grundlinien der lutherischen Ethik* (Tübingen: Furche-Verlag, 1949). (*The Christian Ethics*).
Elert, Werner, *Zwischen Gnade und Ungnade. Abwandlungen des Themas Gesetz und Evangeliums* (Munich: Evangelischer Presseverband, 1948). (*Between Grace and Disgrace*).
Elert, Werner, *Abendmahl und Kirchengemeinschaft in der alten Kirche, hauptsächlich des Osten* (Berlin: Lutherisches Verlagshaus, 1954). (*Eucharist and Communion in the Old Church*).
Elert, Werner, *Der Ausgang der altkirchlichen Christologie. Eine Untersuchung über Theodor von Pharan und seine Zeit als Einführung in die alte Dogmengeschicht* (Berlin: Berliner Verlagshaus, 1957). (*The Conclusion of Christology in the Primitive Church*).
Elert, Werner, *Ein Lehrer der Kirche. Kirchlich-theologische Aufsätze und Vorträge von Werner Elert* (Berlin and Hamburg: Lutherisches Verlagshaus, 1967). (*A Doctor in the Church*).

Secondary Literature

Althaus, Paul, 'Elert, Werner,' *RGG* 3rd ed. 2 (Tübingen: J.C.B. Mohr, 1959), 418.
Beyschlag, Karlmann, *Die Erlanger Theologie* (Erlangen: Martin Luther Verlag, 1993).
Hamm, Bernd, 'Werner Elert als Kriegstheologe. Zugleich ein Beitrag zur Diskussion 'Luthertum und Nationalsozialismus'.' *Kirchliche Zeitgeschichte*, 11 (1998), 206–54.
Hübner, Friedrich (ed.), *Gedenkschrift für D. Werner Elert: Beiträge zur historischen und systematischen Theologie* (Berlin: Lutherisches Verlagshaus, 1955), 411–24.
Krötke, Wolf, *Das Problem "Gesetz und Evangelium" bei W. Elert und P. Althaus* (Zurich: EVZ-Verlag, 1965).
Langemayer, Leo, *Gesetz und Evangelium. Ein Grundanliegen der Theologie W. Elerts*, Konfessionskundliche und kontroverstheologische Studien 20 (Paderborn: Verlag Bonifacius-Druckerei, 1970).
Peters, Albrecht, "Gesetz und Evangelium." *Handbuch der systematischen Theologie* 2 (Gütersloh: Gütersloher Verlag, 1981).
Peters, Albrecht, "Elert, Werner." *TRE* 9 (Berlin: Walter de Gruyter Verlag, 1982), 493–7.
Slenczka, Notger, *Selbstkonstitution und Gotteserfahrung. Werner Elerts Deutung der neuzeitlichen Subjektivität im Kontext der Erlanger Theologie* (Göttingen: Vandenhoeck & Ruprecht, 1999).
Schmidt, K.D. (ed.), *Die Bekenntnisse und grundsätzlichen Äußerungen zur Kirchenfrage. I. 1934. II. 1935 (Texte und Dokumente)* (Göttingen: Vandenhoeck & Ruprecht, 1936).
Wiebering, Joachim E., 'Kirche als Bruderschaft in der lutherischen Theologie,' *Kerygma und Dogma*, 23 (1977), 300–315.
Wolf, Ernst, 'Barmen,' *RGG* 3rd ed. 1 (Tübingen: J.C.B. Mohr, 1958), 873–9.
von Loewenich, Walther, *Erlebte Theologie. Begegnungen, Erfahrungen* (Munich: Claudius Verlag, 1979).

Chapter 8
Paul Tillich

Svein Olaf Thorbjørnsen

The importance of Paul Tillich (1886–1965) as a theologian is due more to the fact that he made theology relevant in his days than to any lasting value in the fruits of his theological endeavors. With his theology, he built bridges between people's personal problems and the Gospel. Here, people found answers to questions about the meaning of life. This bridge was created on the basis of a specific conviction, namely, that the question about meaning has its innermost depth in a religious dimension. For Tillich, human life in its uttermost depth is religious.

A conscious link between the Christian message and contemporary questions and problems played an absolutely central role in Tillich's theology. In this way, he became an alternative both to Karl Barth and to the liberal tradition. Tillich held that Barth did not take account of the human situation, while the liberal theology took account *only* of the human situation. Tillich wanted to unite these two traditions.

This duality characterizes all of Tillich's thinking. He moved all the time in borderlands: between two epochs (the harmony of Idealism and the chaotic period between the Wars), between theory and praxis, between theology and philosophy, between church and society, between religion and culture, between Protestantism and socialism.

Tillich's central influence and his position as a theologian are linked to the time he spent in the USA. In the 1960s, he was regarded as one of the most celebrated intellectuals in America, where he is seen as one of the most influential theologians in the twentieth century. His influence went far beyond the theological sphere. His theological approach, taking its starting point in general realities and the fundamental human questions, made him an important figure for art and architecture, for sociology and psychology, and indeed for the whole of American politics and culture.

Tillich was influential, but he was also controversial, especially in theological terms. His methodological starting point in general realities laid him open to the accusation that he allowed the general and the immanent to determine the theological substance to an unacceptably high degree.

Biography

Tillich was born in 1886 in eastern Germany, the son of a pastor who attached great importance to orthodoxy. He began studying philosophy and theology in 1900, in Berlin, Tübingen, and Halle. In particular, his encounter with Martin Kähler in Halle, and Kähler's understanding of justification by faith, were to be very important for Tillich's theological interests and approach. For Tillich, the undeserved justification embraced also doubters and unbelievers, and God is present in them. Both doubt and unbelief are fundamentally human. Tillich later said that it was this interpretation that allowed him to continue to be a theologian.

Tillich took his doctorate in philosophy in Breslau in 1910 and his licentiate in theology in Halle in 1912, each time on a theme taken from the philosopher Schelling. Tillich did not accept the dichotomy between nature and morality that he found in Ritschl (derived ultimately from Kant), and he was more content with the holistic thinking that he found in Schelling's natural philosophy. After two years as pastor in a parish in Berlin (1912–14), Tillich became a military chaplain. His experiences as a military chaplain throughout the First World War led to the collapse of the Idealistic picture of reality that he had held up to that time, and he began to get involved politically, taking a religious-socialist direction.

During the first years of the War, he wrote his professorial dissertation on the concept of the supernatural. He taught in Berlin from 1919 to 1924, and was professor of systematic theology in Marburg in 1924–25, where he was influenced by Heidegger's existentialist philosophy. There is a trajectory that leads from Heidegger's way of thinking to Tillich's methodology of correlation. He had no great opinion of another colleague, Rudolf Bultmann. From 1925 to 1929, he was professor of the science of religion in Dresden and honorary professor of theology in Leipzig. In 1929, he was appointed to succeed Max Scheler as professor of philosophy at Frankfurt am Main, where he attracted notice. He moved across academic boundaries and discussed the urgent questions of the time, including the political questions. He was very active in the Social Democratic Party and published the pamphlet *Die sozialistische Entscheidung* (*The Socialist Decision*) in 1933. This was confiscated, and Tillich was the first non-Jewish scholar to be deprived of his professorship by the new National Socialist authorities.

In his time as a German academic after the First World War, Tillich was interested in religious socialism and the philosophy of science, in cultural theology, and various dogmatic questions. His broad field of interests also included dance, art, technology, and the sociology of religion. This gave him a basis for experimentation with the traditional theological categories. His understanding of God as "that which concerns us unconditionally" (later: "ultimate concern") goes back to this period. At the same time, his cultural theology acquired both a theological and a political content: politically, linked to concern for the human person and for economic justice, and theologically, linked to the idea of a theonomous culture in which the divine can be experienced in the human, and the eternal in that which belongs to time.

The difficult situation in Germany led Tillich to leave for the USA in 1933. He worked at Union Theological Seminary in New York, where he became professor of philosophical theology in 1941. This chair covered both the philosophy of religion and systematic theology. Tillich's academic tasks thus lay in the area he liked best, in the borderland between theology and philosophy. When he retired in 1955, he was appointed professor at Harvard University, one of the most prestigious – and free – academic posts in the USA. His lectures, both at Harvard and elsewhere, were immensely popular, and a kind of personality cult developed around Tillich. He gave up his post at Harvard in 1962 and spent his last years as professor at the Divinity School of the University of Chicago. Tillich died in 1965.

Tillich thus spent more than thirty years at American universities, and was very active in a number of fields. Naturally, he was interested in theological and philosophical questions, but also in literary, aesthetic, homiletic, and social questions, etc. In this period, however, the political was less prominent. The partition of the world after the Second World War stripped Tillich of his illusions, and he recognized that the chances for a democratic and religious socialism were poor.

Theological Writings

In keeping with his program, Tillich's academic writings cover a wide spectrum. Theology should be produced in a broad room, so that the theological answers could correspond to, or correlate with, the questions people were asking. The polarity between question and answer is a fundamental relationship in all of Tillich's thinking. Theology and philosophy were continually involved both on the side of the answers and on the side of the questions. In this way, theology and philosophy were completely integrated into each other.

Tillich's wish to be at all times in correlation with people's questions necessitated shifts in his thinking. This means that the continuity lies not so much in the contents as in the methodology, in his will to work with the intellectual and cultural challenges of the moment.

There are nevertheless some themes and concepts that recur in most of his books and articles. These concepts were meant to capture the relationships between that which was general and that which was revealed. They are found in various forms and nuances of meaning, depending on the context and the period in which they were employed. Accordingly, one cannot employ immutable concepts to describe Tillich's thinking; the development of the concepts indicates a development both in

Tillich himself and in the various periods in which he employed them. One recurrent concept that Tillich coined was *theonomy*.

This concept is found in Tillich for the first time in a lecture he delivered in 1919, *Über die Idee einer Theologie der Kultur* (*On the Idea of a Theology of Culture*), where it functions as an expression of that which is unconditional in human history and intellectual life. As such, it poses a threat to the existing order and bears within itself the possibility of a new unified culture with a completely different intellectual depth. There is thus no antithesis between the theonomous and the autonomous; the opposite is the heteronomous, that which is imposed upon the human person from the outside. In political terms, Tillich saw a theonomous unified culture of this kind realized in a socialist framework.

As early as 1922, however, in *Kairos*, this optimism is dimmed. Tillich no longer believed that change could come about from within. In the course of the 1920s, the socialist optimism waned more and more. In *Die sozialistische Entscheidung* (*The Socialist Decision*), the pamphlet published in 1933 that had such momentous consequences, he completely abandoned the concept of theonomy. And Tillich did not believe that a theonomous culture was a realistic historical possibility in America.

Paradoxically enough, however, Tillich was to develop the concept of theonomy in a somewhat different version. The distance between autonomy and theonomy increased: autonomy was brought into relation with the question, and theonomy with the answer. As an answer, however, theonomy was no longer linked to empirical reality. It was a symbol of an eschatological hope that was linked to Christ.

On the one hand, Tillich produced occasional writings. He took up the questions of the moment and studied them philosophically and theologically, in keeping with his question-and-answer methodology. This meant that he was receptive to the age in which he lived. On the other hand, there was a systematic element in what he did, both methodologically and substantially. Tillich was a restless soul who was continually *en route* towards something new, towards new systems. This meant that the system out of which he worked had only a relative status and was open. Tillich's lectures on dogmatics in Marburg in 1925 point most clearly in the direction of a totality and a system. Here, he divides systematic theology into apologetics, dogmatics, and ethics. He ascribed to dogmatics (almost in the Barthian sense) the function of ensuring the normative and confessional character of theology. Tillich himself regarded these lectures on dogmatics as an important presupposition of the more "final" elaboration of the system that came in the form of his three-volume *Systematic Theology* (1951–63). In the first volume, however, Tillich denied that "dogmatics" was an applicable theological concept: it was now discredited.

Tillich's *Systematic Theology* has a special construction that is meant to serve a special strategy, namely, the wish to create a link between contemporary culture and Christianity as a historical reality. Tillich wants to demonstrate both that the Christian faith is necessary in our contemporary cultural situation and that our cultural situation has something to contribute in relation to faith. This correlation between theology and culture resembles the correlation between asking and answering in a conversation between human persons. The religious traditions answer the fundamental questions that the human person asks on the basis of his or her circumstances. In these traditions, the questions are expressed in religious symbols. The construction in each of the five main sections in the *Systematic Theology* reflects this "question-and-answer" structure. In each part, a central biblical symbol is correlated as an answer to a fundamental human question that finds expression in our culture.

The first Part correlates the Logos symbol (God's Logos reveals our ultimate concerns) with cultural skepticism. The second Part correlates the Creator symbol (God as Creator is present and active) with the human person's understanding of his or her own finitude and the prospective of destruction and death. The third Part correlates the symbol of Jesus as Christ (as the power of the new existence, he is the one who opens the path to the healing of existential alienation) with the human person's feeling of alienation. The fourth Part correlates the symbol of the Spirit (the unconditional and living power of existence that actualizes our potential) with the human person's experience of ambivalence and a lack of authenticity. The fifth Part correlates the symbol of the kingdom of God (an authentic realization of potential existence, understood both as something within history and as something above history) with the question of the meaning of history.

Another aspect of Tillich's writing is his sermons, which were published in three volumes. *The Shaking of the Foundations* (1948) is particularly famous. This book opened many doors to Tillich in the USA and thus prepared readers for his systematic theology. The short popular book on the philosophy of religion, *The Courage to Be* (1952), had the same function.

Some Key Themes

Like the Neo-Protestant tradition, Tillich had an apologetic goal. He wanted to vindicate the truth and validity of the Christian religion. Whereas Neo-Protestantism had an Idealist basis for its apologetics, Tillich himself created a basis for his apologetic activity, in two ways: formally through his method of correlation, and substantially through his ontology.

Ontology

Tillich understood ontology as almost synonymous with philosophy. In philosophy, reality is the object, and ontology entails analyzing the structures of being that confront the human person in every encounter with reality. Like ontology, philosophy is oriented to these questions about being: What does it mean to say that something "is"? What is being itself – the being that is different from, and lies beyond, all the things that have being? What structures are characteristic of all that has being? Understood in this way, philosophy's questions are questions about the structure of existence.

For Tillich, these questions also apply to the human person. If one asks deep questions of this kind about oneself, this generates fear and despair. The human person realizes that he is alienated from his own essential or real being. This is because he is alienated from being itself, or from the very ground (essence) of existence. The distinction between essence and existence is very important for Tillich. The essence is the potential, unrealized perfection of things. The essence is important ontologically, but not factually. Existence is something factual, but also something that has "fallen" from the essence. As such, it is cut off from its own perfection – but remains dependent on this perfection, and herein lies alienation. The real human person cannot exist in a kind of perfect and pure, potential state of being. The factual human person is one who genuinely exists ("ex-ists") through using his freedom. Such an existence is thus ambivalent. On the one hand, it is anchored in the finite and in an inauthentic being; on the other hand, it is continually moving away from such a non-being. The threat of non-being and death is real, and prompts the question where to find something that can give courage to live, to confirm one's own existence. For Tillich, this can be found in only one place. This place – or the answer to the human person's question – is God as the ground of being, as the one whose function is to integrate and unite. In this way, philosophy's questions are linked to a reflection on non-being that actualizes the power of being that overcomes the threat posed by non-being. For the finite human person, there is a path here that leads further, past the threat of non-existence or nothingness. The ontological question about being thus generates a question about the ground of being. Theology's answer about God as the ground of being is incomprehensible unless it is seen from the perspective of the ontological question.

In this way, a close relationship is established between theology and philosophy, especially existentialist philosophy. According to Tillich, it is good for theology that this philosophy exists, because theology has particularly good presuppositions for answering the questions that existentialism poses. Ontology thus becomes the bridge between theology and philosophy, the area in which they have many interests in common.

The Method of Correlation

This relationship between philosophy and theology, between philosophy's questions and theology's answers, was also a completely integrated part of Tillich's basic, pioneering methodology, the method of correlation. We have already seen several examples of how this is put into practice. Tillich believed that this method would ensure that theology would take the original Christian message seriously and that it would be able to express itself in relation to the contemporary situation. This methodology was an alternative to three other theological methods: the "supernatural," the naturalistic or humanistic, and the dualistic. The "supernatural" method does not take sufficient account of the situation of the receivers: it furnishes answers to questions that the human person has never asked. The problem with the naturalistic or humanistic method is that it remains within the human person's situation and attempts to formulate the theological answers on the basis of this situation. This, however, is an Idealistic view of the human person that does not do justice to the fact that he or she is alienated. The dualistic method lies somewhere between the other two. Here, the attempt is made to combine the natural and the supernatural. This natural theology seeks to deduce the answer from the form of the question.

Asking questions about one's existence is an essential aspect of what it is to be human. These are not general questions, but questions that express an existential search for something. According to Tillich, the question is a part of the human person himself, and exists even if it is not uttered. This means that the human person cannot avoid asking the question. To "be" is a question about the very existence of the human person, a question that rises up from his depths, is linked to the individual human person, and is directed to that which concerns us unconditionally (our "ultimate concern"). What concerns us unconditionally is something eternal and absolute, something to which we are in a relationship. This concerns our being as finite, limited human persons who are handed over to non-being. In this sense, the human person's question about his existence is a religious question. In every sphere of life (religion, worldview, art, literature, science), the human person is basically searching for that which concerns him unconditionally. The same themes are actualized all the time: the relationship between the finite and the infinite, between human existence and absolute being.

The answer to such questions does not lie in the question itself, but comes from outside. Just as the human person himself is the question, so too God himself is the answer, completely independent of all that is human. The answers that theology presents must be derived from revelation, but they must have a form that correlates with the existential questions of the human person. In this sense, the Christian message has the character of an answer to the questions that are contained in every human situation.

The question and the answer are both dependent on each other and independent of each other. Here, there is a dialectical relationship in which the independence is related primarily to the content and the dependence to the form. They are independent in the sense that the answers cannot be derived from the questions. The answer must come from outside. Nor can the existential question be derived from the answer. The dependence is linked to the fact that the answer in one sense adopts the formal structure of the question – and this must be so, if the answer or message is to have a function in the situation in which the question is formulated. Something similar applies to the relationship between the question and the answer: the question contains elements that are already found in the answer. The relationship between the existential question and the theological answer can be expressed in the metaphor of an ellipse: both are within the framework of the religious, and both are oriented towards "the ultimate concern." But they are not identical. In relation to God as the one who answers, and the human person as the one who asks, we can say that God answers the human person's questions, and that these questions are posed under the influence of God's answers.

The methodological consequences that Tillich derives for systematic theology from this idea of correlation mean that one begins by analyzing the human person's situation. Existential questions are derived from this analysis, and these questions are then answered with the help of material from the Christian message. Theology's task is to show that the symbols found in the Christian message are relevant answers to these questions. The method presupposes a collaboration between philosophy and theology.

Theory of Symbols

Tillich elaborated the function of symbols in the theological answers in his *theory of symbols*. In his eyes all knowledge of revelation, of the message, has a symbolic character. Symbols have a direct relationship to what is symbolized. For example, a country's flag is a symbol of the country's unity and independence. A religious symbol, however, is different: it points beyond the reality that it expresses. The symbol represents a kind of leap from finite reality to a reality that lies beyond this and that cannot be held fast. In this sense, we can say that a religious symbol is inauthentic, since it transcends itself *qua* symbol. This kind of use of symbols is necessary in a religious context, first and foremost because the divine transcends and goes beyond immanent reality. The revelation of the transcendent-divine is possible only if it is linked to something immanent, something that belongs to this reality. And this is why the fundamental structure of a divine revelation is symbolic. The religious symbol establishes a link between the inauthentic-immanent and the authentic-transcendent. However, Tillich does not see the symbol as only inauthentic. It also participates in the reality it symbolizes, and it is capable of expressing the reality to which it points. This means that the use of symbolic language does not amount to a kind of devaluation of the religious. The symbol and the theological answers that are clothed in symbolic language express something that is transcendent-divine, and give access to an unconditional reality. Only symbolic language is able to express the unconditional and the transcendent.

Talk about God must thus be symbolic, with one exception: when someone says that God is being itself or the ground of being, this is not a proposition that points out beyond itself. It is authentic. All other talk about God is symbolic and builds on an analogy in being (the *analogia entis*) between the authentic and the inauthentic, between the finite and the infinite. Knowledge of God has therefore a dialectical character. On the one hand, there is nothing finite that can be employed to describe the transcendent God; but on the other hand, everything we know about a finite thing also involves God, because God is the ground of being. And this in turn means that the analysis of existence, the analysis of the finite, is a key to understanding the religious symbols. On the basis of Tillich's method of correlation, we may conclude that the validity of symbols depends on the individual symbol's relationship to the situation of the human person.

Doctrine of God

What consequences does this have for Tillich's doctrine of God? For Tillich, God is a religious expression for the ground of being or for being itself. This, however, creates problems. Can we say that God exists? Tillich believes that the answer is "no." Since he is being itself, he is beyond existence and essence. If we take Tillich's starting point in reality, to say that God exists is in reality to deny God. God is in a way the answer to the question that lies in the finitude of the human person, the answer that is an integral dimension of what it is to exist: being itself. In that case, God cannot be something that exists or is; he cannot even be the highest thing that can be thought of, for then he would be a part of existence – and as such, he would be handed over to alienation in finite being. As God, he is behind or "under" that which exists, as its ground, as a kind of power of being or as a power that counteracts non-being. If God were a part of finite being, he could not be an "ultimate concern," nor something that could answer the questions that lie in finite being. God would then be something other than God. In order to express this concern, Tillich coined the expression "God above God": God, as being itself, is higher than the finite, existent God who is found in traditional Christian theism where God is thought of as a person and a being. This strong underlining of God's transcendence is however balanced by the idea of God's immanence, which has its background in the idea, mentioned above, that everything that is finite has to do with God, since God is the ground of being. God and the world participate in each other, because the ground of being supplies the structural presuppositions for being. This makes it meaningful to say something that initially sounds paradoxical: God is immanent in the world, and the world is immanent in God. These ideas have led critics to ask: Does not this amount to pantheism? And how can the human person enter into a personal relationship to the God of whom Tillich speaks here?

Christology

Tillich's Christology is also an answer to questions that are generated by human existence and that are clarified in an analysis of existence. Tillich's understanding of the Fall plays an important role in this analysis of existence. The Fall is the universal transition from essence to existence, an expression of the human person's alienation from God and thereby also from an essential humanity. The question inherent in human being is a question about the new being that breaks through the alienation and reunites the human person with his or her essence. The answer to this question is Christ. The Christ-symbol is the symbol of a new being which participates in existence, but is at the same time capable of overcoming the gulf between essence and existence. The necessary link that is usually assumed between Jesus and Christ is not equally necessary in Tillich's eyes. Christ, as the new being, can be the one who appeared in Jesus of Nazareth; but in principle, Christ can also be someone else. The central christological category for Tillich is therefore "Jesus as Christ." It is only in his relation to Christ as the new being that Jesus has any significance. The decisive christological point in Christianity is that there is a personal life in which the new being has overcome the old being. The historical aspect of Jesus is not needed as a guarantee of this. Accordingly, the special element in Jesus was not his divinity and humanity in the one person. The incarnation must be reinterpreted on the basis of existential categories: in his humanity, Jesus opened the way to a new possibility, an essentialized humanity under the conditions of existence, and he demonstrated this possibility. He lived under the conditions of alienation while at the same time overcoming them. As one who was under the conditions of existence, Jesus could not be God. He did not have the divine nature. The most Tillich would allow was that Jesus had a kind of essential divinity in himself. "Divine" here means that he was the only one who could make the essential human nature, in a non-split form, existentially present. Christ, as the new being, thus makes it possible for the human person too to be essentialized under the conditions of existence. It is this overcoming of alienation that makes him Christ. The power for this, the power for the essentialization of the human person, was from God, but was not itself God. The understanding of Jesus as Christ implies an Adoptionist understanding of Jesus, a docetic understanding of Christ, and something like a Nestorian understanding of the whole. Jesus and Christ are separated from each other.

Tillich as a Theologian in the Twentieth Century

Tillich was very important as a theologian and philosopher in the twentieth century. Naturally enough, his influence was greatest in the United States, but there has also been interest in his thinking in Europe, and especially in Germany, in the period after his death.

Tillich was in many ways an original and alternative thinker who aimed to create an overarching system in his thinking. His originality meant, however, that he did not get involved to any extent in the great theological debates that were going on in Europe. In one sense, he was parked on theological sidelines. Despite his original strategy and his systematic thinking, no school formed around him. He elaborated his theology and philosophy in categories that appealed to many who were remote from the world of professional theologians and philosophers, including both the intelligentsia and people who felt uneasy and alienated, and found help in Tillich's ideas. Here Tillich's great importance for the psychological sciences and for pastoral-clinical thinking and praxis in America should be emphasized.

By opening up theology to the cultural and the political, Tillich created an understanding for theology as an important dialogue partner in society. As such, he was a counterweight to those who emphasized theology's exclusiveness. He was interested in the fundamental questions that ordinary people contended with, and he believed that theology could help answer these. Tillich's enduring theological significance is less strongly linked to the content of the answers that he gave. It is much more connected to his ability to recognize, identify, and present the fundamental concerns of his generation, and to the vigor and vitality with which he met these concerns and worked on them.

Bibliography

Primary Literature

Tillich, Paul and Renate Albrecht, *Gesammelte Werke* (Collected Writings), 14 vols (Stuttgart: Evangelisches Verlagswerk, 1959–75).
Tillich, Paul and Carl Heinz Ratschow, *Main Works = Hauptwerke*, 6 vols (Berlin: de Gruyter/Evangelisches Verlagswerk, 1987–92).
Tillich, Paul, *The Shaking of the Foundations* [sermons] (New York: C. Scribner's Sons, 1948).
Tillich, Paul, *The Courage to Be* (New Haven: Yale University Press, 1952).
Tillich, Paul, *Systematic Theology*, vols 1–3 (Chicago: University of Chicago Press, 1951–63).

Secondary Literature

For an introduction to Tillich's thinking and a comprehensive list of the secondary literature, see:

Clayton, John, 'Tillich, Paul (1886–1965)', *TRE* 23 (Berlin and New York: Walter de Gruyter, 2002), 553–65.

See also:

Berkhof, Hendrikus, *Two Hundred Years of Theology. Report of a Personal Journey* (Grand Rapids, MI: Eerdmans, 1989), 287–98.
Grenz, Stanley J. and Roger E. Olson, *20th-Century Theology. God and World in a Transitional Age* (Downers Grove: IVP Academic, 1992), chapter 4.
Kelsey, David H., 'Paul Tillich', in David F. Ford and Rachel Muers (eds), *The Modern Theologians. An Introduction to Christian Theology since 1918* (Malden, Mass.: Blackwell, 2005), 62–75.
Manning, Russel (ed.), *The Cambridge Companion to Paul Tillich*, Cambridge Companions to Religion (Cambridge: Cambridge University Press, 2009).
Zahrnt, Heinz, *The Question of God: Protestant Theology in the Twentieth Century*, trans. R. Wilson (New York: Harcourt Brace & Co, 1969). (German original: *Die Sache mit Gott*. München: Piper, 1967).

Chapter 9
Dietrich Bonhoeffer

Trygve Wyller

Dietrich Bonhoeffer (1906–45) is one of the best known twentieth-century theologians. In Germany, his fame is obviously linked to his participation in the resistance to Nazism. He spent many years in German prisons, and was finally executed because of his share in the responsibility for the attack on Hitler. Elsewhere, his fame is linked more to his theology, especially to some brief passages in the letters he wrote from prison in the last years of his life. Dietrich Bonhoeffer won his place in the history of modern theology through formulations such as that we "must live as if God did not exist (*etsi deus non daretur*)." This sentence makes a demand that is almost mystical, and theologians and believers throughout the world have worked on interpreting it for more than 65 years. What did Dietrich Bonhoeffer really mean?

Scholars have given an extremely complex answer to this question. There are many interpretations of Bonhoeffer, and these often disagree. One variant focuses on Dietrich Bonhoeffer's piety, and this has much to be said in its favor, since he also published books of meditations and was the head of a seminary for pastors in the non-Nazi German church in the mid-1930s. Another variant sees Bonhoeffer as a liberation theologian, and this too finds support in Bonhoeffer's extraordinary biography: he was involved in the most conspiratorial networks in German anti-Nazism and provided an important theological interpretation of the basis and the value of this resistance. Yet another variant sees Bonhoeffer as a theologian of secularization. This attaches the greatest weight to his letters from prison, where the traditional interpretation of secularization is turned upside-down.

My presentation will emphasize the point that Bonhoeffer's brief but extraordinarily intense theological career was primarily occupied all the time by one single question: How can Christ be the Lord of the world, theologically speaking? Apologetically or homiletically speaking, the answer is in one sense "easy": Christ *is* the Lord of the world. The main task is then to make a list of various biblical passages and central dogmatic statements cohere, and the solution is clear. Theologically speaking, however, the challenge is different. How is one to justify and interpret a claim that is so improbable and that is contradicted by so much else, for example, in every other academic discipline, in politics, and in culture? In Bonhoeffer's days, there were many other lords who could put forward a much more probable claim than Christ; today, there are doubtless even more of them. How then are we to justify Christ's lordship? The simple yet complete answer is that Christ is Lord because he is an executed, but hidden Lord. The hiddenness is not a problem – it is the freedom that the Gospel gives. This is what Bonhoeffer means when he speaks in his letters from prison of a "deep this-worldliness." We can say that, through this expression and the whole of his theology, Bonhoeffer's most important contribution was to develop and renew Lutheranism's interpretation of the world and of the secular dimension.

Academic Work

Dietrich Bonhoeffer's academic work is closely linked to the development of theology, church life, and politics in the dramatic years after the close of the 1920s in Germany, when the Weimar Republic collapsed, the theological optimism about modernity lost support, and the brutal national and racial romanticism in the Nazi movement emerged. The influence and inspiration from the Swiss Reformed theologian Karl Barth on the theological development of the Lutheran Bonhoeffer is an important part of his academic development. The theology of the twentieth century was radically changed when Barth and his colleagues intensely affirmed that theological research could only be a reflection (*Nachdenken*) on faith. Bonhoeffer's theological development and the position he took cannot be understood unless we relate this to Barth and the dialectical theology. According to Barth, the dominant liberal theology in his age had committed the basic error of seeking to investigate Christianity "objectively" and "historically" – something that was impossible. It was possible to understand Christianity only if one reflected on what faith meant. Liberal theology wanted to present Christianity at arm's length, but in that case, one never grasped the power and the significance of the Christian faith. The young Bonhoeffer studied theology precisely during the clash between the new dialectical theology and the liberal theology that was still influential. His doctoral dissertation, *Sanctorum Communio* (1927), was written precisely in this tension. On the one hand, this is a religious-sociological study of the role played by the Christian community, but its conclusion is one-sidedly along the lines of dialectical theology: one cannot understand what a community is unless one presupposes that it is "Christ existing as a community." In 1931, Bonhoeffer published his professorial dissertation, *Akt und Sein* (*Act and Being*), which is a learned philosophical discussion of the relationship between faith (*Akt*) and philosophical ontology (*Sein*). Bonhoeffer then began to teach at the theological faculty in Berlin, and delivered important lecture courses that have since been published.

When Hitler came to power in Germany in 1933, Bonhoeffer's academic "career" changed. He became an important adviser to the new non-Nazi Protestant church in Germany, the *Bekennende Kirche*. In the mid-1930s, he was head of a seminary for the Confessing Church in Eastern Prussia. His close friend Eberhard Bethge was one of those who studied in this seminary, as was Gerhard Ebeling, who was to become a very influential figure later on. Important texts from this period are the meditative book *Gemeinsames Leben*, 1936 (*Life Together*), and *Nachfolge*, 1937 (*The Cost of Discipleship*).

At the close of the 1930s, Bonhoeffer became increasingly involved in the resistance in Germany to Nazism. Via relatives and friends, he was appointed to a post in the German counterespionage service. This was one of the central milieus for the leading

German military officers who planned to overthrow Hitler, since it was precisely in this department that most of those who took part in the plot over a number of years were employed. Bonhoeffer himself was related to some of the leaders of the conspiracy, or belonged to the same background in the haute bourgeoisie or the aristocracy. Much still remains unknown about his activity as an employee in the counterespionage department, but this position allowed him to travel around in most of the German-occupied countries to meet the German occupation authorities, and he made use of these journeys to have illegal contacts with the local resistance groups. He came to Norway on one such occasion and had secret meetings with important church leaders, but it is related that many of them were highly skeptical, since they were unsure about how to interpret Bonhoeffer's double role.

In this period, Bonhoeffer nevertheless managed to write a number of articles, letters, and theological discourses with an academic character. This activity ceased when he was arrested in 1943 under suspicion of involvement in various kinds of resistance work. The two most important books, *Ethik*, 1949 (*Ethics*), and *Widerstand und Ergebung*, 1951 (*Letters and Papers from Prison*), were published by Eberhard Bethge only several years after Bonhoeffer's execution in April, 1945. He had begun working on *Ethik* for several years before his arrest, and it was only partially completed during his imprisonment. *Widerstand und Ergebung* is a collection of letters that Bonhoeffer wrote to his family and to his friend, the theologian Bethge. It is especially in the letters to Bethge that he thinks aloud as a theologian, in an open and easily accessible manner, about the future of faith and theology in an ever more secularized and modernized world. Although the letters from prison are not written in anything like the strict academic form that we find in Bonhoeffer's earlier works, it is these texts that have made him a classic figure in the history of twentieth-century theology.

Overview of His Theological Writings

Bonhoeffer was only thirty-nine years old when he died, but his theological writings are extensive. The central theme in everything he wrote is the tension in the presence of God between hiddenness and concretization. Bonhoeffer was au fait with what his contemporaries were writing about the doctrine of God and the philosophy of religion, and with some of the early sociology of religion. He was well acquainted with the new hermeneutical theology that was presented by Rudolf Bultmann, but what he has to say about this trend is mostly critical and negative. In a good Barthian tradition, the principal question was not whether it is possible to believe in God, but what must be the content of faith, if faith existed.

An important text for the understanding of Bonhoeffer's dogmatic position is the so-called Christology lecture from 1933 (*Christologie-Vorlesung*, DBW), which exists in the form of notes taken by students who attended his lectures on Christology at the Humboldt University. In this lecture, Bonhoeffer remarks that contemporary existential theology works on the "how question": "How is it possible to believe?" He proposes instead another question, which he regards as more important and more appropriate to Christology, the "whom question": "In whom do we believe?" How must Christ be presented, when he is believed to be the Lord of life? From this starting point, Bonhoeffer arrives at a number of important observations that have stood the test of time. The most important is perhaps the idea of Christ as *Mitte*, as the center in life. When we ask the "whom question" from a perspective of faith, we discover that Christ is in the center because he is between me as sinner, and me as reconciled. In the same way, Christ is the "boundary": he is the one who reveals that there is something behind him, and human beings are not to go behind this boundary. Expressions such as "center" and "boundary" lead to the claim that Christology has ontological implications. With our starting point in faith, we discover how ontology is anchored in Christology. This position has been sharply criticized for being speculative in a manner that is incompatible with Lutheran Reformation theology.

Nachfolge is strongly marked by its genesis in the period when Bonhoeffer was head of the seminary at Finkenwalde in East Prussia, where many of those who were to become central theologians and pastors in the non-Nazi Confessing Church studied. The other part of the German Protestant church, the "Deutsche Christen," legitimated National Socialism by appealing to the so-called order of creation. They claimed that the order in society and nature that prevailed at any given time was an expression of God's will and must therefore be obeyed. Bonhoeffer countered this position in *Nachfolge*, where Christ is presented as the only criterion of obedience: "Only the believer is obedient, only the one who obeys is a believer." The book is constructed in part as a study of the Sermon on the Mount (Matthew 6), and thus also illustrates how the Confessing Church and Bonhoeffer understood and used the Bible. The exegesis is not strictly historical-critical. Rather, it applies the German biblical text directly to contemporary German reality. Contemporary readers clearly grasped that Bonhoeffer was working on the elaboration of a theology that represented a clear alternative to the obvious Nazification of the rest of the Protestant church. He used the expression "cheap grace" to characterize those Lutherans who believed that the experience of grace can be separated completely from the praxis in the life of the individual believer. "Costly grace" is the grace that encounters the believer in his activity as a follower of Christ.

Ethik was published by Eberhard Bethge in 1949, after Bonhoeffer's death. Bonhoeffer himself regarded this as his most important book, probably because most of the motifs that he had developed in the years before the War were collected and systematized here. Important new formulations include the distinction between the ultimate and the penultimate things and the idea of two spheres. The expression "penultimate things" refers to praxis in connection with contemporary living. Many Christians attach less importance to this than to the ultimate things, the questions that touch on salvation and eternal life. Bonhoeffer portrays things differently, in two ways. First of all, he ascribes autonomy to the penultimate things. Christians are not to employ the penultimate things as a kind of method to open up the path for Christ. In a celebrated proposition, Bonhoeffer affirms that the penultimate things are not our path to Christ, but his path to us. Secondly, the penultimate things are an expression of the Christian praxis of life. They are to be formed by faith in Christ and to take the form of goodness and kindness. Since Christ was kind and good, the penultimate things of believers are to be marked by these qualities.

His criticism of the idea of two spheres is connected with the same themes, but from a somewhat different angle. Bonhoeffer's theology has a strongly contextual horizon, and it is almost impossible to understand it if we overlook the dramatic context of Nazism and the conflicts about the interpretation of Christianity. For the theologians and pastors who lived in this context, there was a heavy concrete price to pay. The two-spheres thinking is a tradition that is represented by what Bonhoeffer calls "Pseudo-Lutheranism," a tradition that splits reality into two. One part is "the reality of the world," and the other part is "the reality of Christ," and this "Pseudo-Lutheranism" sees the world as the arena where these two realities are locked in permanent combat.

Bonhoeffer regards the idea of an irreconcilable conflict as the great error in this part of Lutheranism. There is no worldly reality that is far from Christ and that must be brought into conformity with him in a kind of perennial battle. The misunderstanding is to think that the world must be "Christianized." This is the great error, because the idea of Christianizing the world ignores the fact that the world is already reconciled and "accepted" by God in Christ's atonement. Accordingly, there are no longer two realities in mutual conflict, but only one reality. Bonhoeffer calls this "the reality of God that has been revealed by Christ in the reality of the world."

Bonhoeffer thus makes it possible to develop a Christian ethic that aims to concretize the praxis that expresses what "the reality of God in the reality of the world" is. This turns out to mean relatively general modes of conduct that do not necessarily display many signs of being "Christian," if one isolates them from the theological context in which they occur. Bonhoeffer's ethic thus seeks to be Christian, but he does not see ethics as a "Christianization" of the world. He regards such an idea as a doctrinal deviation, because it ignores the fact that the atonement has already occurred once and for all.

A Closer Look at Key Themes

Before 1943

The truly central theme in Dietrich Bonhoeffer is the question how faith shapes the world and the church. This theme is already central to his doctoral dissertation in the sociology of religion and to his professorial dissertation in fundamental theology – texts that were written before the breakthrough of undisguised Nazism in German politics. We can say that this theme is just as much a fruit of the Barthian influence on German Protestant theology as a whole (including Lutheran theology) as of the contemporary political context in Germany in the 1930s. Accordingly, the systematic-theological foundations of Bonhoeffer's theological thinking about how faith is to shape the world are strictly academic, rather than directly political. It is however interesting to see that this new Barthian development in German theology took a direction that made it particularly relevant to the contemporary political situation, and not least to the question how Christians and the churches were to meet the new political situation.

One important expression of this question in many of the texts Bonhoeffer wrote after 1933 is the discussion of the so-called first use of the law. In Lutheran theology, there are two "uses" (*usus*) of the law. The first concerns the law as regulator of civil society (*usus politicus legis*), the second concerns the central theme in Luther's development as a Reformer, the law that leads to Christ because it points to a sin that cannot be expiated with one's own resources (*usus theologicus legis*). On the periphery of Lutheranism, there is also a third use of the law (*usus tertius legis*), which concerns the law as an obligatory norm for Christians; this is sometimes called "sanctification." The third use of the law is not mentioned in the Confessio Augustana, but it is specified in the seventeenth-century Formulae of Concord. It is typical of the Danish-Norwegian Reformation that the Formulae of Concord are not a confessional text in these churches, but they have this function in the Swedish and several other Reformation churches. Bonhoeffer's discussion is located within the classic discussion of the relationship between the three uses of the law.

The more contextual background to his approach to this theme involves a critique of, and a confrontation with, those in German Lutheranism who developed the idea of the relative autonomy of the political law in relation to church ethics. In agreement with part of the Lutheran inheritance, a number of German theologians in the generation before Bonhoeffer maintained that the political use of the law was primarily a requirement that Christians respect the political order that prevailed in a society. The Lutheran doctrine of the Christian's freedom made it possible to liberate the political use of the law from the heavy demands made by the conscience, and obligated the individual Christian to follow the laws that were in force at any particular time. The Nazi regime was anchored in the election of 1933, and Adolf Hitler came to power in a way that many saw as democratically legitimate. Leading Lutheran theologians therefore elaborated a position that legitimated the Nazi government and asserted that it was now this political regime that had responsibility for the "orderings of creation." Some went so far as to claim that it was precisely the Nazi ideology of race and creation that was in accord with God's will. It was not so difficult to argue against this explicitly Nazi theology; it was more difficult to deal with the idea (not *per se* sympathetic to Nazism) that the political level must be relatively autonomous for the sake of religious freedom.

Bonhoeffer rejected the idea that one could say on the basis of the Reformation that the political level was autonomous in relation to the Christian faith. For the Christian, faith makes it possible to see the whole of reality, including the societal part of reality, in a completely new way. In terms of dogmatic theology, therefore, Christians must reject a purely rational approach to the political realm. Christians must interpret the world in the light of faith. This, however, does not mean that Christians must see their life's task as a project of Christianization, since that too is a radical misunderstanding of the atonement. This has in fact happened, and Christians must not repeat this error.

They must let all their interpretation and all their actions in the world be formed by faith. They must investigate and discover how faith demands that the world be shaped. One should certainly use the reason in this activity, but this reason must have faith – not some superior reason – as its source. This position is the background to both *Nachfolge* and *Ethik*. Indirectly, this position is also linked to the central idea in the 1933 lecture on Christology, where Bonhoeffer emphasized the importance of maintaining that Christ's presence in the world is a hidden presence. It is precisely the hidden presence that reveals itself through suffering and non-triumphalist actions. Political activity to shape the world in the light of faith can certainly be interpreted as a variant of this comprehensive and hidden presence of Christ. This brings us to the very heart of Bonhoeffer's theology up to 1943.

The Letters from Prison (1943–45)

Bonhoeffer does not abandon his central theme while he is in prison during the last two years of life. He is still interested in what it means to "share in God's suffering in the world." But the new element is a much broader exploration of the significance of the fact that Christ's hidden presence in the world also finds expression through non-religious persons and secular actions. Since it is the letters from prison that gave Dietrich Bonhoeffer his assured place among the classics of Protestant theology, it is important to note how these letters both develop the central theme and contribute something new to it. The presentation in the previous section should indicate where the continuity lies. The letters from prison do not entail a radical breach with the central theme, but they lead to a Protestant accentuation of it.

The starting point for understanding the Protestant element in the letters from prison is always the idea that although Christ is hidden, he is concretely present as the shaping of reality. In these letters, Bonhoeffer discusses whether, given certain presuppositions, even the ever more secularized world can be understood as such a shaping. In the light of the central role that God's concrete but hidden presence played for Bonhoeffer, it is not so surprising that he develops the idea of the secular world as yet another locus of such a presence. As a participant in the conspiratorial opposition to Hitler, Bonhoeffer met a number of non-Christian and non-religious persons who supported the same resistance and who agreed with him about central values for the new Germany. Naturally, personal experiences of this kind did not make up his mind to write that we "must live as if God did not exist (*etsi deus non daretur*)"; but his personal biography helps to provide a contextual perspective for his theology, which is strict, dogmatic, and often rather abstract – but can be understood only as a contextual theology that is concerned primarily to interpret what it means to say that Christ is present in the world, hidden but nevertheless concrete.

Bonhoeffer's analysis concludes that his contemporary context is characterized by a lesser amount of traditional religion and a growing number of people who believe that the human person's autonomy is more important than linking every decision to the will of God. Against this background, Bonhoeffer asks in the letters from prison whether theology should interpret autonomy and secularization as something other than a falling away from the Christian faith. If it is always the case that the Christian faith must concretely shape the world for the good of human beings, it is surely possible that acting autonomously (that is to say, without interpreting one's actions as something other than an expression of the human person's own will) can involve actions that in a hidden manner open the door to the presence of Christ in the world. This important point in Bonhoeffer is thus a breach with deontological ethics, which affirms that if one has a Christian motivation (disposition) for one's actions, these will often have a Christian value, whereas those who do not have a Christian disposition will not be performing Christian actions.

Bonhoeffer rejects this position. It is not the personal disposition that matters most, but rather the question how the world can be shaped and whether theology can interpret the praxis and the shaping as in accordance with God's will in a hidden manner. It is thus not unthinkable that one particular form of contemporary Christianity can be expressed as "living as if God did not exist," that is, as not seeing one's own Christian motivation and disposition as the most important quality in the Christian life. This can be understood as a development of the central theme that Bonhoeffer had already set out in his early writings. The new element is the strongly Protestant tone in the letters from prison. When he affirms that there are no external demands (a religious disposition, specific Christian points of view, and so on), and that even the apparently non-religious life can be Christian in a hidden way, Bonhoeffer initiates a new epoch in Reformation Christianity. Religious freedom is also the freedom not to express oneself in expected Christian or religious forms and figures. One can be non-religious *and* deeply Christian. In terms of dogmatic theology, such a form of Christianity is borne by Jesus' suffering. God dies on a cross, and he still dies today by bearing the non-religious in such a way that faith does not require particular religious or Christian attributes.

On the other hand, even in the letters from prison, Bonhoeffer makes clear demands with regard to praxis, which must "share in Jesus' suffering" and "exist for others." We can say that while Bonhoeffer opens the door in these letters to a Protestant freedom that is borne by the hidden Christ, he also comes close to the third use of the law through the idea that some specific actions correspond better to the Gospel than others. The radical element is that a Christian disposition does not necessarily make these actions Christian; the traditional element is that it is not just any actions that shape the world in the light of faith. In the tension between the three uses of the law, Bonhoeffer's central theme can be interpreted as fruitful and perhaps still relevant.

Bonhoeffer's Place in the Twentieth Century

Bonhoeffer played an important role in international theology for several decades after the publication of *Ethik* (1949) and *Widerstand und Ergebung* (1951). Remarkably, there were two very different receptions of Bonhoeffer. One tendency was linked to the criticism of the Lutheran doctrine of the two regiments, which we have mentioned above. Here at last was a Lutheran theologian who pointed out the decisive importance of actions in the Christian life – and who had paid the price with his own life. This combination of the new interpretation of the doctrine of the two regiments and his role as a Protestant martyr gave Bonhoeffer a central national role in the construction of the new Germany that was the task after the collapse of Nazism in 1945. In the academic world, this naturally also meant that Bonhoeffer was one of the Protestant theologians who played a role in the development of the earliest liberation theology in the 1960s. Many in the first generation of liberation theologians had studied at European theological faculties where the professors lectured on Bonhoeffer, and he was often portrayed as an ecclesial or theological source of inspiration for resistance to other brutal regimes throughout the world.

The other form of reception is linked to Bonhoeffer's apparent acceptance of secularization and to the new openness in the letters from prison to thinking about the presence of God outside of traditional religiosity. The idea that secularization could also be understood as an expression of God's own death and thus as a good (though undesired) result of Jesus' death on the cross has played, and still plays, an important role in discussions of Christology in a contextual perspective. Nearly seven decades after Bonhoeffer's death, there is no doubt that many things turned out differently from what he had thought: there is less secularization and more religion. He had expected the opposite development. Today's situation is characterized both by the dialogue with other religions and by a greater closeness to religious experience. But this does not mean that the academic significance of Bonhoeffer's theology has become less relevant.

This overview has sought to show that the most appropriate way to develop his thinking is perhaps to unite the two differing tendencies in the reception of Bonhoeffer. The idea of the Gospel as a liberation to live without taking account of what is considered as correct in social, cultural, and religious terms (*etsi deus non daretur*), in combination with the idea that it is in these new and uncodified actions that the hidden presence of Christ lies, can stand as Bonhoeffer's contribution to a future discussion in the church and in theology. At the same time, this position can be a reminder to that part of Protestant Europe that remains proudly secularized that the secular is indeed borne by holiness.

Dietrich Bonhoeffer changed the sad traditional view of the secular that had been held for generations. There is a "deep" this-worldliness that is organically linked to the Gospel. When Christ is killed, the gift that God gives is the secular. But this means that the world, the body, and the concrete are not alien to God. And this means that not even Protestant Norway is empty of holiness (as some think). As Bonhoeffer would see it, the secular Norway has a share in God's good gifts.

Bibliography

Primary Literature

Akt und Sein: Transzendentalphilosophie und Ontologie in der systematischen Theologie (Munich: Chr. Kaiser Verlag, 1988). (*Act and Being. Transcendental Philosophy and Ontology in Systematic Theology*), edited by Hans-Richard Reuter (DBW).

Christology, translated by John Bowden with an introduction by Edwin H. Robertson (London: Fontana, 1971).

Ethik, edited by Ernst Feil, Clifford J. Green og H. Eduard Tödt and Ilse Tödt (DBW 6) (Munich: Chr. Kaiser Verlag, 1992). English translation by Neville Horton Smith: *Ethics* (London: Fontana, 1964).

Gemeinsames Leben; Das Gebetbuch der Bibel, edited by Gerhard Ludwig Müller and Albrecht Schönherr (DBW 5). (Munich: Chr. Kaiser Verlag, 1987). English: *The Cost of Discipleship* (London: Macmillan, 1979).

Schöpfung und Fall (*Creation and Fall*), edited by Martin Rüter and Ilse Tödt (DBW 3). (Munich: Chr. Kaiser Verlag, 1989).

Widerstand und Ergebung: Briefe und Aufzeichnungen aus der Haft, edited by Christian Gremmels, Eberhard Bethge and Renate Bethge with Ilse Tödt (DBW 8) (Munich: Chr. Kaiser Verlag, 1998). English: *Letters and Papers from Prison* (London: SCM Press, 2001).

Secondary Literature

Bethge, Eberhard, *Dietrich Bonhoeffer: Theologe – Christ – Zeitgenosse: eine Biographie* (Gütersloh: Gütersloher Verlagshaus, 2004).

Busch Nielsen, Kirsten, *Dietrich Bonhoeffer* (Copenhagen: Anis, 2000).

Green, Clifford, *Bonhoeffer: A Theology of Sociality* (Grand Rapids: Eerdmans, 1999).

de Gruchy, John, *The Cambridge Companion to Dietrich Bonhoeffer* (Cambridge: Cambridge University Press, 1999).

Peck, William J. (ed.), *New Studies in Bonhoeffer's Ethics* (New York: Edwin Mellen Press, 1987).

Chapter 10
Knud Ejler Løgstrup

Svein Aage Christoffersen

Løgstrup was both a theologian and a philosopher, and he must be counted today among the most prominent Scandinavian thinkers of the twentieth century, with an influence in the German- and the English-speaking worlds. His importance is due above all to his work on ethical questions and problems, but he also wrote in the fields of aesthetics, linguistic philosophy, and epistemology. The various works are held together by phenomenological observations and analyses that are able to uncover constitutive traits in human existence. In Løgstrup's eyes, these fundamental circumstances show what it means to say that the human person's existence is given or *created*. In this way, he brings his phenomenological analyses into the discussion of problems in metaphysics and the philosophy of religion.

Løgstrup's philosophical texts have an underlying theological concern. He wants to rehabilitate the Jewish-Christian idea of creation as a critical alternative to the modern age's understanding of the human person as one who freely and independently creates his own existence. At the same time, he insists that the Jewish-Christian idea of creation must be rehabilitated on a philosophical foundation, so that it does not become dependent on the Christian revelation. Løgstrup does not want to develop a *theology* of creation, but a *philosophy* of creation. This makes his thinking also a critical alternative to the various forms of the theology of revelation that want to anchor the idea of creation in revelation.

The fact that one can work on Løgstrup's philosophy independently of his theology is thus a consequence precisely of his theology. The distinction he draws between philosophy and theology also means that theology is not reduced to a philosophy of creation. The philosophy of religion is interested in the conditions of human life in the created realm, whereas the Christian revelation proclaims the kingdom of God that came and comes with Jesus of Nazareth. The proclamation of this kingdom of God cannot be deduced from the created realm. But human experiences in the created realm, which can be described in a purely phenomenological manner, are a presupposition that allows the proclamation of the kingdom of God to be meaningful.

Biography

Løgstrup was born on September 2, 1905 in Copenhagen, where he grew up. He began his theological studies at the theological faculty in Copenhagen in 1923, and graduated in 1930. He continued his studies at a number of universities abroad, especially in Germany, from 1930 to 1935, where he heard the lectures of Martin Heidegger, Hans Lipps, Friedrich Gogarten, Emanuel Hirsch, and other scholars. In 1935, he married the German philosophy student Rosemarie Pauly, whom he had met at Heidegger's lectures. From 1936 to 1945, Løgstrup was pastor in the parish of Sandager Holevad on Fyn. When Denmark was occupied in 1940, he strongly disagreed with the Danish policy of collaboration and became involved in the illegal resistance movement in 1942. He had to live in hiding from August, 1944 until the end of the War in 1945.

Løgstrup was awarded the gold medal of the University of Copenhagen in 1932 for an essay on Max Scheler's ethics, and he worked in the following years on several manuscripts of a doctoral dissertation in theology. Three of these were returned to him for further work. He took his doctorate in 1943 with a dissertation on *Den erkendelsesteoretiske konflikt mellem den transcendentalfilosofiske idealisme og teologien* (*The epistemological conflict between transcendental-philosophical Idealism and theology*). In the same year, he was appointed professor in the philosophy of religion and ethics at the theological faculty of Århus University, a post that he held until his retirement in 1975.

In the 1930s, Løgstrup became involved in the emerging Tidehverv movement, a Danish parallel to the dialectical theology on the Continent. In the post-War years, however, he adopted more and more clearly a position at variance from leading representatives of Tidehverv, especially Kristoffer Olesen Larsen and Johannes Sløk. Løgstrup's clash with Tidehverv led to his *Den etiske fordring* (1956), which is his best known, most widely read and most discussed book. It also reflects the fact that Løgstrup had joined the circle around the literary periodical *Heretica* in 1950. This periodical was a gathering place from 1948 to 1953 for Danish authors and persons active in the cultural sphere who were looking for a new basis of values for society in the aftermath of the cultural collapse in wartime. Løgstrup's literary interests led to his election as a member of the Danish Academy in 1961.

The clash with Tidehverv brought Løgstrup also to part company with Søren Kierkegaard, who provided the basis for the theology of leading Tidehverv theologians. His critique of Kierkegaard already plays an important role in *Den etiske fordring* (*The Ethical Demand*). It was later expanded considerably, with the addition of new perspectives, in the book *Opgør med Kierkegaard* (*Controverting Kierkegaard*).

At the close of the 1960s, Løgstrup broadened his work on the Christian idea of creation in such a way that he accorded central importance to the universe as well. This later development in his thinking finds expression in his work from the close of the 1970s, *Metafysikk I-IV* (*Metaphysics I-IV*); two of these volumes were published posthumously.

Løgstrup received honorary doctorates from the universities of Lund (1965) and Marburg (1977). He received the Amalienborg Prize in 1974. He died on November 20, 1981.

Løgstrup's Thinking

The Phenomenological Starting Point

The manuscripts of Løgstrup's dissertations from the 1930s give interesting insights into the background and the foundation of his later thinking. Together with the dissertation that won the gold medal, the doctoral dissertation, and the posthumously published collection of sermons from his period as pastor of a parish, these manuscripts give a picture of the position he had reached when he began his work as a professor in 1943.

It is above all the first of these dissertation manuscripts that shows how Løgstrup wants to liberate himself from the epistemological structure of transcendental philosophy, which goes back via Neo-Kantianism to Immanuel Kant. This structure is built upon a separation between subject and object that in practice entails that the human person stands outside and above the world that he or she wants to know. The findings of phenomenological philosophy, however (with Husserl, Heidegger, and Lipps), mean for Løgstrup that this epistemological separation between subject and object is an illusion, since the human person is always involved and active in his own existence. This means that the human person's existence is a function of his involvement. At the same time, the conditions for this involvement are not the human person's own work, but are given precisely in virtue of the fact that he is indissolubly woven together with the world.

Phenomenology's dispute with Kantian epistemology does not mean that science's distinction between subject and object must be rejected. Rather, this must be understood on the basis of the pre-scientific involvement of the human person in the world. The scientific way of thinking is not a fundamental mode of human existence, but a derived mode. Phenomenology uncovers precisely the fundamental form of existence, which is given through the human person's pre-scientific experience of life. Phenomenology is thus not an alternative philosophical system or epistemology, but a clarification of the understanding of existence that is given in virtue of the human person's specific form of existence as such.

Løgstrup does indeed believe that Heidegger has broken with the Neo-Kantian epistemology in a more consistent manner than Husserl, but these years also see an increasing distance from Heidegger, because (in Løgstrup's view) he overlooks the fact that the human person's existence has an ethical quality. The human person is "thrown" into a struggle between opposing forces, creation and destruction, good and evil. Not even phenomenology can extricate itself from these forces.

Although the philosophical analyses are dominant in Løgstrup's work in the 1930s, the theological perspective is certainly not absent. On the contrary, it is decisively important that the transcendental-philosophical epistemology builds on a religious motif that is incompatible with the Jewish-Christian idea of creation. This is why Christian theology cannot build on Neo-Kantian philosophy.

The Ethical Demand: Humanism and Christianity

For Løgstrup, the clash with Neo-Kantian epistemology was not only a path to the rehabilitation of the Jewish-Christian idea of creation in general, but also – and perhaps especially – a path to the recovery of the fundamental ethical concepts. In particular, he emphasizes that the human person is confronted through his or her existence with an absolute and unconditional demand. Failure to heed this requirement has consequences for one's own existence. This idea of an unconditional demand played an important role in Løgstrup's resistance to Nazism during the War and in his criticism of the Danish policy of collaboration, as we see not least in his correspondence with his friend and colleague Hal Koch (*K.E. Løgstrup and Hal Koch. Friendship and Controversy*). Løgstrup dismisses Koch's pragmatic defense of the policy of collaboration with a reference to "laws of life": if these are broken, culture loses its ethical sustainability. It may seem that the policy of collaboration pays off in the short term, but it will undermine society and culture in the long term.

After the War, Løgstrup no longer spoke of "laws of life," but he continued to affirm and develop the idea of an ethical demand that is absolute and unconditional. The conflict with Tidehverv, and especially with Sløk and Olesen Larsen, concerns precisely the ethical demand. On the basis of Søren Kierkegaard, they had developed a Christian dialectic of existence that excluded the idea that the human person's existence *per se* contained an ethical demand. It is of course true (they argued) that an absolute demand is made in preaching, but this is not an ethical demand and has nothing to do with the human person's actions. It has a religious character and concerns the human person's existence in relation to God. To love one's neighbor thus means helping one's neighbor to love God.

Løgstrup holds that such an understanding of the Christian faith is in conflict both with a phenomenological description of the human person's existence and with Jesus' own proclamation, which presupposes that it is precisely in relation to our fellow human beings that our relationship to God is decided. This is why Løgstrup understands his phenomenological analyses in *The Ethical Demand* as uncovering the same understanding of human existence that Jesus presupposes in his proclamation. Løgstrup asserts that although Jesus' proclamation is religious, it must be possible to describe in purely human terms the understanding of life that it presupposes. This allows him, in an article published as early as 1950, to describe his position as uniting Christianity and humanism.

Whenever we have dealings with another person, we hold something of his or her life in our hand, says Løgstrup in 1950, and this formulation is the fundamental perspective in *The Ethical Demand*. In other words, our dealings with each other always involve power. We need not have very much of the other person's life in our hand – it can be a passing mood, or the good humor or cheerfulness of the other person that we can undermine or support. But it can also be a terrifyingly great amount, so that it in fact depends on us whether or not the other person's life is to be successful. But whether little or much is at stake, power is always involved.

The power relationship brings Løgstrup back to our mutual dependence, which he also calls our *interdependence*. This is a fundamental element in what it is to be human. We cannot choose whether or not we wish to have dealings with other people. On the contrary: as human beings, we are always exposed to each other. Løgstrup seeks to demonstrate this in *The Ethical Demand* by means of an analysis of the phenomenon of trust.

All dealings and contacts with other people are built to some extent on trust, not only when we meet people we know, but also when we meet strangers. Special circumstances are required, if we are to meet a stranger with distrust: there must be a war, or enmity, or the danger of betrayal of some kind. Under normal circumstances, we do not believe that a person is lying. We do so only when we have reason to believe that he or she may be lying.

Løgstrup's point is not that we are trustful by nature; that is certainly not the case. Nor does he mean that we ought always to be trustful, for that too is certainly not the case. It is often prudent to be on our guard and not to rely on what other people say and do. Løgstrup's point is that trust is one of several fundamental phenomena that are constitutive of what it is to be a human person. It is one thing to believe that particular persons will attempt to deceive us in one specific situation; it is something completely different to believe that *everyone* wants to deceive us at all times and places. Life would be simply impossible, our life would wither and be stunted, if we encountered one another with a basic distrust and believed that everyone whom we met wanted to steal and to lie, to dissimulate and to deceive us.

Løgstrup's analysis of the phenomenon of trust shows that we are exposed to one another, but it does not show that trust is the only phenomenon that exposes us to one another. We are exposed to one another in many different ways, often including distrust. We not only lead our lives with each other, but also against each other, says Løgstrup, and even when we live against each other, a fundamental dependence can become visible. Nevertheless, the analysis of the phenomenon of trust has the advantage of offering a clear access to the ethical demand that makes itself heard in the lives that we lead with and against each other.

Trust means exposing oneself. Exposure is power, and it is in power that a demand makes itself heard: namely, that we take care of the life of our neighbor, which we have in our power. Everyone who has met another person in trust and has laid his life in the hand of another person knows this. But what kind of demand is this?

Løgstrup says that this demand is radical, one-sided, and silent. It is radical, because it demands that we act unselfishly in view of what is best for the other person, not for ourselves. It is one-sided, because it does not demand anything in return. And it is also silent, since it does not tell us what we are to do. It says *that* we should act for the best of our neighbor, but it does not specify *how* we are to do this. The specific action that is required of us depends on the situation. Sometimes, the demand means that we should show another person the path he should take; at other times, it can mean that we should jump into the water to save him from drowning. Here, we must use our common sense and intelligence, empathy and imagination. We ourselves must be able to grasp what is for the best of our neighbor. Often – but not always – we do know this, thanks to general rules for conduct and custom. Sometimes, we must disregard the rules that are in force in society, in order to take care of our neighbor's life. In some situations, we must also work to change the prevalent rules, because instead of protecting the other person's life, they are an invitation to oppression and assault.

Often, we discover what is for the best of our neighbor when we listen to what he asks of us, but this is not always the case. Sometimes, we must also act in a way that contradicts the other person's expectations and demands. This is particularly clear in our relationship to children. In order to act for the best of the child, we must sometimes do the opposite of what the child asks of us. Accordingly, it is neither our neighbor nor society that "possesses" the ethical demand. It exists only as an anonymous demand in our existence.

Ultimately, therefore, we must do what we ourselves believe to be right, even if this may mean that we are obliged to act both against prevailing custom and against what our neighbor asks of us. We must act on the basis of our own judgment and our worldview. This, however, brings us to a conflict between taking care of the other person's life, on the one hand, and acting on the basis of our own judgment and worldview, on the other. If we are to take our own worldview as the starting point, rather than the worldview of the other person, is this not an incitement to assault? Løgstrup argues that we must avoid two pitfalls here. On the one hand, we can pander to one another in a smooth and superficial manner, in mutual admiration or indifference, never contradicting each other, but also never taking one another seriously. On the other hand, we can ride roughshod over the other person without any regard for him, and without paying heed to any worldview other than our own.

Løgstrup believes that there is no solution in principle to this conflict between indulgence and ruthlessness. But we can discover a solution in the concrete situation, using our own judgment. This, however, presupposes that we *grasp* the conflict. This is why humanism is not a basic solution to this problem once and for all, nor a set of rules that tell us what we are to do in every situation. On the contrary, humanism entails precisely an appreciation and an accurate view of a conflict. If this appreciation disappears in a culture, inhumanity is the result, either as indifference to the lives of other people or as ruthlessness.

Christian Faith and Ethics

Chapter 5 in *The Ethical Demand* is entitled: "Gives der en kristelig etikk?" ("Is there a Christian ethics?"). Løgstrup's answer is an unambiguous "no," but this must be understood in the light of what lies behind the question. As we have seen, Løgstrup holds that the ethical demand is silent, since it says *that* I am to take care of my neighbor's life, but not *how* I am to do this. That is something I must discover for myself. But does this apply in a Christian context too? Does not Jesus give us guidelines for how we are to take care of our neighbor's life? Does not Jesus break the silence of the demand?

Løgstrup answers in the negative: everything that Jesus said and that has been handed down to us is a proclamation of the demand that *per se* is silent. There is no special information in Jesus' proclamation about how we are to take care of our neighbor's life. It contains no directives, no precepts, no moral theology, no casuistry. Jesus does not relieve us of the responsibility for personally finding out how the demand is to be met. The Christian who must take a stance on ethical and moral questions is in exactly the same situation as everyone else. This means that the church and theology are not authorized to break the silence in the name of God and to claim a better knowledge than other people of how the life of the individual and of society is to be organized.

What Jesus does, however, is to say that the demand is *God's*. He breaks the anonymity of the demand. This makes ethics an integral part of the Christian faith, even if Christians do not have a quick path to the solution of ethical problems. Christian faith and ethics, faith and works belong inseparably together. Christian faith is a life at the service of one's neighbor. For Tidehverv, the most important thing was to help one's neighbor to love God. For Løgstrup, the most important thing is to help one's neighbor in his or her temporal need.

The Sovereign Expressions of Life

Trust belongs to the group of phenomena that Løgstrup calls *spontaneous* or *sovereign expressions of life*. He does not employ this expression in *Den etiske fordring*. He does so for the first time in *Opgør med Kierkegaard*. But this is because of the change of perspective. In *The Ethical Demand*, the point is to uncover how the demand is anchored in our dependence on one another. In *Opgør med Kierkegaard*, the point is to uncover phenomena (or expressions of life) that support and shed light on the ethical demand, such as mercy, compassion, openness of speech, and hope. They are "spontaneous" because the human person performs them in keeping with the nature of things and of his own accord, without compulsion or ulterior motives.

One characteristic trait of the sovereign expressions of life is that they are not completely subject to our control. Nor are they wholly our own work: on the contrary, they continually creep up on us from behind. A good example is what Løgstrup calls openness of speech. To speak is to speak out openly. Speech and openness go together. This means that we do not need to reflect and then take a decision to speak openly, when we talk with someone else – we do so quite automatically. It is when we want to deceive the other person that we must take a decision; and then we have to concentrate when we speak.

Because to speak is to speak out, we can be overwhelmed by openness of speech even in situations where we have good reasons to simulate. We can experience how trust takes hold of us even in situations where we have reasons to be distrustful. We must strive all the time to keep trust and openness under control. Truth and trust are not phenomena that come into existence through a decision that we take. They are phenomena that continually break into our life despite our decisions. We decide to lie, but our concentration slackens. We betray ourselves, and the truth comes to light.

Another interesting characteristic of the sovereign expressions of life is that they can be enacted, but they cannot be used for other goals. We can be merciful, but we cannot use mercy to attain other goals. It disintegrates if we try to do so. If we are merciful because we wish to obtain something from the person whom we help, because we want to increase our own credibility, or because we want to enjoy the admiration of others, this is no longer mercy. Mercy with ulterior motives is no longer mercy. This characteristic of the sovereign expressions of life allows Løgstrup also to call them the *sovereign expressions of life*.

Our active life is nourished not only by sovereign expressions of life, but also by the feelings that circle around in our thoughts, such as revenge, jealousy, and petty-mindedness. Why should we attribute a special position to the sovereign expressions of life? Why should we emphasize trust rather than distrust, or mercy rather than revenge?

Løgstrup says that the sovereign expressions of life have a different role to play for our active life than the feelings that circle around in our thoughts. The sovereign expressions of life are indispensable. It is they that support our active life. Trust is one of the fundamental conditions of life, whereas distrust presupposes and exploits trust. We can do without hopelessness, but not without hope. We can do without revenge, but not without mercy. It is the lie that is a parasite on the truth, not *vice versa*.

An important point in Løgstrup's analysis of the sovereign expressions of life is that the soil in which ethics grows is not norms, but phenomena that *per se* are ethical in such an elementary way that we do not even think of them as ethical. Trust, mercy, and truthfulness are not primarily demands with which we are confronted, but phenomena that we all, to a greater or lesser degree, experience in our daily life. When we speak, we do not *think* that it is ethical to be open and honest – that thought comes only when dishonesty makes its appearance. This is why the expressions of life are more fundamental than norms.

The Created Realm and the Kingdom of God

In the 1970s, Løgstrup widened his perspective from our dependence on one another to include our dependence on the universe. The basic idea was present in his thinking from the outset, and is expressed clearly in the sermons he delivered in Sandager-Holevad, but it is only now that the perspective is developed systematically, with wide-reaching consequences for his philosophy of religion and his theology.

One important consequence of this systematic broadening of the perspective is that Løgstrup now studies the human person's destruction of nature and the ecological crisis. The universe is the origin of the human person both phenomenologically and biologically, he writes; but in our modern times, we have reduced the universe from being our origin to merely being our surroundings, and to being hence raw material or resources that we can exploit as we think fit. We need not be surprised that such a shameless way of dealing with our origin leads to an ecological crisis – the surprising thing is that we are surprised! And this surprise shows that we have forgotten how closely we are in fact tied to nature.

Through our metabolism and our senses, we are inserted into the universe. Body and mind are connected. Through sense-experience, through light and sound, colors, and forms, the mind is tuned and recharged, although we do not notice this or reflect on it. "The kindling for the fire of the soul is the sensuous bodiliness of all things," says Løgstrup. This perspective leads him in the 1970s to sketch a philosophy of the senses, in which he distinguishes between sense-experience and understanding, claiming that unlike understanding, sense-experience is without distance. Although sense-experience and understanding are inseparably woven together, sense-experience in its lack of distance is an autonomous access to reality. This is why sense-experience is not only capable of recharging the mind: its function here is necessary.

This undeniably surprising development of the philosophy of the senses must be seen against the background of Løgstrup's continuing endeavor to liberate himself from the transcendental-philosophical epistemology that he now calls the "inside-the-skull theory" (B. Russell). The decisive point when we experience the light and shadows, the forms and colors of the landscape, when we hear birdsong, or see the light from a distant lighthouse, is whether this audible world with forms and colors exists only within our head, or on the contrary, it is we who are outside, beside these things, in our sense-experience. Are we outside, beside the things, or are the things inside, in our head? The latter alternative is perfectly possible, says Løgstrup, but it is not at all necessary. Our understanding takes place in the head, but that does not prevent us from living outside, in the world, in our sense-experience. Løgstrup admits that this is a surprising point of view, but it finds support in the fact that we are unable to live for one single moment as if the "inside-the-skull theory" were true.

The cosmological shift in Løgstrup's thinking also leads him to elaborate more clearly than before the difference between the created realm and the kingdom of God. Creation and destruction, kindness and cruelty are woven together in the created realm. Suffering and death are not merely brought about by human beings; they are built into the structure of the created realm. In the kingdom of God, suffering and death are overcome, but we cannot deduce this from the created realm alone. All we can do is to believe in the word that is preached. This, however, does not change the conditions of our life in the created realm, nor does it allow us to look over the Creator's shoulder, to speak, and understand why the created realm is as it is. The kingdom of God belongs to the future. We know it only in faith in the resurrection of Jesus.

Influence

In recent years, there has been a steady increase in interest in Løgstrup's thinking, not least because important books have been translated to German and English. In Scandinavia, he was been influential not only among theologians and philosophers, but also to a large extent in the academic study of nursing, medical and social studies, pedagogy, literary scholarship, the history of ideas, and aesthetics. He is often spoken of in the same breath as Emmanuel Levinas, as a representative of the ethics of closeness, but this is true only up to a point. it is correct to say that Løgstrup anchors ethics in interpersonal relationships, but he expands this perspective when he emphasizes that we are also woven together with the universe, not only with one another. His ethics is thus not limited to interpersonal relationships, but embraces also society, politics, ecology, and nature.

Bibliography

Primary Literature

Bibliography: Karstein M. Hansen: *K.E. Løgstrups forfatterskap 1930–2005* (Århus: Århus University Press, 2006).
Den erkendelsesteoretiske konflikt mellem den transcendental-filosofiske idealisme og teologien (Copenhagen: Samleren, 1942). (*The Epistemological Conflict between Transcendental Idealism and Theology*).
Kierkegaards und Heideggers Existenzanalyse und ihr Verhältnis zur Verkündigung (Berlin: Blaschker, 1950). (*Kierkegaard's and Heidegger's Interpretation of Human Existence with Special Regard to the Proclamation of the Gospel*).
The Ethical Demand. Introduction by Hans Fink and Alasdair MacIntyre (Notre Dame: University of Notre Dame Press 1997).
Kunst og etikk (Copenhagen: Gyldendal, 1961). (*Art and Ethics*).
Kants æstetik (Copenhagen: Gyldendal, 1965). (*Kant's Aesthetics*).
Opgør med Kierkegaard (Copenhagen: Gyldendal, 1968). (*Controverting Kierkegaard*).
Kants kritikk af erkendelsen og refleksionen (Copenhagen: Gyldendal, 1970). (*Kant's Critique of Reason and Understanding*).
Norm og spontanitet. Etik og politik mellem teknokrati og dilettantokrati (Copenhagen: Gyldendal, 1972). (*Norm and Spontaneity. Ethics and Politics between Technocracy and Dilettantocracy*).
Ophav og omgivelse. Betragtninger over historie og natur. Metafysik III (Copenhagen: Gyldendal, 1984). (*Source and Surroundings*).
Kunst og erkendelse. Kunstfilosofiske betragtninger. Metafysik II (Copenhagen: Gyldendal, 1983). (*Art and Knowledge*).
System og symbol. Essays (Copenhagen: Gyldendal, 1982). (*System and Symbol*).
Skabelse og tilintetgørelse. Religionsfilosofiske betragtninger. Metafysik IV (Copenhagen: Gyldendal, 1978). (*Creation and Annihiliation*).

Vidde og prægnans. Sprogfilosofiske betragtninger. Metafysik I (Copenhagen: Gyldendal, 1976). (*Breadth and Concision*).
Det uomtvistelige. Fem samtaler med Helmut Friis (Vejen: Askov Højskole, 1984). (*The Indisputable*).
Solidaritet og kærlighed – og andre essays (Copenhagen: Gyldendal, 1987). (*Solidarity and Love*).
K.E. Løgstrup og Hal Koch. Venskab og strid (Aarhus: Klim, 2010). (*K.E. Løgstrup and Hal Koch. Friendship and Controversy*).
Etiske begreber og problemer (Copenhagen: Gyldendal, 1996). (*Ethical Concepts and Problems*). First published in *Etik och kristen tro* (G. Wingren). (Lund: Gleerups, 1971).
Prædikener fra Sandager-Holevad. Et udvalg (Copenhagen: Gyldendal, 1995). (*Sermons from Sandager-Holevad*).
Martin Heidegger (Frederiksberg: Det lille forlag, 1996).
Beyond the Etical Demand. Introduction by Kees Van Kooten Niekerk (Notre Dame: University of Notre Dame Press, 2007).

Secondary Literature

Andersen, Svend, *Løgstrup* (Frederiksberg: Anis, 2005).
Bugge, D., Böwadt, P.R. and Sørensen, P. Aa. (eds), *Løgstrups mange ansikter* (Copenhagen: Anis, 2005).
Christoffersen, Svein Aage, *Etikk, eksistens og modernitet. En innføring i Løgstrups tenkning* (Oslo: Tano Aschehoug, 1999).
Ewalds, Svante, *Metafysikk och religionsfilosofi* (Åbo: Åbo Akademis förlag, 1993).
Hansen, Karstein M., *Skapelse og kritikk* (Oslo: Universitetsforlaget, 1996).
Hauge, Hans, *Løgstrup. En moderne profet* (Copenhagen: Spectrum, 1992).
Jensen, Ole, *Historien om K.E. Løgstrup* (Copenhagen: Anis, 2007).
Løgstrup archive: htto://www.teo.au.dk/forskning/aktuelt/loegstrup (accessed March 20, 2012).

Chapter 11
Regin Prenter

Ådne Njå

Regin Prenter (1907–90) was born in Frederikssund and grew up in a church milieu that was influenced by Grundtvigianism. His basic Grundtvigian position was marked early on by dialectical theology, ecumenical interests, and Anglican religiosity. After completing his studies, he undertook study trips, in the course of which he met Karl Barth and Michael Ramsey, who played a particularly important role in his early years as a theologian. During his time as pastor in Hvilsager-Lime and Aarhus, he was a member of Arne Sørensen's Grundtvigian-national party "Dansk Samling." He was active in the resistance, and was uncompromising in his defense of the Jews. A Lutheran shift took place in his theology as a result of his dissertation *Spiritus Creator* (1944) and his appointment as professor of dogmatics at Aarhus University in 1945. From this time onward, his colleague K.E. Løgstrup became one of his most important theological dialogue partners. Prenter was active early on in the East Asia Mission and in the ecumenical movement, and held a number of posts in the Lutheran World Federation and the World Council of Churches. From 1961 to 1963, he was a guest professor at the Protestant faculty in Strasbourg, and from this time there occurs what we could call a Grundtvigian shift in his theology, motivated in part by contemporary hermeneutical philosophy and ecumenically oriented Catholic theology. Prenter retired from his professorship in 1972, in a wrathful reaction against the Marxist currents at the universities, which he regarded as incompatible with a Lutheran-Grundtvigian fundamental theology. He was appointed to a parish in Brandrerup, where he continued to work on his Grundtvigian theology with its new orientation. Prenter held many guest lectures at theological faculties in Europe, the USA, Japan, and Africa. He was awarded honorary doctorates at Strasbourg (1960), Reykjavik (1961), Lund (1962) and Helsinki (1980).

Prenter's thinking is much more dynamic and changeable than one might think at first glance, but there are some theological interests and concerns that are present throughout his work. Above all, Grundtvig's view of the church and his emphasis on the popular element play a central role in everything Prenter wrote. His theology as a whole represents a Grundtvigian covenant theology. The striking thing is that this Grundtvigian theology is interpreted in a variety of fundamental-theological holistic concepts. In the early phase, it is Karl Barth and to some extent F.D. Maurice who determine the interpretative framework. From *Spiritus Creator* (1944) onwards, Martin Luther takes on the role of the authoritative church father. This leads to a radical reinterpretation of the Grundtvigian element. In his later writings, Prenter emphasizes more strongly than in the earlier period Grundtvig's words about theological interrelationships. This in turn leads to a new understanding of the Lutheran and Grundtvigian elements. In this movement, Prenter is all the time in dialogue with important contemporary thinkers: Arne Sørensen, Michael Ramsey, Friedrich Gogarten, Rudolf Bultmann, Hans-Georg Gadamer, Yves Congar, Peter Brunner, and not least K.E. Løgstrup. I believe that it is in this intertextual and dynamic context that it is appropriate to speak of Prenter's Barthian-Grundtvigian period, his Lutheran-Grundtvigian period, and his Grundtvigian turn.

Prenter's Barthian-Grundtvigian Period

In his article "Die sogenannte 'kirchliche Anschauung' N.F.S. Grundtvigs als Frage an die evangelische Theologie von heute" ("The so-called 'Ecclesial Understanding' of N.F.S. Grundtvig as a Question addressed to today's Lutheran Theology"), 1954, Prenter's principal concern is to demonstrate the centrality of the "word" for Grundtvig. Prenter argues that the "word" in Grundtvig is not the biblical Word in isolation, but rather this "word of light" linked inseparably to the living "words of life" through the sacraments. In order to hold fast to his Barthian paradigm, Prenter emphasizes that the confessions of faith in the sacraments are "the Lord's own words" (in his later writings, scripture and confession correlate with the distinction between the Word and faith). Prenter developed his Barthian understanding of Grundtvig in the article 'Die Frage nach einer theologischen Grundtvig-interpretation' (*The Question of a Theological Interpretation of Grundtvig*), 1936, which was printed in a Festschrift for Barth's fiftieth birthday. The theme of this essay is not the connection between preaching and the sacramental words, but the relationship between the Gospel, which Prenter calls the "real theology," and the theology of creation, which he calls "the secondary theology." In keeping with his Barthian paradigm, the young Prenter sees a concentric relationship between real theology (the church school), which is the hermeneutic "center," and secondary theology (the Grundtvigian college), which is the "circumference" that is interpreted.

Prenter's Barthian Grundtvigianism is expressed clearly in *Ordets Herredømme* (*Dominion of the Word*), a collection of essays published in 1941. In the article "Sakramentalt livssyn" ("A Sacramental View of Life"), 1941, Prenter's starting point is Augustine's understanding of the term "sacrament." He draws a distinction between "natural" and "given" sacraments. The former term denotes everything in nature that is capable of reflecting God's goodness and power; the latter denotes the church's actions that are instituted by Christ.[1] Prenter argues that if the creation is to regain its rightful place in theology, we must rediscover a broad concept of sacrament that is not limited to the church's actions. This sacramental outlook on life can appropriately be called "natural theology." This term, however, does not mean that this is theological knowledge in the light of natural experience; rather, the sacramental outlook on life

---

[1] Regin Prenter, "Sakramentalt livssyn" ("A Sacramental view of life"), in *Ordets Herredømme* (Copenhagen, 1941), 30–56.

that has its genesis in the Gospel sees the signs of God's grace in the creation. Prenter maintains that it is only in faith that the creation is recognized and revealed as a sign of God's grace. At the same time, however, he maintains that the sacramentality of the creation is not linked to the knowledge of faith, but is effective *per se* in a positive continuity with the sacramentality of the church.

In the article "Den almindelige kirke" (1941), Prenter links the incarnation of Christ to the church as the body of Christ.[2] Prenter writes that to detach Christ from his concrete chosen people is to practice an ecclesiological docetism. This emphasis on the visible church may at first sight appear to clash with his Barthian rejection of "religion," but this is not the case. In these reflections, it is not the church's life of faith that is central, but God's sovereign freedom. God's free grace is revealed when he chooses, on the basis of what Prenter calls "the divine humor," that which is smallest in the world: first the Jewish people, and then the humiliated Christ and a weak and sinful church. The church is not understood as the "locus" of redemption, in the sense that the reality of the redemption would be restricted to the sphere of the church. Rather, the church is understood as a *sign* of God's universal grace. In keeping with this understanding of the church as a sign, Prenter defines the essence of the church primarily as "liturgy." This refers both to the liturgy's reminder of God and to Christ's universal love for the world. This universal theology leads Prenter to support the national church; he dismisses every kind of formation of parties within the church, as well as the Grundtvigian distinction between the national church as a "civil institution" and the community as "the living community." Prenter holds that this replaces the idea of universal solidarity with a cultivation of fractions in the church.

Prenter's thinking in his early theology about the popular dimension is expressed with particular clarity in the essay "Kristus – Danmark" (*Christ – Denmark*), 1941.[3] When he says "Christ – Denmark" rather than "Christianity and Danishness," this is because he wishes to underline that this entails what he calls historically given spheres of power, rather than human qualities. This emphasis on the two external spheres of power is connected to Prenter's theology and to his aversion to what he understands as a neo-pagan nationalism. We should not get obsessed by qualities that exist in the people as such. We should only emphasize the realistic fact that the human person exists in an antecedently existing culture that he has not himself created. When Prenter offers a positive definition of "Danishness," he typically refers to the Pauline image of the treasure in earthen vessels. The treasure (the Gospel) cannot be made Danish; it comes from outside, from the Jewish people. But the earthen vessel that bears the treasure must be Danish – the language and the weak church – for incarnational reasons. Only Christ is the one positive definition of the people in a non-paradoxical sense. This is also the reason why Prenter rejects not only individualism in general, but also what he calls "the individualism of a people," since the peoples are joined together through Christ in a universal fellowship of peoples. This universal fellowship is, however, not an empirically existing reality. It has its

---

[2] Ibid., 57–79.
[3] Ibid., 151–72.

foundation and its justification in the universality of Christ, of which the church is a sign. And this is the reason for this all-embracing fellowship of peoples. In the article 'Frederick Denison Maurice' (1939),[4] in which Prenter largely accepts Maurice's christological universalism and Christian socialism, he calls Christ's universal fellowship the "*mystical* fellowship in Christ."

Prenter's Lutheran-Grundtvigian Period

Prenter's Lutheran shift comes into full force with his dissertation on Luther, *Spiritus Creator* (1944). In opposition to the Augustinian-scholastic doctrine of grace, Prenter affirms that the work of the Holy Spirit consists in the mediation of Christ's own real presence. Christ's righteousness is an alien righteousness (*justitia aliena*) that can never be identified with the human person's "nature." In virtue of what Prenter calls Luther's "pneumatological realism," affirmed *inter alia* in his *Rationis Latomianae confutatio* (1521), this alien righteousness is a genuine struggle against the sin in us. Seen from the perspective of grace (*favor Dei – gratia*), the believer is totally righteous in Christ and totally a sinner in himself (*simul justus et peccator*). At the same time, seen from the perspective of faith and gift (*fides Christi – donum*), the believer is partly righteous and partly a sinner (*partim justus et partim peccator*). Prenter affirms that there is an interrelation between grace and faith, in such a way that they condition each other. But this is an asymmetrical interrelation, since "*gratia* is the greater of the two." With a reference to Rudolf Hermann, Prenter argues that sanctification cannot be understood as a "concept of measurement," but rather as a "concept of time" in which the subjective correlative to the idea of Christ's real presence consists in the human person's continuous dying to himself and entrusting himself to Christ's alien righteousness. Sanctification has, however, also a positive expression that corresponds to the resurrection. This finds expression with Trinitarian necessity in praise and in good deeds, which Prenter here calls "real piety." In keeping with his new Lutheran-Trinitarian viewpoint, he asserts that this real piety cannot be identified modally with righteousness and sanctification. As a "creation," it must be attributed to the Father.

The clash with Barth is implicit in *Spiritus Creator*, and Prenter soon afterwards attacks Barth's theology head-on in a series of articles that discuss the various volumes of the *Kirchliche Dogmatik*. In "Die Einheit von Schöpfung und Erlösung. Zur Schöpfungslehre Karl Barths" (The Unity of Creation and Redemption. On the Doctrine of Creation in Karl Barth), 1946, he criticizes Barth for representing a Platonizing docetism of creation.[5] The title already makes it clear that what is at stake is not the creation seen in the light of Christ, but rather the fundamental distinction between creation and redemption. According to Prenter, Barth's theology is incompatible with a Lutheran concept of faith and with a Lutheran understanding of the autonomy of

---

[4] Ibid., 181–200.
[5] Reprinted in Regin Prenter, *Theologie und Gottesdienst. Gesammelte Aufsätze / Theology and Liturgy. Collected Essays* (Aarhus and Copenhagen, 1977), 9–27.

the creation. He writes: "The transformation of *credo* to an *intelligo* in the noetic sphere corresponds to a transformation of *est* to a *significat* in the ontic sphere".[6] The slogan he launches against Barth is clear: "EST! Not SIGNIFICAT!" (ibid., 26). In accord with this critique of Barth – but wholly at variance with his earlier reflections – Prenter maintains in *Skabelse og Genløsning* (*Creation and Redemption*), 1955, that "it *must* be called 'law and Gospel,' and *cannot* be called 'Gospel and law'."[7] He writes that the principal difference between himself and Barth is whereas in Barth the theology of creation and pneumatology form a "periphery" around a timeless understanding of redemption, in his own thinking these constitute autonomous works of God that follow one another in the course of time: creation – Christology (i.e., the incarnation – atonement) – soteriology.

The starting point for the work on *Skabelse og Genløsning* was Prenter's refusal to accept the transcendental-philosophical foundation of dogmatic theology in Anders Nygren and Gustaf Aulén. On this question, Prenter agrees with Barth. He argues that the "category" of Christianity is not known antecedently. It is known, together with its content, as it is given through the message of scripture. Prenter is aware of the challenge that confronts theology "from the outside" with regard to the comprehensibility and the offensiveness of the message, but he affirms that the real dogmatic challenge comes "from the inside," namely, from the division of the church into mutually exclusive confessions. In the light of this challenge, a presentation of dogmatics must have a "confessional-ecumenical" character. Accordingly, Prenter introduces his dogmatic theology with Lutheran-Grundtvigian prolegomena, and begins the material dogmatics itself with a Lutheran reading of the Nicene creed. In *Skabelse og Genløsning*, however, he very strictly maintains the principle of *sola scriptura*, but he also emphasizes the apostolic testimony to the resurrection. The act of worship does not determine the content of dogmatics in a positive sense; in a negative sense, it sets boundaries to this content, in the sense that all Trinitarian theology must have a concrete correlative in worship. Prenter thus says that the confession of faith is "antecedent to" scripture, while scripture is "over" the confession.

Prenter's ecclesiology in the aftermath of the Lutheran shift is already expressed in the article "Grundtvigs og Einar Billings syn på folkekirken" (*Grundtvig's and Einar Billing's Views of the National Church*), 1948. In Billing, the idea of the national church is motivated by the idea of God's universal grace that is "reflected" (in Billing's view) in an open national church system. Prenter writes that Grundtvig provides no theological motivation for the idea of a national church, but calls it a "civil institution" that contains the community of Jesus Christ. Prenter objects to Billing's idea of the national church that God's grace is understood as an abstract idea that concerns the human person in general, rather than as the living Christ himself in the encounter with the human person's faith or unbelief. Prenter argues that while baptism is constitutive of membership in the national church, it is *the baptismal covenant*

---

[6] Ibid., p. 17.

[7] Regin Prenter, *Skabelse og Genløsning* (Copenhagen, 1955). English: *Creation and Redemption* (Fortress Press, 1967).

(the word and faith) that is constitutive of membership in the community of Jesus Christ. This basic understanding of the baptismal covenant also leaves its mark on the ecclesiology in *Skabelse og Genløsning*. In keeping with the Lutheran tradition, Prenter places ecclesiology after the doctrine of the means of grace, but he maintains that the administration of the means of grace is inseparably connected to the reception of faith. The church is not the church of the Word alone, but the church of *the Word and Faith*. Although the constitutive marks of the church are the Word and the sacraments, the confession and the good works that are the spontaneous expressions of faith are also elements that allow the church to be recognized.

After his Lutheran shift, Prenter's theology is expressed very clearly in the essay "Grundtvigs syn på mennesket" (*Grundtvig's View of the Human Being*), 1948, where he reads Grundtvig's anthropology in the light of his Lutheran thinking. It is striking that he understands the human person as the image of God, not in the light of the created human life *per se*, but rather in the light of *the life of faith* (faith, hope, and love) and *the words or signs of life of the life of faith* (confession of faith, preaching, and praise). The created nature or speech of the human person is only a "passive suitability" for being the image of God in the relationship of faith. This understanding of Grundtvig's anthropology is expressed in more extreme terms in *Skabelse og Genløsning*, where he understands what Grundtvig says about the human person as the abiding image of God in the light of the distinction between law/judgment and Gospel/redemption. The nature of the human person (*qua* species) has not been corrupted by the Fall, but the image of God, which the person possesses through creation and which expresses his existence as person, or his will, in relation to God, has been distorted into its opposite (the image of the Devil) and expresses the human person's existence under the wrath of God. It is only through integration into the redemption that the image of God positively comes into its own and expresses the human person's relationship to God in grace. Prenter interprets the Grundtvigian formula "first a human person – then a Christian" in the light of soteriology: first condemned – then redeemed.

Prenter's Grundtvigian Turn

Prenter's relationship to Løgstrup reflects his theological development as a whole. In the earliest phase, the two theologians held sharply antithetical positions as the principal representatives of a Barthian-church position and a Tidehverv-Grundtvigian position. After they both became professors at Aarhus University, their relationship was marked by increasing mutual recognition and respect, and it became particularly fruitful in academic terms after they both clashed in the 1950s with what they saw as Gogarten's and Bultmann's nihilistic understanding of creation. Prenter was also one of the most vigorous defenders of *Den etiske fordring* (*The Ethical Demand*), 1956, and spoke very appreciatively of Løgstrup's later *Metafysik I-IV*. From time to time, he also made critical remarks on individual points, which Løgstrup regularly acknowledged. His openness to Løgstrup's phenomenology of creation reflects what we could call an ontological shift in Prenter's writings. In *Skabelse og Genløsning*, he was ambiguous about how Luther's doctrine of ubiquity should be understood; but now he accepts Løgstrup's panentheistic explanation of ubiquity. This ontological shift in Prenter's thinking finds clear expression when love and the personal being of the human person are no longer ascribed to the relationship of faith, as in *Spiritus Creator* and *Skabelse og Genløsning*, but are assigned to the reality of the creation.

Prenter's French lectures on Christology (1962–63), published as *Connaître Christ* (1966), represent a Grundtvigian turn. In the light of the Grundtvigian coupling of the resurrection and the act of worship, Prenter speaks of the two sources of Christology, namely, the written source (scripture), which he regards as the "dogmatic" (substantial) norm for Christology, and the oral source (the confession of faith), which he regards as the "hermeneutical" (existential) norm. In drawing this distinction between dogmatic and hermeneutical, Prenter believes that he is basically maintaining the *sola scriptura* principle, but there can be little doubt that he is in reality pushing the Reformation scriptural principle to its limits, since he lets the confession of faith determine the content of the biblical interpretation and the total direction this interpretation is to take. This means that there is an interaction in terms of content between the confession of faith and the interpretation of scripture. One of the most striking features, in comparison with *Skabelsen og Genløsning*, is that the concept of "confession" is no longer oriented to the creeds that were formulated in the early church in the light of scripture, but rather to the contemporary liturgical praxis of the church. Accordingly, Prenter attributes to the liturgy of the Danish church a central methodological role that is not found in his earlier writings. *Connaître Christ* indicates a liturgical shift in his writings.

Prenter's liturgical shift is connected with a corresponding modification in his understanding of the relationship between sanctification and real piety, which he now (with Luther) calls "actual righteousness" (*justitia actualis*). In his article "Luthers 'Synergismus'?" (1964), he affirms not only that piety is generated by sanctification with a Trinitarian necessity, but also that piety "collaborates" with the alien righteousness of Christ.[8] He draws a distinction between a meritorious synergism, which is thought of as a consecutive relationship between God and the human person, and a genuine synergism, in which there is a correlative-collaborative relationship between God and the human person in the relationship of faith. In this article, Prenter underlines that the actual righteousness is the fruit of the alien righteousness, but that it also "fulfills" this alien righteousness. The alien righteousness is given through baptism; the actual righteousness impels sanctification forward through death to oneself and love of one's neighbor. With a reference to Peter Brunner, Prenter writes that it is not the human person *in virtue of* an infused grace who collaborates, but the human person in his creatureliness *under* grace. Accordingly, when he speaks of a collaboration between alien righteousness and active righteousness, this is not due to a modification of pneumatology or of Christology, but rather to his ontological shift with regard to the theology of creation.

---

[8] In Regin Prenter, *Theologie und Gottesdienst* (Aarhus and Copenhagen 1977).

In *Kirkens embete* (*The Church's Ministry*), 1965, Prenter's Grundtvigian shift is expressed in ecclesiology. In his earlier writings, the laity's life of faith came after the Word and the ministry, but now he sees an interrelatedness, and he places a quite different emphasis on the laity and the liturgy. Prenter wants to develop a "theology of the laity" that is inspired by Yves Congar and is in opposition to Anglican episcopalism. One of the most original contributions in this sense is Prenter's plea for a reintroduction of the place of prophecy in the community, *inter alia* as a critical authority vis-à-vis the official church ministry. In his reflections on the *notae ecclesiae*, Prenter's starting point is no longer in the relationship between the Word and faith, but rather in election and in the church's existence *antecedently to* its notes. He believes that these notes are expressed in the term *perpetuo mansura* and in the prepositional clause *in qua* in Confessio Augustana VII. The church is not "created" through the Word and the sacraments. Rather, it is "awakened," "gathered," and "built up." Relying for support on Grundtvig, Prenter asserts now that preaching too – not only the confession of faith and the good works – is a *sign of the life* that is in Christ. He still holds fast to the fundamental importance of the external Word as a representation of Christ's alien righteousness, but he makes election rather than the Word the focal point of the doctrine of justification. This means in fact that he has set a question mark against his earlier view that the Word is temporally antecedent to faith. He has made it possible to speak of a pneumatological-soteriological activity *prior to* the visible church, while at the same time maintaining the bodiliness of the church, in life and in death, as the birthplace of redemption.

It is only in the 1970s that Prenter interprets anthropology in the light of his Grundtvigian shift, and he does so primarily in polemic against what he sees as the blend of creation and redemption in a theology inspired by Marxism. In the article "Grundtvigs udfordring til moderne theologi" (*Grundtvig's Challenge to Modern Theology*), 1973, and in his later book on Grundtvig, *Den kirkelige anskuelse* (*Understanding the Church*), 1983, he reinterprets the Grundtvigian "first a human person – then a Christian" to mean that the image of God neither disappears nor is distorted through the Fall. Prenter still wants to hold fast to his Lutheran view of sin and righteousness by faith; but at the same time, he affirms a positive *theological-anthropological* continuity between God's activity in creation and in redemption. In his book on Anselm, *Guds virkelighet* (*The Reality of God*), 1982, he even writes of the image of God, bestowed in creation, as the *motivation* for God's redeeming work. In *Kirkens lutherske bekendelse* (1978), he expresses this anthropological modification by supplementing his earlier particular idea of atonement with a universal idea of redemption in which the human person who is God's image is redeemed from the superhuman power of sin. It is also striking both in *Kirkens lutherske bekendelse* (*The Lutheran Confession of the Church*) and in other late texts to see that the image of God is no longer linked primarily to the human person's capacity to speak, but rather to the totality of the human person. He now prefers to emphasize the vulnerability and bodiliness of the human person. In the article "Grundtvigs treenighedslære" (*Grundtvig's Doctrine of the Trinity*), 1983, Prenter's theme is not only the "shadow-image" of the Trinity in the soul through the triad of "love, truth, and vital force," but even more clearly the bodily "image, that is to say, in the threefold life of *heart, mouth, and hand.*"[9] Prenter's Grundtvigian turn entails a bodily turn.

Prenter's Theological Relevance

To a large extent, the conservatism of Prenter's basic attitude and his liturgical theology of the covenant have been alien to the dominant currents in academic theology in Scandinavia in recent decades. In my opinion, however, a number of factors mean that Prenter's theology could once again become relevant to theological discourse. First of all, his continuous work on the understanding of the dogma of the Trinity could be of interest today, now that the understanding of the Trinity has become one of the principal themes in modern theology. Secondly, his Grundtvigian-liturgical theology of the covenant could be of interest, now that the unified culture of the national church is becoming fragmented, and both religious identity and liturgical theology have come onto the theological agenda. Finally, his theological anthropology could once again be of interest, now that more and more people are opposed to "a bodily turn" in anthropology, and hence also in epistemology and hermeneutics. I shall now briefly sketch three topics where I believe that Prenter's theology could be fruitful in contemporary theological discourse: the understanding of the Trinity, liturgical theology, and the understanding of bodiliness and suffering in human life.

Prenter's theology after his Lutheran shift in the mid-1940s was very definitely a Trinitarian theology. As early as *Spiritus Creator*, he states his disagreement with what he sees as modalistic tendencies in the way Holl and Seeberg understand Luther, and he affirms that the real piety must be ascribed to the Father. Barth and Rahner have often been criticized as representatives of the modalism of the western church, but one certainly cannot make the same charge against Prenter. Nevertheless, it is only in connection with his Grundtvigian turn in the 1960s that full justice is done to the immanent-Trinitarian concept of person. Inspired by the dialogic personalism of Gogarten and Løgstrup, Prenter now affirms that the Trinitarian concept of Person has its analogy in the general concept of person. He now speaks of the relationship between the Father and the Son as a reciprocal relationship – something very different from what we find in his earlier writings.[10] Unlike much recent Trinitarian theology, however (for example, Jürgen Moltmann, Leonardo Boff, Gisbert Greshake, Elizabeth Johnson), Prenter avoids a tritheistic identification of God's unity with the perichoresis of the Persons: he continues to speak of the one being of God as the *presupposition* of the interwovenness of the Persons. Although he speaks in several texts of the one God as subject(ivity)/person(ality), he also calls God "the power of that which exists" and "the power of love," thereby opening the door to an impersonal understanding of the

---

[9] In Regin Prenter, *N.F.S. Grundtvig – theolog og kirkelærer*, p. 59.
[10] See Regin Prenter, *Kirkens tro* (Copenhagen 1964), 40–48; "Der Gott, der Liebe ist," in *Theologie und Gottesdienst*, 275–91.

unity of God's being that avoids a quadristic misinterpretation of the doctrine of the Trinity. Prenter's late theology likewise opens the door to criticism of the Filioque, since he envisages a reciprocal relationship between scripture and the confession of faith, and thereby also between Christ and the Spirit. He does this in the context of the western church, where the theology of revelation maintains the identity between the economic and the immanent Trinity. Prenter's solution largely agrees with Wolfhart Pannenberg's late Trinitarian theology.[11]

After Prenter's Grundtvigian shift in the 1960s, it is legitimate to call his theology a "liturgical theology," in the sense that the liturgy not only indicates the goal of theology, but is decisively important from now on for the elucidation of the content of theology. Prenter's liturgical theology differs, however, from many recent contributions in the field of liturgical theology, which do not have a background in Lutheran and Grundtvigian fundamental theology, but rely instead on the tradition of the eastern churches.[12] Despite the common aim to restore the role of the liturgy and of the laity in theology, therefore, there also exist fundamental differences between these liturgical theologies. Liturgical theology that is influenced by the eastern churches argues that the relationship between theology and liturgy must be understood unilaterally, but Prenter maintains that this must be understood as a reciprocal relationship. This difference is due to a difference in theologies of creation. The thinking that is influenced by eastern Christianity operates with an ontological theological conception, where ontology is seen as integrated into ecclesiology and theological criticism is primarily carried out within the church; but Prenter rejects what he calls an ontologization of Christology and maintains the autonomy of the creation, with the result that the theological criticism comes primarily from the outside. Prenter sees a liturgical theology influenced by eastern Christianity as a kind of liturgical-ecclesiological variant of revelational positivism (to use the term Bonhoeffer employed in his critique of Barth). This type of liturgical theology appears to presuppose an ecclesiological and liturgical monism, but Prenter's liturgical theology can play a constructive role in the encounter with ecclesiological and liturgical plurality.

Prenter identifies the cross of Christ with what he calls "the cross of creation" in a way that has led some theologians to believe that he supports a liberation-theological understanding of the cross.[13] But this misses the point. The understanding of the cross in liberation theology tends to be based on a distinction between life and death that manifests itself primarily in power relationships in society, where God's identification with "the crucified ones" entails a critical evaluation of the power relationships and a call "to take the crucified ones down from the cross." In Prenter, however, the fundamental distinction is between creation and redemption, and this forbids placing the main focus on the distinction between "rich" and "poor" *per se*. Naturally, Prenter

---

[11] See Wolfhart Pannenberg: *Systematische Theologie* 1, Göttingen 1988, 283–483, where he also refers to Prenter's late reflections on the understanding of the Trinitarian concept of God.

[12] See, e.g., David Fagerberg: *What is Liturgical Theology?* (Minnesota 1991).

[13] See Philip Lawrence Ruge-Jones: *Cross in Tension* (Chicago 1999).

too affirms that the life of faith consists in defending the oppressed, and he even says that the weak and the poor are saints who are to be loved and helped in a special way, since they are representatives of Christ and of the church. But it is clear that he is more interested in the suffering that life as a matter of fact brings, and that ought not to be avoided, but rather borne. This is why he does not speak (as Sobrino does) of "taking the crucified ones down from the cross," but rather of "taking up one's cross." For Prenter, this means leading a down-to-earth life in the struggle against sin's yearning for all kinds of idealizations. From a classic perspective of oppression, of course, this language can appear inadequate. But seen against the background of the experience that Prenter himself has in mind – that is to say, the utopian understanding of life that suppresses suffering and despises weakness – what he says is highly relevant. This perspective correlates well with the tendency in recent theological discourse to seek to supplement the traditional hamartiology based on guilt with a paradigm of shame: not the shame that is a consequence of abuse, but the shame that is a consequence of narcissist tendencies and of an idealized anthropology that is the product not least of commercial interests.

Bibliography

Primary Literature

'Die sogenannte 'kirchliche Anschauung' N.F.S. Grundtvigs als Frage an die evangelische Theologie von heute', *Evangelische Theologie*, 1 (1934), 278–88.

'Die Frage nach einer theologischen Grundtvig-Interpretation', in *Theologische Aufsätze. Karl Barth zum 50. Geburtstag* (Munich, 1936), 505–13. (*The Question of a Theological Interpretation of Grundtvig*).

Ordets Herredømme (Copenhagen, 1941). (*Dominion of the Word*).

Bibelen og vor Forkyndelse (Copenhagen, 1942). (*The Bible and Our Preaching*).

Spiritus Creator. Studier i Luthers Theologi (Copenhagen, 1944). English: *Spiritus Creator: Luther's concept of the Holy Spirit* (Muhlenberg Press, 1953).

"Grundtvigs syn på mennesket," *Kirke og Kultur*, 53 (1948), 209–26. (*Grundtvig's View of the Human Being*).

"Grundtvigs og Einar Billings syn på folkekirken," *Viborg Stifts Årbog*, 1949. (Copenhagen, 1950), 128–44. (*Grundtvig's and Einar Billing's Views of the National Church*).

Skabelse og Genløsning (Copenhagen, 1955). English: *Creation and Redemption* (Fortress Press 1967).

"Sækulariseringens Evangelium. Bemærkninger til Friedrich Gogartens seneste forfatterskab," *Svensk Teologsk Kvartalskrift*, 31 (1955), 170–92. (*The Gospel of Secularization. Comments on Friedrich Gogarten's Most Recent Writings*).

"Nogle bemærkninger vedrørende kristologien i K.E. Løgstrups: Den etiske fordring," *Dansk Teologisk Tidsskrift*, 4 (1962), 219–20. (*Some Remarks Regarding the Christology of K.E. Løgstrup's 'The Ethical Demand'*).

Kirkens tro (Copenhagen, 1964). English: *The Church's Faith: A Primer of Christian Beliefs* (Fortress Press 1968).
Kirkens embede (Copenhagen, 1965). (*The Church's Ministry*).
Connaître Christ (Neuchâtel, 1966).
Luther's Theology of the Cross (Philadelphia, 1971).
"Grundtvigs utfordring til moderne theologi," *Grundtvigstudier* (Copenhagen, 1973), 11–29 (*Grundtvig's Challenge to Modern Theology*).
Theologie und Gottesdienst. Gesammelte Aufsätze / Theology and Liturgy. Collected Essays (Aarhus and Copenhagen, 1977).
Kirkens lutherske bekendelse (Fredericia, 1978). (*The Lutheran Confession of the Church*).
"Skjulte og åpenbare kristologiske forudsætninger i K.E. Løgstrups metafysikk," *Fønix*, 3 (1978/79), 354–70. ('Hidden and obvious Christological Presuppositions in K.E. Løgstrup's Metaphysics').
Guds virkelighed. Anselm af Canterbury. Proslogion oversatt og udlagt som en indførelse i theologien (Fredericia, 1982). (*The Reality of God. Anselm of Canterbury. Proslogion translated and expounded as an Introduction to Theology*).
"Grundtvigs treenighedslære," in *N.F.S. Grundtvig – theolog og kirkelærer* (Sabro, 1983). (*Grundtvig's Doctrine of the Trinity*).
Den kirkelige anskuelse. En indføring i N.F.S. Grundtvigs folkelige og kristelige grundtanker (Christiansfeld, 1983). (*Understanding the Church. Introductions to N.F.S. Grundtvig's Popular and Christian Thought*).
Erindringer (Aarhus 1985). (*Memoirs*).

Secondary Literature

Bjerg, Svend, *Århusteologerne. P.G. Lindhardt, K.E. Løgstrup, Regin Prenter, Johannes Sløk. Den store generation i det 20. århundredes danske teologi* (Viborg, 1994).
Fagerberg, David, *What is Liturgical Theology? A Study in Methodology* (Minnesota, 1992) (Doctoral dissertation, Yale University, 1991).
Kyndal, Erik, "Lutherforskeren og dogmatikeren Regin Prenter, 1907–1990," *Præsteforeningens Blad*, 81(2) (1991), 17–21.
Njå, Ådne, *Det ånder himmelsk over støvet. Faser i Regin Prenters grundtvigske paktsteologi* (Doctoral dissertation, University of Oslo, 2008).
Ruge-Jones, Philip Lawrence, *Cross in Tension: Theology of the Cross as Theologico-Social Critique* (Doctoral dissertation, Lutheran School of Theology at Chicago, 1999).
Root, Michael, *Creation and Redemption. A Study of their Interrelation. With Special Reference to the Theology of Regin Prenter* (Doctoral dissertation, Yale University, 1979).
Schjørring, Jens Holger, "Regin Prenter in memoriam." *Grundtvigstudier* (Copenhagen 1991), 7–19.

Chapter 12
Gustaf Wingren

Jonny Karlsson

Gustaf Wingren (1910–2000) is one of the central figures in twentieth-century Swedish, Scandinavian, and European theology. His bibliography runs to 750 items, and many of his monographs have been translated into English and German, as well as several other languages. He was the last in the line of theologians who created what international theological scholarship tends to call "the Swedish Luther renaissance." Before him came Nathan Söderblom, Einar Billing, Gustaf Aulén, Anders Nygren, Herbert Olsson, and Ragnar Bring. Wingren was influenced by these theologians, but also by the dialectical theology on the Continent, including Karl Barth and Rudolf Bultmann, and by Danish theology, especially by Grundtvig and K.E. Løgstrup. One of Wingren's most important instruments was polemic, not least against several of the theologians who had impressed him (for example, Nygren, Barth, and Bultmann), but also against his high-church and Pietist predecessors. The fundamental starting points for the elaboration of his own theology were Irenaeus, Luther, and above all the biblical texts and the situation of modern people. This combination gave him a voice all of his own, and it is still worth listening to him.

Biography

Gustaf Wingren was born in Tryseum in Östergötland on November 29, 1910, and grew up in nearby Valdemarsvik, where the most important industry was a leather factory. His father, Gustaf Fabian Wingren, was a tanner and foreman. His mother Teresia took care of the five children until her early death in 1921. Despite the tragedy of his mother's death, Wingren had a positive picture of his upbringing in a Free Church working-class home, where his aunts Hilda and Signe overtook his mother's role. Wingren associated her death with the logion in the Gospel of John about the grain of wheat that falls into the earth and dies in order to give a rich harvest. It was from her that he received his trust and his faith. This remained one of the most central biblical passages for Wingren throughout his life, and he returned to it again and again in his sermons and his writings.

A congenital deformation of the right hand made physical work impossible for Wingren, and it was realized early on that he had a "head for study." These factors meant that he was the only one of his siblings who was allowed to continue with his studies after elementary school. After finishing high school in 1927, Wingren was sent to Lund to study at the upper secondary school there. He did this in record time, and took his examination in 1929. In his memoirs, Wingren tells how he met director Lundberg, the owner of the leather factory, on the high street in Valdemarsvik after he had finished his examination. "He stopped, took out his wallet, gave me a thousand-crowns note and said: 'What has happened now is an honor for Valdemarsvik'." This sum covered one year's food and lodgings in Lund! Wingren began his studies in 1929 at the university of Lund, where he took his licentiate in theology in 1939 with a dissertation on *Marcion och Irenaeus* (*Marcion and Irenaeus*). In the same year, he was ordained to the priesthood in the cathedral of Linköping by Bishop Tor Andræ, and was appointed as assistant in the parish of Gamleby for one year. After ten months of ministry, nine in Gamleby and one in Valdemarsvik, Wingren returned to Lund, where he defended his dissertation *Luthers lära om kallelsen* (*Luther on Vocation*) in 1942. In 1943–44, Wingren worked as a priest in the deanery of Motala. He then returned to Lund and took up a teaching position at the university. He married his wife Signhild in the late 1940s. They had two children, Anna and Anders.

After an appointment procedure where the result was uncertain until the very end, Wingren became professor of systematic theology in 1951, as Anders Nygren's successor. He held this position until his retirement in 1977. In 1959, when a new bishop was to be chosen for Linköping, he declined on the grounds that he "could not leave the work he had to do at the university of Lund." Apart from some brief periods deputizing for a professor and as visiting professor in Åbo, Basel, Göttingen, Aarhus, St. Paul, and Toronto, Wingren remained from 1944 until his death on November 1, 2000 in Lund, since this was his place on earth: "It is in Lund that everything is to function well […]. I now hear for the thousandth time in my mind the voice of the conductor as he went along the train on that Sunday morning, July 10, 1927, calling out just one word: Lund, Lund, Lund."

Wingren was active ecumenically both in the Lutheran World Federation and in the World Council of Churches, where he was a member of the Faith and Order Commission for nearly two decades. When the Societas Ethica was founded in 1964, he became its first chairman.

Overview of Wingren's Theological Writings

The books Wingren wrote can be divided into roughly three phases. The first consists of the books *Luthers lära om kallelsen* (1942) and *Människan och inkarnationen enligt Irenaeus* (*Man and the Incarnation*) (1947), where he presents a perspective that he believes has been forgotten, and that runs through all his writings as a fundamental motif. It concerns the first article of the creed: the Creator who gives of his goodness so that the human person can live, the Creator who works in the human person's everyday calling. In this perspective, we may say (with a little exaggeration) that to be saved means nothing other than to be a human person, conscious of one's flaws and yearning for perfection, and with the Gospel as the clear spring from which one can drink. Wingren's perspective thus does not mean that the first article of faith is superior to the second article, but that the creation and the law are the sphere that gives the Gospel, the second article of faith, its full significance. The second article must be conjoined to the first. In these two books, Wingren works in accordance with the historically descriptive methodology of the Lund theologians, from whom he learns "historical primary research." He realized the flaw in their approach during his semester in Basle, where the students confronted him with what he regarded as a justified question about the kerygma, "the meaning of the Bible's word as a word that is preached now."

This introduces the second phase in Wingren's writings, which consists of the books *Predikan* (*The Living Word*) (1949), *Teologiens metodfråga* (*Theology in Conflict. Nygren, Barth, Bultmann*) (1954), *Skapelsen och lagen* (*Creation and Law*) (1958), *Evangeliet och kyrkan* (*Gospel and Church*) (1960) and *Einar Billing* (*An Exodus Theology. Einar Billing and the Development of Modern Swedish Theology*) (1968). The basis for what Wingren writes here is the new orientation that was the consequence of his period as deputy professor in Karl Barth's chair in Basle. When Wingren looks back on Predikan, he believes that the starting point was that it must be possible "to hold fast to the biblical belief in creation, to hold fast to the continuity between the human and the Christian, to hold fast to the understanding of redemption as the restoration of the natural" (a view he had learnt in Lund), "and at the same time to accommodate the justified elements in Barth's position, namely, the interpretation of the biblical word as an address, as the word that is preached now." Wingren understands preaching as God's action in the present moment. It is God's word spoken against destruction and evil (the "antagonistic aspect" of the Word), and at the same time a word that is one element in the history of God's salvation, with roots in history and en route to eternity (the "temporal aspect" of the Word). In this later perspective, preaching holds together God's works in the past and the works that are to come. In Teologiens metodfråga, the theological projects of Nygren, Bultmann, and Barth are sharply criticized. Every theology presupposes something about how the Bible is to be understood and something about human life, about the situation of the person who is struck by the Word. A false picture is given of the center of the Christian faith, when the starting point is not the Bible itself and preaching, but Kant (Nygren), Heidegger (Bultmann), or the critique of liberal theology (Barth). Mistaken methodological starting points lead to the excision of important parts of the content of the Bible, namely, the creation and the law. This means that it is not a question of being wrong on one point or other – something that could easily be corrected – but of a systemic failure. This critical settling of accounts is followed by a positive presentation of the Christian faith in Skapelsen och lagen and Evangeliet och kyrkan. These two books belong together and have been regarded as Wingren's dogmatics, a synthesis of the fundamental ideas in his theological thinking up to this time. In 1968, he wrote Einar Billing, a very modest work running to 157 pages that has often been forgotten. Obviously, it is a discussion of Einar Billing's theology, but it is also a kind of retrospective view of this second phase in Wingren's own production. He writes: "What I myself have written about 'preaching' and about 'the Gospel' from 1949 until the present day has been strongly influenced by Billing's writings, much more strongly than by Continental kerygmatic theology."

The main themes in this book are the view of the Bible, Christology, and ecclesiology. One central idea that Wingren finds in Billing is the tension between the people and the individual. In the Old Testament, to begin with, we find both law and grace linked to the people. With Ezekiel, the demands of the law are individualized, but grace does not acquire an individual form before Jesus. "For Billing, the point in the expansion – that is to say, in the New Testament development – is that the grace of election is individualized when Jesus gives the individual the forgiveness of sins, and that this same forgiveness in the same individually addressed form is given to individuals in 'all peoples' through the world mission that has just begun."

The third phase in Wingren's writings consists *inter alia* of the books *Växling och kontinuitet* (*Change and Continuity*) (1972) and *Credo* (*Credo. The Christian View of Faith and Life*) (1974), where he reformulates his systematic-theological project. The battle cry is raised in *Växling och kontinuitet* (which corresponds to *Predikan*): "There is no Gospel that is above the milieus. The Gospel is always colored by a local, human, restricted milieu." This is why the Gospel must continually be reformulated with the listeners in view (*växling*, "change"), but with the starting point in the Bible's message about salvation in Jesus Christ (*kontinuitet*, "continuity"). This means that references to culture, societal analysis, and Christianity's relationship to other worldviews play a much larger role here than in Wingren's earlier works. The same can be said about *Credo* (which corresponds to *Skapelsen och lagen* and *Evangeliet och kyrkan*). This book has the structure of a traditional doctrinal treatise based on the three articles of faith, but these are understood as three different aspects of the whole. This means, for example, that both the Son and the Spirit are also found in the chapter about the first article of faith. Another special feature is that each section is concluded with a psalm and a prayer written by Wingren, perhaps because he wanted to say that theory and praxis must not be separated in any simple way.

Other books from this phase in Wingren's production that deserve a mention are *Två testamenten och tre artiklar* (*Two Testaments and Three Articles*) (1976), *Öppenhet och egenart* (*Creation and Gospel. The New Situation in European Theology*) (1979), *Tolken som tiger* (*The Interpreter Who is Silent*) (1981), *Människa och Kristen. En bok om Irenaeus* (*Human Being and Christian. A Book about Irenaeus*) (1983), *Gamla vägar framåt. Kyrkans uppgift i Sverige* (*Old Paths Forward. The Mission of the Church in Sweden*) (1986), and *Texten talar. Trettio predikningar* (*The Text Speaks. Thirty Sermons*) (1989).

A Closer Look at Three Themes

Wingren's Argument

Wingren's theology is conducted from the book *Predikan* onwards along two lines of argumentation, one connected with the training of clergy and the other with academic research. Behind both lies a deeper ambition than merely the desire that theology should function in Lund (see the quotation above). It must also function out in the parishes. Wingren's theology has a practical, pastoral concern, motivated by the fact that sermons must be preached in our churches next Sunday.

The training of clergy. When the Swedish philosopher Ingemar Hedenius proposed in 1958 that the theological faculties should lose their independence and be reorganized in such a way that they became part of the Humanities faculties and that that church itself should educate its clergy, Wingren countered with a Schleiermachian argumentation. The wellbeing of society requires the existence of certain functions such as the care of the sick, law courts, and churches. It is therefore also in the interests of society to have professional training for these functions – that is to say, for doctors, lawyers, and priests. This means that the study of theology is a professional training. Faculties are established to provide training in these fields, not because of "research factors," but because of "training factors" – something that Wingren claims is not incompatible with the fact that these are academic trainings.

As the years went by, Wingren gradually became more pessimistic about the competence of the theological faculties to train future priests. He made one last grandiose – and desperate – attempt to influence the faculties with his book *Tolken som tiger* (1991), which resembles a volcanic explosion more than an attempt at dialogue. In his autobiography, *Mina fem universitet* (*My Five Universities*) (1991), he envisages a future situation in which the Swedish church may be forced to take on the full responsibility for training its clergy. This is because dogmatics and biblical theology are being dismantled at the theological faculties in the name of academic scholarship. We sense in Wingren both grief and resignation when he depicts such a future. Indeed, he goes so far as to claim that he "willingly" accepts the verdict that his own activity is not academic. This however, had not always been the case.

The academic argument. Wingren sees no contradiction at all between the demands connected with professional training and the academic demands. I believe that over the years, Wingren constantly and consistently demanded that theology should maintain its academic quality. From *Predikan* (1949) onwards, however, this is formulated to some extent on new premises. Wingren asserts that contemporary systematic theology has methodological defects. These concern its academic quality, and they are the reason why the study of theology does not function satisfactorily in its role of training clergy.

A systematic theology aims to identify what is specifically Christian. The academic argument for beginning this task with a fundamental analysis of preaching is based in biblical theology. One might perhaps suspect that Wingren begins here by giving the Bible a normative status, and that this would bring him into a pre-critical non-academic position, but he holds that the word of the Bible not only contains commands to preach, but itself claims to be an address, a proclamation. He believes that he finds academic support for this affirmation in the research by exegetes of the form-historical school, which has also influenced the dialectical theology. Wingren also holds that the sermon is a phenomenon that "bears traces of the origin," since the sermon as an exposition of the biblical text for persons who listen has been taking place for two thousand years, and still takes place every Sunday in Christian churches. The biblical text has functioned in every period since earliest Christianity, and still functions, as the starting point and norm for preaching, to which both the preacher and the listeners freely submit. Christians themselves regard the biblical text *de facto* as more than merely one in the series of religious statements. The biblical text differs from all other Christian texts, because Christians in all ages have believed that God is the subject in this word, and they regard the word of the Bible as an address by God. This means that they regard all other Christian texts as subordinate to the Bible. And this in turn means that it is not academic scholars who give the Bible its normative status. All they do is to record that Christians themselves give the biblical text this status. Wingren writes that both the character of the biblical texts (that is to say, the claim they make to be a word that is proclaimed), and the normative quality that Christians ascribe to the Bible are facts that can be observed by everyone. Accordingly, they can be recorded in an academic context.

Another way to put this could perhaps be that according to Wingren, the Bible supports the view that the Christian faith is something relational, something that takes place between two living partners and is oriented towards other living human persons – not a theory, an eternal truth, or anything like that. This means that when we wish to describe Christianity, we should also begin in something that does justice to this relationality. Preaching is a phenomenon in which the character of the biblical word as "address" continues to be realized, since it is spoken to listening persons who assume that the word of the Bible is a word from God. The difficult thing is to remember that the sermon too is an address from God, not merely human talking about God, and that the sermon too claims to include an authoritative address.

This does not mean that theology itself should be an exposition of the biblical text. Wingren emphasizes that theology is *not* to devote itself to exposition. There is a frequent tendency to regard this contemporary exposition as the real task of systematic theology, but this is a mistake. Theology has quite simply assumed that exposition *takes place* in our time, and it is in fact taking place when the word is preached and taught, and so on – in other words, thanks to the fact that a Christian community now exists. It is in this community that all exposition of scripture should be carried out: this is its "home." Academic scholarship stands outside and looks on, when preaching actually takes place (*Teologiens metodfråga*, 1954).

Wingren's basic criticism of contemporary theology is that it cuts off important parts of the content of the Bible that form the framework around the preaching of the Gospel. This is because of faulty methodological starting points that lead scholars to prescind from fundamental aspects of the biblical text. The novelty in the new element in the New Testament proclamation, namely, God's work in Christ, becomes clear only in relation to something old, namely, the Old Testament proclamation of God's work through creation and the law. When this is excised in modern theology, one fails to do justice to "the church's inherent positive relationship to the world." Wingren's solution is to dismantle "the speculative antithesis" between God and the human person, and to accept instead the genuine, biblically anchored antithesis between God and Satan, placing the emphasis on the struggle between these two opponents – a struggle into which the human person is drawn. The preacher's aim is thus not an addition – something that is added onto human life – but a subtraction, in the sense of a liberation from captivity.

Wingren's relationship to the Bible is marked by his focus on the Christ who is proclaimed therein and who now, thanks to his death and resurrection, comes to meet the assembled people in the sermon that is being delivered. This sermon is both the word of creation and the word of redemption in confrontation with the destruction and the pressure from the law to which the Bible assumes that everyone is subject. If we begin from the Bible and read it in the same way as Wingren, but drawing adequate support in historical terms from form-critical exegetes, we arrive at an understanding of the sermon as God's action today. It is here that we find the specifically Christian element. On the basis of an academic argumentation, Wingren believes that he has laid the foundations for a theology that can hold together the human and the Christian, and do justice to the demand for both change and continuity that Wingren makes. He believes that this is essential both for a description of Christianity and for the people who sit in church on Sunday and expect to hear the Gospel.

The Role of Experience

In order to understand the new formulation of his systematic-theological project that Wingren undertakes with the book *Växling och kontinuitet* in 1972, I believe that we can usefully draw on his article "Mina ämnesval" ("My Choice of Topics") from 1966. He begins with experiences in the Valdemarsvik of his youth, where the church did not succeed in creating a unity out of "eating, singing psalms, kicking a football, and going to the cinema." The activity in the parishes tended "to cut off the church from human life in general," instead of having an "integrative role in relation to human life as a whole." This means that what takes place in church on Sunday is not linked to everyday life. People's dealings with God take place in a sphere that is separated from everyday life, a special religious sphere. Instead of making people open to the world and to their fellow human beings, the church creates a space that is separated from the world, a place of refuge outside the world. This makes it impossible for the church to have a pastoral function vis-à-vis the individuals who come to church on Sunday with the distress that has its origin in everyday life. Wingren had not written down these experiences before, and the question is whether he had even formulated them in this way for himself before. The use he makes of his experiences from the 1920s suggests that he regarded these as more generally valid than what he had experienced only when he was over 50. This also allows him to reconstruct his thinking as a continuous whole, from his early years to his mature years as a professor. When he formulates his experiences in this way in 1966, this is because he is beginning to reformulate his theological project, in which experiences of everyday life emerge more clearly and play a greater role than in his earlier writings. I believe that it is obvious that Wingren's references to the time in which he is writing, to everyday experiences, culture, the analysis of society, and Christianity's relation to other worldviews play a much larger role in *Växling och kontinuitet* and in *Credo* than in his earlier works. We can see this also in a number of book reviews and articles about literature that he wrote in the 1970s. Lars Ahlin and Sara Lidman seem to have been particularly important authors for Wingren.

Another experience that Wingren seldom mentions, but which presumably must have played a role in his writings, is the experience of preaching. Normally, he preached every Sunday during his time as a priest in Gamleby and Motala, but he was also in demand as a guest preacher during his time at the university. In his sermons, Wingren increasingly makes a conscious link to the experiences he assumes his listeners will have had, not only of life in the church, but also of life in the world and everyday living.

Theology of Creation or Theology of the Cross?

It is striking to see how often Wingren makes a link in his writings and his sermons to experiences of destruction or defeat. He assumes that his listeners have had such experiences, and that they will interpret them as the absence of God. In the light of the cross, however, Wingren himself interprets these experiences as the deepest fellowship with God. He seldom makes a link to positive experiences that could be interpreted in a simple manner as experiences of God, and this may seem strange in one who has been labeled a "theologian of creation." When he makes the link, in the sermons that I have analyzed, to nature and the vegetable kingdom, he does not talk about the beauty and variety of nature behind which "we" can perceive the Creator himself, but about birds that are injured by oil or about the grain of wheat that is laid in the earth so that it may die and give life to new grains of wheat.

Another tendency we note in Wingren's evocations in his sermons of experiences that he thinks the listeners will have had is that he endeavors through such associations to hold together things that otherwise are often separated, such as the spiritual and the profane, worship and work, the church and the world, or "we" and "they." The fundamental experience of destruction, defeat, and the absence of God binds people together. But it also unites people to God through the cross.

In Christ, death and resurrection are both separated and united, and the same is true of the human person: what happened to Christ will also happen to "us." The death that affects us in everyday life concerns the old human being, "the body of sin," in order that selfishness may be crucified; but life, the resurrection, the resurrection of the new human being, is also present. According to Wingren, this death and resurrection would never come about unless we were reached by the Word, the Word that contains both law and Gospel, the Word that both judges and raises up. It is here that the true secret lies: life lies hidden in the Word that wounds and kills. It is when God comes clothed in his opposite, "*sub contraria specie*," that he saves.

In Wingren's writings and sermons, therefore, the Gospel is concentrated on Christ's death and resurrection. At the same time, the creation and the law are the framework in which the Gospel takes on its full significance. The law shares in the Gospel's work of death and resurrection, and carries out the killing. According to Wingren, faith means nothing other than a willingness to die, to go out of oneself in the often unglamorous tasks of daily life; unbelief is unwillingness to die. No human being can determine what in the Word is law, and what is Gospel. When the "voice" reaches the human being, the Word is always double: it is always both law and Gospel. God thus conquers the devil with the latter's own weapon, namely death. And it is in the cross and in lowliness that God has his glory and his majesty.

This prompts the question whether Wingren's theology ought to be described as a theology of the cross. Is it a theology of creation or a theology of the cross? We probably come nearest to the truth if we say that his project ultimately involves holding together the first and the second articles of the creed, being both a human being and a Christian.

Conclusion

Two events in the 1970s caused surprise among those around Wingren, and consternation elsewhere. In October, 1974, he gave up his priestly ministry because of the way the bishops treated women candidates for ordination. This concrete, drastic action, which in some ways was typical of him, was an expression of his untiring struggle against the high church party and their understanding of ministry. He explained his action to the cathedral chapter of Lund as follows: "Recent developments have made the priestly ministry that I received through ordination an object of exchange that can be used to barter and to buy peaceful relationships among brothers without taking the individual's lawful rights into consideration." The second event was his divorce and his marriage to the author and postwoman Greta Hofsten in 1976. He thereby cultivated even more intensely his alienation and the picture of himself as an *enfant terrible*, an uncomfortable critic both of the church and of the theology that was taught at the faculties; but we also find a new tone of societal criticism, a politically radical critique of the consumer society and "the deification of production." The feeling of alienation may also be reflected in the fact that he increasingly came to regard Denmark as the promised land, as a kind of spiritual and theological domicile. In Denmark, he was not the prodigal son who had squandered his theological patrimony.

Gustaf Wingren and his theology never formed a school either in Sweden or abroad. This may be because his theological program was too closely linked to his own mode of expression, an almost poetical language "like an underground tremor" (as Sara Lidman once said in general about her own writings). Although he never formed a school, he had an unmatched influence on theologians, pastors, and laity both in Sweden and abroad. Wingren debated with the great twentieth-century theologians in the Continent and Scandinavia, but his most important concern was "the Gospel and its work among contemporary people" out in the parishes and in the heart of the individual. Those who are involved in this work will always find good reasons to take up Gustaf Wingren's writings anew.

His books have been published in the USA by Wipf and Stock Publishers. *Människa och kristen* was translated into Danish in 2004, and several of his works have been reissued in Sweden by Artos bokförlag.

Bibliography

Primary Literature

For a complete bibliography, see:

Tolkning och konfrontation (*Interpretation and Confrontation*) (Lund: series *Religio*, nr. 47, Skrifter utgivna av av Teologiska institutionen i Lund, 1996 (also includes articles on Wingren's theology)) or http://www.svenskakyrkan.se/default.aspx?id=648288 (accessed November 29, 2012).

Wingren, Gustaf, *Luthers lära om kallelsen* (dissertation) (Lund: C.W.K. Gleerup, 1942/Skellefteå: Artos bokförlag, 1993). English: *Luther on Vocation* (Philadelphia: Muhlenberg Press, 1957/Eugen, Oregon: Wipf and Stock Publishers, 2004).

Wingren, Gustaf, *Människan och inkarnationen enlig Irenaeus* (Lund: Gleerups, 1947). English: *Man and the Incarnation* (Philadelphia: Muhlenberg Press, 1959/Eugen, Oregon: Wipf and Stock Publishers, 2004).

Wingren, Gustaf, *Predikan* (Lund: Gleerups, 1949/Skellefteå: Artos bokförlag, 1996). English: *The Living Word* (Philadelphia: Muhlenberg Press, 1960/Eugen, Oregon: Wipf and Stock Publishers, 2002).

Wingren, Gustaf, *Teologiens metodfråga* (Lund: Gleerups, 1954). English: *Theology in Conflict. Nygren, Barth, Bultmann* (Edinburgh & London/Philadelphia: Oliver and Boyd, 1958).

Wingren, Gustaf, *Skapelsen och lagen* (Lund: Gleerups, 1960). English: *Creation and Law* (Philadelphia: Muhlenberg Press, 1960/Eugen, Oregon: Wipf and Stock Publishers, 2003).

Wingren, Gustaf, *Evangeliet och kyrkan* (Lund: Gleerups, 1960). English: *Gospel and Church* (Minneapolis: Fortress Press, 1964/Eugen, Oregon: Wipf and Stock Publishers, 2006).

Wingren, Gustaf, *Einar Billing. En studie i svensk teologi före 1920* (Lund: Gleerups, 1968). English: *An Exodus Theology. Einar Billing and the Development of Modern Swedish Theology* (Minneapolis: Fortress Press, 1969).

Wingren, Gustaf, *Växling och kontinuitet* (Lund: C.W.K. Gleerup, 1972). (*Change and Continuity*).

Wingren, Gustaf, *Credo* (Lund: Liber läromedel, 1974/Skellefteå: Artos bokförlag, 1995). English: *Credo. The Christian View of Faith and Life* (Minneapolis: Augsburg Publishing House, 1981).

Wingren, Gustaf, *Öppenhet och Egenart. Evangeliet i världen* (Lund: Liber Läromedel, 1979). English: *Creation and Gospel. The New Situation in European Theology* (Toronto: Edwin Mellen Press, 1979/Eugen, Oregon: Wipf and Stock Publishers, 2006).

Wingren, Gustaf, *Tolken som tiger* (Stockholm: Gummessons, 1981). (*The Interpreter Who is Silent*).

Wingren, Gustaf, *Mina fem universitet* (Stockholm: Proprius, 1991). (*My Five Universities*).

Secondary Literature

Anderson, Mary Elizabeth, *Gustaf Wingren and the Swedish Luther Renaissance* (New York: Peter Lang Publishing, 2006).
Aurelius, Carl Axel, 'Gustaf Wingren', *TRE* 36 (Berlin, 2004).
Bexell, Göran, *Teologisk etik i Sverige sedan 1920-talet* (Älvsjö: Skeab, 1981), 144–80. (*Theological Etichs in Sweden since the 1920s*).
Håkansson, Bo, *Vardagens kyrka. Gustaf Wingrens kyrkosyn och folkkyrkans framtid* (Lund: Arcus bokförlag, 2001). (*The Church of Everyday. Gustaf Wingren's Ecclesiology and the Future of the National Church*).
Jensen, Roger, *Modernisering av lutherdommen …? Gustaf Wingrens nye skapelsesteologiske tilretteleggelse av den lutherske kallslære, i et komparativt perspektiv* (Oslo: PTS skriftserie 9, 2003). (*Modernizing Lutheranism …? Gustaf Wingren Creation Theological Clarification of the Lutheran Concept of Vocation, in a Comparative Perspective*).
Karlsson, Jonny, *Predikans samtal. En studie av lyssnarens roll i predikan hos Gustaf Wingren utifrån Michail Bachtins teori om dialogicitet* (Skellefteå: Artos, 2000). (*The Dialogue of the Sermon. A Study on the Role of the Listener in the Sermon of Gustaf Wingren from the view of Michail Bachtin´s Theory on Dialogue*).
Karlsson, Jonny och Larsdotter, Karin (eds), *Gustaf Wingren predikar*. Postilla (Skellefteå: Artos, 2010). (*Gustaf Wingren preaching. Sermons*).
Kristensson Uggla, Bengt, *Gustaf Wingren. Människan och teologin* (Stockholm/Stehag: Brutus Östlings bokförlag, Symposion, 2010).
Tro och liv nr. 4, 1996 (The theme of this fascicle is Gustaf Wingren's theology. Articles by Edgar Almén, Erik Aurelius, Carl Axel Aurelius, Henry Cöster, and others).

Chapter 13
Jürgen Moltmann

Idar Kjølsvik

Jürgen Moltmann is perhaps the best known living theologian in the world today. He is the most important Reformed theologian and one of the most prominent in the ecumenical context. Many theologians are equally famous in Europe, but none is more famous internationally. No one has been translated more frequently than Moltmann, and he rightly won the unofficial "World Championship in Theology" in summer 2006. He is best known for his theology of hope, which made eschatology respectable in university theology; but he is also the "godfather" of liberation theology, has made very important contributions to Trinitarian theology, and was the first modern theologian to write a large-scale work on eco-theology.

Jürgen Moltmann studied under Hans-Joachim Iwand, Ernst Wolf, and Otto Weber. He also counts Karl Barth, Gerhard von Rad, and Ernst Käsemann as his teachers. Many have underlined his closeness to the Jewish-Marxist philosopher Ernst Bloch, but Moltmann himself sees Weber as more important. In his autobiography, he writes that he still consults Weber's *Grundlagen der Dogmatik* (*Foundations of Dogmatics*) when he is unsure what position he should take on certain questions.

Moltmann is often called a "theologian of history" and is mentioned in the same breath as Wolfhart Pannenberg. These two scholars employ the theology of history to put an effective stop to the spread of existential theology. Their shared goal is nothing less than to bring the era of Barth and Bultmann to an end, and one may well say that they succeed in doing so.

Eberhard Jüngel is another theologian who is close to Moltmann, both because they were colleagues and because they are close to Barth. Moltmann's collaboration and theological kinship with Catholic theologians is less well known. He has worked closely with Hans Küng and Walter Kasper in Tübingen, and initially also with Joseph Ratzinger. Johann Baptist Metz was not in Tübingen, but he is Moltmann's closest ally in the work on political theology. In the final analysis, however, it is his wife, Elisabeth Moltmann-Wendel, who has meant more than anyone else. She grew up in the German Confessing Church under the Nazi regime, and she is one of the "mothers" of feminist theology. They have accompanied one another through thick and thin for 60 years, and still do so today.

Biography

Jürgen Moltmann's life is closely knitted together with his theology. In his case, perhaps more than with many other theologians, one must attach due importance to his biography if one is to grasp his theology. He was born on April 8, 1926 in a progressive Hanseatic family of teachers. He grew up with three younger siblings in the alternative community "Volksdorf" in Hamburg. His father, Herbert Moltmann, was rector of a school, and his mother Gerda, née Stuhr, was a housewife. The house was influenced by the secular Enlightenment and by the philosophers of German Idealism, Lessing, Goethe, and Nietzsche. There was no church in the community, and Moltmann writes that even if there had been a church, no one would have attended it. The Christmas service was held in the school, and had little connection to the Christian faith. Moltmann attended an Anthroposophical school, but he was not a good pupil. He describes his grandmother in Schwerin, the capital of Mecklenburg, as "the angel who saved me" in the transition from childhood to adolescence. As a teenager, he did well in the natural sciences and mathematics, but he was not interested in religion or theology.

When he was seventeen, Moltmann was enrolled as an anti-aircraft defense helper in a battery in the Aussenalster district in Hamburg. During the English "Operation Gomorrah" at the end of July 1943, his friend Gerhard Schopper was shot, while Moltmann himself survived. This was a decisive experience in Moltmann's life, and he began to enquire about God. Later on, he realized that many others would have asked why God could permit something like that to happen, but this idea did not occur to him at that time. His first question was: Where is God?

After a brief period studying chemistry and physics in Hamburg, Moltmann came as a recruit to Lithuania, and later as a soldier to Holland. He was taken prisoner by the British on February 15, 1945, and was detained first in Belgium and later in Scotland and England. In the camp, he saw prisoners who collapsed because they had no hope. He himself was given a Bible, and he found that it gave him hope and supplied words for his own experiences. Psalm 39 and Jesus' cry on the cross – "My God, my God, why have you abandoned me?" – were particularly important. Sixty years later, Moltmann wrote that he had been convinced through all this time that Jesus himself had been looking for him, and that he had found him physically in a prisoner-of-war camp in Scotland, and spiritually in "the dark night of the soul." Moltmann received the answer from "Operation Gomorrah": the Jesus who is abandoned on the cross shows us where God is. And he searches for the one who suffers, and finds him.

In June, 1946, Moltmann had the opportunity to study theology in Norton Camp near Nottingham, where the YMCA offered instruction. This was a turning point in his life. He returned to Germany in April, 1948 as a convinced Christian who had completed half of his theological studies. The meeting with the Evangelical Lutheran church in Hamburg, where (despite his progressive home background) he had been baptized, convinced him that he ought to become a member of the Reformed church "for the sake of the Gospel."

Moltmann's father, with his secular outlook, was skeptical about theology, but he allowed him to study for six semesters. Göttingen was well suited to his new Reformed standpoint. Karl Barth's Reformed professorship was held by Otto Weber. On a study trip to Copenhagen, he met his fellow student Elisabeth Wendel from Potsdam (also born in 1926), whose background was in the Confessing Church, the resistance movement in the church in the Third Reich. Delayed by the War, Moltmann had not got as far in his studies as Elisabeth, who was already writing her doctoral dissertation under Weber when Jürgen fell in love with her. In order to get to know her better, he too decided to write his doctoral dissertation under Weber, and he was assigned the theme of predestination. He defended his dissertation, *Prädestination und Heilsgeschichte bei Moyse Amyraut: Ein Beitrag zur Geschichte der reformierten Theologie zwischen Orthodoxie und Aufklärung*, in 1952 (*Predestination and History of Revelation in Moyse Amyraut: A Contribution to the History of Reformed Theology between Orthodoxy and Enlightenment*). His main goal was not, however, to write a dissertation, but to get married, and he succeeded in both of these. They wanted to work in pastoral ministry in East Germany, but the fact that Moltmann had spent time in England led the communist regime to fear that he might be a spy. They refused him a residence permit, and the couple settled in the village of Wasserhorst outside Bremen in West Germany, where he was pastor in a Reformed parish for five years. Elisabeth Moltmann-Wendel is one of the founders of feminist theology, active as author, mentor, and lecturer. She has been immensely important for her husband in every way. They have four daughters and six grandchildren.

In 1957, Moltmann made the acquaintance of the Dutch theologian Arnold van Ruler, and he made his own the Reformed theology of the kingdom of God. In 1958, with the help of Otto Weber, he became professor at the church college in Wuppertal, where one of his colleagues was Wolfhart Pannenberg. It was also here that he met Ernst Bloch for the first time, in 1959. In the following year, something happened that Moltmann has described several times. While he was on holiday in Italian-speaking Switzerland, he read Bloch's *Prinzip Hoffnung* (*The Principle of Hope*) and forgot the beauty of the Swiss Alps. This was a kind of theological conversion, the prelude to *Theologie der Hoffnung* (*Theology of Hope*) and to Moltmann's move to Tübingen, where he was Bloch's next-door neighbor.

He was appointed to a professorship in Bonn in 1963, and to a chair at the Eberhard-Karls-University in Tübingen in 1967, where he remained until he retired in 1994. His retirement and his seventieth, seventy-fifth, eightieth and recently eighty-fifth birthdays were celebrated in great style, each with its own Festschrift. These celebrations played a great role in the "Moltmann family" (not a "Moltmann school"!), and have been discussed in several books. Elisabeth and Jürgen still live in their own house in Tübingen as active senior citizens. They have no intention of stopping their theological activity until they are compelled to do so.

Writings

James L. Wakefield's bibliography (2002) contains 1,217 titles by Jürgen Moltmann and 850 titles about him, ca. 200 of which are doctoral dissertations. It goes without saying that the weightiest works run from *Theologie der Hoffnung* to the six-volume *Systematische Beiträge zur Theologie* (*Systematic Contributions to Theology*), but his writings can usefully be classified in five distinct epochs.

The Early Phase

The time before Bloch's philosophy and his use of concepts became important can be called Moltmann's early phase. The doctoral dissertation on *Prädestination und Heilsgeschichte bei Moyse Amyraut* (1952) (*Predestination and History of Revelation in Moyse Amyraut*) is his first work. It has never been published; a shortened version appeared as an article in the *Zeitschrift für Kirchengeschichte* (*Journal of Church History*) in 1954. Like this work, everything Moltmann wrote in his early phase has a historical orientation with a clear Evangelical-Reformed character, and therefore also a clear systematic-theological potential. The most important works are: *Die Gemeinde im Horizont der Herrschaft Christi* (1959) (*The Church in the Horizon of the Lordship of Christ*), *Calvin-Studien* (*Studies of Calvin*), *Prädestination und Perseveranz* (1961) (*Predestination and Perseverance*), and *Anfänge der dialektischen Theologie I-II* (1962/1963) (*Begginnings of Dialectical Theology I-II*). The early phase is marked by a great admiration of Karl Barth and Otto Weber, but from *Prädestination und Perseveranz* (*Predestination and Perseverance*) onwards, Moltmann writes more independently, as a dogmatic theologian with new ideas.

The Younger Moltmann

The publication of his work on eschatology, *Theologie der Hoffnung* (1964), made him famous virtually overnight. This book has become a classic; the fourteenth edition was published in 2004. He rounded off the principal phase in his theological production with the eschatological work *Das Kommen Gottes* (1995) (*The Coming of God*). This was also the topic he taught in his last semester in 1994, a sign that he himself sees eschatology as the most important theme in his work.

The most important part of Moltmann's activity must however be divided into two parts, the younger and the older Moltmann. In addition to *Theologie der Hoffnung*, the main works by the younger Moltmann are *Der gekreuzigte Gott* (1971) (*The Crucified God*) and *Kirche in der Kraft des Geistes* (1975) (*The Church in the Power of the Spirit*). The younger Moltmann typically employs a dialectical methodology based on the cross and the resurrection. He himself calls this methodology "the whole of theology in one focal point"; the focal point shifts from book to book. The focal point of *Theologie der Hoffnung* is the resurrection, and this book is a theology of hope. The focal point of *Der gekreuzigte Gott* is the cross, and Moltmann sees this book as a development of Luther's theology of the cross. *Kirche in der Kraft des Geistes* can be understood as the Spirit's synthesis of the thesis of the resurrection and the antithesis of the cross – we should note the sequence here. Moltmann himself believed that the "focal point" methodology was no longer useful, since this book has too many themes. He also writes that he was afraid of ending up in a "binitarian" doctrine of the Father and the Son, but that this last-named book saved him from that fate. It points ahead to *Systematische Beiträge zur Theologie*.

The Transitional Phase

The younger Moltmann can be located in the years 1964–75, and the older in 1980–95 and the publication of *Systematische Beiträge zur Theologie*. There is thus a transitional phase between the two main phases, which he himself calls "theology in movement, dialogue, and conflict." He wrote a great deal in this phase, but there is little that is creative in theological terms. He gives the impression of not being content and at peace with himself. He tells the story of a kind of conversion at a conference in Mexico City in 1977, where he became aware that he was unfortunately neither a woman, black, or poor. He gradually accepted the fact that he was a rich white man and he resolved to do what he could do best, namely, to write lengthy theological volumes. This was the beginning of his most important series, *Systematische Beiträge zur Theologie*. Another important event in this period was the encounter with the Rumanian Orthodox professor Dumitru Stăniloae. Their conversations provided the impetus for the development of Trinitarian doctrine; it is now that Moltmann begins to think "in terms of circumincession." His most important books from the transitional phase are *Gottes Recht und Menschenrechte* (1977) (*A Christian Declaration on Human Rights*), *Zukunft der Schöpfung* (1977) (*The Future of Creation*), and *Jüdischer Monotheismus – Christliche Trinitätslehre* (1979) (*Jewish Monotheism and Christian Trinitarian Doctrine*).

The Older Moltmann

One expression of the transition from the younger to the older Moltmann is a change in methodology. The methodology of the younger Moltmann had a dialectical character and looked at the whole of theology from one focal point: first the resurrection and revelation, then the cross and suffering, and finally the Spirit and the church. The intermediary phase is unclear and vague, without any specific methodology. The best way to describe it would perhaps be the concept of "approach methodology." But something decisively new happens in 1980. Moltmann now develops new Trinitarian metaphors and ways of thinking. He himself calls this methodology "parts that contribute to a whole." In this period, he published *Systematische Beiträge zur Theologie*: *Trinität und Reich Gottes* (1980) (*The Trinity and the Kingdom*), *Gott in der Schöpfung* (1985) (*God in Creation*), *Der Weg Jesu Christi* (1989) (*The Way of Jesus Christ*), *Geist des Lebens* (1991) (*The Spirit of Life*), and *Das Kommen Gottes* (1995). This gives Moltmann's theology its definitive form, and it is extremely difficult to overlook his contributions when Trinitarian theology, eco-theology, and eschatology are discussed.

His "messianic Christology" and "holistic pneumatology" are also significant. His contributions in these fields will remain relevant for a long time.

Retirement Phase

It has become clear over the last years that Moltmann has an identifiable retirement phase which is different from the other phases of his life. This begins with his epistemological work *Erfahrungen theologischen Denkens* (1999) (*Experiences in Theology*), which is a synthesis of his work on *Systematische Beiträge* and was published as the final volume in the series. The highpoints in this phase up to now are a book on eschatology, *Im Ende – der Anfang* (2003) (*In the End – the Beginning*), the collection of articles *Hoffnung auf Gott – Zukunft des Lebens* (2005) (*Hope in God – Future of Life*), and the autobiography, *Weiter Raum* (2006) (*A Broad Place*). *Sein Name ist Gerechtigkeit* (2008) (*Sun of Righteousness, Arise!*), *Ethik der Hoffnung* (2010) (*Ethics of Hope*) and *So komm, dass wir das Offene schauen* (2011) (*Then come, that we see Open Spaces*). These are the fruits of a long theological life, expressed in a shorter and more easily understood form than in earlier books. The pastoral voice is clearer here. At the same time, Moltmann's statements are less guarded, and he offers less evidence to back them up. The "approach methodology" is employed again, but this is not a defect in these books, since they display a maturity everywhere here that is very different from the transitional period. We should note that Moltmann once again becomes clearly confessional. For example, he allows himself to use strong words in criticizing the Lutheran doctrine of justification by faith as "held captive by the sixteenth-century doctrine of the sacrament of penance," and he categorically rejects the joint Catholic and Lutheran declaration on justification because it is "bound by Roman penal law" and is oriented to the assailant, not to the victim.

A Deeper Examination

Many labels have been applied to Moltmann's theology: theology of hope, eschatology, dialectical theology, theology of the cross, political theology, liberation theology, Trinitarian theology, eco-theology, Reformed theology, and ecumenical theology. And he is in fact characterized precisely by plurality. He himself can be surprised by the ideas that occur to him, and he can lose the overview over his own writings. Antje Jackelén, formerly professor in Chicago and now bishop in Lund (Sweden), hits the nail on the head when she writes that Moltmann "narrates eschatological history." It is completely wrong to speak, as does József Niewiadomski, of Moltmann's "theologies" in the plural. Moltmann does not write a dogmatic summa, nor does he engage in ontological theology. When the task is to tell a story that is as open as the story of God and his work of creation, it cannot be right to criticize the narrator for failing to provide a logical analysis of the concepts he employs. It is better to understand Moltmann as a theological artist who puts words to what is going on in the world today and who can give this a theological interpretation; eschatology and eco-theology are good examples. But if we wish to identify a leitmotif in Moltmann, we cannot avoid the concept of hope. What can a human person allow himself to hope for? What should a Christian hope for? Moltmann's theology puts words to *the hope that the human person and the work of creation will be recreated in the future, a hope that is based on God's promises and on the resurrection from the dead of the crucified Jesus Christ.*

The Younger Moltmann

The key work, *Theologie der Hoffnung*, contains many of the same themes and the same vocabulary as Ernst Bloch's *Prinzip Hoffnung*, but it is Jean Calvin who supplies the premises on which it is written. This is first and foremost an Evangelical-Reformed eschatology. It is a programmatic work for a confrontation with the dialectical theology – and especially with Bultmann and the existential interpretation – on the basis of the theology of history.

The next main work, *Der gekreuzigte Gott*, is in many ways Moltmann's *chef d'œuvre*, even if it is not as well known as *Theologie der Hoffnung*. It emphasizes the significance of the cross of Jesus and intends to write a theology of the cross in a "Lutheran" manner. It is marked by the dialectic between Jesus' abandonment by God on the cross and God's solidarity with humanity and with the work of creation through the same Jesus on the cross. The tension thus kindled is the beginning of a special development in Trinitarian theology.

Kirche in der Kraft des Heiligen Geistes closes the work of the younger Moltmann and is more self-contained than the first two volumes in this trilogy. Unlike the first two, it is not accompanied by a discussion book. Moltmann's pastoral voice can be heard here, and the book can be recommended to ministers or as a manual of eschatology. It is both Reformed in confessional terms and ecumenical. It emphasizes the image of the church as the people of God, and programmatically avoids using the image of the church as the body of Christ, since that is too "Catholic" for Moltmann.

The Understanding of History

Moltmann's understanding of history and of reality acquires its definitive form through *Theologie der Hoffnung* and *Der gekreuzigte Gott*. In terms of content, this is an extremely important development in the younger Moltmann. The starting point is that the ideas we human beings have about the future influence us to a great extent here and now. The understanding of the future plays a decisive role for our life and for the choices we make. For example, it is of decisive importance whether we have an "archaic" idea of recurrent cyclical time, or an idea of modern linear time. We should note that what Moltmann contrasts is not eastern and western time, but Israelite and Canaanite time. Mircea Eliade and Gerhard von Rad are the sources of his most important theories. Moltmann also shows that the predominant understanding of time in our culture draws the temporal line from the past, through the present, into the future. He calls this a *futuristic* understanding of time.

This in turn can be divided into two categories, depending on whether one is optimistic or pessimistic about development; but both futuristic understandings agree that it is possible to predict the future, at least to some degree. Moltmann draws the temporal line from the opposite direction: namely, from the future via the present to the past. He says that time comes from God and that it is always new. He calls this an *adventistic* understanding of time. The future is always new: it never repeats itself. The future contains something that we do not guess beforehand, something that changes us. It opens us to the reality that both society and every individual will be something other than we are now. This is a Jewish and Christine idea, and derives from God's promise to Abraham that he would become the father of a large people and that the people would receive a holy land.

The core of faith is the belief that God will fulfill his promises. Moltmann says that one of the biblical secrets is that God's promise is always greater than its fulfillment. When the promise has been fulfilled, it changes into a new promise. Accordingly, when the promise of becoming a father is fulfilled, there comes the promise that God's people will consist not only of Jews, but of people from every land in the world. The kingdom is different from, and greater than, one particular people or territory in the Middle East. Christianity builds on this: all the peoples can belong to the people of God, and the Promised Land is the church and eternity. The decisive point for this interpretation is that the crucified Jesus is raised from the dead and that life is therefore stronger than death, the good stronger than the evil, and love stronger than hatred. Justice wins the victory over injustice. This is the core of the Christian faith, and it can be formulated in various ways. This is why there is always hope, and Moltmann's theology can rightly be called a Theology of Hope. Typically, his books are read by ordinary men and women in those countries that seem most hopeless, and in the USA. In Scandinavia, on the other hand, he is relatively unknown, not only among the laity.

Trinitarian Doctrine

With *Trinität und Reich Gottes*, Moltmann follows up the approaches to the theology of the Trinity that he presented in *Der gekreuzigte Gott*. This book is regarded as the beginning of the older Moltmann's theology. We should note that the dialectical tensions and methodologies of the younger Moltmann find their resolution in Trinitarian concepts. Moltmann begins in history, in the history that is shared by God and the work of creation, and that is held together by the history of Jesus Christ. The history of God's Son is the history of an incarnation. According to God, this is a process that begins in God himself and ends on the cross. In this way, the distinction between the immanent and the economy Trinity is abolished. God is a part of history, and history is a part of God. This is true of all three Persons in the deity.

The history of God and of the work of creation is a history of the cross. In the cross of Jesus Christ, God identifies himself in solidarity with the human person and his or her reality. And God's solidarity goes to the uttermost consequence of what it is to be a human being, namely, death. Moltmann claims that Jesus goes further than any human being goes: he goes right into abandonment by God. We are excused from doing this. Jesus' death on the cross is God's death. The divine solidarity with the human person and with the work of creation concerns not only the Son, but the Father and the Spirit too. God the Father becomes "childless" and is no longer Father. God's Spirit, who unites the Father and the Son, becomes "unemployed" and no longer has any function. God's Son is dead and exists no longer. This is the brutal reality of the cross. On the cross, the triune God becomes visible. And when he becomes visible, he no longer exists.

It is decisively important for Moltmann's Trinitarian doctrine that we start in the concreteness of history, not in the philosophical discussions about Person, subject, and substance. It is also important to see the Persons and relationships as a whole, rather than regarding the Persons as more important than their relationships. This gives Moltmann's "social Trinitarian doctrine" its specific character. Person and fellowship are held together in his thinking: they are equally necessary and equally original. The three divine Persons share in each other's life and existence. They are a part of this existence and cannot be thought of independently of each other. The fellowship "is" God; at the same time, each divine Person "is" God – each one individually, and all three together. The three Persons are in each other and share in each other's life and existence. In the same way, the three divine Persons also share in our human existence, in our lives, in our fellowship. And we and the whole work of creation share in the divine reality. Moltmann calls this a "reciprocal circumincession," a concept he has adopted from Orthodox theology and that will perhaps endure longer than the concept of a "social" Trinitarian doctrine.

God's Coming and the Intermediate State

Das Kommen Gottes is the conclusion to his *chef d'œuvre, Systematische Beiträge*. This book is a treatise on eschatology that in many ways sums up 40 years of theological work. He divides eschatology into personal, historical, and cosmic eschatology. Personal eschatology examines the death of the individual and what comes afterwards. Historical eschatology is entitled "the kingdom of God" and explains what millenarianism and chiliasm are. This ends with the question of the end of history and a chapter about the restoration of all things. Cosmic eschatology attempts to break open theological anthropocentrism, but is perhaps not quite successful. The book closes with "divine eschatology."

The most creative element in *Das Kommen Gottes* is probably Moltmann's teaching on the intermediate state. He rejects Luther's theory that the soul sleeps, and develops an idea that goes back to the Catholic doctrine of purgatory. He interprets the intermediate state on the basis of an adventistic understanding of the future, of how we shall be when "God is all in all." With good foundations in the doctrine of creation, this teaches that in the intermediate state, we are allowed to grow until we become the people God intended us to be, until we become as we shall be in eternal life. The aborted fetus is allowed to be born and grow up. The handicapped child will be healthy. The raped woman is restored to her full dignity. The one who is oppressed will get justice and learn to live in this justice. And so we shall be allowed to enter into eternal life.

Problematic Areas

The problem with Moltmann's orientation to the future is that it prevents him from doing justice both to the present, in general, and to the Christ who is present – *Christus praesens* – in particular. It is difficult to find rest in Moltmann's thinking, because it is so powerfully dynamic. My answer has been to emphasize the teaching about *Christus praesens*. Who is Jesus Christ now? What does he do for me, for us? Where is he? Moltmann answers this question only in terms of a spiritual presence, and this is a grave defect, since without a Christ who is really present, the church is empty in a spiritual sense and can be reduced to a gathering place for personal development or for political activism. On this point, a "Moltmannian" type of theology has considerable potential for development.

I believe that Christian theology must operate with at least three ideas about the presence of Christ: not only the idea of "Christ in the least of our brothers and sisters," and the idea of a spiritual presence that we find in Moltmann, but also the traditional Luther and Catholic real presence. Besides this, Jesus Christ is understood as personally present when sin is forgiven, when God's love is revealed, when good conquers evil, and justice defeats injustice. This can be called a personal presence, and it can exploit a potential that already lies in Moltmann's theology.

Moltmann's Place in Contemporary Theology

Moltmann himself never wanted to found a new theological "school." This is an attitude he shares with most of his contemporaries, who had mixed feelings about Lutheran neo-orthodoxy and the schools that formed in dialectical theology. Until he met Bloch, Moltmann belonged to Karl Barth's "school," and the confrontation with Bultmann's "school" has left its mark on everything he wrote. It is precisely in this way that Moltmann himself became the founder of the history of theology along with Pannenberg, who will be remembered as playing an even more important role than Moltmann in the direction taken by this theological school. There is a clear difference between Pannenberg and Moltmann. The group around Moltmann does not speak of a "school" in relation to him, but rather of belonging to a theological "family."

What can we say about the Moltmann family, other than that they enjoy meeting when the "master" invites them to a feast? Some characteristics can be identified.

First, the Moltmann family is *international.* It has members from North and South America, but also from Korea and Japan – and all parts of Europe. In addition to the Germans, there are many Dutch and Swiss members, but perhaps surprisingly few Africans.

Secondly, the Moltmann family is *ecumenical.* Moltmann is a Reformed theologian in a land with a strong Lutheran and Catholic presence. There is a strong Orthodox influence on his work, especially from Romania, and Pentecostal theologians, above all Miroslav Volf, have made a stronger impact here than on other similar theological "families." Moltmann has good contacts to the Mission Church in Scandinavia, especially in Sweden, but is much read also in Norway. The Free Church influence is indeed obvious. At the same time, the Moltmann family tends to have an anti-Catholic orientation, since this form of faith is somewhat foreign to them, and they dislike hierarchies and oppression and other things they regard as typically Catholic. Nor are they fond of what they see as a somewhat "stiff" Lutheranism.

Thirdly, the Moltmann family is *open,* indeed extremely open to new thoughts and ideas. This can lead to the discussion of very strange questions, which need not be mentioned here. In comparison with other families of theologians, there may be a lack of discussion of questions of the philosophy of science and methodology, but *this* family is extremely well informed about what is "going on" in today's world.

The Moltmann family *does not stand on ceremony.* Under the "master's" influence, they retain the polite "Sie" form and cultivate good table manners, but one is allowed to bring up strange topics, to change one's opinion, and to enjoy oneself. I shall never forget Moltmann's seventieth birthday, when so many prominent theologians gathered for a fantastic meal in the Hirsch restaurant at Bebenhausen monastery. The party ended in the small hours with everyone singing German folksongs and children's songs under the baton of Hans Küng, Eberhard Jüngel, and Dorothee Sölle. It was unforgettable – and typical of Moltmann.

Bibliography

Ising, Dieter: *Bibliographie Jürgen Moltmann.* (Munich: Chr. Kaiser Verlag, 1987).
Wakefield, James L., *Jürgen Moltmann: A Research Bibliography.* (Oxford: Scarecrow Press, ATLA bibliography series 47, 2002).

Primary Literature

Prädestination und Heilsgeschichte bei Moyse Amyraut (Dissertation, 1954). (*Predestination and History of Revelation in Moyse Amyraut: A Contribution to the History of Reformed Theology between Orthodoxy and Enlightenment*).
Calvin-Studien, 1959, (Neukirchen: Neukirchener-Verlag, 1960). (*Studies of Calvin*).
Prädestination und Perseveranz, Geschichte und Bedeutung der reformierten Lehre "de perseverantia sancotrum" (Neukirchen: Neukirchener-Verlag, 1961). (*Predestination and Perseverance, History and Significance of the Reformed Doctrine "de perseverantia sanctorum"*).
Anfänge der dialektischen Theologie I-II (Munich: Kaiser,1962–63). (*Beginnings of Dialectical Theology I-II*).
Theologie der Hoffnung. Untersuchungen zur Begründung und zu den Konsequenzen einer christlichen Eschatologie (Munich: Kaiser, 1964). English: *Theology of Hope: On the Ground and the Implications of a Christian Eschatology* (New York: Harper Row, 1967).

Perspektiven der Theologie. Gesammelte Aufsätze (Munich: Kaiser, 1968). Several of these essays were translated from the German text by Margaret Clarkson in *Home and Planning* (New York: Harper Row, 1971).

Der gekreuzigte Gott: Das Kreuz Christi als Grund und Kritik christlicher Theologie (Munich: Kaiser, 1972). English: *The Crucified God: The Cross of Christ as the Foundation and Criticism of Christian Theology* (New York: Harper Row, 1974).

Kirche in der Kraft des Geistes: Ein Beitrag zur messianischen Eschatologie (Munich: Kaiser, 1975). English: *The Church in the Power of the Spirit* (London: SCM Press, 1977).

Gottes Recht und Menschenrechte: Studien und Empfehlungen des Reformierten Weltbundes (Neukirchen-Vluyn: Neukirchener Verlag, 1976). English: *A Christian Declaration on Human Rights. Theological Studies of the World Alliance of Reformed Churches* (Grand Rapids, 1977).

Zukunft der Schöpfung: Gesammelte Aufsätze (Munich: Kaiser, 1977). English: *The Future of Creation* (London: SCM Press, 1979; Philadelphia: Fortress Press, 1979).

Jüdischer Monotheismus – Christliche Trinitätslehre: Ein Gespräch (Munich, Kaiser, 1979). English: *Jewish Monotheism and Christian Trinitarian Doctrine* (Philadelphia: Fortress Press, 1981).

Trinität und Reich Gottes: Zur Gotteslehre (Munich: Kaiser, 1980). English: *The Trinity and the Kingdom* (London: SCM-Press, 1981; San Francisco: Harper & Row, 1981).

Politische Theologie – politische Ethik (Munich/Mainz: Kaiser/Grünewald, 1984). English: *On Human Dignity: Political Theology and Ethics* (Philadelphia: Fortress Press, 1984).

Gott in der Schöpfung: Ökologische Schöpfungslehre (Munich: Kaiser, 1985). English: *God in Creation* (San Fransisco: Harper & Row, 1985; London: SCM Press, 1985).

Der Weg Jesu Christi: Christologie in messianischen Dimensionen (Munich: Kaiser, 1989). English: *The Way of Jesus Christ: Christology in Messianic Dimensions* (San Francisco: HarperSanFrancisco, 1990).

Der Geist des Lebens: Eine ganzheitliche Pneumatologie (Munich: Kaiser, 1991). English: *The Spirit of Life: A Universal Affirmation* (London: SCM Press, 1992).

In der Geschichte des dreieinigen Gottes: Beiträge zur trinitarischen Theologie (Munich: Kaiser, 1991). English: *History and the Triune God: Contributions to Trinitarian Theology* (London: SCM Press, 1991).

Das Kommen Gottes: Christliche Eschatologie (Munich, Kaiser, 1995). English: *The Coming of God: Christian Eschatology* (Minneapolis: Augsburg /Fortress, 1996).

Erfahrungen theologischen Denkens: Wege und Formen christlicher Theologie (Gütersloh: Chr.Kaiser/Gütersloher, 1999). English: *Experiences in Theology: Ways and Forms of Christian Theology* (Minneapolis: Augsburg/Fortress, 2000).

Wo ist Gott? Gottesräume – Lebensräume (Neukirchen: Neukirchener, 2002). (*Where is God? Rooms for God – Rooms for Life*).

Wissenschaft und Weisheit: Zum Gespräch zwischen Naturwissenschaft und Theologie (Gütersloh: Kaiser/Gütersloh, 2002). English: *Science and Wisdom* (London: SCM Press, 2003; Minneapolis: Fortress Press, 2003).

Im Ende – der Anfang: Eine kleine hoffnungslehre (Gütersloh: Kaiser/Gütersloher, 2003). English: *In the End – the Beginning: The Life of Hope* (Minneapolis: Fortress Press, 2004).

Hoffnung auf Gott – Zukunft des Lebens: 40 Jahre "Theologie der Hoffnung" (Gütersloh: Gütersloher, 2005). (*Hope in God – Future of Life: 40 Years of "Theology of Hope"*).
Totentänze – Tanz des Lebens (Frankfurt am Main: Otto Lembeck, 2006). (*Dances of Death – Dance of Life*).
Weiter Raum. Eine Lebensgeschichte (Gütersloh: Gütersloher, 2006). English: *A Broad Place: An Autobiography* (Minneapolis: Fortress Press, 2009).
Sein Name ist Gerechtigkeit: Neue Beiträge zur christlichen Gotteslehre (Gütersloh: Gütersloher, 2008). English: *Sun of Righteousness, Arise!: God's Future for Humanity and the Earth* (Minneapolis, Fortress Press, 2010).
Ethik der Hoffnung (Gütersloh: Gütersloher, 2010). English: *Ethics of Hope* (Minneapolis: Fortress Press, 2012).
So komm, dass wir das Offene schauen: Perspektiven der Hoffnung (Calw: Calwer, 2011). (*Then Come, That We See Open Spaces: Perspectives of Hope*).

Secondary Literature

Bauckham, Richard, *God Will be All in All: The Eschatology of Jürgen Moltmann* (Edinburgh: T&T Clark, 1999).
Bauckham, Richard, *The Theology of Jürgen Moltmann* (Edinburgh: T&T Clark, 1995).
Conyers, Abda J., *God, Hope and History: Jürgen Moltmann and the Christian Concept of History* (Macon, GA: Mercer, 1988).
Gilbertson, Michael, *God and History in the Book of Revelation: New Testament Studies in Dialogue with Pannenberg and Moltmann* (Cambridge: Cambridge University Press, 2003).
Kantzenbach, Friedrich Wilhelm, *Programme der Theologie: Denker, Schulen, Wirkungen. Von Schleiermacher bis Moltmann* (Munich: Claudius-Verlag, 1984).
Kjølsvik, Idar, *Christus Praesens: Jürgen Moltmanns Geschichtsverständnis und die Lehre vom gegenwärtigen Christus* (Neukirchen-Vluyn: Neukirchener Verlag, 2008) (revised edition of "Kreuz und Auferstehung als Geschichte – und Gegenwart?", 2006). (*Christus Praesens: Jürgen Moltmann's Concept of History and the Teaching on the Present Christ*).
Marsch, Wolf-Dieter (ed.), *Diskussion über die Theologie der Hoffnung von Jürgen Moltmann* (Munich: Chr. Kaiser Verlag, 1967).
Matič, Marko, *Jürgen Moltmanns Theologie in Auseinandersetzung mit Ernst Bloch* (Frankfurt am Main: Europäische Hochschulschriften, 1983).
Momose, Peter Fumiaki, *Kreuzestheologie: Eine Auseinandersetzung mit Jürgen Moltmann. Mit einem Nachwort von Jürgen Moltmann* (Freiburg, Basle, and Vienna: Herder Verlag, 1978).
Morse, Christopher, *The Logic of Promise in Moltmann's Theology* (Philadelphia: Fortress Press, 1979).
Niewiadomski, Józef, *Die Zweideutigkeit von Gott und Welt in J. Moltmanns Theologien* (Innsbruck, Vienna, and Munich: Tyrolia Verlag, 1982).
Rasmusson, Arne, *The Church as Polis: From Political Theory to Theological Politics as Exemplified by Jürgen Moltmann and Stanley Hauerwas* (University of Lund, 1994).

Tang, Siu-Kwong, *God's History in the Theology of Jürgen Moltmann* (Berne: Europäische Hochschulschriften 573, 1996).

Welker, Michael (ed.), *Diskussion über Jürgen Moltmanns Buch "Der gekreuzigte Gott."* (Munich: Chr. Kaiser Verlag, 1979).

Chapter 14
Wolfhart Pannenberg

Svein Rise

Pannenberg represents in many ways a paradigm shift in twentieth-century theology. The most characteristic element is the distance he places between himself and the dialectical theology (with Karl Barth at its head) and the so-called Bultmann school. Although Pannenberg was influenced by Barth, he did not accept his theological program, since Barth appears to lose every link between anthropology and faith. Nor did he find Bultmann's theology "from below" a satisfactory starting point. According to Pannenberg, Bultmann transposes the center of gravity in theology from historical facts to the human person's self-understanding, thus making the interpretation of human existence the framework that establishes the norms for theology. The result is an inappropriate individualization of faith. Pannenberg asserts that liberation theology likewise represented a theological one-sidedness. The endeavor to make the Gospel operative in contexts of societal oppression led to an accommodation of the Gospel to secular understandings of reality, and this ultimately sucked the power out of the liberating message of the Gospel. What then is Pannenberg's program in the encounter with these challenges? The short answer is that he wants to overcome subjectivism by means of a theology that entails an intellectual obligation. In a period where the concept of God seems to have lost its meaning, and historical consciousness has made it impossible to believe on the basis of a formal scriptural authority (*à la* Barth), the only way for theology to recover its credibility is through an intersubjective justification of what it does. This inevitably means that we must investigate questions that lie in the point of intersection between theology and other sciences. It also obliges us to discuss theological universality. Few twentieth-century theologians took this task as seriously as Pannenberg, who entered into dialogue with sociologists, physicists, historians, and philosophers. For Pannenberg, systematic theology entails *inter alia* integrating the total reality of human experience into the discussion of the truth of faith. Only under these conditions is it possible to examine whether the God in whom one believes is a reality or an illusion.

Biography

Wolfhart Pannenberg was born on October 2, 1928 in Stettin on the Oder, in the north-eastern part of Germany which is now Polish territory. In 1942, his family moved to Berlin, where Pannenberg was able to develop his interests in music and philosophy. He read everything by Nietzsche that he could get his hands on.

Nietzsche convinced the young Pannenberg that Christianity was the cause of the misery in the world. In January, 1945, Pannenberg had an experience that he later called the most important single event in his life. On his way home from school, he felt that he was totally surrounded by the light from the distant sun. It was as if for one moment he became one with the sunlight. Pannenberg, who was not a Christian at that time, later said that this event played a decisive role in his consciousness of having a theological vocation. Although he continued to read philosophy after this experience of light – he began to read Kant and other thinkers – his interest in Christianity was awakened for the first time, thanks not least to a high-school teacher who did not fit the picture of the Christian mentality that Nietzsche described in his books. In 1947, Pannenberg began to study both philosophy and theology at the Humboldt University in East Berlin. The study of Christianity fascinated him so much that he decided to make theology the basis of his academic career, although he continued to study philosophy. In Berlin, he was particularly interested in Marxism. He read everything with enthusiasm, from the young Marx to *Das Kapital*. It was only later on that Pannenberg became critical of Marxism's ideological aspect and its oppressive function.

In 1948, Pannenberg moved to Göttingen, where he studied under Friedrich Gogarten, Hans Joachim Iwand, and Nicolai Hartmann, whom he describes as the most learned philosopher in Germany at that period. After one year in Göttingen, he went to Basle with a grant from the World Council of Churches, and studied under Karl Barth and Karl Jaspers. Before coming to Basle, he had read the volumes of the *Kirchliche Dogmatik* (*Church Dogmatics*) that had been published up to that point. Pannenberg admired Barth, both then and later on, but even during his time in Basle he found that Barth's thinking lacked philosophical rigor.

Before he began his studies in Heidelberg in 1950, he had attempted several times to get involved in biblical exegesis, in addition to systematic theology, philosophy, and church history, but he was not successful until he heard Gerhard von Rad's Old Testament lectures in Heidelberg. Pannenberg says that these opened a new world for him. The key word in biblical exegesis at that time was *history*, which Pannenberg recognized also in the lectures of the historian of ideas Karl Löwith. The students felt that the systematic theology taught at Heidelberg was not on the same level as the exegetical agenda, and this insight was the beginning of the so-called Heidelberg circle, a group of theologians who made it their goal to carry through the implications for systematic theology of von Rad's exegetical visions. After ten years of discussions, they published the book *Offenbarung als Geschichte* (*Revelation as History*) in 1961.[1] The importance for Pannenberg of his time in Heidelberg was not limited to the understanding of revelation: Hans von Campenhausen's lectures initiated him into patristic theology, which became fundamentally important for his writing. One of the things Pannenberg learned from the church fathers was that theology is ultimately

---

[1] In addition to Pannenberg (systematic theology), the most important members of the group were Rolf Rendtorff (Old Testament), Ulrich Wilkens (New Testament), Trutz Rendtorff (systematic theology and social ethics), and later, Martin Elze (early church history).

concerned with the polarity between life and death. He was for a time the assistant of the Lutheran Edmund Schlink, to whom he also owed significant impulses. It was Schlink who kindled Pannenberg's interest in ecumenical theology and who taught him the importance of dialogue with other academic disciplines, especially with the natural sciences.

Under Schlink's guidance, Pannenberg completed his doctoral dissertation in Heidelberg on the doctrine of predestination in Duns Scotus. This was published in Göttingen in 1954 under the title *Die Prädestinationslehre des Duns Scotus im Zusammenhhang der scholastischen Lehrentwicklung* (*Duns Scotus' Teaching on Predestination in the Context of the Doctrinal Development in Scholasticism*). His doctoral dissertation, *Analogie und Offenbarung. Eine kritische Untersuchung zur Geschichte des Analogiebegriffs in der Lehre von der Gotteserkenntnis* (*Analogy and Revelation. A Critical Investigation of the History of the Concept of Analogy in the Doctrine of the Knowledge of God*), was accepted in 1955. This studies the history of the concept of analogy from classical antiquity to the middle ages; it has never been published. This dissertation qualified Pannenberg for a teaching position at the University of Heidelberg, where he began lecturing on the history of medieval theology, the Lutheran reformation, and the history of modern Protestant theology. In connection with the last theme, he discovered the importance of Hegel for the development of modern theology, and the challenge that Hegel presents for theology today. At the very least, according to Pannenberg, Hegel's sophisticated philosophy ought to provide a pattern for theology's self-reflection and self-presentation.

In 1958, Pannenberg became professor of systematic theology at the theological seminary in Wuppertal, where he was Jürgen Moltmann's colleague for three years. In this period, he began to develop major projects in systematic theology, especially in Christology and anthropology, but it was only after he became professor at the University of Mainz in 1961 that he was obliged to think through the *whole* of dogmatics, including ethics. In 1968, he became professor at the theological faculty in the University of Munich, where he was also director of the ecumenical institute until his retirement in 1994. In addition to active participation in interdisciplinary forums, especially in the dialogue between theology and philosophy, Pannenberg was a member of several ecumenical working groups, including the Working Group of Protestant and Catholic Theologians who established the premises for the much-discussed Joint Declaration on the Doctrine of Justification (1999). He was visiting professor at many of the most influential theological centers, especially in the USA, and he received honorary doctorates from a number of universities throughout the world.

Theological Writings

Offenbarung als Geschichte, which the Heidelberg circle published in 1961, was a programmatic work. Pannenberg contributed the Introduction and "Dogmatische Thesen zur Lehre von der Offenbarung" ("Dogmatic Theses on the Doctrine of Revelation"). He also wrote an Afterword to the second edition in which he comments on the theses in the book and develops them. He agrees with Barth that revelation can take place only where *God himself* makes himself known to the human person. This means that the medium through which God reveals himself is consubstantial with God *qua* revealer. Revelation is always *self*-revelation. This also means that revelation is linked, not to mystical circumstances of a supernatural character, but to concrete facts in time and space. He parts company with Barth precisely in his emphasis on the *place* where revelation occurs. The programmatic element in *Offenbarung als Geschichte* is the transposition from the proclamation of the Word (Barth) to *history*. This opens up the possibility that revelation can take place indirectly, and that it can be recognized and seen by all who have eyes to see. The indirect revelation also makes it possible to think of the whole of history – universal history – as the place where God manifests himself, and this implies that God can become definitively visible only at the close of history.

Pannenberg's second great contribution to the theology of revelation came already in 1964, with his book *Grundzüge der Christologie* (*Jesus – God and Man*) which went through several editions (the fifth in 1976) and was the first of his books to be translated into English. In his book on Christology, Pannenberg consistently argues *on the basis of the theology of revelation* for Jesus' unity with God; the trajectory from *Offenbarung als Geschichte* is clear. The key to understanding what is involved here is the resurrection and the significance of the resurrection for the person of Jesus. Pannenberg's starting point is that Jesus' proclamation of judgment and salvation is an anticipation of God's future definitive decision. Jesus had the authority to proclaim judgment and salvation, but this authority is confirmed only through what will happen at the end of time. It is important to grasp here that Pannenberg understands the resurrection in the light of one particular tradition, namely, *the future expectation of apocalyptic*. There is a close connection between the anticipatory character in Jesus' activity and the understanding of history in late Jewish apocalyptic. The words of the prophets in the Old Testament are confirmed through their future fulfillment, but the historical visions of the apocalypticist are established through the historical events themselves. This explains why apocalypticism is the framework within which we must understand Jesus' activity, despite the difference between Jesus' proclamation and the visionary Jewish apocalyptic. This also explains why the legitimation of Jesus' person depends on the actual occurrence of the events at the end of time. This leads Pannenberg to propose the thesis that the close of history is anticipatorily present in Jesus' life and death.

The justification in terms of the theology of revelation in Pannenberg's book on Christology implies a thinking "from below" – on the basis of the history of Jesus – which Pannenberg already corrected in the Afterword to the fifth edition.

He realized that it is objectively necessary in Christology to begin "from above," that is to say, in the reality of God. This posed the question whether it is at all possible to demonstrate that, and in what sense, God is involved in the human person's lifeworld. Pannenberg has discussed this problem with particular thoroughness in his anthropological writings, such as *Was ist der Mensch? Die Anthropologie der Gegenwart im Lichte der Theologie* (1962), (*What is Man? Contemporary Anthropology in Theological Perspective*) and *Anthropologie in theologischer Perspektive* (1983), (*Anthropology in Theological Perspective*), which is Pannenberg's principal study in anthropology and the most comprehensive presentation in this field since Max Scheler, Helmuth Plessner, Arnold Gehlen, and Richard Rothe. His standpoint is that if God has revealed himself through Jesus Christ, he has also manifested something of himself – his humanity – in all human experiences. In his discussion of themes such as the formation of identity and self-consciousness, sin, guilt, and responsibility, imagination, reason, and language, together with more overarching topics in cultural anthropology, Pannenberg attempts to show that the religious is implied in the total reality of human life. This is why he gives the name "fundamental-theological anthropology" to the investigations in his book on anthropology. The point is not to presuppose apodictically the reality of God, but to study phenomena and experiences in order to uncover the reality of God that is implied in the phenomena. In his investigations, Pannenberg is in a continuous dialogue with the human sciences. On some topics, he agrees with them, but on others, he states his reservations. One principal conclusion is that we must see the identity of the human person in the light of the image of God. Even anthropological discussions are to be interpreted in the light of the understanding of revelation.

The same applies to his methodological study, *Wissenschaftstheorie und Theologie* (1973), (*Theology and the Philosophy of Science*), where he investigates the scientific character of theology. This project seeks to elaborate criteria for how the demand for truth in the Christian revelation can be verified on the basis of all the experiences the human person has of himself and of the world. In effect, this is an attempt to measure the status of Christianity in terms of the theory of science. Pannenberg argues that this is necessary, since God is a hypothesis that all subsequent experience must be able to confirm or negate on the basis of criteria that are relevant to the theory of science. This does not mean (as some have mistakenly thought) that Pannenberg intends to present "proofs" of the existence of God. Verification is a hermeneutical proceeding that entails testing propositions about God on the basis of the implications of these propositions. This does not mean subjecting God to examination by an authority external to him. When propositions about God are confirmed in relation to the reality that God defines, this confirmation occurs when God demonstrates himself as God. This accords with the biblical concept of self-revelation, as this is developed in the whole of Pannenberg's theology. Accordingly, it is only by testing God on the basis of his implications that theology can lay claim to the intersubjective validity that all science claims for itself.

To show that God demonstrates himself in history is to engage in systematic theology. The core of this demonstration is the doctrine of God, which Pannenberg elaborates most explicitly in his three-volume *Systematische Theologie* (*Systematic Theology*) (1: 1988; 2: 1991; 3: 1993). He had already discussed topics from systematic theology (or dogmatics) that are relevant to the doctrine of God: see above all the collected essays in *Grundfragen systematischer Theologie. Gesammelte Aufsätze* (*Basic Questions in Theology. Collected Essays*) (1: 1967, 2nd ed. 1971; 2, 1980) and the books *Gottesgedanke und menschliche Freiheit* (*The Idea of God and Human Freedom*) (1972; 2nd ed. 1978), *Glaube und Wirklichkeit* (*Faith and Reality*) (1975), and *Metaphysik und Gottesgedanke* (*Metaphysics and the Idea of God*) (1988); but it is only in the *Systematische Theologie* that the doctrine of God is set out in its full breadth as the doctrine of the triune God. The Trinitarian doctrine in Pannenberg's work must be understood along the trajectory of the concept of revelation, as a teaching about the dispensation of salvation or as a teaching about the *way* in which the Father, the Son, and the Spirit act in the event of revelation, as this is presented in Jesus' life and message. The whole work is structured on the basis of this fundamental insight, which takes up anew the programmatic text from 1961.

What does the economy of salvation involve? The first point is that God's divinity is based on the fact that he is the power that determines everything that exists and that he has sovereignty over the creation. It is however only through the definitive salvation of God's creatures that we see that God truly has sovereignty. God's reality and power are established definitively at the close of history. This is why the entire process of history, which reaches its final point in the accomplishment of all things, must be interpreted as a self-demonstration of God and of his reality. It is also a demonstration of God's qualities, which belong to his Trinitarian being. If this is granted, it follows that God's actions in the world – the economic Trinity – disclose who God is in himself, as the immanent Trinity. On the other hand, Pannenberg claims that the immanent Trinity is the presupposition of the economic Trinity: the accomplishment of creation depends on salvation in Christ, because God communicates to the creation the saving life that comes into existence through God's nature. According to Pannenberg, God's love reaches its goal when Christ at the accomplishment of all things hands the divine sovereignty back to the Father. It is only through this event that we know who God is as the infinite and eternal One, since the infinite One then encompasses fully that which is finite and draws it into his own infinity. This is why God's identity is described by means of the unity of the immanent and the economic Trinity, and this lets us understand that God demonstrates himself as *the one* when he enters the world as the Father, the Son, and the Holy Spirit, and makes the world his own.

Key Themes in Pannenberg's Theology

Trinitarian Doctrine

My conclusion to the preceding section has touched on one of the most debated topics in systematic theology today, namely, the relationship between the immanent and the economic Trinity. Karl Rahner established the premises for this debate in 1960 with his thesis that there is identity between God as he is in himself (the immanent God) and God as he acts in history (the economic God). All subsequent debate about Trinitarian doctrine has been obliged to take a position with regard to Rahner's thesis, which has also been called "Rahner's rule." In *The Image of the Immanent Trinity. Rahner's Rule and the Theological Interpretation of Scripture,* Fred Sanders maintains that those involved in the debate have made this thesis either more or less radical. As examples of "radicalizers" of this thesis, he mentions the theologians Hans Küng, Jürgen Moltmann, Wolfhart Pannenberg, Robert W. Jenson, and Catherine M. LaCugna. Sanders sees Yves Congar, Hans Urs von Balthasar, Thomas F. Torrance, Paul D. Molnar, and Karl Barth as "restricters" who have made the thesis less radical. In what sense has Pannenberg radicalized Rahner's thesis?

It is essential in Pannenberg's eyes to establish that the relationship between the Persons in the Trinity is not exhaustively described through a terminology ("proceeding," "begetting") that expresses only whence the Persons in the Trinity have their origin. He argues that the weakness in such a conception is that the relationship between the Persons is thought of on the basis of a one-sided, "one-way communication," from the Father to the Son and to the Spirit, while the other relationships between the Persons are not regarded as of decisive significance for the Persons' identity and being. Ultimately, the source of this one-sidedness is that the Father is thought of as the logical subject in the Trinity; this idea received its classical formulation in Hegel, but its structure also finds expression in Barth's Trinitarian theology. Pannenberg's primary accusation against Hegel and Barth is that when God as a logical subject-concept is thought of *antecedently* to the self-unfolding of this concept in history, one inevitably envisages God as the one who is beyond the world, identical with *himself,* and independent of the history to which he communicates his Trinitarian life. This makes it impossible to unite in one's thinking, in a way that is objectively appropriate, both the intra-Trinitarian life and the way in which this life becomes visible in history. Nor can one explain in Trinitarian terms why it is Jesus and his history that reveal God – with the consequence that neither the incarnation nor Jesus' death has constitutive significance for the identity of God. God's identity in his *being* and God's identity in revelation are thus torn apart, although both Hegel and Barth attempted to unite them in their thinking. Their attempt foundered on their *understanding* of Trinitarian doctrine. I shall now illustrate Pannenberg's *alternative* understanding by means of his cautious criticism of Moltmann.

In the German Festschrift for Moltmann's eightieth birthday, Pannenberg shows how Moltmann, drawing on the patristic theology of circumincession, attempts to establish the unity and the difference between the Persons in God.[2] Pannenberg agrees with Moltmann when he differs from Barth, who takes the divine subject, rather than history, as the starting point in Trinitarian doctrine. Unlike Barth, Moltmann intends to justify the doctrine of the Trinity on the basis of the history of Jesus and to show that this history is also the history of the *Son*. But despite this intention, Moltmann draws a distinction between the constituting of the Persons in eternity (the relationships of origin) and the *life* of the Trinity in salvation history. However, this distinction makes the connection between the immanent and the economic Trinity unclear. Pannenberg asks whether Moltmann's distinction is compatible with the presupposition of unity between the immanent and the economic Trinity. In his own Trinitarian doctrine, Pannenberg has emphasized that when the biblical texts describe the Son's proceeding from the Father, the eternal event is confirmed by the distinction that Jesus in his earthly life draws between himself and the Father, and through the fact that he is obedient to the Father just as the Son is obedient in eternity. Certain events in Jesus' life also reflect the connection. Pannenberg writes that the constituting of the Trinity and the life of the Trinity are interwoven when the Gospels relate the conception of the Son to Jesus' baptism (Luke 3:22), when Paul maintains that the installation of "God's mighty Son" takes place through the resurrection from the dead (Romans 1:4), and when Jesus himself says that he received through the baptism the Spirit who, according to the Gospel of John, proceeds from the Father, and whom Jesus will send to those who belong to him (John 15:26). This entails that God's life cannot be reduced to the relationships of origin. If the reciprocal distinction between the Persons in God applies already in the *constituting* of the Persons, Moltmann's distinction between the constitution of the Trinity and the life of the Trinity (the dispensation of salvation) becomes superfluous, since the constituting and the life are coterminous. Pannenberg argues that this does not happen if one gives the *essential* Trinity *priority* vis-à-vis the manifestations of the Trinity in the dispensation of salvation. A Trinitarian doctrine that finds its orientation in the history of Jesus cannot make the constituting of the Trinity an event *antecedent* to the life of the Trinity, for that would mean that the constituting and its realization would part company. For Pannenberg, the constituting takes place *in* and *through* its realization in history.

This sheds light on the sovereignty of God, which in Barth is so closely connected with God's self-revelation in its Trinitarian unfolding. As Athanasius argued, the Father cannot be the Father without the Son, and this also means that God's kingdom cannot be a kingdom without the Son's mediation. It is precisely in the theology of the kingdom of God that the Persons in the Trinity are indivisible: this is what distinguishes God's sovereignty from a tyrannical monarchy, and Pannenberg holds that Moltmann was right to oppose such an idea when he criticized non-Trinitarian monotheism. The sovereignty of God that Jesus proclaimed is the sovereignty of the Father; both Christians and the Jewish people await the full realization of this

---

[2] See Welker, Volf, *Der lebendige Gott als Trinität* (München, 2006), 13–22 (*The Living God as Trinity*).

sovereignty. But it does not come without the mediation of the Son and the power of the Spirit. The liberating element here is that sharing in the Son's relationship to the Father is the same as sharing in the *eternal* life that has its origin in the fellowship between Father, Son, and Spirit. In this way, the life in the economic Trinity is woven together with the life in the immanent Trinity.

There is no doubt that Pannenberg's concept entails a reorientation of Trinitarian doctrine in relation to the tradition. It aims at a greater integration of the events of history, and it is entirely typical that Pannenberg makes the realization of the life of the Trinity one element in that which constitutes the relationships between the Persons in God. The question is whether this alternative interpretation does justice to God's freedom and independence. I believe that this cannot be answered independently of Pannenberg's understanding of time and eternity, which he discusses in greatest depth in connection with eschatology in Vol. 3 of *Systematische Theologie*. He affirms that when God transcends time through the resurrection – it was God who raised Jesus from the dead through the Spirit (Romans 1:4) – by shattering the border of death, it becomes possible to understand the resurrection as the *content* of eschatology. It is the resurrection that establishes that the Trinity anticipatorily bears the full realization in itself and that makes it possible to think of the eternal, infinite God as encompassing time – our time – and making it his own. Life here and now, in eschatological fellowship with Christ, is a manifestation of, and a continuing process towards, the "content" that will be revealed at the end of time, when all is accomplished. God "realizes" himself in this process towards accomplishment. Pannenberg is aware of the problems that are involved in using the concept of "realization" in this context. It seems clear that it cannot be ascribed to finite subjects, since finite subjects are always subordinate to the difference in time between positing the goal for actions and carrying out these actions. This is not the case with God: since he is infinite and eternal, he is not subordinate to differences in time. Pannenberg must be understood to mean that God, as the infinite and eternal, is identical with himself *before* history begins and *after* history ends. God "realizes" himself when he accomplishes his identity as God *in the world*. This takes place when he draws the creation into his own Trinitarian life; and when this takes place, the fellowship of love in God is realized in the creation too. This allows us to say that God's identity becomes visible in the world when God, through his own qualities, makes the world his own. One would misunderstand Pannenberg if one associated his thinking with process theology or with Hegelian ideas of God *becoming* God – God *becoming* himself – in the events of history. "Realization" concerns, not the intra-Trinitarian being of God *per se*, but the intra-Trinitarian being of God in relation to the world and its history. This means that God preserves his divinity when he "realizes himself" in history. But it also means that God's divinity is at stake in the events of the world, just as it was at stake when Jesus died! However, the resurrection demonstrates God's life and reality. According to Pannenberg, the final, decisive demonstration that God *is* takes place only in eschatology. Until then, faith lives in and from anticipation: in the eschatological fellowship with Christ, the future accomplishment of all things is an anticipatory, present reality.

Creation and Redemption

This conclusion sheds light on what is entailed when God in history demonstrates himself as the one: as the one, God is the power who determines all that exists, and is creation's sovereign. God the Father has however entrusted the *full accomplishment* of his sovereignty to the working of the Son and the Spirit. This Trinitarian definition of God's unity is fundamentally important for the understanding of the relationship between creation and redemption. The fact that it is the Son who brings to accomplishment implies that he does this on the basis of his specific character as *Son* in relation to the Father. As the one who brings to accomplishment, the Son has his own autonomous field of activity, which finds expression through the human person's *faith*, as faith lives in the worshiping fellowship, in prayer, in liturgy, and in praise. But despite the Son's autonomous field of activity, Pannenberg does not see this as a sphere that is *added on* by a mathematical addition to the field of activity of the Father as Creator. The life of faith that the Son mediates on the basis of his specific character is mediated for the Father's sake. Since the Son serves the Father in obedience to his will, faith glorifies the Father and his work, thereby communicating the Father's sovereignty to the world. This means that we must envisage both discontinuity and continuity in the relationship between creation and redemption: discontinuity, since the life of faith has its own space; and continuity, because faith glorifies the Father's creative work. This is the substance of what it means to say that God is "realized" in the world through his Trinitarian actions. The question now is what it means to say that *the human person* is "realized" thereby. How does Pannenberg locate the human person between creation and redemption?

According to Pannenberg, the words used in Genesis 1:26 indicate that the human person was not created identical to the image of God (as if the image of God was something that had already been realized). The Hebrew expression in the text must be interpreted to mean that the human person was created to "resemble" or "correspond to" the image of God. In other words, the image was *per se* different from the human person. Although he was created by God, he was subjected from the very beginning to the natural conditions that made it both possible and necessary to *become* something that he initially was not: namely, the fulfillment of what the creation was originally meant to be. This first became a historical reality through Jesus' life and death, and this is why Jesus Christ is identical with the image that the human person was created to resemble. In his identity with the image, Jesus Christ is the new Adam. Patristic theology, represented by fathers such as Irenaeus and Athanasius, developed this idea from the princple that Jesus recapitulates history by making it the dispensation of God's salvation, in order to fulfill history. The vision of the fulfillment of history through the new Adam is incomparably more radical, in Pannenberg's opinion, than the historically later theological notion that the function of the new Adam was to restore the original primal state in creation. It is true that the fathers also say that through the new life of the resurrection, Jesus Christ recapitulates the creation; but neither Irenaeus nor Athanasius says that recapitulation consists simply in bringing the human person back to the original primal state. This is because recapitulation has a dual aspect. On the one hand, it does mean bringing the human person back to the origin of creation; but it also entails perfecting what existed in the origin. When that which is original is restored, the result is something *more than* what existed in the beginning, although the restoration is also a return to the fresh and natural origin. With a reference to Irenaeus, Pannenberg claims that being given a share in the new life of faith is not the same as receiving a supernatural *supplement* to what it is to be human. It means receiving a share in the life that makes it possible to grow and mature naturally. In this sense, the human person is *en route* to his true humanity, although he already *is* a true human person in the image of God. The idea of a dynamic process towards fulfillment is thus something that Pannenberg fully shares with the church fathers, who spoke of *theôsis*, the "divinization" of the human person. If we are to understand Pannenberg correctly, however, we must relate this process to the idea of discontinuity and continuity. In keeping with this idea, Pannenberg frames his entire systematic theology within the antithesis between *life and death*. Like the patristic writers, he ascribes salvific priority to the resurrection, since it alone overcomes death, the threat to life that blocks the human person's natural growth and maturity. This is not contradicted by the fact that Pannenberg's theology also has a place for both the *theologia crucis* and the *theologia gloriae*. The risen Christ conquers through death, and it is only by becoming one with Jesus in death that the Christian can receive a share in the life that conquers the powers of death. This is how Pannenberg attempts to bind the events of salvation together in a unified Trinitarian theology, although he accords theological and historical priority to the resurrection.

Public Discourse

Pannenberg is certainly one of the most prominent and influential twentieth-century apologists. His apologetics include a vigorous attempt to show how it is possible to overcome atheism's accusation that religion does nothing other than suppresses the wishes and needs of the human person. His strategy is not to argue that the Christian message is adaptable, but rather to give plausible reasons for its truth. This is possible only when the universal rational implications of theology are accepted. Pannenberg's concept has not won universal acclaim, and some have accused him of wanting to present "proofs" of God's existence. Others have held that his theological thinking is influenced more or less clearly by the Hegelian metaphysics of history. Pannenberg's reply is that when theology enters a dialogue with philosophy, this conversation derives its legitimacy from faith itself, since faith essentially seeks reasons that also lie *outside* itself. Since faith lives in the hope that God's sovereignty will be fully realized in the *world*, where reason and rationality are at home, faith is not permitted to withdraw to a subjective inner room, isolated from the experiences in the world in which faith in God – and God's reality – is put to the test. In the light of revelation, it is there that God's demonstration of himself as the power that determines everything and as the Lord of creation can be recognized by the human person. But the final answer to the question whether God genuinely *is* the Lord of creation lies in the future.

Pannenberg's influence has probably been as great in the USA as in Germany, where his theses about the theology of revelation and his bold interdisciplinary involvement have been the object of debate. He has found many readers in America among those who appreciate apologetic theology. It was thus fitting that an American anthology was published in 1988, honoring him with articles covering the major areas in his writings.[3] Pannenberg himself contributed to this anthology with an autobiography and "a response to my American friends."

Bibliography

Primary Literature

Die Prädestinationslehre des Duns Scotus im Zusammenhhang der scholastischen Lehrentwicklung (Göttingen: Vandenhoeck & Ruprecht, 1954). (*Duns Scotus' Teaching on Predestination in the Context of the Doctrinal Development in Scholasticism*).
Analogie und Offenbarung. Eine Kritische Untersuchung zur Geschichte des Analogiebegriffs in der Lehre von der Gotteserkenntnis (Göttingen: Vandenhoeck & Ruprecht, 1955). (*Analogy and Revelation. A Critical Investigation of the History of the Concept of Analogy in the Doctrine of the Knowledge of God*).
Offenbarung als Geschichte (Göttingen: Vandenhoeck & Ruprecht, 1961), 4th ed. with Afterword, 1970. English: *Revelation as History* (New York: Macmillan, 1968).
Was ist der Mensch? Die Anthropologie der Gegenwart im Lichte der Theologie (Göttingen: Vandenhoeck & Ruprecht, 1962), 4th ed. 1972. English: *What is Man? Contemporary Anthropology in Theological Perspective* (Philadelphia: Fortress Press, 1970).
Grundzüge der Christologie (Gütersloh: Gütersloher Verlagshaus, 1964), 4th ed. 1972. English: *Jesus – God and Man* (Philadelphia: Westminster Press, 1968), 2nd ed. 1977.
Gottesgedanke und menschliche Freiheit (Göttingen: Vandenhoeck & Ruprecht, 1972), 2nd ed. 1978. English: *The Idea of God and Human Freedom* (Philadelphia: Westminster Press, 1973).
Grundfragen systematischer Theologie. Gesammelte Aufsätze (Göttingen: Vandenhoeck & Ruprecht, 1967), 2nd ed. 1971. English: *Basic Questions in Theology*, 2 vols (Philadelphia: Fortress Press, 1970, 1971).
Metaphysik und Gottesgedanke (Göttingen: Vandenhoeck & Ruprecht, 1988). English: *Metaphysics and the Idea of God* (Grand Rapids: Eerdmans, 1990).
Wissenschaftstheorie und Theologie (Frankfurt am Main: Suhrkamp Verlag, 1973). English: *Theology and the Philosophy of Science* (Philadelphia: Westminster Press, 1976).

---

[3] See Braaten and Clayton, *The Theology of Wolfhart Pannenberg* (Minneapolis, 1988).

Anthropologie in theologischer Perspektive (Göttingen: Vandenhoeck & Ruprecht, 1983). English: *Anthropology in Theological Perspective* (Philadelphia: Westminster Press, 1985).

Glaube und Wirklichkeit (München: Kaiser Verlag, 1975). English: *Faith and Reality* (Philadelphia: Westminster Press, 1977).

Systematische Theologie (Göttingen: Vandenhoeck & Ruprecht, 1: 1988, 2: 1991, 3: 1993). English: *Systematic Theology* (Grand Rapids: Eerdmans, 1: 1991, 2: 1994, 3: 1998).

Theologie und Philosophie. Ihr Verhältnis im Lichte ihrer gemeinsamen Geschichte (Göttingen: Vandenhoeck & Ruprecht, 1996). (*Theology and Philosophy. Their Relationship in the Light of their Common History*).

Problemgeschichte der neueren evangelischen Theologie in Deutschland. Von Schleiermacher zu Barth und Tillich (Göttingen: Vandenhoeck & Ruprecht, 1997). (*History of the Problems of Recent Evangelical Theology in Germany. From Schleiermacher to Barth and Tillich*).

Beiträge zur Systematischen Theologie,1: Philosophie, Religion, Offenbarung, 2: Natur und Mensch – und die Zukunft der Schöpfung, 3: Kirche und Ökumene (Göttingen: Vandenhoeck & Ruprecht, 1999–2000). (*Contributions to Systematic Theology, 1: Philosophy, Religion, Revelation, 2: Nature and Human Being – and the Future of the Creation, 3: Church and Ecumenism*).

Secondary Literature

Braaten, Carl. E. and Clayton, Philip (eds), *The Theology of Wolfhart Pannenberg. Twelve American Critiques, with an Autobiographical Essay and Response* (Minneapolis: Augsburg, 1988).

Grenz, Stanley, *Rediscovering the Triune God. The Trinity in Contemporary Theology* (Minneapolis: Fortress Press, 2004).

Rise, Svein, *The Christology of Wolfhart Pannenberg. Identity and Relevance* (New York: Mellen University Press, 1997).

Rohls, Jan, and Wenz, Gunther, *Vernunft des Glaubens. Wissenschaftliche Theologie und kirchliche Lehre. Festschrift zum 60. Geburtstag von Wolfhart Pannenberg* (Göttingen: Vandenhoeck & Ruprecht, 1988).

Sanders, Fred, *The Image of the Immanent Trinity. Rahner's Rule and the Theological Interpretation of Scripture* (New York: Peter Lang Publishing, 2005).

Schults, F. LeRon, *The Postfoundationalist Task of Theology. Wolfhart Pannenberg and the New Theological Rationality* (Grand Rapids: Eerdmans, 1999).

Welker, Michael, and Volf, Miroslav (eds), *Der lebendige Gott als Trinität. Jürgen Moltmann zum 80. Geburtstag* (München: Gütersloher Verlagshaus, 2006).

Wenz, Gunther, *Wolfhart Pannenbergs Systematische Theologie. Ein einführender Bericht* (Göttingen: Vandenhoeck & Ruprecht, 2003).

Worthing, Mark William, *Foundations and Functions of Theology as Universal Science: Theological Method and Apologetic Praxis in Wolfhart Pannenberg and Karl Rahner* (Frankfurt and New York: Peter Lang Publishers, 1996).

Chapter 15
Eberhard Jüngel

Kjetil Hafstad

Eberhard Jüngel has contributed to the renewal of German theology in the twentieth century through his uncommonly concentrated writings. Above all, he thinks through the theological significance of Jesus' death. As a philosopher, he helps make it possible for faith to speak and think about God, and he draws the consequences of this for anthropology, ecclesiology, sacramental thinking, and ethics, as well as offering many insights that shed light on society from a theological perspective. Jüngel is anchored in tradition both through his work with classical texts from within and outside the Christian tradition, and by developing the inheritance from the dialectical theology. He builds on Rudolf Bultmann and Ernst Fuchs, and renews and develops the thinking of Karl Barth for his own contemporaries, *inter alia* through his understanding of language. His thinking is elegant and strikingly original. With Jürgen Moltmann and Hans Küng and Walter Kasper, his colleagues at the Catholic theological faculty (Joseph Ratzinger gave up his professorship at the time when Jüngel arrived), he helped make Tübingen the most important center of theological studies in Germany over several decades.

Biography

Eberhard Jüngel was born in Magdeburg in 1934 and remained a citizen of the German Democratic Republic for as long as this was possible. His upbringing in East Germany influenced his view of the socialist government of society. The encounter with a state that insisted on obedience to the rules without any appeal to the reason – indeed, that demanded obedience, no matter how preposterous the regulations were – vaccinated the theologian Jüngel against the language of power both in society and in the church. When the communist republic shut in its people behind the Berlin Wall in 1961, Jüngel, who had grown up in the East but was at that time a promising academic assistant at the Church Academy in West Berlin, was asked at a moment's notice to take on the work of a teaching assistant (in name; in reality, he did the work of a professor) in exegesis at the Theological Linguistic College, the church college that was hastily set up in East Berlin. This institute was located in the old apartment block that had been built for female workers in Borsig's iron factory. It had bedsitting rooms, a church, and a refectory, all built in view of the humane treatment of workers, and it functioned in a simple and practical manner as a theological faculty. This church college was set up to prevent the theological faculties at the state universities (which had to conform to the communist system) from having a monopoly of theological research and education.

In 1966, Jüngel began to teach systematic theology. He was appointed to the chair of systematic theology and the history of dogma at the University of Zurich, as Gerhard Ebeling's successor, and the East German government allowed him to leave the country while retaining his East German citizenship. Many who were appointed to positions abroad were deprived of their East German citizenship, but Jüngel did not want to lose the contact with his students and colleagues in the East. In 1969, he was appointed to the chair of systematic theology and the philosophy of religion at the Eberhard Karls Universität in Tübingen, once again as the successor to Ebeling, who had found the behavior of the rebellious students in 1968 intolerable. Now, however, the East German authorities disregarded their agreement, and Jüngel was refused permission to enter East Germany for a number of years. He insisted on retaining his passport, however, and he maintained his intensive contacts with colleagues in the East. When the Wall fell in 1989, many noticed that he laughed more than usual. He himself said that now he could dance on the Wall.

Like his teacher Karl Barth, who rightly called himself a cheerful partisan for the kingdom of God, Eberhard Jüngel is quickly moved to laughter and joy. He bubbles over with stories, and he knows the literary classics inside-out. He likes to insert witty quotations into his texts, and he is an inexhaustible source of humorous commentaries in a relaxed conversation. Unlike his teacher, he is a knowledgeable gourmet who knows his way around the kitchen. He regards cooking as his "ethical behavior." His activity in the lecture room and in the kitchen is marked by the same appreciation of the sublime. His first students almost regarded him as a fellow student. They relate that he lived in two little rooms crammed full of books in the old building with its bedsitting rooms for students, rooms for teaching, a refectory, a lecture hall, and a church. He ate with the students, played bowls and badminton, and sat at the bridge-table until late at night. The difference was that the light in his room then burned far into the night, since he had to prepare the lecture for the next day. He has always treated his students and doctoral students with great generosity, inviting them to lavish meals (and sometimes challenging them to work in the kitchen). He has always praised culinary skills as highly as academic skills.

Eberhard Jüngel began to write at an early age, and he has written copiously on academic subjects. He himself says that Ernst Fuchs was the professor who most strongly kindled his enthusiasm for languages and hermeneutics. Jüngel headed the Institute of Hermeneutics in Tübingen throughout his period as professor. He has also been involved in practical church ministry. For example, he has offered his services as a guest preacher in Tübingen's parish church for many years, and towards the end of his time as professor he was the leader ("Ephorus") of the Evangelisches Stift in Tübingen, where many theological students from Württemberg can live during their studies. In this way, Jüngel returned in the last period of his teaching activity to the kind of student life he had known in the Borsigstrasse in East Germany and remained "Ephorus" long after his retirement.

The theological milieu in Tübingen was very much alive while Jüngel was there, and perhaps especially in the early 1970s in the midst of the great student protests. The university buzzed with activity, and thousands came from the whole of Germany to study theology. Not all the teachers were able to establish contact with the radicalized students. Jüngel's colleague in Protestant systematic theology, Jürgen Moltmann, was in many ways the closest to the radical students, and he was a prominent source of inspiration for liberation theology; but it was Jüngel who had the most lively and committed conversations with the rebel students. He was not cowed by booing in the lecture hall, which could hold between 700 and 1,000 students. He welcomed controversial debates, provided that he was permitted to hold his lecture first. This meant that the students took him seriously, and did not shout him down. His quick repartee and his humorous criticism of young rebels who were full of socialist rhetoric often led to a lively and respectful dialogue. Jüngel had been vaccinated for the rest of his life against socialist propaganda, and his controversies with the authorities in communist East Germany had given him good training over the years. He punctured the rhetoric and concentrated on fundamental anthropological and societal questions in a way that was unmatched by any of his theological colleagues – not even by the great light of the Catholic faculty, Hans Küng. Together, these prominent theologians created the greatest "flock" of theological students in Germany: more than two thousand studied in Tübingen each year in the 1970s.

Academic Writings

Jüngel's first large-scale work qualified him to teach the New Testament. This was a monumental study of the relationship between Paul's proclamation of justification and Jesus' proclamation: *Paulus und Jesus. Eine Untersuchung zur Präzisierung der Frage nach dem Ursprung der Christologie* (*Paul and Jesus. An Investigation to Clarify the Question of the Origin of Christology*) Hermeneutische Untersuchungen zur Theologie 2 (Hermeneutic Investigation to Theology 2), 1962. Jüngel is clearly influenced by the interest of his teacher Ernst Fuchs in the historical Jesus, understood as a "speech event." He analyzes the Pauline and the Gospel texts in order to identify the historical basis of Christology, a topic that was particularly controversial after both Karl Barth and Rudolf Bultmann had rejected the possibility of basing the proclamation of the Gospel on the historical Jesus. Bultmann's pupils Ernst Käsemann and Ernst Fuchs, and at the same time, independently of these scholars, the Norwegian Nils Alstrup Dahl had reopened this question in the early 1950s, and this debate provides the context for Jüngel's work. His chosen field of study is Paul's proclamation of justification, and he attempts to make use of the results of the historical-critical method with regard to Jesus' own proclamation in order to reflect on the relationship between Paul and Jesus, instead of evaluating this question in the light of what one can infer for example from the christological titles – a subject that was intensely debated by other historians at that time, including the Norwegian Ragnar Leivestad.

With *Gottes Sein ist im Werden. Verantwortliche Rede vom Sein Gottes bei Karl Barth. Eine Paraphrase*, 1966 (*God's Being is in Becoming. The Trinitarian Being of God in the Theology of Karl Barth. A Paraphrase*), Jüngel came to his principal theme, which he has since elaborated in innumerable variations and different contexts: the doctrine of God. Initially, the book seems to be only a modest contribution; it even describes itself as a "paraphrase." For a professorial dissertation, it is very short – 120 pages (140 in the third edition), and it looks like a contribution to a debate between Herbert Braun and Helmut Gollwitzer about the being of God that had begun two years earlier. However, the contribution this book makes points far beyond this narrow context. It is one of the most interesting and valuable attempts to offer a new interpretation of Karl Barth's doctrine of God, with a philosophically more tenable foundation than Barth himself achieved. Jüngel does this precisely by holding fast to Barth's concept of God as moving and mobile in history, while expressing his thought comprehensibly in a new understanding of language that Jüngel himself develops in partial reliance on Ernst Fuchs' linguistic categories. Throughout his lifetime, Barth was the object of critical objections by Rudolf Bultmann, who claimed that his doctrine of God had an insufficient anchoring in anthropology; the strategy Jüngel chooses allows him to counter some of these objections. He develops an independent and original methodology to tackle the specific task of theology, namely, to think God. He gradually develops this concept in his writings, and distances himself from the title *Gottes Sein ist im Werden*, which is somewhat open to misunderstanding; in the Foreword, he explicitly says that this is not to be understood to mean that God is ein werdender Gott, ("a God who is coming into existence"). He later says that God's being is im Kommen ("coming"), and links this more clearly to eschatology and, above all, to the understanding of God as coming to our own time in the Word. *Gottes Sein ist im Werden* made a profound impression on research into Barth, and even on the master himself. In connection with his eightieth birthday in 1966, Barth wrote to his young colleague Jüngel that he was happy to welcome him to the celebrations "because I have come to know you among today's younger theologians as one who has studied me thoroughly, but who is also willing and able to continue the work that is necessary today in an independent and fruitful manner."[1]

Like Barth, Jüngel develops his thinking not least in a series of pioneering articles, from "Die Möglichkeit theologischer Anthropologie auf dem Grunde der Analogie. Eine Untersuchung zum Analogieverständnis Karl Barths" ("The Possibility of Theological Anthropology on the Basis of Analogy"), 1962, to the introduction to his principal theme in the doctrine of God in "Vom Tod des lebendigen Gottes – ein Plakat" ("On the Death of the Living God – a Poster"), 1968, to his fascinating new interpretation of anthropology in a christological perspective in "… keine Menschenlosigkeit Gottes … Zur Theologie Karl Barths zwischen Theismus und Atheismus" (" … No God without Humanity … On Karl Barth's Theology between Theism and Atheism", 1971.) The first vigorous collection of such articles was published in 1972: *Unterwegs zur Sache. Theologische Bemerkungen* (*En Route to the*

---

[1] Karl Barth, *Gesamtausgabe V: Briefe 1969–1969* (Zurich 1975), 328.

Matter. Theological Remarks). The second was published in 1980: *Entsprechungen. Gott – Wahrheit – Mensch* (*Correspondences. God-Truth-Human Being*). A collection of studies of Barth was published in 1982: *Barth-Studien* (*Barth-Studies*). In 1990, he published *Wertlose Wahrheiten. Zur Identität und Relevanz des christlichen Glaubens. Theologische Erörterungen,* 3 (*Valueless Truth. On the Identity and Relevance of the Christian Faith. Theological Considerations,* 3); in 2000, *Indikative der Gnade – Imperative der Freiheit. Theologische Erörterungen,* 4 (*Indicatives of Grace-Imperatives of Freedom. Theological Considerations,* 4); and in 2003, *Ganz werden. Theologische Erörterungen,* 5 (*Becoming Whole. Theological Considerations,* 5).

Jüngel has developed his theological theme of the doctrine of God in these and numerous other smaller books, in relation to the understanding of the human person, of death, of the sacraments, of the church, of society, and of politics. He has done important work in anchoring the doctrine of God in a form that can be defended in terms of the philosophy of religion, with profound reflections on hermeneutics, language, and metaphor. The *chef d'œuvre* that gathers all these threads together is undoubtedly *Gott als Geheimnis der Welt. Zur Begründung der Theologie des Gekreuzigten im Streit zwischen Theismus and Atheismus,* 1977 (*God as the Mystery of the World. On the Foundation of the Theology of the Crucified in the Dispute between Theism and Atheism*), a tour de force in which Jüngel engages in a duel with nineteenth-century atheist thinking, represented by Friedrich Nietzsche, Ludwig Feuerbach, and Johann Gottlieb Fichte. He identifies the grains of truth in their critique and uses these constructively in the understanding of God. Although he scoffs at the contemporary "God is dead" theology, he says that talk of the death of God must now return home to theology. He builds here on Georg Wilhelm Friedrich Hegel's idea of a "speculative Good Friday" and on Dietrich Bonhoeffer's idea (in the letters from prison) that one should think of the world *without* God. He sees talk of the death of God as a core element in the Christian understanding of God, with its foundation in the paschal event. He investigates the metaphysical tradition with regard to the doctrine of God (on which atheistic thinking is based in part), and points out how post-Cartesian thinking has created a reversed metaphysics in which the human individual becomes the horizon, metaphysically speaking. Jüngel argues that this means that the traditional metaphysical understanding of God is no longer theologically tenable. After thus clearing the ground, he sets out his original contribution to a defensible understanding of God. He makes a constructive link to the dialectical theology and its understanding of the Word as the locus where God can be thought, and combines this with an original presentation of how God and transience can be thought together on the basis of the history of Christ. This makes possible a new understanding of revelation, as the revelation of God as *Geheimnis* ("mystery"), where language, analogical thinking, and history are united in one single concept that is able to combine thinking about the world and thinking about God. This approach to the doctrine of God also allows Jüngel to hold fast to the words in 1 John, "God is love," and to specify more precisely how they are to be understood. This work is exceptionally rich in observations and stimulating perspectives, and it has influenced the strong focus both at that time and subsequently on the death of God among Jungel's contemporaries from Jürgen

Moltmann to Wolfhart Pannenberg and among the many theologians who have worked with them both in Germany and internationally. This line of thought has gained an unmatched influence on contemporary theology both through Jüngel's many articles and through the presentation on numerous occasions in the late 1960s and early 1970s of the material that was gathered together in *Gott als Geheimnis der Welt*. Jüngel presents the material with clarity and intellectual acuteness, but also with humor and a lively use of language, with innumerable thought-provoking allusions to the history of thought and of literature. This has established his reputation as an outstanding representative of the modern German language. It has not been easy to retain this richness in translations, and the English versions of his books are rather off-putting.

In his book *Das Evangelium von der Rechtfertigung des Gottlosen als Zentrum des christlichen Glaubens*, 1998 (*Justification. The Heart of the Christian Faith*), Jüngel returns to his early work on Paul and Jesus. His analysis brings out the core concern of the Reformation, namely, the justification of the human person by faith alone. This book has a polemical context: the international Catholic-Lutheran dialogue commission had concluded its many years of work in 1994 with the statement "Church and Justification," and a consensus document was drawn up and signed on Reformation Day 1999, the Joint Declaration on the Doctrine of Justification. Like many members in the Lutheran group in the international dialogue commission, Jüngel finds it deplorable that the consensus document fails to undertake the necessary work on the theological foundations. He claims that central insights in the Reformers' thinking are presented in a way that obscures their concern, and that this undermines the very basis for an ecumenical rapprochement. He published a polemical article on this work in 1997: "Um Gottes willen – Klarheit!"[2] His book follows up this involvement and specifies what justification entails in today's theological thinking. We certainly do not need to return to the conflicts of the sixteenth century. Rather, we must understand justifying faith in today's situation, bearing in mind the development in both ecclesial families up to the present time.

Jüngel has also published outside the specialist field of theologians. His best known book is perhaps *Tod* (*Death*), 1971, which had its origin in an open lecture series for students from all the faculties. It is a presentation of death as a phenomenon and as a theme in the Christian faith, and sets out in a simple form the same concept that emerges in Jüngel's *chef d'œuvre*, *Gott als Geheimnis der Welt*. One important genre in his writings is the collection of sermons. During his career as a teacher of theology, Jüngel has always volunteered his services as pastor and preacher, and some of what he has presented in this context is published in *Predigten* (*Sermons*), 1970. Later volumes of sermons were given more substantial titles, all of which bring out characteristic aspects of Jüngel's thinking: *Geistesgegenwart. Predigten*, 1994 (*Presence of Mind. Sermons*), *Schmecken und Sehen. Predigten*, 3, 1983 (*Tasting and Seeing. Sermons*), and *Unterbrechungen. Predigten*, 4, 1989 (*Interruptions. Sermons*, 3).

---

[2] Jüngel, *Zeitschrift für Theologie und Kirche*, 94 (1997), 394–406.

Key Themes

Jüngel's theological thinking has a very simple basic structure, as he himself frequently emphasizes, sometimes with a reference to Boethius, who describes the being of God as a straightforwardly simple being.[3] At the same time, he maintains: "It is in any case difficult to begin with that which is simplest."[4] There are some main lines to which he continually returns, developing them in new and imaginative ways. I believe his thinking is so fascinating and creative because of its specific combination of simplicity, openness, and a wealth of perspectives that touch both the present and the past. The theme to which he continually returns is the meaning of Jesus' death for theology and for thinking in general. His special and original contribution concerns how Jesus' death, and God's presence in this death, open up perspectives that have not been seen in this way before. His theological starting point presupposes revelation. Theology, as faith's thinking, thus means following after revelation and reflecting on it. In this work, where it becomes clear that God himself is exposed to the destructive powers in life, he can concede that the critics of religion are right in their *particula veri*, while at the same time refuting this critique and employing the speculative reflections of the church fathers on God in movement.

When he then introduces into anthropology the idea of God in death through the death of Jesus Christ, he discovers classical Reformation insights, where the idea of the justificatory significance for the human person of the event of the cross becomes fundamental. This event sets the human person free to lead his life in accordance with this event. Here too, Jüngel contributes original insights. He consistently employs the classical theology throughout his work as a toolbox, but he also sees that if one takes one's starting point in revelation, it is both possible and advisable to develop one's thinking phenomenologically. His scholarly training gave him input from Ernst Fuchs and thus also from Fuchs' teacher, Rudolf Bultmann – and not least from Martin Heidegger, whose lectures Bultmann attended and who was a source of inspiration for him. Here, Jüngel adopts a phenomenological approach to existence and develops this in an original way. He presents fundamental human phenomena in order to shed light on revelation, but also in order to work out what revelation means for the conditions of human existence. He has developed a fine sensitivity in this field, and combines observations from literature, art, history, and his own experiences to form an ingenious and creative whole.

The starting point for the entire construction is and remains revelation. Jüngel simply presupposes this, but he also adds that even if this is an axiomatic presupposition that he is neither willing nor able to prove or demonstrate in any way, the event itself can certainly be demonstrated. He can portray the traces left by this event in such a manner that even those who do not believe will grasp what one is talking about in theology, and they will be able to follow his line of thought.

---

[3] Eberhard Jüngel, *Unterwegs zur Sache* (München, 1972), 116.
[4] Ibid., 104.

The principal theme in Jüngel's academic writing is without doubt the conditions and the possibility of thinking about God. His starting point is something that the two great teachers Karl Barth and Rudolf Bultmann, each in his own way, brought to light: that a crisis affects theology's main task, namely, talking about God. Jüngel develops the basic premises beyond the indications of the dialectical theology: that God is the one who is fundamentally other and that it is not truly meaningful to talk about God unless God himself finds expression (Barth), or that one's own existence is involved (Bultmann). He finds orientation in Bonhoeffer's attempt to interpret God on non-religious premises, and he employs tools that few contemporary theologians dare to use. He makes use of the atheistic critique of religion in order to specify how Christians see God. The combination of these central dogmatic themes with hermeneutics and linguistic philosophy and analogous thinking allows him to elaborate the conditions under which it can be possible to speak about God and express this intellectually in the situation of our own times. This is done through meditation on the God who reveals himself as the *mystery* of the world, the God who in revelation makes himself known, but not in such a way that he can be manipulated. The God who shows himself is sovereign, and one cannot exploit him. He is therefore mysterious. The analogy that makes it possible to hold fast to the event of revelation is precisely language as speech. That which is spoken does not exist before it is spoken, and speech resounds only as long as the speaker is speaking. This means that revelation cannot be transmuted into an insight that one can have under one's control. When he is revealed as the mystery of the world, God remains a mystery, hidden until he reveals himself and speaks in the present moment.

Jüngel works to secure a "return home of talking about the death of God in theology" as a starting point for theological thinking. He recognizes the imprints of this idea, for example in Nietzsche's polemical texts, and it forms the interpretative framework for his understanding of God's love as "the unity of life and death in favor of life."[5] This understanding gives faith a sure ground and confidence, and eliminates every attempt to gain power over the object of faith and to "manage" it. In one of the series of theses he propounds, Jüngel writes: "The God who becomes capable of being experienced as the unity of life and death in love calls into question all the values that concern things taken for granted in religion."[6]

Taking his starting point here in the doctrine of God, Jüngel can go on to illuminate human phenomena, just as he employs human phenomena to express the doctrine of God. He claims that when God can find expression in human speech in this way, this leads to a "linguistic gain": language itself is expanded and enriched. Reflection on the necessary conditions for revelation leads to the conclusion that this must be understood as an "elementary interruption."[7] Such interruptions are fundamental and momentous in human existence, and faith is an elementary interruption of this

---

[5] See, e.g., Jüngel, *Ganz werden* (Tübingen, 2004), 247–9.

[6] Jüngel, "Thesen zum Verhältnis von Existenz, Wesen und Eigenschaften Gottes," in *Ganz werden*, 262.

[7] Jüngel, *Gott als Geheimnis der Welt* (Tübingen, 1977), 221.

kind.[8] We give the name "sacramental" to the sphere that includes sacraments in the traditional sense, but the church too is sacramental when it orders its life in keeping with the Gospel – and in that case, the church too is an elementary interruption. When the church functions *as church*, it is an elementary interruption.[9] Love, which transforms reality, is another elementary interruption of this kind. The characteristic article "Das Entstehen von Neuem"[10] opens up another field of interest and presents a complementary approach and a variation on Jüngel's reflection on the conditions that are necessary for change.

From his earliest writings onward, Jüngel has been interested in basic linguistic phenomena such as analogy and metaphor: see *Zum Ursprung der Analogie bei Parmenides und Heraklit*, 1964 (*On the Origin of Analogy in Parmenides and Heraclitus*), and *Metapher. Zur Hermeneutik religiöser Sprache*, 1974 (*Reflectione on Theological Metaphor as a Contribution to a Hermeneutics of Narrative Theology*). One very important influence on his academic thinking is the understanding of analogy in medieval philosophy, with reference to Thomas Aquinas' principle that "no matter how great the dissimilarity may be, a great similarity exists." This makes it possible to think about God and then to shed light on human phenomena. In many of his writings, Jüngel makes use of the analogous thinking that was dominant in science until its place was taken by an empirical and clinical way of thinking. Analogous thinking is elementary and down-to-earth: the imagination and dreams work analogically, and the same is true of hermeneutics. Through his focus on the intellectual resources in analogous and metaphorical thinking, Jüngel helps to develop the understanding of theology's innermost theme, namely, God. This also permits him to open up perspectives on a wider reality for human phenomena such as faith, hope, and love, as well as the understanding of the church, the sacraments, and ethics.

Jüngel's Place in Twentieth-century Theology

Eberhard Jüngel is one of Germany's most original theologians. He has inspired renewed studies of classical theology and has made Karl Barth's theology once again relevant to our age. He differs from colleagues who have tended to form schools, such as Jürgen Moltmann and Wolfhart Pannenberg, since he does not share their focused interest in the future perspective. Jüngel is content to reflect on the basic conditions of existence and is happy to uncover phenomena that illuminate both theology in the strict sense and anthropology – as well as ethics and politics. In this respect, he resembles the Danish philosopher of religion Knud Ejler Løgstrup, although they are otherwise very different. Like Karl Barth, Jüngel has not formed a school; like his great teacher, he is too original for that. But he has been an important source of inspiration for several generations of theologians, both through the rigor and consistency of his

---

[8] Jüngel, *Ganz werden*, 2.
[9] Ibid., 155 and 277.
[10] Jüngel, *Wertlose Wahrheit* (Tübinben, 2003), 132–50.

thinking and by his willingness to learn from the fundamental human phenomena. The title of his third volume of sermons, *Schmecken und Sehen* ("Tasting and seeing"), is highly characteristic and says a great deal about his thinking.

Bibliography

Primary Literature

Paulus und Jesus. Eine Untersuchung zur Präzisierung der Frage nach dem Ursprung der Christologie (Tübingen: Mohr Siebeck, 1962). (*Paul and Jesus. An Investigation to Clarify the Question of the Origin of Christology*).

Zum Ursprung der Analogie bei Parmenides und Heraklit (Berlin: de Gruyter, 1964). (*On the Origin of Analogy in Parmenides and Heraclitus*).

Gottes Sein ist im Werden. Verantwortliche Rede vom Sein Gottes bei Karl Barth. Eine Paraphrase (Tübingen: Mohr Siebeck, 1966). English: *God's Being is in Becoming. The Trinitarian Being of God in the Theology of Karl Barth. A Paraphrase*. John Webster (trans.) (T&T Clark: Edinburgh, 2001).

Predigten (Munich: Kaiser, 1968). (*Sermons*).

Tod (Stuttgart: Kreuz, 1971). English: *Death. The Riddle and the Mystery*. Iain and Ute Nicol (trans.) (The Westminster Press: Philadelphia 1974).

Unterwegs zur Sache. Theologische Bemerkungen (Munich: Chr. Kaiser, 1972). (*En Route to the Matter. Theological Remarks*).

Metapher. Zur Hermeneutik religiöser Sprache, by P. Ricoeur and E. Jüngel. *Evangelische Theologie, Sonderheft* (Munich: Kaiser, 1974). English: "Metaphorical Truth. Reflections on Theological Metaphor as a Contribution to a Hermeneutics of Narrative Theology", in *Theological Essays I*. Translated with an Introduction by J.B. Webster (T&T Clark: Edinburgh, 1989).

Gott als Geheimnis der Welt. Zur Begründung der Theologie des Gekreuzigten im Streit zwischen Theismus und Atheismus (Tübingen: Mohr Siebeck, 1977). English: *God as the Mystery of the World. On the Foundation of the Theology of the Crucified in the Dispute between Theism and Atheism*. Darell L. Guder (trans.) (Grand Rapids: Eerdmans, 1983).

Entsprechungen. Gott – Wahrheit – Mensch. Theologische Erörterungen (Munich: Chr. Kaiser, 1980). (*Correspondences. God-Truth-Human Being. Theological Considerations*).

Barth-Studien (Zürich, Cologne, and Gütersloh: Benziger – Gütersloher Verlagshaus, 1982). English: *Karl Barth. A Theological Legacy*. Garrett E. Paul (trans.) (The Westminster Press: Philadelphia, 1986).

Wertlose Wahrheit. Zur Identität und Relevanz des christlichen Glaubens. Theologische Erörterungen, 3 (Munich: Chr. Kaiser, 1990; Tübingen: Mohr Siebeck, 2003). (*Valueless Truth. On the Identity and Relevance of the Christian Faith. Theological Considerations, 3*).

Das Evangelium von der Rechtfertigung des Gottlosen als Zentrum des christlichen Glaubens (Tübingen: Mohr Siebeck, 1998). English: *Justification. The Heart of the Christian Faith. A theological Study with an ecumenical Purpose.* Jeffrey F. Cayser (trans.), with an Introduction by John Webster (T&T Clark: Edinburgh, 2001).

Indikative der Gnade – Imperative der Freiheit. Theologische Erörterungen, 4 (Tübingen: Mohr Siebeck, 2000). (*Indicatives of Grace-Imperatives of Freedom. Theological Considerations,* 4).

Ganz werden. Theologische Erörterungen, 5 (Tübingen: Mohr Siebeck, 2003). (*Becoming Whole. Theological Considerations,* 5).

Secondary Literature

Aerts, Lode, *Gottesherrschaft als Gleichnis? Eine Untersuchung zur Auslegung der Gleichnisse Jesu nach Eberhard Jüngel* (New York: Peter Lang, 1990).

Ingolf Ulrich Dalferth, Johannes Fischer und Hans-Peter Großhans von Mohr Siebeck "Denkwürdiges Geheimnis. Beiträge zur Gotteslehre," in: Ingolf Ulrich Dalferth, Johannes Fischer und Hans-Peter Großhans von Mohr Siebeck (eds), *Denkwürdiges Geheimnis. Beiträge zur Gotteslehre. Festschrift für Eberhard Jüngel zum 70. Geburtstag* (Tübingen: Mohr Siebeck, 2004), ix–xii.

Gravem, Peder, *Gudstro og virkelighetserfaring. Den metafysiske gudstanke som problem i kristen gudslære, belyst ut fra G. Ebeling, E. Jüngel og W. Pannenberg* (Oslo: Solum, 1992).

Hafstad, Kjetil, *Wort und Geschichte. Das Geschichtsverständnis Karl Barths* (Munich: Chr. Kaiser, 1985).

Holmes, Christopher R.J., *Revisiting the Doctrine of the Divine Attributes. In Dialogue with Karl Barth, Eberhard Jüngel and Wolf Krötke* (New York: Peter Lang, 2007).

Klimek, Nikolaus, *Der Gott, der Liebe ist. Zur trinitarischen Auslegung des Begriffs "Liebe" bei Eberhard Jüngel* (Essen: Die blaue Eule, 1986).

Schulz, Michael, *Sein und Trinität. Systematische Erörterungen zur Religionsphilosophie G.W.F. Hegels im ontologiegeschichtlichen Rückblick auf J. Duns Scotus und I. Kant und die Hegel-Rezeption in der Seinsauslegung und Trinitätstheologie bei W. Pannenberg, E. Jüngel, K. Rahner und H.U. von Balthasar* (St. Ottilien: EOS, 1997).

Thyssen, Peter, *Eberhard Jüngel* (Copenhagen: Anis, 2002).

Webster, J.B., *Eberhard Jüngel. An Introduction to His Theology* (Cambridge: Cambridge University Press, 1986).

Webster, J.B. (ed.), *The Possibilities of Theology. Studies in the Theology of Eberhard Jüngel in his Sixtieth Year* (Edinburgh: T&T Clark, 1994).

PART III
Catholic Theologians

Chapter 16
Henri de Lubac

Fergus Kerr

Henri Joseph Sonier de Lubac (1896–1991) was born on 20 February 1896, at Cambrai, in northeast France, though the family soon returned to Lyons, their home ground. He attended a Jesuit school in Lyons. He studied law for a year, before entering the Lyons province of the Society of Jesus, then in exile in England. His noviciate was interrupted in 1914 when he was drafted into the French army. He saw action in Flanders, receiving the serious head wound that afflicted him for the rest of his life. He returned to the Jesuits, still in England. He seems never to have been regarded by his superiors as a future professor, either of philosophy or of theology. On his own, he studied Thomas Aquinas, in the light of Etienne Gilson's 'fundamental book', which, he notes with some irony, was 'in the bookcase of light reading that was generously unlocked for us during holidays'. He had already begun working his way through the Greek and Latin patrologies and the medieval scholastics, gathering the quotations out of which he would weave his books. As his younger colleague and friend Hans Urs von Balthasar would note, de Lubac preferred 'to let a voice from the great ecclesial tradition express what he intends rather than raising his own voice' — yet, unmistakably, his views 'can be easily discerned in the web of quotations, especially when one pays close attention to the critiques and corrections of the passages cited'.[1]

Retrieving the Twelfth Century

Henri de Lubac re-created the pre-modern Catholic sensibility, which he wanted to inhabit. About 1960, looking back on decades of research in patristic and medieval-scholastic theologies, he claimed that, for him, the 'great century' of the Middle Ages began around the year 1100, with 'the Bayeux tapestry, the murals at Saint-Savin, the sculptures at Toulouse and Moissac, the Heavenly Jerusalem at San Pietro al Monte (Civate), the basilicas of Cluny and Vézelay, the first mosaics at San Marco'.[2] This was the age of Rupert of Deutz (c.1075–1129/1130), of William of St-Thierry (1075/80–

---

[1] Hans Urs von Balthasar, *The Theology of Henri de Lubac: An Overview* (San Francisco: Ignatius Press, 1991), pp. 26–7.

[2] Henri de Lubac, *L'Exegese Mediévale: les quatre sens de l'Écriture*, 4 vols (Paris: Aubier-Montaigne, 1959–64); see vol. II: p. 232.

1148), and of Bernard of Clairvaux (1090–1153, 'the last of the Fathers ... the first of the great moderns'.[3]

What is remarkable about William was his wide knowledge of Eastern as well as of Western patristic literature. In referring to him, de Lubac is reminding us that the Greek fathers remained in the memory of the Latin Church well into the twelfth century. Rupert, on the other hand, though perhaps best remembered for supposedly holding the eucharistic doctrine later known as impanation, also wrote a commentary on the Song of Songs, in which he interprets the beloved as the Virgin Mary, among the earliest to do so.

What no doubt also attracted de Lubac is that Rupert, on several occasions under suspicion by ecclesiastical authorities, is one of the many misunderstood characters in the history of theology whom he seems to have made a deliberate choice to highlight. Against the 'devastating contractions of [modern Catholic] theology', as Balthasar noted, de Lubac chose to write, not about Bonaventure, Nicholas of Cusa, Pascal, Möhler, Newman, and so on, whom one would have regarded as his 'allies'; but on 'other representatives of universal thought, namely, the great among the vanquished who have fallen because of the machinations of smaller minds or of a narrow Catholicism that is politically rather than spiritually mind', from Origen to Teilhard de Chardin.[4]

Catholicisme

In 1929, after the Jesuits were free to return to France, de Lubac began lecturing on fundamental theology at the Theology Faculty of Lyons. He never held a teaching post in any Jesuit formation house, though informally he influenced many of his juniors.

The books that he wove out of his reading were to become major texts in modern Catholic theology. The first, *Catholicisme: les aspects sociaux du dogme*, appeared in 1938 though the outbreak of the Second World War meant that it reached a wider readership only in the expanded edition of 1947. It appeared in English as *Catholicism: Christ and the Common Destiny of Man*, in 1950. Many regarded it as the key book of twentieth-century Catholic theology, the one indispensable text. Against the background of the liberal-capitalist and totalitarian ideologies of the 1930s, de Lubac sought to show that, in Catholic Christianity, the claims of person and of society are equally respected. Very much a tract for those times, primarily directed against the overly individualistic and introspective spirituality of his youth, as he saw it, the book is as relevant for those who might be inclined to over-emphasise the communal nature of Catholic piety.

Insisting that Catholic Christian dogma is a series of paradoxes, de Lubac declares that the greatest paradox of all is that, while the vision of God enjoyed by the blessed

---

[3] Ibid., III: pp. 426–7.
[4] Balthasar, *The Theology of Henri de Lubac*, pp. 30–31.

is a free gift, unanticipated, unmerited, never owed to them, yet the desire for it is, naturally and constitutively, in every human soul.

Corpus Mysticum

De Lubac's life was again interrupted by the German invasion of France. In 1940, after the capitulation, many Catholics were content with the Vichy government: it seemed the restoration of the traditional Catholic France that the anticlericalism of the Third Republic had opposed. De Lubac was one of the minority who resisted.[5] His Jesuit colleague and friend Yves de Montcheuil, arrested among the Maquis at Vercors, was executed by the Gestapo at Grenoble in August 1944.[6]

Ready for publication by 1939, *Corpus Mysticum: essai sur l'Eucharistie et l'Eglise au Moyen Age*, appeared in 1944. This 'naïve book', as he called it, retrieved the doctrine that 'the church makes the eucharist and the eucharist makes the church'. Leafing through volumes of Migne's *Patrologia Latina*, he hit on the phrase 'corpus mysticum' in the work of Florus of Lyons (died around 860). In modern times, and especially since Pope Pius XII's encyclical *Mystici Corporis Christi* (1943), the Church was referred to as the 'mystical Body' of Christ. As he pursued his research in medieval and patristic authors, however, de Lubac concluded that the phrase *corpus mysticum* referred initially to Christ's *eucharistic* body, and *not* to the visible Church as an institution. For de Lubac, discovering this shift in reference marked a breakthrough: according to the pre-modern understanding Christ should be regarded as mystically present and at work where and when the eucharist was being celebrated. In effect, de Lubac's book anticipated the eucharistic ecclesiology adumbrated at Vatican II.[7]

Surnaturel

The third of de Lubac's decisive interventions, *Surnaturel: Etudes historiques*, the most controversial as it turned out, appeared in 1946. According to the standard Thomist reading, Thomas Aquinas taught that human beings have a natural end or destiny, as well as the supernatural end conferred by divine grace. On the contrary, so de Lubac affirmed, Thomas subscribed to the teaching of the Fathers of the undivided Church, namely, that the human creature desires by nature a fulfilment, which can only come 'supernaturally'. The decisive point is that, on de Lubac's reading, Thomas Aquinas did not believe in any destiny for human beings, now that the Incarnation

---

[5] Henri de Lubac, *Christian Resistance to Anti-Semitism: Memoirs from 1940–1944* (San Francisco: Ignatius Press, 1990).

[6] For his memoir of his colleague see Henri de Lubac, *Three Jesuits Speak* (San Francisco: Ignatius Press, 1987).

[7] For de Lubac's ecclesiology see Paul McPartlan, *The Eucharist Makes the Church: Henri de Lubac and John Zizioulas in Dialogue* (Edinburgh: T&T Clark, 1993).

has happened, other than the supernatural end promised in the New Testament dispensation. In short, for Aquinas, there is no destiny for human beings apart from Christ – and, if there are texts in which he seems to suggest the contrary, then Aquinas would only be playing with the thought experiment of a world, a human nature and fulfilment, as if the history of God's intervention in Christ could be bracketed out.

This book gave rise to the most acrimonious controversy in twentieth-century Catholic theology. This 'merely historical' study was a direct challenge to the standard neo-scholastic theology of grace and nature. August Thomist commentators past and present were accused of misinterpreting Thomas Aquinas – a shocking contention! They did so, he claimed, because of their ignorance of traditional patristic and medieval Catholic doctrine. In particular, they misunderstood or even denied the doctrine of natural desire for God. According to traditional Catholicism, human beings were destined by *nature* to enjoy by divine *grace* everlasting bliss with God. Since the sixteenth century, however, allowing themselves to be shaped by opposition to Lutheranism, Catholic theologians made so much of the distinction between nature and grace that they lost all sense of the 'finality' of nature for grace – of the way in which the human and the natural has always already been embraced within the supernatural.

For neo-scholastic Thomists, it was axiomatic that Aquinas did not just entertain the concept of 'pure nature' as a thought experiment, but held it as an indispensable doctrine. However, as de Lubac wrote in a letter to Maurice Blondel, as early as 3 April 1932: 'This concept of a pure nature runs into great difficulties, the principal one of which seems to me to be the following: how can a conscious spirit be anything other than an absolute desire for God?'[8]

The controversy was never purely academic. It needs to be placed against the background of the bitter struggle that dominated politics in France in the early twentieth century between supporters of the Third Republic with their anticlerical 'laicism', as it was called, and adherents of traditional Catholicism with their monarchist nostalgia and papalist-ultramontanist inclinations. The conflict centred on the education system, with one side fearing that Church schools were not forming children in loyalty to the ideals of the Republic ('liberty, fraternity and equality'), while the other side regarded state schools as seedbeds of socialism and militant atheism. In wider theological terms, the problem was how to respect the autonomy of the secular without abandoning the sacred to the realm of the purely private.

In this light, the first book, *Catholicisme*, sought to correct what seemed to de Lubac an extremely individualistic and privatised religious sensibility by reminding Catholics of the inherently social nature of Christianity. He saw a double failure. On the one hand, Catholics were too often satisfied with a purely conventional religion, which was little more than the socially useful 'religion for the people' – religious practice as social control. On the other hand, inside and outside the Church, Christianity seemed to be a religion devoted to saving one's soul. To counter these

---

[8] Cited by Lawrence Feingold, *The Natural Desire to see God according to St. Thomas and His Interpreters* (Florida: Sapientia Press of Ave Maria University, 2001), p. 628.

apparently antithetical deviations, de Lubac sought to show that 'Catholicism' means that the Church addresses all aspects of human life, the social and historical as well as the personal and spiritual.

No World Outside Grace

The central thesis of *Surnaturel*, accordingly, is that, neither in patristic nor in medieval theology, and certainly not in Thomas Aquinas, was the hypothesis ever entertained of a purely natural destiny for human beings, something other than the supernatural and eschatological vision of God. There is only this world, the world in which our nature has been created for a supernatural destiny. Historically, there never was a graceless nature, or a world outside the Christian dispensation.

This traditional conception of human nature as always destined for grace-given union with God fell apart between attempts on the one hand to secure the sheer gratuitousness of the economy of grace over against the naturalist anthropologies of Renaissance humanism and on the other hand resistance to what was perceived by Counter-Reformation Catholics as the Protestant doctrine of the total corruption of human nature by original sin. Ironically, the Catholic apologists, who sought to protect the supernatural, by separating it conceptually from the natural, facilitated the development of humanism, which flowered at the Enlightenment into deism, agnosticism and ultimately atheism. The conception of the autonomous individual for which the philosophers of the Age of Reason were most bitterly criticised by devout Catholics was, de Lubac suggested, invented by Catholic theologians. The philosophies which broke free of Christianity, to develop their own naturalist and deist theologies, had their roots in the anti-Protestant and anti-Renaissance Catholic scholasticism of the late sixteenth and early seventeenth centuries.

The loss of the patristic-medieval sense of the internal relationship between the order of creation and the dispensation of grace led to a conception of grace as something so totally extraneous and alien to human nature that anything and everything natural and human was downgraded and demeaned. In particular, when questions about politics or sexuality (say) were detached from the traditional unitary theology of grace as fulfilling nature, it was not surprising if politics was treated with cynicism and sexuality with suspicion. When the dispensation of divine grace was no longer assumed to have resonance and even roots in some kind of natural desire for God, human nature – and that means reason, feeling, and the body – becomes temptingly easy to denigrate. On the other hand, so de Lubac claimed, the idea of a 'purely natural' human domain, perhaps once only a thought experiment, eventually gave rise to the space of the secular, free of religion and indeed of God.

In effect, de Lubac undermines neo-scholastic dogmatic theology as radically as he destroys standard natural theology. Doctrine remains 'extrinsic', just a set of abstract propositions, perhaps imposed by ecclesiastical authority, yet lifeless, barely relevant, practically unintelligible, unless connected to, and resonating with, the 'intrinsic' desire on the part of the given human nature of the one accepting or teaching the doctrine. Thus, philosophy, we may say, requires the supplement of theology, yet theology equally requires the foundation of philosophy – which cannot be had. De Lubac's paradox, as neo-Thomist critics understandably objected, looks more like an irresolvable *aporia*. Indeed, as John Milbank highlights, we find Balthasar describing de Lubac's writing as occupying a problematic 'suspended middle' – 'De Lubac soon realised that his position moved into a suspended middle in which he could not practice any philosophy without its transcendence into theology, but also any theology without its essential inner structure of philosophy'.[9]

If grace did not fulfil the deepest longing of our nature, of our ethical, contemplative and (even) naturally mystical impulses, then it would be external, alien and irrelevant. The life of the Spirit, instead of its being real (ontological) participation in the divine nature ('divinisation') would become a purely nominal change in the believer's status by the decree of an alien God operating by the external institutions of the Church. So at least the story goes.[10]

From Being Under Suspicion to Being Consulted at Vatican II

In 1950, his Jesuit superiors in Rome, fearing that he was among the theologians anonymously censured, in the encyclical *Humani Generis*, among those, that is to say, who 'destroy the gratuity of the supernatural order, since God, they say, cannot create intellectual beings without ordering and calling them to the beatific vision', asked de Lubac to stop teaching. Never summoned to defend his views in Rome, he always denied being targeted in the encyclical. Nevertheless, his books were removed from Jesuit libraries and withdrawn from sale. He was ostracised for a decade, his views frequently traduced, as the leader of *la Nouvelle Théologie*.[11]

However, de Lubac continued to bring out books, on a range of subjects: a study of Origen's biblical exegesis (1950), three books on Buddhism (1951–5), and, above all, *Méditation sur l'Eglise* (1953). The last of these, not intended as a full-blown treatise on the Church, and not at all 'scholarly', as he insisted, merely the result of talks at days of recollection for the clergy and suchlike, was only an 'echo' of 'essential texts of Tradition', as the introduction tells us. The nine chapters, taking us from 'The Church as Mystery' through to 'The Church and Our Lady', seems

---

[9] Balthasar, *The Theology of Henri de Lubac*, 15; cf. John Milbank, 'The Suspended Middle: Henri de Lubac and the Debate Concerning the Supernatural', in David Ford (ed.) with Rachel Muers, *The Modern Theologians* (Oxford: Blackwell, 2005), and the expanded version, *The Suspended Middle: Henri de Lubac and the Debate concerning the Supernatural* (London: SCM Press, 2005).

[10] The best summary of the issues as he saw them is in de Lubac's *A Brief Catechesis on Nature and Grace* (San Francisco: Ignatius Press, 1984).

[11] See Joseph A. Komonchak, 'Theology and Culture at Mid-century: The Example of Henri de Lubac', *Theological Studies*, 51 (1990), 579–602; Aidan J. Nichols OP, 'Thomism and the nouvelle théologie', *The Thomist*, 64 (2000), 1–19.

to anticipate much that appeared a decade later – in retrospect, it looks like laying out the structure of *Lumen gentium*, the document on the nature of the Church; but of course de Lubac never imagined that he would be involved in drafting such a text. For the immediately pre-Vatican II generation of seminarians and lay people, this was a widely read and much treasured book – a reminder of just how rich pre-Vatican II ecclesiology was.[12]

Teilhard de Chardin died in 1955, which freed his lay friends to start publishing the books, hitherto held back by his being obliged as a priest to have ecclesiastical approval. At the behest of his Jesuit superiors in France, de Lubac set about clearing Teilhard's name of long-standing suspicions of unorthodoxy, and even trying to establish him as a major Catholic thinker.[13] He continued to browse through patristic and medieval theology, the results of which were published between 1959 and 1964, a massive attempt at retrieval of precritical biblical hermeneutics.[14] By then, however, de Lubac was among the first summoned by Pope John XXIII to help draft the texts for Vatican II. In the event, de Lubac had a hand in composing the major documents, *Dei verbum*, *Lumen gentium* and *Gaudium et spes*. Before the Council concluded, however, he saw signs of a growing 'paraconciliar agitation', demanding reforms in the Church quite different from what was envisaged.

Post-Vatican II Distress

In the 1970s de Lubac became increasingly distressed as he saw the achievement of Vatican II undermined, as he believed, principally by 'progressive' clergy, with their craze for liturgical 'experiment' and preference for neo-Marxist sociology over traditional theological study. They sought to bring the Church 'up to date' – *aggiornamento* – without the deep engagement with the sources – *ressourcement* – which he regarded as essential. Moreover, the Catholicism, which he had struggled to free from the 'separist' conception, as he labelled it, separating nature and grace from one another, was now collapsing the dispensation of divine grace into naturalistic humanism, as if nature and grace were one and the same thing.

---

[12] Translated as *The Splendour of the Church* (New York: Sheed and Ward, 1956; San Francisco: Ignatius Press, 1986); not a good title.

[13] *La pensée religieuse du Père Teilhard de Chardin* (1962, English 1967); *La prière du Père Teilhard de Chardin* (1964, English 1965); *Teilhard, missionaire et apologiste* (1966), *L'Eternel féminin* (1968, English 1971), and an edition of Teilhard's correspondence with Blondel (1965, English 1967).

[14] Susan K. Wood, *Spiritual Exegesis and the Church in the Theology of Henri de Lubac* (Edinburgh: T&T Clark, 1998), which has a good bibliography.

In his last two major works, *Pic de la Mirandole*[15] and *La postérité spirituelle de Joachim de Flore*,[16] he continued his rehabilitation of marginalised figures.

In 1983, when he was nearly 87, he accepted Pope John Paul II's decision to make him a Cardinal, reluctantly, on condition that he not be ordained a bishop. He died on 4 September 1991.

Retrieval of Origen

One of the most important achievements of Henri de Lubac's historical study was the retrieval of the long suspected theology of Origen (at least in the West).[17] Inaugurated in 1948 by his colleague and friend Jean Daniélou,[18] this revival was soon confirmed by de Lubac's path-breaking study of Origen's biblical exegesis (1950). By the mid 1950s, in the heyday of neo-scholasticism, when Pope Pius XII seemed to preside over an inviolably monolithic Catholicism, Origen had returned from neglect and long-standing denigration as a near-heretic to centre stage. The themes, developed by de Lubac and others from Origen's fertile speculations, are as follows.

Origen is the source of the nuptial theology, taken up by de Lubac, which was to become a major theme in the Catholic theology by the end of the twentieth century.

The interpretation of the creature's relationship with God on the analogy of marriage is, of course, biblically grounded. In Hosea, particularly, the covenant between the Lord God and the people of Israel is represented as a marriage, memorably introduced by Hosea's being commanded by God to marry Gomer, in

---

[15] Giovanni Pico della Mirandola (1463–94), Italian philosopher and scholar, based his views chiefly on Plato, in opposition to Aristotle; famous for his *Conclusiones philosophicae, cabalasticae et theologicae* (Rome, 1486), including 13 theses identified as 'heretical' (out of 900), defended Christianity against Jews, Mohammedans and astrologers; many editions of his works in the sixteenth century; symbol of Renaissance blend of Christian and Platonic traditions.

[16] Joachim of Fiore (c.1135–202), monk, exponent of a Trinitarian theology of history, in three ages: the age of the Father, 'the order of the married', the dispensation of the Old Testament; the age of the Son, 'the order of the clergy', the New Testament; and the age of the Spirit, 'the order of monks or contemplatives', when new monastic orders would arise to convert the whole world and usher in the 'Ecclesia Spiritualis' — some Franciscans believed they were the ones.

[17] Origen (c.185–c.254), born in Egypt, probably at Alexandria; brought up Christian; his father Leonides martyred; according to Eusebius took Matthew 19:12 literally; well versed in Middle Platonism; ordained priest 230; established school at Caesarea; tortured during the persecution of Decius; confessor of the faith; buried at Tyre; highly controversial figure; denounced as heretic by late fourth century and suspected ever since; see Henri Crouzel, *Origen* (Edinburgh: T&T Clark, 1989).

[18] Jean Daniélou (1905–74), Jesuit 1929; Sorbonne doctorate *Platonisme et théologie mystique* (published 1944) on the spiritual theology of St Gregory of Nyssa; contributed greatly to the revival of patristic theology, thus to the sidelining of neo-scholasticism; backstage operator at Vatican II; Cardinal 1967; died while exercising ministry to fallen women.

full knowledge of her sexual promiscuity, thus allowing her to become the central symbol of the idolatrous people who forsake the Lord. In the Song of Solomon, the virgin who comes in search of the king as her sexual companion is understood as the soul in search of the lover who is God. In Isaiah 61 the soul, no doubt here of a man, exults because the Lord God has 'covered him as a bridegroom decks himself with a garland and as a bride adorns herself with her jewels'; 'as a young man marries a virgin, so the Lord God's sons marry the land, and as the bridegroom rejoices over the bride so shall the Lord God rejoice over the singer's soul'.

The imagery carries over into the New Testament. In the vision with which the New Testament closes, the holy city, the New Jerusalem, appears as beautiful as a bride prepared to meet her husband (Apoc 21:2).

In a major paper on mysticism de Lubac mentions the symbolism of 'spiritual marriage', *pneumatikos gamos*, 'the theme of pursuit-union', in Origen.[19] The union of divine and human natures in the Incarnation is pictured as a marriage – as by Augustine: 'The Bridegroom's bed chamber was the Virgin's womb', because 'in that virginal womb were joined the two, the Bridegroom the Word, and the bride the flesh' – as Isaiah 61:10 prefigures: 'He hath set a mitre upon me as upon a Bridegroom, and adorned me with an ornament as a Bride.' In effect, Christ in the Incarnation makes himself at once Bridegroom and Bride.[20]

In the Christian tradition, from Origen onwards, the relation between the lover and his beloved has been seen as a description of God's relation with the Church (his bride), or with the individual soul (his spouse).

Church as Mother

A theme that attracted Henri de Lubac even more is that of the Church as 'mother' – *mater ecclesia*.[21] He cites a large number of texts. Among the best known come from Cyprian (d. 258), bishop of Carthage: 'it is impiety to abandon the mother' – meaning the Church: 'We are born from her womb, nourished by her milk, animated by her spirit'; 'The Spouse of Christ brings forth sons spiritually for God … He alone can have God as his Father who first has the Church as his mother'.[22] But he returns us to Origen, independently saying much the same thing: 'He who does not have the Church for mother cannot have God for father.'[23]

This repertoire of maternal imagery for the Church de Lubac happily traces back to the cult of the Great Mother – *magna mater* – that dominated Hellenistic paganism, assuring us that this is a legitimate transposition, indeed 'a typical example of

---

[19] 'Mysticism and Mystery' in *Theological Fragments* (San Francisco: Ignatius Press, 1989), pp. 35–69, 60.
[20] Augustine, *On the Epistle of John to the Parthians* 1, 2 PG 36.
[21] See *The Motherhood of the Church* (San Francisco: Ignatius Press, 1982).
[22] Cyprian, Epistle 44.3; *De Ecclesiae catholicae unitate* 4, Epistle 74.7.
[23] Origen, *In Leviticum* 11.3.

the boldness of Christian thought which was strong enough to seize, without contamination, everything which could serve to express it'. In pagan religion the Earth was enclosed in the earth mother; all living creatures issued from her womb and returned to it. Analogously, the new creation, the redeemed world, is 'included' in the Church. In short, the doctrine of creation is contained within the doctrine of the Church.

However, equally numerous, in patristic texts, we hear of the Church as *virgin mother*, for example as early as Eusebius (c.260–c.340).[24] Neglected in recent centuries, de Lubac observes, this image has been taken up by Paul Claudel, Pierre Teilhard de Chardin and Hans Urs von Balthasar, among others. Again, however, 'the voice of the great Origen is here the voice of all Catholic tradition' – the Church father with the best account of the Church as virgin mother.

Moreover, Origen provides the analogy between Church and soul: each Christian soul is virginal and maternal, receptive to the seed of the Word, bearing the Word it has received. As de Lubac documents, this theme of the birth of the Word in the womb of the Christian soul may be traced in the twelfth-century Cistercians, in the Rhineland mystics, among others.

However, the mothering role of every human soul, of the faithful people as a whole, and of the Church, cannot exist except in conjunction with a certain paternity. The bishop is father of one's soul, and father of the Church entrusted to him. We must not set pastors against people, de Lubac insists. Every member of the *ecclesia mater* exercises, or should exercise, the maternal function – but there is also necessarily a paternal role, the authority exercised by the Church's pastors.

Vir Ecclesiasticus?

In sum, the importance of de Lubac's thesis in *Surnaturel* lies in revealing that the space for the emergence of Enlightenment modernity was created by a neo-scholastic theology, which forgot that we have by nature a desire for God. The 'new theology', far from being the retrieval of patristic tradition in which he and others were engaged, was the neo-scholasticism that dominated from the late nineteenth century onwards and which, as de Lubac sought to show, was an entirely modern phenomenon, being a reaction against, or response to, the Reformation, the Renaissance and the Enlightenment.

Choosing to commemorate and celebrate Origen, Amalarius of Metz, Joachim of Fiore, Pico della Mirandola and Teilhard de Chardin among many others, manifestly offbeat and idiosyncratic figures, Henri de Lubac may seem a somewhat paradoxical 'man of the Church', *vir ecclesiasticus*, yet that is how he regarded himself. That many others have come to regard him in the same way says a good deal about the transformation of Catholic theology, which he helped to bring about. It is hard to believe that he did not plan his books in order to displace the hegemony of

---

[24] Eusebius, *Historia Ecclesiastica* 5.1.45–6.

neo-scholastic theology. That was the effect, as we can see; yet he seems never to have seen, let alone intended, it that way.

Bibliography

Primary Literature

Publication of Henri de Lubac's *Oeuvres complètes* (Paris: Cerf, 1998–) is in progress.
L'Exégèse Médiévale: les quatre sens de l'Écriture, 4 vols (Paris: Aubier-Montaigne, 1959–64).
La pensée religieuse du Père Teilhard de Chardin (Paris, 1962).
La prière du Père Teilhard de Chardin (Paris, 1964).
Teilhard, missionaire et apologiste (1966), *L'Eternel féminin* (Paris, 1968).

English Translations

Augustinianism and Modern Theology (New York: Crossroads, 2000): effectively the first part of *Surnaturel*.
A Brief Catechesis on Nature and Grace (San Francisco: Ignatius Press, 1984).
Catholicism: Christ and the Common Destiny of Man (San Francisco: Ignatius Press, 1988).
Christian Resistance to Anti-Semitism: Memoirs from 1940–1944 (San Francisco: Ignatius Press, 1990).
Corpus Mysticum (London: SCM Press, 2006).
The Discovery of God (Edinburgh: T&T Clark, 1996).
Medieval Exegesis, vols I and II, translated by E.M. Macierowski and Mark Sebane (Edinburgh: T&T Clark, 1998).
The Motherhood of the Church, French original 1971 (San Francisco: Ignatius Press, 1982).
The Mystery of the Supernatural (New York: Crossroads 1998, a revised second half of *Surnaturel*).
'Mysticism and Mystery', in *Theological Fragments* (San Francisco: Ignatius Press, 1989).
The Splendour of the Church (New York: Sheed and Ward, 1956; San Francisco: Ignatius Press, 1986).
Three Jesuits Speak (San Francisco: Ignatius Press, 1987).

Secondary Literature

Balthasar, Hans Urs von, *The Theology of Henri de Lubac: An Overview* (San Francisco: Ignatius Press, 1991).
Crouzel, Henri, *Origen* (Edinburgh: T&T Clark, 1989).
Feingold, Lawrence, *The Natural Desire to see God according to St. Thomas and His Interpreters* (Florida: Sapientia Press of Ave Maria University, 2001).
Grumett, David, *De Lubac: A Guide for the Perplexed* (London: T&T Clark, 2007).

Komonchak, Joseph A., 'Theology and Culture at Mid-century: The Example of Henri de Lubac', *Theological Studies*, 51 (1990), 579–602.

McPartlan, Paul, *The Eucharist Makes the Church: Henri de Lubac and John Zizioulas in Dialogue* (Edinburgh: T&T Clark, 1993).

Milbank, John, 'The Suspended Middle: Henri de Lubac and the Debate Concerning the Supernatural', in David Ford (ed.) with Rachel Muers, *The Modern Theologians* (Oxford: Blackwell, 2005).

Milbank, John, *The Suspended Middle: Henri de Lubac and the Debate concerning the Supernatural* (London: SCM Press, 2005).

Nichols, Aidan J. OP, 'Thomism and the *nouvelle théologie*', *The Thomist*, 64 (2000), 1–19.

Wagner, Jean-Pierre, *Henri de Lubac* (Paris: Cerf, 2001).

Wood, Susan K., *Spiritual Exegesis and the Church in the Theology of Henri de Lubac* (Edinburgh: T&T Clark, 1998).

Chapter 17
Yves Congar

Gabriel Flynn

Yves Congar (1904–95) was one of the foremost Catholic theologians of the twentieth century. He was part of a brilliant generation of French churchmen that also included such gargantuan figures as Henri de Lubac (1896–1991), Marie-Dominique Chenu (1895–1990), and Louis Bouyer (1913–2004), to mention just some of the most illustrious. Congar was one of the chief architects of an exceptional renewal in Catholic ecclesiology. He contributed to the recovery of the biblical images of the Church which emphasise its mystical nature rather than the hierarchical and societal aspects that had been given such prominence in the previously dominant post-Tridentine ecclesiology. Congar's vision for ecclesial renewal led to a profound transformation of the Catholic Church, its relationship with the other Christian churches, and the world. Vatican II became the catalyst for this change, and its documents gave authoritative expression to his most important ideas on the Church. Congar was extraordinarily prolific: he published more than thirty books and approximately one thousand six hundred articles. In November 1935, he founded and directed a new series called *Unam Sanctam* that was to become an ecclesiological library running to seventy-seven volumes, published by Éditions du Cerf in Paris. In one of his last works, *Entretiens d'automne* (Paris, 1987), he offers an incisive analysis of the place of religion in European society: 'Europe was made by Christianity. It is impossible to see modern Europe without Christianity.' Congar viewed the twentieth century as 'the century of the expansion of Islam, but among the minority of faithful who truly believe, it is a really evangelistic century'.

Biography

Congar was born on 13 April 1904 at Sedan in the French Ardennes, on the northern frontier with Belgium, and died at the *Hôpital des Invalides* in Paris on 22 June 1995. His life spanned the twentieth century and he participated in some of its most momentous events, including the Second World War (1939–45) and Vatican II (1962–5). Timothy Radcliffe, former Master of the Dominican Order, in his sermon at Congar's obsequies on 26 June 1995, spoke of four moments of grace in his life: the friendships he formed during the Second World War in the prisons of Colditz and Lübeck; membership of the Dominican Order; participation in Vatican II; and the hope of seeing perfect unity among Christians.

From the beginning, Congar regarded his vocation as being 'at once and by the same vein, priestly and religious, Dominican and Thomist, ecumenical and ecclesiological'. In 1925, he entered the Dominican noviciate for the province of France, taking the name Marie-Joseph in religion. He read theology from 1926 to 1931 at *Le Saulchoir* then in exile in Kain-la-Tombe near Tournai in Belgium because of the anti-clerical legislation of the French Third Republic. This exacting 'school of theology',[1] with its harmonious rhythm of work and liturgical prayer, provided him with an ideal of the religious life. It was here that he came under the influence of Chenu and Ambroise Gardeil, professors at *Le Saulchoir*, whom Congar regarded as his masters. Chenu, the single most significant influence, awakened in him an awareness of the historical dimension of reality, and, as Congar acknowledges, also provided the motivation for some of his most important theological endeavours.

In the years 1928–9, Congar experienced the first great interior appeal to dedicate himself particularly to ecclesiology and ecumenism. He always viewed the renewal of ecclesiology in conjunction with 'wide participation in ecumenical activities'. The way had been prepared by childhood friendships with Protestants and Jews, subsequent contact with a Russian seminary at Lille, and a lecture given by Chenu on the *Faith and Order* movement of Lausanne. The decisive point that set his course, however, was his retreat in preparation for ordination: 'To prepare for ordination I made a special study both of John's Gospel and Thomas Aquinas' commentary on it. I was completely overwhelmed, deeply moved, by chapter 17 ... My ecumenical vocation can be directly traced to this study of 1929.' Then, in 1930 and 1931, he visited the chief places associated with the life of Martin Luther (1483–1546). He was convinced that 'nothing really worthwhile with regard to Protestantism will be achieved so long as we [Catholics] take no steps truly to understand Luther'.

By the end of the 1930s, Congar had become one of the leading theologians of the French Church. He became well known, in the first instance, because of his theological conclusion to a survey on unbelief conducted by *La Vie intellectuelle*. The other reason that accounts for his emergence was the launch, under his direction, of the *Unam Sanctam* collection which prepared the way for Vatican II. Congar's intellectual endeavours were enriched by his association with *Action catholique* (1925–39), a highly respected lay organisation in Belgium and France, as well as with the French worker-priests (*prêtres-ouvriers*). These involvements contributed significantly to his formulation of a renewed theology of the laity.

The period 1939–45 was marked by the Second World War which, as Congar notes, interrupted everything for him. Yet even the war became an occasion of grace in comradeship and had an important influence on his view of the laity and, perhaps most important, showed him that modern unbelief was much more complex than he had thought. In 1985, he wrote emotionally of his comrades in arms, 'I was truly one with them ... We were very close, deeply bonded. I had wonderful comrades!' Congar viewed the time immediately after the Second World War as one of the finest in the French Church. There were new initiatives in theology, liturgy, biblical studies, the

---

[1] Marie-Dominique Chenu, *Une école de théologie: le Saulchoir* (Paris, 1985).

laity and pastoral life. Congar and Jean Daniélou, along with other leading Jesuits and Dominicans, spearheaded the movement for a return to the biblical, patristic and liturgical sources in order to present a more animated faith to the modern person confronted by an atheistic worldview.[2] This project was highly controversial; it was subjected to severe criticism by M.-Michel Labourdette,[3] and Marie-Joseph Nicolas, Professor of Dogmatic Theology at the Institut catholique de Toulouse and Provincial of the Toulouse Dominicans,[4] as well as Réginald Garrigou-Lagrange of the Angelicum in Rome, who used the phrase 'la nouvelle théologie' to describe it.[5]

The period 1945–65 includes Vatican II, arguably the most important event in the history of the Catholic Church since the Protestant Reformation; it is certainly at the zenith of twentieth-century ecclesiology. The French ecclesiastical historian Étienne Fouilloux refers to the Council as 'Father Congar's Council'.[6] The far-reaching programme of ecclesial reform executed at the Council is the *de facto* consummation of Congar's whole previous theological *oeuvre*. The true story of the battle for a 'real council' was revealed to the world with the publication of his long awaited conciliar diary, *Mon journal du Concile* (2002). In the diary, Congar provides a precise description of his part in the preparation of the conciliar texts, undoubtedly the most important aspect of the Council's entire enterprise.[7] On 7 December 1965, at the close of the Council, Congar, fully cognisant of the historic nature of the moment, makes a poignant entry in his diary, one which denotes his own stupendous contribution: 'A large number of bishops congratulate me, thank me. It is in large measure my work, they said ... At the Council itself, I worked a lot. I could almost say: "*Plus omnibus laboravi*".' The third period of Congar's career was also his most prolific, with important works on the laity (*Jalons pour une théologie du laïcat*, 1953); reform (*Vraie et fausse réforme dans l'Église*, 1950); tradition (*La tradition et les traditions*, 2 vols, 1960, 1963); ecumenism (*Chrétiens en dialogue*, 1964); Mariology (*Le Christ, Marie et l'Église* 1952); and Christology (*Jésus-Christ*, 1965). His major work on the Holy Spirit, *Je crois en l'Esprit Saint* (1995), is the fruit of the latter part of his career.

Following the ravages of the Second World War, during which Congar was a prisoner of war (1940–5), and of his exile from Paris (1954–5), a result of the restrictive measures taken against the foremost Jesuit and Dominican theologians in the wake

---

[2] See Gabriel Flynn and Paul D. Murray (eds), *Ressourcement: A Movement for Renewal in Twentieth-Century Catholic Theology* (Oxford, 2012).

[3] M.-Michel Labourdette, OP, 'La Théologie et ses sources', *Revue Thomiste*, 46 (1946), 353–71; Labourdette, 'La Théologie, intelligence de la foi', *Revue Thomiste*, 46 (1946), 5–44.

[4] M.-Michel Labourdette, OP and Marie-Joseph Nicolas, OP, 'L'Analogie de la vérité et l'unité de la Science Théologique', *Revue Thomiste*, 47 (1947), 417–66.

[5] Réginald Garrigou-Lagrange, OP, 'La nouvelle théologie où va-t-elle', *Angelicum*, 23 (1946), 126–45.

[6] Étienne Fouilloux, 'Frère Yves, Cardinal Congar, Dominicain: itinéraire d'un théologien', *Revue des sciences philosophiques et théologiques*, 79 (1995), 379–404 (p. 396).

[7] Yves Congar, *Mon journal du Concile*, ed. and annotated by Éric Mahieu, 2 vols (Paris, 2002), II, p. 511; Congar, *My Journal of the Coucil*, trans. by Mary John Ronayne, OP and Mary Cecily Boulding, OP (Collegeville, MN, 2012), p. 871.

of Pope Pius XII's encyclical *Humani Generis* (12 August 1950); Congar was eventually allowed to return to France in December 1956.[8] He immediately recommenced his work which he describes as 'that of an inner renewal, ecclesiological, anthropological and pastoral'. Congar's commitment to truth and to the Church ensured an exceptionally respectful reception for his views among the Fathers of the Council. Congar said that Pope Paul VI alluded to the work he and other theologians had done in his first encyclical, *Ecclesiam Suam*. Pope John Paul II, who admitted him to the College of Cardinals in 1994, also praised Congar for his immense contribution to the work of Vatican II.[9]

Survey

Congar's comprehensive theology of the Church, synthesised in the notion of a 'total ecclesiology' was formulated in response to particular problems within the Church which, in his view, contribute to unbelief. The findings of his 1935 study, 'Une conclusion théologique à l'enquête sur les raisons actuelles de l'incroyance', published as a theological conclusion to a three-year investigation by the journal *La Vie intellectuelle* into the causes of unbelief, and his subsequent deliberations on unbelief and other related issues in an article published shortly before Vatican II, 'Voeux pour le concile: enquête parmi les chrétiens', provide the inspiration for his major works on the Church and motivated him to institute the *Unam Sanctam* collection.[10] Essentially, Congar held that certain ideas of God and faith, together with a 'wholly juridico-hierarchical' image of the Church, were largely to blame for unbelief. He was convinced that the image presented by the Catholic Church is crucial for the evangelisation of the modern world and determines, to a large degree, the chances for the reunion of the Christian churches.[11] In order to transcend the juridical idea of the Catholic Church, Congar, together with his colleagues Marie-Dominique Chenu and Henri-Marie Féret, embarked on an enterprise to eliminate 'baroque theology',[12] a term which they coined to describe the theology of the Catholic Reformation. The accomplishment of this goal was an important reason for the foundation of the *Unam Sanctam* collection.

---

[8] Yves Congar, *Journal d'un théologien (1946–1956)*, ed. and annotated by Étienne Fouilloux and others, 2nd edn (Paris, 2001), p. 443. For an account of his deep sufferings in this period, notably in Cambridge, England, see: Fergus Kerr, *Twentieth-Century Catholic Theologians: From Neoscholasticism to Nuptial Mysticism* (Oxford, 2007), pp. 36–7.

[9] John Paul II, 'Télégrammes du Pape Jean-Paul II à Mgr Jean-Marie Lustiger, et au P. Timothy Radcliffe', *Documentation catholique*, 92 (1995), 690.

[10] See Gabriel Flynn, *Yves Congar's Vision of the Church in a World of Unbelief* (Aldershot and Burlington, 2004).

[11] Congar, 'The Council in the Age of Dialogue', *Cross Currents*, 12 (1962), 144–51 (pp. 146, 149–50); Congar, 'Voeux pour le concile: enquête parmi les chrétiens', *Esprit*, 29 (1961), 691–700 (pp. 694, 697–9).

[12] Jean Puyo, *Jean Puyo interroge le Père Congar: 'une vie pour la vérité'* (Paris, 1975), pp. 45–6.

I shall refer to three major texts by Congar, published in the *Unam Sanctam* series, from the principal domains of his theological enterprise: ecumenism, the theology of the laity, and Church reform.

Chrétiens désunis: principes d'un 'oecuménisme' catholique (1937) is the first volume of the *Unam Sanctam* series and the first contribution in French to Roman Catholic ecumenism. Congar analyses the two historic fractures to Church unity in the eleventh and sixteenth centuries respectively. The chief advantage of this work, in his view, was that 'for the first time it attempted to define "ecumenism" theologically or at least to put it in that context'. Catholicity is viewed in dialectical terms as the universal capacity for the unity of the Church and the guarantee of respect for what is finest and most authentic in the diversity of languages, nations and religious experiences.

Jalons pour une théologie du laïcat (1953) is an attempt to overcome a restricted, clerical view of the Church and to outline the doctrinal elements of a theology of the laity. This book, acknowledged as a classic, must be read in conjunction with his later writings for a full understanding of his thought on the issue. Congar's original and modest intention for this work was simply 'to offer material for further research'. Nonetheless, he attributed permanent significance to the description of laity articulated there. His insistent, positive characterisation of the 'layman' is noticeable: 'I consider that the definition or rather the description of the layman proposed there (it is taken up by *Lumen Gentium*, no. 31) had abiding value.'

Vraie et fausse réforme dans l'Église (1950), Congar's *magnum opus* on reform and one of his most influential works, outlines the conditions for a true reform of the Church, which he says can be reduced to four principles: (1) the primacy of charity and the pastoral; (2) to remain within the communion of all; (3) patience; respect for delays; (4) a true renewal by a return to the principle of the Tradition. These principles for a true reform of the Church without schism have not been surpassed and are of abiding value. The aim of this work is not to propose a programme of reforms for the Church, but to study the place of reforms in the life of the Church, the reasons which eventually make reform necessary, and most importantly, how to carry out a reform without injury to the unity of the Church. 'Reform *of* the Church', must be 'reform *in* the Church'. The strength of Congar's principles for reform without schism which, unlike the proposals formulated by Luther and the Protestant reformers in the sixteenth century, or Döllinger and the Old Catholics in the nineteenth, is that they uphold 'the idea of reform *within* the Church'.

Key Characteristics of Congar's Thought

Ecumenism

Congar's ecumenism is a remarkable achievement. In the overall framework of his ecclesiology, ecumenism rests within the widest possible setting. It has profound implications for theology, worship and the Church's apostolic life. Congar, fully cognisant of inherent weaknesses in the churches, identifies internal Church reform as a precondition of Christian unity, a point he articulates as follows: 'It very soon occured to me that ecumenism is not a speciality and that it presupposes a movement of conversion and reform co-extensive with the whole life of all communions.' He considers that the division of Christendom was a historically significant factor in the origin of modern unbelief, an urgent task for the Church at Vatican II would then be the pursuit of unity in order to redress the indifference and hostility which result from unbelief.

Congar rejected a utilitarian notion of ecumenism viewed in terms of programmes and projects. The manifestation of its true nature is, rather, to be found in the Church animated by the Holy Spirit. A noticeably consistent feature of his ecumenism is the claim that progress towards unity cannot be measured by the criteria of confessional triumphs or the absorption of one communion by another. What is required is, rather, respect, patience and dialogue. It is to his credit that he was open to dialogue with all, including the *integristes* – extreme right-wing conservative Catholics. He viewed dialogue as a permanent element in the Church's mission to the world. It is certain that the failure of ecumenism results in the sequential triumph of religious intolerance, racial discrimination and wars of religion.

Congar acknowledges that ecumenism is not for everyone since, in his view, only the ecumenically-minded can bring it about. But the attitude implicit in his proposed blueprint for ecumenical dialogue, so profoundly influenced by that of Pope John XXIII, is sound: 'Only after eating together, praying and talking together, can the discussion of certain questions be approached in such a way that the other side is both heard and understood. Only then is there any real possibility of rapprochement.'

An important evolution occurred in his ecumenical thought which may be briefly described as follows: in *Diversités et Communion* (1982), the focus is no longer on Catholicity but on the necessity of diversity at the heart of communion. Congar sums up the evolution in his ecumenical thought in the following terms: 'My confrère and friend J.-P. Jossua finally analysed a change in the key concept from 1937, *Chrétiens désunis* and this book [*Essais oecuméniques*, 1984]: the passage from "Catholicity" to "diversities" and "pluralism".' Congar goes even further to give a qualified acceptance to the expression 'reconciled diversities'. The term 'reconciled diversity' (*Versöhnte Verschiedenheit*), was proposed by the Concord of Leuenberg – a statement of concord between the Lutheran and Reformed Churches of Eastern and Western Europe, signed at Leuenberg, Switzerland on 16 March 1973, allowing the joint possibility of different doctrinal theses, previously considered irreconcilable – and adopted by the assembly of the World Lutheran Federation at Dar-es-Salaam in June 1977.

Ultimately, Congar places the ecumenical reality in an eschatological context. He was convinced that the characteristic absence of an eschatological perspective in pre-conciliar Catholic ecclesiology had hindered ecumenical openness. In the course of his lifetime, he was personally responsible for an impressive and wide-ranging series of ecumenical initiatives and is appropriately remembered as the Catholic Church ecumenist par excellence of his era. He is lauded by the distinguished Dutch ecumenist Dr Willem Adolf Visser't Hooft (1900–85), first secretary general of the World Council of Churches, as 'the father of Roman Catholic ecumenism'.

Theology of the Laity

A theology of the laity is problematic. It is criticised as presenting a clerical and canonical view of the Church that is untenable because it necessarily restricts the vocation of the laity to a limited aspect of the total mission of the Church. But this can hardly be the case in Congar's theology of the laity, defined as a 'total ecclesiology', unless this basic principle can be shown to be false. Congar, in fact, is one of a small number of theologians who contributed to a theology of the laity. He returned to the topic in the course of his career and his reflections constitute a genuine contribution to ecclesiology. His thinking on the subject developed considerably over time, providing a picture of developments in twentieth-century theology, the churches, and modern European society.

Consideration of the clear evolution in Congar's thought concerning the relationship of priests and laity is necessary for a full appreciation of his theology of ministry. In the 1953 edition of *Jalons pour une théologie du laïcat*, on the basis of the essential distinction between clergy and laity, Congar refers to three states or conditions: lay, clerical and monastic. In the 1964 revised edition, however, he states that the present movement of ideas, surpassing the classification of the layperson in relation to the cleric, moves to the organic notion of the People of God in which the prophetical, priestly and kingly functions are shared by hierarchy and laity working in harmony. In 1966, Congar presents a description of his proposals for a theology of the laity in which he states that it is difficult to present a positive definition of the laity except by reference to the distinction, willed by God, between ordained ministers and the faithful, as well as to the differentiation within these structures, which arises from the state of life chosen by Christians. It is important to acknowledge that these remarks do not constitute a regression from his position articulated in 1964, as Congar does not depart from his concern to situate the theology of the laity in the context of the People of God. As he writes: 'The laity are, in their place, the Church; they are the People of God.'

In 1970, Congar acknowledges a departure from his original formulation of the question: 'As to terminology, it is worth noticing that the decisive coupling is not "priesthood/laity" (*sacerdoce-laïcat*), as I used it in *Jalons*, but rather "ministries/modes of community service" (*ministères ou services-communauté*).' An important statement, it indicates a maturing of Congar's theology of ministry which, in his view, helps to avoid clericalism and an excessive compartmentalisation whereby laity is defined in opposition to clergy, a danger in all non-declericalised Roman Catholic ecclesiologies.[13] In *Entretiens d'automne* (1987), Congar, reflecting further on *Jalons pour une théologie du laïcat*, points out that 'there is no longer any need to define the laity in relation to the clergy which, I grant, is rather what I did'. The advantage of the 'ministries/modes of community service' coupling is that it contributes towards a more inclusive vision of ministry that acknowledges, not only the contribution of the hierarchical priesthood

---

[13] Congar, 'Ministères et laïcat dans les recherches actuelles de la théologie catholique romaine', *Verbum Caro*, 71–2 (1964), 127–48 (pp. 137–8).

to the mission of the Church, but also those services performed by the laity which, Congar insists, must also be recognised as ministries.

Congar's theology of laity, far from constructing a clerical Church that restricts the mission of the laity to a limited aspect of the total mission of the Church, calls for the full participation of all in the life of the Church. The vocation of the laity is to be the Church in its fullness. The replacement of the notion of 'priesthood/laity' by the concept of 'ministries/modes of community service', founded on the rediscovery of the principle of the co-responsibility of all the baptised, while retaining the distinction between pastors and the rest of the People of God, boldly asserts that the mission of the Church is a responsibility shared by all. This represents a significant advancement in the cause of the laity which is encapsulated in Congar's expression: 'There can only be one sound and sufficient theology of laity, and that is a "total ecclesiology"'. According to Congar, Vatican II was 'a council of the laity'. Guided by *Apostolicam actuositatem*, he urges Church leaders to 'listen willingly to the laity and to allow them a considerable amount of freedom and initiative'. The success of the Church's mission of evangelism in modern, atheistic society requires the co-operation of laity and hierarchy in the establishment of the social foundations for faith (*praeambula apostolatus*).

Reform and Tradition

Looking at the matter historically, Congar holds an eminent place in the history of Church reform. He is careful but effective in his approach to reform and his extensive involvement at Vatican II helped to make reform of the Church the order of the day in practically every domain. Congar, in fact, sees himself as a man of ideas, but it is his idea of reform that dominates his entire *oeuvre* and constitutes his most important and original contribution to Christian theology. It is clear, as the history of Vatican II shows, that his greatest achievement is to have formulated a theory of Church reform that was successfully acted upon at that Council. In *Mon journal du Concile*, he repeats the assertion that Pope John XXIII read *Vraie et fausse réforme dans l'Église* in 1952. The suggestion that he discovered there the intuition for a Council of the Church, along with a vision for ecumenism, is a matter for historians. But it cannot be denied that the genius of Congar's plan of action, as presented in *Vraie et fausse réforme dans l'Église*, lay in the proposed dialectical relationship between unity and reform in the Church, and so we are justified in speaking of its ultimate success at Vatican II.

The Church, in order to conform more closely to Christ, must engage in perpetual self-reform. This is actualised by means of a return to the sources which provided the inspiration for *Vraie et fausse réforme dans l'Église*. This approach facilitates an openness to change and development while exercising a profound fidelity to the tradition. Reform and tradition cannot, then, be considered in isolation. An authentic reform of the Church is, in fact, only possible if there is a clear acknowledgement of the irreformability of its structure. 'The Church is penitential, the Church is called to constant reform, not in its structure, but in its life.' Without reform, tradition is reduced to a mere tract on apologetics, while reform without tradition is flawed and so thwarts the course of true ecclesial renewal.

Congar's formulation of tradition provides a 'new synthesis' of issues at once complex and controversial in Catholic theology. He proposes a dialectical model that links tradition and reform. In this framework, tradition is viewed in its totality while the Holy Spirit is presented as the guarantor of fidelity: 'While it is extension and progress, Tradition remains linked to its roots. The Holy Spirit is the divine guarantee of its fidelity.' A precise relationship between tradition, the Church and the renewal movement based on a return to the biblical and patristic sources is described in *La Tradition et la vie de l'Église* (1963), the most synthetic of Congar's three studies on tradition:

> This process of ecclesiological rediscovery has been very active in the Catholic Church, and indeed her last word on the matter has not yet been said. We have also been witnessing, for some time, beginning in about 1937–8, a widespread renewal of patristic studies and a powerful biblical movement. All of this is bound to lead to a greater comprehension of Tradition and of its relationship with the Church and with Scripture: three inseparable realities which a truly Catholic theology succeeds precisely in uniting and linking together.

Tradition is Janus-faced. A present reality, it comes from the past and is conducted towards the future by men and women under the guidance of the Holy Spirit. In *La Tradition et la vie de l'Église*, Congar makes this point eloquently: 'We have, I trust, recognised the greatness of Tradition … Christianity is essentially an inheritance, passed down by our Fathers in the faith. But Tradition is also present today. Age-old, it is ever fresh and alive; using its inherited riches it answers the unexpected questions of today. It advances through history towards its final consummation.'

Congar influenced the notion of tradition propounded in Vatican II's *Dogmatic Constitution on Divine Revelation, Dei verbum*. The French philosopher Maurice Blondel (1861–1949) exercised a decisive influence on his formulation of tradition. It is thanks to Congar that Blondel's personalistic theory of tradition gained entry to the teaching of the Council.

Congar's Place in Twentieth-century Theology

An undisputed 'Master', honoured belatedly as an intellectual giant of his time, Congar knew well the angst and the triumphs that normally accompany great thinkers. According to the Cambridge scholar, David F. Ford, Congar 'may well have had more influence on church history than any other theologian in this volume' (*The Modern Theologians*, 1997). He contributed to about half of the documents of Vatican II and his role there was praised by Popes Paul VI and John Paul II. Congar's pre-conciliar works on laity, ecumenism, tradition and reform helped to prepare the ground for what came to fruition at the Council. He was part of and contributed to the tensions in post-conciliar Catholic theology, sadly still dominant in Europe and North America, symbolised in the separation in 1972 of the *Communio* group of theologians (principally von Balthasar, Ratzinger, de Lubac and Kasper), from the journal *Concilium* (principally Rahner, Schillebeeckx, Küng and, of course, Congar).

Congar's creative genius was greatly enhanced by a strong work ethic. His immense theological *œuvre* contributed to a renaissance in Catholic theology in the twentieth century; by reaching back to the ancient sources of Scripture, patristics and liturgy, he sought to contribute to a renewed Church for future generations. His blueprint for renewal also includes the hope of reconciliation between the Christian churches and the re-establishment of the social bases of faith, which must be supported by a Christian anthropology that fully embraces life and the world. As the work of renewal and church reform continues into a new century and a new millennium, scholars and church leaders will be helped by a new reception of his great works.[14]

Bibliography

Primary Literature

Chrétiens désunis: principes d'un 'oecuménisme' Catholique, Unam Sanctam, 1 (Paris: Cerf, 1937).
Divided Christendom: A Study of the Problem of Reunion, trans. M.A. Bousfield (London: Geoffrey Bles, 1939).
Vraie et fausse réforme dans l'Église, Unam Sanctam, 20 (Paris: Cerf, 1950). 2nd edn, Unam Sanctam, 72 (Paris: Cerf, 1969).
Le Christ, Marie et l'Église (Paris: Desclée de Brouwer, 1952).
Jalons pour une théologie du laïcat, Unam Sanctam, 23 (Paris, Cerf, 1953). 3rd edn, rev. with additions and corrections, Unam Sanctam, 23 (Paris: Cerf, 1964).
Neuf cents ans après: notes sur le 'Schisme oriental' (Paris: Chevetogne, 1954).
Christ, Our Lady and the Church: A Study in Eirenic Theology, trans. with an introduction by Henry St. John (London: Longmans, Green, 1957).
After Nine Hundred Years: The Background of the Schism between the Eastern and Western Churches, trans. by Fordham University Press and the Russian Center of Fordham University (New York: Fordham University Press, 1959).
La Tradition et les traditions: essai historique (Paris: Fayard, 1960).
'Voeux pour le concile: enquête parmi les chrétiens', *Esprit*, 29 (1961), 691–700.
'The Council in the Age of Dialogue', *Cross Currents*, 12 (1962), 144–51.
La Foi et la Théologie, Théologie dogmatique, 1 (Tournai: Desclée, 1962).
La Tradition et les traditions: essai théologique (Paris: Fayard, 1963).
Sainte Église: études et approches ecclésiologiques, Unam Sanctam, 41 (Paris: Cerf, 1963).

---

[14] See Gabriel Flynn (ed.), *Yves Congar: Theologian of the Church*, Louvain Theological and Pastoral Monographs Series 32 (Louvain, 2005; Dudley, MA, 2006); *Yves Congar: théologien de l'Église* (Paris, 2007).

Chrétiens en dialogue: contributions catholiques à l'oecuménisme, Unam Sanctam, 50 (Paris: Cerf, 1964).

'Ministères et laïcat dans les recherches actuelles de la théologie catholique romaine', *Verbum Caro*, 71–2 (1964), 127–48.

Dialogue between Christians: Catholic Contributions to Ecumenism, trans. Philip Loretz (London: Geoffrey Chapman, 1966).

Tradition and Traditions: An Historical and a Theological Essay (London: Burns & Oates, 1966).

A History of Theology, ed. and trans. Hunter Guthrie (New York: Doubleday, 1968).

L'Ecclésiologie du haut moyen age: de saint Grégoire le grand à la désunion entre Byzance et Rome (Paris: Cerf, 1968).

L'Église de saint Augustin à l'époque moderne, Histoire des dogmes, 20 (Paris: Cerf, 1970).

I Believe in the Holy Spirit, trans. David Smith, 3 vols (New York: Seabury; London: Geoffrey Chapman, 1983).

Martin Luther sa foi, sa réforme: études de théologie historique, Cogitatio Fidei, 119 (Paris: Cerf, 1983).

Lay People in the Church: A Study for a Theology of Laity, trans. Donald Attwater, rev. edn, with additions by the author (London: Geoffrey Chapman; Westminster, MD: Christian Classics, 1985).

Je crois en l'Esprit Saint, new edn, 3 vols (Paris: Cerf, 1995), 1st edn, vols I and II 1979, vol. III 1980.

Journal d'un théologien (1946–1956), ed. and annotated by Étienne Fouilloux and others, 2nd edn (Paris: Cerf, 2001).

Mon journal du Concile, ed. and annotated by Éric Mahieu, 2 vols (Paris: Cerf, 2002).

True and False Reform in the Church, trans. with an Introduction by Paul Philibert, OP (Collegeville, MN: Liturgical Press, 2011).

My Journal of the Council, trans. by Mary John Ronayne, OP and Mary Cecily Boulding, OP (Collegeville, MN: Liturgical Press, 2012).

Secondary Literature

Chenu, Marie-Dominique, *Une école de théologie: le Saulchoir* (Paris, Cerf, 1985).

Dunne, Victor, *Prophecy in the Church: The Vision of Yves Congar*, European University Studies, 23 (Frankfurt: Lang, 2000).

Famerée, Joseph, *L'Ecclésiologie d'Yves Congar avant Vatican II: Histoire et Église*, Bibliotheca Ephemeridum Theologicarum Lovaniensium, 107 (Louvain: Leuven University Press, 1992).

Famerée, Joseph and Gilles Routhier, *Yves Congar* (Paris: Cerf, 2008).

Flynn, Gabriel, *Yves Congar's Vision of the Church in a World of Unbelief* (Aldershot and Burlington: Ashgate, 2004).

Flynn, Gabriel (ed.), *Yves Congar: Theologian of the Church*, Louvain Theological and Pastoral Monographs Series, 32 (Louvain: Peeters, 2005; Dudley, MA: Eerdmans, 2006); *Yves Congar: théologien de l'Église* (Paris: Cerf, 2007).

Gabriel Flynn and Paul D. Murray (eds.), *Ressourcement: A Movement for Renewal in Twentieth-Century Catholic Theology* (Oxford: Oxford University Press, 2012).

Fouilloux, Étienne, 'Frère Yves, Cardinal Congar, Dominicain: itinéraire d'un théologien', *Revue des sciences philosophiques et théologiques*, 79 (1995), 379–404.

Garrigou-Lagrange, Réginald, OP, 'La nouvelle théologie où va-t-elle', *Angelicum*, 23 (1946), 126–45.

Groppe, Elizabeth Teresa, *Yves Congar's Theology of the Holy Spirit* (New York: Oxford University Press, 2004).

Jossua, Jean-Pierre, *Le Père Congar: la théologie au service du peuple de Dieu*, Chrétiens De Tous Les Temps, 20 (Paris: Cerf, 1967).

Kerr, Fergus, *Twentieth-Century Catholic Theologians: From Neoscholasticism to Nuptial Mysticism* (Oxford: Blackwell, 2007).

Labourdette, M.-Michel, OP, 'La Théologie et ses sources', *Revue Thomiste*, 46 (1946), 353–71. Labourdette, M.-Michel, OP, 'La Théologie, intelligence de la foi', *Revue Thomiste*, 46 (1946), 5–44.

Labourdette, M.-Michel, OP and Marie-Joseph Nicolas, OP, 'L'Analogie de la vérité et l'unité de la Science Théologique', *Revue Thomiste*, 47 (1947), 417–66.

Nichols, Aidan, OP, *Yves Congar* (London: Geoffrey Chapman; Wilton, CT: Morehouse-Barlow, 1989).

Pellitero, Ramiro, *La Teología del Laicado en la obra de Yves Congar* (Pamplona: University of Navarre Press, 1996).

Puyo, Jean, *Jean Puyo interroge le Père Congar: 'une vie pour la vérité'* (Paris: Centurion, 1975).

Vauchez, André (ed.), *Cardinal Yves Congar 1904–1995: actes du colloque réuni à Rome les 3–4 juin 1996* (Paris: Cerf, 1999).

Chapter 18
Karl Rahner

Svein Rise

In the early 1950s, critical questions began to be raised about Catholic scholastic theology. Many held that the content in the Catholic dogmas had become inaccessible to people in general because of the old-fashioned, rigid forms of expression. A new consciousness of the problems involved had made it urgently necessary for the believing Christian not only to *learn* the articles of faith, but also to *understand* them. It was necessary now to construct a bridge from the doctrine of faith to ordinary people's experiences, because faith had increasingly become a foreign element – something for Sundays, but irrelevant as a basis for the human person's faith in everyday life. Rahner's theology can be understood as a response to the crisis of faith that had been brewing for a long time in the Catholic church. The challenge he faced was to make faith once again acceptable as a basis for the human person's understanding of life. A central theme in all his writings is thus how historical events of two thousand years ago can be recognized as obligating truths *today*. Accordingly, we may rightly say that Rahner seeks an intellectually obligating *justification* of faith that, at the same time, makes faith an existential truth that can be experienced. His writings are characterized by the combination of theory and praxis, of academic training and theological spirituality, in a way that is matched by few other theologians in the twentieth century. As we shall see, this means that Rahner makes the "edifying" element in his writings an integrated part of the academic.

Biography

Karl Rahner was born on March 5, 1904 in Freiburg im Breisgau. Even before he took his final school examinations in 1922, he was a keen member of a youth movement led by Romano Guardini. He related subsequently that it was above all the meeting with Guardini that made this movement decisively important for him. After finishing high school, he entered the Jesuit order. He studied philosophy in Feldkirch and in Pullach near Munich from 1924 to 1927, and theology at the Jesuit college in Valkenburg in Holland from 1929 to 1933. He was ordained to the priesthood on July 26, 1932 in St. Michael's church in Munich. From 1934 to 1936, he continued his philosophical studies in Freiburg im Breisgau, where his teachers included Martin Heidegger and Erik Wolf. It was Heidegger's lectures that gave Rahner the most important inspiration for his first philosophical work, a fundamental-ontological interpretation of Thomas Aquinas, which he presented for evaluation for the doctorate in philosophy.

Martin Honecker, at that time concordatary professor in the philosophical faculty in Freiburg, rejected the dissertation, arguing that Rahner had moved too far away from the historical interpretation of the texts. The dissertation was however published in Innsbruck in 1939, entitled *Geist in Welt. Zur Metaphysik der endlichen Erkenntnis bei Thomas von Aquin* (*Spirit in the World. The Metaphysics of Finite Knowledge in Thomas Aquinas*).[1]

Rahner's academic career changed after his time in Freiburg: he returned to theology and completed his studies in Innsbruck in 1936 with the dissertation *Die Kirche aus dem Herzen Christi* (*The Church out of the Heart of Christ*). On the basis of this dissertation, he was awarded his doctorate in theology in the same year, and was judged qualified to take up a teaching post in Catholic dogmatics at Innsbruck in 1937. This meant that from 1937 to 1964, he was a member of the same faculty as his brother Hugo Rahner, who was four years older (1900–1968) and was professor of early church history and patrology there.

From 1939 to 1944, Rahner taught in Vienna, where he was also active in the institute for pastoral care and himself was involved in pastoral ministry in Lower Bavaria. This involvement in the practical life of the church in Vienna came to have decisive significance for Rahner's profile as a theologian, since Christian spirituality, practical exercises, series of sermons, and meditations now became an integral part of his academic theological work.

From 1945 to 1948, Rahner taught in Pullach, before returning to Innsbruck in 1949 as professor in dogmatic theology and the history of dogmas. Pope John XXIII appointed him in 1960 an adviser to the preparatory commission "De sacramentis" for the coming Vatican Council (1962–65). During the Council, Rahner was a member of several commissions and sub-commissions. The two dogmatic constitutions *Lumen gentium* and *Dei Verbum,* together with the pastoral constitution *Gaudium et spes*, were particularly important. After the Council, Rahner continued as adviser and secretary in several commissions. In the same period, he was also an active lecturer in Europe, North America, and Latin America. He also wrote and edited, alone or jointly, a number of standard theological works with an international readership, such as *Mysterium Salutis. Grundriss heilsgeschichtlicher Dogmatik* (*Mysterium Salutis. Outline of a Salvation-Historical Dogmatics*), I-III (with J. Feiner and M. Löhrer, 1965), *Sacramentum Mundi. An Encyclopedia of Theology*, 1968–70, *Kleines theologisches Wörterbuch* (*Dictionary of Theology*) (with H. Vorgrimler, 1961), and *Quaestiones disputatae* (with H. Schlier,

---

[1] The second and third editions were prepared by Johann Baptist Metz. See also Rahner's commentary on *Geist in Welt* in *Herausforderung des Christen* (Freiburg im Breisgau, 1975), 120–22. (*The Challenge Facing the Christian*).

first volume in 1957). With Edward Schillebeeckx, he took the initiative of founding the international theological periodical *Concilium* in 1965. In 1967, he initiated the *Internationale DIALOG Zeitschrift*, which first appeared in 1968.

In 1964, Rahner succeeded Romano Guardini as professor of "Christian philosophy and worldview" in Munich. In 1967, he was appointed head of teaching in dogmatics and the history of dogma at the University of Münster. He retired in 1971, and died at eighty in Innsbruck on March 30, 1984.

Theological Writings

Rahner's writings are voluminous. He wrote more than thirty books, and if we include everything he published, his bibliography runs to more than four thousand titles! He was a master of various literary genres, from the strictly academic dissertation to letters, meditations, interviews, devotional literature, and personal prayers. The variety in his publications reflects Rahner's wish to set up an encounter between the reality of everyday life and the mystery in faith. Although his works constitute a theological and literary whole, I have chosen, for the sake of an overview, to divide them into four main categories: (1) the philosophical academic writings; (2) occasional writings published in his collective volumes *Schriften zur Theologie* (*Theological Investigations*), as well as in the series *Quaestiones disputatae*; (3) writings on pastoral work, praxis, and spirituality; and (4) *Grundkurs des Glaubens* (*Foundations of Christian Faith*).

Geist in Welt (1939) is Rahner's philosophical *chef d'œuvre*. Here, *Geist* ("spirit") means the human person's possibility of knowing the transcendental, that which is higher than the senses – in the tradition, this is also called the metaphysical. *Welt* ("world") designates reality as this is immediately accessible to the senses (experience). Rahner's intention is to demonstrate the basic insight in Thomas that the experience of God (in the world) is the fundamental human experience. According to Thomas, God is the unfathomable horizon of meaning that gives a context to everything we experience. In Rahner's interpretation, the anthropological aspect of this insight entails that through the knowledge of God, the human person also receives the possibility of a conscious, reflected relationship to his own self and to his existence. By taking this approach, Rahner wants to make Thomas comprehensible to readers who are acquainted with the kind of modern philosophical problems that are discussed conceptually by thinkers such as Heidegger (Heidegger's philosophy of being). Rahner also makes use of Heidegger's way of thinking in order to give a more modern and inviting form to the old-fashioned face presented by scholasticism. In this way, his main philosophical work already establishes the premises for a renewal of Catholic scholastic theology.

In 1937, he held 15 lectures in Salzburg on the theme "Zur Grundlegung der Religionsphilosophie" ("On the foundation of the Philosophy of Religion"). These were published in book form during the Second World War, under the title *Hörer des Wortes. Zur Grundlegung einer Religionsphilosophie* (*Hearer of the Word. On the Foundation of a Philosophy of Religion*) (1941). This is not a justification of the philosophy of religion as a theological science, but a discussion of the basis of the human person's relationship to God. It takes concrete form as a question about whether and in what sense the human person is "open" for God's revelation. This question in *Hörer des Wortes* takes up anew the problem posed in *Geist in Welt*: the human person is "spirit" in space and time, and can be so only when he or she becomes visible in the world as true humanity. The truly human finds expression in the fact that the human person is a receptive and listening "spirit" who *in freedom* stands over against his fellow human being and God's free self-communication. When this self-communication is received, it is received in history as *word*. It thus makes sense to see the human person as a "hearer" of the word (a *Hörer des Wortes*) both in relation to his fellow human being and in relation to God.

Rahner wrote a large number of sermons, meditations, reflections, translations, and book reviews, but his best known works are probably the articles in the sixteen collective volumes *Schriften zur Theologie* (1954–84). He did not write a systematic theology, but the various individual themes he discusses in the collective volumes must be regarded as concretizing developments of his fundamental theological conception.[2] Many of the collective volumes are devoted to theological reflections on spirituality; we may mention *Zur Theologie des geistlichen Lebens* (*On the Theology of the Spiritual Life*), *Im Gespräch mit der Zukunft* (*In Dialogue with the Future*), *Frühe Bußgeschichte in Einzeluntersuchungen* (*The Early History of Penance: Individual Investigations*), *Theologie aus Erfahrung des Geistes* (*Theology out of the Experience of the Spirit*), *Humane Gesellschaft und Kirche von Morgen* (*Human Society and Tomorrow's Church*). Many of these volumes have been translated into numerous European languages.

In 1956, with the exegete Heinrich Schlier, Rahner launched a book series called *Quaestiones disputatae*. The idea was to publish books on vital themes in the Catholic faith, in order to breathe new life into questions that the so-called scholastic theology had long regarded as settled once and for all, and to arouse interest in such questions. From 1958, when the series was launched, Rahner wrote eight of the books and was joint author of the next twelve. Some of the best known are *Zur Theologie des Todes* (*On the Theology of Death*) (1958), *Das Dynamische in der Kirche* (*The Spirit in the Church*) (1958), *Die vielen Messen und das eine Opfer* (*The Many Masses and the One Sacrifice*) (1966), and *Zur Reform des Theologiestudiums* (*On the Reform of the Study of Theology*) (1969). The series still exists, although its character has changed somewhat.

Rahner's earliest publications include studies of the church fathers. It was not by chance that he translated and revised early on in his career a book by Marcel Viller, *Aszese und Mystik in der Väterzeit.Ein Abriss der frühchristlichen Spiritualität* (*Asceticism and Mysticism in the Patristic Age. A Sketch of Early Christian Spirituality*) (1939).[3] Rahner maintained that the publication of this type of literature was a special task incumbent upon him. The "pious" books (as he liked to call them) were more important than

---

[2] It was Richard Gutzwiller SJ, the student chaplain in Zurich, who encouraged Rahner to collect and publish the numerous articles, lectures, and essays he had written over the years.

[3] Now in *Sämtliche Werke* (Düsseldorf and Freiburg im Breisgau, 1995) 3, pp. 123–390 (*Collected Works*).

the "learned" books. This is why he himself attached importance to books such as *Die Worte im Schweigen* (*Encounters with Silence*) (1940), *Von der Not und dem Segen des Gebetes* (*Happiness through Prayer*) (1949), and *Das kleine Kirchenjahr* (*The Church Year in Miniature*) (1954). Rahner clearly shows in his meditative book *Betrachtungen zum ignatianischen Exerzitienbuch* (*Spiritual Exercises*) (1965) that mysticism's experiences of God play a fundamental role in his writings. Rahner emphasized in many different contexts that the spirituality of Ignatius of Loyola was the unifying element in his life.[4] He believed that the religious experience of God cannot be captured appropriately by theological reflection, and this explains his polemic against the division of theology into two categories, a theoretical-academic part and a spiritual part that is interested in praxis. For Rahner, "All theology must be theology of salvation." The collective volume *Sendung und Gnade* (*Mission and Grace*), with the subtitle *Beiträge zur Pastoraltheologie* (*Essays on Pastoral Theology*) (1959), is typical of this approach. After the publication of this book, Rahner was asked to contribute to a handbook of pastoral theology. Five volumes of the *Handbuch der Pastoraltheologie* (*Theology of Pastoral Action*), all bearing the imprint of Rahner's thinking and his theological style, were published between 1964 and 1972.[5] They make it very clear that Rahner sees dogmatics and spirituality as two sides of the one coin: spirituality makes dogmatics come alive, and dogmatics makes spirituality normative. The same is true in Christology, which I shall discuss separately below.

When Rahner succeeded Guardini in an interdisciplinary professorship (philosophy of religion and worldview) in Munich, he held his first lectures on the theme "Einführung in den Begriff des Christentums." ("An Introduction to the Idea of Christianity"). He already had the idea of turning these lectures into a book, but it was only in 1976, 12 years later, that this project was realized under the title *Grundkurs des Glaubens. Einführung in den Begriff des Christentums* (*Foundations of Christian Faith. An Introduction to the Idea of Christianity*). Both the lectures and the book are influenced by the fact that the audience in Munich was made up not only of theologians, but of students from all the faculties. The title (literally: "Foundational course in faith") was suggested by the publisher, Herder, and Rahner thought it might be misunderstood as suggesting that this is a popular presentation of the Christian faith in a traditional form, reminiscent of a catechism. This was not his intention. Nor was the book meant as a summary of Rahner's thinking or a condensed version of his theology; he always refused to produce texts of that kind. In a lecture in Freiburg im Breisgau in 1979, Rahner claimed that the intention of this book was "to think through the fundamental unity and the specific interconnectedness in what Christianity proclaims."[6] The subtitle indicates that he wants to find a *concept* for Christianity in this book, and this means that he is looking for *the ultimate reasons* for faith. Rahner wanted to

---

[4] See, for example, *Karl Rahner im Gespräch* (München, 1978–82), II, pp. 211f. (*Karl Rahner in Dialogue*).

[5] From 1968 to 1969, Rahner was joint editor with F.X. Arnold, F. Klostermann, and V. Darlap. He was the only scholar who edited all five volumes.

[6] See *Schriften zur Theologie* (Einsiedeln, 1982), XIV, pp. 48–62.

indicate theological reasons for the *life-praxis* of the individual Christian, and at the same time to indicate the premises for an intellectual account of faith. He argued that a continually more specialized academic knowledge and an increasing number of worldviews made it urgently necessary to look for the *wholeness* of faith, which also gave *thinking* believers encouragement and a perspective for their lives. *Grundkurs des Glaubens* was a fruit of this fundamental determination. In a review in 1978, Cardinal Ratzinger wrote that this book "will remain a source of inspiration when large portions of today's theological production are forgotten."[7]

Finally, we should note that all of Rahner's publications are being collected and published in *Sämtliche Werke* (*Collected Works*), an academic edition of his writings by the Karl Rahner Foundation under the guidance of Karl Lehmann, Johann Baptist Metz, Karl-Heinz Neufeld, Albert Raffelt, and Herbert Vorgrimler that is planned to run to thirty-two volumes.

Themes in Rahner's Theology

Jesus Christ – True God and True Man

The best way to grasp the innermost core in Rahner's theological thinking is to study Christology. "Grant, infinite God, that I may always hold fast to Jesus Christ, my Lord. May his heart reveal for me who you are for me. I wish to look to his heart when I wish to know who you are. God of our Lord Jesus Christ, I shall look to his human heart, for it is only then that I know that you love me."[8] These words give us a glimpse of what Christology is about. The first and fundamental question is: How can the divine and the human in Jesus exist alongside each other, without each of these designations becoming meaningless, or being reduced to merely external designations? On the one hand, we must prevent Jesus' humanity from being understood as a meaningless "shell" around his divinity; and on the other hand, Jesus' divinity must not be devoid of inherent, real significance for his humanity. The problem found a classic and acute formulation at Chalcedon in 451, which says that the Son is "with regard to his divinity, consubstantial (*homoousios*) with the Father, and with regard to his humanity, consubstantial with us," and declares that the Son's (two) natures and the natures (in the Son) are "without confusion and unchanged, not divided, and not separated."[9]

Rahner's main concern here seems to be that the problem is seen in connection with what he called *the fundamental determination* or *fundamental constitution of the human person*, which is identical with the conditions for being a human person in the world – or, in Rahner's terminology, for being spirit in the world (see *Geist in Welt*). This means that the best way to answer the christological question is to show how the

---

[7] *Theologische Revue*, 74 (1978), pp. 171f.
[8] *Worte gläubiger Erfahrung* (Freiburg im Breisgau: Herder, 2004), p. 20. (*Words of Faith*).
[9] See J.N.D. Kelly, *Early Christian Doctrines* (New York: Harper, 1978), pp. 338–43.

human person is determined fundamentally as one who exists with particular regard to his *relationship to God*. For Rahner, Christology is not independent of *anthropology*: as a spiritual being, the human person towers over all other creatures. This is because the human person is a questioning being, created with freedom and consciousness. Since the human person is questioning, without himself possessing the answer, he lives with the totality of himself in an openness vis-à-vis a greater mystery, which is God. This can also be formulated, with Thomas, as follows: the human person is *one who exists* and puts questions vis-à-vis God, but God is *Existence* and the answer to the one who exists. The questioning openness does not mean that the human person's freedom is restricted, or that his humanity is weakened. God must not be thought of as an alien "authority" above the human person, as if God came from the outside and "added" something onto the human person's existence – for God is not a "rival" to the human person and his freedom, but is himself the indwelling guarantee of freedom. This is expressed as follows in the *Betrachtungen zum ignatianischen Exerzitienbuch*: "The call to follow Christ does not reach us first and last in words that come from the outside and that can put us onto a path that does not correspond to our being. This call is the necessary development and unfolding of what we have always been: free persons, determined of our very nature to live with Christ."[10]

This is a brief formulation of the *basic definition* of the human person. The point is that this definition gives us insight into the reality of Jesus' life. Since all live in openness vis-à-vis God, in the expectation that God's gracious self-communication will come to meet this openness, it is possible to believe in God's gift to Jesus and to come to know this gift. It is only on the basis of that which is specifically *human* in the human person that the human person can sense what is involved in Jesus' unity with God. Unity is present as an inherent *possibility* in every human person. In Jesus Christ, this unity is visible and *realized*. Rahner maintains that there is a double truth in this: one truth thought of "from above," and the other truth thought of "from below." What happens in Jesus' reality "from above"? God, on the basis of his inner being, addresses the human person – and the world – with his gracious, unlimited self-communication. And what happens "from below"? Jesus, as a human person in free obedience and the gift of himself, receives the self-communication in a definitive and total manner. According to Rahner, the reciprocal relationship between "from above" and "from below" can best be understood in the light of the basic definition of the human person. Since God and the human person are not "rivals" in the sphere of freedom, we can grasp that full justice is done to *Jesus'* humanity in relation to God, although Jesus *is* divine. Rahner believes that this parallelism helps us to understand anthropology as an imperfect Christology and Christology as a visible and definitive exposition of anthropology, since it is God *himself* who through the incarnation made true humanity possible. Rahner calls this Christology *transcendental*.

In order to ward off misunderstandings, we must note that what Rahner calls *transcendental Christology* – Christology in the light of anthropology – is based ultimately in the de facto experience of the God-man Jesus Christ. The christological

---

[10] *Betrachtungen zum ignatianischen Exerzitienbuch* (München, 1965), p. 121 (*Spiritual Exercises*).

"grammar" that is involved here, which thinks of Jesus on the basis of God's gracious self-communication to him, can be traced directly back to the human person Jesus of Nazareth, and is therefore utterly unthinkable independently of the real historical events in Jesus' life. Christology is thus the criterion for anthropology – not *vice versa*. And this makes it possible to understand that the events that take place in the history of Jesus are unique and unparalleled. "Christology is the end and the beginning of anthropology. And this anthropology, in its most radical realization – namely, in Christology – is theology for all eternity. […] This is the theology we ourselves follow in faith, provided that we do not think that we can find God by simply ignoring the human person Christ."[11] This is a typically Rahnerian formulation of the relationship between Jesus (Christology) and the human person in general (anthropology).

We cannot however overlook the tension that remains in Rahner's thinking between the unique, historical Christ-event and the transcendental Christology that I have attempted to present here.

Jesus as the One Who Brings Salvation

The second aspect I wish to bring out is Jesus' function as the mediator of salvation. Rahner attempted, above all in the first phase of his writing career, to shed light *phenomenologically* on Jesus' significance in the history of salvation, on the basis of three fundamental experiences. This means that Christology is addressed to all persons of good will, even to those who have said "yes" to Christ but are not aware that the historical Jesus is the fulfillment of their (transcendental) search. Rahner speaks in this context of an unreflected and *anonymous* Christianity. It is this that makes it both necessary and possible to shed light phenomenologically on the significance of Jesus in the history of salvation. To put it simply: the main point is to bring the unconscious to consciousness, so that what is unreflected and anonymous can become the object of reflection and consideration.

The first fundamental experience that Rahner describes is the experience of *love*. He recalls that love presupposes familiarity and that the one to whom love is shown must be trustworthy and true. But since love is subject to the basic conditions of the world, it is continually overshadowed by disappointments and defeats. This is why love seeks a stable fixed point that makes it possible to live in an unconditional and unreserved fidelity. This fidelity is found only in *the absolute, perfect love* that manifests itself in Jesus' life and death. Through Christ, we have been shown how divine and human life intersect and how love of one's neighbor reflects the love of God. Since the love of neighbor always seeks its radical fulfillment in the love of God, we can understand that the concrete *manifestation* of the fulfillment of the love of neighbor is the God-man Jesus Christ. Rahner expresses this as follows in *Worte gläubiger Erfahrung* (*Words of Faith*): "We know that all our love for God is poor and weak, but that always wish with our best will to love him, even if we do not manage to say that his love must fill all our heart, all our soul, all our mind, and all our strength.

---

[11] Ibid., 112.

But one thing is certain: the one who sincerely wants to love God, loves him already. For one could not want this, unless God's grace had already touched the human heart and taken possession of it in its uttermost yearning for love."[12]

The second fundamental experience, which Rahner presents in terms akin to Heidegger's philosophy of being, concerns the ambiguity of life, namely, death. The human person is continually confronted by the riddle of death, since the human person in his freedom lives face to face with death as a phenomenon of life and must therefore take a position with regard to death. Besides this, the encounter with death unmasks the human person's own powerlessness and the self-contradictoriness of life. The existential problem for the human person is how he can escape from the conflictual antithesis between freedom and powerlessness. The human person in history looks for the "place" where this antithesis is resolved. The historical "place" is the life, death, and resurrection of Jesus, for where is the antithesis between freedom and powerlessness resolved, if not precisely there? "Death is either the powerlessness that is the uttermost result of the sin that took hold of Adam, or else a share in Christ's self-surrender, which was never greater and more exhaustive than in his death on the cross."[13]

Rahner relates the third fundamental experience to the human person's search for the fulfillment of life. In reality, this fundamental experience includes the two preceding examples, but it is related more explicitly to the consciousness of the meaninglessness and fragmentariness in human life. The human person's path through history is incessantly marked by the attempt to reduce the distance between what the human person *is* and what he or she *ought to be*. If there is no hope that history will one day attain its fulfillment, it is difficult to understand what is meaningful in life and in one's actions. Here too, however, it is impossible for the human person *himself* to achieve the fulfillment. This is why the human person looks for the totality that the Christ-revelation brings, since this revelation concretizes the unfathomable, divine totality of meaning.

Theology and Spirituality

The fundamental experiences make it clear that what the human person is looking for in history is a bringer of salvation who is absolute and definitive. It also becomes clear that Rahner makes Christology the key to anthropology, since the answer to the human person's search is the historical human being Jesus of Nazareth, who is perfectly human in his mediation of God's self-communicating grace. On the other hand, the anthropological approach – beginning from the basic definition and the basic experiences of the human person – has also shed light on the *universal* significance that Jesus has as the bringer of salvation. It is, however, easy to misunderstand Rahner here. He does not place a one-sided emphasis on Jesus' *significance*, independently of Jesus' identity. When Rahner shows the significance of Jesus as the definitive mediator

---

[12] *Worte Gläubiger Erfahrung*, p. 30.
[13] *Betrachtungen zum ignatianischen Exerzitienbuch*, p. 92.

of salvation, light is shed at the same time on the person of Jesus. The one perspective is indissolubly linked to the other. This means, for example, that Jesus' function as redeemer is also an exposition of the miracle of the incarnation. This makes clear the inherent unity between the salvation-historical and the personal perspectives in Christology. "The demand that is put to us through his unique life is an incalculable revelation of God's sovereign grace. [...] He revealed it for us through his life and his words, as we can read it in the history of his life."[14]

This brief sketch of Rahner's project of a Christology for our time – which he himself calls a transcendental Christology – has shown that anthropology plays an important role in the elaboration of Christology. It seems clear that this approach is connected to Rahner's attempt to clarify christology's "for us" or "for the human person." Despite this, however, the accent shifts in Rahner's final writings. In the first phase, he draws on transcendental thinking and aims chiefly to shed light on what is specific to the God-man Jesus Christ. In his last publications, he is more interested in the universal *salvific significance* of Jesus. The shift in accent is probably connected with Rahner's increasing spiritual and pastoral interest. In his last phase, he affirms in countless interviews that the spiritual and the pastoral are the *driving force* in what he writes. It is not always easy to notice this, since the edifying element in his writings is integrated into the academic element. According to Rahner himself, the spirituality of Ignatius of Loyola is the fundamental motivation for everything he writes. This explains why he employs Ignatius' *Spiritual Exercises* as directives for the immediate encounter between the Creator and the creature, between God and the human person.

Let me conclude this presentation with a quotation from the *Betrachtungen zum ignatianischen Exerzitienbuch* in which Rahner emphasizes precisely this point: "We are created by God, set before him, made for him, called to an immediate participation in his glory. But we are still in the world, and are not yet where we shall be eternally. This demands humility of us (the acknowledgement of the fact that we are still only 'en route') and courage (by striving for the future fellowship with God). Out of this human situation come what Ignatius calls *praise, reverence, and service*."[15]

Rahner in Theological Discourse

Rahner was certainly controversial as a theologian and writer. Not everyone approved of the way in which he attempted to renew Catholic scholastic theology; many even of his close friends had reservations, and the number of his critics gradually grew. In this section, I shall present three of his contemporaries who were close to him for a period. The fact that they parted company with him (in various ways) meant that Rahner felt a certain loneliness and isolation in his last years.

Johann Baptist Metz, who had worked early on in his career with Rahner on revisions and new editions of *Geist in Welt* and *Hörer des Wortes,* began to criticize Rahner's transcendental theology so severely in the late 1960s that Rahner was hurt.

---

[14] Ibid., 224.
[15] Ibid., 21.

This did not prevent Metz from giving Rahner his full support some years later, when Rahner rejected the theology of a suffering God. On this question, they stood together against theologians such as Karl Barth, Eberhard Jüngel, Dietrich Bonhoeffer, Jürgen Moltmann, and Hans Urs von Balthasar. Metz also declared his agreement with Rahner on certain aspects of Trinitarian theology.

Urs von Balthasar's critique was every bit as sensational as that by Metz. After he had praised Rahner in the early 1960s, the friendship was put to the test when von Balthasar claimed, several years later, that Rahner's theology approached atheism and heresy! He argued that Rahner too one-sidedly anchored theology in philosophy, thereby reducing Christianity to humanism, and that he lost the historical Christ-event as the premise for faith's personal encounter with absolute love. Many will doubtless agree with Vorgrimler, who was Rahner's close friend and collaborator for many years, that von Balthasar's critique involved slogans rather than arguments, and that his harsh denunciations betrayed a lack of knowledge of what Rahner had actually written. Despite his criticism, however, von Balthasar had great respect for Rahner's creative power and intellectual ability.

The third critic who deserves a mention here is Joseph Ratzinger, now Pope Benedict XVI. Ratzinger and Rahner worked together in 1962 during the Council, *inter alia* on a new draft of a text about the sources of revelation. In his memoirs, Ratzinger reveals that as their collaboration progressed, he saw with increasing clarity that he and Rahner were on two different theological planets, despite their agreement on conclusions and on theological goals.[16] According to Ratzinger, Rahner propounded a speculative and philosophical theology in which neither scripture nor the church fathers ultimately played any great role, and where the historical dimension of theology was relatively unimportant. Ratzinger's criticism does not hit the nail on the head, as far as the content of Rahner's theology is concerned. Through his innumerable meditations, texts about the church year, biblically-based sermons, and not least through his meditations on Ignatius of Loyola's manual, Rahner demonstrates the source of his inspiration, namely, scripture and the fathers, of whom Rahner had a wider knowledge than most theologians. As I have shown, Rahner's theology lives from the experiences of God in mysticism that are the core of the theology of grace and of ecclesiology. Rahner did not really form a school, but he was certainly a pioneer and a renewer. He brought about a vigorous renewal of that which is genuinely Christian by demonstrating the contribution that the Christian faith can make to an age that does not ask the fundamental questions. Rahner did this by doing into the depths and writing about an uncommonly wide spectrum of topics. He always treated the topics of the day in the light of the sources and the historical reception, and not least, in the light of their contemporary relevance. He was an academic theologian, a pastor, and a preacher all at the same time. He was a great intellectual, but he behaved with modesty and humility. It was this combination that

---

[16] *Aus meinem Leben. Erinnerungen* (München: Kösel Verlag, 2002), pp. 156f. (*Milestones: Memoirs, 1927–77*).

made Rahner an influential theologian before, during, and after the Second Vatican Council.

Bibliography

Primary Literature

Schriften zur Theologie, I-XVI (Einsiedeln: Benziger Verlag, 1954–84). English: *Theological Investigations*, 23 vols (Baltimore: Helicon Press, 1961–92).
Geist in Welt. Zur Metaphysik der endlichen Erkenntnis bei Thomas von Aquin (München: Kösel Verlag, 1957). English: *Spirit in the World. The Metaphysics of Finite Knowledge in Thomas Aquinas* (New York: Continuum, 1994).
Hörer des Wortes. Zur Grundlegung einer Religionsphilosophie (München: Kösel Verlag, 1941). English: *Hearer of the Word. On the Foundation of a Philosophy of Religion* (New York: Herder and Herder, 1969).
Grundkurs des Glaubens. Einführung in den Begriff des Christentums (Freiburg im Breisgau: Herder, 1976). English: *Foundations of Christian Faith. An Introduction to the Idea of Christianity* (New York: Seabury Press, 1978).
Betrachtungen zum ignatianischen Exerzitienbuch (München: Kösel Verlag, 1965). English: *Spiritual Exercises* (New York: Herder and Herder, 1965).
Zur Theologie des Todes. Mit einem Exkurs über das Martyrium, Heinrich Schlier (ed.) (Freiburg: Verlag Herder, 1958). English: *On the Theology of Death* (New York: Seabury Press, 1973).
Die vielen Messen und das eine Opfer (Freiburg im Breisgau: Herder, 1966). Quaestiones Disputatae, 31 (*The Many Masses and the One Sacrifice*).
Herausforderung des Christen (Freiburg im Breisgau: Herder, 1975). (*The Challenge Facing the Christian*).
Das Dynamische in der Kirche (Freiburg im Breisgau: Herder, 958) Quaestiones Disputatae, 5. English: *The Spirit in the Church* (New York: Seabury Press, 1979).
Wagnis des Christen. Geistliche Texte (Freiburg im Breisgau: Herder, 1974). English: *Christians at the Crossroad* (New York: Seabury Press, 1975).
Gnade als Freiheit. Kleine theologishe Beiträge (Freiburg: Herder, 1968). English: *Grace in Freedom* (New York: Herder and Herder, 1969).
Karl Rahner im Gespräch, I-II. Paul Imhof, Hubert Biallowons (eds) (München: Kösel Verlag, 1978–82). English: *Karl Rahner in Dialogue. Conversations and Interviews, 1965–82* (New York: Crossroad, 1986).
Sämtliche Werke (Düsseldorf and Freiburg im Breisgau: Benziger and Herder, 1995). (*Collected Works*).

Dictionaries and Encyclopedias

Mysterium Salutis. Grundriss heilsgeschichtlicher Dogmatik I-III, J. Feiner and M. Löhrer (eds) (Einsiedeln: Benziger, 1965). *(Mysterium Salutis. Outline of a Salvation-Historical Dogmatics)*.
Sacramentum Mundi. An Encyclopedia of Theology (New York: Herder and Herder, 1968–70).
Handbuch der Pastoraltheologie, I-IV, F.X. Arnold, F. Klostermann, and V. Darlap (eds) (Freiburg, Basle, and Vienna: Herder, 1964–69). English: *Theology of Pastoral Action* (New York: Herder and Herder, 1968).
Kleines theologisches Wörterbuch, H. Vorgrimler (ed.) (Freiburg im Breisgau: Herder, 1961). English: *Dictionary of Theology* (New York: Crossroad, 1981).
The Practice of Faith. A Handbook of Contemporary Spirituality, K. Lehmann and A. Raffelt (eds) (New York: Crossroad, 1986).

Secondary Literature

Eicher, Peter, *Die anthropologische Wende. Karl Rahners philosophischer Weg vom Wesen des Menschen zur personalen* (Freiburg Switzerland: Universitätsverlag Freiburg-Schweiz, 1970).
Farrugia, Edward G., *Aussage und Zusage. Zur Indirektheit der Methode Karl Rahners. Veranschaulicht an seiner Christologie* (Rome: Editrice Pontificia Università Gregoriana, 1985).
Fischer, Klaus, *Der Mensch als Geheimnis. Die Anthropologie Karl Rahners* (Freiburg im Breisgau: Herder, 1974).
Lehmann, Karl, "Karl Rahner," in H. Vorgrimler and R. Vander Gucht (eds), *Bilanz der Theologie im 20. Jahrhundert. Bahnbrechende Theologen* (Freiburg im Breisgau: Herder, 1970).
O'Donovan, Leo (ed.), *A World of Grace. An Introduction to the Themes and Foundations of Karl Rahner's Theology* (New York: Seabury Press, 1980).
Rise, Svein, *The Academic and the Spiritual in Karl Rahner's Theology* (Frankfurt am Main: Peter Lang, 2000).
Vorgrimler, Herbert, *Karl Rahner. Gotteserfahrung in Leben und Denken* (Darmstadt: Wissenschaftliche Buchgesellschaft, 2004).
Weger, Karl-Heinz, *Karl Rahner. Eine Einführung in sein theologisches Denken* (Freiburg im Breisgau: Herder, 1978). English: *Karl Rahner. An Introduction to His Theology* (New York: Seabury Press, 1980).

Chapter 19
Bernard Lonergan

Kirsten Busch Nielsen

Bernard Lonergan (1904–84) is frequently described as one of the most important Catholic theologians in the twentieth century. This description may or may not be correct, but at any rate it is somewhat imprecise, for although one of Lonergan' ambitions was to modernize theology and bring it up to date, he believed that this project demanded that he went beyond his own period and included history – since contemporary thinking cannot renew itself. New thinking presupposes a tradition. On the one hand, Lonergan could claim that "[a]ny present is powerful in the measure that past achievement lives on in it." On the other hand, he adopted – without contradicting this claim – Pope Leo XIII's dictum that one should increase and perfect the old by means of the new: *vetera novis augere et perficere* (1879). Lonergan thus resolved to develop Neo-Thomism's interpretation of Thomas Aquinas' thinking with the help of Kant's critique of knowledge and in the form of the so-called Transcendental Thomism with which the name of Karl Rahner is also associated. In this way, he resolved to develop the First Vatican Council's intentions with the help of the principles of the Second Vatican Council.

Lonergan made it his life's work to promote a renewal of Catholic theology that consisted in integrating old and new, classical and modern. This meant that his own thinking had an integrative character. He saw not only philosophy and theology as two sides of the same coin; the same applied to metaphysics and criticism, hermeneutics and self-consciousness, culture and religion, rational knowledge and religious experience, objectivity and subjectivity, and insight and conversion. Lonergan took up many of the theological and philosophical questions that confronted his colleagues both inside and outside the Catholic church in the middle and later decades of the twentieth century. Characteristically, he takes up the wide spectrum of challenges in a vigorous effort to make a synthesis and achieve wholeness. Lonergan thought in terms of unity, and this is one reason why his thinking had to go beyond the time in which it came into being.

Bernard Lonergan, SJ – Biography

Lonergan was born in the province of Quebec in Canada in 1904, in a family that had emigrated from Ireland. He attended school in his hometown, Buckingham, and in Montreal. After finishing his schooling in 1922, he decided to enter the Jesuit order. The first four years of training took place in Guelph near Toronto. In the first two years, Lonergan was introduced to the spirituality and tradition of the order; in the next two years, he studied the classical disciplines. This laid the foundations of the religious praxis and the form of life that Lonergan led until he died, almost 80 years old, in 1984. His relationship to the order was subsequently described as a love-hate relationship. His loyalty was tempered by a criticism above all of what he regarded as the poor academic quality of the training and the studies that were required of the young Jesuits.

After his novitiate, Lonergan came to Heythrop College in England, which had just been taken over by the Jesuits. Here he studied philosophy for three years, concluding his studies in 1930 with a degree in Latin, Greek, French, and mathematics from the University of London. He was able to put these qualifications to good use when he worked as a teacher at Loyola College in Montreal for three years, until 1933. It was only after this period that Lonergan underwent the classical Jesuit training, so that he was almost thirty years old when he began a specifically theological study.

After a few months at the Collège de l'Immaculée-Conception in Montreal, Lonergan was sent to the Gregorian University in Rome, where he spent nearly seven years studying theology, with a break of one year's tertianship in Amiens in France (1937–38). In the next two years in Rome (1938–40) – to Lonergan's disappointment, this was to be his last period in the city for now – he prepared his doctoral dissertation, *Gratia operans. A Study of the Speculative Development in the Writings of St. Thomas Aquinas.* After taking his doctorate, he was called back to Canada, not because of theological tasks and challenges that awaited him there, but because of the outbreak of war and the ensuing turbulence.

Until the beginning of 1947, Lonergan worked once more in Montreal, now as a teacher at the Collège de l'Immaculée-Conception where he had earlier studied. From 1947 to 1953, he was professor of theology at the institute in the University of Toronto that is now called Regis College.

In 1953, Lonergan was called back to Rome and lived in post-War Europe. He spent the following 12 years, the most fruitful part of his career in theological and academic terms, at the Gregorian University, where he lectured on classical dogmatic themes, such as Trinitarian theology, until 1965. It was also here that Lonergan returned to the question of human knowledge. This did not entail bidding farewell to his studies of Thomas; on the contrary, Thomas provided the starting point. In *Insight. A Study of Human Understanding,* a book of 800 pages that caused a sensation on its publication in 1957, Lonergan approaches this theme both from the perspective of the theory of consciousness – a "modern" approach in the true meaning of the term – and from a metaphysical perspective. He later said that he wanted to answer, or more correctly, to move his reader to find his or her own answer to three questions: "What am I doing when I am knowing? Why is doing that knowing? What do I know when I do it?" But it was also during his period at the Gregorian University that Lonergan moved into the field where he believed that he could make his own special contribution to the aggiornamento of theology, namely, through the development of a theological method that both made use of and further developed what he had put forward in *Insight*. The leitmotiv up to and including *Insight* had been the question of "the act of human understanding," but now he was guided by the wish to present a methodology that takes its starting point in "what human authenticity is" and that intends to appeal to this authenticity in an intellectual, a moral, and a religious sense.

After an operation for cancer in which one lung was removed, Lonergan's health was permanently weakened. He moved back across the Atlantic and spent the rest of his life in North America. He worked in Toronto until 1975, where he continued the work he had begun in Rome and wrote his second major work, *Method in Theology* (1972). After this, he was Visiting Distinguished Professor at Boston College for eight years, until 1983. During this period, he took up again some of the academic interests of his youth, including the study of economic theory.

Lonergan died in 1984 in Pickering near Toronto, after a return of his serious illness.

Aquinas – The Human Person's Knowledge and Consciousness – Theological Method

Lonergan's thinking has its starting point in an interpretation of Thomas Aquinas. It then moves from the question of "human understanding" to the development of a theory about authenticity as the backbone in a theological method. In order to understand the inner consistency in this thinking, we must return to the theme with which I began: tradition and renewal. When this is taken as the superscription for Lonergan's work, it tells us something about the basic core of his project and about the perspectives he believed this project opened up.

Lonergan's starting point is his conviction that the human person's consciousness works in a dynamic, immutable, and repeated pattern that consists of a number of different functions, which he classifies in *Insight*. In *Method in Theology*, which I follow here, Lonergan affirms that there are four such steps: experience, understanding, reflection or evaluation, and finally, taking a position. Let us hear Lonergan himself on this point, because a quotation can show something that applies to much of his writings. He writes so beautifully and simply that one risks overseeing the complexity and (we must add) the potential problems in his texts:

> There is the *empirical* level on which we sense, perceive, imagine, feel, speak, move. There is an *intellectual* level on which we inquire, come to understand, express what we have understood, work out the presuppositions and implications of our expression. There is the *rational* level on which we reflect, marshal the evidence, pass judgment on the truth or falsity, certainty or probability, of a statement. There is the *responsible* level on which we are concerned with ourselves, our own operations, our goals, and so deliberate about possible courses of action, evaluate them, decide, and carry out our decisions (p. 9).

The specific characteristic of consciousness is precisely that it is *conscious*. It can relate to itself. We not only experience, understand, reflect, and act. We can also experience that we experience, understand, reflect, and take a position. We can understand this, we can reflect on this, and we can take a position with regard to this. Nor does the consciousness work only in the pattern formed by these four functions. We can also look behind each one of the ways in which the consciousness works. If we do so, we learn something about ourselves and something about reality. In his epistemology, Lonergan is a realist or, more precisely, a so-called critical realist. The world in its being *is* as we make it our own in our incessant and unlimited asking. We do not make our own the things as they appear in relation to our own selves, but as they simply *are*, independently of us.

Lonergan emphasizes the dynamism of the consciousness, which continually seeks beyond itself. "One … is not locked up in oneself," Lonergan says. One incessantly transcends oneself by making one's surroundings one's own not only through sense perceptions, but also through an intelligent, reflective, and evaluative asking. For Lonergan, therefore, turning to the subject thus also entails the idea that the subject turns away from himself, that is, a kind of decentering of the subject. This is an aspect that has attracted particular attention for some decades from a so-called post-modern perspective, since it is akin to what theoreticians of subjectivity have identified as a central element in a theory about the subject. When the consciousness seeks beyond its own self in this way, it follows what Lonergan calls "transcendental notions," directives inherent in the consciousness, a sequence of imperatives: "Experience!," "Understand!," "Reflect!," and "Take a position!" Lonergan says that the consciousness works authentically when it listens to these imperatives; if it fails to do so, it degenerates into inauthenticity.

As one may suspect, Lonergan is not particularly interested in negative phenomena such as despair, hopelessness, and lack of love, or falsehood, hatred, and wickedness. Lonergan gathers these aspects of humanity under the heading of "inauthenticity" and describes it as the alienation of the human person from what he or she is meant to be. Accordingly, he writes that "[sin] is alienation from man's authentic being, which is self-transcendence, and sin justifies itself by ideology," while forgiveness and reconciliation mean that the person who is alienated and ideologically hardened is reconciled to his or her "true being."

The theological method that Lonergan develops is built on his analysis of the human consciousness as destined for self-transcendence. Theology, like all the other sciences, must follow the structure indicated by the four different operations of the consciousness. Besides this, Lonergan retains a traditional distinction between so-called indirect and direct theology, mediating and mediated theological thinking, or analytic and systematizing theological thinking. This distinction means that one phase of theology concerns work on data, sources, and texts in their historical genesis and in the meaning that they derive from this genesis, while the other phase concerns the elaboration, formulation, and communication today of theological affirmations and creedal propositions. Lonergan argues that each of these phases includes all the four levels of consciousness that his analysis has uncovered, in such a way that one specific theological element belongs to each level of consciousness, and theology as a whole has a total of eight different special functions. In the first phase, the functions follow the levels of consciousness "upwards," from experience via understanding and reflection to taking a position. In the second phase, the functions follow these levels in the reverse order, from taking a position via reflection and understanding to experience.

In the names that Lonergan gives to these eight functions, we can see traces of the classification of theology into exegesis, history, systematic theology, and practical theology (a classification well known in Scandinavian theology too). Lonergan's eight functions are "research," "interpretation," "history, "dialectic," "foundations," "doctrines," "systematics," and "communications." We should note "foundations," the theological function that deals with the basis of theology. A change takes place here in the matter on which theology works, since it is in "foundations" that "conversion" is "made thematic and explicitly objectified." "Conversion" (a concept to which I shall return) is a religious phenomenon and thus cannot be a part of theology, since one must draw a distinction between religion and theology. Nevertheless, conversion is necessary, in order to give the theologian a qualified, personal relationship to the material on which he or she works. A conclusion is thus drawn in "foundations" from conversion, which is thereby objectified (as Lonergan says). This basis provides guidelines for dealing with the material that the first four functions have registered, interpreted, analyzed historically, and classified. But conversion, as a subjective religious phenomenon, is kept at arm's length from theology here. Accordingly, "foundations" comes not *before*, but *during* the theological work, *after* the investigation of theology's texts and sources from a historical perspective. This is one of the ways in which Lonergan parts company with classical "theological" theology. He believes that fundamental theology, the reflection on the foundation and starting point of theology, can no longer be a set of dogmatic propositions about religion, the church, scripture, and tradition. It must be "the horizon within which the meaning of doctrines can be apprehended." Lonergan is not interested primarily in theological content, but in theology as a process, as something that the theologian *does*. It is through this process that the content comes into the picture.

The decisive point in this holistic view of theology as a science is not whether one can use it as a basis for writing teaching manuals and drawing up plans for study. Lonergan's method is not only a method *for* or *in* theology, and what he writes is not a manual that tells one what to do step by step in order to acquire theological knowledge. Lonergan's method is an expression of his ambition to change theology radically, in such a way that one would now need to speak of theology *as* method.

Lonergan writes that what he wants to bring about is nothing less than the launching of "a second Enlightenment." This entails a criticism of Catholic theology. He asserts that it was only well into the twentieth century that it grasped the challenges of the age of the Enlightenment, and this means that Catholic theology has not yet encountered the modern age. Lonergan's leap forward to the second age of the Enlightenment, which consists in the switch from theology to method, is intended to make it suitable for a world in which one can no longer presuppose a more or less permanent unified culture. The task is to do justice to the new cultural and social contexts of theology, aware of both historical anchoring and cultural plurality. Lonergan holds that this transformation of theology comes about precisely where one goes all the way to the subject, as he himself did in his theological development from his studies of Thomas in the 1930s and 1940s to *Method in Theology,* and where one takes the consciousness' way of working as the starting point for theology – for theology *as* method. If this transformation is allowed to take place, the new age of Enlightenment is realized. And this in turn means that one has transposed the decisive "past achievements" and "vetera" to the present day.

Conversion

If we are to point to one single concept in Lonergan's theological method that is central both to the theory of consciousness (of which the method in general is an expression) and to the method itself in its theological identity – and a concept that is an interesting object of study in its own right – the most obvious candidate is the concept of *conversion.*

The fact that the human person is capable of transcending himself and reaching out to something that lies outside himself does not mean that this actually happens. Lonergan offers a very simple explanation in *Method in Theology* for why what is possible becomes real: "… our capacity for self-transcendence […] becomes an actuality when one falls in love. Then one's being becomes being-in-love" (p. 105). To love means not only reaching out beyond oneself, but *being* out of oneself. It is self-transcendent. In keeping with the fact that there are no limits on the human person's asking – and that this asking, in Lonergan's view, must ultimately be an asking about God, because God is the uttermost and the ultimate – he sees love for God as the uttermost and most comprehensive realization of the human person's possibility of self-transcendence.

We can thus say that there are two elements in Lonergan's philosophy of religion, which underlies the theological method. The first is the human person's fundamental asking and longing. The second is the love of God as the fundamental fulfillment of this longing. This love of God goes in both directions: it is the human person's love for God and God's love for the human person. It is the love for God that the human person bears with all his heart and all his soul and all his mind and all his strength (Lonergan refers here to the quotation from Deuteronomy in Mark 12:30). And it is the love from God that is "poured out into our hearts through the Holy Spirit who is given to us" (Romans 5:5, one of Lonergan's favorite biblical texts).

In short, the human person's asking represents a universal structure that Lonergan maps and describes philosophically and psychologically. It is an essentially human trait to ask the questions in which self-transcendence consists. This universal structure is a possibility that can be realized. And Lonergan holds that it is in fact realized in religious experience, and more precisely in the love of God. Philosophy and theology, anthropology and religion, the universal and the specific merge here. Lonergan also underlines that his view of religious experience as simultaneously universal and specific makes him a theological partner of Ignatius of Loyola ("consolation without cause"), Rudolf Otto ("mysterium fascinans et tremendum"), and Paul Tillich ("ultimate concern"). His kinship to the great nineteenth-century theologian Friedrich Schleiermacher is also obvious.

Lonergan moves here on the border between a general, anthropologically based method and a specific, theologically based method. Ever since the publication of *Method in Theology*, Lonergan's interpreters have debated whether he betrays the purely anthropological element by introducing a specifically theological and Christian element into the method (so that the theological method comes into existence in a kind of "state of emergency"), or whether on the contrary, we must say that in Lonergan's thinking, the anthropological element is "fulfilled in a natural manner" by the theological. I believe that this is not an "either/or," but a "both/and." As I read Lonergan, it is not in the least remarkable that he, as a Roman Catholic theologian who wants to promote renewal, but who also wants to hold fast to the central insights of the tradition (including the dogmatic insights) and who understands himself as "a Roman Catholic with quite conservative views on religion and church doctrines," should establish a parallel between the abstract, general dimension of his method and a concrete theological doctrinal content. As the reader will certainly guess, the position one takes on this question necessarily depends on how one grasps the relationship between the natural knowledge of God and revelation, and in many cases this will also reflect one's confessional starting point. We should add that there are Catholic theologians today who criticize Lonergan on the grounds that his method is *too* abstract, *too* subjective, and therefore *too little* dogmatic.

It is indisputable that Lonergan's argumentation is constructed in such a way that his philosophy of religion contains points of view and concepts that actually belong to theology. One of the most central and frequently used concepts is "conversion."

The background to this concept is the biblical and theological tradition, and Lonergan understands conversion in the New Testament sense, as primarily the conversion to which Jesus calls when he proclaims that God's kingdom is at hand. But conversion is also a concept that Lonergan develops in such a way that it belongs to his modern theory of consciousness that takes shape in the 1960s, and that thus has its place in a transformed, modern theology that he wants to elaborate. He holds that conversion must be seen in connection with the subject and with the subject's experience. In *Insight*, he formulated the idea that all knowledge of the truth, and therefore all objectivity, is the fruit of authentic subjectivity. In *Method in Theology*, he expanded this to include not only intellectual truth, but also moral and religious truth. The subject is not only a subject who knows, but also a subject who makes moral decisions, that is to say, who decides in favor one particular kind of conduct and action vis-à-vis other persons. And this subject is also religious, with a relationship to God. Lonergan employs the concept of conversion in speaking of this fully rounded subjectivity, which is intellectual, moral, and religious.

What is conversion? As I have said, the fact that the human person possesses the capacity for self-transcendence says something only about what is possible for the human person. This mere possibility is realized in love. And Lonergan describes by means of "conversion" how this realization takes place. Conversion is an event, a process of maturing, that results in a very profound change. This change means that one moves in conversion into a new horizon which is completely incompatible with the previous horizon: "the movement into a new horizon involves an about-face [...]. Such an about-face and new beginning is what is meant by a conversion" (pp. 237–8). This movement entails authenticity, because one leaves a horizon that contains incorrect understandings and that blocks the path to self-transcendence.

A Look Ahead

By the time of his death, Lonergan had been awarded honorary doctorates at a large number of universities throughout the world, and his name featured prominently in academic conferences, a series of books, several periodicals, and many research institutes. The *Collected Works of Bernard Lonergan* in 21 volumes bring together most of his writings, both those already published and archive material, and some of his books have been translated into German and Italian. This means that what some of his students have called the "Lonergan movement" was already under way at his death, and it is very active today, nearly 30 years later. But it has not become easier, as time goes by, to point to one area as the focal point of Lonergan's extensive and lifelong involvement as Catholic priest, Jesuit, Thomist, teacher, philosopher, historian of dogma, mediaeval scholar, economist, and critic of culture and society, although (as I have said) all these different facets were exceptionally well integrated in his work.

It is impossible to know whether future generations will still regard Lonergan as one of the most important twentieth-century Catholic theologians. It is of course improper to speak of rivalry in this field, but it seems that it is Karl Rahner – a Jesuit, a transcendental Thomist, a theologian at the Second Vatican Council (like Lonergan himself), who was born and died in the same years as Lonergan – who comes closest to rivaling his importance. It is at any rate certain that Lonergan has a central position in twentieth-century Catholic theology. His *œuvre* is an obvious place to begin the study of twentieth-century theology, because it relates to a number of different currents in Catholicism and discusses both dogmatic and fundamental questions. It is also certain that his future "fate" will depend on whether he continues to live on as a classic in theology – that is to say, as a "past achievement." According to Lonergan's own understanding of the dynamic relationship between tradition and renewal, the correctness of such an evaluation will depend on *future* theological proposals.

Biography

Primary Literature

Lonergan, Bernard J.F., *Insight. A Study of Human Understanding* (Toronto: University of Toronto Press, 1992).
Lonergan, Bernard J.F., *A Second Collection* (Philadelphia: Westminster, 1974).
Lonergan, Bernard J.F., *Method in Theology* (New York: Seabury, 1979).

Lonergan, Bernard J.F., *A Third Collection* (London: Geoffrey Chapman, 1985).
Lonergan, Bernard J.F., *Collection* (Toronto: University of Toronto Press, 1993).
Lonergan, Bernard J.F., *Word and Idea in Aquinas* (Toronto: University of Toronto Press, 1997).
Lonergan, Bernard J.F., *Grace and Freedom. Operative Grace in the Thought of St. Thomas Aquinas* (Toronto: University of Toronto Press, 2000).

Secondary Literature

Crowe, Frederick E., *Lonergan* (London: Geoffrey Chapman, 1972).
Gregson, Vernon (ed.), *The Desires of the Human Heart. An Introduction to the Theology of Bernard Lonergan* (Mahwah: Paulist Press, 1988).
Kanaris, Jim and Mark J. Doorley (eds), *In Deference to the Other: Lonergan and Contemporary Continental Thought* (Albany: University of State New York Press, 2004).
Lamb, Matthew L., 'Lonergan', in *Theologische Realenzyklopädie*, vol. 21, pp. 459–63 (Berlin/NY: de Gruyter, 1991).
McGuckian, Michael C., 'The Role of Faith in Theology: A Critique of Lonergan's Method', *Irish Theological Quarterly*, 71 (2006), 242–59.
Meynell, Hugo A., *An Introduction to the Philosophy of Bernard Lonergan. Second Edition* (Toronto: University of Toronto Press, 1991).
Nielsen, Kirsten Busch, *Teologi og omvendelse. Introduktion til Bernard Lonergan* (Copenhagen: Akademisk Forlag, 1996).
Rende, Michael L., *Lonergan on Conversion. Development of a Notion* (Lanham/London: University Press of America, 1991).

Chapter 20
Hans Urs von Balthasar

Staale Johannes Kristiansen

The Swiss Hans Urs von Balthasar (1905–88) has a central place among the great Catholic theologians of the last century. He taught for some periods at a number of European universities, but unlike the other theologians who left their mark on contemporary Catholic thinking, Balthasar never held an academic professorship in theology. This gave him both the freedom and the time to produce a very remarkable body of theological writing that in many ways went far beyond the boundaries of the academic theology of that period. Balthasar seeks to open up theology for a conversation both with modern philosophy and with the thinking of the church fathers. On this point, he is closest to Jean Daniélou and especially Henri de Lubac, the main representatives of the so-called "new theology" (*la nouvelle théologie*). He was also close to Joseph Ratzinger, who belonged to the next generation, and they published several books together. His encounter with Karl Barth also provided important impulses. Balthasar's most original and creative contribution to twentieth-century theology is his *theological aesthetics*, which he presents as a challenge to theological methodology.

Balthasar's work is marked by an ideal of *holistic theological thinking*. This does not mean that he always writes about the major issues in theology. But when one reads his more detailed studies and his acute analyses of individual theological themes, one always senses that this points outwards to a larger context. As we shall see, this approach draws its inspiration from the Romantic philosophers, from the church fathers who draw on the Alexandrian tradition, and from Saint Thomas Aquinas. This holistic thinking has its foundations in a theology of creation that centers on the Logos – just as in Balthasar's greatest theological model: "In Origen, I discovered the brilliant sense for what is Catholic …" Here, the personal piety nourished by scripture (the Logos – the Word) is combined with an openness to seeking the truth wherever it is to be found (the *logos spermatikos*). Balthasar's theology agreed with the endeavor of the *nouvelle théologie* to open up the church to the world. As de Lubac once said, Balthasar was the theologian who most precisely and comprehensively anticipated all the great themes of the Second Vatican Council. He also became involved in the debate about the reception of the Council, not least when he launched the periodical *Communio* with Ratzinger in 1972, as a counterweight to the *Concilium* of Schillebeeckx, Küng, and Rahner.

Balthasar's *chef d'œuvre*, his trilogy in sixteen volumes, is the only work by a Catholic theologian that can be mentioned in the same breath as Barth's comprehensive *Kirchliche Dogmatik*. But Balthasar can be called a systematic theologian only in a certain sense, since he is always critical of every form of systematization of the Christian revelation, which is always greater and richer than anything that theology can embrace and express. When he brings the thinking of the church fathers, especially their basic apophatic attitude, up to date, he anticipates the post-modern critique of an unambiguous concept of truth – or, to put it more correctly, he renews the classical Christian insight on this point. *The truth is symphonic,* as the title of one of his finest short books affirms. This use of metaphors from music and musical theory is typical of Balthasar, and it too is connected to his ideal of a holistic perspective. Great music, such as the Masses and symphonies of Mozart, has a specific ability to hold a complex plurality together in such a way that the individual voices do not lose their significance and their freedom. At the same time, music reminds us that such visions can be received only in the moment. The notes disappear in the very instant in which they are heard, but they hold together a unique wholeness in their temporary expression. In this way, music provides a model that Balthasar attempts to attain in his own theological style.

Biography, Intellectual Training, and Early Writings

Hans Urs von Balthasar was born in a pious Catholic family in the Swiss town of Lucerne on August 12, 1905. His own accounts of his life give us a picture of a childhood and adolescence completely surrounded by music; he showed a special sensitivity to music and an ability to memorize at an early age. Both his talent as a pianist and his first book, *Die Entwicklung der musikalischen Idee. Versuch einer Synthese der Musik* (*The Development of the idea of Music. Attempt at a Synthesis of Music*), 1925, might have suggested that music would be his vocation in life, but when he came to choose the path for his life during his studies, he devoted himself to the study of German literature and studied at the universities in Vienna, Berlin, and Zurich. In 1928, he took his doctorate with the dissertation *Geschichte des eschatologischen Problems in der modernen deutschen Literatur* (*History of the Eschatological Problems in Modern German Literature*). This was published in 1930. It was reissued in three volumes, with revisions and deeper studies of individual themes, in 1937–39, under the title *Apokalypse der deutschen Seele*. Both the early book on music and the revised doctoral dissertation provide important approach routes to Balthasar's later theological and philosophical thinking. The fascination he shows here for the Romantic thinkers was to follow him all his life, but with the passing of time, their religious philosophy was more strongly balanced by a fundamental incarnational principle that is characteristic of von Balthasar's theology.[1]

---

[1] See Aidan Nichols, *Scattering the Seed. A Guide through Balthasars's Writings on Philosophy and the Arts* (London, 2006).

The tendencies to disintegration in European intellectual life at this time offered an interesting humus for new thinking and new interconnections, and the young Balthasar profited from this during his studies. He heard Romano Guardini's lectures on Kierkegaard in Berlin and became a friend of Freud's pupil Rudolf Allers, who had parted company with Freudian reductionism and converted to Catholicism. In 1929, shortly after his mother's early death, Balthasar entered the Jesuit order. He began his two-year novitiate in southern Germany; one of his fellow novices was Alois Grillmeier. This was followed by two years studying philosophy at Pullach near Munich – a study he later described as a "desert of neo-scholasticism." However, it was in Munich that he met Erich Przywara, who became Balthasar's mentor: "He made you learn the scholastic philosophy with an open, free-style approach, and then go on to modern philosophy, to compare Augustine and Thomas with Hegel, Scheler, and Heidegger." Przywara's thinking about the *analogia entis* was especially important for Balthasar. Next came four years studying theology at Forvière near Lyons. Even here in France, Balthasar and the other students heard little about the *nouvelle théologie* and the burgeoning renaissance of interest in the liturgy and theology of the early church. The exception among the teachers was Henri de Lubac, who showed the students the path that led "behind the scholastic teaching-matter to the church fathers." This does not mean a general rejection of the scholastic thinkers of the middle ages, where both de Lubac and Balthasar find many of their highest theological ideals realized. It means first and foremost a criticism of the rigid methods of neo-scholasticism and the theology of the handbooks, which did not work historically with the source texts from the early church and the middle ages, but simply copied the one-sided readings of Saint Thomas from the previous century. De Lubac's book *Catholicisme* was a breath of fresh air for Balthasar, who felt a strong need to bring the insights from thinkers of the past up to date in a dialogue with modern thinking. In this book, he encountered "Catholicism in its fullness," completely free of the fear of modernity that was prevalent at that time. Balthasar worked closely together with his fellow students Henri Bouillard and Jean Daniélou. All three were fired with enthusiasm for de Lubac's vision of the church's youthful openness and creativity. De Lubac made his patristic library available to the students: "So while the others went off to play football, Daniélou, Bouillard, and I myself, and a few others with us, sat down with Origen, Gregory of Nyssa, and Maximus ..." Balthasar used earplugs during the other lectures, in order to be able to read through all the works of Augustine. Together with Augustine, it was precisely the trio of Origen, Saint Gregory, and Saint Maximus who remained his favorite theologians. They are present to varying degrees in everything he wrote.

Balthasar wrote important monographs on his three favorite theologians. He wrote two early articles on Origen in 1936–37, later collected in *Parole et mystère chez Origène* (*Word and Mystery in Origen*, 1957).[2] This work was an important contribution to the rehabilitation of Origen, which was promoted above all by de Lubac, Daniélou, and Balthasar, and which has had a great influence on recent patristic research. Balthasar himself claimed that of all his books, the anthology *Origenes, Geist und Feuer* (*Origen. Spirit and Fire*) was the one he looked back on with the greatest joy. This translation, with an introduction to Origen, was first published in 1938, and then in a revised edition in 1956. His monograph on Gregory of Nyssa, *Présence et Pensée* (*Presence and Thought*), was published in 1942, and his monograph on Maximus, *Kosmische Liturgie* (*Cosmic Liturgy*), came in 1941 (expanded edition, 1961). Another important input he received in France came from the fiction of Charles Péguy, Georges Bernanos, and Paul Claudel. He later wrote a large-scale monograph on Bernanos (*Gelebte Kirche: Bernanos*, 1954/1988. English: *Bernanos: An Ecclesial Existence*), and translated both him and Claudel into German.

After finishing his studies with the licentiate in theology and in philosophy, Balthasar was allowed to choose between a professorship at the Gregorian University in Rome, where they wanted him to set up an institute for ecumenical theology, and the position of student chaplain in Basle. It was typical of the man that he chose the latter. As a student chaplain, he also taught in a number of theological fields, and the list of guest lecturers invited by him indicates the renewal that was beginning in this milieu: Hugo Rahner, Martin Buber, Karl Rahner, Yves Congar, Henri de Lubac, and many others. In this period, Balthasar also made contact with Karl Barth, who was working at the theological faculty in Basle. He held a lengthy series of lectures on Barth's theology in 1949–50, which led to the book *Karl Barth. Darstellung und Deutung seiner Theologie* (*The Theology of Karl Barth*), 1951. Barth himself heard these lectures and took a positive attitude to the younger Catholic theologian's approach to his theology. This book shows how fascinated Balthasar was by Barth's Christocentric thinking. It also contains important theological discussions of nature and grace. After Przywara and de Lubac, Barth was the third great source of inspiration for Balthasar, although he had clear objections to certain parts of Barth's theology. Their shared love and knowledge of Mozart played an important role in their long-lasting friendship.

The meeting with the doctor and mystic Adrienne von Speyr was even more significant. Balthasar affirmed that his work must not be understood separately from hers. They founded the Johannes Community, a secular institute, in 1945, and the Johannes Verlag was set up at about the same time. When the Jesuit order refused his request to continue his work with Adrienne von Speyr and the Johannes Community as a Jesuit, he decided – with great regret – to leave the order. When he did so in 1950, this put him in a difficult position vis-à-vis the church hierarchy. Initially, no bishop was willing to allow Balthasar to celebrate Mass (with one single exception). He became even more suspect because of his links to the theologians associated with

---

[2] Hans Urs von Balthasar, *Parole et Mystère chez Origène* (Paris, 1957).

the so-called *nouvelle théologie*. It was in this period that Balthasar realized that the church's true vocation is not the introverted centering on the clergy, but the laity and the world.

In the following years, Balthasar held lectures at many European universities. He turned down a number of professorships, including the invitation to succeed Guardini in Munich. His nomadic life led to exhaustion and several periods of grave illness. The suspicions about Balthasar in these years meant that he was not called as a *peritus* (theological expert) to the Second Vatican Council in 1962 – unlike de Lubac, Daniélou, Rahner, Ratzinger, and Congar. We should note the obedience that Balthasar displayed in this period. One of the Lutheran observers at the Council, George A. Lindbeck, has described how deeply he was impressed by Congar, de Lubac, and the other theological specialists: several of them had been muzzled for years before the Council, but they had waited patiently for the renewal that was now established by Pope John XXIII.[3] Balthasar displayed the same patience, and he too was rehabilitated after the Council. He was appointed a member of the papal International Theological Commission when it was founded in 1969, and remained a member until his death. He was awarded the Paul VI prize for theology in 1984. He was John Paul II's favorite theologian, and the pope honored him in 1988 by creating him cardinal. Balthasar died two days before the ceremonies in Rome, while he was preparing to celebrate Mass on the morning of June 26, 1988.

A Further Overview of His Writings

The literary part of Balthasar's life's work includes 85 books, more than five 500 articles, and nearly 100 translations of other authors.[4] His bibliography alone runs to 200 pages in book form.

I have already mentioned several of the most important works from the 1930s and 1940s. From early in the 1940s, von Speyr's inspiration can be clearly seen in Balthasar's theology, both in the fundamentally Trinitarian vision and in the emphasis on the Marian element – an integrated Mariology.[5] He wrote several monographs in the 1950s, on Barth, Bernanos, Reinhold Schneider, and Martin Buber. His work on Teresa of Lisieux (1950), which shows his incipient fascination with Carmelite spirituality, is also important for his more mature christological thinking.

---

[3] George Weigel, 'Re-Viewing Vatican II', *First Things*, December (1994). Also published on http://www.firstthings.com/article/2007/01/re-viewing-vatican-iian-interview-with-george-a-lindbeck-2 (accessed February 22, 2012).

[4] Henrici, Peter: 'Hans Urs von Balthasar: A Sketch of his Life", in David L. Schindler (ed.), *Hans Urs von Balthasar: His Life and Work* (San Francisco, 1991), 31.

[5] See Andrew Louth, 'Hans Urs von Balthasar,' in Alistair McGrath (ed.), *Modern Christian Thought* (Oxford, 1993) and Brendon Leahy's thorough discussion of von Balthasar's Marian theology in Brendon Leahy, *The Marian Profile – in the Ecclesiology of Hans Urs von Balthasar* (London: New City, 2000).

In different ways, all the earliest works point ahead to Balthasar's *chef d'œuvre* in the trilogy *Herrlichkeit. Eine theologische Ästhetik* (*Glory of the Lord. A Theological Aesthetics*), 1961–69, *Theodramatik* (*Theo-Drama: Theological Dramatic Theory*), 1971–83, and *Theologik* (*Theo-logic*), 1985–87, where he seeks to re-establish the unity between the three classical transcendentals: *the beautiful, the good, and the true*. He worked on this project from early in the 1960s until a few years before his death. Other important theological work from the same period is collected in the five volumes of his *Skizzen zur Theologie* (*Explorations in Theology*), 1960–86.

It is difficult to systematize the voluminous body of writings from Balthasar's pen. The Johannes Verlag makes the following suggestion for a thematic classification of his writings:[6] (a) the trilogy; (b) *Skizzen zur Theologie*; (c) the monographs; (d) expositions of scripture; (e) presentations of the church fathers; (f) contemplative texts; (g) "Mary – church"; (h) "Christ today"; (i) the understanding of time and the last times; (j) commentaries on his own writings; (k) the collected edition of his early writings. The most important works under point (i), on the understanding of time and the last times, are *Theologie der Geschichte* (*A Theology of History*), 1950/1959, *Das Ganze im Fragment* (*Man in History*) 1963, and *Theologie der drei Tage* (*Mysterium Paschale*), 1969. Under point (k), we should – in addition to his early work on music and his doctoral dissertation – mention his Nietzsche anthology (1942), and the extensive essay 'Von den Aufgaben der katholischen Philosophie in der Zeit' ('On the Tasks of Catholic Philosophy in Our Time'), 1946.

The Main Ideas in Balthasar's Writings

"The Truth is Symphonic"

The whole of Balthasar's theological thinking is based on a sensitivity towards truth as something mystical. This sensitivity has its origins in the early influence of the Romantic religious philosophy on Balthasar, but even more strongly in the writings of the church fathers. Another important factor is his recognition of the ability of music to gather complex voices around a unified counterpoint, and the parallels he draws from this. What, then, does his celebrated affirmation that *the truth is symphonic* mean? Balthasar sees revelation as a form in which the triune God, who is perfect unity, moves out into plurality in order to communicate with the human person, who belongs to the created plurality. The truth of revelation (in the work of creation, in God's actions in history, and in the word of scripture) is therefore plural, but at the same time unified (one), because it has its source in God himself. Revelation is the one truth spread out in plurality, in order to gather that which is spread back into unity with God. But "the truth is too overwhelming to be captured in a net of finite concepts." This means that truth can never be adequately revealed in the world by means of

---

[6] http://www.johannes-verlag.de/jh_hans_werke_t.htm (accessed February 22, 2012).

uniform expressions.[7] (Here, Balthasar is much indebted to the thinking of Dionysius the Areopagite in *On the Divine Names*.) Truth's unity in plurality has to be expressed symphonically and polyphonically. In order for revelation to be "comprehensible," we must listen to the whole polyphony of revelation, says Balthasar. At the same time, he affirms that the revelation is not a sweet harmony. It is dramatic, like all great music. Its unity is not obvious, so truth can never be grasped in its fullness by any human being. It is inexhaustible.[8] These perspectives are presented in *Die Wahrheit ist symphonisch* (*The Truth is Symphonic: Aspects of Christian Pluralism*), and are developed in *Theologik* (*Theo-logics*).

Die Wahrheit ist symphonisch was written in 1972, but this line of thinking is already set out in the monograph on Karl Barth, twelve years before the Second Vatican Council, which was an implicit criticism of the systematic theology of the church theologians at that time. This book also shows how Balthasar anticipated the dynamic thinking about the nature of truth that we find in the conciliar texts about the church's relationship to the world (*Gaudium et spes*), ecumenism (*Unitatis redintegratio*), and the relationship to the world religions (*Nostra aetate*). The truth that the church serves can never be a closed system: the church is open to the truth, wherever it may be found. This does not mean that everything is fluid, for the church administers the special revelation and is guided by the tradition. But Balthasar attempts to show that the patristic thinking about truth – with reference especially to Augustine, Maximus, and Origen (whom he also calls a "father of the church") – was marked by an awareness of the *semper major* of the revelation. In a section that bears the imprint of Maximus' theology about the relationship between the Logos and the created *logoi*, he writes:

> This means that the content in revelation, as the highest ratio – the personal, divine Logos himself – needs all the forms of worldly logoi of the truth in order to present its inexhaustible fullness: the abstract and general just as much as the concrete and individual. Theology must work from below, where, as Newman loved to show, all the truths in culture and in the people are gathered up by the church and made accessible to theology.[9]

In other passages too, Balthasar clearly takes up Newman's idea of an organic perspective on doctrinal development. He holds fast to the idea of a *philosophia perennis*, a truth that is unchanged through the ages. But this *philosophia perennis* is understood as a *form* that lives and therefore develops, and that makes itself available for the form of revelation. Balthasar makes "form" (*Gestalt*) a key concept in his approach to the history of thinking. Like beauty, truth too has a "history of styles." The great philosophies come into existence through dialogue with one another, writes Balthasar,

---

[7] Hans Urs von Balthasar, *Karl Barth. Darstellung und Deutung seiner Theologie* (Einsiedeln, 1951), p. 251.

[8] Hans Urs von Balthasar, *Die Wahrheit ist symphonisch. Aspekte des christlichen Pluralismus* (Einsiedeln, 1972), p. 42.

[9] Balthasar, *Karl Barth*, pp. 264–5.

through agreement but also through marking boundaries. And it is through this dialogue that new forms of thought are shaped. Plato presupposes both Parmenides and Heraclitus; Aristotle and the Stoics are unthinkable without Plato; and Plotinus creates a synthesis of them all. Balthasar says that this dialogue has nothing to do with eclecticism: this is "humanity, as it thinks symphonically, polyphonically."[10] He sees Thomas Aquinas as "the most extreme example" in this history. Thomas' originality consists in the elaboration of a universal form that integrated all the preceding intellectual traditions. Great thinking is comparable to great architecture, which does not copy the form of the past, but develops that which is still of value in the tradition. Great thinkers ("the great architects of the spirit") characteristically give a new form to the truth that does not change in its essence. This applies to theological thinkers too, since theology must make use of all the various philosophies and forms of thought "in order to be able to express the fullness in revelation."[11] Balthasar gives a positive description of Roman Catholic theology by agreeing with Karl Barth's critical assessment of it as "dialectical through and through."

Balthasar does not in any way dismiss the clarity in the church's dogmas, but he maintains that these must be read in the light of the church's mystical experience. He points out that the theologians who elaborated the church's fundamental dogmas, such as the Cappadocians or Maximus the Confessor, always combined positive language with a fundamental apophatic insight. This was why they were so careful (in principle) to employ scripture's own formulations. Besides this, the dogmatic formulations were understood in the context of the liturgy, as a part of the hymnic, doxological language. Balthasar's emphasis on mystical theology is connected to his insight that revelation is essentially infinite and mystical, just like God himself. All divine revelation is linked to that which is concrete; this is especially true of the incarnation. The truth is personal – "I am the truth" (John 14:6) – and can therefore ultimately be known only in a personal dialogue with the Word, the Logos. But God's Logos also works in all that is created, in all living structures, in all cultures.

Theology and Spirituality

Balthasar's theology of truth must be seen in connection with his wish for a revitalization of the link between theology and spirituality. This is one of the keys that unlock his theological thinking.[12] He traces the loss of the link back to the separation between scholastic and monastic theology, while at the same time pointing to the "scholastic" thinkers and mystics, from Saint Bonaventure and Saint Thomas onwards, who succeeded in holding theology and spirituality together. The break in the link has led to an impoverishment of both theology and spirituality. One the one hand, the language of theology has lost its ability to express the "existential" character of

---

[10] Balthasar, *Die Wahrheit ist symphonisch*, p. 42.
[11] Balthasar, *Karl Barth*, p. 264.
[12] See Mark McIntosh's discussion of this theme in Mark A. McIntosh, *Christology from within. Spirituality and the Incarnation in Hans Urs von Balthasar* (Notre Dame and London, 2000).

the mystery of faith, and on the other, modern mystical authors lack the interpretative framework in Trinitarian theology for their experiences. As a theologian, Balthasar points out above all the dangers entailed by "regarding historical revelation as an event in the past, as something given, rather than as something that is continually happening, something that must be listened to and followed."[13] In his revitalization of this attitude to revelation, Balthasar points to the church fathers and Saint Ignatius of Loyola as the foremost models. Origen and the Cappadocians are the best example of a theology that is able to express personal experience in a dogmatic language, in an existential-objective synthesis. Accordingly, he sees spirituality as "the subjective aspect of dogmatic theology, the Word of God as it is received by the bride and grows in her."[14] It is precisely in this context that Mariology is given a central place in Balthasar's theological thinking, along with reflection on the saints as "the real theologians," those who allow the Word to dwell in them.

Mark A. McIntosh has shown how Balthasar seeks to bring the doctrine of the incarnation up to date in the light of these perspectives. Balthasar upholds a typically "high Christology." He always emphasizes the eternal nature of the Son as the Logos of God. But he avoids presenting Christology as a "Christology from above" with its starting point in Christ's divine nature. He holds fast to the concrete element as the starting point for knowledge, and he follows Origen in seeing Jesus' humanity as the revelation of his divine nature. Balthasar develops here the Christology of Chalcedon, the Christology of Saint Maximus with its Trinitarian foundation, and the mysticism of obedience in Saint Ignatius of Loyola. In his book on Maximus the Confessor, Balthasar underlines what he regards as Maximus' existentialist innovation in Christology. The unity in the person of Christ is not seen as a unity of natures, but as a unity on the level of existence: the divine and the human in Christ cooperate in a unique form of the gift of self, obedience, and love. It is this that characterizes the Son's *form of existence*, as distinct from those of the Spirit and the Father.[15] This insight is developed in Balthasar's *Theodramatik* and is found in a more compact form in *Theologie der Geschichte* (1959), where he writes: "The incarnation is not the umpteenth presentation of a tragedy that was already laid down in the archives of eternity. It is a totally original event [...]."[16] The incarnation was a real drama, where everything was at stake: everything depended on the Son's total gift of himself to the Father. It is in this way that the original sin of the human person is overcome; Balthasar takes up the interpretation of the Fall by Clement and Irenaeus as a refusal to wait for God's hour, as an untimely snatching of the gift that God had wanted to give when the human person was mature enough to receive it. The Son's gift of himself is the complete opposite of this: "The form of existence of the Son, which makes him the Son from

---

[13] Hans Urs von Balthasar, "Theologie und Heiligkeit," in *Verbum Caro (Skizzen zur Theologie I)* (Einsiedeln, 1960), p. 211.
[14] Ibid.
[15] McIntosh, *Christology from Within*, 39ff.
[16] Hans Urs von Balthasar, *Theologie der Geschichte* (Einsiedeln, 1950, new edition 1959), p. 17.

all eternity (John 17:5), is the uninterrupted receiving of all that he is, of his own self, from the Father [...]."[17]

In this way, Balthasar combines Maximus' christological insight with Saint Ignatius' spiritual directive about the imitation of Christ's descent. The believer becomes one with God through entrusting himself to the obedience that Christ showed in the form of his existence, which is expressed concretely in the Gospel narratives and is understood as a continuous event in the present. Balthasar thus attempts to get behind the metaphysical language in the classical Christology and Trinitarian doctrine by transposing the focus from an essentialistic to an actualistic terminology. As with other important theologians in the last century (Pannenberg, Moltmann), the starting point of the Christology he writes is the Jesus-event, but he links this indissolubly to the mystics' reception of Jesus' life as something that takes place in the present. Faith is thus seen primarily as a reception of God's deed in Christ. At the same time, this receptivity has its origin in the human person's longing to be united with God, the natural longing for God. The human person must open himself freely in love vis-à-vis God. But there is no contradiction here, since Balthasar is developing de Lubac's reminder that classical Catholic theology sees nature as sustained by grace: the creation always "has its ground in the Logos, or more exactly, in Jesus Christ."[18]

The Trilogy, with the Emphasis on Theological Aesthetics

Hans Urs von Balthasar's *chef d'œuvre* is the voluminous trilogy *Herrlichkeit. Eine theologische Ästhetik* (1961–69), *Theodramatik* (1971–83), and *Theologik* (1985–87), a theology about *the beautiful, the good, and the true.* In many respects, his theological aesthetics is his most important work. He maintains that God does not come to the human person first and foremost as the great teacher (the true) or as the redeemer (the good). God comes above all in order to give us himself, as a revelation and an irradiation of his Trinitarian love. God teaches us the truth and carries out the work of salvation *in order to* bring the human person back to unity with himself, to make us sharers in the life of the Trinity. It is above all beauty that kindles in the human person this longing to be united to God, this longing for him who is the source of all earthly beauty. In his theological aesthetics, however, Balthasar is not primarily interested in *the beautiful* in the modern philosophical sense of this term, but in the theological meaning of beauty: beauty as *Herrlichkeit*, "glory." This glory finds expression in a paradoxical manner, both in the harmony of the work of creation and in the beauty of the kenosis, that is to say, in the Son's descent and in his handing over of himself on the cross.

Balthasar himself disagreed with the assertion that the first part of the trilogy was his true life's work – for theological aesthetics points out beyond itself (as beauty always does) to "theodramatics" (the good). He says that the manifestation of God, the theophany, is only the prelude to the most central event, the historical drama

---

[17] Ibid., p. 12.
[18] Balthasar, *Karl Barth*, 297.

into which God himself enters ("while at the same time remaining behind the stage") and in which we all must take part. God does not only want to be known and contemplated: his actions prepare the ground for a response on our part. Drawing on the insight he had gained through his study of Western fiction and drama (not least, Greek tragedy), Balthasar attempts in the *Theodramatik* to demonstrate the dramatic character of revelation and the response it demands from us. In Christ, God gives himself to the human person in order to kindle our love. The core in the drama of creation and redemption is the encounter between the infinite divine freedom and the limited human freedom. In this perspective, Balthasar elaborates christological, ecclesiological, and liturgical interpretations of the relationship between grace and free will, or between the Bridegroom and the bride. We can sense behind much of Balthasar's *magnum opus* Origen's bridal mysticism and his theology of God's pedagogy (*paideusis*). His dramatical perspective has interesting parallels to Hans-Georg Gadamer's philosophy of art in the first and paradigmatic part of *Truth and Method*.[19]

Theologik discusses the possibilities of communicating in human language this existential drama that takes place in scripture, and especially in the life of Jesus. Balthasar works here with a specifically Christian understanding of truth or the true. Since God has spoken his Word in time, the core in *Theologik* is a *Christologik* that focuses on the theology of the Logos. The fact that God created the world through the Logos makes a theological language possible. But the Logos is always greater than the words.

The main concern of the trilogy is thus the indissoluble *unity* between the beautiful, the good, and the true. This is why he calls the trilogy a *triptych* in which each of the three main pictures has its own meaning, but the pictures must be seen as a unity, if one is truly to grasp the iconographic program.[20] However, the sequence in which the trilogy was published is not a matter of chance. It was precisely the desire to rehabilitate the unity between the three transcendentals that led him to write the theological aesthetics first:

> Beauty shall be our first word here. Beauty is the last thing the thinking intellect dares to approach, for it is only beauty that dances like an ungovernable irradiation around the double constellation of the true and the good and their inseparable relationship to each other.[21]

In its approach to the Christian revelation, most modern theology seems to have lost sight of the aesthetic dimension and to have concentrated instead on the ethical

---

[19] See the comparative study of these two thinkers in Jason Paul Bourgeois, *The Aesthetic Hermeneutics of Hans-Georg Gadamer and Hans Urs von Balthasar* (New York, 2007).

[20] See the *Prolegomena* to *Theodramatik*, and his retrospective *Rechenschaft* (1965), also published with other similar essays in Hans Urs von Balthasar, *Mein Werk – Durchblicke* (Einsiedeln and Freiburg, 1990). English: *My Work in Retrospect* (San Francisco, 1993).

[21] Hans Urs von Balthasar, *Herrlichkeit. Eine theologische Ästhetik* I (Einsiedeln, 1961), p. 16.

and logical dimensions. Theological methodology must take into consideration the fact that these three are indissolubly interwoven in the biblical understanding of reality. Balthasar sees the integration of theological aesthetics in theology as the only appropriate method and approach to the fullness of revelation. There is an inherent link between the three transcendentals, a relationship in which the loss of one always leads to an impoverishment of the other two: "In a world without beauty [...] the good too loses its attractiveness." The same thing occurs with our relationship to the truth, when this is no longer seen as beautiful. Balthasar identifies the broken link to the beautiful as the root of the inner separation between the good and the true in modern thinking. His wide-ranging work traces the history of the "alienated beauty," focusing on those pre-Christian and Christian philosophers, theologians, and authors who hold fast to the integration of the beautiful in art and thinking. The principal emphasis is on Plotinus and Vergil, the church fathers Saint Irenaeus, Saint Augustine, and Dionysius, and on Saint Anselm, Saint Bonaventure, Dante, Saint John of the Cross, Pascal, Hamann, Soloviev, Hopkins, and Péguy.

While the beautiful has been dismissed as mere appearance in Modernity, Balthasar's understanding of beauty is linked directly to Saint Thomas Aquinas, who speaks of the beautiful as *both* form (*forma*) and glory (*splendor*). These two concepts play an important role throughout Balthasar's writings, not only in the theological-aesthetical texts, but also in Christology. The idea of the *form-character of the Christian revelation* is absolutely central.[22] The climax of revelation – the incarnation – is a drama in which God himself becomes *form* (or assumes form into himself) for the sake of the human person. The concrete appearance is decisive here. In the Son, we see God himself; but Christ also conceals something of his own glory. Here, once again, we sense the underlying importance of Origen and of his insight that God reveals as much as the individual person can receive at any particular time. For Balthasar, beauty is an appearance, but at the same time, it is more: it is a sign that always points towards something deeper. The beautiful is the bearer of "a hidden spiritual deep dimension" that is expressed in the sensuous realm, as he writes later on in an article about art and preaching.[23]

In Christ, we see God's own form, God's beauty (*Gestalt Gottes/forma Dei*). But can one say that Jesus was beautiful during his earthly life? Balthasar reports the patristic discussion of this question.[24] With reference to Psalm 45:2 ("You are the fairest of the children of men"), Saint John Chrysostom and Saint Jerome emphasize Jesus' physical beauty; but with reference to Isaiah 53:2 ("He had no glorious form"), Saint Justin, Clement of Alexandria, Tertullian, and Saint Ambrose reject this. For Saint Augustine, there is no contradiction here. Drawing on an idea of Origen, he writes that the one

---

[22] Aidan Nichols calls this "the master idea" in von Balthasar's theological aesthetics: Nichols, *Scattering the Seed*, 61.

[23] Hans Urs von Balthasar, 'Christliche Kunst und Verkündigung, in Johannes Feiner and Magnus Löhrer (eds), *Mysterium Salutis: Grundriss heilsgeschichtlicher Dogmatik*, I (Einsiedeln, 1965), pp. 708–26.

[24] Hans Urs von Balthasar, *Herrlichkeit. Eine theologische Ästhetik* I (Einsiedeln, 1961), p. 136f.

who loves Christ, and sees him with pure eyes, beholds the inner beauty of Jesus, the invisible beauty in the visible.[25] This brings us to the essence of Balthasar's own understanding of beauty as glory. According to the Gospel of John, God's glory reveals itself on the cross, in Christ's sacrifice for all. It is here that the human person sees God's own beauty in Christ – but in the form of kenosis, the form of descent. God reveals his being through the sacrificial love, the beauty of kenosis. Love is always beautiful – even our own weak attempts to imitate Jesus' life – because it goes out beyond itself. And in this way, love binds all things together.

When Balthasar forms his trilogy on the transcendentals in this sequence, beginning with the beautiful, he reverses Kant's sequence in his critical studies of the reason, ethics, and aesthetics. Kant perfects the autonomization and the downplaying of aesthetics which were already widespread in his days. In keeping with this downplaying, recent thinkers have simplified the problem of knowledge, so that it becomes a question of analyzing individual phenomena. Balthasar pleads for a renewal of an aesthetic way of thinking (in a manner that is clearly parallel to Hans-Georg Gadamer's philosophy of art). Confronted with the "symphony of truth" in the world and in the special revelation (scripture, the incarnation), theology can learn from the experience people have when they encounter a work of art. What happens when a piece of music or a picture captivates us and touches our soul? A complexity of meaning is embraced in one expression, in one single moment. We are given an intuitive knowledge of reality itself, of *the true*, when the form in its appearance shows itself as beautiful. The form awakens a well-being in us that reminds us that reality in its essence (despite all falsehood and wickedness) is both good and true. Reality is infinitely valuable.[26] Here, we glimpse one of several interesting parallels between Balthasar's theological aesthetics and the existentialistic philosophy of art of the Neo-Thomist Jacques Maritain.

Balthasar wants to challenge theology's optimistic confidence in approaching the divine by means of concepts and analyses. In one of his retrospective essays, he writes that he has attempted to construct a philosophy and a theology that take their starting point in an analogy: not in abstract being, but in Being as this finds expression in a concrete form. In addition to the more direct inspiration from the Thomist thinkers Erich Przywara and Gustav Siewerth, we can sense here the link to Martin Heidegger's existentialist philosophy, although Balthasar also disagrees with Heidegger on central points.[27] Balthasar writes that a newborn baby can come to self-knowledge only through love, through the smile from its mother. Through this smile, reality opens up for the child, revealing four things:

---

[25] Enarrationes in Psalmos 127.8. See also Commentary on 1 John, tr. 9.9.
[26] See Balthasar, *Herrlichkeit* I, 111.
[27] See Oliver Davies, 'The Theological Aesthetics,' in Oakes, T. and Moss, D. (eds), *The Cambridge Companion to Hans Urs von Balthasar* (Cambridge, 2004), pp. 137ff; and Fergus Kerr, 'Stories of Being', in Fergus Kerr, *After Aquinas. Versions of Thomism* (Oxford, 2002), pp. 73–96.

(1) that he is united in love with its mother, even if he is another than his mother. Accordingly, all Being is one. (2) That this love is good. Accordingly, all Being is good. (3) That this love is true. Accordingly, all Being is true. And (4) that this love kindles joy. Accordingly, all Being is beautiful.[28]

Balthasar is making an anti-Kantian point: "The revelation of existence, of Being, is meaningful only if we grasp in the appearance the essence (*Ding an sich*) that manifests itself. The little child attains knowledge, not through a pure appearance, but from the mother herself." This analogy reminds us that the human person exists only in "interpersonal dialogue." The Word that creates and sustains the world speaks many times and in many ways. Theology's methodology is the conversation with this Word, which is the path to the ultimate goal, union with the triune God.

Influence

In many ways, Hans Urs von Balthasar's theology breaks through the boundaries of the perspectives of modern contemporary theology. His thinking also confuses those who are eager to classify theologians into categories along an ecclesial right-left axis. Before the Council, the traditionalists dismissed him along with the main representatives of the *nouvelle théologie*, the pioneering theologians who turned out to stand for a much more comprehensive renewal of the tradition than the traditionalists themselves, since they went behind the one-dimensional interpretation of Saint Thomas and placed him within a richer Catholic tradition. At the same time, they listened to the truth where it could be found, even outside the church – and not least, in modern philosophy. After the Council, Balthasar was honored as one of the most important forerunners of the conciliar renewal, but he disappointed many of those who wanted to radicalize the Council when he cautioned against positing an antithesis between ecclesial renewal and classical Christian doctrine (for example, on the question of women's ordination). But those who wanted to claim him as a champion of conservative theology were startled when he published a new book on the *apokatastasis*, the "restoration of all things." Although he did not defend this doctrine, he pleaded that it was important that theological thinking should bear the imprint of the *hope* of universal salvation.

Balthasar is becoming increasingly important for Catholic theology today, not least through the reception of his work in the English-speaking world. It is interesting, though not entirely unproblematic, to note that many speak of a decisive parting of the ways between the theologies of Rahner and Balthasar after the Second Vatican Council. It is true that in today's dialogue between theology and late-modern philosophy, Balthasar seems to have much more to say than the theologians associated with *Concilium*. Still, one should not forget that Balthasar initially expected great things of Rahner's work for the renewal of Catholic theology, although he later became very

---

[28] Hans Urs von Balthasar, *Mein Werk – Durchblicke*, 92--3.

critical of the premises of Rahner's thinking. On the basis of a distinction drawn by Balthasar himself, it has been said that Rahner follows Kant and the scholastics, while Balthasar follows Goethe and the church fathers.

Balthasar is read and discussed outside Catholic academic circles too. Many Protestant theologians find here a Catholic theology with direct relevance to the discourse in their own tradition. His book about Karl Barth and his conversation with him remain highly relevant. This encounter in a theological dialogue between two of the most prominent representatives of their traditions is a unique event in twentieth-century theology, and their conversation had considerable influence on Balthasar's elaboration of a late-modern Catholic thinking. What would the result have been, if he had also been able to work more closely with one of the most prominent contemporary Orthodox theologians, such as Vladimir Lossky or Dumitru Stăniloae?

Balthasar is the founder of modern theological aesthetics, and his thinking in this field bears clear fruit in recent theological discourse, far beyond Catholic circles. For example, he plays an important role for the founders of the English *Radical Orthodoxy* movement. As we have seen, he anticipates much of the post-modern criticism of an unambiguous concept of truth. His idea of reality (truth) and revelation as an inexhaustible mystery demands an expectant openness both in relation to the truth that is given to us and in relation to those truths whose deepest meaning God is continually disclosing. If one sees so-called post-modern thinking as an initial breach with the reductionism of modernity (that Balthasar himself traced back all the way to scholasticism), there is much to indicate that the coming decades will see a more balanced and mature implementation in theology of this breach. Balthasar's work will play an important role in the Catholic elaboration of a more holistic post-modern thinking – as we already see in a recent philosopher like Jean-Luc Marion.

Bibliography

Primary Literature

For a complete bibliography, see *Hans Urs von Balthasar. Bibliographie 1925–2005* (Einsiedeln: Johannes Verlag, 2005).

Herrlichkeit. Eine theologische Ästhetik (Einsiedeln: Johannes Verlag, 1961–69), English: *The Glory of the Lord: A Theological Aesthetics* (Edinburgh: T&T Clark, 1982–91).
Theodramatik (Einsiedeln: Johannes Verlag, 1971–83). English: *Theo-Drama: Theological Dramatic Theory* (San Francisco: Ignatius Press, 1988–94).
Theologik (Einsiedeln: Johannes Verlag, 1985–87). English: *Theo-logic* (San Francisco: Ignatius Press, 2000–2005).
Die Entwicklung der musikalischen Idee. Versuch einer Synthese der Musik (Braunschweig: Fritz Bartels Verlag, 1925) (*The Development of the Idea of Music. Attempt at a Synthesis of Music*).

Apokalypse der deutschen Seele. Studien zu einer Lehre von letzten Haltungen (Salzburg: A. Pustet, 1937–39). (*Apocalypse of the German Soul*).

Glaubhaft ist nur Liebe (Einsiedeln: Johannes Verlag, 1963). English: *Love Alone is Credible* (San Francisco: Ignatius Press, 2004).

Karl Barth. Darstellung und Deutung seiner Theologie (Einsiedeln: Johannes Verlag, 1951). English: *The Theology of Karl Barth* (San Francisco: Ignatius Press, 1992).

Kosmische Liturgie: Höhe und Krise des griechischen Weltbilds bei Maximus Confessor (Freiburg: Herder, 1941). English: *Cosmic Liturgy. The Universe According to Maximus the Confessor* (San Francisco: Ignatius Press, 2003).

Mein Werk – Durchblicke (Einsiedeln and Freiburg: Johannes Verlag, 1990). English: *My Work in Retrospect* (San Francisco: Ignatius Press, 1993).

Origenes, Geist und Feuer. Ein Aufbau aus seinen Schriften, übersetzt und mit einer Einführung (Salzburg: Otto Müller Verlag, 1938/1956). English: *Origen. Spirit and Fire. A Thematic Anthology of His Writings* (Edinburgh: T&T Clark, 1984).

Parole et Mystère chez Origène. Paris: Cerf, 1957. (Word and Mystery in Origen).

Présence et pensée. Essai sur la philosophie religieuse de Grégoire de Nysse (Paris: Beauchesne, 1942). English: *Presence and Thought. An Essay on the Religious Philosophy of Gregory of Nyssa* (San Francisco: Ignatius Press, 1995).

Skizzen zur Theologie (5 vols) (Einsiedeln: Johannes Verlag, 1960–86). English: *Explorations in Theology*, 4 vols (San Francisco: Ignatius Press, 1989–95).

Theologie der drei Tage (Einsiedeln: Johannes Verlag, 1969). English: *Mysterium Paschale* (San Francisco: Ignatius Press, 2000).

Theologie der Geschichte (Einsiedeln: Johannes Verlag, 1950, new edition 1959). English: *A Theology of History* (San Francisco: Ignatius Press, 1994).

Die Wahrheit ist symphonisch. Aspekte des christlichen Pluralismus (Einsiedeln: Johannes Verlag, 1972) English: *The Truth is Symphonic: Aspects of Christian Pluralism* (San Francisco: Ignatius Press, 1988).

'Von den Aufgaben der katholischen Philosophie in der Zeit', in *Annalen der Philosophischen Gesellschaft Innerschweiz*, 3. Jahrg., Nr. 2/3 (Dez./Jan. 1946–47). English: 'On the Tasks of Catholic Philosophy in Our Time', in *Communio*, 20 (1993), 147–87.

'Theologie und Heiligkeit,' in *Verbum Caro (Skizzen zur Theologie I)* (Einsiedeln: Johannes Verlag, 1960). English: 'Theology and Sanctity', in *Explorations in Theology*, 4 (The Word Made Flesh) (San Francisco: Ignatius Press, 1989–95).

'Christliche Kunst und Verkündigung, in Feiner, Johannes and Löhrer, Magnus (eds), *Mysterium Salutis: Grundriss heilsgeschichtlicher Dogmatik*, I (Einsiedeln: Benziger, 1965), 708–26.

Secondary Literature

Bourgeois, Jason Paul, *The Aesthetic Hermeneutics of Hans-Georg Gadamer and Hans Urs von Balthasar* (New York: Peter Lang 2007).

Davies, Oliver, 'The Theological Aesthetics,' in Oakes, T. and Moss, D. (eds), *The Cambridge Companion to Hans Urs von Balthasar* (Cambridge: Cambridge University Press, 2004).

Henrici, Peter, "Hans Urs von Balthasar," in Walter Kasper (ed.), *Lexikon für Theologie und Kirche* (Freiburg: Herder, 2006).

Henrici, Peter, 'Hans Urs von Balthasar: A Sketch of his Life", in David L. Schindler (ed.), *Hans Urs von Balthasar: His Life and Work* (San Francisco: Ignatius Press, 1991), 7–43.

Kerr, Fergus, *After Aquinas. Versions of Thomism* (Oxford: Blackwell Publishing, 2002), 73–96.

Leahy, Brendan, *The Marian Profile – in the Ecclesiology of Hans Urs von Balthasar* (London: New City, 2000).

Louth, Andrew, "Hans Urs von Balthasar," in Alistair McGrath (ed.), *Modern Christian Thought* (Oxford: Blackwell Publishing, 1993).

McIntosh, Mark A., *Christology from Within. Spirituality and the Incarnation in Hans Urs von Balthasar* (Notre Dame and London: University of Notre Dame Press, 2000).

Nichols, Aidan, *The Word Has Been Abroad: A Guide Through Balthasar's Aesthetics* (Edinburgh: T&T Clark, 1998).

Nichols, Aidan, *Divine Fruitfulness: A Guide to Balthasar's Theology Beyond the Trilogy* (Washington: Catholic University of America Press, 2007).

Nichols, Aidan, *Scattering the Seed. A Guide through Balthasar's Early Writings on Philosophy and the Arts* (London and New York: T&T Clark, 2006).

Oakes, Edward T., *Pattern of Redemption. The Theology of Hans Urs von Balthasar* (New York: Continuum, 1994).

Oakes, T. and Moss, D., *The Cambridge Companion to Hans Urs von Balthasar* (Cambridge: Cambridge University Press, 2004).

Quash, Ben: "Hans Urs von Balthasar," in David F. Ford (ed.), *The Modern Theologians* (Oxford: Blackwell Publishing, 2005).

Schindler, David L., *Hans Urs von Balthasar – His Life and Work* (San Francisco: Ignatius Press, 1991).

Weigel, George, 'Re-Viewing Vatican II ', *First Things*, December (1994).

Chapter 21
Jean Daniélou

Aidan Nichols

Jean Guenolé Marie Daniélou was born on 14 May 1905 into a cultured family closely linked to the elites of early twentieth-century France. His father, Charles, a politician of the Centre Left, several times achieved ministerial office in the administrations of Aristide Briand. The elder Daniélou's Republicanism and disapproval of clerical interventions in politics made him, for the period, an unlikely believer. Daniélou's mother, Madeleine, a more traditional Catholic, was a professional educationalist, much involved in projects to secure the entry of women into higher learning. Daniélou deemed her religious faith, which was both intelligent and deeply spiritual, the chief formative influence on his own.[1] The attraction to her of Ignatian spirituality heralded her eldest son's eventual entry into the Society of Jesus.[2]

His childhood was divided between homes in Paris and Brittany. To the latter, with its wild Atlantic coastline, he ascribed his love of nature, and sense of the disclosure of God through the cosmos. Also owed to the Breton contribution to his upbringing was his respect for popular Catholicism. A 'militant' Gospel – the reference might be to 'Catholic Action', or, later, 'political theology' – was not, he thought, the only way of embodying the evangelical impulse. Christianity 'expressed in the sacralisation of the chief moments of existence' – the traditional way of life of Breton fisherfolk and farmers – was equally valid.

In his university years, spent in Paris, Daniélou was caught up in the literary renaissance, both general and more specifically Catholic, of the 1920s, an 'epoch of *détente* and cultural enchantment' after the sufferings of the First World War. In this period he acquired his extremely rich literary culture, as well as his principal orientations in the intellectual life at large. At the Sorbonne, his love affair with the Hellenic world began. This would bear fruit in his studies of not only the Hellenistic Jewish philosopher Philo but also – and more importantly for theology – the Greek Fathers and ecclesiastical writers, notably Gregory of Nyssa and Origen of Alexandria, much of whose approach to mystical theology and biblical exegesis he retained. He was deeply influenced by the writings of the poet and critic Charles Péguy, who confirmed him in his primarily *symbolic rather than conceptual* approach to the

---

[1] For his spirituality, see the notebooks published 20 years after his death: Marie-Joséphe Rondeau (ed.), *Jean Daniélou. Carnets spirituels* (Paris, 1993).
[2] Jean Daniélou, *Et qui est mon Prochain? Mémoires* (Paris, 1974), p. 48.

expression of faith.[3] He ascribed to Péguy his continuing confidence in the value of historic culture, as well as a distrust of appeals to 'progress', and, more positively, the notion of hope as 'surmounted despair'. A still closer spiritual affinity linked him, he considered, to the novelist François Mauriac, whose principal theological emphasis lay not, as with Péguy, on the virtues (whether natural or supernatural), but on the dialectic of sin and grace.

In this formative period of his life, Daniélou also admired the Neo-Thomist layman Jacques Maritain for his refined spiritual-intellectual personality, which found expression in such programmatic statements for Catholic life as *Art et Scolastique*, an essay on the revival of, especially, the visual arts, and *La Primauté du spirituel*, a counterblast to the rallying cry, 'Politics first!', of the nationalist-monarchist movement *Action française*. (In the ultra-activist years immediately following the Second Vatican Council Daniélou looked back on this work as a plea for putting contemplation prior to action.) But he could not stomach the systematic quality of Maritain's Thomism – or indeed any *thorough-going* Thomism for that matter. All systematisations, he considered, distorted the real. Unfortunately, he failed to notice that the role of Aristotelianism in Aquinas is to concentrate attention on the native intelligibility *precisely of the real*, rather than to stimulate construction of conceptual systems.

In point of fact, Daniélou would maintain, despite himself, some clear emphases from the Thomist tradition. In epistemology, he treated – as did the Thomists – the conformity of mind with being as a sine qua non for the validity of thought. In theology, he accepted Thomas's account of the inter-relation of the *via affirmativa* and the *via negativa* in the knowledge of God – and indeed much else besides. His argument for divine being as infinite personality was sheer Maritain. But his opposition to any notion of Thomism as *the* Catholic philosophy and theology to the effective exclusion of all others would play a major part in the Church conflict over 'la nouvelle théologie' in the 1930s, 1940s and 1950s.[4]

Daniélou considered his personal philosophical sympathies to lie as much or more with the vitalist philosopher Henri Bergson and the phenomenologist Max Scheler. He certainly profited from Bergson's reflections on memory and time, and Scheler's notions of love and sympathy. More broadly he appealed to these figures to license the intuitive element in his thinking.

Among lesser known luminaries of the French Catholic revival who played a part in Daniélou's life and education as a layman, it is well worth mentioning the Egyptian-born Dominican Orientalist Jean de Menasce. Daniélou was deeply interested in the ancient religions of the Near and Middle East; his most original scholarly contributions, which place early Jewish Christianity in a wider setting, bear witness to this lasting passion.

It was, then, an unusually well-formed young Catholic with an exceptional religious culture who in 1929 entered the novitiate of the Society of Jesus at Laval

---

[3] He expressed his continuing attachment to poetry as a tool of meaning in a work co-authored as *Actualité de la Poésie: études, témoignages, poèmes, extraits et documents* (Paris, 1956).

[4] Aidan Nichols, OP, 'Thomism and the *nouvelle théologie*', The Thomist, 64 (2000), 1–19.

(north-west France). His basic orientation to the Church Fathers was already in place, as was his concept of his mission as an intellectual-spiritual apostolate. Not that the lengthy Jesuit training left no mark. To his years as a Jesuit ordinand on Jersey (in the Channel Islands) he ascribed the acquisition of a discipline of prayer and, through the reading of Emmanuel Mounier's journal *Esprit*, a higher estimate of the importance of economic, social and political issues than of speculatively philosophical ones. The period 1936 to 1939, which included his priesting in 1938, were spent at Fourvières, the house erected in Lyons to give young French Jesuits closer contact with contemporary currents of thought. He was in full sympathy with this project. An earlier generation of Francophone Jesuit stars – Pierre Rousselot, Joseph Maréchal – by dancing pirouettes, however brilliant, on the Neo-Scholastic stage had left their secular contemporaries unmoved. Daniélou had a tendency to be over-impressed at first by the positive elements in innovatory thinking, and only subsequently discover the negative accompaniments (examples from the history of his mind are Jean-Paul Sartre and Karl Marx). So he was delighted to be in close proximity to such fellow-Jesuits as Pierre Teilhard de Chardin, who was seeking a natural scientific version of the Christian narrative, from the origins to the Eschaton, and Gaston Fessard, who was investigating the usefulness to theology of a Hegelian analysis of history.

It is notable that both of these examples concern giving a greater place than had Scholasticism to the dimension of *temporality* – for this would be the key to Daniélou's own most distinctive theologising. As he wrote, 'For me, the theology of history is the most important aspect of contemporary theology'. However, neither Teilhard nor Fessard but Henri de Lubac was his real master. De Lubac consolidated Daniélou's conviction that patristic *ressourcement* should be Catholic theology's most important *form*. De Lubac also gave him the idea that the theology of history should be its most important *content*. In an encomium of de Lubac in his posthumously published *Mémoires* Daniélou declared:

> [A] theology of history allows us to gather together, while ordering in a hierarchy, the various currents that criss-cross religious history, to make a synthesis of them, a vision of the whole, by integrating into theology the dimension of temporality which all the great modern systems have included in one way or another.[5]

That is what made de Lubac's thought for Catholics the most 'important' of the twentieth century, the most potent for the formation of a truly 'actual' theological synthesis.

The pupil praised the master for the revival of the fourfold sense of Scripture in de Lubac's *Exégèse mediévale*, a crucial confirmation of Daniélou's own intuition of the importance of typology. He shared de Lubac's emphasis on the need to understand modern thought, as represented (for de Lubac) by the trio of Nietzsche, Marx and Kierkegaard. Of those three, the frequent recurrence of the term 'existence', or 'mystery of existence', in Daniélou's theological work strongly suggests that the

---

[5] Daniélou, *Et qui est mon Prochain?*, p. 91.

influence of Kierkegaard had touched him, in part no doubt indirectly through the Catholic Existentialist Gabriel Marcel.[6] He admired de Lubac's studies of Eastern religion – chiefly Buddhism, whereas Daniélou was more interested in Hinduism. He was not in the least troubled by de Lubac's (as Daniélou judged) total lack of any systematic impulse. Quite rightly, de Lubac preferred to disengage, rather, the most genial insights of past and present. Far in the future, in the conflictual situation of the post-Conciliar Church, another ground for rejoicing came to be de Lubac's alignment with Hans Urs von Balthasar's journal *Communio* – which possessed, so Daniélou would comment, 'all that is solid in present-day theology in a common line' joining de Lubac, Louis Bouyer, and Daniélou himself.

The influences of childhood, precocious young manhood, and de Lubac's powerful example furnished Daniélou with the principal convictions he took to the Parisian Institut Catholique when at the young age of 37 he was presented to the chair of the History of Christianity, thus following in the footsteps of the great historian of the early Church, Louis Duchesne, his predecessor but one. Daniélou's patristic monographs, and the massive 'History of Christian Doctrine before the Council of Nicaea', as well as his panoramic study of the early Church co-authored with the historian of ancient philosophy and culture Henri Marrou, would fully justify his selection to this prestigious post. The fine Festschrift entitled *Epektasis* bore witness to the esteem in which other patristic scholars held him.[7]

Outside of his professional remit he also gave a great deal of time to dialogue with representatives of other religions (and none), through such means as the ecumenical review *Dieu Vivant* and the missiologically oriented 'Cercle Saint Jean-Baptiste' (both in Paris), as well as, internationally, the high-powered 'Rencontres de Florence', and the Eranos colloquia organised by an admirer of C.G. Jung's in Canton Ticino (Switzerland). These in no way diminished his sense of the uniqueness of Christianity, and the claims of Catholic orthodoxy. But they served to expand his sense of the variety of idioms in which Gospel and doctrine can be expressed, as well as the possibility of acquiring nuggets of real gold from cultures beyond the Church's limits.

He would remain at the Institut Catholique for 25 years – with intervals of enforced absence through his dangerous work for the French Resistance during the Second World War, as well as, on a very different note, Roman sojourns for the sessions of the Second Vatican Council, 1962–5, where he acted as a *peritus* or theological expert. His influence on the Conciliar texts may be found in the doctrine of revelation in *Dei Verbum*, the Dogmatic Constitution on Revelation, in the overall caste of *Nostra Aetate*, the Declaration on the Relation of the Church to Non-Christian Religions,

---

[6] Daniélou could be treated, with de Lubac, as marrying the neo-patristic orientation of 'la nouvelle théologie' with 'existential theology': thus Dieter Hoffmann-Axthelm, *Anschauung und Begriff: zur historischen Einordnung von 'Nouvelle Théologie' und 'Existentialer Theologie'* (Munich, 1973).

[7] J. Fontaine and C. Kanengiesser (eds), *Epektasis. Mélanges patristiques offers au cardinal Jean Daniélou* (Paris, 1972).

and in the eschatological emphases which sit in somewhat uneasy tension with the 'theology of earthly realities' in the Pastoral Constitution on the Church in the Modern World, *Gaudium et spes*.

Only his appointment as a cardinal by Pope Paul VI in 1969 brought his university-level teaching to an end – whereupon his encounters with others became more irregular but not necessarily less frequent. He developed a surprising talent – and popularity – in television interviews and debates, at a time when the foundations of both Church and State in France were shaking. And he continued to animate groups of students, declaring to critics of his acceptance of Episcopal orders that, indeed, despite their denials, he had 'a church': not a diocese (as they would have preferred) but something equally important – 'les jeunes': the Parisian young. Much of the last period of his writing was concerned to reinstate credal and ethical certainties, and a proper sense of the rightful authority of the Church, in a French Catholicism profoundly troubled by the post-Conciliar crisis. He was elected to membership of the *Académie Française* – for the 'immortals' of high culture – in November 1972.

Jean Daniélou died on 20 May 1974 – in the unlikely setting of a brothel which the septuagenarian was visiting in the course of his priestly ministrations. It was a supreme monument to the total freedom of movement Paul VI had given him as a cardinal. It was also an indication of a certain lack of prudence. He had always said and done what he thought right, regardless of reactions. The following year, a 'Société des Amis du Cardinal Jean Daniélou' was founded in Paris, with an annual bulletin, to 'promote the study of his writings and the continuance of his influence'.[8]

Theological Vision and Method

Daniélou assisted students of his thought by directing them for its essentials to his first book, *Le signe du Temple*, written as early as 1941. All his other books, he opined, were no more than commentaries on this opusculum. Given the ambitious character of the dossiers that make up his history of Christian doctrine until the Council of Nicaea, it is hard to take this judgement literally. But nonetheless, for what concerns the great lines of his own thinking – and that would include his instinctive manner of organising the content of the texts left by ancient authorities in the Church, the comment is fair enough. As he himself (again) remarked, his patristic monographs, which are, so far as bulk is concerned, his chief output, were not written merely as 'scientific' analysis – though they are also that – but in order to express his own concerns. In this, as in all his theological writing, he took it for granted that Scripture and Tradition constitute what he called the 'regulative basis to which the theologian must always refer on pain of making arbitrary constructions'.

Le signe du Temple identifies itself as a theology of history which considers a succession of religious epochs, each of which is characterised by a distinct modality

---

[8] [Anon.], 'Daniélou, Jean', in F.L. Cross and E.A. Livingstone (eds), *The Oxford Dictionary of the Christian Church* (Oxford, 1997, 3rd edn), p. 450.

of divine presence. To some degree, these epochal modes of presence overlap yet they also constitute a narrative which runs from God the Alpha to God the Omega. The divine 'temple' is in turn cosmic (in nature); Jewish (in Jerusalem); 'Christic' (in the Word incarnate); ecclesial (in the Church, and most notably in the Holy Eucharist), and eschatological (at the End). In some versions of this list Daniélou will also include – in connexion with the ecclesial 'temple' – a *mystical* condition of the polyvalent divine indwelling. This is the temple of God in the hearts of redeemed human beings, justified and sanctified by the blood of the Lamb.

Two key presuppositions help explain Daniélou's presentation of the God–world relationship in the various modes of its realisation. The *first* concerns what he liked to call *correspondances*, 'correspondences'. In symbolic thinking, by a poetic grasp of the real, certain affinities declare themselves for the purpose of articulating the sacred. Granted Daniélou's literary sensitivity, one can detect here an influence from the Symbolist aesthetic influential among late nineteenth and early twentieth century French poets. But how was that aesthetic set theologically to use? At one level, these correspondences concern the harmony which governs the inter-relations of the economy of creation with that of salvation. Some features of the cosmos constitute natural epiphanies which provide a 'vocabulary' – both ontic and, through the mediation of human interpreters, linguistic – for the saving events of the divine redemptive plan. Obvious examples are the meteoreological phenomena associated with the Sinai revelation in the book of Exodus where a storm expresses the concentrated intensity of God's existence, or, in the same book, the vagaries of the flood-waters at the Red Sea which entail death by drowning for oppressors, a way of escape for victims.

At another level, these 'correspondences' concern the inter-relations of events within the divine plan to secure creation definitively through redeeming it in Jesus Christ and by his Spirit. That can be so because the same Saviour God – gradually revealed as Trinity – is at work at all the stages of the economy, in both Old and New Testaments. As a close student of Jewish Christianity it was the latter which especially concerned Daniélou though, to be sure, the principles of biblical typology are common to writers in the non-Semitic traditions of Greek East and Latin West as well.

Daniélou was convinced that the typological exegesis of Scripture was no mere patristic (and mediaeval) curiosity, which subsequently, with the advent of the historical-critical method, the Church, heaving a sigh of relief, could lay aside. On the contrary: whatever gains the historical-critical method might bring, the Church's fundamental way of reading the Scriptures must remain that of the Fathers. Only the typological method allows the unity of the Testaments to be concretely affirmed: this Daniélou would seek to show in his study of that subject, *Sacramentum futuri*. Only that same method can validate the use of Scripture in the traditional Liturgies: this was the burden of his *Bible et Liturgie*, a work so appreciated by the Eastern Orthodox as to be translated into modern Greek. Only an openness to typology, again, enables twentieth-century scholars, and a wider public, to rediscover the earliest 'reception' of the Gospel which took place in the world of early Jewish Christianity, long lost to consciousness in the Great Church but thanks to the energy of researchers and sometimes their good luck, now available again through the meticulous re-composition of a jigsaw. Thus the theology of highly condensed symbols – the palm and the crown, living water, Elijah's chariot, the star of Jacob and the like – he explored in *Les Symboles chrétiens primitifs*. Only typology – this was his conviction – allows Scripture to interpret Scripture through the hermeneutical complementarity of distinct but 'corresponding' events and texts. Where typology is suppressed, the art of the Church ceases to be legible, and the capacity to write theology in the spirit of the Fathers withers away. From his standpoint, Daniélou can pay the Fathers no greater compliment than when he writes, 'They had an extraordinary perception of the sacred symphony'.[9]

The *second* key presupposition which throws light on Daniélou's rich account of divine modes of presence in the world does not concern this organic inter-relating of distinguishable economies (creation and salvation) or differing phases of saving time (whether the time of 'holy pagans', or the times of the Old Covenant and the New) by the invocation of such instructive 'correspondences'. The second key presupposition entails a contrasting insistence on maintaining due distinctions where levels of reality and manners of investigation are concerned.

Daniélou was very taken by the seventeenth-century philosopher and mathematician Blaise Pascal's plural 'orders' of the real and of appropriate enquiry therein. In the *Pensées*, Pascal had applied to physical, rational and cordial understanding – senses, reason, heart – a notion he had earlier worked out in his mathematical writings. In mathematics, lines, squares and cubes cannot be added together, since – so Pascal explained – they belong to different orders. Pascal himself made different applications of the orders doctrine. Similarly, Daniélou's concern with multi-dimensionality is constant in emphasis but flexible in application.

The scheme Daniélou most characteristically offers is a triple one which takes the form: cosmos, interiority, revelation – each irreducible and with approaches suited to itself.

> My universe is ... multidimensional. I respect the immense richness of the real. Only the distinction of orders allows one to explore the real in its totality, an inexhaustible reality, moreover, in whose discovery we can always advance.[10]

The scientific exploration of the cosmos discloses the real – stupendously so – in the organisation of matter. Art, literature and philosophy, by contrast, show us the 'inner man' – another world of inexhaustible richness, though sadly impoverished by those who measure the human through quantitative analysis. And finally there is revelation: the order of 'charity and prophecy, the universe of the divine dimension of man and history as that is in its essence revealed in Christ'. Here too there are riches beyond words.

---

[9] *Et qui est mon Prochain?*, p. 135.
[10] Ibid., p. 122.

In his philosophical essay collection *Scandaleuse Vérité* Daniélou compares these three orders to Teilhard's biosphere, noosphere and Christosphere, while insisting – presumably against Teilhard – that there is 'no passing from one to another of these', since each is an 'irreducible universe'. No process of evolution joins them, but rather passages to different planes. On the level of the noosphere, personalist humanism can be as much a prison as is materialism on the level of the biosphere. Here too man must go beyond himself to discover the divine Spirit who not only energises one's existence in creation but raises it above itself in salvation and theosis.

The Pascalian doctrine of the multiple orders of the real, and their cognitive instruments, enabled Daniélou to distinguish between various strata in the realm of being. So far as the interpretation of the Bible is concerned, the natural-scientific, historical-humane and revelatory-salvific orders and the intellectual disciplines which appropriate these are simply not identical. Theologically synthetic thinking can respect natural scientific considerations and humane historiography as aids in its enquiry, but it need not be confined to their methods. Nor indeed should it, since the disclosure of the real represented by the cosmic and human orders can and does serve revelation as *Hilfsmittel*: auxiliaries to the unique self-disclosure of the Uncreated.

Daniélou found this principle of the distinction of orders helpful more widely in the making of Catholic theology. It served above all to differentiate the *various modes of divine presence* to human understanding. And that interest in the modalities of God's presence to humanity, as *Le signe du Temple* and all Daniélou's subsequent writing bears witness, constitutes the heart of his theological sensibility and thought.

Particular Theological Themes

How did Daniélou's theological vision and method lead him to treat particular theological themes? The centre of Christian theology is the mystery of God in Jesus Christ as revealed in the history of salvation. Daniélou's awareness of the wider world of human religion in its cosmic setting in creation will prevent him from treating these topics in a spirit of revelational positivism. Yet at the same time, he will insist that only a theology of history can do full justice to a revelation expressed in saving events.

God

Daniélou's *de Deo*, entitled *Dieu et nous*, proposes three basic ways of knowing God: via 'the religions', via philosophy and via faith – though to do justice to the last of these he finds he must add a trio of supplementary essays, which take as their subject the different manners in which, for faith, God makes himself known in Christ, in the Church Christ founded, and in the mystical witnesses to Christian living. Among these various modalities Daniélou is concerned to establish *order*: to show how religions and philosophies, Old and New Testaments, theology and mysticism, have a proper relation to the knowledge of God and so to each other.

On *the religions*: he treats a general disclosure of God through creation and human conscience as furnishing the valid elements in the world-religions beyond Israel and the Church. Though in the post-lapsarian situation cosmic religion tends to be vitiated by three profound errors – polytheism, pantheism and dualism – the Letter to the Romans (1:20) expects a genuine knowledge of God to issue from what Daniélou terms, with the Rumanian anthropologist of religion Mircea Eliade, 'hierophanies' in the natural order. Cosmic religions possess 'theologies' in the form of myths, most of which are cosmogonic in object: they bear on the primal origin of all the essential realities of life, and of the world as a whole. Their natural mysticism may be considered the interior manifestation of cosmic process. The symbolism in which they convey their sense of the sacred can serve the historic revelation, but the grave misconceptions about the God–world relation into which paganism falls shows the need for a new divine initiative in saving history.

Daniélou detected a similar ambivalence in *philosophy*. Rational argument about God's existence and nature is necessary: without it, man falls prey to obscurantism and superstition. But both Gregory of Nyssa in the East and Thomas Aquinas in the West insist on the limitations of a purely rational approach to the mystery of God: philosophy can affirm God's existence but it transgresses its own limits if it claims a complete grasp of the intelligibility of his being. Appeal to analogy-thinking is in place here – but it does not suppress the character of this issue as a 'limit-problem'. Such 'problems' (other examples of this kind of aporia are freedom and suffering) compel man towards conversion, since they engage his existence. Daniélou stresses the importance of a philosophical opening towards the idea of divine personality, and thus communicativity and self-giving in God. Without that, there can be no existential encounter such as biblical revelation posits.

The God of *faith* is the same God yet known now not as a transcendent principle behind the world but as actively involved in it through unique interventions in its course, the sum-total of which constitutes a 'plan': the design of 'sacred history', the 'history of salvation'. Insofar as these events are, on their empirical side, humanly chronicled, they can be investigated by the historical method. But their divine character is known only through revelation to intelligence in its supernaturally elevated prophetic mode, as the mind rests on the self-evidence – Daniélou emphasises the rock-like nature of this, signalled by the Hebrew term for truth, *emeth* – of the Word of God. In a series of *covenants* – Daniélou accepts from the Protestant exegete Walter Eichrodt the importance of this concept for the Old (and indeed the New) Testament, but emphasises, with the Catholic doctors and mystics, its *nuptial* quality – that Word discloses not only what is, the divine being, but also what shall be, the future realisation of the promises of God to his beloved corporate human partner. The Word received in faith invites human persons to draw near to the sovereign reality which is God's holiness, at once his beauty and his ethical demandingness.

This divine self-revelation climaxes in Jesus Christ as the disclosure of God the Holy Trinity. Daniélou takes as axiomatic a principle proposed by St Gregory Nazianzen in his fifth Theological Oration: revelation of the Persons is by stages. In the Old Testament, revelation is primarily of the Father: appropriately, since the literature of Israel deals chiefly with origination (the origin of creation, of election, of mission). That is so even if there is also in its pages a 'dark' disclosure of the Word and the Spirit who theophanise mysteriously in the events of creation and salvation. In that manner – here it is Irenaeus of Lyons who is key for Daniélou – the way is prepared by mutual 'accommodation' of God and man as they 'get used to' one another – for the manifestation of the Son in the New Testament and of the Spirit as that Testament gives way to the time of the Church.

In the remainder of *Dieu et nous* Daniélou asks how, in the Church, which is the fruit of the Ascension, harvested at Pentecost, the theologian and, equally or more importantly, the ordinary believer – can be aware of this, the sole veridical, interpretation of the biblical data. His answer is: through the Church's Tradition which was responsible for the written deposit of the biblical witness in the first place. And here discerning the truth expressed in the documents is one thing; articulating it in a variety of idioms is another. Thus Daniélou justifies his writing a history of Christian doctrine in its Semitic, Hellenic and Latin phases – to which he hopes to see added at some future date of Catholicism's story an Indian, and a Chinese. With his debt to such mystical theologians as Gregory of Nyssa, he does not hold, however, that Christian God-talk is limited to learned forms of retrieval of a past revelation. By sheer faith, beyond all concepts, the individual soul can seize the mysterious divine reality through the communication God makes of himself *hic et nunc* in the new creation of baptismal grace, which is a sharing in the triune life on the basis of the death and resurrection of Christ.

Christ

If Daniélou's Christology in *Dieu et nous* is really a Triadology, that is because he planned to write a *De Christo* in the form of a companion volume, which appeared in 1961 as *Approches du Christ*.

In that work, Daniélou affirms the real, but limited, value of the historical-critical approach to Jesus of Nazareth. He places it at the head of his account, arguing ingeniously that, since the entry of the Word into the empirical order by birth as Jesus in a Palestinian-Jewish environment at the time of the Roman principate was *also* the beginning of his salvific manifestation, mentioning first the order of investigative historical knowing suits likewise the order (in a quite different sense of the word 'order') of the saving events.

In the Gospels, just as the Infancy Narratives use Jewish literary techniques to pattern their materials by reference to Old Testament examples, so the rest of the text stylises, possibly through liturgical use, the common tradition of the primitive community going back to the apostles. 'The Gospels are the outward expression of what for the apostles Jesus *was*.' This is why they are necessarily testimony and not dispassionate biography. In entering his historical milieu in all its particularity, Jesus also overflowed it, surpassing the limits of his period and country in such a way as to fulfil the image of God in man. *Ecce homo*! People of every sort identify with him and his message. Modern ideologies of freedom and the person are, remarks Daniélou in a fashion that looks ahead to the late twentieth-century Anglo-Saxon movement 'Radical Orthodoxy', merely 'secularized "left-overs"' of the Sermon on the Mount.

The question ultimately raised by Jesus's personality and behaviour is whether his transcendence of his time and place does not indicate as well a unique identification with the creative Word, the *archetypal* Image of God. Jesus's re-working of the Torah, including the Sabbath, which for Jews, was inscribed in the very structure of creation,[11] his assumption of the divine prerogative of forgiveness, his self-identification with the Temple, the place of the *Shekinah*, his Lordship over death as shown in the raising of Lazarus, and his emphasis on a unique I – different from the modes of 'normal' prophetic utterance and coming to its climax in the 'I Am' sayings of St John's Gospel: all these amount convergently to a claim to divinity which can only be explained by saying he was mad, bad or God.

In retrospect, the Pauline literature – emphasised by Daniélou partly because he treats Johannine thought as an echo of the *ipsissima vox* of Jesus himself and not as theological reflection – finds in the mission, the sacrificial death and the Resurrection of Jesus the Word the final irrevocable fulfilment of the divine promises. As the One 'to whom the world belongs [Christ] re-takes possession of it ... in such a way as to establish the world in its final condition, thus fulfilling the divine design'. In a theology of the mysteries of the life of Christ indebted to the Fathers and the Liturgy, the Incarnation and Baptism of the Lord are essential to this, as are his Passion, death and descent into Hell. Above all, it is the Resurrection, the consummation of the Incarnation, the outcome of the Cross – it means the ending of man's slavery to death and sin, and the communication to him of an endless share in divine life – that is the central moment of human history. Here there can be absolutely no comparison with other religious founders or thinkers, a claim the Pascalian distinction of orders helps to articulate. Daniélou contrasts the 'order of wisdom', to which, say, Gautama and Socrates, belong, with the 'order of holiness' where Christ is situated. He 'is not primarily a great religious personality, He is primarily an act of God among men'.

The events in which that divine act was manifested are not only world-changing. They are also world-fulfilling. Thus the Ascension, towards which the Resurrection leads, is the climax of cosmic process: 'not only does the glorified Christ become the Head of the Church which is his Body, but he becomes the Lord of all creation'. There can be – here we have Daniélou's eschatological emphasis – 'nothing beyond' this. This is, after all, the new and eternal Covenant. To these events, and to this goal, the Old Testament points forward by means of its 'prophecies and types'. Within the specific order of the revelation to Israel, something, however, could not be foreseen. It was not to be predicted that the fulfilment of the expected divine act of deliverance and consummation, on the one hand, and, on the other, of the coming of a human Messiah to be its instrument, would coincide. Jesus Christ is God now turned towards man, and man now turned towards God, and these two movements are one.

---

[11] One might refer here to Daniélou's study of the opening chapters of Genesis: *Au commencement: Génèse I-III* (Paris, 1963).

In post-Resurrection time the contents and power of these events are unfolded by the development of the Conciliar dogmas, which for Daniélou have at their heart the reconciliation of two freedoms, God's and man's, in the person of the incarnate Word; by the Church's preaching; by her celebration of the sacramental mysteries, and by her mission which Daniélou portrays in studiedly unfashionable terms: it is first and foremost a mandate to make known the message of salvation, in view of the Judgment to come. More gently, the work of the Word in history is also continued through the progress of individuals in spiritual life with Christ as their 'interior Master'. That is a reminiscence of the writings of St Augustine, though Daniélou draws into his account of Christ in the life of the soul Greeks – Clement of Alexandria and Gregory of Nyssa, mediaeval Latins – Bernard and Tauler, Counter-Reformation saints – Teresa of Avila and Ignatius Loyola, and to represent the nineteenth and twentieth centuries, Jean-Marie Vianney, the Curé d'Ars, and Abbot Columba Marmion who a quarter of a century after Daniélou's death would be declared 'blessed' by Pope John Paul II.

Conclusion

Jean Daniélou was or became – whatever anxieties Toulouse Thomists may have felt for his role in the dispute over *la nouvelle théologie* – a classically Catholic theologian. That was so in his concern to integrate into theology as many as possible of the themes of Scripture, while seeing the two Testaments in their reciprocally interpreting unity. It was so in the amplitude of his appeal to Tradition – to the Fathers of both East and West, to the historic Liturgies, to the Councils and other major magisterial declarations of the Church. He was classically Catholic too in his robust metaphysical realism, expressed in a fundamentally Thomasian ontology of creation, and in the equally vigorous realism with which he described the events of salvation for what they are: God's self-involvement in divinely initiated acts.

If much of his theological work comes under the heading of *ressourcement* – going back to the sources, at once biblical, patristic and liturgical, he was no mere antiquarian. His Gallic concern for coherence and clarity – this too was also 'classical', but in the sense of typical of France's *grand siècle* – sought to exhibit the wholeness of the revelatory pattern, set against its wider creational backcloth. The twin principles of 'correspondence' and 'order' enabled him to bring this wholeness yet distinctiveness to light.

Daniélou's existentialism, unlike that of Bultmann against which he maintained unceasing enmity, did not cancel out his theological concern for objectivity (which link him, sometimes despite himself, to the Neo-Thomists), or for totality thinking about revelation, not least in its relation to the cosmic and human End (which suggest an affinity with Bouyer and Balthasar). The rooting of that existentialism in a profound sense of corporate process (owed to de Lubac), and (via an ecumenical range of exegetes) in a Scripturally founded theology of covenant, saved him from the snares of individualism. Yet through the language of encounter, at once biblical and existentialist (here one might compare the early Schillebeeckx), he was able to combine communitarianism with personalism, and to treat his readers, as he did his pastoral clients, as unique selves, invited to an equally journey of discovery and, ultimately, growth in union with God.

This combination of theological and spiritual qualities he brought sharply to bear on the rather disoriented French Catholicism of the post-Conciliar years. The example was not perhaps lost on another, if much younger, *peritus* at Vatican Council II: Joseph Ratzinger.

Bibliography

Primary Literature

A. Historical Theology (including exegesis and background studies to Scripture)
Platonisme et théologie mystique: doctrine spirituelle de Saint Grégoire de Nysse (Paris, 1944).
Les divers sens de l'Écriture dans la tradition chrétienne primitive (Louvain, 1948).
Origène (Paris, 1948).
Sacramentum futuri. Études sur les origines de la typologie biblique (Paris, 1950).
Bible et Liturgie. La théologie biblique des sacrements et des fêtes d'après les Pères de l'Église (Paris, 1951).
Des origines à saint Grégoire le Grand (Paris, 1953 = Nouvelle histoire de l'Eglise, 1).
Les saints 'païens' de l'Ancien Testament (Paris, 1956).
Les Manuscrits de la Mer morte et les origines du Christianisme (Paris, 1957).
Philon d'Alexandrie (Paris, 1958).
Histoire des doctrines chrétiennes avant Nicée (Paris, 1958–78).
Études d'exégèse judéo-chrétienne: les Testimonia (Paris, 1966).
La Colombe et la ténèbre. Textes extraits des 'Homélies sur le Cantique des Cantiques' de Grégoire de Nysse (Paris, 1967).
Les Évangiles de l'enfance (Paris, 1967).
[Grégoire de Nysse] Vie de Moïse, ou, Traité de la perfection en matière de vertu. Introduction, texte critique et traduction (Paris, 1968, 3rd edn).
Être et le temps chez Grégoire de Nysse (Leiden, 1970).
Le Judéo-christianisme: les textes, les doctrines et la vie spirituelle (Paris, 1982).

B. Doctrinal Theology
Le signe du Temple ou de la présence de Dieu (Paris, 1942).
Le Mystère du salut des nations (Paris, 1946).
Le Mystère de l'Avent (Paris, 1948).
Essai sur le mystère de l'histoire (Paris, 1953).
Les Anges et leur mission, d'après les Pères de l'Église (Paris, 1953).
Dieu et nous (Paris, 1957).
Approches du Christ (Paris, 1961).

Scandaleuse Vérité (Paris, 1961).
Jean-Baptiste, témoin de l'Agneau (Paris, 1964).
La Catéchèse aux premiers siècles (Paris, 1968).
La Trinité et le mystère de l'existence (Paris, 1968).
La Résurrection (Paris, 1969).

C. Pastoral Theology
Les laïcs et la mission de l'Église: etudes et documents du Cercle Saint Jean-Baptiste (Paris, 1962).
Évangile et monde moderne: petit traité de morale à l'usage des laïcs (Tournai, 1964).
L'Oraison, problème politique (Paris, 1965).
L'avenir de la religion (Paris, 1968).
Autorité et contestation dans l'Église (Geneva, 1969).
La Foi de toujours et l'homme d'aujourd'hui (Paris, 1969).
L'Eglise des apôtres (Paris, 1970).
Crise de l'Eglise, crise de l'homme (Paris, 1972).
Pourquoi l'Église? (Paris, 1972).
Contemplation: croissance de l'Église (Paris, 1977).

D. Inter-religious Dialogue
Dialogues avec les Marxistes, les Existentialistes, les Protestants, les Juifs, l'Hindouisme (Paris, 1948).
Les Juifs: dialogue entre Jean Daniélou et André Chouraqui (Paris, 1960).
Mythes païens, Mystère chrétien (Paris, 1966).

Secondary Literature

Fontaine, Jacques (ed.), *Actualité de Jean Daniélou* (Paris: Cerf, 2005).
Fontaine, Jacques and Kanengiesser, Charles (eds), *Epektasis. Mélanges patristiques offers au cardinal Jean Daniélou* (Paris: Beauchesne, 1972).
Hoffmann-Axthelm, Dieter, *Anschauung und Begriff: zur historischen Einordnung von 'Nouvelle Théologie' und 'Existentialer Theologie'* (Munich: Kaiser, 1973).
Jacquin, Françoise, *Histoire du Cercle Saint-Jean-Baptiste: l'enseignement du Père Daniélou* (Paris: Beauchesne, 1987).
Lebeau, Paul, *Jean Daniélou* (Paris: Fleurus, 1967).
Nichols, Aidan, OP, 'Thomism and the nouvelle théologie', *The Thomist*, 64 (2000), 1–19.
Pizzuto, Pietro, *La teologia della rivelazione di Jean Daniélou: influsso su 'Dei Verbum' e valore attuale* (Rome: Pontificia Università Gregoriana, 2003).
Rondeau, Marie-Josèphe Rondeau (ed.), *Jean Daniélou. Carnets spirituels* (Paris: Cerf, 1993).
Societe des amis de Jean Danielou (ed.), *Jean Daniélou 1905–1974* (Paris: Cerf, 1975).
Veliath, Dominic, *Theological Approach and Understanding of Religions: Jean Daniélou and Raimundo Panikkar, a Study in Contrasts* (Bangalore: Kristu Jyoti Publications, 1988).

Chapter 22
Edward Schillebeeckx

Olav Hovdelien

Edward Schillebeeckx (1914–2009) studied under Yves Congar. From the mid-twentieth century onwards, he elaborated his own characteristic theological thinking, which has often led scholars to mention him in the same breath as influential Catholic theologians such as Henri de Lubac, Karl Rahner, and Hans Urs von Balthasar, in addition to Congar. Like these men, Schillebeeckx helped to lay the foundations for the Second Vatican Council (1962–65), and he played an active role, *inter alia* through the periodical *Concilium*, in the post-conciliar debates. Schillebeeckx, who was influenced by existentialism and other currents of thought, focused especially on the problematical aspects of the way of thinking and living that are typical of modern life. This means that he must be regarded as a modern theologian in more than one sense: not only because he lived through two World Wars, the Cold War, and the period of rebuilding after the Second World War, but also because of his concentration on the theological discussion of the conditions of modern life. He was a theologian who knew the age in which he lived, while at the same time wishing to remain anchored in the church's life.

Biographical Sketch

Edward Cornelis Florent Alfons Schillebeeckx was born on November 12, 1914 in Antwerp in Belgium, the seventh of fourteen children. The autumn of 1914 was a fateful hour for Europe. The First World War had begun only a few months earlier, and just before Edward's birth, his family fled before the German army, and were evacuated to Antwerp from their home town of Kortenberg in Flanders. They belonged to the middle class, and they returned to their home town after the War. Schillebeeckx attended a boarding school conducted by the Jesuits in Turnhout. After his schooling, he joined the Dominican order in Ghent in 1934, with the intention of working as a priest. He received his basic theological and philosophical training from the Dominicans in Louvain, where he was influenced by Dominic De Petter, who sought to combine Neo-Thomist philosophy with a strong interest in Husserl's phenomenology. This was an important source of inspiration for Schillebeeckx' later theological thinking. He was ordained to the priesthood in 1941, and began teaching

Thomist theology at the seminary in Louvain in 1943, after the outbreak of the Second World War made it difficult for him to pursue further theological studies.[1]

After the War, he was sent to Paris to continue his studies at Le Saulchoir, the Dominican house of studies, where he was influenced by celebrated theologians such as Yves Congar and Marie-Dominique Chenu. In parallel to his studies of Catholic theology, he attended lectures at the Sorbonne, where those he encountered included Albert Camus and Maurice Merleau-Ponty. The theology that Schillebeeckx encountered in Paris in the 1940s is often called *la nouvelle théologie* ("the new theology"). This may be described in simple terms as a theology that sought to achieve an equilibrium between a new emphasis on historical studies on the one hand, and the traditional theology inspired by scholasticism on the other, with its emphasis on a deductive synthesis in the light of Thomist philosophy. The study of the church fathers played a central role for these theologians.

After his return to Louvain in 1947, Schillebeeckx wrote a dissertation on sacramental theology, with a renewed understanding of the sacraments that he had gained from his studies of sacramental theology in the church fathers and in mediaeval theologians. This was published in Dutch in 1952 as *De sacramentele heilseconomie* ("The sacramental dispensation of salvation") and is still regarded as an important contribution in this field. Six years later, Schillebeeckx was appointed to a professorship in dogmatic theology and the history of theology at the University of Nijmegen, a position he held until his retirement in 1983.

In addition to his work as professor, Schillebeeckx was an adviser to Cardinal Alfrink and the Dutch bishops, and he accompanied them to the Second Vatican Council (1962–65), where he exercised considerable influence and attracted international attention as one of the leading progressive theologians at the Council. Although he did not have the formal status of a *peritus*, Schillebeeckx held a number of lectures in English for the participants in the Council, and he gave active support to the Dutch bishops.

After the Council, he was closely associated with the reform movement, together with Congar, Karl Rahner, and Hans Küng, and he was one of the founders of the periodical *Concilium* in 1963.[2]

In addition to his academic theological studies, Schillebeeckx always studied secular thinkers, and he was well acquainted with the most important philosophical currents: the hermeneutical philosophy in the tradition that followed Heidegger and Gadamer, Anglo-American analytical philosophy, and the critical theory of the Frankfurt school. In this way, he always sought to be *au courant* with contemporary thought, and this gave him a greater ability than many other Catholic theologians to

---

[1] Erik Borgman, *Edward Schillebeeckx. A Theologian in his History* (London and New York, 2004), pp. 18–54. Robert J. Schreiter, "Edward Schillebeeckx," in David F. Ford (ed.), *The Modern Theologians. An Introduction to Christian Theology in the Twentieth Century* (Oxford: 1997), p. 152. The Edward Schillebeeckx Foundation, http://schillebeeckx.nl (accessed November 16, 2012).

[2] Borgman, *Edward Schillebeeckx*, pp. 103–11, 125, 135–8. Schreiter, "Edward Schillebeeckx," pp. 152–3. The first issue of *Concilium* was published in 1965.

elaborate a theology in dialogue with the zeitgeist. This was a strength in his theological thinking, but perhaps also a weakness. From the 1960s onward, Schillebeeckx was regarded as the leading Dutch-language modernizing theologian.

He was a controversial theologian who continually encountered skepticism and opposition, because of his tendency to incorporate secular philosophy into his thinking. The Congregation for the Doctrine of the Faith questioned his orthodoxy on several occasions. He was, for example, accused of denying the resurrection of Jesus as an objective fact and of proposing an understanding of the eucharist that was close to the Zwinglian Protestant tradition. However, no point in his theology was ever officially rejected by the church.[3]

A number of American and European universities recognized his work by awarding him honorary doctorates. He is also the only theologian to have received the Erasmus Prize (1982) for his work in promoting European culture. He died in Nijmegen on December 23, 2009.

Overview of Schillebeeckx' Most Important Books

This overview will indicate some of Schillebeeckx' most important studies, but far from all his works are mentioned here. He published more than 800 articles and books over more than 60 years, and he has been translated into 13 languages. More than 100 of his works have been translated into English and German, including his most important books.[4]

One recurrent interest for Schillebeeckx through his entire career was the relationship between the church and the world, and what it means to be a Christian in the modern age. This theme is treated more indirectly in his doctoral dissertation, since this work is about the theology of the sacraments, but as early as 1959, he published the study *Christus, sacrament van de Godsontmoeting* ("Christ, sacrament of the encounter with God"), in which he develops an understanding of the sacraments that is influenced by existentialist philosophy. In this book, Schillebeeckx employs perspectives from the existentialist philosophical analysis of the human person's existence in the world to stake out an alternative to the more mechanistic understanding of the sacraments and of grace that he saw as typical of scholastic theology. This cautious challenge to the dominant scholastic theology, in the light of insights drawn especially from existential philosophy and phenomenology, is very characteristic of Schillebeeckx' writings before the Council, and recurs in many of his studies.

The Second Vatican Council brought considerable changes for the Catholic Church in many fields. For Schillebeeckx, it also brought a change in the way he wrote, both in the themes and in the form. He now abandons the scholastic vocabulary almost

---

[3] Schreiter, "Edward Schillebeeckx," p. 153.
[4] Schreiter, "Edward Schillebeeckx," p. 155. For a complete bibliography of his publications from 1936 to 1996, drawn up by Ted Schoof OP and Jan van de Westelaken.

completely, and begins even more strongly to construct on the basis of the dominant thinking in twentieth-century philosophy. This makes his theology less accessible, since it requires his readers to have not only traditional theological competence, but also a thorough knowledge of both Continental and Anglo-American analytical philosophy.[5]

In connection with the discussions before and after the Council, Schillebeeckx published a wide-ranging five-volume work, *Theologische Peilingen*. I: *Openbaring en Theologie* ("Revelation and Theology" I and II, 1964); *God en mens* ("God and the human person," 1965); III: *Wereld en Kerk* ("World and Church," 1966); IV: *De zending van de kerk* ("The Mission of the Church," 1968); and V: *Geloofsverstaan* ("The Understanding of Faith," 1972). This work is a holistic investigation of the most central themes in dogmatic theology.

After he completed this *magnum opus*, another shift took place in his writings in the mid-1970s when he turned to New Testament exegesis and published the first two volumes of his extensive christological trilogy: *Jezus, het verhaal van een levende* ("Jesus. An Experiment in Christology," 1974), and *Gerechtigheid en liefde, genade en bevrijding* ("Christ. The Christian Experience in the Modern World," 1977). In these books, he discusses New Testament research and insights from the study of the early Christians, in order thereby to offer his own independent contribution to very central questions of fundamental theology. His combination of New Testament exegesis with perspectives of systematic theology means that no academic discussion in the Catholic sphere can overlook him. At the same time, however, this way of working has made him controversial within the church.

In the first volume of his christological work, Schillebeeckx' starting point is the discussion of the historical Jesus, whom he describes, in agreement with leading New Testament scholarship, as an eschatological prophetic figure. The key to this understanding of Jesus is his proclamation of an imminent kingdom of God. He is thus understood in the light of his situation in a Jewish context, and Schillebeeckx shows how Jesus' words and actions intend to point to the coming kingdom of God.[6] In the second volume, the focus shifts to how the first Christians experienced salvation as a reality. This book therefore contains a thorough discussion of the concept of "grace" against the background of the New Testament concept of grace, before Schillebeeckx looks more closely at the meaning of salvation in the world and at the consequent social-ethical responsibility.[7] The narrative of Jesus, as a personally lived life in the imitation of Christ, is at the center of the first two books in the christological trilogy: in other words, we must learn to know the God to whom Jesus bears witness by taking

---

[5] See Edward Schillebeeckx, *Christ the Sacrament of the Encounter with God* (New York, 1963). Edward Schillebeeckx, *The Understanding of Faith. Interpretation and Criticism* (London, 1974).

[6] Edward Schillebeeckx, *Jesus. An Experiment in Christology* (New York, 1979). See Schreiter, "Edward Schillebeeckx," pp. 154–5.

[7] Edward Schillebeeckx, *Christ: The Experience of Jesus as Lord* (New York, 1980). See Schreiter, "Edward Schillebeeckx", p. 155.

Jesus' life as our model. Schillebeeckx thus understands Jesus' life as a paradigm both for our own humanity and in the struggle for the *humanum*. This leads him to emphasize strongly our social-ethical responsibility in the encounter with suffering and injustice in the world. He explores this theme more deeply in *Als politiek niet alles is. Jezus in de westerse cultuur* ("On Christian Faith. The Spiritual, Ethical, and Political Dimensions," 1986).

After publishing the first two volumes of his wide-ranging christological trilogy, Schillebeeckx then wrote a study of church ministry, *Pleidooi voor mensen in de kerk* ("The Church with a Human Face," 1985). He published the third volume in the Christological trilogy, *Mensen als verhaal van God* ("The Human Story of God") in 1989. This continues the first two volumes. Its emphasis is on the Gospel message and the Christian faith, and it develops themes such as revelation, experience, God, Christ, and the church.[8] Schillebeeckx wrote this trilogy on the basis of his interest and active participation in fields such as the relationship between the church and political work, women's position in the church, and liberation theology. Each of these themes has been controversial in its own way.

Through his academic writings, Schillebeeckx left his mark on academic theological discussion throughout the post-War period, especially in connection with the Second Vatican Council and the post-conciliar debates. His pastoral books, his sermons, and his lectures have reached an audience far wider than the professional theological readership. Although he himself admitted that several of his books were hard to read, he insisted – for example, in the first volume of the christological trilogy – that he was writing in order to bridge the gulf between academic theology and the concrete needs of ordinary Christians. His last project before his death in 2009 was a book on the sacraments from an anthropological perspective.

Some Central Themes in Schillebeeckx' Theology

Edward Schillebeeckx touched on many different themes in the course of his extensive writings, but one central and recurrent theme in his thinking was the relationship between the church and the world. A great of his writing consists of theological discussions of what it means to be a Christian in the modern world, with the focus *inter alia* on how modern people can experience salvation personally in today's society. Schillebeeckx' fundamental theological conviction is that it is possible to acquire knowledge of God in the light of the world and in this world. He sees no contradiction between divine revelation and human experience. And it is this conviction that has led Schillebeeckx to the religious and theological view of the world and of culture that he has elaborated in many of his academic theological works.

---

[8] Edward Schillebeeckx, *On Christian Faith. The Spiritual, Ethical and Political Dimensions* (New York, 1987).

According to his biographer, Erik Borgman, Schillebeeckx' theological project aims to find the saving God in the heart of the complex reality in which people lead their lives today, in a world that we cannot grasp in an overview. This is why the core in his theology is the idea that the Christian faith should be a constructive element in today's society. In order for this to be possible, we must engage in a theological discussion of the conditions under which modern people live. Schillebeeckx attempts to do this by relating to the various intellectual currents that play a dominant role in society in each particular age. He is profoundly convinced that theology has much to learn from secular thinking about the fundamental conditions of human existence and about the human person's situation as a member of society. As a theologian, Schillebeeckx had seen that many of the old answers were no longer experienced as adequate for modern Christians who had grown up in a time marked by war and violence, and by new scientific and technological achievements. It was therefore important for Schillebeeckx to ask: What does salvation mean in today's secularized society? What kind of role does eschatology play in the understanding of human history today? And how should Christians live as members of society in the light of the Gospel?

Schillebeeckx' aim is "to do theology," as he says – in other words, to take his stance in the continuous dialogue between the church's tradition, on the one hand, and today's cultural and intellectual climate, on the other, while all the time seeking to answer the questions that concern people today. He himself calls his inductive critical-hermeneutical project the "theology of culture." He describes this as follows: he is not writing "for eternity," but for men and women of today who are located in one particular historical situation, and he endeavors to answer their questions. This means that his theology has a specific date, and is thus contextual. At the same time, he goes behind this concrete situation, since the goal in all his writings is to take a position with regard to the questions of *all* men and women.[9]

The central idea is that each person must individually take responsibility for his or her own life. This responsibility must be taken in solidarity with one's fellow human beings, especially with those on the margins of society. This is understood as a central aspect of faith in God. Existential philosophy clearly influences Schillebeeckx here. He affirms that God can be grasped only indirectly. This means that revelation is closely linked to human experience in a broad sense – not only to the experience of God's presence, but also to the experience of being a human person situated in the world.

Schillebeeckx develops this idea, and claims that God is so mighty that no single religion can possess a complete understanding of who he is. He refers in this context to the "family likeness" between all the various traditions of religious experience and to Wittgenstein's use of concepts.

Nor can God be grasped by building upon the best elements in all religions, because God continually appears as new, and he is greater than all religions. No human perspective can grasp God completely as he is, and all religious traditions are

[9] See Borgman, *Edward Schillebeeckx*, p. 470.

able, to a greater or lesser degree, to experience God. Schillebeeckx calls the various religions "schools of wisdom."[10] It is this kind of fundamental epistemological presupposition that has led to what can be seen as a relativization in Schillebeeckx of the church's place in the world in the light of God's kingdom. He believes that the church must reflect anew on the relationship between Christianity and other religious traditions. He counters the traditional proposition: "There is no salvation outside the church," with a proposition of his own: "There is no salvation outside the world." On the relationship between Christianity, Judaism, and Islam, he writes that all three religions are seriously concerned about ethical conduct. The goal of all three is to establish the kingdom of God as a kingdom of righteousness among human persons.[11] He appears to go very far in juxtaposing different religions as "schools of wisdom," and it is thus not surprising that Schillebeeckx has been a controversial theologian and that this was a major charge leveled against him by the Congregation for the Doctrine of the Faith. They understood this part of Schillebeeckx' theology as a rejection of fundamental dogmas of the church that had been drawn up at the Councils of Nicaea and Chalcedon.

Another important idea in Schillebeeckx' theology emerges in connection with his strong focus on the church's responsibility in the encounter with human suffering, sin, and injustice. This has played a central role in his thinking from the early 1960s onwards. He calls the encounter with the suffering and injustice of the world "contrast experiences," that is to say, experiences that point to the opposite of what is experienced and to the world as it was meant to be. This means that experiences of meaningfulness, joy, love, justice, and peace are interpreted as experienced "fragments of salvation." There is a *humanum*, an ideal of how human life is meant to be. This *humanum* is not yet realized, but it will be revealed at the coming of God's kingdom, when Jesus Christ, the paradigm of humanity, once again dwells among human beings. In this way, Jesus' suffering and death are the ultimate contrast experience, while at the same time they point to an eternal life without suffering and injustice. Only God knows the definitive meaning of history. Schillebeeckx develops these ideas above all in his christological trilogy.[12]

Schillebeeckx' emphasis on the anthropological in his theological thinking must not be misunderstood to mean that God is a "human projection." Here, he is still influenced by Thomist thinking. He holds fast to God's sovereignty with regard to

---

[10] Edward Schillebeeckx, "Prologue: Human God-Talk and God's Silence," in Mary Catherine Hilkert and Robert J. Schreiter, *The Praxis of the Reign of God. An Introduction to the Theology of Edward Schillebeeckx* (New York, 2002), pp. ix–xviii. See Mary Catherine Hilkert "Experience and Revelation," in Mary Catherine Hilkert and Robert J. Schreiter, *The Praxis of the Reign of God. An Introduction to the Theology of Edward Schillebeeckx* (New York, 2002), p. 60.

[11] Edward Schillebeeckx, *God is New Each Moment. In Conversation with Huub Osterhuis and Piet Hoogeveen* (London and New York, 2004), p. 119; see Edward Schillebeeckx, *The Human Story of God* (New York: Crossroad Publishing, 1990), p. 12.

[12] See especially the third volume, Edward Schillebeeckx, *The Human Story of God* (New York: Crossroad Publishing, 1990). See Hilkert, *The Praxis of the Reign of God*, p. 61.

the course of history and the sustaining of the world; at the same time, however, it is important for him to affirm that God is also a loving God, a God who has made the human person's cause his own. God wants everything that is good for human beings. This is expressed in a special way through Jesus' suffering and death. In the light of this, Christians are called to work for a better and more just world.

This brings us to what is perhaps the most controversial point in Schillebeeckx' thinking, namely, his use of Marxist philosophy. He writes that we must take the best that Marx has to offer and use this to develop a new form of Christianity. The "best" in Marx is his deep concern for humanity. Schillebeeckx also affirms that Marxism must be a constant source of inspiration for Christians.[13]

It is very difficult to follow him here, when he equates working for a better and more just world with his adoption of Marxist analyses of society. Many historical examples show that this is a false conclusion.

Schillebeeckx' Theological Testament

Schillebeeckx' theology did not lead to the formation of a school in the narrow sense in the Dutch-speaking area, like (for example) Karl Rahner's theology in Germany. Nevertheless, his theology has been very influential, although it is of course difficult to assess exactly how important his thinking was for the new ecclesiological ideas of the Second Vatican Council, with the new emphases on the role of the laity, the bishops' collegiality, and the description of the church as a "sacramental sign." It is nevertheless possible to demonstrate a significant agreement in vocabulary between the conciliar documents and Schillebeeckx' thinking in the years before the Council. Although it cannot be said that he was a dominant figure during the sessions, he was certainly one of the most important participants in the post-conciliar debates, *inter alia* through the periodical *Concilium*.

Schillebeeckx' theological method, which builds bridges between systematic theology and biblical exegesis, is exemplary and constitutes an important corrective to today's specialized academic theologians (both systematic theologians and exegetes). This was also an important contribution to theological hermeneutics, as was his insistence that academic theology must be structured in such a way that it is experienced as relevant to ordinary believers.

In the Catholic church, Schillebeeckx' insistence on the importance of a theological discussion of human experience has helped to put this on the theological agenda. Ordinary believers have also been helped to take this part of the faith seriously. This central part of his holistic theological project remains valid, as does his insistence on bringing about a closer dialogue between the church and the world. Schillebeeckx saw himself as a man who thought things through, and although much of what he wrote was naturally colored by the context in which it was written, it can still be

---

[13] Schillebeeckx, *God is New Each Moment*, pp. 99–100.

fruitful to read his theological works. He was without doubt a creative and pioneering theologian, a man of great intellectual depth who was committed to the church.

Bibliography

Primary Literature

Ted Schoof O.P. and Jan van de Westelaken, *Bibliography 1936–1996 of Edward Schillebeeckx O.P.* (undated), http://schillebeeckx.nl/wp-content/uploads/2008/11/Bibliografie-Sx-nwe-versie.pdf (accessed November 16, 2012).

De sacramentele heilseconomie. Theologische bezinning op S. Thomas' sacramentenleer in het licht van de traditie en van de hedendaagse sacramentsproblematiek (Antwerpen: 't Groeit; Bilthoven: Nelissen, 1952).

Christus sacrament van de Godsontmoeting (Bilthoven: Nelissen, 1959). English: *Christ the Sacrament of the Encounter with God* (New York: Sheed and Ward, 1963).

Openbaring en Theologie. Theologsiche Peilingen I (Bilthoven: Nelissen, 1964). English: *Revelation and Theology* (I and II. London: Sheed and Ward, 1967–68).

God en mens. Theologische Peilingen II (Bilthoven: Nelissen, 1965). English: *God and Man* (London: Sheed and Ward, 1969).

Wereld en Kerk. Theologische Peilingen III (Bilthoven: Nelissen, 1966). English: *World and Church* (London: Sheed and Ward, 1971).

De zending van de kerk. Theologische Peilingen, IV. (Bilthoven: Nelissen, 1968). English: *The Mission of the Church* (London: Sheed and Ward, 1973).

Geloofsverstaan. Interpretatie en kritiek. Theologische Peilingen, V (Bloemendaal: Nelissen, 1972). English: *The Understanding of Faith. Interpretation and Criticism* (London: Sheed and Ward, 1974).

Jezus, het verhaal van een levende (Bloemendaal: Nelissen, 1974). English: *Jesus: An Experiment in Christology* (New York: Seabury Press, 1979).

Gerechtigheid en liefde. Genade en bevrijding (Bloemendaal: Nelissen, 1977). English: *Christ: The Experience of Jesus as Lord* (New York: Seabury Press, 1980).

Pleidooi voor mensen in de kerk. Christelijke identiteit en ambten in de kerk (Baarn: Nelissen, 1985). English: *The Church with a Human Face. A New and Expanded Theology of Ministry* (New York: Crossroad Publishing, 1985).

Als politiek niet alles is. Jezus in onze westerse cultuur. Abraham Kuyper-lezingen 1986 (Baarn: Ten Have, 1986). English: *On Christian Faith. The Spiritual, Ethical and Political Dimensions* (New York: Crossroad Publishing, 1987).

Mensen als verhaal van God (Baarn: Nelissen, 1989). English: *The Human Story of God* (New York: Crossroad Publishing, 1990).

"Prologue: Human God-Talk and God's Silence," in Hilkert and Schreiter (2002), ix–xviii.

God is New Each Moment. In Conversation with Huub Osterhuis and Piet Hoogeveen (London and New York: T&T Clark Publishing, 2004).

Secondary Literature

Borgman, Erik, *Edward Schillebeeckx. A Theologian in his History* (London and New York: Continuum, 2004).
Ford, David F. (ed.), *The Modern Theologians. An Introduction to Christian Theology in the Twentieth Century* (Oxford: Blackwell, 1997).
Hilkert, Mary Catherine and Robert J. Schreiter, *The Praxis of the Reign of God. An Introduction to the Theology of Edward Schillebeeckx* (New York: Fordham University Press, 2002).
Kerr, Fergus, *Twentieth-Century Catholic Theologians. From Neoscholasticism to Nuptial Mysticism* (Oxford: Blackwell, 2007).

Chapter 23
John Paul II/Karol Wojtyła

Michael Waldstein

A characteristic theological vision informs John Paul II's pontificate as a whole, a vision Karol Wojtyła developed already in the 1940s on the basis of his encounter with the writings of St John of the Cross. Although Wojtyła tends to be seen as a philosopher, four of the seven books he published before his election are theological. His magnum opus, written before his election but published as a cycle of Papal catecheses, is the great *Theology of the Body* (TOB), in which the many strands of his philosophical and theological thought come together. As a rule, Papal writings involve much collaboration with advisors and departments of the Curia so that one cannot automatically attribute them to the Pope personally. The case of John Paul II seems to be different although some of his writings bear the marks of collaboration more than others. Throughout his many documents one can see the stamp of a single coherent vision that Wojtyła articulated in its outlines already in his 1948 doctoral dissertation on St John of the Cross. It is a vision of Christian life as a spousal gift of self of God to the human person and an answering spousal gift of the person to God, both rooted in the communion of persons in the Trinity. Following St John of the Cross, John Paul II pays particular attention to the *experience* of faith, to the manner in which faith permeates and changes the lived experience of personal subjectivity.

The Beginning of the Vision under Nazi Occupation

Karol Wojtyła was born in Wadowice, a small city near Krakow, on May 18, 1920. His mother died in 1929 and his father in 1941. Upon graduation from high school in Wadowice (1938), he enrolled in the course of Polish literature and linguistics at Krakow's Jagiellonian University. He also began formal training as an actor in the theatrical group *Studio 38*.

After invading Poland in 1939, Hitler attempted to liquidate the Polish intelligentsia, killing more than 70,000 in the first year. To avoid execution or deportation, Wojtyła had to find manual labor. He worked first in a quarry and then in the Solvay chemical plant. His co-workers supported him secretly to allow him to keep up his studies.

The Gestapo removed the majority of Polish priests from their parishes in order to decapitate Polish resistance. About 3,600 priests were killed. Lay ministry became a necessity. Thus in 1940 Wojtyła came under the pastoral care of a layman, Jan Tyranowski, who was a glowing admirer of St John of the Cross.

"Even before entering the underground seminary, I read the works of that mystic, especially his poetry. In order to read it in the original, I studied Spanish. That was a very important stage in my life" (*Crossing the Threshold of Hope*, 142). "To [St. John of the Cross] I owe so much in my spiritual formation. I came to know him in my youth and I entered into an intimate dialogue with this master of faith ... Ever since then I have found in him a friend and master who has shown me the light that shines in the darkness for walking always toward God" (Homily at Segovia, November 4, 1982).

At the core of St John of the Cross's vision of human life stands self-surrender to God, leading to spousal communion with God. "It was an approach to the human condition as radically opposed to the Nazi will-to-power as could be imagined. Under the tutelage of the unexpected apostle, Jan Tyranowski, and amid the madness of the Occupation, the imitation of Christ through the complete handing over of every worldly security to the merciful will of God seized Karol Wojtyła's imagination. Over time, it would become the defining characteristic of his own discipleship" (Weigel, *Witness to Hope*, 61–2).

St John of the Cross develops the image of bride and bridegroom as the central image for understanding Christian life as a union of love with God. The key concept he uses to grasp this image theologically is the "gift of self." "There he [God] gave me his breast; / there he taught me a sweet and living knowledge; / and I gave myself to him, / keeping nothing back; / there I promised to be his bride."[1] In his commentary on this stanza, St John of the Cross writes, "She most willingly and with intense delight surrenders herself wholly to him in the desire to be totally his and never to possess in herself anything other than him ... she is really and totally given to God without keeping anything back, just as God has freely given himself entirely to her."[2] Wojtyła speaks a similar characteristic language about spousal love between man and woman. "The essence of spousal love is self-giving, the surrender of one's 'I' ... The fullest, the most uncompromising form of love consists precisely in selfgiving, in making one's inalienable and non-transferable 'I' someone else's property" (Wojtyła, *Love and Responsibility*, 96–7). In his *Theology of the Body*, John Paul II expands this intuition into a comprehensive theological method which he calls "hermeneutics of the gift" (TOB 13:2).

Hitler treated Poles like grains of sand. On the level of the individual, he placed them in a position in which they would be small, insignificant, isolated and without personal dignity; on the social level, he massed them together in great heaps, to be

---

[1] St John of the Cross, *Spiritual Canticle*, stanza 27.
[2] Ibid. *Commentary*, 27.6.

shoveled here or there according to grand designs. Wojtyła encountered an opposite sense of the person in St John of the Cross. On the level of the individual, persons are endowed with vast personal interiority, capable of the infinite, of great dignity above all because each person is uniquely loved by God for his or her own good; on the social level, persons are destined for an unrepeatable relation of spousal union with God, which gives rise to organically differentiated membership in the Church as the bride of Christ after the pattern of the communion of persons in the Trinity. These two principles, the personal (unique personal subjectivity) and the social (the communion of persons), were to become the two pillars of Wojtyła's and John Paul II's theological vision.

Wojtyła participated as actor and playwright in the underground "Rhapsodic Theater," an act of cultural resistance punishable by execution. The group performed classical plays (*Oedipus, Antigone, Hamlet,* etc.) as well as more recent plays in the tradition of Polish Romanticism with its distinctive view of history. "History had a spiritual core; the deterioration of traditional national virtues had caused Poland's political collapse; reestablishing Polish independence required recovering those virtues as the foundation of a new Polish state" (Weigel, *Witness to Hope*, 34). Among the aims of Polish Romanticism, freedom ranks very high: "Nothing about us without us!" It is a freedom that goes hand in hand with a Catholic-inspired communitarian concept of the common good.

The "Rhapsodic Theater" was based on the conviction that the power of drama lay in the spoken and received word, which had the strength to alter what the world of power considered unalterable facts by inspiring non-violent revolutions. John Paul II was to observe this power of the word in the revolutions that brought about the downfall of communism in Central and Eastern Europe with remarkably little bloodshed.

In 1942 Wojtyła entered the clandestine seminary set up by Cardinal Adam Sapieha, archbishop of Krakow. One of his fellow seminarians, Jerzy Zachuta, was caught and shot by the Gestapo. After the defeat of the Nazis in 1945, Wojtyła continued his studies in theology at the reopened Seminary and at the Jagiellonian University. He received a thorough formation in Thomistic philosophy and theology. "We in the Thomistic school, the school of 'perennial philosophy'" he writes about himself as if this were a matter of course.[3]

The Unfolding of the Vision under Communist Domination

World War II was a war Poland lost twice, first to Nazi Germany, then to Soviet Russia. Wojtyła's experience of both totalitarian regimes deeply shaped his thought by turning it increasingly in the direction of "the mystery of the person."

---

[3] Karol Wojtyła, "The Human Person and Natural Law," in *Person and Community: Selected Essays*, 279–99 (New York: P. Lang, 1993), 181.

Ordained a priest by Archbishop Sapieha in Krakow on November 1, 1946, Wojtyła was sent to Rome to earn a Doctorate in Theology. Under the direction of Reginald Garrigou-Lagrange OP, he wrote a dissertation on faith as the proximate and proportionate means for a union of love with God according to St John of the Cross (June 1948).

In his first assignment, university chaplain in Krakow, he focused in particular on the pastoral care of young couples, with many of whom he built lasting friendships. "As a young priest I learned to love human love … If one loves human love, there naturally arises the need to commit oneself completely to the service of 'fair love,' because love is fair, it is beautiful" (John Paul II, *Crossing the Threshold of Hope*, 123). From this time on, marriage and the family lay at the heart of Wojtyła's theological and pastoral work.

In 1951 he began work on a habilitation thesis in Moral Theology. The thesis takes Max Scheler's account of the imitation of Christ as the point of departure to argue that it is not possible to build a Christian ethics on the basis of Scheler's philosophy. Wojtyła advances three main criticisms of Scheler, organized according to the four Aristotelian causes minus matter. Scheler's philosophy fails to grasp (1) that moral goodness is a real attribute of the person: the formal cause of the imitation of Christ; (2) that the person is a truly responsible causal origin of acts: the efficient cause of imitation; (3) that God in the infinite goodness of his nature is the end: the final cause of imitation. "The whole difficulty is the result of the phenomenological premises of the system and we must assign the blame to these principles" (Wojtyła, *Scheler*, 115). Among these premises, Wojtyła criticizes in particular the bracketing of real being and the consequent reduction of the object of philosophy to phenomena in consciousness.

Wojtyła also sees a positive contribution in Scheler that resembles the attention to lived experience in St John of the Cross.

> [Theologians] should not forego the great advantages which the phenomenological method offers their work. It impresses the stamp of experience on works of ethics and nourishes them with the life-knowledge of concrete man by allowing an investigation of moral life from the side of its appearance. Yet, in all this, the phenomenological method plays only a secondary assisting role … At the same time, these investigations convince us that the Christian thinker, especially the theologian, who makes use of phenomenological experience in his work, cannot be a Phenomenologist. (Wojtyła, *Scheler*, 196)

In 1954, the year the communist authorities closed the Faculty of Theology in Krakow, Wojtyła began teaching at the Catholic University of Lublin and two years later accepted the chair of ethics at Lublin in the Department of Christian Philosophy, which he kept until his election in 1978. Three courses (1954 to 1957) have been published as *The Lublin Lectures*. The 1957/8 course of lectures appeared in 1960 under the title *Love and Responsibility*. Wojtyła unfolds in this book what he had learned about the gift of self and the beauty of spousal love from St John of the Cross and from the young couples he befriended as university chaplain.

In 1958 Wojtyła was appointed auxiliary bishop, then Archbishop of Krakow (1964). He continued teaching part-time in Lublin, mostly on the doctoral level. First as auxiliary, then as Archbishop of Krakow, he participated in the Second Vatican Council and made a substantial contribution as member of the redaction committee of *Gaudium et spes*. Paul VI named him a Cardinal in 1967.

During the Council Wojtyła wrote his main philosophical work, *The Acting Person*. The experience of Nazi and Soviet totalitarianism played a significant role in the shaping of this book. Wojtyła responds to the violence committed against the person by delving into the metaphysical foundations of personhood.

> I devote my very rare free moments to a work that is close to my heart and devoted to the metaphysical sense and mystery of the PERSON. It seems to me that the debate today is being played on that level. The evil of our times consists in the first place in a kind of degradation, indeed in a pulverization of the fundamental uniqueness of each human person. This evil is even much more of the metaphysical order than of the moral order. To this disintegration, planned at times by atheistic ideologies, we must oppose, rather than sterile polemics, a kind of "recapitulation" of the inviolable mystery of the person.[4]

In this way, the experience of the person's "pulverization" under Nazi and communist domination shaped Wojtyła's account of the inviolable mystery of the person both on the level of the individual (self-possession and integration in action) and on the social level (self-gift and the common good).

Wojtyła's experience at the Council is reflected in a book on the implementation of the Second Vatican Council (1972) that highlights the Trinitarian and experiential aspects of Christian life along the lines of his dissertation on St John of the Cross and *The Acting Person*. Quite similar in theological orientation is the Easter retreat he preached to Paul VI and his household in 1977.

Elected bishop of Rome in 1978, he carried out his ministry in an evangelical and missionary spirit, which is reflected already in the number of his pastoral visits: 104 visits outside Italy, 146 within; 317 visitations in Roman parishes; 984 meetings with heads of state and prime ministers. He proposed and unfolded the Gospel in many writings, among them 14 Encyclicals, 15 Apostolic Exhortations, 11 Apostolic Constitutions, 45 Apostolic Letters and five books.

In the first five years of his Pontificate, he set down seven major reference points for the pastoral care of marriage and the family: *Theology of the Body*; Synod about the family (1980); Pontifical Council for the Family (1981); post-synodal exhortation *Familiaris consortio* (1981); John Paul II Institute for Studies on Marriage and Family

---

[4] Letter to Henri de Lubac; see Henri de Lubac, *At the Service of the Church: Henri de Lubac Reflects on the Circumstances that Occasioned his Writings* (San Francisco: Ignatius, 1989), 171–2.

(1981); Charter of the Rights of the Family (1983); new ordering of marriage and family in the new Code of Canon Law (1983).

The involvement of the KGB in the assassination attempt on May 13, 1981 has not been proved, but remains a plausible hypothesis. The attempt occurred after his first major impact on the Soviet bloc during his first pastoral visit to Poland (June 1979). Renewed during his next two visits (June 1983 and June 1987), the impact contributed to the largely non-violent downfall of communist domination and the transition to democracy in 1989.

In his particular love for young people John Paul II established World Youth Day. Since the days of his friendship as a child and adolescent with Jerzy Kluger, son of the head of the Jewish community in Wadowice, he had a special love for the Jewish people. He labored to advance the cause of ecumenism particularly with the Orthodox Church. He celebrated the great Jubilee of the Incarnation in 2000, the highpoint of his pontificate, to promote the spiritual renewal of the Church. He died on April 2, 2005. The cause for his beatification was opened three months later.

The Theological Principles of the Vision

In John Paul II's theology, *Gaudium et spes* 24:3 plays a key role. It supplies the two key principles on the basis of which one can understand "the inviolable mystery of the person," both on the level of the individual and on the social level. "Indeed, the Lord Jesus, when he prays to the Father, 'that all may be one … as we are one' (Jn 17:21–22) and thus offers vistas closed to human reason, indicates a certain likeness between the union of the divine Persons, and the union of God's sons in truth and love. This likeness shows that man, who is the only creature on earth God willed for itself, cannot fully find himself except through a sincere gift of self (cf. Lk 17:33)."

Two principles are contained in the final sentence. (1) On the level of the individual person, man is the only creature on earth God willed for its own sake. (2) On the social level, man can only find himself in a sincere gift of self. For the second principle, the council quotes Luke 17:33, "Whoever seeks to make his life secure will lose it, and whoever loses his life will make it live." John Paul II sees these two principles as containing "the whole truth" or "the integral truth" about the human person (TOB 15:2–3).

Already in *Love and Responsibility*, published five years before *Gaudium et spes*, Wojtyła articulates these two truths as a comprehensive pair of principles. He calls the first truth "the personalistic norm." Kant's formulation provides him with a point of departure. "In all of creation, everything one might want and over which one has power can be used *as a mere means*. Only man himself and with him every rational creature is *end in itself*."[5] In explicit contrast to this formulation, Wojtyła sees the personalistic norm as turning on the person "having" ends rather than "being" an

---

[5] Kant, *Critique of Practical Reason*, Ak 5.87, cf. 5.131; see also *Groundwork for the Metaphysics of Morals*, Ak 4.429; *The Metaphysics of Morals*, Ak 6.434.

end. "This principle should be restated in a form rather different from that which Kant gave it as follows: whenever a person is the object of your activity, remember that you may not treat that person as only the means to an end, as an instrument, but must allow for the fact that he or she, too, *has, or at least should have, an end*" (*Love and Responsibility*, 28). The difference between being an end and having an end is highly significant, particularly when one considers God as the final end. Being God and having God as an end are different. In his Thomistic reformulation of the Kantian norm, Wojtyła sets it into a more encompassing teleological account of human life as ordered to union with God.

One can restate the personalistic norm in a positive form. "The person is a good toward which the only proper and adequate attitude is love" (*Love and Responsibility*, 41). This positive formulation shows why the personalistic norm can be one of two principles that express "the whole truth" about man. "For the whole law is summed up in a single commandment, You shall love your neighbor as yourself" (Gal 5:14).

While the personalistic norm concerns the *beginning*, the *nature* of the person as person, the second principle, the law of the gift, concerns the *end*, the *fully unfolded life* of the person. Together, the two principles encompass the whole life of persons from beginning to end. They are the fundamental laws of the life of persons.

> One person can give himself or herself, can surrender entirely to another, whether to a human person or to God, and such a giving of the self creates a special form of love which we define as spousal love. This fact goes to prove that the person has a dynamism of its own and that specific laws govern its existence and development. Christ gave expression to this in a saying that is on the face of it profoundly paradoxical: "The one who finds his life shall lose it and the one who loses his life for my sake will find it" (Matt 10:39) ... This is doubly paradoxical: first in that it is possible to step outside one's own "I" in this way, and secondly in that the "I" far from being destroyed or impaired as a result is enlarged and enriched, of course in a super-physical, a moral sense. The Gospel stresses this very clearly and unambiguously: "loses – finds; finds – loses." You will readily see that we have here not merely the personalistic norm, but also bold and explicit words of advice, which make it possible for us to amplify and elaborate on that norm. The world of persons possesses its own laws of existence and of development. (*Love and Responsibility*, 97)

The only point lacking in this remarkable passage from *Love and Responsibility*, which anticipates the core of John Paul II's teaching, is the Trinitarian exemplar. According to *Gaudium et spes* 24:3, what explains the law of the gift is the similarity between the union of divine persons and the union of human persons in truth and love. Wojtyła explicitly discusses the Trinitarian exemplar in his 1948 dissertation on St John of the Cross (see p. 230), but he does not return to it in his theological writings until after Vatican II when he develops his theological method as a "hermeneutics of the gift" on the basis of *Gaudium et spes* 24:3.

In the encyclical *Dominum et vivificantem* (1986), John Paul II lays down the deepest foundation of his hermeneutics of the gift.

> In his intimate life, God "is love," the essential love shared by the three divine Persons: personal love is the Holy Spirit as the Spirit of the Father and the Son. Therefore he "searches even the depths of God," as uncreated Love-Gift. It can be said that in the Holy Spirit the intimate life of the Triune God becomes totally gift, an exchange of mutual love between the divine Persons and that through the Holy Spirit God exists in the mode of gift. It is the Holy Spirit who is the personal expression of this self-giving, of this being-love. He is Person-Love. He is Person-Gift. Here we have an inexhaustible treasure of the reality and an inexpressible deepening of the concept of person in God, which only divine Revelation makes known to us. (*Dominum et vivificantem*, 10)

On this Trinitarian foundation, John Paul II builds his teaching on the image of God. He sees the image not only in each individual person, in the rational nature of the person, but in the communion of persons. "Man becomes an image of God not so much in the moment of solitude as in the moment of communion. He is, in fact, 'from the beginning' an image in which not only the solitude of one Person, who rules the world, mirrors itself, but also the inscrutable, essentially divine communion of Persons" (TOB 9:3). "Being a person in the image and likeness of God thus also involves existing in a relationship, in relation to the other 'I'. This is a prelude to the definitive self-revelation of the Triune God: a living unity in the communion of the Father, Son and Holy Spirit" (Mulieris dignitatem, 7).

It is in light of this Trinitarian image that John Paul II approaches the theology of the human body. The highest purpose of the human body, male and female, is to express the gift of self of bride and bridegroom to each other. Ultimately, this gift is a sacramental sign by which the life of the Trinity itself becomes present in the world.

> Man appears in the visible world as the highest expression of the divine gift, because he bears within himself the inner dimension of the gift. And with it he carries into the world his particular likeness to God ... Thus, in this dimension, a primordial sacrament is constituted, understood as a sign that efficaciously transmits in the visible world the invisible mystery [of Trinitarian communion] hidden in God from eternity ... The body, in fact, and only the body, is capable of making visible what is invisible: the spiritual and the divine. It has been created to transfer into the visible reality of the world the mystery hidden from eternity in God, and thus to be a sign of it. (TOB 19:3–4)

In his *Theology of the Body*, John Paul II unfolds this vision of human sexuality in much detail.

The two principles of *Gaudium et spes* 24:3 can be seen at work also in other areas of John Paul II's theology. The greatness of this theology lies in the disciplined and creative application of an experiential, spousal and Trinitarian vision to the broad range of issues discussed by John Paul II.

Bibliography

The Standard Biography with Extensive Bibliography

Weigel, George, *Witness to Hope: The Biography of John Paul II 1920–2005* (updated edition with new preface, New York: HarperCollins, 2005).

The Seven Books of Karol Wojtyła before his Election:

1948: Doctoral Thesis: *Faith according to St. John of the Cross* (San Francisco: Ignatius Press, 1981). The original Latin text with facing Italian translation: *La dottrina della fede in S. Giovanni della Croce: Doctrina de fide apud S. Joannem a Cruce* (edited by Massimo Bettetini; Milan: Bompiani, 2003).

1953: Habilitation Thesis: *Evaluation of the Possibility of Constructing a Christian Ethics on the Assumptions of Max Scheler's System of Philosophy* (no English translation available). German translation: *Über die Möglichkeit eine christliche Ethik in Anlehnung an Max Scheler zu schaffen*, in Juliusz Stroynowski (ed.), *Primat des Geistes: Philosophische Schriften* (Stuttgart-Degerloch: Seewald, 1980).

1954–7: *Lublin Lectures* (no English translation available). German translation: *Lubliner Vorlesungen* (Stuttgart: Seewald Verlag, 1980). Wide-ranging discussion of the anthropology and ethics of Plato, Aristotle, Augustine, Thomas Aquinas, Utilitarianism, Kant and Scheler.

1957–9: *Love and Responsibility* (San Francisco: Ignatius Press, 1993).

1969: *The Acting Person* (This definitive text of the work established in collaboration with the author by Anna-Teresa Tymieniecka for publication in the Reidel book series Analecta Husserliana, Dordrecht, Boston and London: D. Reidel, 1979). Tymieniecka altered the text substantially, with Wojtyła's generous and general approval, yet in a direction that often distorts Wojtyła's thought.

1972: *Sources of Renewal: The Implementation of the Second Vatican Council* (San Francisco: Harper & Row, 1980).

1976: *Sign of Contradiction* (retreat preached to Paul VI and his household; New York: Seabury Press, 1979).

An authoritative edition of the first five books plus a number of important essays appeared in a single volume in Italian as Karol Wojtyła, *Metafisica della persona: Tutte le opere filosofiche e saggi integranti*, edited by Giovanni Reale and Tadeusz Styczen (Milan: Bompiani, 2003).

The Five Books of John Paul II

1979–84: *Man and Woman He Created Them: A Theology of the Body*, trans. and intro. by Michael Waldstein (Boston: Pauline Books and Media, 2006). John Paul II's main theological work was written before his election (1978) and delivered as a series of catecheses from 1979 to 1984.

1994: *Crossing the Threshold of Hope* (edited by Vittorio Messori; New York: A.A. Knopf, 1994).
1996: *Gift and Mystery: On the Fiftieth Anniversary of My Priestly Ordination* (New York: Doubleday, 1996).
2004: *Rise, Let us be on our Way* (London: Jonathan Cape, 2004).
2005: *Memory and Identity: Personal Reflections* (London: Weidenfeld & Nicolson, 2005).

The Fourteen Encyclicals (Four Trilogies, One Pair)

1979: *Redemptor hominis*: programmatic encyclical, first in the Trinitarian trilogy, on the Son.
1980: *Dives in misericordia*: second in the Trinitarian trilogy, on the Father.
1981: *Laborem exercens*: first in the trilogy of social encyclicals.
1985: *Slavorum apostoli*: first of the two ecumenical encyclicals.
1986: *Dominum et vivificantem*: third in the Trinitarian trilogy, on the Spirit.
1987: *Redemptoris mater*: first in the Christological trilogy.
1987: *Sollicitudo rei socialis*: second in the trilogy of social encyclicals.
1990: *Redemptoris missio*: second in the Christological trilogy.
1991: *Centesimus annus*: third in the trilogy of social encyclicals.
1993: *Veritatis splendor*: first in the fundamental moral trilogy.
1995: *Evangelium vitae*: second in the fundamental moral trilogy.
1995: *Ut unum sint*: second of the two ecumenical encyclicals.
1998: *Fides et ratio*: third in the fundamental moral trilogy.
2003: *Ecclesia de Eucharistia*: third in the Christological trilogy.

Chapter 24
Benedict XVI/Joseph Ratzinger

Gösta Hallonsten

A theologian on Peter's chair is something unusual, at least in modern times. Joseph Ratzinger's thinking can be followed through his voluminous writings on a variety of subjects. He has continued to write after his election as Pope Benedict XVI. It is difficult to draw a distinction between "the Pope's theology" and "Ratzinger's theology"; but this is necessary only to some extent, since the problem did not arise only with the outcome of the conclave on April 18, 2005. It arose already in 1977, when Ratzinger was appointed archbishop of Munich, and then became head of the Congregation for the Doctrine of the Faith in Rome in 1981. During his time as cardinal, Joseph Ratzinger continued to publish extensively. He frequently gave lectures in his own name (so to speak) on topics that were being discussed at the same time in statements and texts issued by the Congregation for the Doctrine of the Faith. This double role was a departure from the tradition, as was John Paul II's manner of exercising the papal ministry. Despite this, one should not treat the texts of the Congregation for the Doctrine of the Faith as a part of Ratzinger's writings. They have their genesis in a lengthy period of consultations with theologians, members of the curia, and the cardinals who make up the Congregation itself. The situation with Pope Benedict XVI is somewhat different. In addition to the publication of two volumes of his study of Jesus, which according to the foreword "is not in any sense an act of the magisterium, but is only the expression of my personal seeking 'the face of the Lord' (cf. Psalm 27:8),"[1] his first encyclical, *Deus Caritas Est*, is strongly marked by his own theology. These texts must therefore be included among his own writings. Although his other discourses, sermons, and official texts certainly have a clearly "Ratzingerian" profile, we leave them out of this presentation.

Style and Originality

One who studies Joseph Ratzinger's writings faces a number of problems. To begin with, he has written an enormous amount, and the perspectives in his writings are numerous. Ratzinger is a Catholic theologian in every sense of the term. He lives in and from the tradition, and he has been able to discuss most of the themes that a Catholic theologian might conceivably be interested in. Every presentation of his theology

---

[1] *Jesus von Nazareth*, I, 22 [All quotations from Benedict XVI/Joseph Ratzinger and other German authors are translated from the German originals by Brian McNeil].

must therefore to some extent be selective. Another problem that we encounter is a paradox. Few contemporary theologians are as easy to read, and write in such a delightful style, as Joseph Ratzinger, but a closer analysis encounters difficulties that are connected precisely with his language and style. There is a tone in the argument and discussion that sometimes conceals what the author himself thinks. The reader feels that he is being invited to accompany the author on a journey; but at the end, it can be difficult to know what conclusions have been drawn. Besides this, there is a strongly polemical note from the end of the 1960s onwards. The author seems to need to set up an opposing position, against which his own arguments are then directed. At the same time, one cannot deny that Joseph Ratzinger has an acute eye for the weaknesses in contemporary trends.

A third problem is more far-reaching, and is necessarily a major theme in the present essay: How is Joseph Ratzinger to be characterized as a theologian? What is his contribution, wherein lies his originality? For many reasons, it is too early to answer this question; but a few points can be made. Joseph Ratzinger has not formed a school, although his "Schülerkreis" has come together with their former teacher every year since 1970. He has no theological system "of his own," like Karl Rahner, nor can he be compared to Hans Urs von Balthasar, a theologian to whom he is close. It is very difficult to detect any striving for originality in Ratzinger. There is no single fundamental idea or theme around which he systematically constructs his theology. The only systematic-theological monograph (in the narrower sense of this term) that he wrote as Vol. 9 of the series *Kleine katholische Dogmatik*, edited by Alfons Auer: *Eschatologie – Tod und ewiges Leben* (*Eschatology: Death and Eternal Life*), 1977. In the same year, Ratzinger was appointed archbishop of Munich. In his autobiography, *Aus meinem Leben. Erinnerungen* (*Milestones. Memoirs: 1927–1977*), 1998, he writes that he had long planned to write a dogmatic theology of his own and that he had been ready to start this task in Regensburg, before the appointment came: "I was looking forward to say something of my own, something new – yet something that had grown totally within the faith of the church. But obviously, this is not what I was meant to do."[2] Joseph Ratzinger certainly had his own "vision of the whole,"[3] but it is characteristic of his theological self-understanding that this vision should have grown totally within the framework of the church's faith. As a theologian, therefore, Joseph Ratzinger/Benedict XVI can be called a *vir ecclesiasticus*. And he became more and more of a "man of the church" as time went on; this can help explain his polemical digressions, which seem to be dictated by a passionate desire to defend the church's faith against the innovations of theological fashion. His pupil H.-J. Verweyen has written: "Unlike many of his theological contemporaries, he adopted from the beginning of his teaching activity the principle that he would not say anything that could sow confusion about the doctrine that the Catholic church teaches as universally binding. He did not allow his passion for asking academic questions about prevailing doctrinal opinions to lead

---

[2] Joseph Ratzinger, *Aus meinem Leben. Erinnerungen* (1927–77) (München, 1998), p. 176.
[3] Ibid.

to the neglect of his pastoral ministry, which he had received through his ordination as a 'simple priest'."[4]

From Renewer to "Reactionary"

The difficulty about describing Joseph Ratzinger's theology has a lot to do with the picture of him as "conservative," an adjective that has been applied to him since the end of the 1960s. What counts as "conservative" is, however, something that varies in accordance with specific circumstances; and those who follow Ratzinger's thinking from his 1954 doctoral dissertation, *Volk und Haus Gottes in Augustins Lehre von der Kirche* (*The People and House of God in Augustine's Doctrine of Church*), up to the present day will encounter an extremely consistent thinker. The shifts and changes in his theology, for example in ecclesiology, are relatively slight. The fact that Ratzinger was characterized as a "progressive" before and during the Second Vatican Council says more about the fundamental direction in this theology than the later label "conservative." For one thing is beyond doubt: Joseph Ratzinger turned his back from the outset on the neo-scholastic theology which was dominant at that period. His theology is deeply anchored in history, and he can be seen as a representative (though an independent representative) of the *ressourcement* movement ("back to the sources"). Henri de Lubac influenced him early on in his career, and he was close to Hans Urs von Balthasar. But he had "an interesting position of his own"[5] in the context of this new interest in historical thinking in Catholic theology that can be observed in the mid-twentieth century. Like de Lubac and von Balthasar, Ratzinger began with the church fathers, and more specifically with Augustine. It is easy to trace the trajectories from his doctoral dissertation to his later ecclesiological thinking, and to themes such as truth and reason, or the understanding of society and of history. After his dissertation, he began to study scholasticism, and chose, in agreement with his supervisor Gottlieb Söhngen, to study Bonaventure's concept of revelation and theology of history. When he presented his professorial dissertation to the faculty in Munich in 1955, however, he encountered resistance. The well-known dogmatic theologian Michael Schmaus wrote a critical report, and the faculty sent the manuscript back to Ratzinger, requesting him to submit an improved version. When it was finally approved in 1957, it amounted to only one-third of the original manuscript. It was published in 1959 under the title *Die Geschichtstsheologie des Heiligen Bonaventura* (*The Theology of History in St. Bonaventura*). This event played an important role in Joseph Ratzinger's biography, since he had already begun his career as an academic teacher at Freising near Munich, and a professorial dissertation (*Habilitation*) is a presupposition for a tenured professorship at a German university. Ratzinger himself has described the drama in his autobiography, where he also gives the theological explanation for

---

[4] Hans-Jürgen Verweyen, *Joseph Ratzinger – Benedikt XVI. Die Entwicklung seines Denkens* (Darmstadt, 2007), p. 82.
[5] Ibid., p. 33.

Schmaus' opposition. This concerns the concept of revelation. Neo-scholasticism generally identified revelation with the revealed truths, and this is why scripture could sometimes be referred to as "revelation" *tout court*. The young Dr. Ratzinger claimed that such an identification was unthinkable for the high middle ages, where "'Revelation' was always the concept of an act: this word designates the act in which God shows himself, not the objectified result of this act. And because this is so, the concept of 'revelation' always includes also the receiving subject."[6] Revelation thus necessarily entails receiving by someone. As Ratzinger himself notes, this discovery was important for him, when the Second Vatican Council debated revelation. The more dynamic concept of revelation contained in the conciliar constitution *Dei Verbum* is completely in accord with Ratzinger's discovery. In his commentary on this constitution in the supplementary volume to the *Lexikon für Theologie und Kirche*, it is easy to discern the link. And it is easy to agree with Hans-Jürgen Verweyen's evaluation of the two first parts of Ratzinger's study of Bonaventure, which were not published: "It is a sad curiosity that Joseph Ratzinger of all people, whose dangerous concoction (at least, that is how Michael Schmaus saw it) was not allowed to see the light in published form, was soon afterwards a respected representative of the theological avant-garde at the Second Vatican Council. Yet he was regarded only a few years later as a member of the group of the worst reactionaries."[7]

The Early Ratzinger

Joseph Ratzinger was ordained to the priesthood with his brother Georg in 1951. He had completed his doctoral dissertation even before his ordination; it was submitted for an essay prize awarded by the theological faculty in Munich. The fundamental theologian Gottlieb Söhngen had proposed the topic for this competition, which Ratzinger won; his essay was thereby automatically accepted as a doctoral dissertation. It was published in printed form in 1954 (see above). After his ordination, he worked for one year as curate in a parish in Munich, and was then appointed to teach at the seminary in Freising. In 1954, he became professor of dogmatics and fundamental theology at the Philosophical-Theological University College in Freising. His academic career then took him to Bonn, where Ratzinger was professor of fundamental theology from 1959–63; to Münster, where he was professor of dogmatics until 1966; to Tübingen, where he was professor of dogmatics until 1969; and finally to Regensburg, where he held the chair of dogmatics until 1977.

---

[6] Ratzinger, *Aus meinem Leben*, p. 84.

[7] Verweyen, *Joseph Ratzinger – Benedikt XVI*, p. 25. Now that the professorial dissertation in its entirety has been published in 2009 in *Joseph Ratzinger. Gesammelte Schriften,* Vol. 2, it is possible to study the early Ratzinger's theology in greater depth. There is good reason to believe that his study of Bonaventure left a lasting mark on Ratzinger's theology, both in its content and in its form. See also Marianne Schlosser, "Zu den Bonaventura-Studien Joseph Ratzingers," 35–7, in *Joseph Ratzinger. Gesammelte Schriften*, Vol. 2.

Joseph Ratzinger's initial research had been into historical material, but as professor he had to lecture on all the themes of dogmatic theology, as well as on fundamental theology, including what today is called the theology of religions.

Three of his early writings, which were reprinted later, deserve special mention. His inaugural lecture in Bonn, "Der Gott des Glaubens und der Gott der Philosophen. Ein Beitrag zum Problem der Theologia Naturalis," (*"The God of Faith and the God of the Philosophers. A Contribution to the Problem of Theologia Naturalis"*) takes up a theme that often recurs in his writings: the rationality of faith and Ratzinger's positive view of the early church's synthesis between biblical and Greek thinking. There is a direct trajectory from this lecture to Pope Benedict's lecture in Regensburg in 2006.

In a festschrift for Karl Rahner in 1964, Ratzinger discusses "Der christliche Glaube und die Weltreligionen" ("The Unity and Truth of Religions: The Place of Christianity in the History of Religions") He assesses Rahner's idea of "anonymous Christians" – the tone is friendly, but the substance is critical. He also anticipates today's discussion in the theology of religions, and rejects the attempt by Christians to look at the religions from the perspective of the question of salvation. This is pursued in a number of lectures delivered from the 1990s up to his election as pope; these are collected in the book *Wahrheit, Glaube, Toleranz* (*Truth and Tolerance: Christian Belief and World Religions*). For Ratzinger, the relationship between the religions is not static, but changes through exchange and reciprocal influence. Religion cannot be seen as separated from culture. In this context, he also rejects the idea of the "inculturation" of the Gospel as misleading. There is no "pure" Gospel devoid of culture, and this means that the relationship between the Gospel and various cultures ought rather to be considered in the framework of what he prefers to call "interculturality."

A third important essay was "Ein Versuch zur Frage des Traditionsbegriffs" ("An Essay on the Question of the Concept of Tradition") published in 1964, where Ratzinger interprets the decree on tradition promulgated by the Council of Trent and takes a position in the lively discussion about scripture and tradition that was going on in Catholic theology just before and during the Second Vatican Council. This is followed up in the important commentary on the first two chapters of *Dei Verbum*.

Theologian at the Council

During Ratzinger's time as a young and promising theologian in Bonn, he attracted the attention of the archbishop of Cologne, Cardinal Joseph Frings, who took him with him as his personal adviser during the Council. From the end of the first session onwards, Ratzinger was an official conciliar theologian (*peritus*). He worked closely with Karl Rahner, Yves Congar, and other celebrated theologians. Ratzinger played an important role in the work on the texts about revelation, the church as sacrament, episcopal collegiality, and mission. Already during the discussion of *Gaudium et spes* – on the church in today's world – Ratzinger criticized the text. He has repeated this criticism many times, beginning with his commentary in the *Lexikon für Theologie und Kirche*. He found the text far too optimistic about human progress, and held that its statements about sin and its consequences did not go far enough. During the Council, Ratzinger also worked together with Hans Küng, who ensured that he was appointed to a professorship in Tübingen in 1966. With Küng and the other well-known conciliar theologians, Ratzinger was from the beginning a member of the team behind the periodical *Concilium*, founded in 1965, until he broke with them in 1969 and founded *Communio* with Hans Urs von Balthasar and others. It became ever clearer in these years that the paths of Ratzinger and Küng would diverge. In relation to Rahner, too, Ratzinger (according to his own account) had realized early on in the Council years that they "lived on two different planets, in theological terms."[8] The student protests in Tübingen were a turning point for Ratzinger. He experienced the turbulence when students occupied the lecture rooms. In his autobiography, he attacks the "destruction of theology in keeping with the Marxist messianism," which led to an ideologization of faith and an instrumentalization of the church for political goals.[9] Ratzinger's criticism of political theology runs like a leitmotiv through his later writings. The critique of Marxism occurs surprisingly often, most recently in his first encyclical; but the foundations are already laid in his study of Augustine's *City of God* and of Bonaventure's debate with Joachim of Fiore's vision of an "age of the Spirit" when the poor would reign. Aidan Nichols writes: "Before the name 'liberation theology' was ever heard of, Ratzinger had to arrive at some judgment about this uncanny thirteenth-century anticipation of liberationalist eschatology."[10]

The Creed and Eschatology

Before the student revolution broke out, Ratzinger had delivered a series of lectures in Tübingen, entitled *Einführung in das Christentum* (*Introduction to Christianity*). In published form, this was to become the most widely read of his books, at least until his election as pope, and it remains the best introduction to his theology. Ratzinger's beautiful prose and argumentative power plead on behalf of the truth of the Christian faith, as this is formulated in the Apostolic Creed. Although Ratzinger appears here as a Catholic theologian whose primary aim is to expound the church's faith, there are two things in this book that are rather striking. First, it is clear that the center of gravity lies in the common content of faith that is shared by all Christians. He deals only briefly with ecclesiology, and the polemic in the book does not take the form of controversial theology, but is directed against the "demythologization" and relativization of the historicity of faith. Secondly, Ratzinger displays great skill in explaining the meaning of the traditional articles of faith. This meaning lies in their existential, almost personalistic understanding. Ratzinger writes that the biblical concept of God is paradoxical, since it combines two antithetical ideas, "since it is

---

[8] Ratzinger, *Aus meinem Leben*, p. 131.
[9] Ibid., pp. 139 and 150.
[10] Aidan Nichols, *The Thought of Pope Benedict XVI. New Edition. An Introduction to the Theology of Joseph Ratzinger* (London and New York, 2007), p. 65.

believed that Being is Person and that the Person is Being; that only that which is hidden is believed to be the one who is totally near; that only that which is inaccessible is believed to be the one who is accessible; that *that* One is believed to be *the* One who is for everything and for whom everyone is."[11] Ratzinger writes positively about the early church's use of Greek philosophy; but the biblical faith in God has broken through the general element and emphasizes the special and personal elements that are characteristic of the concept of God and of anthropology. Although the Christian faith in God is no less monotheistic than other religions, the unity in God is a relational unity. "Father," "Son," and "Spirit" are relational concepts. They are characterized by a reciprocal "gift of self" (*Hingabe*). This is not something that is added onto the Person externally; rather, the Person "is identical with the act of self-giving."[12] This is entailed by the fact that God is love (the title Benedict XVI later gave to his first encyclical). The key to the interpretation of *Einführung in das Christentum* is the "principle of love" that runs through the book, and Ratzinger himself has stated that he was influenced by the early philosophy of Max Scheler and by the Augustinian personalism of the Catholic theologian Romano Guardini.

The main tendency in *Einführung in das Christentum* is found in Ratzinger's *Eschatologie* too. He vigorously attacks contemporary attempts to get away from "outdated" elements in classical eschatology, such as belief in an intermediate state and in the immortality of the soul. Apart from the polemic, however, Ratzinger's presentation is marked by a thorough discussion of German exegesis, a wide knowledge of the history of eschatology, and a subtle discussion of what the traditional ideas, which he accepts, can be thought to mean. Ratzinger holds that we cannot have any concrete ideas about the new world. The confession of faith in "the resurrection of the flesh" entails specifically the certainty that the cosmos has a goal: spirit and matter are to be united in a new and definitive manner.[13]

The Church, Ecumenism, and Liberation Theology

Ratzinger has often returned to ecclesiology after he completed his doctoral dissertation on Augustine's understanding of the church. Important books in this field are *Die christliche Brüderlichkeit* (*Christian Brotherliness*), 1960; *Das neue Volk Gottes. Entwürfe zur Ekklesiologie* (*The New People of God. An Outline for Ecclesiology*), 1969; and *Weggemeinschaft des Glaubens. Kirche als communio* (*Pilgrim Fellowship of Faith: The Church as Communion*), 2002. The basic thrust of his ecclesiology is constant. He consistently maintains a eucharistic *communio*-ecclesiology with an emphasis on the sacramentality of the episcopal ministry. Ratzinger finds the priority that was given to the idea of the "people of God" in the post-conciliar period problematic.

---

[11] Joseph Ratzinger, *Einführung in das Christentum. Vorlesungen über das Apostolische Glaubensbekenntnis* (Munich, 8th ed., 2006), p. 125.

[12] Ibid., p. 171.

[13] Joseph Ratzinger, *Eschatologie – Tod und ewiges Leben* (Regensburg, 1977), p. 160.

He had already anticipated this discussion in his doctoral thesis. The church as the people of God can be understood only on the basis of the idea of the body of Christ. The Council's emphasis on the church as a sacrament is also fundamental. There are only slight shifts of emphasis in Ratzinger's ecclesiology, but they are important in terms of church politics. These concern his view of collegiality and the relationship between the universal and the local church.

The collected essays in Theologische Prinzipienlehre. Bausteine zur Fundamentaltheologie (Principles of Catholic Theology), 1982 and in Kirche, Ökumene und Politik (Church, Ecumenism and Politics: New Essays in Ecclesiology), 1987, are particularly important. A number of these essays show that Ratzinger is a well informed and competent ecumenist. He was for many years a member of the "Ecumenical Working Group of Evangelical and Catholic Theologians," and he was one of those who took the initiative for the discussion of a Catholic acceptance of the Confessio Augustana (1976–80). He has an extensive knowledge of Luther and Lutheran theology, and despite a number of critical statements in this field, it must be acknowledged that he played a decisive role in the final stages of the genesis of the Joint Declaration on the Doctrine of Justification in 1999. His election as pope was greeted by the Orthodox churches with certain expectations that naturally had their basis in his earlier participation in the dialogue with the Eastern churches and in his theological anchoring in the early church. This is shown by the frequently quoted – and frequently misunderstood – statement that Ratzinger made in 1976: "In terms of the doctrine of primacy, Rome need not [muss nicht] demand of the East more than what was formulated and lived in the first millennium."[14]

The clash with the theology of liberation that was expressed in the two documents of the Congregation for the Doctrine of the Faith (1984 and 1986) is, of course, reflected in Ratzinger's writings. As I have mentioned, this clash has a much longer pre-history in his thinking. During his time as cardinal, Joseph Ratzinger took up ever more frequently questions about the church and politics, often interwoven with themes such as faith and reason, tolerance, and the conscience. The question of Europe's identity is also important for Ratzinger. This theme is reflected in book titles such as *Wendezeit für Europa, Werte in Zeiten des Umbruchs* (*A Turning Point for Europe: The Church in the Modern World – Assessment and Forecast*), *Glaube – Wahrheit – Toleranz* (*Truth and Tolerance: Christian Belief and World Religions*), and *Dialektik der Säkularisierung* (*The Dialectics of Secularization: On Reason and Religion*). The last-named book contains his famous dialogue with the German philosopher Jürgen Habermas. It is less well known that Cardinal Ratzinger took part several times in public debates with secular Italian intellectuals such as Marcello Pera and Paolo Flores d'Arcais. It is worth looking somewhat more closely at the group of themes that are discussed, especially because these concern basic issues in Joseph Ratzinger's understanding of theology and philosophy.

---

[14] Joseph Ratzinger, "Die ökumenische Situation – Orthodoxie, Katholizismus und Reformation," in *Theologische Prinzipienlehre. Bausteine zur Fundamentaltheologie* (Munich, 1982), p. 209.

Enlightenment Thinking and the Crisis of the West

When the Second Vatican Council promulgated its decree on religious freedom, *Dignitatis humanae*, Joseph Ratzinger greeted this as "the end of the middle ages, indeed the end of the Constantinian era."[15] He laments in many passages that the Christian faith's claim to truth and universality was obscured by the demand that the institutional church should enjoy political domination. The late Ratzinger affirms that the Enlightenment critique of reason performed an important function in view of the correct distinction between religion and politics. At the same time, he continues to defend Christianity's place in the public sphere. Its function is to remind society that the political order is not the ultimate foundation of society. Here, the conscience plays an important role; on this point, Ratzinger was influenced early on by John Henry Newman. The conscience is more than a subjective conviction. It is the authority that reminds the human person of the truth. Ratzinger insists on what he called, in his dialogue with Habermas, "the pre-political fundamental moral values for the free society." In the same dialogue, he admitted that the doctrine of the natural law is problematic in its traditional form. Nevertheless, it is of course in this direction that he argues. Freedom must not be allowed to become a formal, empty concept that is at the mercy of shifting majorities. Freedom needs content. "We can define it as the safeguarding of human rights, but we can also describe it more broadly as the guarantee that things will go well both with society and with the individual ..."[16] Ratzinger explicitly appeals to secular opinion. On the one hand, he criticizes what one can call "instrumental rationality" or "the self-mutilation of the reason."[17] It is thought that empirical-positivistic science can offer endless technical possibilities; but Ratzinger believes that the restricted concept of reason that this science bears means that it risks abolishing the human person in the long term. On the other hand, Ratzinger maintains that Enlightenment thinking and Christianity have common roots, and that the Enlightenment reason includes the recognition of inalienable universal values. Rationality belongs to the essence of Christianity.[18] Christianity and Enlightenment thinking share the original faith in the rationality of the world, and this means faith that reason, in a broader sense, can arrive at norms that guide the defense of human dignity. Whereas the Enlightenment defended universal morality *etsi Deus non daretur* ("as if God did not exist"), Ratzinger proposes that we should reverse this today: "Even the one who cannot affirm God's existence should be able to live and to attempt to shape his life *veluti si Deus daretur* – as if God existed."[19] This does not pose

---

[15] Joseph Ratzinger, *Ergebnisse und Probleme der dritten Konzilsperiode* (Köln: 1965), p. 31.

[16] Joseph Ratzinger, *Werte in Zeiten des Umbruchs. Die Herausforderungen der Zukunft bestehen* (Freiburg im Breisgau, 2005), p. 52. English trans. by B.McN.: *Values in a Time of Upheaval*, 54.

[17] Joseph Ratzinger, *Ohne Wurzeln. Der Relativismus und die Krise der Europäischen Kultur* (with Marcello Pera) (Augsburg, 2005), p. 74.

[18] Joseph Ratzinger, *Glaube, Wahrheit, Toleranz. Das Christentum und die Weltreligionen* (Freiburg im Breisgau, 2003), p. 68.

[19] Ratzinger, *Ohne Wurzeln*, 82.

a threat to the individual's freedom to believe what he or she will. Rather, "that which is held in common receives a criterion and a point of reference that we desperately need."[20] Behind this attitude lies Ratzinger's solid conviction, which has remained constant over the years, that European culture is built upon a synthesis between faith and reason, between biblical and Greek thinking, and that this synthesis cannot be renounced. The relationship between faith and reason is reciprocally critical: "Without faith, the reason is not complete; but faith without reason is not human."[21]

The Role of Philosophy

With this view of Enlightenment thinking, faith and reason, etc., Ratzinger/Benedict XVI has a clear goal when he takes part in debates. Commentaries on philosophy and philosophical reasoning also play a large role in his theology, but it is striking that he has never explicitly and methodologically given a philosophical or fundamental-theological exposition of his theology. One can indeed to a certain extent regard the Introduction to *Einführung in das Christentum* as a brief fundamental theology, but it is precisely in this context that Ratzinger has been described philosophically as an "Idealist" and "Platonist." It is clear that he operates in this Introduction with the dichotomy between "visible" and "invisible": "Christian faith [...] is the option that takes the invisible as more real than the visible. It is the profession of faith in the primacy of the invisible, as that which is truly real."[22] In combination with his explicitly personalistic interpretation of the Christian faith, these words prompt the suggestion that he is influenced by Idealism, and this charge has been leveled by Walter Kasper and others. Ratzinger rejected this, and the discussion between these two theologians was not made any easier by the fact that it took place while Marxism was going from strength to strength at the western European universities. Another important factor here is the very clear emphasis on history in Ratzinger's theology. In the Introduction to the *Einführung*, the offensiveness of the Christian faith lies not only in the primacy of the invisible, but also in the fact that this faith is tied to a specific history. The break with the domination of neo-scholasticism in Catholic theology also gives Ratzinger's thinking an emphasis on history; but the foundations of his view of theology and history were laid in his studies of Augustine and Bonaventure, two thinkers in the Christian Platonist tradition.

There can be no doubt that Ratzinger's relationship to modernity is strangely ambivalent. One reason for the surprisingly strong opposition between Ratzinger and the majority of German Catholic theologians is probably that the latter see German Idealism as a natural starting point and dialogue partner. The German variant of Enlightenment thinking, with the history of its Romantic-Idealist reception, has never

---

[20] Ibid.
[21] Ratzinger, *Glaube, Wahrheit, Toleranz*, p. 110.
[22] Ratzinger, *Einführung in das Christentum*, 8th ed., p. 66.

played any constructive role in Ratzinger's theology. This is one of the difficulties in classifying him, because in one sense, he too comes from the same context.

The Interpretation of Scripture

Finally, the question of the relationship between theology and philosophy in Joseph Ratzinger also recurs when we look at his attitude to historical-critical biblical scholarship. On the one hand, it is clear that Ratzinger has looked at critical biblical research with a positive eye from the beginning of his studies. He has applied and taken up the results of exegesis on his own theology, both constructively and with critical acuteness. In his commentary on *Dei Verbum*, Ratzinger notes that one of the main questions behind this conciliar constitution was how the historical-critical method can be applied to the exposition of sacred scripture. One cannot say that the Council resolved the question of the relationship between the church's exposition of the Bible and critical exegesis; but Ratzinger adds: "One thing, at any rate, is certain: that one cannot pass by the historical-critical method, and that it responds to a demand that theology itself makes."[23] In practice, Ratzinger has followed this line, as can be seen most recently in *Jesus von Nazareth I* (*Jesus of Nazareth I*): "Seldom has the historical-critical method been given such a central position in the construction of Christian doctrine as here. According to the Pope, it is as it were a defense of the incarnational principle of faith."[24] At the same time, Ratzinger/Benedict criticizes the limitations of the historical-critical method and employs what is known as "canon criticism" in his book: the starting point for the interpretation is the canon and a christological hermeneutic that sees a direction and a goal in the various texts. The exposition is strongly influenced by the patristic interpretation of the Bible, though it is not identical to this. Joseph Ratzinger had earlier set out his criticism in the important essay "Schriftauslegung im Widerstreit" ("Interpretation of Scripture in Antagonism"), 1989, where he criticizes first and foremost the philosophical presuppositions of the historical method. An exegesis that employs a completely inner-worldly explanatory model and the presupposition that history is always homogeneous – in other words, that what does not happen now cannot have happened in the past – cannot reach the message and the claim of scripture. Ratzinger proposes a dual method of exposition: "Obviously, the texts must first be placed in their historical context and expounded on the basis of this context. But in a second exposition, they must also be seen from the perspective of the entire historical development and must be understood on the basis

---

[23] Joseph Ratzinger, "Dogmatische Konstitution über die göttliche Offenbarung (Dei Verbum). Einleitung und Kommentar zu Kap. I und II," *Lexikon für Theologie und Kirche*, 2nd ed. Vol. 13, 1967; p. 499.

[24] Martin Ebner, in Söding, Thomas, (ed.), *Das Jesusbuch des Papstes. Die Antwort der Neutestamentler* (Freiburg, 2007), p. 33.

of Christ as the midpoint of the events. Only the two methods together allow one to understand the Bible."[25]

A Creative Exponent of the Tradition

It is clear that Joseph Ratzinger/Benedict XVI will be regarded by history as one of the most important theologians of the twentieth century. One cannot pass him by, if one wants to understand the break with neo-scholastic theology and the breakthrough for the ideas that leave their mark on the documents of the Second Vatican Council. The reception of important councils always proves problematic, and it is therefore very difficult to get a perspective on Ratzinger's theology, since it came to be seen very largely as a controversial contribution to the post-conciliar discussion. A somewhat different and perhaps even more difficult question is whether Ratzinger/Benedict is an original theologian. He has scarcely ever endeavored to be original, although he has passionately defended his own positions. Despite the polemic, he himself has always seen this as a defense of the given truth and of the tradition. But he is a creative exponent who thinks his own thoughts.

Bibliography

Primary Literature

Volk und Haus Gottes in Augustins Lehre von der Kirche (Munich: Zink, 1954; reprinted 1992). (*The People and the House of God in Augustine's Doctrine of Church*).
Joseph Ratzinger Gesammelte Schriften, hg. v. Gerhard Ludwig Müller, in *Verbindung mit dem Institut Papst Benedikt XVI.*, Regensburg. Band 2: *Offenbarungsverständnis und Geschichtstheologie Bonaventuras. Habilitationsschrift und Bonaventura-Studien* (Freiburg: Herder, 2009). (*Understanding of Revelation and Theology of History in Bonaventure*).
Die Geschichtstheologie des Heiligen Bonaventura (Munich: Schnell und Steiner, 1959; reprinted 1992). English: *The Theology of History in St. Bonaventure* (Chicago: Franciscian Herald Press, 1971).
"Der Gott des Glaubens und der Gott der Philosophen. Ein Beitrag zum Problem der Theologia Naturalis," 1960 (reprinted in Vom Wiederauffinden der Mitte. Texte aus vier Jahrzehnten, 1997). (*The God of Faith and the God of the Philosopphers. A Contribution to the Problem of Theologia Naturalis*).

---

[25] Joseph Ratzinger, "Schriftauslegung im Widerstreit," 1989. Reprinted 2005 in *Wort Gottes. Schrift – Tradition – Amt* (Freiburg im Breisgau, 2005), pp. 111–12. The books about Jesus by Benedict XVI/Joseph Ratzinger have already generated an extensive debate and secondary literature, especially in German. See Gunnar Anger and Jan-Heiner Tück, "Vorstudien und Echo."

Die christliche Brüderlichkeit (München: Kösel-Verlag, 1960). (*Christian Brotherliness*).

"Der christliche Glaube und die Weltreligionen," 1964. Reprinted in *Vom Wiederauffinden der Mitte. Texte aus vier Jahrzehnten* (Freiburg im Breisgau: Herder, 1997) and as ch. 1 in *Glaube, Wahrheit, Toleranz*). English: "The Unity and Truth of Religions: The Place of Christianity in the History of Religions", in *Truth and Tolerance: Christian Belief and World Religions* (San Fransisco: Ignatius Press, 2004).

"Ein Versuch zur Frage des Traditionsbegriffs," 1965. Reprinted in *Wort Gottes. Schrift – Tradition – Amt* (Freiburg im Breisgau: Herder, 2005). ("An Essay on the Question of the Concept of Tradition").

Ergebnisse und Probleme der dritten Konzilsperiode (Köln: 1965). (*Results and Problems of the Third Period of the Council*).

"Dogmatische Konstitution über die göttliche Offenbarung (Dei Verbum). Einleitung und Kommentar zu Kap. I und II," *Lexikon für Theologie und Kirche*, 2nd ed. Vol. 13, 1967. ("Dogmatic Constitution on the Divine Revelation (Dei Verbum). Introduction and Commentary to Chs. 1 and II").

Einführung in das Christentum. Vorlesungen über das Apostolische Glaubensbekenntnis (Munich: Kösel, 1968). English: *Introduction to Christianity* (San Fransisco: Ignatius Press, 2004. Second ed.).

Das Neue Volk Gottes. Entwürfe zur Ekklesiologie (Düsseldorf: Patmos, 1969). (*The New People of God. An Outline of Ecclesiology*).

Eschatologie – Tod und ewiges Leben (Regensburg: Pustet, 1977) Auer and Ratzinger, Kleine katholische Dogmatik, IX. English: *Eschatology: Death and Eternal Life* (Washington, D.C.: Catholic University of America Press).

Theologische Prinzipienlehre. Bausteine zur Fundamentaltheologie (Munich: Erich Wewel Verlag, 1982). English: *Principles of Catholic Theology* (San Fransisco: Ignatius Press, 1987).

Kirche, Ökumene und Politik. Neue Versuche zur Ekklesiologie (Freiburg im Breisgau: Johannes Verlag, 1987). English: *Church, Ecumenism and Politics: New Essays in Ecclesiology* (Slough: St. Paul Publications, 1988).

"Schriftauslegung im Widerstreit," 1989 (reprinted 2005 in Wort Gottes. Schrift – Tradition – Amt) ("Interpretation of Scripture in Antagonism").

Wendezeit für Europa? Diagnose und Prognosen zur Lage von Kirche und Welt (Freiburg im Breisgau: Johannes Verlag, 1991). English: *A Turning Point for Europe: The Church in the Modern World – Assessment and Forecast* (San Fransisco: Ignatius Press, 1994).

Aus meinem Leben. Erinnerungen (1927–1977) (München, 1998). English: *Milestones. Memoirs: 1927–1977* (San Francisco: Ignatius Press, 1998).

Weggemeinschaft des Glaubens. Kirche als Communio (Augsburg: Sankt Ulrich Verlag, 2002). English: *Pilgrim Fellowship of Faith: The Church as Communion* (San Fransisco: Ignatius Press, 2005).

Glaube, Wahrheit, Toleranz. Das Christentum und die Weltreligionen (Freiburg im Breisgau: Herder, 2003). English: *Truth and Tolerance: Christian Belief and World Religions* (San Fransisco: Ignatius Press 2004).

Werte in Zeiten des Umbruchs. Die Herausforderungen der Zukunft bestehen (Freiburg im Breisgau: Herder, 2005). English: *Values in a Time of Upheaval* (New York: Crossroad; San Fransisco: Ignatius Press, 2006).

Dialektik der Säkularisierung. Über Vernunft und Religion (with Jürgen Habermas) (Freiburg: Herder, 2005). English: *The Dialectics of Secularization: On Reason and Religion* (San Fransisco: Ignatius Press, 2007).

Ohne Wurzeln. Der Relativismus und die Krise der Europäischen Kultur (with Marcello Pera) (Augsburg: Sankt Ulrich Verlag, 2005). English: *Without Roots: The West, Relativism, Christianity, Islam* (New York: Basic Books, 2007).

Deus Caritas Est. Encyclical (Vatican City: Libreria Editrice Vaticana, 2006). English: *God is Love* (San Fransisco: Ignatius Press, 2006).

Jesus von Nazareth, 1: Von der Taufe im Jordan bis zur Verklärung (Freiburg: Herder, 2007). English: *Jesus of Nazareth: From the Baptism in the Jordan to the Transfiguration* (San Fransisco: Ignatius Press, 2008).

Jesus von Nazareth, 2: Vom Einzug in Jerusalem bis zur Auferstehung (Freiburg: Herder, 2011). English: *Jesus of Nazareth: Holy Week: From the Entrance into Jerusalem to The Resurrection* (San Fransisco: Ignatius Press, 2011).

Secondary Literature

Nichols, Aidan, *The Thought of Pope Benedict XVI. New Edition. An Introduction to the Theology of Joseph Ratzinger* (London and New York: Burns and Oates, 2007). With extensive bibliography.

Verweyen, Hans-Jürgen, *Joseph Ratzinger – Benedikt XVI. Die Entwicklung seines Denkens* (Darmstadt: Primus Verlag, 2007).

Rowland, Tracey, *Ratzinger's Faith. The Theology of Pope Benedict XVI* (Oxford: Oxford University Press, 2008).

Meier-Hamidi, Frank, and Ferdinand Schumacher, (eds), *Der Theologe Joseph Ratzinger* (Quaestiones disputatae 222) (Freiburg: Herder, 2007).

Marianne Schlosser, "Zu den Bonaventura-Studien Joseph Ratzingers", pp. 29–37, in: Joseph Ratzinger Gesammelte Schriften, hg. v. Gerhard Ludwig Müller, in *Verbindung mit dem Institut Papst Benedikt XVI. Band 2: Offenbarungsverständnis und Geschichtstheologie Bonaventuras. Habilitationsschrift und Bonaventura-Studien* (Regensburg: Herder, 2009).

Söding, Thomas, (ed.), *Das Jesusbuch des Papstes. Die Antwort der Neutestamentler* (Freiburg: Herder, 2007).

Pro Ecclesia. A Journal of Catholic and Evangelical Theology. Volume XVII, Number 2, Spring 2008: "A Book symposium on Pope Benedict XVI, Jesus of Nazareth."

Anger, Gunnar and Tück, Jan-Heiner, "Vorstudien und Echo. Ein erster bibliografischer Überblick zu Joseph Ratzingers Jesus-Buch," in Tück, Jan-Heiner (Hg.), Annäherungen an "Jesus von Nazareth." *Das Buch des Papstes in der Diskussion* (Mainz : Matthias-Grünewald-Verlag, 2007), pp. 182–99.

Most of Joseph Ratzinger's books have been translated into English and are published by Ignatius Press (San Francisco).

Chapter 25
Hans Küng

Hermann Häring

Hans Küng is one of the best known contemporary Catholic theologians. His name is closely linked to the Second Vatican Council (1962–65) and stands both for Christian ecumenism and for a consistent reform of the church in accordance with scripture. He has published comprehensive works on the renewal of ecclesiology, Christology, and the doctrine of God in accordance with scripture. His discussions of these topics have lost none of their relevance; this also applies to the difficult questions of the Petrine ministry and infallibility. The ecclesiastical sanctions against Küng only served to enhance his celebrity and influence. There have been no substantial discussions or refutations of his disputed theses up to the present day.

After the election of Hans Küng's former colleague, Joseph Ratzinger, to the papacy in April, 2005, the two are often regarded as theological antipodes. Hans Küng has written about this in the second volume of his memoirs *Umstrittene Wahrheit*, 2007.

Küng's name also stands for dialogue with the world religions and for the program of a "global ethic" in commitment to peace and the reconciliation of the peoples. This project includes thorough investigations of the world religions. As the founder of the "Global Ethic Foundation," he promotes the idea of a global ethic. This has led to numerous works that study the world religions, questions of world peace, questions concerning world ethics in economy, society, and politics, and the role of the United Nations. In this way, Küng has ensured that the creed by which he lives has found a lively echo among Christians and others: "I hope for the unity of the churches. I hope for peace among the religions. I hope for fellowship among the nations."

Biography

Hans Küng was born in 1928 in Sursee in German-speaking Switzerland. He studied from 1948 to 1955 at the Gregorian University of the Jesuits in Rome, taking his Licentiates at the close of three years of philosophy and four years of theology. He was ordained to the priesthood in Rome in 1954. After further studies, especially in Paris, he took his doctorate in 1957 at the Institut Catholique in Paris with a thesis on Karl Barth's doctrine of justification. After brief periods in pastoral work and at the University of Münster, he became professor of Fundamental Theology in 1960 at the Catholic Faculty of the University of Tübingen, where he became professor of Dogmatics in 1964. After Pope John XXIII summoned the Second Vatican Council in 1959, Küng worked in lectures and publications to spread the ecumenical idea, and had intensive contacts with Protestant colleagues (H. Diem, E. Käsemann, E. Schlink; later, J. Moltmann and E. Jüngel). In 1962, he was appointed an official adviser to the Council ("peritus"). He was present at all four sessions of the Council and committed all his energies to the reform of the church, in drafts of texts, lectures, and conferences attended by bishops. In 1963, with Y. Congar, K. Rahner and E. Schillebeeckx, he founded the international theological periodical *Concilium*, which appeared in seven languages and was for a long time the mouthpiece of Catholic renewal. In 1964, he founded the Institute for Ecumenical Research in Tübingen, and was its director until his retirement. In the following period, he held many lectures and was visiting professor in Europe and the USA. He spoke about numerous aspects of the renewal of theology and of the church. The monograph on the church, in which he gives a detailed justification of his ecclesiology, was published in 1967 and was important for his subsequent work. In view of the stagnating situation in the church, he put the question of papal infallibility up for discussion in 1970; the Roman curia never forgave him for this, and this led to decades of disputes on the theological and church-political level. At the same time, Küng devoted a decade to extremely intensive research, which broadened the sphere of ecumenical questions and supplied these with a basis in Christology and the understanding of God. Together with five ecumenical university institutes, Küng drew up a memorandum on the recognition and reform of church ministries.

In 1979, John Paul II (1978–2005) launched a strictly conservative course within the church. At the same time, under Roman influence, German bishops made objections in letters, discussions, and public statements to Küng's Christology and his doctrine of God. Küng experienced his deepest crisis at Christmas 1979, when Rome decided to withdraw his ecclesiastical authorization to teach. After fruitless attempts at mediation, he finally left the Theological Faculty, but retained a place in the university as "Professor of theology" with his own Institute. This caesura was the beginning of a new and successful theological path for Küng. His unwavering positions, oriented to scripture and to the context of faith today, made him a credible champion in many people's eyes. The lecture rooms were fuller than ever, and he continued to travel through Europe and other continents giving lectures. From now on, however, his consistent concentration on the themes of the world religions assumed a greater importance than this lecturing activity. He began by holding dialogue lectures with scientists of religion on Hinduism, Buddhism, Islam, and Chinese religions. He developed his Institute systematically into a center for encounters with other cultures and religions, but also with specialists in economics and politics. He undertook many journeys to other continents and applied to public Foundations for financial support. The basis of all these activities remained study and academic work. Between 1991 and 2004, he published three large monographs of his own, besides the important monographs and publications of his collaborators. All these works are written in such a way that they are academically responsible and correct, but are at the same time accessible to a wide readership.

Other momentous developments followed. In 1989, Küng held a lecture at UNESCO in Paris on the theme: "No world peace without religious peace," and a lecture in

1990 at the World Economic Forum in Davos (Switzerland) on ethical questions of economics. These and other programmatic lectures were brought together in a little book with a title that was to determine the coming period: *Projekt Weltethos* (*Global Responsibility*). In 1995, he was enabled to found the "Global Ethic Foundation," which has been the basis of his work since his retirement in 1996. In 2011, the University of Tübingen established a World Ethic Institution (WEIT) with a professorship for a global economic ethic, once again thanks to generous donations. In 1993, together with members of other religions, he drew up a declaration for the Parliament of World Religions in Chicago, which became the classic text for his subsequent work. His activity now knew no bounds, with conferences, exhibitions, and personal encounters that gave him contact with representatives of great cultures and religions, the world economy, and world politics. Nor should we forget the great television documentary on the world religions in seven parts (also a multimedia project), "Tracing the Way," into which he poured his energies from 1995 to 2000. Küng elaborated the concept, traveled through all the contents with his collaborators and the television team, and helped to ensure that the material could be used didactically and pedagogically. In this period, he continually returned to his desk; Tübingen remained the center of his activity. The project of a global ethic was further developed in a wealth of studies and publications, and its basic idea was articulated through the examination of questions about human obligations and the obligations of institutions, questions about the consequences to be drawn for the communication of the global ethic in schools, about economic ethics and political ethics, and proposals for a political world order that would be capable of bringing peace. The considerable interest that this project, inspired by a theologian, has found outside theological and ecclesiastical institutions is something new and unexpected.

Survey of Theological Thought and Production

Küng's biography and his theological development are closely interwoven, and are well documented in his publications. His books alone run to ca. 15,000 pages, without taking account of other articles and essays.[1] His dissertation on Karl Barth's doctrine of justification *Rechtfertigung*, 1957 (*Justification*, 1964) already sounded an ecumenical note. It concludes that the doctrine of justification does not separate the Catholic and the Protestant churches. This thesis attracted attention. Catholics were slow to discuss it, but it was confirmed 42 years later through the Joint Declaration on the Doctrine

---

[1] Since Hans Küng's bibliography is documented with extraordinary detail and reliability on the homepage of the Foundation World Ethos (see www.weltethos.org, accessed February 20, 2012), only the main title and date of publication are mentioned in this essay. Only the most important publications can be mentioned. Other titles, as well as the sometimes complicated bibliographical information (new editions and translations, often into numerous languages, and the editorship or joint editorship of collective volumes and documentary works), can be found on the homepage.

of Justification (Augsburg, 1999). The ecumenical theme is studied in greater depth in the books that prepared the way for the Council, *Konzil und Wiedervereinigung*, 1960 (*The Council, Reform and Reunion*, 1961); *Strukturen der Kirche*, 1962 (*Structures of the Church*, 1964). This reaches its high point in the book *Die Kirche*, 1967 (*The Church*, 1967), which takes account both of the state of exegetical knowledge and of the group of ecumenically sensitive topics that remain critical even today. The memorandum *Reform und Anerkennung kirchlicher Ämter*, 1973, which was drawn up by Küng in cooperation with five other university institutes, is one of the important studies that followed. During this period, there were initiatives concerning eucharistic fellowship, the election of bishops, the abolition of celibacy, and the admission of women to ordination. *Unfehlbar? Eine Anfrage*, 1970 (*Infallible? An Enquiry*, 1971) is a small book that had far-reaching consequences. Here, Küng asks for a cogent and exegetically tenable theological justification of the papal claim to infallibility.

The 1970s were devoted to Christology and the doctrine of God. In 1970, Küng published his monograph on Hegel, *Menschwerdung Gottes* (*The Incarnation of God*, 1987). This manuscript, completed in 1964, analyzes Hegel's picture of Christ against the background of classical Christology, indicates its limitations, and proposes a Christology that can be justified exegetically. After very intensive exegetical studies and systematic theological reflection, he presented this Christology in a challenging book that became a bestseller: *Christ sein*, 1977 (*On Being a Christian*, 1977). Küng brings the story of Jesus (his message, praxis, death, and resurrection) into the context of its own time and of our time. He does not deny the divine dimension of the Christian message, nor does he reject an ontological reflection. This becomes clear in the second great monograph of this decade, *Existiert Gott?*, 1978 (*Does God Exist?*, 1980). This examines the history of thinking about God in the modern period and analyzes the question of faith as being a question of basic trust. With the book *Ewiges Leben?*, 1982 (*Eternal Life?*, 1984), Küng closes the epoch of the 1970s. He understands this book as the final volume of a trilogy.

Küng's new orientation in the 1980s also finds expression in large-scale publications. In two books, he documents his dialogue with scientists of religion and the results of his initial investigations of the theme. These are *Christentum und Weltreligionen*, about Islam, Hinduism, and Buddhism, 1984 (*Christianity and the World Religions*, 1986), and *Christentum und chinesische Religion*, 1988 (*Christianity and Chinese Religions*, 1989). At the same time, his own theological convictions become ever clearer in these encounters, and this leads in a regular sequence to small clarifying studies and expositions such as *Credo*, 1992 (*Credo*, 1993) or *Die Hoffnung bewahren*, 1990 (*Reforming the Church Today*, 1990). However, his main interest remains constant. In the framework of the research project "The religious situation of the world," initiated after the dramatic changes in world politics in 1990, three fundamental works appeared on *Das Judentum*, 1991 (*Judaism*, 1992), *Das Christentum*, 1994 (*Christianity*, 1995), and *Islam*, 2004; I do not mention here the numerous articles that present analyses of individual aspects and their implications for theology. These monographs are elaborated in accordance with the method of "paradigm analysis" that Küng had earlier developed (see the volumes edited by H. Küng and D. Tracy, *Theologie – wohin?*, 1984, and *Das neue Paradigma von*

Theologie, 1986). Paradigm analysis allows Küng to identify the deep structure and epochal organizations of the religions over the course of history and to compare them with one another.

From 1989 onwards, Küng has devoted his energies to the "world ethos project" *Projekt Weltethos*, 1990 (*Global Responsibility*, 1991). Faced with the contemporary situation of the world and the menacing effects of globalization, Küng is convinced that the world religions and their cooperation are taking on an outstanding political importance. He was intensively involved in drawing up the declaration on the global ethic, which counts as the classic text of this project: the *Erklärung zum Weltethos* (*Declaration Toward a Global Ethic*), which was adopted by the Parliament of World Religions in Chicago in 1993. This declaration shows the extent of the consensus of the world religions on basic ethical questions concerning world society and world peace. Publications in various fields followed, including:

1. Numerous documentations of the project, such as *Wissenschaft und* Weltethos, 1998, *Globales Unternehmen – globales Ethos*, 2001, and *Wozu Weltethos?*, 2002 and 2006, as well as the following books by H. Küng: *Weltethos für Weltpolitik und Weltwirtschaft*, 1997 (*A Global Ethic for Global Politics and Economics*, 1997) and *Spurensuche. Die Weltreligionen auf dem* Weg, 1999 (*Tracing the Way. Spiritual Dimensions of the World Religions*, 2002); see also H. Schmidt (ed.), *Allgemeine Erklärung der Menschenpflichten*, 1998 (*A Global Ethic and Global Responsibilities. Two Declarations*, 1998), and the *Aufruf an unsere führenden Institutionen*, 1999 (*Call to our Guiding Institutions*), adopted by the Parliament of World Religions in Cape Town in 1999: Küng collaborated in drawing up this text. In *Anständig wirtschaften. Warum ökonomie Moral braucht*, 2010, he reacts to the prolonged world financial crisis.
2. Large-scale studies of the three monotheistic world religions and of Hinduism by collaborators of the Global Ethic Foundation: K.-J. Kuschel, *Streit um* Abraham, 1994, *Vom Streit zum Wettstreit der Religionen*, 1998, *Juden – Christen – Muslime*, 2007, and other works; S. Schlensog, *Der Hinduismus*, 2006; in addition to numerous studies and collective volumes on the world religions, on the ethical education and training of young people, and on ethical questions in society, economy, and politics (bibliographies in www.weltethos.org. February 20, 2012).
3. The manifesto *Crossing the Divide. Dialogue among Civilizations*, 2001, which is inspired by the basic idea of the Projekt Weltethos, was the result of an initiative by Kofi Annan. H. Küng collaborated in drawing it up.

Nor should we forget the numerous publications on other topics, such as religion and art, religion and literature, women in Christianity, and humane dying *Menschenwürdig sterben*, written with Walter Jens, 1995 (*A Dignified Dying* 1995). His book on the relationship between theology and the natural sciences won a wide readership: *Der Anfang aller* Dinge, 2005 (*The Beginning of All Things*, 2007).

Küng's highly informative memoirs are indispensable for the understanding and interpretation of his life and work. Two volumes have appeared: *Erkämpfte Freiheit*, 2002 (*My Struggle for Freedom* 2003) and *Umstrittene Wahrheit*, 2007.

Again and again, he allows the reader to see the spiritual background that is the motivating force in his work. Testimonies to this are the very personal book *Was ich glaube*, 2009 (*What I Believe*, 2010) and a combative publication that is permeated by his passionate commitment: *Ist die Kirche noch zu retten?*, 2011.

The Theology of Hans Küng: Key Aspects

As early as his youth, when he was confronted with German National Socialism, Hans Küng took an interest in issues of society and world politics. His studies in the cosmopolitan city of Rome also gave his theological thinking a worldwide horizon. This background has left a profound mark on his theological work.

His *first productive phase* (from 1957 onwards)[2] is devoted to ecumenism among Christians, which he believes must begin with a reform of the Catholic church in accordance with scripture. He learned from Karl Barth and Protestant exegesis to take scripture seriously as the source of Christian identity and to read his own tradition anew against the background of the Bible. The Second Vatican Council (1962–65) gave impulses that confirmed the ecumenical goals he had pursued since writing his dissertation. He was thus the first Catholic theologians to elaborate a comprehensive ecclesiology that is consistently inspired by scripture. He understands the church primarily as the people of God, called by God. It is provisional: it does not act out of its own power or for itself, but must follow the message and the cause of Jesus and subordinate itself to the kingdom of God. All the institutional questions that have developed a high dynamic of their own within the Catholic church must be answered in the light of this goal. Topics that were ecumenically sensitive, and soon became the object of debate, were the relationship between scripture and tradition, the question of the foundation of the church by Jesus, the meaning and interpretation of the eucharist, and a fundamentally new reflection on priesthood and hierarchy, on the papacy and Roman centralism, and on the history of the Catholic church's guilt in relation to heretics and Jews. Other topics that Küng soon raised were the demand for mutual recognition of ecclesial ministries, eucharistic fellowship, the introduction of democratic elements (especially the election of bishops), women's ordination, and the abolition of celibacy.

In view of the stagnation within the church, the questions about reform were initially narrowed down to cover secondary questions such as the Roman claim to infallibility. Unfortunately, the discussion has overlooked the methodological background and the consequences that this generates for a Christian theology and an

---

[2] No final date is given for the productive phases, since Küng never revises earlier concepts, but integrates them into his later concepts. This is why one can speak of a continuous expansion of boundaries, leading to a greater complexity in his thinking.

appropriate criticism of the church. This is shown by the monograph on Hegel, which was published in the same year. These methodological clarifications are one reason why it is important. Greek metaphysics (from Plato to Idealism) thinks ahistorically, and this makes it unable to speak appropriately of the person and the cause of Jesus. This does not amount to a simple disqualification of the classical Christology with its metaphysical tone; but Küng does relativize its Hellenistic-metaphysical form, opening up a new space for the biblical profession of faith in Christ. Since the church's magisterium identifies itself unreservedly and in an authoritarian manner with this Christology, Küng simultaneously prepares the path for a hermeneutic that is critical of the system and is fundamentally different from the customary hermeneutic of an ecumenism that reconciles everything and is thus ineffective. The significance of this hermeneutic could already be seen in the discussion of infallibility.

Second productive phase (from 1970): The books on the Christian existence and faith in God, mentioned above, bring further clarification. Küng does not transpose the truth and the will of God into the ontological system of a divine and a human "nature": rather, these are immediately present in Jesus' proclamation and action and in his fate. This means that Küng de facto elaborates a Christology that can adopt the great formulae of the tradition, but understands them on the basis of the event of Jesus. This demands the cautious reconstruction of the figure of Jesus from the biblical sources, that is to say, from the wealth of material that academic exegesis has compiled in the last decades. Alongside E. Schillebeeckx, Küng was the first Catholic theologian to carry out this work so extensively. He expounds faith in Jesus not metaphysically, but by means of a narrative, and this allows him to reach people today. They receive an answer to the decisive question of what it means to be a Christian today: "The decisively Christian element is Christ Jesus himself."

Although the Christian concept of God is revealed through the figure of Jesus Christ, the question about God is not simply absorbed into the story of Jesus. This is why Küng's second great monograph reconstructs the question about God as a disputed, but fascinating and inalienable question that decides the fate of the modern period. He analyzes the history of thought in the modern period (including Descartes, Pascal, Hegel, Kierkegaard, Feuerbach, Marx, and Freud) and discovers in Nietzsche's nihilism the greatest challenge – to which a reply must be given. It is true that God's existence cannot be proved, and faith in God remains always exposed to the risk of doubt and refutation. But on the basis of a fundamental trust in reality, and by living out a rationality that involves inner participation and cannot be objectified, we can grasp that faith in God is a meaningful decision that is certainly rational and inherently consistent. This acknowledges the reason in keeping with its abilities, and we see once and for all that as soon as we situate the historically reliable memory of the human being Jesus in this context, this memory can become trust and faith in Jesus Christ. Looking back, we can see that the two books are related to each other; they complement and explain each other, not in the sense of a reason that offers external proofs, but of a reason that understands from within. If the hierarchy of the Catholic church was unable to accept this distinction, that may be because it still insists on the rationally irrefutable proof of its own "truths" and of its exclusive claim to truth.

This is why the disturbing success of these books too, with their implicit systemic criticism, was bound to lead to the Roman reaction that attempts even today to discriminate against Küng. The fact that he has nevertheless not thought of leaving the Catholic church even for one minute, despite the many who have advised him to do so, bears witness to the inherent consistency of his own concept.

Third productive phase (from 1980): Already during the Council, Küng not only pleaded for a rehabilitation of Judaism, but also posed the question of the world religions.[3] Later, he parted company with K. Barth by demanding that there should be not only an ecumenism within Christianity, but also an ecumenism of the world religions. Küng sees this as a consequence of his approach, which is biblical-narrative but also entails systematic reflection. The idea of Christian superiority must be relativized. Küng's vision is of a theology that makes possible an undistorted view of other religions, without thereby succumbing to relativism. Throughout the world, religions are places of very varied, but always concrete experiences of God in fellowship. This is why Küng believes in the value of a concrete, well-informed dialogue by participants who enjoy talking to one another. Such a discussion presupposes knowledge of other religions. This dialogue intensifies from 1980 onwards.

Küng also sees this new approach as a test of the foundations of his earlier theology. Looking back, we can see that this experiment was successful. Küng's earlier approaches to a theology oriented both to scripture and to contemporary experience prove viable. On the one hand, he continues to appeal to Jesus of Nazareth, whose unique history and message prove their worth in the dialogue of the religions. This includes Jesus' experience of security in God, his solidarity with other people, which had its foundation in God, as well as his failure – which was linked to this solidarity. On the other hand, he understands faith in God as a radical trust in an ultimate and ineffable source that gives human beings their dignity, binds them together from within, and ultimately relativizes all earthly reality. There are testimonies to such a faith outside of Christianity too. It is against this background of a great respect for other religions that Küng initiates the interreligious dialogue. He does not engage in dialogue in a neutrally empirical manner, in accordance with the criteria of an uninvolved phenomenology; nor does he do so from the standpoint of a superior faith or knowledge. He initiates this dialogue as a committed Christian who gives an account of his experience of faith and is willing to criticize himself. His intention is to take note of that which is different in other religions, and he includes all the world religions here.

Interreligious dialogue thus takes place as an enriching exchange of experiences of faith that are shared and heard by the other partner; sometimes, this is a critical exchange. In none of his books does Küng perceive other religions as rivals or as a contradiction of his own faith, but rather as a complement that challenges his faith. For example, we have something to learn from the Buddhist reservation with regard

---

[3] Christenheit als Minderheit. Die Kirche unter den Weltreligionen, in J. Neuner (ed.), *Christian Revelation and World Religions. The World Religions in God's Plan of Salvation* (1965), pp. 25–66.

to the name of God and from the Muslim criticism of a naïve deification of Jesus; we can learn from the oriental concept of compassion and from the Jewish prohibition of images. In this way, Küng learns a differentiated way of looking at the religions; in the course of the years, he draws ever more complex pictures of them. In each religion, he traces systematically not only an original period and abiding core elements, but also epochal figures, "paradigms" that arise in new cultural contexts, develop their own stability and convincingness, and develop over lengthy periods of time. These often exist alongside other paradigms of one and the same religion, so that the complexity of a religion increases with its age.

Let us mention some examples. In the case of Judaism, this applies to the paradigms of (1) the tribes, (2) the Davidic kingdom, (3) the post-exilic theocracy, (4) a rabbinic-synagogal period, and (5) assimilation in the modern period. Something comparable is true of Christianity, with the various paradigms of (1) a Jewish-apocalyptic, (2) a Hellenistic-Orthodox, (3) a Roman Catholic, (4) a Protestant, and (5) a modern post-Enlightenment period. In Islam, Küng reconstructs (1) the paradigm of the first Islamic community, (2) the paradigm of the Pan-Arabic kingdom, (3) the Pan-Islamic paradigm of the world religion, (4) the paradigm of the Ulama and Sufis, with a tendency to traditionalism, and (5) the paradigm of modernization.

Fourth productive phase (from 1989): For the first time, it is possible to speak of the formation of a school of collaborators of Küng who adopt this working model and its goals with a considerable autonomy. Increasingly, the methodological impulses generated by Küng's investigations of religion are not only at the service of theological and comparative-religious analyses, but enter the public sphere. He seeks with ever greater emphasis to communicate his insights and to create trust through encounters. The worldwide horizon, which was already established in his early years, now becomes an explicit theme. From the beginning of the "Projekt Weltethos," we consistently find in his books the motto: "No peace among the nations without peace among the religions. No peace among the religions without dialogue between the religions. No dialogue between the religions without basic research into the religions." Küng ultimately sees in all the religions that are important today one single criterion that is at work in them and that also makes them comprehensible to outsiders. This criterion can be described by means of the concept of "humanity" (*Menschlichkeit*). True religion is always a religion that despite all egoisms and potential for violence aims at the well-being, the salvation and rescue of the human person and of the world, and at a worldwide reconciliation of human beings. On the basis of this experience, Küng does not see "humanity" as a non-religious or secular concept. It already played an important role in *Christ sein*, and one of Küng's great discoveries in the 1980s is that it is precisely as a religiously motivated praxis of life that "humanity" can develop intensively, but without excluding secular concepts of humanity. In other words, this approach is not the uncritical humanistic supplement of a modernistic mood, but is the consequence of a well thought out Christology and image of God.

For Küng, therefore, religions (and theology) have an outstanding formative power in politics and culture. They bear in themselves not only a great potential for violence, but also tremendous power to promote humane living in society, peace, and reconciliation. The "Projekt Weltethos" is not a call for self-absorption on the part of the religions. On the contrary, it summons them to concern for the future of a world that is being turned upside down in military, societal, and power-political terms. After the end of the Cold War (1945–90), Küng discovered the necessity of this project, and he has elaborated it even more intensively after September 11, 2001. Religious dialogue is indispensable, since the threat to the future means that we must be able to reach agreement about a global ethic. This term does not mean an ethics that is elaborated theoretically, but an ensemble of attitudes and standards, criteria and positions that is already lived or at least acknowledged by innumerable persons today.

The Chicago declaration points to "a common set of core values," to a "fundamental consensus concerning binding values, irrevocable standards, and fundamental moral attitudes" that have long been alive in the religions. To general surprise, it was discovered that all the great religions share as their common property not only the Golden Rule, but also very ancient criteria that can be translated with astonishing ease into the present day. The declaration speaks of a culture of (1) non-violence and respect for all life, (2) solidarity and social justice, (3) tolerance and truthfulness, without manipulation and corruption, and (4) a culture of equality and partnership between men and women. These criteria are to be understood and lived in the spirit of the Golden Rule. There can be no doubt that this ethic can also be justified and understood in secular terms. Accordingly, the collaboration with religious worldviews is desired, and a secular effect is intended.

This proceeding has immense consequences with regard to the world religions. They are led out from their defensive self-isolation. The threat to the future generates a common responsibility, and the cultural and political dimensions of the religions and of their faith are strengthened. All the religions are to be evaluated in terms of their ability to join in shaping the future of the world, which is imperiled. Küng is convinced that the religions not only have the obligation to achieve this: rather, thanks to their profoundly humane faith in God, they are also capable of achieving this. They can create religious motivations for this task, as well as the indispensable "conversion of the heart" in which a consciousness of ultimate and definitive responsibility arises. Secularized and highly differentiated societies increasingly lack this consciousness, because their legal systems insist ever more one-sidedly on strengthening individual rights.

This program also has great consequences for the future of a reconciled humankind, because it activates the most important arsenals that influence people's actions and conduct in the various cultures. The fear that this program reduces the religions to a kind of moral armament is unjustified, since the program understands the political potency of the religions as emanating from the Spirit of God and as a demonstration of the power of faith in God. This program cannot be abstracted from the concrete encounter with all the religions that continues to be promoted in the "Projekt Weltethos." Accordingly, there is a symbiosis between the third and the fourth productive phases in Küng himself and in the Foundation Global Ethic. The problems of an intercultural and interreligious culture in western Europe illustrate every day the necessity and the fruitfulness of promoting encounters that aim to secure peace between people.

It is difficult to determine whether a fifth phase will follow. One would have to call it a phase of the final integration that begins with the writing of his memoirs (from 2002 onwards). His personal motivation is displayed openly in the book *Was ich glaube*, 2009 (*What I Believe*, 2010), and *Ist die Kirche noch zu retten?*, 2010, recalls his committed involvement within the church in the first decades of his writing activity.

Küng and the Theological Discourse of the Twentieth Century

Küng has made his mark on the discourse of Catholic theology above all through the following substantial and methodologically relevant interventions: the acceptance of the doctrine of justification, the leading role of scripture in doctrine and theology, the historical discussion of ecumenically sensitive themes such as the eucharist, the question of ecclesial ministries, and papal primacy. Since 1970, the doctrine of infallibility has been recognized as highly problematical, both substantially and hermeneutically. Only E. Schillebeeckx has written a comparable Christology that is consistently reliable in exegetical terms.

Küng's interventions on behalf of ecumenical theology are closely linked to this. They concern above all questions of the Catholic-Protestant relationship: the biblically and historically justified acknowledgment of ministries and of other churches, and the new shape to be taken by the papacy. We should not underestimate Küng's wide-reaching activities in support of church renewal, through his writings, his collaboration in the periodical *Concilium*, through the formation of a critical public consciousness by personal interventions and initiatives for the collection of signatures, and finally his personal resistance to the church leadership, which is theologically responsible and is honestly maintained wherever he believes that scripture and human rights demand this resistance on his part.

Küng's most lasting influence is as a champion of interreligious dialogue and of the inclusion of other religions in Catholic ecumenical thinking. Through this activity, and through the "Projekt Weltethos," he has finally succeeded in getting a more attentive hearing in the secular public sphere for Christian theology and the religions. His address to the plenary assembly of the United Nations in November, 2001, attests this, as do the many speakers who have come to Tübingen to deliver the annual lecture on global ethic: Tony Blair, Mary Robinson, Kofi Annan, German President Horst Köhler, the Iranian winner of the Nobel Peace Prize, Shirin Ebadi, the IOC President Jacques Rogge, Helmut Schmidt, the former Federal Chancellor of Germany, Archbishop Desmond Tutu, winner of the Nobel Peace Prize, and Stephen K. Green, former President of HSBC Holding. The Christian churches would do well to take up the impulses generated by this work and to put their message at the service of a reconciled humankind.

Bibliography

Primary Literature

Rechtfertigung. Die Lehre Karl Barths und eine katholische Besinnung. Mit einem Geleitbrief von Karl Barth (Einsiedeln, 1957).
Die Kirche (Freiburg, Basle, and Vienna, 1967).
Menschwerdung Gottes. Eine Einführung in Hegels theologisches Denken als Prolegomena zu einer künftigen Christologie (Freiburg, Basle, and Vienna, 1970).
Christ sein (Munich and Zürich, 1974).
Existiert Gott? Antwort auf die Gottesfrage der Neuzeit (Munich and Zürich, 1978).
With others, *Christentum und Weltreligionen. Hinführung zum Dialog mit Islam, Hinduismus und Buddhismus* (Munich and Zürich, 1984).
Projekt Weltethos (Munich and Zürich, 1990).
Das Judentum (Munich and Zürich, 1991).
Das Christentum. Wesen und Geschichte (Munich and Zürich, 1994).
Weltethos für Weltpolitik und Weltwirtschaft (Munich and Zürich, 1998).
Der Islam. Geschichte, Gegenwart, Zukunft (Munich and Zürich, 2004).
Der Anfang aller Dinge. Naturwissenschaft und Religion (Munich and Zürich, 2005).
Erkämpfte Freiheit. Erinnerungen (Munich and Zürich, 2002).
Umstrittene Wahrheit. Erinnerungen (Munich and Zürich, 2007).
Was ich glaube (Munich and Zürich, 2009).
Anständig wirtschaften. Warum Ökonomie Moral braucht (Munich and Zürich, 2010).
See also www.weltethos.org.

Secondary Literature

Häring, H., *Hans Küng. Breaking Through* (London, 1998).
Kuschel, K.-J. and H. Häring (eds), *Hans Küng: New Horizons for Faith and Thought* (London, 1993).
Kuschel, K.-J. and W. Jens, *Dialogue with Hans Küng* (London, 1997).
Nowell, R., *A Passion for Truth. Hans Küng: A Biography* (London, 1981).

Chapter 26
Elisabeth Schüssler Fiorenza

Annelies Moeser

Elisabeth Schüssler Fiorenza, one of the foremost biblical scholars of the twentieth century and beyond, has had a significant impact on not only the field of scholarship itself, but also on widening the circle of those who are included in the conversation. She has been recognized by the academy as the first female president of the Society of Biblical Literature (1987), recipient of numerous awards and guest professorships and honored by her colleagues in three Festschriften. She is known for her feminist critical analysis bringing women to the center and her deconstructions of what may appear to have been normative, value-free (what she calls "scientific") interpretations. Her creative use of neologisms (such as "kyriarchy," "malestream," or "wo/men") and her regular use of "G*d" to express the Divine are evidence of her recognition of the power of language to construct reality. She investigates how biblical texts and scholars use language to *construct* rather than simply describe a picture of the early Christian community. The task of scholarship, then, is to recognize these dynamics in order to bring to light evidence of other voices and experiences of the early Christians. Schüssler Fiorenza disputes the idea of "pure, disinterested" scholarship. She calls on scholars to recognize how their work supports or contests political, ethical, and ecclesiastical interests. She is deeply committed to do scholarship engaged in the struggle for liberation and justice. She states her own agenda clearly in the Preface of *Rhetoric and Ethic: The Politics of Biblical Studies* when she writes, "I propose a fundamental change in how we understand and employ the biblical text, based on a critical understanding of language as a form of power. I ask readers to re-envision biblical studies as a theory and practice of justice."[1]

Biographical Sketch

Elisabeth Schüssler was born to German parents in Tschanad (Cenad), Romania in 1938. As fighting neared the area in September 1944, she fled with members of her family through Hungary, Austria and finally, to Germany. She remembers the family was housed in a cow barn outside Dachau when the war ended.

Schüssler Fiorenza has herself reflected on the significance of her experiences as a seven-year-old refugee upon her thought and theological work as a feminist liberationist. She writes that she "learned early to insist that wo/men must be

---

[1] Schüssler Fiorenca, *Rhetoric and Ethic: The Politics of Biblical Studies* (1999), Preface, ix.

respected as people."[2] These experiences of war and displacement instilled in her a strong sense of a claim to justice. She later learned of the injustices perpetrated at Dachau and elsewhere. Identifying as both victim and victimizer, she committed herself to working against dehumanization, prejudice, and every type of structural oppression that diminishes human dignity.

Her academic path was marked by success in the face of great challenges. She graduated from gymnasium in 1958. She received her Theologicum (the equivalent of a Master of Divinity) as a Catholic theologian in 1962 from the University of Würzburg. In 1963 she earned her Licentiate degree in Theology *summa cum laude* in Würzburg. She left Würzburg after Rudolf Schnackenburg refused her a fellowship because he felt that, as a woman, she had no future in theology. She then earned her doctorate *summa cum laude* at the University of Münster in 1970 writing her dissertation on Revelation (later published as *Priester für Gott: Studien zum Herrschafts- und Priestermotiv in der Apokalypse* [*Priests for God: Studies of the Motif of Lordship and Priests in the Apocalypse*]). During her years of study, she was often the only woman studying theology at that level, an experience which was to make her even more sensitive to the fact that much scholarship assumed a male perspective as normative.

She moved to the United States and taught at the University of Notre Dame from 1970 to 1984. It was here that she wrote *In Memory of Her: A Feminist Reconstruction of Christian Origins* (1983). It is hard to overestimate the tremendous excitement this book raised among both scholarly and lay readers. However, the author was not allowed to use the book in her own classes at Notre Dame. Still under the impression that non-ideological, "objective" scholarship was a possibility, Notre Dame could not accept her clear commitment to feminist and liberationist perspectives.

Schüssler Fiorenza left Notre Dame to teach at the Episcopal Divinity School in Cambridge, Massachusetts for the next four years (1984–8). It was a fruitful period. She co-founded the pioneering *Journal of Feminist Studies in Religion* with Jewish feminist theologian Judith Plaskow in 1985 and remains an editor of the journal to this day.[3] This not only provided her a forum for her own theology but launched the career of many feminists whose work did not fit the male perspective of other academic journals.

Another pioneering moment came as Schüssler Fiorenza was elected as President of the Society of Biblical Literature. Serving the 1987 term, she was the first woman to serve as President since the Society's foundation in 1880 She used her presidential address (published in the *Journal of Biblical Literature* and later developed into the book *Rhetoric and Ethic: The Politics of Biblical Studies*) to call scholars to adopt a "double ethics." The "ethics of historical reading" searches for the meanings of the text in its historical context (against later dogmatic interpretations). An "ethics of accountability" asks scholars to take responsibility for contemporary political and ethical consequences of interpretation, such as legitimatization of war and

---

[2] Schüssler Fiorenza, "Wartime as Formative," *The Christian Century*, August 16–23 (1995), p. 778.

[3] http://www.sbl-site.org/assets/pdfs/pastpresidents.pdf (accessed September 20, 2011).

anti-Judaism. Schüssler Fiorenza's core theological principles came to the fore again as she asked the Society to "constitute a responsible scholarly citizenship that could be a significant participant in the global discourse seeking justice and well-being for all."[4] In 1988, Schüssler Fiorenza joined the faculty of Harvard Divinity School as the first Krister Stendahl Professor of Divinity; a position she holds to this day. Her career has been studded with awards, scholarships, guest professorships, and other signs of academic recognition. Most recently, she received the 2011 Jerome Award from the Catholic Library Association—"awarded in recognition of outstanding contribution and commitment to excellence in scholarship which embody the ideals of the Catholic Library Association."[5] Her ongoing activity has not only borne fruit in her own academic work but has shaped the work of many other scholars who continue to interact, contest, and further develop her initial insights.

In Memory of Her

Schüssler Fiorenza's *In Memory of Her: A Feminist Theological Reconstruction of Christian Origins* (1983) must count as one of the most exciting and significant works of twentieth-century theological scholarship. It generated tremendous interest and critique from both the academy and the churches. At the center of her reconstruction is a view of women as historical agents whose presence and activities are often not recognized or are actively suppressed in androcentric texts that have been preserved including the New Testament. Schüssler Fiorenza argues that "women were not marginal in the earliest beginnings of Christianity; rather, biblical texts and historical sources produce the marginality of women."[6] Thus, she attempts to map not only the history of women's oppression but also of their leadership and authority. She utilizes a hermeneutics of suspicion with regard to the biblical text, identifying both it and historical male scholarship as rhetorical constructions of reality. All scholars and texts construct reality; there is no "objective" or "purely factual" recounting of the early Christian communities. Her goal is to proclaim the gospel, but in a way that will not be oppressive but liberative to women and men. Biblical revelation is not limited to or always found in the biblical text but its locus "is found in the life and ministry of Jesus as well as in the discipleship community of equals called forth by him."[7]

Schüssler Fiorenza stresses that attempts to find Jesus as liberative in contrast to Judaism miss the mark. The early Jesus movement is an inner-Jewish renewal movement. Jesus is identified as prophet and child of Sophia (a topic she would develop in greater depth in her book *Jesus: Miriam's Child, Sophia's Prophet*) who calls

---

[4] Schüssler Fiorenza, "The Ethics of Biblical Interpretation," *Journal of Biblical Literature* 107 (1988), p. 17.
[5] http://www.hds.harvard.edu/news-events/2011/05/13/hds-faculty-recognized-for-scholarship-teaching (accessed September 20, 2011).
[6] Schüssler Fiorenza, Intro to 10th anniversary edition of *In Memory of Her* (1983), p. xx.
[7] Ibid., p. 34.

forth a "discipleship of equals." In this community no one is called "father" (Matt 23:9) and discipleship "abolishes the claims of the patriarchal family and constitutes a new familial community."[8] The missionary Christian movement was not initiated by Paul and his writings show that his views were not always seen as normative. Paul joined a movement in which women were already active as leaders and participants. Schüssler Fiorenza examines the evidence for women as missionaries, house church leaders, and patrons. She reconstructs the theology of the early movement as rooted in experience of the Holy Spirit, understanding Jesus as the Sophia (Wisdom) of God (e.g. 1 Cor 1:24, 30) and the new community as the people and "temple" of God.

Paul's teachings are in tension with each other at times. Paul recognizes women as equal with men in the community, through baptism in Christ (Gal 3:28). He knows women in leadership roles, such as Prisca, Chloe, and Phoebe, and assumes women will pray in the Corinthian assembly. But he is concerned that the outside world will misinterpret the Corinthian worship as orgiastic ceremonies of oriental cults, such as the Isis cult that was well-established in Corinth. Hence his stress on order and proper appearance, insisting that women will pray only with their hair veiled (1 Cor 11:5). Schüssler Fiorenza is aware that some exclude 1 Cor 14:33b–36 as an interpolation but she treats this as an original Pauline statement. She interprets it in light of Paul's concern for the community's reputation in the eyes of the outside world for "order." She understands Paul to limit the participation of married women, not all women, thus subordinating their right to rights in favor of his missionary theology. Paul's claims to be a father to the communities to whom he ministered (e.g. 1 Cor 4:15) and to his role in presenting the church as a bride of Christ (2 Cor 11:2) reflect patriarchal images. These tensions will be used in post- and pseudo-Pauline traditions reflected in the household codes to subordinate women and slaves in Christian families and assemblies.

Feminist analysis must recognize the concrete political aims of the patriarchal Greco-Roman household as a model for the state. The fear of being labeled seditious drives Jewish apologists Philo and Josephus to stress the subordination of women in Judaism. Household codes are introduced in Colossians, 1 Peter, and Ephesians. This "strategy for survival gradually introduced the patriarchal-societal ethos of the time into the church."[9] However, it is important to note for reconstructing Christian origins these codes are *prescriptive for*, and not *descriptive of*, Christian life in Asia Minor.

Schüssler Fiorenza posits a shift in the second century from charismatic leadership to administrative office in the Christian community. The Pastoral Epistles describe leadership in terms of age and gender stratification rather than charismatic "giftedness." 1 Clement stresses "order" while Ignatius of Antioch goes further by stating that the bishop presides in the place of God. The second- and third-century struggles between prophetic and administrative types of authority are finally resolved in favor of local bishops. In the following centuries, the church was never entirely successful in repressing women's activity in preaching and teaching or in its control over groups of women such as the "widows." Schüssler Fiorenza contrasts these

---

[8] Schüssler Fiorenza, *Jesus: Miriam's Child, Sophia's Prophet* (1994), p. 147.
[9] Ibid., p. 266.

post-Pauline and post-Petrine developments to the gospel narratives, specifically to those of Mark and John. The evangelists continue to witness to the role women played as exemplary disciples in service and ministry.

Finally, Schüssler Fiorenza reflects on the reconstruction of Christian origins she has outlined. She calls for recognition of the *ekklēsia* (assembly) of women (a term she develops more fully in her subsequent work and begins to call "*ekklēsia* of wo/men") as the place in which all can decide on their own spiritual welfare. Women are called through their baptism into a discipleship of equals and empowered by the Spirit to proclaim the God's vision of an alternative community. This model of church seeks to live in solidarity with the oppressed, poor, and marginalized. Women must not only overcome patriarchal oppression but reclaim their heritage of a continuing struggle for liberation.

Theology and Language

This introduction has stressed Schüssler Fiorenza's commitment to liberation and justice and her unveiling of the impossibility of "disinterested" or apolitical scholarship. One of the methods she uses is the reconstruction of the historical origins of early Christian communities and the historical suppression of wo/men's voices. Another key method for troubling presuppositions and worldviews is her use of language to express the instability of concepts otherwise taken for granted. In this section, we examine some of the new terms Schüssler Fiorenza has created and some existing language to which she has given special significance in her work.

Kyriarchy—one of Schüssler Fiorenza's fundamental insights was the identification of "kyriarchy" as a system of dominance over others. She created the word by joining the Greek words *kyrios* (lord/master) and *archō* (to rule) and first used it in *But She Said: Feminist Practices of Biblical Interpretation*. This represented a major step forward from early feminism's view of the binary structure of patriarchy as purely a power dynamic of men over women. Kyriarchy represents the interlocking grid of multiple social locations and sources of power, including gender, social status, material possession(s), race, ethnicity, and other factors. Because kyriarchy is based on multiple factors, wo/men of higher status, wealth, etc. may share in the oppression of wo/men who lack these traits.

Wo/men—the broken form of the word immediately calls attention to itself, thereby inviting the reader to reflect on its meaning. The term means "people" in a broad sense, including men, women, feminists of any gender, and non-feminists and it is meant to convey diversity. Schüssler Fiorenza stresses the diversity of factors by which wo/men are defined; not only by gender but by race, class, and colonization.[10] In line with Schüssler Fiorenza's sensitivity to the effects of language, she also means

---

[10] Schüssler Fiorenza, *Rhetoric and Ethic* (1999), p. ix.

it to counteract the effects of using male language as "generic" language, e.g. using the word "men" to designate all people.[11]

G*d—Schüssler Fiorenza stresses the way in which language constructs reality. She insists that human language is inadequate for expressing the divine reality. Therefore, she uses this incomplete form of the word to highlight the fact that "God" is not fully representable or describable in our limited language. This is similar to Jewish usage of not fully spelling out the name "God."

Discipleship of Equals or Ekklēsia of Wo/men—the use of these terms reflect Schüssler Fiorenza's own use of "double ethics." On the level of the "ethics of historical reading," she focuses attention on the discipleship and leadership of women in the early Christian communities and disputes that either was limited to the 12. On the level of "ethics of accountability," Schüssler Fiorenza investigates the meaning of ekklēsia of wo/men for the contemporary church, in particular for the Roman Catholic church. First, it means that wo/men (a term inclusive of men) *are* church, not separate from it, and while the institutional church is patriarchal so are wo/men who collaborate in the patriarchal church. For example, the division between lay-women and "nun-women" is part of the male hierarchicalism that must be overcome. Second, the ekklēsia of wo/men is meant to be a democratic assembly of equals who share in decision-making. In the Roman Catholic debate about women's ordination, she underlines the need to transform the clerical hierarchy, not simply insert women into the existing structures. Women must press to be ordained bishops before seeking ordination to lower ranks of clergy so as to have the power to effect structural and theological transformation of the church.[12]

Sophia, Sophiaology—although Sophia is clearly not a term unique to Schüssler Fiorenza, it nevertheless is important for her portrayal of Jesus. Using her work from *In Memory of Her* as a basis, she explores feminist Christologies in her book *Jesus: Miriam's Child, Sophia's Prophet: Critical Issues in Feminist Christology*. She critiques both traditional "heroic" savior types of Christology as well as feminist relational Christologies which are purely individual and depoliticized. Neither type is liberative to women, especially to marginalized women. With her customary focus on justice, Schüssler Fiorenza calls for feminist Christology to "test out the implications and elaborate the power of Christological discourses either for legitimating or for changing kyriarchal relations of domination."[13] Schüssler Fiorenza acknowledges Judith Plaskow's critique of anti-Judaism feminist Christologies that portray Jesus as a feminist over against Judaism (for example, that he alone would heal women on the Sabbath). Instead, Jesus, as a Jew, is a part of the contemporary array of Jewish holiness and emancipatory *basileia tou theou* movements (she often translates this Greek term as "commonweal" or "empire of God" to demonstrate its opposition to the Roman empire).

---

[11] Ibid., p. 6.

[12] Schüssler Fiorenza, *Discipleship of Equals: A Critical Feminist Ekklēsia-Logy of Liberation* (1993) pp. 15, 88–9.

[13] Schüssler Fiorenza, *Jesus: Miriam's Child* (1994), p. 61.

Schüssler Fiorenza identifies two levels in early Christian reflection: one in which Jesus is understood as a "messenger and prophet of Sophia" and another which "identifies Jesus with Divine Wisdom."[14] Jesus's prophetic ministry includes all of Israel, especially the poor and marginalized in an inclusive table ministry that shows how "Sophia is justified by all her children" (Luke 7:35). He is one of a line of prophets sent by Sophia (Luke 11:49) and his death is a result of this ministry (Matt 11:12). Sophia's invitation for rest and easy yoke are placed in the mouth of Jesus by Matthew (Matt 11:28–30) as a part of this early Christological reflection on Jesus as Divine Wisdom. In John's Gospel, the themes of Sophia are utilized but articulated under masculine titles such as "Logos" (grammatically masculine in Greek and meaning "word") or "Son."

Schüssler Fiorenza wants to draw on "Jesus messenger of Sophia" traditions because they allow her to highlight the particularity of Jesus without ceding to anti-Judaism or to Christian claims of superiority over Judaism. She also calls on feminists to reflect on sophiaology in terms of language used to express divine reality. She is not asking for a reintroduction of first-century language; rather for feminists to create new terms for the divine that are based on a critical reassessment of androcentric and kyriarchal language. For example, the term "lady" in an expression such as "Lady Wisdom" betrays a class origin and a framework of domination (think of a white female plantation owner and her black female slave—only one of which is considered a "lady"). She encourages feminists to re-vision language for G*d and Christ. Thus, sophiaology is an important resource in Schüssler Fiorenza's theological work.

Schüssler Fiorenza's Ongoing Engagement in Twenty-first-century Scholarship

Elisabeth Schüssler Fiorenza remains an active teacher, author, editor, and speaker. Her work continues to engage scholars in a variety of established areas, such as historical-critical studies and feminist theology/approaches, as well as emerging approaches to biblical interpretation.

Her initial theorization of kyriarchy within feminist analysis was extended (by her and others) to deconstructing other inequalities such as colonialism in postcolonial (or as she prefers the term "decolonizing") criticism and empire studies (the border between those two fields is porous). In her book *The Power of the Word: Scripture and the Rhetoric of Empire*, Schüssler Fiorenza warns against an unnuanced view of Paul as "counter-imperial" that does not recognize that Paul also uses imperial language and concepts to reinscribe imperialism, albeit in service to his vision of God. Her emphasis on the complexity of unequal structures of privilege has also allowed her to engage in a critique of empire-studies and postcolonial scholarship that ignore the feminist dimension and normalizes the masculine social location and experience. She also responds to her critics in the postcolonial field, such as Musa W. Dube and

---

[14] Ibid., p. 139.

Stephen D. Moore. Moore, for his part, acknowledges he finds her response persuasive and likewise encourages her to further develop certain aspects of her critique.[15] The influence of her work can also be seen in a series such as "Paul and Critical Contexts" (Fortress Press) where authors such as Brigitte Kahl, Neil Elliott, and especially Joseph A. Marchal engage her work. Marchal's *The Politics of Heaven: Women, Gender, and Empire in the Study of Paul*[16] deliberately pulls together feminist and postcolonial approaches with an emphasis on rhetorical analysis in a way that shows the influence of Schüssler Fiorenza on his methodology.

Her colleagues and students have recognized her in three Festschriften. These include: *Toward a New Heaven and a New Earth: Essays in Honor of Elisabeth Schüssler Fiorenza* edited by Fernando F. Segovia; *Walk in the Ways of Wisdom: Essays in Honor of Elisabeth Schüssler Fiorenza*;[17] and *On the Cutting Edge: The Study of Women in Biblical Worlds: Essays in Honor of Elisabeth Schüssler Fiorenza*.[18] These volumes, edited by and containing essays by many of the most well-known and influential scholars in the areas of feminist and postcolonial biblical criticism, is a mark of respect for the contributions of Schüssler Fiorenza in this area.

A newly emerging approach in biblical studies is "intersectionality" (a termed coined by legal scholar Kimberly Crenshaw) which considers identities that are formed at the intersection of race, ethnicity and gender. With Laura Nasrallah, Schüssler Fiorenza organized a symposium highlighting an intersectional analysis to Early Christian studies at Harvard Divinity School in 2007. The two collected and published papers from that symposium in a book titled *Prejudice and Christian Beginnings: Investigating Race, Gender, and Ethnicity in Early Christian Studies*.[19] Schüssler Fiorenza's introduction explains how an intersectional analytic uses the concept of kyriarchy to analyze the multiple forms of domination present in the social world of early Christianity both to critique prejudice and to formulate an alternative vision of justice and tolerance.

Finally, what is often less recognized is Schüssler Fiorenza's profound impact on future generations of pastors and her deep involvement with education of laity. While at the Episcopal Divinity School, Schüssler Fiorenza initiated a doctor of ministry program for Feminist Liberation Theology and Ministry (in the United States, this degree program is designed to facilitate further theological and academic reflection for active ministers). The Festscrift *Walk in the Ways of Wisdom: Essays in Honor of Elisabeth Schüssler Fiorenza* speaks of the intensity with which master's students at Harvard Divinity School engage in her classes and are empowered to develop their own theologies.[20] In these new areas of discussion, and through her legacy of student

---

[15] See his review in *Biblical Interpretation*, 18(1) (2010), p. 77.
[16] Minneapolis: Fortress Press, 2008.
[17] Edited by Shelly Matthews, Cynthia Briggs Kittredge and Melanie Johnson-DeBaufre.
[18] Edited by Jane Schaberg, Alice Bach and Ester Fuchs.
[19] Minneapolis: Fortress Press, 2009.
[20] Shelly Matthews, Cynthia Briggs Kittredge and Melanie Johnson-DeBaufre (eds), *Walk in the Ways of Wisdom: Essays in Honor of Elisabeth Schüssler Fiorenza* (2003), pp. 4–5.

formation and lectures to laity, Schüssler Fiorenza's work continues to be a valuable theoretical resource for twenty-first-century biblical interpretation.

Bibliography

Primary Literature

Der vergessene Partner: Grundlagen, Tatsachen und Möglichkeiten der Beruflichen Mittarbeit der Frau in der Heilssorge der Kirche (Düsseldorf: Patmos, 1964) (*The Forgotten Partner: Foundations, Facts and Possibilities of Woman's Professional Collaboration in the Church's Pastoral Ministry*).
Preister für Gott: Studien zum Herrschafts- und Priestermotiv in der Apokalypse. Neutestamentliche Abhandlungen n.s. 7 (Münster: Aschendorff, 1972) (*Priests for God: Studies of the Motif of Lordship and Priests in the Apocalypse. New Testament Studies*).
The Apocalypse (Chicago: Franciscan Herald Press, 1976).
Hebrews, James, 1 and 2 Peter, Jude, Revelation. With Reginald H. Fuller et al. Proclamation Commentaries (Philadelphia: Fortress, 1977).
Invitation to the Book of Revelation: A Commentary on the Apocalypse, with Complete Text from the Jerusalem Bible (New York: Doubleday, 1981).
Lent. With Urban T. Holmes. Proclamation II: Aids for Interpreting the Lessons of the Church Year, Series B (Philadelphia: Fortress, 1981).
In Memory of Her: A Feminist Reconstruction of Christian Origins (New York: Crossroad, 1983); tenth anniversary edition, 1994 (with new introduction); 2nd edn (London: SCM Press, 1995).
The Book of Revelation: Justice and Judgment (Philadelphia: Fortress, 1985); 2nd edn with new epilogue, 1998.
Bread Not Stone: The Challenge of Feminist Biblical Interpretation (Boston: Beacon, 1985); tenth anniversary edition, 1995.
Revelation: Vision of a Just World. Proclamation Commentaries (Minneapolis: Augsburg Fortress, 1991).
But She Said: Feminist Practices of Biblical Interpretation (Boston: Beacon, 1992).
Discipleship of Equals: A Critical Feminist Ekklēsia-Logy of Liberation (New York: Crossroad, 1993).
Jesus: Miriam's Child, Sophia's Prophet: Critical Issues in Feminist Christology (New York: Continuum, 1994).
Sharing Her Word: Feminist Biblical Interpretation in Context (Boston: Beacon, 1998).
Rhetoric and Ethic: The Politics of Biblical Studies (Minneapolis: Fortress, 1999).
Jesus and the Politics of Interpretation (New York: Continuum, 2000).
Wisdom Ways: Introducing Feminist Biblical Interpretation (Maryknoll: Orbis, 2001).
En la senda de Sofía. Hermeneutica feminista critica para la liberación. Translated and edited by Severino Croatto and Cristina Conti (Buenos Aires: Lumen-Isedet, 2003).

Grenzen überschreiten. Der theoretische Anspruch feministischer Theologie. Ausgewählte Aufsätze (Münster: LIT Verlag, 2004) (*Crossing Boundaries: The Theoretical Claim Made by Feminist Theology*).

Die vier Mirjams: die Schwester Mose, die Mutter Jesu, die Schwester des Lazarus und Mirjam von Magdala aus feministisch-theologischer Sicht (Luzern: Romero Haus, 2004) (*The Four Miriams: The Sister of Moses, the Mother of Jesus, the Sister of Lazarus, and Miriam of Magdalena from the Perspective of Feminist Theology*).

The Open House of Wisdom: Critical Feminist Theological Explorations (Tokyo: Shinkyo Shuppansa, 2005) (appeared only in Japanese).

The Power of the Word: Scripture and the Rhetoric of Empire (Minneapolis: Fortress Press, 2007).

The Dance of Interpretation. Compiled and edited by Yeh Pao-Kuei (Cecilia Yeh) (Taipei, Tawain: Yeon Wang, 2007) (appeared only in Chinese).

Democratizing Biblical Studies: Toward an Emancipatory Educational Space (Louisville: WJK Press, 2009).

Transforming Vision: Explorations in Feminist The*logy (Minneapolis: Fortress Press, 2011).

Secondary Literature

Enander, Glen, *Elisabeth Schüssler Fiorenza*. Spiritual Leaders and Thinkers series (Philadelphia: Chelsea House Publishers, 2005).

Journal of Feminist Studies in Religion, 25(1) (2009). Special issue in honor of Elisabeth Schüssler Fiorenza.

Kim, Nami and Deborah Whitehead, "Elisabeth Schüssler Fiorenza and Feminst The*logies/Studies in Religion." Editors' Introduction. *Journal of Feminist Studies in Religion*, 25(1) (2009), pp. 1–18.

Marchal, Joseph A., *The Politics of Heaven: Women, Gender and Empire in the Study of Paul* (Minneapolis: Fortress Press, 2008).

Matthews, Shelly, Cynthia Briggs Kittredge, and Melanie Johnson-DeBaufre (eds), *Walk in the Ways of Wisdom: Essays in Honor of Elisabeth Schüssler Fiorenza* (Harrisburg, London and New York: Trinity Press International, 2003).

Moore, Stephen D., "The Power of the Word: Scripture and the Rhetoric of Empire" (a review), *Biblical Interpretation*, 18(1) (2010), pp. 77–9.

Nasrallah, Laura and Elisabeth Schüssler Fiorenza. *Prejudice and Christian Beginnings: Investigating Race, Gender, and Ethnicity in Early Christian Studies* (Minneapolis: Fortress Press, 2010). Schaberg, Jane, Alice Bach, and Ester Fuchs (eds). *On the Cutting Edge: The Study of Women in Biblical Worlds: Essays in Honor of Elisabeth Schüssler Fiorenza* (New York and London: Continuum, 2004).

Schüssler Fiorenza, Elisabeth, "The Ethics of Biblical Interpretation: Decentering Biblical Scholarship," *Journal of Biblical Literature*, 107 (1988), pp. 3–17. This is the published form of her 1987 SBL Presidential Address.

Schüssler Fiorenza, Elisabeth, "Wartime as Formative," *The Christian Century* (August 16–23, 1995), pp. 778–9.

Segovia, Fernando F. (ed.), *Toward a New Heaven and a New Earth: Essays in Honor of Elisabeth Schüssler Fiorenza* (Maryknoll: Orbis Books, 2003).

For additional bibliography, including books edited and co-edited by Schüssler Fiorenza, as well as her very numerous contributions to books of essays and articles the reader may find information in "Published Works of Elisabeth Schüssler Fiorenza" in the *Journal of Feminist Studies in Religion*, 25(1) (2009), pp. 221–40 or to her curriculum vitae attached to the Harvard Divinity School website: http://www.hds.harvard.edu/sites/hds.harvard.edu/files/schusslerfiorenza0510.pdf (accessed September 20, 2011).

PART IV
Orthodox Theologians

Chapter 27
Sergei Bulgakov

Andrew Louth

Among the Russian émigrés who settled in Paris in the 1920s, Bulgakov was already an established theologian and, as Dean of the newly-established Institute of Orthodox Theology dedicated to St Sergii (the Institut St-Serge), he rapidly assumed theological leadership (equally famous contemporaries among the émigrés, such as Nikolay Berdyaev and Lev Shestov, were not such committed theologians). He became one of the voices representing Russian Orthodoxy in the burgeoning ecumenical movement, and was particularly active in the newly-founded Fellowship of St Alban and St Sergius. He spent the rest of his life in Paris, and during this period his theological interests predominated, issuing in two trilogies that represent a comprehensive attempt to set out the theological perspective of those Russian theologians who had sought to respond to the intellectual concerns of the nineteenth-century West, and who had been profoundly affected by German idealism (and also by the Kierkegaardian reaction, something of which can be found, quite independently, in Dostoevsky). In these theological works, Bulgakov sought to engage with the theological world of the West, particularly as he encountered it among the Western intellectuals who welcomed him in Paris. Bulgakov's *œuvre*, then, represents a distinctive moment in an engagement between Russian Orthodoxy and the West, at the point at which the Russians of the emigration found themselves established there, and anxious to seize the opportunity to communicate to their Western contemporaries, in terms they could understand, the distinctive vision of Russian Orthodoxy.

Early Years and Life in Russia

Sergei Nikolaevich Bulgakov was born in 1871 in Livny, a small provincial town in the Orël province about 400 km south of Moscow. His father was a priest serving the cemetery chapel and belonged to a priestly ('levitical') family, stretching back several generations. After schooling, Sergei was sent to the local theological seminary, where he was unhappy, lost his faith and, as a young Marxist, went to Moscow University, where he studied economics and law (1890–94). By the turn of the century, although still confessedly a Marxist, he was beginning to develop his own ideas and in his thesis, submitted unsuccessfully for a doctorate in 1900, on agriculture and economics, he had broken with Marxism, though without developing any clear alternative. In the early years of the twentieth century, he began, like many of the intelligentsia, to turn back to his childhood faith. He was one of the contributors to the volume of essays, published in 1909, *Vekhi* ('Landmarks'), in which a group of intellectuals made clear their dissatisfaction with Marxism and its neglect of spiritual and metaphysical questions. By this time, Bulgakov occupied the chair of Political Economy at the Institute of Commerce in Moscow University, a position he held until 1911, when he resigned over government interference in university matters. Writing of his return to Christianity, Bulgakov acknowledged the influence of Dostoevsky and the Russian philosopher and historian, Vladimir Solov'ev; he also wrote about various experiences that unsettled his Marxist convictions, and drew him back to his childhood faith. As early as 1895, his first sight of the mountains of the Caucasus made him aware of the 'dull pain of seeing nature as a lifeless desert' to which a Marxist analysis of reality had committed him, and convinced him that he could not be 'reconciled to nature without God', with the realisation that the 'pious feelings of his childhood' might be true.[1] A few years later, during his period of study in Germany, his encounter with Raphael's Sistine Madonna in the Zwinger Gallery in Dresden brought him to tears and with them 'the ice melted from my soul';[2] thenceforth, his regular early morning visits to the gallery led him to an experience of prayer. His final conversion, 10 years later in 1908, took place in a solitary hermitage deep in a forest. His return to the Christian faith was an ecclesial awakening, too, leading him to participate in the movements seeking reform in the Church that were to culminate in the reform synod of Moscow in 1917–18, and also to his involvement in the controversy over the invocation of the divine name among the Russian monks on Mount Athos, which had led to their condemnation and the removal of most of them by Russian naval vessels in 1913. Bulgakov, like his friend Pavel Florensky, had great sympathy for the 'venerators of the Name' among the monks. For Bulgakov, the presence of Jesus was experienced by the invocation of his name, 'of which every human heart is the temple, and every believer the priest, bearing the seal of the Name'.[3] The book Bulgakov wrote on the philosophy of the name remained, however, unpublished until after his death. Bulgakov's commitment to Church reform led to his being a delegate at the synod of 1917–18, which was cut short by the October Revolution and of which the only lasting result was the restoration of the patriarchate that had been abolished by Peter the Great. The very fact of the synod was decisive for Bulgakov: this act of independence gave the lie to the charge of caesaropapism and freed Bulgakov to seek ordination to the priesthood. On the feast of Pentecost ('Trinity Sunday'), 1918, Bulgakov was ordained deacon in the Danilov Monastery and the next day, the Monday of the Holy Spirit, ordained to the priesthood (thereafter, as was the custom, adopting the more archaic spelling of his name: Sergii). The turmoil of last years had not left him, however, and while a priest serving in Yalta in the Crimea, he wrote a dialogue called *From the Ramparts of Cherson* ('Cherson' being the Byzantine

---

[1] Sergei Bulgakov, *Avtobiograficheskie Zametki*, pp. 61f. (Eng. trans., *A Bulgakov Anthology*, p. 10).

[2] Ibid., p. 64 (*Anthology*, p. 11).

[3] Sergei Boulgakov, *La Philosophie du Verbe et du Nom* (Lausanne: L'Age d'Homme, 1991), pp. 200–201.

– and ecclesiastical – name for Sevastopol in the Crimea), again not published in his lifetime, with the significant subtitle 'The "Catholic Temptation" of an Orthodox Theologian', in which he rehearsed the arguments of the various sides in the debate over the Russian Church, and finally exorcised the temptation to abandon Russian Orthodoxy for Roman Catholicism.

Exile and Controversy

In December 1922, Lenin issued a decree exiling most non-Marxist intellectuals from Russia, and in January 1923, Bulgakov left the Crimea for Europe. After a brief period in Prague, he settled in Paris where he became the first Dean of the Institut de St-Serge and professor of dogmatic theology. On his way to Prague, Bulgakov passed through Constantinople and visited the church of Hagia Sophia, then a mosque. There he had another remarkable experience, which he identified with the figure that had become, and was to remain, central to his theology: the figure of Sophia, the divine wisdom. The church of Hagia Sophia he experienced as 'the artistic and tangible proof and manifestation of holy Sophia—of the Sophianic nature of the world and the cosmic nature of Sophia ... neither heaven nor earth, but the vault of heaven above the earth ... neither God nor man, but divinity, the divine veil thrown over the world.'[4] In Paris, Bulgakov sought, through his writings, his lectures, and perhaps above all through celebrating the Divine Liturgy and preaching and spiritual counsel, to make Russian Orthodoxy a living presence in the West. The Russian Church in the West rapidly became divided. There were those who repudiated the Revolution and the patriarch's acquiescence with the Communist authorities, most stridently those who formed the Russian Orthodox Church Abroad at a synod in Sremski-Karlovci in Yugoslavia in 1921 (the so-called 'Synodal Church'). Then in 1930, Metropolitan Evlogy, the Russian Orthodox exarch in Europe, broke off relations with the Russian Church and placed the parishes of the exarchate under the jurisdiction of the Œcumenical Patriarchate. Finally there were those – a minority – who remained faithful to Moscow, whatever the difficulties. The Institut St-Serge remained with Metropolitan Evlogy. Bulgakov's theology, as we shall see, was largely rooted in nineteenth-century Russian religious philosophy, in particular the thought of Solov'ev. Central to this was the notion of the divine wisdom, the Sophia Bulgakov had experienced so deeply in Constantinople. The notion of Sophia, save as a title for Second Person of the Trinity, was an innovation in theology and attracted criticism: partly for the confusion it introduced to the doctrine of God (was it a fourth person or something else?), partly as a symbol of a theology rooted in German idealism. In 1935 both the Synodal Church and the Moscow Patriarchate condemned Bulgakov's 'sophiology'. Metropolitan Evlogy sought advice on the issue, and commissioned a report which, though unhappy about sophiology, declined from condemning Bulgakov personally. For two of Bulgakov's opponents in Paris – Georges Florovsky, who, like Bulgakov, belonged

---

[4] Sergei Bulgakov, *Avtobiograficheskie Zametki*, p. 95 (*Anthology*, p. 14).

to the exarchate, and Vladimir Lossky, who supported and had advised the Moscow Patriarchate – 'sophiology' was a theological dead-end, and they sought to renew Orthodox theology by a return to the theology of the Fathers of the Church, especially the Greek Fathers (including Gregory Palamas), a position that came to known as the 'Neo-Patristic synthesis'. This controversy clouded Bulgakov's last years, but he continued with his theological writing until his death from cancer in 1944.

Bulgakov's Works: A Survey

Bulgakov's earliest works were studies in economics, culminating in his *Philosophy of Economics* (1912), where the notion of Sophia first appears in connexion with the engagement between human beings and their natural environment, manifest in the cultivation of the land, the husbanding of animals, and the edifices of culture and civilisation, from homesteads to the achievements of art. In this engagement between human effort and nature, the human builds on the divine work of creation (and in some way shares in it): it is in this realm that Bulgakov first spoke of Sophia. From this time on, Bulgakov's work became more distinctively theological, and the first major product of this theological turn was the massive work, *The Unfading Light* (1917; literally: the 'light without evening', a common term in Orthodox liturgical texts), a work of philosophical theology in which Bulgakov displayed his wide-ranging learning, leading from religious consciousness to the notion of *sobornost'*, to God and nothingness, with a long discussion of negative theology, to consideration of the cosmos and Sophia, taking on the way the nature of evil, and finally to a discussion of humankind under the headings of 'The First Adam', covering creation in the divine image, sexual differentiation, the Fall and human search for God, 'The Second Adam', covering creation, Incarnation and salvation, and 'Human History', covering economics, art, politics and the end of history, with a final eschatological chapter – close to the traditional structure of dogmatic theology, but more inclusive. His time in Paris was dominated by his two trilogies: the first, 'little' trilogy (1927–9), consisting of *The Burning Bush* (on the Mother of God), *The Friend of the Bridegroom* (on St John the Baptist) and *Jacob's Ladder* (on the angels), and the great trilogy, 'On Divine Wisdom and Godmanhood [or: Divine-humanity]', consisting of *The Lamb of God*, *The Comforter* and *The Bride of the Lamb* (1933–45, the last volume being published posthumously). Alongside these major works, there were a host of smaller works, lectures and articles: on literature, art and sociology; on theological topics such as the doctrine of the Eucharist and the related notion of the Holy Grail, icons, final restoration ('apokatastasis'), and an extended discussion (conceived of as an appendix to *Unfading Light*) 'on hypostasis and hypostaticity'; and on Christianity and the Jewish question. Some of these works engaged with the Roman Catholic theology he had encountered in Paris; others were conceived in the context of the early ecumenical movement, in connexion with which he proposed the possibility of *communio in sacris* for those who had advanced along the road of ecumenism. Two books appeared in English: one expounding his ideas on Sophia (*The Wisdom of God*,

1937), and an introduction to Orthodoxy for the interested Westerner (*The Orthodox Church*, 1935), which makes no reference to 'sophiology', suggesting that the notion was not indispensable in his thought.

Priest and Spiritual Father: The Importance of the Liturgy

Bulgakov's works are densely written and their argument often hard to follow, in this following the example of nineteenth-century idealist philosophy. Even those most exasperated with theology speak of his personal presence much more warmly; Alexander Schmemann, who studied at the Institut St-Serge during Bulgakov's time there, spoke of 'the incomprehensible gulf which he and many others perceived between the saintly and luminous personality of Bulgakov on the one hand, and his ponderous philosophical edifice on the other'.[5] This 'saintly and luminous personality' revealed itself above all in his celebration of the sacraments, especially the Divine Liturgy and the sacrament of confession. Here is perhaps the most profitable way into his theology, for his theology is impregnated with echoes of the Orthodox liturgy (in the broader sense of the word, not just the Eucharistic liturgy), and he frequently develops his thought by taking examples from the liturgical services. The very title of the *Unfading Light* recalls a phrase frequently found in liturgical texts, referring to the light of the 'day without end of the Kingdom'. Another example can be found in the subjects of his so-called 'little trilogy' – *The Burning Bush, The Friend of the Bridegroom, Jacob's Ladder* – on the Mother of God, John the Baptist and the Angels. The choice of the Mother of God and St John the Baptist is certainly influenced by the iconographic tradition, and especially the icon called the *Deisis* – 'Intercession' – in which a seated Christ is flanked by the Mother of God and St John with their hands raised in an attitude of prayer. They are the two who are closest to Christ, and this closeness is manifest in prayer. These considerations are already liturgical, but the final volume on the Angels makes these considerations more precisely Eucharistic, for all these volumes are concerned with the conjunction of the two worlds – the earthly and the heavenly – a conjunction manifest in different ways in the Mother of God and St John, but realised most immediately for us in the celebration of the Divine Liturgy, when we join together with 'thousands of Archangels and tens of thousands of Angels, the Cherubim and the Seraphim, six-winged and many-eyed'. But considering together the Mother of God and the Baptist has a more precisely Eucharistic reference, as Bulgakov himself makes clear when he recalls that in the preparation service, the *Proskomidi*, as the priest cuts fragments to set beside the Lamb, the bread to be consecrated, the first two fragments are in honour of the Mother of God and then of the Baptist. Similarly in the Eucharistic prayer, after the epiclesis, the first to be commemorated by name is the Mother of God, followed immediately by St John the Baptist.[6] The way in which such

---

[5] Alexis Klimoff, 'Georges Florovsky and the Sophiological Controversy', *St Vladimir's Theological Quarterly*, 49 (2005), pp. 67–100, here p. 81.

[6] Sergei Bulgakov, *The Friend of the Bridegroom*, p. 136.

precise liturgical references feed Bulgakov's theological reflection is very striking. A final point: Boris Bobrinskoy recalls a saying of Bulgakov's to the effect that 'the whole of his theological vision he had drawn from the bottom of the eucharistic chalice'.[7] That remark may well be a traditional priestly proverb, but, even so, it is striking that Fr Bobrinskoy specifically attributes it to Bulgakov. We may deduce from all this that, despite the somewhat forbidding form of his theology, Bulgakov's theological reflection is rooted in his prayer and especially in his liturgical prayer. It is right here to recall the experiences through which he traced his journey back to the faith of his childhood, already quoted above, experiences that evoked in his heart a sense of prayer and wonder, something confirmed and sealed by his priestly ordination, when, as he says, passing through the holy doors and approaching the holy table 'was like going through fire, scorching, cleansing, and regenerating. It was entrance into another world, into the kingdom of heaven. It initiated for me a new state of being in which I have lived ever since'.[8]

The Wisdom of God – Sophiology

And here, we find the kernel of the importance for Bulgakov of Sophia, the divine wisdom. The idea of Sophia has long roots, going back to the Wisdom literature of the Old Testament, where Wisdom appears as God's companion from before creation, working with him in the work of creation as a master workman (Prov. 8:30), a female figure intimate with both God and man, later apparent in distorted reflexions in gnostic literature, and a striking dedication for churches in the Byzantine and Slav traditions; in the West Wisdom emerges again in the esoteric mystical tradition found in Jacob Boehme and others, and becomes crucial figure, this time highly sexed, for Solov'ev, who passed the tradition on to his disciples, Florensky and Bulgakov. In this latter manifestation, Sophia represents both the coherence of creation, still bearing the touch of the divine creator, but also representing what the persons of the Trinity have in common, what they manifest in the created order. Sophia mediates between God and cosmos, but is not strictly something 'in between', for there is nothing in between the created and the uncreated; rather Sophia is the point of contact, facing both ways – to God and to humankind. She corresponds in significant ways to the Mother of God, a creature turned towards God, receiving God in her being. Bulgakov knows the tradition of Wisdom well, but in contrast to Solov'ev, his vision of Wisdom is not of a woman 'with eyes full of an azure fire', though still for Bulgakov her gaze is 'like the first shining / Of universal and creative day'.[9] Wisdom speaks to Bulgakov of the

---

[7] Boris Bobrinskoy, *La compassion du Père* (Paris, 2000), p. 160, cf. 173; *La mystère de la Trinité* (Paris, 1986 (1996 imprint), p. 149 (presumably from an oral tradition, as no reference is given).

[8] Bukgakov, *Avtobiograficheskie Zametki*, p. 41 (*Anthology*, p. 8).

[9] Quotations from Solov'ev's poem, 'Three Meetings': *Vladimir Solovyov's Poems of Sophia*, trans. Boris Jakim and Laury Magnus (Chicago: The Variable Press, 1996), pp. 34f.

'divine veil thrown over the world', so that nothing in creation is bereft of the touch of the divine, nothing created barren of holiness. This sense of the holiness of the world, the holiness of nature, Bulgakov felt as a painful nostalgia during his Marxist days, and its recovery followed on the realisation that he could not be 'reconciled with nature without God'. Moreover, it is this that lies behind Bulgakov's not altogether fair criticism of the Western Catholic idea of nature and grace that he encountered among his Western friends in Paris. There he found – in a curious way anticipating de Lubac's later criticism of traditional Latin theology in his work, *Surnaturel* (1946) – a notion of pure nature, that is, created nature devoid of grace or the touch of God, which was for Bulgakov quite abhorrent and incomprehensible. It is this notion of pure nature that lies at the basis of his criticism of Roman Catholic Mariology in *The Burning Bush*, since he maintains, perhaps oddly but shrewdly, that it is implicated in the doctrine of the Immaculate Conception.

The Great Trilogy: *On Divine Wisdom and Godmanhood*

Bulgakov's mature theology is set out comprehensively in his later trilogy, *On Divine Wisdom and Godmanhood*. The first volume is called *The Lamb of God*, which deals with the Son of God, in the Trinity, in creation, as incarnate, and concludes with an exposition of the threefold work of Christ, as prophet, priest and king. It is perhaps the most explicitly sophiological of his works, the first three sections, in particular, expressed in terms of divine wisdom, created wisdom and their conjunction in the God-man. The second is entitled *The Comforter*, and deals with the Holy Spirit, with an epilogue on the Father. The final volume, *The Bride of the Lamb*, deals with the created cosmos; the Church, history and the afterlife; and eschatology. This final volume was published posthumously in 1945, although it was ready for the press in 1939, and contains a number of addenda, that might have been incorporated in the main text, had Bulgakov had the energy to rework them; they constitute, as his French translator, Constantine Andronikov, put it, a 'final Amen'.

This trilogy, considered as a comprehensive work of dogmatic theology, has an unusual structure. A traditional structure might be: (Revelation,) doctrine of God, Trinity, doctrine of creation, the Fall, Christology, redemption, Church and Sacraments, eschatology – a structure that can perhaps be traced back to St John Damascene, and is found in dogmatic treatises in both the East and the West. Bulgakov's structure is significantly different: Son, Spirit, Church and humanity. For he sees theology as the human response to the revelation of God the Father through the Son and the Spirit, a revelation manifest in the created order and discerned within the Church in its prayer and worship. It is a strikingly Irenaean vision of theology, with the Son and the Spirit as the two hands of God, fashioning and redeeming the world, and forming the Church. The Father is the ultimate source of all, known only through the Son and the Spirit; hence the short epilogue on the Father in *The Comforter*, for everything about the Father is revealed through the Son and the Spirit. The mention of St Irenaeus points to another element in Bulgakov's methodology: the importance of the Fathers.

In one of his shorter treatises, Bulgakov summarises his theological method in these words: 'it is necessary, first of all, to return to the theology of the Fathers (one thousand years into the past), to the patristic doctrine, and to use it as a true guide, creatively to unfold it and apply it to our time'.[10] There is tendency to accept uncritically the accusations against Bulgakov of an ignorance of the Fathers by the espousers of the 'Neo-Patristic synthesis', but this assertion of Bulgakov's suggests a theological methodology not that different from theirs. In fact, the sources of Bulgakov's theology are clear, however indebted he is to Solov'ev and the nineteenth-century Russian reception of German idealism: they are the Scriptures and the Fathers, often mediated through the prayers and songs of the liturgical offices. Bulgakov is often quite painstaking in his citations from the Fathers (though this is disguised by the French and, especially, the English translators who often curtail or omit altogether Bulgakov's patristic material). He also makes good use of nineteenth-century Russian historical and patristic scholarship (though not the dogmatic textbooks), particularly in the discussion of the doctrine of the procession of the Holy Spirit, of the work of V.V. Bolotov.

Sophia–Kenosis–Eschatology

The theology Bulgakov draws out from Scripture, the Fathers, and the liturgical prayer and worship of the Church is one of immense richness that can scarcely be summarised in a brief chapter. There are, however, several features of it that may perhaps be commented on. First, obviously, the question of Sophia. We have already said something of this in connexion with Bulgakov's experience of the wonder of nature and art that he could only resolve by returning to the faith of his childhood: his sense that nature, because created by God, can never be bereft of the sense of the touch of the Creator – a touch, almost a caress, that he designated Sophia, the divine wisdom. So, in exploring the contact between God and human kind culminating in the Incarnation, he finds himself compelled to talk of Sophia, turning towards God a created face, and to the creation an uncreated countenance. There flows from this a sense of the immanence of God in creation (he uses the word 'panentheism'), so that creation itself may be seen as a manifestation of God, a theophany: this leads him to relate Sophia to the Platonic notion of the divine ideas, that are embodied in the cosmos, and brings him close to the notions of the *logoi* of creation (developed by St Maximos the Confessor, apparently unknown to Bulgakov) and of the divine energies or activities (explicitly linked to St Gregory Palamas by Bulgakov). A culminating example of this is found in the close relationship between Sophia and Mary, the Virgin Mother of God. In *The Burning Bush*, he puts it like this:

> The Mother of God is sophianic to the highest degree. She is the fulness of Sophia in creation and in this sense she is created Sophia ... Sophia is the foundation, the pillar

---

[10] Sergei Bulgakov, *The Holy Grail and the Eucharist*, p. 82.

and ground of the truth, in its fulness revealing the Mother of God, and in this sense She is, as it were, the personal expression of Sophia in creation, the personal form of the earthly Church ... In the God-mother, heavenly and created Wisdom are united, the Holy Spirit living in Her, with a created human hypostasis. Her flesh becomes completely spiritual and transparent to heaven, in Her is fulfilled the goal of the created world ... She is also, in this sense, the glory of the world.[11]

Second, the doctrine of self-emptying, *kenosis*. Phil. 2:5–11 says that Christ 'emptied himself [*ekenosen*], taking the form of a slave'. This has generally been taking as affirming that the divinity of Christ was tempered in the Incarnation, so that his humanity was not overwhelmed. In nineteenth-century Russian thought, the idea is taken more radically. In his self-emptying Christ does not temper or diminish his divinity, but *reveals* it, for the essence of divinity is love, and love makes space for the other, defers to the other. This is true, Bulgakov maintains, within the Trinity itself: in their mutual love, the persons of the Trinity could be said to defer to one another. But the act of creation is also an act of *kenosis*: God, as it were, makes space for creation, allows it to be itself; God does not in any way absent himself from creation, but his loving presence does not overwhelm it, he grants it freedom. Similarly, parallel to the *kenosis* of the Son in the Incarnation, there is a *kenosis* of the Spirit in creation, or more specifically in history; divine providence does not direct the course of history in a deterministic way, but works with the free decisions of men and women.

Finally, Bulgakov's theology has a strong sense of eschatology, which is rooted in his fundamental theological stance, of the human response in the Church to the coming of God as Son and Spirit. His trilogy ends with the Church reaching out as the Bride in the Spirit to the coming Lord Jesus, whom it awaits with eager hope, not fear. Not surprisingly, Bulgakov holds out a hope that all may be saved, though hesitates about the term *apokatastasis*, as perhaps detracting from the creature's free response to God in deification.

Conclusion

Bulgakov can be seen as perhaps *the* Russian theologian who sought to grasp the *kairos* of the encounter of Orthodoxy with the West and unfold the riches of the Orthodox tradition for the benefit of a Western Christendom that had lost so much of the original Christian vision. Although he was more aware than most of the need to engage with philosophical issues, his theology is fundamentally liturgical, the theology of one standing in the Spirit and beholding the glory of God in the face of Christ.

---

[11] Sergei Bulgakov, *Kupina Neopalimaya*, pp. 189, 191.

Bibliography

Primary Literature

Bulgakov's Principal Works

Filosofiya Khosyaistva (Moscow, 1912; *Philosophy of Economics the World as Household*, trans. Catherine Evtuhov, New Haven: Yale University Press, 2000).

Svet' Nevecherniy [*The Unfading Light*] (Moscow, 1917).

Tikhie Dumy [*Quiet Thoughts*] (Moscow, 1918).

Drug Zhenikha (Paris, 1927; *The Friend of the Bridegroom*, trans. Boris Jakim, Grand Rapids: William B. Eerdmans, 2003).

Kupina Neopalimaya (Paris, 1927; *The Burning Bush On the Orthodox Veneration of the Mother of God*, trans. Thomas Allen Smith, Grand Rapids: William B. Eerdmans, 2009).

Iakova Lestitsa (Paris, 1929; *Jacob's Ladder. On Angels*, trans. Thomas Allen Smith, Grand Rapids: William Eerdmans, 2010).

Evkharisticheskiy Dogmat (in *Evkharistiya*, Paris: YMCA Press; Moscow: Russkiy Put', 2005, pp. 138–205, together with *Evkharisticheskaya Zhertva* [*Eucharistic Sacrifice*]; *Eucharistic Dogma*, trans. Boris Jakim, in *The Holy Grail & the Eucharist*, Hudson: Lindisfarne Books, 1997, pp. 63–138, together with *The Holy Grail*).

Agnets Bozhiy (Paris, 1933; *The Lamb of God*, trans. Boris Jakim, Grand Rapids: William B. Eerdmans, 2007).

The Orthodox Church (London: The Centenary Press, 1935).

Utishitel (Paris, 1936; *The Comforter*, trans. Boris Jakim, Grand Rapids: William B. Eerdmans, 2004).

The Wisdom of God (London: Williams and Norgate, 1937).

Nevesta Agntsa (Paris, 1945; *The Bride of the Lamb*, trans. Boris Jakim, Grand Rapids: William B. Eerdmans, 2002).

Avtobiograficheskie Zametki [*Autobiographical Notes*] (Paris, 1946; portions translated by Natalie Duddington in *A Bulgakov Anthology*, edited by James Pain and Nicolas Zernov, London: SPCK, 1976, pp. 3–27).

Filosofia Imeni [*Philosophy of the Name*] (Paris, 1953).

Dukhovniy Dnevnik [*Spiritual Journal*] (Paris, 1973).

On the Ramparts of Cherson (published in Russian, *Trudy sotsiologii i teologii*, 2, Moscow: Nauka, 1997; *Sur les remparts de Chersonèse*, trans. Bernard Marchadier, Geneva: Ad Solem, 1999).

Since 1989 many of these works have been republished in Russia. All the above (save for *Autobiographical Notes*, *Spiritual Journal* and *Sur les Remparts*) have been translated into French by Constantine Andronikov (Collection SOPHIA, Lausanne: L'Age d'Homme).

Bibliography of Bulgakov's works in English in *A Bibliography of Russian Idealist Philosophy in English* (Variable Readings in Russian Philosophy 7, Jordanville: The Variable Press, 1999, pp. 16–22).

Secondary Literature

Arjakovsky, Antoine, *Essai sur le Père Serge Boulgakov* (Paris: Parole et Silence, 2006).
Bobrinskoy, Boris, *La compassion du Père* (Paris: Éditions du Cerf, 2000).
Bobrinskoy, Boris, *La mystère de la Trinité* (Paris: Éditions du Cerf, 1986/1996 imprint).
Evtuhov, Catherine, *The Cross and the Sickle: Sergei Bulgakov and the Fate of Russian Religious Philosophy, 1980–1920* (Ithaca and London: Cornell University Press, 1997).
Louth, Andrew, 'Sergii Bulgakov and the Task of Theology', *Irish Theological Quarterly*, 74 (2009), pp. 243–57.
Nichols, Aidan, *Wisdom from Above. A Primer in the Theology of Father Sergei Bulgakov* (Leominster: Gracewing, 2005).
St Vladimir's Theological Quarterly, 49(1–2) (2005) [issue devoted to Bulgakov].
Vallière, Paul, *Modern Russian Thought: Bukharev, Soloviev, Bulgakov: Orthodox Theology in a New Key* (Edinburgh: T&T Clark, 2000), pp. 227–403.
Vladimir Solovyov's Poems of Sophia, trans. Boris Jakim and Laury Magnus (Chicago: The Variable Press, 1996).
Williams, Rowan, *Sergii Bulgakov: Towards a Political Theology* (Edinburgh: T&T Clark, 1999).

Chapter 28
Georges Florovsky

Brandon Gallaher

'To follow' the Fathers does not mean just 'to quote' them.
'To follow' the Fathers means to acquire their 'mind,' their phronema.[1]

If the greatness of a theologian is determined by his influence, Georges Florovsky is undoubtedly the greatest Eastern Orthodox theologian of the twentieth century as, indeed, is often claimed. His theological programme and method of a spiritual return to, and renewal in, the Byzantine heritage (i.e. Greek Patristic corpus, the monastic and liturgical tradition) – in the well-worn slogan, 'neo-patristic synthesis' – has increasingly become the dominant paradigm for the Orthodox theology and ecumenical activity. As a teacher, his students included some of the best-known names in modern Orthodox theology: John Meyendorff (1926–92), John Romanides (1928–2001) and John Zizioulas (b. 1931). In addition, he mentored others who are also now key figures in modern Orthodox thought: Archim. Sophrony Sakharov (1896–1993), Vladimir Lossky (1903–58), Alexander Schmemann (1921–83) and Kallistos Ware (b. 1934).[2] Given that his influence has been so profound, it becomes difficult to discern what Florovsky may or may not have taught in contradistinction from the contemporary assumptions upheld by most Orthodox theologians. Florovsky's literary work, moreover, is almost entirely occasional and essayistic in nature although he wrote widely in Patristics, Russian history and culture and Christian doctrine. Nowhere in his writing will one find a sustained systematic treatment of 'neo-patristic synthesis'. Arguably, the unsystematic nature of Florovsky's literary work and the institutionalisation of key areas of his theological vision has, as it were, locked away for the student until quite recently both an understanding of his writings as a creative whole and a proper evaluation of his contemporary theological legacy. One possible hermeneutic 'skeleton key' in this process may be found in an analysis of his writings in their Russian émigré context. When read in this context, both the fundamentally polemical nature of his thought and the basic appeal of his theology to a Pan-Orthodox identity (i.e. not bound by any nationality) come to the foreground. Florovsky's polemicism, above all, can be seen in his attempt to articulate a theology of the 'traditional' identity of Eastern Orthodoxy *against* the 'sophiology' of the great Russian economist, philosopher and theologian Sergii Bulgakov (1871–1944).

---

[1] Georges Florovsky, *The Byzantine Fathers of the Fifth Century*, p. 38 and 'St Gregory Palamas and the Tradition of the Fathers', p. 109.

[2] Schmemann and Meyendorff followed Florovsky in the deanship of St Vladimir's Orthodox Theological Seminary, Crestwood, New York.

A Voyage into Exile and towards Pan-Orthodoxy[3]

Georges Vasilievich Florovsky was born on 28 August 1893 (Old Style Julian Calendar = 9 September 1893 by the Gregorian Calendar) into a clerical and highly academic family in the provincial town of Elisavetgrad in the Russian Empire (now Kirovohrad, Ukraine) and at six months moved south with his family to Odessa. He was a precocious but sickly child with a voracious appetite for reading and an aptitude for learning languages, which would later earn him the reputation, even amongst his critics, as a genuine theological encyclopaedia. Florovsky studied philosophy (with an emphasis on history) at the University of Odessa from 1911 to 1919. However, in January 1920 the threat of an offensive of the Red Army forced his family to flee Odessa via Istanbul for Sofia, Bulgaria. He remained in Sofia for a year during which time he became briefly allied with the 'Eurasians'. The Eurasians were a Russian movement critical of the West who looked to Asia and the Tatars in their quest for Russian identity, although Florovsky would typically emphasise Russia's Byzantine-Orthodox heritage. In December 1921, he took up a Czechoslovak government scholarship to study and teach in Prague. He soon began teaching the philosophy of law as a teaching assistant in the Russian Law Faculty, Charles University as well as the history of Russian literature at the Russian Institute of Commercial Knowledge (or simply, Russian Institute). In Prague, he completed and in June 1923 successfully defended before the Russian émigré academic organization, the Russian Academic Group (RAG in Czechoslovakia), a higher research Masters thesis (roughly equivalent to a present day Phd dissertation) on the historical philosophy of the Russian social and political thinker Alexander Herzen (1812–70).[4] The Masters degree was confirmed in October of 1923 and the diploma was issued on 30 April 1925 by the Board of the Russian Academic Organizations Abroad.[5] Herzen's attack on all forms of historical determinism, emphasis on the freedom of man as an historical

---

[3] For biography see Andrew Blane (ed.), *George Florovsky: Russian Intellectual and Orthodox Churchman* (Crestwood: St Vladimir's Seminary Press, 1993) and Paul L. Gavrilyuk, *Georges Florovsky and the Russian Religious Renaissance* (Oxford: Oxford University Press, forthcoming).

[4] See recently Derek Offord, 'Alexander Herzen' in *A History of Russian Philosophy 1830–1930: Faith, Reason, and the Defense of Human Dignity*, edited by G.M. Hamburg and Randall A. Poole (Cambridge: Cambridge University Press, 2010), pp. 52–68.

[5] See Paul L. Gavrilyuk, 'Georges Florovsky's Monograph "Herzen's Philosophy of History": The New Archival Material and the Reconstruction of the Full Text', Forthcoming *Harvard Theological Review*.

actor and vision of the movement and creativity of history in terms of perpetually opposed antinomies would later influence Florovsky's hermeneutics and practice as an historical theologian. In Prague (1921–6), in reaction to Bulgakov's sophiology (who was then oddly also his confessor), he formed a study circle devoted to the Fathers which he saw even then as the wellspring of Orthodoxy. It is on the basis of his interest in the Fathers that Florovsky was offered in 1926 a post in patrology at the newly formed l'Institut de Théologie Orthodoxe Saint-Serge in Paris, which became the seminary for the Patriarchal Exarchate of Russian Parishes under the Patriarchate of Constantinople led by Metropolitan Evlogii (Georgievskii) (1868–1946). Florovsky lived and taught in Paris for some 16 years (1926–39 and 1945–8); broken only by the Second World War which he spent in Belgrade teaching and acting as a school chaplain. During his Paris years the foundations of all his later academic and ecumenical work were laid. Ordained to the priesthood in 1932, he became intensively involved with the life of his own church as an assistant chaplain for the Russian Student Christian Movement and entered deeply into the ecumenical movement (with the Fellowship of St Alban and St Sergius and the nascent World Council of Churches (WCC)), including a long-running dialogue with Karl Barth, and adapted for Orthodoxy the first ferment of what would later become the *ressourcement* movement or return to the patristic and medieval sources which preceded and grounded the work of Vatican II. Florovsky developed his theology during a period of ecclesial confusion in the Orthodox Church. For centuries the Orthodox, under a succession of 'yokes' (Tartar, Muslim, Turkish, etc.), had Westernised their theology so that it was at odds with their distinctively Eastern spiritual character. The confusion wrought by this Western 'pseudomorphosis' of Orthodox consciousness (which Florovsky detailed in his massive 1937 work, *The Ways of Russian Theology*)[6] came to the crisis point in the twentieth century in a long succession of national tragedies including the Armenian Genocide of 1915, the Russian Revolution of 1917 and subsequent civil war and the 1923 'Asia-Minor catastrophe'. Florovsky's theology, which calls for a renewal of the Orthodox Church by a return to its Patristic, liturgical and monastic sources, is a response to this confusion.

---

[6] Cf. Florovsky, *Ways of Russian Theology*, I, *The Collected Works of Georges Florovsky* [hereafter cited as *CW*, I, *CW*, II etc.], Gen. Ed. Richard Haugh (Vaduz, Liechtenstein and Belmont, MA: Büchervertriebsanstalt, 1974–89), V, p. 85 and 'Western Influences in Russian Theology', *CW*, IV, p. 170; the term is derived from mineralogy via Oswald Spengler's *Decline of the West* (1915/22). A pseudomorph is a crystal of one mineral with the form of another (George Hunston Williams, 'Father Georges Florovsky's Vision of Ecumenism', *Greek Orthodox Theological Review*, 41(2–3) (1996), p. 154 and see F.J. Thomson, 'Peter Mogila's Ecclesiastical Reforms and the Ukrainian Contribution to Russian Culture: A Critique of Georges Florovsky's Theory of the Pseudomorphosis of Orthodoxy', *Slavica Gandensia*, 20 (1993), pp. 67–119.

The Bulgakovian Context and the Final American Years

These years also saw two controversies with Bulgakov (then dean of St Serge) that would confirm Florovsky in his theological project: the 1933–35 controversy concerning Bulgakov's Proposals for Limited Episcopally Blessed Intercommunion between the Anglican and Orthodox Churches in the Fellowship of St Alban and St Sergius, of which Florovsky was a vocal opponent, and the 1935–37 controversy concerning sophiology in which he mostly opposed Bulgakov through non-public measures. Florovsky opposed what he saw as the ecclesially universalist and pantheist tendencies of Bulgakov's sophiology in both these episodes by a contrasting maximalist insistence on what he understood to be the maintenance and defence of traditional doctrinal and ecclesial boundaries. Ultimately, the memory of Florovsky's trenchant opposition to the well-beloved Bulgakov (d. 1944) and his sometimes imperious manner led to hostility from his colleagues and in 1948 he eagerly took up a professorship in Dogmatic Theology and Patristics (and from 1949, the deanship) at the newly formed St Vladimir's Orthodox Theological Seminary then in New York City.

As dean of St Vladimir's, he formed the seminary into a Pan-Orthodox institution with the highest academic standards and an international reputation gained through his well-publicised ecumenical labours within the WCC. However, in the process, he alienated both his faculty and his own students who found him overbearing, demeaning and short-tempered. A series of missteps, including firing the popular young lecturer in church history and liturgics and Dean of Students, the theologian and liturgist Alexander Schmemann (1921–83), led to his dismissal by the bishops in early 1955. Following St Vladimir's, Florovsky taught part-time at a variety of schools in Boston and New York[7] until he landed a position at Harvard Divinity School in early 1956 where he was its first ever Orthodox theologian to hold a post. At Harvard, he was to spend many years teaching Patristics and Russian culture and history, working at the highest ecumenical levels and writing a series of essays on tradition, Patristics and ecumenism, which, after having been collected in the first four volumes of his *Collected Works*, became widely influential and formative of the contemporary notion of Orthodox theology and identity. In the autumn of 1964 he retired to Princeton as a Visiting Professor of Slavic Studies and Religion. His remaining years are notable for his work on the first volumes of his *Collected Works*. On 11 August 1979, Florovsky died at 85 years old in Princeton, New Jersey; having retained his own sense of himself as an Orthodox Christian to the end through revolution, exile, war, displacement and life in a score of countries.

---

[7] Interestingly, Florovsky taught part-time from 1955 to 1965 at the Greek seminary in Boston, Holy Cross Greek Orthodox School of Theology, until he was fired by then Bishop (later Greek Orthodox Primate of the Archdiocese of North and South America) Iakovos (Coucouzis) (1911–2005) in a faculty dispute concerning Florovsky's advice on fasting to some conservative students.

Identity and Polemicism – The Florovskian Vision

As was mentioned earlier, Florovsky's neo-patristic synthesis is fundamentally polemical. John Meyendorff, in his important preface to an edition of Florovsky's *Ways of Russian Theology*, relates that in his lectures Florovsky frequently argued that the Fathers theologised for the refutation of heretics (p. ii). This Patristic approach to theology, Meyendorff continues, was the 'fundamental psychological method of Florovsky in his critique of Russian culture' and, more particularly, his refutation of the sophiology (pp. ii–iii) of the philosopher, critic, poet and mystic, Vladimir Solov'ev (1853–1900) and, especially, that of Bulgakov who attempted to more thoroughly 'orthodoxise' Solov'ev's thought. At almost every point of his theology, Florovsky is, arguably, silently responding to the sophiology of Bulgakov (pp. ii–iii). Neo-patristic synthesis, therefore, is best understood as a positive assertion of Orthodoxy identity by means of a negative polemic against heterodoxy.[8] But what is the positive aspect of the programme?

'Christological Concentration'

The fundamental thematic unity of neo-patristic synthesis is its assertion of the identity of the Orthodox Church and Orthodoxy more generally. Florovsky's synthesis, not unlike the theology of Barth, is a sort of 'Christological concentration'[9] where all Christian doctrine and spirituality is wholly determined by 'the central vision of the Christian faith: Christ Jesus, as God and Redeemer, Humiliated and Glorified, the Victim and the Victor on the Cross' (Florovsky, 'The Ethos of the Orthodox Church', p. 192). Florovsky's Christology begins with a meditation on the definition (and inheritance) of Chalcedon which he saw not as a metaphysical but an 'existential statement' of faith describing our Redeemer as a divine Person, God Himself who takes on human nature and thereby 'enters human history and becomes an historical person' ('The Lost Scriptural Mind' [1951], p. 13). Florovsky's Christology is crucial for understanding his neo-patristic synthesis because Christ is the personal centre of the identity of the Church or, more methodologically, 'The theology of the Church is but a chapter, and a principle chapter of Christology' (*Le corps du Christ vivant*, p. 12). Furthermore, Florovsky's Christology grounds the two basic poles of his

---

[8] For a more detailed account of Florovsky's polemicism and his appeal to a pan-Orthodox identity see Brandon Gallaher, '"Waiting for the Barbarians": Identity and Polemicism in the Neo-Patristic Synthesis of Georges Florovsky', *Modern Theology*, 27(4) (October 2011), pp. 659–91 (and in expanded form: 'A Re-envisioning of Neo-Patristic Synthesis?: Orthodox Identity and Polemicism in Fr Georges Florovsky and the Future of Orthodox Theology', *Theologia*, forthcoming 2013 (in Greek)) and, more recently, in direct response to our reading, Matthew Baker, 'Neopatristic Synthesis and Ecumenism: Towards the "Reintegration" of Christian Tradition', in Andrii Krawchuk and Thomas Bremer, ed., *Eastern Christianity in Encounter* (NY: Palgrave-MacMillan, forthcoming).

[9] Karl Barth, *How I Changed My Mind* (Edinburgh: The Saint Andrew Press, 1969), p. 43.

Christocentric theology, which are the *historical* and the *personal*. Theology must be *historical* because the Christian faith bears witness to a God who has acted, acts and will act in history from creation in Christ until His coming again. Theology, however, is also eminently *personal* insofar as the Truth in whom we live abundantly (John 10:10) is a Person, our Master, Redeemer and Head, Jesus Christ.

Ecclesiology and Living Tradition

The headship of Christ of His Church, as His personalised human Body, makes the Church into a 'kind of continuation of Christ' ('The New Vision of the Church's Reality', p. 108); a notion he adapted from Johann Adam Möhler (1796–1838) of the Catholic Tübingen School (whose influence is pervasive).[10] We are redeemed and saved by living and dwelling within the fullness and unity of this risen Divine person incarnate in the world who is the Church as Christ 'in both His head and His body', in Florovsky's favourite Augustinian phrase.[11] The Body of Christ, as a divine-human organism, is 'knit together' and 'grows' (Col. 2:19) in unity of the Spirit and love through its perpetual renewal in the Eucharist, guaranteed by the uninterrupted sacramental succession of the hierarchy. Being a divine–human unity, the Church is not bound by time, but, in the celebration of the Eucharist by the bishop, eternally embraces the living and the dead who are all one and alive in Christ through His Spirit. This time-conquering aspect of ecclesial unity is symbolised by 'tradition' which is the living ever renewed connexion to the plenitude of the Church's experience in all ages as founded on the experience of the Apostles in being breathed on by Christ in the Upper Room and in their participation at Pentecost: 'Tradition is the constant abiding of the spirit and not only the memory of words. Tradition is a *charismatic*, not a historical, principle' ('Sobornost: The Catholicity of the Church', p. 47). Hence, tradition, for Florovsky, is not merely a guarding of the apostolic deposit or a conservative principle, but 'it is primarily the principle of growth and regeneration' (p. 47). Throughout his work, to describe the dynamism, creativity and freedom of the life of the Body of Christ as animated by His Spirit, he constantly uses a phrase that was common amongst his Russian émigré contemporaries – 'living tradition' (*zhivoe predanie*). Once again, Florovsky adapts this idea from Möhler as well as such Slavophile writers as Aleksei Khomiakov (1804–60) and Ivan Kireevsky (1806–56).

Within the life of tradition, through which the Spirit moves, witnesses, reveals and proclaims, the shape and form of the unity of the Church becomes visible as the Gospel itself given within Scripture as a 'God inspired scheme or image (*eikon*) of truth, but not truth itself' (p. 48). Scripture only lives and breathes within tradition. It exists in

---

[10] Möhler, *Symbolism: or, Exposition of the Doctrinal Differences between Catholics and Protestants as Evidenced by their Symbolical Writings*, 2 vols, second edn, trans. James Burton Robinson (London: Charles Dolan, 1847), Vol. 2 (Chap. 5, §36): p. 6 and see 1: p. 35; see Gallaher, '"Waiting for the Barbarians"', pp. 669ff.

[11] See Augustine, *In Iohannis evangelium tractatus CXXIV*, PL 35. c.1622.

the Body of Christ, who is truth Himself, and in this Body Christ 'unchangeably and unceasingly reveals Himself' (p. 48). The unity of the Church (and here one might easily replace 'unity' with 'identity'), therefore, is simultaneously salvific, cariative, eucharistic, traditional-Scriptural and pneumatic in character. It is a unity of the One whole Jesus Christ in both His head and His body through His Spirit, that is, Christ is one both in Himself and in us also. The divine–human unity of the Church above all reflects the unity of the Trinity in whom many become one, which Florovsky referred to as *sobornost'* or catholicity. The idea of the Church as *sobornost'* – completeness, integrality, conciliarity and difference-in unity – is largely adapted by Florovsky, once again, from Möhler, the Slavophiles as well as his contemporaries in the emigration.[12]

The Churching of Being – The Catholic Consciousness of the Fathers

This catholicity, completeness in the life of grace by being bonded together in a union of common life and love with one's fellows reflecting the Trinity, is a call to all Christians in the 'glorious liberty of the children of God' (Rom. 8:21) to participate, in the famous émigré coinage, in the 'churching' (*otserkovlenie*) of their very being. Florovsky, in a notion popular in the period, variously refers to 'the catholic transfiguration of personality', 'catholic consciousness' and 'the catholic regeneration of the mind'. Each Christian is commanded to freely love his neighbour as himself by rejecting, denying and even dying to himself. He sees himself so wholly in the other because, in the other, he is freely responding to Christ Himself. The Christian life consists of the free cultivation in history of an ecclesial consciousness whereby in faith in Christ 'we enclose the many within our own ego' imaging the Holy Trinity in whom many become one ('Sobornost', pp. 43–4). In taking on Christ through treating our brother as our life, we become incorporated into Christ and 'become inheritors of the divine nature' (II Peter 1:4).

The free historical process of creative striving and ecclesial becoming in Christ is described by Florovsky, following the Fathers, as 'divinization' (*theosis*) and 'deification' (*theopoiesis*). Man is created in the 'image of God' which itself reflects, is a likeness, of the Proto-image or image of creation in God. This Proto-image transcends created nature and in no way coincides with the *imago dei*. It serves as a 'supra-natural challenging goal' set above created nature for man to freely participate in union with God and to become himself by transcending himself in a 'leap from the plane of nature onto the plane of grace ... this realization is the acquisition of the Spirit, is participation in God' ('Creation and Creaturehood', p. 74). Given his Christocentrism and the importance of freedom and creativity in the process of divinisation or the churching of the mind, it is not surprising that he saw history as a field of action where behind contingent events stand free personalities. The course of singular events from Creation to the Second Coming does not 'follow evolutionary schemes and patterns' ('The Predicament of the Christian Historian', p. 48) but moves forward by breaks that

---

[12] See Sergii Bulgakov, *The Orthodox Church*, trans. Lydia Kesich (Crestwood, NY: St. Vladimir's Seminary Press, [1932] 1988), pp. 60ff.

are linked to new developments by creative bursts of inspiration in the form of heroic feats (*podvig*) of free personalities.[13] Here once again can be seen his polemic against the determinism of sophiology as well as the influence of Herzen with his rejection of a teleology to history. However, for Florovsky, there is, contra Herzen, an end and direction to history, which is the ever-persuading but utterly non-coercive grace of God given to us in the Spirit of Christ (Rom. 8:9). At the centre of history, therefore, stands Jesus Christ and His Church composed of a union of free personalities. Christ calls all men to become free agents in a 'history of the spirit, the story of man's growth to the full stature of perfection, under the Lordship of the historical God-man, even of our Lord, Jesus Christ' ('The Predicament of the Christian Historian', pp. 58 and 64).[14]

If the identity of the Church as catholicity (sc. unity in Christ) is described as a form of consciousness which Christians are in the process of acquiring in their growth into the full stature of Christ, in becoming truly free, then it is not surprising that Florovsky uses a variety of psychological imagery to discuss its internal life. Throughout his work he speaks of a primary set of terms as subjects (e.g. Church, Fathers, tradition) undergoing, being characterised by or possessing a second set of terms (e.g. 'experience', 'faith', 'image', 'vision', 'witness', 'memory', 'freedom' and especially 'mind') in stock phrases such as 'the experience of the Church', 'the mind of the Fathers', 'the vision of the Fathers' etc. He will likewise combine the second set of terms within itself treating one as a subject of another, such as, the 'experience of faith'. Florovsky's psychology of catholic consciousness begins with a silent internal faith (as an 'experience' or 'vision'), which revelation, which is the Word of truth, addresses to man. This comprehension of the truth of Christ cannot remain silent but must be expressed noetically as a dogma. Dogma, therefore, witnesses to what has been experienced or seen by faith in a vision.

The saints, and, in particular, the Fathers, are the pre-eminent instances of this catholic consciousness. The Fathers have attained to such a fulness of catholicity, such a completeness of a life full of grace, that their faith once expressed is no mere personal profession but, as Florovsky expressed it in his *Ways of Russian Theology*, 'precisely the testimony of the Church. They speak from the depths and fullness of its catholicity: they theologize within the element of *sobornost*" (II, p. 295). The Fathers, who witness to the testimony of the Church and its life as tradition, are accordingly described everywhere in Florovsky as not just teachers but 'guides and witnesses' to the identity of the Church whose '*vision* is "of authority", not necessarily their words'.[15] The Fathers neither present to us 'ready-made' answers, nor can one look to them for a simple *consensus patrum* as a binding empirical agreement of individuals.

---

[13] See Florovsky, 'Evolution und Epigenesis (Zur Problematik der Geschichte)', *Der russische Gedanke*, 1(3) (1930), pp. 240–52.

[14] See Matthew Baker, 'Georges Florovsky (1893–1979) – *Agon* of Divine and Human Freedom' in *Creation and Salvation: A Medley of Essays on Recent Theological Movements*, Vol. II, edited by Ernst M. Conradie (Münster: LIT Verlag, 2012), pp. 29–35.

[15] Brandon Gallaher, 'Georges Florovsky on Reading the Life of St Seraphim', *Sobornost*, 27(1) (2005), p. 62 (an annotated archival letter of Florovsky).

The Fathers help us face the problems that are of true importance in the new age and to construct a contemporary synthesis. We must follow the Fathers creatively and not through what Florovsky often referred to as a 'theology of repetition' quoting their sayings outside the context of their meaning and life. We are called, then, to *creatively* and *spiritually* return to the sources, to follow the Fathers by acquiring their mind (*phronema*), which is a *consensus* reflecting the very 'catholic mind' or fundamental identity of the Church.

Christian Hellenism and Dogmatics as a Perennial 'Christian Philosophy'

Florovsky was quite explicit that the vision of the Fathers was coextensive with the teaching and lives of the Greek Fathers understood as a 'Christian Hellenism'. In direct contradiction to the prevailing opinion of Adolf von Harnack (1851–1930) that dogma in Christianity was an 'acute Hellenisation' of the faith,[16] Florovsky argued that the Hellenisation of revelation in the Fathers was by no means accidental but part of the providential action of God in the calling of the Gentiles (cf. 'Revelation, Philosophy and Theology', p. 32). Hellenism, Florovsky admitted, is itself 'ambiguous' and 'double-faced', as can be seen in the pagan revivals of the Renaissance and German Romanticism ('The Predicament of the Christian Historian', p. 23). Pagan philosophy, in particular, and Hellenism, more generally, had therefore to be 'baptised' in the Church. This Christian Hellenism is coextensive with the Byzantine heritage and Florovsky regarded it as the common tradition of the Church in East and West, which is embodied above all in the Orthodox Church. Florovsky called the Orthodox specifically, but also all Christians regardless of tradition, to return to this 'Hellenism under the sign of the cross' ('The Christian Hellenism', p. 9) by means of a 'spiritual Hellenisation (or re-Hellenisation)' of theology: 'let us be more Greek to be truly catholic, to be truly Orthodox' ('Patristics and Modern Theology', p. 232).

---

[16] The phrase in Harnack initially was a medical metaphor used to refer to Gnosticism where Gnosticism is the 'acute hellenisation' and the 'chronic condition' (a 'gradual process' of hellenisation leading to the acute state but still retaining the Old Testament faith) is Catholicism/Orthodoxy (*History of Dogma*, 3rd Ed., 7 vols., trans. Neil Buchanan (London: Williams & Norgate, 1894–1899 [1886–90]), I, pp. 226ff.). Harnack later applies the phrase more generally to the dogmatic orthodoxy of the (especially Greek) Fathers and Florovsky is reacting to this broader use. Harnack and his ilk argued that dogma in Christianity was an inessential Greek 'husk' (an 'acute Hellenisation') which covered an essential Jewish 'kernel' (i.e. fatherhood of God, the brotherhood of man and infinite value of the human soul). Christianity had been infected by Greek metaphysics which distorted the simple Hebraic message of the Gospel so de-Hellenisation (not Florovsky's re-Hellenisation!) was needed (See Adolf von Harnack, *What is Christianity?*, 2nd edn, trans. Thomas Bailey Saunders (London and Oxford: Williams and Norgate; New York: G.P. Putnam's Sons, 1901), pp. 13ff., 51ff., 199ff., espec. 205 and see (on Greek Orthodoxy) p. 221; cf. Paul L. Gavrilyuk, 'Harnack's Hellenized Christianity or Florovsky's "Sacred Hellenism": Questioning Two Metanarratives of Early Christian Engagement with Late Antique Culture', *St Vladimir's Theological Quarterly*, 54(3–4) (2010), pp. 323–44).

Through the gracious choice of specific 'eternal words, incapable of being replaced' in their dogmatic definitions, the Fathers, forged a perennial albeit eclectic 'Christian philosophy' which was 'enclosed' within Christian dogmatics ('Revelation, Philosophy and Theology', p. 34). Bulgakov, in contrast, believed that dogmas were truths of religious revelation that had metaphysical content and therefore were expressed differently depending on the language of the philosophy of the day whether that was the Greek philosophy used by the Fathers or our own contemporary philosophy.[17] In reaction to this view, Florovsky asserted that it was wholly illegitimate, as he believed Bulgakov had attempted with Idealist thought in his sophiology, to express Christian teaching in any other philosophy but that forged by the Fathers. Christianity 'is history in its very essence' and there exists no abstract general Christian message that can be detached from its historical context and there likewise is no eternal truth 'which could be formulated in some supra-historical propositions' ('The Eastern Orthodox Church and the Ecumenical Movement', p. 75). The philosophy that the Fathers used in expressing Christian dogma was in fact unique and differed greatly from that of Aristotle and Plato and so it was wholly absurd to attempt to reinterpret 'traditional doctrine in terms of categories of a new philosophy, whatever this philosophy may be' ('Patristics and Modern Theology', p. 231). The 'presuppositions and categories' of this new 'philosophy of the Holy Spirit' ('Revelation, Philosophy and Theology', pp. 34–5) included the resurrection, history as a non-circular once for all creative fulfilment involving free acts of free personalities, man as a free person and God's absolute freedom (divine and human voluntarism) and, by extension, a radical distinction between God and creation (cf. 'Creation and Creaturehood', pp. 43–78). This last presupposition was aimed tacitly at Bulgakov's sophiology, which blurred the line between the created and the uncreated.[18]

---

[17] For Bulgakov's thinking on the relation of theology to philosophy and Church tradition see his 'Dogma and Dogmatic Theology' [1937], trans. Peter Bouteneff, *Tradition Alive: On the Church and the Christian Life in Our Time-Readings from the Eastern Church*, edited by Michael Plekon (Lanham, MD: Sheed & Ward, 2003), pp. 67–80.

[18] See, in Florovsky's exegesis of Origen, the polemical allusion to a 'fourth hypostasis' (which Bulgakov's sophiology was routinely accused of upholding): Florovsky, 'Appendix: The Idea of Creation in Christian Philosophy', p. 65. On sophiology and its problems see the following works by myself: Brandon Gallaher, 'Graced Creatureliness: Ontological Tension in the Uncreated/Created Distinction in the Sophiologies of Solov'ev, Bulgakov and Milbank', *Logos: A Journal of Eastern Christian Studies*, 47(1–2) (2006), pp. 163–90 at 174–82, 'The Christological Focus of Vladimir Solov'ev's Sophiology', *Modern Theology*, 25(4) (October 2009), pp. 617–46 and Review of Bulgakov's *The Lamb of God* (Grand Rapids: Wm. B. Eerdmans Publishing Company, 2008), *Logos*, 50(3–4) (December 2009), pp. 543–8 and *Freedom and Necessity in Modern Trinitarian Theology*, Oxford Theological Monographs Series (Oxford University Press, forthcoming), Part I [this is a revised version of the following: '*There is Freedom*: The Dialectic of Freedom and Necessity in the Trinitarian Theologies of Sergii Bulgakov, Karl Barth and Hans Urs von Balthasar', DPhil Thesis, University of Oxford, 2011].

Romantic Roots and Theological Limitations

Florovsky developed in his neo-patristic synthesis a whole constellation of philosophical and theological sources from late Romanticism but notably the theologies of Johann Adam Möhler and Ivan Kireevsky. From Möhler he drew, most importantly, the notion of the life of the Church as a 'living tradition' in which the saints and doctors of the Church are bound together in a common 'vision' of unity in which they share the same 'catholic consciousness'.[19] Kireevsky was perhaps, next to Herzen, the Russian thinker whose influence is the strongest in Florovsky. Kireevsky's Hellenism and Anti-Western (particularly, Anti-Idealist) polemic were conjoined with a call for the restoration of the 'philosophy of the Holy Fathers' which he understood as a transformation of classical pagan philosophy, but, more importantly, as a product of the 'superior vision' or 'immediate, inner experience' of the Fathers.[20] Today, such a Romantic approach to the Fathers, even amongst some Orthodox, is decidedly unpopular because it not only largely ignores the importance of the non-Greek Patristic corpus with its collapse of 'Byzantinism' with Orthodoxy, but it far too hastily resolves the differences of the Patristic writers into a reified whole ('the mind of the Church'). Furthermore, it ignores the Patristic writers' distinct contexts (Greek, Latin, Syriac, Coptic, Armenian, etc.) and uses categories (tradition, experience, vision, faith, etc.) which, while by no means alien to the Fathers, have a content that largely reflects Florovsky's Russian émigré theological project. Florovsky's work is hampered by its 'Easterncentric' vision of theological O/orthodoxy and, therefore, unsurprisingly often (but certainly not always) exhibits an anti-Western bias, which sees the Western theological tradition as a falling away from the ecclesial truth of Eastern Orthodoxy and not a distinct and equally valid development of the 'vision of the Fathers'. This rather partisan approach to theology though by no means universal has proved (sadly) vastly influential in contemporary Orthodox theology.

Orthodox Ecumenism as Missionary Activity and the Limits of the Church

Florovsky's essential ecumenical position, as was mentioned earlier, was forged in the mid-1930s in reaction to Bulgakov's ecumenical work. Bulgakov believed both that the churches might be led to unity by limited episcopally blessed intercommunion

---

[19] Johann Adam Möhler, *Unity in the Church or The Principle of Catholicism Presented in the Spirit of the Church Fathers of the First Three Centuries*, trans. Peter C. Erb (Washington, D.C.: Catholic University of America Press, [1825] 1996), pp. 107–11, 117, 127ff., 177 and 175–81; see also Aleksei Khomiakov, 'The Church is One', *On Spiritual Unity: A Slavophile Reader*, trans. and edited by Boris Jakim and Robert Bird (Hudson: Lindisfarne Books, 1998), pp. 31–53 at 36 and see pp. 33ff.
[20] Ivan Kireevsky, 'Fragments' [early 1850s] in *On Spiritual Unity: A Slavophile Reader*, trans. and edited by Boris Jakim and Robert Bird (Hudson: Lindisfarne Books, 1998), pp. 276–91 at 283.

and that although the Orthodox Church most fully embodied the Church Universal or *Una Sancta*, that the Church Universal was not bound by its limits and included to a lesser degree other ecclesial bodies as true churches.[21] Throughout his work, in contrast, Florovsky is clear that he believed that the Orthodox Church is *the true and only* Church which does not witness to a 'local tradition of her own' but witnesses to 'Patristic tradition' or 'the common heritage of the Church universal' (Florovsky, 'The Eastern Orthodox Church and the Ecumenical Movement', p. 72). Nevertheless, he argued that not everything that had been held or was even then held by the Orthodox Church was the 'truth of God' and so she could be said to be still imperfect although she embodied the fulness of truth: 'The *true Church* is not yet the *perfect* Church' ('Confessional Loyalty in the Ecumenical Movement', p. 204). All other churches, he argued, had defected from Orthodoxy as the common tradition of the Undivided Church or were 'schismatic' and were consequently called to return and be healed (i.e. 'conversion') within the unity of the Orthodox Church (pp. 204–5). Intercommunion, between the Orthodox and the heterodox, whose faith and life were so radically different, was naturally inconceivable and as a *means* to unity it was 'a blind alley from which there is no escape'.[22] Future progress on the road to unity would only come from supplementing an 'ecumenism in space' (the discovery and registry of the various agreements and disagreements amongst the churches) with an 'ecumenism in time', which was the reintegration of the East and the West in their return to their common tradition in Orthodoxy ('The Challenge of Disunity', p. 36); although he tended to see this common tradition as essentially 'Eastern', 'Christian Hellenist' and 'Greek' in character. Florovsky, not surprisingly, saw the involvement of the Orthodox Church in the ecumenical movement as a kind of 'missionary activity' ('Une vue sur l'Assemblée d'Amsterdam', p. 9) or as the witness of the truth of Orthodoxy to the whole Christian world: 'Christian reunion is just universal conversion to Orthodoxy … What is beyond [the Church's norm of the rule of faith and order] is just abnormal. But the abnormal should be cured and not simply condemned. This is a justification for the participation of an Orthodox in the ecumenical discourse, in the hope that through his witness the Truth of God may win human hearts and minds' ('Confessional Loyalty in the Ecumenical Movement', pp. 204–5). He largely enunciated this vision of ecumenism in successive ecumenical

---

[21] See the following works by myself: Brandon Gallaher, 'Bulgakov and Intercommunion', *Sobornost*, 24(2) (2002), pp. 9–28 (sequel to 'Bulgakov's Ecumenical Thought', *Sobornost*, 24(1) (2002), pp. 24–55), *Catholic Action: Ecclesiology, the Eucharist and the Question of Intercommunion in the Ecumenism of Sergii Bulgakov*, MDiv thesis, St Vladimir's Orthodox Theological Seminary, 2003 and 'The Contribution of Sergii Bulgakov to Modern Ecumenism' in *"That they all may be one" (John 17,21). Orthodoxy and Ecumenism – A Handbook for Theological Education*, Eds. Pantelis Kalaitzidis et al. (Geneva/Volos: WCC, CEC, and the Volos Academy for Theological Studies, forthcoming).

[22] 'Report of Conference held at High Leigh June 26–28, 1934 on "The Healing of Schism"'. Found in Oxford Archive of The Fellowship of St Alban and St Sergius. Folder labelled 'The Fellowship Conference Policy Before 1940', p. 6.

meetings of the WCC in the late 1940s and early 1950s. Florovsky's ecumenical theology has since become the core of the present rationale for Orthodox involvement in the ecumenical movement – ecumenism as a sort of tacit evangelism.

Furthermore, although Florovsky believed the One, Holy, Catholic and Apostolic Church *is* (not merely, in a weak sense, 'subsists in') the Orthodox Church, he did not hold that only Orthodox were therefore Christians. He contended, most famously in the 1933 essay 'The Limits of the Church',[23] which itself is dependent on an earlier little known essay of Bulgakov,[24] that *individual Christians* in various schismatic bodies existed outside of the canonical but inside the spiritual bounds of the Orthodox Church. This quasi-membership of certain heterodox in the Orthodox Church is by virtue of such elements as right belief, the preaching of the Word of God and true devotion. Above all, and here he adapts Augustine, the heterodox could be said to be Christians due to the 'validity' of their Trinitarian baptism whose graciousness and ecclesiality, albeit lacking full efficacy outside the canonical bounds of the Church, the mainstream tradition of the Orthodox Church acknowledges by receiving the heterodox believers not by a 'new baptism' but by the sacraments of Confession or Chrismation.

The Post-Florovsky Era: The Need to Re-envision Neo-Patristic Synthesis

Many of the key insights of Florovsky's neo-patristic synthesis, as has been mentioned, are simply his development of ideas already found in late Romanticism, especially Alexander Herzen, Johann Adam Möhler, the Slavophiles and its legacy in the Russian emigration more broadly. Nearly 30 years ago, Rowan Williams wrote in his prescient obituary of Florovsky that 'it is easy to forget that [Florovsky] was not a walking textbook but an original and radical mind' (p. 70). While time may have shown that Florovsky was perhaps not as 'original' thinker as had previously been thought, he was most certainly a 'radical' one (in its root meaning: *radix*) whose genius consisted in his awareness that the time was ripe in the so-called 'Orthodox diaspora', in the context of the *ressourcement* movement and in the light of a stream of national tragedies, for the construction of a Pan-Orthodox theological identity founded on a return to the roots of Orthodoxy in the Eastern Patristic corpus and the liturgical and spiritual tradition. The future of Orthodox theology is presently widely discussed by those contemporary Orthodox theologians following in the wake of Florovsky.[25]

---

[23] Cf. Florovsky, 'The Doctrine of the Church and the Ecumenical Movement', *The Ecumenical Review*, 2(2) (Winter 1950), pp. 152–61.

[24] Bulgakov, 'Ocherki ucheniia o tserkvi. (III). Tserkov' i "Inoslavie"', *Put'*, 4 (June–July 1926), pp. 3–26. Abridged translation: 'Outlines of the Teaching about the Church: The Church and Non-Orthodoxy', *American Church Monthly*, 30(6) (1931), pp. 411–23 and 31(1) (1932), pp. 13–26.

[25] See especially Paul L. Gavrilyuk, 'The Orthodox Renaissance', *First Things*, December 2012, pp. 33–7.

It would seem that the resolution of the current discussion depends much on a frank acknowledgement that a common Christian identity for both East and West and an effective response to the various versions of modernity cannot be constructed from a theological synthesis that retains a romantic Byzantinism and an anti-Western polemicism. A re-envisioning of neo-patristic synthesis is then certainly needed, if not indeed a greater openness in Orthodoxy to other theological methodologies, in what is now a secular, pluralistic, global and western age of the world. However, such a proposed pre-modern theology will only be a theology of repetition if, in being steeped in the mystery of the patristic faith, it does not then return to the pre- and post-Reformation Western sources with humility. Such humility in the face of another is characterised, to adapt a phrase of Florovsky, by a 'daring of spiritual assurance' ('Foreword' to *The Undistorted Image*, p. 5) that in light of this encounter is willing to consider fundamental doctrinal change in the search for an ecumenical Orthodoxy that can respond to our time.

Bibliography

Primary Literature

Collected Works

The Collected Works of Georges Florovsky [hereafter cited as *CW*, I, *CW*, II, etc.], Gen. Ed. Richard Haugh (Vaduz, Liechtenstein and Belmont, MA: Büchervertriebsanstalt, 1974–89).[26]

The Patristic Witness of Georges Florovsky: Essential Theological Writings, edited by Brandon Gallaher and Paul Ladouceur, Foreword by Kallistos Ware (Continuum/T&T Clark, forthcoming 2013).

Individual Works

'Appendix: The Idea of Creation in Christian Philosophy', *Eastern Churches Quarterly*, 8(2) (1949), pp. 53–77.

The Byzantine Fathers of the Fifth Century [1933], *CW*, VIII.

---

[26] The volumes of the *Collected Works* should be treated with caution after Volume II as there are extensive translation and editorial problems in almost all the volumes especially the last two volumes on ecumenism (XIII–XIV). Arguably, excluding his monograph *Ways of Russian Theology*, Florovsky's most seminal works are essays and they are collected in the first four volumes of his *Collected Works*. When available, the original publication is to be preferred. For a detailed bibliography see Andrew Blane (ed.), *George Florovsky: Russian Intellectual and Orthodox Churchman* (Crestwood: St Vladimir's Seminary Press, 1993), pp. 341–436. For secondary literature see Matthew Baker and Nikolaos Asproulis, 'Secondary Bibliography of Scholarly Literature and Conferences on Florovsky', *Theologia*, 81(4) (October–December 2010), pp. 357–96.

'The Challenge of Disunity', *St Vladimir's Seminary Quarterly*, 3(1–2) (Fall–Winter 1954–5), pp. 31–6.

'The Christian Hellenism', *Orthodox Observer*, 442 (January 1957), pp. 9–10.

'Confessional Loyalty in the Ecumenical Movement' in *Intercommunion*, edited by Donald Baillie and John Marsh (New York: Harper and Brothers Pub., 1952 [1950]), pp. 196–205.

Le corps du Christ vivant: Une interprétation orthodoxe de l'Église in *La Sainte Église Universelle: Confrontation oecuménique*, Cahiers Théologiques de l'actualité protestante, Hors-Série 4 (Neuchatel and Paris: Dalachaux et Niestlé, 1948), pp. 9–57.

'Creation and Creaturehood' [1928], *CW*, III, pp. 43–78.

'The Doctrine of the Church and the Ecumenical Movement', *The Ecumenical Review*, 2(2) (Winter 1950), pp. 152–61.

The Eastern Fathers of the Fourth Century [1931], *CW*, VII.

'The Eastern Orthodox Church and the Ecumenical Movement', *Theology Today*, 7(1) (April 1950), pp. 68–79.

'The Ethos of the Orthodox Church', *The Ecumenical Review*, 12(2) (January 1960), pp. 183–98 [also at *CW*, IV, pp. 11–30].

'Evolution und Epigenesis (Zur Problematik der Geschichte)', *Der russische Gedanke*, 1(3) (1930), pp. 240–52.

'Foreword' in Archimandrite Sophrony's *The Undistorted Image: Staretz Silouan: 1866–1938*, trans. Rosemary Edmonds (London: The Faith Press, 1958), pp. 5–6.

'The Limits of the Church', *Church Quarterly Review*, 117(233) (October 1933), pp. 117–31.

'The Lost Scriptural Mind' [1951], *CW*, I, pp. 9–16.

'The New Vision of the Church's Reality' in *John XXIII Lectures*, Vol. 2, 1966 Byzantine Christian Heritage (New York: John XXIII Center for Eastern Christian Studies, Fordham University, 1969), pp. 107–12.

'Patristics and Modern Theology', *Diakonia*, 4(3) (1969 [1937]), pp. 227–32.

'The Predicament of the Christian Historian' [1959], in *CW*, II, pp. 31–65.

'Revelation, Philosophy and Theology' [1931], *CW*, III, pp. 21–40.

'Sobornost: The Catholicity of the Church' [1934], *CW*, I, pp. 37–55.

'St Gregory Palamas and the Tradition and the Tradition of the Fathers' [1960], *CW*, I, pp. 105–20.

'Une vue sur l'Assemblée d'Amsterdam', *Irénikon*, 22(1) (1949), pp. 5–25.

Ways of Russian Theology [1937], I–II, *CW*, V–VI.

'Western Influences in Russian Theology' [1937] in *CW*, IV, pp. 157–82.

Secondary Literature

Amaral, Miguel de Salis, *Dos visiones ortodoxas de la Iglesia: Bulgakov y Florovsky*, Colección teológica 111 (Pamplona: Ediciones Universidad de Navarra, 2003).

Baker, Matthew, 'The Eternal "Spirit of the Son": Barth, Florovsky and Torrance on the Filioque', *International Journal of Systematic Theology*, 12(4) (October 2010), pp. 382–403.

Baker, Matthew, 'Georges Florovsky (1893–1979) – *Agon* of Divine and Human Freedom' in *Creation and Salvation: A Medley of Essays on Recent Theological Movements*, vol. II, edited by Ernst M. Conradie (Münster: LIT Verlag, 2012), pp. 29–35.

Baker, Matthew, Matthew Baker, 'Neopatristic Synthesis and Ecumenism: Towards the "Reintegration" of Christian Tradition', in Andrii Krawchuk and Thomas Bremer, ed., *Eastern Christianity in Encounter* (NY: Palgrave-MacMillan, forthcoming).

Baker, Matthew, *'Neo-Patristic Synthesis': An Examination of a Key Hermeneutical Paradigm in the Thought of Georges V. Florovsky*, ThM. Thesis, Holy Cross Greek Orthodox School of Theology (Brookline, MA, 2010).

Baker, Matthew, '"Theology Reasons" – in History: Neo-Patristic Synthesis and the Renewal of Theological Rationality', *Theologia*, 81(4) (October–December 2010), pp. 81–118.

Baker, Matthew and Nikolaos Asproulis, 'Secondary Bibliography of Scholarly Literature and Conferences on Florovsky', *Theologia*, 81(4) (October–December 2010), pp. 357–96 (this whole issue, edited by Nikolaos Asproulis, is on Florovsky with Greek and English articles).

Barth, Karl, *How I Changed My Mind* (Edinburgh: The Saint Andrew Press, 1969).

Blane, Andrew (ed.), *George Florovsky: Russian Intellectual and Orthodox Churchman* (Crestwood: St Vladimir's Seminary Press, 1993).

Bulgakov, Sergii, 'Dogma and Dogmatic Theology', trans. Peter Bouteneff, *Tradition Alive: On the Church and the Christian Life in Our Time-Readings from the Eastern Church*, edited by Michael Plekon (Lanham: Sheed & Ward, 2003), pp. 67–80.

Bulgakov, Sergii, *The Orthodox Church*, trans. Lydia Kesich (Crestwood: St. Vladimir's Seminary Press, [1932] 1988).

Bulgakov, Sergii, 'Outlines of the Teaching about the Church: the Church and Non-Orthodoxy', *American Church Monthly*, 30(6) (1931), pp. 411–23 and 31(1) (1932), pp. 13–26.

Cohen, Will, 'Sacraments and the Visible Unity of the Church', *Ecclesiology*, 4(1) (2007), pp. 68–87.

Gallaher, Brandon, 'Bulgakov and Intercommunion', *Sobornost*, 24(2) (2002), pp. 9–28.

Gallaher, Brandon, 'Bulgakov's Ecumenical Thought', *Sobornost*, 24(1) (2002), pp. 24–55.

Gallaher, Brandon, *Catholic Action: Ecclesiology, the Eucharist and the Question of Intercommunion in the Ecumenism of Sergii Bulgakov*, Mdiv thesis, St Vladimir's Orthodox Theological Seminary, 2003.

Gallaher, Brandon, 'The Christological Focus of Vladimir's Solov'ev's Sophiology', *Modern Theology*, 25(4) (October 2009), pp. 617–46.

Gallaher, Brandon, *Freedom and Necessity in Modern Trinitarian Theology*, Oxford Theological Monographs Series (Oxford University Press, forthcoming).

Gallaher, Brandon, 'Georges Florovsky on Reading the Life of St Seraphim', *Sobornost*, 27(1) (2005), pp. 58–70.

Gallaher, Brandon, 'Graced Creatureliness: Ontological Tension in the Uncreated/Created Distinction in the Sophiologies of Solov'ev, Bulgakov and Milbank', *Logos: A Journal of Eastern Christian Studies*, 47(1–2) (2006), pp. 163–90.

Gallaher, Brandon, 'A Re-envisioning of Neo-Patristic Synthesis?: Orthodox Identity and Polemicism in Fr Georges Florovsky and the Future of Orthodox Theology', *Theologia*, forthcoming 2013 (in Greek).

Gallaher, Brandon, 'Review of Bulgakov's *The Lamb of* God (Grand Rapids, MI: Wm. B. Eerdmans Publishing Company, 2008)', *Logos*, 50(3–4) (December 2009), pp. 543–8.

Gallaher, Brandon, 'The Contribution of Sergii Bulgakov to Modern Ecumenism' in *"That they all may be one" (John 17,21). Orthodoxy and Ecumenism – A Handbook for Theological Education*, Eds. Pantelis Kalaitzidis, Thomas FitzGerald, Cyril Hovorun, Aikaterini Pekridou and Nikolaos Asproulis (Geneva/Volos: World Council of Churches, Conference of European Churches, and the Volos Academy for Theological Studies, forthcoming).

Gallaher, Brandon, '"Waiting for the Barbarians": Identity and Polemicism in the Neo-Patristic Synthesis of Georges Florovsky', *Modern Theology*, 27(4) (October 2011), pp. 659–91.

Gavrilyuk, Paul L., 'Florovsky's Neopatristic Synthesis and the Future Ways of Orthodox Theology' in *Orthodox Constructions of the West*, edited by Georges Demacopoulos and Aristotle Papanikolaou (New York: Fordham University Press, forthcoming).

Gavrilyuk, Paul L., *Georges Florovsky and the Russian Religious Renaissance* (Oxford: Oxford University Press, forthcoming)

Gavrilyuk, Paul L., 'Georges Florovsky's Monograph "Herzen's Philosophy of History": The New Archival Material and the Reconstruction of the Full Text', Forthcoming *Harvard Theological Review*.

Gavrilyuk, Paul L., 'Harnack's Hellenized Christianity or Florovsky's "Sacred Hellenism": Questioning Two Metanarratives of Early Christian Engagement with Late Antique Culture', *St Vladimir's Theological Quarterly [=SVTQ]*, 54(3–4) (2010), pp. 323–44.

Gavrilyuk, Paul L., 'O polemicheskom ispol'zovanii kategorii "zapad" v pravoslavnom bogoslovii na primere neopatristicheskogo sinteza prot. Georgiia Florovskogo' ['The "West" as a Polemical Category in Eastern Orthodox Theology: the Case of Fr. Georges Florovsky's Neopatristic Synthesis'], *Vestnik pravoslavnogo sviato-tikhonovskogo gumanitarnogo universiteta*, 29 (2010), pp. 61–78.

Gavrilyuk, Paul L. 'The Orthodox Renaissance', *First Things*, December 2012, pp. 33–7.

Gudziak, Boris, 'Towards an Analysis of the Neo-Patristic Synthesis of Georges Florovsky', *Logos: A Journal of Eastern Christian Studies*, 41–2 (2000–1), pp. 197–238.

Harnack, Adolf von, *History of Dogma*, 3rd Ed., 7 vols., trans. Neil Buchanan (London: Williams & Norgate, 1894–1899 [1886–90]).

Harnack, Adolf von, *What is Christianity?*, 2nd edn, trans. Thomas Bailey Saunders (London and Oxford: Williams and Norgate; New York: G.P. Putnam's Sons, 1901).

Khomiakov, Aleksei, 'The Church is One', *On Spiritual Unity: A Slavophile Reader*, trans. and edited by Boris Jakim and Robert Bird (Hudson: Lindisfarne Books, 1998), pp. 31–53.

Kireevsky, Ivan, 'Fragments' [early 1850s], in *On Spiritual Unity: A Slavophile Reader*, trans. and edited by Boris Jakim and Robert Bird (Hudson: Lindisfarne Books, 1998), pp. 276–91.

Klimoff, Alexis, 'Georges Florovsky and the Sophiological Controversy', *SVTQ*, 49(1–2) (2005), pp. 67–100.

Künkel, Christoph, *Totus Christus: Die Theologie Georges V. Florovskys* (Göttingen: Vandenhoeck and Ruprecht, 1991).

Meyendorff, John, 'Predislovie' in Georgii Florovskii, *Puti Russkogo Bogosloviia* (Vilnius: Vilnius Orthodox Diocesan Council, 1991), pp. i–vi.

Möhler, Johann Adam, *Symbolism: or, Exposition of the Doctrinal Differences between Catholics and Protestants as Evidenced by their Symbolical Writings*, 2 vols, 2nd edn, trans. James Burton Robinson (London: Charles Dolan, 1847).

Möhler, Johann Adam, *Unity in the Church or The Principle of Catholicism Presented in the Spirit of the Church Fathers of the First Three Centuries*, trans. Peter C. Erb (Washington, DC: Catholic University of America Press, [1825] 1996).

Nikolaev, Sergei V. 'Spiritual Unity: The Role of Religious Authority in the Disputes between Sergii Bulgakov and Georges Florovsky Concerning Intercommunion', *SVTQ*, 49(1–2) (2005), pp. 101–23.

Offord, Derek, 'Alexander Herzen' in *A History of Russian Philosophy 1830–1930: Faith, Reason, and the Defense of Human Dignity*, edited by G.M. Hamburg and Randall A. Poole (Cambridge: Cambridge University Press, 2010), pp. 52–68.

Payne, Daniel P., 'Barth and Florovsky on the Meaning of "Church"', *Sobornost*, 26(2) (2004), pp. 39–63.

'Report of the Conference held at High Leigh June 26–28, 1934 on "The Healing of the Schism"'. Found in Oxford Archive of The Fellowship of St Alban and St Sergius. Folder labelled 'The Fellowship Conference Policy Before 1940'.

Shaw, F. Lewis, 'The Philosophical Evolution of Georges Florovsky: Philosophical Psychology and the Philosophy of History', *SVTQ*, 36(3) (1992), pp. 237–55.

Tanev, Stoyan, 'Energeia vs. Sophia: The Contribution of Fr. Georges Florovsky to the Rediscovery of the Orthodox Teaching on the Distinction between the Divine Essence and Energies', *International Journal of Orthodox Theology*, 2(1) (2011), pp. 15–71.

Thomson, F.J., 'Peter Mogila's Ecclesiastical Reforms and the Ukrainian Contribution to Russian Culture: A Critique of Georges Florovsky's Theory of the Pseudomorphosis of Orthodoxy', *Slavica Gandensia*, 20 (1993), pp. 67–119.

Williams, George Hunston, 'Father Georges Florovsky's Vision of Ecumenism', *Greek Orthodox Theological Review*, 41(2–3) (1996), pp. 137–58 [the whole issue is devoted to Florovsky and his legacy].

Williams, Rowan, 'Obituary of Georges Florovsky', *Sobornost*, 2(1) (1980), pp. 70–71.

Chapter 29
Nicolas Afanasiev

Michael Plekon

Many have said that the twentieth century, the century of two world wars, the Holocaust, the Great Depression, the atom bomb, was also the century of the rediscovery of the church. Over against such massive events as these, such a rediscovery might seem small. Yet it would not be too much to say that the recovery of the sense that the church is the people of God, not the hierarchy, not the canons or other rules, not simply texts and structures, is a most significant reappraisal. And perhaps even more important was the work of Nicolas Afanasiev (1893–1966) in restoring the "eucharistic ecclesiology," that is, the understanding that the church makes the Eucharist but that the Eucharist also makes the church. Afanasiev's groundbreaking work in many ways opened up ecclesiology once more in the twentieth century, and while he has had his critics and while revived ecclesiological directions have diverged from his—those of Henri de Lubac, Georges Florovsky, his own younger colleague Alexander Schmemann, John Zizioulas, J.M.R. Tillard, Paul McPartlan—the vision he retrieved of the church in the early centuries remains precious and invaluable, not only for thinking about the liturgy and the ordained ministries but especially about the priesthood of all the baptized.

An "Ecclesial Soul": A Life

Nicolas Nikolaievitch Afanasiev was a lawyer's son, born in Odessa in 1893, who first wanted to be a physician (his only child eventually became one), then a mathematician and finally a historian. Having fought in the White Army, he knew early on in life the horrors of war, death and displacement. Fleeing the Revolution he first settled in Belgrade where he did his degree with historian A.P. Dobroklonsky and was forever after influenced by his teacher's demanding sense of doing history. He also studied with Basil Zenkovsky, the philosopher, psychologist and later priest who would teach with him on the faculty of St Sergius Institute. His closest friend in Belgrade was another future colleague, Fr Cyprian Kern, and he was part of the Brotherhood of St Seraphim with him and the future Bishop Cassian (Bezobrazov), also to be a professor and dean at St Sergius. The very first dean, the great theologian Fr Sergius Bulgakov, invited Afanasiev to teach canon law in Paris. Afanasiev would soon distinguish himself by his pioneering work on the historical contexts and forces shaping the councils and their canons. Like his later protégé, Alexander Schmemann, it was Bulgakov who had an enormous impact on his theology.

While by no means invested in the pursuit of Divine Wisdom as was his dean, not a "sophiological" thinker, Afanasiev became an unusual blend of rigorous historian and eschatological theologian. Bulgakov's single-handed eucharistic revival stamped Afanasiev as it did many others in the Russian émigré community. Not only was Fr. Bulgakov singular in chanting aloud the prayers formerly said *mystice*, quietly, he also set the Eucharist again at the center of liturgical and church life, recognizing all the dimensions liturgical specialists would later rediscover—the cosmic, the communal, the ecclesial.

From 1930 until 1940 Afanasiev taught as a lay theologian at St Sergius. He was one of the faculty who defended Fr Bulgakov when accused of questionable theological writing by Vladimir Lossky and Patriarch Sergius of Moscow. He contributed a now classic article on whether the canons are changeable or not to the 1937 manifesto of progressive Orthodoxy, the anthology *Zhivoe predanie* [*Living Tradition*] and was a member of the Brotherhood of St Sophia gathered around Fr Bulgakov. He was ordained a priest on January 8, 1940 by Metropolitan Evlogy, that remarkable bishop whose dedication to freedom allowed intellectual life to flourish at St Sergius and through the "Russian Paris." During the war he served the Orthodox parish in Tunisia only returning to St Sergius in 1947. Despite the lack of a research library, he continued to plan what would be his major works—the study of the early church's structure and spirit, its "eucharistic ecclesiology." This would become *Tserkov Dukha Sviatogo* [*The Church of the Holy Spirit*], defended as his doctoral dissertation at St Sergius in 1948, many of the chapters published as journal articles and only brought together and published posthumously in 1971. The companion volume, though not published as a book, *Granitsy Tserkvi* [*The Limits of the Church*], studies in the ecclesiologies of St Paul, Ignatius of Antioch, Cyprian and other of the fathers would likewise emerge in his classes as well as in theological journals as essays. His wife, Marianne, described his dedication to pastoral ministry in Tunisia, a love for his community that knew no religious or ethnic boundaries. Both Marianne Afanasiev and Dominican scholar Aidan Nichols document the wide range of courses Afanasiev took responsibility for at St Sergius, from liturgy and the sacraments, including marriage and holy orders, to church history and New Testament along with the history of the councils and canons.

It is remarkable that Afanasiev published as much as he did because in addition to his teaching he was also the treasurer of St Sergius and the consultant to the hierarch and diocesan council with respect to the canons. As if all these obligations were not enough, Afanasiev was prominent in the last years of his life in the intense ecumenical activities surrounding the Second Vatican Council. He was an official Orthodox observer at the Council and his mark is to be found in the dogmatic constitution on the Church, *Lumen gentium*, which recognizes a eucharistic ecclesiology. Aidan Nichols cites Afanasiev as the only Orthodox theologian whose name and worked were referenced in the Synodal Acts of the Council.

Afanasiev's 1950 essay on the need for renewal of the divine liturgy, *Trapeza Gospodnia* [*The Lord's Supper*] became both the inspiration and model for Alexander Schmemann's work in liturgical theology, the debt acknowledged in footnotes as well as in the latter's obituary essay on the former. Afanasiev was present at the laying down of the condemnations of the eleventh-century schism by Pope Paul VI and Ecumenical Patriarch Athenagoras I. He would dedicate one of the last of his essays, "Una sancta," on the history, character and healing of the great schism to the "pope of Love," John XXIII. In failing health during the last decade of his life, Fr Afanasiev died on December 4, 1966 after a brief hospitalization.

"The Church Makes the Eucharist, the Eucharist Makes the Church": Rediscovering Ecclesiology

"The Church of God is in Christ" since the people of God are gathered by God "in Christ", and thus it belongs to God as Christ belongs to him. From this follows the identity of the Church with the Eucharist and the identity of the local Church with the Church of God, which is actualized each time during her Eucharistic assembly. On the strength of this double identity, the members of a local church, gathered at the Eucharistic assembly, are revealed as the Church of God. Members of the local church become members of the body of Christ and all that are gathered together for the Eucharistic assembly are "The Church of God in Christ". Thus to gather together for the Eucharistic assembly means to gather "in the Church". "When you assemble in the Church ...". Christ is present in the Eucharist in the fullness of his body, one loaf and one cup, but his body is the Church. The Church is where the Eucharist is celebrated, and where the Eucharist is celebrated, there is the Church. This is the fundamental principle of the Eucharistic ecclesiology revealed by Paul.[1]

Afanasiev's theological significance can be summarized in the now very familiar ecclesiological principle: "*The Church makes the Eucharist, the Eucharist makes the Church.*" John Zizioulas has become the principle voice in ecclesiology in the last decades but without Afanasiev's journey "back to the sources" of church life, the flourishing of ecclesiology would not have happened. We now take the centrality of the Eucharist for granted, the rooting of all ecclesial offices in the liturgy as a given. We cannot see the church except as eucharistic nor the Eucharist as anything but ecclesial, even defining of the church. See for example *The Catechism of The Catholic Church*, paragraphs 1118, 1166–7, 1343, 1396, 1407, 2177.[2] The church was ordinarily defined

---

[1] Nicolas Afanasiev, *The Lord's Supper*, in *The Limits of the Church*, trans. Vitaly Permiakov and Alvian Smirensky, edited by Michael Plekon (forthcoming).

[2] *The Catechism of the Catholic Church* (New York, 1995).

by the canons and the hierarchy, that is by the formal ecclesiastical organization, as primarily an historical and social institution.

Afanasiev sought the structure elsewhere, in the communion that created community. The clerical stratification system was to come later, but in the first five centuries every bishop, presbyter, deacon, prophet, evangelist, teacher or other role in the church was charismatic, inspired by the Spirit. The assembly took from its own those who were blessed with the gifts to lead, teach, organize. It was not a question of who was in charge, who could do or not do this action, of power granted by the laying on of hands but of responsibility, service, all summed up in the "rule of love," not of law or of status. Every Christian however was a priest by baptism as well as a prophet and king/queen of the kingdom of heaven. Thus every believer had a place. The liturgy was celebrated or concelebrated by all—hence all the prayers in the plural. While today some traditionalists might reject Afanasiev as an "innovator" in his vision of the church and ideas for liturgical reform, he was anything but that. Reform was restoration of tradition and since that tradition was living, it was authentic renewal.

Much was accomplished at Vatican II in renewing the liturgy, in returning to the sources in ecclesiology, with respect to the mission of the church and its relationship to the world, in the place of the ordained and those in religious life in the church and, last but not least, in the reappropriation of the most biblical ecclesiological definition of all, namely of the church as the people of God. Afanasiev was in good company in his efforts both in ecclesiological and liturgical renewal. Both before World War II and during it, strong relationships were forged among an ecumenical company of theologians—Romans Catholic such as Jean Daniélou, Yves Congar, I.-H. Dalmais, M.D. Chenu, Henri de Lubac, Bernard Botte, the Reformed Oscar Cullmann, Anglicans Gregory Dix and Michael Ramsay and Walter Frere, among others. Contacts through the philanthropic work of the American YMCA, the ecumenical activities of the fledgling World Council of Churches, through meetings of the Fellowship of St Alban and St Sergius and through cooperation in the Resistance enabled Christians to encounter other Christians beyond their ecclesial boundaries. Academic work also supported this. A look at photographs of participants in the annual St Sergius Liturgical Weeks confirms this ecumenical interaction. The weeks were started by Afanasiev and Kern in 1952. More recently Afanasiev's name is cited by Paul Evdokimov, Frs Schmemann, Boris Bobrinskoy, John Meyendorff and Bishop Hilarion Alfayev who were St Sergius graduates, also by Aidan Kavanagh, J.M.R. Tillard, Robert Taft and Bishop Kallistos Ware. Paul Bradshaw's work also confirms the eucharistic shape of ecclesiology and even Afanasiev's critics indicate a debt to his pioneer work in returning to the ecclesiology of the ancient church. Relatively few critics outrightly dismiss Afanasiev's framework.

The Church of the Holy Spirit, the Church of Love

The Church of the Holy Spirit, Afanasiev's principal work, is a careful historical investigation of the early church's eucharistic ecclesiology. Afanasiev begins with the initiation rites of *baptism and chrismation*, namely the consecration of each member of the church as priest, prophet and king. In contradiction of later theological vision which separated the clergy from the laity on the basis of ordination, Afanasiev inspects the baptismal texts themselves as well as those of ordination and the Eucharist. These show that all the baptized are consecrated to priestly ministry. All the people of God celebrate the Eucharist. Afanasiev also scrutinizes not only the ordination texts but the testimonies of such fathers as Ignatius of Antioch and Irenaeus of Lyons in pursuit of the emergence of the office of bishop from that of first presbyter/presider. The Eucharist is concelebrated not just by the presider but by the entire assembly. Thus the calling and setting apart of the presiders must be for service not for greater status or power. Every Christian is consecrated in baptism and chrismation for service to God in the liturgy and in life. All are also consecrated service in the church and the world, the service depending on one's place (*topos*) or position in the assembly.

The presence and work of the Holy Spirit is foundational for the church. He cites Irenaeus of Lyon: "Where the Spirit is, there is the Church and all grace." As a careful historian and theologian, Afanasiev ruthlessly criticizes the neglect or subordination of the church's divine nature to empirical variables, yet he also faulted those who overspiritualize the church, forgetting the material and human dimensions. He saw these as Nestorian tendencies. The communal nature of the church is paramount for him. It is not just the sum of its members. The church has a social reality *sui generis*. Echoing Tertullian (from whom comes the phrase "the church of the Holy Spirit"), we recall: *Solus christanus, nullus christianus*—"You cannot be a Christian by yourself." In the church, no one ever spoke or acted alone but "always and everywhere together" with the others, the *epi to auto* of Acts that punctuates his writings. Fundamental to his vision is *the royal priesthood of all the baptized*.

The Holy Spirit's most precious gift, for Afanasiev, as one can read in the last chapter of *The Church of the Holy Spirit*, was the rule or "authority of love" (*vlast' lyubvi*). The Spirit's love governed the early church, not laws, clerical elites or political figures. Yet this charismatic sense of community did not last long. Afanasiev retells the fairly familiar church history of the rise of the rule of law and of a clerical caste. My colleague Alexis Vinogradov points out that for Afanasiev the elements (*panta*) of the church that were not formed by love, would really never be "of" the church nor integral to its life, even if they endured for centuries.

The most misinterpreted and thus controversial emphasis of Afanasiev is his insistence that *the local church is fully the church*. The local church, the immediate community that celebrates the Eucharist and from this extends itself in ministry to the world however is never isolated, but always in communion with the rest of the church that comprise the universal "Church of God in Christ." The only church known in the early centuries was the "local church" of this household or this city. While fully the church itself, Afanasiev insists that the local church is *only the church in communion with,* along with all the other churches. In formulaic terms, 1+1+1=1. The aggregation of many local churches does not constitute a church greater than any one of them. This said, it is impossible to fault Afanasiev for a reduction of the church to its smallest local expression. The contemporary "parish" is in a sense the "local church" for its members but even they realize there is much more church beyond their assembly. One cannot in a "congregationalist" manner pit the "local church" against say the deanery, diocese, national church or the church catholic and ecumenical (*oikumene*). There is a most profound ecumenical sensitivity here, allied to Bulgakov's conviction that God has retained elements of unity despite the division among the churches.

Afanasiev's Legacy Today

One must locate the eucharistic ecclesiology of *The Church of the Holy Spirit* within the scholarly context of its time, admitting that research has progressed, that other studies would have to be consulted and perhaps even some perspectives modified. Perhaps Afanasiev's understanding of Cyprian's "universal ecclesiology" is skewed, taking what Cyprian judged to be a description of the local church in Carthage for the church worldwide. Some of the criticism of Afanasiev may come from more than misinterpretation or his own misreadings. There may be some ecclesial uneasiness, interpreting his critique of the emergence of a clerical caste as simply anti-clericalism. It may also be that the decentralized, localized ecclesiology Afanasiev sketches, one still evident in the Eastern churches, is still confusing if not problematic to some Western Christians, particularly Roman Catholics. Afanasiev was critical of the reforming Moscow Council of 1917–18's use of the representation of the lower clergy and laity by delegates. He also objected to the delegates' roles in council deliberations as a distortion of roles and places in the church. He appears to put down very rigid and definitive lines around the particular ministries of bishops, clergy and laity, lines that have been blurred virtually on a regular basis through church history. With Fr John Meyendorff we might argue that despite the model of the early church, the empirical church in the early twentieth century in Russia desperately required participation by all of the assembly, after years of clerical domination. Other would maintain that the conciliar character of the early church simply was more inclusive than Afanasiev admits.

Yet despite these and other criticisms, Afanasiev's ecclesiological study is still significant and perhaps even more relevant than when he was writing a half century ago. The appearance of *The Church of the Holy Spirit* in translation will allow both further analysis and criticism as well as assimilation of its conclusions. There is for example at present among the Orthodox (members of the episcopate in particular) significant ecclesiastical opposition to the essential conciliar or sobornal nature of the church's liturgy and structure. But when faced with the empirical history of the church, it is hard to imagine scholarly refutation of its conciliar nature, East or West. Thus while the restorations and reforms of the Moscow Council of 1917–18 were implemented in only a few local churches, it is still difficult to dismiss the Council's appeals to the liturgy, the scriptures, patristic writings and the structure and actions of many earlier general and local councils.

It is also difficult to reject the communal, charismatic and eucharistic shape of the church that Afanasiev presents. So many other sources support it such as the Pauline letters, the gospels, the writings of Ignatius of Antioch as well as Cyprian of Carthage whom he views as a proponent of a "universal ecclesiology." One can also find this vision of the church in John Chrysostom, Augustine, the Didaché, Justin Martyr and later Augustine, Basil the Great, the Gregories of Nazianzus and Nyssa. Perhaps the most creditable and convincing sources are the ancient and present texts of the eucharistic liturgy themselves.

Afanasiev's recovery of the eucharistic ecclesiology of the early church in *The Church of the Holy Spirit* is still relevant for us today, almost over a half century after he completed the first draft of it. Similarly, the drift away from the communal and communing celebration of the Eucharist to the intensely personal piety of the first half of the twentieth century that Afanasiev sketched out in *The Lord's Supper* was and remains most instructive. In both the Eastern and Western churches there are the challenges of external indifference as well as internal ones of extremism and despair. Afanasiev's vision of the church as eucharistic community is the constructive model, an image that can still be imitated. His criticism of ecclesiastical legalism and of clerical authoritarianism remains powerful. His is a voice seldom heard in Protestant, Catholic or Orthodox theological scholarship and debate. His vision is rooted in the bread and cup on the holy table and in the Spirit-filled community gathered round it in love. His colleague and protégé Alexander Schmemann took his lead from the ecclesiological vision of *The Church of the Holy Spirit* and a sense and urgency for liturgical renewal from *The Lord's Supper*. Many graduates of St Vladimir's Seminary who were Fr Schmemann's students put into practice the return to frequent communion and communal celebration of the liturgy they learned from him as well as from his teacher, Fr Nicolas Afanasiev.

Afanasiev concluded *The Church of the Holy Spirit*'s introduction as his colleague and teacher Sergius Bulgakov ended many of his books—with the church's eschatological cry heard in the last book of the New Testament, the name of the One who was to come and always is coming: "the name of the Lord Jesus Christ." Fr Afanasiev's voice deserves to be heard, his vision of the church read and considered.

Bibliography

Primary Literature

"Canons and Canonical Consciousness," www.orthodoxresearchinstitute.org/articles/canon_law/afanasiev_canonical_consciousness.htm (accessed January 14, 2011).
The Catechism of the Catholic Church (New York, 1995).
"The Church Which Presides in Love," in *The Primacy of Peter*, edited by John Meyendorff (Crestwood: St. Vladimir's Seminary Press, 1992), pp. 91–144.

The Limits of the Church, including *The Lord's Supper*, trans. Vitaly Permiakov and Alvian Smirensky, edited by Michael Plekon (forthcoming).

Tserkvo Dukha Sviatogo (Paris: YMCA Press, 1971) (*The Church of the Holy Spirit*), trans. Vitaly Permiakov, edited by Michael Plekon (Notre Dame: University of Notre Dame Press, 2007).

"Una sancta," *Irenikon*, 36 (1963), pp. 436–75 and "The Eucharist: The Principal Link between the Catholics and the Orthodox," *Irenikon*, 3 (1965), pp. 337–39, "The Church's Canons: Changeable or Unchangeable," *Zhivoe predanie* (Paris: YMCA Press, 1937), pp. 82–96, 31–44 in *Tradition Alive: On the Church and the Christian Life in Our Time-Readings from the Eastern Church*, edited by Michael Plekon (Lanham: Sheed & Ward/Rowman & Littlefield, 2003), pp. 3–30, 47–9. Website: www.golubinski.ru/academia/afanasieffnew.htm (mostly in Russian) (accessed January 14, 2011).

Secondary Literature

Alexandrov, Victor, "Nicholas Afansiev's Ecclesiology and Some of its Orthodox Critics," *Sobornost*, 31(2) (2009), pp. 45–69.

Barbu, Stefanita, "Charism, Law and Spirit in Eucharistic Theology: New Perspectives on Nikolai Afanasiev's Sources," *Sobornost*, 31(2) (2009), pp. 19–43.

Kolumzine, Nicolas, "L'ecclésiologie eucharistique du Père Nicolas Afanasieff," in *La liturgie, son sens, son esprit, sa méthode*, Conférences Saint-Serge XXVIIIe Semaine d'études liturgiques (Rome: Edizioni liturgiche, 1982), pp. 113–27 and "Le rôles liturgiques dans l'assemblée de l'Eglise primative selon le Père Nicolas Afanasieff," in *L'assemblée liturgique et les différents rôles dans l'assemblée*, Conférences Saint-Serge, XXIIIème semaine d'études liturgiques (Rome: Edizioni liturgiche, 1977), pp. 209–24.

Nichols, Aidan, *Theology in the Russian Diaspora: Church, Eucharist, Fathers in Nikolai Afanas'ev 1893–1966* (Cambridge: Cambridge University Press, 1989).

Plekon, Michael, "Bishops as Servants of the Church," *Sobornost*, 31(2) (2009), pp. 70–82.

Plekon, Michael, *Living Icons: Persons of Faith in the Eastern Church* (Notre Dame: University of Notre Dame Press, 2002).

Wooden, Anastacia, "Eucharistic Ecclesiology of Nicholas Afanasiev and its Ecumenical Significance: A New Perspective," *Journal of Ecumenical Studies*, 45(4) (2010), pp. 543–60.

Chapter 30
Vladimir Lossky

Matti Kotiranta

The group of émigré theologians of the period following the Russian revolution that came to be known as the neo-Palamist school made a significant conquest in their discovery of an 'existentialistic emphasis' in the writings of St Gregory Palamas (1296–1359), 'the Thomas of the East'. One of the principal architects of this school may be said to have been Vladimir Lossky (1903–58), who was undoubtedly one of the most significant Orthodox theologians of the twentieth century. He became known above all as a major interpreter of Palamas' theology and a representative of the Eastern personalist doctrines.

Although the distinction between *ousia* and *energeia* gained its final form in connection with the Hesychast Controversy in the fourteenth century, Lossky and the other neo-Palamists claimed that it had incorporated from the outset an 'existentialistic emphasis' according to which God is not solely *ousia*, an essence as such, but also *energeia*, a personal being, capable of expressing Himself dynamically in free personal acts.

The neo-Palamist claim that we can speak of God only by virtue of His actions, or 'effects', aroused considerable cross-denominational debate in the field of Orthodox theology. Some scholars were able to detect a trace of the modern concept of *person* in this, and the distinction between the unknowable essence of God and His known 'effects', which resembles certain themes put forward by the Ritschl school, has become a real stumbling block for Palamist theology. Scarcely any other subject in Orthodox theology – apart from the *filioque* question – has attracted so much attention in recent centuries as this neo-Palamist insistence that the original Palamist view contained an 'existentialistic emphasis', in spite of the fact that problems have arisen at the ecumenical level over what precisely is meant by this emphasis.

Lossky's personalist thinking may be regarded as summing up the whole of the neo-Palamist doctrine that has coloured Orthodox theology for almost the last 60 years, and his influence is clearly to be seen in the ideas of some of the best-known Orthodox theologians of the period: *Georges Florovsky, Dumitru Staniloae, Olivier Clément, Christos Yannaras* and most especially *John Meyendorff*.[1]

---

[1] See Meyendorff, *St. Gregoire Palamas et la Mystique orthodoxe* (1959a), p. 290 also Meyendorff (1959b), p. 131.

Vita

Vladimir Nikolaievich Lossky was born at Göttingen on 26 May 1903 and died in Paris on 7 February 1958. His father, Nikolai Onufrievich Lossky, and his mother, Ludmila Vlamirovna, belonged to the liberal, aristocratic wing of the Russian intelligentsia, and it was in this academic atmosphere of the arts and learning that Vladimir grew up in St Petersburg. His father was in fact one of the major Russian philosophers of the early years of the twentieth century, an intuitivist with a personalist slant that undoubtedly helped to shape Vladimir's theological thinking.

Vladimir Lossky did not follow in his father's footsteps in his philosophical views, however, and he later publicly distanced himself from the metaphysics of Nikolai Lossky, i.e. the personalist philosophy that stemmed from the monadology of *Leibniz*. In his youth his main interest was in history, which he studied at the University of Petrograd in 1919–22. Of his teachers during these formative years, particular mention should be made of *Lev Karsavin*, a specialist in medieval history under whose supervision his interests turned to the religious and social history of Western Europe. It was the combination of Karsavin's guidance and the pro-Western atmosphere that prevailed in academic circles in St Petersburg – by contrast with the strictly Slavophil spirit that reigned in the University of Moscow – that ensured that the Western Europe of the Middle Ages, including figures such as *St Bernard of Clairvaux* and *St Francis of Assisi*, together with the theology of the Roman Catholic Church, remained lifelong objects of interest for him.

Vladimir Lossky's studies at the University of Petrograd came to an end when his family was forced to leave Russia in November 1923, in the second wave of exile following the revolution. They had previously refused to leave in 1922, when Lenin allowed those non-Marxist intellectuals who had not been involved in the civil war to flee the country. This first wave of exile had included *Fr Sergius Bulgakov* and *Nikolai Berdyayev*, for instance.

The family first took refuge in Prague in 1923, from where Vladimir went on to Paris a year later, to begun studying at the Sorbonne under the historian *Ferdinand Lot* and also *Etienne Gilson*, who introduced him to medieval philosophy. It was through Gilson's lectures that his attention turned to *Meister Eckhart*, his first object of theological interest. Eckhart's consistent emphasis on God's incomprehensibility led him in turn to the apophatic theology of the Alexandrians, the Cappadocian Fathers and above all the *Corpus Areopagiticum*. His earliest publications, in 1929 and 1930, concerned the negative theology of *St Dionysius the Areopagite*, and it was in these that he introduced his view of the theology of *St Gregory Palamas* as a synthesis of the whole preceding Orthodox tradition.

In 1928 Lossky, together with his close friend *Evgraph Kovalevsky* and a number of other young Russian émigrés, founded the 'Brotherhood of Saint Photius', an informal organisation devoted to defending the universality of Orthodox Christianity against local emphases, e.g. exclusive identification with either the Greek or the Russian tradition. The paradoxical element in all this was that it was precisely Lossky's independence of all Slavophil tendencies that bound him more closely than ever to the Patriarchate of Moscow. The majority of the emigrants exiled in 1922 and 1923 were of the opinion that the Patriarchate of Moscow under *Metropolitan Sergei* (*Stragorodsky*) was going too far in its loyalty to the new Soviet administration and the policy of oppression that it had pursued in relation to the church. It was this atmosphere of mistrust that prevailed between Metropolitan Sergei and the majority of the emigrants that eventually led in 1930 to Sergei's refusal to recognise the Patriarchate's French exarch *Metropolitan Evlogi*, upon which the Exarch, together with the majority of the émigrés and the leaders of the Institute of St Sergius, including Berdyayev and also Bulgakov, who was its principal at the time, applied to be taken under the jurisdiction of the Ecumenical Patriarchate. Only a small minority, represented by the Brotherhood of St Photius, to which Lossky belonged, retained their ties with the Patriarchate of Moscow and its head, Metropolitan Sergei.

Unlike many other emigré theologians, Lossky remained faithful to the French Exarchate of the Patriarchate of Moscow throughout his life. The schism between those who retained their loyalty to the Patriarchate and those who followed Metropolitan Evlogi culminated in the sophiological controversy of 1935 and 1936, as a consequence of which Lossky published his *Debate on Sophia* (Russ. *Spor o Sofii*), at the request of Metropolitan Sergei and in the name of the Brotherhood of St Photius. This was his first literary work that was specifically directed against Bulgakov's main Christological publication *The Lamb of God* (1933),[2] in which the latter presented his highly controversial doctrine of *Sophia*, the Divine Wisdom, that was subsequently condemned as a heresy by the Holy Synod of the Russian Church, largely on the basis of Lossky's assessment.

Lossky's Written Works as Manifestations of His Principal Theological Ideas

In *Spor o Sofii* (*The Debate on Sophia*), published in 1936, Lossky discussed, as mentioned above, the sophiology, or doctrine of the Divine Wisdom, put forward by Sergei Bulgakov in his book *Agnets Bozhi* (*The Lamb of God*), which had aroused such a controversy at that time. His primary criticism was that Bulgakov assumed in his thinking that one could come to know God's essence, his divine nature, through

---

[2] Unlike Lossky, Fr Georges Florovsky never publicly spoke out against Bulgakov's sophiology, although he did criticise it in his *Ways of Russian Theology* (Russ. *Puti Russkogo Bogosloviya*).

His Wisdom, or Word (*Sophia* = *Logos*). Lossky sets out in his work to dismiss all interpretations of the Trinity that lead to God's divine nature (*ousia*) being knowable through His Wisdom (*Sophia*). At the same time he attempts to show that the elements in this theory that are traceable to the influence of German idealism are alien to the original theology of the Holy Fathers as contained in the *Philokalia*.

Lossky's book also has a wider background, in that it is connected with the Neopatristic School that flourished in the late 1930s and early 1940s. This school's sharpest criticism at the early stage was directed at the Russian 'sophiologists', *Vladimir Solovyov, Fr Sergius Bulgakov* and *Fr Pavel Florensky*, whose metaphysical speculations had imbibed influences from the German idealism of *Kant, Hegel* and *Schelling*.

It is important to note that without sophiology as a catalyst the emergence of neopatristic thinking and Palamist theology would not have been by any means as pronounced a development as it in fact was. The sophiological controversy confirmed the apophatic approach in the theological thinking of both Lossky and the neo-Palamists who followed him, and in accordance with the mystical theology of St Gregory Palamas the possibility for conceptualisation of the essence of God was categorically denied. This also stimulated a new approach to defining the Orthodox doctrine of the Trinity more precisely and in a manner which clearly excluded the sophiological interpretation.

Essai sur la Théologie Mystique de l'Église d'Orient (*The Mystical Theology of the Eastern Church*), dating from 1941–2, is regarded by many as Vladimir Lossky's principal work. It is in a sense a 'neopatristic synthesis', as Georges Florovsky points out, and it serves to underline in the best possible way its author's belief that all theology is mystical by nature and that without mystique there can be no theology. The second outstanding characteristic of the book is that it emphasises the apophatic, or negative, path to a knowledge of God, in connection with which it presents an extensive analysis of the patristic doctrine of deification and the *ousia–energeia* distinction that lies at the centre of the Palamist theology.

This distinction that exists in the theology of the Eastern church has been illustrated by saying that cataphatic theology puts forward affirmations regarding the essence of God (*ousia*), such as 'God is love, goodness, life, etc.', even though these do not actually reveal the true inner nature of the divinity, whereas apophatic theology is based on the fact that the essence of God is hidden from us and is thus in the Orthodox understanding the only correct way of approaching the question. Furthermore, as Lossky explains, apophatic theology distinguishes two interpretative traditions, one of which attributes the hidden nature of God to the finite capacity of human reasoning and conceptualisation, while the other, which may be regarded as typical of Eastern Orthodox theology – and especially of that associated with the name of Gregory Palamas – maintains that this hidden nature is an inherent property of God Himself.

In summary, it may be said that Lossky's *Mystical Theology of the Eastern Church* contains the apophatic Greek patristic doctrine of the Trinity, especially that preached by the Cappadocian Fathers, in a nutshell, maintaining that the relations between the persons of the Trinity (*hypostasis*) and their essence (*ousia*) cannot be analysed because they cannot be separated conceptually. It is for this reason that the Greek patristic model of the Trinity examines the unity of the divine essence (*ousia*) 'metaontologically' via the hypostases of the Trinity. The persons are conceived of as engaged eternally and inseparably in motion and interaction, forming a single, triune God. These persons of the Trinity exist only in their relations to one another. This Greek model of the Trinity which arose out of the Cappadocian equivalent was later summed up, in Lossky's view, in the concept of eternal *perichoresis* as put forward by St John of Damascus (d. 749) in his *De Fide Orthodoxa*, which brings forth the essence of the persons of the Trinity in terms of a structure: the Father exists in the Son, the Son exists in the Father and both exist in the Spirit, just as the Spirit exists in both the Father and the Son.

À l'Image et à la Resemblance de Dieu (*In the Image and Likeness of God*) is a collection of 12 essays written in 1947–57. The title is especially apt as it expresses one outstanding feature of Lossky's doctrine of images: man is not to be understood in the Platonic sense as the image of God, but rather as created *in* the image of God. This image is a man or woman, a person with a body and soul. The majority of the book is concerned with the nature of God, His person and His divine providence. The only chapter, in fact, that fits the title of the book is the seventh, 'The Theology of Images'. In many respects this book repeats the same ideas as were raised in the *Mystical Theology of the Eastern Church*, but it deals with them in more detail.

Théologie dogmatique represents a series of lectures on this topic given by Lossky for the Paris Exarchate of the Russian Orthodox Church and was published posthumously as a set of separate papers in the journal *Messager de l'Exarchat du Patriarche russe en Europe occidental* in 1964 and later in book form, including an English edition under the title *Orthodox Theology* in 1978. It consists of a brief basic course in dogmatic theology, and as such does not differ greatly from his *Mystical Theology*, except that the treatment of the topics is more systematic. The book proceeds in accordance with the history of the Salvation of Mankind and deals, in this order, with doctrines concerned with God, the Creation, Original Sin, Recapitulation in Christ and final Deification. Thus it is deification, participation in the triune life of God, that becomes the focal point of the whole account.

Vision de Dieu (*The Vision of God*), published in 1962, is a historical survey of the tradition of 'seeing God' which is so powerfully present in Lossky's theology and which he refers to as the 'Palamist synthesis', the roots of which the author is not afraid to trace back from St Gregory Palamas as far as St John the Evangelist and St Paul the Apostle. Lossky regards this 'seeing God' as the most perfect state of communion with the personal life of God, as becomes evident when he likens seeing God in this life (*in via*) to seeing God in eternity. The former, as an ecstatic experience of the light of God (= *energeia*), means for him participation in the life of the Trinity in this world, so that in his way of thinking the divine light and its synonyms '*energeia*', 'grace' and 'will' become a particular principle and capability that guides the realisation of the human personality, which in turn is a question of achieving eternal light, or participation in the triune God.

Special mention among Lossky's posthumously published works should be made of his doctoral thesis *Théologie négative et connaissance de Dieu chez Maître Eckhart* (*Negative Theology and Knowledge of God in Meister Eckhart*, 1960), an analysis of Eckhart's theology that he had been working on for virtually the whole of his life and which was published only after his death. In it Lossky criticises Eckhart for the impersonal nature of his apophatic theology, and above all for the fact that his theocentric speculation leads to an apophaticism in which the impersonal nothingness of the divine being takes precedence over the Trinity, placing the essence of God before His person. Lossky describes Eckhart's thinking as a synthesis of Aristotelian-Scholastic and neo-Platonic elements.

Lossky's Personalistic Mode of Thought as the Foundation of His Neo-Palamite Synthesis[3]

Lossky's personalistic mode of thought stands on the foundation of his own postulate concerning the theology of St Gregory Palamas (1296–1359). He considers that Palamas' thought itself already subsumes an 'existentialistic emphasis' that is linked in its point of departure to both the *ousia–energeia* distinction and the concepts of God's transcendence (*ousia*) and participation (*energeia*) included in it. Thus God is not solely *ousia*, an essence as such, but also *energeia*, a personal being capable of expressing Himself dynamically in free personal acts. Certain researchers have detected in these statements of Lossky a trace of the concept of person which is central to existentialist thinking. This interpretation has been strengthened by its resemblance to certain themes presented by post-Kantian theologians, i.e. the distinction between the unknowable essence of God and His recognisable 'effects'. Problems have arisen both as to what is denominated as the 'existentialistic emphasis' and by the fact that it is referred to using this term.

For reasons derived both from the history of ideology and from ecumenics, the above assertion concerning the 'existentialistic emphasis' included in Palamas' theology put forward by Lossky and by the neo-Palamites following him such as Fr Georges Florovsky, Fr John Meyendorff and Fr Dumitru Staniloae has risen to the forefront of interest among researchers. Certain researchers salute this 'existentialistic emphasis', which is held to be quite rare in the area of Orthodox theology, but they are suspicious as to its origins. Both Roman Catholic and Protestant research concerned with Palamas directs attention to the existentialistic features of neo-Palamite thinking, while concurrently asking whether this is of genuine Palamite origin. This line of research is represented, among others, by Dorothea Wendebourg, a Lutheran theologian, who deems neo-Palamite theology to be ecumenically fruitful as such due to the 'modern' features involved in it. Nevertheless, she calls its Palamite origin into

---

[3] The findings detailed in this section are based on the author's doctoral thesis *Person as Perichoresis: Vladimir Lossky's Trinitarian Mode of Thought in Relation to the Palamite Heritage and the Russian Philosophy of Religion*.

question.[4] She maintains that the *ousia–energeia* distinction that is essential to Palamite theology does not include the concept of a personal God, as Palamas understands *ousia* as a metaphysical principle of being from which the *energeia* can be inferred.[5] Rowan D. Williams, an Anglican researcher and the present Primate of All England, also understands Palamite theology as being founded on a materialistic-physical ontology, which in his view excludes emphasis on the personal characteristics of existentialist thought.[6] Fr Bernhard Schultze, a Roman Catholic researcher, in turn defines real participation as lying in the realm of the mental, detaching it from physical participation, which in his view is what is represented in Palamas.[7]

In the light of the starting points mentioned above, both Roman Catholic (Schultze) and Protestant (Wendebourg) research has reached the conclusion that the fourteenth-century theology of St Gregory Palamas cannot include a 'genuine' concept of person. The only option left open to these researchers for explaining the existentialistic features in neo-Palamite theology is therefore the notion that the neo-Palamites acquired this decisive impact on their thinking from modern existentialism. For that reason, it would appear that the existentialistic emphasis does not belong to the genuine Orthodox tradition, and that the neo-Palamites consequently do not represent authentic Orthodox theology in the context of ecumenical dialogue.

Research paradigms springing from modern existentialism have failed to yield a plausible analysis of the delineation of the relationship between the neo-Palamite concepts of person and nature. Similar difficulties arise in the interpretation of the *ousia–energeia* distinction which is so essential to Palamite theology, and in the ecumenically significant concept of participation. As a result, the explanations proffered alternate between emphasising either the option of 'nature' or that of 'person'. When the classical, i.e. Aristotelian, concept of nature is taken as the principle of interpretation, the neo-Palamite emphasis on person does not fit coherently. Furthermore, researchers who have adopted this classical approach have concluded that Palamas represents a 'static' ontological concept of *ousia*. In this perception, participation is primarily concerned with the linkage of the physico-materialistic to the energies emanating from the deity. Yet, modern existentialist viewpoints on the neo-Palamite concept of person fail to seriously consider the discussion of the divine nature, an area nonetheless taken for granted by the neo-Palamites themselves. It should also be noted that within modern existentialism, in which person as an epistemological principle precedes nature, person is defined simply in terms of the criticism of the classical concept of nature.

---

[4] Wendebourg, 'Gregorios Palamas', *Klassiker der Theologie*, 1 (1981), p. 268; see also p. 265.

[5] Wendebourg, 'From the Cappadocian Fathers to Gregory Palamas', *Studia Patristica*, 12 (1982), p. 196, and Wendebourg, 'Person und Hypostase: Zur Trinitätslehre in der neueren orthodoxen Theologie', in *Vernunft des Glaubens* (1988), p. 513.

[6] Williams, 'The Philosophical Structures of Palamism', *Easter Church Review*, 1–2 (1977), p. 41.

[7] Schultze, 'Grundfragen des theologischen Palamismus', *Ostkirchliche Studien* (1975), pp. 109–10.

How should Vladimir Lossky's mode of thought be characterised in the light of the starting points mentioned above? Lossky's mode of thought can in some sense be designated as 'personalistic'. This holds good when consideration is afforded to the fact that his concept of person does not conform to that of modern existentialism. Lossky's personalistic mode of thought follows the solution of apophatic theology, where person and nature are not polarised as they were in the modern Continental thinking of the early twentieth century. The issue at hand is a trinitarian-personalistic mode of thought based on an apophatic approach in which the concept of the relation between person and nature in the polarisation of ontological vs. existentialist is on the whole not established. Nor does this concept yield to analysis in the manner of the recognised options for the concept of person, since the definition of the relation between nature and person in Lossky is not based on the modern concept of person any more than on the classical Western, i.e. Aristotelian, concept. The analysis of the relation between nature and person, whereby person is either differentiated from nature as a separate, autonomous principle or is considered to be the existence of nature, therefore leads the interpretation of Lossky's concept astray even from its very point of departure.

Lossky's concept of person and its relation to nature can best be understood on the basis of an apophatically conceived trinitarian theology and the understanding of the perichoresis of the Persons of the Trinity contained in that view. In their interpenetration, the Persons are mutually equivalent, sharing all the attributes which may be relegated to the unknown *ousia* of the Deity. It can therefore be stated that neither person nor essence (nature) alone enjoys the status of an ontological principle in the Trinity. This idea of Lossky's rests on the thought included in the concept of person in his neo-Palamism, i.e. that a person is not an independently subsistent being but is characterised by reciprocity and sharing. An aseitic substance cannot be person. The Persons were begotten in the Trinity simultaneously, so that the hypostases are both eternally independent and indivisibly divided.

According to Lossky it is inconceivable that the unknown *ousia* could precede the Persons of the Trinity as their basis or principle and remain unknown as such. In his application of the Palamite argument that God is unknown in His *ousia* but recognised in His *energeia*, Lossky takes as his self-evident point of departure the concept involved in the perichoresis of person that the *ousia* cannot be detached from the unity of persons into a separate nature. God, anonymous in His *ousia*, is the mystery of the entire inner Trinity, while in the economic Trinity, God is manifest in His energies, or activities.

According to Lossky's exegesis of Palamas, the Palamite concept of the transcendence of the *ousia* originates in the salvatory economy of the Trinity and from the experiential knowledge of such. From the experiential apperception, it can be explained that Palamas, as he proceeds forward from the salvatory economy, is not interested in speculation on the Trinity, but rather he expresses the activities of God's salvatory economy 'in the gifts of the energies, i.e. creation, incarnation and theosis'. The purpose of the *ousia–energeia* distinction is not, however, to deny the presence of the Triune God in the energies, but its primary focal point is avoidance of the Pantheistic concept that theosis makes man *in unio* into a god by nature. When Palamism addresses the essence of God and the energies separately, this is a means of stating simultaneously – thus avoiding the Pantheistic idea of fusion – that the Triune God as an entity (in His *ousia*) is inaccessible to man's realm of knowledge but that God in His energies (or *energeia*) has made Himself experientially reachable.

Furthermore, as stated in Lossky's exegesis of Palamas, the experiential justification of the Trinity is also the point of departure for the fact that St Gregory Palamas' theology distinguishes between two meanings of *ousia*, i.e. in which the relation of essence, *ousia*, to *energeia* (singular), or to the energies (plural), is discussed in two separate modes. First, the distinction between *ousia* and *energeia* is a distinction existent in God as an entity (the 'immanent Trinity'),[8] whereby essence, *ousia*, denotes all of God, the true essence of the Trinity, inaccessible and transcendental. Thus, the true essence of the Trinity, the unity of the *ousia*, is based on the unity of the *energeia*, and the singular use of the *energeia* functions as a basis for the consubstantiality of the Trinity. The origin of the *energeia*, like that of the *ousia*, is the hypostasis of the Father, in whose activity both the Son and the Holy Spirit identify themselves.[9] In this sense of *ousia* there is no particular need to emphasise persons, as the unknowable *ousia* means God as an entity, the Trinity, not God's nature '*an sich*' as presented in the interpretations of Palamas arising from the background of Western theology.

Second, the distinction between *ousia* and *energeia* explains the relation of God to the world, where the energies appear as the temporal acts of God's essence, i.e. *ousia*.[10] In this sense the Trinity is unknown in its essence, but manifest in the temporal acts, or energies, of its hypostases. Consequently, *ousia* refers to the inner structure of the Trinity ('God in Himself', the 'immanent Trinity'), whereas *energeia* refers to the outer structure ('God for us', the 'economic Trinity'). In this sense of *ousia*, the Trinity creates the world and is accessible, or as Lossky put it, will 'come to abide in man' in the economic action of the Trinity, the energies.[11] This act by the hypostases follows the order of the trinitarian salvation history, i.e. from the Father through the Son in the Spirit.

The essential prerequisite for the above two meanings of *ousia* is the concept of triadic unity, where the persons on the one hand sustain nature, and on the other hand *energeia*, or the energies. From the viewpoint of the concept of triadic unity, the distinction between *ousia* and *energeia* in God (i.e. the Trinity) does not sever the divine unity as erroneously presumed in the critique of the neo-Palamite image of God. The trinitarian model of the triadic unity, the tri-personality, as expressed in Greek patristics, is in Lossky based specifically on the Greek pre-understanding of *hypostasis*, which is not to be translated with the Latin word *persona*. The Greek word signifies a similarity of essence, not a unity of essence. This is seen especially

---

[8] Lossky, *Essay sur la thélogie mysticue* (1944), pp. 62–3 (*The Mystical Theology* (1976), pp. 63–4). See also Palamas, *Triads* III, i, 8; *Triads* III, i, 29.
[9] Lossky, *Essay sur la thélogie mysticue*, pp. 79–80 (*The Mystical Theology*, p. 82).
[10] Lossky, *Essay sur la thélogie mysticue*, p. 83 (*The Mystical Theology*, p. 86).
[11] Lossky, *Essay sur la thélogie mysticue*, p. 83 (*The Mystical Theology*, p. 86).

in the fact that in the neo-Palamite concept of person the Aristotelian distinction of *substantia prima* (i.e. *hypostasis*) vs. *substantia secunda* (i.e. *ousia*) is applied to the trinitarian *ousia–energeia* distinction in a manner which is an inversion of the Aristotelian view. When theologies based on Aristotelian philosophy consider that *the Godhead gives form to the persons*, then each person as *substantia prima* represents the Godhead as to what it is. By contrast, in neo-Palamite thinking, the *persons give form to the godhead*. Each person of the Godhead, i.e. the Father, the Son and the Holy Spirit, is *substantia secunda* to the essence which makes God what He is.[12] Western research into Palamas launches out from the former, i.e. the Latin, Aristotelian, meaning, and therefore leads from its very inception to a variant interpretation of Palamas' concept of the Trinity. Basing his thought on the meaning of the Greek concept of *hypostasis*, however, Palamas reaches his understanding from the idea of the similarity of essence. This means that *ousia* is no longer a 'static' concept in Palamas' thought, but a statement of connectedness, a relationship.

Due to the fact that the hypostasis concept so strongly emphasises similarity of essence, the unknown essence of God, i.e. *ousia*, signifies the Trinity in its entirety. The unknowableness of God is always the unknowableness of the Trinity. This observation made by Lossky is of such fundamental significance that the distinction between the *ousia* and *energeia* of God cannot be dealt with as a separate concept or 'locus' of the Trinity, as Roman Catholic and Protestant theology have attempted to do. This emphasis does, however, require observation of the fact that Palamite theology does not contain a concept of God's essence as such (*an sich*), an idea very characteristic of Western thinking. Furthermore, it is to be noted that Lossky's concept has its origins in the triadic unity pattern of the Trinity found in Greek patristics, in which the persons are not separated from the essence but uphold the essence. Hence, nature is not sovereign but always exists within the hypostases. The Godhead, i.e. the Trinity, is internally in communion.

It can therefore be held, in Lossky's theology, that the apophatically perceived perichoretic concept of person also establishes, conceptively, the *ousia–energeia* distinction, the cardinal dogma of Palamite theology. In accordance with apophatic theology, God can then only be discussed on the level of His energies, i.e. effects. The primary cause, i.e. the triune God, and the 'effect' are however not 'ontologically' separable from each other. God is at the same time both unknown (*ousia*) and knowable (*energeia*). In His energies, God is also accessible totally, i.e. as the Trinity. Even though distinctions should be maintained between the cause, the effect and the person or thing acted upon, these do not all form separate realities. This becomes understandable only from the viewpoint of the neo-Palamite concept of person, where 'nature' and 'person' are not understood to be alternative options. By offering a true option in the discussion on the relation between person and nature, Lossky's

---

[12] Lossky, *Essay sur la théologie mysticue*, p. 49 (*The Mystical Theology*, p. 50). Vrt. Lossky, *Essay sur la théologie mysticue*, pp. 52–4 (*The Mystical Theology*, pp. 53–5). See more closely Kotiranta, *Vladimir Lossky's Trinitarian Mode of Thought in Relation to the Palamite Heritage*, pp. 38–41, especially reference p. 39.

concept of person evokes new thought. Furthermore, it can also be claimed that this concept is ecumenically fruitful, since in previous research all attempts to bridge the gap between the Eastern and Western concepts of participation have foundered upon the dispute over an ontological conceptualisation based on nature or an existentialist consideration grounded in person.

Lossky's understanding of the Persons of Trinity as perichoretic means a repudiation of all those interpretations of the doctrine of the Trinity in which nature (i.e. divinity; *ousia*) is considered the basis, or starting point, for the Trinity. The placing of nature as an ontological principle would in Lossky's understanding entail a corruption of the genuine concept of the Trinity as well as that of person. Further, from the viewpoint of apophatic theology, this understanding of nature would lead to a problematic solution in which the divine nature (*ousia*) would in principle be knowable. The sophiological interpretation of *Solovyov, Florensky* and *Bulgakov* in particular entails this difficulty. The apophatic theological solution which considers person as perichoresis also signifies rejection of the other model of interpretation, as it repudiates the concept of an absolute Spirit 'above' the Trinity. This emphasis is in turn visible in the statements issued by Nikolai Berdyayev[13] concerning the doctrine of the Trinity. According to Lossky it is the patristic model of the Trinity, i.e. that of triadic unity, that attempts to make a strong statement of repudiation concerning the concept of a distinct, separable Spirit or person detectable behind or above the Trinity. This line of thought is particularly bound up in the issue of how the primary position of the person of the Father is to be understood.

In the trinitarian-personalistic pattern of thought, which is what Lossky's thought can properly be termed, person obtains the primary position in a sense. Yet this has to do with the triadic unity of the persons, not a person. According to his concept, the Persons of the Trinity are in a perichoretic and reciprocal interpenetrative relation, where one person (the person of the Father) cannot be regarded as having the status of an ontological principle from which nature (the deity) could be defined. The person of the Father is nevertheless the 'reason' for the differentiation of the Son and the Holy Spirit, but this is true only in the sense of the differentiation of the persons and their identifiability (*gnoristikon idioma*). The Person of the Father is not the cause of the existence of the Son and the Holy Spirit, however. This is not a causal relation in the philosophical sense, since the Persons of the Trinity exist eternally and only in perichoresis, sustaining one deity (*ousia*) and participating in shared action (*energeia*).

The ontological implications of the trinitarian-personalistic pattern of thought are concretely manifested in the manner in which the trinitarian doctrinal solution of triadic unity steers the substance of theology and anthropology in Lossky's

---

[13] Furthermore, Lossky does not accept solutions reached in accordance with modern Western personalism and existentialism (Berdyayev), in which the existentialism so characteristic of post-Kantian philosophy guides the interpretation of the theological understanding of God. This leads to a rejection of the apophatic model of the Trinity, based on the perichoretic concept of person propounded by the Cappadocian Fathers. In Lossky's understanding, neither person nor nature forms the ontological principle for the perichoresis of person. In person sharing perichoretically with the other triadic persons, the common nature together upholds the nature.

scholarship. The most significant content which Lossky confers on the personality of man in conjunction with his anthropology is that man is the image of the Trinity, *Imago Trinitatis*.

The most far-reaching and fundamental outcome of this brief analysis is a demonstration of the fact that the concept of person can be genuinely discussed in neo-Palamism, can be considered Palamite and can even be seen to be in conformity with the classical trinitarian formulation. Thus the personalistic mode of thought expressed by Vladimir Lossky and the neo-Palamites is not to be rejected as an Eastern version of modern personalism, which would really be quite foreign to Orthodox theology. In Lossky's concept, person, or rather the persons, uphold nature, making it what it is. Thus nature and person are closely related concepts, in keeping with the usage of the Eastern terminology.

Lossky's Place and Significance in Orthodox Theology

In addition to becoming well-known as one of the most significant Orthodox theologians of the twentieth century and above all as a notable interpreter of St Gregory Palamas, Vladimir Lossky was also active ecumenically, playing a prominent part in the ecumenical movement in the years following the Second World War. In particular, he attempted to foster contacts between Orthodox and Anglican Christians, and his activities in the Fellowship of St Alban and St Sergius and in ecumenical circles soon raised him to the position of a 'mouthpiece' for Orthodox beliefs in Western Europe, a position that had automatically belonged to Bulgakov during the pre-war period. Lossky's *Essai sur la Théologie Mystique de l'Église d'Orient* (*The Mystical Theology of the Eastern Church*) may be regarded as his ecumenical manifesto, for it was in this that he attempted to demonstrate that the *filioque* had not been merely an addition of secondary importance for East–West relations but rather had been the underlying cause of most of the differences of opinion. Ironically, as Lossky's reputation as a theologian was growing abroad, his personal isolation was increasing in Paris, on account of the Bulgakov debate, until eventually it was so restricted that he was lecturing informally to small but lively groups of theological students who remained under the jurisdiction of the Patriarchate of Moscow. It is both revealing and tragic that Lossky was never allowed to teach at the Institut St-Serge, and it was undoubtedly this that caused him to be overshadowed for a long time by scholars who had progressed from that institute to the American Orthodox community, such as Georges Florovsky and Alexander Schmemann.

Bibliography

Primary Literature

For an exhaustive bibliography on Lossky, see *In the Image and Likeness of God* (1974), pp. 229–32.

Spor o Sofii. Debate on Sophia, Russ (Paris, 1936).
Essai sur la théologie mystique de l'Église d'Orient (Paris, 1944).
Der Sinn der Ikonen. In Zusammenarbeit mit Leonid Ouspensky (Bern and Olten, 1952).
Théologie négative et connaissance de Dieu chez Maître Eckhart (Paris, 1960).
Vision de Dieu. Préface de Jean Meyendorff (Neuchatel, 1962).
'Théologie dogmatique', in *Messager*, 46–7 (1964), pp. 85–108; 48 (1964), pp. 218–33; 49 (1965), pp. 24–35; 50 (1965), pp. 83–101. In English: *Orthodox Theology: An Introduction*. Transl. by Jan and Ihita (Kesarcodi-Watson: Crestwood, 1978), pp. 27–118.
'Foi et théologie', in *Contacts*, 13 (3–4/1961), pp. 163–76. In English: *Orthodox Theology: An Introduction* (Kesarcodi-Watson: Crestwood, 1978), pp. 13–25. Translated by Jan an Ihita.
A l'Image et a la Ressemblance de Dieu. A collection of 12 essays written in 1947–57 (Paris, 1967).

English Translations

The Mystical Theology of the Eastern Church (London, 1957). Trans. by a small group of members of the Fellowship of St. Alban and St. Sergius, Reprint (Crestwood and New York, 1976).
The Vision of God (The Library of Orthodox Theology 2. Aulesbury, 1963). Trans. Asheleigh Moorhouse. Preface by John Meyendorff.
In the Image and Likeness of God (Crestwood, 1974). Edited by John H. Erickson and Thomas E. Bird, with an Introduction by John Meyendorff.
Orthodox Theology: An Introduction (Crestwood and New York, 1978). Trans. Jan and Ihita Kesarcodi-Watson.

Secondary Literature

Coffey, David, 'The Palamite Doctrine of God: A New Perspective', *St. Vladimir's Theological Quarterly*, 32 (1972), pp. 329–358, 1988.
Florovsky, Georges, *Puti Russkogo Bogosloviya*. Ways of Russian Theology, Russ. (Paris, 1937/1983).
Kotiranta, Matti, *Persoona perikoreesina. Vladimir Losskyn kolminaisuuskäsitys ja sen suhde palamistiseen perinteeseen ja venäläiseen uskonnonfilosofiaan* [*Person as Perichoresis: Vladimir Lossky's Trinitarian Mode of Thought in Relation to the Palamite Heritage and the Russian Philosophy of Religion*] Diss. (Helsinki, 1995).

Laats, Alar, *Doctrines of the Trinity in Eastern and Western Theologies: A Study with Special Reference to K. Barth and. V. Lossky. – Studien zur interkulturellen Geschicte des Christentums – Studies in the Intercultural History of Christianity*, vol. 114. Diss. (New York: Peter Lang, 1999).

Meyendorff, John, *Introduction a l'etude de Gregoire Palamas* (Paris, 1959a).

Meyendorff, John, *St. Gregoire Palamas et la mystique orthodoxe* (Paris, 1959b).

Papanikolaou, Aristotle, 'Divine Energies or Divine Personhood: Vladimir Lossky and John Zizioulas on Conceiving the Transcendent and Immanent God', *Modern Theology*, 19(3) (2003), pp. 357–85.

Schultze, Bernhard, 'Grundfragen des theologischen Palamismus', *Ostkirchliche Studien* (1975), pp. 105–35.

Wendebourg, Dorothea, 'Gregorios Palamas (1296–1359)', *Klassiker der Theologie* 1. Hrsg. von Heinrich Fries und Georg (München: Kretschmar, 1981), pp. 252–68.

Wendebourg, Dorothea, 'From the Cappadocian Fathers to Gregory Palamas. The Defeat of Trinitarian Theology', *Studia Patristica*, 12 (1982), pp. 194–8.

Wendebourg, Dorothea, 'Person und Hypostase. Zur Trinitätslehre in der neueren orthodoxen Theologie'. *Vernunft des Glaubens. Wissenschaftliche Theologie und kirchliche Lehre*. Festschrift zum 60. Geburtstag von Wolfhart Pannenberg. Hrsg. Jan Rohls und Gunther Wenz (Göttingen: Vandenhoeck & Ruprecht, 1988), pp. 117–60.

Williams, R.D., 'Person and Personality in Christology', *OR* (1975a), pp. 253–60.

Williams, R.D., *The Theology of Vladimir Nikolaievic Lossky. An Exposition and Critique*. Diss. Bodleian Library, Interlibrary Loans, Oxford. (Microfilm) (1975b).

Williams, R.D., 'The Philosophical Structures of Palamism', *Easter Church Review*, 1–2 (1977), pp. 27–44.

Chapter 31
Dumitru Stăniloae

Calinic Berger

Dumitru Stăniloae (1903–93) was the foremost Romanian Orthodox dogmatic theologian and patristic scholar of the twentieth century. He was a pioneer of Palamite studies, having been the first to publish any translation or major study of Palamas, and can be included among contemporary "neo-Patristic" scholars in his emphasis on a return to patristic sources. Stăniloae was extraordinarily prolific: he published over 40 books, including several major dogmatic studies, 30 volumes of Greek patristic translations, a 12-volume translation of the *Philokalia*, 200 theological articles (many of them major studies), and over 400 editorial and periodical articles, besides reviews, introductions and other miscellany. His theological synthesis is similarly vast in scope: it fully integrates later Byzantine theology (Dionysius, Maximus, Palamas), also incorporating insights from contemporary theology (Catholic, Protestant and Orthodox) and philosophy, all combined in his "personalist" emphasis. His academic writings are imbued with a pastoral concern which gives them an inspirational dimension, making them traditional and contemporary simultaneously, engaging scholars, clergy and laymen.

Biography

Dumitru Stăniloae was born in the village of Vlădeni (near Brașov), Romania, in 1903. His parents were deeply religious, and from a young age he desired to become a priest. He entered the Cernăuți Seminary in 1922. However, being dissatisfied with the scholastic manuals of theology (which "detached theology from the life of the people"), he left the seminary to spend two years (1923–4) at the Faculty of Literature in Bucharest. He later returned to Cernăuți, graduating in 1927 with a thesis entitled, "The Baptism of Children." During this second period he began to study the Greek Fathers, and learned Russian in order to read Bulgakov.

Under the guidance of Metropolitan Nicolae Bălan, he spent the years 1928–9 abroad, in Athens, Munich, Berlin and Paris. His doctoral thesis was completed in 1928, entitled "The Life and Work of Patriarch Dositheus of Jerusalem and his Relations with the Romanian Lands." In Athens he studied (and later translated) the *Dogmatics* of Christos Androutsos, whom he greatly respected. Yet he grew more dissatisfied with the theology of his day. "The doctrine ... *Deus est actus purus* ... was unfortunately introduced into our textbooks, and has created serious difficulties for the religious spirit of our theologians, who lose their habit of reckoning God as a living person."

From Athens, Stăniloae studied in Germany where he was exposed to Barth and also to dialectical theology. It was during this period that he turned decisively to Palamite thought. "In the dialectical theology I found an image of a separate and distant God, while in the Palamite one I met a God who comes towards man, opens Himself to him like light, through prayer. He fills him with His energies, yet remaining incommunicable with respect to His essence, incomprehensible, apophatic." In the libraries of Europe, Stăniloae copied unpublished Palamite manuscripts, acquiring a detailed knowledge of his thought that he would retain for the duration of his career.

In 1929, Stăniloae began teaching at the Theological Academy in Sibiu, becoming rector in 1936. He also became the editor of a major Romanian newspaper, *Telegraful Român*, for which he would write almost 350 articles on theological and cultural topics from 1934 to 1945. In 1930, he married his wife Maria and started a family (two of his three children died young). In 1932, he was ordained a priest.

His first major study appeared in 1938, *The Life and Teaching of St. Gregory Palamas*, which included translations of previously unpublished texts. It was followed in 1942 by a study of the metaphysics of the Romanian philosopher, Lucian Blaga, and in 1943 by a major study in Christology, *Jesus Christ, or the Restoration of Man*. Also in this period Stăniloae commenced his translation of the *Philokalia*. This life-long project had a pastoral goal of making patristic thought accessible to both clergy and laity, giving it practical expression in life and sermon. "I became convinced that there is an organic unity between patristic thought and the thought which must respond to the problems of today." Between 1946 and 1948, Stăniloae published four of what would become 12 volumes.

After World War II, Stăniloae was moved from Sibiu to Bucharest where he began teaching at the Theological Institute in 1947. He published over 30 articles before 1958, most being studies in comparative theology. In Bucharest, Stăniloae associated with "The Burning Bush" movement, a group of Romanian intellectuals with a common interest in hesychasm and the *Philokalia*. In 1958, together with members of this group, Stăniloae was arrested by the Communist authorities and spent the next five years in prison. He never spoke about this experience except to say, "I carried my cross, as is normal for any Christian."

Stăniloae returned in 1967 to the Institute in Bucharest where he remained until his retirement in 1973. The next 20 years of his life proved incredibly productive. Stăniloae wrote over a dozen major studies in ecclesiology. From 1976 to 1981, another six volumes of the *Philokalia* were published. In 1978, the first component of his *magnum opus* appeared, the three-volume *Orthodox Dogmatic Theology*. In 1981 this was followed by *Orthodox Spirituality: Asceticism and Mysticism*, and in 1987, by *Spirituality and Communion in the Orthodox Liturgy*. All three works are exceptional for their breadth of subject matter, wealth of patristic citations, and full incorporation of Byzantine theology, combined with Stăniloae's own profound "personalist" reflections.

Stăniloae reposed on October 5, 1993. Thousands, including the entire synod of the Romanian Orthodox Church, attended his funeral.

Survey

Jesus Christ, or the Restoration of Man (1943) is a comprehensive Christological treatise, incorporating the insights of Leontius of Byzantium, St. Maximus the Confessor and St. John Damascene, in dialogue with contemporary thinkers from Bulgakov to von Balthasar. Topics include the hypostatic union of two natures, the communication of properties, the two wills of Christ and concept of γνώμη, and the various aspects of redemption.

Especially important is Stăniloae's detailed discussion of "hypostasis" or, person. Admitting that "person" is ultimately a mystery, Stăniloae seeks to provide definitions of "person" and "nature" which conform to Chalcedonian Christology, insisting upon a balance in which neither can exist without the other. The "contents" of the "hypostasis-person" and of "nature" are the same, but the person exists for himself, whereas the nature exists for the person. The "nature" answers the question "what?"; the "person" answers the question "who?" Therefore, "hypostasis" is a completed nature with the character of subject (that which says "I" to another "thou").

Stăniloae notably distances himself from the then-current position of Bulgakov and others, in which the "I" or person is the source of freedom, existing in a certain disjuncture from "nature." This latter teaching he proves untenable in the Christology of St. Maximus, in which freedom is part of nature. The book provides a dogmatic foundation of Stăniloae's apophatic notion of personhood and the integral relation between "person" and "nature," which would appear in his subsequent work. He would revisit these themes in *The Immortal Image of God* (1978) and *God and Man* (1990).

Orthodox Dogmatic Theology (1978) is notable in both scope (topics include revelation, knowledge of God, the attributes of God, Trinity, cosmology, Christology, Pneumatology, ecclesiology, sacraments and eschatology) and content (a neo-Patristic dogmatics which fully incorporates later Byzantine theology into its synthesis). The work is a comprehensive collection of Stăniloae's major insights, but is by no means a repetition of previously published content. It is simultaneously a theological treatise and a spiritual reflection: "We have sought in this synthesis ... to uncover the spiritual significance of the dogmatic teachings, to point out their truth as it corresponds to the deep needs of the soul."

One major theme throughout the work is the *personhood* of God. Stăniloae reflects on every topic from a "personalist" perspective. For example, God is both transcendent and immanent—"being," "being itself" and "beyond being"—not only on account of the divine "super-essence" (Stăniloae uses Dionysius' term), but because He is *person*, or rather, the "Supreme Personal Reality." As with his Christology, Stăniloae is careful not to create a disjuncture between "person" and "nature" in the Trinity. The *hypostasis* "cannot be understood either emptied of nature or separated from relationship." Stăniloae's reflections on the divine "super-essence" and "divine intersubjectivity" (John Damascene's notion of *perichoresis*), as on the relations among Persons, are unique for their creativity.

Another major theme is the role of the world as a means of revelation and interpersonal communion. The world has a *personal* dimension—without which it would have no meaning—on account of each thing having a reason, or "logos," which connects it to the one personal *Logos* or Word of God.

Orthodox Spirituality (1981) is a comprehensive theological exposition of the *philokalic* spiritual life. The book is divided into sections corresponding to the Dionysian scheme of the stages of the spiritual ascent: purification, illumination and deification.

Stăniloae points out that the goal of spiritual life is twofold: the healing of our nature and our union with God, the former requiring ascetic discipline, the latter, a mystical experience of God. Both of these goals are inseparable, simultaneous and unending processes. The fact that the healing of our nature is a goal of spiritual life implies that we cannot ignore the world or our neighbor in this process. Orthodox spirituality is not only integrally connected to the material dimension of reality, but totally inseparable from it. Our actions affect our spiritual development, serving to either enclose us in egotism or open us for interpersonal communion. Stăniloae equates this process to a working out of gifts received in Baptism and Chrismation, and thus to an ever-deepening union with the Persons of the Trinity. He thereby sees Orthodox spirituality as having a Christological, pneumatological and ecclesial character simultaneously.

The spiritual ascent begins with *purification*, as the process of reorienting the self from egotism to love, and of the powers of human nature from serving the passions to inculcating the virtues. *Illumination* is the intensification of the spiritual and intellectual gifts (given in Chrismation), through which one becomes sensitive to the presence and activity of God in all things. This is simultaneous with a growth in communion with God through prayer, culminating in "pure prayer," through which one sees God reflected in depth of one's being, or "heart." *Deification* is both a process of being filled with God's presence, and an ecstatic experience of union with God. Our deification begins in this life, but will continue for all eternity. In the future age the Saints will participate in the Trinitarian intersubjectivity, being simultaneously one with God and each other, in an unconfused manner, and all creation will become the transparent bearer of the uncreated energies.

Also discussed are the interrelation of human faculties (reason, heart, will, etc.), their role in various stages, and the contents of the seven hesychastic manuals (from Symeon the New Theologian to the Russian Pilgrim).

Spirituality and Communion in the Orthodox Liturgy (1987) is a theological commentary on the texts and ritual actions of the Orthodox Liturgy. Stăniloae highlights the theological themes which have been layered together in the history of the Liturgy, elucidating their harmony. The book is rich with citations from Byzantine theologians and engages contemporary scholarship.

Stăniloae wrote this book as a sequel to *Orthodox Spirituality* in order to convey the reciprocal relationship between the sacraments and spiritual gifts, the life of the community and of the individual, and the work of Christ and the Spirit in the Liturgy and outside of it. The book is divided into sections corresponding to the sections of the Liturgy. In the introduction, Stăniloae comments on Orthodox architectural arrangement, in which the church building is seen as an image of the cosmos and of the human being, in each of which Christ serves as High Priest. It is thus the central location of the work of Christ in the cosmos, the Church, and the life of each individual, from baptism to burial.

One central theme is the Liturgy as a participation in and a making present of Christ's sacrifice, but not a re-offering of what was once offered on Golgotha. In the Liturgy, all members of the community and the Church are represented by crumbs on the *diskos*, and hence all offer themselves in a state of sacrifice to the Father, along with Christ's perfect sacrifice, as co-heirs and brothers in Christ—or rather, Christ offers their sacrifice along with His, that they might experience the Father's love, expressed by His sending the Holy Spirit, who rests "upon us and these gifts," as He rests upon the Son. Throughout the work, one sees Stăniloae's integration of Byzantine Pneumatology, in which the Spirit proceeds from the Father, rests in the Son, and shines forth from the Son to the Father. The Liturgy thereby brings us into a relationship with the entire Trinity in the position of adopted sons and co-heirs with Christ in the most accentuated manner. It integrates, in his view, the entire economy of the Son and the Spirit, uniting cross, resurrection and Pentecost, a fact demonstrated in the Liturgy by the priest making the sign of the cross over the gifts at the moment of the invocation of the Spirit.

The book contains notable commentary on the details of the rites. For example, when a particle of bread is cut for the Mother of God and placed next to the lamb, the priest prays, "by her prayers, O Lord, accept this sacrifice upon Thine heavenly altar." Stăniloae explains: "The most pure life and prayers of the Mother of God created the possibility of the Lord taking His flesh from her, in order that He might bring it as an offering for our salvation." Likewise now, this unique prayer is offered because the Body of Christ is always the Body taken from the Virgin. The Mother of God is thereby integrally connected to each Eucharistic celebration.

Philokalia, Translations, Studies

Stăniloae's translation of the *Philokalia* (with exceptional, copious footnotes) has been hailed as a monumental event in the cultural life of Romania. His version did not follow the Greek or Russian content, but added other works and authors, including substantial additions from St. Maximus the Confessor. Stăniloae's goal was to inspire a renewal of Church life at all levels.

Additionally, Stăniloae translated almost the entire fundamental *corpus* of Greek Patristic literature, including SS. Maximus, Gregory of Nyssa, Athanasius, Cyril of Alexandria and Dionysius the Areopagite—all with copious footnotes. Some of these notes have been translated and published separately due to their own value.

His dogmatic studies contain a wealth of patristic content, which Stăniloae places into dialogue with contemporary thought. Of special interest are his substantial ecclesiological studies of the 1960s and 1970s.

Key Characteristics of Stăniloae's Theology

Person and Nature, Divine and Human

As mentioned above, Stăniloae developed his notion of "person-hypostasis" not only from patristic Trinitarian theology but also from Chalcedonian Christology (mainly of St. Maximus), and in many points in contradistinction to modern personalism, resulting in a double emphasis on "person" and "nature" as integral and inseparable. For Stăniloae *both* nature *and* relation/communion are constitutive to "person." This balanced approach is a defining characteristic of Stăniloae's theological synthesis.

Throughout Stăniloae's works the theme of personhood is central as the quintessential characteristic of both God (the "Supreme Personal Reality") and man (the "image" of God). Stăniloae incorporates the Cappadocian understanding of "image" and the bold assertions of Maximus (e.g. "God and man are paradigms of one another") into his theological synthesis. Human personhood not only reflects divine personhood (thereby possessing an apophatic and transcendent character), but also reveals it, without anthropomorphism. This allows Stăniloae to frequently use analogies between human and divine personhood, resulting in some of his most creative and fruitful reflections.

In Stăniloae's view, interpersonal communion occurs only in and through the elements of nature. Likewise in the divine–human relationship: the uncreated energies therefore have a personal character, revealing the Divine Persons, but never the Divine Essence. Stăniloae, following the Cappadocians, sees *common nature* as foundational for interpersonal communion (both in the Trinity and human life), and following the Christology of St. Maximus, sees freedom as a part of *nature*. Therefore, a person is free *because of* and *through* his nature, not in spite of it.

Logos and Logoi: The World as Revelation

In Stăniloae's synthesis, the material creation plays a central role in the divine–human dialogue. His vision is based on Maximus' notion of the "reasons" (*logoi*) of creation, Dionysius' concept of symbol/*logos* and participation, and the Palamite doctrine of the uncreated energies, all synthesized in Stăniloae's personalist emphasis. In this vision, the goal of knowledge is always "person" (interpersonal communion), and the means of attaining this goal is always found in "nature." By "nature" is included human nature, the created world, and even the uncreated energies. All of these things constitute the energies and elements which give persons, divine and human, the ability to commune with one another. It necessitates a spirituality that leaves out no aspect of reality.

Central in Stăniloae's synthesis are the *logoi*, a modality of divine immanence. Every created reality (every tree, bird, etc.) has its associated *logos*. The *logoi* correspond to the divine activity through which God creates, sustains and guides all things towards Himself. As the models/goals of all things, the *logoi* pre-exist in an eternal, undifferentiated and unchanging unity in God Himself, the one *Logos*, and become differentiated through creation. This is not an impersonal emanation in Stăniloae's thought, but a manifestation of the *personal* providence of God, which ensures that each thing in the world is a personally-willed expression of the *Logos*. The *logoi* are "rooted in God as Person, or as a supreme loving communion of Persons" and reflect "the presence of God as Person in all things."

There is no dualism in Stăniloae's notion of the *logoi*. The "symbol" (or, created reality) *is* the manifestation of the (uncreated) *logos*, and the *logos* cannot be known apart from the symbol. In manifesting the *logoi*, the symbols themselves do not disappear, but become "transparent," revealing something, or Someone, beyond themselves. Stăniloae is careful to avoid the two extremes of an identification of the uncreated with the created (pantheism) and of a mutually exclusive separation of God and the world. Stăniloae uses Gregory Nazianzus' analogy comparing the world to a finely crafted lute: God does not simply make the lute (showing us His skill) but plays music on it. The world has a potentially infinitely-dimensional depth of meaning as the medium of the divine–human dialogue, a sacred, gnoseological and *personal* dimension, revealing not only a rational, but a personal God. Ultimately, the *logoi* point to Christ, the incarnate *Logos* of God, who is thereby the fulfillment and destiny of both man and the world.

Asceticism and Knowledge

As an expression of the personal *Logos* of God, the world is both gift and task. God communicates through the things of the world, and man must freely respond to this communication, A person does so by changing his relation to the world through asceticism (removing egotism), thereby seeing God manifested through the *logoi* more and more, until even the distinction between subject and object is transcended: one sees the Giver more than the gift in all things. Man thereby develops his natural powers and communes with the thoughts and intentions of God. Thus, bodily asceticism is integrally connected to spiritual growth.

Therefore, Orthodox asceticism is a fight not against nature, but for it, that it might enable interpersonal communion. Asceticism is not a scorn of the world, but a discovery of the world. One does not reject the world to see God, but only "a world narrow and exaggerated by the passions, to find a world transparent which becomes a mirror of God and a ladder to Him." Far, then, from removing a person from the world and other persons, asceticism leads to a heightened sense of responsibility towards them. Asceticism does not lead to disinterest, but to an exclusion of egotistical self-interest. It includes and promotes the interest of love.

The Integration of Theology and Spirituality

Stăniloae's person/nature synthesis, and its extension into the structure of the world through the *Logos-logoi*-symbol relation, are foundational for his integration of theology and spirituality. By underlining the personal character of both the Orthodox dogmatic and ascetic (*philokalic*) tradition, Stăniloae reveals their profound unity. All of our goals and actions are always oriented ultimately toward another *person*, and the means of actualizing these goals is provided by *nature*. The growth of interpersonal communion is thus simultaneous with the healing of nature.

Stăniloae's theological vision can be described as one great synthesis. All realities contribute to man's deification, all progress together, mutually assisting and interpenetrating each other. There is no dialogical opposition between, nor total separation of, theology and spirituality, person and nature, *logos* and symbol, essence and energy, body and soul, mind and heart, cataphatic and apophatic, purification, illumination and deification, the world and God, and finally, even the created and uncreated. But neither is there an identification of these realities. They all exist together in Chalcedonian manner. Through and beyond all things, God as Personal Reality works to bring man into an ever deeper communion with Himself.

Triadology: The Christological/Pneumatological Synthesis

Above all, Stăniloae's synthesis is profoundly *Trinitarian*. Stăniloae makes the triadological element of the *philokalic* tradition explicit. For him, "deification is nothing other than the extension to conscious creatures of the relations that exist between the divine Persons." The communion and deification we receive from God are never abstract, but always in the specific relationship of adopted sons to the Father, who sends His Spirit to rest in us, and return our prayer to the Father. In this, the uncreated energies, as an extension of God's essential love and communion, have a *personal* character, serving always to reveal the Divine Persons. An "unipersonal god would not have within himself that eternal love or communion into which he would wish to introduce us."

Stăniloae's synthesis between Christology and Pneumatology, which fully incorporates later Byzantine theology, has two main components: first, the inseparability of the Son and the Spirit. The Holy Spirit "proceeds from the Father" and the Son is "begotten of the Father" simultaneously and inseparably—meaning *not alongside of* but internal to each other. Second, he adheres to the Byzantine interpretation of the phrase "through the Son" as referring not to a causal act, but to the eternal relationship between the Son and the Spirit, namely, the "manifestation" or "shining forth" of the Spirit through the Son. Specifically, the Holy Spirit proceeds from the Father *to* the Son. He proceeds no further than the Son, but *rests* in the Son, and is "manifested" or "shines out" from the Son, specifically *toward* the Father.

This relationship between the Son and the Spirit is found throughout Stăniloae's writings. It is prominent in his ecclesiology, in which it allows Stăniloae to avoid a disjuncture between the institutional and charismatic, universal and local, authority and freedom, tradition and inspiration, and liturgy and ministry. In everything the Spirit builds up the Body of Christ; in everything, the Body of Christ breathes the Spirit.

We should note that Stăniloae is careful not to depersonalize any Person of the Holy Trinity in his synthesis. The procession/manifestation of the Holy Spirit is the foundation of the Trinitarian *perichoresis*. The unity of the Holy Trinity is thus monarchical (the Father as *arche*), essential (*homoousios*) and hypostatic (*perichoresis*) simultaneously.

Place in Twentieth-century Theology

Stăniloae has created a theological synthesis which carefully preserves the balances of patristic thought, fully incorporates later Byzantine Pneumatology and Palamite theology, dialogues with contemporary theological and philosophical thought, and combines all with his own personalist emphasis. His work demonstrates the profound unity of the Orthodox dogmatic and ascetic (*philokalic*) traditions, and thus of theology and spirituality, with the goal of inspiring a renewal of Church life on all levels.

Stăniloae was as prolific as he was creative. He was a pioneer in Palamite studies and the Patristic revival in contemporary Orthodox theology and gave Romanian theology, which formerly followed scholastic methodologies, a decisively patristic and Palamite foundation. His synthesis found expression throughout his groundbreaking theological studies, translations and articles, translations of which are yet lacking. Due to this, as due its vast content and synthetic character, a full reception of Stăniloae's work has yet to occur. As it does, it will certainly contribute to the enrichment of contemporary theological thought.

Bibliography

Primary Literature

For an exhaustive bibliography: Păcurariu and Ică, pp. 16–67.

Teologia dogmatică ortodoxă, 2nd edn (3 vols, București: Institutului Biblic și Misiune, 1996); French: *La génie de l'orthodoxie*, trans. Dan Ilie Ciobotea (Paris: Desclée de Brouwer, 1985); German: *Orthodoxe Dogmatik*, trans. H. Pitters (Cologne: Gütersloh, 1985); English (in process): *The Experience of God*, trans. Ioan Ioniță and Robert Barringer (6 vols, Brookline: Holy Cross, 1994–).

Spiritualitatea ortodoxă (București: Institutului Biblic și Misiune, 1981); reprinted as *Ascetica și Mistica Ortodoxă*, 2 vols (Alba Iulia: Editura Deisis, 1993); English: *Orthodox Spirituality*, trans. Archm. Jerome Newville and Otilia Kloos (South Canaan: St. Tikhon's Seminary Press, 2002).

Theology and the Church, trans. Robert Barringer (New York: SVS Press, 1980).

Secondary Literature

Baconsky, Teodor and Tătar-Cazaban, Bogdan (eds), *Dumitru Stăniloae sau Paradoxul Teologiei* (București: Anastasia, 2003).
Berger, Calinic, "Does the Eucharist Make the Church? An Ecclesiological Comparison of Stăniloae and Zizioulas," *St Vladimir's Theological Quarterly*, 51(1) (2007), 23–70.
Bielawski, Maciej, *The Philocalical Vision of the World in the Theology of Dumitru Stăniloae* (Bydgoszcz: Wydawnictwo homini, 1997).
Costa de Beauregard, M., *Dumitru Stăniloae: Ose comprendre que Je t'aime* (Paris, 1983).
Păcurariu, Mircea and Ică, Ioan I. Jr. (eds), *Persoana si Comuniune. Prinos de Cinstire Preotului Profesor Academician Dumitru Stăniloae* (Sibiu: Editura Arhiepiscopiei Ortodoxe, 1993).
Roberson, Ronald G., *Contemporary Romanian Orthodox Ecclesiology: The Contributions of Dumitru Stăniloae and Younger Colleagues* (Rome: Pontificium Institutum Orientale, 1988).
Toma, Ștefan L., *Tradiție și actualitate la pr. Dumitru Stăniloae* (Sibiu: Agnos, 2008).
Turcescu, Lucian (ed.), *Dumitru Stăniloae: Tradition and Modernity in Theology* (Iași: Center for Romanian Studies, 2002).
Ware, Kallistos, Introduction, *The Experience of God*, vol. 1, pp. ix–xxvi.

Chapter 32
Alexander Schmemann

Sigurd Hareide

The liturgical movement must be accorded a very prominent place in any overview of the theological movements that set their mark on church life in the twentieth century. Almost all the great churches were influenced by the results of its scholarship and ideals when they revised their liturgy in the last forty years. Even more important than the liturgical changes that followed in the wake of the liturgical movement was however its influence on "theology itself." This was due not least to the ability of the liturgical movement to free the old questions that had divided the churches from their closed positions in controversial theology and abstract dogmatics and to transpose these questions into a context where they could be understood in a way that was more ecumenically fruitful. It was above all in sacramental theology that this movement often contributed to fresh theological thinking and brought the churches closer together. Not only orders of service have drawn closer to one another in their form and content: the same is true of theologies.[1] The continuing validity of the ancient maxim *lex orandi est lex credendi* ("the law of praying is the law of believing") has been demonstrated.

The Orthodox theologian Alexander Schmemann (1921–83) maintained vigorously in a number of books and articles from the end of the 1950s until his much too early death in 1983 that the primary concern of the liturgical movement was *theological* reform – not liturgical changes. He believed that his own contribution to the theological reorientation that he saw as a necessary consequence of the liturgical movement was his important coining of the concept of "liturgical theology" as a holistic theological vision. Today, when the liturgical movement is evaluated critically, especially in the Catholic church, together with the liturgical reform that came in the wake of the Second Vatican Council,[2] it is well worth listening to Schmemann's theological contribution

---

[1] See *Baptism, Eucharist and Ministry*, World Council of Churches, 1982.
[2] See, for example, Aidan Nichols, *Looking at the Liturgy* (San Francisco, 1996).

Alexander Schmemann and the Liturgical Movement

It is an interesting fact that a theologian like Alexander Schmemann, whose starting point was in Russian Orthodoxy, should have become such an important interpreter and inspirer of a movement that began in the Western church.[3] But Schmemann saw the liturgical movement as "a kind of 'Orthodox' movement in a non-Orthodox context."[4] He himself grew up as an Orthodox Christian in a "non-Orthodox context," in the Orthodox exile milieu in France, and there is no doubt about the decisive role this played in his theological development. He received his theological training at the Orthodox theological institute of Saint-Serge in Paris, where he was particularly influenced by the patristic scholar Cyprian Kern and by the professor of canon law, Nicholas Afanasiev, who is best known for his "eucharistic ecclesiology," which Schmemann developed further in his liturgical theology.

Schmemann also encountered a larger theological milieu in Paris, which was the center of the liturgical movement in the 1940s and 1950s. The prominent liturgical scholars Jean Daniélou and Louis Bouyer worked at the Catholic Centre de Pastorale Liturgique, which had been founded in 1943 by one of the great pioneers of the liturgical movement, Dom Lambert Baudouin, and others.[5] It was not least in his contacts with this milieu that Schmemann formed his theological worldview and laid the foundations of what he was later to write in and about liturgical theology.

In 1951, Schmemann and his family moved to the USA, where he helped build up Saint Vladimir's Orthodox seminary in New York. One major reason for this move was his wish to arrive at a more consistent Orthodox ecclesiology than was possible in France at that period. Schmemann was concerned about the problematical aspects of the overlapping Orthodox jurisdictions, and he was one of the main architects behind the establishing of the Orthodox Church in America as an autocephalous church in 1970.

At Saint Vladimir's seminary, he was greatly fascinated by the theology of the dean, Georges Florovsky, who had earlier taught at Saint-Serge. Florovsky had a vision for the Orthodox mission in the West; he criticized the accepted nationalistic Orthodox stereotypes and unmasked Orthodox theology's "Western captivity." Florovsky had the ability to be both rooted in the past of the Orthodox church and completely open to the best theological movements in Western Christianity. Many of these descriptions of Florovsky could also be employed to describe Schmemann. When the seminary moved in 1962 from New York City to its present location in Crestwood, half an hour by train from the city, Schmemann became dean and held this position until he died of cancer in 1983.

---

[3] This biographical sketch is based largely on John Meyendorff's article, "A Life Worth Living," in Fisch (ed.), *Liturgy and Tradition* (Crestwood, 1990), pp. 145ff. (Originally published in *St. Vladimir's Theological Quarterly* 28 (1984): 3–10).

[4] Schmemann, *Introduction to Liturgical Theology* (Crestwood, 1996), p. 15.

[5] See Byström and Norrgård, *More than Words* (Stockholm, 1996) pp. 32–3 and p. 42.

During his period as dean of Saint Vladimir's, Schmemann succeeded fully in integrating the seminary into the life of the church. Under his leadership, it became the center of a wide-reaching liturgical and eucharistic renewal in the Orthodox church, both in the USA and in the wider world. This meant, for example, an increase in the reception of Communion from once a year to once a week; the eucharistic prayer was prayed aloud, not in silence as was the custom; the new vernacular (American English) was used in the liturgy, and the sermon in the liturgy underwent a renewal. Many of the liturgical changes took place as follows: they were practiced first in the seminary's liturgical life, and then spread to other places. There was often strong opposition, and Schmemann has been given both the honor and the blame for many of the liturgical changes that American Orthodoxy experienced during his time at Saint Vladimir's.[6] It was also in the USA that he elaborated the liturgical theology for which he is best known, although he had taken his doctoral degree in liturgical theology at Saint-Serge in Paris in 1959, with Nicholas Afanasiev and John Meyendorff as his examiners.

In addition to his work as dean at Saint Vladimir's, Schmemann delivered many lectures in other contexts. He was also assistant professor at Union and General, the two great theological seminaries in New York. He took part in the Second Vatican Council as one of the Orthodox observers. In the mid-1970s, he was one of the seventeen persons from a wide variety of churches who put their signatures to the Hartford Appeal, a theological protest against various currents in contemporary Christianity; its initiators were Professor Peter L. Berger and Richard John Neuhaus, then a Lutheran pastor and later a Catholic priest.[7] Schmemann's ecumenical involvement was wide and varied, and he was particularly celebrated as a good speaker. He lacked patience as a researcher, but he made up for this through his ability to formulate and his commitment. I believe that Jeffrey Gros' description of Alexander Schmemann as "a great scholar and pastoral activist" sums up well his theological and ecclesial service.[8]

Liturgical Theology as a Holistic Vision

Alexander Schmemann's theological *chef d'œuvre* is his doctoral dissertation (1959), which was published in Russian in 1961 and in English in 1966 with the characteristic title *Introduction to Liturgical Theology*. In his subsequent books and articles on liturgical theology, he builds further on the fundamental insights in his dissertation. There is nevertheless a certain development in the understanding of liturgical theology in his writings. In his earliest works, he positions liturgical theology as one theological discipline alongside other disciplines. In this connection, he compares

---

[6] See John Meyendorff, "The Liturgical Path of Orthodoxy in America" (1996), pp. 49ff.
[7] See Schmemann, *Church, World, Mission* (Crestwood, 1979), p. 193: "The Ecumenical Agony."
[8] In a book review of Fisch (ed.), 1990 in *Worship*, 65 (1991), 92.

liturgical theology with biblical theology in their relationship to dogmatics. Both analyze theological sources (worship and the biblical text) which are then employed in the doctrine of the faith. Liturgical theology and biblical theology are thus a kind of ancillary disciplines between the theological sources and systematic theology.[9] Gradually, Schmemann came to assert more clearly that liturgical theology is a holistic theological vision. All the theological disciplines, including "systematic" theology, must be seen in relation to liturgical theology. In the process towards this understanding, the distinction between "liturgical theology" and "theology of the liturgy" is an important step. Here, he was able to build upon and develop insights from the earlier liturgical movement.

Schmemann was not the first to use the concept of "liturgical theology." It occurs already in 1937 in M. Cappuyen's lecture *Liturgie et théologie*, delivered at one of the most important meetings in the early liturgical movement, the "liturgical week" at Mont César in Belgium.[10] But both Cappuyen and other representatives of the liturgical movement before him use the concept of "liturgical theology" in parallel to the concept of "theology of the liturgy." For example, Louis Bouyer, under whom Schmemann studied in Paris, writes as follows in his book *Liturgical Piety* (1955) about the theological study of the liturgy:

> The *theology of liturgy* is the science which begins with the liturgy itself in order to give a theological explanation of what the liturgy is, and of what is implied in its rites and words. Those authors are not to be accounted *liturgical theologians*, therefore, who go on to work the other way round and seek to impose on liturgy a ready-made explanation which pays little or no attention to what the liturgy says about itself.[11]

Bouyer employs "theology of the liturgy" and "liturgical theologians" as corresponding expressions. One of Schmemann's primary theological contributions was the distinction between these two. He argues that they stand for two completely different understandings of the relationship between theology and liturgy. Although Bouyer employs the two concepts interchangeably, Schmemann can build on his distinction between two different approaches to the relationship between liturgy and theology. For Schmemann, the "theology of the liturgy" is an approach in which theology is an object for theology. The theologian's task is then to give a theological explanation of the nature and function of the liturgy. The result is the attempt to extract a "theology of worship" that can then be used against the liturgy, in order to demand liturgical reform (where necessary). This means approaching the liturgy from the outside, with a ready-made theological theory about worship.[12]

---

[9] See Schmemann, *Introduction to Liturgical Theology*, pp. 18–19.

[10] See Fisch, (ed.), *Liturgy and Tradition* (1990), p. 5: "Schmemann's Theological Contribution."

[11] Quoted from Fisch, ibid., p. 6.

[12] Schmemann, in Fisch (ed.), *Liturgy and Tradition* (1990), pp. 11–12: "Theology and Liturgical Tradition" (1963). In what follows, I refer without detailed bibliographical references

"Liturgical theology" is an approach to the liturgy in which it becomes "the basic source of theological thinking, a kind of *locus theologicus par excellence.*" This means, according to Schmemann, that liturgical theology is not primarily about liturgy or liturgical reform, but about theology. Its concern is theological, because the liturgy itself is theological. Liturgy is theology's fundamental source, because it is in the liturgy that the church's faith is revealed and manifested – theology in the deepest sense, as the doctrine and knowledge of God. This makes it clear that liturgy is more than just one source of theology, and liturgical theology is more than just one theological discipline. It is "the very source of theology, the condition that makes it *possible.*" This leads Schmemann to express a general skepticism about the Western division of theology into disciplines, and claims that "All theology, indeed, ought to be 'liturgical'."

Although all theology ought to be liturgical, this does not mean that worship is the only object that theology studies. The point is, rather, that theology must have its point of reference in the church's faith, as this is manifested and communicated in the liturgy. Schmemann describes the liturgy as "the ontological condition of theology" and "the living norm of theology," the place where the sources of faith and of theology – scripture and tradition – function as sources by becoming a living reality. According to Schmemann the liturgy or the *lex orandi* is "the *sui generis* hermeneutical foundation" of theology.

The Double Crisis of Theology and Liturgy

According to Schmemann, liturgy and theology have been separated. He claims that one finds in the theology of the church fathers the correct relationship between liturgy and theology, "an organic connection between their theological thought and their liturgical experience" in which the axiom *lex orandi est lex credendi* ("the law of praying is the law of believing") implies that "that the liturgical tradition, the liturgical life, is a natural milieu for theology, its self-evident term of reference." This patristic approach has been replaced in Western Catholic theology, and later in Eastern Orthodox theology too, by what he calls a "scholastic" approach. He does not however use this term to refer exclusively to one particular theological school or period in the history of theology, but rather to "a theological structure which existed in various forms in both the West and the East, and in which all 'organic' connection with worship is severed." He agrees with his predecessor as dean at Saint Vladimir's, Georges Florovsky, that this phenomenon is the "Western captivity" of Orthodox theology.

Schmemann writes that the scholastic model has enjoyed a monopoly from the close of the patristic age to the twentieth century, and that the liturgical movement

---

to a number of articles by Schmemann in Fisch (ed.) 1990: "Liturgical Theology: Remarks on Method" (1981), "Liturgical Theology, Theology of Liturgy and Liturgical Reform" (1969) and "Liturgy and Theology" (1972).

is "the first attempt to break this monopoly, to restore to liturgical tradition its own theological status."

The challenge to liturgical theology today is the change in the understanding of both liturgy and theology that is a result of the scholastic approach. Schmemann's vigorous insistence on the need for liturgical theology is based on what he calls the double crisis of theology and liturgy (in an article published in 1970). He identifies this crisis as early as 1949, before he came to America, in the article "On Understanding the Liturgy."[13]

The liturgical crisis is characterized by the believers' deficient understanding of the liturgy: "They love worship, not for its meaning, but for something else […] They even sometimes say that you don't have to understand worship: it's enough to love it and sense it." The dignity of worship thus lies not in the meaning it expresses, but "its 'effect' on the soul and psychology of the believer and the strengthening in him of a prayerful attitude." Schmemann calls this Orthodox "liturgism" a "reduction [of worship] to 'feeling' and 'emotional experience' [… the] fundamental illness of contemporary liturgical consciousness." This crisis in the liturgical consciousness of the faithful has serious consequences for theology, and this is the other part of the crisis:

> … the refusal to understand worship, to search in it for the 'rule of faith', often has a pernicious effect on theology itself: it loses the firm ground from beneath its feet and turns either into a 'pure science', 'science for the sake of science', or into the expression of 'private theological opinions' which do not dare to present themselves as a witness to the catholic tradition of the Church.

"On Understanding the Liturgy" is an appropriate title not only for this early article, but for everything Schmemann wrote. It points first of all to the problem: the liturgy is not understood, and this also means that the faith of the church, the *lex credendi*, is not understood. At the same time it also articulates the solution to the problem: the liturgy must again be understood in a proper way, for then, it is not only the liturgy that is understood, but the faith of the church too, her *lex credendi*. Liturgical theology therefore involves "a slow and patient bringing together of that which was for too long a time and because of many factors broken and isolated – liturgy, theology and piety, their reintegretion within one fundamental vision."[14]

As we have seen, Schmemann's liturgical-theological vision was developed on the basis of central concerns in the liturgical movement before him. A debate at the end of the 1960s between Schmemann and two important actors in the movement at that period helped to refine his theological and non-activist understanding of liturgical

---

[13] Since Schmemann wrote this article in Russian, I am dependent here and in what follows on the account in English by Walter Ray, *Lex orandi est lex credendi* (Crestwood, 1992).

[14] Schmemann in Fisch, (ed.), *Liturgy and Tradition*, p. 46.

theology.[15] Against the background of the reforms of the Roman rite after the Second Vatican Council, the Benedictine Bernard Botte wrote an article in *Saint Vladimir's Seminary Quarterly* in which he challenged Schmemann by asking if the time had not come for a reform of the Byzantine liturgy too. W. Jardine Grisbrooke, the Anglican historian of liturgy, joined in the debate after Schmemann's initial response and warned against waiting too long for a reform of the Orthodox liturgy.

Schmemann insisted that this was not the time for "an external liturgical reform but for a theology and piety drinking again from the eternal and unchanging sources of liturgical tradition." He also claimed that liturgy always changed, because it is living, and that the liturgical reform, with the necessary purifications and changes, would come organically without a break in continuity. From his perspective, the "romantic and nostalgic pathos of liturgical restoration" was just as bad as the continuous busy endeavor to make the liturgy more "understandable," "relevant," and "closer to the people." He believed that both approaches lacked the fundamental understanding of the liturgy, not as "an end in itself," but as the "'epiphany' of the Church's faith, of her experience in Christ of herself, the World and the Kingdom." As I have mentioned, Schmemann himself nevertheless contributed to the renewal of the praxis of worship in Orthodox churches in the USA and far beyond the American context. This debate at the end of the 1960s is interesting, not only because it sheds light on Schmemann's theological position and its development, but also because it takes the pulse of central problems that are posed in today's debate about what Cardinal Ratzinger has called "the reform of the [liturgical] reform."

The Theologian – A Witness

Schmemann's theological writings can be divided roughly into two parts. One part is a fundamental-theological reflection on the relationship between liturgy and theology, focusing on the concept of "liturgical theology." The other part puts into practice the holistic theological vision for which he argued in his *Introduction to Liturgical Theology* and that he developed later, especially in the articles he wrote in the 1960s. When he writes about the fundamental-theological problems, he continually brings in experiences from the Orthodox liturgical tradition; and when he writes about the concrete rites and sacraments, for example, in his large works on baptism and the eucharist,[16] he continually presents small excursuses on the relationship between theology and liturgy and the unfortunate separation of things that belong together "in one fundamental vision." As a theologian, Schmemann is very definitely a synthesizer. Sometimes this leads him to indulge in very broad generalizations where the historical processes are complicated, and historians of liturgy may criticize him for

---

[15] See the articles by Schmemann and the two opponents in Fisch (ed.), *Liturgy and Tradition*, pp. 21–48.

[16] Schmemann, *On Water and the Spirit* (Crestwood, 1974) and *The Eucharist* (Crestwood, 1988).

this. At the same time, it is precisely this continuous holding together of liturgy and theology, church life and academia, that expresses his theological vision, to which he continually returns and which marks his entire theological approach.

This also means that Schmemann goes beyond the frameworks of purely professional or academic theology. Schmemann is present in what he writes as priest, theologian, and scholar, and this too is in keeping with his theological ideals. He sees theology as much more than an academic activity (although it is that too). Theology is ultimately a charism with the task of service, and the theologian himself is a witness. This is because we see the real objects of theology – God, the world, the human person – in their true light, "in Christ," in the celebration of the eucharist, and "we receive this truth in participation of the Body and Blood of Christ, in the unending Pentecost that 'guides us into all truth and shows us things to come' (John 16:13)." The eucharist is "the moment of truth" for the theologian and for theology.[17]

Secularism and the Christian Worldview

Given this pastoral concern in Schmemann's theological approach, it is not surprising that his works of popular theology have found a wide readership. His best known book is probably *For the Life of the World. Sacraments and Orthodoxy*, first published in 1963 as a study guide for a conference in the interdenominational national Christian student fellowship in the USA. It has been translated into eleven languages and even circulated in a samizdat translation in the Soviet Union. In a foreword to the 1973 edition of this book, Schmemann explains its popularity by reference to the theme it takes up: "secularism ... and the deep polarization which secularism has provoked among Christians themselves." He points out that some regard secularism "as the best fruit of Christianity in history," while others see it as "the justification for an almost Manichean rejection of the world." The first group "reduce the Church to the world and its problems," while the second group see only the wickedness in the world while they "morbidly rejoice in their apocalyptic gloom." The uncovering of dichotomies of this kind is typical of Schmemann's rhetoric. It often makes reading his books both thought-provoking and entertaining.

For the Life of the World can be read as Schmemann's response to the theologies of secularization in the 1960s, but it is also a response to a theology that barricades itself in the trenches when the world changes and Christianity loses cultural influence. However, this book was not written for theologians in the conventional sense of the term, but for Christian students, and his message is that the theology and the worldview that are revealed in Christian worship are the best answer to the problem of secularization. He consistently speaks of "secularism" as an "ism," an ideology, and proposes as a contrast the Christian sacramental worldview in which the world is "very good" because it is created by God. It is true that the world lies in wickedness because of the Fall, but it is called to salvation "in Christ." Schmemann writes with

---

[17] Schmemann in Fisch (ed.), *Liturgy and Tradition*, p. 87: "Theology and Eucharist."

conviction that the answer to the problem of secularism and to the polarization among Christians when they encounter secularism is not to be found in "neat intellectual theories," but in the living liturgical experience of the church. It is here that the believer meets the true Christian worldview and the correct relationship between the "world," the "church," and the "kingdom of God." All Christians are called to bear witness to this in the world, and this is the basic task of theology and of the theologian.

Schmemann's Influence

It is difficult to discern any unified "Schmemann school" among later theologians. Although some Orthodox circles mounted a rather intense opposition to his theology, he has certainly been very influential in the Orthodox world.[18] But it is not so much his internal appeal in the Orthodox world that is typical of Schmemann, but rather the fascination and challenge his theology have presented to theologians from a great number of other confessions. This is true above all in the "academic field" of liturgical theology – if we disregard Schmemann's intentions and establish this new theological discipline.[19] Let me therefore mention here some of the non-Orthodox theologians who have found inspiration in Schmemann and who stand in varying degrees in his tradition.

As examples of the ecumenical influence of Schemann's writings I will begin by mentioning two Scandinavian books of a more popular-theological character that have communicated central ideas of Schemann to a Scandinavian context. My first example is *Evighet i Tiden. En bok om jødisk sabbatsglede og kristen søndagsfeiring* ("Eternity in Time. A book about the Jewish Sabbath joy and the Christian celebration of Sunday") by Ole Christian Kvarme, now the Lutheran bishop of Oslo. In this book, Kvarme gives an account of Schmemann's theology of Sunday, a very central aspect in his theological thinking. Sunday is the eighth day, the day of resurrection, when eternity breaks into time. In Schmemann's theology, cosmology (the doctrine about the world), ecclesiology (the doctrine about the church), and eschatology (the doctrine about the kingdom of God and the age to come) are held together in the church's celebration of the eucharist on the eighth day. Another proof of Schmemann's ecumenical influence is the Swedish Pentecostal pastor Peter Halldorf. In his books he refers several times to Schmemann's theology. For example in the book *Drikk dypt av Ånden* ("Drink deeply of the Spirit"), he is clearly inspired by Schmemann's theology of baptism and of Sunday.

---

[18] See the chapters on Schmemann in A. Nichols, *Light from the East.* (San Francisco, 1995),"Alexander Schmemann and Liturgical Theology" and in M. Plekon, *Living Icons* (Indiana, 2002), "Alexander Schmemann. Teacher of Freedom and Joy in the World as Sacrament".

[19] See, e.g., K. Irwin, *Liturgical Theology* (Collegeville, 1990) and D. Vogel, *Primary Sources of Liturgical Theology*, (Collegeville, 2000). Schmemann is of course included in both presentations of the field of liturgical theology.

In his book *What is Liturgical Theology? A Study in Methodology* (1992), David W. Fagerberg, a former Lutheran pastor who later converted to Catholicism, compares Schmemann's position on the relationship between liturgy and theology with the positions taken by other theologians, including Regin Prenter and Peter Brunner. Fagerberg concludes that Schmemann holds liturgy and theology together in an organic definition. He gives an interesting classification of the various positions and an excellent presentation of Schmemann. Another writer who shared Schmemann's radical view of the relationship between liturgy and theology, and indeed even radicalized this view, was Professor Aidan Kavanagh, OSB (1929–2006), who is especially well known for his books *The Shape of Baptism* (1978) and *On Liturgical Theology* (1984). Apart from his remarkable rhetoric, Kavanagh is best known for his insistence that "the law of praying" takes precedence in theology over "the law of believing."

Another theologian who is clearly inspired by Schmemann is the Lutheran Professor Gordon Lathrop (Philadelphia). In his imposing liturgical-theological trilogy, *Holy Things. A Liturgical Theology* (1993), *Holy People. A Liturgical Ecclesiology* (1999), and *Holy Ground. A Liturgical Cosmology* (2003), he repeatedly refers to Schmemann, especially to his *Introduction*. He is obviously inspired by (the early) Schmemann, but unlike Schmemann, Lathrop also strongly criticizes liturgical tradition and recommends radical breaches where necessary, for example in the question of ministry.[20] This may perhaps be an aspect of Lathrop's Lutheran inheritance. Despite the position they take on this and on other theological questions of the present time, both Lathrop and the other theologians who are inspired by Schmemann share a capacity to challenge customary ways of thinking and sequences of argumentation. I believe that this is due to their ability to hand on in a genuine manner one central aspect of Alexander Schmemann's liturgical theology: this is a theological approach that can challenge because it attacks the theological problems from a different angle (so to speak).

And perhaps this is the best summary of Alexander Schmemann's activity: he was a theologian who challenged, and who continues to challenge, in everything he wrote. This is why one can always find material in his texts to fire one with enthusiasm and to provoke one, whether one loves worship or is critical of it, whether one is a Western or an Eastern Christian, Catholic, Orthodox or Protestant, an academic theologian or a "theologian in the pews." He himself lived with the pain of being a "sign of contradiction." The only place where he felt completely at home in ecclesial terms was the Divine Liturgy; he often reflects on this theme in his posthumously published diaries.[21] We who read him can nevertheless be glad that he experienced this, and we can allow ourselves to be challenged by his writings, so that we break

---

[20] He breaks clearly with Schmemann's own position on this matter. See the debate book edited by Schmemann with a foreword by Schmemann: *Women and the Priesthood* (1983; revised edition, (ed.) by Th. Hopko: *Women and the Priesthood*, (Crestwood, 1999).

[21] Juliana Schmemann (trans.) *The Journals of Father Alexander Schmemann* (Crestwood, 2000).

through theological and confessional categories as did Schmemann and the liturgical movement of which he was a child.

Bibliography

Primary Literature

For a complete bibliography, see Paul Garrett: "Fr Alexander Schmemann: A Chronological Bibliography," *St. Vladimir's Theological Quarterly*, 28 (1984), 11–26.
Fisch, (ed.), *Liturgy and Tradition. Theological Reflections of Alexander Schmemann* (Crestwood: St. Vladimir's Seminary Press, 1990). A collection of texts by Schmemann.
Schmemann, Alexander, *Introduction to Liturgical Theology* (Crestwood: St. Vladimir's Seminary Press, 1996).
Schmemann, Alexander, *Of Water and the Spirit* (Crestwood: St. Vladimir's Seminary Press, 1974).
Schmemann, Alexander, *Church, World, Mission. Reflections on Orthodoxy in the West* (Crestwood: St. Vladimir's Seminary Press, 1979).
Schmemann, Alexander, *The Eucharist. Sacrament of the Kingdom* (Crestwood: St. Vladimir's Seminary Press, posthumous 1988).
Schmemann, Juliana (trans.), *The Journals of Father Alexander Schmemann 1973–1983* (Crestwood: St. Vladimir's Seminary Press, 2000).

Secondary Literature

Baptism, Eucharist and Ministry. World Council of Churches, 1982.
Byström, Jan, and Leif Norrgård, *Mer än ord – liturgisk teologi och praxis* (Stockholm: Verbum Förlag, 1996). (*More than Words – Liturgical Theology and Praxis*).
Fagerberg, David, *What is Liturgical Theology? A Study in Methodology* (Collegeville Minnesota: The Liturgical Press, 1992).
Halldorf, Peter, *Drikk dypt av Ånden. Den Hellige Ånds nærvær og gaver i den kristnes personlige liv* (Oslo: Luther Forlag, 2003). (*Drink Deeply of the Spirit. The Presence and Gifts of the Holy Spirit in the Personal Life of the Christian*).
Hareide, Sigurd, *Liturgien som teologiens kilde. En analyse av Alexander Schmemanns liturgiske teologi* (Oslo: Det teologiske Menighetsfakultetet (MF Norwegian School of Theology), special dissertation, spring 1998). (*Liturgy as the Source of Theology. An Analysis of the Liturgical Theology of Alexander Schmemann*).
Hopko, Thomas (ed.), *Women and the Priesthood* (Crestwood: St. Vladimir's Seminary Press, 1999).
Irwin, Kevin W., *Liturgical Theology. A Primer* (Collegeville: The Liturgical Press, 1990).
Kavanagh, Aidan, *The Shape of Baptism: The Rite of Christian Initiation* (Collegeville: The Liturgical Press, 1991) (first ed. 1978, Pueblo Publishing Company).

Kavanagh, Aidan, *On Liturgical Theology* (Collegeville: The Liturgical Press, 1992) (first ed. 1984, Pueblo Publishing Company).

Kvarme, Ole Christian, *Evighet i Tiden. En bok om jødisk sabbatsglede og kristen søndagsfeiring* (Oslo: Verbum Forlag, 1992). (*Eternity in Time. A Book about the Jewish Sabbath Joy and the Christian Celebration of Sunday*).

Lathrop, Gordon, *Holy Things. A Liturgical Theology* (Minneapolis, Minnesota: Fortress Press, 1993).

Lathrop, Gordon, *Holy People. A Liturgical Ecclesiology* (Minneapolis: Fortress Press, 1999).

Lathrop, Gordon, *Holy Ground. A Liturgical Cosmology* (Minneapolis: Fortress Press, 2003).

Meyendorff, John, "The Liturgical Path of Orthodoxy in America," *St. Vladimir's Theological Quarterly*, 40/1–2 (1996).

Nichols, Aidan, *Light from the East. Authors and Themes in Orthodox Theology* (London: Sheed & Ward, 1995).

Nichols, Aidan, *Looking at the Liturgy. A Critical View of its Contemporary Form* (San Francisco: Ignatius Press, 1996).

Plekon, Michael, *Living Icons. Persons of Faith in the Eastern Church* (Indiana: University of Notre Dame Press, 2002).

Ray, Walter Dean, *Lex orandi est lex credendi: Fr. Alexander Schmemann and Liturgical Hermeneutics* (Crestwood: St. Vladimir's Orthodox Theological Seminary, Master thesis, 1992).

Vogel, Dwight W., *Primary Sources of Liturgical Theology* (Collegeville, Minnesota: The Liturgical Press, 2000).

Chapter 33
Matta El-Meskeen

Samuel Rubenson

Matta El-Meskeen ("Matthew the Poor"), or Father Matta as he came to be known throughout the world, is by far the most discussed and most influential theologian in Arabic-speaking Christianity today. While other theologians from the non-Chalcedonian (or Oriental Orthodox) tradition, such as the Indian Metropolitan Paulos Gregorios and the Armenian Catholicos Aram Keshishian have had a great influence on church politics and within the ecumenical movement, the texts that Father Matta sent out from his monastery in the Egyptian desert have reached a wide public both in his own church and internationally. Despite this, his person and his writings have scarcely been noticed at academic theological institutions.[1] The most important reason for this is, of course, linguistic. Father Matta wrote all his voluminous works in Arabic, and only small parts of his writings have been translated into modern Western languages. Besides this, he was not an academically trained systematic theologian, but a spiritual writer who had read deeply both patristic and modern theological literature. His books and articles cover every conceivable theme and genre, from biblical commentaries and theological tractates to historical investigations and contemporary questions of church politics and society.

Naturally enough, Father Matta was most influential in Egypt. He was a leading figure at an early date in the monastic revival that began in the 1940s, and he soon became an uncompromising spokesman for a radical reform, on the basis of a fresh reading of the patristic literature in harmony with the new orientation that was taking place in Greek and Russian Orthodox theology. A deep-rooted conflict with the leadership of the Coptic church meant that he was excommunicated for a period; and he was marginalized in church politics up to the time of his death, assigned to a life as

---

[1] In addition to the introductions to the European translations, the most important information about him in non-Arabic literature can be found in O.F.A. Meinardus, especially in his "Zur monastischen Erneuerung in der koptischen Kirche," *Oriens Christianus*, 61 (1977), 59–70, *Die Wüstenväter des 20. Jahrhunderts*, Würzburg 1983, and "Zeitgenössische Gottesnarren in den Wüsten Ägyptens," *Ostkirchliche Studien*, 36 (1987), 202–6; and in Gottfried Glassner, "Erneuerung im Zeichen der Mönche. Das Aufblühen der koptischen Klöster und das Reformwerk des Matta al-Maskin," *Die koptische Kirche. Einführung in das ägyptische Christentum*, (Stuttgart: Kohlhammer 1994, 93–104). An overview and analysis of Father Matta's role can be found in Samuel Rubenson, "Tradition and Renewal in Coptic Theology," in Nelly van Doorn-Harder and Kari Vogt (eds), *Between Desert and City: The Coptic Orthodox Church Today* (Oslo: Novus Forlag 1997, 35–51). [Translator's note: Father Matta's name is transliterated into English in a variety of ways (see Internet). I use the form that is given in *Orthodox Prayer Life*.]

hermit and later as the abbot of a desert monastery. Nevertheless, his writings found a wide readership, first in Egypt and later in the Middle East, and finally in Europe thanks to translations into English, French, Greek, Italian, Russian, and Spanish. In a unique manner, he attracted the attention of the Egyptian state authorities and in Muslim intellectual circles in Egypt, where he was spoken of as an important cultural personality and a social reformer.

Biography

Father Matta was born in Benha in the Egyptian delta in 1919 and received the name Yusuf Iskandir.[2] He studied pharmacy and set up his own pharmaceutical company. During the Second World War, Egypt was one of the most important strongholds of the Allies in the eastern Mediterranean, and this meant good business for Yusuf Iskandir. His pharmaceutical company boomed. But like many younger Egyptians, he turned against the secular Western influence and against what he regarded as modern decadence, as well as against the Western military presence and their indifference to the situation and the interests of the Egyptians themselves.[3] Muslim men joined the Muslim Brotherhood; Yusuf joined the radical monastic reform movement that began in some of the desert monasteries. Its most prominent figurehead was Mina al-Mutawahhid ("Menas the hermit"), who was elected patriarch in 1959 and took the name Kurillus VI.[4] Kurillus combined a very radical ascetic lifestyle with an openness to the age in which he lived and an insight into the necessity of higher studies. Father Mina had himself given up a career in the civil service in Alexandria in the 1920s to become a monk and later a hermit. He was a disciple of the legendary Ethiopian monk 'Abd al-Masih ("the servant of Christ"). His radical following of Christ in the life of a desert hermit, his assiduous silence, and his utter lack of compromise left a profound mark upon the entire monastic renewal in the 1940s – including Father Matta. The centers of the renewal early on were Deir al-Suryani in Scetis, today's Wadi Natrun, with its tradition of studies, and the monastery of Saint Samuel in the desert to the south of the Fayum oasis under Father Mina as abbot; this was the strictest of the Coptic monasteries.

In August, 1948, Yusuf Iskandir sold his pharmaceutical business and went to Saint Samuel's monastery and Father Mina. On this occasion, he received the monastic name Matta (Matthew), with the addition of *el-Meskeen*, "the poor man" or "beggar." Father Matta had already encountered in Alexandria the spiritual and theological renewal that was flowing through the Orthodox churches in Europe and

---

[2] A comprehensive biography of father Matta in Arabic, *Abûnâ Mattâ al-Miskîn. As-Sîra al-tafsîliyya*, was published by the monastery of St. Macarius in 2008.

[3] The role of the Copts in the history of modern Egypt and in political life is discussed in B.L. Carter: *The Copts in Egyptian Politics* (London: Croom Helm 1986).

[4] For an insightful account of his life and work, see Nelly van Doorn-Harder, "Kyrillos VI (1902–1971): Planner, Patriarch and Saint," in *Between Desert and City*, 231–43.

the reawakened interest in the literature of the early church. In Saint Samuel's, he was able to get to know this tradition and study it in depth. He had brought to the monastery a handwritten anthology of sayings about prayer, translated from Russian by Archimandrite Lazarus Moore, and a collection of texts by Isaac the Syrian (Isaac of Nineveh) in an Arabic translation. The monastery itself possessed only one book in addition to the Bible and the liturgical books, a collection of sayings of the desert fathers that was read aloud during meals. While Father Matta was training himself in the spiritual tradition of prayer that these texts communicated, he translated Moore's anthology into Arabic. He added his own reflections and experiences of the life of prayer. His translation thus grew slowly into an extensive manuscript.[5]

After two hard years, illness (due primarily to the excessively high mineral content in the water) and famine forced the monks to leave Saint Samuel's. Father Matta was sent by Father Mina to Deir al-Suryani. This monastery had a good library and a well-educated abbot, Bishop Tawfilus. With other young and dedicated monks, Father Matta was able to study the classical texts of the Orthodox tradition. Father Matta's voluminous handwritten spiritual guidance in prayer was printed for the first time in the monastery's own printing press, under the title *Hayat as-salat al-urthuduksiya* ("The Orthodox life of prayer"). The printing was paid for by a young university teacher named Nazir Gayed, who calls Father Matta his spiritual father in the foreword to the book. Shortly afterwards, Nazir Gayed became a monk in the monastery. Much later on, he became a bishop, and then patriarch of the Coptic church as Pope Shenouda III.[6]

Father Matta's radical and uncompromising ascetic lifestyle and his teaching made him a natural leader for the younger monks, but he gradually withdrew, since he was disturbed by the interruptions to his contemplation. He left the monastery for a hermit's grotto further into the desert. Others soon followed him. They led a life in solitude during the week, and visited the monastery to take part in the community worship at the weekends. In an attempt to promote the reform of the church in connection with the abdication of Patriarch Yusab in 1954, Father Matta was appointed the Vicar of the patriarch in Alexandria, but his stay in the city was brief; after eighteen months, he gave up. He returned to Saint Samuel's in an attempt to avoid the conflicts and to concentrate on his own spiritual exercises, his studies, and his writings. It did not take long before a group of his closest disciples from Deir al-Suryani followed him. Some of these (including Pope Shenouda) were to be among the most prominent leaders of the Coptic church at a later date. Father Matta gradually emerged as the spiritual leader of the revival. Thanks to his writings, people began to talk about him in the Egyptian parishes and monasteries. At the same time, however, the revival itself, the radical monks' disobedience of the bishops, and their attraction to Father Matta were a source of turbulence.

---

[5] Father Matta himself describes this process in the foreword to *Hayat as-Salat al-Urthuksiya*. See the English translation (*Orthodox Prayer Life*, 9–12).

[6] On Shenouda and his biography, see John Watson, "Signposts to Biography – Pope Shenouda III," in (*Between Desert and City*, 244–54).

When the abbot of Saint Samuel's, Father Mina, was elected patriarch in April, 1959, the situation changed completely. Father Matta and the other monks from Deir al-Suryani were ordered to return to their monastery. In his zeal to reform the church, the new patriarch wanted to tighten up the rules for monastic life, especially with regard to obedience and submission to community life. Some of the radical young monks, including Shenouda, obeyed and returned to Deir al-Suryani, Father Matta and his closest followers disobeyed the patriarch's order and moved to Helwan, a dirty suburb of Cairo, to a community of intellectual friends of the reform, where he continued to teach and write. The tension between the ecclesiastical authority and the charismatic leadership soon became too strong, and Father Matta and his disciples were excommunicated in 1960. In order to avoid involving others in this situation, they immediately left the community and went off to Wadi Rayan, a little oasis in a valley far into the desert, south of the great Fayum oasis.

Father Matta and his closest followers lived for nine years in Wadi Rayan, until he was pardoned in spring 1969 and was called to take over the St. Macarius monastery, an ancient community in Wadi Natrun that at that time was on the brink of ruin, and to renew life there. During his time in Wadi Rayan, Father Matta wrote indefatigably on various subjects. His treatises were then printed by the brothers in Helwan and were diffused in monasteries and churches by well-educated young Copts who desired renewal and church reform. Father Matta, who lived in total separation from the world and the church, gradually emerged as the conscience and the guide of the Christians in Egypt, and soon in other countries too. Every attempt to get him to compromise or to be silent had failed.

From 1969 until his death in 2006, Father Matta was the spiritual father and undisputed leader of the St. Macarius monastery. Immediately after he and his disciples moved in, extensive restoration work on the buildings began. In the course of the 1970s, the monastery was restored and extended, and many novices entered. In ten years, the number of monks rose from scarcely ten to well over a hundred. The new monks had all studied at university and were enthusiastic disciples of Father Matta, whose articles and books circulated among young Copts at the university. The old buildings were renovated and completely new cells were built into a monastery wall, thus increasing the area of the monastery tenfold. Outside the monastery proper, large tracts of the desert were cultivated with modern methods, and the monastery soon carried out intensive agriculture, including the raising of cattle. A modern printing press was set up in the monastery, producing both the monthly periodical *St. Mark* and Father Matta's writings. The monastery quickly established good contacts with both Orthodox and Catholic reform monasteries and also became a center for an ecumenical monastic movement.

Before this development had really got off the ground, Pope Kurillus VI died in March, 1971, and Father Matta was put forward as a candidate for the patriarchal office. His name was highly controversial, and when finally lots were drawn to decide which of the three nominees should become patriarch, the lot fell on Shenouda, at that period curial bishop with responsibility for educational questions. Father Matta's reluctance to submit to the church's leadership soon became a problem for the new patriarch, who was disturbed not least by the fact that the monastery built up its own direct and close relationships to the Egyptian government and to monasteries outside the Coptic church. Shenouda reacted strongly when Father Matta opposed him by defending President Anwar Sadat in connection with the latter's visit to Jerusalem in 1977, and when Matta defied canon law by receiving a Coptic Catholic monk into the community at the end of the 1970s. Their relationship deteriorated even further when Father Matta gave his clear support to Professor George Bibawi, a prominent Coptic theologian, when he criticized traditional Coptic theology, including the theological instruction that the patriarch gave, on the basis of the church fathers and of contemporary Orthodox theology.[7] When President Sadat attempted to depose Shenouda III in August, 1981, and sent him to a monastery under house arrest, the conflict escalated. Father Matta's good relations to the President, his critical attitude to the patriarch's political conduct, and the fact that several of the bishops who temporarily took over during the Patriarch's absence were close to Father Matta disqualified him completely in the Patriarch's eyes.[8] When the Patriarch some years later not only excommunicated Professor Bibawi for heresy, but also succeeded in having him banished, the conflict took on a more clearly theological character, in which the Patriarch's right-hand man, Bishop Bishoy of Damietta, who was general secretary of the Holy Synod, came to play a decisive role.

While others assumed responsibility for the building activities and the agriculture, Father Matta devoted himself gradually from the 1980s onwards exclusively to writing. He left the monastery and moved with a few monks to a hermitage of his own near the sea, in the desert to the west of Alexandria. He concentrated now on writing detailed commentaries on the New Testament texts, but he also continued to write articles for the monastery's periodical. He won respect by refraining from direct polemic against the Patriarch or Bishop Bishoy, and also from defending himself against accusations of heresy, although these accusations gradually became more pointed.[9] His health declined seriously at the end of the 1990s, and he returned to the St. Macarius monastery, where he died in summer 2006.

---

[7] George Habib Bibawi emerged in the late 1970s and early 1980s as the most significant theologian of the Coptic church in international terms. His most important work, *Al-Qiddis Athanasiyus al-Rasuli fi Muwajaha al-Dini ghair al-Urthuduksi* (Cairo, 1985), is in the field of soteriology and investigates critically how contemporary Coptic theology has taken over Anselm's soteriology in its Protestant form.

[8] There was a lively discussion in the Egyptian press of the conflict between Father Matta and Shenouda. This is also mentioned in Mohamed Heikal's comprehensive biography of President Sadat. He writes that Father Matta was Sadat's principal adviser on church questions. See Mohamed Heikal, *The Autumn of Fury* (London: André Deutsch 1983, 156–60, 238, 257).

[9] The accusations against Father Matta culminated in a series of writings by Pope Shenouda that were published in 2004 under the title *Al-Lahut al-Muqarin* ("Comparative theology"). For a comparative study of the theologies of Father Matta and Shenouda, see Jacques Masson, "Théologies comparées: Shenouda III et Matta al-Miskin," *Proche-Orient Chrétien*, 55 (2005), 52–61.

Theological Writings

Father Matta's theological writings are very extensive and cover a wide spectrum. In addition to the larger works on prayer, the eucharist, monastic life, the theology of Paul, and a series of biblical commentaries, there are roughly one hundred shorter books in various fields, as well as the articles in the periodical *St. Mark* and a large collection of recorded sermons. Typically, many of Father Matta's texts make extensive use of texts from the early church and from modern Orthodox and Western theology. What gives his writings weight is not primarily anything original or theologically creative, but the clear anchoring in his own spiritual experience of a monastic and liturgical life, on the one hand, and the radical edge to his language, on the other.

There can be no doubt that the most widely read part of Father Matta's production is the spiritual direction in his various writings about prayer, fasting, the liturgy, Bible reading, and the feasts of the church's year. His first and fundamental work, *Orthodox Prayer Life*, appeared in 1952 and has since gone through nine editions in Arabic; it has also been translated into French, English, and other languages. In this book, Father Matta employs the literary genre we know from the collections of the aphorisms of the desert fathers and from early Christian writers such as Evagrius of Pontus and John Climacus, as well as from Olivier Clément today. In 28 systematically arranged chapters, we find Father Matta's own reflections on the essence of prayer, finished off with a total of 395 short quotations from the tradition. Father Matta's strong predilection for Isaac the Syrian is reflected clearly, but he also quotes frequently from the homilies of Pseudo-Macarius, the letters of Antony, the *Ladder* of John Climacus, and the writings of the Syriac mystic John of Dalyatha. We also find a number of quotations from Irenaeus, Augustine, and John Cassian, as well as from modern authors such as John of Kronstadt, Seraphim of Sarov, and Vladimir Lossky. For Father Matta, the center is the experience in prayer of God's presence, of the fullness of eternal life, and of unity with all that is created. Similarly, the doctrine of *theôsis*, divinization, and its presupposition in the incarnation, are the basis both here and in many of his other texts for Father Matta's teaching about prayer as an exercise in transformation.

The other writings about spiritual guidance include a large number of brief works about the great feasts in the church's year, especially Lent and Easter, some shorter texts about prayer, and an important little work about reading the Bible. Despite their small format and the relatively simple form of direct address, they contain in concentrated form the most important of Father Matta's thoughts. They show his strong emphasis on the church as a formative fellowship, its importance for solidarity across time and space, and his underlining of the necessity of spiritual training (asceticism). His pamphlet on reading the Bible points in concentrated form to the set of hermeneutical rules that we then encounter in the large-scale works of biblical theology and exegesis.

The large book on the eucharist is the most comprehensive of his works in systematic theology. Here, Father Matta takes up the liturgical renewal in the Catholic church from the mid-twentieth century onwards and in the works of the exiled Orthodox theologians; he also offers a historical and liturgical-theological analysis of the Coptic liturgy. Some of Father Matta's brief Christological texts are more fundamental, with their strong emphasis on the mystical presence of Christ in the believer's life. A number of short writings on the Holy Spirit and on the Spirit in the Christian's life are also important. Like the book on the eucharist, these belong to the group of writings that Shenouda, with his strongly Protestant starting point, criticized most sharply for not being faithful to the Bible. Some of Father Matta's ecumenical writings have attracted considerable attention, not least his two pamphlets on Christian unity,[10] in which he criticizes the official ecumenical movement with its innumerable dialogue meetings, and pleads for a deeper Christian unity based on the unity of creation and reconciliation. He gives an account of the fundamental view of the church that lies behind these writings in his most important work on ecclesiology, *Al-Kanisa al-Khalida* ("The eternal church"), first published in 1960 and since reprinted many times.

Internationally, it was Father Matta's spiritual guidance and his ecumenical appeals that attracted the greatest attention. In Egypt, the greatest debate concerned his interventions in social questions and his view of the church's role in society and in politics. He strongly criticized the Coptic church's ambitions to play a political role and the church leaders' wish to see themselves as the spokesmen of Christians in the world and their striving for secular goals. He is also critical of the establishing of ecclesiastical social institutions of various kinds. According to Father Matta, the church is a spiritual reality, and its task is of a spiritual nature. Church social welfare expresses precisely that distinction between rich and poor, between educated and uneducated, between healthy and sick that Christ abolished. Alms are only degrading and spiritually dangerous both for the one who gives and for the one who is compelled to receive. As a member of society, the Christian must do his best to work in the imperfect political and secular context in which he lives; but in the church, there must be no separation, and thus nothing that shows the poor person that he or she is poor. Father Matta urgently warns against the religious fanaticism and sectarian spirit that risks following in the tracks of an excessively politicized church. In a number of other pamphlets, Father Matta also set out his position on such controversial questions as contraception and women's role in society and in the church.

The most important of Father Matta's historical writings is his large volume on early Coptic monasticism (1972) and his large book about Athanasius of Alexandria (1981). To these we should add his little edition, with a commentary, of the Arabic version of the letters of Antony (1979). His strong commitment to patristic studies is also reflected in the solid manual *Dirâsât fî abâ al-Kanîsa* ("Manual of the church

---

[10] *Al-Wahda al-Masihiyya* (1965) and *Al-Wahda al-Haqiqiya* (1984). These have been translated into many languages.

fathers") which the monastery published in 1999. He carried out the most important basic work for this volume.

During the last twenty years of his life, Father Matta gradually devoted himself more and more to biblical theology and exegesis. The most important of these works is his commentary on the Gospel of John (1990). After an introductory volume in which Father Matta discusses the basic questions about the character and limitations of language and presents his own hermeneutic, the commentary consists of two large volumes. In the Egyptian context, it is very remarkable to see that Muslim literary scholars in academic circles took note of his hermeneutical and literary analyses of the Gospel of John.[11] Father Matta followed the publication of his three volumes on John with a number of commentaries on the Acts of the Apostles and the epistles, as well as a book about Paul.

Without claiming in any way to have offered an exhaustive description of everything Father Matta wrote, I believe that there are three central themes in his work: the incarnation, prayer, and unity. In close agreement with Athanasius and Cyril of Alexandria, Father Matta emphasizes the incarnation as the reconciliation between heaven and earth, between the divine and the human. Through the incarnation, it is possible for the human person to transform the transience of life into the history of salvation. Time's power to kill is abolished, since the world is sanctified in the mystery of the incarnation and the atonement. Like many other Orthodox theologians, Father Matta underlines the importance of the incarnation for an understanding of the creation and of nature as made holy. The fact of the incarnation is also the basis of Father Matta's strong emphasis on the church as a historical phenomenon. He insists with unusual vigor, and in agreement with modern missiology, on the importance of the inculturation and the plurality of faith in Christ. He says that it is not the church's task to appear united in itself, but rather to bring about a deeper unity in the world.

An essential key to Father Matta's theology is the strong emphasis on prayer. The human person is called to an active life, but this is meaningless if it is not grounded in prayer and contemplation, which give human life its power and its direction. It is in prayer and contemplation that the human person can keep his gaze set on the goal and prepare himself for death, which is inevitable, and for eternal life. Prayer transforms and sanctifies the one who prays and forms him or her into a true human being. In agreement with the early monastic tradition, Father Matta sees prayer as a path from practical exercises to an ability to see through things, and then to spiritual insight and seeing. His mysticism, like that of many of the monastic fathers, emphasizes joy and rest, and the possibility of seeing God that is given to us in contemplation.

For Father Matta, unity is not only a fundamental aspect of ecclesiology: it is also central to anthropology. The human person is created for unity – unity with God and with all creation. This unity presupposes equality and participation, which are continuously challenged by sin and death and must therefore be restored and sustained through active participation. This means that to acquire the virtues in

---

[11] See, e.g., the interview with Father Matta in *Alif: Journal of Comparative Poetics*, 12 (1992), 200–209.

obedience to the commandment and to strive for righteousness through humility and service, but also through suffering, tears, and prayer, is to participate in Christ's life and thus to be formed into unity. Neither Christian unity nor unity in the world is something that must be created and decided upon. This unity exists, but it must be lived. What is needed is not agreements but a living love for other persons.

Father Matta in Contemporary Theology

Father Matta's theology grew out of the life of a continuous outsider. As a young man, he encountered not only Western material and technical superiority, but also the contemptuous view that the European churches – Orthodox, Catholic, and Protestant – held of the Coptic church, which they called "Monophysite." In his own church, he soon clashed with the established hierarchy and with much of the popular religious piety on which their position was based. Even within the reform movement, he became controversial because of his reluctance to subordinate himself to the reform program of Pope Kurillus VI. Although his theological production took shape above all in the St. Macarius monastery during the 1970s and 1980s, its foundations were laid in the more isolated circumstances of Saint Samuel's and Wadi Rayan.

It is too simple to see the conflict with the church leadership, and especially with Pope Shenouda, which came to dominate the last twenty-five years of Father Matta's life, as only a personal conflict based on the path he chose for his life. On the contrary, his radicality and his theological learning – unusually broad in the Coptic context – and his literary gifts accentuated a latent tension between different groups in the twentieth-century Coptic reform movement. The reform endeavors that began in the nineteenth century under Western influence, especially from the Anglican mission, provoked a strong reaction at the turn of the century. Many of the young reform-minded Copts abandoned the church for politics at the beginning of the twentieth century, and the church leadership came into the hands of strongly conservative forces until a group of younger Copts, inspired by the 1952 revolution, kidnapped Pope Yusab III and forced him to abdicate in 1954. Those who favored reform found a home in the Sunday school movement, with its strong focus on teaching about the Bible, which had developed in the Coptic church on the Protestant model.[12] Many of the zealous young monks came from this movement, but they left the parishes and moved to the desert because they were not given the scope they wanted in parish life. The entire reform movement got wind in its sails when Kurillus VI was elected patriarch in 1959 after a long vacancy. Young and well-educated monks, especially from the Syrian monastery, were appointed to important offices and given the task

---

[12] The Sunday school movement, which is important for the Coptic church today, not least with regard to the strong Protestant influence, is presented by Wolfram Reiss: "Die Erneuerung begann in der Sonntagsschule. Geschichte und Entwicklung der Sonntagsschulen in der Koptischen Orthodoxen Kirche," *Die koptische Kirche. Einführung in das ägyptische Christentum* (Stuttgart: Kohlhammer 1994, 84–92).

of reforming the church's traditional theological education in order to meet the contemporary challenges both from Islam and from the secular West; one such monk was Shenouda III. Naturally enough, the basis for this reform was the Sunday school movement and the older Western catechetical models, which now came to be applied to the mediaeval Christian-Arabic tradition that had set its seal on the church since the Arabization in the twelfth and thirteenth centuries. This meant that the choice was made to encounter the modern age with a strategy that was completely different from Father Matta's use of modern Orthodox theology in combination with the monastic fathers.

The severest criticism of Father Matta concerns the Bible. He learned and applied modern historical-critical exegesis combined with traditional Alexandrian hermeneutics, but Pope Shenouda and other leaders in the church claimed that the way to counter Islamic accusations that the Christians had a falsified, unreliable, and contradictory sacred text was to posit the Bible as a simple, clear, and absolute norm. They argued that it was only by encouraging a strict fidelity to the Bible that the Christian minority could hold its own against both Islam and Western secularism. This is why the very severe criticism of Father Matta for being unfaithful to the Bible also crops up in the ecumenical dialogues in which the Coptic church has taken part in recent decades.

The second point on which Father Matta has been harshly criticized concerns his anthropology and the doctrine of *theôsis*. Here, it is clear that while Father Matta (like much of modern Orthodox theology) largely follows the teaching that permeates the Pseudo-Macarian Homilies, he is the object of the same kind of criticism as the Messalians in the early church. The very strong emphasis on the human person's sharing in the divine nature, on the indwelling power of the Spirit, and on the atonement as a radical liberation from the power of evil have been seriously questioned by Shenouda, whose theology is marked more by a classic Western doctrine of the atonement that strongly emphasizes the Fall, guilt, forgiveness, and grace.

Select Bibliography

Hayat as-salat al-urthuduksiya, 1952 and later. English: *Orthodox Prayer Life. The Interior Way* (Crestwood: St. Vladimir's Press, 2003).
Al-kanisa al-khalida (1960) (*The Eternal Church*).
Al-kanisa wa-l-dawla (1963) (*The Church and the Nation*).
Al-wahdah al-Masihiya (1965) (*Christian Unity*).
Kalimat Allah: shihadah wa khidmah wa hayah (1965) (*God's Word: Testimony, Service, and Life*).
Al-masih fi-l-mujtama'a (1968) (*The Christian in Society*).
Al-Qiddis Antuniyus nasik injili (1968) (*Saint Antony, an Ascetic in Keeping with the Gospel*).
Al-iman bi-l-Masih (1970) (*Belief in Christ*).

Al-Rahbana al-Qibtiyya fi asr al-Qiddis Anba Maqar (1972) (*Coptic monasticism at the time of Saint Macarius*).

Al-Ruh al-Quddus wa-amalahu dakhil al-nafs (1972) (*The Holy Spirit and his Work in the Soul*).

Maqalat bayn al-siyasa wa-l-din (1972) (*Articles about Politics and Religion*).

Al-afkharistiya wa-l-Quddas (1977) (*Eucharist and Liturgy*).

Al-Taqlid wa-ahamiyatihu fi-l-iman al-Masihi (1978) (*Tradition and its Significance for the Christian Faith*).

Rasa'il al-Qiddis Antuniyus: Talkhis al-mabadi ar-ruhiyya al-hamma (1979) (*Letters of Antony. A Summary of the Important Spiritual Foundations*).

Al-Qiddis Athanasiyus al-rasuli (1981) (*Saint Athanasius the Apostolic*).

Al-wahda al-haqiqiyya satakunu ilhaman li-l-'alam (1984) (*True Unity*).

Al-madkhal li sharh injil al-Qiddis Yuhanna (1990) (*Introduction to the Commentary on John*).

Sharh Injil al-Qiddis Yuhanna (1990) (*Commentary on John*, 2 vols).

Sharh risalat al-Qiddis Bulus al-rasul ila ahl Ruma (1992) (*Commentary on Romans*).

Al-Qiddis Bulus al-rasul (1992) (*Saint Paul the Apostle*).

Al-risala ila Ibraniyeen (1993) (*Letter to the Hebrews*).

Sharh al-risala ila Afasos li-l-Qiddis Bulus al-rasul (1994) (*Commentary on Ephesians*).

Sifr Amal al-Rusul (1995) (*Acts of the Apostles*).

Sharh risalat al-Qiddis Bulus al-rasul ila ahl Ghalatiya (1996) (*Commentary on Galatians*).

The Communion of Love (Crestwood: St. Vladimir's Press, 1984).

Chapter 34
Emilianos Timiadis

Gunnar af Hällström

Thanks to their work in the World Council of Churches, many great Orthodox theologians have become known outside the Orthodox community. Georges Florovosky made an important contribution to the preparations for the first General Assembly of the World Council of Churches in Amsterdam in 1948. John Meyendorff was the chairman of Faith and Order. Nikos Nissiotis was for many years a member of the central committee of the World Council of Churches. This group of Orthodox leaders in the ecumenical movement also includes Metropolitan Emilianos Timiadis of Silivria, who was the emissary of the patriarchate of Constantinople in Western Europe for most of his active ministry (1959–84).

At the time of Timiadis' birth in Konya (Iconium) in Turkey in 1916, there were very grave tensions between Greeks and Turks. His family was subject to harassments, and his father disappeared under mysterious circumstances. The widow and her children fled to Greece. Despite their poverty, Timiadis received a good education, first in economics in Athens and then in theology at the Halki Academy near Istanbul. After he took his doctorate in Salonika, his path turned westward, and he studied literature in Oxford. He was professor of theology at the Ecumenical Institute in Bossey in Switzerland for a time, but also at Holy Cross theological institute in the USA and at Joensuu University in Finland. Holy Cross awarded him an honorary doctorate. His lengthy period as the Genevan representative of the patriarchate of Constantinople for 25 years made Timiadis a Western European. Nationalism of every kind was alien to him. Without any doubt, his homeland was Europe, especially Western Europe. Even in his nineties, he commuted between Greece and Italy, which had become his second home. He never visited his titular diocese of Silivria, although it lies in Europe; this city to the south-west of Istanbul is now Turkish, and there is no longer any Orthodox community there. "Emilianos" is the official name that Timiadis adopted together with the title of Metropolitan. He published his writings under the name of Emilianos Timiadis. He died in February, 2008 at Egion in the Peloponnese, and was buried there.

A Theology Based on the Church Fathers

Timiadis' bibliography comprises 47 books and a hundred articles. His writings discuss everything from the problems of immigrants to contraception, but there are certain emphases that return in everything he wrote. One such emphasis is the importance of the church fathers for modern theology. Orthodox theologians operate in general with a number of well-known quotations from the Cappadocian fathers and John Chrysostom, but Timiadis lives in the whole wealth of the Greek patristic writings and builds his own theology on this. He was also very familiar with Augustine of Hippo, about whom he wrote a lengthy monograph. Other Western church fathers whom he frequently mentions with approval include Hilary of Poitiers.

According to Timiadis, the wisdom of the church fathers is both diachronic and transhistorical. It is applicable in every age. But this does not mean that theologians in every age are to repeat the old formulae of the fathers. Culture and context change, and this means that a theologian must "draw out" the applications from the patristic principles. The fathers have indicated a path, and we must continue further along this path without either trying to go backwards or standing still. Old truths must "be incarnated anew." Timiadis makes an interesting analogy between the church fathers and the eucharist: both are given, historical realities, but they continuously create something new in new human beings and new situations. This analogy illustrates well the way in which Timiadis believes the church fathers are to be applied afresh to each new generation of Christians.

Timiadis was for a long period the spokesman of the Orthodox group in the doctrinal discussions between Orthodox and Lutherans under the aegis of the World Council of Churches. He was aware that both Luther and Calvin – and indeed Karl Barth too! – often referred to the fathers. He sometimes criticizes the "sola scriptura" principle, but he acknowledges that Christians who adhere to this principle have on occasion attained greater depths than those who superficially quote the church fathers. Strictly speaking, the wisdom of the fathers is not a complement to the Bible. Rather, wisdom consists first and foremost in a correct, spiritual insight into the scriptures. To understand (Greek: *sun-ienai*) God's Word is not primarily an intellectual process, but a going (Greek: *ienai*) together with the Word. "In other words, the Bible will make sense only while travelling together with the insight, the hidden context and the very meaning along their road. The Fathers were always conscious of this key which opened the inner part of the Bible." He agrees with Athanasius of Alexandria when he affirms that scripture contains certain *ennoiai*, that is to say, meanings or ideas, that later Christian generations must uncover, interpret, and formulate anew. This is what the fathers themselves did, and every new Christian generation should do the same. Timiadis does not admit that Orthodoxy accords the church fathers the same authority as the Bible. But he holds that the fathers are "the only certain teachers of scripture." His frequent use of the fathers led to the accusation by Protestants that he had a "minimalistic use of the Bible."

The patristic inheritance includes also the Councils of the early church. Timiadis frequently comes back to this theme. He does not wish to change the dogmatic formulations of the Councils, but he returns again and again to the idea that all theology is bound to its own time and place. The theologians must express the truth of Christianity in the language of their own time – letting the propositions of the faith "be incarnated" anew, as Timiadis puts it. He also discusses in detail the so-called "canons," the practical directives laid down by the conciliar fathers. He is convinced that these canons have a pastoral and therapeutic significance for all times, but one must not have a mechanically literal relationship to them. The disciplinary decisions of the early church are edifying, provided that one looks for the love and the pastoral principles that underlie the formulations.

The liturgies of the early church also form a part of the patrimony from the church fathers. They mediate a great wealth of biblical material from one generation to the next. Timiadis holds that Luther and Calvin put an end to the liturgical tradition, with the consequence that the Reformation churches were deprived of many spiritual blessings. Thanks to the liturgical inheritance, the Orthodox church lives closer to the Bible than Protestants think.

Orthodoxy's Gift to Christendom

Timiadis makes no secret of the fact that he represents the Orthodox church. His understanding of Orthodoxy can be seen most clearly in the book *What the Orthodox Church Owes to the West* (1991). This work is marked by concern for the whole of Christendom and by an ecumenical interest. Its theme is "fraternal diakonia," help and support among brothers and sisters. A person who belongs to *one* church belongs to *all* the churches. Orthodoxy too has received many good things from the West, that is to say, from Catholic and Protestant Christians. In today's world, no church can solve the problems on its own: the contributions of all the churches are needed. But alongside this "democratic" view of the denominational church, Timiadis has another view that he emphasizes even more strongly. He sees the Orthodox church as the "Church" with a capital letter. It is there that the inheritance from the apostles has been preserved. Although the church fathers are the common possession of all the denominations, it is Orthodoxy that has preserved their teaching and spirituality. Timiadis gives some examples of this: an anthropology that emphasizes the "spiritual man," a spirituality that emphasizes God's presence, a Christianity that is contemplated and experienced as the great mystery, with continuity instead of confusion, and a rich Christology instead of an "anemic" Christology. Precisely those points that Timiadis regards as the most important aspects of Christianity have been best preserved by Orthodoxy. His argument is thus based on practical considerations, not on canon law. Deprived of fellowship with the Orthodox church, the Catholic church became legalistic, and Protestantism ended up in an overemphasis on the apostolic period. This meant that Protestantism lost many centuries of spiritual blessing. The Orthodox church has many gifts for Christendom, but Timiadis repeats one special aspect again and again, namely, holism. He writes that the Orthodox church is permeated by a basic holistic view. Christ is a wholeness; Christendom is a wholeness consisting of the Christians in heaven and the Christians on earth; and humanity is a wholeness in which the Christians are pioneers who are a leaven for the culture in which they live. Timiadis' description of Western humanity and Western Christianity emphasizes the opposite of this: individualization, atomization, and so on. One example is the

Western ideal of science, where a global and catholic view of knowledge was lost, and knowledge was thus fragmented.

Timiadis' book about Orthodoxy's contribution to Christendom contains a lengthy chapter on the physical world, on nature. He himself had a great interest on botany and zoology up to a certain level. Here, he may perhaps be following the example of Basil the Great, a church father whom he often mentions. In the *Hexaemeron*, a commentary on the creation narrative, Basil gives detailed descriptions of animals and plants and their qualities, since he is convinced that every little part of the creation has its own meaning, bestowed by the Creator. Timiadis mentions in passing that he has taken part in a world congress about spiders – something that surely very few theologians have ever done! His emphasis on the importance of nature for the Christian and for humankind in general accords well with the interest in nature that the patriarchate of Constantinople displays in modern times. Timiadis speaks of a "cosmic redemption," a restoration of the whole of creation. He also mentions a "cosmic doxology," a praise of God in which even "wild animals and stones" can take part. The human person can help bring about this cosmic event through his or her attitudes and commitment to the good of nature. Asceticism too, defined as a voluntary limitation of one's own needs, benefits the creation. But Timiadis underlines only to a small extent the meaning of the ascetic exercises for the divinization of the human person.

"Homo Oecumenicus"

Ecumenism entered Timiadis' life in a practical form already during his student days. As a young student in Istanbul, he had contact with the YMCA and the local Catholic church. As a chaplain to seafarers in Belgium and Holland from 1952 to 1959, he worked together with other denominations for the sailors' welfare. Even before that, he had listened to Reformed preachers in Scotland in order to learn how to preach central Christian truths in a living way. Interestingly enough, Timiadis never (as far as I know) mentions preaching as one of the points on which the Orthodox church is allegedly superior. As the representative of the patriarchate of Constantinople at the World Council of Churches, he came into close contact with another type of ecumenism. Work at the World Council entailed active participation in innumerable conferences and many general assemblies. Timiadis was, for example, present at the general assemblies of the World Council in Amsterdam in 1948 and Uppsala in 1968, and he was an observer at the Second Vatican Council in 1964. He had dealings with great Christian personalities such as John Paul II, Shenouda III, Visser't Hooft, Johannes Willebrands, Hamilcar Alivisatos, and Karl Barth.

There are not many Orthodox theologians who make a thorough study of Lutheran theology, but Timidias did so as a part of his official work. During his time at the World Council of Churches, he led the Orthodox delegation in the doctrinal dialogue with the Lutherans. It was during this period that he wrote his memorandum on the Confessio Augustana, entitled "Un texte inachevé." As this title indicates, his attitude was surprisingly critical. Although the Confessio Augustana is indeed "vital and creative," and contains ecclesial elements (*notae ecclesiae*), Timiadis indicates (without discussing this in detail) that there is a decisive difference in terms of the history of ideas between his own interpretation of Christianity and that found in the Confessio Augustana. This text has overlooked the important Platonic tradition and prefers something that reminds one of Stoicism. Presumably, what Timiadis misses is Christian mysticism; but the very existence of the Confessio Augustana is something of a problem in his eyes. Confessional documents may be necessary in an emergency, but this very fact means that they cannot be the normative texts for all time to come. Strictly speaking, confessional documents are not necessary. Timiadis calls them "reference points" that can exist alongside an oral interpretation of Christianity. Doxology is superior to theology. Timiadis seems to think that the Confessio Augustana is an isolated measure taken in the sixteenth century, the ideas of a group of theologians that are no longer definitive. He writes that even during the Reformation period, the Confessio Augustana was "irresolute" and "inconsistent." From Timiadis' perspective, it is not clear to what extent the Confessio Augustana wants to promote reformation or deformation, loyalty to the tradition or a rejection of the tradition once and for all. The Reformers are not content merely to correct abuses in the Catholic church; they also change the praxis of the early church. Timiadis refers here to the doctrine of confession, where a general and unconditional absolution replaces the "therapeutic" institution of penance in the early church. The Confessio Augustana makes no contribution of any kind to the liturgy, claims Timiadis, but only to doctrine; in his system of values, this is extremely negative. He regards taking part in each other's liturgy as a necessary element in ecumenical work, not least during the times of crisis that the endeavor to achieve unity will always undergo here and there.

Ecumenical work cannot build upon a downplaying of the importance of one's own denomination or upon a willingness to make compromises. As he got older, Timiadis also valued less and less the significance of doctrinal dialogues. Indeed, he sees a certain danger in "unspiritual doctrinal dialogues." Many a heresy began through the wish to define and regulate everything. In this way, many Christians have become people who wait for directives from above. For Timiadis, the ideal is as much freedom as possible. The church may well be a *complexio oppositorum* in which all the expressions of faith that are not explicitly forbidden are allowed to exist. Using a musical metaphor, Timiadis claims that polyphony is not the opposite of symphony. Nor does freedom apply only to the Christian life: it should also come into play in doctrinal questions. For example, Timiadis writes that it is not necessary for everyone to think in exactly the same way about creation and redemption. But it is clear that he finds it difficult to envisage any great flexibility on questions such as Trinitarian doctrine or Christology.

In addition to a greater openness to plurality, Timiadis affirms that work on language and terminology is an ecumenical necessity. Theology has been influenced to a large degree by the terminology of the surrounding culture. This makes it necessary to go behind the terminology to what the terminology intends to say.

Naturally, Timiadis is familiar with the idea of the bishop as guarantor of the church's unity, but he almost completely neglects this aspect of unity. This is understandable, since it is not the bishop, but the monk at prayer who comes closest to his ideal. It is above all in his book *Le monachisme orthodoxe* (1981) that he presents monasticism as "Christianity in Christianity" and the "heart" of Christianity. And according to Timiadis, it is not the individual bishop who means most for the church's unity, but the Council with both bishops and laity. He regards an ecclesiology that overemphasizes the hierarchical structure as "monophysite"; he regards an underemphasis as "Arian."

Theology of Metamorphosis

The transfiguration (*metamorphôsis*) of Christ plays an especially great role in Byzantine Christianity, not least in its iconography. Timiadis applies the idea of metamorphosis to humanity in general and to the individual Christian in particular. Christ came in order to "transform both the world and ourselves," to transform everything and everyone. Christ's church is a "workshop for sanctification on earth," an instrument for the reshaping of the world. Timiadis' interpretation of Christianity strongly emphasizes spiritual transformation, which he often calls "sanctification." In his book *Lebendige Orthodoxie* (1966), he presents the Orthodox faith for outsiders, with the concept of sanctification as his starting point. There is no standstill in the spiritual life: either it goes forward, or it goes backward. The individual human being must be transformed into the likeness of Christ; this is the same as *theôsis*, divinization. This entails that the human being makes God's moral qualities his or her own; but we cannot attain or understand God's innermost being. Timiadis holds that the church possesses all the means that a human being needs for sanctification.

Timiadis regards infant baptism as a problem. It is possible only because the godparents take the responsibility of caring for the child's spiritual growth. This reasoning is logical, if (like Timiadis) one sees Christianity primarily from the perspective of sanctification. It is easy to impose on an adult candidate for baptism the obligation to seek sanctification, but the question of children is not so simple. Nevertheless, Timiadis does not just leave the child to sit around empty, waiting for a time when it will be able to strive consciously for sanctification. He wrote a whole book about children and their spiritual development, *La croissance spirituelle de l'enfant* (1989).

The Orthodox clergy do not always grasp how important they are for the spiritual development of the parish. They often want to "hide" behind their solemn functions, such as the celebration of the liturgy. But they should not only be celebrants; they should also be pastors, that is to say, shepherds who lead the parish forward. The pastors should care for their parishes like the fathers of the church, who were passionate about teaching. However, it is the individual Christian who bears the decisive responsibility. God has "invested" a great deal in every Christian, and he expects to receive the "profits." The human person's weakened will and sin cause serious disturbances in the process towards holiness. Confession – to which Timiadis returns often, and which he discusses in detail in no less than six of his books – involves a renewed contract with God. Prayer and participation in the liturgy (especially in the eucharist) give new strength to the weakened will. Besides this, the entire church can fall into sin and be in need of improvement. Timiadis does not hesitate to speak in some passages of the church as a sinner. But the church is a sinner that brings forth saints.

Metamorphosis always occurs through the individual person, but it aims at the whole of humanity, and ultimately at the whole of creation. Everything is to be sanctified, since the whole creation is a theophany, an expression of God's being. The Orthodox custom of blessing water and praying for animals is rooted in this global view of the transformation of all things. Timiadis likes to use the word "transfiguration," and he employs an eloquent image to illustrate what he means. The evening sun beautifully gilds a landscape, but it does not change it. Metamorphosis means a new light on the individual and the world, but it does not change their innermost being. A sanctified human being is no less a human being; rather, he or she is more of a human being than one who lacks sanctification. The human being who is not sanctified is a menace to himself, to his fellow human beings, and to nature. Peoples and cultures too belong to the realities that the church wants to preserve and sanctify, although Timiadis is not unaware of the contrary examples from the colonial period. Timiadis makes special mention of the Russian and Greek cultures. It is obviously not intended that the Greek-Byzantine culture, excellent though it is, should swallow up all the other cultures. There are many people in the West who wrongly equate Byzantium with Orthodox faith in general. Science, technology, and art must likewise be brought into a relationship to God: Timiadis uses here the German noun *Gottbezogenheit*, "relatedness to God." The tragedy of the modern world is the neglect of the relationship to God. But the great privilege of Christians is that they are allowed to put everything in relation to God.

Bibliography

Primary Literature

The Relevance of the Church Fathers for Today: An Eastern Orthodox Perspective (Brookline: Holy Cross Orthodox Press, 1994).
Le monachisme orthodoxe. Hier-Demain (Paris: Buchet-Chastel, 1981).
What the Orthodox Church Owes to the West (Brookline: Holy Cross Orthodox Press, 1991).
The Ecumenical Councils in the Life of the Church (Joensuu: Joensuu University Press, 2003).
Who is our God? (Joensuu: Joensuu University Press, 2006).

Secondary Literature

"Que tous soient un!" Mélanges offerts en hommage par la Fraternité Saint-Élie à Son Éminence le Métropolite de Silyvria Emilianos Timiadis (Editura Trinitas. IASI, 2005).

Emilianos Timiadis, *Chiamati alla libertà. I fratelli e le sorelle di Bose in dialogo con il metropolita Emilianos di Silyvria* (Edizione Qiqajon. Magnano: Comunità di Bose, 2004).

Chapter 35
Johannes Zizioulas

Lars Erik Rikheim

Johannes D. Zizioulas (born January 10, 1931) is certainly one of the best known twentieth-century Orthodox theologians. His ecumenical involvement has also made him one of the theologians who are most frequently quoted and commented upon across denominational boundaries. Yves Congar called him "one of the most original and profound theologians of our age."[1] This description is due not least to Zizioulas' fundamental familiarity with both the Eastern and the Western theological traditions. He came to know Western theology *inter alia* during his studies in the USA and while he held academic positions in Great Britain. But his writings are not marked only by knowledge of various theological schools, but also by the respectful way in which he speaks of other traditions than his own. There is a striking absence of denominational arrogance and contemptuous simplifications in what he writes. Accordingly, McPartlan, who is one of the foremost interpreters and communicators of Zizioulas' theology, can write: "He has been a man of dialogue, and not only by his writings but also by his personal presence has enabled many in the West to discover and be enriched by the Orthodox tradition."[2] But Zizioulas' principal aim is not only to enrich the West with Orthodox ideas. He addresses those who experience the tragedy of the division of the church between East and West, the fact that the church does not "breathe with both its lungs." He writes for those who long for a reunion of the two.

Biography

Zizioulas began his theological studies at the Universities of Salonika and Athens in the early 1950s.[3] He spent a semester doing further studies at the ecumenical institute in Bossey near Geneva in 1954–55. This was his first encounter with the West, and proved to be a decisive year of study for the 20-year-old theologian, since it was here

---

[1] Yves Congar, *Bulletin d'écclésiologie* (1982), p. 88.
[2] From a letter to the author.
[3] There is little available written material about Zizioulas' academic career. The following overview is based largely on the presentations by Patricia A. Fox and Paul McPartlan. For more biographical information about Zizioulas' formative years as a theologian, see Gaëtan Baillargeon, *Perspectives Orthodoxes sur l'Eglise-Communion, L'œuvre de Jean Zizioulas* (Paris: Médiaspaul, 1989).

that he became seriously involved in ecumenism, which was to shape the future course of his life and work. In the same year, he received a grant from the World Council of Churches, and went to the USA at the end of the semester to take his Master's degree at Harvard. The teachers whom he encountered included Georges Florovsky in patristics and Paul Tillich in philosophy.

The Russian Orthodox émigré theologian Florovsky had played a central role in ensuring an Orthodox presence in the World Council of Churches in 1950. He came to have a powerful influence on Zizioulas, whose studies he directed as patristic scholar and ecumenical theologian. Both men are spokesmen for the same agenda: modern Orthodox theology must work to achieve a *neo-patristic synthesis* that can lay the foundations for a re-established unity between East and West. These theologians are deeply convinced that the authentic catholicity of the church must embrace both traditions. The expression "neo-patristic synthesis" is borrowed from Florovsky and is used by Zizioulas in *Being as Communion*.

After his military service, Zizioulas returned to Harvard with a three-year grant. In this period he worked simultaneously in two fields of research, with the intention of submitting two doctoral theses, one at Harvard on the Christology of Maximus the Confessor under the guidance of Florovsky, the other at the University of Athens on the church's unity in the bishop and the eucharist under the guidance of A.G. Williams, who was professor of church history at Harvard.

During his stay in the United States, Zizioulas also taught at the Russian Orthodox seminary of Saint Vladimir in New York, where he met two other prominent theologians, John Meyendorff and Alexander Schmemann, who, like Florovsky, had earlier worked at Saint-Serge in Paris. They had studied under Nicolas Afanasiev, who is best known for his eucharistic ecclesiology (which Zizioulas was later to criticize for fundamental reasons).[4]

In 1964, Zizioulas returned to Athens, where he was appointed professor of church history in 1965. In 1966, he defended his doctoral dissertation *Enotes tes Ekklesias en te Theia Eucharistia kai to episkopo kata tou treis protous aionas* ("The unity of the church in the divine eucharist and in the bishop during the first three centuries"). At this time, he was also active as a member of two working groups in the Faith and Order commission of the World Council of Churches. Later, he was also elected a permanent member of the commission, and he spent two and a half years in Geneva, where the contact with Protestants, Catholics, the Pre-Chalcedonian churches, and the Orthodox churches were strengthened and developed. While he was learning about these various traditions, he was gradually consolidating his own position as spokesman for his own tradition. In 1970, he left Geneva to teach patristics at the University of Edinburgh. Three years later, he became professor of systematic theology at the University in Glasgow, where he remained until 1986, when he was "summoned

---

[4] What Zizioulas criticizes is not the choice of the eucharist as the decisive ecclesiological principle, but the imbalance between the local and the universal church in Afanasiev's presentation.

from the ranks of the laity" to be ordained and assume the task of Metropolitan of Pergamum, becoming a member of the Ecumenical Patriarchate in Istanbul.

Zizioulas has also taught at the University of Salonika and has held guest professorships at universities in Geneva and London and at the Gregorian University in Rome. He was also one of the founders of the International Commission for Theological Dialogue between the Orthodox and the Roman Catholic churches in 1979. He remains a member of this Commission, and is also a participant in the international Anglican-Orthodox dialogue.

Theological Writings

Zizioulas did most of the work on his dissertation *Enotes tes Ekklesias* in the USA. It was published already in 1965, the year before he defended it at the University of Athens. It was subsequently translated into French, and an English translation was published in 2001 (see bibliography).

His first publication after his dissertation was the article "La vision eucharistique du monde et de l'homme contemporain," in the periodical *Contacts* (1967). This was originally a lengthy lecture that Zizioulas held at a congress in Salonika in 1966 about "The Orthodox church and the world."

During his time at the universities of Glasgow and Edinburgh, Zizioulas published numerous articles in various periodicals. Some of these, reflecting his patristic and ecumenical interests, were collected later and published in French in the book *L'Être ecclesial*. He revised a number of these articles and published them in the book *Being as Communion: Studies in Personhood and the Church* (1985), which is certainly his best known and most influential work, and must indeed be regarded as his *chef d'œuvre*. This was followed up in 2006 by a new study, *Communion and Otherness. Further Studies in Personhood and the Church*, edited by Paul McPartlan, who is himself an important interpreter and communicator of Zizioulas' theology.

In addition to these books, Zizioulas has written a number of articles; a complete overview up to 1993 will be found in Paul McPartlan's *The Eucharist Makes the Church*. With regard to Zizioulas' view of the church's apostolicity, which I discuss and comment upon in the present chapter, we should mention an article published in 1996, in which he explores this theme more deeply: "Apostolic Continuity of the Church and Apostolic Succession in the First Five Centuries."

In his article "The Early Christian Community," Zizioulas briefly comments on several of the themes he discusses more comprehensively elsewhere. For those who have not read him and want to get to know Zizioulas better, this article is a good place to start.

Important Secondary Literature

Several books are devoted in part to the study of Zizioulas' theology. Two of the best known are Paul McPartlan's thorough analysis of Zizioulas' ecclesiology in *The Eucharist Makes the Church. Henri de Lubac and Johannes Zizioulas in Dialogue* and Patricia A. Fox's *God as Communion. Johannes Zizioulas, Elisabeth Johnson, and the Retrieval of the Triune God*. Fox has written an interesting book from the perspective of feminism and liberation theology about Zizioulas' Trinitarian theology and the relevance of this theology to our modern understanding and interpretation of the profession of faith in the triune God. A collection of articles about various aspects of Zizioulas' writings was published in 2007. There are 12 essays in *The Theology of John Zizioulas – Personhood and the Church*. Several of the contributors discuss the criticism that has been made, above all in the Orthodox Anglo-Saxon context, of Zizioulas' reflections on Trinitarian theology and his defense of the ontology of a person. This book also gives bibliographical references to other studies of Zizioulas' work.

The Principal Themes in His Writings

Zizioulas discusses a large number of themes in his books and articles. He reflects on Trinitarian theology, Christology, and pneumatology; theological anthropology; the theology of the ministry and of the sacraments; and above all, the eucharist. He comments on these themes in an ecumenical spirit, in the light of the church fathers and of the challenges posed by modernity, and in the framework of one particular understanding of the ontology of community and of the person. The themes are almost always related to his understanding of the church. It is primarily in connection with ecclesiology that Zizioulas has attracted attention.

The tradition from the Greek fathers plays a central role. A return to the patristic sources means that theology finds its orientation and is anchored in the assembly that celebrates the worship of God: in the liturgy. This is a central perspective in Zizioulas' writings. Among the writers of the Greek patristic tradition, he refers with particular frequency to Ignatius of Antioch, the Cappadocian fathers, and Maximus the Confessor. He argues that their contributions have a strongly ecumenical character and relevance. As we shall see in connection with Zizioulas' presentation of the church's apostolicity and ministries, the tradition from Ignatius of Antioch is a decisive corrective to an excessively institutionalized concept of the church. In the case of the Cappadocian fathers, it is above all their contribution as bridge-builders between the Antiochene and the Alexandrian worlds that make them "catholic" and "ecumenical" teachers.[5] References to the fathers also bring equilibrium to the classical controversy about the relation of the Spirit to the Father and the Son. One example is the way in

---

[5] "The teaching of the 2nd Ecumenical Council on the Holy Spirit in Historical and Ecumenical Perspective," in J.S. Marins (ed.), *Credo in Spiritum Sanctum* (Rome: Libreria Editrice Vaticana, 1983), Vol. 1, p. 39, n. 29.

which Maximus the Confessor refutes the Byzantines' suspicion that the Romans had fallen into heresy with regard to the Filioque. According to Zizioulas, Maximus the Confessor is a very important figure who can help us make progress towards our goal of understanding one another better, and of finally achieving a definitive unity between East and West in the understanding of pneumatology.

Isolation, radical individuality, or total autonomy – this is not the human person's vocation. The human person is called to fellowship and to reciprocal relationship with others. Just as God is a fellowship of Persons, so too the church is a fellowship of persons. In the light of this idea of fellowship, the concept of *koinônia* is fundamentally determinative of Zizioulas' ecclesiology. He proposes an ontological understanding of fellowship, and thus also of the person. There is a Western tradition that largely gives priority to the individual, understood as substance and being. Zizioulas counters this by emphasizing the patristic insight (which is developed especially in the Trinitarian theology of the Cappadocian fathers) that being and substance must be transcended by a person's ontology – an ontology that is necessarily anchored in the idea of a fellowship. The confession of faith in the one God is a consequence of the confession of faith in God as Father, that is to say, as Person.

This ontology of the person and of fellowship is a recurrent theme in Zizioulas' writings, and lays down very specific paths for his theological reflection. The significance of the church's fellowship or of the local eucharistic fellowship cannot be reduced to a practical arrangement whereby the sacraments are celebrated and received in view of the sanctification of the individual. On the contrary, the fellowship is ontologically determinative of the *ekklêsia*. In other words, the church as *koinônia* ("fellowship") belongs to the very definition of the church's nature. This has far-reaching consequences. One area in ecclesiology that is directly affected here is the view of apostolicity. I shall now attempt to specify what such an ontological definition of the church implies for ecclesiology by presenting some aspects of Zizioulas' interpretation of the church's apostolicity, continuity, and succession. This is one of the most central themes in his principal work, *Being as Communion*, and he discusses it in detail in other articles.

First, however, I must draw attention to the framework or fundamental structure of ecclesiology in Zizioulas, namely, the relationship between pneumatology and Christology. The individual ecclesiological themes, including the question of the church's apostolicity, are anchored in this context, and the account he gives of this is one of the most characteristic aspects of Zizioulas' writings. We find a detailed presentation in *Being as Communion*, where one chapter is entitled "Christ, the Spirit and the Church."[6]

---

[6] Zizioulas, *Being as Communion* (New York, 1985), pp. 123–42.

The Church in Christ and in the Spirit

According to Zizioulas, the different ways of thinking about the church in the Eastern and the Western traditions are reflected in the relationship between Christology and pneumatology. Where the West has given the priority to Christology, the East has emphasized pneumatology and eschatology. The result is that the West has come to regard the church much more strongly as a continuation of the incarnation, and has evaluated the church on the basis of innerworldly categories. Zizioulas sees this way of thinking as typified by concepts such as *history* and *tradition*. The pneumatological accentuation that has been prominent in the East has given ecclesiology a predominantly eschatological character. He argues that the emphasis on this aspect has however sometimes tended to detach the church from history, with catastrophic consequences *inter alia* for the church's missionary task. Nevertheless, the Eastern church's emphasis on pneumatology, especially as this is expressed in the church's liturgical life, has saved it from various forms of clericalism and anticlericalism that have played such a disastrous role in the history of the Western church.

According to Zizioulas, the relationship between Christology and pneumatology raises two questions that are decisive for ecclesiology. The first concerns the priority between the two. Is Christology to be determined by pneumatology, or should the opposite be true? The second question concerns content. When we speak about Christology and pneumatology, what specific areas in Christian doctrine do we have in mind? The problem posed by the first question can already be seen in the earliest part of the tradition, both in the New Testament and in early Christian liturgies. In the New Testament, we find affirmations that the Spirit is given or mediated by Christ ("For the Spirit had not yet come, because Jesus had not yet been glorified," John 7:39), but also the view that Christ does not exist before the Spirit is active, as we see in connection with the texts about the baptism of Christ (in Mark) and his biological conception (in Matthew and Luke). According to these texts, the Spirit is not only a forerunner who announces the coming of Christ, but also the one who brings about his very identity as Christ.

Zizioulas recalls that the early church's Trinitarian faith entails that God's action vis-à-vis his creation *ad extra* is one and indivisible. Where there is the Son, there are also the Father and the Spirit; and where the Spirit is, there are also the Father and the Son. However, each of the divine Persons contributes in his own way to the realization of God's redeeming plan in the dispensation of salvation. God's action is one and indivisible, but at the same time Trinitarian; it is one and indivisible, but not undifferentiated.

The characteristic of the Son is that he has become incarnate. He has become *history*. This cannot be said of the Father and the Spirit. They are involved in history, but they have not become history as the Son has.

With regard to the Spirit, there are two characteristics that Zizioulas especially emphasizes. The specific activity of the Spirit in the history of salvation is to free the Son from the limitations of history. The Son dies on the cross and shows that he is subject to the conditions of existence in history, but the Spirit raises the Son from the dead (cf. Romans 8:11). The Spirit is the one who is *outside* history, and the Spirit's work is to bring into history the "fulfillment," the *eschata* of God. The basic mark and specific quality of pneumatology is its eschatological character. The Spirit makes the Son an eschatological reality, the last Adam or (as Paul says) "the new Adam." In other words, the Spirit makes the Son the representative of humankind. He makes him exemplary.

Another characteristic of the Spirit and of the Spirit's presence in history is that he not only makes Christ one, one individual. He makes him many. It is because of the Spirit that we can say that Christ has a body, and thus that we can speak of the church as Christ's body. "For through one Spirit we were all baptized to become one body," writes Paul (1 Cor 12:13), and he links the Spirit directly to *koinônia* at 2 Cor 13:13: "The grace of our Lord Jesus Christ, the love of God, and the fellowship [*koinônia*] of the Holy Spirit be with you all." The fellowship into which the Spirit leads and which he sustains is the body of Christ, the church. In this sense, the mystery of Christ is also a mystery of fellowship. The unity between Christ and his members, between the one and the many, is understood in the light of a so-called corporative personality that is determinative of the identity of Christ. Zizioulas refers to this corporative unity in a variety of contexts. This idea has fundamental consequences for ecclesiology; indeed, it is a key to understanding his ecclesiology.

For Zizioulas, it is not enough to say that eschatology and fellowship are "fundamental" for pneumatology and ecclesiology. These pneumatological elements must be made *constitutive* of ecclesiology. In other words, the church's very nature, or its ontology, must be described in terms of eschatology and fellowship. The Spirit does not breathe life into a church that already exists: the Spirit *creates* the church. This means that pneumatology concerns, not the church's *bene esse*, but its *esse*. The Spirit is not a power that is added onto the being of the church: the Spirit *is* the very being of the church. The church is constituted by means of eschatology and fellowship. In this sense, pneumatology is an ontological category in ecclesiology.

Despite his positive evaluation of the Second Vatican Council, Zizioulas points out that a pneumatology of this kind is not to be found in the conciliar documents. Several Orthodox theologians have criticized the ecclesiology of the Second Vatican Council for giving the impression that the church and its structures are already established before the Spirit comes into the picture.[7]

Apostolicity

What are the consequences of Zizioulas' understanding of the place of pneumatology in ecclesiology for his view of apostolic continuity? In the light of what he writes about the relationship between Christology and pneumatology, it is not surprising that he draws a distinction between two fundamental and different meanings of the term "apostolic" as applied to the church. He calls one meaning "historical" and the other "eschatological." The Western church has favored the historical meaning, but the

---

[7] See Zizioulas, *Being as Communion*, pp. 123 and 141–2.

eschatological understanding has been dominant in the Eastern church. However, the eschatological understanding of the church has been communicated, not in manuals of theological doctrine, but in liturgy and iconography. He explicitly states in *Being as Communion* that this disproportion between the *lex orandi* and the *lex credendi*, between liturgy and theological reflection, in Zizioulas' own Orthodox tradition is one of the reasons that prompt him to make his theological contributions. And we cannot fail to see the ecumenical relevance of emphasizing this perspective, which has largely been forgotten. The two perspectives, the historical and the eschatological, are not mutually exclusive, but if each is taken on its own, it leads to different views about how a church understands its apostolicity. Zizioulas proposes a synthesis between the two, and he claims that this was the case in the early church.

When he speaks of the historical meaning of apostolicity, Zizioulas points to a missionary context. The apostles are presented as autonomous individuals, to some extent independent of one another. They are entrusted with a message, they are furnished with authority, and they are sent out to all the peoples. The essential point in this context is that the apostle represents a point of contact between Christ and the church. Continuity is described here as a movement that begins in God. God sends Christ, Christ sends the apostles, and the apostles communicate the message of Christ by establishing churches and appointing overseers (*episkopos – presbuteros*). Within this linear and historical understanding of continuity, Christ can also be called an "apostle" (Hebrews 3:1). And it is in such a historical or "missiological" context that the handing over of apostolic authority to other persons, in order to carry out this mission, is mentioned (cf. Acts 20:17–35; 1 Timothy 5:22; 4:4; 2 Timothy 2:2; Titus 1:4; 2:1–15; etc.).

The eschatological understanding of apostolic continuity is different. This tends to speak of an anticipation of the accomplishment of history. Here, the apostles are not depicted as single individuals who hand on the Gospel and their authority to other single individuals, but as a college gathered around Christ who carry out their function under his supervision. Zizioulas refers here to the New Testament texts that depict the apostles as *the twelve* or as a *college* linked to their eschatological function, that is to say, in relation to that time in salvation history when the kingdom of God is revealed and accomplished. The most important passages here include the Gospel accounts of Jesus' Last Supper (especially the pericope in Luke) with their clearly eschatological tone (cf. Matthew 19:28; Luke 22:30; Acts 1:12–26; 2:17). The apostles are not those who follow Christ and are sent by him, but those who accompany him and are gathered around him *in the same place*. According to Zizioulas, the difference between the depiction of the apostles as individuals and as a college corresponds to the difference between mission and eschatology. Mission presupposes that the apostles are sent to all the peoples who are spread over the face of the earth, while the *eschata* entail a *gathering together* of these peoples. This does not mean that Zizioulas overlooks the eschatological character of mission; but he draws a distinction between eschatology, understood as a movement and a direction, and eschatology understood as a state. As a movement, eschatology is the result of a historical process: it is the high point of mission. As a state, eschatology confronts history with a presence of the kingdom of God here and now, and this presupposes that God's scattered people – and the apostles – are gathered together.

The apostles' relationship to Christ and to the church is very different in the two models. In the historical model, they follow Christ and function as a link between Christ and the church. In the eschatological model, they do not follow him, but are gathered around him. Nor do they function as a link between Christ and the church within a historical process; on the contrary, they are themselves the ground and foundation of the church in the presence of the kingdom of God here and now.

Zizioulas writes in several places about the development of these two models in the post-apostolic church. He interprets Clement of Rome, the author of the First Letter of Clement at the close of the first century, as an example of the historical approach to apostolicity, where it is viewed as a linear movement. Clement writes that the apostles appointed presbyter-bishops as their successors (1 Clement 42.1–4; 44.1–4), and these texts have played an important role in the contemporary discussion of the apostolic succession.

The eschatological model, which can be seen especially in the Syrian-Palestinian tradition, has a formative and normative function for the early church. Zizioulas writes that Ignatius of Antioch (at the close of the first and the beginning of the second centuries) is an early representative of this tradition. The pictures of the eucharistic assembly to which Ignatius points is drawn, not from history, but from the eschatological state of the church gathered *in the same place* in order to share in God's eternal life, which is mediated to creation at the eucharistic altar. Zizioulas argues that the ministries and their structure in the eucharistic assembly in the letters of Ignatius must be understood on the basis of their eschatological background.

The one bishop in the assembly – it is in Ignatius that we encounter the so-called monarchical episcopate for the first time – is surrounded by a college of presbyters, but also by the deacons and the rest of the assembly. Ignatius identifies the bishop with Christ and the Father. He thus sees the apostles as present, not in the bishop, but in the college of presbyters, who are (logically enough) described as a council of apostles. This picture reflects precisely the structure that we find in the New Testament texts mentioned above. However, this does not mean that the presbyters are charged with the "apostolic succession." The individual ministries are defined by their relationship to one another, and this is an ontological relationship. Accordingly, if we wish to speak of the church or of its apostolicity, it is not enough to speak of the bishop. We must also include the presbyters, the deacons, and the ministry of the believers. "Without these, one cannot speak of a 'church'," says Ignatius. It is thus the eucharistic assembly as a whole that can be said to constitute the church's apostolicity.

Zizioulas writes:

> Continuity here is guaranteed and expressed not by way of succession from generation to generation and from individual to individual, but in and through the convocation of the Church in one place, i.e. through its *eucharistic structure*. It

is a *continuity of communities and Churches* that constitutes and expresses apostolic succession in this approach.[8]

The eschatological understanding of apostolicity thus entails that it is the fellowship as a whole, and the relationships between the individual ministries – rather than one particular ministry alone – that express the church's apostolicity. Zizioulas accords a prominent and normative place to Ignatius' thinking. Each Christian is assigned one particular place (*ordo*, from which "ordination" is derived) and has a role to carry out in the eucharistic assembly. The structuring of this assembly is not fortuitous, but is determined by the eschatological picture of the church, of the apostles who are gathered around Christ and the whole of God's people. This excludes every form of causality whereby the ministry of the one is the cause of the ministry of the other. The episcopal ministry itself would be completely incomprehensible if it were not seen in its eucharistic context and in relation to the other ministries (see *Being as Communion*, pp. 192–3). The ministries, including the ministry of the believers, must thus be regarded as contemporaneous realities, for it is only in this way that they can manifest the church's eschatological state. Contemporaneity is one of the most central concepts in Zizioulas' conceptual apparatus. This perspective also makes it clear that the fellowship as such is constitutive of the church, and hence also of the church's apostolicity.

Some important and interesting conclusions are drawn when Zizioulas compares the historical and the eschatological understandings of apostolicity, which are expressed in these and other texts. He begins by pointing to the understanding of continuity. In the historical approach, there is a transmission from the past to the present, and on into the future. This may involve the transmission of power and authority, or of something normative that is to be imitated, and continuity is to be understood as retrospective in relation to the past. The apostolicity of the church comes from the past.

According to the eschatological understanding, one cannot speak of transmitting authority or of copying a normative period. Here, the church's apostolicity comes not from the past, but from the future, as an anticipation of the church's nature in its fully realized state. Zizioulas underlines that such an anticipation must not be confused with a feeling of expectation. This is not a psychological anticipation. It communicates a real presence of the *eschata* here and now, in the sense that lies in the Johannine *nun*, "now." Apostolicity is thus related to the full realization, and thus on the deepest level to the risen Christ – that is to say, to the ultimate goal of all things.

As I have mentioned, the relationship between Christology and pneumatology is the framework of reference for ecclesiology in Zizioulas. This relationship is directly affected by the two ideas about the church's apostolic origin. In the historical understanding of continuity, Christology dominates. The church's apostolicity is anchored in an event or in an act of institution from the post that is transmitted by means of specific structures. In this context, the Spirit must be understood both as the

---

[8] "Apostolic Continuity and Succession," in Zizioulas, *Being as Communion*, p. 177.

one who is transmitted by Christ, and is dependent on him, and as the divine power that gives life to structures that already exist. "Here Christology indicates a self-defined event and so does the notion of the apostolate" (*Being as Communion*, p. 179).

In the eschatological understanding, it is the Spirit himself who creates these structures and who makes the church apostolic through the structure of fellowship. The Spirit creates or constitutes the church. The Spirit is not only a life-giving power in the history of salvation. He is also the Lord – *Kyrios* (cf. the Nicene creed) – who makes the *eschata* present in history. History thus becomes not merely a distant past that we remember, but also a presence of the future. Zizioulas typically points in this context to the early church's eucharistic anamnesis (the "remembrance" in the eucharistic prayer; cf. the liturgy of Saint John Chrysostom) where not only Christ's cross, death, resurrection and ascension are recalled, but also his second coming. This paradox of a memory of the future, where that which is remembered is made present through the Spirit, also determines how the church's apostolicity is understood. This comes to us not only from the past, but also from the future. This means that apostolic continuity cannot be reduced to an arrangement that takes the form of a transmission of authority from one person to another or within an apostolic college, as is the case in the historical view of apostolicity.

When the historical, linear understanding of apostolicity became dominant in the church, it was sufficient to speak of an unbroken chain of episcopal ordinations, since this established the apostolic succession (as if this were a mechanical activity). It also led to a detachment of the apostolic college from the church's eucharistic fellowship and the idea that this college stood outside and above the eucharistic fellowship. This made it possible to see titular and auxiliary bishops as an ecclesiological normality.

The understanding of continuity that Zizioulas proposes must be understood as:

> ... a continuity of identity of each local Church with the eschatological community as it was originally expected in and through the original church of Jerusalem and as it is, ever since the destruction and dispersion of this community, experienced in the New Jerusalem coming down from heaven, in the community of the Eucharist. Faithfulness to this eschatological community was in this case [i.e. in the first centuries of the church] the main requirement in the search for apostolic continuity and succession.[9]

According to Zizioulas, a pneumatological ecclesiology entails that the church cannot find any absolute guarantees in history, neither in ministries nor in sacraments nor in the apostolic succession. The church must invoke the Spirit continually, in order to become what it is in Christ. The church must do what the apostles did: they had received the Spirit from the risen Christ and they continued to invoke the Spirit. The epicletic dimension in the church's liturgy bears witness to a corresponding logic. "[...] the 'words of institution' and the entire anamnetic dimension of the Church

---

[9] "Apostolic Continuity of the Church and Apostolic Succession in the First Five Centuries," p. 164.

are placed at the disposal of the Spirit, as if they could not constitute in themselves a sufficient assurance of God's presence in history."[10]

There is however no contradiction between history and the *eschata*. The incarnation shows us that history can be the bearer of the definitive and the absolute. Indeed, history can be the bearer of God's life. This is why the synthesis between history and eschatology finds its most sublime expression in the eucharist, which is at one and the same time tradition (*paradosis*) and remembrance (*anamnesis*), the past and the future. According to Zizioulas, it is this synthesis between history and eschatology that constitutes the church's sacramental nature.

This means that the eucharist activates the church's historical consciousness in a retrospective way. At the same time, the eucharist is the church's eschatological moment *par excellence*, a remembrance of the kingdom of God. The eucharist is the space where God's scattered people, spread over the whole earth, are gathered in one and the same place, where "the many" are united in "the One," and where God's eternal life is tasted here and now.

Zizioulas writes that in the eucharistic celebration, the church in its fully accomplished – eschatological – state is both present and formative for the earthly church on its pilgrimage. It follows that no ordination can take place outside the local eucharistic assembly, since it is in this assembly that God's eschatological assembly is present. The historical or institutional continuity is thus determined by the eucharistic assembly. This in turn means that every *ordo* or ministry in the church, including the ministry into which one is introduced by baptism, is a bearer of apostolic continuity. The ministry of the laity is thus also ontologically indispensable for the apostolic character of the church.

With his focus on the eschatological and eucharistic fellowship, Zizioulas has contributed a necessary and fruitful new perspective to the ecumenical debate, and not least to Western theology, which has largely been marked by an apparent contradiction between institution and charism, between Spirit and ministry. As one who transmits the shared Christian tradition, a builder of bridges between East and West, and a man with roots in the tradition from the fathers of the undivided church, Zizioulas helps shed a new and fresh light on traditional theological problems.

Bibliography

Primary Literature

A complete overview of publications up to 1993 will be found in McPartlan, *The Eucharist Makes the Church* (Edinburgh: T&T Clark, 1993).

---

[10] Zizioulas, *Being as Communion*, pp. 187–8.

Enotes tes Ekklesias en te Theia Eucharistia kai to episkopo kata tou treis protous aionas (Athens, 1965). English: Elisabeth Theokritoff (trans.), *Eucharist, Bishop, Church: The Unity of the Church in the Divine Eucharist and the Bishop During the First Three Centuries* (Brookline: Holy Cross Orthodox Press, 2001).

Being as Communion. Studies in Personhood and the Church (New York: St. Vladimir's Seminary Press, 1985).

Communion and Otherness. Further Studies in Personhood and the Church, Paul McPartlan (ed.), (London: T&T Clark, 2006).

"Apostolic Continuity of the Church and Apostolic Succession in the First Five Centuries," in James F. Puglisi and Dennis J. Billy (eds), *Apostolic Continuity of the Church and Apostolic Succession* (Louvain Studies, 1996).

"The Early Christian Community," in Bernard McGinn, John Meyendorff and Jean Leclercq (eds), *Christian Spirituality – Origins to the Twelfth Century* (New York: Holy Cross Odtodox Press, 1993).

Secondary Literature

Paul McPartlan, *The Eucharist Makes the Church. Henri de Lubac and Johannes Zizioulas in Dialogue* (Edinburgh: T&T Clark, 1993).

Patricia A. Fox, *God as Communion. Johannes Zizioulas, Elisabeth Johnson, and the Retrieval of the Triune God* (Collegeville: Liturgical Press, 2001).

Douglas H. Knight, (ed.), *The Theology of John Zizioulas – Personhood and the Church* (Burlington: Ashgate, 2007).

PART V
British and American Theologians

Chapter 36
Austin Farrer

Margaret Yee

Although Austin Farrer would not ever have considered himself "a great theologian," he has been deemed by distinguished thinkers as *"the one genius"* of twentieth-century Anglican theology. Amongst those who have publicly accredited him with honour is The Most Revd Dr Rowan Williams, former Archbishop of Canterbury, whose tribute to Farrer remains indisputable—"Possibly the greatest Anglican mind of the 20th century."

This chapter will seek to pinpoint the primary reasons why Farrer's contribution to metaphysics and theological thought has been seen as not only important for *twentieth-century* modern theology, but indeed *likely to have even greater impact in the twenty-first century*.[1]

At his untimely death in 1968, aged 64, Farrer was Warden of Keble College, Oxford. He had first come to Oxford as a Scholar of Balliol, where he took firsts in Honour Moderations in 1925, in Literae Humaniores in 1927, and in Theology in 1928. His exceptional capacities had won him the Craven Scholarship in 1925 and the Liddon Studentship in 1927. In 1931 he became Chaplain and Tutor at St Edmund Hall; was Speaker's Lecturer from 1937 to 1940, and from 1935 to 1960 was Fellow and Chaplain of Trinity College. In 1960 he was appointed Warden of Keble.

Unknown to him, on December 22, 1968 he was to preach his last sermon at St Andrew's Church, Headington, entitled "The Ultimate Hope," which was broadcast on BBC Radio. His unexpected death seven days later came as a dreadful shock to colleagues, friends and family alike. The significance of his words on Resurrection Hope resonated in sombre remembrance:

> My precious truth is this: that Christian hope is not one thing, but two. It works on two levels, and they are equally vital. There's hope for this world; and there's hope for a world beyond it. There's hope for this world so long as it lasts ... For our God is a God who does nothing in vain. He has not put us here to waste our time, or to suffer mere frustration; there's something to be done here for God's glory, and for man's well-being. [...]

---

[1] Margaret Yee, "The Human Person – Picking up the Dropped Baton," in Ian Weeks and Duncan Reid (eds), *A Thoughtful Life: Essays in Philosophical Theology* (Adelaide, 2006), pp. 177–80.

There's hope on the short view, hope within the world, that something can be made of it. But beyond that there's hope in the long view ... So there are two levels of hope.[2]

"A Bigger View of the World"

Throughout his life, Farrer's thought engaged with what may be described as *"a bigger view of the world."* The philosophical complexities, arising from such *inclusive* thinking in which spiritual things were incorporated, remained problematic. How was one to state in a rational and credible manner the perceptions which theologians affirmed were intrinsic to divine revelation, but which *logical positivists* (a school of philosophers, mathematicians and scientists emanating from the 1930s Vienna Circle) had argued were unverifiable?

In such an academic climate, the demise of metaphysics appeared inevitable, though clearly not for all! In 1947, a group of scholars in Oxford known as *"The Metaphysicals"* began meeting together. Austin Farrer was one of its foundation members. As he was often to say, whatever one's starting point inevitably one will be confronted with theological concerns, for the divine/human relation is integral to life itself.[3]

His persistent and illuminative endeavours to re-state in credible terms the relation of the "short" and "long views," namely the human and the divine, are what ultimately led to his being recognized as a *formative theologian* of the twentieth century. Two characteristic descriptions of his understanding of the divine/human relation emerged, which he referred to as (1) "the causal joint" and (2) "double personal agency" acting. This terminology, specially chosen by Farrer, provides the *clue* to the particular approach he adopted for tackling the enigmatic factors which had long baffled the most learned of minds.

As a *practical* man, as he was often to describe himself, he realized that in day to day living one was at times conscious that there was "something more" to sheer human existence. However, the impossibility of reconciling human and divine realities continued to prove perplexing. This was not only true for theologians but virtually for any person interested in establishing the nature of human existence or the meaning of ultimate reality. Even in our contemporary world, as the sciences explore evolution and consciousness via *reductionist* methods in search of a unified theory of reality, the re-emergence of *emergence* is becoming increasingly unavoidable. As Farrer was prone to argue, in the very living out of one's life, a *non-reductionist* account seemed a more likely explanation. Could this apparent *hiatus* between the divine and the human be overcome?

---

[2] Austin Farrer, "The Ultimate Hope," in *A Celebration of Faith* (London, 1970), pp. 117 and 118–19.

[3] Austin Farrer, "A Starting-Point for Philosophical Examination of Theological Belief," in Basil Mitchell (ed.), *Faith and Logic* (London, 1957).

Reconciling the Divine and the Human

As early as 1943, Farrer's first major work in philosophical theology, entitled *Finite and Infinite*,[4] was published. The possible reconciliation of concepts of divine nature with human nature was explored in different ways. His earlier philosophical writings, however, restricted by Aristotelian *formalism*, did not encompass the personal aspects of *voluntarism*. Thus, in his later revised preface to the second edition of this book, published in 1959, his adoption of a personal metaphysics was made explicit. Whilst the idea of God had been understood in Aristotelian thought as *Actus Purus* or "Absolute Being," Farrer argued that the Analogy of Being needed instead to be understood in *voluntarist* terms. This shift represented what in modern-day terms would be described as *a philosophy of action*. Thereafter, *Divine Being* came to be expressed as *"agency acting"* and *"being as becoming"* in contrast to more static concepts.[5] As a consequence, an immeasurable vitality was introduced into his philosophical writings.

Implementing Three Innovative Steps

Metaphysical personalism Farrer held that theological reflection needed to depart from a rigid Aristotelism which he found prevalent in Thomism, though he remained committed to the formalist demands of rational enquiry to which Thomists adhered and of which he fully approved. In his revised preface to *Finite and Infinite*, we find the *first* of a number of innovative moves. His shift to metaphysical personalism marks a prime emphasis which he considered essential in order to re-state traditional theology credibly without loss of its essential richness.

This initial move methodologically to bring vitality to his philosophical writings was concurrent with the liveliness in his biblical thought and hermeneutical tasks. In fact, one may well surmise that in his daily plumbing of the depths of St Mark, St Matthew or St John, the dynamic force of the texts were themselves making a considerable impact on his reflection. In his book on biblical interpretation, *A Rebirth of Images*, he made clear that in such engagement new insights continued to emerge. We find him arguing that academic acuteness of thought would be lost if such developments of thought, often requiring adaptation or change, were not treated as seriously as new learning in any other discipline, be this in the sciences or the humanities.

A multi-disciplinary and inclusive approach In 1948, in his second major philosophical writing entitled *The Glass of Vision* we discover the very heart of his theological thought. The "turning point" rests in his method of approach to what he described

---

[4] Austin Farrer, *Finite and Infinite* (London, 1943; second edition, 1959 with revised preface, London, 1966). Please note: hereafter, full details of all Farrer's major publications mentioned in this article are provided in the bibliography.

[5] Ibid., p. 21; Austin Farrer, *The Glass of Vision* (London, 1948), pp. 3–11, 40–43; Austin Farrer, *Faith & Speculation* (London, 1967), pp. v, 61–7, 140–41.

as the *"Images of Revelation."* Confronted with investigating the form of revelation in Christian thought, the images of revelation in which he espied divine/human action were what led him to devise a *second* innovative move. His decision to centre on the *human imagination* with its symbolic capacities provided him with the required arena. The shift envisaged also engendered a broader, multi-dimensional framework of thought conducive to theological explanation.

In retrospect, this innovative approach can be described as *multi-disciplinary* and *inclusive* in form:

1. It was *multi-disciplinary* as it was extended to ensure exchange with other disciplines such as history, psychology and ethics to test the full legitimacy of theology's own subject matter. Insights and knowledge from other disciplines needed to be addressed. The rational demands of such exchange could test the legitimacy of theological thought. Nevertheless, theology still retained its own subject matter.
2. It was *inclusive*, as it enabled discussion of theological concepts to be pursued critically and rationally without exclusion, thereby avoiding any likely distorted outcome in one's findings.

His adventurous move heralded the means by which the multi-dimensional character of theology could be critically assessed and its contribution to academic learning appropriately considered.

Farrer's illuminative method, carefully crafted and presented in his eight Bampton Lectures, is articulated with exemplars in *The Glass of Vision*. He states that three things – the sense of metaphysical philosophy, the sense of scriptural revelation and the sense of poetry *"rubbing against one another in my mind, seem to kindle one another, and so I am moved to ask how this happens."*[6] Recognizing that the major stumbling-block for theologians in a rational world was their claim to "Revelation," his central attention in the lectures was given to investigating *"the form of revelation"* and its possible justification.

In order to appreciate the import of his methodological approach, a more detailed account is necessary to indicate why these innovative moves proved so significant for theology.

The human imagination and the images of revelation   Along with his *second* move to study Revelation using what in the modern world can be described as a *multi-disciplinary* approach, Farrer introduced a *third* innovative step. In so doing, he shifted attention to two *very different* areas of thought for exploring how apprehension of divine revelation was possible. These were: (1) the human imagination per se and (2) how the human mind is able to perceive "something more" than mere human things. From these two very different perspectives he was able to argue that just as the human mind is able to reach heights of inspiration, distinguishable from psychologically weird

---

[6] Farrer, *The Glass*, p. ix.

and abnormal phenomena, similarly in discerning spiritual things, characteristic of their own particular form, one could be inspired to apprehend, through the human imagination, the "images of revelation."

Here, it is important to note that Farrer was in no way appealing to "guaranteed proofs" for scriptural claims; nor did he wish to appeal to the rigidity of a legalistic approach as others had done. Further, whilst well aware of the old propositional revelation, he himself sought to describe the dynamic character of scriptural revelation as "images" and not "propositions" per se.

There is a paramount reason for this distinction. His purpose may virtually be seen as the *key* to his theology. Having shifted attention to the *human imagination* as the central focus of his reflection on Revelation, it followed that the term "images" was best able to describe the *form of that revelation* which he argued was apprehended by *a movement of thought*. He considered the term "images" to be more appropriately representational of the poetical sense by which the dynamic meaning of divine/human action in scriptural revelation was conveyed than the term "propositions." Revelation was perceived by the human imagination in the form of "lively images," actively engaging the human mind to apprehend divine/human action. Once apprehended, such reflection could be portrayed in language, which was capable of encapsulating this sense of meaning. Thereafter, the metaphorical capacity of language enabled the lively character of Revelation to be more adequately referred to and communicated. As discussed more fully by recent writers such as Janet Martin Soskice in her book *Metaphor and Religious Language*[7] the capacity of metaphor to *refer to* or *signify* spiritual things was a function that had been well understood by Farrer:

> The images themselves are not what is principally revealed: they are no more than instruments by which realities are to be known. The inspired man ... does not think <u>about</u> the images, but about what he takes them to signify.[8]

Whilst therefore language could refer to things that were human, finite and confined to this world (Farrer's "short view"), at one and the same time it had the capacity of pointing to things beyond, to recognition of spiritual things such as the divine, the infinite, the transcendent (the "long view"). Thus, he maintained that in Revelation, the "infinite" is *shadowed forth* in the "finite":

> When finite objects happen to have been brought into such a mental focus that they are capable of acting as symbols of the infinite, then the mind's power to know the infinite leaps into actualisation, seeing the finite in the infinite, and the infinite in the finite.[9]

---

[7] Janet Martin Soskice, *Metaphor and Religious Language* (Oxford, 1985).
[8] Farrer, *The Glass*, p. 57.
[9] Ibid., p. 90.

Divine Action, History and Revelation

Hence, for Farrer, in the actions of Jesus, the distinctive characteristics of divine action are revealed. In the sayings, parables, teachings and actions of Jesus, his earthly life, his trial, his suffering, his crucifixion and death, are portrayed the lively images and significance of divine revelation. These take place in a historical context.

Just as major concepts are developed and formed in ordinary everyday living, similarly major spiritual concepts, which he came to name as "dominant images," develop, giving breadth and depth to theological understanding.

They are apprehended and lived out in action in what he was later to describe as "the life-in-grace." It is in interpreting the images of revelation that we also engage with the mind of Christ, which is transforming of human thought and action.

The language and literature of scripture, understood in this poetical sense as the "images of revelation," are able to convey these living images from generation to generation. As such, a long tradition of lived belief unfolds as divine action, functioning concurrently with human action, is apprehended. The *locus* of inspiration is the human mind. Its subject matter is the "images." The "images" are the *instruments* of Revelation. The action, expressing the Revelation takes place in human history. Its significance is recognized by human minds. Here we have divine/human coincidence.

From the above discussion, it should now be obvious why in 1959 Farrer considered it necessary to affirm explicitly his emphasis on *action and activity* in his revised preface to *Finite and Infinite*. Once the *form of revelation* was understood as a function of the human imagination, a personal metaphysics was indispensable. Revelation was in essence a divine action apprehended by human minds as they came into focus with the mind of Christ, lived out in the life, teachings and action of Jesus.

The significance of such action rested in the close interaction of images and events, when actual happenings in a historical context bore the marks of divine/human activity. "Images" fusing together, signified meaning in a way mere concepts derived from propositions could not encapsulate. The primary mode of revelation, once understood as images, signified the reality being lived out.

> Poetry and divine inspiration have this in common, that both are projected in images which cannot be decoded, but must be allowed to signify what they signify of the reality beyond them.[10]

Images and Christian Doctrine

In wrestling with the nature of divine/human coincidence emanating from the Doctrine of Incarnation, Farrer was well aware that an even greater hurdle was awaiting him with the Doctrine of the Trinity. How was one to account for the

---

[10] Ibid., p. 148.

paradoxical statements concerning the three-in-one or for that matter the one-in-three?

It is at this point that the full impact of his *second* and *third* innovative moves can be demonstrated poignantly. In using a *multi-disciplinary approach* and identifying the *locus of inspiration as the human imagination* with its *"lively images" as the mode of Revelation*, he had, in effect, mapped a voluntarist metaphysic for theology in which the relations of the Godhead in the Doctrine of the Trinity as well as the relation of divine/human coincidence in the Doctrine of Incarnation could be credibly accounted for. In what can be described as his *theology of action*, the rationally problematic relations in the Godhead of Father, Son and Holy Spirit, and the lively activity implicit in divine/human action in the Person of Jesus could effectively be shown as made manifest in an imaged form:

> The great images interpreted the events of Christ's ministry, death and resurrection, and the events interpreted the images; the interplay of the two is revelation.

Divine/human meaning is conveyed through Jesus' actions:

> the primary revelation is Jesus Christ himself ... The actions of Christ's will, the expressions of his mind: these, certainly, are the precious seeds of revelation.

Hence, he described the revelatory significance of this "seamless" divine/human action as follows:

> Christ does not save us by acting a parable of divine love; he acts the parable of divine love by saving us.[11]

Incarnational theology is set in place. The perplexities of divine/human coincidence are no longer rationally problematic once understood in the form of images rather than propositions. Similarly, unless understood as "images of revelation," the doctrine of the Trinity would remain obscure. The old scholastic way *"to hunt for propositions"* or the new scholastic way of painfully seeking *"to count and classify all the texts in St. Paul or St. John"* where the three Persons of the Trinity were found to be mentioned or connected with one another he considered simply futile. Religious experience itself or religious formulae were judged also as inconclusive in substance or unhelpful. Alternatively, to recognize that the *locus* of inspiration was the human mind, where the liveliness of such understanding is conveyed from the Mind of Christ to the mind of the Apostles and to the mind of believers engaged in the "life-in-grace," enabled one to account for how such richness and divine fullness of the great and dominant images of revelation came to be apprehended. In addition, he reminded his readers that some dominant images are given wholly as dominant, as in the case of the great image of the Holy Trinity, in which the relations of Godhead are at once signified:

---

[11] Ibid., p. 43, p. 40; and Austin Farrer, "Revelation" in Mitchell, *Faith and Logic*, p. 99.

> If we want to find the Divine Trinity in the New Testament, we must look for the image of the Divine Trinity ... The Trinity is one of the images that appear, it is not a category of general application. When we have isolated the image of the Trinity, and studied it in itself, we can then proceed to ask what place it occupies in the world of the New Testament images – whether dominant or subordinate, vital or inessential: and how other images are affected by it.[12]

First and Second Causes—"Double Personal Agency"

Farrer's biblical, metaphysical and poetical skills continued to enlighten and illuminate his theological reflection. At the metaphysical level he could equally be engaged with expounding how second causes (human action) were contingent on first causes (divine action). The Creator (divine agent) creates the creature (human agent). The creatures are capable of acting individually, each to their own will. Independent beings exclude other beings. A created human individual is not an ass, any more than an ass is a human being. Finites exclude one another. However, the individual mind is capable of both finite and infinite thought at the one time. These are not in contradiction. Finite minds (human action) in particular focus with Divine Will (divine action) are capable of reaching heights of inspired excellence. This he called "Double Personal Agency" acting. The "Causal Joint" described the causal relation of divine/human action by which such action was enacted:

> We can set no limits to the supernatural enhancement God can bestow. He who has by a first act created us, harmoniously extends our operation by a second. There is nothing non-human in what we are thus enabled to do: it is not the act of some other creature tacked on to us; it is simply the act of man enabled to receive divine communication ...
>
> Thus, in exercising such an act, we are aware of going into a new dimension, but we are aware of no discontinuity.[13]

Given such understanding it becomes clear that, for Farrer, the divine/human coincidence was a *seamless garment* in which the "causal joint," exhibiting "double personal agency" acting was made manifest. He argued that difficulties only arose when the divine/human relation was addressed as a *temporal* instead of a *logical* relation.

---

[12] Farrer, *The Glass*, p. 47.
[13] Ibid., p. 33.

A Science of God?

Meeting Empirical Demands

Such implications were often spelled out more fully in his sermons of which there are many in which academic thought and practical living were intertwined. Most significant among these for contemporary thought are his Lenten Sermons, published in Europe in 1966 as *A Science of God?* and in the United States as *God is not Dead*; and re-issued as *A Science of God?* by SPCK, London, with a new foreword by Margaret Yee in 2009. In succinct form, Farrer made explicit the empirical demands of scientific enquiry which are incumbent on all critical research, theology included. In *A Science of God?* he gives a full explication of the Creation of Life and the God of Nature. At the scientific level, he grappled with cosmological arguments relating to the origin of life and the universe, persuaded that the *theory of evolution* could be encompassed within theological reflection. On the other hand, he maintained that an argument based solely on astrophysics lacked adequacy of explanation for that "something more" observed in practical, everyday life. Indicating the reasons for what in contemporary times may be described as *emergence*, he extrapolated from such to explanations of possible origins. This inevitably engaged him in discussions of a Creator and the relation of God and Nature. As a consequence, kernels of thought in his writings foreshadow ways to approach issues concerning human personhood, which in a technologically advanced scientific world have become central issues for theology.

A Seamless Whole

Farrer also addressed the wider issue of human consciousness in *The Freedom of the Will* and questions concerned with evil, suffering and the Love of God in his book *Love Almighty and Ills Unlimited*. However, his major importance as a *formative* theologian of the twentieth century rests in his distinctive methodological approach. In maintaining the richness of tradition, he ensured continual renewal in theology by pinpointing its dynamic activity. Most significant of all, his innovative moves, as discussed above, enabled him to articulate the relation of *human* and *divine* action as a *seamless whole*. From this lively base, he was able to open up an academically meaningful arena for theologians to continue exploring transcendent, multi-dimensional horizons using critical skills. The outcome achieved bore a mark of uniqueness, suggesting a route by which perplexing concerns of divine/human relation could be addressed rationally.

In a highly secular and scientific world, in which biotechnology is changing the face of humanity with regard to cloning, chimeras and embryonic stemcell research, the question of "what it means to be human" is becoming increasingly unavoidable. Undoubtedly the benefit of an innovative approach such as Farrer's opens up a positive direction for dealing with complexities in human personhood. His methodology provides a more inclusive outcome in which divine conditions would not necessarily be overlooked. By proposing "a bigger view of the world," in which both empirical and cognitive factors are also kept in close interaction, as is fulfilled in scientific exploration, Farrer mapped a route by which theology could make its contribution effectively to interdisciplinary debates. His approach made it possible for notions of transcendence to be taken into account seriously as ongoing explorations into human life were pursued. He thereby showed how a more holistic understanding of "what it means to be human" could be pinpointed and its implications followed through. Once a multi-disciplinary, inclusive and critical appreciation of "what makes a human person human" is achieved, such outcomes are capable of (1) universal application, and (2) offering a more comprehensive account of human life than "reductionist" or "utilitarian" approaches seem able to do.

Concluding Thoughts

The above reconsideration of Austin Farrer's methodological approach to theological reflection has attempted to demarcate the principles of enquiry which place him amongst the formative theologians of the twentieth century. It has been suggested that the marked significance of his studies may well have an important bearing on theology in the twenty-first century. In expounding tradition and renewal for his own age, Farrer's illuminative method of approach has continued to inspire a number of learned scholars ever since, and may well "come into its own" deservedly in our contemporary times.

There has been a long-standing *Anglophilic* interest in his thought which has engaged theologians and philosophers in North America and the United Kingdom. In 2004 an international conference in celebration of the centenary of his birth was held in Oriel College, Oxford, and papers published in the book *The Human Person in God's World*. In addition, there is a growing interest in Farrer in continental Europe, following papers presented on specific areas of his thought at the *Sophia Europe* 2005–8 conferences. Implanting of his metaphysics and philosophical theology globally has been initiated in wider fields via exchange with academics in Australasia, India, Africa, South Africa and Japan. In Oxford, a small group of scholars from biblical, theological and philosophical areas, who have benefited from the inspiration of Farrer's thought and learning, continue in reflection. Numbered amongst these are two of his last students, Professor John Barton, Oriel and Laing Professor of the Interpretation of Holy Scripture, Oxford, and Dr John Muddiman, New Testament Studies, Oxford.

In contemporary times, it is suggested that Farrer's thought, especially his emphasis on the images of revelation and the human imagination, could prove particularly valuable for scholars working in the field of Patristics, and wrestling with methodological questions related to Christian Doctrine. His work has importance also for the sciences, life sciences and social sciences in which issues related to the origins of life and the universe still remain enigmatic. It is hoped that studies such as these and similar areas of development will attract scholars in the future to take up yet unexplored implications of the riches of Farrer's metaphysics and philosophical theology. The establishing of The Austin Farrer Fund in memory of a distinguished former Chaplain was made with one such intention in mind.[14]

Whilst controversy may well emerge from an undertaking of this kind, especially with those who have vigorously maintained that Farrer was ultimately a "process theologian" influenced by Charles Hartshorne and A.N. Whitehead's philosophy, there are just as many at present who would resist any such ascription, believing him to have been more concerned with tradition and renewal. Interestingly, Farrer simply described himself as involved in a "theology of process" rather than explicitly in "process theology" per se. Thereby hangs a yet unresolved tale! What can be affirmed with confidence is that his innovative moves and their impact on serious thought continue to prove extraordinarily illuminative in the most unexpected ways.

It is perhaps fitting, therefore, to close this chapter with words spoken in tribute to him by Basil Mitchell:

> Austin Farrer was by common consent, one of the most remarkable men of his generation. He possessed the qualities of originality, independence, imagination and intellectual force to a degree amounting to genius, and the word was sometimes used of him ... His scholarship was immense ... his intellectual activity was like a flame ... sometimes fierce, sometimes wayward, but always casting unexpected light.[15]

Bibliography

Primary Literature

Finite and Infinite (London: Dacre Press, 1943) (2nd edition, 1959 with revised preface; also published by Macmillan and Humanities, 1966).
The Glass of Vision (London: Dacre Press, 1948) (Bampton Lectures).
A Rebirth of Images, the Making of St. John's Apocalypse (London: Dacre Press, 1949).
A Study in St. Mark (London: Dacre Press, 1951).
St. Matthew and St. Mark (The Edward Cadbury Lectures 1953–4; London: Dacre Press, 1954) (2nd edition, 1966; also by Macmillan).
The Freedom of the Will (London: A. & C. Black, 1958) (Gifford Lectures for 1957).
"A Starting-Point for Philosophical Examination of Theological Belief," in Basil Mitchell (ed.), *Faith and Logic* (London: Allen & Unwin, 1957).

---

[14] The Austin Farrer Fund was launched on the occasion of the celebration of the 400th anniversary of the consecration of the Trinity College Chapel in 1994 in memory of a distinguished former Chaplain. Intended to support candidates for postgraduate study in Theology or Philosophical Theology who have not secured awards from major funding bodies. Offered alternate years, sufficient to cover college fees (about £1,500 GBP p.a.). Priority given to internal candidates.

[15] Austin Marsden Farrer Tribute in Farrer, *A Celebration*, p. 13.

Love Almighty and Ills Unlimited: An Essay on Providence and Evil; Containing the Nathaniel Taylor Lecture for 1961 (New York: Doubleday, 1961).

"The Ultimate Hope," in *A Celebration of Faith* (London: Hodder & Stoughton, 1970), pp. 117 and 118–19.

A Science of God? (London: Bles, 1966) (published in the United States as *God is not Dead* (New York: Morehouse-Barlow, 1966); re-issued *A Science of God?* (London: SPCK, 2009) with new foreword by Margaret M. Yee).

Faith and Speculation: An Essay in Philosophical Theology, Containing the Deems Lectures for 1964 (London: A. & C. Black, 1967).

Secondary Literature

Hebblethwaite, Brian, *The Philosophical Theology of Austin Farrer* (Leuven: Peeters, 2007).

Hebblethwaite, Brian and Douglas Hedley (eds), *The Human Person in God's World: Studies to Commemorate the Austin Farrer Centenary* (London: SCM Press, 2006).

Hebblethwaite, Brian and Edward Henderson (eds), *Divine Action* (Edinburgh: T&T Clark, 1990).

Hein, David and Edward Henderson (eds), *Captured by the Crucified: The Practical Theology of Austin Farrer* (New York and London: T&T Clark International, 2004).

Loades, Ann and Robert MacSwain, *The Truth Seeking Heart* (Norwich: Canterbury Press, 2006).

Slocum, Robert B., *Light in a Burning-Glass: A Systematic Presentation of Austin Farrer's Theology* (Columbia: University of South Carolina Press, 2007).

Soskice, Janet Martin, *Metaphor and Religious Language* (Oxford: Clarendon Press, 1985).

Yee, Margaret, "The Human Person – Picking up the Dropped Baton," in Ian Weeks and Duncan Reid (eds), *A Thoughtful Life: Essays in Philosophical Theology* (Adelaide: ATF Press, 2006), pp. 177–80.

Yee, Margaret, "Austin Farrer's Science of God" in Miklos Vetö (ed.) *Philosophie, Théologie, Littérature. Hommage à Xavier Tilliette, SJ pour ses quatre-vingt-dix ans.* (Éditions Peeters, Louvain-Paris, 2011).

Chapter 37
Michael Ramsey

Rowan Williams

"For God ... made his light to shine in our hearts to give us the light of the knowledge of the glory of God in the face of Christ." (2 Corinthians 4:6) It is a text that could plausibly stand as a summary of everything Michael Ramsey[1] believed mattered most in Christian life and theology.[2] The best work to be written on his theology to date has the simple title *Glory: The Spiritual Theology of Michael Ramsey*, and anyone at all familiar with his writing will know the omnipresence of this theme. But Ramsey's theology was not just a celebration of the divine radiance or beauty; or rather it was a celebration of divine beauty which assumed that 'the knowledge of glory' was more than merely a metaphor for the enjoyment of that beauty. Ramsey spelled out in several places the sense in which the Pauline phrase was a quite specific prescription for doing theology. And in this, as in many other ways, he stood close to perhaps the greatest theological mind in twentieth-century Roman Catholicism, the Swiss Hans Urs von Balthasar, whose first major multi-volume work on theological method was entitled *Herrlichkeit*, 'Glory'. Indeed, as we shall see, the connection was more than a matter of parallels: Balthasar uses Ramsey's work in some key sections of his discussion of the New Testament, and helps us see where the Archbishop's fundamental theological insights might lead if developed more systematically.

The Glory of Christ's Face

The implication of Paul's words is that the face of Christ – not just the narrative of Christ or the words of Christ or even the work of Christ – is a source of knowledge because it is the bearer of glory. And early in his work on *The Glory of God and the Transfiguration of Christ*, Ramsey undertakes a careful study of the basic meanings of 'glory' in Jewish Scripture that begins to make sense of this in a way that takes

---

[1] Michael Ramsey (1904–88) was the Archbishop of Canterbury from 1961 to 1974. In addition to the influence he had as a Church leader, Ramsey also published many important theological works. He became Canon Professor of Theology at Durham University in 1940 and Regius Professor of Divinity at Cambridge in 1950. In 1961 he was appointed Archbishop of York, and five years later Archbishop of Canterbury.

[2] Rowan Williams, 'Theology in the Face of Christ', in *Glory Descending: Michael Ramsey and His Writings*, edited by Douglas Dales, John Habgood, Geoffrey Rowell and Rowan Williams (Norwich: Canterbury Press, 2005), pp. 176–87. Reprinted by permission.

it beyond a simply aesthetic response to revealed beauty. Like Balthasar again, he is concerned – though he would not have expressed it in these terms – to create a theological aesthetic, a doctrine of beauty anchored in consideration of God's own nature. 'Glory' is a word that expresses the internal solidity of some reality – it may be wealth or power or reputation, as in various passages from the Psalter and Isaiah, but it may also be the internal life of a person, as in Psalms 16 and 108, and Genesis 49:6. The root *kbd* expresses weight or magnitude; the verb *kabed* means to be heavy, to be many, to possess honour (just as we call someone a weighty person) – though also, by a quite understandable paradox, it can mean being dull or sad.

God's glory is thus, in this context, not only God's radiance, the visible form of God's power; it is inextricably linked with some idea of God's character, God's life. As Ramsey points out in these early pages of his book, the promise in the prophets that God will in the last days or in the new age manifest his glory is connected with the manifesting of God's justice: what is revealed is who God is. 'In the kabod of Yahveh,' he writes, 'radiance, power and righteous character are inextricably blended.' It is as if the word described the inner 'resource' of God, that which grounds and informs God's substantial, objective presence, a presence that is fleetingly uncovered in theophanies in the Hebrew Scriptures but whose full manifestation in the world awaits the last days. In the meantime, however, there is one setting in which we can say that the glory of God is regularly present and effective in ancient Israel – the Temple, upon which glory descends at its consecration (2 Chronicles 5.13–14), in which Isaiah encounters the glory that confers on him his prophetic vocation (Isaiah 6), from which glory departs in Ezekiel's vision (Ezekiel 11.22–3). In the Priestly writings, this is first associated with the tabernacle in the wilderness and then with the Jerusalem Temple – a perceptible presence, whose virtually physical quality is vividly expressed in the statement in 2 Chronicles that the priests could not stand to perform their duties when the cloud of God's presence descended. Although this manifestation seems less to do with character than some others, as Ramsey points out, it is worth noting that it functions in the texts referred to as a sort of intermittently visible sign of divine fidelity to Israel, so that it is not exactly neutral in respect of God's character. Against this background, it is clear that the conception of glory in the face of Christ immediately speaks of Christ as revealing the divine character, the inner integrity of God, as we might put it, in the promised last days. If we say that we have seen glory in him, we recognize that the messianic age has come. Ramsey shows how both Paul and John work with this idea. Paul declares that Jesus already fully inhabits and diffuses glory, so that believers are promised both the vision of that glory and a share in its light: they too will be radiantly transfigured presences. Already we reflect glory when our faces are turned to Jesus; in the age to come we shall do so completely in our whole (renewed) material identity. For John, Jesus' journey towards the Cross is the record of a gradual unveiling of glory, moving in exact step with the outward closing in of Jesus' mortal fate: the Cross is in this sense the eschatological moment, the new age breaking in as its *kairos* arrives, and the followers of Jesus who have seen his glory gathering throughout the ministry have been made ready to receive the outpouring of the Spirit on the day of resurrection. They begin thereby to enter the state of glory promised them in Jesus' prayer in John 17; the mission that was Jesus' now becomes theirs by the gift of the Spirit, and if Jesus is glorified by the performance of his mission from the Father, so believers, working and witnessing in the Spirit, are equipped to share the same glory.

Glory and the Cross

What is new in John, and decisive for Ramsey's theology here and elsewhere, is the focus upon John's association of glory in its fullness with the Cross. The glory of Jesus in the Fourth Gospel is always related to what might be called the 'other-directedness' of Jesus' vision: he receives glory from the Father because he does what he sees the Father doing, he accepts his identity, his destiny, from the Father's hand, so that his glory is always that of a Son whose being is derived from the Father's (John 1:14). Since the Cross is the climax of Jesus' obedience to the Father's will, it is the moment in which he is most entirely receptive to the glory given by the Father. On the Cross, he has nothing of his own: he 'hands over his spirit' (19:30) and becomes wholly transparent to the divine presence and action in that moment of self-dispossession. Already in *The Gospel and the Catholic Church*, Ramsey had emphasized that in the New Testament the distinctive sense of 'glory' was given by its association with 'self-giving',[3] with a self having 'its centre in Another',[4] so that the disciples are summoned to share in the divine unity by sharing in the divine 'self-negation'. And while this may be disputable as a general judgement on the New Testament's vocabulary, it is obvious that Ramsey sees the Fourth Gospel as providing the ultimate integrative principle for the rest of that vocabulary. It is perhaps also worth noting that he will have known the passing comment of his teacher, E.C. Hoskyns, on John 1:14, that two texts in Leviticus (9:6 and 9:23) associate the manifestation of God's glory in the Tabernacle with the hour of sacrifice.[5] Given that, as Hoskyns also noted, the incarnate Word in the Fourth Gospel is understood as one 'whose Body is the numinous Temple of God',[6] the connection of thought is very plain.

Ramsey as an Exegete

This is already a rich vein of exegetical reflection, and it was to be steadily mined in various ways by Ramsey in practically everything he wrote in the rest of his career. My question is how these themes can now help us 'plot' the locus and path of theology in a time when the biblical theology of Ramsey's era is largely forgotten

---

[3] Michael Ramsey, *The Gospel and the Catholic Church* (London: 1936/1956. Reprinted in 1990), p. 92.
[4] Ibid., p. 25.
[5] Edwyn Clement Hoskyns, *Fourth Gospel* (London, 1940), p. 148.
[6] Ibid., p. 149.

or rejected. Ramsey's method of exploring and aggregating the meanings of key words in Scripture has long been overtaken by new techniques of textual analysis and historical research; as John Court observes in a critical essay on Ramsey as exegete, the theological dictionary is the typical deposit of this style of theology, with its assumptions that 'biblical' concepts in general are naturally distinctive and that they have a sort of intrinsic directedness towards a full and normative explication in the pages of the New Testament. The effect is to obscure the real distinctiveness of specific texts and traditions from each other and to flirt with a supersessionist attitude to Jewish words and meanings.[7] While there may be some debate about how just this assessment is overall, it is certainly true that Ramsey's approach seems to reflect a 'dictionary' method. I want to ask how seriously this affects the essence of what he is arguing, before going on to see what further development of his basic ideas may be possible.

First of all, it is indisputable that, for example, *kabod* in Hebrew has precisely the physical connotations that are important to Ramsey and that we understand something of the word's use when we grasp this; and Paul's passing use of the phrase 'the weight of glory' suggests that he is not unaware of this background. Equally, it is clear that many of the texts of Christian Scripture under discussion are consciously reflecting on the complex of uses and meanings in Hebrew Scripture. Indeed, the truth is that, for the writers of the New Testament, the theme of God's glory is already a literary and theological datum; as Ramsey notes, it is something discussed in Jewish literature of the period. For the early Christians, it is, so to speak, already a 'dictionary' issue – that is, it has become one aspect of the literary unity that is 'Scripture' for Paul and his contemporaries. They are doing biblical theology: they are treating the texts of Hebrew Scripture as a synchronic reality, something that can be engaged with as a coherent whole. Of course there are differences between Hebrew usages and between different New Testament responses to them. But there is more of a continuum than a critic might at first allow. And one of the interesting features of some recent New Testament scholarship is, ironically, the recovery of certain lost or obscured themes that draw diverse material together: the significance of the ritual and myth of the Temple for the entire period, to take a pertinent example, has been identified more decisively than ever.

So it would be a mistake to conclude that Ramsey's method is as artificial as Court seems to suggest. Undoubtedly, scholarship has moved on; but its movement has not nullified the idea of searching for thematic connections. Reference to the Temple in recent exegesis points up very clearly the significance for first-century Jewish people of the building and the sacrificial system as concrete embodiments of divine presence. That Temple-related language is so widely spread in the New Testament writings implies that it was indeed debates over the location of divine *kabod* that fuelled much of the earliest Christological reflection. Certainly for Johannine thought, the actual material presence of Jesus is in the strongest possible sense the habitation of *kabod*; and it is not fanciful to see in the falling-back of the soldiers confronted with Jesus in

---

[7] R. Gill and L. Kendall (eds), *Michael Ramsey as Theologian* (London 1995), p. 97.

Gethsemane a serious echo of Old Testament imagery such as that in 2 Chronicles: here too glory has a presence as powerful and exclusive as that of a material other, it impinges on those in its field of force. We are not dealing with a simple manifestation of divine radiance, but with something apprehended as both more continuous and more active. Granted the reservations that may be entered against certain versions of 'dictionary theology', the fact is that John's Gospel in particular is a complex single text reflecting on a complex scriptural heritage that is seen as a unified whole. It is not an arbitrary exercise to trace theological continuities and implications in such a setting.

John's Gospel famously lacks a transfiguration narrative: when those around Jesus see or are invited to see his glory, it is not an exceptional visual phenomenon that they are directed to. They see (or fail to see) in the context of Jesus' human activity – and ultimately in the context of his human suffering. In other words, to see glory in the Johannine world is to be given a possibility that is not just inherent in ordinary human capacity. The believer sees that God's solid, resistant objectivity, God's activity that 'pushes' at our own boundaries, is wholly identified with the physical presence of Jesus: not with particular works of power, though these may trigger recognition, nor with words of wisdom or prophetic insight, though these may be seen to be fitting to the underlying reality, but with the entirety of Jesus' identity, and most particularly his unequivocally human and finite moment, his death. And such a vision depends upon some modification in the believer's capacity, depends, in fact, upon the believer's 'death': John's Gospel ends with the enigmatic recommissioning of Peter for a future in which he will be bound and delivered up like his master. As we have seen, Ramsey insists, in *The Gospel and the Catholic Church*, on the Johannine linkage between unity and death: the trinitarian communion into which believers are introduced is a life in which all believers have relinquished their own centre in themselves so as to be centred in Christ and in the human other.[8] Thus the truthful vision of Jesus that is given to the believer is a vision from somewhere other than the natural centre of the ego: it is the truth given by the Paraclete.

Ramsey and Balthasar

I have already mentioned von Balthasar's citations of Ramsey; and it is specially in the context of these themes that Balthasar most suggestively refers to him. Balthasar's discussion of the way in which God's life is present in the entirety of Jesus' humanity notes Ramsey's stress on the 'quasi-physical' character of glory in respect of Jesus' human story in making the point that the *Hoheit*, the exalted splendour, of Jesus is not something that can be separated, even by the most sensitive surgical tools of research, from the facts of his life.[9] It is not a literary device or a matter of psychological

---

[8] Ramsey, *The Gospel and the Catholic Church*, pp. 24–7.
[9] Hans Urs von Balthasar, *Herrlichkeit*. (Einsiedeln, 1962). English: *The Glory of the Lord* (Edinburgh: 1982), III.2.ii, pp. 300–306.

reaction. It is the sense of divine freedom permeating Jesus' human identity; and it is recognizable only by gift, the gift of what Balthasar calls a *Sensorium*, a transformed sensibility, or, in scholastic language, a *connaturalitas*, a community of nature and instinct that allows us to see God's freedom in the light of or in virtue of a freedom granted to us. A little later,[10] Balthasar again refers to Ramsey to bear out his argument that Luke's Jesus is in fact set before us in a narrative in which it is just as clear as in John that his entire existence is to be seen as manifesting glory. Interestingly, Balthasar also refers to Kierkegaard's great meditation in the *Philosophical Fragments* on the anonymity of God in Jesus; though he (rightly, I think) identifies what is missing in Kierkegaard's reflections as the trinitarian dimension, which alone gives its full (and positive) sense to the Johannine narrative. The hidden glory is not simply an arbitrary paradox or simply a consequence of the impossibility of God appearing as God in the created order: it is the outworking in finite form of the eternal self-yielding, self-hiding we might almost say, of the Son before the Father, the Son who does not will to be 'visible' except as the living act of the Father – which takes us back to Ramsey's repeated emphasis on the eternal and inner-trinitarian ground of the Johannine sense of glory.

In the light of Balthasar's elaborations of the same basic motif, we can perhaps see more clearly how and why the glory of God is, for Ramsey, a reality that is about knowledge – as the Pauline text with which we began implies. The relinquishing of a centre in the self, the drawing out of love and faith towards Christ actually makes possible the understanding of who God is in Jesus – of the trinitarian life and the incarnational sacrifice. As the believer begins to be free of self-absorption, s/he begins to see a little of what might be thinkable about a God wholly free of self-interest. Such a God is, on the one hand, free to be present without self-protection or reserve in any place, including the places most remote from 'heaven': he can be in the hell of suffering and abandonment without loss of self, since the divine self is utterly invested in the other; and, on the other hand, such a God cannot be conceived as an eternal individual self, but as a life lived eternally in that 'investment' in the other. Thus the believer perceives what I have called the interiority and integrity of God, the resource and solidity of divine life: what is indestructibly solid in God is this life-in-the-other.

To see the freedom of God to be in the Cross is to see glory, because it is to see how God's utterly non-negotiable presence and action can be real in the physical body of the tortured and dying Jesus.

The Jesuit theologian Edward Oakes, writing about von Balthasar, quotes a French Catholic philosopher as saying that, in the life of faith, 'Perception of credibility and belief in truth are identically the same act'.[11] Oakes explains why this is not in fact a wholly adequate formula, but there is a point here that illuminates Ramsey's thinking once again. Seeing why Christian belief is credible is inseparable from that transformation of the self and its habitual ways of working that is prompted by

---

[10] Ibid., p. 328.
[11] Edward T. Oakes, *Pattern of Redemption: The Theology of Hans Urs von Balthasar* (New York: 1994), p. 141.

grace; when you see that the gospel is believable, you do so because you have in the same moment believed, that is, trusted yourself to the presence that decentres and dispossesses the self. The judgement that the gospel is believable is an act of self-commitment. Oakes's reservation is that this initial act is a sort of submission before it is really vision; *fides ex auditu*, 'faith comes from hearing', because there is a sense in which we hear before we see, we are addressed, affected, acted on, in a way that the language of 'seeing' doesn't quite capture. I think, though, that this is in fact some of the force of speaking about 'glory' and beauty in the way that Balthasar and Ramsey do, and the force of their stress upon the physical resonance of such words. Precisely because glory is not something that is capable of being mastered and because beauty is not something that can be domesticated into the self's agenda, encounter with glory and beauty might be said to be more like hearing than some kinds of seeing. Ramsey would have referred us to the proximity in 2 Chronicles of 5:13–14 and 6:1: the glory of the Lord is perceptible as a cloud, and God is one who 'dwells in thick darkness'. Similarly, Balthasar's theology of aesthetics turns on the fact that the crucified Jesus has no 'form' that is attractive to our expectations. The seeing of glory in the Cross and the crucified is not a panoptic sweep of the landscape, but a synoptic moment of grasping together unreserved love and unqualified pain and abandonment – seeing the Cross as an event whose 'centre' is an eternal and infinite stripping of self. It is the sole finally convincing demonstration of freedom, the vision of God's liberty to be not only for but in the other; as such it is the vision of glory, the inner resource, the inner logic, of God's life.

The Cross of the Risen One

And the way in which Ramsey and Balthasar alike reach for the apparently crude and mythological imagery of the oppressive material cloud in the sanctuary is not only that it secures the notion of an otherness as starkly 'in the way' as any bodily presence, but that it also evokes that aspect of physical encounter which tells us that sheer material contact does not and cannot offer us a finished conceptual picture, an object or thought, but primarily an occasion for thought, the beginning of a process that will not ever supplant the encounter itself. Thought begins only when we have first been interrupted by encounter with the non-negotiable. This is true of all intellectual activity worth the name; but it is clear that where theology is concerned it is true in a very particular way which asserts that the 'object' of theology continues always to have this character of interrupting and resisting any possible attempt at conceptual finality. The bare thereness of Jesus as part of the material history of the world tells us that in no way can God be less resistant to our minds and agendas than the rest of the material order. Yet the unbreakable association of the infinite God with the material Jesus underlines, paradoxically, that God is never part of the system of the universe because he is absolutely and unreservedly free in his love to be, to live, in the place of death and hell. Seeing God in Jesus is at once to see that there is no way around or even 'through' the concreteness of the Incarnation, and that it is this very fact that establishes as nothing else could the complete liberty of God, and thus his radical difference from all finite reality, caught up in the balances of action and passion, initiative and response, conditioning and creativity. These polarities are somehow transcended in the fusion of Jesus' helpless passion with God's most supremely free action.

This is why, for Ramsey, there is nowhere else for a theologian to begin but with the paschal event.[12] The Word made flesh is never an object for theology; the Word on the Cross is the actual condition for the perception, Balthasar's *Sensorium*, of theology's business. Yet it is at the same time the Cross as proclaimed, not as bare event – and so the Cross as the Cross of the Risen One. God's own witness to, God's 'owning' of, the Cross as the place he has made uniquely his place is part of what makes glory visible (which is why Ramsey could never have managed to settle for a mental, internalized account of the Resurrection; its witness is again as non-negotiably mysterious as any other moment in the material world). We do not – as some, including Ramsey, would say a theologian like Rudolf Bultmann does – present the Cross and appeal to some intense inner drive of blind trust and self-projection that allows us to acknowledge the Lordship of the crucified. We are overtaken by the Resurrection as the event that will not allow us to ignore the Cross or mourn it or regard it as a past event of failure and shame. Here again, I suspect Ramsey had in mind some of the most complex and demanding pages of Hoskyns on the Fourth Gospel, where he develops the idea of the Spirit in John as God holding before us, inescapably, the events of Jesus' life and death, as well as the text of Scott Holland that he quotes about the whole earthly life of Jesus being raised in the event of Easter.[13]

'The Church is Pointing beyond Theology'

The theology that is revealed in the face of Christ, in the perception of glory in humiliated humanity, thus determines that our theology has to be done 'in the face of Christ'. It is necessarily a theology that is rooted in relation to the concrete Christ – the historical figure as held before us through the event of the Resurrection and the continuing action of the Spirit. And for it to be a truthful activity, manifesting somehow in words what it is talking about, it has to be a kenotic activity, a speech that is 'dispossessed' by the encounter with Christ. As such, following through the logic of Ramsey's whole scheme, it does not happen outside the Body of Christ, which is, as *GC* puts it, the 'expression' here and now of the paschal event of death and Resurrection. Theology in the Body does not only talk about this event or seek to understand it; it seeks to embody it.

What precisely this must mean in practice Ramsey does not say – though some would say he succeeds in showing. It is certainly, in intention, a relativizing of

---

[12] Ramsey, *The Gospel and the Catholic Church*, pp. 5–7.
[13] Michael Ramsey, *The Resurrection of Christ: A Study of the Event and its Meaning for the Christian Faith* (London: Collins, 1961), pp. 9–10.

theology. 'The Church is pointing beyond theology', as he says in *GC*; the theologian's work and 'ideal' has to be lost in the reality of the Body for it to find its proper meaning. It also demands what *GC* so emphasizes, a penitential clarity about the Church's failings, the sense of a community under judgement as the only credible sign of the true presence of the Body; if theology is in some sense lost in the life of the Body, this is not at all to say that the concerns of an institution are now allowed to absorb or neutralize the asking of unwelcome questions. The unwelcome questions, however, are not speculative but moral and spiritual, questions about whether the paschal mystery is in fact honoured and lived among those who call themselves believers. If theology has a role in this, it is again and again to recover the vision of the Church as it fundamentally must be, as witness to the Cross and Resurrection. Hence Ramsey's surprising and insightful comment[14] that Barth and Brunner have restored to Protestant theology a proper understanding of the Church's function – a Church always characterized by 'tribulation' because it is always the meeting place of sin with the love and judgement of God. Ramsey refers to Barth's Romans Commentary on this point, to a passage where Barth insists that we discuss the manifest failings and betrayals of the Church only within a strictly theological context: to see the tribulation of the Church clearly is to see the scope of divine love. It is in fact a sort of echo of Ramsey's own central theme. Seeing God in the middle of Godlessness is to see glory; to apprehend the liberty of God in the Godlessness of the Church is to be at the heart of the one theological mystery, the paschal freedom of God to be where love insists on being, in the depths of what is other.

Kenotic Theology

Gradually some sense of what Ramsey might mean by a 'dispossessed', self-losing theology comes into focus. It is not and cannot be a systematic edifice, constructing a picture of the universe and of God's action in it that could be contemplated as an object (and remember that Barth always denied being a systematic theologian). It is a constantly renewed struggle to keep the paschal reality at work in the Church's language – for praise and thanksgiving (which is why the Eucharist is always a fundamentally theological occurrence) and for self-scrutiny on the part of the community and acknowledgement of failure. Theology has to spell out what it can of how and why the face of Christ is what transforms the human world; having done that, it does not seek any further place or dignity, but stands ready to resurrect the question when the Church's practice and speech have overlaid it. Hence Ramsey's approving reference, at the end of *GC*, to Maurice's description of theology as digging rather than building, removing debris, undermining the partisanships of believers so as to unite at the foundational level where the act of God is at work.

And it is Maurice who gives Ramsey one of his most evocative pictures, in an address delivered in Cambridge for the centenary of Maurice's death. Maurice, he

---

[14] Ramsey, *The Gospel and the Catholic Church*, pp. 202–3.

reminds us, believed that theology was everyone's business. Sometimes he allowed this to lead him into rather ambitious generalizations about what the ordinary person knew or believed. But behind this lay a solid awareness that the subject matter of theology is every man, woman and child, so that the struggling and not very articulate awareness of even the poorest and least intellectual Christian living in the face of Christ has as much claim to be theology as the 'professional's' work. On his deathbed, Maurice 'began talking very rapidly but indistinctly ... about the Communion being for all nations and peoples, for men who were working like Dr Radcliffe (his physician). Something too about it being the work of women to teach men its meaning ...'.[15]

Neither Maurice nor Ramsey is the most obvious recruit to feminist or liberation theology; but the picture of the dying Maurice pouring out those barely intelligible words about those who are able to uncover the meanings of the mystery brings us momentarily into a similar world. It addresses the 'professional' theologian in a way that sobers and challenges. Ramsey very evidently believed that theology needed doing and doing well, with the tools of historical and linguistic and philosophical expertise. But the doing of it well was never to be thought of as the successful polishing of argument or refinement of concepts; whatever of this needed doing was subordinate to the work of the Body – not as a directive and inquisitorial overseer, but as the environment in which the transforming seriousness of God's glory in Christ was definitively at work. Theology would have to begin, just as Luther argued, with the knowledge of the Cross; but the Cross always as that place in creation where we may find God's integrity made plain. And that integrity is made plain only as the theologian's mind is converted – lost to the ambitions of a patternmaking ego or an ideological programme.

It is not, in the nature of things, a job description, a set of conditions that must be met by anyone professing to make contributions to a subject conventionally called theology. It is something recognized in and by the Body, recognized in gratitude for the way in which it digs down to what is alone truly generative of the common life and the common prayer. In the long run, the Church discerns those who are in a particular sense its theologians. Few would doubt that Michael Ramsey has been and still is discerned as such.

***

This lecture, given at Lambeth Palace, was sponsored by the Trinity Institute of Christianity and Culture.

---

[15] *CTP*, p. 44.

Bibliography

Primary Literature

The Gospel and the Catholic Church (London: 1936/1956. Reprinted in 1990).
'The Significance of Anglican-Orthodox Relations', *Sorbonst*, 1938.
The Church of England and the Eastern Orthodox Church: Why their Unity is Important (London: 1946).
The Glory of God and the Transfiguration of Christ (London: 1949).
F.D. Maurice and the Conflict of Modern Theology (London: 1951).
Introducing the Faith (London: 1961).
The Resurrection of Christ: A Study of the Event and its Meaning for the Christian Faith (London: Collins, 1961).
Constantinople and Canterbury: A Lecture in the University of Athens (London: 1962).
Christ Crucified for the World (London: 1964).
Rome and Canterbury (London: 1967).
God, Christ and the World: A Study of Contemporary Theology (London: 1969).
Come Holy Spirit (New York and London: 1976).
The Holy Spirit (London: 1977).
The Cross and this World (London: 1980).
Jesus and the Living Past (Oxford: 1980).
Be Still and Know (London: 1982).

Secondary Literature

Chadwick, Owen, *Michael Ramsey – A Life* (Oxford: 1990).
Coleman, D. (ed.), *Michael Ramsey: The Anglican Spirit* (London: 1991).
Court, John, "Michael Ramsey and Biblical Theology" in Gill, R. and Kendall, L., *Michael Ramsey as Theologian* (London: 1995).
Dales, D.J., *Glory: The Spiritual Theology of Michael Ramsey* (Norwich: 2003).
Gill, R. and Kendall, L. (eds), *Michael Ramsey as Theologian* (London: 1995).
Hoskyns, Edwyn Clement, *Fourth Gospel* (London: Faber and Faber, 1940).
Oakes, Edward T., *Pattern of Redemption: The Theology of Hans Urs von Balthasar* (New York: 1994).
Von Balthasar, Hans Urs: *Herrlichkeit* (Einsiedeln: 1962). English: *The Glory of the Lord* (Edinburgh: 1982).

Chapter 38
Henry Chadwick

G.R. Evans

Henry Chadwick's achievement was to help to clarify the ways in which the writing of the 'history' of theology can be a mode of 'doing theology'. It was his presumption that the continuities and discontinuities in the history of the faith and life of the Church theology are not merely episodes in a story but weave the very fabric of the faith. As an ecumenist and ecumenical theologian he felt a responsibility to make the method 'work' in applied as well as academic theology so that the one faith in the future united Church will also be manifestly the faith of the Church through the ages.

He was a major influence in shaping the field of ecumenical theology. In this context he treated a number of key topics in ecclesiology (particularly questions of authority, primacy and ministry), the theology of the sacraments (most notably the Eucharist), the theology of salvation (especially the doctrine of justification). He explored some of the special problems of theological language raised by ecumenical dialogue. The originality of this work, for example in framing the concept of 'substantial agreement' (Final Report of ARCIC I), is slowly becoming clear as the ecumenical movement matures, rides out a period of discouragement and it begins to be possible to take stock of the long-term achievement.

His ecumenical writing was often done in collaboration with others serving with him on ecumenical commissions where his personal contribution may have been decisive to a degree which was not always apparent until later.

Biography with Focus on Theological (and Ecclesial) Work

Henry Chadwick (b. 23 June 1920) was the fourth child and the third son of a barrister and a pianist. An elder and a younger brother were both ordained as Anglican priests, and William Owen Chadwick (b. 1916), became an ecclesiastical historian of comparable distinction, writing mainly on the early modern and modern periods. The brothers, excellent friends, regularly turned to one another for comment and criticism.

Henry Chadwick won a King's Scholarship to Eton. From there he went to Magdalene College, Cambridge, on a Music Scholarship, for he was himself a considerable pianist. He trained for the Anglican ministry at Ridley Hall, Cambridge, a theological college with 'evangelical' sympathies, though his own Churchmanship later tended towards what he called the 'top of the candlestick'. From 1946 to 1958 he was a Fellow of Queens' College, Cambridge. He served as Junior Proctor in the academic year 1948–9 (a role to which the Colleges elect in rotation and which carries responsibilities for the discipline of students throughout the university).

Chadwick was elected to the Regius Chair of Divinity in the University of Oxford in 1959, which prompted his election as a Fellow of the British Academy in 1960. His inaugural lecture, 'The Circle and the Ellipse; Rival Concepts of Authority in the Early Church', delivered before the University of Oxford on 5 May 1959, took as its underlying theme that interaction of ecclesiology and politics, the ideal and the reality in the Church's life, which became a lifetime interest, and increasingly reflected the balance of Chadwick's own working life. He was still known primarily as a patristic scholar. He published *The Early Church*, the first volume of the Pelican History of the Church, in 1967.

The move to Oxford brought a steady stream of invitations to give high profile lectures. The Hewett Lectures given in New York and Boston in 1962 became *Early Christian Thought and the Classical Tradition* (1966, reprinted 1984). He gave the Gifford Lectures in St Andrews in 1962–4; the Birkbeck Lectures in Cambridge in 1965.

A number of scholarly responsibilities filled these years, of the kind he liked to refer to as 'midwifery'. Chadwick had been editor of the *Journal of Theological Studies* since 1954 and was to remain so until 1985. When he gave up the editorship after 31 years, a note from his then fellow-editors Maurice Wiles and Morna Hooker, published in the April 1986 issue, spoke not only of the growth of the journal 'in academic standing and international repute' under his guidance but also of 'many a scholar whose early offerings for publication have had the benefit of his kindly but searching eye'. He was made a Delegate of the Oxford University Press in 1960 and served until 1979. The Delegates, senior scholars representing the various disciplines, form the link between the publisher and its parent university, give formal approval for publication and remain the ultimate guardians of the scholarly reputation of the Press. There was a line of doctoral students and Chadwick was punctilious in giving time to young scholars from all over the world.

This period of Chadwick's life culminated in his appointment as Dean of Christ Church, where he remained from 1969 to 1979. The Dean of Christ Church is not merely the head of an Oxford College but the Dean of a Cathedral Chapter, since the College 'chapel' is also the cathedral of the diocese of Oxford. The notoriously heated politics of the cathedral chapter were combined with those of the College governing body with an intricacy perhaps unparalleled in any other community. This was something of which Chadwick was actively aware, and had indeed already experienced, since the Regius Professorship had included a canonry at Christ Church. He consciously connected the realities of this microcosm of modern ecclesiastical politics with the problems in theoretical and practical ecclesiology with which he grappled as a theologian.

The administrative load increased, and included a period as Pro-Vice-Chancellor of the University of Oxford (1974–5). Yet these were not by any means barren years when it came to the writing of scholarly monographs. *Priscillian of Avila: The Occult and the Charismatic in the Early Church*, appeared in 1976. Chadwick kept up with what was always for him the 'real world' of scholarship. He could be seen walking about the streets of Oxford in scholarly discourse in which he as well as his colleague would find stimulus (for example with M.T. Gibson, as he explained the issues she would need to consider with reference to the Eucharist while she was working on her book on *Lanfranc of Bec* (1978); and he wrote his own study of Boethius as she began work on the edition of collected essays on *Boethius: His Life, Thought and Influence* which also appeared in 1981). He would walk across in the intervals of university and college meetings to the Bodleian Library, where he would browse for half an hour through the rack on new accessions in the Lower Reading Room and exchange a word with readers who happened to be at work there.

When he lectured on 'The Role of the Christian Bishop in Ancient Society' at the Center for Hermeneutical Studies in Hellenistic and Modern Culture's thirty-fifth colloquy in 1979, he spoke with some personal understanding of the difficulties of managing the tensions between the active and the contemplative life. Nevertheless, he himself is not known to have been put forward for episcopal office. He was the first to acknowledge that he lacked the necessary ordinary pastoral skills as well as pastoral experience.

Chadwick began to emerge as an ecumenical theologian after the Second Vatican Council. He served on the first Anglican-Roman Catholic International Committee (ARCIC I) from 1969 to 1981 and on ARCIC II from 1983 to 1990. He began in high optimism and considered this to be among the most important passages of work of his life as a theologian, and was often heard to say that it was a cause worth dying in.

He was offered the Regius Professorship of Divinity in Cambridge in 1979 and made the decision to return, although by now Oxford had become his intellectual home. The return to the purely academic life was intended to lift some of the administrative burden of heading an Oxford college and a cathedral chapter. This time his inaugural lecture, delivered before the University of Cambridge on 5 May 1981, took as its subject 'Frontiers of Theology'. Books appeared. *Boethius: The Consolations of Music, Logic, Theology and Philosophy*, in 1981; the *Atlas of the Christian Church* (1987), co-edited with the present author. A few years of academic contentment followed, in the room at Magdalene College which still had C.S. Lewis's carpet on the floor and was so densely packed with the books which had arrived from the deanery at Christ Church that there was scarcely room for arriving students to squeeze between the bookshelves. Cambridge expected two lectures a week on patristic subjects in term. The fortnightly Patristic Seminar flourished under his chairmanship with the regular attendance of Caroline and Ernst Bammel, Nicholas Lash, Christopher Stead and sometimes William Frend. Academic 'missions' included a trip to Geneva to examine the Isaac Newton papers at the Fondation Hardt. Chadwick the musician took special pleasure in leading the publisher of Hymns Ancient and Modern through its development into the Canterbury Press, the takeover of the *Church Times*, and the launch of hymn-books with modern experimental hymns. His Presidency of the Henry Bradshaw Society marked a related interest in liturgy.

During this second 'Cambridge' period he was chosen by Cambridge to be the university's representative member of the Church of England General Synod, where he sat in the House of Clergy. He became an active member of the Faith and Order

Advisory Group (FOAG) of the Church of England General Synod. The FOAG was chiefly concerned with ecumenical questions at this time, preparing documents about the reception of the bilateral dialogues which were reaching their final form and being sent to the Church of England for response.

The University of Cambridge introduced an 'early retirement' scheme in the early 1980s, as an economy measure. Chadwick and his wife went back to live in Oxford, which they had come to prefer to Cambridge. But he was soon to receive an invitation from the Fellows of Peterhouse, among the oldest of the Cambridge Colleges, to become its Master. He was moved to accept partly by pleasure that the College had been willing to invite a priest to be its head. He held the post for six years from 1987 to 1993, becoming the only person ever to occupy the Regius Chairs of Divinity in both the ancient universities of England and also to be head of a college in each of them.

The administrative burdens were not as heavy at Peterhouse as they had been at Christ Church. There was time for writing. A series of works on Augustine had already begun to appear. The brief *Augustine*, in the Oxford Past Masters series, had been published in 1986. A translation of the *Confessions* into English came out in 1991. *Augustine: A Very Short Introduction* emerged in 2001. An essay on Augustine appeared in a little volume *Founders of Thought* (1991) in collaboration with Jonathan Barnes (Aristotle) and Richard Hare (Plato).

Two important books were published after Chadwick's ultimate retirement and return once more to Oxford, in which he was consciously 'rounding things up'. *The Church in Ancient Society: From Galilee to Gregory the Great* (2001) was the work he had been planning for many years. *East and West: The Making of a Rift in the Church: From Apostolic Times until the Council of Florence* (2003), a slimmer volume, drew together a number of studies on the relationship between Orthodoxy and the Church of the Latin West.

Survey: On Theological Thought/Production

'Critical Scholarship': Finding a Direction

Discovering one's interests as a young scholar in England at this period was not a clear-cut process. Henry Chadwick's brother Owen had written a book on *John Cassian* (1950) before settling to his long-term interests in the ecclesiastical history of a much later period. There was no normative expectation in Oxford and Cambridge in the 1950s that a promising young Fellow of a College would undertake doctoral studies as an 'apprentice' academic. A doctorate usually came much later in life in the form of a 'higher doctorate', which is awarded in England for publications and not for a thesis.

Chadwick's first major academic project, the translation of Origen's *Contra Celsum* (1953, with a new edition in 1980), made his name largely for the scholarly quality of its annotation. *Alexandrian Christianity: Selected Translations of Clement and Origen with Introductions and Notes*, with J.E.L. Oulton (1954). *The Sentences of Sextus* was published in 1959. A translation from an early modern German theologian, *Lessing's Theological Writings: Selections in Translation*, came out, with an introductory essay, in 1956, and although it did not lead to the development of a specialist interest in more modern theology it did establish a lasting affection for the German language, for German theology and for Germany itself, culminating in the award of the Humboldt Prize in 1983, and the Lucas Prize at Tübingen in 1991.

In the Bishop Westcott Memorial Lecture in 1960, published in 1961 as 'The Vindication of Christianity in Westcott's Thought', Chadwick remarked that 'to Westcott, Lightfoot and Hort Cambridge theology owes perhaps one thing above all – its standards of critical scholarship'. 'Critical scholarship' had a particular meaning in the Cambridge theological tradition of the time. Chadwick learned his trade as a textual critic and intellectual historian in this tradition by giving time as a young academic to the humbler services of scholarship such as translation and annotation, which included Origen and Lessing. Chadwick said of Westcott what he could equally have said of himself. 'It corresponded to his view of the very nature of Christian doctrine that it should be studied historically.'

The subsequent trajectory of the development of his interests was, as he himself acknowledged, marked as much by response to requests as by personal interest, and increasingly so as time went on. In the Introduction to the items collected in *Tradition and Exploration* (1994), Chadwick writes: 'Many of the papers were originally composed because an authority or a Church committee or an international congress specifically asked for a paper on a particular problem.'

Themes of Ecumenical Theology

Ecumenical committees in particular had a need for position papers, and the kind Chadwick was regularly invited to supply were of the sort which attempted to explain the way history had shaped a problem and made it Church-dividing. The choice of topics for study by ARCIC I and later by ARCIC II led to studies on 'authority' (especially the question of 'primacy'), 'Eucharist' and 'ministry' as well as on 'justification' and the theology of salvation.

The problem of 'authority' had attracted him from his youth. He was writing on the subject in the *Journal of Theological Studies* in 1957. His was principally an ecclesiological interest, centred on the question how authority works within the institutional framework of the Church, but he was well aware that authority has an intimate relationship with power. His own understanding of the operation of 'communities' was always heavily influenced by the experience of the power-struggles of a series of Oxford and Cambridge colleges, and the Oxford cathedral chapter.

A paper on 'Full Communion', written in the context of the work of ARCIC in 1981, is conceived almost entirely in terms of the ecclesiological mechanics which enable Christians in divided communities to 'do things together', especially those which affect sacramental life. This was an area of language and concept which Chadwick helped to make familiar in Europe but which has penetrated less fully into ecclesiological writing in the United States. Similarly, Chadwick's work on primacy has had its greatest importance in the context of the long European history of relations with Rome. He stressed the distinction between the Anglican 'primacy of honour' and the Roman Catholic 'primacy of jurisdiction'.

The Eucharist was a subject in which he had been interested at least since he published an edition of the *De sacramentis* of Ambridge of Milan in 1960. He set out to articulate the theology of the Eucharist in the context of the work of ARCIC I in such a way as to enable Anglicans and Roman Catholic to recognise the essential unity of their beliefs. In 1989, stimulated by a commemorative conference on Berengar of Tours and the emergence of the doctrine of transubstantiation, he published an article, 'Ego Berengarius', in the *Journal of Theological Studies* (1989), his principal piece of 'medieval' research.

Mutual recognition and reconciliation of ministry has again and again proved to be the breaking point in ecumenical bilateral dialogue. Chadwick went back to the New Testament texts and the problems which have resulted down the ages from the use of the terms *presbyter* and *episcopos*. The movement for the ordination of women introduced a wholly new dimension during the period of the work of ARCIC I and the reception of the Final Report, as provinces of the Anglican Communion began to ordain women to the priesthood and to talk of allowing women to be bishops. Chadwick's position was that this was not a question of doing justice, nor one of equality of opportunity; what mattered was the threat of schism, for, like Augustine, he was strongly of the view that schism is heresy. Ordination of practising homosexuals was not then the burning issue it has since become in the Anglican Communion.

The second Anglican–Roman Catholic International Commission asked Chadwick to write a paper on 'justification'. He went back to the sixteenth century, but to Trent rather than to Luther. Justification, he argued, 'was not only intricate, but had not previously been a matter considered by such a council', when it was considered by the Council of Trent in the second half of 1546. Chadwick found this an exercise challenging to his methodology which had usually worked from a solid base of patristic material.

Content: More Thorough Presentation of Key Aspects of His Work

Chadwick designed his theological methodology in the course of a lifetime's work, which he saw as itself forming a continuum, first as a patristic scholar in the tradition of the seventeenth-century Anglican divines, and subsequently as an ecumenical theologian balanced at the dividing line between Rome and Canterbury, which, for him, was really no line at all.

In the ecumenical area of his work, Chadwick was always most strongly committed to the Anglican–Roman Catholic dialogue. Chadwick had a sympathy with John Henry Newman, which was important to his self-understanding as a theologian. Newman made the journey from the Church of England to Rome which Chadwick himself never made, though many observers half-expected him to do so. Chadwick was never drawn into the work of the World Council of Churches like the great Roman

Catholic ecclesiologist Jean Tillard, a fellow-member of ARCIC I and II. And despite his extensive travels to lecture, especially in the United States, he saw the project above all from an English vantage-point. The essay on the Lambeth Quadrilateral written for the 1888 Lambeth Conference centenary notes the importance of the call for Home Reunion by which 'the English bishops meant the reconciliation of Protestant Nonconformists to the ministry and liturgy of the Church of England'. Chadwick suggests, with hindsight, that the Lambeth Conference saw this as playing 'a significant part in the formation of Anglican policy toward ecumenism'. Yet he himself concentrated on the dialogue with Rome which was expressly excluded by the early Lambeth Conferences. He took an active interest in the dialogues with the Orthodox, both Roman and Anglican, but never entering with the same passion into the dialogues with the churches of the Home Reunion agenda.

The Emergence of an 'Ecumenical Method'

In many respects Chadwick remained a man of the nineteenth century. He found in John Henry Newman a mind both congenial and concerned with questions of the deep workings of faith, on which he himself did not speak with ease. 'Deep personal convictions ... are discovered on the far side of a gulf which is crossed by what Newman calls "the illative sense" ... a capacity of the mind to discern truth in an accumulation of probabilities', he wrote in a paper on 'Romanticism and Religion', which he frequently offered to undergraduate societies who asked him to talk to them, and kept in a drawer for the purpose. It was published among the collected papers in the Canterbury Press volume 'Tradition and Exploration' in 1994.

Yet Chadwick the ecumenist had to design a methodology for this relatively new branch of theology. Theological questions have, for the most part, proved to be perennial. Most have proved capable of making a fresh appearance in the slightly adjusted dress of a new period. The historian of theology, unless he is writing on a narrow topic as it was treated within a brief span of time, has too much evidence; he finds himself obliged to 'illustrate' rather than to 'prove'. Chadwick chose his evidence to support conclusions he believed to accord with the consensus of the Church through the ages. He was open to the charge that he used evidence selectively to lead to a preferred conclusion. Nevertheless, he actively sought, like a latter-day Vincent of Lérins, to discover the truth where it had been recognised always and everywhere and by everyone.

He never questioned that it would be necessary to the success of the endeavour to make the history work out right. What had happened and what had been said in the past, however divisive or polemical, was not to be discarded or rejected; it was to be interpreted so that it could be seen to be not discordant, but merely one view of what had been a shared position all along.

Chadwick's method of working, even when he was asked to produce a piece of work such as a position paper for a committee, which would necessarily be brief and without footnotes, was to go back to the sources and create a patchwork of extracts from authors who would be regarded as authorities by those who were to use the paper. This was itself a problem area. In many respects, Chadwick's assumptions resembled those of the Western Middle Ages, when *auctoritates* were routinely used as supports for premises in the construction of syllogisms with limited distinctions of weight and reliability.

It was not that he did not put Scripture first, but he was far from regarding early Christian and even much later texts as necessarily greatly inferior authorities. The allocation of editorial responsibilities on the *Journal of Theological Studies* marked a decision not to be a Biblical scholar. Chadwick chose to deal with the articles and reviews which fell outside the arena of Biblical studies and to hand that part of the editing to a series of fellow-editors, although he remained General Editor of Black's New Testament Commentaries.

He drew from the web of extracts he assembled the principle that 'harmony in the Church is preserved by adhering to authority and by respect to law and good discipline'. In that context, he believed, it would rarely be necessary to accept that something could legitimately be Church-dividing. In the case of Justification, he wrote, 'it is enough to feel astonishment that the western Church should split in the sixteenth century on a theologoumenon of immense technicality, engendering a library of huge folio tomes'.

He would then tell the history of the way a problem had been treated in the past, in a way which was designed to bring out the theological emphases now seen to be necessary to the mending of division.

He regarded this not as a device for getting over a difficulty but as a road back to reality and forward to consensus. As he wrote in 'Disagreement and the Ancient Church', a paper contributed to a Festschrift for his friend Martin Hengel in 1996, even the early Church's texts were full of controversies but these 'were stages on a road towards greater consensus'.

As an ecumenist, he became profoundly interested in the problem of theological language. During the period of his service as a member of the General Synod of the Church of England, he gave an address to the Synod at its summer meeting at York in 1983 on the reception of the Lima Report on Baptism, Eucharist and Ministry of the World Council of Churches, and on the Final Report of ARCIC I. He began by reminding the Synod that the participating Churches had had a say in the shaping of both but 'if the Church of England now indicates a wish to pursue the path their two documents invite participant Churches to follow, some changes will come about'. He was well aware that the documents were being met with a mistrust that threatened their success. 'Ecumenical conversation is not an exercise in diplomacy.' It should not be assumed that 'if anything actually moves in the deadlock, this is because some poor fool has made a concession, has compromised with principles, has watered down the truth'.

This was not, he was to argue, a matter of politics. Paul Avis's book on ecumenical theology came out in 1986, making challenging claims that ecumenical agreements almost inevitably involved some slipperiness with language. Chadwick was conscious of several dimensions of this difficulty. In a much less hopeful treatment some years later, he reflected on the reasons why the reunion of the Roman Catholic and Anglican Churches which had seemed to be 'possible' within a generation 'now looks a vain hope'. 'Ecumenical Stock-Taking: Unfinished Business' is a gloomy piece, written after the Vatican's negative response of 1991 to the Final Report of ARCIC I. He claimed that the text had surprised its first readers by not depending 'on foggy or subtle ambiguities' but 'incisively articulated the essence of the matter as shared doctrine'. 'The point about language is not a new one to surviving members of ARCIC I; for the commission explicitly and consciously sought to avoid terms that carry a heavy polemical load of association.'

There is an irony in this exploration of the problem of language. Though *The Early Church* became a standard work, frequently reprinted, it is not an easy read. Though a considerable stylist Chadwick was not an author who found it easy to write accessibly. Even in his writings which lack footnotes their place is taken by scholarly asides, invitations to those who know a little about the subject to plunge in much further.

Ethics

Chadwick was at home in the microcosm of Oxbridge politics and in the macrocosm of Church politics. He was an honourable 'fixer' who took pleasure in the warfare and liked to win; he was a good judge of whether a battle could be won and held back from those which could not. So it came naturally to him to consider how things had been affected by such considerations in the emerging young Church. His bent for politics and his consciousness of the play of political thought in the shaping of events derived not from a desire for personal power but from an interest in the problem of authority which had begun in his youth.

It was, as he recognised, one of the classic dilemmas of the patristic world that a leading churchman who wished to be a serious theologian and to have a meaningful intellectual and spiritual life would have to work hard to strike a balance. Gregory the Great wrote an influential book on the subject and it was never far from Chadwick's mind once he was subject to similar pressures himself from the early age at which he became Oxford's Regius Professor. He remained a private man, one effect perhaps of the repressive education delivered in English public schools such as Eton in the 1930s. He was able to speak of his own inner world only in the terms of the history of thought. From time to time, asides reveal the man and his personal moralities. In 'Romanticism and Religion' he explored a polarity perhaps more important in his own life than he cared to say. 'On the literary side Lessing's polemic against the artificial perfections of Corneille and Racine and his advocacy of the full-blooded naturalism of Shakespeare, set up the ideal of free expression of natural feelings … Lessing, himself a simple child of the Enlightenment, must be reckoned one of the major influences making Romanticism possible.' 'The traditional affirmations were held because men believed that they stated what is the case. The Romantic view of religious and moral affirmations was to change that profoundly. They were on the way to being personal moral judgements, statements of moral policy, or aesthetic appreciations.' 'The later Romantics of the second half of the nineteenth centry are much inclined to use religious vocabulary for describing an aesthetic attitude' (he has in mind Ruskin, Rossetti, Walter Pater, the pre-Raphaelites and Yeats). 'A religion of good taste is not very good religion if that is all it is.' The Romantics 'were in search of mystery', but 'Mystical theology has normally taught that feelings of deep exaltation and emotion are to be distrusted in the spiritual life'. 'Newman's *Grammar of Assent* illustrates simultaneously the power and the vulnerability of the Romantic view of religion … it is never clear how the subjective illative sense differs from a blind guess.'

He recognised the importance of the conflict in the modern West between the emphasis on individual freedoms and 'self-determination' and accepting external constraints. As he remarked in an essay on 'Truth and Authority', 'in … reasoning, moral judgment, and innermost feeling, authority can be in tension with the freedom of the individual'.

A cluster of works on questions of ethics remained peripheral to the main stream of his work. *The Sentences of Sextus* (1959) was subtitled *A Contribution to the History of Early Christian Ethics*. Chadwick turned to the subject of 'conscience' when he was invited to write on *Gewissen* for the *Reallexikon für Antike und Christentum* (1978). He chose the title of '*The Originality of Early Christian Ethics*' for the James Bryce memorial lecture delivered at the Wolfson Hall, Somerville College, Oxford, on Friday 28 October 1988 (published 1990). He wrote a paper on Augustine's ethics.

Placing the Theologian in Relation to the Theological Discourse of the Twentieth Century

Henry Chadwick was the honorand of two Festschriften, one published by the Oxford University Press and one by the Cambridge University Press: *Christian Authority: Essays in Honour of Henry Chadwick* (1988), edited by G.R. Evans; *The Making of Orthodoxy: Essays in Honour of Henry Chadwick* (1989), edited by Rowan Williams, later Archbishop of Canterbury. The first emphasised his achievement as an ecumenical theologian, the second his work as a patristic scholar.

It is worth asking how he himself saw the matter. In one of his last books, *The Church in Ancient Society*, he wrote with undimmed confidence in the endurance of the Christian faith. 'Initially belonging to the ancient world, Christianity remains the faith of a high proportion of this planet's population. Its characteristic teachings and ideals still speak universally to mind and conscience in individuals and still bond together communities across chasms of differences in education and race. To study the ancient Church is to watch the Christian society forming structures and social attitudes that have remained lasting and in the main permanent.'

Bibliography

Primary Literature

Origen, *Contra Celsum*, translation (Cambridge: Cambridge University Press, 1953). New edition in 1980.

Lessings' Theological Writings (Stanford: Stanford University Press, 1956). Selections in translation came out, with an introductory essay.

The Sentences of Sextus: A Contribution to the History of Early Christian Ethics (Cambridge University Press, 1959).

The Early Church (Harmondsworth: Penguin, 1967).

Early Christian Thought and the Classical Tradition (Oxford: Oxford University Press, 1966). Hewett Lectures given in New York and Boston in 1962. Reprinted 1984.

Priscillian of Avila: The Occult and the Charismatic in the Early Church (Oxford: Clarendon Press, 1976).

'Gewissen', in *Reallexikon für Antike und Christentum* (Stuttgart: Hiersemann, 1978).

Boethius: The Consolations of Music, Logic, Theology and Philosophy (Oxford: Clarendon Press, 1981).

Augustine (Oxford: Oxford University Press, 1986). Past Masters Series.

Augustine, *Confessions*, translation (Oxford: Oxford University Press, 1991).

The Church in Ancient Society: From Galilee to Gregory the Great (Oxford: Oxford University Press, 2001).

East and West: The Making of a Rift in the Church: From Apostolic Times until the Council of Florence (Oxford: Oxford University Press, 2003).

Secondary Literature

The Making of Orthodoxy: Essays in Honour of Henry Chadwick, edited by Rowan Williams (Cambridge: Cambridge University Press, 1989).

Christian Authority: Essays in Honour of Henry Chadwick, edited by G.R. Evans (Oxford: Oxford University Press, 1988).

Chapter 39
Jaroslav Pelikan

Jan Schumacher

"The church lives by the past, but for the future."

Early in the 1950s, Karl Barth published a book about nineteenth-century Protestant theology. One of the negative developments that Barth diagnosed in this epoch of the history of theology was that the most gifted theologians had fled into history, where they found a secure space that allowed them to pursue their academic research far from the challenges of the present day. When the first English translation of Barth's book about nineteenth-century Protestant theology was published in 1959, the forward was written by Jaroslav Pelikan, at that time professor of church history at the University of Chicago and a member of the American Lutheran church. Pelikan responded to what Barth had said by remarking that when Karl Barth decided to become a systematic theologian, Protestant historical theology had lost a man who could have become a great historian of dogma, on the same level as Adolf von Harnack![1]

Pelikan himself was in a close dialogue with Adolf von Harnack's writings throughout his entire life as a scholar, and he would surely have reacted strongly against any selection of the greatest twentieth-century theologians that failed to include Adolf von Harnack and his highly distinctive interpretation of the development of dogma in the early church. There was a biographical element in this link to Harnack: Jaroslav Pelikan's teacher and mentor in church history was Wilhelm Pauck, who, like Barth, had studied under Harnack. But Pelikan's relationship to Barth went deeper than this. It was through an uninterrupted dialogue with Harnack's writings that Pelikan developed his own understanding of what it means to be a historian and of the historian's task among the theological disciplines.

Jaroslav Pelikan's Academic Career

Jaroslav Pelikan (1923–2006) was born in Akron, Ohio, and belonged to a family that had emigrated from Slovakia to the USA. Both his grandfather and his father were pastors in a Slovakian Lutheran Synod in America. He completed his studies and took his doctorate when he was 22 years old. His career took him to both kinds of academic environments, to those linked to the church and those that were independent.

---

[1] Karl Barth, *Protestant Thought: From Rousseau to Ritschl* (New York, 1959), p. 311. For Jaroslav Pelikan's presentation of the American edition, see pp. 7–10.

From 1946 to 1949, he taught at the University of Valparaiso, and from 1949 to 1953 at Concordia Theological Seminary. In 1953, he moved to the University of Chicago. He concluded his academic career at Yale University, where he was Sterling Professor of History. When he reached retirement age in 1996, he could look back on almost 25 years at this prestigious institution. During this period, he was dean of the Historical-Philosophical Faculty for five years.

It was as professor at Chicago and Yale that Pelikan carried out his greatest literary project, the presentation of the history of the Christian tradition in five volumes. The first volume of *The Christian Tradition* was published in 1971, and the last volume came out eighteen years later, in 1989 – exactly 100 years after Harnack published the first volume of his *Lehrbuch der Dogmengeschichte,* as Pelikan naturally noted! He describes this work as something he had regarded as his vocation from his student days onwards, namely, to write a follow-up to Harnack's work. It was prepared in a series of lectures and seminars on "The History of Christian Thought" while he was professor at Chicago. He gave an account of what the history of dogma is, and of the methodological choices that historical theology faces, in two separate works, *Historical Theology: Continuity and Change in Christian Doctrine* (1971) and the prestigious Jefferson Lectures in 1983, published as *The Vindication of Tradition* (1984). Pelikan himself described this latter essay as "some systematic reflection on my lifelong study of continuity and change in the development of tradition." The Canadian literary critic Northrop Frye hailed it as a "classic" for all who were interested in exploring the questions concerning tradition – a concept that also played an important role in the school of literary studies that Northrop Frye represented.

Pelikan spent most of his life as a theological teacher and writer in a free academic context. The significance of the university was that it allowed him to reflect on the church's history without being influenced by the guidelines for practical academic work, and not least the results of this work, which (he believed) easily got the upper hand in ecclesiastical seminaries and in universities with strong ties to the church. His period at Concordia was brief. It may be that he sensed even then that his literary activity not only would produce a considerable volume of important academic studies, but also was a personal "quest" that would end forty years later with his conversion to the Orthodox church in the USA.

The Historian's Challenge

The foreword to Karl Barth's book about Protestant theology in the nineteenth century is a good example of how Pelikan reflects on the task of the historian, which can be described briefly as creating the interest or the irritation in the readers that is necessary, if they are to open their minds for the fathers and brothers – today, we would add: "the mothers and sisters" – who speak through the historian, provided of course that these fathers (and mothers) have succeeded in establishing a dialogue with the historian himself or herself.[2] It is this that makes Barth's book so important in Pelikan's eyes. Barth has communicated an epoch to us in such a way that it seizes hold of the reader. Pelikan argues that this power is due to Barth's ability to open himself up to the past in a way that is best described by saying that the past will speak through the historian only if the past has spoken to the historian. Barth displays the ability that is utterly decisive for a historian, and that Pelikan described in another context as "polyglot."[3] On this point, Barth shows his greatness, in contrast to the small-mindedness displayed by his inferior imitators. After reading the master, they had no interest in studying the past; why should one read liberal theologians who, like Harnack, had got lost in the mists of history, when one had seen the light itself in Karl Barth's theology? Harnack was to prove a fruitful dialogue partner throughout Pelikan's life, and everything that he wrote bears the traces of this conversation.

The Historian is "Polyglot"

Why ought theologians to take an interest in the past and spend time on thinkers who belong to a different age? Pelikan's writings are sustained by the conviction that every thinking person and every institution, whether religious or cultural, needs history as a liberator from inappropriate influences. He refers here not only to influences from the past. A conscientious investigation of the past is required in order to counter the forms of influence to which we are subject, and which derive both from our own selves and from the air we breathe. This is why the historian's task cannot be compared to the task of an auditor. The auditor examines the accounts from the past in order to show again and again how far we ourselves have come, in comparison with those who lived before us. The historian must learn other languages. Pelikan has in mind not only ancient languages like Latin, mediaeval English, and Norse, although this too can prove necessary. Rather, he refers to the ability to get into a conversation with another age. This is absolutely essential, if the historian is to be able to function as an interpreter between the past and the present.

The significance for theology of this kind of historical thinking ought to be obvious. One cannot get away from the fact that the churches are the bearers of a tradition;

---

[2] Pelikan in Barth, *Protestant Thought*, p. 10.
[3] Jaroslav Pelikan, "The Historian as Polyglot," *Proceedings of the American Philosophical Society*, 137 (1993), pp. 659–68.

and this is true, irrespective of how far out on Christianity's left wing one may be.[4] A church that allows the past to remain uninterpreted will inevitably incur the risk that its current faith and praxis will slowly but surely lose their meaning. Pelikan himself formulated an aphorism that has often been quoted: "Tradition is the living faith of the dead; traditionalism is the dead faith of the living."[5]

For Pelikan, tradition means "What the church of Jesus Christ believes, teaches, and confesses on the basis of the word of God."[6] His working hypothesis as a historian was that such a tradition exists throughout the whole of the church's life and history, but it was important for him that this tradition should be studied from the perspective of *development*.[7] He gained this insight from his study of development as an intimate interplay between continuity and change – an interplay that traditionalism is unable even to grasp, still less to take seriously.

Liturgy and Tradition

Where is this tradition present in the churches' life in such a way that it can be made the object of historical investigation? Some would reply by pointing to confessional documents that contain summaries of Christian doctrine, others to preaching as the place where tradition comes alive, while others again prefer to investigate the development in the theologians' studies. None of these answers is wrong, but Pelikan believes that they become wrong if one forgets to point to the liturgy. The presentation of the history of the Christian tradition is not the same as the "history of dogma." This is what Harnack did, but his perspective was too narrow. Nor did Pelikan want to write a "history of theology," because that would attribute too much importance to the theologians' role. This does not mean that their contribution to the history of the Christian tradition was insignificant; but Pelikan's chosen perspective has no place for a continuous search for their originality, in order to organize the material around this. The theologians were important as participants in a dialogue that runs through the whole of the church's history. And this is why those aspects of the Christian tradition that the theologians felt compelled to reflect upon were given

---

[4] See Jaroslav Pelikan's own reflections on this in Jaroslav Pelikan, 'The Will to Believe and the Need of a Creed', in V. Hotchkiss and P. Henry (eds), *Orthodoxy & Western Culture. A Collection of Essays Honoring Jaroslav Pelikan on His Eightieth Birthday* (New York, 2005), pp. 165–84.

[5] Jaroslav Pelikan, *The Vindication of Tradition* (New Haven, 1985), p. 65.

[6] Pelikan introduces his presentation of the history of the Christian tradition with this "definition". Jaroslav Pelikan, *The Christian Tradition: A History of the Development of Doctrine: The Emergence of the Catholic Tradition*, Vol 1 (Chicago and London, 1971), p. 1.

[7] See his retrospective remarks in Hotchkiss and Henry (eds), *Orthodoxy & Western Culture*, p. 40: "[I]ncreasingly I came to believe that every theological system, even a heretical theological system, emphasizes one valid aspect or dimension of orthodoxy defined as 'the whole counsel of God' (Acts 20.27), but at the expense of others. Therefore I also found, not in theological liberalism … but in tradition and orthodoxy, the presupposition from which to interpret any portion or period."

a prominent place in Pelikan's narrative; indeed, they determined the structure and the course of this narrative. In chapter after chapter, through the shifting epochs of the church's history, his aim was not to present the plurality of theological schools. Rather, the themes that were central in each period came to form the structure in the great narrative of the Christian tradition that Pelikan gradually wrote. He wanted to base this on the church's doctrine, not in the form of defined articles of faith, but as the living interplay between faith and adoration, preaching and teaching, discussion, dialogue, debate, and polemic.

Is there anything that holds this plurality together? Is it possible to make the basic assumption of a tradition or (to use another expression frequently found in Pelikan) an "orthodoxy"? The American historian of ideas Arthur O. Lovejoy had almost totally dismissed the idea of any inherent cohesion in Christianity.[8] Pelikan himself writes positively about the author of *The Great Chain of Being* in *The Christian Tradition*, but his own position was the exact opposite of Lovejoy's. He claimed that the duality between "doctrine" and "praise" that is found in the term "orthodoxy" itself was a clear enough indication of where this unity and coherence were to be found.[9] To speak of the Christian tradition while prescinding from the liturgy is due to an erroneous conclusion that forgets that "doctrine" is certainly not the only activity of the church, nor even its primary activity. "The church worships God and serves mankind, it works for the transformation of this world and awaits the consummation of its hope in the next."[10]

When Pelikan undertook the great task of writing a history of dogma, the role of the liturgy in this history was one of the elements that meant that his researches formed a counterpart to Harnack's work. Harnack had claimed that the formation of the church's dogma was unconnected to the liturgy, but Pelikan made the ancient formula *legem credendi statuat lex orandi*, "the law of praying is to constitute the law of believing," a methodological strategy in his studies of the history of dogma. He wished to demonstrate that the growth and development of the Christian dogma was a clarification and articulation of the faith that lived in and through the liturgy.[11]

It follows that the liturgy is the most important "locus" of tradition in the church's history. It is here that faith is contemporary, and history shows examples again and again of how worship, prayer, and praise have generated genuine theological problems. To use an image that Pelikan himself employs, we may say that the church's tradition is present in the liturgy in a way that recalls the letters demanding ransom money that we see in detective films. As we know, they are cleverly put together from words and letters cut out of newspapers and magazines. The skillful investigator is able to discover the sources and thus find out what the kidnapper is up to; but

---

[8] Arthur O. Lovejoy, *The Great Chain of Being. A Study of the History of an Idea* (Cambridge, Mass. and London, 1964 [1936]), p. 6.

[9] Pelikan refers to Lovejoy's book in Pelikan, *The Emergence of the Catholic Tradition*, p. 361.

[10] Pelikan, *The Emergence of the Catholic Tradition*, p. 1.

[11] On this, see Jaroslav Pelikan, 'The Predicament of the Christian Historian', http://www.ctinquiry.org/publications/pelikan.htm (accessed January 23, 2012), *Center of Theological Enquiry*.

it is the combination of words and letters that are intended to be meaningful here and now for the one who receives the ransom demand. At the same time, the liturgy preserves another important characteristic of tradition, that is to say, the openness that means that when we read the past, we must bear in mind that unity is not the same as uniformity. One final point: the correct relationship between theology and liturgy is important for Pelikan simply because it is the language of the liturgy – and strictly speaking, only this language – that preserves the profound paradox that we cannot speak of God, and yet we do so.

Development and Continuity

The term "polyglot" is also important when we wish to grasp Pelikan's understanding of the concept of tradition.[12] The Christian tradition speaks with many tongues. Both prose and poetry are necessary – both prayer and praise, both speech and silence. And the usual demands for logical consistency do not get us very far. Tradition represents a blend of continuity and change, and these two concepts are the most important building bricks in Pelikan's understanding of the "development of doctrine."[13] On this point, he acknowledged his debt to another important nineteenth-century theologian alongside Harnack, namely, John Henry Newman. Pelikan maintained that "development of doctrine" was Newman's concept. "I have adopted – and adapted – John Henry Newman's concept of the development of doctrine, and I have sought for the elements of continuity as well as for those of change, in fact, for the elements of continuity in the change, as I have learned to see, in Newman's brilliant oxymoron, that 'great ideas change … in order to remain the same'."[14]

In parallel to his *magnum opus*, the five-volume *The Christian Tradition: A History of the Development of Doctrine*, Pelikan also published a number of individual studies in which he applied the methodology in *The Christian Tradition* to a wide field in the history of ideas and of culture, always with the explicit intention of identifying links between culture and the church's tradition. He had already studied the history of philosophy in the modern age from this perspective in one of his earliest books, *From Luther to Kierkegaard* (1950). Plato's influence on the Christian tradition was the theme in a study of the dialogue *Timaeus* (*What Has Athens to do with Jerusalem?*, 1997). The book *Bach among the Theologians* (1986) was about music. In *The Mystery of Continuity* (1986) and *The Excellent Empire* (1987), he studied the understanding of history in the Western tradition. The first of these two books has its starting point in Augustine, while the latter looks at Edward Gibbon's classic *Decline and Fall of the Roman Empire*. Pelikan tells us that he had read this book regularly since his boyhood!

---

[12] A good introduction to this subject is his own essay: Pelikan, *The Vindication of Tradition*.
[13] See the subtitle to *The Christian Tradition*: "A History of the Development of Doctrine."
[14] Pelikan, "The Predicament of the Christian Historian," 3. http://www.ctinquiry.org/publications/pelikan.htm (accessed January 12, 2012).

Theological Writings with a Wide Perspective

Many passages in Pelikan's writings demonstrate his conviction that historical theology must transcend the traditional boundaries of this discipline, and must include fields such as art and literature. Studies of this kind include Pelikan's *Imago Dei: The Byzantine Apologia for Icons* (1990) about visual art, while the Christian tradition and literature are the theme in his studies of Dante (*Eternal Feminines*, 1990) and Goethe (*Faust the Theologian*, 2001); the latter book is dedicated to Northrop Frye. Pelikan's experience as a university teacher forms the background to *The Idea of the University – A Reexamination* (1992), in which he reflects on developments in higher education in America, in a dialogue with John Henry Newman and his book *The Idea of the University* (1852).

We should also mention individual studies of the history of theology that have a more traditional character. Pelikan's book about *Luther the Expositor* (1959) is an introduction to Luther's exegetical writings, and was published as a supplementary volume to the great American edition of Martin Luther's works, of which Pelikan was one of the chief editors. His study *Obedient Rebels* (1964) deals with the theology of the Reformation period, with a subtitle that expresses Pelikan's approach: *Catholic Substance and Protestant Principle in Luther's Reformation*. Three of Pelikan's books are in a group by themselves, since they were written for a wider readership. *Jesus through the Centuries: His Place in the History of Culture*, first published in 1985, found many readers and has gone through numerous editions. He followed this up in 1996 with *Mary through the Centuries*, a book with the same broad intention of giving information about her place in the history of culture. The third book of this kind was published in 2005, with the Bible as its theme: *Whose Bible is it? A History of the Scriptures through the Ages*. The ecumenical perspective, which had been fundamental in all his writings up to that point, was now broadened to include the other "peoples of the book," the Jews and Muslims.

In the last years of his life, Jaroslav Pelikan was involved in a large project that aimed to make the confessional documents of Christian churches from all epochs available in modern language. The three-volume work *Creeds and Confessions of Faith in the Christian Tradition*, with a CD-ROM containing the confessional texts in their original languages, was published in 2003. He wrote an introduction to this comprehensive collection of confessions of faith, in a large volume entitled *Credo* (2003). Here, as also in his own contribution to the Festschrift that was published to mark his eightieth birthday – "The Will to Believe and the Need for Creed" – he underlines a prominent motif in his writings, namely, the untenability of the widespread antithesis between personal faith, on the one hand, and the common confession of the church, on the other. It was this sense of unease that led him finally to leave the Lutheran church in America.

The Path to Orthodoxy

Many of those who reviewed Pelikan's five-volume work on the Christian tradition drew special attention to the wide place that the Orthodox tradition receives in his presentation. Pelikan devoted the whole of the second volume, with the subtitle *The Spirit of Eastern Christendom (600–1700)*, to a period in the history of the Eastern tradition in which – according to customary opinion – very little had happened that was worthy of a historian's interest. Pelikan begins this volume with two quotations (p. 1). The first is from Adolf von Harnack, who had in effect asserted in his history of dogma that "the history of dogma in the Greek church came to an end, [so that] any revival of that history is difficult to imagine." The second is from Edward Gibbon, who wrote that the Christians in the East "held in their lifeless hands the riches of their fathers, without inheriting the spirit which had created and improved that sacred patrimony."

For Pelikan, such statements illustrated all too well the prejudices that had led Western historians to ignore Eastern Christianity, apart from those episodes in which the so-called Western church was also involved. He seeks to amend this state of affairs by showing that the Orthodox line was not a dead traditionalism, but a living tradition to which one could meaningfully apply the perspective of continuity and change.

In 1992, Pelikan was invited to deliver the prestigious Gifford Lectures on Natural Theology at the University of Aberdeen. Here, he stepped back from the presentation in *The Spirit of Eastern Christianity*, and sought to depict the Eastern theological patrimony as the result of the encounter between Christianity and the Hellenistic classical culture, an encounter that found expression in the so-called Cappadocian fathers, Gregory of Nyssa, Gregory Nazianzen, and Basil the Great, all of whom lived in the second half of the fourth century.[15] He gave the printed version of these lectures the title *Christianity and Classical Culture*, and in retrospect, this must be said to be his intellectual and literary *tour de force*. The book has two parts, each of which studies "natural theology" from two perspectives, that of "apologetics" and that of "presupposition." These two perspectives are referred to in the book's subtitle: *The Metamorphosis of Natural Theology in the Christian Encounter with Hellenism*. Each of the two principal parts is divided into 10 chapters, in such a way that each of these chapters has its counterpart in the other principal part. Pelikan thus elegantly gives the book a mirror-structure.

Pelikan himself said that he had brought about, by means of these lectures, a profound change in the perspective on the Eastern tradition in comparison with Harnack's celebrated statement that "dogma is basically a work of the Greek spirit on the ground of the Gospel." Pelikan regards this as an excessively simple description of what came out of the encounter between Christianity and Hellenism. Where Harnack saw a "Greek spirit" that was easily discernible in the theology of the fourth and later centuries, Pelikan saw an "influence" that itself had been influenced by this encounter

---

[15] Jaroslav Pelikan, *Christianity and Classical Culture. The Metamorphosis of Natural Theology in the Christian Encounter with Hellenism* (New Haven and London, 1993).

– indeed, an "influence" that had undergone a transformation or *metamorphosis* as a result of this cultural encounter. In Hellenism, there was a philosophical tradition that had emerged as an alternative, or even as an antidote, to the traditional religion with its cultic acts and sacred narratives. But the Greek church fathers were not only philosophers and apologists. They were also priests and preachers, and they could not think of theology detached from Christian praxis – a praxis that for them was identical with the liturgy. This is why the classical natural theology did not form a synthesis with Christianity, but itself underwent a metamorphosis. How was it possible for Harnack to take such a different view? What was the decisive factor in the tradition to which he himself belonged? Pelikan has no doubts about what is at stake here: it is a question of the importance of the liturgy in the Christian tradition. Harnack and academic theology lacked a vital sensitivity to what Pelikan (borrowing an expression from an Eastern patriarch) liked to call "the melody of theology." In an article published in 1973, he goes into this matter as follows:

> A disciple of St. Augustine formulated the Western Latin version of this 'melody of theology' in the principle that 'the rule of prayer should lay down the rule of faith'. The supreme instance of this principle was, of course, the dogma of the Trinity. It is not, in the strict sense, a doctrine of the New Testament; it is, rather, the church's way of saying what it had to say to be faithful to the New Testament and to its own fundamental pattern of worship. If it was right to speak to Christ as the worship of the church did, and if the monotheism of the Bible was to be preserved, something like the dogma of the Trinity seemed to be the only way for 'the rule of faith' to be conformed to 'the rule of prayer' and for 'the melody of theology to be sung in harmony with both.[16]

Five years after the publication of his book on the Cappadocians, Jaroslav Pelikan was received into the Orthodox church. He wrote that while others read their way into a conversion, he wrote his way into the Orthodox church. And he added that if an airplane had circled over the runway for as long as time before it landed, it would have run out of fuel long ago. He fell asleep in the Orthodox faith on May 13, 2006.

The Church Lives by the Past, but for the Future

It is not easy to classify Pelikan in the same category as other historians. Most church historians choose one small area of the past, which they gradually master, but Pelikan had much larger ambitions from the very outset. He wanted to interpret the whole of Christianity's past and to describe the development of Christianity from the earliest times down to the present day. And he did this in a continuous dialogue with the two nineteenth-century thinkers who, in his opinion, had made the greatest contribution

---

[16] Jaroslav Pelikan, "Worship between Yesterday and Tomorrow," *Studia Liturgica*, 9 (1973), p. 205.

to reflection on Christian tradition and history, Adolf von Harnack and John Henry Newman.

Pelikan's writings can be seen as a protest against the development in church history towards an ever more specialized discipline in academia. His work is also characterized by a profound conviction that many ecclesial traditions today want to wash their hands of the past, and that this can only lead in the long term to irreparable damage. He remarked, with the Lutheran church in America particularly in mind: "Too often we have supposed that the knowledge of God is something that the church possesses once and for all – or, at any rate, something that our particular church has come to possess once and for all."[17] Pelikan believed that it was both immature and harmful to think that one particular epoch in the church's history had been entrusted with Christian doctrine in its complete form. In the same way, it would be presumptuous to claim that one part of the church no longer needed to grow in the knowledge of God. It is here that history plays the important role of working against a collective loss of the church's memory. This differs from Harnack's view of the task of the history of dogma, namely, to correct the past in order to make the church's message more comprehensible to the German bourgeoisie. The historian must be a spokesman for the past, and this means that his task – unenviable, but very important – is to disturb ecclesial self-satisfaction in all its forms. To be a spokesperson means allowing the voices from the past to be heard in a church that tries to forget them, but that needs to hear them afresh. This also means that one avoids claiming the support of the past for one's own positions. Martin Luther should not be studied because he was a "Lutheran" (something he certainly was not), nor should Calvin be studied because he allegedly was a Barthian! "[T]he church can have authentic creativity in her theology and her worship only if she overcomes the dread disease of amnesia which, especially in the modern world, does so easily beset us all." Ultimately, this means that Pelikan wrote his important works not for his own age alone, but just as much in view of the future, for the twenty-first century. "The church lives by the past, but for the future."[18]

Bibliography

Primary Literature

A comprehensive bibliography of Jaroslav Pelikan's writings will be found in:

Hotchkiss, V. and Henry, P. (eds), *Orthodoxy & Western Culture. A Collection of Essays Honoring Jaroslav Pelikan on his Eightieth Birthday* (New York: St. Vladimir Press, 2005), pp. 185–228.

---

[17] Ibid., p. 207.
[18] Ibid., p. 205.

His most important works include the following:

The Riddle of Roman Catholicism: Its History, Its Belief, Its Future (Nashville: Abingdon Press, 1959).
Luther the Expositor: Introduction to the Reformer's Exegetical Writings [Luther's Works, Companion volume] (St. Louis: Concordia Publishing House, 1959).
Spirit versus Structure: Luther and the Institutions of the Church (New York: Harper & Row, 1968).
Historical Theology. Continuity and Change in Christian Doctrine (New York: Corpus Books / London: Hutchinson, 1971).
The Christian Tradition: A History of the Development of Doctrine:
   Vol. 1: *The Emergence of the Catholic Tradition (100–600)*.
   Vol. 2: *The Spirit of Eastern Christendom (600–1700)*.
   Vol. 3: *The Growth of Medieval Theology (600–1300)*.
   Vol. 4: *Reformation of Church and Dogma (1300–1700)*.
   Vol. 5: *Christian Doctrine and Modern Culture (since 1700)* (Chicago: University of Chicago Press, 1971–89).
"Worship between Yesterday and Tomorrow," *Studia Liturgica*, 9 (1973), pp. 205–14.
The Vindication of Tradition (New Haven: Yale University Press, 1984).
Jesus through the Centuries: His Place in the History of Culture (New Haven: Yale University Press, 1985).
Bach among the Theologians (Philadelphia: Fortress Press, 1986).
The Mystery of Continuity: Time and History, Memory and Eternity in the Thought of Saint Augustine (Charlottesville: University of Virginia Press, 1986).
Eternal Feminines: Three Theological Allegories in Dante's Paradiso (New Brunswick NJ: Rutgers UP, 1990).
The Idea of the University: A Reexamination (New Haven: Yale University Press, 1992).
Christianity and Classical Culture. The Metamorphosis of Natural Theology in the Christian Encounter with Hellenism (New Haven: Yale University Press, 1993).
"The Predicament of the Christian Historian," 3. http://www.ctinquiry.org/publications/pelikan.htm (accessed January 12, 2012).
Faust the Theologian (New Haven: Yale University Press, 1995).
Mary through the Centuries: Her Place in the History of Culture (New Haven: Yale University Press, 1996).
What has Athens to do with Jerusalem?: Timaeus and Genesis in Counterpoint (Ann Arbor: University of Michigan Press, 1997).
Divine Rhetoric: The Sermon on the Mount as Message and as Model in Augustine, Chrysostom, and Luther (Crestwood, NY: St. Vladimir Seminary Press, 2000).
Credo: Historical and Theological Guide to Creeds and Confessions of Faith in the Christian Tradition (New Haven: Yale University Press, 2003).
Whose Bible is it? – A History of the Scriptures through the Ages (New York: Viking, 2005).
"The Will to Believe and the Need of a Creed," in V. Hotchkiss and P. Henry (eds), *Orthodoxy & Western Culture. A Collection of Essays Honoring Jaroslav Pelikan on His Eightieth Birthday* (Crestwood, NY: St. Vladimir Seminary Press, 2005).

Secondary Literature

David A. Lotz, "The Achievement of Jaroslav Pelikan," *First Things*, 23 (1992), 55–65.
Darrell Jodock, "Christian Doctrine and Modern Culture," *Journal of the American Academy of Religion*, 61(2) (1993), 321–38.

Chapter 40
George Lindbeck

Roland Spjuth

From time to time, a book is published that becomes point of reference to which everyone is obliged to relate, since it provides clear categories for the interpretation of theology's sometimes complicated discourse. One such book appeared in 1984 when the American Lutheran theologian George Lindbeck published *The Nature of Doctrine: Religion and Theology in a Postliberal Age*. Lindbeck and Hans Frei, his colleague at the theological faculty in Yale, had already attracted attention as mentors for several young theologians who were looking for new paths for theology outside the established alternatives. Lindbeck's book now made the term "postliberal" a collective designation of these currents in Anglo-Saxon theology. Not everyone agreed with Lindbeck in his description or in the categories he applied, but everyone was compelled to relate to these. In the last years of the twentieth century, this book set the agenda for much of the theological debate, especially in Anglo-Saxon theology.

Lutheran Theology in the Universal Church

George Lindbeck was born in 1923 in China, the son of Swedish-American Lutheran missionaries. He came to the USA at the age of 17 and began his studies, which led to his doctoral dissertation at Yale University on the mediaeval theologian Duns Scotus (1955). Even before he had completed his doctorate, he was appointed to the faculty in Yale and remained there until his retirement in 1993.

As an expert on mediaeval theology, Lindbeck was appointed as one of three official representatives of the Lutheran church at the Second Vatican Council (the others were Vilmos Vatja and Kristen Skydsgaard), and this was a very important experience for him. He attended the Council from 1962 to 1965. Between the sessions, he informed Lutheran churches about this historic process of transformation. During these years, he came increasingly to sense that he and other observers shared with Catholics a common mission to renew the church. According to Lindbeck himself, this ecumenical fellowship became the primary context for his theology.

After the Council, Lindbeck devoted a considerable amount of time to ecumenical theological work, not least in the dialogue between Lutherans and Catholics. In his books *The Future of Roman Catholic Theology* (1972) and *Infallibility* (1971), he attempted to find paths that led beyond the doctrinal differences that separated the Catholic and Lutheran churches. His starting point was that the necessary renewal of the church must build on scripture and on the traditions of the church prior to the modern period.

This was the common point of departure both for the Catholic *nouvelle théologie* and for Karl Barth's theology, which influenced Lindbeck's early theological milieu. One proof of the fruitfulness of this starting point is that it explains why the Second Vatican Council went much further in its efforts to renew the church than most people believed beforehand. According to Lindbeck, the bishops' attitude changed because they became convinced in the course of the conciliar process that the church's sources did not support the conservative stance of the curia. The return to the sources (*ressourcement*) necessitated both the aggiornamento of the church and an ecumenical openness. Lindbeck regrets that after the Second Vatican Council, the ecumenical scene was split to such a degree between traditionalists who merely repeated the traditional doctrines and renewers who began directly with the churches' social involvement. In his polemic against much of the liberation theology that dominated the World Council of Churches, he sees it as an ecumenical impoverishment to begin directly in God's work in the world for peace, justice, and the environment, rather than in the church's own sources.

Lindbeck's ecumenical commitment did not lead to a downplaying of his identity as a Lutheran theologian. Ecumenism is built on the seriousness with which the participants take their own tradition. But he replaced the conservative, pietistic, and low-church Lutheranism in which he had grown up with a more church-centered and historically anchored interpretation. He reads the Lutheran Reformation on the basis of its original intention of being "a reformation within the Catholic church," and he sees the Confessio Augustana as the clearest expression of this intention.

The book *The Nature of Doctrine*, which made Lindbeck celebrated, was born of his reflections on the function that doctrines played in the ecumenical dialogue. The book describes three different ways of understanding Christian doctrines. The first interpretation, which is predominant in conservative theology, holds that the articles of the Christian faith are informative propositions about objective facts. The second interpretation, which Lindbeck calls the liberal strategy, sees doctrines as symbolic interpretations of inner experiences. Lindbeck believes that neither of these models can explain the situation that arises *de facto* in the encounter between Christian traditions. The conservative view makes it impossible to understand how Christians can achieve genuine unity while belonging to different doctrinal traditions, while the liberal model doubtless enables us to speak about unity in shared inner experiences, but does not do justice to the fact that the doctrinal differences are just as obvious. In contrast to these conservative and liberal strategies, Lindbeck developed a "cultural-linguistic model." This compares religions to a culture or a language, that is to say, to the interpretative patterns that form both the total life-world of a society and the identity of its members.

Lindbeck does not regard the cultural-linguistic model as a controversial creation of his own. Rather, he attempts to sum up dominant contemporary views of religion, as these are expressed, for example, by the anthropologist Clifford Geertz and the linguistic philosopher Ludwig Wittgenstein. These views agree that identity and experience are to a high degree social and cultural constructions. His own contribution is to clarify the consequences of this religious paradigm for the understanding of the Christian faith and ecumenism. The decisive point is that a cultural-linguistic model does not make doctrines the primary thing. Lindbeck compares them rather to "secondary" grammatical reflections about how language should be used correctly. The most important task of doctrines is not to "provide information," but to ensure that the Christian life is constructed in a way that is faithful to the grammar in its fundamental narratives. This position allows Lindbeck to show how a grammatical rule can be expressed in changing ways in different contextual situations. For example, the rule "that a Christian always gives thanks to God for the gift of salvation" is expressed by means of different doctrines in different contexts, without thereby infringing the same fundamental grammatical rule for the formation of the Christian life. Lindbeck hopes that this theory about rules will allow him to get beyond the polarization between a stable grammatical structure and a varying theological vocabulary.

Lindbeck wrote little after *The Nature of Doctrine*, despite the enormous interest kindled by this book. He was strikingly silent in the debates about the interpretation of postliberal theology. Instead, his theology has focused on arguing that ecumenical work must find a connection to the church's Jewish roots. In a number of articles, he says that the church must be understood "like the people of Israel." Some of these later articles were collected by James J. Buckley in *Church in a Postliberal Age* (2002). This book also includes representative articles from Lindbeck's theological career and is the best starting point for one who seeks an overview of his theology as a whole.

Postliberal Theology

Truth and Scripture

By means of his cultural-linguistic model, Lindbeck underlines that religion is based on various cultural constructions. These differ, and there is no neutral ground that would allow us to test which of these cultures best corresponds to reality. Lindbeck thus accepts the epistemological position that rejects "foundationalism." Although this is something he learned through his philosophical studies, he believes that it may be his upbringing in northern China, far away from the harbor cities that were influenced by the West, that taught him this respect for the varieties of cultures. His anti-foundationalism leads him to call into question the liberal project that has dominated theology since the Enlightenment and that seeks to translate, correlate, or revise theology in relation to modern experiences. A cultural-linguistic model does not begin with modern experience as a given and unquestionable point of departure. Instead, Lindbeck asks what tradition and what culture ought to construct the Christian's identity. And with this starting point, it is natural for Lindbeck to emphasize that the church should be formed primarily by the sources and narratives of its own tradition.

Lindbeck's emphasis on the narratives of one's own tradition is strongly influenced by his colleagues at Yale – for example, Brevard Childs' canonical reading of the Bible, David Kelsey's argument that the authority of the Bible is based on the community's use of the text, and not least, Hans Frei with his interpretation of scripture as a realistic narrative. Frei holds that modern hermeneutics has destroyed the ability to let Bible's own interpretative framework be determinative of the Christian faith. The Bible's world became a foreign world that had to be explained through scholars' references to something outside the text itself, either to its historical reference or to a spiritual experience or a moral truth that lies behind the text. Against this, Frei claimed that the Bible should be read as a realistic narrative with its own inherent meaning. Lindbeck strongly agrees with this, and argues against the liberal strategy of translation that theology ought instead to absorb the world. The biblical narrative must be internalized as the interpretative framework on the basis of which the Christian understands and attempts to lead his life. Or, as Lindbeck puts it in words that have often been quoted, "it is the text, so to speak, which absorbs the world, rather than the world the text." This proposition has often been criticized, but it does not contain any absurd assertion that the Bible gives the true explanation of all phenomena. Nor does Lindbeck downplay the importance of the context: this must be taken seriously, with all the insights that can influence faith. His words mean that every culture has an overarching interpretative framework, and according to Lindbeck, the aim of the church's struggles and argumentation is to establish that the Christian's interpretative framework should be the biblical narrative rather than the modern secular narrative.

Lindbeck's logic means that the test of the truth in the Christian affirmations is whether they are faithful to the fundamental grammar of the Christian faith – in other words, whether they are intertextually true. For example, the truth in the proposition "Jesus is Lord" primarily means that the Christian should form his or her life through prayer, adoration, and lifestyle in such a way that it reflects Jesus' lordship. The fundamental test is thus whether the belief is coherent with one's own tradition. This means that a crusader who smashes the head of an unbeliever because "Jesus is Lord" falsifies the Christian grammar, irrespective of whether the crusader is in fact correct when he says that "Jesus is Lord" is a statement about facts. This intertextual understanding of truth has perhaps been the most disputed point in Lindbeck's postliberal theology. Does it not succumb to a relativism? And does it not make the critical testing of religious language impossible? Lindbeck certainly believes that faith is tested above all through the fruit and the attractiveness that lie in faithfully living the Christian faith on the basis of its own center. But it is wholly incorrect to say that he is uninterested in whether faith is true in a more ontological sense. This ontological truth cannot, however, be tested by measuring individual doctrines against external facts or internal experience. Since faith is a "cultural-linguistic totality," its reference to ontological reality must be discussed as a totality, as "a single gigantic proposition." A testing of this kind between different cultural life-worlds is naturally immensely complex, and Lindbeck's reflections in *The Nature of Doctrine* leave several questions unanswered. He stated subsequently that his endeavors resembled Alisdair MacIntyre's reflections on the rational testing of different traditions. The important test here is whether a tradition is able to open up reality for those who share in it, whether it can integrate new insights and absorb challenges from other traditions. Basically, Lindbeck holds that the Christian argumentation on behalf of faith (apologetics) must have a humble attitude when the representatives of various traditions begin to talk together and to examine their life-worlds in those areas where common points of contact exist. He describes this strategy, in a term borrowed from William Werpehowski, as *ad hoc apologetics*.

The Israel-like Church

Lindbeck was convinced early on that the church's contemporary situation is undergoing radical change through the ever more comprehensive secularization and individualization of the West. He agrees with the Catholic theologian Karl Rahner that Christendom as an era is over and that Christians, like the early church, will exist as a minority movement in a diaspora. This makes it self-destructive to continue the liberal strategy of accommodating faith to an increasingly non-Christian culture. Instead, Lindbeck says that the church must recover a pre-Constantinian structure. Faith is intensified in a post-Christian age. Church membership demands a personal step and the willingness to live in contrast to the surrounding society. A church in a diaspora no longer speaks from a position of power; it speaks as the Lord's suffering servant for the world. Lindbeck is convinced that an ecclesial identity of this kind can be sustained only by more closely-knit communities. A church like this is not the same as a fundamentalist and closed movement. Lindbeck sees the early church as an ecumenical and international church that was open to the world.

Throughout his theological career, Lindbeck has insisted that it is good that Christendom as an era is over. He has, however, reservations about what this means for the formerly Christian societies in the West. He is increasingly uneasy about the development in a society that lacks religion and that is gradually being dominated by an unchecked neoliberal market economy and by the consumption of wares and of values. He identified himself at one point with the more radical Reformation theology of Stanley Hauerwas, but he later came to take a more ambivalent attitude to Christendom as a phenomenon. Today, he asks whether it is possible to strengthen the necessary shared identity in Western society without the collaboration of the church.

Lindbeck's unease about the effects of the collapse of Christendom does not however call into question his basic idea that the church must return to the early church's visible fellowship of local churches in the diaspora. His continued reflections on this theme have led to a strong emphasis on the church as "Israel-like." One of the great problems with Christendom was its sharp break with its Jewish roots. The church replaced the literal Israel as the people of God. Against this, Lindbeck holds that theology must regain the New Testament view that the church is a continuation and an expansion of God's one people. This means not only a new relationship to Judaism, but also a strong corrective to the tendency to spiritualize and individualize the Christian faith. When the church is thought of as "God's people like Israel," it is clear that the noun "people" designates an empirical and historical reality. Lindbeck takes offense at the fact that so many Christian theological terms and models for the church shift the focus from this crystal-clear content and emphasize rather a suprahistorical, mystical reality. A renewed ecclesiology must regain the Old Testament insight that its primary level is the narrative of the history of God's people rather than a systematic theological account of what the church is.

An Israel-like church is also of central importance for Lindbeck's ecumenical endeavors. "Israel-like" means that all who belong to Israel belong to the people of God, irrespective of their internal differences. Just as all "Jews" belong to the people of Israel, irrespective of their internal distinctions, so too all Jews and Christians belong together in the people of God, simply because they have been chosen by God. The history of Israel also shows how important it is both to accept change in new situations and to preserve continuity and tradition. When the church is seen as the history of one people, it can integrate change, plurality, and tradition. In concrete terms, Lindbeck believes that this cannot be carried out without an emphasis on the episcopal ministry. But this ministry must be understood on the basis of the structure of the pre-Constantinian church, as a reciprocal network of local communities where the bishops worked together to acknowledge each other's leadership and apostolic fidelity.

A Cultural-linguistic Understanding of Religion

A third area in which Lindbeck's postliberal theology has played a very important role is religious dialogue. The liberal tradition which had previously been dominant in America saw religion as an almost universal phenomenon, the expression of a sacred dimension in all human life, but with varying symbols and rites. Christianity could thus be explained as a symbolic expression of this mysterious deep dimension in existence. William Placher has pointed out that there was another tradition at Yale, where only the individual religions were studied, not "religion" in general. It is in this context that Lindbeck elaborates his "cultural-linguistic model."

This model says that we cannot understand the different religions by pointing to a common core. According to Lindbeck, the human person does not relate to any experiences or dimensions outside his or her language or culture. Religions are different cultural and linguistic worlds that are nourished by their own memories and narratives. This is why the religions construct their worlds in different ways. Lindbeck regards the view that all religions are about salvation, or are based on religious experiences, as grave reductions that fail to see how – and with similar terminology – much that is different can be constructed within different religious interpretative frameworks. The consequence of this holistic understanding is that religions cannot be translated into each other, or into some third supposedly neutral (secular) language, without losing something fundamental to their own interpretation of life. Lindbeck believes that the assertion of untranslatability clearly exists in classical Christian hermeneutics. The language that Christians employ declares that the community that reads the Bible is one unique and chosen testimony to God's saving will. If the Bible is given a secondary position in regard to some other interpretative framework, it is also loses something essential in its content.

Lindbeck's understanding of religion can be read as an early expression of the late-twentieth-century celebration of plurality that came to be a commonplace in so-called postmodernism. Critics interpret it as a concession to relativism and say that the idea of untranslatability makes religious dialogue impossible. Lindbeck claims that the opposite is true, and that the genuine dialogue was disturbed by the idea, promoted by a liberal religious discourse, that all the religions, despite their differences, are expressing the same common core. This idea denies both the genuine differences that exist between the religions and their universalistic claims. It reflects, not a genuine dialogue, but a concealed Christian or secular agenda. But if the dialogue begins with the insight that religions are unique, this dialogue makes possible the difficult art of understanding the others on their own terms. This probably also means that the religious dialogue cannot take the form of a universal religious dialogue, and that this must be replaced by bilateral conversations.

Lindbeck does not only emphasize the differences between the religions. He also speaks in favor of a "peaceful coexistence." Faith's claim to be a unique testimony is not the same as what Lindbeck calls an arrogant claim that salvation is found only in the church. His emphasis on an "Israel-like church" means that he marks his distance from the interpretation of the church's mission as saving souls. God has chosen his people so that through its narrative – which, like the story of Israel, also includes the church's failures – it may bear a testimony to who God is. As far as the human person's salvation and the improvement of the world are concerned, God is free to use any means that he wishes. Lindbeck also holds that the Christian faith has a vocation to serve all the societies in which it exists. And since most communities are held together by a religious conviction, Christians are called to serve non-Christian societies too, and to seek the best for them. From the first apologists onwards – who addressed a pagan religious Rome – the Christian tradition has affirmed that it is important for the church to seek the peace and progress of society, if for no other reason than because this gives the church the freedom it needs in order to be a testimony to God.

Postliberalism as a Research Program

Scholars have discussed whether the term "postliberal" applies to the formation of a school. A number of important theologians in America wrote their doctoral theses under Lindbeck and Frei in Yale, for example, William Placher, Bruce Marshall, James Buckley, Ronald Thiemann, Kathryn Tanner, David Yeago, Joseph DiNoia, and George Hunsinger. Despite a clear family likeness in this group, there are also many differences, and most of these theologians dislike being labeled as postliberals. Besides this, few of them follow Lindbeck's theology completely; one point on which they differ is his interpretation of doctrines as grammatical rules without an ontological reference. And other categories, such as postmodernity and radical orthodoxy, have moved higher up on the theological agenda in America today. Lindbeck himself believes that postliberalism should be read as a kind of research program with a number of shared starting points. In this sense, there is a rather large group of scholars who continue their work in a postliberal direction.

Lindbeck has also had considerable influence on the renewal in Protestant Evangelical theology. Although many here have their reservations about Lindbeck's view of truth, a growing number hold that postliberalism shows how the church can be a community formed by scripture without being fundamentalist, and how they can combine the idea of being a countercultural church in the diaspora with ecumenism and openness to the needs of society. Important theologians in this group include Stanley Grenz, Nancey Murphy, Clark Pinnock, and Kevin Vanhoozer.

The most important consequence of Lindbeck's postliberal agenda is perhaps that it helped to end the dominant position of liberal and revisionist theologians at American universities at the beginning of the 1980s. The criticism of pre-linguistic experiences and of a universal religious dimension has helped change the theological discourse. This can be seen, for example, in the transition made by David Tracy (one of Lindbeck's earliest critics) from a liberal to a postmodern theology. Theologians of religion who were active at an earlier date, such as Paul Knitter and John Hick, have been balanced by a new group who are closer to Lindbeck, such as Gavin D'Costa, Paul Griffiths, and J.A. DiNoia. The changes within the liberal tradition, together with the postmodern conditions in which today's theology is carried out, have not completely abolished the differences between the various theological schools. But perhaps these factors mean that some elements in Lindbeck's description of the polarizations have lost their actuality.

Bibliography

Primary Literature

Infallibility (Marquette University Press, 1971).
The Future of Roman Catholic Theology. (Philadelphia, 1972).
The Nature of Doctrine: Religion and Theology in a Postliberal Age (Louisville and London, 1984).
"The Story-Shaped Church: Critical Exegesis and Theological Interpretation," in Garrett Green (ed.), *Scriptural Authority and Narrative Interpretation* (Philadelphia, 1987), pp. 161–78.
The Church in a Postliberal Age, edited by James J. Buckley (Grand Rapids, 2002).

Secondary Literature

Buckley, James J., "Postliberal Theology: A Catholic Reading," in Roger A. Badham (ed.), *Introduction to Christian Theology: Contemporary North American Perspectives* (Louisville, 1998), pp. 89–102.
DeHart, Paul J., *The Trial of the Witnesses: The Rise and Decline of Postliberal Theology* (Oxford, 2006).

Fodor, James, "Postliberal Theology," in David F. Ford and Rachel Muers (eds), *The Modern Theologians: An Introduction to Christian Theology since 1918*, 3rd ed. (Oxford, 2005), pp. 229–48.

Hunsinger, George, "Postliberal Theology," in Kevin J. Vanhoozer (ed.), *The Cambridge Companion to Postmodern Theology* (Cambridge, 2003), pp. 42–57.

Marshall, Bruce D., "Aquinas the Postliberal Theologian," in *The Thomist*, 53 (1989), pp. 353–406.

Marshall, Bruce D. (ed.), *Theology and Dialogue: Essays in Conversation with George Lindbeck* (Notre Dame, 1990).

Phillips, Timothy R. and Okholm, Dennis L. (eds), *The Nature of Confession: Evangelicals and Postliberals in Conversation* (Downers Grove, Illinois, 1996).

Vanhoozer, Kevin J., *The Drama of Doctrine: A Canonical Linguistic Approach to Christian Theology* (Louisville, 2005).

Chapter 41
Robert W. Jenson

Olli-Pekka Vainio

One of the major events in twentieth-century theology was the new interest in Trinitarian themes. The mainstream of nineteenth-century Protestant theology had criticized the doctrine of the Trinity for being tied to Hellenistic ontology and therefore deviating from authentic, original Christianity. Especially after Immanuel Kant, skepticism about theological ontology increased dramatically. The general spirit of the post-Enlightenment era was to interpret religion increasingly from the viewpoint of the human person and experience. The whole Trinitarian endeavor seemed, to borrow Colin Gunton's blunt statement: "a matter of mathematical conundrums and illogical attempts to square the circle."

A number of things changed this downward trend. The birth of the ecumenical movement and consequent discussions with Protestant, Orthodox, and Catholic churches brought the issue back to the table. The works of prominent theologians, such as Karl Barth (1886–1968) and Karl Rahner (1904–84), engaged extensively with Trinitarian themes. Wolfhart Pannenberg, Jürgen Moltmann, Eberhard Jüngel and Robert W. Jenson continued this movement in their own studies. While occasionally disagreeing with each other, they more or less subscribe to Rahner's famous maxim: "the economic Trinity is immanent Trinity and vice versa," meaning that God's works in the history reveals the essence of God for us.

From this insight arose the renaissance of Trinitarian theology. The doctrine of the Trinity was no longer seen as an unauthentic and rationalistic scheme forced upon vivid religious experiences of the first Christians, which stagnated the imaginative beliefs to a dead formula, as was supposed by liberal Protestantism. Instead, Trinitarian theology was again seen as the articulation of the Church's experience of being encountered by God Himself and joined in Him, manifested through God's works in history and crystallized in the person of Christ.

Life

Robert W. Jenson was born August 2, 1930 at Eau Claire, Wisconsin, into a pastor's family of the then Norwegian Lutheran Church. In his college years in Luther College in Decorah, Iowa, he studied classics and philosophy before beginning theological studies at Luther Seminary, St Paul, Minnesota, in 1951. There he became familiar with traditional confessional Lutheran theology and patristics, and the thought of the modern historical-critical school. During an intership at the

University of Minnesota, he met Blanche Rockne, a young seminary counselor, who later became his wife and "co-author" of many of his books. In 1957 Jenson moved to Heidelberg for doctoral studies with preliminary plans to write his dissertation on Rudolf Bultmann. His supervisor in Heidelberg, Peter Brunner (1900–81), however, encouraged him to work on Karl Barth's doctrine of election instead. At that time, he also studied nineteenth-century German theology and philosophy, with the help of Wolfhart Pannenberg, who was a lecturer in Heidelberg. He attended a seminar held by Martin Heidegger and later one by Hans-Georg Gadamer. In Heidelberg, he made friends with another American student, Carl Braaten, who would later become his closest theological collaborator. In 1959 Jenson moved to Basel in order to study under the tutelage of Karl Barth.

After completion of his dissertation, which was approved by Barth himself, in 1959 (*Alpha and Omega: A Study in the Theology of Karl Barth*, published in 1963), Jenson returned to Luther College. One of the most notable events in the 1960s was establishing the theological journal *dialog* in order to free American Lutheranism from the theological and cultural isolation from which it then suffered. In the 1960s, Jenson spent a three-year period at Mansfield College, Oxford University. There his encounters with Anglicanism and ecumenical worship put him on a track which would lead to a number of ecumenical efforts, and theologically in an increasingly Catholic direction. In 1968, Jenson returned to the United States and a teaching position at the Lutheran Seminary in Gettysburg. As a result of his experiences with Anglicanism in Oxford, Jenson was appointed to the Lutheran-Episcopal ecumenical dialogue in the same year, and later through collaboration with George Lindbeck (born 1923), he became involved in the Roman Catholic–Lutheran dialogue as well. In 1988 Jenson moved to the religion department of St Olaf College in Northfield where he worked until his retirement in 1998. In 1991, he and Braaten founded together the Center for Catholic and Evangelical Theology. In connection with the newly established Center, the colleagues began publishing the ecumenical theological journal *Pro Ecclesia*, after recognizing that their previous journal *dialog* had moved too far from its original mission. After his retirement Jenson became the Senior Scholar for Research at the Center for Theological Inquiry, Princeton, New Jersey.

Major Works

After his dissertation, his first major volume was *A Religion against Itself* (1967), a critique of current American religious culture. In this volume Jenson partly joined with the contemporary "secular" or "death of God" theology, which considered all metaphysical theological language to be meaningless. Simultaneously he was critical toward the extreme forms of the movement, which were in danger of lapsing into nihilism. In *The Knowledge of Things Hoped For: The Sense of Theological Discourse* (1969), he sought to integrate the (classically rival) traditions of continental and analytical philosophy. In *God after God: The God of the Past and the God of the Future, Seen in the Work of Karl Barth* (1969), he engaged again with the "death of God" theology, siding with the thought of Jürgen Moltmann and Wolfhart Pannenberg. In the 1970s, Jenson engaged with distinctively Lutheran themes, especially in the books *Lutheranism: The Theological Movement and its Writings* (with Eric Gritsch, 1976) and *Visible Words: The Interpretation and Practice of Christian Sacraments* (1978). At that time, he also began to study patristic thought (especially the writings of Gregory of Nyssa, Cyril of Alexandria, and Maximus the Confessor), which led him to develop a creative new proposal for Trinitarian theology in *The Triune Identity: God According to the Gospel* (1982), which he has later developed in his other studies. At the end of the 1980s, he engaged with the religious heritage of his own continent, which resulted in a publication of creative exposition of Jonathan Edwards' (1703–58) theology (*America's Theologian: A Recommendation of Jonathan Edwards*, 1988).

Over the years Jenson has collaborated extensively with Carl Braaten. They have produced a co-authored two volume *Christian Dogmatics* (1984) and numerous jointly edited volumes on a wide array of subjects including ecumenism, culture, and fundamental issues of Christian life and dogmatics. At the end of the 1990s, Jenson completed his *magnum opus*, the two-volume *Systematic Theology* (Vol. 1: *The Triune God*, 1997 and Vol. 2: *The Works of God*, 1999), which has been widely regarded as one of the most important and creative works in modern theology. In these volumes Jenson presents his central theological thinking in systematic form. *Systematic Theology* is written "in the anticipation of the one church," trying thus to be a genuinely ecumenical exposition of Christian doctrine.

Jenson's engament with issues of current culture can be found in the collected works *Essays in Theology of Culture* (1995) and *On Thinking the Human: Resolutions on Difficult Notions* (2003). Lately Jenson has also produced two commentaries, one on *Song of Songs* (2005) and the other on *Ezekiel* (2009), in connection with the new movement of "theological interpretation," where Scriptures are read from the perspective of credal faith. A theoretical treatise of this project is *Canon and Creed* (2010). One of the most amusing pieces of his work is *Conversations with Poppi about God: An Eight-Year-Old and Her Theologian Grandfather Trade Questions* (2006), where Jenson discusses spiritual matters with his granddaughter. In *Lutheran Slogans: Use and Abuse* (2011) he defends Lutheran theology against reductionistic readings that result from the abuse of well-known slogans used to define the core of Lutheran theology, such as *sola* and *simul* principles.

Main Themes of Scholarship

Since his dissertation, the question of time has permeated much of Jenson's work. Drawing from the discussions around "death of God" theology, Jenson builds his notion of God in relation to the central existential and philosophical questions of the twentieth century. If there is no transcendence beyond our realm of experiences, which would connect earthly events in a continuum thus creating a purpose and goal for everything, are we left alone with nihilism and relativism?

While trying to give an answer to this great question of the twentieth century, Jenson starts to build his theological method in post-foundational manner. There are no neutral vantage points from which to answer these kinds of questions and it is not possible to give warrant to theology with supposedly independent criteria. For example, philosophy, as it has traditionally been understood in Western thought, is only one *theological* way of thinking of a particular faith differing in some central points from Christian thought. Here Jenson departs from the method of earlier liberal Protestantism, which used hundreds of pages for theological prolegomena, trying to ground theology in, for example, universal reason (Enlightenment) or human experience (liberal Protestantism). On the other hand, while following some leads given by George Lindbeck's and Hans Frei's postliberal school of thought, Jenson seeks to connect theology more closely with extra-linguistic realities. Theology and theological doctrines do not speak only about theological language but about God's works within our history. According to Jenson, true knowledge of God is not available without special revelation. However, special revelation consists of particular events in history being therefore capable of being presented in a universal way. While Jenson sees that no universal criterion or rationality is needed in the Church in order to ground its particular way of thinking and reception of revelation, the particular theology of the Christian Church is a prerequisite for universal rationality.

While somewhat critical of natural theology, Jenson, however, uses as a universal starting point a kind of inverted natural theology. Jenson claims that there exists a formal, conceptual set of questions, which structure the particular contents of our belief systems. Every human being wrestles with certain common questions, which are universally shared. These questions gather around the question of time. According to Jenson, "all human self-understanding and action is ineluctably tensed"; we cannot live without the categories of "will be" (future), "was" (past) and "is" (present). On the one hand, human life is shaped by the past, which is always beyond our reach and therefore determined to be as it is forever. On the other hand, humans look forward to what is to come, this future being free from the past and yet to be disclosed. Human life "happens" in the intersection of the past and the future, that is, in the present; this experience of waiting for the open future is, according to Jenson, shared by all cultures.

This self-understanding creates religions and their counterpart, nihilism. What unites all religions is the attempt to merge events in history as a continuum, or as a story, and give meaning to the present. If human beings cease in this endeavor, they practice nihilism: human life is interpreted as a plotless series of disconnected events without any direction or meaning. Generally, religions are reactions to the possibility of nihilism. Jenson claims that in all that we do, we rely upon some *particular* way to make sense of our lives: "we seek a certain kind of eternity." (As a sidenote, the inability of the Bultmannian School to give any particular answer to the nature of "future" caused Jenson to distance himself from it; openness to mere and undefined future just does not make sense.) When this seeking takes a particular and recognizable form, we "practice religion." This way all religions and even nihilism are always connected to some kind of self-revelation of the Triune God, who is encountered in the phenomenon of time.

These existential questions do not, however, contain yet any specific content which is able to be answered within all kinds of belief systems. Jenson sharply criticizes the kind of positivistic theology of religions where sheer abstract forms or questions shape the content of religions. Jenson believes that the answers given to these questions differ a great deal from each other. It is either *the past* or *the future*, which shapes the transcendence. In the first case, it is not time which defines reality. Time and all events of history are eventually less important, and what really *is*, is not shaped by contingency and change. Beyond time and change there is something necessary, static, immovable and eternal, which is in religion and philosophy defined as "God." In the latter case, temporal and particular events of history open up the future beyond determinism, which looms behind the former model and threatens to render the acts of God in history meaningless or merely redundant.

The doctrine of the Trinity is the particularly Christian answer to the universal question of being in time. The Christian answer in the form of the Triune God is not a human projection (*à la* Feuerbach) but the depiction of reality. For Jenson, there is no transcendence detached from historical and temporal reality. Consequently, the doctrine of the Trinity cannot identify anything if God had not identified himself earlier in history. Thus, the doctrine of the Trinity is a contextual expression of the acts where God identifies himself. To be precise: God does not only self-identify *by* certain events so that he would be ontologically something different than, or outside of, those events. Instead, God identifies himself *with* those events as well. This indicates that God is ontologically bound to those events, the two most important events of identification being the Exodus and the person of Jesus Christ, especially his Resurrection. Still, God is in a certain sense *other* than the reality, which He uses to identify himself but He nevertheless is the *same* as these events. In addition to particular identifying events, God's self-revelation takes places through "personal names" and "identifying descriptions." These include God's proper name YHWH, and the answer to the question "who is God?" as it is given in the New Testament: "Whoever raised Jesus from the dead." Since Jenson believes that God is really identifiable "by and with" the Exodus and the Resurrection, then it naturally follows to ask what sort of being he is. Jenson's answer is that "God's hypostatic being is constituted in *dramatic coherence*." The noticeable feature of dramatic coherence (or, the story or life within history) is that it must be complete before one can truly identify it; the story must reach its temporal end. In other words, God's very being and identity are united with history in such a way that it is not merely established in the past who he will be, but rather his eternal identity can be grasped only from the end of the story. This feature sets him against some metaphysically rigorous trends of Thomistic theology.

Jenson's major thesis, tangling up the nature of God and our history, creates some problems, which form the basis of the major criticisms of Jenson's thought. Traditionally, even while acknowledging the necessary identity of the economic Trinity and immanent Trinity, Christian theology has fought to maintain that while what happens in the story of salvation is the perfect expression of God in His immutable essence, God would still be the same God even if there were no creatures and created world at all. In keeping with this, it has been thought that between the temporal expression of God's identity and its source (God as He is) the relation exists not of necessity, but of grace. One of the most disputed consequences of Jenson's thought is that he must reject many of the classical perfections ascribed to God, at least as they are traditionally understood, such as impassibility, unchangeability, and timelessness.

Jenson, however, presumes that God *could* have been the same God without the creation of this particular world—in principle—although we have no way of knowing how this could have taken place. After choosing this reality, there is no independent reality of God outside this temporality. All other claims are counterfactual; merely play with abstract possibilities. Additionally, God does not identify himself by and with everything that exists (as has been claimed in process theology); only a limited number of events and descriptions are revelatory.

The Current Place in Theological Discussion

Jenson's theology is not confessionally restricted so that he could be regarded as a Lutheran theologian only. His theological style and efforts to produce dogmatic theology for the whole Church joins him with the movement sometimes known as "Evangelical Catholics": Protestants who appreciate and work with the sources of the Church undivided. Jenson's works are primarily read among traditional Catholic and Evangelical theologians. Although his approach is ecumenical, some aspects of Jenson's project create problems for the reception of his thought. The radical subordination of metaphysics to a Trinitarian doctrine of God cuts against traditional Catholic philosophical theology and its use of the *analogia entis*. On the other hand, most Evangelical low-church theologians have a hard time accepting Jenson's high views of the Church and the Sacraments—views that flow directly from his primarily Trinitarian theology.

Jenson sides with a number of influential theological movements of his time. These include, among others, narrative theology and postliberalism. While Jenson takes advantage of these schools of thought, he goes further and develops their ideas at many fundamental points. Issues such as the analysis of postmodern culture, the deconstruction of modernity, the metaphysics of participation, and an understanding of philosophy as inherently theological are all themes shared with the Radical Orthodoxy movement. Jenson, however, relying more upon the Biblical narrative than philosophical metaphysics, provides a coherent and clear account, which can probably be considered more approachable than the vast and complex corpus of Radical Orthodoxy.

Jenson can be classified as one of the major players in the post-foundational theological game and one of the few pan-theologians of our time. Mastering all the central fields of theology, he has been able to create an interpretation of Trinitarian theology, which is interesting in existential, philosophical, and exegetical senses.

Bibliography

Primary Literature

The Knowledge of Things Hoped For: The Sense of Theological Discourse (New York: Oxford University Press, 1969).
The Triune Identity: God According to the Gospel (Philadelphia: Fortress, 1982).
Essays in Theology of Culture (Grand Rapids: Eerdmans, 1995).
Systematic Theology, Vol. 1: *The Triune God* (New York: Oxford University Press, 1997) and Vol. 2: *The Works of God* (New York: Oxford University Press, 1999).
On Thinking the Human: Resolutions on Difficult Notions (Grand Rapids: Eerdmans, 2003).
Song of Songs (Louisville: John Knox Press, 2005).
Canon and Creed (Louisville: John Knox Press, 2010).

Secondary Literature

Aran Murphy, Francesca, *God is Not a Story: Realism Revisited* (Oxford: Oxford University Press, 2007).
Bentley Hart, David, "The Lively God of Robert Jenson," *First Things* (October 2005).
Gunton, Colin E. (ed.), *Trinity, Time, and Church: A Response to the Theology of Robert W. Jenson* (Grand Rapids: Eerdmans, 2000).
Watson, Francis, "'America's Theologian': An Appreciation of Robert Jenson's Systematic Theology, with Some Remarks about the Bible," *Scottish Journal of Theology*, 55 (2002), 201–3.
Yeago, David, "Catholicity, Nihilism, and the God of the Gospel: Reflections on the Theology of Robert Jenson," *Dialog*, 31 (1992), 18–22.

Chapter 42
Sallie McFague

Ellen T. Armour

Sallie McFague, E. Rhodes and Leona B. Carpenter Professor of Theology Emerita from Vanderbilt University, is currently Distinguished Theologian in Residence at Vancouver School of Theology in Vancouver, B.C.[1] After graduating *magna cum laude* from Smith College in 1955, McFague became one of a very few women of her generation to seek graduate training in theology. She earned the B.D., M.A., and Ph.D. degrees from Yale University (awarded in 1959, 1960, and 1964, respectively). She assumed a teaching post at Vanderbilt in 1970, serving as the Divinity School's dean from 1975 to 1979. She retired from Vanderbilt in 2000 and moved to Vancouver.

There is little doubt that McFague merits inclusion in any list of great theologians in the twentieth century. She firmly established her place at the forefront of contemporary theology with the publication of her fourth book, *Models of God: A Theology for an Ecological, Nuclear Age* (1987), which received the American Academy of Religion's Award for Excellence of Books in the Field in 1988. Her subsequent work, which has grown out of the methodological and ethical concerns articulated in *Models*, has continued to garner positive attention in the academy and beyond. Her work has been reviewed not only in top tier academic journals in North America and Europe, but also in publications like *Christian Century* that are aimed at lay audiences in the United States. Most recently, Willie James Jennings included McFague in his list of the five most important theologians of our time (on the strength specifically of *The Body of God: An Ecological Theology*).[2] Her work has also been translated into a number of European languages and is widely taught in colleges, seminaries, and graduate programs throughout the world. But perhaps the most significant indicator of her standing as a public theologian is her recent collaboration with the Dalai Lama.

---

[1] This chapter is based on my earlier essay, "Sallie McFague," in *A New Handbook of Christian Theologians*, edited by Donald L. Musser and Joseph R. Price (Nashville: Abingdon Press, 1996), pp. 278–86. Adapted and used by permission.

[2] Willie James Jennings, "Willie James Jennings 5 Picks: Essential Theology Books of the Past 25 Years," *Christian Century*, 127/21 (October 19, 2010), 39–22. *ATLA Religion Database with ATLASerials*, EBSCO*host* (accessed January 30, 2012).

McFague was the only Christian theologian to be invited to address a group of scholars from a variety of disciplines gathered by His Holiness in Dharamsala, India, on the issue of climate change.[3]

In the video of her presentation, McFague is introduced as "the mothership" of Christian eco-theology—and rightly so. She was one of the first theologians to bring together ecological issues and concerns about human liberation. The nuclear and ecological crises are particularly crucial issues facing today's world, she argues, but they are not separable from issues of gender oppression, racial prejudice, or economic injustice. Because the impact of—and responsibility for—ecological problems differs with socioeconomic location, solutions to ecological problems must take social and economic justice into account. McFague is certainly keenly aware that she writes from a particular socioeconomic location; that of a white-middle-class, feminist, first-world theologian. She addresses her work specifically to other first-worlders, calling them to acknowledge a special responsibility for the ecological crisis as largely a creation of the first world's pattern of consumption.

McFague also acknowledges that, to call itself Christian, constructive theology must hold itself accountable to what is essential about the Christian tradition. Her normative vision of Christianity centers on the claim that there is a personal power in the universe that is on the side of life in all its forms and against whatever impedes life's flourishing. Therefore, rather than supporting relationships of domination, Christianity should be destabilizing, inclusive, and nonhierarchical. This vision of Christianity is, she argues, coherent with the portrayal of God's activity in the Hebrew Scriptures and in the New Testament, especially in the life of Jesus. However, McFague is not a narrow Biblicist. She rejects any strong division between the three traditional sources of Christian theology: scripture, tradition, and experience. Scripture is the earliest layer of tradition, she argues, and both scripture and tradition are codified experience. McFague prefers to think of scripture (and tradition) as a Christian classic—that is, a collection of paradigmatic experiences with the divine that serves as a model for subsequent generations of believers. While content matters, she also takes as normative for theology the *form* of scripture. All theology should be "risky, adventurous interpretation of the salvific love of God for our time."[4]

---

[3] "Ecology, Ethics and Interdependence," Dharamsala, India, October 17–21, 2011. Dr. McFague's talk can be viewed at http://www.youtube.com/watch?v=_NDSt7Xe O8w&feature=youtu.be (accessed October 2, 2011).

[4] McFague, *Models of God* (Minneapolis, 1987), p. 44.

This way of construing theology's traditional sources allows her the freedom to broaden the stream of what counts as "tradition." Although maintaining her grounding in biblical and theological texts, McFague also mines poetry, novels, and religious autobiographies as resources for theological reflection. Her concerns for social and ecological justice have led her to educate herself in science and economics, which she brings into conversation with theology.

Metaphorical Theology and the Christian Imagination

The most distinctive feature of McFague's seminal work is the level at which she engages in theological construction. She is far more concerned therein with how Christianity *imagines* the relationship of God and the world than with working out a coherent *conceptual* account of that relationship. McFague's work mediates between second-order theological reflection (abstract conceptual argumentation) and first-order religious language (symbols, images and stories). From her early interests in literature and story as a resource for Christian life and thought (see her dissertation, published in 1966 as *Literature and the Christian Life*) to the mode of reflection exemplified in *Models*, which she describes as "remythologizing" Christianity,[5] McFague has tried to stay close to the stories, symbols, and images that fund theological reflection while keeping clearly in view the issues that motivate theology—how to construe the relationship between God and the world, how to conceive the problem of the existence of evil, and how to comprehend what salvation means.

McFague found a rich methodological resource for this work in Paul Ricoeur's theory of metaphor. The theory of religious language she devises using his account of metaphor initially appears in her second book, *Speaking in Parables: A Study in Metaphor and Theology* (1975), and it lays the groundwork for her subsequent work. According to Ricoeur, metaphors produce meaning in a unique way. Where analogies work on the basis of a presumed similarity between the referent and its analogue, metaphors exploit the *difference* between the referent and what figures it. Metaphors produce meaning through a "twist"; metaphorical meaning appears through the rupture of literal meaning. The metaphor, "war is a chess game," creates the similarity between "war" and "chess game" through the difference between them. War involves people (who risk and sometimes lose their lives) and weapons rather than game pieces. However, viewing war through this metaphorical twist highlights the aspect of strategy in war.

In McFague's view, Ricoeur's theory provides the best account of how religious language works. All language for the divine is metaphorical, she argues. Images for God do not work on the basis of a presupposed similarity between the divine and the mundane, but create a resemblance through a twist produced when the image is transposed from its appropriate context to an unexpected one. Language for God

---

[5] McFague, *Models*, p. xi.

does not describe God's being, but attempts to articulate human beings' *experience* of God in terms that, by definition, do not fit.

Speaking in Parables reads the parables of Jesus through the lens of Ricoeur's theory. The parables are not allegories reducible to moral messages, McFague argues; rather they are radical redescriptions of reality. The conventional setting of the parable draws its readers into the narrative only to turn their world upside down. In the parable of the prodigal son, for example, the father subverts ordinary expectations by rewarding the profligate son rather than the dutiful son. This re-vision of God's love occurs in and through the details of the parable, through its "twist" on conventional expectations. God's love both "is" and "is not" like that of a father's love for his children.

Speaking in Parables focuses on the quality and character of primary religious language, but her subsequent work, for which she is best known, turns our attention to what she argues mediates between first-order and second-order religious language. Her next book, *Metaphorical Theology: Models of God in Religious Language* (1982) uncovers the bridge between the two kinds of religious discourse, models of God. Models are extended metaphors that, because of their explanatory power and fit, have become paradigms within which Christianity thinks and lives. Models are drawn from primary religious language but shape and fund second-order theological reflection. The parable of the prodigal son makes use of a central metaphor for God in Christianity; that of God as father. McFague argues that this metaphor has combined with other central metaphors-cum-models (lord and king) to become *the* dominant model in Christian theology.

Metaphors become models because they are able to provide a coherent framework for fleshing out theological concepts. The Christian tradition has derived an entire theology from the paternal-monarchical model. Imaging God as Father-King organizes Christianity's conception of the divine–human relationship. If God is Father, then human beings are his children. Within that model, sin comes to be conceived as the rebellion of the child against the father. Redemption requires the sacrifice of an elder sibling who pays for the wrongdoing of the other children.

McFague acknowledges the structuring power of the monarchical model, but she recommends that Christianity seek out other models because the monarchical model has become idolatrous and irrelevant. Christianity has come to assume that "Father" is literally God's name; thus, the model has lost its metaphorical character. It is, furthermore, irrelevant to our contemporary context—and dangerously so, given the threat of ecological and nuclear disaster. Given that Christianity developed in a patriarchal and monarchic culture, it is no coincidence that these metaphors for God dominate. However, most of us no longer live under monarchies. And imaging God as Father-King allows human beings to abdicate responsibility for the created order. It encourages us to assume a childlike position before God in which we simply trust that God, as Lord of Creation, will take care of his own.

McFague is not the first to criticize masculine language for God; this was a central claim of second wave feminist theologians beginning with Mary Daly's groundbreaking book *Beyond God the Father*. For some (including Daly), the seeming intractability of this language and its consequences for women and for nature required abandoning Christianity altogether. Thus, few have matched McFague's constructive contribution to *Christian* feminist God-talk. At the close of *Metaphorical Theology*, she proposes a "thought experiment": what if Christianity were to think within *different* models for God? She takes the preliminary steps toward working out one such model, God as friend; her next book, *Models of God*, takes up this "thought experiment" as its primary task. All models run the risk of losing their metaphorical character, especially when one model is allowed to dominate the scene, as has been the case with the monarchical model. For that reason, McFague advocates developing a plurality of models for God. In *Models*, McFague offers three fully articulated models (God as mother, lover, and friend) as alternatives to the dominant paternal-monarchical model. The text explores distinctive aspects of the God–world relationship opened up by each model. Her portraits of these models include careful assessments of each model's claim to being Christian and of its ability to accommodate critical issues in Christian theology. Of particular concern to McFague are the ways the models voice divine love and articulate divine activity. All three models stress the radical interdependence of all life, including the divine life in which all life is embedded. Her primary aim is to develop models that will support Christian *involvement* in caring for the world; thus, she considers as well the ethic implied by each model.

To function as good models, these metaphors must be rich in symbolic resources and must speak to human experience at its deepest level. Because these models are drawn from the most basic relationships in human life, they are rich in symbolic connotations. Yet no matter how rich their resources, all models are limited, and McFague calls her readers' attention to those limits in each case. Rather than reducing the divine to the mundane, metaphorical theology underscores the gap between them thus drawing attention to the tentativeness of all naming of the divine.

Space does not permit me to offer an account of all three of these models, so I will focus only on the first, the model of God as mother. McFague grounds this model in Christianity's claim that God is the ground of being and source of all that is. Indeed, she argues, God as mother models the creative love of God particularly well because of the model's associations with birth and gestation. She acknowledges that some Christians will resist this model because it seems explicitly sexual. She reminds us, though, that the model of God as father also has sexual connotations, although they have receded from view. Imagining God as mother *seems* more sexual only because our culture associates women more closely with sexuality. In any case, God as mother is a model, not a description. To image God as mother is not to claim that God *literally* gave birth to the cosmos, but that God "bod[ies] forth" the world.[6] God's creative activity is continuous. The world, rather than being separate from God, is part of God's very being.

McFague refuses to limit divine activity as seen through this model to stereotypically feminine attributes such as nurturing. This process advances her

---

[6] McFague, *Models*, p. 110.

claim that the Christian tradition needs *female* (rather than *feminine*) models for the divine to counter the dominance of male models. God as mother is concerned with promoting the just treatment of her creation. McFague notes that this model's association with justice has precedent in scripture and tradition. Divine wisdom has been personified as female and described as the source of order and justice in creation (see, for example, Proverbs 9).

God as mother joins together with the other models (lover and friend) to form the trinity. As mother models God's creative activity, lover and friend model God's redemptive and sustaining activity. Together the three promote a common ethic (solidarity and justice) and common understanding of salvation as working to overcome alienation and suffering. If the world is "bodied forth" by God, human beings cannot love God without loving the rest of the world. Loving the world involves working for a just order that will balance the needs of different forms of life for the good of the whole. This ethic, McFague argues, is particularly appropriate for an ecological, nuclear age.

This gesture toward ethics will bear concrete fruit later in McFague's *oeuvre*, but the book that follows *Models* moves in a more conceptual—even metaphysical—direction while still insisting on the metaphorical nature of even those claims. *The Body of God: An Ecological Theology* (1993) develops more fully the model of the world as God's body as a way to ground the relationship between God and the world evoked by the models of God as mother, lover, and friend. *Body* also pursues another valuable aspect of McFague's work begun in *Metaphorical Theology*, bridging theology and science. There, she drew on recent literature in the philosophy of science (most notably, Thomas Kuhn's research on paradigm shifts in science) to suggest that science and theology are both dependent on models. For example, wave-particle theory in physics uses what is known (the behavior of waves and particles) to explain the unknown (the behavior of electrons).

In *Body*, McFague brings science and theology into even closer proximity. Science, she argues, can enrich the religious imagination as it thinks through the implications of imagining the world as God's body. To the degree that Christianity has spoken positively about embodiment (a surprisingly rare event, she notes, given the centrality of incarnation), those bodies have tended to be only human—and paradigmatically white male—bodies. Contemporary science encourages Christianity to expand its notion of embodiment to encompass the enormous variety of physical life in the cosmos. Becoming familiar with biologists' account of the enormous diversity in a tidal pool inspires a sense of wonder and awe.

That sense of wonder extends to contemporary cosmology, as well. McFague finds theological value in exploring the "loose fit" between the scientific picture of the origin, growth, and function of the cosmos and theological claims. That "loose fit" emboldens her to speak of a common (scientific) creation story that enriches the religious imagination by refiguring the relationship between unity and diversity. According to that story, all life is literally unified by the fact that it is all made of matter-energy. Though it originates in one source, contemporary physics tells us that matter-energy-life tends toward ever greater diversity, dispersion, and variety.

In other words, organic unity lies in the cosmos' past, not in its future. On the other hand, science also makes it clear that all elements of the ecosystem are linked together in interdependency.

McFague is not attempting to resurrect a natural theology; that is, she is not turning to the natural world in order to discern God's activity in initiating and directing its emergence and maintenance. Science will not support claims that God constitutes the *telos* (end, goal, origin) of the created order. Rather, she proposes that we start with what we know: a sense of wonder at the complexity and diversity of creation. Regardless of *how* creation happened, it *did* happen—and in a most marvelous way. Christianity claims that God was and is involved in that marvelous process, but McFague willingly leaves behind "how" and "why" questions about God's involvement in favor of the more pragmatic question of what Christians should do in light of the claim about God's involvement.

Reimagining Nature and Ourselves

By McFague's own account, her sixth book, *Super, Natural Christians* (1997) completes the project launched by *Metaphorical Theology* of reorienting theological language away from ways of thinking and being that are environmentally destructive and socially unjust toward more sustainable and just ways of thinking and being. Where the first three books focused on Christian language for God, *Super, Natural Christians* focuses on Christian conceptions of nature. In large part thanks to modernity's influence, Christianity has tended to view nature as a means to an end; as resource and raw material provided by God for humanity's use and, in actual practice, abuse. Instead, McFague urges us to image nature as subject rather than object. Drawing again on contemporary cosmology and biology, she notes the various dimensions of nascent subjectivity present in the natural world. Though we may not be able to ascribe consciously directed agency to most other beings (as we do human beings), the organisms that comprise much of nature are centers of self-directed teleological activity. Considered on a larger scale, both nature and cosmos also exhibit complex and multivalent teleological activity, as well.

McFague is no closet creationist; nor has she become the pantheist that some have accused her of being all along. This is not a claim that nature *is* a subject—divine or mundane. Rather, she retains the insistence first articulated in *Metaphorical Theology* on the metaphorical nature of theological language. That is, nature both is and is not (accurately spoken of as a) subject. But how we speak of nature affects how we see it and, thus, how we live in relationship to it. If we continue to see it as (mere) object, it will be all too easy to perpetuate our long-established patterns of using nature until we finally use it up. Conceiving of nature as subject, on the other hand, demands a reorientation of our relationship to nature from subordination, if you will, to partnership based on recognition of our interdependence.

For all of its continuity with the three books that immediately precede it, *Super, Natural Christians* also inaugurates an important shift in McFague's writing; that is, a turn toward articulating more explicitly the ethical implications of her theological claims. Living into and out of this new relationship between humanity and nature requires more than new ways of thinking; it also requires of us new ways of doing. Thus, fittingly, the book concludes with very concrete suggestions for practice with a particular focus on those first-worlders who live in urban settings (and who, as a result, might feel most distant from nature).

The ethical dimensions of her theology occupy center stage in McFague's next book, *Life Abundant: Rethinking Theology and Economy for a Planet in Peril* (2001). Motivated primarily by the realization that the main barrier standing between North American Christians' largely unthinking but deep commitment to unsustainable patterns of consumption is the rampant individualism at the heart of much theology and economic theory, McFague tackles the difficult task of rendering both accessible to ordinary readers with the hope of changing hearts, minds, and lifestyles. Appropriately, given that the book was written as she was preparing to retire from Vanderbilt after 30 years of teaching, but certainly given the importance of religious autobiographies to her teaching life, she begins the book with her own. In brief but moving compass, she charts the various moments of conversion in her own life. This way of opening *Life Abundant* grants the book an authenticity and a humility that takes McFague's remarkable accessibility of style to a new level. It invites the reader into a process of self-opening toward potential transformation through the theological education that follows (in many ways, *Life Abundant* is a primer in theological reflection) in the service of individual and systemic reform.

Retirement in 2000 meant a change of scenery from the southern United States to western Canada, but it did not mean the end of either her publishing or teaching careers. As Distinguished Theologian in Residence at Vancouver School of Theology, she continues to teach on a part-time basis and to write. In 2008, Fortress published *A New Climate for Theology: God, the World and Global Warming*. Her focus here is on theological anthropology, a logical turn given the diagnosis of rampant individualism as the cause of our unsustainable lifestyles in *Life Abundant*. The more personal and (relatively) optimistic tone of *Life Abundant* is replaced here with a sober—and sobering—account of the science behind claims about global climate change. Rendered with McFague's usual clarity and elegance, that account highlights the signal importance of our mundane practices of consumption as a matter for theological consideration. She confronts the reader with the very real effects of those practices, as scientists understand them. We are—incontrovertibly, according to climate science (though some will continue to deny it)—interconnected to all that is at every level. If we continue to live out that interconnection through unchecked consumerism, we will find ourselves undone with and by the radical changes to the planet we call home that we have launched. Thus, it is imperative that we find our way into a lived understanding of what it means to be human that is—literally—life sustaining rather than death dealing. McFague then sets about the task of articulating an ecological theological anthropology that acknowledges deep relationality (to the world, God, and one another). In her careful hands, we find the resources for hope in the face of despair in the very interrelationality that we have exploited at our peril to this point. Once again, McFague turns to the "lives of the saints"—the autobiographies of such luminaries as John Woolman, Martin Luther King, and Dorothy Day—all of whom recognized interrelationality and the obligation to others that comes with it as fundamental. Interrelationality and its concomitant obligations are ultimately rooted in God as the one in whom we live, move and have our being, McFague claims, wherein lies our ultimate hope even in the face of very real fragility. Not because God will rescue us regardless, but because, in the lives of these "saints," we see that taking up our place as the hands and feet of God (so to speak) is possible and impactful.

McFague's latest, *Blessed are the Consumers* (2013), continues her engagement with climate change, but moves from a theological anthropology to a theologically grounded practice. Written in the wake of the Great Recession of 2008, McFague returns again to the connection between economics and ecology first articulated in *Life Abundant*. Climate change, she argues, is a spiritual crisis rooted in over-consumption (itself rooted in the quasi-religious belief that in accumulating more "things" lies abundant life). Unless we cut back radically, we can expect worsening global warming and with it, more serious economic challenges. A spiritual crisis demands a spiritual cure, which McFague offers in the form of kenosis; a move from ego-centeredness to world-centeredness that issues in actual practices of relinquishment. We take up such practices—whether large (giving up our cars) or small (reconnecting with nature on short hikes) not in pursuit of ascetic self-denial, but of life abundant for all. As models, she turns once again to the "saints" (here Simone Weil in addition to Woolman and Day) whose lives she has studied for so long. In each case, relinquishment reflects reprioritization and results in new joys, not a sense of deprivation.

Though it recapitulates certain insights and themes from previous work, *Blessed* also breaks new ground—not least in offering a feminist retrieval of kenosis. Since the 1970s, feminist theologians have criticized the asymmetric kenotic theology that defined normative femininity *as* willing self sacrifice for the sake of husband and family. McFague is careful to craft her retrieval around that critique. Secondly, this is the first of McFague's texts to explicitly (if only tentatively) engage with other religious traditions (Buddhism in particular, perhaps reflecting her time with the Dalai Lama). Though grounded in Christian theology, McFague claims that the fundamental insights about the nature of reality developed in *Blessed* are to be found across the religious traditions—and even outside them. Its basic insight—life's interconnectedness, interdependence, and fragility—and the practices it grounds can be embraced not only by the "spiritual" as well as the "religious" but by those who claim neither. That said, though, turning to kenosis also offers Christianity, at least, a path toward renewed relevance and resonance, McFague asserts, by returning to its founding claim; that in self-emptying (kenosis) lies abundant life.

McFague in Context

McFague's work sits at the convergence of a number of important trends in twentieth-century theology. Her focus on religious language is part of a larger "turn to language" that occurred in twentieth-century philosophy and, through both its Wittgensteinian and Heideggerian channels, influenced theology. Though typically (and rightly) read as a "liberal" theologian, McFague was trained at Yale in the theology of Karl Barth, who was a formative influence on her. In theme if not in method or substance, one can see certain resemblances between her work and that of the so-called "postliberals" usually identified as his more direct heirs. Like them, McFague is deeply concerned with the "grammar" of Christian theo-logic as it plays out in lived religiosity. However, she tacks toward liberal theology in her treatment of both. Christianity is and ought to be inextricably connected to the world and to larger currents in contemporary culture, in her view. Its theological grammar is in need of reformation, not just reinforcement.

McFague's work also reflects the signal and sanguine influence of liberation theologies—including but not limited to feminist theologies, to which she is a major contributor. Finally, though her metaphorical method necessarily entails reticence on matters metaphysical, her work also exhibits deep affinities with process theology (which she acknowledges) and, well before the publication of *Blessed*, had even been taken up by theologians of religious pluralism. In the last analysis, however, McFague's approach to the theological task through the Christian imagination makes hers a distinctive voice in contemporary theology that will continue to sound in the years to come.

Bibliography

Primary Literature

TeSelle, Sallie (McFague), *Literature and the Christian Life* (New Haven: Yale University Press, 1966).

McFague, Sallie, *Speaking in Parables: A Study in Metaphor and Theology* (Minneapolis: Fortress Press, 1975).

McFague, Sallie, *Metaphorical Theology: Models of God in Religious Language* (Minneapolis: Fortress Press, 1982).

McFague, Sallie, *Models of God: Theology for an Ecological, Nuclear Age* (Minneapolis: Fortress Press, 1987).

McFague, Sallie, *The Body of God: An Ecological Theology* (Minneapolis: Fortres Press, 1993).

McFague, Sallie, *Super, Natural Christians: How We Should Love Nature* (Minneapolis: Fortress Press, 1997).

McFague, Sallie, *Life Abundant: Rethinking Theology and Economy for a Planet in Peril* (Minneapolis: Fortress Press, 2000).

McFague, Sallie, *A New Climate for Theology: God, the World and Global Warming* (Minneapolis: Fortress Press, 2008).
McFague, Sallie, *Blessed are the Consumers* (Minneapolis: Fortress Press, 2013).

Secondary Literature

Davaney, Sheila Greeve, and John B. Cobb, Jr. "Models of God: Theology for an Ecological, Nuclear Age," *Religious Studies Review*, 16/1 (January 1, 1990), 36–42.
Jennings, Willie James, "Willie James Jennings 5 Picks: Essential Theology Books of the Past 25 Years," *Christian Century*, 127/21 (October 19, 2010), 39–22.
Malone, Nancy H. (ed.), "A Discussion of Sallie McFague's *Models of God*," *Religion and the Intellectual Life*, 5/3 (Spring 1988), 9–44.
Peters, Ted, "McFague's Metaphors," *Dialog*, 27/2 (March 1, 1988), 131–40.
Ray, Darby (ed.), *Theology That Matters: Ecology, Economy, and God* (Minneapolis: Fortress Press, 2006).
Reynolds, Terrence, "Two McFagues: Meaning, Truth, and Justification in Models of God," *Modern Theology*, 11/3 (July 1, 1995), 289–313.
Reynolds, Terrence, "Parting Company At Last: Lindbeck and McFague in Substantive Theological Dialogue," *Concordia Theological Quarterly*, 63/2 (April 1, 1999), 97–118.
Rieger, Joerg, "Theology and Economics," *Religious Studies Review*, 28/3 (July 1, 2002), 215–20.
Ross, Susan A., "Women, Beauty, and Justice: Moving Beyond von Balthasar," *Journal of the Society of Christian Ethics*, 25/1 (March 1, 2005), 79–98.
Schrein, Shannon, *Quilting and Braiding: The Feminist Christologies of Sallie McFague and Elisabeth Johnson* (Collegeville: The Liturgical Press, 1998).
Trexler, Melanie E., "The World as the Body of God: A Feminist Approach to Religious Pluralism," *Dialogue & Alliance*, 21/1 (March 1, 2007), 45–68.
Webb, Stephen H., "Should We Love All of Nature? A Critique of Sallie McFague's *Super, Natural Christians*," *Encounter*, 59/3 (Summer 1998), 409–19.
Wells, Harry L. "Taking Pluralism Seriously: The Role of Metaphorical Theology Within Interreligious Dialogue," *Journal of Ecumenical Studies*, 30/1 (December 1, 1993), 20–33.

Chapter 43
David Tracy

Jan-Olav Henriksen

Among living Roman Catholic theologians, David Tracy is perhaps the most original and influential American theologian in the second half of the twentieth century. He is well known not least because of his high-profile and emphatic insistence that theology has its place in the public arena. This emphasis has led him to develop a reflection on theological principles that counteracts the risk that theology can become a purely inner-churchly and isolationist activity. In this context, he is celebrated not least because of his debate with the Yale theologian George Lindbeck, who has elaborated a position that is in many ways the exact opposite of Tracy's. At the same time, however, Tracy – unlike many in both the Catholic and the Protestant camps – is aware that theology is a hermeneutical activity that cannot be carried out independently of the conditions in contemporary culture that make understanding possible. This is why the theologian Tracy has had a strong influence on recent generations of American theologians, and he is respected far beyond the boundaries of his own church for his pioneering work on the questions mentioned here. It was thus no surprise that he was invited a few years ago to deliver the celebrated Gifford Lectures, an honor bestowed only on the most influential and pioneering of modern theologians. Tracy's theology has also inspired and furthered the development of a more social-critical form of thinking. This prompted many of those involved in liberation study to travel to study under him.

Biography, with Emphasis on His Academic Work

Tracy was born in New York in 1939 and studied philosophy and theology at St. Joseph's Seminary in that city. After his ordination to the priesthood in 1963, he continued his theological studies at the Gregorian University in Rome, during the Second Vatican Council. He took his licentiate in theology there in 1964 and his doctorate in 1969. He wrote his dissertation on his teacher, Bernard Lonergan. Tracy then taught for most of his career at the University of Chicago Divinity School. When we bear in mind the length of his career, Tracy has not written many books, and it is well known that he writes in a compressed manner and is sometimes difficult to understand. He has nevertheless been very influential, not least because many people have found in his writings a greater clarity about the conditions that make it possible to practice theology in, and in dialogue with, a postmodern culture.

Overview of His Theological Writings

Throughout his writing career, Tracy has taken up questions linked to methodological and hermeneutical problems. Originally, he was influenced by Bernard Lonergan's transcendental Thomism, as we can see in *The Achievement of Bernard Lonergan* (1970), but it is in his next two books, *Blessed Rage for Order* (1975) and *The Analogical Imagination* (1981), that he develops his own more original and creative contributions in this field. In the former book, he explains how theology must develop a critical correlation between the values and experiences that exist in the experiential world of modern and postmodern human persons, on the one hand, and what the text in the Christian tradition can mean in the encounter with such experiences, on the other hand. This is done by means of a thorough and critical examination of various ways of doing theology. Through this structure, which leads him to raise problems with regard to both orthodox and more liberal ways of doing theology, Tracy creates a debate and posits a new agenda for the discussion of the activity of theology in our days. At the same time, the book contains a discussion of many themes in fundamental theology, linked above all to the understanding of the religious dimension in experience and in language.

In *The Analogical Imagination*, Tracy develops comprehensively his understanding of how theology, as a hermeneutical activity, must relate to various forms of public arenas. We shall look at central points in this book below. It attracted extra attention because it was drawn into the above-mentioned debate about the Yale theologian George Lindbeck's book *The Nature of Doctrine*, which presents Lindbeck's basic understanding of what theology is in a completely different manner from Tracy. Many scholars have subsequently presented these two accounts of fundamental theology as examples of two paradigmatically antithetical ways of thinking about basic problems in theology (corresponding to some extent to the antithesis that could be seen in German theology between Eberhard Jüngel and Wolfhart Pannenberg).

Two books on which Tracy worked and that he published at the close of the 1980s show a revision of his basic thinking about fundamental theology in the light of the interreligious dialogue. Both *Plurality and Ambiguity* (1987) and *Dialogue with the Other* (1990) emphasize the necessity of such a dialogue and attempt to establish the importance of articulating a Christian understanding of God in a pluralistic religious context of this kind. This accords with Tracy's underlying concern to develop theology in the encounter with the contemporary cultural climate.

Tracy has long planned to write a large-scale and comprehensive systematic theology. The first studies in this project that were made accessible to the public were the lectures entitled "This side of God" that he delivered as the Gifford Lectures in 1999–2000; these have never been published in book form. In recent years, he has become increasingly interested in the tragic visions that are found in the classic Greek dramas and in Nietzsche. He has also moved more in the direction of apophatic theology, thereby signaling a greater openness for thinkers such as Luther who underline God's hiddenness. This development in the direction of mysticism in Tracy has not met with universal approval.

The Public Sphere, Language, and Hermeneutics – Basic Elements in Tracy's Fundamental Theology

In his fundamental theology, Tracy emphasizes how important it is for theology to be conducted as a public conversation. Theologians cannot withdraw to an innerchurchly sphere and remain there, dispensed from all responsibility vis-à-vis a larger public sphere. This means that theology must also possess public criteria (not merely private or sectarian criteria) for what it may reasonably say and do. Tracy thus demands that theologians justify themselves and make themselves accessible in a larger context, and in relation to a public sphere that is larger than the ecclesiastical sphere.

Tracy says that it is important for theology to develop in relation to the following three public spaces: society, academia, and the church. The most complete and nuanced treatment of this question will be found in *The Analogical Imagination* (1981), where he also describes why and how theological activity is necessarily related to these three public spaces.

Tracy defines the pluralistic situation of theology in our days in a way that attempts to build a bridge that links different dimensions of reality. He thereby prevents theology from being isolated in a sphere all by itself, and ensures that it is a form of "public theology." Tracy's starting point is the differentiations that must be made between different forums or institutions in a modern world. When he then goes on to speak of the church and academia as two institutions to which theology must relate, it is relatively simple to grasp what he means. These institutions are delimited and well known, and they are the normal "places" for theological activity in our part of the world, if we include theology in what goes on at universities. But what does Tracy mean when he says that theology should also be conducted in relation to "society"?

Tracy sees society as a combination of what he calls the techno-economical, the political, and the cultural areas. The first area organizes and distributes goods and services in order to attain particular goals. The political area is concerned with social justice and the use of power, with the aim of using power legitimately and overcoming conflicts in a just manner. The third dimension in society, where art, religion, and reflection have their place in a special manner, investigates and expresses the meaning and the value in various expressions of individual, group-based, and communal forms of life. This is also the locus of reflection on the connection between worldview and morality (see *Analogical Imagination*, 7). Tracy holds that theology must speak with a clear voice in relation to all these dimensions in society. It must prevent the technoeconomical rationality, which attaches importance to achieving strategic goals, from gaining a monopoly. The way to ensure this is to employ insights into a variety of traditions (including religious and theological traditions) when negotiating questions of social justice. This allows theology to contribute to a living and critical relationship to the values that exist in any given cultural setting.

Tracy's basic point is that if *theology* does not take seriously its task with regard to these various dimensions of society, there is a risk not only that theology itself may be privatized, but that *religion* too may be marginalized in society. This is his response to a situation that in many ways increases the chances that theology and religion will withdraw to the private sphere or to closed institutional spaces. Theology, as Tracy understands it, cannot only exist in a religious form of life that is clearly marked off from other societal dimensions, nor can it only express what is found in such a form of life.

Tracy holds that a good theologian or religious thinker helps to clarify the way in which one can live *de facto* as a believer and a participant in society. The contribution made by such thinkers is so important because they are able to formulate something that not only applies to their own selves; and this is why their writings are often regarded as *classics*. If theologians (and other scholars in the humanities) fail to see that they have this role, they are marginalized, and we risk ending up with a society that is governed by the instrumental reason, a society in which there is no longer anyone who can explain why something is just and right (see *Analogical Imagination*, 14). This emphasis on the fact that works by such thinkers belong to the classics suggests that he is taking up central motifs in the hermeneutics of Hans-Georg Gadamer, where the classics are those works that across distances of space and time still seem able to inform us about important aspects of human existence and help us to understand these. The classics help to interpret experience.

We notice two points in Tracy's position here. First of all, he begins directly with a description in which culture and cultural values and interpretative patterns (including religion) are a part of a greater whole. Secondly, Tracy also claims that if one sees religion and theology as an autonomous dimension of society, one fails to grasp that that which finds expression as religion must be understood as woven into a greater totality that also influences the shaping of theology and the concrete leading of a religious life. He looks at theological activity, not only from the perspective of theology itself, but also on the basis of the role it has in a larger context. In other words, he sketches a picture of religion and theology as obliged to encounter that which is other than itself and to communicate with this. By putting things in this way, Tracy ensures that theologians and other thoughtful and reflecting believers, by relating to something outside faith, can also gain a more distanced foundation for understanding faith, since this makes it possible to see faith more from "the outside."

In many ways, there is a natural path that leads from looking at theology's relation to society to identifying one of theology's public spaces as academia. This follows almost automatically, even when one has argued (as Tracy does) that theology shares a common room with other dimensions of society. It cannot be taken for granted today, however, that theology belongs in an academic context. Paradoxically, there are two groups with diametrically opposed interests that concur here: both those who are secular critics of theological activity, and those who understand theology first and foremost as an expression of the Christian confession of faith, can agree that theology need not have a place in an academic context. Both groups see theology as the expression of a form of private conviction that has nothing to do with public discourse. On this question, Tracy joins company with a theologian such as Pannenberg, and emphasizes that if theology is to claim to say something true about reality, it must also put forward claims that can be tested to determine whether they are universally valid. Truth is by definition something that is valid for everyone. This makes it all the more important that theology should not be privatized.

Tracy claims that theological work on questions of truth also helps to clarify the difference between theology and the science of religion. He draws a distinction between working on *meaning* and working on *truth*. In the science of religion, one can be content with clarifying the contexts of meaning within and in relation to a given religious view, but theology cannot be content with a limitation of this kind. It must also ask about the conditions under which that which is asserted or practiced in a given praxis of faith can count as *true*. Tracy says that theologians are compelled to put forward affirmations that can lay claim to be true. If they do not take seriously this claim and this task, they will soon betray their own inheritance (see *Analogical Imagination*, 20).

The final public space in which Tracy believes a theologian is anchored, and to which he must relate in his formulations, is the church. Provided that one does not identify the church with the kingdom of God (and there are good reasons for *not* doing so), this public space is the place where theological reflection can be very important both in a constructive and in a critical sense, and in a great variety of ways. This, however, presupposes that the individual theologian has a relationship of positive commitment to the church and does not distance himself completely from it; for in such a case, the theologian's work is much less capable of exercising an influence. But Tracy holds that the greater challenge to theology occurs when some theologians make the church the *only* framework of reference for their work. This priority is based on a misunderstanding, since society and academia will always be a part of what theology necessarily relates to. Theologians are a part of society, and the theological tradition is a part of the history that has led to modern academic activity. Accordingly, Tracy argues (doubtless correctly) that when the theologian functions as an interpreter of the ecclesial tradition, the relationship to the other two public spaces will play a role in the way in which he or she works. This means that it would be wrong to regard society and academia as something to which theologians relate only externally. Theologians will always be socialized into a larger context, in which these public spaces play a role and leave their traces on attitudes and opinions.

This leads Tracy to understand the theologian's relationship to the church as determined by the fact that the church is both a theological and sociological reality. The church thus needs theological work that clarifies the fundamental elements that can make theology credible or appropriate in relationship to all three public spaces. Theology must also continue to interpret and reinterpret resources that are found in the ecclesial tradition, in order to apply these appropriately today. Tracy sees the task of theology as the combination of these two elements (*Analogical Imagination*, 31).

He thus makes it clear that theology cannot consist only of unfolding the inherent grammar of faith or in creating new and coherent expressions of faith – something that is possible within the framework of a given cultural-linguistic fellowship (as in the thinking of George Lindbeck, his partner in discussions in the 1980s). Theology has public tasks that are greater than this. Theology must be articulated in ways that are comprehensible to persons who are not believers. The content of theology cannot be elaborated within a world of its own that is uninfluenced by knowledge and conditions that exist outside the religious sphere.

Tracy believes that theology possesses two different forms of conceptual language for reflection on human experience, as this is expressed (for example) in the encounter with the testimony about Christ. The first of these languages is the analogical, which attempts to link together, in a convincing and organic manner, elements in this experience and other events and elements in experience. This language is continuously employed in the attempt to set out more adequately the connection between Jesus Christ and the rest of history. And although these expositions are never complete, Tracy affirms that there is nevertheless in principle a continually growing harmony in the ways in which this totality is presented (see *Analogical Imagination*, 408 ff.). Thomas Aquinas, Schleiermacher, Rahner, and Pannenberg are examples of theologians who elaborate theology on the basis of this type of language.

The other type of theological language is the dialectical, which emphasizes that there is an antithesis between the human reason and God's revelation, and that there therefore cannot be any simple continuity between God and the human person. This is the language that unmasks every human attempt to redeem oneself (ibid., 414 ff.). Tracy finds representatives of this use of language in the dialectical theology (Barth), but also in recent forms of liberation theology, with which Tracy himself has shown sympathy (thereby locating himself on another wing in the Catholic camp than a theologian like Ratzinger).

Tracy refuses to see any absolute antithesis between these two forms of language. He emphasizes that both are necessary and that each has its own legitimate context for use. It is in the interplay between these two languages that a living theology can develop. It follows that both forms of language are ultimately expressions of an analogical idea that attempts to formulate a theological understanding of the meaning in the events that create faith in God, and of how these events are connected to other elements in the human world. In the nature of things, Tracy sees faith in Jesus Christ as the decisive starting point for this work.

In *Blessed Rage for Order*, Tracy proposes five theses that sum up the insights that structure theological work (pp. 43–63). I present these here because this list shows how he identifies the central elements in theological work and defines their relationship to one another.

First, the two most important sources for theology are Christian texts and shared human experience and language.

Second, the task of theology consists in a critical correlation of the results of an investigation of these two sources.

Third, the most important method for investigating the source called "human experience and language" is a phenomenological description of the religious dimension that is present in both everyday and scientific experience and language. Tracy thus presupposes (not unlike Pannenberg) that such a dimension exists. And if one believes that religion has something to do with the reality and experience of human life, this is a perfectly reasonable thing to do.

Fourth, the most important method in the investigation of the sources of the Christian tradition is a historical and hermeneutical examination of *classic Christian texts*. In Tracy's classification, these are first and foremost the biblical texts, but it is also reasonable to include the church's confessional documents in this category.

Fifth, in order to determine the status of truth in the results of the investigation of both these sources, the theologian must employ an explicitly transcendental or metaphysical form of reflection that explicitly attempts to combine the results of theological investigations in a totality where the various elements can provide the foundation for each other, and where they take their places in an integrated totality. In other words, the question of truth cannot be decided by experience alone, or only by what the texts say. It is in the combination of these two elements that we can draw conclusions about the truth in theological affirmations.

Tracy's theses are a good and comprehensible presentation of important components in a process of theological work. They are well thought through with regard both to various objects of investigation and to various methods. At the same time, this presentation emphasizes that the collecting and synthesizing of knowledge that is formulated by theology entails a responsibility that today's "constructors" of theology cannot ignore. Theologians cannot be content with repeating constructions from the past as if these were solutions to the theological problems of the present day, or as if they could contribute straightforwardly to an interpretation of our experiences.

Conclusion

Tracy's theological edifice rests upon his continuous emphasis that theology is a hermeneutical activity anchored in the present day and characterized by dialogue, an activity that draws on classical sources. He has also exercised a great influence through his insistence on the public character of theology and by pointing to the necessity of encountering the pluralistic culture. This makes Tracy's fundamental theology a corrective to those understandings of theology that prefer theological work to take place in a relatively closed and inner-churchly space where the decision about what counts as adequate expressions of Christian doctrine is not taken on the basis of universally acceptable criteria.

One critical point is that up to now, Tracy's interest in methodological questions and fundamental theology has prevented him from publishing large-scale systematic contributions that can follow up his own programmatic insights. It is uncertain whether this criticism will remain valid in future, since Tracy has regularly signalized that we can expect more from his hand. There is little reason to suppose that if he does publish, his writings will be met with indifference.

Bibliography

Primary Literature

The Achievement of Bernard Lonergan (New York: Herder and Herder, 1970).
The Analogical Imagination: Christian Theology and the Culture of Pluralism (New York: Crossroad, 1981).
Plurality and Ambiguity: Hermeneutics, Religion, Hope (San Francisco: Harper & Row, 1st ed. 1987).
Blessed Rage for Order: The New Pluralism in Theology (San Francisco: Harper & Row, 1988).
Dialogue with the Other: The Inter-Religious Dialogue (Grand Rapids, Michigan: Eerdmans, 1991).
On Naming the Present – Reflections on God, Hermeneutics, and Church (Maryknoll, N.Y.: Orbis Books, and London: SCM Press, 1994).
Tracy, David, and John B. Cobb, *Talking about God: Doing Theology in the Context of Modern Pluralism* (New York: Seabury Press, 1983).

Secondary Literature

Jeanrond, Werner G. and Jennifer L. Rike, *Radical Pluralism and Truth: David Tracy and the Hermeneutics of Religion* (New York: Crossroad, 1991).
Martinez, Gaspar, *Confronting the Mystery of God: Political, Liberation, and Public Theologies* (New York: Continuum 2001).
Ray, S. Alan, *The Modern Soul: Michel Foucault and the Theological Discourse of Gordon Kaufman and David Tracy. Harvard Theological Dissertations in Religion*, 21 (Philadelphia: Fortress Press, 1987).
Stell, Stephen Lawson, *Hermeneutics and the Holy Spirit: Trinitarian Insights into a Hermeneutical Impasse* (PhD thesis, Princeton Theological Seminary, 1988).

Chapter 44
Stanley Hauerwas

Arne Rasmusson

In its issue of September 10, 2001 the American news magazine *Time* declared that the pacifist Stanley Hauerwas was "America's best theologian." Hauerwas himself held that "best theologian" was not something a Christian theologian should endeavor to be; but the accolade attests the central – but also controversial – place Hauerwas occupies in contemporary theology. The theological world looks different today compared with the situation some 40 years ago, when Hauerwas completed his theological education. Many theologians have contributed to this development, and other factors are involved as well. But few have had such a great influence as Hauerwas. His many books, his dynamic lectures, and now also his influential former students have led to a redrawing of the theological map. He has set the agenda even for many of his critics. He is also widely read outside the sphere of academic theology, both inside and outside the Christian church.

Biography

Stanley Hauerwas was born in 1940 in Pleasant Grove in northern Texas and worked in his youth alongside his father as a bricklayer. He has often returned to the bricklayer's craft as a model of what moral training aims at. He grew up in a Methodist community, but he abandoned the Christian faith until he realized, during his college studies in philosophy, that he did not know enough to allow him to reject the faith. He relates that he then began to study theology at Yale Divinity School precisely in order to get more knowledge. In 1968, he took his doctorate with a dissertation on character and virtue in theological ethics. When he began his theological studies, he was very sympathetic to theologians such as Paul Tillich and the Niebuhr brothers. He himself says that he was moved to rethink his theological position by the insight that it was not theological liberals, but figures such as Karl Barth and Dietrich Bonhoeffer who played the decisive role in the church's resistance to Nazism. The time at Yale not only brought an encounter with Barth's theology; Hauerwas was also profoundly influenced by philosophers such as Wittgenstein and Aristotle and their emphasis on the concrete, on the common actions that maintain human life and thinking. Also classic theologians, such as Augustine and especially Thomas Aquinas, assumed a central importance for him.

After teaching for a couple of years at the Swedish Lutheran Augustana College in Rock Island, Illinois, he began to teach at the Roman Catholic University of Notre

Dame in South Bend, Indiana, in 1970, although he was a Methodist. He has said that he did not think of himself as a specifically Protestant ethicist, either then or later. The Catholic tradition was a part of his own tradition, although he was not a Catholic. He has always been profoundly influenced by Catholic theology, and has written in dialogue with it. In 1994, he moved to Duke University in Durham, North Carolina, where the Divinity School is Methodist. It is clear that the Methodist inheritance too has formed him, although he is now active in an Episcopal church. As we shall see, the same is true of the Anabaptist tradition. In one text, he calls himself jokingly a "high church Mennonite."

Theology as Ecclesial Practice

Hauerwas has worked as a professor of theological ethics, but he sees himself as a theologian, since Christian ethics is, for him, a form of theology. One decisive reason why he chose to work in the modern field of ethics is his belief that the truth of Christian convictions cannot be evaluated independently of their practical application. His question is: Does the Christian language function? Can one use it to describe and to live in the world that actually exists? In this sense, he defends a theological realism. He has not written systematic theology in the usual meaning of this term, and he is critical of the idea that theology is analogous to a philosophical system. Besides this, he usually writes in the form of essays; most of the thirty books he has published are collections of essays. This makes it difficult to summarize his "thinking." He is a coherent thinker, but it is above all his frequently brilliant, creative, and critical descriptions and analyses of questions, developments, and events that make it so enthralling (and often entertaining) to read him.

His dissertation, which was later developed into book-form as *Character and the Christian Life*, discusses the moral nature of the Christian life. Hauerwas believes that a one-sided emphasis on a doctrine of justification, understood in forensic terms, has made it difficult for Protestant theological ethics to describe the bodily and social nature of the Christian life, where the human person shares in God's activity. There has been a fear that an emphasis on sanctification would undermine the fact that the Christian life is based on God's grace. On the other hand, the moral philosophy Hauerwas encountered was concerned with the relationship between determinism and freedom. In order to give space for moral freedom, morality was often located in a non-determined sphere separated from the determinist world of the body and society. In both cases, it is difficult to deal with the bodily and social nature of human life, and hence also with the continuity of this life over time.

Hauerwas' response to these two problems was to take up anew the concepts of "character" and "virtue" as a way to describe how God's activity is mediated in bodily and social terms in human life, where "being in Christ" means sharing in the divine life. God's grace is not something that flows above *de facto* human life, or that expresses itself only in one isolated action. This continuity is indicated by the way in which God's activity forms a human person's character. But this happens in a social context. It is in the social communities in which we live that we learn the practices and the symbols and metaphors that form our character and that help us to see the world in an adequate manner.

We can describe Hauerwas' subsequent writings as a development and concretization of the basic ideas he had formulated in *Character and the Christian Life*. If our character is formed in social communities, it is important to analyze how such communities function. Another of his early books is entitled *A Community of Character*. For Christians, the primary community is the church, and ecclesiology becomes increasingly central in his theology. God acts to save and sanctify in and through the church, Christ's body, and in and through the community and the practices that constitute the church. It was in the encounter with the Mennonite theologian John Howard Yoder in the early 1970s that Hauerwas received the instruments he needed to develop a type of ecclesiology that is present implicitly in *Character and the Christian Life*. Along with Yoder's ecclesiology came something else that Hauerwas initially found hard to accept, namely, a different way of understanding the relationship between church and world and the church's social ethics, as well as the idea that non-violence is a constitutive part of Christian theology and Christian discipleship. Yoder's theology has continued to exercise a profound influence on Hauerwas, and he often describes Yoder as a much more important theologian than himself.

In a similar way, the category of "narrative" helped him to speak more concretely of the clear continuity of life that lies in the concept of character, and to hold this together with the idea that our "vision" is formed by the narratives we live with. He is however critical of the concept of "narrative theology." "Narrative" is not a concept that organizes his theology, but it is a serviceable instrument that helps us understand how vision, character, and community function together. This does not apply only to Christian theology, but it is particularly applicable there, since the Christian faith presupposes a fundamental narrative.

Hauerwas can say that Christian discourse is about God, the world, and oneself as narratives, or as parts or subplots that are woven together in a large narrative. The church can thus be described as a continuation of the biblical narrative. To be a Christian is to be a part of, and to be formed by, this socially mediated narrative. One learns to know God, the world, and oneself by being initiated into a tradition, an embodied narrative that includes a set of practices, linguistic usages, and moral skills. It follows that Christian theology and ethics cannot be separated from the practices into which Christian convictions are woven. Hauerwas and Samuel Wells edited *The Blackwell Companion to Christian Ethics*, which is completely structured around the practices of Christian worship (with more than thirty articles) from the initial salutation and the sign of peace to prayer, baptism, and the Lord's Supper. It is through such practices, lived in everyday worship, that the Christians' convictions, emotions, and desires are formed.

In the same way, according to Hauerwas, the Christian use of the Bible is woven into the church's life. Christians believe that God has promised to speak through scripture, so that the church can live in fidelity to God. But scripture should not be understood as first and foremost an object for study. Rather, scripture is something the church lives with, and something through which it sees the world. This is why discipleship is necessary before one can read scripture aright. And discipleship is not an individual project: the Christian life takes shape in a community, and one learns from others. He criticizes both fundamentalism and the historical-critical method for separating the Bible from the church: in practice, the context for reading the Bible is *de facto* the nation and the liberal subject. Hauerwas also believes that hermeneutical theory can function as a way of replacing the church with theory. The Bible can be used in a Christian way only as a part of the shared life of the church. It is not the abstract "text" that addresses the church or the individual Christians, questioning and challenging them. Rather, God's address is mediated through human beings who attempt together to live in fidelity to the Christ to whom the Bible bears witness.

He understands theology in a similar manner, as a practical activity that is connected with the theological convictions that ought to be central to the life of the Christian church, an activity in which these convictions can be understood to be true. This means that Christian theology of its very nature is political. It concerns the life and convictions of the Christian people, not the worldviews of individuals. Theologians are not autonomous "thinkers" who analyze the concept of God in abstraction from how human beings live with God. Instead, Hauerwas argues that theology is an activity that analyzes and develops the linguistic skills that help the church to understand better, and to do better, what it does. This does not mean that theology is not a theoretical activity; it means that the goal of theology is to serve the church's life. And since the church lives in the world, theology is carried out in relation to other intellectual activities and traditions. The question of truth has always been central for Hauerwas, although he has been critical of many of the intellectual strategies that are used in discussing this question. He himself has always written theology with the help of, and in a critical dialogue with, other intellectual disciplines, such as philosophy, social and political theory, sociology, political science, history, and so on. There is no "purely" theological or religious dimension." A theology that is serviceable must transcend the boundaries of academic fields. This means that Hauerwas' theological work is done in a continuous discussion with non-Christian thinkers. For example, one of his latest books, *Christianity, Democracy, and the Radical Ordinary*, is written as a dialogue book with the secular political scientist Romand Coles.

As I have said, Hauerwas has not written a systematic presentation of his "theology." His discussions of the concrete life of the church in the world, or his way of describing the world, allow us to discern the theological convictions that are at the center of his theology. He presupposes a Trinitarian theology with an eschatological orientation. In the center of the Christian narrative stands Jesus' life, death, and resurrection, understood in continuity with the history of Israel. The resurrection means that this Jesus is now present in the church and in the world through the Spirit. Christians, as a church led by the Spirit, learn to know God and God's way in the world through following Jesus Christ in their life as the church in the world. This also means that God as creator and the world as creation cannot be understood correctly, independently of how we meet God in Israel, Jesus Christ, and the church. Hauerwas thus understands the doctrine of creation as a part of the entire Trinitarian narrative. And this means that the creation must be understood christologically and eschatologically. In the same way, one cannot speak about Christ and the Christian hope independently of our understanding of God as the one who creates and sustains the world.

Hauerwas holds that the life, death, and resurrection of Jesus show that God governs the world through love and forgiveness – and this in turn means that love and forgiveness are a real possibility in this world. His understanding of redemption is both historical and social. Sin and death are embodied in the history of humankind, and this is why redemption had to take the form of a historically and socially mediated alternative narrative and practice: this is called "the church." God acts salvifically by creating a people who are called to be bearers of, and witnesses to, the life that God has made possible through Jesus Christ. In this sense, salvation is of its very nature political, and Hauerwas is critical of privatized forms of Christianity or ideas about the salvation of the individual that are detached from God's action in and through the church. But this is a politics determined by the reality of God's kingdom, which can be seen in Jesus' life. It is the church's embodied alternative narrative that gives us instruments to understand and describe the world in which the church lives.

This is why, in his Gifford Lectures *With the Grain of the Universe*, Hauerwas described Karl Barth as the most prominent twentieth-century representative of "natural theology," since a natural theology can only be a part of the entire Christian doctrine of God. To understand the church's faith is to understand how the world is, if these convictions are true. But we cannot understand this without the testimony given by human beings who embody these convictions and point to a possible world in which we can live. When the practice of the Christian church takes a wrong turn, the same often happens to theology (and *vice versa*). The weakness in Barth's theology – seen from Hauerwas' perspective – is precisely his fear of specifying the material conditions for the embodiment of the Christian faith in the life of the church and the Christian. In this context, Yoder has more to offer.

The Church as Politics

If the church is a new *polis* that is the bearer of an alternative narrative and practice, the great challenge for the church is political: How is it to live as a church that is faithful to Jesus Christ in the world in which it finds itself? This is the background to Hauerwas' frequently quoted claim that "The church does not *have* a social ethic, but rather *is* a social ethic." The church's primary vocation is not to formulate social strategies for the state or for those who may come to hold power in future. The church is called to witness to the new reality that is the kingdom of God, a reality that makes possible the beginning of a new social and political order. If the church only adopts the understanding of power and of politics that is dominant in a world that itself does not know this new reality, it abandons its witness and allows its politics to be determined by an understanding of reality that is foreign to the kingdom of God.

Hauerwas holds that it is precisely by being an ecclesial theology, by taking its starting point in the faith and practice of the Christian church, that theology can make fruitful contributions to the general political discussion. The Christian interpretation is not something that is applied to a neutral "reality" that everyone understands in exactly the same way. The social and political questions that the church confronts, and the way in which they are understood, depend on the kind of community that the church is, on the narratives it tells, on its localization in society, and on the social practices with which the church lives. This does not apply only to theology; all forms of social theory and political description are situated socially and politically. A large part of Hauerwas' writings therefore consists of theologically determined descriptions of questions and situations. He focuses both on what kind of church the church ought to be, in order to be able to relate and live the Christian narrative, and on how one can interpret and describe the world in which we live on the basis of the Christian faith. This is why his books largely consist of "thick" social and political analysis. He has analyzed a wide spectrum of questions: war and peace; how the church and society meet people with intellectual disabilities; marriage and the family; various bioethical questions; the modern university; the Holocaust; poverty; race; liberal political philosophy; the language of rights, etc.

Traditional political theology often adopts the opposite strategy. One takes for granted the descriptions that are dominant in the social movements one supports, the social theories on which one builds, or the descriptions one encounters in the general public debate, and then one discusses how theology can become relevant in relation to these interpretations. But for Hauerwas, the "description of the situation" is in itself a theological, ethical, and political task. Theology, formed within the framework of the church's practice, becomes the lens through which the world is seen. This allows theology to challenge the narratives that have a formative and dominant role in a society, and to point to new possibilities. He criticizes the church and theology for allowing its thinking to be taken captive so frequently by what Christians ought to see as false ideas about reality and about what is possible. He writes: "Christians are a people whose imagination has been challenged by a God who has invited us into an otherwise unimaginable kingdom. For only God could have created a world in which forgiveness rather than force could be both a possibility and a duty."

His criticism of the church's "Constantinian inheritance" is related to this. When Christianity functions as the religion of an empire, a state, or a nation, and the church is totally integrated into one particular society and the elites of the church are closely linked to the other elites in society, the Christian way of understanding the world has been taken captive, and that which "now" exists is regarded as natural and given. Even in a modern, secular, post-Constantinian society, Hauerwas believes that the church and theology are often held captive today, just as much as in the past, by ideas about normality that Christians ought to question. If Christian theology and ethics allow themselves to be determined primarily by the question of what the government or the state ought to do, or of how the processes of societal change ought to be directed, the church's ability to see other possibilities is limited.

Hauerwas says that Christians should bear witness to a God who governs the world not through coercion, but through love and forgiveness. The social sphere and the context out of which theology and Christian social ethics are written should not be those who believe that they have power, or those who attempt to take power, but a church that does not attempt to control history. He writes that the truth about reality is seen better by those who know that they lack control. To "live without control" is therefore one of the central Christian virtues; and this virtue in its turn demands hope and patience. Patience is demanded of a church that is called to live in peace in a world full of violence. Without patience, the Christian hope risks turning into fanaticism or – as a disappointed optimism – into cynicism and despair. As a patient people, the church does not lose its hope that what God has promised will be fulfilled. God has given human beings time. Hope thus helps the church to see the world as it is and to seek alternatives to violence and other instruments of power. The simple fact that one does not think in terms of control ("What should those in power do, or what ought we to do if we had power?") strengthens the "imaginative" ability, since it creates a space for moral and social experiments that could otherwise easily be judged unrealistic and ineffective. This is particularly important for one who defends an attitude of non-violence, and Hauerwas therefore underlines the significance of presenting society with alternative descriptions and practices and of making social experiments that can have a lasting importance. There are many examples of this in history.

This allows us to understand what he means by "the politics of gesture," the political significance of everyday life and of the Christians' local reality. The church is not a representative of a utopian ideal, nor is it an agent for the implementation of this ideal. Behind such ideas lies the conception of politics as a struggle for control over the processes of social change. Hauerwas sees "the church's politics" as the actions that fill the shared daily life. Through these actions, one embodies one's world, and human beings receive a moral formation in order that they can envisage and live out alternative attitudes. Hauerwas believes that such a politics is more significant in political terms than the struggle for power and large-scale social and political strategies. He says that one reason for the poverty of contemporary Christian social ethics is that it tends to set up church committees for social justice instead of making the local church's life the primary context of theological work.

Although he claims that the church serves the world best by being "church" – a church that forms human beings and communities, and thereby is able to see things differently – this does not mean that he thinks that the church and theology should never make statements on questions of policy. If a church lives in this way, it can also contribute different perspectives. And he himself has participated in government inquiries on bioethical issues and has been active in the general political debate, most recently with regard to the wars in Afghanistan and Iraq. But this is a result of the former emphasis; it is not the center.

Influence

As was the case with Karl Barth, Hauerwas' view of church and theology involves a critical clash with large sectors of modern theology and with theological ethics in both its conservative and its liberal forms. Analyses of historical and contemporary theologians and philosophers, and dialogues with these thinkers, form an important part of his writings. Above all, he has sought to indicate the interplay between theology, political practice, and the theory of knowledge, and especially how liberal political practice and the claim to knowledge within the framework of the modern nation-state have transformed Christian theology's self-understanding. His criticism and his prominent position have therefore also led to intensive criticism from various sources. One customary objection is that his position leads to ecclesial and theological sectarianism in which theology isolates itself from public debate and Christians withdraw from political involvement. Many of his critics believe that his Christian pacifism reinforces this tendency, since pacifism and political responsibility are seen as incompatible – at the very least, one ought not to make any statements about foreign policy. Many also think that his criticism that the church has allowed itself to be determined too much by the dominant liberal ideas is not only excessively sweeping; it also isolates Christianity in a world culture that is increasingly liberal, and where liberalism is the best hope for a better world. A number of Protestants criticize him for an excessively "Pelagian" attitude. And it is often claimed that his view of the church's possibilities is unrealistic.

Hauerwas does not agree, of course, and he has often, together with his numerous theological allies, attempted to counter these criticisms, which he believes are often based on precisely the assumptions that he criticizes. One can also point out the paradox that a theologian who is accused of promoting the isolation of the church is read and discussed outside the theological and churchly world to a greater extent than most other theologians. At any rate, his influence on contemporary theology is considerable and extends beyond all church boundaries, from various kinds of Protestants to Catholics and Orthodox. Even his critics often carry on the discussion on *his* premises. Many of his former students are now themselves influential theologians. He is one of the sources of inspiration of radical orthodox theology, and many of his former students contributed to the anthology *Radical Orthodoxy*. His way of writing theology does not create a closed system or the formation of a narrow school. Rather, he gives space for a broad ecumenical theology and church practice. Hauerwas has also written a number of more popular books, often with his former colleague at Duke, William Willimon, now a bishop in the United Methodist church. These have found a wide readership. The best known is *Resident Aliens: Life in the Christian Colony*. This is in accordance with his conviction that theology must first and foremost serve the church in its life in the world.

Bibliography

Primary Literature

Vision and Virtue: Essays in Christian Ethical Reflection (Notre Dame: Fides Publishers, 1974).
Character and the Christian Life: A Study in Theological Ethics (San Antonio: Trinity University Press, 1985 [1975]).
A Community of Character: Toward a Constructive Christian Social Ethic (Notre Dame: University of Notre Dame Press, 1981).
The Peaceable Kingdom: A Primer in Christian Ethics (Notre Dame: University of Notre Dame Press, 1983).
Against the Nations: War and Survival in a Liberal Society (Minneapolis: Winston Press, 1985).
Suffering Presence: Theological Reflections on Medicine, the Mentally Handicapped, and the Church (Notre Dame: University of Notre Dame Press, 1986).
Christian Existence Today: Essays on Church, World, and Living in Between (Durham: Labyrinth Press, 1988).
After Christendom? How the Church Is to Behave If Freedom, Justice, and a Christian Nation Are Bad Ideas (Nashville: Abingdon Press, 1991).
Unleashing the Scripture: Freeing the Bible from Captivity to America (Nashville: Abingdon Press, 1993).
In Good Company: The Church as Polis (Notre Dame: University of Notre Dame Press, 1995).
Wilderness Wanderings: Probing Twentieth-Century Theology and Philosophy (Boulder: Westview Press, 1997).
With the Grain of the Universe: The Church's Witness and Natural Theology (Grand Rapids: Brazos Press, 2001).
The Hauerwas Reader, eds John Berkman and Michael G. Cartwright (Durham: Duke University Press, 2001).
Matthew. Brazos Theological Commentary on the Bible (Grand Rapids: Brazos Press, 2006).
The State of the University: Academic Knowledges and the Knowledge of God (Oxford: Blackwell, 2007).
Hannah's Child: A Theologian's Memoir (Grand Rapids: W.B. Eerdmans, 2010).
War and the American Difference: Theological Reflections on Violence and National Identity (Grand Rapids: Baker Academic, 2011).
with Charles Robert Pinches, *Christians among the Virtues: Theological Conversations with Ancient and Modern Ethics* (Notre Dame: University of Notre Dame Press, 1997).
with Romand Coles, *Christianity, Democracy, and the Radical Ordinary: Conversations between a Radical Democrat and a Christian* (Eugene: Cascade Books, 2008).
with Jean Vanier, *Living Gently in a Violent World: The Prophetic Witness of Weakness* (Downers Grove: IVP Books, 2008).

with Samuel Wells (eds), *The Blackwell Companion to Christian Ethics* (Oxford: Blackwell, 2004).

with William H. Willimon, *Resident Aliens: Life in the Christian Colony* (Nashville: Abingdon Press, 1989).

with William H. Willimon, *The Truth About God: The Ten Commandments in Christian Life* (Nashville: Abingdon Press, 1999).

Secondary Literature

Albrecht, Gloria H., *The Character of Our Communities: Toward an Ethic of Liberation for the Church* (Nashville: Abingdon Press, 1995).

Hütter, Reinhard, *Evangelische Ethik als kirchliches Zeugnis: Interpretationen zu Schlüsselfragen theologischer Ethik in der Gegenwart* (Neukirchen-Vluyn: Neukirchener, 1993).

Jones, L. Gregory, Reinhard Hütter and C. Rosalee Velloso da Silva (eds), *God, Truth, and Witness: Engaging Stanley Hauerwas* (Grand Rapids: Brazos Press, 2005).

Kallenberg, Brad J., *Ethics as Grammar: Changing the Postmodern Subject* (Notre Dame: University of Notre Dame Press, 2001).

Katongole, Emmanuel, *Beyond Universal Reason: The Relation between Religion and Ethics in the Work of Stanley Hauerwas* (Notre Dame: University of Notre Dame Press, 2000).

Nation, Mark and Samuel Wells (eds), *Faithfulness and Fortitude: In Conversation with the Theological Ethics of Stanley Hauerwas* (Edinburgh: T&T Clark, 2000).

Pinches, Charles Robert, Kelly S. Johnson, and Charles M. Collier (eds), *Unsettling Arguments: A Festschrift on the Occasion of Stanley Hauerwas's 70th Birthday* (Eugene: Cascade Books, 2010).

Rasmusson, Arne, *The Church as Polis: From Political Theology to Theological Politics as Exemplified by Jürgen Moltmann and Stanley Hauerwas* (Notre Dame: University of Notre Dame Press, 1995).

Wells, Samuel, *Transforming Fate into Destiny: The Theological Ethics of Stanley Hauerwas* (Carlisle: Paternoster, 1998).

Chapter 45
Sarah Coakley

Linn Marie Tonstad

Sarah Coakley's work takes place at the intersection of systematic theology, feminist theology and analytic philosophy of religion. Her innovative, yet deeply traditional, theological method is grounded in the practice of contemplative prayer as a practice of unsaying (or un-mastery) that undoes human tendencies towards idolatry. Coakley's development of a *théologie totale*, an approach to systematic theology that offers a vision for life as a whole using engagements with disciplines outside theology and focusing especially on artistic forms, is an unchastened claim to the priority of God that rejects, in its own performance of fragmentation (in method and language) and ascesis (through prayer), the outsize versions of the will-to-power that classical systematic theologies have often been accused of offering. Her argument for a specifically Christian, and feminist, form of power-in-vulnerability through kenotic submission to God rejects the aspersions secular feminist theory casts on Christianity while emphasizing the centrality of experience and the body to any Christian theology whatsoever. As a theologian engaged in presenting the rational and affective logic of Christianity in conversation with science, theory and the church, Coakley's *oeuvre* moves beyond, without avoiding, the characteristic aporias and contradictions of foundationalism vs. non-foundationalism, modernism vs. post-modernism, systematicity vs. *bricolage*, and reason vs. suspicion. Ambitious and controversial, contentious and elegant, Coakley's project stands at the very fore amongst contemporary practitioners of systematic theology in its most expansive sense.

Biographical Sketch[1]

Sarah Coakley was born in Blackheath, London in 1951. Already from the age of 12, she knew that she wanted to be a theologian – initially, she was influenced by the few books on theology she could find in her parents' home, which included Simone

---

[1] This biographical sketch is based on the following sources: Elaine Williams, 'Sarah Coakley', in Sian Griffiths (ed.), *Beyond the Glass Ceiling* (Manchester, 1996), pp. 36–43; Mark Oppenheimer, 'Sarah Coakley Reconstructs Feminism', *Christian Century*, 120/13 (2003), pp. 25–31; Rupert Shortt, 'Sarah Coakley: Fresh Paths in Systematic Theology', in *God's Advocates* (Grand Rapids, 2005), pp. 67–85, as well as personal communications from Sarah Coakley, who graciously answered questions about her theological development and relationships in the preparation of this sketch.

Weil on attentiveness, J.A.T. Robinson's *Honest to God*, and Evelyn Underhill's letters. She studied at the Blackheath School before going up to Cambridge, where she was disappointed to discover that theological study mostly meant Scripture alone. As a result, she gained a thorough grounding in scriptural interpretation and the relevant languages mostly under the supervision of J.A.T. Robinson. She trained in philosophy of religion with Don Cupitt, Brian Hebblethwaite and especially Donald MacKinnon. Towards the end of her undergraduate studies, much to her relief, she had the opportunity to read systematics with Stephen Sykes, who put her onto Ernst Troeltsch. Friendships with David Ford and, especially, Rowan Williams developed already in this period. It was also at this time that she met her husband, James F. (Chip) Coakley, who was reading theology as a Marshall scholar and is a scholar of Syriac. (The couple has two children, Edith and Agnes Etheldreda.) Coakley recalls that during this time in Cambridge, no one ever expressed so much as a feminist thought in her hearing.

It was when she came to Harvard Divinity School as a Georgia Harkness fellow in 1973–5 that her characteristic preoccupations began to emerge through greater embeddedness in liturgy and the practices of the church. She began to attend daily Eucharist, and she rediscovered practices of prayer and the bodied nature of the spiritual and religious life. It was, ultimately, through such practices of prayer that Coakley came to identify as a feminist, through the experience of the entanglement of divine and sexual desire. This move to practices set her on a path that would lead to her eventual ordination as a priest of the Church of England (a process begun in 1998, and completed in 2001), a path that has brought together her most passionate theological interests with her form of life.

Coakley returned to Cambridge for her doctorate, spending only one year in residence before moving to Lancaster to teach. Her doctoral degree was supervised by Maurice Wiles and was the basis of her influential first book, *Christ Without Absolutes: The Theology of Ernst Troeltsch*, which cemented her sense of the possibilities and, eventually, the limits of 'liberal' approaches to Christology and theology. She took up her first post at Lancaster University in 1976, in the first 'religious studies' department in England, where she taught with John Milbank. Coakley remained at Lancaster until 1991. During this period, she spent 10 years as a member of the Doctrine Commission of the Anglican Church, and it was in this work that her interest in experience, particularly charismatic and prayerful experience, as a source and resource for theological reflection emerged.

Coakley taught at Oxford from 1991 to 1993, but some in the department viewed her with some suspicion as far too liberal – lecturing on feminist theology seemed especially odd, although she drew large numbers of students. She returned to Harvard in 1993, and became Mallincrodt Professor of Divinity there in 1995. Coakley's pursuit of ordination, frequent celebration of the Eucharist, and particularly the experience of teaching contemplative prayer in prison combined to further develop her conviction of the inseparability of Christian practice, contemplation and the transformation of relationships to self, other and God. Coakley's interdisciplinary approach to theology was furthered in these years by a major grant from the Templeton Foundation (received with the evolutionary biologist Martin Nowak) for the study of the relationship between theology and evolutionary science. She also collaborated with Kay Shelemay on an edited volume entitled *Pain and its Transformations*. Harvard Divinity School was, especially towards the end of this period, driven by debates over the relationship between the analytic study of religion and its confessional practice. Coakley, now a prominent practitioner of the confessional approach to the study of religion – indeed, she refuses even the intimation that the confessional status of a Christian theologian might be thought to detract from rather than to advance the academic status of the work – found herself in an increasingly conflictual relationship with others in the Divinity School. She returned to Cambridge as Norris-Hulse Professor of Divinity in 2007, the first woman to hold that position. She gave the Gifford lectures in the spring of 2012 and is currently completing her four-volume systematic theology, the first volume of which is appearing in 2013.

Overview of Her Thought

Coakley's wide-ranging theological, philosophical and scientific interests converge around the central issues of gender, desire, theological method, knowledge of God and the role of the body in religion and religious practices. At the heart of her work stands the integration of systematic and 'practical' theology – indeed, Coakley refuses that disjunction absolutely – through the practice of silent prayer, a contemplative 'waiting on God' that works as a purgation of idolatry.

The process of 'waiting on God' in contemplative prayer effects a radical transformation of the person while confronting her with the limitations of her understanding of God. This transformation of the person into 'sonship' in the image of Christ involves a form of gender fluidity that requires movement into those 'dark' continents of the human person stereotypically associated with the racial and sexual other: the body, affect and un-mastery. Coakley rejects what she identifies as the restless longing for one-knows-not-what in secular gender theory – the fulfillment of the body, a God in feminine form – in favour of the transformation of all aspects of personhood, including gender and sexual difference, through engagement with the God who is closer to the person than she is to herself. This transformation, pursued through contemplation, does not lead the soul in ascent away from the body but rather directs attention 'downward', into the vulnerability and 'femininity' of the body as the very locations in which the person encounters God.

In this process, the person will undergo suffering as she is transformed into Christ, and that suffering may be willingly and freely embraced as a form of commitment to the world and its ambiguities of sin and death. Such embrace does not valorise suffering for its own sake; instead, it takes seriously the relationship between contemplation and social transformation, the way that the 'other' is encountered and loved as other as the contemplative is taken up into the curlicues of divine desire. At the centre of this theological method is the decision to make oneself vulnerable to God, to trust God as the divine 'Other' who (also the non-other) transforms the self into the person she is meant to be, a Christ. This process, an interruption of the normal patterns of selfhood by the ambush of the divine other (Spirit), will throw up in confusing and destabilising manner many abjected (refused) aspects of self and personhood. Characteristically, from the perspective of a theological diagnosis of sin, persons are deluded about their own independence, invulnerability and 'masculine' self-possession. The therapy of this delusion requires its undoing through the work of God in the waiting contemplative. The clarity of 'masculine' reason thus finds itself led into the 'dazzling darkness' of 'femininity' in the encounter with God, in analogy to Moses' ascent on the mountain in Gregory of Nyssa's *Life of Moses*.

Coakley's work on figures like Gregory of Nyssa and pseudo-Dionysius recovers resources in their thought for envisioning richer visions of life and the God-relationship contained in classical Christian traditions, particularly in their mystical-theological incarnations. Rightly refusing a disjunction of the mystical (or the apophatic) from the doctrinal (or the cataphatic), Coakley views doctrine as a grammar of Christian life that does not reduce to internal justification according to radically relative standards, but rather may be tested and examined for its rationality and consistency using reason, through practice, and in dialogue with other traditions and modes of analysis, particularly evolutionary biology. In her inaugural lecture as Norris-Hulse professor, for instance, Coakley argues that analyses of the importance of reciprocal altruism in the evolution of humans and human sociality may serve to recover the priority of sacrifice in the Christian life while offering a 'moral-teleological' argument for God as the one 'who has set up the whole cooperation game to climax in free participation in his love'.[2]

Coakley's commitments to rigour, justification, clarity and reason are characteristic of analytic philosophy of religion, while her interests in gender and the dark continents of the human person in her relation to God are usually associated with Continental philosophy of religion and French feminist theory. From this perspective, Coakley may be understood as an analytic philosopher of religion who has taken the insights of feminist theory and criticism seriously – she is one of the first to do so. At the same time, her work refuses a radical disjunction between these forms of discourse. Significantly, Coakley has critiqued analytic philosophers of religion for envisioning freedom and the God–self relation in ways that seem to equate God with the Enlightenment 'man of reason' while valorising independence, freedom as a power for opposites, and self-sufficiency in the human being. These latter values install incompatibilist understandings of human freedom before God while taking for granted an ideal of 'masculine' independence rather than 'feminine' vulnerability of the human self in relation to God.

For Coakley, knowledge of God is a deepening darkness into which the feminist is invited; the dazzling of all 'light' (masculine cognition) renders her, and indeed all persons, rightly 'feminised' in relation to God. '"Can a feminist call God Father", then? One might more truly insist that she *must*; for it lies with her alone to do the kneeling

---

[2] Sarah Coakley, *Sacrifice Regained: Reconsidering the Rationality of Religious Belief* (Cambridge, 2012). This argument is developed further in her Gifford lectures.

work that slays patriarchy at its root.'[3] The ambiguity of this theme must be noted. It is clear that Coakley wishes to argue that the 'feminisation' of creation and the pray-er in relation to God is not to be considered an essentialist assertion about the nature of femininity itself. Rather, this assertion inverts cultural stereotypes about whether the human who relates to God becomes 'man' in the image of God. For Coakley, the person becomes, as it were, woman, in entering that 'dark continent' of willed submission and vulnerability to the only 'Father' (of the 'Son') who may dangerously be trusted to batter the sinful submissive into the only kind of chastity that will free her from her sexed vulnerability to sinful human structures of patriarchy. 'She' (and 'he', who must become like 'her'), must abandon herself to the control of the Spirit in analogy to the way in which the self loses control to the other in the darkness of sexual desire and relationship. At the same time, can femininity be installed (even non-essentially) as the shape of a God-relation without installing masculinity on the divine side of the relationship?

This brings us to another aspect of the complicated relation between consent and control in Coakley's theology. On the one hand, self-abandonment to God in her theology submits the pray-er to God's uncontrollable and unpredictable primacy: God cannot be identified with any social programme in particular, nor can one safely hold some part of oneself in reserve in submission to God, for it is the emptying of the self in waiting upon God that allows the process of purgation of idolatry to take place in the self. At the same time, that self-emptying is thoroughly and deeply intentional and consensual. One has and gains a self through the concreteness of the practices of what Coakley repeatedly terms 'willed' submission to God. The very practice of wordless prayer, a material practice of directing one's time (and un-directing one's thought, as it were) is a practice of 'having' the self that one abandons (the central paradox of all kenotic accounts of selfhood). But beyond this, the self is not to be abandoned to other selves in direct analogy or consequence of the way one is abandoned to God. It is precisely the self that is gained through the practice of self-abandonment to God that finds itself 'empowered' to resist human hierarchies of one over the other, the transformation of functional hierarchies into injustice, and the slippage between 'Father' and fathers. And this self experiences in the practices of prayer a relation to the 'communion of saints', living and dead, that transforms the practice of contemplative prayer into a deeply social (and political, in analogy to the 'personal is the political' slogan of 1970s feminism) relation to the other. This social relation must then be brought, also, into the 'bedroom'; indeed, it is inside this space of divine and divinely directed desire that the sexual relation will take its right shape, as the enactment of processes of gender fluidity that move through and beyond the various forms of heterosexual approaches to human relationality and that are ultimately, like all else in human life, oriented towards God.

---

[3] Sarah Coakley, *God, Sexuality and the Self: An Essay 'On the Trinity'* (Cambridge, 2013), chapter 7.

Key Themes

Experiencing the Trinity in Prayer

The ferment around Coakley's theological work, especially in the United States, came to a head around her qualified assertion that God may be experienced as Trinity. Trinitarian theology in the twentieth century has been in one form or another a response to Karl Barth's placement of the doctrine at the heart of the Christian message and Karl Rahner's assertion that the Trinity is a doctrine so far removed from the spiritual lives of ordinary Christians as to be utterly irrelevant for them. Coakley takes on Rahner's challenge, foregrounding the *experiential* quality of access to the Trinity, an experience grounded in the shape of the 'conversation' into which the self is caught in the practice of silent prayer. Romans 8 is absolutely central to Coakley's work in this regard. Four central themes emerge from this nexus of experience, contemplative prayer and God.

First, the practice of silent prayer brings the individual up into 'a movement of *divine* reflexivity a sort of answering of God to God in and through the one who prays'.[4] Specifically, Romans 8:14–15 and 26 identify the Spirit as one who teaches the 'pray-er' to call God 'Father'. In this process, the Spirit is implicitly distinguished from the Father. This is 'the only valid *experiential* pressure towards hypostasizing the Spirit'.[5] The Spirit prays in and for the pray-er, purging her idolatries while transforming her into the image of Christ as an adopted 'Son' of the 'Father'. This is a process of kenotic vulnerability in which the pray-er is delivered to God.

Second, this practice brings about a relation to the 'Son' (irreducible to, yet never departing from, the historical Jesus and the risen Christ), the one into whom all of creation is being 'progressively transformed'.[6] It is not, then, that the person praying has qualitatively different experiences of the three persons; rather, 'the pray-er's total "experience" of *God* is here found to be ineluctably tri-faceted. The "Father" is both source and ultimate object of divine desire; the "Spirit" is that (irreducibly distinct) enabler and incorporator of that desire in creation – that which *makes* the creation divine; the "Son" *is* that divine and perfected creation'.[7] The differentiated, single experience of transformation in prayer – finding oneself prayed in, encountering the Source of divine desire to whom prayer is directed, and being transformed anew – is a holistic triune experience of God.

Third, the Spirit is not a shapeless 'feminine' third (the 'other' of the male Father and the male Son) or a location of the relation between Father and Son as the bond

---

[4] Sarah Coakley, 'Can God Be Experienced as Trinity?' *The Modern Churchman*, 28 (1986), p. 21.

[5] Sarah Coakley, 'Why Three? Some Further Reflections on the Origins of the Doctrine of the Trinity', in Sarah Coakley and David A. Pailin (eds), *The Making and Remaking of Christian Doctrine: Essays in Honour of Maurice Wiles* (Oxford, 1993), p. 37.

[6] Ibid.

[7] Ibid., pp. 37–8.

of love, as in much historical and contemporary trinitarian theology. Coakley was one of the earliest theologians to recognise the deeply sexist nature of the much-praised recovery of the femininity of the Holy Spirit in Yves Congar and Leonardo Boff, for instance. Indeed, Coakley identifies the indeterminate 'place' of the Spirit, its forgetting, as a failure of trinitarian theology which she (admittedly speculatively) connects with the Spirit's history of drawing women and the marginalised into (unregulated) speech. Instead, the Spirit comes 'first' as the one who draws the person into God. The Spirit's experiential priority must, then, be reflected in doctrine, above all at the level of the Spirit's purgative work in relation to the idolatries of the pray-er who finds her sexual and gendered self brought forward for examination (shaken out, as it were), and painfully reformed through a continual process of de-idolisation in which she learns to distinguish between fathers and *the* 'Father': 'in the same silence we learn to use "Father" *proprie*, and *only* as "Father"-in Trinity.'[8] The place of the Spirit in a *théologie totale* is first in experience and first in engendering the validity of theological language as it is used by the contemplative feminist theologian on her knees (and, presumably, in her writing – but can such writing 'safely' be read by those who have not experienced such purgation of idolatry, especially the non-feminist?). Simultaneously, Coakley's adaptation of the Troeltschian sect/church distinction allows for the identification of a necessary relationship between the organised, 'safe' grammar of church doctrine and the Spirit's corrective and purgative capacity at the edges of the space of church. The distinction is analogous, one might argue, to the right functioning of the relation between cataphatic and apophatic language in theology, in which the assertion of apophasis accompanies the throwing up or, as Coakley says, 'bombardment' of non-sanctioned images for God that displace and destabilise what might otherwise become idolatrously calcified: for this too the invitation comes from the Spirit.

Fourth, this experience leads directly into the depths of sexuality, gender and desire – of and for God. In *God, Sexuality and the Self*, Coakley offers a sophisticated and subtle examination of trinitarian iconography to show the ways in which, despite the avowals of Christian theologians, the maleness of God (Father and Son) and the exclusion of the symbolically and literally feminine (Spirit, Mary, Church) have indeed characterised the history of attempts at representing the unrepresentable. Coakley consistently emphasises the priority of desire in human existence, yet unlike most theorists of sex, gender and sexuality she refuses to assign priority to any other form of desire than that for God. Indeed, it is God's desire for us that takes priority in grounding and ordering human desire towards its right ends. That, however, does not mean that she excludes human desire and sexuality from theological significance. Instead, all human desires and forms of relationship take their places in transformative relations to the priority of Christ and God. The Spirit 'interrupts' understandings of gender as relations between the two, just as the priority of the Spirit interrupts any assumptions about a paternal Trinity constituted by Father and Son with the Spirit as their feminine other and supplement. This transgressive interruption is grounded

---

[8] Coakley, *God, Sexuality, and the Self*, chapter 7.

theologically in the incarnation which moves across the boundary of the difference between God and creation.

Sacrifice and Ascesis as Fundamental Human Postures

For Coakley, the priority of God's gracious initiative elicits the response of sacrifice from the human person under the conditions of sin. While the logic of God's action is a graced logic, the reality of sin and idolatry means that the sacrifice required to gain 'participation in this [trinitarian] reflexivity-in-God involves purgation into life rather than sacrifice-as-death', and this kind of sacrifice installs 'a theonomous self which is authentically free because authentically submitted to God'.[9] Note the significance of this kind of interrelation between theonomy, freedom and authenticity: the self, which is authentically God-related, is bent against itself in its own claims to possession and mastery, and must sacrifice (abandon itself) in order to gain itself rightly. This sacrifice is not death, nor the gift of death, but transformation towards life, a feminist call for sacrifice 'as a purgation of desire for the sake of love' in which 'desires are sorted and idolatry purged' and the self learns to identify with God's desires '*for* life and joy, not for their suppression'.[10]

Théologie Totale as Method

The *théologie totale* that Coakley develops as a method for systematic theology brings together several different elements:

- Theology as a way of life, where systematic theology is grounded in the particular and specific practice of contemplation.
- Systematic theology in (relatively) ordinary language; a systematic theology that refuses the disjunction of the systematic and the pastoral.
- Intertwining of theology and cultural forms, or a multi- and interdisciplinary approach to theology (using art and art history, fieldwork in church communities, experiences of teaching theology in prison or working as a hospital chaplain) as legitimate resources for systematic reflection.
- The priority of 'un-mastery' for the theologian, a practice of 'un-mastery' that cannot be achieved by 'good intentions' or by 'fiat'.[11]
- And which results in an unsystematic systematic theology – a series of pieces, pictures of a total (but not totalising) theology that is *underway* (in via).

---

[9] Sarah Coakley, 'In Defense of Sacrifice: Gender, Selfhood, and the Binding of Isaac', in Linda Martín Alcoff and John D. Caputo (eds), *Feminism, Sexuality, and the Return of Religion* (Bloomington, 2011), p. 23.

[10] Ibid., pp. 28–9.

[11] Coakley, *God, Sexuality, and the Self*, chapter 1.

Coakley's Significance

Ultimately, Coakley's significance for the contemporary theological scene cannot fully be assessed until the completion of her four-volume systematic theology. Nonetheless, the importance of her work is already apparent in several ways. First, there is a sense in which she still stands alone in the contemporary theological scene in the particular 'shape' that her theology, and its method, has taken. It would be interesting to speculate as to why her theology has found greater resonance among more methodologically conservative theologians and philosophers of religion than among feminist theologians and feminist philosophers of religion, a fact that one suspects both mystifies and delights Coakley herself. Her 'agent provocateur' approach to theology may, on occasion, provide 'cover' for theologians who wish to allow the basic programme of systematic theology to go untouched at its foundations (making only minor adjustment, perhaps in the use of pronouns) by the sorts of critiques that feminist philosophers and theologians of various ideological camps have offered. At the same time, and as Coakley herself would aver, if certain assumptions and arguments she offers are convincing – particularly with respect to the relationship between sexuality and God and the purgation of idolatry learned, and deployed, by a feminist on her knees – such 'covering' reflects an inadequate engagement with the total programme of her work.

Second, for a time it was taken for granted at the cutting edge of theology that no more systematic theologies of the 'old' kind could, or should, be written. If Coakley's systematics fulfils its promise, it will require a rethinking of the assumptions and conditions under which a *théologie totale* may be written, rather than a jettisoning of the possibility of such projects, from 'postmodern' directions. Third, Coakley's work participates in, and furthers, the movement of feminist theology beyond relegation to the margins ('from margin to center' in bell hooks' memorable formulation) as a particularist or identitarian form of theology relevant only to (white, Western) women. Whether it is possible to succeed in such a project using the method and conditions Coakley has set for herself will have to be tested particularly by the volume on race forthcoming later in her systematics. Finally, her turn to the evolutionary basis of the logic of sacrifice offers a new way forward in conversations about Christianity, evolution and theology.

Bibliography

Primary Literature
(Selected Works by Sarah Coakley (a complete bibliography is available on her Cambridge website))

Books
God, Sexuality, and the Self: An Essay 'On the Trinity' (Cambridge: Cambridge University Press, 2013).
Powers and Submissions: Spirituality, Philosophy and Gender (Oxford: Blackwell, 2002).
Sacrifice Regained: Reconsidering the Rationality of Religious Belief (Cambridge: Cambridge University Press, 2012).

Articles and Book Chapters
'Can God Be Experienced as Trinity?', *The Modern Churchman*, 28 (1986), pp. 11–23.
'Dark Contemplation and Epistemic Transformation: The Analytic Theologian Re-Meets Teresa of Ávila', in Oliver D. Crisp and Michael C. Rea (eds), *Analytic Theology: New Essays in the Philosophy of Theology* (Oxford: Oxford University Press, 2009), pp. 280–312.
'Feminist Theology', in James C. Livingston, Francis Schüssler Fiorenza, with Sarah Coakley and James H. Evans, Jr. (eds), *Modern Christian Thought*, volume II: *The Twentieth Century* (Upper Saddle River: Prentice-Hall, 2000), pp. 417–42.
'God as Trinity: An Approach through Prayer', in *We Believe in God: A Report by The Doctrine Commission of the General Synod of the Church of England* (London: Church House Publishing, 1987), pp. 104–21.
'In Defense of Sacrifice: Gender, Selfhood, and the Binding of Isaac', in Linda Martín Alcoff and John D. Caputo (eds), *Feminism, Sexuality, and the Return of Religion* (Bloomington, 2011), pp. 17–38.
'Living into the Mystery of the Holy Trinity: Trinity, Prayer, and Sexuality', *Anglican Theological Review*, 80/2 (1998), pp. 223–32.
'Providence and the Evolutionary Phenomenon of "Cooperation": A Systematic Proposal', in Francesca Aran Murphy and Philip G. Ziegler (eds), *The Providence of God: Deus Habet Consilium* (London: T&T Clark, 2009), pp. 179–93.
'What Does Chalcedon Solve and What Does it Not? Some Reflections on the Status and Meaning of the Chalcedonian "Definition"', in Stephen T. Davis, Daniel Kendall, SJ and Gerald O'Collins, SJ (eds), *The Incarnation: An Interdisciplinary Symposium on the Incarnation of the Son of God* (New York: Oxford University Press, 2002), pp. 143–63.
'Why Three? Some Further Reflections on the Origins of the Doctrine of the Trinity', in Sarah Coakley and David A. Pailin (eds), *The Making and Remaking of Christian Doctrine: Essays in Honour of Maurice Wiles* (Oxford: Clarendon Press, 1993), pp. 29–63.

Secondary Literature

Byassee, Jason, 'Closer Than Kissing: Sarah Coakley's Early Work', *Anglican Theological Review*, 90/1 (2008), pp. 139–55.
Hallonsten, Gösta (ed.), 'Sarah Coakley: A Symposium', *Svensk Teologisk Kvartalskrift*, 85/2 (2009), pp. 49–92.
Oppenheimer, Mark, 'Sarah Coakley Reconstructs Feminism', *Christian Century*, 120/13 (2003), pp. 25–31.
Shortt, Rupert, 'Sarah Coakley: Fresh Paths in Systematic Theology', in *God's Advocates* (Grand Rapids, 2005), pp. 67–85.
Williams, Elaine, 'Sarah Coakley', in Sian Griffiths (ed.), *Beyond the Glass Ceiling* (Manchester, 1996), pp. 36–43.

Chapter 46
Alister E. McGrath

Olli-Pekka Vainio

In the twentieth century, the rapid progress of natural sciences created a need for theology to relate itself to both scientific method and particular findings of modern science. Broadly speaking, the dialogue between theology and sciences has taken place within two different ways of understanding the nature of theology. On the one hand, there have been revisionist approaches that have tried to shape theology to accommodate the implications of science. This stance, exemplified by, for example, David Griffin and Ian Barbour, has usually been closely related to process philosophy originating from Alfred North Whitehead (1861–1947) and developed in a more theological direction by Charles Hartshorne (1897–2000). On the other hand, some theologians do not necessarily seek to shape theology to accommodate science, but instead concentrate more on the relationship between scientific methodology and theological method. Representatives of this approach include Thomas F. Torrance, John Polkinghorne and J. Wentzel van Huyssteen. In the last decade, Alister McGrath has emerged as one of the leading theorists of this approach.

Life

Alister McGrath (b. 1953, Belfast) began his academic career as a scientist. In college, he majored in pure and applied mathematics, physics and chemistry. McGrath moved to Oxford in 1971 to study chemistry at Wadham College, and after graduation continued as a researcher in molecular biophysics at the Department of Biochemistry. One of the most decisive moments in McGrath's life was his conversion from atheism to Christianity, which he mentions in many of his books. In the 1960s, following the trend of the time, he had become convinced of the superiority of a Marxist form of atheism and the claims made by A.J. Ayer in his famous and popular book *Language, Truth and Logic*, according to which all talk about God was unverifiable and therefore meaningless. Consequently, it was believed that as a result of scientific and technological progress religion would fall into oblivion and atheism would prevail.

In the course of his studies, McGrath began to extend the same critical attitude to atheism, which he had formerly directed toward Christian religion. In 1971, he started to have doubts about the intellectual substance of the atheist worldview. Eventually, he came to realize that instead of being a factual, or scientific, statement about reality atheism was a philosophical system among others. Additionally, he came to see that he had not read Christian theology enough in order to understand it properly, and thus had rejected only a straw man. This led McGrath to immerse himself in the world of theology, receiving permission to do a degree in theology alongside his research in biophysics. While carrying out research in Utrecht, the Netherlands, in 1976 he had an idea which would shape his life and academic career. In the preface of his *A Scientific Theology: Nature*, he writes:

> the idea that shot through my mind was simple: explore the relation between Christian theology and the natural sciences, using philosophy and history as dialogue partners. It would be grounded in and faithful to the Christian tradition, yet open to the insights of the sciences. This would be more than a mere exploration of a working relationship; it would be a proposal for a synergy, a working together, a mutual cross-fertilization of ideas and approaches – in short, a scientific theology.

In 1977, McGrath received a D.Phil. for his research in the natural sciences and in the following year he gained a first class honours in Theology. In 1981, he was ordained priest (Church of England) and served in this role for a short period before going back to Oxford in 1983, where he was appointed lecturer in Christian doctrine and ethics at Wycliffe Hall. McGrath was the Principal of Wycliffe Hall from 1995 to 2004, and Professor of Historical Theology at Oxford University from 1999 to 2008. Since then, McGrath has worked at King's College, London, as the Professor of Theology, Ministry and Education.

McGrath has delivered several named lectures, such as the Bampton Lectures at Oxford University in 1990, where he examined the formation of Christian creedal formulations. The lectures were published as *Genesis of Doctrine*. He was the Gifford Lecturer at the University of Aberdeen and Hulsean Lecturer at the University of Cambridge in 2009. The lectures were published under the titles *A Fine-Tuned Universe: The Quest for God in Science and Theology* and *Darwinism and the Divine*. McGrath was elected a Fellow of the Royal Society of Arts in 2005.

Major Works

Alongside the dialogue with natural sciences, McGrath has written extensively on the development of theological doctrines. One of his major works is the monumental exposition of the history of the doctrine of justification (*Iustitia Dei: A History of the Christian Doctrine of Justification*), which describes all major interpretations of justification from biblical concepts to modern ecumenical discussions. McGrath's reading is not limited to a certain confessional viewpoint and is open to insights from different traditions and to ecumenical convergence.

Themes of historical theology are discussed in *Luther's Theology of the Cross*, *Reformation Thought: An Introduction*, *Intellectual Origins of the European Reformation* and *Making of Modern German Christology* as well. In these volumes McGrath's style is rather general. He offers trajectories of development and classifications. In light of his earlier career, McGrath is perhaps most well known as an educational writer.

In keeping with this, one of the most widely used textbooks of theology in the world is his *Christian Theology: An Introduction*.

In *Genesis of Doctrine: A Study in the Foundations of Doctrinal Criticism*, he engages critically with George Lindbeck's postliberal theology and especially his account of "doctrine," claiming that Lindbeck's idea of theological doctrine as cultural-linguistic entity suffers from fundamental shortcomings. According to McGrath, Lindbeck's view that doctrine does not make first-order truth claims about reality but being only a description of the use of religious language within a specific liturgical community gives a reductionistic account of theological language. McGrath claims that theological language is first and foremost about reality. It is grounded in the acts of God within our reality, not only in the coherence of intertextual concepts, as Lindbeck claims. His engagement with Lindbeck forms a starting point for his *A Scientific Theology* series as well. The relationship of theology and the natural sciences is given a preliminary treatment in *Science and Religion: A New Introduction* and *The Foundations of Dialogue in Science and Religion*. His latest books on theology and science deal especially with the questions of natural theology, such as *The Open Secret: A New Vision for Natural Theology*.

In addition to academic textbooks and introductions, McGrath is known for books written for a popular audience. These include, among others, books dealing with pastoral issues such as doubt and self-esteem, handbooks of apologetics and popular introductions to particular Christian doctrines. In recent years he has argued against well-known atheist Richard Dawkins in two books (*Dawkins's God: Genes, Memes, and the Meaning of Life*; *Dawkins Delusion?*). McGrath has also authored biographies of T.F. Torrance, Jean Calvin and C.S. Lewis, and written a series of children's fiction, *The Aedyn Chronicles*. Few academic theologians have managed to gain so wide a popular and academic audience as McGrath.

Main Themes of Scholarship

In the first three volumes of his *A Scientific Theology* series (2001–3)—subtitled "Nature", "Reality" and "Theory," respectively, and summarized in *The Science of God* (2004)—McGrath outlines a project, which, on the one hand, gives theology its own space, and, on the other hand, looks for the points of contact with the natural sciences. The project is one of the most ambitious attempts to explore the interface between theology and science to date. While the work can be read both as a treatise on the relationship of Christian theology and the natural sciences and a work on theological methodology, McGrath regards it as a defence of the entire theological enterprise itself, which is a legitimate intellectual discipline in its own right. Christian theology "has its own sense of identity and purpose that are linked with an appreciation of its own limitations and distinctive emphases within the human quest for wisdom as a whole."

But why choose the natural sciences as dialogue partners for theology? According to McGrath, these two disciplines share the same approach to reality, which they understand as both rationally structured and intelligible. In short, both are committed to "realism." First, reality is what it is independently of what we happen to think about it. We do not create or construct facts about reality, instead we discover them as we engage with reality (ontological realism). Second, we are able to get in touch with reality and gain knowledge about it (epistemological realism). Third, it is possible to form sentences that can be understood in terms of correspondence with reality (semantic realism).

McGrath identifies himself as a part of critical realist school of thought, which he has adapted from T.F. Torrance (1913–2007) and Roy Bhaskar (born 1944). Critical realism presents a middle way between naïve realism and postmodern anti-realism. According to the former, our knowledge about realism is objective, self-evident and not corrupted by the observer. This was the typical modernist notion of knowledge. The latter claims that there is no knowledge outside specific contexts: all claims are bound to certain time and place. Additionally, there are no universal criteria to evaluate different claims about reality. Critical realism denies both relativism and naïve realism by claiming that although our knowledge is always partial and progressive, we have ways to distinguish between true and false representations of reality. Generally speaking, theories and claims about reality can be assessed with the criteria of success and explanatory scope: some accounts are more successful than others if they explain more than others.

Concerning the criteria of evaluation of differing interpretative traditions, McGrath sides with Alasdair McIntyre. Accordingly, we are able to evaluate competing traditions and their interpretations by assessing how internally coherent and convincing the given the tradition is and how it is able to deal with its intra-systemic problems. Second, we can ask whether the tradition offers an account of why the competing traditions exist, and whether it is able to answer to the questions posed to it by other traditions. Thus, it is possible to evaluate the viability of traditions without adapting a third, superficially neutral, point of view, which would eventually be in the same epistemological boat as the two other traditions.

McGrath's stance is "post-foundational": there is no neutral God's eye viewpoint from where reality could be observed objectively and without interest. As a consequence, theology is given its own space and autonomy as a scientific discipline, at least *prima facie*. Theology is autonomous in the sense that its claim to truth cannot be rejected on *a priori* grounds (as Ayer insisted). Human beings are not in a position in which they could confidently say, for instance, "physical reality is all there is." It is impossible to restrict *a priori* the methods or norms that can be used to gain knowledge in theological matters without unwarranted limitation of theology's vision of reality. However, McGrath emphasizes that this epistemic space for theology should not result in a theology that becomes an intellectual ghetto separated from general scientific discussion. Conversely, only post-foundationalism makes a genuine interaction with the scientific disciplines possible by enabling a dialogue between various sciences and locating common factors between them. McGrath states that the goal of scientific theology is not to merge theology with the natural sciences but to find *resonance* between them. In this way, it is possible for theology to communicate its contents to non-theological audiences and fulfil its apologetic function.

One central tenet of McGrath's critical realism is the notion of "stratified reality." Reality is multi-leveled to such an extent that different methods for acquiring knowledge are needed at different levels. We have different methods in physics, sociology and psychology, for example. Similarly, within medicine we can study a cancerous tumour, which is a physical entity, sociological effects of cancer, or mental effects of cancer to the patient and his or her family. All these strata are both separate and linked with each other but there is no one single method for all of them. McGrath thus denies methodological reductionism, according to which there is one single scientific method shared by all academic disciplines.

Second, it must be recognized that each method of investigation cannot be determined *a priori* by, for example, philosophers or physicists, but only *a posteriori* as a result of engagement with some specific strata of reality. In critical realist terminology: ontology determines epistemology. First, we encounter the phenomenon, and only afterwards we can begin to test which method is the best possible one.

This means that we have no *single* theological method, but multiple methods engaging different strata of theological reality. According to McGrath, for instance, the basic error of previous methodological discussions has been the attempt to reduce all theological strata to one singular notion, such as feeling (Schleiermacher) or community (Lindbeck). But clearly there is more to theological or religious spheres of life than mere feelings or the uses of language within communities.

In theology, we are not able to study God per se. Even God's revelation took place in the past, and today we only have access to the *effects* of this revelation. We have at our disposal multiple effects of revelation, such as texts witnessing about Christ, ancient liturgies, prayers and creeds, communal structures (such as offices of deacon, pastor and bishop), formation of theological concepts (such as "*homouusios*") and images, and accounts of religious experiences, supreme weight being in the Holy Scriptures. Together they form the data of theological inquiry. Different aspects of this data require different methods. Theology approaches revelatory strata abductively by inference from things to which we now have access to the best possible explanation for their existence. The question theology asks is, what do we need to explain this state of affairs? In keeping with this, theology should always think about the big picture—that is, how the different strata are mutually connected and how they form a whole.

McGrath's project is one of natural theology, yet it is more in line with what is nowadays called "theology of nature," in order to distinguish it from, for example, a more Thomistic kind of natural theology. In this theology of nature model, "nature" does not always and everywhere mean the same thing. The theoretical framework in which we observe and interpret nature fixes what we mean by "nature" and what we consider "natural." Therefore, nature as such is not something that explains (*explicans*) but something that demands explanation (*explicandum*). Thus theology of nature cannot mean that nature "as it is" offers an objective ground for theology (as suggested by some stronger forms of natural theology). The Christian reading of nature sees nature as creation. Because God created everything that exists, we are able to discern the fingerprints of God in nature. However, we are not able to come to know God only by observing nature. For example, theistic proofs may support the coherence of the Christian worldview and communicate something of it to outsiders. Similarly, theology of nature does not provide independent proof for Christian revelation. Instead, theology of nature provides resonance, "a realization that what is being proclaimed by theology makes sense of things." Theology thus offers a "prism through which nature can be viewed and understood."

According to McGrath's view of theological language, we are able to speak about God through analogies. The phenomena in our world have a potential to represent God, but they must always be authorised by God to perform this function. By looking at the shepherd on a field, for example, we do not come to understand more about God if there is no record of Christ saying: "I am the Good Shepherd." Analogies rest upon a covenant between the signifier and signified, not upon nature as such. Still, the ontological emphasis of God's revelation is in created reality itself. Human beings need special revelation to discern the revelatory nature of historical events as God's revelation for human beings. Thus special revelation does not rise above the natural world but brings us back to it. Nevertheless, analogies are not identical with the systems with which they are associated. Simultaneously, different analogies form a network of interlocking images, whose interpretative use is determined by their mutual relationship. Our language about God is not perfect but asymptotic, always coming closer but never becoming identical.

But how can Christian theology be sure that it has given an authentic account of reality? McGrath sets out two variables which help to see the heart of problem and its solution. First, according to *the underdetermination of theory by evidence*, if the evidence about the event is not conclusive, the event is open to differing and even contradicting interpretations. Second, according to *the dynamics of the reception of theory*, it is possible for theories to be initially widely accepted and later modified or even abandoned when the inquiry produces new evidence and better theories. Within the history of early Christology, which ultimately sets the agenda for orthodox Christian theology, we are able to see both of these variables at work. The Scriptures do not articulate a clear Christological or Trinitarian dogma, and during first Christian centuries there existed a number of Christological models, some of which were later condemned as heretical. This process of doctrinal development, where some doctrinal formulations were affirmed while others were ruled out, is for McGrath analogous to the progress of scientific theories. Radical theologies see this process as a power play where the strong oppress the weak. McGrath claims that it is simply the way through which all intellectual communities develop. Before Copernicus, it was commonly believed that the Sun revolves around the Earth. Nevertheless, this fact is not used by anybody as a proof for the plurality of legitimate interpretations of the composition of the cosmos. Christianity is based on public events and publicly addressed words of witness, which were later subjected to theorization. It is only natural that a number of competing theories will emerge, and some of them will prevail (and others perish) according to their ability to explain the original events.

One of the starting points of McGrath's project is the rejection of "fideistic" approaches to theology. In fideist approaches, theology becomes incommensurable with other "language games," such as science. But is it not more natural for religious persons to think of God as the best explanation for the effects of the alleged original revelation? While McGrath admits this, he sees that an atheist and a Christian engage with the same reality in their attempts to make sense of the world. Both have the same evidence as to what the world is like, but they interpret it differently. This does not, however, lead them to inhabit two separate worlds and language games. When two competing interpretations are offered, we must evaluate which interpretation has more explanatory power. Nonetheless, only faith can see revelatory acts as God's actions performed for my sake.

Current Place in Theological Discussion

As a former atheist, McGrath has written about both historical and contemporary atheism, and he regularly debates with leading atheists. His strategy is not so much to concentrate on convincing atheists about the truth claims of Christianity as it is about the deconstruction of the premises of atheist argumentation and worldview, and the unwarranted rivalry between religion and science. Although McGrath is highly appreciated within contemporary evangelical theology, some more conservative evangelical scholars criticize him because of his positive attitude toward ecumenism and use of critical realism as the auxiliary principle of Christian theology. This is seen to open theological doctrines to development, error and corrections, and the use of pragmatist criteria in evaluation of the meaning and use theological doctrines. McGrath's global influence consists mostly of his educational output, his textbooks covering almost all areas of Christian systematic theology and appearing in numerous languages. However, his greatest scholarly contribution to the dialogue between theology and the natural sciences is likely to have the most lasting influence.

Bibliography

Primary Literature

The Genesis of Doctrine: A Study in the Foundations of Doctrinal Criticism (Oxford and Cambridge, MA: B. Blackwell, 1990).
The Foundations of Dialogue in Science and Religion (Malden, MA: Blackwell Publishers, 1998).
A Scientific Theology, Vol. 1. *Nature* (Grand Rapids: W.B. Eerdmans Pub 2001); vol. 2. *Reality,* 2002; vol. 3. *Theory,* 2003.
The Science of God: An Introduction to Scientific Theology (London: T&T Clark 2004).
The Dawkins Delusion? Atheist Fundamentalism and the Denial of the Divine. Alister McGrath with Joanna Collicutt McGrath (London: SPCK, 2007).

Secondary Literature

Chung, Sung Wook (ed.), *Alister E. McGrath and Evangelical Theology: A Dynamic Engagement* (Carlisle: Paternoster Press; Grand Rapids: Baker Academic, 2003).

Colyer, Elmer, "Alister E. McGrath, a Scientific Theology, Volume 1, *Nature*," *Pro Ecclesia*, 12 (2003), 226–31.

Colyer, Elmer, "Alister E. McGrath, a Scientific Theology, Volume 2, *Reality*," *Pro Ecclesia*, 12 (2003), 492–7.

Colyer, Elmer, "Alister E. McGrath, a Scientific Theology, Volume 3, *Theory*," *Pro Ecclesia*, 13 (2004), 244–40.

Keating, James F., "The Natural Sciences as an *Ancilla Theologiae Nova*: Alister E. McGrath's *A Scientific Theology*," *The Thomist*, 69 (2005), 127–52.

Myers, Benjamin, "Alister McGrath's Scientific Theology," *Reformed Theological Review*, 64 (2005), 15–34.

Shipway, Brad, "The Theological Application of Bhaskar's Stratified Reality: The Scientific Theology of A.E. McGrath," *Journal of Critical Realism*, 3 (2004), 191–203.

PART VI
Theological Movements and Developments

Chapter 47
Postmodern Theology

Jayne Svenungsson

For almost 40 years the seemingly harmless term "postmodern" has sown discord and ruffled feathers in the intellectual world. Mere sight of the term has caused some commentators to see red in more than one sense: "postmodernism" for them embodies the utter degeneracy of the 1960s Left. For their part, more than a few commentators on the left have associated the term with the neoliberal climate of the 1980s, viewing its essence as an appeal to a kind of anything-goes-philosophy: you choose your truth, I choose mine, and neither of us can lay claim to a truth value beyond the endless droning of the market. When the formulation "postmodern theology" first emerged in American theological circles in the mid-eighties, eyebrows were understandably raised. Not least because for most people, inside as well as outside traditional religious boundaries, theology and religion stand for something that postmodernism would seem to repudiate: belief in some form of comprehensive and lasting truth.

What is concealed by the term postmodern theology? To answer this question we need first to clear up a number of points relating to the caricatures of postmodernism just mentioned. Few if any of the commentators usually associated with the term "postmodernism" have made the sterile assertion that everything is relative. What an array of academics in different disciplines have sought to problematize, however, is our blind faith in the transparency of truth; that there exists a clear access to reality above and beyond our historical and cultural context. This deepened understanding of our socially and culturally conditioned existence is reflected in a series of dislocations in our view of what knowledge and language are, of how the human subject should be understood in relation to its environment, and of the significance of historical and scientific developments. A summary and preliminary definition of postmodern theology would be, quite simply, that it concerns the kind of theology which rests on the theoretical and methodological premises brought into being by those dislocations. But before examining the growth of postmodern theology in more detail, let us consider the constituent elements of these modernity-critiquing dislocations.

The Crisis in Western Modernity

One of the most fundamental insights which postmodern thought has enabled is that all cognitive activity must be understood in its original historical context. This insight holds especially true for postmodern philosophy itself. Several of the philosophers conventionally associated with postmodernism emerged during a period that in many regards can be characterized as a time of crisis but also of self-scrutiny. More precisely, to return to that moment is to find oneself in the immediate aftermath of a half-century defined by a succession of fascist and totalitarian movements, two devastating world wars, and the accelerating collapse of colonial rule.

With such a background it can hardly be coincidental that at this very moment critical questions began to be asked of the ideals which had propped up Western modernity: Was there a link between a philosophical tradition centred squarely on the human subject, and the relentless conquest and subordination of other continents and peoples by modern Europeans? To be sure, modern faith in development and progress has in many regards been confirmed by the achievements of technology and medicine. But what are we to make of the fact that this same "progress" has also produced gas chambers and nuclear weapons? Has our erstwhile faith in metaphysical and theological truths simply been translated into an equally indiscriminate faith in Science, Reason, and Utility?

It is as an extension of these grounded critiques that the first dislocations in Western philosophy in the latter half of the twentieth century should be understood. In an attempt to provide a general description of these dislocations, we can take our point of departure in two of postmodernism's most frequent, but also most misinterpreted, slogans. First, Jacques Derrida's declaration *il n'y a pas de hors-texte*—"there is no reality beyond the text".[1] Time and again, this laconic statement has been taken as evidence that postmodern philosophy asserts a position of hopeless subjectivism and relativism. And yet this is a far cry from what Derrida meant. In order to appreciate the real meaning of his words it is vitally important to grasp that "text" here must not be understood in the narrow sense of the term. Rather, it denotes the entire socio-cultural grammar in which we are nurtured as we grow up in a given culture.

Derrida's assertion is directed, quite simply, against the dualism between subject and object that is definitive of much modern thought, in which the human *ego* is presumed to exist apart from its surrounding reality, indeed, apart even from its own physical body. In contrast to this view, Derrida and many other philosophers have contended that our self-consciousness is always mediated by the concrete reality in which we live, through our corporeality, through memories (collective as well as individual), through narratives, through other people's lives, and many other factors. To claim that there can be no reality beyond the text or language is thus a way to point out that our whole capacity for thought is intimately tied to our linguistically structured experience.

The other slogan which is often mentioned in descriptions of postmodern thought is "the death of metanarratives". The phrase originated in Jean-François Lyotard's reference to "incredulity towards metanarratives" in his celebrated work *La condition postmoderne* (1979).[2] Lyotard's argument in this book is that modern philosophy is

---

[1] Jacques Derrida, *Of Grammatology*, trans. Gayatri Spivak (Baltimore, 1976), p. 158.
[2] Jean-François Lyotard, *The Postmodern Condition: A Report on Knowledge*, trans. Geoffrey Bennington and Brian Massumi (Manchester, 1989), p. XXIV.

defined by the fact of having derived its legitimacy from a series of comprehensive ideologies or "metanarratives," such as the Enlightenment view of knowledge as the key to human liberation from the prejudices of earlier generations. What makes such metanarratives problematic is their tendency to remain blind to their own existence. In their eagerness to differentiate new, scientific knowledge from premodern forms of knowledge—fables, myths, or legends—they fail utterly to see that they are relying on narrative or even mythical forms of knowledge grounded in specific suppositions and prejudices.

According to Lyotard, what distinguishes the postmodern condition is that increasingly these metanarratives are beginning to fracture. At this point it should be noted that Lyotard's view of the disintegration of metanarratives was not a matter of normative proclamation. Rather, it was an attempt to capture in words the process of decolonization: as new views on knowledge and truth gain ground, people gain a new perspective on the dominant attitudes in their own cultural sphere. By way of summarizing postmodernism against the background of Derrida's and Lyotard's slogans, we might therefore describe it as a heightened critical and hermeneutic awareness.

The Growth of Postmodern Theology

It should be clear from this sketch that postmodern thought is not a clearly delineated philosophical school. Even if several of the names usually cited in accounts of postmodernism belong to the French phenomenological tradition, corresponding dislocations in the view of knowledge, language, history, and human subject can be discerned in Anglo-American philosophy as well as in the German hermeneutic tradition. Turning to postmodern theology, we similarly discover that the rubric in no way describes a homogeneous theological movement. On the contrary, it can be seen as an umbrella term for a diverse array of theological currents whose common denominator is that they have their starting point to a greater or lesser degree in these philosophical developments, which they strive to integrate into theological argument.

Although it was not until the 1980s that the term "postmodern theology" became current, it was possible to discern a number of developments in North American theology during the preceding decade which indicated that these dislocations were about to force their way into theology. Of particular relevance in this regard is Yale theologian Hans Frei's attack on modern biblical hermeneutics, which Frei sees, like modern philosophy as a whole, as characterized by a dualism between subject and object—between our reality and that of the text. To bridge this gap, conservative and liberal theologians alike have sought to give meaning to the text by reinserting it into a reality outside the text itself; one in the form of actual historical relations (biblicism), the other in the form of abstract moral truths (liberal theology). Paradoxically, in doing so they have created further dualisms. By contrast, Frei proposes a holistic approach and rejects, first, any idea that the meaning of a biblical text might be found by means of references external to the text. On the contrary, the meaning is *in* the text itself—in the narrative it relates and in the characters it portrays. Second, Frei rejects the distinction between the world of the text and the world of the reader; for Christians, the Bible's narratives are quite simply the reality through which they shape their own lives.[3]

Another line of development during the 1970s, which in a number of aspects anticipated postmodern theology, was the so-called God-is-dead theology, a loosely affiliated grouping of theologians (including Gabriel Vahanian and Thomas J.J. Altizer) motivated by a desire to formulate a radical, anti-metaphysical, and intra-worldly theological system. They drew inspiration from Hegel as well as Nietzsche, who in different ways—and with quite different significances—had announced the death of a transcendent God. Among contemporary philosophers they found support in Derrida, whose semiotic reflections seemed to confirm their theological challenge to the notion of a transcendent reality. Although their visions had little in common with Frei's, these theologians were united, broadly speaking, by their shared challenge to modern philosophy's ascription of linguistic meaning to a reality beyond the text. It is also in this sense that God-is-dead theology anticipates significant elements of postmodern theological argument. Even so, it should be noted that in another sense it remained decidedly modern: while several of these theologians aimed to reject the traditional dichotomy between transcendence and immanence, their goal could only be attained by dissolving the first term. Moreover, such a manoeuvre entailed indirect acceptance of the validity of the dichotomy, remaining bound, as it were, to the dualism of modern thought.

A third important precursor of postmodern theology was feminist theology, which achieved a major breakthrough during the 1970s. Like the God-is-dead theologians, several pioneering feminist theologians—Mary Daly being perhaps the best-known—were motivated by a desire to deconstruct the transcendent Father. Yet their primary critique was addressed not to the very concept of transcendence but to the fact that God in the Judeo-Christian tradition had so unequivocally been associated with masculine attributes and thereby sanctioned men's subordination of women in both the church and the culture at large. Feminist theology constitutes an important link in the emergence of postmodern theology precisely because it reveals the extent to which theology has unreflectively taken man as its norm. To be sure, early feminist theology did not explicitly take aim at *modern* theology; on the contrary, most of these theologians saw themselves as working within an extension of the liberal tradition that is ultimately traceable to Friedrich Schleiermacher. Nevertheless, the feminist critique touched a central nerve in modern liberal theology: the notion of universal religious experience. By showing how experience supposed to be common to all humanity was in fact *men's* experience, feminist theology rocked modern theological methodology to its foundations.

---

[3] See also Hans Frei, *The Eclipse of Biblical Narrative: A Study in Eighteenth- and Nineteenth-Century Hermeneutics* (New Haven, 1974).

While each of these of developmental strands in 1970s theology provided elements that would be important for the emergence of postmodern theology, it was, as already noted, not until the 1980s—1984, to be precise—that the first references to postmodern theology appeared. That year saw the publication in the United States of two theological works that were to attract a great deal of attention. The first of these was Mark C. Taylor's *Erring: A Postmodern A/theology*. Taylor had a background in the God-is-dead theology movement of the 1970s, but in this book he turned his attention to the remaining modern (as opposed to *postmodern*) elements of God-is-dead theology, that is to say, the dialectical interpretation of transcendence and immanence as outlined above. Despite the radical ambitions of God-is-dead theology, this interpretation seemed to him merely another expression of the Western tradition's inability to live with what is other and ambiguous. As an alternative, Taylor instead argued for postmodern *a/theology*, a term by which he sought to define a position neither "*purely* theological or non-theological, theist or atheist, religious or secular, believing or non-believing."[4]

Taylor concluded his a/theological manifesto by celebrating an endlessly *erring* reinterpretation of Christian symbols that refused to be confined by traditional ecclesiastical or theological authorities. Although there was an obviously postmodern aspect to Taylor's ambition of rupturing the polarizations created by modern theological debate, it was also clear that Taylor retained a firm foothold in the liberal theological tradition. By the mid-1980s, thanks not least to the major influence of Paul Tillich, the latter had become the dominant tradition in North American academic theology. Turning now to the second widely-noted work published in 1984, George Lindbeck's *The Nature of Doctrine: Religion and Theology in a Postliberal Age*,[5] we note directly how its subtitle announces the author's intention to change the theological agenda of this tradition.

Like Frei, Lindbeck was at Yale, one of the few leading theological institutions to take its bearings from Karl Barth rather than Paul Tillich. In the same way as Barth had criticized modern liberal theology and modern biblicism during the first half of the twentieth century, Lindberg sought to expose how the modern view of dogma had led theology into two impossible culs-de-sac. More liberal commentators had attempted to preserve the academic status of theology by understanding dogma as the symbolic expression of a more fundamental, religious experience. As a countermove, conservatives had presented dogma as informative propositions about objective relations of fact. Drawing a parallel with Frei's text-integrated understanding of the meaning of biblical texts, Lindbeck instead argued for what he dubbed a *cultural-linguistic* understanding of religious dogma. In order to grasp the real significance of a dogma, in other words, it was necessary above all to attend to how it was actually used within the relevant context—in the case of Christian dogma, preferably the Christian community. Underneath such reasoning can be heard not only Barth's community-

---

[4] Mark C. Taylor, *Erring: A Postmodern A/theology* (Chicago, 1984), p. 12.

[5] George A. Lindbeck, *The Nature of Doctrine: Religion and Theology in a Postliberal Age* (Philadelphia, 1984).

oriented theology but also Ludwig Wittgenstein's theory of language games. Like late Wittgenstein, Lindbeck rejects the possibility of prelinguistic human experience, thereby distancing himself from a founding premise of modern liberal theology.

Notwithstanding their several important similarities, a quick comparison leaves no doubt that Taylor's and Lindbeck's pioneering works of postmodern theory were actuated by quite different theological motives. While Taylor's intention can be described most easily as a desire to radicalize the legacy of modern liberal theology, Lindback's intention was to bring about a radical break with this legacy. In stark contrast to Taylor, Lindbeck in several respects grapples with more traditional theological concepts, not least by returning theology to Christian practices and thereby giving the church a more or less normative role in theological work.

Ongoing Developments in Postmodern Theology

On several counts Taylor's and Lindberg's works are symptomatic of the ongoing development of postmodern theology. Though the terms "liberal" and "conservative" remain awkward in theological contexts, it is reasonable to suggest that more liberal vis-à-vis more conservative veins exist within postmodern theology, too. The former— encompassing Taylor and the "deconstructive" theology which emerged in the wake of God-is-dead theology—in a broad sense discharges the legacy of Schleiermacher and Tillich, while the latter—encompassing Frei and Lindbeck—has its roots in the theological resurgence effected by Barth in the early twentieth century.

Even if this sketch is accurate, it remains insufficient, primarily because it presents Taylor and God-is-dead theology as the sole or principal representatives of the liberal tradition during the latter half of the twentieth century. In actual fact, far greater influence was exerted by those theologians—David Tracy, Gordon Kaufmann, and Sallie McFague, to name just a few—who came together in the mid-1980s under the banner of "revisionists." Just as Jürgen Habermas had cautioned against premature rejection of the modern philosophical tradition, so, too, did these theologians acknowledge the importance of defending the gains made by modern theology. This gesture contained an implied criticism of Taylor's erring postmodernism but also— and perhaps primarily—of Lindbeck's stated ambition of abandoning the liberal tradition.

At the same time, growing numbers of theologians were rallying to Frei and Lindbeck during the course of the 1980s, which soon resulted in the emergence of a loosely affiliated school of "postliberalism." Uniting these theologians was a number of fundamental theoretical premises that in several respects broke with the liberal theological paradigm. First, they—like Lindbeck—rejected the idea of a prelinguistic universal religious experience that could form a basis for theology. Instead, they argued that theology must be practised *ad hoc*, that is to say, without any pre-established methodological basis. To the extent that any given starting point existed for theology, it was rather to be found in the particular context provided by Christian practices. Such arguments revealed another characteristic feature of postliberal theology:

the prioritizing of the particular above the universal. This aspect was reflected not least in the attitude of many postliberal theologians towards other religious traditions, rejecting the goal of modern theology of religions—to stipulate a core shared by all religions—and instead seeking dialogue among the different characteristics of religions. One final aspect which warrants mention as a defining feature of postliberal theology is its strong emphasis upon narrative, with biblical narrative being held up as constitutive of Christian theology and practice alike.

However, as has been indicated, postliberal theologians did not go unopposed. One of the most influential debates in North American theology in the 1980s was an exchange between revisionism and postliberalism—or between "Chicago" (where David Tracy was working) and "Yale." This debate has often been portrayed as a tug of war between a surviving modern agenda and the new postmodern perspectives erupting into theology in the 1980s. Although there may be something to this view, it is noticeable in retrospect that the debate was actually about fundamental differences of position on a series of key theological questions, such as the relation between theology and church, the character and status of the biblical texts, and the issue of what theology's primary audience should be. While the metonyms Chicago and Yale still have a significance in theological discourse, it should also be noted that by the late 1980s the tension was on the wane. A main reason for this was that from an early stage Tracy—arguably the most important representative of revisionism—began moving in a more postmodern direction as a consequence of an ongoing dialogue with several of the postliberal theologians as well as with Jean-Luc Marion, one of the most important representatives of the "theological turn" in French phenomenology during the last decades of the twentieth century.

For those wishing to trace the development of postmodern theology in the 1990s and up to the present day, it is thus a highly differentiated picture that emerges, in which the more or less well-defined factions of the 1980s (deconstructionists, revisionists, postliberals) have taken on different significations. To this can be added an array of important developments in European philosophy and theology which left visible traces on the conversation taking place within international theology. One could here adduce the aforementioned theological turn in French phenomenology (possibly also in the continental tradition more broadly) and likewise the influential and keenly debated Anglo-Catholic current *Radical Orthodoxy*, which carries on essential aspects of postliberal theology even as it finds inspiration to a far greater extent in postmodern European philosophy.

Even so, in order to illuminate something of the complexity that is a hallmark of postmodern theology, two lines of development may be highlighted. First, the ongoing development of the deconstructive tradition whose early obvious representative was Mark C. Taylor. The term "deconstructive" originates in Derrida's philosophy and indicates the important role played by deconstruction both for God-is-dead theology and for Taylor's own attempts to undermine the same. Yet what none of these radical theologians foresaw was the explicitly "theological" turn that Derrida's philosophy would take at the end of the 1980s. Even as Derrida's interest in theological questions grew, it became increasingly clear that his own understanding of deconstruction had relatively little to do with either the immanentism of God-is-dead theology or Taylor's aimlessly erring a/theology. On the contrary, in his later works Derrida was to portray deconstruction in increasingly ethical-political and even messianic terms — as the hope of future justice, as a cry for the possibility of the impossible.

As a result of this development, Taylor soon found himself competing with a succession of theologians and philosophers who found in Derrida's works the potential for a new and more constructive theological reorientation. Australian philosopher of religion Kevin Hart and English theologian Graham Ward are among the more notable of the names that deserve mention in this context. The most important, however, was undoubtedly American philosopher of religion John D. Caputo, who wrote a number of theological studies of Derrida as well as arranging a series of high-profile conferences on the theme of *Religion and Postmodernism* at which Derrida was a frequent guest during his final years. Yet there is anything but unity among these deconstructively-oriented theologians and philosophers of religion On the contrary, their interest in deconstruction cuts directly across theological traditions as well as denominations. For example, Caputo, who is Catholic, explicitly positions himself within the liberal tradition — which does not prevent him from at the same time adopting a highly critical position towards Taylor's a/theological reading of deconstruction. No less wide is the distance to Ward, who is in fact a prominent figure in the aforementioned neo-Barthian current *Radical Orthodoxy*. Naturally, there are also considerable differences among their respective attitudes towards deconstruction; while Caputo sees it as fully compatible with Christian theological thought, Ward acknowledges its methodological appeal but adopts a critical stance towards the extreme consequences which Derrida's philosophy entails for a theological understanding of reality.

The second development which needs to be noted in order to illuminate the complexity of postmodern theological discussion is the continued development of feminist theology. As previously outlined, the questioning of universal religious experience by early feminist theology anticipated in important aspects the postmodern critique of modern theological methodology. Despite this questioning, several of the first generation of feminist theologians did not hesitate to establish "women's experience" (for example, the experience of being oppressed on the basis of one's gender) as the new norm according to which theology should be shaped. That this notion was not unproblematic became apparent, however, when feminist theology differentiated during the course of the 1980s. With black ("Womanist"), Latina ("Mujerista"), and lesbian theologians joining the theological discussion, it became clear that "universal" female experience in fact reflected white heterosexual middle-class women's experiences rather than experience shared by all women.

Alongside this differentiation, particularly during the 1990s, feminist theology underwent a theoretical reorientation in a more postmodern direction. Inspired by poststructuralist theorists such as Julia Kristeva and Luce Irigaray as well as queer theorists such as Judith Butler, a series of theologians have launched a radicalized critique of that problematic universalism which anchors itself to the concept of experience in early feminist theology as well as of its notion of a stable female subject. In its place, they have underscored that the subject should rather be understood as a set of relations in which identity is created by means of a series of limitations and exclusions and in which gender identity is not necessarily more fundamental than that of ethnicity, class, or sexuality. Although it is possible to locate a postmodern change of perspective within feminist theology since the 1980s, this should not be taken to mean that there is any prevailing unity in approach or values. Just as with postmodern theology at large, theologians working in a more barthian or postliberal vein (for example, Serene Jones and Mary McClintock Fulkerson) may be found alongside theologians who position themselves more explicitly in the liberal tradition (for example, Rebecca S. Chopp and Catherine Keller).

Theology beyond Cartesian Dualism

Given this background of proliferating diversity, is it still possible to identify any common features that make it meaningful to refer to an entity called postmodern theology? To extend Richard J. Bernstein's celebrated diagnosis of modernity's dilemma as "Cartesian anxiety"—produced by the dualisms to which modern thought has been shackled—I would like to answer the question in the affirmative and refer to postmodern theology's goal of overcoming these dualisms.[6] This ambition finds expression not least in the changed methodological approach that, theological differences of opinion notwithstanding, unities the various theorists discussed in this essay. Thus it is possible to discern a thoroughgoing scepticism towards all forms of linguistic dualism—in the form of reference either to a prelinguistic religious experience (a methodological cornerstone of the modern liberal tradition) or to an objectively accessible revelation (as has been presupposed by the biblicist traditions). Instead, theorists now assert the *hermeneutic* character of theology, even if opinions remain highly divided over the role that should accordingly be assigned to Scripture, tradition, and living Christian practices in theological work.

Closely tied to this break with subject-object dualism is a repudiation of another of modernity's dualisms, that of body and soul, or theory and practice. It is closely reflected in the growing interest in actual human bodies (and sexuality), which feminist theory in particular has helped to put onto the theological agenda. Alongside this interest in the physical body, however, can be observed a growing interest in the corporal or material aspects of theology in a more general sense. Postmodern theology, in other words, in contrast to the lack of context that has defined much modern thinking about religious ideas, emphasizes the fact that religious faith is in the first instance something lived and embodied by concrete individuals in particular contexts. This interest in concrete religious practices is perhaps most visible in neo-barthian currents such as postliberalism and *Radical Orthodoxy*, where theological reflection is partly regarded as commentary on already existing Christian practices. But even among more liberal thinkers such as Tracy and Caputo—who are critical

---

[6] See Richard J. Bernstein, *Beyond Objectivism and Relativism: Science, Hermeneutics and Praxis* (Philadelphia, 1983).

of the tendency to allow a particular Christian practice to become normative of theology—there is a clear emphasis upon the significance for our theological heritage of living traditions.

In conclusion, however, it should be stressed that the goal of overcoming the dualisms of modern thought must not be confused with a desire to abolish *differences* (for example, between God and humankind, transcendence and immanence, matter and spirit). The former directs its critique at the tendency to present these differences in negative, dialectical, or precisely dualistic terms. Among the most illuminating of these is the modern contrast between spirit and matter in which spiritual reality is associated with the divine and raised above the material, with the result that nature is increasingly regarded as dead matter available for human exploitation. Admittedly, dualistic understandings of spirit and matter can be found in thinkers of earlier periods, but rarely in such categorical terms as in Western modernity. It is therefore significant that many postmodern theologians, in an attempt to overcome the dualism of spirit and matter as well as other dualisms, seek inspiration in premodern thought. Accordingly, a growing interest can be observed in the biblical, earth-oriented understanding of the divine as well as in the Patristic and medieval sacramental view of life. And it is perhaps here that the true value of the turn to postmodern theology lies: in the recovery, prompted by curiosity, of approaches and insights that modern theology in its eagerness to be *modern* has sometimes too hastily consigned to the oblivion of history.

Bibliography

Bornemark, Jonna and Hans Ruin (eds), *Phenomenology and Religion: New Frontiers*, Södertörn Philosophical Studies 8 (Huddinge: Södertörn University, 2010).

Burnham, Frederic B. (ed.), *Postmodern Theology: Christian Faith in a Pluralistic World* (Eugene: Wipf & Stock Publishers, 2006).

Caputo, John D. and Michael J. Scanlon (eds), *God, the Gift and Postmodernism* (Bloomington: Indiana University Press, 1999).

Chopp, Rebecca S. and Sheila Greeve Davaney (eds), *Horizons in Feminist Theology. Identity, Tradition, and Norms* (Minneapolis: Fortress Press, 1997).

Courtine, Jean-François, Jean-Louis Chrétien, Michel Henry, Dominique Janicaud, Jean-Luc Marion, Paul Ricœur, *Phenomenology and the "Theological Turn": The French Debate* (New York: Fordham University Press, 2000).

Depoortere, Frederiek, *Christ in Postmodern Philosophy: Gianni Vattimo, René Girard and Slavoj Zizek* (London and New York, T&T Clark, 2008).

Henriksen, Jan-Olav, *Desire, Gift, and Recognition: Christology and Postmodern Philosophy* (Grand Rapids: Eerdmans, 2009).

Murphy, Nancey, *Beyond Liberalism and Fundamentalism: How Modern and Postmodern Philosophy Set the Theological Agenda* (Valley Forge: Trinity Press International, 1996).

Penner, Myron B. (ed.), *Christianity and the Postmodern Turn: Six Views* (Grand Rapids: Brazos Press, 2005).

Robbins, Jeffrey W. (ed.), *After the Death of God* (New York: Columbia University Press, 2007).
Vanhoozer, Kevin J. (ed.), *The Cambridge Companion to Postmodern Theology* (Cambridge: Cambridge University Press, 2003).
Ward, Graham (ed.), *The Postmodern God: A Theological Reader* (Cambridge, Mass./Oxford: Blackwell, 1997).
Ward, Graham (ed.), *The Blackwell Companion to Postmodern Theology* (Cambridge, Mass./Oxford: Blackwell, 2001).
Westphal, Merold (ed.), *Postmodern Philosophy and Christian Thought* (Bloomington and Indianapolis: Indiana University Press, 1999).

Chapter 48
Radical Orthodoxy

Ola Sigurdson

One of the most lively, most discussed, and most criticized schools formed in contemporary Western theology in the decades around the turn of the millennium is the originally English movement of "Radical Orthodoxy." From its modest beginnings at Cambridge University – officially dated to May 1, 1997 – it has succeeded in the course of a few years in exercising a sensational influence on theological debate. The following are usually said to be the founders of the movement: Graham Ward, formerly Dean of Peterhouse, the oldest college in Cambridge; Catherine Pickstock, at that time Research Fellow at Emmanuel College; and John Milbank, who formerly taught at the Faculty of Divinity in the University of Cambridge. Of these three, it is only Pickstock who has remained faithful to Cambridge up to now. Ward later became professor of contextual theology at Manchester University and has, at the time of writing, just been appointed as Regius Professor of Divinity in Oxford. Milbank, after a period at the University of Virginia, became professor of religion, politics, and ethics at the University of Nottingham, where he also started "The Centre of Theology and Philosophy." The book series "Radical Orthodoxy" (Routledge) also played an important role, but it has now been replaced by a new series with the same editors, "Illuminations: Theory and Religion" (Blackwell). Two other series of publications linked to the Centre founded by Milbank have also been launched: "Interventions" (Eerdmans) and "Veritas" (SCM Press). The importance of these series, especially the first, has consisted not only in spreading the ideas of the movement, but above all in giving a relatively clear form to the movement as such. Radical Orthodoxy is not a movement that one can apply to join. Rather, it expresses one particular theological standpoint that finds expression in a variety of projects and contexts.

Peterhouse in Cambridge played an important role in the emergence of radical orthodoxy. This college has a lively group with the concise name of "Theory Group" that organizes discussion evenings on theoretical topics. It is all very sophisticated, with leather armchairs, a fire blazing in the open hearth, and a glass of wine during the discussion that follows the guest lecturer's address. It was in circumstances such as these that what was later to become radical orthodoxy took shape. Peterhouse's neighbor in Trumpington Street is the Anglican church of Little St. Mary's, with a clearly Anglo-Catholic profile. This little church too influenced, or at least exemplified, the ecclesiology in the radical orthodox movement. This means that radical orthodoxy, in terms of its origin, is a very English undertaking that displays a number of similarities to other English theological movements. However, the Anglo-Catholic origin does not mean that this movement is limited to Anglicans.

Rather, it involves a catholicity that can be embraced by several denominations, and it is scarcely surprising that the original group included several of England's most interesting Roman Catholic theologians. Several of the movement's original teachers also have links to Cambridge, including Rowan Williams, the former Anglican archbishop of Canterbury, and Nicholas Lash, the first Roman Catholic professor of theology at Cambridge since the Reformation, who retired in 1999.

Orthodoxy and the Critique of Modernity

What then does the radical orthodox movement stand for? The easiest way to find an answer to this question is to consult the manifesto written by the three original members of radical orthodoxy. This was published in 1999 in the first volume in the series: *Radical Orthodoxy: A New Theology*. Let us begin with the "orthodox" in radical orthodoxy. This entails first and foremost a fundamental affirmation of the kind of Trinitarian and christological Christianity that is formulated in the classic creeds. The various members of the radical orthodox movement agree in seeing patristic and mediaeval theology as a resource for contemporary theological work. They believe that one can find resources here for a richer theology that is more open in both confessional and societal terms than the theology in the late middle ages and the modern period, which is marked by conflicts with the nation-state and strife between the denominations. They are, of course, aware that we live under different circumstances today, and this means that the mere repetition of this theology does not *per se* solve our problems. Nor do they claim – although the movement is sometimes accused of doing so – that the Christian church was in any simple sense better in the past. Rather, they argue that since historical theology was not marked by the antithetical pairs that are the scourge of modern thinking and of modern society, it offers possibilities of overcoming these antitheses in our thinking.

John Milbank's *Theology and Social Theory: Beyond Secular Reason* (1990) must be regarded as the most important text in radical orthodoxy. He shows, by means of a genealogical investigation of modern sociology and philosophy, how these presuppose what they exclude, that is to say, a theological perspective, and how the theological thinking that generated them was from the very outset unable to live up to its own best ambitions. The postmodern critique has already uncovered how the binary oppositions on which modernity is based – faith and knowledge, private and public, female and male, emotion and reason – are secretly dependent on each other. At the same time, however, the postmodern critique has not succeeded in showing any way of escaping from this destructive dilemma. Milbank sees the solution in an ecclesiology, that is to say, a Christian sociology, inspired by Augustine's *City of God*, but also by his *De musica*. He writes:

> Christianity is peculiar, because while it is open to difference – to a series of infinitely new additions, insights, progressions toward God, it also strives to make of all these differential additions a harmony, "in the body of Christ," and claims that if the

reality of God is properly attended to, there can be such a harmony. And the idea of a consistently beautiful, continuously differential, and open series, is of course the idea of "music."[1]

Milbank identifies here social and intellectual resources for an ontology that builds on an original harmony, not – as in modern or postmodern thinking – on an original conflict. In the Christian narrative, it is love (the harmonious relationships), not war (the disharmonious relationships) that is the origin of all things. In order to avoid the dichotomies of modernity, therefore, Milbank wishes to go back to the period before the modern age, to Augustine, to Dionysius the Areopagite, and even to Thomas Aquinas, about whom Milbank has co-authored a book with Pickstock. One of the antitheses that radical orthodoxy wants to deconstruct is the modern dichotomy between life and teaching: the Christian view of God is not primarily a question of ideas, but is articulated also in the practices in which the Christian takes part. Fellowship with God takes place in and through a social fellowship among human beings.

The deconstruction of the dichotomy between life and doctrine is closely connected to a theme that radical orthodoxy shares with much of postmodern philosophy, namely, the critique of the modern subjectivity. Instead of envisaging the human person's subjectivity as if it were an independent core inside the human person that enters into relationships with other persons only at a secondary stage – Descartes' *cogito* is the classic example here – the modern subjectivity is the nodal point in a network of relationships. This means that subjectivity cannot be thought of independently of, or antecedently to, these relationships. It is above all Catherine Pickstock who has asserted that the Christian subjectivity is formed by a liturgy that abolishes the modern dichotomy between private and public, passive and active. All of everyday life ought to be incorporated into this liturgy, and should thereby be understood as liturgy. Thus, what she is advocating is not a liturgy *alongside* everyday life, but rather a liturgical understanding of life *as a whole*. The emphasis on the liturgy also contrasts with a static understanding of the relationship between God and the human person. The relationship cannot be established or controlled by means of a theoretical formula. This means that the human person's identity can be open, without thereby being dissolved: "there is no other way to be than to be on the way."[2] Pickstock draws on a new reading of Plato's *Phaedrus* when she expounds such a "doxological" understanding of the human person's subjectivity, which entails an understanding of existence as a *gift* to be received rather than as something *given* that can be quantified and manipulated, something that loses the relationship to its transcendental source.

---

[1] John Milbank, "Postmodern Critical Augustinianism: A Short Summa in Forty-two Responses to Unasked Questions," in Graham Ward (ed.), *The Postmodern God: A Theological Reader* (Cambridge, Mass., 1997), p. 268.

[2] Catherine Pickstock, *After Writing: On the Liturgical Consummation of Philosophy* (Oxford, 1998), p. 185.

This means that many of the books that are published in the series and elsewhere by theologians and philosophers who are associated with the radical orthodox movement offer new readings of patristic or mediaeval theologians in the light of contemporary challenges. The radical orthodox thinkers are all at home in a Christianity that goes back to the Christianity that was influenced by Platonism, and above all to Augustine. Swedish Lutheran theology in the twentieth century, with Anders Nygren leading the charge, accused patristic and mediaeval theology of being influenced by Platonic thinking. Radical orthodoxy accepts in principle that Nygren is correct on this point, but it claims that this is a strength – not a weakness. Here there is a clear affinity to the *nouvelle théologie*, the French movement in the early part of the twentieth century. The clearest difference between radical orthodoxy and the *nouvelle théologie* is that the former has a more explicit interest in philosophy. The radical orthodox movement has made use of contemporary postmodern philosophy to uncover more clearly the philosophical presuppositions in large areas of modern philosophy which also (as radical orthodoxy maintains) influenced the *nouvelle théologie*. Radical orthodoxy therefore has a clearer critique of modernity. This critique is not limited to the philosophical legacy, but also extends to the ecclesiological, social, and political spheres. At the same time, it is obvious that these thinkers are building further on insights drawn from writers such as Henri de Lubac, Hans Urs von Balthasar, and Maurice Blondel.

Another parallel might be the theology of the Swiss Reformed theologian Karl Barth in his *Kirchliche Dogmatik* (*Church Dogmatics*), but although the radical orthodox thinkers also refer to Barth, they are skeptical of the distinction he draws between theology and philosophy. Barth's emphasis on revelation threatens to establish a *modus vivendi* between theology and philosophy that only strengthens the modern distinction between faith and knowledge. This is merely an arbitrary truce; what radical orthodoxy wants to do is to investigate critically the presuppositions of philosophy. The postmodern critique of Western philosophy showed that it does not in the least take an "objective" and "neutral" attitude; on the contrary, it implies a specific way of looking at the world. This means that various philosophies can potentially come into conflict with the Christian way of looking at the world, and this makes it important to trace their genealogy. This link to the postmodern critique does not, however, mean that the radical orthodox thinkers themselves embrace postmodern philosophy. This should rather be seen as a strategic alliance. According to Milbank and Pickstock, Jacques Derrida's philosophy is basically nihilistic. Postmodern philosophy is thus a negative contrast that makes clear the need of a genuinely Christian philosophy. Ward has a more nuanced evaluation of Derrida, for example in the book *Barth, Derrida and the Language of Theology* (1995), where he reads Barth as a linguistic philosopher with the help of Derrida, and thereby attempts to show both the necessity and the impossibility of speaking theologically about a God about whom nothing can be said. Ward believes that without the theological dimension, Derrida risks sinking down into nihilism – but without Derrida's philosophical supplement, Barth's theology risks repeating modernity's gulf between faith and knowledge. This means, according to Ward's reasoning, that we cannot really choose between Derrida and Barth.

Here, we discern a distinction in the radical orthodox movement between what we could call an impatient and a more patient attitude to other philosophical or theological movements than their own. I shall return to these points below.

Radicality and Postsecularity

Let us now turn to the "radical" in radical orthodoxy. This comprises various elements. First, it aims at a return to the patristic and mediaeval roots – for the word "radical" is derived from the Latin *radix*, "root." Secondly, it aims at an ethical, political, and aesthetic vision that is critical of modern society. The radical orthodox movement, at least in England, has roots in an earlier Anglican movement known as "Christian socialism" that attempted to emphasize a Christian socialist tradition which differed both from academic Marxist socialism and from reformist (and secular) social-democratic socialism. This means that a great deal of societal criticism is embedded in the radical orthodox critique of modernity, both implicitly and explicitly. Thirdly, "radical" also points to a need to think about the tradition. Although they took up the patristic and mediaeval tradition, they realized that it never succeeded in making use of its own best insights. In relation to their own tradition, therefore, they grasp the value of being self-critical. One example of this is their conviction that patristic and mediaeval theology never makes sufficiently clear that the bodiliness of the human person is the way in which he or she communicates with God too; subsequently, in modernity, the body simply fell outside theology's field of vision. Several of the representatives of radical orthodoxy also hold that it is perfectly reasonable to envisage same-sex marriage as a genuine expression of the Christian tradition. In their manifesto, Milbank, Ward, and Pickstock write that the radical orthodox movement endeavors to articulate "a more incarnate, more participatory, more aesthetic, more erotic, more socialized, even 'more Platonic' Christianity."[3] In one sense, this is a Christianity of which only glimpses have been seen up to now. Here, radical orthodoxy offers a vision not only of a different theology, but also of a different church, and consequently of a different society.

It is interesting to compare briefly radical orthodoxy with what is usually called "postsecular" philosophy, that is, the trend among contemporary philosophers of turning their backs on secularism as a natural starting point and instead – without themselves necessarily professing adherence to any religious fellowship – recognizing the significance of religion for humankind, and of theology for Western thinking. A postsecular philosophy of this kind can be found in the new self-confidence with which some philosophers, who themselves have a religious conviction, have returned to theology in the contemporary philosophical discussion (for example, Emmanuel Lévinas, Paul Ricoeur, Gianni Vattimo, and Jean-Luc Marion), but also among philosophers who themselves profess to be agnostics or atheists, but who recognize

---

[3] John Milbank, Graham Ward, and Catherine Pickstock, *Radical Orthodoxy: A New Theology* (London/New York, 1999), p. 3.

that theological thinking contains intellectual resources that are philosophically indispensable (for example, Giorgio Agamben, Alain Badiou, Jacques Derrida, Luce Irigaray, and Slavoj Žižek). Although this constitutes a theoretical discourse in which much of the argumentation of radical orthodoxy is at home, the movement in general is skeptical of the attempts in some postsecular philosophy to mediate between theology and philosophy. A correlation of this kind always risks presupposing a modern distinction between theology and philosophy, and thereby conducting the discussion within the framework of precisely those "rules of the game" that radical orthodoxy wants to call into question. Since radical orthodoxy's vision is genuinely theological, it is more reminiscent (paradoxically enough) of the resolutely Marxist and atheist attempts by Alain Badiou or Slavoj Žižek to make use of Christianity for their own intentions, although of course radical orthodoxy works the other way round. According to Milbank, only theology is able to deal with the dichotomies that are generated by the modern tradition, since it is born of an ontology that is characterized by harmony rather than conflict, by love rather than war. At the same time, one can claim that radical orthodoxy is at home in this movement, since it largely shares with postsecular philosophy the same methodology (genealogy, discourse analysis) and important themes (gift, the body, the social situatedness of knowledge) and critical lines of battle (the unambiguous, instrumental, and bodiless reason of modernity). Like contemporary postsecular and postanalytical philosophy, Ward and Gerard Loughlin (at Durham University) and others are interested in analyzing popular culture as one of the most important expressions of contemporary thinking and values.

Theology and Nihilism

For a further exemplification of radical orthodox thinking, I turn to Ward, who has attempted in several books to make a diagnosis of the contemporary Western culture that he wishes to call "postmodern." Ward uses this difficult concept to speak of a social change that has meant *inter alia* the implosion of modern secularism. In his seventh thesis about Feuerbach (1845), Karl Marx claimed that "religious sensibility [*das religiöse Gemüt*] is itself a societal product";[4] Ward would claim that the credibility of secularism in our days is just as precarious as the credibility of religion was in Marx's days. The forces that built up the secular world-system of modernity have collapsed from within, and this means that the dichotomies that built up the modern system – public/private, reason/emotions, nature/culture, object/subject – have collapsed, since the principles of their mediation have turned out to be constructions that emerged in the course of history, rather than something given by nature. The death of God which Nietzsche announced has meant that all references to some external ground –

---

[4] The following presentation of Ward's arguments is based on his book *True Religion* (Oxford, 2003) and on the article "Introduction: 'Where We Stand'," in Graham Ward (ed.), *The Blackwell Companion to Postmodern Theology* (Oxford, 2001), pp. xii–xxvii.

God, nature, the reason – have been obliged to recognize their arbitrariness. This also means the disappearance of the principles that allow one to keep separate the natural and the cultural. All the hierarchies of values on which one relies in order to be able to say whether something is good or bad collapse, once there is no longer any authority outside the system that supports their weight. It is not simply that everything could have been otherwise; everything that exists is already otherwise, depending on the perspective that one adopts. This implosion produces what Ward, with the Jesuit Michel de Certeau, the French theoretician of culture, psychoanalyst, and scholar of mysticism, calls a "hollow" – a vacuum without values. This vacuum leads to a nihilism that is both longed-for and suppressed.

Ward describes the nihilism with the help of Karl Marx and of Jacques Lacan's analysis of commodity fetishism (here, Žižek's influence is noticeable). The fetishistic longing does not seek to be satisfied, for that would quench the longing. Instead, it seeks a goal that entices but never supplies what is longed for. This makes the commodities the cause of our longing, rather than the object of our longing. The longing wanders about, unceasingly enticed by new commodities. In God's absence, God's presence too becomes a commercial product that is marketed by means of angels and miracles. The commercial culture is a flirt with nihilism as a half-serious, half-playful yearning for obliteration, for the total absence that is the definitive non-fulfillment of longing. This is why Ward describes our contemporary culture as a culture of death. But a culture is never monolithic. The implosion of secularism means that the dualism between the secular and the religious also disappears, making it possible to think anew of God and religion, as an alternative to commercialism's flirt with nihilism.

Here, it may seem that Ward is painting contemporary culture in somber colors in order that his theological response may appear all the brighter. Theology would then fill this hollow in a demystified world after the collapse of this demystified world. But Ward is not the spokesman of an authoritarian Christianity as the answer to contemporary culture's loss of all legitimate authorities. Nor is it the point that everything in secular culture is bad. Ward's goal is to found a critical theology that is capable of being critical even in the postmodern situation and that does not merely re-establish the authoritarian aspects of the collapsed secularism by setting up yet another absolute and unambiguous authority, this time under the sign of theology. The distinctive contribution of theology to the discussion of contemporary culture is the idea of a position that is outside the prevailing system of values, yet does not lack communication to this system. The doctrine of the incarnation speaks of a God who reveals himself in the world, yet is not a part of it. This means that there is an external reason for a radical critique by theology, since it is not only a part of this system of values. Theology breaks with the cultural logic of our age by refusing to let itself be integrated as yet another modulation of the prevailing system of values.

Ward holds that without the idea of a God who in some sense is outside the system, it is difficult to see what possibilities of a radical critique are in fact accessible. Accordingly, the theological discourse can function as a critical analysis of a remystified world, not just as a product of this world. Although theology shares the mediated status of all discourses, and therefore cannot lay claim to a privileged position, the idea of God means that theology envisions a world that is not ruled by the laws of commodity fetishism. Theology speaks of an alternative way out of the system of values that became established after the implosion of secularism. Or perhaps, inspired by Augustine, theology speaks of another city – a city that is built not on the longing for obliteration, but on the longing for God. This city exists here and now, not only in the Christian church, but in many communities. Ward does not aim to create a Christian enclave alongside contemporary society. Rather, he thinks of the city of God as a presence in and through the secular city. This makes the presence of the city of God ambiguous, but at the same time it affirms the decisive role of the possibility of criticizing both the secular city and the postmodern city.

How Radical is Radical Orthodoxy?

Critics have not found the self-designation "radical orthodoxy" wholly satisfactory. The North American Catholic philosopher of religion John D. Caputo, one of the first to introduce Derrida's philosophy to theology and the philosophy of religion in the United States, believes that radical orthodoxy is more orthodox than radical. This is the impression given by their critique of modernity and by their attempt to revalidate the earlier tradition.[5] How is radicality to be weighed up against orthodoxy? Doubtless, there is no answer to this equation; but in more general terms, it is certainly arguable that there are some problems, at least in the articulation of radical orthodoxy's program that can easily lead to the impression voiced by Caputo. Several of these problems concern the realism and exclusivism of the movement's ecclesiology. As far as realism is concerned, one can ask to what extent the radical orthodox movement succeeds in getting to grips with a problem that confronts all church preaching and praxis in a multicultural society, namely, the distinction between what the sender intends and what use the receiver makes of what he is given. In principle, even the most perfectly celebrated liturgy at a Mass in Little St. Mary's risks being used by people whose views strongly diverge from the intention of the Christian church. In other words, it is difficult to understand how one specific liturgy and one specific ecclesiology can be as determinative for a person's conduct in life as some of the leading representatives of radical orthodoxy hope. In purely theoretical terms, this problem may not be insoluble; but I would imagine that it is a great practical problem for most parish communities in today's society.

The second trait I have mentioned is the exclusivism that finds expression both in ecclesiology and in the critique of modernity, but perhaps more strongly in Milbank and Pickstock than in Ward. Milbank has constructed his theology with the help of contrasting categories: the nihilistic-secular tradition *versus* the Platonic-Christian tradition. With regard to this manner of argumentation, several philosophers who have points in common with radical orthodoxy's way of working – for example,

---

[5] See John D. Caputo, *On Religion* (London/New York, 2001), p. 61.

the postmodern Jewish philosophy around Peter Ochs, Robert Gibbs, and *Scriptural Reasonings* – have pointed out that the radical orthodox rhetoric has an exclusive effect that makes a genuine critique of the movement impossible. This trait led Milbank's former teacher, Nicholas Lash, to speak of "Cardinal Milbank" in a polemical article.[6] Where Milbank and radical orthodoxy are interested in going beyond the antithetical pairs one finds in modern philosophy and modern society, this position runs contrary to their own intentions – and this is a significant criticism. Others in the radical orthodox movement, such as Ward in his christological-ecclesiological book *Cities of God*, have more clearly attempted to think outside these binary distinctions. I do not wish to deny that there is an exclusivist problem in radical orthodoxy, but it is conceivable that this trait is to some extent generated by a theology that refuses to accommodate the poor self-confidence in the modern reason, and that was schooled at a university where to some extent the disputation still survives as a pedagogical method.

One attractive trait in radical orthodoxy is that this movement offers a theology that is willing and able to conduct a discussion with the most advanced thinking of our age, while at the same time succeeding in preserving its unique theological voice. It intends to be an attempt to win back theology's public status without feeling obliged to legitimate its existence on the basis of some allegedly neutral philosophical or scientific method. Like much other contemporary philosophy, it finds its academic legitimacy in the critical discussion of the presuppositions of knowledge. But the claim radical orthodoxy makes and the field in which it works extends far beyond academia. Why has the radical orthodox movement attracted so much attention, both among its supporters and among its detractors? This may be because we see once again a holistic theological vision that is able to articulate a position with regard both to the church and to academia, politics, and culture. It remains to be seen how critical and constructive radical orthodoxy will be in these fields; but here, for the first time for many years, a meaningful theological alternative challenges us to say where we stand.

Bibliography

Caputo, John D., *On Religion* (London/New York: Routledge, 2001).
Hankey, Wayne J. and Douglas Hedley (eds), *Deconstructing Radical Orthodoxy: Postmodern Theology, Rhetoric and Truth* (Aldershot: Ashgate, 2005).
Hemming, Laurence Paul, *Radical Orthodoxy? A Catholic Enquiry* (Aldershot: Ashgate, 2000).
Lash, Nicholas, "Where Does Holy Teaching Leave Philosophy? Questions on Milbank's Aquinas," *Modern Theology*, 15/4 (1999).

---

[6] Nicholas Lash, "Where Does Holy Teaching Leave Philosophy? Questions on Milbank's Aquinas," *Modern Theology*, 15/4 (1999), p. 437.

Loughlin, Gerard, *Alien Sex: The Body and Desire in Cinema and Theology* (Oxford: Blackwell, 2004).
Milbank, John, *Being Reconciled: Ontology and Pardon* (London and New York: Routledge, 2003).
Milbank, John, *The Future of Love: Essays in Political Theology* (London: SCM Press, 2009).
Milbank, John, *Theology and Social Theory: Beyond Secular Reason* (Oxford: Blackwell, 1990; revised ed. 2006).
Milbank, John, *The Word Made Strange: Theology, Language, Culture* (Oxford: Blackwell, 1997).
Milbank, John and Catherine Pickstock, *Truth in Aquinas* (London and New York: Routledge, 2001).
Milbank, John, Graham Ward and Catherine Pickstock, *Radical Orthodoxy: A New Theology* (London and New York: Routledge, 1999).
Milbank, John and Simon Oliver (eds), *The Radical Orthodoxy Reader* (London and New York: Routledge, 2009).
Milbank, John, Slavoj Žižek and Creston Davies (eds), *Theology and the Political: The New Debate* (Durham and London: Duke University Press, 2005).
Milbank, John, Slavoj Žižek and Creston Davies (eds), *The Monstrosity of Christ: Paradox or Dialectic?* (Cambridge, Mass. and London: The MIT Press, 2009).
Milbank, John, Slavoj Žižek and Creston Davies (eds), *Paul's New Movement: Continental Philosophy and the Future of Christian Theology* (Grand Rapids: Brazos Press, 2010).
Pickstock, Catherine, *After Writing: On the Liturgical Consummation of Philosophy* (Oxford: Blackwell, 1998).
Smith, James K.A., *Radical Orthodoxy: Mapping a Post-secular Theology* (Grand Rapids and Milton Keynes: Baker Academic/Paternoster Press, 2004).
Ward, Graham, *Barth, Derrida and the Language of Theology* (Cambridge: Cambridge University Press, 1995).
Ward, Graham, *Christ and Culture* (Oxford: Blackwell, 2005).
Ward, Graham, *Cities of God* (London and New York: Routledge, 2001).
Ward, Graham, *Cultural Transformation and Religious Practice* (Cambridge: Cambridge University Press, 2005).
Ward, Graham, *The Politics of Discipleship: Becoming Post-material Citizens* (Grand Rapids: Baker Academic, 2009).
Ward, Graham, *True Religion* (Oxford: Blackwell, 2003).
Ward, Graham (ed.), *The Blackwell Companion to Postmodern Theology* (Oxford: Blackwell, 2001).
Ward, Graham (ed.), *The Certeau Reader* (Oxford: Blackwell, 2000).
Ward, Graham (ed.), *The Postmodern God: A Theological Reader* (Cambridge, Mass.: Blackwell, 1997).
Ward, Graham and Michael Hoelzl (eds), *The New Visibility of Religion: Studies in Religion and Cultural Hermeneutics* (London: Continuum, 2008).

Ward, Graham and Michael Hoelzl (eds), *Religion and Political Thought* (London: Continuum 2006).

Ward, Graham and Michael Hoelzl (eds), *What is Political Theology?* (London: Continuum, 2012).

Chapter 49
Feminist Theology
Astri Hauge

Feminism is not a new phenomenon, as many people seem to think. It arose long before equality between women and men became an important political theme in Norway. The background to feminism, or to the feminist struggle, is a patriarchal culture that has existed for many millennia. From ancient times down to our own days, the man has been defined as the standard human being, and the woman as his subordinate helper. Spirit, reason, creativity, strength, authority, and dominance characterized the man, while the woman represented matter, feeling, reproduction, weakness, obedience, and submissiveness. The man's place was in society, the woman's place in the home as the man's servant. A patriarchal gender ideology of this kind has been dominant in the past and continues to hold sway today in many places, for example, in conservative Christian milieus in the USA.

History: The Emergence of Feminist Theology

Human Rights – For Whom?

"All men are born equal ...," according to the constitution of the USA (1776). This language makes women invisible and has given rise to doubts and discussions about whether or not women are included; and these doubts and discussions have not abated. At the close of the eighteenth century, the ideas of the age of the Enlightenment inspired many women and men to argue that women should have the same human rights as men. There have been many active feminists in the USA and in many European countries from the eighteenth and nineteenth centuries onwards. Early in the twentieth century, women were given voting rights in most Western countries, but the views about women's and men's nature and tasks changed little. Right up to our own days, the church's men have carried the banner of patriarchal ideology, while women in the church have argued that the Gospel or the Christian faith opens the way to a more equal praxis in church and society.[1]

Two books became important sources of inspiration in the 1950s for women in many lands who desired a change.

Simone de Beauvoir's *Le deuxième sexe* (1949; English translation: *The Second Sex*, 1953) was a critical analysis of the dominant gender ideology that defined the man as

---
[1] See Clark and Richardson, *Women and Religion* (San Francisco, 1977).

the *first* and the standard human being and the woman as the *second,* who diverged from normality and was the man's servant. In the USA, Betty Friedan's *The Feminine Mystique* (1963) was a catalyst for the dissatisfaction many felt with the narrow role as wife, mother, and housewife.

The Pioneers of Feminist Theology

At the end of the 1960s, the Western world experienced both an antiauthoritarian student protest and a growing radical women's movement. Feminists looked critically at male-dominated structures and institutions in society, and not least at religion: its view of women, its gender ideology, and the patriarchal church government. Many abandoned the churches, while others became active critics inside them. Feminist theology emerged first in the USA, where church membership is more important and the religious plurality is greater than in other Western lands. Feminist theology was partly a grassroots movement and partly formulated by well-educated feminist theologians.

There can be no doubt that Mary Daly was the most important pioneer of feminist theology in the USA. She was a Catholic theologian with doctorates in philosophy and theology. During the Second Vatican Council (1962–65), which was open to reform, she optimistically began writing her book *The Church and the Second Sex* (1968), a feminist critique that demanded reforms of Catholic theology and church life. When she returned to the USA, she taught at Boston College, which was run by the Jesuits. She has described the following years as a dramatic and traumatic change of consciousness from a radical reforming Catholic to a post-Christian feminist. *Beyond God the Father* (1973) is her academic rupture with Catholic (and to a large extent, with Christian) theology: the church's dogmas reflect the essence of patriarchy, that is to say, contempt for women, violence, and imperialism. It is only when these dogmas are turned upside down that women can find freedom and "salvation." The radical feminist sisterhood is the healing and strengthening fellowship for women ("sisterhood as anti-church").[2]

This book gave fresh impetus to a consciousness-raising process and to a reflection on women's liberation and the Christian faith that was already going on. Many left the churches and became post-Christian (revolutionary) feminists, while others remained in the churches as "reformists" and worked on the criticism and change of a theology, a liturgy, and a preaching that bore the imprint of patriarchy.

Latin American liberation theology was an important source of inspiration for many theologians in the USA. Rosemary Radford Ruether, a reforming Catholic, was one of the most influential feminist theologians from the end of the 1970s onward.

---

[2] [Translator's note: In this essay, "fellowship" translates the Norwegian noun "fellesskap." The Norwegian noun has no gender associations. Some women writers prefer to avoid "fellowship" because of the masculine associations of "fellow" (= man), but I have used it here in order to avoid other words that have either stronger or weaker associations than "fellowship" (e.g., "community," "group").]

Letty Mandeville Russell, a Presbyterian who was strongly influenced by Barthian/neo-orthodox theology, laid the basis for her theology of liberation through many years of pastoral ministry in a New York slum (*Human Liberation in a Feminist Perspective – A Theology*, 1974).

These women belonged to a white middle class of European origin. Women from the Afro-American and Latin American population experienced that their existential situation, their experiences of faith, and their problems with faith were absent from feminist theology, and they began to write theology on the basis of their own context (Jacqueline Grant, Ada-María Isasi-Díaz, and others).

What is theology? In the strongly pluralistic American context, the word "theology" is not necessarily related to Christianity. There is a feminist theology related (for example) to Judaism, Buddhism, Islam, and (neo-)paganism. Attitudes to religion are often marked by relativism, pragmatism, and individualism: What works for me is true and right.

What is feminist theology? The following definition takes account both of the broad understanding of "theology" and of the plurality in feminist theory.

Feminist theology is a reflection on the content and meaning of religion, with special attention to the relationship between women and men in theory (doctrine, sacred writings) and praxis (organization; societal consequences), on the basis of the insight that religion has been used/misused to oppress women. The goal is to make a contribution to women's liberation.

Feminist theology in Europe was inspired by American feminist theology, the secular women's movement, and the Second Vatican Council. It received an extra impetus from the World Council of Churches, especially thanks to the comprehensive study project "Community of women and men in the church." University posts in feminist theology were established early on in the Netherlands and Germany, and somewhat later in Great Britain too. In Scandinavia, especially in Sweden and Denmark, a considerable number of women have taken their doctorates with theses in feminist theology or women's and gender studies.[3]

The present essay will concentrate on feminist theology in Western culture with roots in Christianity.

---

[3] Women's and gender studies in theology in the five Scandinavian countries have expanded greatly and cover a wide thematic range, as can be seen from the 20-page bibliography in "Scandinavian Critique of Anglo-American Feminist Theology" (see bibliography below). A number of Norwegian women have taken their doctorates in feminist theology or women's studies. Old Testament: Hanne Løland; New Testament: Turid Karlsen Seim, Jorunn Økland, Marianne Bjelland Kartzow; church history: Kari Elisabeth Børresen, Lisbeth Mikaelsson, Gunvor Lande, Synnøve Hinnaland Stendal, Ingunn F. Breistein, Kristin Norseth; systematic theology: Jone Salomonsen. We must also mention Dagny Kaul, a doctoral student at the theological faculty in the University of Oslo in the 1970s, who introduced feminist theology to women theologians and has been a driving force in feminist theology in Norway. Anne Louise Eriksson (systematic theology) and Eva Lundgren (science of religion) in Sweden have also had considerable influence in Norway.

What are the Characteristics of Feminist Theology?

"Women's experience is the source and norm of feminist theology." These or similar formulations were often heard in the early phase of feminist theology. In feminist groups and other conversations among women, stories with typical shared traits emerged: experiences of being overlooked, of not being heard (in the church, in academia), of being steamrollered and exploited (in work and in private life), of being made to look ridiculous or being corrected by the teacher if they asked questions about women's status and roles, for example, in church history. When women shared experiences of marginalization and broke with male society's definitions of women, they found freedom and strength: *"Sisterhood is powerful!"*[4] Theology was faced with an increasing number of new questions about "what," "why," and "how" – questions that "normal theology" ignored or laughed at. This led Daly to declare that feminists must commit "methodicide," because the established methods of theology and the man-centered perspective that it took for granted had become an idol that prevented new discoveries. Women must begin to ask non-questions and to discover and analyze non-data. In other words, they must focus on that which is ignored, reduced to silence, and defined against the background of normal theology.

But what is women's experience? It was white middle-class women in America who first appealed to "women's experience" as an argument or as a basis for theological or political affirmations. When Afro-American women and women in other cultures began to put words to their experiences, the differences between women became clear. Some live under a double or triple oppression because of gender, race, and social class. By sharing experiences across social/ethnical boundaries, they discovered both common traits and specific characteristics that were important in the elaboration of strategies of liberation.

Feminist theory investigates the causes of women's oppression and tries to find strategies to abolish this. Some types of feminist theory are related to more general political theories or ideologies: liberal feminism, socialist feminism, and Marxist feminism have differing views of what causes oppression and what strategies can remove it. Radical feminism is profoundly skeptical about the entire structure of society, which is based on men's power over women. It is often separatist: that is to say, the attempt is made to live with the greatest possible degree of separation and independence vis-à-vis male-governed society (see Daly). Feminist theology often has a rather general feminist standpoint, but some texts may be more or less clearly based on one particular feminist theory.

Feminist Theology's Relationship to Women's and Gender Studies

The academic context of feminist theology is partly women's studies and partly "traditional" academic theology. The women's movement inspired research into topics in a great variety of academic disciplines, such as the understanding

---

[4] This is the title of a feminist anthology edited by Robin Morgan (1970).

and ideology of gender, structures that oppressed women, and the cause of male dominance. Women's or gender studies gradually became established as a specific field in many disciplines. The gender ideology and cultural role in Christianity and other religions was also analyzed outside theology. Women's studies, and not least feminist philosophy (including gender theory and the philosophy of science), became important dialogue partners for feminist theology.

Women's studies have developed through a number of specific phases. First of all, it was important to *make visible* the conditions under which women live and to make individual women visible, since women were largely invisible (absent) in virtually all the spheres of male-centered research. Historians and sociologists described and analyzed the conditions under which women lived in the private sphere and in society, and the structural oppression in various fields; they uncovered the existence of extensive violence against women in marriage/partnership.

Secondly, the *gender perspective*. Women's studies switched the focus from women's life and history to understandings of gender. How is gender defined, and what significance is ascribed to biological gender? What kinds of gender *ideologies* have found their spokesmen in the great philosophers, psychologists, theologians, etc.? What forces have contributed to changes in women's and men's roles?

Gender theory became the basis and starting point for women's studies in the third phase. Feminists agree that women have been oppressed because of their gender. But what *is* gender? What meaning does gender have? From the beginning of the feminist movement roughly 200 years ago, the dominant view has been that there is one single human nature, although women and men have different functions in procreation. Differences between women and men in behavior and personal characteristics were regarded as the result of the ways in which culture socialized and treated the two genders. "Femininity" and "masculinity" are seen as cultural constructions, ideological straitjackets that form and cripple the development of boys and girls. This is a *humanistic and constructionist theory of gender*.

From the 1980s and 1990s onwards, *poststructuralism* has radicalized the constructionist view. Here, two-gender thinking is regarded as a heterosexist ideological construction that is based on, and serves, certain social/political interests. Genders exist only as linguistic, societal, and cultural constructions.

Within feminism and feminist theology both past and present, there have been currents that think in *essentialist* terms. In other words, they assume that there are male and female qualities inherent in nature. Male qualities and values (competition, power, profit, etc.) have dominated culture, politics, and life in society, and are driving the world or the ecosystem to the point of destruction. This is why the female qualities must be accorded a higher value and must be translated into praxis: care, empathy, altruism, and the will to create peace and egalitarian relationships between human beings.

A Feminist Look at the Picture of God

God Created in the Image of the Man

"If God is male, the man is God. The divine patriarch castrates women, as long as he is permitted to go on living in human beings' imagination." Daly argues that a masculine picture of God necessarily creates a patriarchal society: if God in heaven is a father who governs his people, the governance of society by men is in accordance with the divine plan and the order of the universe. The husband who takes decisions that affect his wife represents God himself, and she has no right to think and act autonomously.

The church's language about God as Father, Son, and Spirit is understood by most people as a gendered definition of God. Daly claims that traditional pictures of God's transcendence, holiness, and supremacy (God as king, lord, judge, etc.) reflect the power structure of patriarchy and have contributed to the infantilization and oppression of women and of lower-class persons. Since they are the primary victims of patriarchal pictures of God, women have a special vocation to *iconoclasm*, that is to say, to tear down the false gods by means of the critique of religion – and indirectly, by changing the patriarchal social structures.

Old Tradition – New Experience of God

This found an echo in many women. Some followed Daly's example, leaving the church and declaring themselves to be *post-Christian feminists*. They held that a genuine knowledge of God could emerge in this new sisterhood. Many religious fellowships of women were founded, ranging across a very wide spectrum of faith and lifestyle. Feminist "witch movements" (feminist Wicca) looked back to ancient rituals and to ideas about faith that the church had condemned as heresy. Women's groups that were more loyal to tradition read the Bible with women's eyes in search of an egalitarian (non-patriarchal) message, and worked for a change in the view of women in theology, liturgical language, and symbols.[5] Between these two extreme points, many groups sought a new experience of God in very different ways. The anthology *Womanspirit Rising* (1979) documents this plurality.

Liberating Talk about God

"The Bible talks about God in masculine imagines, and the church has always talked about God as 'He' – Father, Son, and Spirit. Only heretical movements have talked about God as Mother." This has often been asserted by theologians who are critical of feminist theology and who reject all use of female images to speak of God. But feminist theology has shown long ago that the Bible's picture of God is drawn using metaphors and images from the lives of both men and women. Feminist theology

---

[5] See Cochran, *Evangelical Feminism* (New York, 2005).

continually searches for images and a new language that can liberate women from pictures of God that can cripple them. Some look in the Bible and the Christian tradition, and find a rich treasure of names, images, metaphors, and comparisons that have been swept aside by the one-sided focus on God the Father, Son, and Spirit. Some look among religious movements that have been labeled as heresies by the dominant church. Some look in other religions.

But what or who is God? A transcendent, omnipotent being, or a symbol of our highest values? Is it possible for us to know anything at all about God? How can we address and speak about the deity? There are widely divergent opinions on all these issues, and I shall present some of them briefly here.

Mary Daly: God is Not God the Father

Mary Daly claims that women need ideological, psychological, and religious liberation from the religion that has brought them guilt and self-contempt. When women reject traditional definitions of roles, live a new androgynous life, and develop their consciousness, this points to God's infinite development/revelation. For God is living and dynamic. God's self-revelation and self-development take place in the universe and in human history (cf. Tillich; process theology). Women's liberation thus creates a qualitatively new understanding of the divine; Daly sees this as a kind of quantum leap in the development of the human person. Anthropomorphous symbols of God (father, lord, king, and so on) make God a "thing." God must be given a new name, since God is active and dynamic *Be-ing*, the opposite of not-being. God/transcendence is the Verb in which we share and in which we live.

However, Daly changed her view and argued that the term *God* is indissolubly linked to patriarchal orderings and patterns of thought, and is therefore unusable. In later books (*Gyn/Ecology*, *Pure Lust*, etc.), she claims that there is a total conflict between radical separatist feminism on the one hand and the world religions on the other. They are an expression of men's hatred of women and are instruments for the necrophile patriarchy, whereas radical feminism is biophile and lives in harmony with all of nature. Despite her sharp criticism of theology, she has held fast to the traditional Catholic concept of God (God as Being, from Thomas Aquinas), but with the feminine form: Goddess.

Rosemary Radford Ruether: God/ess – Everywhere

Rosemary Radford Ruether's book *Sexism and God-talk: Towards a Feminist Theology* (1983) discusses the traditional theological themes in the light of the broad Christian tradition (including so-called heretical movements) and of other religious traditions. She claims that Israelite religion (the Old Testament) and Christian theology have postulated an essential distinction between God and the world, between nature and spirit. Monotheism and the patriarchy thereby created the dualistic patterns of thought that mark Western culture. We need to acquire alternative and more fruitful models from outside this context. She presents as positive examples the ancient religions in the Near East and elsewhere, in which power and status were ascribed to both goddesses and gods (unlike later views about "female" and "male" qualities).

Ruether takes up Tillich's concept of the "ground of being" as a metaphor for the deity, the vital force that is immanent in all that lives and that transcends all that lives. But she underlines more strongly the immanence of the deity, and finds that the religion of the Indians and ancient fertility religions have a more adequate understanding of God than the Bible and the Christian tradition. She has proposed God/ess as a name or symbol of the original good nature and humanity. God/ess is not a personal deity, but can be thought of in personal terms, as something that is manifested in and through living beings in the world. God/ess as "thou" corresponds to a "thou-ness" in all that lives. Conversion to God/ess entails conversion to the earth and to one's own authentic self, according to Ruether. Her concept of God is close to pantheism: God is in everything, the deity and the world/universe are woven together and inseparable. It can also be understood as a type of religious naturalism that raises the status of "the creation"/the universe by means of the symbol God/ess.

Elizabeth A. Johnson: The Triune Sophia-God – She Who Is

Johnson and several other Catholic feminist theologians find more of value in the Christian tradition than Daly and Ruether. In the book *She Who Is: The Mystery of God in Feminist Theological Discourse* (1997), she employs the narratives and images of the Bible as the most important source of symbols that can open the way to a new talking about God. She also points out that there are hidden treasures in the Christian tradition.

Johnson claims that the image of "mother" is better suited than masculine images to symbolize God as creator of the universe and origin of all life. The essence of motherhood is a relationship that never ceases to exist: and such is God's relationship to the world. However, these are analogies rather than exact descriptions. Johnson maintains a *panentheistic* understanding of God: God is both near at hand, present in the creation and in the world of human beings, and at the same time infinitely greater and other than we can grasp. God is in the world, and the world is in God – while at the same time they are radically different.

Johnson strongly emphasizes that God is incomprehensible, a mystery that we cannot grasp. How is the church – the people of faith – to express this? She finds the solution in the story of God's revelation to Moses in the burning bush (Exodus 3). When Moses asked what God's name was, he received an answer that confirmed God's mysterious, incomprehensible being: "I am who I am." This God is a mystery, and at the same time a personal character. God expresses compassion, promises liberation, and strengthens the human being who is to carry out God's plan.

Johnson refers to Aquinas' interpretation: the divine essence is identical with divine existence, so that *qui est* ("the one who is") is the most exact name for God.

Although God is one, we experience God's presence and action in the world in three different ways. This is why Christians from the early church onwards have professed faith in a triune God: Father, Son, and Spirit. The qualities and actions that the tradition ascribes to each of them are also attributed to wisdom (*Sophia* in Greek) in the Book of Proverbs and the apocryphal Book of Wisdom. On this basis, Johnson speaks of the Trinity as *Spirit-Sophia, Jesus-Sophia, and Mother-Sophia*. New language about God must first of all express something that characterizes the living God, mediated through scripture, tradition, and the contemporary experience of faith; and it must also combat sexism. Johnson concludes that *She Who Is* is a good and accurate name for God. The female pronoun will provoke reactions and unmask the fact that God is male in people's consciousness. Since women too are created in God's image and have a share in the divine life, the female name is theologically legitimate.

The Goddess Movement: "I Found God in Myself, and I Loved Her Fiercely"

This quotation from the early phase of feminist theology expresses a mood and an experience that were very typical of the non-churchly part of feminist theology. A common element in a large number of various religious fellowships of women is that they speak of the *Goddess* rather than of a gender-neutral God. Theologians in the movement elaborated *thealogy* (= doctrine of the Goddess) as a counterpart to patriarchal *theology*. The *Goddess* confirms the female body and women's fellowship, culture, and power. The Goddess contributes to harmonious relationships both between individuals and between human beings and nature.[6]

This movement won many adherents among women who were not (or were no longer) connected to the dominant monotheistic traditions. It contains every type of faith in God, from belief in a *personal deity* (as in the Jewish and Christian tradition), via *polytheism* (belief in goddesses and gods) to *pantheism* (everything is divine). The goddess can serve as a symbol of the goodness of women's strength and power, and of the energy in the processes of life, death, and rebirth in nature.

Postmodern Feminist Theology

Here, the question is not about God's existence and being in the ontological sense, but about the origin of the symbol of God and its meaning and function in the symbolic order and in the societal order. This is strongly influenced by Luce Irigary, who has written about the theory of gender difference and is in turn influenced by Feuerbach. God and religion are seen as a projection of human and cultural values; "God the Father" shows that the father-son relationship has a high status. In order to become autonomous as *female human persons*, women need female representations of God, and this means that they must develop new images of the divine. God is experienced as a greater power or force that is at work in the fellowship among women. But God is that which each individual woman is and does; in other words, there is a reciprocal identification of God and the woman.

---

[6] Carol P. Christ, "Why Women Need the Goddess," in *Womanspirit Rising* (New York, 1979).

Christology: What does Jesus mean? Christa, a bronze sculpture depicting a crucified woman, was exhibited in a cathedral in New York several years ago. This attracted considerable attention and gave rise to a vigorous discussion. Was this blasphemy? Were the suffering and the sacrificial death being taken away from Jesus and laid upon a woman? Or was the sculpture meant to affirm that Jesus, who is claimed to be the Son of God and the world's redeemer, represents both women and men? Irrespective of what the artist had in fact intended, the name *Christa* was adopted by a number of feminist theologians. For some, Christa is a symbol or name of the sacred, liberating, creative, and erotic spirit of God/dess, which is deeply rooted in women's lives. In that case, Jesus is one among many others who can be bearers of this spirit. *The body of Christa* is experienced powerfully in women's fellowship. *Christ/Christa*, as a positive symbol of power, liberation, and new life, is thus separated from Jesus as a historical person. Other feminists claim that the Christa symbol can glorify women's sufferings instead of fighting against injustice.[7] Daly's criticism is more radical. She calls the church's faith that Jesus is Christ/Messiah, the Son of God, *Christolatry* (the blasphemous adoration of Christ).

Gender and the Representation of God

The Christa statue actualizes an important theological question: Can a male representative of God or redeemer-figure mediate God's presence or salvation to both men and women to the same degree? Many who take an essentialist view of gender answer this question in the negative: women need a female Christ/Christa, because Jesus Christ represents maleness and patriarchy. For constructionists, gender is fundamentally unimportant; a human being of male or female gender can represent everyone. But in a patriarchal context, a male representative of God will inevitably legitimate men's dominance. The challenge for feminist theology is to elaborate a Christology that confirms and demonstrates that women are created in the image of God on equal terms with men. The background to feminists' strong opposition to "normal church" Christology is the strongly patriarchal imprint that Christology has had in most churches down through the centuries. Theologians have claimed that the incarnation of God *had to* take place in the form of a man, because God himself is masculine in his being; because maleness is ontologically superior to femaleness; and because the man is the standard human being, and the woman is a deviation from the norm (Thomas Aquinas). A man can represent humankind, but a woman represents only herself or her gender.

Jesus Seen with "Black" and "White" Eyes

Conflicts, oppression, and an unequal distribution of resources among ethnic groups have left their traces on liberation theology in the USA. Afro-American women call their theology *womanist theology*. It has its starting point in an analysis of the triple

---

[7] Elisabeth Gössmann, *Dictionary of Feminist Theology* (Gütersloh, 1991), pp. 39f.

oppression under which they suffer, because of gender, race, and social class. This means that they distance themselves from the *feminist theology* that is dominated by white middle-class women. There are considerable differences in the way they view Jesus.

Jesus is our brother and friend, say Afro-Americans. Their culture bears the marks of a long history of oppression. In slavery and distress, they found consolation in the thought that Jesus, who had suffered, was with them in their suffering. One day, God would give them freedom, peace, and joy. This is continued by the womanist theologians.

The Jesus of the whites is white and racist, and is therefore inadequate for black women. For them, Jesus is black – and, as the least of the least, a black woman. Jesus' life and actions are the keys to understand what it means to say that Jesus is Christ: he brings God down upon to earth and is God's presence in their difficult lives. Jesus is friend, brother, and helper; he knows them, he heals them and cares for them. He suffers with them in a society that is hostile to both black people and women. He is also the liberator who works through, for, and with them to free Afro-Americans from their complex oppression. Jesus' death on the cross shows his solidarity, and the resurrection is the basis of their faith and trust. The fact that Jesus was a man is unimportant. He is Christ because of what he did.[8]

Jesus is one prophet among many, claims Rosemary Radford Ruether. Jesus was a fearless messianic prophet who criticized patriarchal relationships and other forms of oppression, one who lived in solidarity with the poor and oppressed, and who set people free. He was a genuine human being, not a divine figure. To regard him as God's definitive revelation is to replicate the attitudes against which he protested. Ruether holds that this is a contradiction of Jesus' spirit. She formulates the problem of many feminists: "Can a male savior save women?" For her, *Christ* is a symbol of the liberated human person and the liberating word of God, both of which can and should be represented by other human beings, both women and men.

Jesus is Sophia's prophet, according to Elisabeth Schüssler Fiorenza. In the book *In Memory of Her* (1983), she portrays Jesus as a prophet for Wisdom (*Sophia*). He proclaimed a vision of the kingdom of God and gathered around himself a flock of disciples in which men and women were equal. These disciples opposed in word and deed the patriarchal structures of dominance and subordination. In this way, Jesus and the Jesus movement are a potential model for women who fight for freedom today.

Jesus is more than a prophet – he is God's unique self-presentation, according to Letty Mandeville Russell. Like liberation theology, she sees Jesus as a radical prophet and liberator, but also as far more than this: Jesus is the servant of God and of humankind. His life, death, and resurrection are stages in God's plan of salvation. He is the risen and exalted *Kyrios* ("Lord": Philippians 2:5ff.) who lives in order to bring to completion the new creation of God. Russell wants to free Christology from its patriarchal captivity.

---

[8] *Dictionary*, pp. 38f., and pp. 40–42.

Jesus is God's presence in the world. Elizabeth A. Johnson describes Jesus as God's incarnate Wisdom (*Jesus-Sophia*). God is compassionately present in Jesus' words and actions when he teaches, heals, and calls women and men to an inclusive table fellowship. Jesus' suffering and death show God's identification with those who suffer in all ages, including the women who are raped and abused. After the resurrection, he is recognized as Christ, and the fellowship of disciples continues his redeeming and liberating activity. *Jesus-Sophia* neutralizes sexist Christology, because this symbol removes the link between maleness and divinity.

What are the Special Characteristics of Feminist Theology? What are its New Contributions to Theology?

Feminist theology speaks explicitly of situations that are "taken for granted" or reduced to silence on the part of people in general and of theologians. It uncovers and criticizes the massive patriarchal inheritance in theology and church life. Feminist theology sees women's experience and the situations in which they live as relevant and significant for theology. The differences between women and men in society with regard to status, income, power, and influence are not seen as "natural," but as structural oppression. Violence against women in partnerships is a non-theme in some writings about sexual ethics and pastoral literature, but it is made visible here as a gender-determined oppression.

Feminist theology focuses on the relationship between society and theology – like other types of liberation theology, but unlike "normal theology." Feminist theology investigates how theology directly or (through silence) indirectly legitimates unjust power structures. Feminist theology looks at gender ideologies and gendered power structures in society and in academia/theology (something that is seldom done by men's liberation theology). One example is men's authority and position as subject, something that it is taken for granted. Feminist theology uncovers the gender blindness and the androcentric orientation in men's theology.

Feminist theology has a stronger interdisciplinary orientation than "normal theology." The latter splits up problems that are a complex totality in women's lives, and the parts are treated in different disciplines. This, however, means that the problem complex, the bad totality, disappears. For example, a woman whose image of God, image of "father," image of herself, and her family relationships have been destroyed through sexual abuse is sent to a pastor, and the problems can be discussed in pastoral-theological literature – or ignored. Dogmatics, ethics, preaching, liturgy, hymns, etc. will continue to mediate a massively masculine image of God that creates arrogance in many men and problems about faith in many women. Feminist theology insists that experiences of abuse and oppression are relevant to the whole of theology.

After this brief presentation of the criticism and new formulation of theology by various feminist theologians, I conclude this essay with some reflections of my own.

Critique of Theology and Faith

The task of theology, and especially of dogmatics, is to interpret God or the divine in a way that contemporary people can experience as true and relevant. Many think that theology too *is* true, and in that case, the critique of theology by feminist theologians or others can be perceived as an attack on Christianity itself. But since every human being "understands in part" (1 Corinthians 13), *all* theology is fallible and limited. Theological work can be influenced by one's own interests or those of a group, and this is why we need correctives in the form of theology and the critique of theology from a variety of contexts. Even theologies that have a basis, a fundamental outlook, and a content that one criticizes can have perspectives and substantial elements that open the door to new insight and reflection.

The Bible is strongly criticized by many feminist theologians who have experienced its use as a weapon against women's autonomy. I see the Bible as the fundamental source of faith in God and of faith in myself as a human being, as a woman created in the image of God (Genesis 1:26). It is the most important testimony to God's revelation in the history of human beings. It must be read in the light of the time and the culture and the human beings who communicated the message. The Bible is not infallible, but it is a good "map." The Bible contains mutually contradictory views of women, from clearly patriarchal statements and ordinances (mostly in the Old Testament) to more egalitarian texts (mostly in the New Testament).

The high point of the Bible is the Gospel stories about Jesus of Nazareth, God's Son and our brother. He rebukes the values of patriarchy and every mentality that seeks domination. In his deeds and his words, he reflects God's love, mercy, and holiness. The Bible's message gives a basis for equal dignity and equality between women and men. But conventional thinking and "natural" male dominance mean that the theology that sets the tone continues to ignore women's experience, their living situations, and their position in church and society. This is why a critical feminist theology is necessary.

Bibliography

Børresen, Kari Elisabeth (ed.), *Image of God and Gender Models in Judaeo-Christian Tradition* (Oslo: Solum Humanity Press, 1991).

Cheopp, Rebecca S. and Sheila Greeve Danavey (eds), *Horizons in Feminist Theology: Identity, Tradition, and Norms* (Minneapolis: Fortress Press, 1997).

Christ, Carol P. and Judith Plaskow (eds), *Womanspirit Rising: A Feminist Reader in Religion* (San Francisco: Harper and Row, 1979).

Clark, Elizabeth and H. Richardson (eds), *Women and Religion: A Feminist Sourcebook of Christian Thought* (New York: Harper and Row, 1977).

Cochran, Pamela D., *Evangelical Feminism; A History* (New York: New York University Press, 2005).

Daly, Mary, *Beyond God the Father. Toward a Philosophy of Women's Liberation* (Boston: Beacon Press, 1973).

Fiorenza, Elisabeth Schüssler, *In Memory of Her* (New York: Crossroad, 1983/1994).

Elisabeth Gössmann, Helga Kuhlmann, Elisabeth Moltmann-Wendel und Ina Praetorius (eds), *Wörterbuch der feministischen Theologie* (*Dictionary of Feminist Theology*). (Gütersloh: Gütersloher Verlagshaus, 1991).

Johnson, Elizabeth A., *She Who Is: The Mystery of God in Feminist Theological Discourse* (New York: Crossroad, 1997).

Parsons, Susan Frank (ed.), *The Cambridge Companion to Feminist Theology* (Cambridge: Cambridge University Press, 2002).

Ruether, Rosemary Radford (ed.), *Religion and Sexism: Images of Women in the Jewish and Christian Tradition* (New York: Simon and Schuster, 1974).

Ruether, Rosemary Radford, *Sexism and God-Talk: Toward a Feminist Theology* (Boston: Deacon Press, 1983).

Russell, Letty Mandeville, *Human Liberation in a Feminist Perspective – A Theology* (Philadelphia: Westminster Press, 1974).

Russell, Letty Mandeville, *The Future of Partnership* (Philadelphia: Westminster Press, 1979).

Russell, Letty M. and Shannon J. Clarkson (eds), *Dictionary of Feminist Theologies* (Louisville, KY: Mowbray, 1996).

Sawyer, Deborah F. and Diane M. Collier (eds), *Is There a Future for Feminist Theology?* (Sheffield: Sheffield Academic Press, 1999).

"Scandinavian Critique of Anglo-American Feminist Theology," *Journal of the ESWTR* 15, (Louvain, 2007). Yearbook.

Chapter 50
Ecumenical Theology

Peter Lodberg

Ecumenical theology belongs to the twentieth century. It was created by the divisions, conflicts, and wars of the bloodiest century the world has ever experienced, and its response to social, political, ecclesial, and economic conflicts was the healing of differences and work for unity among peoples, churches, religions, and nations.

Ecumenical theology starts at home with the historical and theological divisions among the Christian churches. It looks upon church history as a history of separation that has divided 20 centuries of Christianity into six major streams: Orthodox, Roman Catholic, Anglican, Protestant, Independent, and Marginal Christian. Across these denominational divisions are found different identities such as: Evangelicals and Revivalists (Pentecostals, Charismatics, and Neocharismatics). The irony of church history from an ecumenical perspective is that the efforts to maintain the purity and unity of Christian faith have always developed into disunity and strife among Christians. Ecumenical theology, thus, is the counter-movement against this development of church conflict, because it considers the disunity of the church as a "scandalon," e.g. as a matter of faith and order that goes against the unity of the apostolic faith, the unity of the church, and faith in the "Spirit of truth" who "will guide you into all the truth" (John 16:13).

The interest of ecumenical theology in matters of church division is not only an interest in organizational matters of the visible church, but is also very much linked to a renewed interest in ecclesiology and the relationship between the church and the world. Special emphasis is placed upon the church's responsibility for justice, peace and creation, e.g. "for the life of the world" (liturgy of John Chrysostom). This includes understanding mission as *missio Dei* to all of creation and diakonia as *the liturgy in society after the liturgy*. The unity of the church, thus, is very closely linked to issues related to the unity of humankind, and ecumenical theology includes issues related to all of human existence.

Ecumenical theology was formulated during the twentieth century by persons and institutions belonging to the ecumenical movement that found its organizational expressions in a number of ecumenical organizations such as the World Council of Churches and regional and national council of churches. The confessional organizations like the Lutheran World Federation or the World Alliance of Reformed Churches have seen themselves as committed to the ecumenical cause and theological agenda.

The Resources of Ecumenical Theology

Theology is the necessary reflection on the continuing content and relevance of an already established Christian faith and its practice. Theology is therefore on the one hand related to intellectual knowledge, reflection, and criticism, but it is also on the other hand related to a community (church, family, friends) that is able to transmit the faith and be the place for the sharing of the experience of faith, in order to build up the community of believers.

Ecumenical theology stresses the importance of the church and the worshipping community as the place where the Christian faith and tradition are handed over to new generations and individuals. The apostolic tradition is a living tradition that is maintained down through the ages and all over the world through the preaching of the good news, in the confession of faith and in liturgical prayer. The New Testament shows very clearly that maintaining and living the unity of the church expressed in the confession of the one faith is the core of the Christian belief.

The basic principle that opened especially the Protestant theology to ecumenical theology in the twentieth century was the rediscovery in Karl Barth's dialectical theology of the Christological principle. In the words of the German ecumenical theologian Edmund Schlink, the Christological principle introduced a Copernican change in the relationship among the churches.[1] In the old theological world view the churches were regarded as revolving around each other, but in the new Christological world view all churches were revolving around Christ. The consequence was important. All churches must be seen as churches that sharet in the Christ-event, and no church can any longer maintain that it alone is the full and only realization of the body of Christ. The Roman Catholic Church accepted the consequence of this important shift in the theological paradigm during the Second Vatican Council (1962–5).

According to Cardinal Walter Kasper, the decisive element of the Second Vatican Council's ecumenical approach is the fact that the Council no longer identifies in *Lumen Gentium 8* the Church of Jesus Christ simply with the Roman Catholic Church, as had Pope Pius XII in his 1943 Encyclical *Mystici Corporis*.[2] The Second Vatican Council replaced *"est"* (the Catholic Church "is" Jesus Christ's Church) with *"subsistit,"* i.e. the Church of Jesus Christ can historically and concretely be met as a present reality in the Catholic Church. The Catholic Church at the same time recognizes the existence of elements of the church (*elementa ecclesiae*) outside the Catholic Church.

It is interesting that the Second Vatican Council made use of Calvin's concept of *"elementa"* or *"vestigia"* in order to describe the relationship between Christ, the Roman Catholic Church, and Non-Catholic Christians. The World Council of Churches in its *Toronto Declaration* from 1950 also referred to the concept of elements, when it had to describe the relationship among its member churches and the meaning of membership in the World Council of Churches. *The Toronto Declaration* states that

---

[1] E. Schlink, *Ecumenical Dogmatics* (Göttingen, 1983).
[2] W. Kasper, www.vatican.va (accessed January 15, 2012).

"(T)he member churches of the World Council recognize in other churches elements of the true Church."[3] These "vestigia ecclesiae" are then identified as the preaching of the Word, the teaching of the Holy Scriptures and the administration of the sacraments. They are described as "a fact of real promise and provide an opportunity to strive by frank and brotherly intercourse for the realization of a fuller unity."

From its inauguration in 1948 the World Council of Churches was eager to avoid any criticism of being a superchurch that would negotiate unions between the churches on the basis of one particular conception of the church. It should not prejudge the ecclesiological problem, and over the years the World Council and the Commission on Faith and Order have established themselves as places for the discussion of a common understanding of ecclesiology and its relationship to issues such as baptism, Eucharist, and ministry that divide the churches.

Seen from the perspective of the Roman Catholic Church, which is a member of the Faith and Order Commission, but not of the World Council of Churches, there is still a need for clarification on ecclesiological issues, especially on the ordained ministry. Of special interest to the Roman Catholic Church is, however, the recent development in ecumenical theology within some Protestant churches as it is reflected in the understanding of apostolicity and the apostolic succession in the episcopate. In the Lima document on "Baptism, Eucharist and Ministry" (1982), published by the Faith and Order Commission, the apostolic succession in the episcopate is considered "as a sign, though not a guarantee, of the continuity and unity of the Church." The issue of the historical episcopate is also taken up in the ecumenical dialogue among the Lutheran churches in Northern Europe and the British and Irish Anglican churches that in 1992 produced *The Porvoo Common Statement*. In the conversation there is a common understanding of the apostolicity of the whole church and the apostolic ministry, understood as the succession in the episcopal office, and the historic succession as a sign.

In some Protestant circles, the ecumenical dialogue on apostolicity and historical episcopacy is criticized because it puts too much emphasis on the church as an institution with its own hierarchy at the expense of seeing the church as a community of people gathered around Word and sacraments. The tradition of the Reformation has always favoured community and not episcopacy, as in the synodal and presbyteral constitution of the Lutheran and Reformed churches. Theologically, the episcopate is a pastorate with the function of church leadership. The legitimate plurality of the episcopal and synodal-presbyteral order is important to the *Leuenberg Agreement* from 1973 that unites a group of Lutheran, Reformed and Methodist churches in continental Europe. Some churches like the Church of Norway and the Evangelical-Lutheran Church in Denmark have signed both the *Porvoo Common Statement* and the *Leuenberg Agreement* in order to stress the importance of maintaining the plurality of church order.

---

[3] M. Kinnamon, *The Ecumenical Movement* (Geneva, 1997).

Ecumenical Theology and Statements

The Lima document, the *Leuenberg Agreement* and the *Porvoo Common Statement* are examples of results of ecumenical theological dialogues and have themselves produced ecumenical theology, e.g. a new way of reflecting on cooperation among Christian churches. Lima is the result of a multilateral discussion among representatives from a number of churches, while Leuenberg and Porvoo belong to the category of bilateral conversation between two confessional churches.

The Roman Catholic Church too takes part in bilateral dialogues. Three documents were produced between 1980 and 1990 by the "Joint Catholic-Orthodox Commission" on a common understanding of faith, church, and sacraments. In cooperation with the Lutheran World Federation, the Roman Catholic Church has produced a "Joint Declaration on the Doctrine of Justification" that was signed by the parties in 1999.

The dynamic of these dialogues is, first, to agree on the disagreements; second, to study together the historical and theological reasons behind the disagreements. An important part of this study is to agree on the degree of the theological problem and decide if the theological disagreements are an issue that divides the churches, or if the disagreements belong to the necessary pluralism of theological freedom. It is also important to try to understand the issue in question as it is understood by the dialogue partner. A change in mutual understanding, attitude, and language, thus, is part of the dialogue process.

The next step is to formulate a common statement and say together what can be said on the issues that divide the churches, in order to express agreement, convergence, or even consensus. According to Nicholas Lossky, perhaps the greatest difficulty for ecumenical theology is the fact that while it is relatively easy to agree about doctrinal problems in the light of a common acceptance of Jesus Christ as the sole criterion of truth, it is much harder to reach a common mind about the reading of the historical context in which theology and belief is to be expressed.[4] Here, Lossky touches upon the important question of the reception by the churches of the results of the ecumenical dialogues. Most of the dialogue results have not let to substantial changes in the individual churches toward more church unity (meaning sacramental fellowship). The results are often met with a "hermeneutic of mistrust," because the ecumenical documents are written in a non-recognizable way compared to the confessional tradition. The writers of the documents often develop a common trust and understanding of the words and concepts they are using, while the final product looks like a "third language" that is unfamiliar to the ordinary church member. The understandable reaction from people outside the ecumenical discussion is mistrust and a spirit of suspicion; behind each word, suspicious readers tend to see the old heresies of the other(s).

Another difficulty is the fact that the ecumenical dialogue is seen as a Western phenomenon that does not address the issues of importance for Christians of the global South. It is a fact that the need for ecumenical dialogue and church unity grew out

---

[4] N. Lossky, *Dictionary of the Ecumenical Movement* (Geneva, 1991).

of Europe and the way confessional disagreements were (mis)used by churches and political parties during World War I and II in Europe. The geographical unevenness must be regarded as a serious challenge to ecumenical dialogues, because the center of gravity in Christianity has moved to the global South in the twentieth century.[5] The confessional pluralism of Europe has been transported to the South from Europe and North America, and one result is perhaps that the interest for ecumenical dialogues will vanish from the theological agenda, because the churches in the global North will be more and more preoccupied by their own institutional survival in an age of secularism and atheism, while the churches in the global South will concentrate on evangelism, mission to the North, and social issues at home. Thus, the future of ecumenical theology will be very much related to the theology of mission, peace, and social justice.

Ecumenical Theology of Mission

Ecumenical theology is closely related to the theology of mission, because the ecumenical movement started as an outcrop of the Protestant missions of the nineteenth century.[6] Since 1961, World Mission and Evangelism has been an integral part of the structure of the World Council of Churches. This has led to some important shifts in missionary thinking under the overarching concept of *missio Dei* (God's mission) that is related to the new Christological emphasis in ecumenical theology as shown above. The International Missionary Council at its Assembly in Achimota, Ghana, in 1958 formulated the new mood in the following way: "The Christian world mission is Christ's, not ours."[7] The churches changed from being the sender to being the one sent. All churches had the same missionary task, and mission became a partnership among equal churches; the dichotomy between "us" and "them," "home" and "abroad" was no longer part of the missionary vocabulary.

In the ecumenical theology of mission, the church is understood as essentially missionary. The church is mission, and missionary activity is not so much the work of the church as the church at work. Church and mission have been changed to the mission of the church. This means that the church is dynamic as the people of God that is permanently underway in space and time toward the end, that is, the Kingdom of God. As the people of God on the move toward the Kingdom of God, the church becomes a sign and instrument of this new reality that is coming to life through the mission of the church. At the General Assembly of the World Council of Churches in Uppsala, Sweden, in 1968 the key formulation was: "The Church is bold in speaking of itself as the sign of the coming unity of mankind." The church became a dynamic critical force challenging policies and traditions in church and society which kept people apart or avoided addressing the root causes of injustice, violence and ecological

---

[5] T.M. Johnson, *Atlas of Global Christianity* (Edinburgh, 2009).
[6] D. MacCulloch, *A History of Christianity* (London, 2009).
[7] D.J. Bosch, *Transforming Mission: Paradigm Shifts in Theology of Mission* (Maryknoll, 1993).

disaster. The member churches decided in Uppsala to give priority to combat racism, and especially apartheid in Southern Africa, as a matter of faith, e.g. *status confessionis*.

The inspiration came from Martin Luther King, who was invited to speak at the Assembly in Uppsala, but was killed, and from Dietrich Bonhoeffer, who coined the phrase "the church for others" in his letters from a Nazi prison in 1944: "The church is the church only when it exists for others ... The church must share in the secular problems of ordinary human life, not dominating, but helping and serving." The theology of Dietrich Bonhoeffer became an important source of inspiration for many churches and theologians who had to understand and act in the age of secularization and social development after World War II. Instead of speaking about "the church *for* others," theologians like Theo Sundermeier and Johannes Aagaard would rather talk about "the church *with* others" in order to stress the solidarity among people and avoid the helper-syndrome. The church is not above or outside secular society, but an integral part of society in critical solidarity with the people and its aspirations for justice, peace, freedom, and mutual respect. This opened the door to several ways of formulating the role of the church in modern society. A significant example is the former GDR and bishop Albrecht Schönherr, who coined the phrase "Kirche im Sozialismus" as a leading ecclesiological concept during the Communist regime, but also in South Africa, Dietrich Bonhoeffer became an important source of inspiration for thelogoans like David J. Bosch, John de Gruchy, C.F. Beyers Naudé, and Desmond Tutu.[8]

In the ecumenical theology of mission, *humanization* became the goal of mission, and mission was understood as an overarching concept for social services, political activism, international development work, and the struggle to protect human rights. The distinction between church and world disappeared, because it was considered meaningless.

The emerging ecumenical mission paradigm was harshly criticized by Evangelical groups like the Lausanne Movement, who wanted to maintain a difference between church and world, salvation and humanization, and social work and evangelism. A parallel series of mission conferences were held since the early 1970s, organized by the World Council of Churches and the Lausanne Movement. During the last decade tensions have eased and new forms of cooperation are looked for, but the organizational split still exists.

Ecumenical Social Ethics

The ecumenical movement was born in an atmosphere of optimism. The First International World Mission Conference in Edinburgh in 1910 celebrated the idea of Christianizing the whole world within one generation. The ideals and superiority of Western Christianity were accepted without any discussion.[9] The scramble for Africa, organized around the three Cs: Christianization, Civilization, and Commerce, was

---

[8] P. Lodberg, *Faith and Power in the Holy Land* (København, 2010).
[9] T.M. Johnson, *Atlas of Global Christianity* (Edinburgh, 2009).

about the power struggle among European nations and Christian churches—not about the right of Christianity to consider itself as the civilizing force of modernity.

But the twentieth century took a dramatic new direction just four years after the jubilant atmosphere of 1910. World War I and its devastating consequences not only for Europe, where the war began, but for the whole world, was not clear from the beginning, but after World War II a totally new political situation was established. Old empires like the Ottomans or the British had disappeared or were declining, and they were replaced by new empires: the USSR and the United States. After World War II, new words like the Cold War and the Iron Curtain were invented to describe the new situation, and the United Nations was established as an arena for maintaining world peace through negotiation among the nations of the world. The Universal Declaration of Human Rights became an important instrument to avoid a repetition of the dehumanization and extermination of religious and political minorities in the Nazi concentration camps.

Ecumenical social ethics was developed in a constant dialogue with the unfolding political issues of the troublesome times of the twentieth century. Churches took an active part in peace keeping efforts prior to World War II and made a huge effort in refugee relief work after the war. The World Council of Churches was established in 1948 just like the United Nations, and leading ecumenists took an active part in the development of the Universal Declaration of Human Rights that was declared in 1948. Later on, many churches involved themselves in international relief work and humanitarian assistance to people living in poverty and under difficult economical situations.

A main issue in ecumenical social ethics has been to walk the fine line between theology and politics, church and state, in order to formulate the co-responsibility of the churches for society without being a political institution themselves. Prior to World War II, the concept of *middle axioms* (freedom, order, and peace) was established as the values that the churches should stand and work for in society. A leading idea about the relationship between state and church was formulated by Dietrich Bonhoeffer in his new interpretation of the Lutheran ideas of two kingdoms/regiments. Instead of a defensive understanding of the church's subordinating to the state under all circumstances, he called the churches to challenge the state when people were suffering—not for the churches to play a political role, but to challenge the state to live up to its responsibility as a proper state, e.g. a state that cares for the weakest and poorest of society.

After World War II the issue of decolonization and democratization of society became very important in ecumenical social ethics. In the history of ecumenical social ethics, the World Council of Churches Conference of 1966 in Geneva was a milestone and prompted a new discussion regarding the theological dimensions of "the secular." This was a move from strictly confessional theology, whether Orthodox, Roman Catholic, or Protestant, to theology that was praxis-oriented and took its material from the actual socio-economic and political challenges of the global situation. At the Geneva conference a theology of revolution formulated largely by Richard Shaull, a North American with considerable experience in Latin America, was extremely influential. Subsequently, social ecumenical ethics was inspired both by the theology of liberation represented by Ruben Alves and the political theology of hope espoused by Jürgen Moltmann. With an expression borrowed from Yves Congar and Gustavo Gutiérrez, these theologies can be characterized as "theologies of temporal realities," even though their advocates did not necessarily agree among themselves on every issue.[10] Nevertheless, they all shared a similar hermeneutic that sees the *humanum*, as it is revealed in the history of Jesus Christ, as the cornerstone both for theology and ecclesial practice. Theologies of revolution and liberation and other political theologies, which after the Uppsala assembly provided the basis for the World Council of Churches' activity with respect to justice and peace, agree that human experiences of suffering and injustice are essential to a proper understanding of the biblical story of salvation. Shaull, Alves, and Moltmann point to actual history as the place where all theology must begin and end.

The center of theology became "the people" and especially "the poor people from the underside of history." Thus, ecumenical social ethics was measured on the yardstick: what serves the poorest of the poor people, and what are the root causes that keep poor people in poverty. This allowed the ecumenical movement to support the process of decolonization in Africa and Asia together with the establishment of local governance and the establishment of national councils of churches that often became the social and political instruments of the local churches. New national identities were established through the struggle for political independence, and the churches took their part in building up new societies. Many of these African societies were ruled by one-party systems, but after the 1989 many of the African churches began to work for multi-political party-systems. Some of the inspiration came from the democratic struggle in South Africa and its first democratic election in 1994. But also the pressure from international donors was felt in many countries, and the concept of neo-colonialism was coined to understand the continuing dependency of African countries on the West. In recent years a theologian like Emmanuel Katongole from Uganda has challenged the fact that modern Africa has been especially vulnerable to chaos, war, and corruption.[11] He sees the African people caught in a seemingly endless cycle of violence, plunder, and poverty. Their resources are exploited and their lives wantonly sacrificed time and again to the greed and ambition of oppressive regimes. Katongole maintains that the nation-state as the successor of the colonial state has stood in the way of the development aspirations of Africans.

Today the issue of a real democratic state is not only linked to politics and economy, but also to the issue of climate change and ecology. Many people from the global South are on the move to the North because of drought as a consequence of climate change in their home countries. They are looking for personal and financial security in Europe and North America and they represent in blood and body the process of globalization: migration. When people move, they bring their culture and religion to a new place. Today, we realize that globalization and migration are challenging

---

[10] J. Briggs (ed.), *A History of the Ecumenical Movement* (Geneva, 2004).
[11] E. Katongole, *The Sacrifice of Africa: A Political Theology for Africa* (Grand Rapids, 2011).

political systems in many places, but they are also changing the cultural and religious environment in many old nation-states in Europe. The dramatic consequences of globalization are already challenging ecumenical social ethics and the churches that often play an important role for maintaining both tolerance in the society and a cohesive local or national culture.

Conclusion

Ecumenical theology is a child of the many social and political revolutions in the twentieth century. It has helped the churches to cope with the issues of strife, war, cold war, decolonization, secularization, migration, and globalization. Ecumenical theology has set a new standard in a pluralistic and globalized world: theology is a critical reflection on established practices in order to change an unjust world to the benefit of the ordinary person, and the theological work has to be done ecumenically, e.g. together and across confessional lines. The answers to new challenges are not necessarily found in the old confessional dogmatic formulations that worked on the principle of strife, disunity, and conflict, but in a corporate theological enterprise where confessional theology is an important resource for discussion, but not necessarily the answer to present challenges. Today, ecumenical theology is more important than ever in a globalized, pluralistic, and vulnerable world, because it helps us to think globally and act locally.

Bibliography

Bosch, D.J., *Transforming Mission: Paradigm Shifts in Theology of Mission* (Maryknoll: Orbis Books, 1993).

Briggs, J. (ed.), *A History of the Ecumenical Movement, Vol. 3: 1968–2000* (Geneva: World Council of Churches, 2004).

Gros, J. (ed.), *Growth in Agreement II. Reports and Agreed Statements of Ecumenical Conversations on a World Level, 1982–1998* (Geneva: World Council of Churches, 2000).

Gros, J. (ed.), *Growth in Agreement III. International Dialogue. Texts and Agreed Statements 1998–2005* (Geneva: World Council of Churches, 2007).

Johnson, T.M., *Atlas of Global Christianity 1910–2010* (Edinburgh: Edinburgh University Press, 2009).

Kasper, W., *Current Problems in Ecumenical Theology.* www.vatican.va.roman (accessed January 4, 2012), pp. 1–11.

Katongele, E., *The Sacrifice of Africa: A Political Theology for Africa* (Grand Rapids: Eerdmans Publishing Company, 2011).

Kinnamon, M. (ed.), *The Ecumenical Movement: An Anthology of Key Texts and Voices* (Geneva: World Council of Churches, 1997).

Lodberg, P., *Tro og magt i Det hellige Land. Palæstinensisk teologi og kirke i et transformationssamfund efter 1967* [*Faith and Power in the Holy Land. Palestinian Theology and Church in a Society in Transformation after 1967*] (København: Aros, 2010) (including an English summary).

Lossky, N. (ed.), *Dictionary of the Ecumenical Movement* (Geneva: World Council of Churches, 1991).

MacCulloch, D., *A History of Christianity* (London: Penguin Books, 2009).

Meyer, H. (ed.), *Growth in Agreement. Reports and Agreed Statements of Ecumenical Conversations on a World Level* (New York and Ramsey: Paulist Press, 1984).

Raiser, K., *Religion, Macht, Politik. Auf der Suche nach einer zukunftsfähigen Weltordnung* [*Religion, Power, Politics: In Search of a Sustainable World Order Ecumenical Dogmatics*] (Frankfurt a. Main: Verlag Otto Lembeck, 2010).

Schlink, E., *Ökumenische Dogmatik* [*Ecumenical Dogmatics*] (Göttingen: Vandenhoeck & Ruprecht, 1983).

Tjørhom, O. (ed.), *Apostolicity and Unity: Essays on the Porvoo Common Statement* (Grand Rapids: Eerdmans Publishing Company, 2002).

Chapter 51
Liberation Theology

Sturla J. Stålsett

What does faith mean when it is interpreted in the light of the experience of suffering, injustice, and the fight for liberation and better living conditions? This is the basic question in the theological current that has emerged under the name of "liberation theology." The question goes in both directions: What light does the experience of suffering shed on the sources and traditions of faith? And what insight and inspiration does faith provide for the everyday struggle in the encounter with poverty, discrimination, and oppression?

Liberation theology can be called a result of a double shift in theological reflection in the second half of the twentieth century. The first involves a contextual shift, and we can call the second a victimological shift.

The contextual shift enquires into the "where" of theology. Within philosophy, literary studies, and theology, there has been a renewed hermeneutical interest in the presuppositions and character of interpretation and understanding. This has led sociologists of knowledge to undertake a critical examination of the societal presuppositions and conditions for the development of new knowledge. In tandem with this, contextual theology emerges, with a critical awareness of how context and theological writing influence each other, even in terms of content.[1]

The "where" of theology is necessarily linked closely to a question about "who," that is to say, about theology's biographical anchoring and presupposition. Who is the theological subject? Whose life experiences are allowed to form the questions and the perspectives?

The victimological shift investigates this question about the "who" of theology. Its aim is to make theology a concrete service of the poor and the outcast. The question about God is posed from the perspective of the victims. The basic presupposition of liberation theology is a position with regard to injustice and distress that is often summed up in the phrase "a preferential option for the poor."[2]

---

[1] S.B. Bevans, *Models of Contextual Theology* (Maryknoll, N.Y.: 1992); S. Bergmann, *Gud i funksjon* (Stockholm, 1997).

[2] This was the title of the concluding document of the third Conference of Latin American bishops at Puebla in 1979, see A.T. Hennelly (ed.), *Liberation Theology* (Maryknoll, N.Y.: 1990), pp. 253–8. It has been seen as a summary and a confirmation of what had been the principal concern of liberation theology from the outset. See G. Gutiérrez, *Teología de la liberacion* (Salamanca, 1984), p. 15.

This necessarily entails a pluralization of theological perspectives and expressions. There are potentially as many theologies of liberation as there are contexts and forms of poverty in a broad sense – oppression, discrimination, and marginalization.

Why then is it meaningful to operate with a collective term such as "liberation theology"? The primary reason is the common concern to allow faith to be heard and to be put into practice as a critical and constructive power in the encounter with marginalization. At the same time, we can say that the many different theologies of liberation have their genesis in the same theological renewal that took place in the 1960s and 1970s; and one of the most important places of origin of this renewal was the Latin American continent. Together with feminist theology and Black theology in South Africa and the USA, Latin American liberation theology has given both form and content to basic elements in the subsequently elaboration of a variety of liberation theologies. In the present essay, accordingly, we shall concentrate on Latin American liberation theology as representative and largely normative for what is meant by the term "liberation theology."

Among the most trendsetting liberation theologians in the Catholic church, we find Juan Luis Segundo, Enrique Dussel, Gustavo Gutiérrez, Leonardo Boff, Clodovis Boff, Franz Hinkelammert, Hugo Assmann, Ignacio Ellacuría, Jon Sobrino, José Severino Croatto, Maria Pilar Aquino, and Ivone Gebara. In the Protestant churches, we have names such as Rubem Alves, José Míguez Bonino, Elsa Tamez, Jorge Pixley, and Victorio Araya.

Context: From Development to Liberation

The new theological orientation that occurred in the Latin American continent in the course of the 1960s took the form of a step away from a harmonizing paradigm of development to a more critical and conflictual paradigm of liberation.

Poverty was widespread on the continent, and had been so for generations. In the 1950s, however, there was a new optimism that modernization would also bring prosperity and development to most Latin Americans too. Poverty had long been seen primarily as a deficiency disease: poverty was due to a lack of development. The solution to this predicament would lie in a supply of knowledge and capital from the rich countries to the poor countries, which would in this way catch up with the living standards and level of development of the rich. Development would come about through imitation of the political and economic strategies of the rich countries. At the same time, this would not entail any loss or decline in living standards in the rich countries. On the contrary, a better economy in the South would stimulate world trade, and would thus benefit the countries in the North too. It was a harmony-model of this kind that lay behind President John F. Kennedy's large-scale plan for Latin America at the beginning of the 1960s, the so-called "Alliance for progress."

In the course of the 1960s, however, there was a break with this widespread understanding. The optimistic climate of the 1950s was contradicted by the evidence in the 1960s that prosperity for all was not an automatic consequence of modernization. One of the first who broke fundamentally with the whole paradigm of modernization was the Mexican Rodolfo Stavenhagen, in his essay on "seven mistaken theses about Latin America" (1966).[3] He was soon joined by others (F.H. Cardoso, T. Dos Santos, O. Sunkel, and not least A. Gunder Frank). These *dependistas* (theoreticians of dependence) focused more strongly on the political and historical aspects of the negative relationship of dependence between the center and the periphery. Sunkel claimed that underdevelopment in the poor nations must be seen as the *normal* effect of existing international relations, and that it has a *concrete* history that requires a thorough analysis. It is useless for countries on the periphery to copy the modernization strategy of the rich lands, unless something is done both internationally and nationally to change the political-structural conditions.

This means the abandonment of optimism with regard to development and the modernization paradigm. Latin America cannot develop itself out of dependence. What is needed is "liberation." In reality, the breakthrough of the "dependence school" entails a transition from harmony to conflict, from reform to revolution, and from development to liberation.

This break with the development paradigm had consequences for other academic disciplines too. One particularly pioneering move was the introduction of liberation as a central concept in pedagogy by the Brazilian Paulo Freire (Freire 1972). In the same way, this concept came to set its mark on the emerging theological reflection in Latin America in this period.

Gutiérrez: Liberation as the Primary Theological Concept

The Peruvian Catholic theologian Gustavo Gutiérrez was one of the first to enact this transition from *development* to *liberation* in theology too. In his book *Teología de la Liberación. Perspectivas*, published in Lima in 1971, Gutiérrez clearly aligns himself with the *dependista* school. Gutiérrez claims that while development has become synonymous with reform politics and modernization, there is an increasing recognition in Latin America that something else is needed. The poor countries must fight to break the dominance by the rich countries, to which they are subjected.[4]

In this perspective, it is more exact, and more humane, to speak of a process of liberation, even if this is necessarily more conflictual. Gutiérrez points out that every liberation contains an inevitable element of rupture that is not present in the idea of development. Liberation cannot be a mere repetition of the internal ruptures that are known from the rich countries in the center,[5] because the situation of the poor countries is different. The Latin Americans must form their *own* liberation. What is at stake in all processes of liberation – in the North as in the South, in the East as in the

---

[3] "Siete Teses Erróneas sobre América Latina," first published in the Mexican newspaper *El Día* in June, 1965.

[4] G. Gutiérrez, *Teología de la liberación*, pp. 51ff. (cited from the 10th ed., Salamanca, 1984).

[5] Gutiérrez (1984), p. 53.

West – is "the possibilities of leading an authentically human existence; a free life, a freedom that is process and historical conquest."[6]

Gutiérrez thus widens the perspective. The liberation of which he speaks is not just the break by the poor countries and groups with domination by the rich. It is a comprehensive historical process in which human beings take their destiny into their own hands and form their future through a raising of consciousness and goal-oriented praxis.

Gutiérrez shares this analysis with a number of contemporary sociologists. The original point is that he makes it the basis of a theological study: What is the relationship between the liberation process that is necessary in society and the salvation that Christianity proclaims?[7]

Gutiérrez claims that there is a connection. He distinguishes three levels of meaning in the concept of liberation.[8] First, there is the *historical-political* level. The term "liberation" designates what the oppressed social classes and peoples need and strive to attain. It underlines the conflictual aspect in the economic, societal, and political process. Secondly, there is a deeper level that we could call *historical-existential*. Here, the term is used about the understanding of history as the process of the human person's liberation, in which one acquires a conscious relationship to one's own situation in the framework of the changes that history brings. Liberation in this sense expresses a demand for a free unfolding of all the human dimensions, "a gradual conquest of real and creative freedom [that] leads to a permanent cultural revolution, to the forming of a new human person, of a society that is qualitatively different."[9]

Thirdly, Gutiérrez introduces the *soteriological* level. Liberation in the biblical sense is what Christ brings to the human person.

Christ the Redeemer liberates the human person from sin, which is the deepest cause of all hostility, all injustice and oppression, and he gives the human person authentic freedom. That is to say, he brings the human person into fellowship with himself. This is the foundation of all human brotherhood.[10]

It is important for Gutiérrez to underline that these three levels of meaning are not parallel or chronologically successive. Instead, this is "a unified and complex process that finds its profound meaning and its definitive accomplishment in the redeeming work of Christ." Gutiérrez affirms that the levels cannot be separated; they imply each other reciprocally.

Here, we catch sight of a centrally important mark of liberation-theological reflection, which it shares with postmodern theology (see Jayne Svenungsson's essay in the present book), namely, the opposition to the classical dualism, the refusal to accept the traditional idea of two sharply distinct spheres, a spiritual and a worldly

---

[6] Ibid., 47.
[7] Gutiérrez (1984), p. 73.
[8] Gutiérrez (1984), pp. 68–9.
[9] Gutiérrez (1984), p. 68.
[10] Gutiérrez (1984), p. 69.

sphere. The history of salvation is nothing that is different from or outside the history of human beings. Rather, it comes to expression in and through this history. This means that theology's task is to interpret "the signs of the times,"[11] that is to say, to look for God's (absence and) presence in human history. The goal is to provide inspiration for liberating action in faith and in solidarity with those chosen by God – the poor and the victims – thereby taking part in and receiving God's salvific action.

Liberation theology arises through this confluence of critical societal analysis and theological reflection, and very quickly attracts considerable attention, even outside Latin America. At roughly the same time, a specifically Black liberation theology and feminist theology emerge, and many claim that this signals a paradigm shift in theology, especially in a methodological sense.

Method and Structure: Theology in Two Acts

According to Gutiérrez, liberation theology is "critical reflection on praxis in the light of God's Word." This means that the theological reflection comes here as "the second act," following one particular type of historical experience and action.[12]

The "first act" can in turn be divided into two parts. First comes experience, then a reaction to experience, which is expressed in action. One of the first academic theologians in Scandinavia to be inspired by liberation theology, Per Frostin, borrowed Edward Schillebeeckx' concept of "contrast experience" to describe the starting point of liberation theology's work.[13] This can be an experience of one's own suffering and exclusion, or an encounter with other people's experience. This is initially a passive experience, a discovery of how reality looks "from the reverse side." Immediately, however, there is a reaction to this experience, a mobilization, a working and struggling for change – "liberation." This can be an organized political struggle, or the daily endeavor to survive and to achieve worthy living conditions.[14] It is not based *a priori* on a religious conviction or conversion, but is generated by an "ethical indignation,"[15] a raising of the socio-political consciousness with regard to an "injustice that cries out to heaven,"[16] or a spontaneous act of mercy and solidarity when faced with the suffering of another person.[17]

---

[11] See J.L. Segundo, *Liberation of Theology* (Maryknoll, N.Y.: 1976), p. 40; Gutiérrez (1984), p. 30.

[12] Gutiérrez (1984), p. 35.

[13] P. Frostin, *Liberation Theology in Tanzania and South Africa* (Lund, 1988).

[14] In Latin American feminist theology, "daily life" (*la vida cotidiana*) receives particular emphasis as a hermeneutical starting point. See M.P. Aquino: *Our Cry for Life. Feminist Theology from Latin America* (Maryknoll, N.Y.: Orbis Books, 1993).

[15] L. Boff, *La fe en la periferia del mundo* (Santander, 1981), p. 14. See C. Boff and L. Boff, *Introducing Liberation Theology* (Tunbridge Wells: Burns & Oates, 1987), pp. 1–4.

[16] See the document on justice issued by the Latin American episcopal conference at Medellín in Colombia in 1968. A.T. Hennelly, *Liberation Theology* (Maryknoll, N.Y.: 1990), p. 97.

[17] J. Sobrino, *The Principle of Mercy* (Maryknoll, N.Y.: 1994).

This discovery of the poor person does not always happen automatically. Often, it must be forced to happen. It is this that Gutiérrez means when he speaks of "the breaking-in of the poor person" (*irrupción del pobre*) into the public sphere of society.[18] It is through active organization and action that the poor person achieves his goal, makes his voice heard, and calls others to give an account of themselves. For Gutiérrez, this is the most outstanding and important sign in our times, and it is a summons to conversion and to a new praxis with regard to the one who is excluded. Neutrality is challenged. In the encounter with the suffering of the poor person, one cannot remain an onlooker – for otherwise, one becomes a sharer in guilt.

Here, we see the provocative partisanship of liberation theology. It presupposes that one takes a stance that is ultimately anchored in the belief that God has taken the side of the poor person. God is the God of the poor, and thereby – *only* thereby – the God of all human persons.

This is also a call to the poor themselves to rediscover their own dignity and demand their rights.[19] They must be the principal agents in their own process of liberation.[20] They must be recognized and constituted as subjects. The influence from Freire is clear here.

These are two aspects of the first act in a liberation-theological method. It is in principle "pre-theological." Being personally affected by – or allowing oneself to be affected by other people's experience of – injustice and suffering, and then acting in order to overcome this situation is not something based *a priori* on any religious insight or faith. But in a continent like Latin America, where secularization has made so few inroads, this will most often take place *de facto* in the framework of one or other form of spirituality or praxis of faith.

This first step consists in a discovery and interpretation of the historical and societal context. This means that to a greater degree than other theological currents, liberation theology finds its most important dialogue partners in the social sciences. In many ways, sociology, political science, economics, and social anthropology take over the dominant role that philosophy had in theology in the past.

The many critics of liberation theology have seized precisely on this point, since it is clear that much in the analysis of society, especially in the sociology that was dominant in the 1960s (for example, the "dependence school" or Freire's *Pedagogy of the Oppressed*), was inspired by Marxism. This caused considerable skepticism (to put it mildly) in the two centers of power in relation to the poor in Latin America, namely, Washington and Rome. The liberation theologians were met with massive criticism, and sometimes persecution, both within and outside the church. Documents of military strategy drawn up in the USA saw liberation theology as a threat to security.[21] Thousands of liberation theologians, priests, nuns, and deacons have paid with their

---

[18] Gutiérrez (1984), p. 30.
[19] Gutiérrez, *La fuerza histórica de los pobres* (Salamanca, 1982), p. 52.
[20] Gutiérrez (1984), p. 387.
[21] See especially the so-called Santa Fe documents; see, e.g., Ph. Berrymann, *Liberation Theology* (London, 1987), p. 3.

lives in assassinations and acts of war since the emergence of liberation of theology. Among the best known are the murders in El Salvador, first of Archbishop Romero in 1980 and then of Ignacio Ellacuría and five of his Jesuit confrères and two of their colleagues in 1989.

It is in the midst of this experience of injustice and the struggle to overcome it that theological reflection comes in – but as the *second* step (re-flection). The basic intuition is simple: "the societal situation in Latin America is in conflict with the Gospel."[22] The task of theological reflection is to undergird this intuition and to unfold its implications, thus contributing to inspiration and to insight into what can be done to tackle the problems. This takes the form of a critical and constructive analysis of the praxis that aims to create change. The criteria of evaluation are found in the sources of faith: "reflection on praxis in the light of God's Word."

The programmatic goal is not only to integrate theology into the work on behalf of liberation, but also to liberate theology from its captivity in one particular cultural and political context – namely, the European context, the bourgeois and male-dominated (or patriarchal) church.[23] The focus lies more on correct action (orthopraxis) than on correct doctrine (orthodoxy).

The Content of Theology: Principal Characteristics and Core Points

What are the characteristics and the content of this theological reflection? One important ecclesial presupposition for the emergence of liberation theology was certainly the Second Vatican Council (1962–65). At least three factors have left clear traces.

First, the Council represented an opening to the modern world, an aggiornamento. This involves a contextualization. But unlike the situation in Europe, where this entailed a positive new orientation in relation to the good things of the modern age and an acknowledgement of the mature, autonomous subject in society, aggiornamento in Latin America meant a focus on the reverse side of the modernization project and a discovery of those persons who had not been accorded the status of subjects in practical politics. This was the first time that the church took serious note of the widespread poverty on the continent as a problem that also affected the church. The conference of Latin American bishops at Medellín in 1968 marked a breakthrough, or indeed a societal conversion, for the Catholic church in Latin America.

Secondly, much of the theology that inspired the Vatican Council (Karl Rahner, Yves Congar, and many others) contained a new thinking about the relationship between immanence and transcendence that made possible liberation theology's close coupling of liberation and salvation – which was also expressed in the slogan of "only one history."

---

[22] Gutiérrez, Liberation Praxis and Christian Faith (London, 1980), p. 27.
[23] Segundo, *Liberation of Theology*, 1976.

Last but not least, the Vatican Council contributed to a contextualization and popularization of the Bible in Latin America. The priests' monopoly on biblical interpretation was abolished, and the Mass was no longer celebrated in Latin, but in the local languages. This opened up the sources of faith in a new, more direct, and non-hierarchical way for the numerous poor believers.

In a number of places, the shortage of priests meant that laypersons played the central role in the life of the communities, undisturbed by priestly or episcopal interference. Basis communities emerged in which the Bible was read and interpreted in the light of concrete experiences of a shortage of water and electricity, unemployment, violence, and political oppression.[24] The Exodus narrative became a much appreciated account of the God who intervenes on the side of the oppressed and leads them to a new land in freedom. Jesus was called Christ the Liberator, the one who brings "good news to the poor." They read with a sense of recognition about how he was persecuted, tortured, and killed, like so many poor people in Latin America who fight for liberation. Christ's resurrection was no longer seen as a sign that poverty and suffering find their solution only on the far side of the gates of death, but rather as a sign that by raising up the crucified Jesus, God shows that he is on the side of the victims. And the kingdom of God was understood as the promise of a society in which the oppressed receive freedom – not one day far off, but here and now.

This made the life of faith and the exegesis of scripture in the basis communities a primary context for the development of a popular liberation theology. The more academic and systematic theology at the academic institutes developed in a reciprocal interplay with this popular theology.[25]

This means that we have already mentioned some of the fundamental themes in liberation theology. Since its primary contribution is a new method and a new perspective, all the classic themes of theology are in principle taken up and discussed.[26]

The popular Bible reading has led to – and has in turn been shaped by – a liberation-theological biblical hermeneutics. The leading figures here are José Severino Croatto,[27] Jorge Pixley, and Carlos Mesters (Mesters, 1989). In recent years, this hermeneutics has been taken to a deeper level and differentiated in many creative readings from various socio-cultural and sociopolitical positions (Indian, Afro-Caribbean, Latin American feminist).

The starting point for reflection on the being of God is that God reveals himself as the God of the poor.[28] God's partisanship and solidarity with "the poor, foreigners, widows, and orphans" is a basic theme. God is a God who shows himself in history in absence and presence, in a dialectic between a God who is *semper maior* and

---

[24] G. Cook, *The Expectation of the Poor* (New York, 1985).
[25] Boff, *Epistemología y métode de la teología de la liberación* (San Salvador, 1991).
[26] J. Ellacuría and J. Sobrino (eds), *Mysterium Liberationis* (Maryknoll, N.Y., 1993).
[27] J.S. Croatto, *Biblical Hermeneutics* (Maryknoll, N.Y., 1987).
[28] Sobrino, *Dios* (Madrid, 1983); Gutiérrez, *On Job* (Maryknoll, N.Y., 1987); Gutiérrez, *The God of Life* (Maryknoll, N.Y., 1991).

semper menor, writes Jon Sobrino. The mystery of God is concealed in the tension between the continued presence of suffering and the promise of freedom and salvation, between cross and resurrection, between theodicy and Gospel. This tension can be resolved only in a concrete praxis of discipleship where one walks with God in the midst of history's ambiguity. This means that the possibility of knowing God has a practical presupposition, and the work for justice, inspired by faith, becomes a form of mystagogy, an introduction to the mystery. Perhaps the most original aspect of liberation theology's elaboration of the doctrine of God is linked to the antithesis between God and idol.[29] This theme occurs relatively early on, as a criticism of European theology's one-sided focus on the challenge from atheism. The liberation theologians claim that the challenge in Latin America is not the lack of worship of God, but the idols that hide themselves in the political and economic structures. This sharp criticism has been amplified above all by the ecumenical research center Departamento Ecuménico de Investigaciones (DEI) in Costa Rica under the guidance of the economists and philosophers Hugo Assmann and Franz Hinkelammert. They reacted to the triumph of neoliberalism in Latin America and the rest of the world in the course of the 1990s by formulating a theological analysis in which economics is presented as a quasi-religious system.[30] The market is given divine status in dominant political and economic thinking. The economic laws have taken over the role of God's commandments, and the social costs of the structural economic adjustments imposed by the International Monetary Fund and the World Bank on all the debtor lands become "necessary human sacrifices." From a characteristically Protestant starting point, the Mexican Methodist Elsa Tamez has pointed out a liberating potential in the Pauline idea of justification by faith precisely in the context of a market-fundamentalist system like this.[31]

The major detailed studies of Christology are by the Brazilian Franciscan Leonard Boff[32] and the Basque-Salvadorian Jesuit Jon Sobrino.[33] The contextual approach leads in both these theologians to a strong focus on the connection between the suffering people and the suffering Jesus. In keeping with the historical-transcendental approach inspired by Karl Rahner, it is accordingly the human, historical Jesus who is at the center of the interpretation, although this (in the view of the liberation theologians themselves) does not weaken Jesus' divine side.

This means that the cross is given a central place in a context in which, as they see it, "Good Friday continues." Perhaps the most audacious new formulation in this field

---

[29] P. Richard, *La lucha de los dioses* (San José, Managua, 1980).

[30] F.J. Hinkelammert, *The Ideological Weapons of Death* (Maryknoll, N.Y., 1985); H. Assmann and F.J. Hinkelammert, *A Idolatria do Mercado* (Petrópolis, 1989); H. Assmann (ed.), *Sobre ídolos y sacrificios* (San José, 1991).

[31] E. Tamez, *The Amnesty of Grace* (Nashville, 1993).

[32] Boff, *Jesus Christo libertador* (Petrópolis, 1972); Boff, *Passion of Christ* (Maryknoll, N.Y., 1987).

[33] Sobrino, *Christology at the Crossroads* (Maryknoll, N.Y., 1978); Sobrino, *Dios* (Madrid, 1993); Sobrino, *Christ the Liberator* (Maryknoll, N.Y., 2001).

comes from Jon Sobrino, under inspiration from I. Ellacuría, Archbishop Romero, and others, when he reflects on those who suffer and are oppressed today as "the crucified people," that is to say, the crucified body of Christ in history.[34]

The orientation to the cross and the noticeable influence from Jürgen Moltmann, not least on Sobrino's early work, have led to accusations that the Jesuit Sobrino has become something of a Protestant. In this context, we should note that liberation theology has in principle a naturally ecumenical character. It is not concerned with the classical boundary lines between the confessions. The decisive point is whether or not the perspective and the fate of the poor are allowed to exercise a genuine influence on how we speak about God. There is also a considerable potential for religious dialogue here, but this has developed only to a small extent in the relatively homogeneous religious context in Latin America.

Liberation-theological ecclesiology has its starting point in the emergence and the experiences of the basis communities. Here, it is above all Leonard Boff who has done the pioneer work, and who has had to pay the price. In his books *Church, Charism and Power* and *Ecclesiogenesis*,[35] he criticizes the hierarchical church model in the Catholic church and points to the basis communities as representing a renewal and a challenge. These see the church as born from below with a flat structure and with the full participation of the entire people of God. This is a remedy for a number of pathological traits in the church that has its center in Rome.

Boff did not have to wait long for an answer from Rome. Cardinal Joseph Ratzinger, at that time prefect of the Congregation for the Doctrine of the Faith, initiated a severe reprimand of Boff. After many years of negotiations, disciplinary measures, and a great deal of public attention, Boff finally gave up his priestly ministry.[36]

Criticism and Renewal

The Vatican's opposition to liberation theology has had both theological and more administrative and church-political expressions. The most important theological critique is formulated in the two Instructions that were published in 1984 and 1986,[37] but the administrative and church-political measures to tame the liberation theologians and silence them were the more effective weapon. Liberation-theological seminaries were closed, and the most radical bishops were wing-clipped and then slowly but surely replaced by conservative successors.

This massive opposite from the central church authority was one of the reasons why liberation theology, after its most productive phase in the 1970s and 1980s, lost

---

[34] See S.J. Stålsett, *The Crucified and the Crucified* (Berne et al., 2003).
[35] Boff, *Church, Charism and Power* (New York, 1985); Boff, *Ecclesiogenesis* (Maryknoll, N.Y., 1986).
[36] *Congregation for the Doctrine of the Faith* in A.T. Hennelly (ed.), *Liberation Theology* (Maryknoll, N.Y., 1990); see K. Nordstokke, *Ekklesiogenese* (Oslo, 1990).
[37] See Hennelly, *Liberation Theology* (Maryknoll, N.Y., 1990).

much of the interest it had attracted, and much of its influence, in the 1990s. Another reason was the societal development.

As in the rest of the world, the year 1989 was a decisive caesura for the radical forces in Latin America. The neoliberal wave washed over this continent too, and all the alternatives to the existing social order were judged to be dead and powerless after the fall of the Berlin Wall. Although liberation theology as a theological orientation assuredly had a greater distance vis-à-vis concrete leftwing political projects than many of its critics alleged, there can be little doubt that the new zeitgeist drained liberation theology of strength and popular support. Liberation theology had been inspired by the vision of a societal change that would benefit the poor and the oppressed, but there was little sign of this now. Instead of the liberation of the poor, there came the liberalization of market forces. In the religious sphere, it seems that it was the Pentecostals who succeeded in putting forward an answer to the needs of the poor majority of the population in a neoliberal age. If we may exaggerate somewhat, we may say that whereas the liberation theologians had taken a position in favor of the poor, the poor themselves chose to become Pentecostals.

The character of the popular resistance struggle changed in the same period, and became less explicitly political. The civil wars ended and the military dictatorships disappeared. Party politics gradually became discredited in the wake of technocratic and corrupt regimes with the neoliberalism of the 1990s. But new popular movements emerged. The most prominent were the movement of those without land in Brazil and the Indian movements in Chiapas (Mexico) and Bolivia.

As a counterpart to the World Economic Forum in Davos, The World Social Forum in Porto Alegre in southern Brazil was founded, representing a global force and a renewal of popular opposition to globalization. At the start of the new millennium, after terrible examples of misjudged neoliberalism, the political pendulum swung back to the left, with Social Democratic and socialist presidents in a number of countries: Brazil, Argentina, Chile, Uruguay, Venezuela, Bolivia, and Nicaragua.

This situation has led liberation theology to a refreshing self-criticism and renewal. One of the most important objections to the "classic" liberation theology was that its subject was too one-dimensional (despite somewhat different intentions). "The poor person" was placed in the center; but socio-economic exclusion is far from the only mechanism of oppression. The poor are many and various, and they have different needs and projects.

This generates a great plurality: Indian theology, Latin American feminist theology (which criticizes both Western feminist theology and male-dominated liberation theology), Afro-Caribbean theology, earth theology, etc. An old and a new generation of liberation theologians from the whole world met at a World Forum on Theology and Liberation that was arranged for the first time in 2003 in connection with the World Social Forum.[38]

We may leave open the question whether it is because of this renewal that the Vatican continues to look at liberation theology with critical eyes. It reached the title

---

[38] See http://www.pucrs.br/pastoral/fmtl/ (accessed November 3, 2011).

of a Vatican document again in March, 2007, when the Congregation for the Doctrine of the Faith published a *Notificatio*, a serious warning, in connection with Jon Sobrino's Christology, asserting that this contains "serious errors" and can be "a danger" for the faithful. In other words, Cardinal Ratzinger (now Pope Benedict XVI) has not abandoned his vigorous campaign against liberation theology.

There are above all two concerns that guide the Vatican's criticism of Jon Sobrino's books and raise the temperature in its documents. First, there is the question of who is entitled to produce theology, who has the right to interpret the texts and the tradition. The monopoly on interpretation in the church is at stake here. In keeping with the liberation-theological principle of the "position in favor of the poor," Sobrino chooses what he calls "the church of the poor" as the privileged locus of interpretation for his theological work. The Congregation for the Doctrine of the Faith rejects this totally. The only proper locus for theology is the apostolic faith, as this is transmitted by the church through all the generations. Every other starting point for theological work risks distorting the content of faith. This amounts to a rejection of the basic stance of contextual theology, and the magisterium's monopoly on interpretation is upheld in the strongest possible terms.

The second point is the question of the radicality of God's humanity in Christ. Sobrino is criticized for overemphasizing the human and historical Jesus. These two accusations are closely linked, and point very precisely back to the specific starting point of liberation theology, to what I have called the contextual and victimological shift. By starting in the daily life of the one who is poor and excluded, and insisting that it is not only possible, but also necessary for Christian theology to choose the victims' perspective, liberation theology continues to prompt debate, opposition, and renewal.

Bibliography

Aquino, M.P., *Our Cry for Life. Feminist Theology from Latin America* (Maryknoll: Orbis Books, 1993).

Assmann, H. (ed.), *Sobre ídolos y sacrificios. René Girard con teólogos de la liberación* (San José: Departamento Ecuménico de Investigaciones, 1991).

Assmann, H. and F.J. Hinkelammert, *A Idolatria do Mercado. Ensaio sobre Economia e Teología* (Petrópolis: Vozes, 1989).

Bergmann, S., *Gud i funktion. En orientering i den kontextuelle teologin* (Stockholm: Verbum, 1997).

Berrymann, P., *Liberation Theology. The Essential Facts about the Revolutionary Movement in Latin America and Beyond* (London: I.B. Tauris & co LTD, 1987).

Bevans, S.B., *Models of Contextual Theology* (Maryknoll, N.Y.: Orbis Books, 1992).

Boff, C., *Epistemología y método de la teología de la liberación. Mysterium liberationis. Conceptos fundamentales de la teología de la liberación. I. Ellacuría y J. Sobrino* (San Salvador: UCA Editores, 1991), 1:79–113.

Boff, L., *Jesus Cristo libertador: ensaio de cristologia crítica para o nosso tempo* (Petrópolis: Editora Vozes, 1972).
Boff, L., *La fe en la periferia del mundo. El caminar de la iglesia con los oprimidos. Presencia Teológica* (Santander: Sal Terrae, 1981).
Boff, L., *Church, Charism and Power: A Radical Ecclesiology* (New York: Crossroad, 1985).
Boff, L., *Ecclesiogenesis: The Base Communities Reinvent the Church* (Maryknoll, N.Y.: Orbis Books, 1986).
Boff, L., *Passion of Christ, Passion of the World. The Facts, Their Interpretation, and Their Meaning Yesterday and Today* (Maryknoll, N.Y.: Orbis Books, 1987).
Congregation for the Doctrine of the Faith, "Notification Sent to Fr. Leonardo Boff regarding Errors in His Book, 'Church: Charism and Power'" (March 11, 1985), in A.T. Hennelly (ed.), *Liberation Theology* (see below).
Cook, G., *The Expectation of the Poor. Latin American Base Communities in Protestant Perspective* (New York: Orbis Books, 1985).
Croatto, J.S., *Biblical Hermeneutics. Toward a Theory of Reading as the Production of Meaning* (Maryknoll, N.Y.: Orbis Books, 1987).
Ellacuría, J. and J. Sobrino (eds), *Mysterium Liberationis. Fundamental Concepts of Liberation Theology* (Maryknoll, N.Y.: Orbis Books, 1993).
Freire, P., *Pedagogy of the Oppressed* (London: Harmondsworth), 1972.
Frostin, P., *Liberation Theology in Tanzania and South Africa* (Lund: Lund University Press, 1988).
Gutiérrez, G., *Liberation Praxis and Christian Faith. Frontiers of Theology in Latin America.* R. Gibellini (London: SCM Press, 1980), 1–33.
Gutiérrez, G., *La fuerza histórica de los pobres* (Salamanca: Ediciones Sígueme, 1982).
Gutiérrez, G., *Teología de la liberación. Perspectiva* (Salamanca: Ediciones Sígueme, 1984).
Gutiérrez, G., *On Job. God-Talk and the Suffering of the Innocent* (Maryknoll, N.Y.: Orbis Books, 1987).
Gutiérrez, G., *The God of Life* (Maryknoll, N.Y.: Orbis Books, 1991).
Hennelly, A.T. (ed.), *Liberation Theology. A Documentary History* (Maryknoll: Orbis Books, 1990).
Hinkelammert, F.J., *The Ideological Weapons of Death. A Theological Critique of Capitalism* (Maryknoll, N.Y.: Orbis Books, 1985).
Mesters, C., *Defenseless Flower: A New Reading of the Bible* (Maryknoll, N.Y.: Orbis Books, 1989).
Nordstokke, K., *Ekklesiogenese. Konsil og kontekst i Leonardo Boffs ekklesiologi* (Oslo: Diakonhjemmets høgskolesenter, 1990). English: *Council and Conflict in Leonardo Boff's Ecclesiology* (Lewiston: Edwin Mellen Press, 1996).
Richard, P., *La lucha de los dioses. Los ídolos de la opresión y la búsqueda del Dios liberador* (San José, Managua: Departamento Ecuménico de Investigaciones/Centro Antonio Valdivieso, 1980).
Segundo, J.L., *Liberation of Theology* (Maryknoll, N.Y.: Orbis Books, 1976).
Sobrino, J., *Christology at the Crossroads. A Latin American Approach* (Maryknoll, N.Y.: Orbis Books, 1978).

Sobrino, J., *Dios. Conceptos fundamentales de la pastoral.* C. Floristán y J.-J. Tamayo (Madrid, 1983), pp. 248–64.

Sobrino, J., *El principio-misericordia. Bajar de la cruz a los pueblos crucificados* (Santander: Sal Terrae, 1992). English: *The Principle of Mercy. Taking the Crucified People from the Cross* (Maryknoll, N.Y.: Orbis Books, 1994).

Sobrino, J., *Jesus the Liberator. A Historical-Theological Reading of Jesus of Nazareth* (Maryknoll, N.Y.: Orbis Books, 1994).

Sobrino, J., *Christ the Liberator: A View from the Victim* (Maryknoll, N.Y.: Orbis Books, 2001).

Stålsett, S.J., *The Crucified and the Crucified. A Study in the Liberation Christology of Jon Sobrino* (Berne et al.: Peter Lang, 2003).

Tamez, E., *The Amnesty of Grace: Justification by Faith from a Latin American Perspective* (Nashville: Abingdon Press, 1993).

Chapter 52
Pentecostal Theology: Historic Accents and Current Trends

Frank D. Macchia

William J. Seymour, the son of former African slaves, was the key figure in the Apostolic Faith Mission at Azusa Street in Los Angeles from which Pentecostalism expanded near the turn of the twentieth century as a global movement, and he was arguably one of the most creative thinkers of the movement's early years.[1] He captured well the cluster of pneumatological themes that formed the early nucleus of Pentecostal beliefs. The "crown jewel" of that cluster had to do with what was termed the "baptism in the Holy Spirit." Seymour described the repentant sinner's experience of Spirit baptism this way:

> The Lord has mercy on him for Christ's sake and puts eternal life in his soul, pardoning him of his sins, washing away his guilty pollution, and he stands before God justified as though he had never sinned ... Jesus takes that soul that has eternal life in it and presents it to God for thorough cleansing and purging from all Adamic sin ... Now he is on the altar for the fire of God to fall, which is the baptism with the Holy Ghost. It is the free gift upon the sanctified, cleansed heart.[2]

This Spirit baptism or gift of heavenly fire upon the sanctified life for Seymour was the gift of power for witness in the world (Acts 1:8). Following the nineteenth-century Wesleyan Holiness Movement, Seymour was conditioned to think of one's participation in the Christian life and mission as a series of crisis experiences (conversion, sanctification, Spirit baptism or empowerment) by which one is fully cleansed and consecrated for one's divinely-ordained vocation in the world, the epitome of which was to bring the goodness of God to the peoples of the world. Unlike the Holiness Movement, however, Seymour and other early Pentecostals defined Spirit baptism as the empowerment of the sanctified life (its release in the world as a force for witness) rather than as sanctification itself.

---

[1] Though Seymour developed his early theology of Spirit baptism from the teachings of Charles Parham in Kansas City, he elaborated on it creatively and was influential in leading the Azusa Street mission in Los Angeles, which functioned as a kind of hub for the spread of global Pentecostalism.

[2] William J. Seymour, "The Way into the Holiest," *The Apostolic Faith*, 1(2) (1906), p. 4.

Was he splitting hairs between sanctification and empowerment? Perhaps. Singaporean Pentecostal Pastor, David Lim, noted that Spirit baptism for Pentecostals was actually an enhancement of sanctification, as a "vocational sanctification."[3] Pentecostals viewed the church from the beginning as a missionary fellowship sanctified and empowered by the Spirit to bring the blessings of God to the nations before Christ returns. Speaking in tongues and other extraordinary spiritual gifts such as prophecy, word of knowledge and divine healing (1 Cor. 12:8–10) were highlighted as signs that the church is in the latter-day outpouring of the Spirit very near to the coming of the kingdom of God at Christ's return. Opinions varied as to the necessity and meaning of tongues as a sign of the church's empowerment to bear witness to the nations, with the white American Pentecostal denominations tending to insist on tongues as the characteristic or initial evidence of the experience. But not all Pentecostals agreed. Seymour insisted that the only sure sign of the Spirit's empowerment was love. In fact, he understood the Bible evidence of speaking in tongues in this light as a sign that the Spirit was crossing barriers between peoples, making them a reconciled and reconciling movement. He wrote concerning the sign value of tongues in the church: "God makes no difference in nationality, Ethiopians, Chinese, Indians, Mexicans, and other nationalities worship together."[4] Tongues were an eschatological sign that brought to visible expression the ultimate realization of the kingdom of God in the diverse communion of saints.[5] Kimberly Alexander notes further concerning the Pentecostal accent on healing that their Wesleyan background oriented them towards a healing metaphor of salvation and of the Christian life that involved both body and soul.[6] Pentecostal eschatology in this light was not wholly otherworldly (as it sometimes seemed) but involved hope for the healing of creation.[7] It was thought that the battle with the powers of darkness would intensify as the end draws near, calling for extraordinary spiritual gifts (powers of the age to come, Heb. 6:5) for the victory of the mission of God in the world, a conviction that is especially vibrant today in the Pentecostalism of the Southern Hemisphere.[8] As Veli-Matti Kärkkäinen has shown, Pentecostal ecclesiology celebrates the charismatic structure

---

[3] Shared with the author in person.

[4] William J. Seymour, "The Same Old Way," *Apostolic Faith* (1906), p. 3. See also, Cecil M. Robeck, "William J. Seymour and the Bible Evidence," in Gary McGee (ed.), *Initial Evidence* (Peabody, 1992), pp. 72–95. See Murray Dempster's provocative development of this understanding of glossolalia: "The Church's Moral Witness: A Study of *Glossolalia* in Luke's Theology of Acts," *Paraclete*, 23 (1989), pp. 1–7.

[5] Frank D. Macchia, "Sighs too Deep for Words: Towards a Theology of Glossolalia," *Journal of Pentecostal Theology* (1992), pp. 47–73. See also Frank D. Macchia, "Tongues as a Sign: Towards a Sacramental Understanding of Pentecostal Experience," *Pneuma* (1993), pp. 61–76.

[6] Kimberly Alexander, *Pentecostal Healing: Models in Theology and Practice* (Blandford Forum, 2006).

[7] Murray W. Dempster, "Christian Social Concern in Pentecostal Perspective: Reformulating Pentecostal Eschatology," *Journal Pentecostal Theology*, 2 (1993), pp. 53–66.

[8] See Kingsli Larbi, "African Pentecostalism in the Context of Global Pentecostal Ecumenical Fraternity: Challenges and Opportnities," *Pneuma*, 24(2) (2002), pp. 138–66.

and missionary nature of the church in which ordained ministries of oversight join with other gifted members of the people of God to participate in the mission of God in the world.[9]

An Expanding Diversity

This early cluster of pneumatological emphases raised a number of issues and debates in the first 25 years of the Movement's history. Pentecostals coming in to the Movement from outside of the narrow confines of the Holiness Movement saw no need to view sanctification as a crisis experience sandwiched in between the initial moment of personal faith in Christ and the empowering experience of Spirit baptism. Rather, in tension with their Wesleyan Pentecostal brothers and sisters, they understood sanctification as a progression that spans the entire Christian life. This view of sanctification, which tended over time to dominate global Pentecostalism, was more Reformed than Wesleyan. As noted above, debates also broke out over the exact role of speaking in tongues in the Spirit baptismal experience. Other issues were more significant. Early in the history of the American Assemblies of God denomination, which would become one of the largest Pentecostal denominations globally within the more Reformed wing of the Pentecostal Movement, a schism occurred (ca. 1916) over the proper formula and role of water baptism. About one-third of the membership held that baptism was to be in Jesus' Name (rather than in the name of the Trinity) and that repentance, water baptism, and Spirit baptism (as evidenced by speaking in tongues) were an inseparable cluster of events that constituted Christian initiation, rather than Christian initiation being limited to repentance (conversion to Christ by faith in the gospel) with water and Spirit baptism occurring afterwards as post-conversion events (the more common Pentecostal viewpoint). The minority faction that insisted on baptism in Jesus' Name even went so far as to deny the validity of the Trinitarian doctrine, since baptism in Jesus' Name implied for them that the church is baptized into Christ who is the manifestation in flesh of the one God who has no distinction of persons. This faction, called apostolic or oneness Pentecostals, now represents about one-fifth of the global Pentecostal Movement and is growing rapidly in China, Mexico and the United States. Recent ecumenical conversations between the oneness and Trinitarian branches of Pentecostalism have explored the dangers of tritheism on the Trinitarian side and Nestorianism on the oneness side.[10]

---

[9] Veli-Matti Kärkkäinen, *Towards a Pneumatological Theology: Pentecostal and Ecumenical Perspectives on Ecclesiology, Soteriology, and Theology of Mission* (edited by Amos Yong) (Lanham, 2002). See Gary Tyra, *The Holy Spirit in Mission: Prophetic Speech and Action in Christian Witness* (Downer's Grove, 2011).

[10] The danger of Nestorianism comes from the tendency in oneness theology to describe Jesus' relating to the Father as a relating to the God who resides within him, as though Jesus in his humanity can act independently of his divine nature. For the entire report, see: "Oneness-Trinitarian Pentecostal Final Report," *Pneuma*, 30 (2008), pp. 203–24.

I raised the question as to whether or not it was possible in the oneness Pentecostal theological "grammar" to see in the Father, Son and Spirit more than mere adverbs (describing the divine self-disclosure in history) so as to see these names as in some sense adjectives as well (describing who God is eternally), so long as we avoid the tritheistic implications of viewing these three as "persons" in the modern sense of the term.[11]

Enacting Theology

Pentecostalism expanded globally both theologically and culturally. Such expansive diversity raises the question as to what if anything is distinctive about Pentecostal theology beyond the experience of the Spirit's power for witness or mission. Walter J. Hollenweger concluded that what is most distinctive to Pentecostalism theologically is not any particular doctrine but rather an experience of the Spirit and a way of expressing it. He recognizes the importance of Wesleyan Holiness theology in the rise of the Pentecostal doctrine of Spirit baptism but locates the distinctiveness of Pentecostal theology not in concepts but rather in the nonliterary way of expressing and mediating a dynamic experience. Noting the roots of Pentecostal theology in William J. Seymour (son of former African slaves) and the proliferation of Pentecostalism in the global South, Hollenweger proposed that Pentecostal theology is typically African (or at least non-Western), or is done most characteristically in the form of stories and other media close to the heart of human experience, such as the dance, the song and the healing ritual, what the expert on African Pentecostalism, Allan Anderson, terms "enacting theology."[12] Though Pentecostals did write popular theological treatises, Pentecostal theology gained expression most typically in such enacted dramas rather than in written texts. One can still call Pentecostal theology a critical discipline Hollenweger insisted, since such expressions of belief tended to be implicitly critical and reflective, but without following the modernist rules of Western intellectual analysis. Hollenweger understood that Pentecostals were not the only ones who stood in this oral, narrative, or what we may term "performative" stream of theological reflection, but he was quick to note that Pentecostals tended to flourish in those areas of global Christianity that did.[13]

Hollenweger's work showed that Pentecostal theology was not a fundamentalist reaction to the openness of liberal Protestant theology to the enlightenment challenges

---

[11] Frank D. Macchia, "The Oneness-Trinitarian Pentecostal Dialogue: Exploring the Diversity of Apostolic Faith," *Harvard Theological Review*, 103(3) (2010), pp. 329–49.

[12] Allan Anderson, *Zion and Pentecost* (Pretoria, 2000), p. 253.

[13] Hollenweger has been prolific, but a good place to start would be his classic, *The Pentecostals* (reprint; Peabody, 1988). On Pentecostalism and narrative theology, see also, Jerry Camery-Hoggatt, "The Word of God from Living Voices: Orality and Literacy in the Pentecostal Tradition," *Pneuma*, 27(2) (2005), pp. 225–55, and Kenneth J. Archer, "Pentecostal Story: The Hermeneutical Filter for the Making of Meaning," *Pneuma*, 26(1) (2004), pp. 36–59.

of Western culture, as those exposed to white middle-class Pentecostalism in the United States (most influenced by Fundamentalism) tended to think was the case. He highlighted Pentecostal groups that were critical of social injustice on theological grounds[14] (which, as Douglas Petersen and, more recently, Amos Yong, have shown, is not based primarily on secular social analysis but rather on the Pentecostal community's distinctive loyalty to the gospel and its subversion of the larger culture[15]). Gerald Sheppard showed in a similar vein that while Fundamentalists were trying to beat the modernists at their own game by proving the veracity of scripture using science, Pentecostals were seeking to discern the power of the scriptural witness in life.[16] More recently, Harvey Cox has written that Pentecostalism holds promise for an approach to theology that takes seriously "primal" religious experience and various forms of reflection that are more artistic and embodied than merely rational. He looks at the presence of speaking in tongues in Pentecostal churches as a sign that Pentecostal worship is not limited to rational thought and words (in ways oriented as well to the intuitive and the aesthetic as Edmund Rybarczyk reminds us[17]). Cox argues that the experiential nature of Pentecostalism tends to make it easily adaptable to various cultural settings, implying ecumenical possibilities and challenges on a global scale.[18]

---

[14] See for example, Walter J. Hollenweger, *Pentecost between Black and White: Five Case Studies on Pentecost and Politics* (Belfast, 1974).

[15] Douglas Peterson has written on this theme in the context of Latin America, popularizing the idea that Pentecostals do not advocate a social program, they *are* a social program. Douglas Peterson, *Not by Might Nor by Power: A Pentecostal Theology of Social Concern in Latin America* (Carlisle, 1997). Amos Yong has written a thorough theology of political and social transformation from a Pentecostal perspective, incorporating also the typical Pentecostal emphases on sanctification, Spirit baptism, healing, and defeating the dark powers: Amos Yong, *In the Days of Caesar: Pentecostalism and Political Theology* (Grand Rapids, 2011). See also Donald Miller, *Global Pentecostalism: The New Face of Christian Social Engagement* (Berkeley, 2007).

[16] Gerald T. Sheppard, "Word and Spirit: Scripture in the Pentecostal Tradition," part 1, *Agora*, 1(4) (1978), pp. 4–5, 17–22, and part 2, *Agora* 2: I (1978), pp. 14–19.

[17] Edmund Rybarczyk, "Reframing Tongues: Apophaticism and Postmodernism," *Pneuma*, 27(1) (2005), pp. 83–104.

[18] Harvey Cox, *Fire from Heaven: The Rise of Pentecostal Spirituality and the Reshaping of Religion in the Twenty-First Century* (Reading, 1994). Terry Cross also notes the broadly experiential nature of Pentecostal theology: "The Rich Feast of Theology: Can Pentecostals Bring the Main Course or Only the Relish?" *Journal of Pentecostal Theology*, 16 (2000), pp. 33–4.

A Pentecostal Doctrinal Grammar

Not all Pentecostal theologians would find Pentecostal testimonies and rituals theological in the "regular" sense of the term (Karl Barth called such practices "irregular" theology).[19] James K. Smith, for example, distinguishes between spiritual practices that shape the Pentecostal worldview, on the one hand, and, on the other hand, the related Pentecostal philosophy that explores fundamental theological issues like epistemology and ontology (how we know) and Pentecostal theology (what we know) both of which are "theoretical modes of reflection."[20] Granted that Pentecostal theology has its social base in the enacted dramas and narratives of Pentecostal communities, there is also a place for a second order critical reflection on Pentecostal enactments or performances from the standpoint of the Scriptures.

The question posed here is whether there is a distinctive doctrinal configuration typical of the Pentecostal Movement that directs what is or is not appropriate speech or enactments about God and the divine economy. Donald W. Dayton reached back into the original Wesleyan Holiness influence to discover a Pentecostal doctrinal framework, which consisted of four major points of emphasis: Christ as Savior, Spirit Baptizer, Healer, and Coming King (one could add "Sanctifier" as well to form a fivefold gospel).[21] One need only add to this fourfold gospel the belief in the "Bible evidence" for Spirit baptism, tongues and other spiritual gifts, and one has the major points of doctrinal emphasis. Dayton is convinced that this fourfold gospel regulated Pentecostal theology from the beginning of the Movement and still does throughout its global diversity.

I proposed some years ago that Hollenweger and Dayton framed the initial debate over what is distinctive to Pentecostal theology, the former stressing the typically-non-Western medium of theological reflection (oral or enacting theology) and the latter reflecting on the typically-Wesleyan/Holiness cluster of doctrinal emphases in the form of a fourfold gospel (with charismatic signs following). Hollenweger's work spawned a significant amount of research on the global diversity of Pentecostal theology, especially with regard to its non-Western roots. A significant debate was spawned from Dayton's work over the precise nature of Pentecostal theological distinctives. A revision of Dayton's fourfold gospel schema was offered by David William Faupel who agreed with this framework but held that eschatology (the emphasis on Jesus as the coming King) was key to the entire cluster. In other words, the intense experience of Christ in the power of the Spirit highlighted in the Pentecostal fourfold gospel centered on the coming Christ who called the church to Spirit-empowered mission (along with the entire span of extraordinary spiritual

---

[19] Karl Barth, *Die Christliche Dogmatik im Entwurf*, Bd. 1 (1927), Gerhard Sauter (ed.) (Zürich, 1982), p. 151.

[20] James K. Smith, *Thinking in Tongues: Pentecostal Contributions to Christian Philosophy* (Grand Rapids, 2010), pp. 1–4.

[21] Donald W. Dayton, *The Theological Roots of Pentecostalism* (Grand Rapids, 1988).

gifts) in preparation for the fulfillment of the kingdom of God on earth.[22] Deeply influenced by this eschatological accent, Pentecostal theologian, Steven J. Land, wrote a seminal work in which he argued that Pentecostal theology was characteristically a more robustly eschatological version of the Wesleyan emphasis on the sanctified life. Pentecostal theology reflected on spirituality, namely, the sanctified affections as "passions" for the coming kingdom of God in power. Though Land embraced all four points of the fourfold gospel, he followed Faupel in viewing all of them within the overarching context of eschatological hope.[23]

The Return to Spirit Baptism as the Key Distinctive

I became convinced when reviewing this entire debate that Pentecostal theology from the beginning was more explicitly and distinctively focused on pneumatology than is indicated by making eschatological hope the primary focus. Though I agree with the significance of the fourfold gospel (including the eschatological emphasis) for Pentecostal theology, Pentecostalism from the beginning concentrated most intensely on what was termed the "baptism in the Holy Spirit." I agree with Singaporean Pentecostal theologian, Simon Chan, that Pentecostals do not agree on many points of doctrine but "what comes through over and over again in their discussions and writings is a certain kind of spiritual experience of an intense, direct, and overwhelming nature centering on the person of Christ which they schematize as 'baptism in the Holy Spirit.'"[24] Borrowed from the Holiness Movement, this term "Spirit baptism" was uniquely made the concentration of Pentecostal theology. This concentration implied that the Pentecostals typically emphasized most the question of how humanity was to become the dwelling place of God for the purpose of participating in God and in the divine mission or plan for the world in Christ.[25]

Interestingly, the most erudite ecumenical responses to Pentecostal theology in the 1970s during the heyday of the so-called "Charismatic Movement" also directed their reflections to the unique Pentecostal root metaphor of Spirit baptism. Charismatics from mainline churches were drawn to the charismatic spirituality of the Pentecostal Movement but strove to understand the distinctively-Pentecostal accent on Spirit baptism in ways that were consistent with their own denominational traditions. British Evangelical theologian, James D.G. Dunn, though embracing the charismatic spirituality of Pentecostalism, held that Spirit baptism was theologically the reception

---

[22] David William Faupel, *The Everlasting Gospel: The Significance of Eschatology in the Development of Pentecostal Thought* (Sheffield, 1996).

[23] Steven J. Land, *Pentecostal Spirituality: A Passion for the Kingdom* (Sheffield, 1991).

[24] Simon Chan, "Evidential Glossolalia and the Doctrine of Subsequence," *Asian Journal of Pentecostal Studies*, 2 (1999), p. 196.

[25] See Dale Coulter, "Delivered By the Power of God: Toward a Pentecostal Understanding of Salvation," *International Journal of Systematic Theology*, 10(4) (2008), pp. 447–67.

of the Spirit that comes at one's initial faith in Christ.[26] Catholic theologians, Killian McDonnell and George Montague, also centered their response to Pentecostalism on Spirit baptism but in a way that upheld a sacramental interpretation (against Dunn). Spirit baptism for McDonnell and Montague was the means by which one is incorporated into Christ through water baptism. The typically-Pentecostal doctrine of baptism in the Holy Spirit, redefined sacramentally, was thus in their view to be regarded as normative for Catholic theology. Like Dunn, they did not wish to discount the significance of Pentecostalism's charismatic spirituality. They noted that there is a widespread connection forged in the first eight centuries of the church between initiation to the life of the Spirit at baptism and the "release" of the Spirit in the charismatically-diverse life of the church. Though Pentecostals were "theologically" incorrect in their understanding of Spirit baptism by separating it from Christian initiation through baptism, they were "experientially" correct in their appreciation of the consequences of Spirit baptism for Christian experience and gifted practice.[27]

In response to these and other ecumenical partners in dialogue, I noted that this quarrel over the meaning of Spirit baptism in relation to Christian initiation was to some extent internal to Pentecostalism as well. Though the majority of Pentecostals classically held that Spirit baptism was distinct from Christian initiation, not all did (as I noted above). In my view, Spirit baptism in the New Testament is arguably fluid and expansive enough to include all of the accents raised among the opponents in this debate, both within and outside of Pentecostalism. The verb "baptizing" in the Holy Spirit as used in the New Testament concerned primarily the eschatological realization of the kingdom of God on earth. The proclamation of the Kingdom was the context for John the Baptist's description of Jesus as the one who will baptize in the Spirit (Mt. 3:1–12). According to Luke, Jesus discussed John's usage of the term in the context of the kingdom of God as well, noting that the Spirit will come as the disciples gather in Jerusalem, the city traditionally identified as the place where the kingdom of God will be established (Acts 1:3–8). The outpouring of the Spirit in Jerusalem on the Day of Pentecost is then described with far-reaching eschatological implications (2:17–21). To think more foundationally about this, we may say that the Son as the man of the Spirit descended into alienation from God on the cross in order to bring humanity more profoundly into the realm of the Spirit, the realm of Christ's sonship. Raised from the dead and ascended to the Father, Christ received the Spirit from the Father and poured the Spirit upon the disciples (2:33) (an act that resembled John's pouring water over the heads of the repentant in baptism), which sets in motion their participation in the mission of God and its eschatological fulfillment in the new creation. Even Paul's use of the term points to the eschatological destiny of the church as a unity of diverse members in Christ (1 Cor. 12:13).[28] Spirit baptism emerges in my

---

[26] James D.G. Dunn, *Baptism in the Holy Spirit* (Minneapolis, 1970).

[27] Killian McDonnell and George Montague, *Baptism in the Holy Spirit and Christian Initiation: Evidence from the First Eight Centuries* (Collegeville, 1991).

[28] The use of *eis* in this verse points to the purpose or end to which all are baptized into the Spirit. See also the so-called Pauline description of Pentecost in Eph. 4:7–13.

reconstruction as the most distinctive accent of the fourfold gospel, Spirit baptism now expanded to function as the root metaphor by which the other accents are to be understood, an eschatological event of divine self-giving that constitutes the church, opens it to the mission of God in the world, and leads to the divine indwelling and healing of creation in Christ's image. Highlighting Spirit baptism supports my contention that pneumatology is the most emphasized theological concern among Pentecostals. Such a reconstruction might be a helpful Pentecostal rejoinder to our ecumenical respondents.[29]

Amos Yong has recently explored the broader ecumenical significance of Pentecostalism's pneumatological accent. Yong pushes Pentecostal theology beyond its historic focus on salvation through Christ to explore more fully the universal expanse of its pneumatological emphasis (thus implying a cosmic Christology as well). In relation to a theology of religions, the economy of the Spirit relates most explicitly to diversity and otherness. While remaining inseparable from the mission of Christ, the Spirit also includes the "other" on a variety of levels including, but not limited to, the narrower concern over salvation in the explicit name of Jesus. There is breathing room within the Pentecostal accent on pneumatology for a theology of religions that takes into consideration a variety of hospitality situations involving the church in its relationship to other religious faiths in a way that respects their otherness in relation to the Spirit.[30] Yong also pushes Pentecostal pneumatology beyond its narrower commitment to the supernatural. From the vantage point of his universal pneumatology, Yong has worked on the cutting edge of a Pentecostal theology of science in which the Pentecostal concentration on the Spirit expands to involve engagement with a variety of "tongues" or discourses about the nature and teleological ends of creation. The Pentecostal penchant to highlight the extraordinary work of the Spirit in nature implies a dynamic world that is orderly and predictable but also open to surprises that signify its *telos* in God.[31]

Conclusion

Pentecostal theology is still in the making. As a movement, Pentecostalism is only a century old. It has been blessed by its Wesleyan and Reformed roots as well as

---

[29] See Frank D. Macchia, *Baptized in the Spirit: A Global Pentecostal Theology* (Grand Rapids, 2006), and Frank D. Macchia, *Justified in the Spirit: Creation, Redemption, and the Triune God* (Grand Rapids, 2010). See also Amos Yong, *The Spirit Poured Out on All Flesh: Pentecostalism and the Possibility of Global Theology* (Grand Rapids, 2006).

[30] Amos Yong, *Beyond the Impasse: Towards a Pneumatological Theology of Religions* (Grand Rapids, 2003). See also, Amos Yong, *Hospitality and the Other: Pentecost, Christian Practices, and the Other* (Maryknoll, 2008).

[31] Amos Yong and James K. Smith, *Science and the Spirit: A Pentecostal Engagement with the Sciences* (Bloomington, 2010). See also Amos Yong, *The Spirit of Creation: Modern Science and Divine Action in the Pentecostal-Charismatic Imagination* (Grand Rapids, 2011).

by ecumenical partners who have come alongside from other traditions to help the Movement practice its theological reflection. The gift of the outpoured Spirit through Christ for the accomplishment of the divine mission in the world remains its enduring accent. Those who are working to develop this accent do so with the hope of enriching other conversations as they have been enriched in the past. In the process of enriching other conversations, Pentecostal theology will itself be expanded but, hopefully, without losing its own distinctive gifts.[32]

Bibliography

Anderson, Allan, *Zion and Pentecost* (Pretoria, 2000).

Alexander, Kimberly, *Pentecostal Healing: Models in Theology and Practice* (Blandford Forum, 2006).

Archer, Kenneth J., "Pentecostal Story: The Hermeneutical Filter for the Making of Meaning," *Pneuma*, 26(1) (2004), pp. 36–59.

Barth, Karl, *Die Christliche Dogmatik im Entwurf, Bd. 1* (1927), Gerhard Sauter (ed.) (Zürich, 1982).

Camery-Hoggatt, Jerry, "The Word of God from Living Voices: Orality and Literacy in the Pentecostal Tradition," *Pneuma*, 27(2) (2005), pp. 225–55.

Chan, Simon, "Evidential Glossolalia and the Doctrine of Subsequence," *Asian Journal of Pentecostal Studies*, 2 (1999), 195–211.

Coulter, Dale, "Delivered By the Power of God: Toward a Pentecostal Understanding of Salvation," *International Journal of Systematic Theology*, 10(4) (2008), pp. 447–67.

Cox, Harvey, *Fire from Heaven: The Rise of Pentecostal Spirituality and the Reshaping of Religion in the Twenty-First Century* (Reading, MA: Addison-Wesley Publishing Company, 1994).

Cross, Terry, "The Rich Feast of Theology: Can Pentecostals Bring the Main Course or Only the Relish?" *Journal of Pentecostal Theology*, 16 (2000), pp. 33–4.

Dayton, Donald W., *The Theological Roots of Pentecostalism* (Grand Rapids: Zondervan, 1988).

Dempster, Murray W., "The Church's Moral Witness: A Study of Glossolalia in Luke's Theology of Acts," *Paraclete*, 23 (1989), pp. 1–7.

Dunn, James D.G., *Baptism in the Holy Spirit* (Minneapolis, 1970).

Faupel, David William, *The Everlasting Gospel: The Significance of Eschatology in the Development of Pentecostal Thought* (Sheffield: Sheffield Academic Press, 1996).

Hollenweger, Walter J., *Pentecost between Black and White: Five Case Studies on Pentecost and Politics* (Belfast, 1974).

Walter J. Hollenweger, *The Pentecostals* (reprint; Peabody: Hendrickson, 1988).

---

[32] See Wolfgang Vondey, *Beyond Pentecostalism: The Crisis of Global Christianity and the Renewal of the Theological Agenda* (Grand Rapids, 2010).

Kärkkäinen, Veli-Matti, *Towards a Pneumatological Theology: Pentecostal and Ecumenical Perspectives on Ecclesiology, Soteriology, and Theology of Mission* (edited by Amos Yong) (Lanham, 2002).

Land, Steven J., *Pentecostal Spirituality: A Passion for the Kingdom* (Sheffield: Sheffield Academic Press, 1991).

Larbi, Kingsli, "African Pentecostalism in the Context of Global Pentecostal Ecumenical Fraternity: Challenges and Opportnities," *Pneuma*, 24(2) (2002), pp. 138–66.

Macchia, Frank D., *Baptized in the Spirit: A Global Pentecostal Theology* (Grand Rapids: Zondervan, 2006).

Frank D. Macchia, *Justified in the Spirit: Creation, Redemption, and the Triune God* (Grand Rapids: Eerdmans, 2010).

Frank D. Macchia, "The Oneness-Trinitarian Pentecostal Dialogue: Exploring the Diversity of Apostolic Faith," *Harvard Theological Review*, 103(3) (2010), pp. 329–49.

Frank D. Macchia, "Sighs too Deep for Words: Towards a Theology of Glossolalia," *Journal of Pentecostal Theology* (1992), pp. 47–73.

Frank D. Macchia, "Tongues as a Sign: Towards a Sacramental Understanding of Pentecostal Experience," *Pneuma* (1993), pp. 61–76.

McDonnell, Kilian and George Montague, *Baptism in the Holy Spirit and Christian Initiation: Evidence from the First Eight Centuries* (Collegeville, 1991).

Miller, *Global Pentecostalism: The New Face of Christian Social Engagement* (Berkeley, 2007).

Peterson, Douglas, *Not by Might Nor by Power: A Pentecostal Theology of Social Concern in Latin America* (Carlisle, 1997).

Robeck, Cecil M., "William J. Seymour and the Bible Evidence," in Gary McGee (ed.), *Initial Evidence* (Peabody, 1992), pp. 72–95.

Rybarczyk, Edmund, "Reframing Tongues: Apophaticism and Postmodernism," *Pneuma*, 27(1) (2005), pp. 83–104.

Seymour, William J., "The Way into the Holiest," *The Apostolic Faith*, 1(2) (1906), 4.

Seymour, William J., "The Same Old Way," *Apostolic Faith* (1906), 3.

Sheppard, "Word and Spirit: Scripture in the Pentecostal Tradition," part 1, *Agora*, 1(4) (1978), pp. 4–5, 17–22, and part 2, *Agora*, 2: I (1978), pp. 14–19.

Smith, James K., *Thinking in Tongues: Pentecostal Contributions to Christian Philosophy* (Grand Rapids, 2010).

Tyra, Gary, *The Holy Spirit in Mission: Prophetic Speech and Action in Christian Witness* (Downer's Grove, 2011).

Yong, Amos, *Beyond the Impasse: Towards a Pneumatological Theology of Religions* (Grand Rapids, 2003).

Yong, Amos, *Hospitality and the Other: Pentecost, Christian Practices, and the Other* (Maryknoll, 2008).

Yong, Amos, *In the Days of Caesar: Pentecostalism and Political Theology* (Grand Rapids: Eerdmans, 2011).

Yong, Amos, *The Spirit of Creation: Modern Science and Divine Action in the Pentecostal-Charismatic Imagination* (Grand Rapids, 2011).

Yong, Amos, *The Spirit Poured Out on All Flesh: Pentecostalism and the Possibility of Global Theology* (Grand Rapids: Baker Academic, 2006).
Yong, Amos, and James K. Smith, *Science and the Spirit: A Pentecostal Engagement with the Sciences* (Bloomington, 2010).

PART VII
Theology, Philosophy and Literature

Chapter 53
G.K. Chesterton

Torbjørn Holt

"A real kindness and sympathy, never quite hidden even when he was most intolerant, gave charm to everything he said. The flow of quaint imagery showed a quick receptive mind: the love of old fixed certainties a shrinking from the unknown future."[1] This is how the English writer Gilbert Keith Chesterton is described in an interview published in 1919. The interviewer was not the first to discover Chesterton's warmth and generosity – nor his polemic. And it was precisely the combination of warmth and polemic that was typical of Chesterton. In his book *Heretics* (1905), he writes polemically against many of the intellectual elite of the period, including George Bernard Shaw, H.G. Wells, and Bertrand Russell; at the same time, most of them remained his friends, and they would certainly have protested vigorously if anyone had described him as "intolerant". Chesterton as well as his adversaries saw their debates as honest and fair fights, something that was absolutely necessary when important issues were at stake. They all took the same delight in their incessant crossing of swords, and they preferred a fair fight to being knocked senseless with intellectual sandbags.

The question of whether Chesterton met the future with his back to it, thanks to his love for the old and well-tried truths, should be left until we have got to know him better.

G.K. Chesterton is one of the most important writers in the English-speaking world in the first half of the twentieth century. Chesterton was a colossus in more than one sense. He was 1.90 meters tall and weighed around 140 kilograms. He was a striking figure in literary London, a journalist and author with a passionate commitment to all kinds of causes between heaven and earth (both these places included). He was always on his way to one of his innumerable activities, his coat and hat crumpled, a cigar in the corner of his mouth, and his walking stick swinging like a crusader's sword. He was a man with a big heart, a sharp intellect, brilliant wit, and generous humour. He saw himself as a happy and carefree Christian mendicant friar who had no other cares than the salvation of the whole world.

Many people today have never heard of him, but more and more are reading his books, and they often mention him as one of the authors who have meant most to them. Although he never pretended to be a theologian, he was extremely important for many of those who wrote and lived in the interface between faith and literature later in the twentieth century, and who are still read by millions. This applies above

---

[1] Hugh Lunn, Interview with G.K. Chesterton, *Hearth and Home*, October 17, 1919.

all to C.S. Lewis, but also to Dorothy L. Sayers, Evelyn Waugh, J.R.R. Tolkien, Graham Greene, and a number of other authors.

Chesterton was a master of contemporary relevance, a man who described the wisdom and the folly of his age with great precision. This means that some of his journalism requires footnotes, if the reader is to get the point of what he is saying – since we no longer know the age in which he lived. But there are pearls to be found among the up-to-date commentaries that now no longer seem up-to-date. The humour in Chesterton's paradoxes is a part of the argument itself. He could be just as witty as the great humourists of his age, but he went far deeper than most of them. In a book like this, which discusses great theologians and their academic writings, Chesterton is in many ways a strange bird. Virtually nothing in his extensive writings can be called "academic." Unlike C.S. Lewis, for example, who was one of the leading academics in the history of English literature in his age, Chesterton had little formal academic training. He is usually described as a journalist. He was a writer of detective stories on a par with Agatha Christie, a humourist on a par with Oscar Wilde, a travel writer on a par with Robert Byron, and a Christian apologist on a par with C.S. Lewis. Besides this, he was a literary critic, a biographer, an author of science fiction, a Catholic polemicist, a historian, an illustrator, a Christian humanist, and a social reformer – and many of these things all at once, and in the same books.

Chesterton's Biography

Chesterton was born in Campden Hill in Kensington in London on May 29, 1874. He was a pupil at St. Paul's School, and then studied at the Slade School of Art, where he took parts of the training in illustration. He also attended courses in English literature at University College in London, but he did not complete a university degree. In 1896, he began to work for a London publisher, and he set out on his own as a freelance journalist and literary critic in 1902. This was to be his profession for the rest of his life. He married Frances Blogg in 1901, and they were inseparable throughout their happy marriage until Chesterton's death. From 1902 onwards, he wrote a weekly commentary column in *The Daily News*, and a weekly column in the popular weekly magazine *The Illustrated London News* from 1905 onwards – a column that was to last for 30 years. He was forbidden to write about politics and religion, but he gradually became an expert in getting round this prohibition. He sniffed: "Religion and politics are the only subjects that could possibly interest sane men" when anyone brought up this prohibition. In 1926, he was given his own magazine, *G.K.'s Weekly*, which was published until his death in 1936. His fame grew with the years. Chesterton wrote between 80 and 100 books, several hundred poems, around 200 short stories, several plays, and nearly 4,000 essays and articles. His essays are an inexhaustible source of lively quotations and profound thoughts. We shall look in more detail below at some of Chesterton's more theological works, but it is important to bear in mind that his theology is found everywhere, often in a compact form in quotations, in poems, in short detective stories, or in articles that deal with quite different topics than religion.

Chesterton has a very characteristic style. At first sight, he can seem like a younger edition of Oscar Wilde – a *flaneur*, witty, and with a hailstorm of striking formulations. He is famous for his paradoxes: "Thieves respect property. They merely wish the property to become their property that they may more perfectly respect it."[2] This is typical Chesterton. Another example, from the sphere of religion, was later to become the heartbeat in his writings: "The Christian ideal has not been tried and found wanting; it has been found difficult and left untried."[3] When we move on from individual quotations and read his books or articles in context, we soon discover the depths in Chesterton.

He is one of the Christian authors who were admired and read by both liberal and conservative Christians, and by many outside the Christian ranks. Although his theological position was that of a traditional Catholic, it is not easy to locate him on a modern right/left spectrum when we look at his writings as a whole. He himself put it as follows:

> The whole modern world has divided itself into Conservatives and Progressives. The business of Progressives is to go on making mistakes. The business of the Conservatives is to prevent the mistakes from being corrected.[4]

In his younger years, Chesterton was fascinated by occult phenomena, and he was sympathetic to Unitarianism for several years. But in the first years of the twentieth century, he became ever clearer in his defense of the Catholic faith, which he propagated with great breadth and insight long before he finally converted to the Catholic church in 1922. It is important to note that "Catholic" is how English Anglo-Catholics generally describe their faith, then and now. It did not at first mean Roman Catholic for Chesterton. His thought and faith developed in a Roman direction slowly, as it did and does with so many other converts to Roman Catholicism.

Chesterton's closest friend and literary ally was the poet and essayist Hilaire Belloc (1870–1953). Shaw coined the name "Chesterbelloc" for the two of them, and this name stuck. He also described them as two parts of a pantomime elephant, a friendly and unambiguous allusion to their weightiness (in both senses of the word). Belloc rejoiced when Chesterton finally entered the church to which he himself had belonged for the whole of his life. They discovered more and more that they had shared interests in theology, literature, and social questions.

Chesterton's best known literary figure is the detective priest Father Brown, who appears in fifty-two short stories published between 1911 and 1935. Father Brown is a small, bashful Catholic priest, with curly hair and an umbrella, with a warm heart, a sharp intellect, and a great insight into the many alleyways of the human mind and the various labyrinths of evil. Father Brown's pastoral-criminological moves usually mean not only that the crime is cleared up, but that the perpetrator saves his soul.

---

[2] G.K. Chesterton, *The Man Who Was Thursday* (Wordsworth Classics, 1907), Ch. 4.
[3] G.K. Chesterton, *What's Wrong With the World* (Kessinger Publishing, 1910), Ch. 3.
[4] *The Illustrated London News*, April 19, 1924.

In one of his cases, Father Brown says: "I caught him (the criminal) with an unseen hook and an invisible line which is long enough to let him wander to the ends of the world, and still bring him back with a twitch upon the thread."[5] Through Father Brown, Chesterton shows how cynicism and sarcasm destroy wisdom in the same way as they destroy innocence. With cynical eyes, we cannot see with objective clarity. Dark clouds cause us to lose perspective. It is only with innocent eyes that we see clearly.[6]

Chesterton died on June 14, 1936, in his home in Beaconsfield in Buckinghamshire, to the north-west of London. In the telegram that he sent on the occasion of Chesterton's death, Pope Pius XI called him "Defensor Fidei" ("Defender of the Faith"), the same title that Pope Leo XI had bestowed on Henry VIII in 1521, and that is still used by the British monarchs.[7] Several groups are working to promote Chesterton's canonization.

Chesterton's Theological Writings

We shall now look briefly at a few of Chesterton's more theological books, and then explore some of the ideas in his writings.

Orthodoxy and The Everlasting Man

Orthodoxy (1908) is Chesterton's first presentation of what he positively upholds. "I will not call it my philosophy; for I did not make it. God and humanity made it; and it made me."[8] Another quotation is very characteristic of Chesterton's theological argumentation, in its use of striking metaphors to compare Buddhism and Christianity:

> Buddhism is centripetal, but Christianity is centrifugal: it breaks out. For the circle is perfect and infinite in its nature; but it is fixed for ever in its size; it can never be larger or smaller. But the cross, though it has at its heart a collision and a contradiction, can extend its four arms for ever without altering its shape. Because it has a paradox in its

---

[5] From the Father Brown short story "The Queer Feet." Evelyn Waugh uses this point in *Brideshead Revisited*, when Lord Marchmain returns from his Bohemian existence in Venice towards the end of his life, and is reconciled to God and the church on his deathbed. The image of the fishing line is particularly apt in its original appearance in Chesterton as the story is about a club called "The Twelve True Fishermen".

[6] Joseph Pearce, Pearce, Joseph, *Wisdom and Innocence – A Life of G.K. Chesterton* (London, 1996), p. 161.

[7] The full text of the Pope's condolence telegram reads: "Holy Father deeply grieved death Mr Gilbert Keith Chesterton devoted son Holy Church gifted Defender of the Catholic Faith. His Holiness offers paternal sympathy people of England assures prayers dear departed, bestows Apostolic Benediction" (quoted from Pearce, *Wisdom and Innocence*, p. 485).

[8] G.K. Chesterton, *Orthodoxy* (Hendrickson Christian Classics, 1908), chapter 1.

centre it can grow without changing. The circle returns upon itself and is bound. The cross opens its arms to the four winds; it is a signpost for free travellers.[9]

The point of view that he expresses here is typical of his writings as a whole, namely, that orthodox faith and theology are not limiting, but liberating. The cross is fixed in its form, but infinite in its extent.

The Everlasting Man (1925) is an attempt at a religious longitudinal section through the whole history of humanity from the cave-dwellers up to the last days. Chesterton wrote it partly as a corresponding work to H.G. Wells' book *The Outline of History*. He reflects in the introductory chapter on the difficulty of evaluating Christianity when one is close to it – as everyone in European civilization is, more or less: "The next best thing to being really inside Christendom, is to be really outside it."[10] Christianity's popular critics are not really outside. They do not see clearly. "Now the best relation to our spiritual home is to be near enough to love it. But the next best is to be far enough away not to hate it."[11]

The first part begins in chapter 1 with the cave-dwellers. He defends them against the traditional accusation of being primitive (using clubs to woo their brides, who were dragged by the hair to the cave, etc.).

> The only thing we know about them, is that they made drawings on the cave walls. (…) The more we see man as an animal, the less he resembles one. (…) When all is said, the main fact that the record of the reindeer men attests, along with all other records, is that the reindeer man could draw and the reindeer could not.[12]

The cave-dweller was different from all other creatures "because he was creator in addition to creation". This idea of "subcreation" was developed further by J.R.R. Tolkien and C.S. Lewis, but it is already prominent in *The Everlasting Man*. In the next chapters, he follows civilization from the Near East to the Mediterranean region, and observes the culture and religion of classical antiquity:

> To me it is a very strong impression made by pagan literature and religion. I repeat that in our special sacramental sense there is of course, the absence of the presence of God. But there is in a very real sense the presence of the absence of God.[13]

People in antiquity were conscious of the Fall. Chesterton asserts that those who have fallen are conscious of their fall, even though they have forgotten how deep they have fallen.

---

[9] Ibid., chapter 2.
[10] Chesterton, *The Everlasting Man*, introduction.
[11] Ibid.
[12] Ibid., chapter 1.
[13] Ibid., part 1, chapter 4.

The second part of the book, which deals with Christ, also begins in a cave. Here too there were beasts, and Christ was born in the cave or grotto under the floor of the world. Here, down in the cave, the shepherds found their Shepherd.[14]

Chesterton emphasizes that the Jesus of the Gospels is far from being only gentle. When he drives out demons he is like "a very business-like lion-tamer or a strong-minded doctor dealing with a homicidal maniac."[15] In principle, it made sense that Caiaphas, the high priest in what was at that time the most consistently monotheistic religion in the world, rent his garments in protest when "a strolling carpenter's apprentice said calmly and almost carelessly, like one looking over his shoulder: 'Before Abraham was, I am.'"[16] Was this Jesus only a normal human being, or was he something more? This idea is developed further in the next chapter:

> Normally speaking, the greater a man is, the less likely he is to make the very greatest claim. (…) No modern critic in his five wits thinks that the preacher of the Sermon on the Mount was a horrible half-witted imbecile that might be scrawling stars on the walls of a cell. No atheist or blasphemer believes that the author of the Parable of the Prodigal Son was a monster with one mad idea like a Cyclops with one eye. Yet by all analogy we have really to put him there or else in the highest place of all.[17]

The story of Jesus also ends in a cave. The dead Christ was laid to rest in this second cave, and he took all the old world with him into the grave. When he rises again on the third day, the disciples meet him:

> Even they hardly realized that the world had died in the night. What they were looking at was the first day of a new creation, with a new heaven and a new earth; and in a semblance of the gardener God walked again in the garden, in the cool not of the evening but the dawn.[18]

Christ crossed the great gulf between our world and the world to come.

> It was that abyss that nothing but an incarnation could cover; a divine embodiment of our dreams; and he stands above that chasm whose name is more than priest and older even than Christendom; Pontifex Maximus, the mightiest maker of a bridge.[19]

The Christian faith has passed through various epochs in the course of history: "At least five times, therefore, with the Arian and the Albigensian, with the Humanist

---

[14] Ibid., part 2, chapter 1.
[15] Ibid., part 2, chapter 2.
[16] Ibid., *The Everlasting Man*, part 2, chapter 2.
[17] Ibid., part 2, chapter 3.
[18] Ibid., part 2, chapter 3.
[19] Ibid., part 2, chapter 5.

sceptic, after Voltaire and after Darwin, the Faith has to all appearance gone to the dogs. In each of these five cases it was the dog that perished."[20]

Chesterton employs in several passages in his books the image of Christianity as the key that perfectly fits the keyhole that is the universe. "We are Christians and Catholics not because we worship a key, but because we have passed a door; and felt the wind that is the trumpet of liberty blow over the land of the living."[21]

Readers of Chesterton's texts over many generations often discover this fresh wind. It gives many of his texts a relevance that we often look for in vain when we read his contemporaries – and this relevance is a sign that he is a classic.

Distributism

Chesterton also got involved in social politics and economics, a commitment that he shared with Hilaire Belloc. They were critical both of capitalism and of socialism in the forms that these two competing societal systems took in the years after the Russian Revolution. They called the third way in economic philosophy, which they themselves supported, distributism. Their aim was to apply Catholic principles of social justice in the debate about society. Pope Leo XIII's encyclical *Rerum Novarum* (1891) and later Pius XI's *Quadragesimo Anno* (1931) affirm that the means of production in a society should not be under the control either of a few state bureaucrats or of a few rich private persons. Instead, as many persons as possible should own the means of production – land, machines, etc. (Pope John Paul II also took up the same tradition in his encyclical *Centesimus Annus*, which marked the hundredth anniversary of *Rerum Novarum* in 1991). The Third Way Campaign in the United Kingdom, which promotes the widest possible extension of ownership, is one example of a movement inspired by distributism.

In Chesterton's view, the problem with capitalism is not that there are too many capitalists, but too few. The smallest and most important unit in society is the family. The distributists promoted the principle of subsidiarity: nothing that can be taken care of by small units should be handed over to larger units. Chesterton's most important books on distributism are *What's Wrong with the World* (1910) and *The Outline of Sanity* (1927). Both Chesterton and Belloc wrote a number of articles about distributism in *The American Review* in the 1930s. He states the need for more than theories about credit or corporative power. There is a need for a new theory and practice about pleasure.

> The vulgar school which teaches bread and circus, gives people circus only. It doesn't even teach people to enjoy circus. Our task is not only to teach them to enjoy circus, but to enjoy enjoyment.[22]

---

[20] Ibid., part 2, chapter 6.
[21] Ibid., part 2, chapter 5.
[22] G.K. Chesterton, *G.K. Weekly*, December 13, 1934.

Chesterton and the Theological Tradition of the Twentieth Century

Chesterton was not a professional theologian. Throughout his active life, he was a representative of traditional Catholic theology, first in its Anglo-Catholic, and later in its Roman Catholic form. He always believed what the church believed. He had no ambitions to be an original dogmatic theologian – he regarded originality as something reserved for the heretics. At the same time, most of what he wrote bears the marks of his own distinctive style. His self-description is also a good description of the relationship between the orthodox and the original: "I am the man who with the utmost daring discovers what was discovered before."[23] The *Oxford Dictionary of the Christian Church* sums up Chesterton's theological and literary position with great precision: "His defence of orthodoxy and conventionality in an individual and unconventional style soon established his literary reputation."[24]

Chesterton's thinking was an original mixture of fun and philosophy. The humour was largely his own, while his philosophy is greatly indebted to Thomas Aquinas, the great doctor of the church. He has links to the Aquinas renaissance that neo-Thomist currents in the Catholic church had created in Chesterton's lifetime. Leo XIII (pope from 1878 to 1903) worked actively to promote a renewed study of Thomas in the Catholic church, and Chesterton has his place in this tradition. His biography of Thomas Aquinas (1933) was not original, but it is one of the best simple presentations of the great mediaeval theologian and philosopher. Chesterton is marked by Thomist realism. "When he (H.G. Wells) says (…) 'All chairs are quite different', he utters not merely a misstatement, but a contradiction in terms. If all chairs were quite different, you could not call them 'all chairs'."[25]

Chesterton had an enormous influence on a wide spectrum of authors. It is difficult to see how C.S. Lewis' Narnia books or Evelyn Waugh's *Brideshead Revisited* could have been written without his influence. He probably helped Lewis to find the path to the Christian faith.[26] He also had a significant influence on Graham Greene and J.R.R. Tolkien. Dorothy L. Sayers states clearly how important Chesterton was for her. Other authors who emphasize the significance of Chesterton are Ernest Hemingway, Fredrick Buechner, Jorge Luis Borges, Gabriel Garcia Márquez, Karel Čapek, Paul Claudel, Agatha Christie, Sigrid Undset, Ronald Knox, Kingsley Amis, W.H. Auden, Anthony Burgess, E.F. Schumacher, Orson Welles, Dorothy Day, and Franz Kafka. Chesterton was such an all-round writer that they all find something in him that inspires them. Some are attracted and influenced by his apologetics, others

---

[23] Michael Ffinch, *G.K. Chesterton* (London, 1986), p. 5.
[24] *The Oxford Dictionary of the Christian Church*, edited by F.L. Cross (Oxford: Oxford University Press, 2005), p. 330.
[25] Chesterton, *Orthodoxy*, Ch. 3.
[26] In a letter to Sheldon Vanauken (December 14, 1950), Lewis calls *The Everlasting Man* "the best popular apologetic I know." In a letter to Rhonda Bodle (December 31, 1947), he says that "the [very] best popular defence of the full Christian position I know is G.K. Chesterton's *The Everlasting Man*."

by his humour, others again by his detective stories or his aphorisms. Some are struck by Chesterton's humanity, his deep respect for the ordinary person. Chesterton has something for everyone.

Conclusion

Did Chesterton meet the future with old, irrelevant answers to new questions? The interviewer in 1919 implicitly applied the much-used chronological argument that new things are better than old. Chesterton would have disagreed strongly with such an idea. He would have regarded it as a form of chronological snobbery. The test of relevance is not whether an idea is new or old, but whether it actually does justice to the contemporary situation. Much that is old does not do so, but much that is old does in fact do justice, sometimes well, to today's situation. The chaff must be separated from the wheat – a task for alert persons in every age. The test of truth is not whether the message is old or new, but whether it is in fact true or not: "My attitude toward progress has passed from antagonism to boredom. I have long ceased to argue with people who prefer Thursday to Wednesday because it is Thursday."[27]

Many of Chesterton's observations of social life and politics are still highly relevant, and some are prophetic. Chesterton keeps on making an appearance, more than 75 years after his death, in the role of the child who shouts out when the theological and political emperors of our time have no clothes. But it is not Chesterton the polemist who should have the last word. In one of his earliest books, *Charles Dickens* (1906), Chesterton describes what he calls "The Common Mind":

> The common mind means the mind of all the artists and heroes; or else it would not be common. Plato had the common mind; Dante had the common mind. Commonness means the quality common to the saint and the sinner, to the philosopher and the fool; and it was this that Dickens grasped and developed. In everybody there is a certain thing that loves babies, that fears death, that likes sunlight: that enjoys Dickens. And everybody does not mean uneducated crowds; everybody means everybody.

"Common" means "ordinary" both in the sense of "unsophisticated" and in the sense of "that which is common to everyone." Around the turn of the last century, England had an elite culture that was, if possible, even more snobbish than in our own days. To be "common" was an insult. The elite were sophisticated, highly articulate, rich, and arrogant (as elites often are). In his encounter with all this, Chesterton was the apostle of the ordinary. And "common" meant for him the same as *catholicam* in the creed: that which is for everyone, at all times and in all places. Here, Chesterton's theological and human programme coalesces: in a religion where God became a human being, the highest mark of nobility is to be an ordinary human being.

---

[27] *New York Times Magazine*, November 11, 1923.

Bibliography

Primary Literature (with dates of first publication)

Ignatius Press has begun the publication of Chesterton's Collected Works. Roughly two-thirds of the volumes have appeared.[28]

The Napoleon of Notting Hill (Penguin, 1904).
Heretics (Dover, 1905).
Charles Dickens (Wordsworth Literary Lives, 1906).
The Man Who Was Thursday (Wordsworth Classics, 1907).
Orthodoxy (Hendrickson Christian Classics, 1908).
What's Wrong With the World (Kessinger Publishing, 1910).
"The Ballad of the White Horse," in G.K. Chesterton, *Early Poetry* (Inkling Books, 1911).
Magic (Dodo Press, 1913). (Chesterton's most popular play, on which Ingmar Bergman based his film "The Magician").
The New Jerusalem (Indypublish, 1920).
St. Francis of Assisi (Bantam Doubleday Dell Publishing Group, 1923).
The Everlasting Man (Dover Books, 1923).
The Catholic Church and Conversion (Ignatius Press, 1927).
Robert Louis Stevenson (House of Stratus, 1927).
Father Brown (5 collections of detective short stories, published by Penguin between 1911 and 1935).
Chaucer (House of Stratus, 1932).
St. Thomas Aquinas (The Echo Library, 1933).
Autobiography (House of Stratus, 1936).

Secondary Literature

Cooney, Anthony, *G.K. Chesterton, One Sword at Least* (London: Third Way Publications, 1999).
Coren, Michael, *Gilbert: The Man Who Was G.K. Chesterton* (New York: Paragon House, 1990).
Ffinch, Michael, *G.K. Chesterton* (London: Weidenfeld & Nicolson, 1986).
Kenner, Hugh, *Paradox in Chesterton* (London: Sheed and Ward, 1947).
Ker, Ian, *Chesterton. A Biography* (Oxford University Press 2011). (This is possibly the new standard biography).

---

[28] The most important writings are still in print. Many of his books were published in very large editions, and they can often be found in second-hand bookshops, especially in Great Britain and the USA. His newspaper articles are the most difficult to get hold of, but many of these were printed in collected works.

Oddie, William, *Chesterton and the Romance of Orthodoxy. The Making of GKC 1874–1908* (Oxford University Press 2008). (A groundbreaking and probably definitive biography on the young Chesterton).

Paine, Randal, *The Universe and Mr. Chesterton* (Sugden, Sherwood & Co, U.S., 1999).

Pearce, Joseph, *Wisdom and Innocence – A Life of G.K. Chesterton* (London: Hodder & Stoughton, 1996). (The best biography of Chesterton).

Ward, M., *Gilbert Keith Chesterton* (London: Sheed & Ward, 1944).

The Oxford Dictionary of the Christian Church, edited by F.L. Cross (Oxford: Oxford University Press, 2005).

There is also a good article about Chesterton on Wikipedia, and the American Chesterton Society has one of the best homepages about him: www.chesterton.org (accessed March 20, 2013).

Chapter 54
Jacques Maritain

Gregory M. Reichberg

It is not without paradox that Jacques Maritain (1882–1973) has been included in a book on contemporary *theologians*. He consistently called himself a *philosopher* and, with the exception of some writings at the very end of his life, was never willing to accept the label "theology" as a description of his intellectual output. It remains true however that among the philosophical writings of the last century there are few more intertwined with the discourse of faith than Maritain's. Throughout a philosophical career that spanned over 60 years, Maritain kept to the conviction that far from being an impediment to reason the Christian faith (and the discipline that issues from it—theology) would strengthen philosophy, much as grace perfects nature. Hence, "ascending" to the knowledge of God from the naturally knowable truths of this world, he sought to show how the perennial questions of philosophy would receive a deeper and fuller response if examined in vital contact with the "descending" wisdom which God communicated to humankind in the Hebrew and Greek scriptures.[1]

> The philosopher's experience itself has been revitalized by Christianity. He is offered as a *datum* a world that is the handiwork of the Word, wherein everything bespeaks the Infinite Mind to finite minds who know themselves as minds. What a starting point! Here is, as it were, a fraternal attitude toward things and reality, – I mean insofar as they are *knowable* – for which the progress of the human mind is indebted to the Christian Middle Ages.[2]

In joining philosophy to faith Maritain's aim was not "apologetic," if by this term is meant an attempt at using reason to draw non-believers beyond reason to the Christian faith. While Maritain did indeed play an important role in the conversion of quite a few of his contemporaries—including leading artistic figures such as Jean Cocteau—he maintained nonetheless that his work was ordered first and foremost to extending our philosophical knowledge of human existence and destiny. His contribution, arguably unrivaled by any other contemporary philosopher, was to explore how these philosophic truths are in constant and close connection with the

---

[1] On the contrast between the "ascending" wisdom of philosophy, and the "descending," wisdom of revealed theology, see Jacques Maritain, *Science and Wisdom*, trans. Bernard Wall (New York, 1940), pp. 3–33.

[2] Jacques Maritain, *An Essay on Christian Philosophy*, trans. Edward H. Flannery (New York, 1955), p. 22 (translation modified).

revealed truths of the Christian faith. This connection he exhibited in all major fields of philosophy: metaphysics, epistemology, ethics, aesthetics, and political theory. Within the confines of this chapter we will focus especially on the last-named field, since it is here that Maritain's influence has extended most broadly. But first, let us consider some essentials about his life and writings.

Life and Writings

Born in Paris on 18 November 1882 to a prominent bourgeois family (his maternal grandfather, Jules Favre, was a leading politician who had been Minister of Foreign Affairs under the Third Republic) Maritain was raised in the context of liberal Protestantism. Indeed, as a young student at the Lysée Henri IV, his best friend was Ernest Psichari, the grandson of Renan. Maritain's mother had socialist leanings; a close friend of Charles Péguy, she would communicate her political ideals to her son, who became an ardent supporter of Dreyfus during the famous affair of 1898.

A student in philosophy and natural science at the Sorbonne in the early 1900s, it was there that Maritain met the young Jewish émigré, Raïssa Oumançoff, who would later become his wife. A close intellectual and spiritual bond quickly developed between them. Together they experienced a deep distress at the positivism (and accompanying skeptical relativism) that reigned in French academic circles at this time. Sitting together on a park bench in the Jardin des Plantes (the large public garden that lies close to the Sorbonne), the two made a fateful decision. If, in the months ahead, no glimmer of enduring truth should appear on their horizon, they would take their own lives: "We wanted to die by a free act if it were impossible to live according to the truth."[3] Soon thereafter (the winter of 1901–2), Charles Péguy, although unaware of their decision, proposed that the young couple attend the lectures that Henri Bergson was then giving across the street from the Sorbonne at the independent Collège de France. The philosopher's vigorous repudiation of scientific materialism, and his ardent espousal of freedom and other metaphysical realities that could be known by the intuitive human mind,

Jacques Maritain (right) during his years at Princeton, talking to Georges Florovsky (left) and David Marsh.

---

[3] Raïssa Maritain, *We have been Friends Together and Adventures in Grace*, trans. Julie Kernan (New York, 1961), p. 68.

provided Jacques and Raïssa with a glimpse of the absolute that they so ardently desired.

Another decisive encounter occurred three years later, when, in 1905, the newly married couple met the Catholic writer Léon Bloy, after having read his novel *La Femme pauvre*. Bloy brought Jacques and Raïssa into contact with a Catholicism radically different from the bourgeois religiosity then prevalent in Parisian society. Bearing witness to Christ as an impoverished (married) laymen, and writing books that spoke of the mystery of the redemption, while severely chastising the ambient culture of superficial and smug materialism, Bloy's example prepared the way for the Maritains' conversion to the faith. Baptized in 1906, the young convert Jacques assumed that this path required the renunciation of his earlier philosophical aspirations. It was not until several years later, upon reading Thomas Aquinas's *Summa theologiae*, that he recovered his earlier commitment and decided to pursue a philosophical vocation as a disciple of the great medieval theologian.

Maritain did not approach Aquinas in the spirit of a historian, as would, for instance, his fellow Catholic philosopher Étienne Gilson. Maritain sought rather to find in Aquinas a set of principles which could be creatively applied to contemporary problems. In so doing, Maritain did not intend to amend Aquinas' principles, or to construct a new system out of them that would bear a more or less close resemblance to their original articulation in the master's own text. Even less did he intend to reconcile Aquinas' thought with the philosophical postulations of modernity, born of Descartes' vision of a new "method" and continued by thinkers such as Kant and Hegel. Such an effort, would, in Maritain's opinion, be doomed to failure and would conceal the deep chasm that separated the metaphysical realism of Aquinas' philosophy from the misguided idealism of the moderns. He did not however believe that the task of Christian philosophy could adequately be accomplished by a simple exposition of Thomistic principles as they might be found in the writings of Aquinas, since processes of historical change had brought real advances to human life and culture, including the human being's moral and political self-understanding. Progress was no mere illusion, although a careful effort of philosophical (and theological) reflection was required to "liberate" these advances from the errors which, parasitically as it were, had placed modernity on a collusion course with the Catholic faith.

> Christian humanism, integral humanism, is capable of assuming all, because it knows that God has no opposite and that everything is irresistibly carried along by the movement of the divine government. It does not reject into darkness all that which, in the human heritage, relates to heresies and schisms, to the aberrations of the heart and of reason ... It knows that the historical forces invaded by error have served God despite themselves, and that despite themselves there has passed through them all along modern history, at the same time as the surge of the energies of illusion, the surge of Christian energies in temporal existence. In the scheme of Christian humanism there is a place not for the *errors* of Luther and Voltaire, but *for* Voltaire

and Luther, according as, in spite of their errors, they have contributed in the history of men to certain advances (which belong to Christ, as does every good among us).[4]

Professor from 1914–40 at the Institut Catholique of Paris, where he occupied the chair of history of modern philosophy, Maritain exhibited his conception of "philosophizing in the faith" with a series of groundbreaking works, including *Art et scholastique* (1920), *Les degrés du savoir* (1932), *De la philosophie chrétienne* (1933), *Science et sagesse* (1935), and *Humanisme intégral* (1936). During this period, the Maritains' home in Meudon (a suburb of Paris) became a central meeting place for poets, philosophers, theologians, and others who sought to carry out their creative and intellectual endeavors in vital connection with faith. This was the seat of the "Cercles Thomistes" where research papers were presented, and where, in addition, a yearly retreat was held, usually preached by Fr. Garrigou-Lagrange, which at its peak assembled upwards of 300 participants.

Residing in New York City during World War II (where, for a time, he led the École Libre de Hautes Études at the New School for Social Research), Maritain sought to elucidate the philosophical and spiritual foundations of the French resistance movement. He also undertook numerous practical endeavors in support of persons fleeing Nazi occupied Europe. Voicing strong opposition to the Vichy regime (his *À travers le désastre* (1941) was one of the first books to be distributed clandestinely in occupied France), Maritain rejected not only its collaboration with National Socialism but also the paternalist social model which it represented. In its place he proposed a form of democracy (*Christianisme et démocratie*, 1945), wherein the recognition of fundamental human rights would serve as a basis for civic communion. This vision of the Christian sources of freedom, rights, and justice would later find expression in the documents of Vatican II, and would exercise an important influence on the Christian Democratic movement in Latin America (most notably in Chile under Edwardo Frei). In late 1944 De Gaulle appointed Maritain as France's ambassador to the Holy See, a post which he occupied until 1948, and during which time he urged (unsuccessfully) Pope Pius XII to issue an encyclical condemning anti-Semitism. Alongside his official duties he also managed to write a Thomistic rejoinder to the existentialist philosophies that were very much in vogue at the time, *Court traité de l'existence et de l'existant* (1947), which explored the metaphysics of existence, human personhood, and freedom.

From 1948 to his wife's death in 1960 Maritain was professor of philosophy at Princeton University in New Jersey. It was during this period that he produced some of his largest and most systematic works, several of which were written directly in English: *Man and the State* (1951), *Creative Intuition in Art and Poetry* (1953), *On the Philosophy of History* (1957), and *La philosophie morale* (1960).

In the final decade of his life Maritain turned increasingly to theological topics. Having moved to Toulouse in order to live in close proximity to the Little Brothers

---

[4] Jacques Maritain, *Integral Humanism*, trans. Joseph Owens in Otto Bird (ed.), *The Collected Works of Jacques Maritain*, vol. 11 (Notre Dame: Notre Dame University Press, 1996), p. 210 (translation modified).

of Jesus (a religious order that followed the example and teaching of Charles de Foucauld), eventually taking vows at the ripe age of 89, he first published *Dieu et la permission du mal*, which explored human initiative in evil and its relation to the divine will. This was followed by *Le Paysan de la Garonne* (named from the river which runs through Toulouse), that offered a positive vision of the Church in continuity with Vatican II, yet which warned against some of the excesses which were then being committed in the name of the council. After a short work on the grace and humanity of Jesus (*De la grace et de l'humanité de Jesus*, 1967), that probed the special conditions which supervene on human nature (especially with respect to cognition) by virtue of its union with the divine nature in the person of Jesus Christ, Maritain continued the ecclesiastical reflections of the *Peasant* with a treatise *De l'Église du Christ: La personne de l'Eglise et son personnel* (1970). As indicated by its subtitle, this book aimed to show how the Church is more than a loose assembly of individuals; it enjoys a supernatural unity, an authentic personhood, by reason of its identity as the Mystical Body of Christ. Pure and spotless in itself the Church nevertheless cannot fulfill its mission without the contribution of fallible human beings, whose errors and sins can sometimes reach all the way to the top of its chain of authority. To disentangle this apparent paradox (elucidated by reference to the Inquisition, anti-Semitism, the Galileo incident, and other such historical "black marks"), Maritain distinguished two sorts of causality exercised by ecclesiastical personnel, one, *instrumental*, wherein the Church in its fullness acts through and in its members, and the other *proper*, wherein these members act from their own initiative and can therefore fail in carrying out their duties, thereby separating themselves from the Church's invisible, inner life.

Maritain's last book, *Approches sans entraves*, was published six months after his death on 28 April 1973. It included numerous essays of a theological cast. Among them is an analysis of the effects of original sin on the workings of human intelligence ("Réflexions sur la nature blessée") and a meditation on eschatological themes. In the latter, he advanced the hypothesis that, after the final judgment, the damned would be offered a kind of reconciliation with God. This will not be redemption through Christ (whom they have irrevocably rejected); as a consequence for all eternity will they be denied access to the beatific vision and the communion of saints. Rather God, in his mercy, will put end to their punitive suffering, and will allow them the sort of limited felicity which can spring from the natural knowledge of his existence.

Christianity and the Secular State

Today it is often taken for granted that Christian faith is compatible with pluralist representative democracy. Yet it must be said that belief in this compatibility is in fact quite recent. Its widespread acceptance within Catholicism, especially on the European continent, dates from the period after World War II. Within France in particular, the ideal of a lay state (*l'État laic*), existing in separation from the established Church, was long viewed with suspicion by traditionalist Catholics, who equated this ideal with the rejection of revealed religion by the free thinkers of the

French revolution. The assertion of religious tolerance, and the neutrality of the state vis-à-vis the competing claims of different religions, was viewed as a dangerous form of relativism that would undermine public and private morality. Indeed, in the two decades after his conversion Maritain shared this traditionalist viewpoint. Yet with the papal condemnation of the monarchist movement *l'Action Francaise* in 1926, Maritain began to question the traditionalist Catholic understanding of the political order. The result was a series of works, beginning with *Primauté du Spirituel* (1927) and culminating in *Man and the State* (1951), in which he sought to show how the modern idea of a pluralistic, secular state could be placed in vital continuity with, and even be informed by, religious principles drawn from the Christian faith.

Maritain's most famous and influential elucidation on this theme was undoubtedly his book *Humanisme intégral* (1936), which was originally delivered as a series of lectures in Spain, where the heated political conflict between traditionalists and republicans would soon escalate into civil war. Acknowledging that Christianity has always upheld a distinction between the temporal order of the earthly city, on the one hand, and the spiritual order of the Church and the kingdom of God, on the other, Maritain showed how the relationship between these two orders must not be represented as fixed and unchanging throughout history. Thus, in the Christian Middle Ages, the unity of the temporal order was conceived of as dependent upon a shared faith (the "ideal of a Holy Empire"). On this "sacral conception" of the terrestrial city, goods associated with the human being's temporal existence were deemed valuable in light of the assistance that they provided for the achievement of spiritual ends. From such a standpoint, religious pluralism would be viewed as an inherent evil; and religious minorities, while tolerated, would never be accepted into the temporal community as fully-fledged citizens.

By contrast, under the historical conditions of modernity, Maritain maintained that a new model of the relationship between the spiritual and the temporal (and by extension between Church and state) would have to be elaborated. This model could not be premised on a pure and simple separation of the two orders. Rightly understood, the two should be conceptualized as in vital interaction with each other. But on such a conception, shared theological faith would no longer provide the primary bond of unity between citizens, nor would the temporal order be valued chiefly for its instrumentality vis-à-vis man's spiritual end. Under this new model of humanity's *earthly* destiny, fundamental Christian truths would be reflected into the temporal order, where they would function as sources of inspiration for the promotion of human dignity, freedom, equality and civic brotherhood. This humanism "open to the divine," Maritain termed an "integral humanism," and the value thus placed on the achievement of the human being's *temporal* good would manifest (better perhaps than the instrumentalist conception of the Middle Ages) the *natural* effects of God's providential guidance for humanity. Maritain thereby sought to identify a middle way between a theocratic (and authoritarian) conception of politics on the one hand, wherein the authentic dynamism of human freedom is rejected, and, on the other hand, the naturalist humanism of secular liberalism or Marxism, wherein the path to human perfection is deemed to be fully achievable by human forces alone.

Central to his theorizing on this middle way was the idea, developed by Maritain at some length, that the temporal good of mankind has its own inherent value. As such, it should not be thought of as a pure means to man's higher religious end (this is the error of theocratic authoritarianism). To the contrary, human flourishing in the earthly city has more than a merely instrumental worth; it represents an end to which our best efforts and deepest sacrifices are rightly ordered. Yet, despite its importance and dignity, the temporal end of mankind is not the ultimate, absolutely final end to which we are ordained (neglect of this point is the key error of secular humanism). This ultimate end is the Kingdom of God, which will achieve its fullness in the world to come. As a result, a key task of the Christian philosopher consists in articulating the exigencies of these two ends, temporal and eternal, so that each is understood in its proper relation to the other.

In virtue of a process of differentiation normal in itself, though vitiated by the most erroneous ideologies, the secular or temporal order has in the course of modern times been established, as regards the spiritual or sacred order, in such a relation of autonomy that in fact it excludes instrumentality. In short, it has come of age.

> And this too is a real historical gain which a new Christendom should preserve. Certainly this does not mean that the primacy of the spiritual would be ignored. The temporal order would be subordinate to the spiritual, no longer, of course, as an instrumental agent, as was so often the case in the Middle Ages, but as a *less elevated principle agent*; and above all, the earthly common good would no longer be taken as a mere means in relation to eternal life, but as what it essentially is in this regard, namely, as an *intermediary or infravalent end*. A real and effective subordination—that is the contrast with modern Gallican and "liberal" conceptions; but a subordination which no longer takes a purely ministerial form—this is the contrast with the medieval conception.
>
> In this way there is disengaged and made precise the notion of a *vitally Christian lay body politic* or a *Christianly constituted lay state*.[5]

The Benefits of "Christian Philosophy"

Maritain's views on the role of religion in the temporal sphere developed in close continuity with his investigation into the relationship between philosophy and faith. In the years which immediately preceded his writing of *Humanisme intégral* Maritain had participated in a debate among French philosophers on the notion of "Christian philosophy." The debate was launched in 1931 by Émile Bréhier, a leading professor at the Sorbonne, who maintained in his article "Y-a-t-il une philosophie chrétienne?"[6]

---

[5] Ibid., p. 264.
[6] Émile Bréhier, "Y-a-t-il une philosophie chrétienne?" *Revue de métaphysique et de morale* (April–June 1931), pp. 133–62.

[Is There Such a Thing as Christian Philosophy?]) that the Middle Ages contained no intellectual movement that could rightly be called a "Christian philosophy." He argued that during this period philosophy enjoyed no real autonomy as a discipline; for it was controlled by dogma and other specifically religious interests. Moreover, due to its inherent fragility (a result of original sin), human reason was viewed by thinkers of this period as incapable of being its own proper measure and rule. No historian of philosophy, Bréhier concluded, who had asked the right questions could possibly conclude from sound principles that that there had had ever been a Christian philosophy.

Bréhier's article was in fact an attack on his junior colleague at the Sorbonne, Étienne Gilson. In a series of works on Augustine, Bonaventure and Aquinas, Gilson had maintained that these medieval thinkers could be found postulating a number of original philosophical ideas that were not reducible to the speculations of Aristotle, Plotinus and other ancient philosophers. To designate the original philosophical notions that had appeared in medieval theology under the influence of Judeo, Christian, and Islamic faith traditions, Gilson employed the term "Christian philosophy" (thereby emphasizing the Christian thinkers who were the main focus of his research). His main thesis was that in the Middle Ages philosophy had indeed achieved new insights, and did so precisely because it was exercised in the context of monotheistic, scriptural revelation.

Entering this debate, Maritain gave several lectures which resulted in his book *De la philosophie chrétienne*, which was published in 1933. Unlike Gilson, who has argued for "Christian philosophy" largely as a descriptive–historical thesis about the development of philosophy in the Middle Ages, Maritain adopted a more systematic–normative approach to the question. The core of Maritain's analysis was to distinguish the "nature" and "state" of philosophy. Vis-à-vis its intrinsic nature or essence, speculative philosophy reflects an inherently natural functioning of reason; in this sense it depends on the Christian faith neither for the principles from which it demonstrates its conclusions, nor for its basic methods. In this respect philosophy differs decisively from theology, since the latter discipline takes the revealed truths of faith as its starting point, necessitating, as a vital part of its methodology, acquiescence to divine authority (speaking through the ministry of the Church). From this perspective, there can be no sense in calling philosophy "Christian," no more than there could be a Christian biology or a Christian chemistry.

Maritain did however qualify these comments somewhat to fit the special case of moral philosophy, and this would have important implications for his political theory (since, in line with Aristotle, Maritain conceived of political philosophy as a branch of ethics). As a practical discipline—the purpose of which is to provide sound guidance for human action—moral philosophy would need to take into account the special features which attach to human action under the present phase of salvation history. These features Maritain listed as three in kind (1) the ultimate end or goal of the human being is eternal life in the world to come, an end that entirely transcends our current temporal existence; (2) human beings have been prevented from attaining this end by a disaster that occurred at the dawn of history, i.e. the "original sin" of Adam and

Eve; and (3) the effects of original sin have been overcome by the redemptive action of Jesus Christ, whose voluntary sacrifice on the cross again made the attainment of eternal life possible for human beings. If moral philosophy is to be adequate to its task of guiding human action, it would have to take into account this threefold datum of the New Testament economy of salvation. Hence, alongside the natural principles that form the substance of moral philosophy (principles articulated by Plato, Aristotle and subsequent thinkers), this discipline stands in need of principles drawn from the higher science of theology. Moral philosophy is not thereby transmuted into theological ethics, since it retains its distinctive methodology and sphere of application; moreover the revealed principles that it receives from theology merely complement the corpus of naturally knowable principles which stand at the core of the discipline. True, a certain loss of methodological purity results from this reception of principles from "above"; yet the great gain in practical efficacy (since in action the end is paramount, and without knowledge of man's true end moral philosophy would give faulty guidance) is, in Maritain's estimation, more than worth the cost.

Whether speculative or practical, philosophy does not designate an abstract essence only. Viewed concretely as the activity of a human subject, the exercise of philosophy is affected by the historical and existential condition of the whole person who engages in this activity. Moreover, taking into account the fact that philosophy represents *wisdom*, the highest and best, but also the most difficult exercise of "natural" reason, it follows that any impediments suffered by the human being as a result of primordial "original" sin will inevitably influence our access to the most fundamental philosophical truths: those that concern human nature, destiny, and God. Similarly, the "fact" of our redemption in Jesus Christ will have a positive effect on the exercise of human reason vis-à-vis the highest and most important objects of speculation, since grace heals nature. Historically and existentially, then, the "state" or concrete condition in which one philosophizes can augment one's ability to succeed in this activity. Following this line of argumentation, Maritain concludes that Christianity provides the optimal condition (or "state") for philosophical reflection.

Maritain amplified on this conclusion by explaining how Christian faith (and the theology that issues from it) strengthens the activity of philosophy in two different ways. First of all, faith provides philosophical reason with a set of "objective reinforcements" (*apports objectifs*). In this connection Maritain mentioned creation *ex nihilo*, God as subsistent being, moral fault as an offense against God, and metaphysical personhood, as fundamental concepts that were brought to the attention of philosophers by the influence of Christianity. Unlike the trinity of divine persons in God, or our participation in God's nature through grace—ideas that entirely exceed the unaided "natural" capacity of the human mind—the concepts mentioned above (creation *ex nihilo*, etc.) are *de jure* accessible to human reason without positive divine revelation, yet, *de facto* they were introduced into Western philosophical discourse only after having been revealed in the Hebrew and Greek scriptures. Maritain cites these examples as evidence that philosophy can be stimulated to reach new heights of speculation under the impact of Judeo-Christian revelation.

Second, Maritain noted that Christian faith (and theology) also strengthens philosophy by the conferral of "subjective reinforcements" (*apports subjectfs*). Viewing philosophy as an inner vital disposition (a "*habitus*") by which the cognitive faculties of an individual person are rendered fit for grasping metaphysical and moral truths, Maritain sought to show how the vitality of such a disposition would be greatly aided by the healing power of grace. Exercised concretely by an individual in a state of grace, the natural philosophical *habitus* will benefit from its conjunction with supernatural disposition of faith, which rectifies the person's ordination to divine truth.

> [G]race produces more than its strictly supernatural effects in us: the divine life which it engrafts in our souls is endowed with a healing power with respect to our nature ... It would be absurd to expect the *gratia sanans* to supply for the philosophic *habitus*, or to preclude aberrations, even of the gravest kind. Yet it is certain that the more the philosopher remains faithful to grace, the more easily will he free himself of manifold futilities and opacities, which are as a mote of self-love on the eye of reason.

> In sum, we understand that the state of philosophy has been changed and lifted up by Christianity, not only with respect to the objective material proposed but also with respect to the vitality and deepest dynamism of the intellect. On all these counts it must be affirmed that faith guides or orientates philosophy ... without thereby violating its autonomy; for it is always in keeping with its own proper laws and principles and by virtue of rational norms alone that philosophy judges things.[7]

Conclusion

Maritain concludes his discussion of "Christian philosophy" by emphasizing how the adjunction of these two terms should in no way be read as calling into question the rightful autonomy of philosophy. In this vein, he warns against the temptation—which readily arises when philosophy is exercised in a Christian context—to make philosophy inherently dependent upon faith, such that the advent of Christianity is thought to result in a form of philosophy entirely different from what had been recognized by the ancient Greeks. While conceding their important contributions to Western thought, Maritain nevertheless cites Kierkegaard, Boëhme, Jacobi, and even Nietzsche, as thinkers who too closely identified philosophy with Christian "stimulations," thereby compromising its inherently rational character.

---

[7] Maritain, *An Essay on Christian Philosophy*, pp. 28–9 (translation modified).

Bibliography

Primary Literature

Cahiers Jacques Maritain, published biannually by the Cercles d'Etudes Jacques et Raïssa Maritain (Kolbsheim, France). Includes primary and secondary source materials.

Collected Works of Jacques Maritain, edited by Ralph McInerney, Frederick Crosson and Bernard Doering (Notre Dame: University of Notre Dame Press, 1995–), 20 volumes.

Oeuvres complètes de Jacques et Raïssa Maritain, edited by Cercle d'études Jacques et Raïssa Maritain (Fribourg: Academic Press, 1982–2008), 16 volumes.

Maritain, Jacques, *Science and Wisdom*, trans. Bernard Wall (New York, 1940).

Maritain, Jacques, *An Essay on Christian Philosophy*, trans. Edward H. Flannery (New York: Philosophical Library, 1955).

Maritain, Jacques, *Integral Humanism*, trans. Joseph Owens, edited by Otto Bird, in *The Collected Works of Jacques Maritain*, vol. 11 (Notre Dame: Notre Dame University Press, 1996).

Secondary Literature

Barré, Jean-Luc, *Jacques et Raïssa Maritain: Les mendiants du Ciel* (Paris: Stock, 1995).

Bréhier, Émile, "Y-a-t-il une philosophie chrétienne?" *Revue de métaphysique et de morale* (April–June 1931), pp. 133–62.

Maritain, Raïssa, *We have been Friends Together and Adventures in Grace*, trans. Julie Kernan (New York: Image Books, 1961).

Sweet, William, "Jacques Maritain," *Stanford Encyclopedia of Philosophy*, http://plato.stanford.edu/entries/maritain (revised July 8, 2008, accessed March 3, 2012. Includes a list, with references, of Maritain's principal works).

Chapter 55
Edith Stein

Tor Martin Møller

Phenomenology was one of the strongest philosophical currents in Europe in the first half of the twentieth century. Its leading figures included Edmund Husserl (1859–1939), Max Scheler (1874–1928), and Martin Heidegger (1889–1976). Edith Stein (1891–1942)[1] was one of the many young students who were fascinated by Husserl's philosophy and his slogan "To the thing itself!," and who went to Göttingen to study under the Master (as Husserl's students liked to call him).

Edith Stein saw the object-oriented phenomenology as a liberating reaction to the contemporary Neo-Kantian philosophy and psychology, which focused on the subject. Like several of her close friends among the students in Göttingen – including Roman Ingarden (1893–1970) and Hedwig Conrad-Martius (1888–1966) – Edith Stein engaged in a lifelong debate with the Idealist approaches in Husserl's later philosophy. It was also in the Göttingen milieu that she received important impulses that helped to lead her to Christianity. When she converted, her philosophical investigations took a religious turn. And after she became a Carmelite nun, they took a mystical turn.

Life

Edith Stein was born in 1891 in a Jewish family in Breslau, at that time a city in the German empire (now Wrocław in Poland). She was born on Yom Kippur, the great Jewish Day of Atonement, which fell on October 12 that year. Her mother, who observed the Jewish religion strictly, is said to have emphasized the symbolic importance of this date. Edith Stein was the youngest of eleven children, four of whom had died before her birth. Before her second birthday, her father died of heatstroke on a business trip, at the age of 48. Her mother died in 1936, shortly before her eighty-seventh birthday.

Edith Stein was always a good pupil, but she tired of school after her primary schooling and began work as a governess in the house of her aunt in Hamburg. After eight months there, when she was 13 years old, she went back to school in Breslau. She had become a convinced atheist, and renounced her Jewish religion. After completing her secondary schooling, she intended to study history, German, and psychology, but

---

1 [Translator's note: Edith Stein was canonized by the Catholic church in 1998. In the English-speaking Catholic world, she is mostly known by her religious name: Saint Teresa Benedicta of the Cross.]

she found weaknesses in the courses that were offered, especially in the foundations of the study of psychology.

When a fellow student drew her attention to Husserl's *Logische Untersuchungen* (English: *Logical Investigations*), this was such a momentous experience for her that she left Breslau after two years at the university there to study under Husserl in Göttingen from the spring semester of 1913 onwards. War broke out in 1914, and after taking a state examination qualifying her as a teacher in 1915, she volunteered for military service as a nursing auxiliary. She followed Husserl to his new professorship at Freiburg, where she defended her doctoral dissertation on August 3, 1916. She then became his personal assistant, with the task of editing the lengthy second volume of his *Ideen zu einer reinen Phänomenologie und phänomenlogischen Philosophie* (English: *Ideas Pertaining to a Pure Phenomenology and to a Phenomenological Philosophy*). This was a thankless task, since Husserl had lost interest in it. Accordingly, she resigned after two years. Nevertheless, it is principally thanks to her that the work was published posthumously.

One of the younger professors in Göttingen of whom Edith Stein thought highly was the Jewish scholar Adolf Reinach, who fell on the frontline in Flanders in November, 1917. He had had powerful religious experiences during the War, and had been baptized together with his Jewish wife. Edith Stein was profoundly affected by Reinach's death, and when she visited his widow in Göttingen shortly afterwards, she was struck by the strength that Mrs. Reinach found in her newly acquired Protestant faith. Already in 1914, Max Scheler, who was interested in Catholic ideas at that time, had opened her otherwise rationalistic eyes to religious phenomena that could not simply be dismissed. Edith Stein's own religious awakening coincided in part with a difficult period in her life, since she suffered because of her unrequited love for Ingarden, which she admitted to him in a letter written on Christmas Eve, 1917. In 1919, she encountered professional resistance to her academic career in Göttingen, because she was a woman. In the same year, she fell in love with the philosopher Hans Lipps, but this too remained unrequited.

During a visit to Conrad-Martius in summer 1921, she came across the autobiography of Teresa of Avila (1515–82). She read this book in one single night and immediately realized that she would become a Catholic. She at once bought a Catholic catechism and missal and began to study them carefully. She then went to the priest in Bergzabern, Eugen Breitling, and asked to receive baptism. This took place on January 1, 1922; with the permission of the bishop, Conrad-Martius was her godmother, although she was a Protestant. Edith Stein claimed that at this point, she already saw the Carmelite order as her destiny, but that she postponed entering this strict order out of consideration for her mother. In any case, the conversion came as a shock to her family.

In 1923, she began to teach at the girls' school run by the Dominican sisters in Speyer. In 1932, she took up a position at the Institute for Academic Pedagogy in Münster, but she lost this in the following year, after the National Socialists came to power. She had had contact with the Benedictine abbey of Beuron from 1927 to 1933. Now that she no longer had access to jobs in public life, her mother's resistance ceased to be a sufficient reason for not entering religious life. Finally, on October 14, 1933, the Vigil of the feast of Saint Teresa of Avila, Edith Stein took the religious name of Teresa Benedicta of the Cross and entered the Carmelite order in Cologne, where she took her vows on April 21, 1935.

After Kristallnacht on November 9, 1938, it was clear that Edith Stein had to escape, and she moved to the Carmelite convent in Echt in the Netherlands on New Year's Eve 1938. After the Catholic bishops in the Netherlands condemned the deportation of Jews in a pastoral letter, Hitler issued an order on July 26, 1942 that all Catholics of non-Aryan origin were to be arrested. The Gestapo came to the convent in Echt and fetched Edith Stein on August 2, 1942. She said to her terrified sister, who had converted in 1936 and had followed her to Echt: "Come, we are going for our people!"

Writings

Edith Stein's conversion forms a boundary line in her writings. Before this date, she wrote purely philosophical works; after her baptism, she wrote either religious works or philosophical works with a clearly religious or theological intention. During her lifetime, virtually only what she wrote before or around the time of her conversion was published. Almost of all the later religious works were published posthumously, beginning in 1950.

Before Baptism

The first phase in her writings is the period when she belonged to the phenomenological circle around Husserl in Göttingen and Freiburg, from 1915 until she moved to Speyer in 1923. All of these works, which are classic phenomenological dissertations, are concerned with questions about the nature of the human person.

Only a part of the doctoral dissertation, *Zum Problem der Einfühlung* (English: *On the Problem of Empathy*), was published, because she herself had to pay for the publication. The following studies were published in Vols 5 and 7 of the *Jahrbuch für Philosophie und phänomenologische Forschung,* which was edited by Husserl himself. The first was "Beiträge zur philosophischen Begründung der Psychologie und der Geisteswissenschaften" (English: *Philosophy of Psychology and the Humanities*), which consisted of two separate articles on "Psychische Kausalität" ("Sentient Causality") and "Individuum und Gemeinschaft" ("Individual and Community").[2] The second study was "Eine Untersuchung über den Staat" (English: "An Investigation Concerning the State"). These essays were published in 1922 and 1925 respectively, but it is probable that they were completed a few years before publication, since the printing process took a long time. The titles show that these writings form parts of a larger-scale and complex project that has its roots in Edith Stein's search for insight

---

[2] [Where works by Edith Stein have not yet been published in an English translation, I give my own translation in square brackets.]

into the basic structures of human existence. In this way, as Ingarden has pointed out, she was one of the phenomenological forerunners of Martin Heidegger's *Sein und Zeit*.

The theme of her doctoral dissertation was the human person's direct encounter with other persons and the possibility of understanding them as thinking and feeling beings. In the following two works, she focused on the human person's mental constitution *per se* and the person's relationship to a larger fellowship. Finally, in the last essay from this period, she attempted to clarify the foundation of the existence of the state as the overarching social entity. These works thus make up an interesting whole. They all deal with human existence as this appears in various contexts: in itself, in relation to other individuals, in relation to a fellowship of individuals, and in relation to the overarching societal structure. In addition to these ontological investigations of the person and society, Edith Stein also prepared a series of lectures in this period, *Einführung in die Philosophie* [*Introduction to Philosophy*]. This was first published in 1991, but it was probably completed as early as 1921. It gives an account of her view of philosophy and of the phenomenological method.

After Baptism

During her years in Speyer, from 1923 to 1932, Edith Stein devoted herself to translations and to intensive studies of Thomas Aquinas' philosophy. It is clear that she was in a transitional phase in this period and that she was looking for a new basis for her Christian thinking. It is characteristic that the next philosophical essay from her hand is a comparison of the philosophies of Husserl and Thomas, or rather, a confrontation between their systems of thought, in the article "Husserls Phänomenologie und die Philosophie des hl. Thomas v. Aquino: Versuch einer Gegenüberstellung" (English: "Husserl's Phenomenology and the Philosophy of St. Thomas Aquinas: Attempt at a Comparison"). This was her contribution to a Festschrift marking Husserl's seventieth birthday in 1929. This is a modest article, running to 30 pages, and it was published after nearly six years of withdrawal from the philosophical landscape; but it is the result of a long and intense process of maturation. This finds expression in the book-length manuscript entitled *Potenz und Akt* (English: *Potency and Act*), which she prepared in 1931 as her professorial dissertation, intending to submit it to Heidegger in Freiburg. The aim of this dissertation was to achieve an understanding of Thomas' Aquinas methodology. It thus represents the definitive transition in Edith Stein from a pure phenomenology to an approach to philosophy that was inspired by Thomism. In the preparatory phase, she had studied these questions in depth and translated Thomas' great work about "truth," the *Quaestiones disputatae de veritate*.

The new work as a lecturer at university level in Münster allowed Edith Stein to return to the topics that she had studied in her early period. She completed a lengthy manuscript of lectures for the winter semester of 1932/33 on *Der Aufbau der menschlichen Person* [*The Composition of the Human Person*]. Here, she revised her earlier thinking in the light of the new methodological approach she had acquired through her work on Thomas Aquinas. Nevertheless, this was a *philosophical* anthropology. She elaborated a *theological* anthropology in spring 1933 in a book manuscript entitled *Was ist der Mensch?* [*What is the Human Being?*], with the explicit goal of presenting the anthropology that is inherent in the Catholic doctrine of faith. This is thus the natural culmination of her thinking up to this date. It was unfortunately also the end of her academic career, since the Nazis' anti-Aryan laws excluded from public positions all who were of Jewish ancestry.

After she entered the Carmelite order, she was encouraged to continue her academic work. Her *chef d'œuvre*, a revised and greatly expanded version of what she had planned as her professorial dissertation, entitled *Endliches und ewiges Sein* (English: *Finite and Eternal Being*), was written in the mid-1930s. It was, of course, impossible to publish it under the regime at that period, and the fact that she called this work her farewell gift to Germany, when she was forced to flee in 1938, says much about how highly Edith Stein valued the German tradition and culture.

Even after her flight to Echt in the Netherlands, Edith Stein continued her academic work, *inter alia* with translations and a study of Pseudo-Dionysius. She was also asked to write a book to mark the four-hundredth anniversary of the birth of John of the Cross in 1942. She was not able to finish her last great work, *Kreuzeswissenschaft* (English: *The Science of the Cross*); the manuscript was found open on her writing desk after the Nazis had arrested her. In this book, she goes through the writings of Saint John of the Cross and offers a running commentary. Given the political situation in Europe, it is unlikely that it was planned to publish it in her own name.

Principal Themes

Positivistic philosophy assumed that the consciousness assembled its complex experiences out of simpler sense-impressions, but a central starting point for Edith Stein and other realistic phenomenologists was that the object itself is directly given for the consciousness. The original element in experience is not only sense-impressions, but the things themselves. Although human knowledge is limited and fallible, the objects of experience show themselves as they are – not as constructions of the consciousness or as mental replacements for something that is alien to the consciousness.

The Human Person and Empathy

In her doctoral dissertation *Zum Problem der Einfühlung*, the focus is on the deepest presuppositions for relationships between persons, since Edith Stein wanted to contribute to a better basis for the scientific study of the person and of society. Empathy, which is the foundation of the understanding of other persons and fellowship with them, thus was a natural starting point for her investigation. What kind of empathy is involved here?

At that period, the problem of empathy was well known from aesthetics. Empathy finds expression in art when the public who look at a given object of art see how the human persons who are depicted pass through certain mental states. This happens despite the fact that the object that communicates this impression is made of dead matter – stone, bronze, or oil on canvas. The same thing happens in the theater, even though we know that what we are watching is a play. This problem can be seen to be derived from the underlying philosophical question about how it is at all possible for us to have knowledge, through our own experience, of other persons' experiences. One expression of the fact that such a form of knowledge exists is our ability to see that other people are happy, angry, or sad. Edith Stein's starting point was that this is a special form of experience that is obvious in the same way as other phenomena in the real world. It is not the case that we see certain physical facts – that someone laughs, raises his voice, or weeps – and then infer by means of a special mental operation that he is happy, angry, or sad. According to Edith Stein, the experience of other people's moods is originally given as a holistic experience.

The philosophical problem is: How are we to account for this possibility, since the experiences of the individual cannot be experienced by anyone other than that person himself? This can be difficult for one whose starting point is in private experiences; but Edith Stein's starting point was the opposite of this. She saw experiences of empathy as an experience of genuine phenomena, not as inferences from vicarious sense-experiences. However, empathy does not involve a direct experience of the other person's feelings, since the experience of these feelings is a privilege of the one who has them "in the first person." If however we have an immediate experience of other persons' moods, this (according to Edith Stein) must be due to a form of experience that can be compared in one sense to the experience we have of the non-observable parts of physical objects.

For example, one does not see the back side of a ball that is lying in a basket, but when one sees the ball, one sees a wholly round object and one takes the "back side" of the ball for granted in the experience of the object. The round ball, and the whole person with both an outer and an inner appearance, thus emerge immediately as parts of the reality to which we relate. The special characteristic of living persons is that their mood becomes immediately present for the one who sees them – unlike, for example, the visual arts. It is possible to lift Edvard Munch's painting "Puberty" up and take it down from the wall without being affected by its human motif. But for most people, it would not be possible to enter a room in which a real person in such a mood was present, without being affected by this. The fact that we can be led astray by illusions is not some special characteristic of empathy; it applies to all experience.

One example that Edith Stein herself uses is that we know a friend's pain if we comes to us and tells us that he has lost his brother. The question that interests her is: What kind of knowledge is this? She is not interested in how we arrive at this knowledge. It is clear that one could have arrived at this knowledge also by means of a third person's account or through a photograph that showed the surviving brother grieving. But the direct encounter of the grieving person with a fellow human being has a different ontological character that makes the pain a present reality for the one whom he encounters. It is not simple to tear oneself away from such a presence of a fellow human being, where his state is experienced immediately – though without being given directly (or originally, as Husserl said) in a first-person perspective. On the other hand, one can easily see pictures of a far-off catastrophe on television and then lose consciousness of this as soon as the bell rings to tell us that the frozen pizza is ready to be eaten. The special characteristic of empathy is that it seizes the onlooker and holds him fast in such a way that the onlooker cannot exempt himself from it. Empathy can thus be seen as an underlying structure that makes possible a genuine human fellowship and personal relationships.

Realism versus Idealism

Of all Husserl's students, Edith Stein was the one who reacted most strongly, already during her studies, when the Master's thinking took an apparently Idealist direction in his *Ideen zu einer reinen Phänomenologie* (1913) and in subsequent writings. Later, thanks to her study and translation of Thomas Aquinas' philosophical works, she was able to take a critical position with regard to Husserl's phenomenology. Let me attempt to sum up her criticism, on the basis of the article she wrote for the Festschrift marking Husserl's seventieth birthday, where she indicates areas in which Husserl's phenomenology and Thomist philosophy take divergent paths.

She begins by pointing out that Husserl and Thomas agree in their view of *philosophy as a strict science*, with reason as its guide. However, the concept of rationality in Thomas also includes the supernatural. The consequence is that while Thomas' thinking has a place for *faith*, Husserl as a philosopher seeks only *knowledge*, since his philosophical starting point is that which is immediately *given* for the knowing consciousness – whereas Thomas' philosophical starting point is reality as a whole, *independently* of every such process of knowledge. Faith thus aims at truth, but the truth lies beyond what one can attain with natural experience, and is thus regarded as a gift of grace rather than as an epistemological achievement. Thomas sees *critical* philosophy as a pointless project, since it seeks to take the human person himself as the basis for a first philosophy. Since human knowledge is limited, the human person can never attain certain knowledge of any totality or of the total context in which the individual things have their place. *Dogmatics* is necessary, in order that the one who seeks can find solid answers that are independent of his own self. Ultimately, dogmatics points back to God as absolute existence. This makes Thomism a *theocentric* philosophy, the antithesis of the *egocentric* phenomenology that has its starting point in that which exists, as something that is given for the consciousness. This is unsatisfactory for a Thomist, because consciousness too is based on an underlying reality. The phenomenological *ontology* teaches how the objects of which we have consciousness, or their ideal picture, are structured. Husserl claims that in this exercise, we must put brackets around the real existence of the objects and only direct the consciousness to the acts of the consciousness itself; one must leave to *metaphysics* the question about the existence of the things. All the time, however, Thomas, who also draws a distinction between being and fact, is interested in the being or state of the real world.

The points of comparison that Edith Stein establishes between Husserl and Thomas show that the confrontational position that she took up vis-à-vis Husserl was based on the question of Idealism versus realism. Philosophically speaking, Thomas' Christian philosophy, which points to something primary that is greater than human consciousness, is closely related to the type of objections raised by Husserl's early students, with their Idealistic orientation, to the Master's later Idealist tendencies. Her confrontation with the phenomenological methodology does not amount to a rejection, but rather to a systematic modification. Her article in the Festschrift concludes with a lengthy discussion of the *concept of intuition*, on which Thomas and Husserl largely agree. In this case, "intuition" is not mystical knowledge. While logic tells us how we are to think and arrive at valid conclusions, it is intuition that gives us insight into specific circumstances and into what one is talking about.

Faith and Knowledge

Edith Stein's Thomist critique of Husserl's phenomenology opened the way for her own Christian philosophy, which she elaborated in *Potenz und Akt* and later set out more deeply in her *chef d'œuvre*, *Endliches und ewiges Sein*. In the introduction to the latter work, in which she expresses her view of the meaning and possibility of a Christian philosophy, she observes that it is the task of philosophy to give an account of the basis of all the sciences. Since the domain of faith is an expansion of the conceptual and epistemological sphere of conventional philosophy, the task of Christian philosophy is to give an account of the totality and of the possible unified understanding of everything that is embraced by knowledge and faith *together*. One of Edith Stein's principal concerns is therefore to demonstrate that there is a place for faith and revelation in an otherwise strictly scientific ontology. As the title indicates, she attempted in *Endliches und ewiges Sein* to bring about a meeting between two worlds in a fundamental teaching about Being. The subtitle – *Versuch eines Aufstiegs zum Sinn des Seins* (English: *An Attempt to an Ascent to the Meaning of Being*) – also suggests that the book is virtually an alternative to Heidegger's *Sein und Zeit*, which was published in 1927.

Edith Stein's approach is metaphysical, in the sense that she aims to give an account of Being and of the existent as such, not limited (as she understood Heidegger's fundamental ontology) to human existence. Instead of rejecting Heidegger's analysis, she points out that it is defective. Her starting point as a Christian philosopher is that not everything can be explained on the basis of human existence alone. Revelation and faith come into action at the point where natural knowledge no longer gives us answers.

One example of how she presents such connections is the relationship between time and eternity in the light of the temporal structure in human existence, which shows that we are finite beings. Both human life as such and our personal experiences belong to a short period or moment, and exist only between a moment in which we and our experiences "do not yet exist" and another moment in which they "no longer exist." Our finite existence, between being and not-being, thus appears as an isolated point and can reveal for us "the idea of pure being, which does not contain non-being at all, [...] which is not temporal, but eternal".[3] Our concept of the finite can be understood only in the light of its opposite, and thus opens our mind to the concept of eternity.

Another example is the human person's *Geworfenheit* ("thrownness"). According to Heidegger, this is what characterizes our existence, and Edith Stein largely agrees with this. "[A] human being finds itself in existence (*im Dasein*) without knowing how it got there, it does not exist in and by itself and from its own being it cannot expect to get any information about its purpose. However, that does not do away with the question about the purpose."[4] According to Edith Stein, existence in the form of thrownness is not something for which the individual himself is responsible. It can therefore be interpreted as the work of creation. There is a corresponding alternative interpretation of what Heidegger describes as the fear of nothing, which is a basic attitude in the human person, since one stands all the time before one's own death and nothingness. She sees this is as only one aspect of the matter: fear of death can be real enough, but it is very often accompanied by a joyful confidence, since we trust that our existence is sustained in a manner beyond our own control and comprehension.

As these examples show, *Endliches und ewiges Sein* is the work of a Christian philosopher, in the sense that the dogmas are taken for granted. Edith Stein writes in the preface that she writes like "a student for fellow students", not in order to convert anyone. Her task is to demonstrate the metaphysical and ontological connections and phenomena that provide the background for the understanding of the theological elements.

Edith Stein Today

Edith Stein was not a thinker who founded a school, but she was a central figure in the original phenomenological milieu around Husserl, the Göttingen school. In the course of the twentieth century, however, the phenomenology with its realistic orientation, to which Edith Stein adhered, was overshadowed in the philosophical landscape early on by the existential direction that Heidegger represented and that Sartre developed further. At the time of Edith Stein's death, she was still relatively unknown outside a narrow academic and Christian milieu.

Her philosophical, religious, and personal writings created an increasing interest in her life and work after they began to be published in the 1950s. This is due not least to Karol Wojtyła (1920–2005), later Pope John Paul II, who had a profound academic and personal interest in the phenomenological movement in general and in Edith

---

[3] Edith Stein, *Endliches und ewiges Sein. Versuch eines Aufstiegs zum Sinn des Seins,* in *Edith Stein Gesamtausgabe* (Freiburg 2000–), Ch. II § 2.

[4] Ibid., *Anhang* I B 2.

Stein specifically. Before he became pope, Wojtyła had begun his own activity as a theological-philosophical writer at the point where Edith Stein had left off, namely, with a dissertation on faith in the writings of John of the Cross. He followed this with a dissertation about the possibility of basing Christian ethics on Max Scheler's phenomenological system. Edith Stein's fellow student Ingarden was the future pope's philosophical teacher, and he is quoted frequently in the revised edition of Wojtyła's *chef d'œuvre, Osoba i czyn* (English: *Person and Act*). When he was cardinal archbishop of Cracow, Wojtyła invited Ingarden in 1968 to hold a lecture on Edith Stein as a philosopher.

In addition to their shared philosophical interest in the human person, Edith Stein's own faith journey, and her tragic end in a concentration camp not far from the town in which he spent his childhood, must have spoken strongly to the future pope. When he canonized her on October 11, 1998, Pope John Paul II presented her as a reminder of the Nazis' attempt to wipe out the Jews. On October 1, 1999, Pope John Paul II then named her one of six patron saints of Europe. He affirmed that these six saints had overcome through faith the divisions of the times in which they lived, and that they represented the cultural basis of Europe and its national and spiritual plurality. He pointed out that Edith Stein had engaged in a dialogue with contemporary philosophy and that she had finally borne witness to God through her martyrdom.

The great general interest in Edith Stein in our own days arose after her beatification on May 1, 1987. The most important event that will allow future generations of theologians and philosophers to continue their study of Edith Stein is the publication of her Collected Works in 25 volumes, beginning in 2000. The new critical "Edith Stein Gesamtausgabe" (ESG) replaces "Edith Steins Werke" (ESW), which was published from 1950 onwards (in both cases by Herder Verlag).

The feast of Teresa Benedicta of the Cross is kept on August 9, the date on which it is assumed that Edith Stein was killed in Auschwitz-Birkenau in 1942. Her death and her posthumous reputation are paradoxical. The story of Edith Stein, the defenseless woman who became Europe's protector, contains to the full the dark and the bright sides of the symbol of the Cross with which she herself was preoccupied.

Bibliography

Primary Literature

Edith Stein Gesamtausgabe (ESG) (Freiburg: Herder, 2000–).

English translations (except where otherwise noted):

The Collected Works of Edith Stein (CES) (Washington: ICS Publications, 1986–).
Aus dem Leben einer jüdischen Familie und weitere autobiographische Beiträge (ESG 1, 2nd ed. 2007). English: *Life in a Jewish Family* (CES 1, 1986).

Zum Problem der Einfühlung (see ESG 5). (Halle: Waisenhauses, 1917). English: *On the Problem of Empathy* (CES 3, 1989).
"Beiträge zur philosophischen Begründung der Psychologie und der Geisteswissenschaften" (see ESG 6). *Jahrbuch für Philosophie und phänomenologische Forschung* 5 (Halle: Niemeyer, 1922). English: *Philosophy of Psychology and the Humanities* (CES 7, 2000).
"Eine Untersuchung über den Staat" (see ESG 7). *Jahrbuch für Philosophie und phänomenologische Forschung* 7 (Halle: Niemeyer, 1925). English: *An Investigation Concerning the State* (CES 10, 2006).
Einführung in die Philosophie (ESG 8, 2004).
"Husserls Phänomenologie und die Philosophie des hl. Thomas v. Aquino: Versuch einer Gegenüberstellung." *Jahrbuch für Philosophie und phänomenologische Forschung, Ergänzungsband* (Halle: Niemeyer, 1929). English: "Husserl's Phenomenology and the Philosophy of St. Thomas Aquinas: Attempt at a Comparison," in Mary Catharine Baseheart, *Persons in the World: Introduction to the Philosophy of Edith Stein* (Dordrecht: Kluwer, 1997).
Potenz und Akt. Studien zu einer Philosophie des Seins (ESG 10, 2005). English: *Potency and Act. Studies Toward a Philosophy of Being* (CES 11, 1998).
Der Aufbau der menschlichen Person. Vorlesungen zur philosophischen Anthropologie (ESG 14, 2004).
Was ist der Mensch? Theologische Anthropologie (ESG 15, 2005).
Endliches und ewiges Sein. Versuch eines Aufstiegs zum Sinn des Seins, including "Martin Heideggers Existenzphilosophie" and "Die Seelenburg," (ESG 11/12, 2006). English: *Finite and Eternal Being. An Attempt to an Ascent to the Meaning of Being* (CES 9, 2002).
Kreuzeswissenschaft. Studie über Johannes vom Kreuz (ESG 18, 3rd ed., 2007). English: *The Science of the Cross* (CES 6, 1983).

Secondary Literature

Arborelius, Anders, *Edith Stein: biografi – texter* (Tågarp: Karmeliterna, 1983).
Berkman, Joyce Avrech (ed.), *Contemplating Edith Stein* (Notre Dame, Ind.: University of Notre Dame Press, 2006).
Gerl, Hanna-Barbara, *Unerbittliches Licht. Edith Stein – Philosophie, Mystik, Leben* (Mainz: Matthias Grünewald Verlag, 1991).
Macintyre, Alasdair C., *Edith Stein: A Philosophical Prologue, 1913–1922* (Oxford: Rowman & Littlefield, 2006).
Müller, Andreas Uwe, *Grundzüge der Religionsphilosophie Edith Steins* (Freiburg: Alber, 1993).
Møller, Tor Martin and Mette Nygård (ed.), *Edith Stein – filosof og mystiker* (Oslo: Emilia forlag, 2000).

Chapter 56
C.S. Lewis

Oskar Skarsaune

When he wrote, Lewis never used his two Christian names, Clive Staples. He disliked them, and always shortened them to "C.S.," just as Gilbert Keith Chesterton was known only as "G.K." Of all modern books, it was to Chesterton's book *The Everlasting Man* that Lewis ascribed the greatest significance for his own development as a Christian apologist.

He was very well aware that he had no theological training and that he had read very little modern theology. He writes in a letter that he knows nothing of Tillich, Barth, and Brunner, and that although he had read something of Maritain, Niebuhr, and Berdyaev, he had got nothing important out of them. "Kierkegaard still means nothing to me." He reacted positively to Buber, and he says that Rudolf Otto's *Das Heilige* is one of the books that has been important for him. Nygren's *Eros och Agape* supplied him with a useful analytical tool, and "I liked, but could make no use of, Aulen's *Christus Victor* … You would hardly, among literate people, find a man who is less "in the know" or "up to date" than I am."[1]

The impression of an author whose access to Christian tradition and thinking was via belles lettres rather than works of theology is strengthened when one sees which authors meant the most for his journey to the Christian faith: G.K. Chesterton, Dorothy L. Sayers, George MacDonald, and J.R.R. Tolkien.

But Lewis was no ignoramus in theology. Like so many who had received a classic English education, he had read a good deal of patristic and mediaeval theology. His favorite authors were Augustine, Athanasius, Boethius, Thomas Aquinas, and Dante; among the English classics, he mentions Richard Hooker (1554–1600), George Herbert (1593–1633), John Bunyan (1628–88), William Law (1686–1761), Joseph Butler (1692–1752), and others. Butler's *The Analogy of Religion, Natural and Revealed, to the Constitution and Course of Nature* (1736) is probably the closest one comes to a literary model for Lewis' own books in the apologetic genre. It is scarcely necessary to mention that as a literary scholar, he was familiar with the poetry of Donne (1572–1631) and Milton (1608–74).

---

[1] In a letter to Corbin Scott Connell, October 31, 1958, quoted from Griffin, *C.S. Lewis*, 369f.

Biography and Writings[2]

He was born in Belfast in 1898, the younger of two brothers. His father was a lawyer, his mother the daughter of a pastor. He received a "normal" Christian upbringing. His parents were Protestants, and Lewis himself later found his natural place in the Anglican Church. On one point, however, his parents' interests were perhaps somewhat unusual, and this was to prove very significant for the boy's development. They were very well read, and their house in Belfast had an unusually large collection of books. Young "Jack" was a voracious reader, and he disappeared into the world of books.

He was especially fascinated by Norse mythology. He was deeply moved by the story of Balder, which he found infinitely beautiful and at the same time terrifying. He later described the strong emotion that this and similar stories evoked in him as "longing" or *Sehnsucht* (his choice of vocabulary was doubtless inspired by Otto's *Das Heilige*).

In his adolescence, Lewis lost his childhood faith, and his atheist conviction was strengthened somewhat later on, when he became a private pupil of the atheist and logician W.T. Kirkpatrick, who taught his young pupil to become a sharp analyst and rationalist who could pitilessly dissect pompous and high-flown utterances and demonstrate that they were at best meaningless for a more penetrating logic.

This childhood and adolescence produced a young man who lived with an inner conflict. On the one hand, there was a highly cultivated and trained appreciation of the aesthetic beauty of the myths, an uncommon ability to create images, and a productive poetic imagination. On the other hand, there was an unbending rationalism that did not acknowledge any reality other than what could be described and measured and weighed by exact science. "The two hemispheres of my mind were in the sharpest contrast. On the one hand a many-islanded sea of poetry and myth; on the other a glib and shallow 'rationalism.' Nearly all that I loved I held to be imaginary; nearly all that I believed to be real I thought grim and meaningless" (*SbJ* 138). He still delighted in the myths, but he "believe[d] in nothing but atoms and evolution and military service" (*SbJ* 140).

Lewis was appointed to the position of Fellow and tutor in English at Magdalen College in Oxford in 1924, with English Renaissance literature as his specialty. His colleagues here included John Ronald Reuel Tolkien (1892–1973), who was later to

---

[2] I give brief references in brackets in the text to Lewis' works, with the following abbreviations: *FE* = *Fernseeds and Elephants*; *GD* = *God in the Dock*; *M* = *Miracles*; *MC* = *Mere Christianity*; *PP* = *The Problem of Pain*; *SbJ* = *Surprised by Joy*. Page references are to the editions listed in the bibliography below.

write *The Hobbit*, *The Lord of the Rings* trilogy, and *The Silmarillion*. Thanks to many long conversations with Tolkien and other colleagues and friends in Oxford, Lewis felt that cracks were beginning to appear in his intellectual defenses of atheism. Two points were of particular importance. The first was an increasing recognition that if its principal argument was the complete meaninglessness of the universe, atheism had great problems in explaining where the human being found his concepts about meaning – *if* the universe as a whole was truly meaningless. On this point, Lewis the rationalist and logician experienced a growing problem with his atheism.

But there was also another point in the argumentative wall of defense around his atheism that began to show cracks. He had been convinced by the historian of religion James G. Frazer (in his celebrated work *The Golden Bough*) that the Gospel narratives about a Son of God who dies and rises again were nothing more than a myth about a fertility god, like stories about Balder and others. Now, he read the Gospels and was struck by the fact that "They had not the mythical taste" (*SbJ* 188). One of his atheist friends surprised him one day by saying: "All that stuff of Frazer's about the Dying God. Rum thing. It almost looks as if it had really happened once" (*SbJ* 179). During a long nocturnal conversation with Tolkien and another literary friend, Tolkien succeeded in convincing him that pagan myths too should not be regarded simply as lies.

In 1929, Lewis converted from atheism to a Hegelian type of theism, and in 1931, he began to profess the Christian faith. He published his first Christian book in 1933: *The Pilgrim's Regress: An Allegorical Apology for Christianity, Reason and Romanticism*, an allegorical autobiography inspired by John Bunyan's *Pilgrim's Progress*. He later followed up this book by four other apologetic works: *The Problem of Pain* (1940), *Mere Christianity* (1952; first edition 1942–43), *The Abolition of Man* (1943), and *Miracles: A Preliminary Study* (1947). In these books, the reader encounters both sides of Lewis' natural talent: the rationalist and logician on the one hand, and the poet, the creator of images, and the enthusiast for myths on the other.

He developed the last-named aspect of his talent through the series of fictional works that made him world-famous, especially after his death: the science fiction trilogy *Out of the Silent Planet* (1938), *Perelandra* (1943), and *That Hideous Strength* (1945), and the seven books for children about the fantasy land of Narnia (published from 1950 to 1956). His most ambitious attempt to compete with Tolkien as a modern creator of myth came in the book *Till We Have Faces: A Myth Retold* (1956). Lewis cultivated his writing in the framework of a literary club, The Inklings, who met regularly in the Eagle and Child pub in St. Giles Street in Oxford. In addition to Lewis, his brother Warren, and J.R.R. Tolkien, the journalist and dramatist Charles Williams was a core member of The Inklings.[3]

Lewis' academic career proceeded undramatically. In 1954, he was appointed professor of mediaeval and Renaissance English literature at Cambridge University and was offered a fellowship at Magdalene College. He moved there in that year, and held this position until shortly before his death in 1963.

---

[3] On the club and its leading personalities, see Carpenter, *The Inklings*.

His writings are more extensive than the titles I have mentioned, and they display a high degree of intellectual consistency across the large differences in their genres. In my presentation of the principal ideas in Lewis' apologia for Christianity, I concentrate on three of the apologetic books, *The Problem of Pain*, *Mere Christianity*, and *Miracles*.

Principal Ideas

As I have said, Lewis presented his conversion to Christianity as an event in two phases. First, he became a theist: he accepted the first article in the Christian faith. But it took another two years before he was also ready to accept the second and third articles in the Christian creed. This is reflected in his apologetic writings, which are variations on two main motifs.

Argumentation on Behalf of Theism

When Lewis wanted to present his arguments on behalf of theism, he often took as his starting point his earlier argumentation on behalf of atheism. In a very compressed form, these arguments took the following form – the quotation comes from *Mere Christianity*, which is built on popular talks he gave on BBC radio in 1942:

> My argument against God was that the universe seemed so cruel and unjust. But how had I got this idea of just and unjust? A man does not call a line crooked unless he has some idea of a straight line. What was I comparing this universe with when I called it unjust? If the whole show was senseless from A to Z, so to speak, why did I, who was supposed to be part of the show, find myself in such violent reaction against it? […] Thus in the very act of trying to prove that God did not exist – in other words, that the whole of reality was senseless – I found I was forced to assume that one part of reality – namely, my idea of justice – was full of sense. Consequently atheism turns out to be too simple. If the whole universe has no meaning, we should never have found out that it has no meaning; just as, if there were no light in the universe and therefore no creatures with eyes, we should never know it was dark. *Dark* would be a word without meaning (*MC* 41f.).

In a manner similar to Immanuel Kant, Lewis operates with a kind of "moral proof of God." In *The Abolition of Man*, he argues in detail for the view that moral imperatives cannot be explained as merely subjective feelings or social conventions. They appear as absolute laws, or as specifications of one absolute law, and it is not we ourselves who produce this law, either individually or collectively. The existence of the law points to a Lawgiver. It is impossible to explain the existence of a moral law of this kind in a materialistic universe in which matter is all that exists.

Lewis' second starting point is our ability to recognize with our reason that something is true. Let me attempt to sum up in a very simplified form his highly acute and detailed arguments. In a purely material universe, every event – including a mental state in our brain – will be a material event, and it will be caused by the immediately preceding event that is its physical cause. The same must apply to the states in our brain. State B must be caused by state A, which immediately preceded it, and the causal relationship must be purely physical. Let us now suppose that state B expresses itself in a statement about a state of affairs. This statement may be true or mistaken, but in any case it will be a necessary consequence of the preceding state A, irrespective of whether it is true or false. And the results of our attempts to test whether statement B was true or false would in turn be predetermined physically, irrespective of whether they were true or false – and so on, *ad infinitum*. I would be predetermined physically to have all the views I have, just as my adversary who holds the opposite views would likewise be predetermined physically to have his views. If one thinks this through to its logical conclusion, this chain of thinking ends up by dissolving the entire concept of reason. We would have no possibility of checking whether our views were true or false, for we would never get behind or beyond the physical regularity that governs our thoughts.

Lewis sums up in a quotation from J.S. Haldane the dilemma that is inherent in a naturalistic explanation of the world: "If my mental processes are determined wholly by the motions of atoms in my brain, I have no reason to suppose that my beliefs are true … and hence I have no reason for supposing my brain to be composed of atoms" (*M* 19). Pure materialism corrodes; it saws off the branch that supports it.

In other words, it is precisely in the human person's reason, in the laws of logic – which are different in kind from physical causality – that another reality than the physical regularity in the created universe reveals itself. We encounter a regularity that has to do with consciousness, thought, and intellect. We encounter here too a regularity that we ourselves have not created, something that simply exists and that must be obeyed if we wish to attain true knowledge. And this brings us to the conclusion that human reason is a reality that occupies a position all by itself, a reality that indicates that the intellectual and mental realities in the world are not secondary phenomena that accompany matter. The mental and intellectual aspects of the human person bear witness to a spiritual origin that (to put it somewhat metaphorically) must be at least a match for its product. In other words, must be at least a match for the human person, and it is reasonable to suppose that it far transcends the human person in intellect and power.

But what about atheism's argument against God, based on evil in creation? Since a good God cannot will what is evil, and evil exists, it follows either that God is not good or that he is not omnipotent – or perhaps that he is neither one nor the other. Lewis takes up this challenge in *The Problem of Pain*, and begins with a discussion of the concept of omnipotence. His starting point is the usual definition as the "power to do all, or everything," and he makes the important point here that "everything" must mean the "power to do all that is intrinsically possible." This sounds like a limitation on God's omnipotence, but this is not the case. For example, the concept of a "square circle" is logically meaningless, because we have combined two concepts with mutually exclusive definitions. There will never be any reality that corresponds to the concept of a square circle, because this concept is a meaningless combination of sounds, a nonsensical concept. Lewis makes an important point here: sentences that contain nonsensical words and nonsensical affirmations are every bit as nonsensical when we put "God" as the subject. The proposition: "X can draw a square circle" is meaningless for every "X," even when we say: "X = God."

> You may attribute miracles to Him, but not nonsense. This is no limit to His power. If you choose to say 'God may give a creature free will and at the same time withhold free will from it,' you have not succeeded in saying *anything* about God: meaningless combinations of words do not suddenly acquire meaning simply because we prefix to them the two other words 'God can.' It remains true that all *things* are possible with God: the intrinsic impossibilities are not things but nonentities. It is no more possible for God than for the weakest of His creatures to carry out both of two mutually exclusive alternatives; not because His power meets an obstacle, but because nonsense remains nonsense even when we talk it about God (*PP* 16).

This purely linguistic clarification may have a greater apologetic potential than one initially realizes. When we find the world that God has created to be evil and unjust, we must ask: "What world are we actually comparing this world to?" Is it not the case that many of the alternatives that we envisage entail in reality – whether or not we are aware of this – logical nonsense of this kind, square circles (so to speak)? Naturally, we know little about this, but Lewis presents an interesting argument to illustrate the logical necessities that (probably!) exist as a result of the creation of conscious beings like the human person. God wanted to create beings who had the ability to love him of their own free will. If the human person is to have a genuine possibility of choosing the good, he or she must also have an equally genuine possibility of choosing evil. If God were to eliminate immediately the consequences of all evil actions, the possibility of doing evil would not be real.

> We can, perhaps, conceive of a world in which God corrected the results of this abuse of free will by His creatures at every moment: so that a wooden beam became soft as grass when it was used as a weapon, and the air refused to obey me if I attempted to set up in it the sound-waves that carry lies or insults. But such a world would be one in which wrong actions were impossible, and in which, therefore, freedom of the will would be void; nay, if the principle were carried out to its logical conclusion, evil thoughts would be impossible, for the cerebral matter which we use in thinking would refuse its task when we attempted to frame them (*PP* 21).

Lewis believes that these are good arguments in support of the claim that the necessary framework for a genuine fellowship among God's creatures, especially human beings, is a *stable* creation that behaves in accordance with fixed laws. In this creation, no immediate dispensation from these laws is given when parts of the creation are misused by evil wills, or human beings are affected by the powers of nature thanks to a lack of foresight and insight on their part. "Fixed laws, consequences unfolding by causal necessity, the whole natural order, are at once limits within which their [*sc.* souls'] common life is confined and also the sole condition under which any such life is possible. Try to exclude the possibility of suffering which the order of nature and the existence of free wills involve, and you find that you have excluded life itself. [...] Perhaps this is not the 'best of all possible' universes, but the only possible one" (*PP* 22f.).

The Gospels' Narrative – Myth became Fact

In his discussion of the second article of faith, Lewis has a completely different starting point from that in his apologia for theism. It is important for him to underline that in the incarnation, where the Son of God becomes a human being, we encounter something totally unexpected, something that no wise man could ever construe with his reason. The story of the incarnation

> ... is not transparent to the reason: we could not have invented it for ourselves. It has not the suspicious *a priori* lucidity of Pantheism or of Newtonian physics. It has the seemingly arbitrary and idiosyncratic character which modern science is slowly teaching us to put up with in this willful universe, where energy is made up in little parcels of a quantity no one could predict, where speed is not unlimited, where irreversible entropy gives time a real direction and the cosmos, no longer static or cyclic, moves like a drama from a real beginning to a real end. If any message from the core of reality ever were to reach us, we should expect to find in it just that unexpectedness, that willful, dramatic anfractuosity which we find in the Christian faith. *It has the master touch – the rough, male taste of reality, not made by us* ... (*PP* 13, my italics).

He returns to this point in *Mere Christianity*:

> Reality, in fact, is something you could not have guessed. That is one of the reasons I believe in Christianity. It is a religion you could not have guessed. If it offered us just the kind of universe we had always expected, I should feel we were making it up. But, in fact, it is not the sort of thing anyone would have made up. It has just that queer twist to it that real things have (*MC* 44).

Nevertheless, God did not leave us *wholly* without premonitions of the mystery of the incarnation. God sent his prophets to the Jews, the chosen people, and they proclaimed beforehand the one who was to come. Lewis notes this, but he gives it only a modest place in his writings; what he continually returns to is his fascination in his childhood and adolescence with the non-Christian myths about the dying and rising god, whom Lewis often calls the "corn god": Baal, Osiris, Adonis, Balder.

> In this descent and re-ascent everyone will recognize a familiar pattern: a thing written all over the world. This is the pattern of all vegetable life. It must belittle itself into something hard, small and deathlike, it must fall into the ground: thence the new

life re-ascends. It is the pattern of all animal generation too. There is descent from the full perfect organisms into the spermatozoon and ovum, and in the dark womb a life at first inferior in kind to that of the species which is being reproduced, then the slow ascent to the perfect embryo, to the living, conscious baby, and finally to the adult. […] Death and rebirth – go down to go up – it is a key principle (*M* 116).

This general theme of life has become a narrative, a *myth,* in the myths about the dying and rising fertility god. – What then of the Gospels' story about the Son of God who became man and who died and rose again for human beings? *"Is not Christ simply another corn-king?"* (*M* 117, my italics).

At this point, according to Lewis, we encounter something utterly surprising when we read the Old and New Testaments. In both Testaments, the world of myth in which we normally encounter the fertility god is totally absent. Or more correctly, there is an intense fight, using every weapon available, against Baal, the corn-god who was ancient Israel's closest neighbor. For the God of Israel was not a god of nature, a fertility god who was one with nature. He was the *creator.* Nature was his work, but it was not identical with him. This is why the Israelites had to learn to think differently about him than the Canaanites thought about their Baal. They had to learn to think differently – that is to say, *in accordance with the truth* – about God, *inter alia* because it was precisely in *this* people that God wanted the incarnation to take place. If God had in fact become a human being and had died and risen again in another people, in a people with a natural religion, all this would have been "swallowed up" in the world of the myths. The world would have been enriched with yet another myth. – This is why it is profoundly significant that the only *real* death and resurrection of God took place in the one people that stood completely outside the magic circle of the myths.

> The records, in fact, show us a Person who *enacts* the part of the Dying God, but whose thoughts and words remain quite outside the circle of religious ideas to which the Dying God belongs. The very thing which Nature-religions are all about seems to have really happened once, but it happened in a circle where no trace of Nature-religion was present. It is as if you met the sea-serpent and found that it disbelieved in sea-serpents … (*M* 118).

Now … we can understand why Christ is at once so like the Corn-King and so silent about him. He is like the Corn-King because the Corn-King is a portrait of Him. The similarity is not in the least unreal or accidental. For the Corn-King is derived (through human imagination) from the facts of Nature, and the facts of Nature from her Creator; the Death and Re-birth pattern is in her because it was first in Him. On the other hand, elements of Nature-religion are strikingly absent from the teaching of Jesus and from the Judaic preparation which led up to it precisely because in them Nature's Original is manifesting Itself. In them you have from the very outset got behind Nature-religion and behind Nature herself. Where the real God is present the shadow of that God do not appear; that which the shadows resembled does. The Hebrews throughout their history were being constantly headed off from the worship of Nature-gods; not because the Nature-gods were in all respects unlike the God of Nature but because, at best, they were merely like, and it was the destiny of that nation to be turned away from likenesses to the thing itself (*M* 119f).

Accordingly, we should not be troubled in our faith when we hear that there are parallels to the Gospel narratives in other, pagan myths. Lewis writes in one passage: "… 'parallels' and 'Pagan Christs': they *ought* to be there – it would be a stumbling block if they weren't" (*GD* 45).

The story that the Gospels tell about Jesus is the one single myth that has genuinely occurred: *Myth became Fact.* This is why there are parallels to it in the history of religion; but this does not in the least mean that it is unhistorical. This makes it meaningless to "demythologize" the Gospel narratives or to peel off the mythical in the hope that what remains is the historical. Lewis explicitly challenged the German theologian Rudolf Bultmann and his school. They held that they were obliged to characterize the Gospels as partly unhistorical because they were partly mythical:

> [W]hatever these men may be as Biblical critics, I distrust them as critics. They seem to me to lack literary judgment, to be imperceptive about the very quality of the texts they are reading. It sounds a strange charge to bring against men who have been steeped in those books all their lives. But that might be just the trouble. A man who has spent his youth and manhood in the minute study of New Testament texts and of other people's studies of them, whose literary experience of those texts lacks any standard of comparison such as only can grow from a wide and deep and genial experience of literature in general, is, I should think, very likely to miss the obvious things about them. If he tells me that something in a Gospel is legend or romance, I want to know how many legends and romances he has read, how well his palate is trained in detecting them by the flavor; not how many years he has spent on that Gospel…. I have been reading poems, romances, vision-literature, legends, myths all my life. I know what they are like. I know that not one of them is like this [the Gospel of John] (*FE* 106–108).

Influence

It is not simple to locate Lewis in the theological discourse of the twentieth century, since he was too much of an outsider. In one sense, he did form a school, since he won a great number of adherents, some of whom were able philosophers and writers who in various ways continued his apologetic project. But few of them were theologians, and none of them played a leading role in the theological discourse of the twentieth century.

Bibliography

Primary Literature

For an extensive bibliography, see Colin Duriez, *C.S. Lewis Encyclopaedia* (Toronto: Azure Publishing, 2002).

The Abolition of Man (Riddel Memorial Lectures, 15th series) (London: Oxford University Press, 1943; paperback, Glasgow: Collins, Fount Books, 1978).
Mere Christianity (London: Geoffrey Bles, 1952; quotations from paperback, Glasgow: Collins, Fontana Books, 1955).
Miracles: A Preliminary Study (London: Geoffrey Bles, 1947; quotations from paperback, Glasgow: Collins, Fontana Books, 1960).
The Pilgrim's Regress: An Allegorical Apology for Christianity, Reason and Romanticism. (London: J.M. Dent, 1933; paperback, Grand Rapids: Eerdmans, 1958).
The Problem of Pain (London: Geoffrey Bles, 1940; quotations from paperback, Glasgow: Collins, Fontana Books, 1957).
Surprised by Joy: The Shape of My Early Life (London: Geoffrey Bles, 1955; quotations from paperback, Glasgow: Collins, Fontana Books, 1959).

Secondary Literature

Beversluis, John, *C.S. Lewis and the Search for Rational Religion* (Grand Rapids: Eerdmans, 1985).
Carpenter, Humphrey, *The Inklings: C.S. Lewis, J.R.R. Tolkien, Charles Williams, and their Friends* (London: Allen & Unwin, 1978).
Griffin, William, *C.S. Lewis: The Authentic Voice* (Tring: Lion Publishing, 1988).
Wielenberg, Eric J., *God and the Reach of Reason* (Cambridge: Cambridge University Press, 2007).

Chapter 57
Northrop Frye

Jan Schumacher

"But you can't believe things because they're a lovely idea."
"But I do. That's how I believe."

(Evelyn Waugh, *Brideshead Revisited*)

The scene could have been taken from Evelyn Waugh's novel *Brideshead Revisited*. One day in early summer, 1937, a group of American students appeared in the doorway of a room in Merton College in Oxford where a "genius" sat and worked conscientiously on yet another essay on English literature that he had to hand in to his tutor. He came from Toronto and was about 25 years old. The intruders wanted to entice him away from his books and take him on an outing in the countryside. One of them had borrowed an old Chevrolet, and they wanted to visit St. Mary's church in the village of Fairford. This was famous as one of the few churches in England where all the mediaeval stained glass windows had survived unscathed during the Protestant iconoclasm in the seventeenth century.

The young student's full name was Herman Northrop Frye. He was born in 1912 in the federal state of Québec in Canada and arrived in Toronto at the age of 17, where he matriculated as a student at Victoria College. This was to be his place of study and his future workplace until his death in January, 1991. Frye came to Oxford in the autumn of 1936 after taking the examinations for the Bachelor's degree in philosophy and English literature at the University of Toronto. He had also taken the theological examinations that made it possible for him to be ordained as a pastor in the Reformed United Church of Canada, but it was not theology that had moved him to come to Oxford for further studies. His interests were in literature. Frye went to Oxford with a conviction that can be compared to a religious vocation: he wanted to study the highly eccentric poet William Blake. This choice could well need support from something like a consciousness of vocation, since the dominant school in literary scholarship in the 1930s, modernism, had largely dismissed the Romantic literary canon – and William Blake was regarded as an early representative of this canon. Romanticism had broken with the tradition, and replaced it with faith in the power of the poetic inspiration to set the genius free. In the course of the 1930s, the great prophet of modernism in England, Thomas Stearns Eliot, attempted to reinstate the canon.

William Blake and the Tradition

Frye had already begun working on a comprehensive study of William Blake's literary universe. This was published ten years later as *Fearful Symmetry: A Study of William Blake*. Frye's reading of Blake came to the conclusion that this poet was certainly not eccentric. On the contrary, Blake was planted in the tradition; but (to borrow Eliot's expression) Blake's greatness consisted in the fact that he gave the tradition a new form and thereby expanded it. It was through reading Blake in the light of the Bible that Frye grasped how this poet too could be taken as a representative of the expansive possibilities of the tradition. Frye was later to publish a book about Eliot, who was much older. Their relationship is a clash between a "Protestant" and a "Catholic" way of understanding the tradition. Frye had a very complicated relationship to Eliot, as far as politics and religion were concerned. In religious terms, Eliot had traveled a long way from his background in an extreme Protestant tradition (Unitarianism) to the Anglo-Catholic wing in the Church of England. Frye's background lay in Protestant fundamentalist revival Christianity, but he had experienced a religious breakthrough in his early teens that he later compared, without irony, to the scene in John Bunyan's *Pilgrim's Progress* where the burden of sins falls from his shoulders into the empty grave. The burden that had fallen from the young Frye's shoulders was, however, the demand that he adore and submit to a God who acted in a way that was unacceptable to human moral sensibility. Eliot submitted to religion as an external ordering and discipline, and saw religion essentially in the light of his own shortcomings. For Frye, religion was primarily linked to liberation, and he was unwilling to present this liberation as an antithesis to the human person's deep longing to realize life to the full. This was the tradition from Milton and Bunyan that was developed by Blake, and this was a religion that needed no ecclesiastical authority. On the contrary, it had emerged in opposition to established, organized religion.

Blake and the Modern Period

Let us return to the stained glass windows in St. Mary's church in Fairford, which were something of a revelation for the young Frye. He had already read Emile Mâle's pioneering work on the Gothic cathedrals in France, *L'art religieux du XIIIe siècle en France* (1898; the first English translation was published in 1913, and many later editions followed under the title *The Gothic Image*). The visit in the church lasted several hours, and Frye saw a number of things that fascinated him. This was the first time he had the opportunity to see how things that Mâle had described in such detail looked in reality: first of all, how the whole of mediaeval doctrine appeared as a coherent universe or as a structure, thanks to the iconography of the cathedral. Secondly, he saw how this construction made of images consisted of narratives from the Old and the New Testaments, and that it was the same narratives – or more correctly, their inherent literary relationships – that also held the building together as a meaningful whole. The images must have evoked familiar narratives in Frye's memory, and he had in fact no problems about reading what he saw: it was the same narratives that he had heard again and again during his upbringing in a small Methodist parish out in the Canadian province. But he also recognized the pictures because he was already so thoroughly immersed in his study of Blake's poetry. As is well known, many of these poems were illustrated by Blake himself, who had studied under a graphic artist and had spent much of his time during his apprenticeship in Westminster Abbey, where he made sketches of the church's Gothic decoration. These motifs contributed to Blake's illustrations of the biblical personages.

Emile Mâle had called the cathedrals "books in stone and glass," and he claimed that the intention of such books was didactic. They were constructed first and foremost to meet the needs of the great majority of the population, who were illiterate. One hundred years after Mâle, this claim is highly disputable. One must juxtapose text and picture. To restrict the function of the pictures to their didactic use is not an accurate description of the religious mentality of the middle ages, if one means thereby that the content of Christianity can be described better and more exactly than through the Bible's universe of narratives and metaphors. The program of images in St. Mary's church in Fairford postulated the unity of the Bible by depicting the symmetry of the narratives and metaphors; Frye was to do the same by means of his highly distinctive writings about the Bible and its significance, not only for the graphic arts or the mentality of the middle ages, but also for the modern epoch and for literature in an age where art and culture had gradually won their autonomy vis-à-vis religion. And William Blake – the visionary poet whom Frye had chosen to study, despite the improbability of such a choice at that date – was important because he lived in the midst of a great paradigm shift in Europe. The old existential world, largely a product of an ideological use of the Bible, had worn out like an old garment: "The older construct wore out because it repressed the sense of human autonomy, the awareness that there are more things in man than any church or government can recognize or accommodate" (*Creation and Recreation*).

Blake was one of the first to grasp this dramatic shift, and he employed harsh words when he accused traditional religion of being oppressive. When one looks more closely, however, one sees that Blake's poetry is certainly not a product of self-generated fantasies and original metaphors. It is securely anchored in the tradition and permeated by biblical substance. This is why Blake was so important for Frye, and why he dedicated so much of his time, his research, and his writings precisely to the Bible: "Blake's reading of the Bible is so deeply rooted in the structure and imagery of the Bible that it is perhaps worth asking what principle his reading is based on" (*Creation and Recreation*).

Frye's Course on the Bible

Creation and Recreation, from which these quotations are taken, is the title of three lengthy lectures that were published in 1980. In a brief foreword, Frye says that these lectures build on older material, some of which had been published earlier. Many of his students at Victoria College in Toronto were familiar with these ideas. A course in the Bible had been offered there since the early twentieth century, and after Frye began to teach at the College in the late 1940s, he took over these lectures. Their character changed gradually, in keeping with his own reflection on the theme of the Bible and literature. In part, his biblical teaching involved enabling the students to recognize the influence of the Bible in literature, thanks to a thorough familiarity with biblical narratives and metaphors; in part, it was also a clear alternative to the way in which the Bible was taught in theology. Frye's aim was not to attack theologians for the way they read the Bible. Given their close relationship to ecclesiastical Christianity, the theologians had no real choice in the matter. But theology's dilemma, as Frye saw it, was that it was compelled to prescind from the fact that the Bible is wholly permeated by a literary language. For Frye, this meant a figurative language, myths, and metaphors. The problem with the theologians' use of the Bible was that it was inadequate in the eyes of a literary scholar. Theology regarded the form of the Bible as secondary and subordinate to its content. This was true both of the biblical scholarship that attempted to create confidence in its own reconstruction of what had "really" taken place "behind" the texts (which were treated as historical sources), and of the traditional dogmatics that used the Bible primarily as an arsenal of "proofs" that were to be used to justify doctrines that had been propounded in accordance with the laws of logic.

By the early 1970s, Frye's course on the Bible had developed a profile of its own. It sought to present the Bible as a part of the mythological framework of Western culture. He also began to collaborate with another scholar at Victoria College, Jay McPherson, whose interests lay in Greek and Roman mythology. The course thus gave a general introduction to the "mythological framework" of Western culture.

Creation and Recreation not only contained older material. It was also connected to a larger project on which Fry was working and which he called "a study of the narrative and imagery of the Bible and its influence on secular literature." This "larger book," *The Great Code: The Bible and Literature*, which is perhaps the best known of Frye's books (at least among theologians), was published in 1982. In the foreword, he reveals that he was planning a sequel to this book, but it took another eight years before this second part appeared: *Words With Power: Being a Second Study of The Bible and Literature.* Together with the short essay *The Double Vision: Language and Meaning in Religion, Words with Power* was Frye's literary "swansong." He died in the following year, 1991.

Frye's Legacy

A great deal of ambitious work has been done since Northrop Frye's death to develop the inheritance from this distinctive thinker, whom theologians found too strange and literary critics too religious. One result has been the publication of several volumes of his posthumous papers. Even the numerous notebooks that he filled over the years are now available in a scholarly edition. In the present context, it is especially valuable to have texts in which Frye deals with biblical and religious questions in a separate anthology entitled *Northrop Frye on Religion*. This includes the important essay *Creation and Recreation*, which was long out of print. Similarly, the manuscripts of the lectures from the course that he and McPherson taught jointly have recently been made available in the book *Biblical and Classical Myths*.

What, then, does Frye's contribution to the discussion of the Bible in the twentieth century amount to? It goes without saying that it is impossible to present in the space of a few pages the many nuances in his numerous books and articles. But let us return to what happened in the church in Fairford nearly eighty years ago, and see where this starting point leads us. The young Frye was overwhelmed by seeing with his own eyes the demonstration of a symmetry. This symmetry was the product of many things: first of all, of narratives that were very similar. All these narratives – Frye prefers the word "myths" – were framed by a great myth that spoke about creation, fall, and new creation, a "comedy" that begins when the human person loses the tree of life and the spring of life in Genesis, and finally, in the closing book of the Bible, gets them back in a form that far surpasses what had been lost. The beginning is fulfilled, and at the same time transcended, in the conclusion. Within the framework of this great narrative, there are many narratives that reveal the same structure as the great narrative. They concern the unfaithfulness of the people of Israel, which is followed by disaster – which in turn is followed by a sudden and undeserved rescue. We recognize this sequence in the New Testament, in the Gospels' narratives about Jesus, although the sequence of events here is not launched by any "fall." Some of the most luminous individual narratives in the Bible likewise have this structure; Frye refers *inter alia* to the Book of Job and to the parable of the prodigal son.

Finally, this symmetry was so easy to see because it consisted of a set of metaphors that could equally clearly be given their place in a common space or universe. And this universe coincides with one of the most universal realities that can be thought of, namely, the world we see around us – or more correctly, the way our lifeworld looks in our hopes and longings, or in our anxiety and fear. This can be described as a continually repeated cycle, or seasons (spring, summer, autumn, and winter) – cyclic myths that Frye had put into circulation in *Anatomy of Criticism*, a book about literary criticism, in 1958. But the world we describe as cyclical also appears as hierarchical, as a chain of "realms": the mineral realm, the plant realm, the animal realm, and the human realm. It is in these realms that we find the "raw materials" for the metaphors the Bible employs. One who is familiar with the Bible's use of images will, however, know that these "realms" always make their appearance in an "adapted," transformed form, as a product of human beings' ability to create culture.

Accordingly, the metaphors for the kingdom of God are the city, the garden, the flock, and the feast (or wedding). The kingdom of God is metaphorically identical with paradise and the Promised Land, and with spring and summer.

The Bible and Literature

The visit to St. Mary's church that morning confirmed Frye's surmise that the mediaeval iconography and the underlying interpretation of the Bible on which this program of images was based offered a fruitful hypothesis about the Bible as a book. And this was exactly the working hypothesis he needed as a future literary scholar and an insatiable reader who was familiar with the history of the Bible's influence. As he himself put it in the introduction to *The Great Code*, "the more traditional approaches of medieval typology and certain forms of Reformation commentary […] were more congenial to me because they accepted the unity of the Bible as a postulate. They do tell us how the Bible can be intelligible to poets […]."

None of the poets, nor any of the great classical preachers in the tradition, was seriously interested in how the narratives came into the Bible. Their approach to the Bible was "poetical," like that of the anonymous craftsmen behind the program of images in the cathedrals. Their attention was directed to something that called forth their creative abilities, namely what the narratives and metaphors had become after they had been given a place in the Bible, the meanings the new literary context had given them, and what they in turn had done with other narratives and metaphors (so to speak). It was precisely this that emerged so clearly through the mediaeval illustrations to the Bible. The evangelist Luke's narrative of the stable in Bethlehem was made more credible by the prophecy in the first chapter of Isaiah about the ox and ass who know their master. When the painters depicted this or the poets sang about it, the two texts coalesced – as in the mediaeval Christmas carol *Puer natus in Betlehem*: "Both ox and ass, though beasts they be, Alle Alleluya. / Yet in that Child their Master see. Alleluya."

"A Lovely Idea"

It may seem strange to use the word "credible" in this context, but that is because this word has undergone a "double-glazing" in our consciousness, in order that it can be kept separate from everything that involves aesthetics. To believe in Christianity because it is *"a lovely idea"* is perceived as dilettantish and childish. The antidote to this that organized religion has offered consists in translations of the biblical message. When Frye speaks of "translations," he has in mind, not new translations of the Bible, but the fact that Christianity is presented in a binding fashion in a different linguistic mode than that which is dominant in the Bible. There are numerous examples of this in the modern history of Christianity, largely because organized Christianity either has not understood the dominant linguistic mode in the Bible, or else has been profoundly distrustful of it. The churches have communication problems, not because religious language has become obsolete, but because of this ingrown distrust, which shows that the relationship between language and reality is extremely unclear. One good example of this is the spread of fundamentalism in recent years. Fundamentalism pretends to show respect for the biblical text, but it betrays its true nature when it combines this respect for the text as God's Word with the demand that one particular interpretation be accepted. The form of "clarity" that is ascribed to the Bible in this manner is the opposite of the "unity" that Frye ascribes to the Bible and that he regards as the only appropriate way to speak of the literal meaning of the Bible – that is to say, its mythical and metaphorical meaning.

When we think about the Bible and language, we meet the question of the relationship between the original language and a translation. Frye sees the great linguistic problem of Christianity in recent years as connected with something other than the many languages. Every language has many ways of speaking. We do not write in the same way as we speak; and we speak in different ways depending on whom we are speaking to and what we want to attain through what we say. It is important to hear the difference between Greek and Norwegian, but it is equally important to perceive and master the difference between persuading and convincing – to say nothing of the culturally determined agreements that have been made about the relationship between our words and reality.

The Various Phases of Language

In both *The Great Code* and *Words with Power*, Frye has described this linguistic plurality as a variety of phases in the history of language. "Language" here refers to the shifting versions of the relationship between language and reality. Each of these phases presupposes an understanding of what the "power" of language entails. At the extreme end of the scale of what words can perform, Frye adduces the story of Jephthah in the Book of Judges, who was unable to revoke the promise that turned out to seal his daughter's fate. At the other end of the scale, Frye locates the descriptive language that derives its power from its similarity to the external world and thus has no magic beyond its resemblance to reality. Between these two extreme points, we find linguistic modes such as dialectic and rhetoric, each of which represents its own version of the power that lives in words. Frye concludes his reflections by claiming that there is a close link between the language of the Bible and poetic language.

Frye's sketch of the history of language is not about phases that have been superseded. The closer we come to our own time, the greater is the linguistic differentiation. Descriptive language may seem predominant, but it faces competition from other ways of speaking. The fact that language *has* power does not mean that language *exercises* power. The language of power is at home in the world of ideologies; but if we are looking for the true humane powers of language, we must identify the words that people use to express their fear and their longings. Remnants of the past continue to play a role here – also as a criticism of the power that has been and still is exercised by means of language.

Frye sees poetical language and literary fiction as remnants of this kind, as a language that is powerful but has little ideological and political power. Why does official Christianity display a tendency to reduce poetry to a second-rate form of speech? Frye believes that this is because Christianity in the modern age has let itself be influenced by the idea of the progress of culture, where the position of one's own age is seen as the result of enlightenment, whereas the thinking of earlier ages lies in darkness. Academic paradigms for the study of the Bible are a good example of how modern Christianity has struggled to bring old texts up to the level of our own age. In this instance, the fundamentalism that we have already mentioned is extremely modern, since it has taken a position that is in accordance with the premises in a descriptive understanding of language, and has thus been compelled to construct a bible that is remote from what the Bible actually is. When Frye reconstructs the Bible as a coherent literary universe, he is challenging such attempts to accommodate Christianity to our age, where these endeavors have been made at the cost of the specific literary character of the bible text. At the same time, the insight into how the Bible was the universe of meaning for Augustine, Dante, Luther, and Blake shows how modern theological conceptions and interpretations of Christianity locate reality in frameworks that are determined by linguistic structures. If the goal is to make Christianity accessible and comprehensible for modern people, one runs the risk that faith becomes a mirror in which the believer loses himself, as in the myth of Narcissus. The fact that Christianity, like literature, has an imaginative and autonomous life forces us to enter into a tension between so-called reality and the vision of other worlds. We must not shun this tension; Christianity is obliged to enter into it, for otherwise the risk being self-confirming. Frye compares this with Jacob's wrestling with the Angel of the Lord (Genesis 32) in which we must hold out: "Somehow or other, the created scripture and the revealed scripture, or whatever we call the latter, have to keep fighting each other like Jacob and the angel, and it is through the maintaining of this struggle, the suspension of belief between the spiritually real and the humanly imaginative, that our own mental evolution grows" (*The Secular Scripture*).

Frye's "View of the Bible"

If we wish to describe Frye's view of the Bible, we must go back to his two great books on the Bible, *The Great Code* and *Words with Power*, in order to see what he actually does with the Bible. Frye's books are not the result of one particular view of the Bible that is antecedent to what he later came to write about. The basis of his writing is a literary competence that can be acquired only by the repeated reading of the work – in this case, of the Bible itself. His "view" of the Bible came into being while he was writing and teaching, primarily because he wanted to find the answer to one simple but momentous question: How is it possible that such a composite collection of literary texts came *de facto* to exercise such an enormous influence on the literature in our cultural sphere? Frye introduces *The Great Code* by calling the book "an attempt to study the Bible from the point of view of a literary critic." What is literary criticism about? Frye answers by means of the word "tradition." Criticism is "the conscious organizing of a cultural tradition," and has thus primarily a practical function, that is, to make us more conscious of how much we are conditioned by the Bible's myths (or narratives) and metaphors (or pictures). The Bible is like the Giant Troll Snake in Ibsen's *Peer Gynt*: no matter how much we twist and turn, we cannot escape from it, if we want to understand the language in which literature has found expression, and which it continues to use.

Frye believes that there is little help to be found in the modern theological views of the Bible, if one wishes to read it as a literary critic. He writes that there are two modern views of the Bible. One has been called the historical-critical view, while the other is fundamentalist (which is "modern" because it is elaborated as a reaction to the former view, and hence is marked by its polemical counterpart). Typically, fundamentalism has only one answer to the question of the literal meaning of the Bible – namely, the descriptive meaning. It also suffers from a fear of taking the Bible seriously as it actually is. "The Bible is far too deeply rooted in all the resources of language for any simplistic approach to its language to be adequate" (*The Great Code*). This is Frye's main objection to a view of the Bible as a simple form of descriptive text. Such a position betrays an ear that is insensitive to both literary and religious language.

Frye clearly sees the usefulness of modern biblical criticism, but this has not yet been able to shed any light worth mentioning on how a poet could get the idea of reading the Bible and making the world of biblical ideas his own, in order thus to be liberated for creative thinking and writing. If a literary-critical presentation of the Bible essentially consists in a constructive systematization of literary observations, based on repeated reading, the end product of the long and laborious process whereby the Bible came into being plays an important role for the literary critic; and nothing in the traditional paradigm of biblical criticism corresponds to this.

This must not be taken to mean that the Bible has an obvious unity. The impression it makes on the reader is that one of being "home-made." As a book, it unites very different material, and it has also been put to very different uses, such as presenting dogmas, justifying doctrines, and promoting intolerance. The study of church history reveals a use of the Bible that has often been buttressed by powerful affirmations about the Bible's authority. Ironically enough, one can see how each time the use of the Bible in religious institutions has succeeded in transforming its literary and rhetorical high voltage into low voltage, with clearly negative consequences for the Bible's creative potential.

When Frye discusses how the attempt has been made again and again in institutional religion to "tame" the Bible, he prefers an ironic distance, rather than entering into theology's precincts. This is not what interests him; Frye's concentrates on showing us how narratives and metaphors in the Bible display an explosive creative power, in the sense that new texts are generated all the time. Frye regards as a genuinely literary datum the Bible's ability to recreate itself.

Two concepts are important when Frye, towards the close of *The Great Code*, sums up what he experiences as a literary critic when he hands himself over to the Bible. First, it is a question of the *resonance* of the biblical texts. "Through resonance a particular statement in a particular context acquires a universal significance." We should recall the story of the prophet Elijah, who hears "the sound of a still, small voice" on Mount Horeb after the storm, the earthquake, and the fire (1 Kings 19). In the context, the voice tells the prophet that he should not be afraid, for all the prophets of Baal will be destroyed! "But the wonderful phrase has long ago flown away from this context into many new contexts, contexts that give dignity to the human situation instead of merely reflecting its bigotries."

Frye links the second fundamental literary datum to the theory of *polysemy*, "the sense of further discoveries to be made within the same structure of words." This is not a case (as theological traditions have claimed) of arbitrary and disparate meanings, but of "different intensities or wider contexts of a continuous sense, unfolding like a plant out of a seed." On this point, Frye holds that Dante and the polyvalent biblical interpretation in the middle ages still have a role to play.

This is the Bible's "great code." It is this that has recurred through the long history of the Bible's influence. We could describe this by paraphrasing some words of Paul: "[texts] are sown in dishonor, they are raised up in glory. They are sown in weakness, they are raised in power" (cf. 1 Corinthians 15). And it is still possible for the following to occur: "The normal human reaction to a great cultural achievement like the Bible is to do with it what the Philistines did to Samson: reduce it to impotence, then lock it in a mill to grind our aggressions and prejudices. But perhaps its hair, like Samson's could grow again, even there" (*The Great Code*, 233).

Bibliography

The works by and about Northrop Frye are very numerous. The University of Toronto Press publishes his *Collected Works*. As of 2009, 27 volumes had appeared; in all, 30 are planned.

Primary Literature

Bibliographies by Robert D. Denham: *Northrop Frye: An Annotated Bibliography of Primary and Secondary Sources* (Toronto, 1987); [updated version:] *Northrop Frye: A Bibliography of His Published Writings,* 1931–2004 (Toronto, 2004).

The following works are particularly useful in the context of the present essay.

Lee, A.A., and J. O'Grady (eds), *Northrop Frye on Religion* [Collected Works of Northrop Frye vol. 4.] (Toronto, 2000).

Frye's most important works on the Bible are the following:

The Great Code. The Bible and Literature (San Diego, New York, and London, 1982).
Words with Power: Being a Second Study of the Bible and Literature (San Diego, New York, and London, 1990).

Secondary Literature

For a presentation and discussion of various aspects of Northrop Frye's view of literature, see the following works:

Hamilton, A.C., *Northrop Frye: Anatomy of his Criticism* (Toronto, 1990).
Hart, J., *Northrop Frye: The Theoretical Imagination* (London, 1994).

See also the following collections of essays:

Cook, E., C. Hosek, J. Macpherson, P. Parker and J. Patrick (eds), *Centre and Labyrinth: Essays in Honour of Northrop Frye* (Toronto, 1983).
Lee, Alvin A. and Robert D. Denham (eds), *The Legacy of Northrop Frye* (Toronto, 1994).

Chapter 58
Paul Ricoeur

René Rosfort

Paul Ricoeur is not a theologian but a philosopher, and it is important that a theologian who uses his texts should bear this in mind. He repeatedly made it clear that he was not a Christian philosopher, but a philosopher with theological interests. He also emphasized that his philosophical writings possess autonomy in relation to his theological writings and his Christian conviction. He was, however, deeply interested in theology and religion throughout his life.

His first and abiding source of theological inspiration is Karl Barth, and this is particularly important in connection with the problem of evil. Rudolf Bultmann's existential hermeneutical theology is both an inspiration and a polemical starting point for Ricoeur's own methodological approach to theology. Finally, Jürgen Moltmann's theology of hope is decisively important for Ricoeur's reflections on the relationship between theology, evil, and ethics.

Biography and Academic Career

Ricoeur was born in 1913 in Valence in north-eastern France. He was orphaned at an early age and grew up in his grandparents' Protestant household. After studying at the University of Rennes, he completed his philosophical studies at the Sorbonne in 1935. The years before the outbreak of war were spent partly in teaching at a secondary school and partly in military service. In 1940, he was taken captive by the Germans and sent to a prisoner-of-war camp, where he remained until the end of the war in 1945. Ricoeur wrote a great deal in this period, since his position as officer gave him special privileges, and thus the opportunity to deepen his knowledge of German philosophy and theology (Husserl, Jaspers, Heidegger, and Barth).

In the years immediately after the war, he lived in the village of Chambon-sur-Lignon, where he taught philosophy at the Cévenol College and made the acquaintance of a group of American Quakers, who later, from 1954 onwards, often invited him to lecture in the USA. In 1948, he moved with his family to Strasbourg, where he worked first as lecturer and then as professor in the history of philosophy. He studied classic works of philosophy in depth and systematically. He dedicated each year to one particular philosopher, including Plato, Aristotle, Spinoza, Kant, and Hegel. He also took part actively in the life of the Protestant community and wrote innumerable articles for Christian periodicals. At the same time, he played an important role through the philosophical periodical *Esprit*.

His influential doctoral dissertation on the voluntary and the involuntary (1950) and his numerous publications led to an invitation from the Sorbonne in 1957, where he became professor of metaphysics. He settled in a Protestant milieu in Paris. The progressive leftwing politics of this group sometimes brought him into conflict with the authorities. He also lectured regularly at the theological faculty. This activity, together with his interest in the philosophy of religion, made him unpopular at the philosophical institute in the Sorbonne. His philosophy was labeled spiritual and crypto-theological, and this led him to leave the Sorbonne in 1965 to take part in the foundation of a new university on the outskirts of Paris, Paris X – Nanterre. He was elected dean of this university in 1969, but he renounced this post the following year as a consequence of the riots and the political power games in connection with the student uprising.

After the dramatic events of 1970, Ricoeur left France. He first taught for three years at the University of Louvain in Belgium, but then he returned to Nanterre. Shortly afterwards, however, he decided to put a final stop to his academic career in France. He had already been associated with the University of Chicago, and in 1971, he succeeded Paul Tillich in his professorship at the theological faculty there, while continuing to teach in the philosophical institute. He achieved great success and fame until he retired in 1991 and returned home to France. In the intervening years, he had never turned his back on France; he divided his time for lengthy periods between the two continents. His position in Chicago committed him to work for only one semester each year, and he spent the other half of the year in France, where he continued his influential work as editor of an important philosophical periodical and as joint editor of a series of philosophical volumes, *L'Ordrephilosophique*, at the leading publisher Éditiondu Seuil. He also played a vigorous part in the philosophical and theological debate on the old continent. This transcontinental activity made possible an uncommon breadth in his publications in this period, since he drew on both Anglo-American and continental sources at a time (1970–90) when this was extremely rare in the philosophical debate.

He returned to France as a world-famous philosopher and finally achieved in his homeland the recognition that he had long been accorded elsewhere. Despite his advanced age, he continued to publish books and articles. Until only a few years before his death, he traveled all over the world to give lectures, and when he died in 2005, he had received honorary doctorates from more than thirty universities worldwide.

Overview of his Philosophical and Theological Writings

As already mentioned, Ricoeur was a philosopher rather than a theologian. This means that his theological writings are indissolubly linked to his philosophical development. He never wrote a specifically theological book, but he produced a large number of articles that shed light on the theological implications of his philosophy. Over a period of 69 years, from 1935 to 2004, he wrote around 140 theological articles (his bibliography is not yet complete) in the following fields: practical theology (approx. 50), the relationship between theology and ethics (approx. 60), and hermeneutics and exegesis (approx. 30).

The articles in practical theology dominate the period up to 1960, and are often written in connection with contemporary social and political problems. From 1960 to 1985, he is primarily concerned with the relationship between theology and hermeneutics, while the final period up to 2004 is marked by a renewed interest in the relationship between theology and ethics.

It is difficult to impose sharp chronological dividing lines on his theological writings, since he returned to the same problems again and again throughout his life. With a few exceptions, these fall under three thematic headings. (1) The first and most persistent theme is the problem of evil in the dialectic between the voluntary and involuntary, and in relation to hope; (2) the relationship between hermeneutics and theology, especially in connection with religious symbols and biblical exegesis; and (3) the relationship between theology and ethics.

In order to get an overview of his writings, it can be helpful to follow this thematic division and to connect each theme to his philosophical development. I select those theological articles that are of the greatest importance in relation to the respective themes and that are available in an English translation.

The Problem of Evil and Hope (1950–1970)

Ricoeur's early philosophy is defined by his great unfinished work on the human will. Ricoeur examines in three books the relationship between the voluntary and the involuntary, and attempts to find an answer to the question of how evil comes into the world. Is evil already present in the world, or does it enter the world through human actions? His first two books are exclusively philosophical. They attempt to sketch a philosophical anthropology that uncovers the being of the human person as a perennial conflict between the realm of the senses and reason, and that defines the *possibility* of evil precisely as a consequence of this fragile constitution. It is however impossible to understand the evil that exists *de facto* in the world without an interpretation of the symbols through which evil makes itself known in the human person's existence. This is therefore the theme of his third book, *The Symbolism of Evil* (1960), which is of particular interest to theologians because it assumes that the biblical symbols and myths are needed in order to understand the modern human person's relationship to evil. Ricoeur develops an idea about the problem of evil that sees evil as a challenge to human thinking. The problem of evil cannot be reduced to a theoretical question about freedom and nature, that is to say, neither to the biological origin of original sin, nor to theodicy's rational explanation, nor to a purely moral question about responsibility and guilt. Rather, the problem of evil, through the polyvalence of the symbols, compels thinking to understand its own limitation. Thinking cannot resolve the dialectic between the voluntary and the involuntary in relation to evil, but it can transform the problem of evil into a practical question about the action of the human person in the openness to the future that is hope's gift: How can I in hope allow good to overcome evil in my actions?

The most important articles for this project are: "Christianism and the Meaning of History" (1951), "The Image of God and the Epic of Man" (1960), "Original Sin: A Study in Meaning" (1960), "The Demythization of Accusation" (1965), "Interpretation of the Myth of Punishment" (1967), "Freedom in the Light of Hope" (1968), "Guilt, Ethics, and Religion" (1969), and "Hope and the Structure of Philosophical Systems" (1970).

But before Ricoeur takes up the practical question of how the human person is to fight against evil, he spends many years on what he calls "the long detour." This detour goes via the symbols, metaphors, and myths of the Bible. The Bible speaks to me about good and evil, about the human person's fragile finitude, and about God's infinite goodness. But how do I as a modern person make my own this way of speaking about the fundamental circumstances of the human person?

Theology and Hermeneutics (1965–1981)

After his investigation of the fragile structure of the will in relation to freedom and nature, Ricoeur's philosophical interest turns to language and interpretation as fundamental conditions in the existence of a human person. The human person understands herself and the surrounding world through language, and attains this understanding only through an interpretation of the language in which she expresses herself and of the cultural symbols and traditions in which she finds himself situated. Language and culture conceal innumerable meanings and significations that go beyond the immediate understanding of one's milieu. These meanings lie fallow in the symbols, metaphors, and myths that we find *inter alia* in the biblical narratives. An attentive interpretation of the linguistic constructions opens up new dimensions and possibilities in our relationship to the world and to the other human person. This is why Ricoeur spends many years on developing a theory of interpretation that is able to bring out the many different meanings that lie fallow in the biblical narratives, from symbols via metaphors to the mythical stories. Exegesis is a necessary first step on the path to an understanding of how the Bible still speaks to us modern human persons; exegetical work must be complemented, however, by a more general theory of interpretation that examines how the human person understands himself in the encounter with the text. Ricoeur therefore seeks to unite biblical exegesis with a philosophical analysis of the structure of understanding. This is closely linked to his earlier work on a philosophical anthropology.

The fundamental works in which he elaborates a theory of interpretation and its relationship to a theological hermeneutics are: *Freud and Philosophy* (1965), *Biblical Hermeneutics* (1975), and *Interpretation Theory* (1976).

To these, we must add the following articles: "The Hermeneutics of Symbols and Philosophical Reflection" I-II (1961, 1962); "Preface to Bultmann" (1968); "Fatherhood: Phantasm to Symbol" (1969), "Philosophy and Religious Language" (1974), "Philosophical and Biblical Hermeneutics" (1975), "Manifestation and Proclamation" (1978), and "The Bible and the Imagination" (1981).

As I have mentioned, Ricoeur's theory of interpretation is not exclusively a theoretical matter. He envisages it as a practical instrument for dealing with the problem of evil and with the human person's task in life. This is why Ricoeur returns in his later writings to evil, but this time as part of an ethical project.

Theology and Ethics (1979–1998)

How is the human person to relate to the evil that is a concrete part of the life he or she shares with other persons? Most of Ricoeur's late philosophical and theological writings are concerned with the relationship between good and evil and with the significance of this relationship for the human person's conduct. His theory of interpretation leads to an understanding of the human person as something more and other than immediate interaction with his surroundings. We are a part of a cultural tradition, and this means that our understanding of the world is always influenced by how others before us have thought and written about the world. Our ethical understanding of good and evil is especially linked to the Christian symbols, metaphors, and myths that have formed our cultural horizon. Through its interpretation of the Christian symbols, theology should break with the anthropocentric view of ethics and point to the origin that is greater than the individual's understanding of good and evil. The human person is a part of a continuous creation that is good, and is more original and greater than the human understanding. This shows that the individual human being is radically dependent on a greater power. We are dependent on God, who in his goodness has given us life, and our actions are meant to reflect our love for God's creation *despite* the many forms of wickedness that we encounter in our existence. We are not to act on the basis of our human understanding of profit, happiness, and justice; we are meant to act as collaborators in the continuation of God's good creation, in faith in goodness *despite* evil. Ricoeur holds fast to the idea of the creation as God's gratuitous gift to the human person. He elaborates a theory that attempts to unite an economy of the gift with the logic of justice that leaves its mark on the life of the modern person. The suffering and death of the innocent, injustice, and inexplicable hatred are nothing other than individual concrete proofs that our endeavors to construct a rational shield of reciprocal justice against the radicality of evil do not succeed. We cannot make the good secure by means of our calculations. All we can do is attempt to do what is good and to care for the other person, without thinking of what one gets out of it, in faith in the good *despite* evil.

The two central books in this connection are *Oneself as Another* (1990; chapters 8 and 9) and *Thinking Biblically* (1998; written with André LaCocque). I also mention the following articles: "The Logic of Jesus, the Logic of God" (1979), "'Whoever loses their life for my sake will find it'" (1984), "Evil, a Challenge to Philosophy and Theology" (1986), "The Summoned Subject in the School of the Narratives of Prophetic Vocation" (1988), "The Memory of Suffering" (1989), "Ethical and Theological Considerations on the Golden Rule" (1989), "Pastoral Praxeology, Hermeneutics and Identity" (1989), "Love and Justice" (1991), and "Philosophical Hermeneutics of Religion: Kant" (1992).

Basic Themes

Two themes deserve a closer look, since they constitute the core in Ricoeur's theological work: theological hermeneutics and the relationship between the problem of evil and the economy of the gift.

Theological Hermeneutics

Theological hermeneutics is a regional hermeneutics in relation to a more general theory of interpretation, which allows theological hermeneutics to apply the general theory of interpretation as an instrument to achieve a better understanding of the relationship between the Bible and the interpreter. At the same time, however, theological hermeneutics is a hermeneutics of a special kind, because the biblical texts speak of a unique and universal message that concerns the whole of humankind.

Ricoeur emphasizes interpretation so strongly that he actually regards the Christian faith as something that is constituted hermeneutically. As a convinced Protestant, Ricoeur sees the biblical texts as the only legitimate basis for theology, and this means that a theology that does not relate constantly to the Bible is, and remains, empty speculation. The human understanding of God must therefore rest on our understanding of the texts that speak of God by means of symbols, metaphors, and myths.

Ricoeur thus sets about elaborating a theological hermeneutics that takes account both of the historical and social horizon of the text (the Bible is written down by human beings who lived in another cultural context) and the universal message in the text (the kerygma). His theory of interpretation has four distinct but closely linked steps: (1) the structure of the text; (2) the distancing of the text; (3) the world of the text; and (4) the appropriation of the text. In order to understand what the biblical texts' language about God means for human beings today, we are obliged to open up the text by passing through these four interpretative stages.

The structure of the text. This level is the first step in every interpretation. What is said about God is linked to various forms of linguistic constructions from the simplest forms such as symbols and metaphors, via parables, hymns, and prophecies, to larger narratives such as the Pentateuch and the Gospels. The theological significance is indissolubly interwoven with the form of the text, since God and the creation make themselves known in various ways, depending on which text one is reading. God's nature, or the relationship between God and the human person, is not unambiguous in the many texts of the Bible. These articulate a variety of meanings that must be classified through a patient work of exegesis that can thus allow the complex universe of the Bible to emerge for the modern reader.

The distancing of the text. The next task is to understand the difference between the spoken and the written word. The spoken word always has a priority over the written word, since the human person speaks before he or she writes. The Gospels are the best example of this relationship, since they seek to preserve and hand on Jesus' spoken words by writing them down. But an essential change takes place in speech when it is written down. As soon as the text leaves the author's hand and finds a reader, the nature of the text is changed, since its meaning is no longer bound to the intentions and aims of the author, but merges with reader's horizon of understanding. We encounter God's Word in a text that is no longer bound to one particular time and one particular place or to the intention of one particular author. The text speaks to us through our understanding of the text, and this means that the text distances itself from its author and addresses us to speak about something that transcends both the original intention of the author and our horizon of understanding.

The world of the text. This step is the core in Ricoeur's theory of interpretation, since it attempts to define what the text is talking about and how this address transcends the author's intention and the reader's horizon of understanding. The text opens up a world that does not resemble the world in which the reader lives. The text *creates* something that did not exist before, since it opens the door to hidden possibilities. Ricoeur calls this "the reality of possibility," since the human person's grasp of reality is nuanced and expanded through meanings that otherwise would not have been permitted to exist within a given view of the world. In this way, the text can create for the reader possibilities that were not previously accessible in his or her daily relationship to the world.

The appropriation of the text. This last step follows close upon the heels of the previous step, and shows the existential significance of every interpretation. When the reader finds himself confronted with the reality of possibilities that is the world of the text, this does something to the way in which the reader understands his own self. The reader cannot understand the text on the basis of his own horizon of understanding without thereby reducing the text to something that it is not – namely, a product of the reader himself. Texts speak to the reader and create imaginary variations on the reader's self-understanding, since they awaken the reader's imagination and thereby create new possibilities to which the reader can relate. In this final step, the most important thing is to understand that although the world of the text speaks to *my* imagination, it cannot be reduced to me. It is not I who determine how the text is to be understood. Rather, my understanding is influenced by the possibilities that the text opens up for me.

This final existential step in Ricoeur's theological hermeneutics is an expression of a general attitude in his theological writings, namely, their primarily practical orientation. The interpretation of the biblical texts is not merely an intellectual activity, but is directed towards a change of the individual person's conduct. This practical orientation is treated most thoroughly in his analysis of the human person's conduct in the relationship between the reality of evil and the economy of the gift.

Evil and the Economy of the Gift

Ricoeur's early analyses of the problem of evil had shown that evil cannot be thought away or coped with rationally in view of a higher justice. Evil exists as an abiding problem in human existence, and must, as such, be integrated into our understanding of God and of creation. In his late writings, Ricoeur discusses in depth the relationship between the problem of evil and human conduct. What ought we as human beings to do in a world where evil appears to overshadow good in our actions?

Ricoeur is particularly interested in the tragic dimension of evil, which allows the innocent to suffer. It is not possible to understand the relationship between evil and good on the basis of a rational logic that says if that if you do good, you will be rewarded with good (and the same applies to evil). On the contrary, we are confronted all the time with innocent and unjust suffering – which underlines that our attempts to prevent evil through social and legal measures do not achieve success over the concrete reality of evil. Evil does not distinguish between guilt and innocence, and is blind to good works. Our relationship to cannot be based on a narrow understanding of reciprocal justice. We must learn from the semantic richness that lies fallow in the symbols of evil. The biblical symbols and metaphors enable a different understanding of evil, which does not see evil as an unambiguous phenomenon, but in a constant connection with good. Evil exists, but in a relationship of dependence on the good. This relationship cannot be calculated and summed up in a logical system of reciprocal justice ("if you do something good for me, then I do something good for you").

The Christian symbols and narratives open the possibility of thinking about evil in a different way, since they show the possibility of another reality where people do good deeds not *because of* the profit that is linked to these good deeds, but *despite* the tragic reality of evil. Hermeneutics is thus indissolubly linked to the practical dimension of human existence, since the interpretation of the narrative and symbolic constructions of the text has its practical correlation in what the human person does with the meanings uncovered through interpretation.

Ricoeur gives an example of a practical application of hermeneutics in his analysis of the relationship between the Golden Rule and the Bible's commandment to love. On the one hand, we have a rule that demands that we treat our neighbor as we wish our neighbor to treat us. On the other hand, we have a commandment that says that we must love our enemies, turn the other cheek, and give our cloak as well, if anyone steals our coat. The Golden Rule appears to agree with our *de facto* reality, where our actions are shaped by our interests and profit, while the commandment to love goes against everything that one can expect of general human existence in society.

It is this general understanding of reality that is challenged by the commandment to love, when the biblical texts open up a new and different possibility for human existence in society. Love has no eyes for profit: love gives, with no thought of gain or of one's own interests. Ricoeur calls this *the economy of the gift*, since this is a perspective on human action that creates a new meaning for human existence in society. The gift transcends the action of the individual person and points to life as an original gift that is bestowed on the whole of creation. We are meant to understand life as a well-intentioned gift. We ought to continue to sustain this life and hand it on to others in our actions. Ricoeur speaks of an "economy," because the meaning of the gift cannot be reduced to individual actions or particular views about life, but is a transformation of our entire way of looking at existence. Instead of seeing life as the enforcement of our own private interests and goals in the best possible interplay with other people's lives, we are meant to see life as the possibility of continuing and protecting a meaning that is larger than our own life.

Naturally, Ricoeur does not hold that the commandment to love should replace the principle of justice in the Golden Rule, on which our contemporary societal structure is roughly based. He is too pragmatic to take such a view. He believes that the symbolic richness in what the Bible says about love opens up a possibility to reinterpret and nuance the general principle of justice, on the basis of the reality of possibility that we find in the symbols. This reinterpretation should build on the tension between two fundamental principles: a love that goes one way (that is to say, that gives without any thought of profit and interest) and a justice that goes both ways (that is to say, that constructs the idea of equality and reciprocity). Under ideal circumstances, a continuous interpretation of this kind can pave the way for a Christian ethic, or (as Ricoeur prefers to call it) a general ethic in a religious perspective.

Ricoeur's Place in Twentieth-century Theology

It is difficult to place Ricoeur in twentieth-century theology. He is a philosopher and calls himself a theological apprentice. This means that he does not claim to occupy a place in one particular theological tradition; nor does he seek to create a new current in theology. As we have seen, his theological writings are concerned more with the sources of theology (the Bible, the Christian tradition, and religious experience) than with theology itself. He is inspired by great theologians such as Barth, Bultmann, and Moltmann (in addition to Ebeling and Tillich), but he does not explicitly state his own views about their overarching theological positions. He draws on them primarily with regard to the methodological and practical problems that he is investigating: How do I understand the Bible's metaphors and symbolic narratives, and how do I appropriate the message that this understanding articulates? And what does this message mean for my life with other people?

Ricoeur's theological hermeneutics, exegesis, and religiously inspired ethics always aim at a universality that seems difficult to combine with one specific Christian theology. Ricoeur the philosopher always plays the dominant role in his theological writings and attempts to draw the general anthropological implications out of the Christian texts, without wishing to express a view or relate to specifically Christian dogmas such as the Trinity, life after death, or the definitive truth of Christianity.

This does not mean that Ricoeur the Christian fails to have a relationship to these dogmas; it means only that they are not a part of his theological reflections.

Accordingly, his importance for theology lies mostly in the methodological and practical fields. He did not form a specific school, but he has certainly had an influence on theological thinking in the last four decades. His theory of interpretation has been important for the methodology of exegesis, and his fundamental hermeneutical understanding of human nature has formed a decisively important background to the development of postmodern theologies such as narrative theology and the hermeneutical theology of the Yale school, although it has been important, especially for the latter school, to emphasize their distance vis-à-vis Ricoeur.

Ricoeur's philosophical and theological writings have not yet yielded up all their riches; they still await a thorough examination and represent in many ways an important source for future theologians. His reflections on the relationship between text and action are, and remain, decisively important for a religion that finds its basis in textual traditions and its goal in an effective influencing of contemporary human conduct.

Bibliography

Primary Literature

The Symbolism of Evil, trans. E. Buchanan (Boston: Beacon Press, 1967). French: *Philosophie de la volonté II. Symbolique du mal* (Paris: Aubier, 1960).

Freud and Philosophy: An Essay of Interpretation, trans. D. Savage (New Haven: Yale University Press, 1970). French: *De l'interprétation. Essaisur Sigmund Freud* (Paris: Seuil, 1965).

"Biblical Hermeneutics," *Semeia*, 4 (1975), 29–148.

Interpretation Theory. Discourse and the Interpretation of Meaning (Fort Worth: Texas University Press, 1977).

Oneself as Other, trans. K. Blamey (Chicago: University of Chicago Press, 1992). French: *Soi-mêmecommeunautre* (Paris: Seuil, 1990).

Thinking Biblically: Exegetical and Hermeneutical Studies (with A. Lacocque) (Chicago: University of Chicago Press, 1998).

History and Truth, trans. C.A. Kelbley (Evanston, Ill.: Northwestern University Press, 1965). French: *Histoire et Vérité* (Paris: Seuil, 1967).

The Conflict of Interpretations, trans. K. McLaughlin ed. D. Ihde (London: Continuum, 1989). French: *Conflit des interprétations* (Paris: Seuil, 1969).

From Text to Action, trans. K. Blamey and J.B. Thompson (Evanston, IL: Northwestern University Press, 1991). French: *Du texte à l'action. Essaisd'herméneutique II* (Paris: Seuil, 1976).

Figuring the Sacred: Religion, Narrative, and Imagination, trans. D. Pellauer, ed. M.I. Wallace (Minneapolis: Fortress Press, 1995).

Secondary Literature

Greisch, J., *Le cogito herméneutique. L'herméneutiquephilosophique et l'héritagechrétien* (Paris: Vrin, 2000).
Greisch, J., *Paul Ricoeur. L'itinérance du sens* (Grenoble: J. Milton, 2001).
Kearney, Richard, *On Paul Ricoeur: The Owl of Minerva* (Aldershot: Ashgate, 2004).
Rasmussen, David, *Mythic-Symbolic Language and Philosophical Anthropology: A Constructive Interpretation of Ricoeur* (The Hague: Martinus Nijhoff, 1971).
Uggla, Bent Kristensson, *Kommunikation på bristningsgränsen. En studie i Paul Ricoeurs projekt* (Stockholm/Stehäg: Brutus Östlings Bokförlag Symposion, 1994).
Vanhoozer, Kevin J., *Biblical Narrative in the Philosophy of Paul Ricoeur. A Study in Hermeneutics and Theology* (Cambridge: Cambridge University Press, 1990).

Chapter 59
Thomas Merton

Henning Sandström

Those who have played a decisively important role in the theological debate can by and large be divided into two groups. One group is, of course, those who can be called theologians in the strict sense. The second group consists of men and women who can best be called religious personalities, but who have not produced any important systematic-theological writings. Instead, these persons have inspired and enriched various religious traditions by means of works that are more similar to the works of a creative artist.

Thomas Merton is a typical example of a religious personality of this kind. He was one of the converts to Roman Catholicism and mystics who attracted most attention in the twentieth century. Through his extensive and many-faceted writings, he has exercised an increasing fascination on Roman Catholics, high church Protestants, pacifists, enthusiasts for mysticism, and representatives of the dialogue between Christianity and Buddhism. One aspect of this fascination is the foundation of a number of Thomas Merton Societies, where the academic interest in Merton plays the central role. There are thus good reasons why Merton should be included in a work that discusses the most important theological thinkers of the twentieth century.

Thomas Merton's Life

Thomas Merton's life can be divided into two periods, his life in the "world" (1915–41) and his monastic life (1941–68).[1] He was born in France in 1915, the oldest son of an artist couple. He was baptized in the Anglican church, but he spent his youth without any formal ecclesiastical or religious contacts. After attending school in France and Great Britain, he pursued academic studies in Cambridge and at Columbia University in New York. He concluded these studies with the M.A. degree and a dissertation on William Blake.

---

[1] There are several biographies of Merton. The most detailed is Michael Mott, *Seven Mountains* (Boston, 1984).

Thomas Merton and the Dalai Lama

One characteristic of Thomas Merton is his endeavor to affirm his vocation. His life and the positions he took are marked to a high degree by the choice between two different forms of vocation, the vocation to the artistic life and the vocation to the religious life. As a young man, he felt drawn to become an author, although this attitude cannot be wholly explained as an expression of an idea of vocation; he believes that since he came from an artistic family, it was natural for him to turn against a bourgeois lifestyle. The importance of writing for Merton is clearly shown by the fact that he spent his whole life with a pen in his hand.

During his time as a student at Columbia University, Merton converted to the Roman Catholic church. His path to the church was long and winding, but it was to a large extent his own experiences of art and philosophy that enabled him to take this step. He had already visited Rome in 1933, and after visiting one of the churches in the city, he said that the artists had made him understand who Christ was.[2] But he did not convert until 1938, and by then, the inspiration from neo-Thomist philosophy had acquired just as much significance. Merton's position certainly had a philosophical and intellectual foundation, but there is also a deeper emotional and psychological side. When he visited churches in New York, Merton believed that it was only in Catholic churches that people truly prayed; this did not happen seriously in Protestant churches.

After converting in 1938 and taking his MA examination in 1939, Merton planned to write a doctoral dissertation on the English Jesuit and poet Gerard Manley Hopkins. In this period, his longing to respond to his vocation to a contemplative religious life grew stronger. His first idea was to enter a Franciscan community, but he was not accepted. In April, 1941, he made a retreat in the Trappist monastery of Our Lady of Gethsemane in Kentucky. He was overwhelmed by his experience during this retreat, and the monastery became his home from December that year.

The years between 1941 and 1968 are not particularly rich in external experiences, but Merton's life as a Trappist monk, and as a priest from 1949 onwards, are not particularly typical of that order. He was allowed to continue his writing, and he wrote a couple of books that are more of interest to the historian of religious life; but the decisively important event was the publication of his autobiography, *The Seven Storey*

---

[2] Thomas Merton, *Seven Storey Mountain* (New York, 1948), p. 109.

Mountain,[3] which became nothing less than a world sensation. In purely practical terms, it transformed Merton's life in the monastery. He was able to concentrate on writing, while at the same time his correspondence grew to enormous proportions.[4] The fact that Merton was able to devote himself so intensively to writing, while simultaneously affirming his religious vocation, can be seen as a union of the two forms of vocation. Merton saw writing as an active form of contemplation.

Writing also gave him the possibility of actively developing his own theology. After converting to the Roman Catholic church and becoming a Trappist monk, Merton sought to interpret reality on the basis of Roman Catholic standpoints. This meant, *inter alia*, that mysticism was seen as legitimate, since it had a natural place in the Roman Catholic church. But Merton's development meant that he did not feel completely at home in the church's dogmatics. He looked for models who were acceptable from the church's standpoint and who had a fruitful influence on his own spiritual development. He found one such model in John of the Cross, who is the object of one of Merton's more systematic works.[5] His horizon widened in the 1950s and 1960s. He became more open and more positive in regard to the world outside the monastery walls. Naturally, many factors were at work here, but Merton's mystical experience during a brief visit to Louisville in 1958 was decisively important.[6] This "vision" resulted in a feeling of fellowship with all the living, both with the divine and with humankind. After this experience, Merton's experience of mysticism and contemplation was interpreted less and less from a Roman Catholic perspective. In short, we can say that whereas Merton had earlier affirmed mysticism as a legitimate expression of the Roman Catholic church, he now turns around, and hereafter affirms the Roman Catholic church since this is a legitimate expression of mysticism.

Towards the close of the 1950s and in the course of the 1960s, Merton's theological profile changed, and he came to appear as the very opposite of a typically introverted Trappist. This is particularly noticeable in three areas. First, Merton gets involved in social and political questions. He takes a position against racism in the Southern states and against the American involvement in the Vietnam War. Secondly, his theology is enriched by modern imaginative literature; one example of this is his correspondence with Boris Pasternak. His wide-ranging activity in this area allows us to speak of a fully developed theology of art, or a theological aesthetics. Thirdly, Merton's interest in mysticism and contemplation develops further, but this is now accompanied by a more universalist attitude. This leads him to study Buddhism, especially Zen Buddhism. His interest in Buddhism went rather far, and some held that one could

---

[3] This was published in Great Britain under the title *Elected Silence*.
[4] Well known persons who corresponded with Merton include Jacques Maritain, Erich Fromm, Mark Van Doren, Boris Pasternak, Czeslaw Milosz, Rosemary Radford Ruether, and D.T. Suzuki.
[5] Merton, *The Ascent to Truth* (New York, 1951).
[6] This event is described in Merton's journal, *Conjectures of a Guilty Bystander*, pp. 156ff.

speak of Merton's Zen Catholicism.[7] This, however, signifies rather an emphasis on personal experience, and can be seen as a "meta-religion"; Zen is not exclusively an expression of Buddhism. Nothing indicates that Merton had plans to leave the monastery or to convert to Buddhism. But his religious position developed in such a way that he could accept various different designations as appropriate expressions of a correct affirmation of the Absolute. This is why Merton found it natural to call himself both Catholic and Buddhist. It is, however, clear that leading Buddhists too thought that Merton had attained a deeper understanding of Buddhism than most Westerners achieved.[8]

In 1968, Merton was given permission to attend a congress in Bangkok that was organized by Roman Catholic monasteries in Asia. En route to Thailand, Merton took the opportunity to visit India and Sri Lanka. His journal during this journey contains very illuminating insights into his understanding of Eastern spirituality. On the day after he delivered his lecture on "Marxism and Monastic Perspectives," he died suddenly in his hotel room, exactly twenty-seven years after he had made the Trappist monastery his home.

Thomas Merton's Theological Writings

Since Merton was not a systematic theologian, but can better be described as a mystic who lived with a pen in his hand, it is of course possible to maintain that everything he wrote can help in one way or another to shed light on his theological profile and his religious development. In the present context, however, we prescind from his literary writings, his personal journals, diary notes, and correspondence, although many of these books – especially *The Seven Storey Mountain* – were very important and reached a wide readership. These works, however, cannot be characterized as theology.

It is not completely easy to define the genre of Merton's writings, but I believe that we can classify them in three main sections: *theology; political and social writings; aesthetics and criticism*.

The theological writings can be subdivided into *academic* works, *confessional theological* works, and *personally creative* works. The most academic work is Merton's study of John of the Cross, *The Ascent to Truth* (1951), in which he gives an account of the mysticism in John of the Cross. He contrasts John's respected mysticism with what he sees as false mysticism, false Quietism, and Gnosticism.[9] We can make two observations about Merton's theological profile here: he finds it important to stand within an accepted Roman Catholic tradition, and he emphasizes that all mysticism is active and life-affirming. It is the confessional theological works that, alongside *The Seven Storey Mountain*, have made the principal contribution to the general picture

---

[7] See for example Chalmers McCormick, "Zen Catholicism," in *Journal of Ecumenical Studies*, 9 (1972).
[8] Both the Dalai Lama and Thich Nhat Hanh have expressed such ideas.
[9] Merton, *Ascent to Truth*, pp. 49ff.

of Merton as a monk who recognized his pastoral responsibility, a man with a great need for solitude, and the defender of contemplation and of the Roman Catholic church. *Seeds of Contemplation* was published in 1949, and this book is particularly important for those who wish to investigate Merton's development, since he had come so far when he revised it in 1961 that what he produced was a new version, published in 1962 as *New Seeds of Contemplation*. The earlier version bears the marks of Merton's inner-church confessionalism; in the later version, we see clearly his growing interest in the world outside the monastery and his newly-gained theological independence. In his understanding of contemplation, Merton has now developed a non-dualistic vocabulary in which his use of the terms "consciousness" and "enlightenment" reveals influences from Zen Buddhism. Another work that went through a similar revision is Merton's study of the Psalter, *Bread in the Wilderness*, which was published in 1953. This relatively pious book is the basis of the posthumously published *Opening the Bible*, where a great devotion to the biblical texts is accompanied by a non-confessional interpretation of their value. Merton holds that while no other work actually reaches the level of the Bible, it is not in principle impossible to say that this might have been the case.[10]

The personal creative works are marked by a gradually increasing independence and by a new orientation in terms of their themes. These works too are certainly the expression of a theology of contemplation, but their specific characteristic is that contemplation is now located in a universal context where the focus is on Zen Buddhism. The most important works here are *Mystics and Zen Masters* and *Zen and the Birds of Appetite*. The posthumously published journals from Merton's Asian journey, *The Asian Journal of Thomas Merton*, are also illuminating in this context. In these books, Merton displays a good knowledge of Zen, and the confessionalism of his early years has been replaced by a universalist and experiential understanding of reality.

In his political and social writings, Merton takes up questions concerning racism and social justice. It was above all in the late 1950s and the early 1960s that Merton began to focus on these problems. Chronologically, these writings come after his more traditional period, and they are published at the same time as creative books about Zen. He drew critical attention to questions about racism in the Southern states in the USA and to America's war in Vietnam. The most important books in this area are *Seeds of Destruction* and *Faith and Violence*.

During the 1950s, Merton returned to his early interest in literature and wrote a great deal in the field of aesthetics and criticism. Under the inspiration of Jacques Maritain and others, he wrote extensively about art, creativity, and the holy, but his most important contributions in this field are his interpretations of some of the most prominent contemporary authors, especially Boris Pasternak, Albert Camus, and William Faulkner. Here, Merton shows himself to be a creative and independent author. Through writing about these authors and presenting his own aesthetic ideas,

---

[10] Merton, *Opening the Bible*, (New York, 1948), pp. 16ff.

Merton discovered a new possibility of uniting his two forms of vocation, the artistic vocation and the vocation to the religious life.

Two Principal Themes in Thomas Merton's Theology

One can, of course, discuss which of Merton's works is the most important, and what picture of him future generations will have. I believe that the areas in which Merton's independence is more clearly expressed are his dialogue with Zen Buddhism and his theological literary criticism, especially in what he writes about Pasternak, Camus, and Faulkner.

As a young man, Merton had a certain interest in eastern religions, but he rejected them in his confessional zeal. When he returned later to this area, in the course of the 1950s, his starting point was completely different. Now, his focus is primarily on Zen and Buddhism. In *Zen and the Birds of Appetite*, Merton writes that Zen is not to be understood as a doctrine or as something that belongs exclusively to Buddhism. Zen is something common to all human beings; Zen is at home in all religions, but it cannot be explained by means of religious or dogmatic concepts. Zen is often explained as meditation, but Merton believes that Zen is *direct experience*, which results in a unity between the invisible and the visible.[11] To attain this unity entails liberating oneself from the empirical "I," from the false "self." These ideas may strike some people as rather Buddhist, but Merton also speaks of the *person*, of that which constitutes the true identity of the human being, as opposed to the empirical "I" that is only an expression of the human being's defective understanding of oneself and of reality.

Those who regard Zen as antithetical to Christianity cannot find their starting point anywhere else than in dogma. One who sees Zen as exclusively Buddhist and as a theoretical system that is a rival to Christianity has misunderstood Zen. This is not unusual in those who come from Western culture, but Merton holds that there are early examples of theologians and mystics who represent an understanding of mysticism that is close to what the representatives of Zen believe. He finds the clearest example in Master Eckhart; and there are also similarities between Zen and the Christian existentialist Gabriel Marcel. Although Merton certainly does not want to attach labels to Zen, he believes that it can be understood as an Asian form of existentialism.[12]

Merton sees nirvana as something *dynamic*, close to Tillich's understanding of *the ground of being*.[13] Zen and Buddhism should not be seen as an expression of a flight from life and from social responsibility. In *Mystics and Zen Masters*, he writes that Thich Nhat Hanh is the most typical example of social responsibility that he knows in Buddhism. Thich Nhat Hanh is important in his own right for the understanding of Merton, since Merton strongly underlines the feeling of fellowship that he experiences

---

[11] Merton, *Zen and the Birds of Appetite* (New York, 1968), p. 37.
[12] Merton, *Mystics and Zen Masters* (New York, 1967), p. 219.
[13] Ibid., pp. 284ff.

with this monk, poet, and existentialist. Both Thich Nhat Hanh and Merton emphasize that when they take a political position, this has nothing to do with party politics, but is generated by a contemplative understanding of the whole of reality, based on wisdom. Merton sees his own positive evaluation of Thich Nhat Hanh as a criticism both of conventional Christianity and of conventional Buddhism.

Conventional forms of religion typically have their starting point in dogmas and in a theoretical understanding or confession, whereas all genuine religion that gets behind the empirical self is based on experience. And Merton and Thich Nhat Hanh hold that precisely this experience is the only possible starting point for a meaningful interreligious dialogue. A correct understanding of *Zen* can facilitate such a dialogue. Merton certainly wrote about Buddhism and Zen with great insight even before he came to Asia in 1968, but during this journey (which is described in *The Asian Journal of Thomas Merton*), his understanding of Buddhism deepens. Above all, the giant Buddhist statues in Polunnaruwa on Sri Lanka bring his "pilgrimage" to its final achievement. He believes that he has encountered the perfect, and that time must pass before he can write about this. Naturally, this experience deepens Merton's interest in Buddhism, although the Buddhist statues belong to the Theravada tradition.

Merton's search for spiritual inspiration led him not only to a deeper understanding of Zen, but also to imaginative literature. As a young man, Merton had dreamed of becoming a writer. As a monk, his interest finds expression both in an intensive study of modern authors and in the elaboration of a theological aesthetics or theology of art. Merton's theology of art is not a wholly pioneering work; he builds to a large extent on Maritain's ideas. But what he does is to integrate the significance of art into a theology of contemplation. Contemplation and creativity are the central concepts in Merton's theological aesthetics.

Contemplation is an expression of a human activity, an endeavor to discover one's own true identity. The contemplative state that is the result of this endeavor makes it possible for the artist to be inspired by the divine, and it is an affirmation of the human person's true identity.[14] All this of course is perfectly compatible with official Roman Catholic theology, but there is a difference of degree: Merton has a tendency to choose precisely the artist-poet as an example of a contemplative existential attitude. Although creativity presupposes human activity, this is not sufficient to permit us to speak of any genuine creativity. For Merton, the source of creativity originates in the divine. The theology of creativity is first and foremost an understanding of the activity of the Holy Spirit; but this activity wishes to use the human artist as an inspired instrument. Neither animals nor nature can function as an instrument of this kind. Both the divine and the human are presupposed, if we are to speak of art as a result of creativity. The relationship between contemplation and creativity in Merton's thinking can thus best be summarized as follows: contemplation is an expression of a human activity and attitude, while creativity is linked to God's activity, with the inspired human artist as God's instrument.

---

[14] Merton, "Poetry, Symbolism and Typology," in *Literary Essays* (New York, 1981), p. 332.

Merton doubtless sees writing as a form of prayer and contemplation, but it is important that the poet does not sacrifice his originality and innocence in order to serve a conscious purpose. A true poet can never give his conscious religious confession priority over his originality. Merton clearly believes that a true poet represents a deep dimension that receives its nourishment from the unconscious and must not be degraded to a confessional program.

Merton actively helped to introduce several Latin American authors to the USA, but his most important contribution in the field of theological aesthetics is his interpretations of Boris Pasternak, Albert Camus, and William Faulkner. Here, he follows his aesthetic program. When he writes about Boris Pasternak's *Doctor Zhivago*, he finds it to be a masterpiece, a work that is not marked by a party-political or confessional distancing from the Russian Revolution. Naturally, this way of understanding the novel is very different from that of many other interpreters. Merton believes that Pasternak's basic attitude is one of *faith in life* – not faith in any specific ideology. No doubt, Merton finds points of agreement between Pasternak and Orthodox Christianity, but Pasternak does not represent this form of Christianity. His spirituality can rather be understood as an expression of an original contact with God. His ability to construct a story is marked by wisdom and by a contemplative understanding of life that is congenital, not something taught by the church or by theology.

Merton calls Albert Camus a "post-Christian" writer. This means that although Camus has a negative attitude to Christian institutions, he represents certain Christian values. Merton sees the French author as an agnostic; but this does not prevent Camus from representing an unconscious faith in creation, a faith that leads him to defend life and love. Merton holds that Camus' work has a moral and pedagogical function. Camus describes a reality that he himself has experienced, and he exhorts us to act. It is only when the human person does not dare to take a position, and becomes passive, that evil and the absurd get a foothold in our existence.[15]

Like Pasternak, William Faulkner represents an original wisdom. Merton doubtless finds similarities between the Old Testament and Faulkner, but this is not because Faulkner is influenced by the biblical writings. Instead, Merton affirms that Faulkner's wisdom is derived from the same source that inspired the Bible too. Faulkner's creativity is so strong that he succeeds in giving life to archetypical patterns.[16] He is able to create myths in such a way that the reader can identify with the "hero" of the narrative. Faulkner represents a confessionless faith in life, and Merton holds that much of his writings are different from typical modern literature, in which much bears the sign of alienation. Merton sees Faulkner as something of a prophet.

One main point in Merton's theological aesthetics is that imaginative literature can very well give expression to deep existential truths, to a much higher degree than conventional theology is able to do. The value in imaginative literature lies in its ability to influence the reader, and Merton speaks of its cathartic effect. What unites

---

[15] See, e.g., "The Plague of Albert Camus: A Commentary and Introduction," in *Literary Essays*, pp. 181–217.

[16] "Baptism in the Forest," in *Literary Essays*, pp. 101f.

Pasternak, Camus, and Faulkner is their creativity and the confessionless and almost unconscious position they take on behalf of life. The fundamental point for Merton is that no religion or confession has a monopoly of the truth. The writer must safeguard his originality, and must not subjugate himself to any political or propagandist purpose. The fundamental theological attitude that we find in Merton's understanding of Zen and of Buddhism can be clearly seen in his theological literary criticism too.

Thomas Merton's Legacy

A many-faceted person like Thomas Merton naturally inspired many people, but since he must be regarded as a religious personality rather than as a theologian in the accepted sense of the word, it is not completely easy to place him in any theological tradition or to claim that he formed a school. The most typical trait in Merton is his personal mystical experiences, which played a decisive role in the formation of his theology of contemplation.

I believe that the area in which his theology of contemplation has had the greatest importance, and where it will most probably have an even greater importance in the future, is the religious dialogue between Christianity and Buddhism. Merton takes his place in a tradition in which the necessary starting point is religious experience; it is not possible to attain a shared understanding of reality if religions are regarded as dogmatic systems. Merton was, of course, not the first spokesman of a more existential and dogmatic understanding of Zen; one of those who inspired him was Aelred Graham. An interreligious dialogue that takes its starting point in experience, and where the only genuinely fruitful experience is mysticism or the contemplative understanding of life, is thus not something that originates with Merton – but he was most certainly one of the pioneers of such an attitude. His position developed from affirming a religion based on faith to affirming a religion based on personal experience. A later theologian who stands in this tradition is the Jesuit William Johnston, who has worked in Japan for many years.

Thomas Merton's significance for the dialogue between Christianity and Zen Buddhism does not, however, lie only in the fact that other representatives of Christianity have followed in his footsteps. It is equally important that representatives of Buddhism see him as an insightful dialogue partner. This applies to several of the most prominent representatives of Buddhism, such as D.T. Suzuki and Thich Nhat Hanh, but respect for Merton is not confined to the representatives of Zen. The Dalai Lama too saw Merton as one who had come very far in his understanding of Buddhism.

Bibliography

Primary Literature

The Ascent to Truth (New York: Harcourt, Brace & Co., 1951).
The Asian Journal of Thomas Merton, Naomi Stone, Patrick Hart, and James Laughlin (eds), (New York: New Directions, 1973).
Bread in the Wilderness (New York: New Directions, 1953).
Faith and Violence: Christian Teaching and Christian Practice (Notre Dame: University of Notre Dame Press, 1968).
The Literary Essays of Thomas Merton, Patrick Hart (ed.) (New York: New Directions, 1981).
Mystics and Zen Masters (New York: Farrar, Straus and Giroux, 1967).
New Seeds of Contemplation (New York: New Directions, 1962).
Opening the Bible (Collegeville: Liturgical Press, 1970).
Seeds of Contemplation (New York: New Directions, 1949).
The Seven Storey Mountain (New York: Harcourt, Brace & Co., 1948).
Zen and the Birds of Appetite (New York: New Directions, 1968).

Secondary Literature

Carr, Anne E., *A Search for Wisdom and Spirit. Thomas Merton's Theology of the Self* (Notre Dame: University of Notre Dame Press, 1988).
Furlong, Monica, *Merton. A Biography* (London: Collins, 1980).
Johnston, William, *The Still Point. Reflections on Zen and Christian Mysticism* (New York: Fordham University Press, 1970).
King, Robert H., *Thomas Merton and Thich Nhat Hanh. Engaged Spirituality in an Age of Globalization* (New York: Continuum, 2001).
Kramer, Victor A., *Thomas Merton* (Boston: Twayne, 1984).
Labrie, Ross, *The Art of Thomas Merton* (Fort Worth: Texas Christian University Press, 1979).
McCormick, Chalmers: "The Zen Catholicism of Thomas Merton," *Journal of Ecumenical Studies*, 9 (1972).
Mott, Michael, *The Seven Mountains of Thomas Merton* (Boston: Houghton Miffin, 1984).
Ott, Elizabeth, *Thomas Merton, Grenzgänger zwischen Christentum und Buddhismus. Über das Verhältnis von Selbsterfahrung und Gottesbegegnung* (Würzburg: Echter Verlag, 1977).
Sandström, Henning E., *Ars gratia Dei. En studie i Thomas Mertons teologiska estetik* (Lund: Lund University Press, 1992).
Shannon, William H., Christine M. Bochen and Patrick F. O'Connell (eds), *The Thomas Merton Encyclopedia* (Maryknoll: Orbis Books, 2002).
Stenqvist, Catharina, *Nu – är verklig. Thomas Merton och kontemplativa erfarenheter* (Tollarp: Studiekamraten, 1996).
Woodcock, George, *Thomas Merton. Monk and Poet. A Critical Study* (Edinburgh: Cannongate Publishing, 1978).

Chapter 60
Christos Yannaras

Norman Russell

Christos Yannaras is a highly original thinker who does not fit easily into any 'school'. A philosophical theologian influenced by Heidegger, Wittgenstein and the French existentialists, he is best known as the exponent of an ontology of the person rooted in the Greek patristic tradition. He is also known for a strongly apophatic approach to the knowledge of God hostile to the rationalist theology long dominant in the West, which he regards as a fundamental distortion of the Gospel kerygma. He is nothing if not controversial. Conservative Orthodox are upset by his bold restatement of traditional teaching in a contemporary language that makes use of such expressions as 'mode of existence', 'relation', 'reciprocity', 'ecstasy' and 'eros'. Many Western Christians are offended at the way their tradition is represented in his writings. His books have nevertheless had huge sales. They began to be translated into Western European languages in the early 1970s, and since the collapse of the communist system have also been translated into Romanian, Russian and other Eastern European languages.

Biographical Sketch

Christos Yannaras was born in Athens in 1935. At the age of 19, he entered the Zoe Movement, an association of lay theologians dedicated to promoting personal piety through study circles and popular publications which for several decades had exerted enormous influence in Greece. Yannaras entered Zoe at the beginning of a troubled period when the Movement was torn apart by internal strife. He nevertheless persevered in it for the next 10 years.

In 1964 Yannaras left the Movement, disillusioned with what he had come to see as its non-Orthodox character. In his autobiography he mentions the works of Nicolas Berdyaev, Paul Tournier and Igor Caruso as opening his eyes to other dimensions of Orthodoxy. But the turning-point came with the publication of the Greek translation of Vladimir Lossky's *Mystical Theology of the Orthodox Church* (Thessalonica 1964). An important catalyst for this change of outlook was a charismatic personality called Demetrios Koutroubis, who had recently returned to Orthodoxy after some years with the Jesuits in France and the Lebanon. Koutroubis introduced a group of Zoe's best young minds to new theological currents then stirring in Western Europe, particularly the revival of patristic studies in France and the work of the Paris-based Russian émigré theologians who, besides Lossky, included Florovsky, Schmemann and Meyendorff. It was through these authors that the Greeks were able to recover the tradition of hesychast spirituality, whose greatest exponent was St Gregory Palamas.

For the next three years, from 1964 to 1967 (when it was closed down after the Colonels' coup), Yannaras was editor of a journal called *Synoro* ('Frontier'). This innovative forum brought young theologians who were later to make a name for themselves together with leading figures in literature and the arts. It was at the forefront of the theological 'renaissance' that changed the nature of religious discourse in Greece in the 1960s and led to the renewal of monastic life on Mount Athos and the strengthening of patristic studies in Greek universities.

While he was still a member of Zoe, Yannaras had been pursuing theological studies at the University of Athens. In 1964, in tandem with his editorship of *Synoro*, he went abroad to complete his studies, first in Germany and then in France, receiving a doctorate in philosophy from the Sorbonne with a work entitled *Metaphysics of the Body: A Study on John Climacus* (published later in Greek in 1971). When this work was presented as a thesis at Athens it was rejected because of its emphasis on Christian love as 'erotic'. The University of Thessalonica, however, was altogether more receptive to Yannaras's ideas. It awarded him a doctorate in theology for a thesis entitled: *The Ontological Content of the Theological Concept of the Person*.

Yannaras's first teaching appointment was at the University of Crete. He was refused a post at the University of Athens, ostensibly because of his theological views but in reality because he had attacked the university's theological faculty as narrow and backward-looking. He returned to Athens in 1981, when he was appointed, after some controversy, to the chair of philosophy at the Panteion University of Social and Political Sciences. His election had been opposed by the left, who did not want to see a theologian occupy a secular chair.

His retirement from his chair at the Panteion in 2002 has not led to any diminution in his writing or lecturing. He continues to be a prophetic voice denouncing the egocentric culture of the modern age and calling for participation in an authentic Christian experience able to reach out in ecclesial communion to the source of real life.

Survey of His Thought

A prolific author, Yannaras is the most widely read theologian in Greece today. His 51 books, most of them still in print, cover a broad range of genres from technical philosophical treatises to volumes of essays on political and cultural themes. His first work, *The Theology of the Absence and Unknowability of God*, written in Bonn and published in Athens in 1967, was the product of his encounter with the thought of Heidegger. Five years later it was reissued with a new title: *Heidegger and the Areopagite* (Athens 1972). This book contains the kernel of all that Yannaras has written subsequently. His key conviction, following Heidegger, is that the Western philosophical tradition from the Scholastics to Nietzsche has led inexorably to the 'Death of God' and the triumph of atheistic secularism. Against this Yannaras sets the apophatic tradition of the Greek East, which holds that God cannot be known by an intellectual ascent to a first cause, for our minds cannot grasp what God is in his essence. We can only know him by his energies, or operations, which means that knowledge of God comes from the experience of relation, not from discursive reasoning.

The themes sketched out in *Heidegger and the Areopagite* are developed more fully in two of Yannaras's most important works, *Person and Eros* (first published under the title *The Ontological Content of the Theological Concept of the Person*, Athens 1970), which explores the ontological implications of our participation in the divine energies, and *The Freedom of Morality* (Athens 1970), which argues that ethics is not about codes of behaviour but about our free response to God's erotic summons, a response that allows us to be transformed into his divine image. These books have both been greatly expanded since their first appearance in 1970. But even in their initial form they immediately established Yannaras's reputation as one of the few Greek theologians who could speak to people on religious matters in a meaningful contemporary language.

He has continued to develop these themes. In *Postmodern Metaphysics* (Athens 1993) he argues that the new physics, which has overturned the old Newtonian certainties in the natural sciences, also suggests fresh possibilities for a metaphysics based on the idea of relation. In *What Can be Said and What Cannot be Said* (Athens 1999) he continues the discussion he began in *Person and Eros*, this time (as the title suggests) using Wittgenstein rather than Heidegger as a springboard. The topics covered range from the role of language in defining experience to the metaphysical distinction between illusion and reality. *Relational Ontology* (Athens 2004) concludes this discussion with a further 20 topics, focusing now on ontological rather than epistemological concerns, to support the argument that our fundamental mode of existence is relational.

We return to 1970 to pick up another important theme in Yannaras's thinking, for it was in the same year that *Person and Eros* and *The Freedom of Morality* were first published that he read a paper at an Inter-Orthodox Conference held at Brookline, Massachusetts, in which he set out trenchant views on the nature of the Church. This was 'Orthodoxy and the West', first published in 1971, which stands in the same relation to his ecclesiology as *Heidegger and the Areopagite* does to his philosophy. In this paper he contrasts what he sees as a Western drive to dominate the physical reality of the world on the basis of an individualistic intellectualism going back to medieval scholastic thinkers, with an Orthodox approach that relies on a personal relationship with the world expressed in eucharistic-liturgical terms.

The views expressed in 'Orthodoxy and the West' and also in the provocative eighth chapter of *The Freedom of Morality* ('Pietism as an Ecclesiological Heresy') and an article on 'Theology in Present-Day Greece' published originally in French in 1971, have been brought together in *Orthodoxy and the West*. Like his other key works, this book has been issued in increasingly expanded versions. It was first published in 1972 as *Orthodoxy and the West: Theology in Greece Today*, and most recently, much enlarged and with a new title, *Orthodoxy and the West in Modern Greece*, in 1992. The most important themes are on the one hand the deviations of Western theology along intellectualist lines, and on the other the 'Babylonian captivity' of the Orthodox Church under Greek Westernisers until the theological renaissance of the 1960s. The aim of the work, in Yannaras's own words, is 'to study in Westernized modern Hellenism a cultural tragedy which is perhaps of general human interest, and to highlight the real spiritual problems that have been created by the Western "religionizing" of the Church'.[1]

In his latest ecclesiological work, *Against Religion* (Athens 2006), Yannaras develops further his notion of 'religion' as a perversion of the ecclesial communion that is the proper expression of the Christian faith. A 'religionised' Christianity is one which has been reduced to an ideological system satisfying an instinctual need for security. Yannaras sees such a Christianity not only as characteristic of the West but also as permeating Orthodoxy. Even the recent translations of the *Philokalia*, far from spreading a knowledge of Orthodox spirituality, only promote an individualistic approach to faith, a fact he attributes to the Westernising mentality of its chief compiler, Nikodemos of the Holy Mountain.

Yannaras has also written in other genres: autobiography, journalism, systematic theology and prose-poetry. Two works in the last two categories, *Elements of Faith* (Athens 1983) and *Variations on the Song of Songs* (Athens 1990) have been widely read both in Greece and abroad. *Elements of Faith* is not a systematic theology in the conventional sense, beginning with first principles arrived at by a rational process – the oneness of God – and then working down through the Trinity to the Church and moral conduct. It begins with the search for truth and discovers that truth is found only in personal relationship. It offers an experiential approach, culminating in Jesus Christ and how he is to be found in a Church which is first and last a eucharistic community.

Variations on the Song of Songs is a poetic meditation on a book of the Bible that has long been a favourite with mystics. It is about love and failure, our thirst for life, and our reciprocal relations with each other and with God. The 'mode of life' is contrasted with the 'mode of nature', the latter mode expressing our disordered, instinctually-driven selves, while the 'mode of life' is the love that 'transforms our existence into relation'. The book is a lyrical restatement of the themes more austerely discussed in *Person and Eros*; when the two are read in conjunction with each other, the one illuminates the other. Indeed all of Yannaras's books are interrelated, the whole corpus forming a coherent structure.

Key Themes

The Apophatic Character of Knowledge

Although a traditionalist, Yannaras is not a conservative. In his youth he rejected the academic style of theology then current that relied on Western European, particularly

---

[1] *Orthodoxy and the West* (2004), p. viii.

German, models and went back to the philosophical tradition of Dionysius the Areopagite, Maximus the Confessor and Gregory Palamas, and beyond these to Heraclitus, Plato and Aristotle. This tradition, with its emphasis on apophaticism, is particularly sensitive to the limitations of language. 'Apophaticism', says Yannaras, 'is the denial that we can exhaust the truth in its expression, a denial that we can identify the knowledge of truth simply with an understanding of its declamatory logic'.[2] The purpose of this denial is to ensure that we do not mistake language – even the sophisticated language of symbol and myth – for reality. We cannot say that we know God when all we have done is construct an intellectual model of him. Quoting Dionysius, Yannaras insists that apophaticism points towards a union with God that 'is superior to anything available to us by way of our own abilities or activities in the realm of discourse or intellect'.[3] Apophaticism thus refers ultimately to our deified mode of existence, our transformation through union with the source of life in a manner transcending all conceptual knowledge.

Apophaticism and Personal Existence

If we cannot encounter reality through conceptual knowledge, what other approaches are available to us? The answer is through immediate experience. Experience is not simply the raw material that we process mentally to give us our picture of the external world. Before anything else it is relational and personal: 'We know beings as presence (*par-ousia*), not as essence (*ousia*).'[4] With this as his starting-point Yannaras develops an ontology of the person as relational event. We are conscious of persons phenomenologically and this consciousness signifies an *a priori* relationship before we define it by the 'semantics' of language.

The relation that constitutes us as persons is not a static one. It requires a dynamic movement which Yannaras discusses in terms of *ekstasis* and *eros*, a going out of the self in love. In his more technical works he describes this as 'self-transference from the naturally given capacity for intellectualization to the otherness of its personal actualization, from the self-evidentness of noetic-conscious conceptualization of objective conventionality and the naturally given common understanding of objective essences to universal existential relation'.[5] If such descriptions leave us baffled, here is how Yannaras expresses the same thought in a more literary style:

> The distinction of nature from person is not an intellectual definition. It is the experience of love: the revelation of the uniqueness of the Beloved which is not susceptible to definition. Definitions are only nature, signifiers of a common understanding. They define the objective, the common denominator. The erotic

---

[2] Ibid., p. 25.
[3] *On the Absence and Unknowability of God* (2005), p. 88.
[4] *Person and Eros* (2007), p. 6.
[5] Ibid., p. 20.

revelation remains unbounded, it shines in the otherness of the person, in his or her freedom. Unbounded, that is, inaccessible to touch.[6]

Elsewhere Yannaras speaks of the invitation or summons (*klēsis*) that is the trigger for this movement. The invitation-to-relationship and our free response to it is presupposed by humanity's constitution as *personal* existence. This is one of Yannaras's chief metaphysical arguments for the existence of God.

Persons Human and Divine

If truth is personal relation and knowledge is participation in truth, then the reality of the person and of interpersonal relationships has priority over any intellectual definition of truth. We can understand this with regard to other human beings, but how does it help us to know God? God is personal yet not bounded as we are: 'It is precisely as personal existence, as distinctiveness and freedom from any predetermination by essence or nature that God constitutes being and is the hypostasis of being.'[7] But if God is personal existence as absolute freedom from predetermination, how can we finite human beings also be persons except in a very different sense? Yannaras's reply is this:

> I also define the human subject as *personal* existence even though it expresses its relation existentially with the modes-energies of nature's limitations. Self-awareness, rationality, the power to create, active existential otherness, are also characteristics of the human subject, but dependent on the limitations of created nature. Nevertheless, I also define the human subject as *personal* existence, since the relation's natural expression refers experientially to a pre-natural factor of referentiality: to the relation's 'nucleus' or hypostatic term, which is presupposed by the reference's real-existential character, and which defines itself existentially only by the mode of relation.[8]

Or, as Yannaras goes on to say: 'If there exists a human subject, it exists only as a result of the invitatory energy of the uncreated, which is only loving.' For the uncreated 'exists only in the mode of loving self-transcendence and self-offering'.[9] The human person is therefore the hypostasisation of the uncreated invitatory energies. This is what is meant by 'participation in the divine energies'. Yannaras is perfectly aware of the logical difficulty of holding that the created hypostasises the uncreated. But he insists that the 'energies express the existential fact without being identified with the "essential" or hypostatic otherness of what expresses them'.[10]

---

[6] *Variations on the Song of Songs* (2005), p. 62.
[7] *The Freedom of Morality* (1984), p. 17.
[8] *Postmodern Metaphysics* (2004), p. 177.
[9] Ibid., p. 179.
[10] Ibid.

It is not only the conceptual difficulty of which Yannaras is aware. Translating these insights into the realities of life is painfully hard:

> How can you lay hold of the topmost branches (cf. Song of Songs 7:8) with fingers of clay? The ascent to love resembles a labor of Sisyphus. Yet we exist only as creatures crawling up a trunk to attain heights we cannot grasp. Only by desire which constitutes us as *personal* existence.[11]

Personal existence requires a transition from the mode of finite nature to the mode of real life. The mode of finite nature is self-assertive and self-perpetuating. The mode of real life is the ecstatic reaching out to erotic communion with the Other.

Ethics and the Person

Moral behaviour is the expression of a relation of love; it is not simply conformity to a code, even one that is divinely sanctioned:

> If we accept morality simply as man's conformity to an authoritative or conventional code of law, then ethics becomes man's alibi for his existential problem. He takes refuge in ethics, whether religious, philosophical or even political, and hides the tragedy of his mortal, biological existence behind idealized and fabulous objective aims. He wears a mask of behaviour borrowed from ideological or party authorities, so as to be safe from his own self and the questions with which it confronts him.[12]

Yannaras passionately opposes those moralists who emphasise the satisfaction of God's justice. For him a 'just' God as they conceive him is simply 'a heavenly police constable', a projection of fallen humanity's need for 'supernatural individual security within the reciprocal treachery of collective co-existence'.[13] He sees the 'mode of virtue' as often masking an instinctual drive towards self-assertion:

> [Human n]ature is skilful in the tricks she plays with the unconscious. She plays the game of self-interest even with the mode of virtue. That is why in the iridescent gleam of virtue we often discern the color of a cold hunger for self-regard. It is because 'the dog of sensuality knows very well how to beg for spirit when flesh is denied it'.[14]

So what is virtue? It is 'the abandonment of a self-centred individualism, the active pursuit of self-transcendence and self-offering'.[15] It is the transformation of the mode

---

[11] *Variations on the Song of Songs* (2005), p. 61.
[12] *The Freedom of Morality* (1984), p. 15.
[13] *Elements of Faith* (1991), p. 83.
[14] *Variations on the Song of Songs* (2005), p. 125.
[15] *Postmodern Metaphysics* (2004), p. 155.

of nature into the mode of freedom. And the mode of freedom is attained through communion with the ecclesial body.

The Church

The Church exists to enable us to participate in true life, to exist ultimately in the mode of the personal hypostases of the Trinity. Through baptism we are born into the ecclesial body's unity, which transforms life into communion. And through the eucharistic meal, 'which constitutes and realizes the Church', we participate in a life-giving love, which is the mode of the Son's offering of himself to the Father.[16]

Given the eucharistic reality of the Church, anything that tends to turn it into a vehicle for the exercise of power – the professionalisation of the clergy, the adoption of codes of law, the abuse of political influence – is to be deplored. Yannaras has called this the 'religionisation' of Christianity, the turning of what should be the means of life into an institutionalised ideology. It is his perception of its insidious growth that lies behind his criticism not only of 'the West' but also of contemporary developments in Orthodoxy. The 'Vaticanisation' of the Orthodox hierarchy, in post-communist Eastern Europe as well as in Greece, has led in his view to the prevalence today of 'Orthodoxism' rather than Orthodoxy.

Unsurprisingly, Yannaras identifies the Church with a gathered remnant, a 'tiny "yeast" … of people who continue to be gripped by vital questions about life and death' in a secular world where the Church has become culturally irrelevant.[17] Not that this makes him sectarian. Rather, he is a voice crying in the wilderness, recalling the Church to its true vocation.

Yannaras's Significance Today

When Yannaras first came to the attention of Western theologians in the early 1970s he was recognised as an important new voice. It has disappointed him, however, that while his work has stimulated theologians such as Jürgen Moltmann and Rowan Williams, it has failed to engage professional philosophers. There seem to be two reasons for this, one being the sharp divide existing between philosophers and theologians in Western academic culture, the other being the ambitious nature of the goal Yannaras has set himself. He believes that the distinction between essence and energy is not only of theological importance but also the key to a philosophical epistemology, a conviction he bases on the apophaticism that he regards as a fundamental epistemological principle in Greek philosophy. The West he sees as rejecting the apophatic side of this philosophy (along with the essence/energies distinction that depends upon it) while accepting its intellectualist side. On the foundation of the apophaticism of the

---

[16] *Orthodoxy and the West* (2004), pp. 29–30.
[17] 'The Church in the Postcommunist World' (2003), p. 31.

Greek tradition and philosophical criteria derived from Heidegger, he constructs an ontology of the person which is relational, and finds its fulfilment in God.

Not everyone has found Yannaras's enterprise entirely convincing. Stelios Ramfos, for example, regards it as unrealistic to think 'that modern people nowadays could really be expected to understand the ontological categories of the Christian East in such a way that these should genuinely be able to wean them away from an intellectualist idea of truth'.[18] Yet the attempt is worth making. Basilio Petrà, while conceding that Yannaras's theological conclusions can look like 'the superimposition of arguments from faith rather than developments from the reflections themselves', points out that his thought is actually 'of a kind that uses philosophical categories within a theological understanding of reality'.[19] It is not arguments from faith that are superimposed so much as philosophical reflections that are offered to help us enter into Yannaras's theological vision. In a modern culture where God is increasingly irrelevant, this vision, supported by existential insights into freedom, relation and personhood, is fresh and exciting. Without sacrificing intellectual rigour, Yannaras cuts theological discourse free from its academic straightjacket, as his enormous sales in Greece witness. As more of his books become available in translation, his influence will grow.

Bibliography

Books (date of Greek edition in brackets) and Articles by Christos Yannaras

'Orthodoxy and the West', *Eastern Churches Review*, 3 (1971), pp. 286–300. Also in *Greek Orthodox Theological Review*, 17 (1972), pp. 115–31.
'La théologie en Grèce aujourd'hui', *Istina*, 2 (1971), pp. 129–67. English version in *St Vladimir's Theological Quarterly*, 16 (1972), pp. 195–214.
The Freedom of Morality (Crestwood: St Vladimir's Seminary Press, 1984) (1979).
Elements of Faith (Edinburgh: T&T Clark, 1991) (1983).
Person and Eros (Brookline: Holy Cross Orthodox Press, 2007) (1987).
On the Absence and Unknowability of God (London and New York: T&T Clark International, 2005) (1988).
Variations on the Song of Songs (Brookline: Holy Cross Orthodox Press, 2005) (1990).
Orthodoxy and the West (Brookline: Holy Cross Orthodox Press, 2004) (1992).
Postmodern Metaphysics (Brookline: Holy Cross Orthodox Press, 2004) (1993).
What Can Be Said and What Cannot Be Said (in Greek) (Athens: Ikaros, 1999).
The Church in Post-Communist Europe (Berkeley: Interorthodox Press, 2003). A different version, entitled 'The Church in the Postcommunist World', appears in the *International Journal for the Study of the Christian Church*, 3 (2003), pp. 29–46.

---

[18] *Yearning for Unity* (2011), p. 35.
[19] Basilio Petrà, 'Personalist Thought in Greece in the Twentieth Century', *Greek Orthodox Theological Review*, 50 (2005), pp. 1–48.

Relational Ontology (Brookline: Holy Cross Orthodox Press, 2011) (2004).
Against Religion (in Greek) (Athens: Ikaros, 2006).

Secondary Literature

Louth, Andrew. Introduction to *On the Absence and Unknowability of God* (English trans. pp. 1–14). A brief but perceptive assessment of Yannaras and his significance.
Louth, Andrew. 'Some Recent Works by Christos Yannaras in English Translation', *Modern Theology*, 25 (2009), pp. 329–40. A judicious review article surveying *Postmodern Metaphysics, Variations on the Song of Songs, Orthodoxy and the West* and *Person and Eros*.
Nichols, Aidan. 'Christos Yannaras and Theological Ethics' in his *Light from the East* (London: Sheed & Ward, 1995), pp. 181–93. A useful discussion of *The Freedom of Morality*.
Nissiotis, Nikos. 'Orthodoxy and the West: A Response', *Greek Orthodox Theological Review*, 17 (1972), pp. 132–42. A critical discussion of 'Orthodoxy and the West' by one of Yannaras's leading Orthodox contemporaries.
Payne, Daniel P. *The Revival of Political Hesychasm in Contemporary Orthodox Thought: The Political Hesychasm of John S. Romanides and Christos Yannaras* (Lanham: Lexington Books, 2011). A doctoral thesis which seeks to interpret Yannaras's political writings (at least those available in English) through the application of modern social theory.
Petrà, Basilio. 'Personalist Thought in Greece in the Twentieth Century: A First Tentative Synthesis', *Greek Orthodox Theological Review*, 50 (2005), pp. 1–48. An important article by one of Yannaras's best interpreters today.
Ramfos, Stelios. *Yearning for the One* (Brookline: Holy Cross Orthodox Press, 2011). A major study of Greek personalism, first published in 2000.
Russell, Norman. 'Modern Greek Theologians and the Greek Fathers', *Philosophy and Theology*, 18 (2006), pp. 77–92.
Spiteris, Yannis. 'Christos Yannaras' in *La teologia ortodossa neo-greca* (Bologna: Dehoniane, 1992), pp. 296–322. An excellent overview of Yannaras's *oeuvre* up to 1990.
Ware, Kallistos. 'Scholasticism and Orthodoxy: Theological Method as a Factor in the Schism', *Eastern Churches Review*, 5 (1973), pp. 16–27. A sympathetic but critical response to 'Orthodoxy and the West'.
Williams, R.D. 'The Theology of Personhood: A Study of the Thought of Christos Yannaras', *Sobornost*, 6 (1972), pp. 415–30. Still a very valuable examination of some of the ideas later developed in *Person and Eros*.

Chapter 61
John D. Caputo

Neal DeRoo

John D. Caputo (1940–) is the leading figure in postmodern theology. Employing a deconstructive approach that takes seriously the insights of negative theology, he has reimagined the very purpose of theology itself, moving it from talk about God to talk directed to God and to what God calls us to do. Working within the Christian tradition, he has produced a strand of postmodern theology known as "weak theology" that challenges modern presuppositions within traditional or "strong" theology (most notably, the sovereignty and omnipotence of God) with an eye to re-awakening theology to its practical and ethical aims. His work has exercised considerable influence, not only in philosophical and theological discourse, but also in the "emergent church" and other lay movements. He is a key figure in bridging twentieth and twenty-first century theology.

Biography

John D. Caputo was born to an Italian-American Catholic family in Philadelphia in October of 1940. He was schooled in the Catholic tradition, and joined the order of the de la Salle Brothers of the Christian Schools in 1958, where he followed a rather strict monastic routine during his 15-month novitiate. This time was extremely formative for Caputo, deeply entrenching the affective elements of religious sentiment, and exposing him to the religious thought of the Scholastic masters (most notably Aquinas) and the Medieval mystics. The dynamic between the three elements introduced during his period of monastic silence will drive Caputo's thought for the rest of his life.

During his undergraduate education with the Brothers at LaSalle University, he encountered "existential" philosophy for the first time in the works of Kierkegaard. This, too, would prove to be a hugely formative experience. He sought to pursue his studies of existential philosophy through graduate work in Heidegger, whose project of "overcoming metaphysics" struck him as continuing, in another register, Maritain's *Three Degrees of Knowledge*. However, his desire to pursue doctoral studies in philosophy and teach at the university level, instead of teaching high school religion and English, put him at odds with his Brother Provincial, and he left the order after completing his B.A. in 1962. From there, he followed an academic path, receiving an M.A. from Villanova University, and a Doctorate in philosophy from Bryn Mawr College. In 1968 he began teaching at Villanova University, where he was appointed the David R. Cook chair in philosophy in 1993. In 2004, he retired from Villanova and took up a position as the Thomas J. Watson Professor of Religion and Humanities and professor of philosophy at Syracuse University, from which he retired in 2011.

Caputo's concern for the interrelation between religious experience and philosophical thought manifested itself in his first major works, *The Mystical Element in Heidegger's Thought* (1978; reprinted 1986), *Heidegger and Aquinas: An Essay on Overcoming Metaphysics* (1982), and *Demythologizing Heidegger* (1993), where the limits of systematic philosophical thinking are highlighted by the employment of mystical themes and tropes.

But it is his engagement with the deconstructive thought of Jacques Derrida that really helps Caputo find his own voice in the conversation between philosophy and religion. Beginning with *Radical Hermeneutics* (1987), *Against Ethics* (1993), and *More Radical Hermeneutics* (2000), Caputo's work takes a decidedly deconstructive turn, deepening the hermeneutic insights of H.G. Gadamer into an inescapable aspect of life itself: hermeneutics, and interpretation, go all the way down throughout human experience.

The religious importance of interpretation for human thinking is highlighted most notably in Caputo's landmark re-reading of Derrida's thought, *The Prayers and Tears of Jacques Derrida: Religion with/out Religion* (1997). Here, Caputo reveals Derrida—and deconstruction itself—to be a way of thinking that is essentially inhabited by religious and theological tropes: prayer, the call, love, desire, etc. To further explore the nexus of deconstruction and religion begun in *Prayers and Tears*, Caputo organized a series of biannual conferences at Villanova University designed to bring Derrida personally in dialogue with leading theologians and philosophers on topics like *God, the Gift and Postmodernism* (1997); *Questioning God* (1999); and *Augustine and Postmodernism* (2001). The conferences proved to be essential to the development of postmodern religious thought in North America, and Caputo continued them after Derrida was no longer able to attend, bringing leading European philosophers like Marion, Zizek, Badiou, Vattimo, and Cixous together to explore the distinctly religious themes of *Transcendence and Beyond* (2003); *St. Paul among the Philosophers* (2005); *Feminism, Sexuality and the Return of Religion* (2007); *The Politics of Love* (2009); and *The Future of Continental Philosophy of Religion* (2011).[1]

By engaging non-theological thinkers, such as Derrida, Badiou, and Žižek, in essentially religious conversations, Caputo showed that religious sentiment is not confined to recognized religions, and therefore thought did not need to be denominationalistic in order to be genuinely religious. He develops this insight into

---

[1] The lectures and discussions of these conferences are all collected in volumes, co-edited by Caputo, bearing the titles listed here (see the bibliography at the end of this chapter for more details); *The Politics of Love* and *The Future of Continental Philosophy of Religion* remain forthcoming.

a more sustained, "affirmative"[2] theology with the advent of his "weak" theology of the event in *The Weakness of God: A Theology of the Event* (2006), and *The Fate of all Flesh: A Theology of the Event II* (an as-yet unfinished manuscript that tackles the issue of theological materialism).

In addition to his academic work, he has also published a series of more popular works that were intended to address, and arouse, religious passion and desire in a straightforward and heartfelt way accessible to non-academics. These works, *On Religion* (2001), *Philosophy and Theology* (2006), and *What Would Jesus Deconstruct? The Good News of Postmodernism for the Church* (2007), have had an enormous influence on the development of certain progressive elements in the church, most notably the "emergent church" movement that has applied Caputo's work to issues of ecclesiology, liturgical performance, evangelism, and church structure.

Survey

Given his concern for the relationship between systematic thinking, mysticism, and religious feeling, Caputo's thought can be understood as navigating the treacherous path between negative and positive theology. Early on, Caputo focused especially on the mystical aspects found in negative theology. In *The Mystical Element in Heidegger's Thought* and *Heidegger and Aquinas*, for example, the limited nature of finite human knowledge is supplemented—and even superseded—by the possibility of a direct and immediate intuition of the divine. This intuition, drawn out of the mystical tradition of Eckhart and St Thomas, does not itself fall prey to the limitations that hinder human attempts at thought. The task of the religious person then—including the theologian, it would seem—is to cease thinking and talking *about* God, and instead talk *to* God, and so to let God be (God).

But this positive affirmation of mysticism will not last long. Implicit already in parts of the second edition of *Mystical Element* is a subtle shift in Caputo's theological tune: he sings the same negating stanzas, but he has a little less gusto for the mystical union of the chorus. While he continues to affirm the limitations of human reason, he now starts to apply this limitation also to the realm of human intuition. This increasing wariness of mysticism stems from the fact that even our intuitions of God are affected, necessarily, by human finitude, and are therefore inserted into the necessity of hermeneutics described in *Radical Hermeneutics*. Because radical hermeneutics characterizes human existence, even our mystical experience of God is still, *qua* human experience, an experience of (by) humans, and not God's experience. Human experience, Caputo emphasizes, is constituted within the matrix (*khôra*) of human societal and cultural conditions. This matrix entails that all human experience is contingent, and not founded on eternal truths or the intuition of timeless essences.

---

[2] Caputo prefers to speak of his work as an "affirmative" rather than a "positive" theology, as the notion of positive theology remains tied too closely to the strong, confessional understanding of theology and religion that he critiques.

Therefore, as *More Radical Hermeneutics* makes clear, our task is to realize that what we take as true is always an interpretation and that, when push comes to shove, we do not know some eternal Secret, Truth, or God. Even our experiences of "god" cannot escape this situation.

But this is not such a bad thing. The lack of direct access to Truth enables us to act responsibly in the world. If we had direct access to the Truth, then we would have to do as the Truth tells us to, and this alone could justify our actions: "I'm sorry if you don't like what I'm doing, but it has to be this way. The Truth [or the Bible, or God] tells me to, and it cannot be wrong." It is justifications like this that have led to some of the most horrific abuses in human history. To avoid such horrors, we must embrace our own responsibility, and we are truly only responsible, Caputo argues in *Against Ethics*, when we realize the contingency of our own existence. This entails acknowledging that, if things are bad, it is up to us to fix them—even though our attempt to fix things might make them worse and, without the Truth to fall back on, we have no way of knowing, for sure, what the "right" thing to do is.

While the necessity of interpretation suggested by *khôra* echoes many of the main themes of apophatic theology (e.g. the humility of human reason), Caputo clearly does not echo the affirmation of a direct experience of a transcendent superhuman entity that most often accompanies apophatic theology. Given that Caputo's understanding of *khôra* shows that even an experience of the transcendent cannot escape the contingency (and therefore revisability) that lies underneath all human experience, there would seem to be no room left in Caputo for anything like a positive theology—there is only the negation, only the silence. But Caputo's discussions of *khôra* have an essentially religious dimension, as he argues in *The Prayers and Tears of Jacques Derrida*. In the very desert of our *khôral* contingency we find a hope and yearning that things will get better. This messianic hope stems, not from outside or beyond the world but from within it: rather than Truth and the Good being hard-wired into us, Caputo claims that there are promises that we pick up from our tradition (Justice, Democracy, God) that inspire us to act. The work of deconstruction is done in response to those promises as we attempt to incarnate them more appropriately in our particular context.

In *On Religion*, Caputo continues to develop the religious implications of this affirmative deconstruction. Religion is the loving, the desiring, the hoping that animates our life, rather than a belief in some intellectual propositions. It is not the love of this or that particular God, but is rather the loving or desiring of "God," where "the name of God is the name of love, the name of what we love."[3] Caputo ties this notion of religion to the *cor inquietum* (Book I, ch. 1) and the "What do I love when I love my god" (Book X) of Augustine's *Confessions*, thereby returning to the Catholic tradition from which he began (but to Augustine, not Aquinas), only by significantly questioning it, from within (in keeping with another Augustinian line: "I have become a question to myself"). This questioning from within is done, not in the hope of making

---

[3] John D. Caputo, *On Religion* (London and New York, 2001), p. 6.

the tradition more in line with liberal democracy or European philosophy, but with the intent of helping the tradition live up to the spirit or promises that animate it.

As a theologian, Caputo must explain his own faith tradition in a way consistent with his notions of *khôra* and radical hermeneutics, a project that begins in earnest for him with *The Weakness of God: A Theology of the Event*. In this work, he challenges the traditional picture of God as a sovereign (hyper-)Being of unlimited abilities (omnipotence, omniscience, etc.). In its place, he conceives of God as the "weak force" of desiring or loving described in *On Religion*. Equating God with an event that happens in the name of God, Caputo not only critiques the omnipotence of God, but even questions whether God can "exist," in the traditional sense of that term. Since the promises that drive us are found within our traditions, there is no need for an immaterial or super-natural realm that can be distinguished from the plane of existence, of human experience. Instead, there is only this life here, and the promises and events within it that call to be thought, to be done, to be incarnated or enacted, by things in existence. God is such a call, such a promise, such an event.

Key Themes

Caputo has called his theology a "weak" theology. The notion of a weak theology draws heavily on Derrida's "weak force," as well as the "weak thought" of Vattimo. It entails that, whatever we are doing when we are doing theology, we are not describing, or even trying to describe, the objective structure of what "is." The point of theology is not to talk *about* God, but to talk *to* God and hear what is being said in the name of God. Caputo is interested in what we are doing when we call on the name of God, and not in what answers to that call. In this sense, Caputo neither posits nor denies the existence of God. Instead, he changes the terms of the debate, claiming that theology should focus on what God *insists* that we do, rather than on God's *existence* or *essence*. This focus on insistence rather than existence, on provocation and the call rather than indication and the Being (who is called God), is why Caputo dubs this a theology of the event (rather than a theology of God, properly speaking).

This is not to say that the theology of the event has no implications for our understanding of God. It does—but only in a limited fashion, since its concern is not with positing the existence of God, let alone positing certain characteristics that such an existing God may or may not possess. In this limited fashion, Caputo's weak theology posits a weak God, as well. This is not to say that it suggests a vision of God that is like the traditional picture of God, only with a bit less power: some quasi-powerful being who rules over creation tentatively, insecurely, like a child king; or, even worse, some being who is too weak even to rule, but just lays around, demanding our worship without doing anything. Rather, it re-orients our talk of God entirely, away from something like the philosophical essence of God (as God possesses it) and toward the nature of God as it affects and inspires us in our experience. Caputo takes the phrase "weakness of God," not analogically from Derrida and Vattimo, but directly from Paul (cf. 1 Cor. 1:29) and the notion of Christ's *kenosis*. On the traditional picture of God, *kenosis* cannot be understood apart from the divine nature that demands the satisfaction of both divine justice and divine mercy. To meet these demands, God must become human, be punished as a human, and then be restored again to full divinity: God's weakness, the *kenosis*, is nothing but a temporary affair, a brief dalliance on the "wrong side of the tracks," that remains secure in the knowledge that when it is all over, God's power will be restored and Christ will return home (and wait for us to join him there). Viewed from the perspective of Holy Saturday, however—and the Holy Saturday experience must be our primary interpretive key because it describes also the eschatological condition of the contemporary church: those living in the time after God has been killed and before God's return as the living God—the story of the crucifixion is not that of the son's paying the ransom to the Father for the sins of the people, not a story of power and control at all, but rather the story of "a certain death of God," a very specific kind of death, or rather, the death of a very specific kind of God: "the death of the *ens supremum et deus omnipotens*, the death of the God of power."[4]

What Caputo announces, then, is the deconstruction of God understood according to the attributes of Greek metaphysics like immutability, omnipotence, and omniscience. Unlike the "death of God" offered by Altizer et al. (which did not, in fact, kill God, but only changed his address, granting humanity divine status and metaphysical necessity), Caputo wants to abandon those metaphysical notions altogether. This does not, however, merely leave us "erring" and "destinerrant," wandering alone in the desert, with no guide calling us in one direction or another, as Mark C. Taylor's a/theology might suggest. Rather, the end of the metaphysical God opens up the genuine possibility of a prophetic experience of God. The weakness of God emphasizes the prophetic character of the name of God as a force of disruption in the world. We do not experience God as acting directly in the world so much as God calling or inspiring human actions in the world, actions that challenge the ruling edicts of this world in view of a "sacred anarchy" that always affirms and furthers life. The affirmative nature of the call is evidenced in the creation account of the first chapter of Genesis. In his reading of that story (which draws heavily on the work of Catherine Keller, the Jewish Midrashic tradition, and pre-second century Christian thought), Caputo replaces the *ex nihilo* Creator God with the spirit [*ruach*] that swept over the (already present) deep [*tehom*], bringing light to the (previous) darkness [*pne choshekh*] and life to what was previously a desolate emptiness [*tohu wa-bohu*]. This call for light and life is the call, the provocation, the event, that stirs in the name of God. This is the inspiration of all who talk to God, and should be the inspiration also behind theology, according to Caputo: not "what can we say about God," but "how can we free this inspiration so that it can inspire anew and again." Taylor's a/theology, like the "strong" theology of the traditional metaphysical God, fails to adequately release the event happening in the name of God, and so ends up leaving God behind as a dead name.

---

[4] John D. Caputo and Gianni Vattimo, *After the Death of God*, edited by Jeffrey Robbins (New York, 2007), p. 66.

The call of God does not come from a world beyond our own, then, but from the event, the provocation, that is happening in the name of God. This provides the impetus for Caputo's critique of two-world theology. This critique applies to the very idea of the super-natural or metaphysical, of the existence of "things" called God, the devil, angels, etc., in any world other than the one humans live in. This is not a refutation of the notion of heaven or a kingdom of God, but rather the suggestion that such a place, such a kingdom, must exist, if it exists, in this world. Therefore, the kingdom must be understood eschatologically, not as the theory of a distinct place we will be taken to at the end of time, but as the promise that—as impossible as it may seem—this world will someday reflect the glorious vision of the kingdom of God. The task of God's followers, then, is to work for the coming of the kingdom in this world, here and now, by striving to make this world more like that kingdom: more just, more forgiving, more blessed. This can be done, not by transforming some "inner soul" through piety and devotion, but through inspired action in the world, action that can be sweeping and institutional, but also small and concrete (giving a cup of cold water to a thirsty person, for example).

The affirmations of the material world and our traditions within it are done, not in the name of a naïve realism or a neo- (or radical) orthodoxy, but from what Caputo calls a hyper-realism: everything is not (merely) material, but there is also nothing other than the material. In this manner, Caputo not only challenges the problematic Cartesian dualism that sees the material as essentially in opposition to the mental (spiritual, cultural, etc.), but he affirms a certain eschatological character to reality itself: there are animating forces (events) that work within bodies and things and cannot be separated from them. These forces are not separate entities that exist in their own right, requiring physical bodies in order to be "incarnated" (i.e. in-bodied), like the proverbial ghost in the machine; instead, these forces are constitutive of material reality itself—but in neither a strictly literal (like the midi-chlorians in *Star Wars*) nor a strictly metaphorical sense. Rather than thinking the world from the matter–spirit dualism, and then trying to explain how that dualism can be overcome, Caputo's hyper-realism pushes for an essentially material spirituality or, if you prefer, an essentially spiritualized materiality.

This brings him, practically speaking, in line with theories of the created nature of reality, but without the metaphysical character of a God-Being who is the true Agent in all actions. In place of such an über-Agent we are left with distinct, finite, religious people (not metaphysical entities like "The Church" that function like the Hegelian *Geist*) loving God and desiring to live out that love in the best way they can, but without assurance of success. By focusing on this loving, desiring aspect of religious experience, Caputo re-discovers the specifically "religious" way out of metaphysics that was the focus of his early works on Heidegger, Aquinas, and Eckhart. This can only be a way out of metaphysics, however, if we maintain a "weak" theology and a "weak" religion that does not itself slide back into metaphysics. This moment of negative theology—what in phenomenology would be called the reduction—can never be lost sight of, if one is to properly understand Caputo's positive theological contributions.

Caputo's Place in Twentieth-century Theology

Caputo's "weak" theology re-thinks several theological tropes and themes through a lens that significantly re-casts our understanding of the role and purpose of theology. As such, it bears some affinities with other movements in twentieth-century theology, but cannot be equated with any of them. As we have seen, there are overtones of the eschatological focus of thinkers like Moltmann, Rahner, and Zizioulas at work in Caputo's understanding of the kingdom of God and of the eschatological nature of reality; similarly, Caputo's religious materialism and his project of demythologizing pay clear homage to the work of Tillich. In re-casting theology as "weak" and focused on provocation rather than invocation, Caputo's weak God also closely resembles Bonhoeffer's late discussions of a "religionless Christianity."

However, in focusing on our *khôral* situation, Caputo re-introduces a certain aspect of negative theology into twentieth-century theological discourse. By drawing on the resources of Augustine, Aquinas, and Eckhart in this way, Caputo not only re-shapes how we understand the discourse of positive theology, but he also engages theology with postmodernism, and therefore prepares it to move forward into the twenty-first century, able to tackle anew contemporary issues like materialism from a context steeped in theological themes but not bound by metaphysical orthodoxy. What the consequences of such an engagement will be remain unclear, and therefore Caputo's true place in theology may not be properly understood for several decades. For now, he offers, at the least, a strong warning against the intrusion of modern metaphysics into theology, and, at most, a new picture of Christianity that recovers theology's ability to meaningfully and directly impact the everyday lives of loving, desiring religious people everywhere.

Bibliography

Primary Literature

Books
The Mystical Element in Heidegger's Thought (Athens: Ohio University Press, 1978). Revised, paperback edition with a new "Introduction" (New York: Fordham University Press, 1986).
Heidegger and Aquinas: An Essay on Overcoming Metaphysics (New York: Fordham University Press, 1982).
Radical Hermeneutics: Repetition, Deconstruction and the Hermeneutic Project (Bloomington: Indiana University Press, 1987).
Against Ethics: Contributions to a Poetics of Obligation with Constant Reference to Deconstruction (Bloomington: Indiana University Press, 1993).
Demythologizing Heidegger (Bloomington: Indiana University Press, 1993).

Deconstruction in a Nutshell: A Conversation with Jacques Derrida, edited with a commentary (New York: Fordham University Press, 1997).
The Prayers and Tears of Jacques Derrida: Religion without Religion (Bloomington: Indiana University Press, 1997).
More Radical Hermeneutics: On Not Knowing Who We Are (Bloomington: Indiana University Press, 2000).
On Religion, Thinking in Action Series (London and New York: Routledge, 2001).
Philosophy and Theology (Nashville: Abingdon Press, 2006).
The Weakness of God: A Theology of the Event (Bloomington: Indiana University Press, 2006).
After the Death of God (with Gianni Vattimo), edited by Jeffrey Robbins (New York: Columbia University Press, 2007).
What Would Jesus Deconstruct? The Good News of Postmodernity for the Church (Grand Rapids: Baker, 2007).
How to Read Kierkegaard (London: Granta Books, 2007; New York: Norton, 2008).

Selected Articles
"For the Love of the Things Themselves: Derrida's Phenomenology of the Hyper-Real," *Journal of Cultural and Religious Theory*, 1(3) (2000), n.p.
"The Return of Anti-Religion: From Radical Atheism to Radical Theology," *Journal of Cultural and Religious Theory*, 11(2) (2011), 32–125.

Co-edited Books
Caputo, John D. and Linda Martin Alcoff (eds), *St. Paul among the Philosophers* (Bloomington: Indiana University Press, 2009).
Caputo, John D. and Linda Martin Alcoff (eds), *Feminism, Sexuality and the Return of Religion* (Bloomington: Indiana University Press, 2011).
Caputo, John D. and Michael J. Scanlon (eds), *God, the Gift and Postmodernism* (Bloomington: Indiana University Press, 1999).
Caputo, John D. and Michael J. Scanlon (eds), *Augustine and Postmodernism: Confessions and Circumfession* (Bloomington: Indiana University Press, 2005).
Caputo, John D. and Michael J. Scanlon (eds), *Transcendence and Beyond* (Bloomington: Indiana University Press, 2007).
Caputo, John D., Mark Dooley, and Michael J. Scanlon (eds), *Questioning God* (Bloomington: Indiana University Press, 2001).

Secondary Literature

Dooley, Mark (ed.), *A Passion for the Impossible: John D. Caputo in Focus* (Albany: SUNY, 2003).
Martinez, Roy (ed.), *The Very Idea of Radical Hermeneutics* (Atlantic Highlands: Humanities Press, 1997).

Olthuis, James H. (ed.), *Religion With/out Religion: The Prayers and Tears of John D. Caputo* (New York: Routledge, 2001).

Zlomislic, Marko and Neal DeRoo (eds), *Cross and Khôra: Deconstruction and Christianity in the Work of John D. Caputo* (Eugene: Pickwick, 2010).

Chapter 62
Jean-Luc Marion

Jan-Olav Henriksen

Which contemporary philosophers can be regarded as important contributors to the theological agenda? No answer to this question can overlook Jean-Luc Marion, who is one of the great names among present-day French philosophers – not only as a philosopher of religion, but also as a Descartes scholar and a phenomenologist. This is due not least to the book that was his professional breakthrough, *God Without Being*. Marion is mentioned now in the same breath as Lévinas and Ricoeur, but he has also received impulses from other French philosophers who influence the contemporary agenda in the philosophy of religion, not least from Jacques Derrida. Marion is invited to hold lectures at universities throughout the world today, and he attracts hearers who are interested in both theology and philosophy – not least because he gives the impression of being original but not inaccessible. Marion has proved a fruitful dialogue partner in the development of a position in the philosophy of religion that is anchored in phenomenological philosophy.[1]

Biography, With the Emphasis on His Academic Work

Jean-Luc Marion was born in 1946. He studied philosophy at the École Normale Supérieure in Paris and at other institutes. His teachers included several of the last century's important French philosophers, such as Althusser, Deleuze, and Derrida. Although his academic training is in philosophy, Marion has also cultivated a lively interest in theology throughout his active career. He has also been influenced by several of the most important and trendsetting Roman Catholic theologians during his time as a student, including de Lubac, Daniélou, and von Balthasar (see the articles on these theologians in the section on Catholic theology).

---

[1] In addition to my own reading of Marion's works, this presentation is indebted above all to the information in Horner, Robyn: *Jean-Luc Marion: A Theo-Logical Introduction* (Burlington, VT: Ashgate, 2005). Horner has also written an interesting study in which she compares Derrida and Marion: see Horner, Robyn, *Rethinking God as Gift: Marion, Derrida, and the Limits of Phenomenology* (New York: Fordham University Press, 2001).

Marion first made his name in academia as a thorough and creative Descartes scholar. He devoted himself to an intensive study of the early Descartes while he taught at the Sorbonne from 1972 to 1980. He brought this work to a successful conclusion with his doctoral dissertation on this theme. In addition to his work in this field, he also began early on to publish works with a more theological orientation in theological periodicals. This led many to regard him as part of the conservative wing in French Roman Catholicism after 1968, although he has got involved in inner-theological polemics only to a small extent. It is entirely characteristic of Marion's work that he endeavors to elaborate themes primarily in the framework that is posited by his own philosophical starting point. He has therefore always insisted that he is a philosopher, not a theologian. This applies even to those cases where it is clear that what he says or writes has theological consequences. His thinking is also marked by his refusal to admit that he is working on a theological basis or within theologically informed parameters. It appears that this is because he does not wish to be "defined out of" theological discourse. Rather, he wants to show that a philosophical and phenomenological approach to certain phenomena opens the door to theological interpretation and problems.

After taking his doctorate in 1980, Marion was appointed to a position at the University of Poitiers. This is interesting for various reasons – first of all, because this is where Descartes himself studied, and also because Emmanuel Lévinas taught here from 1963 to 1967. This appointment thus meant that Marion was following in Lévinas' footsteps not only in institutional terms, but also in taking phenomenology in new directions.

Marion's international career took off from the mid-1980s onwards, and his work became celebrated and attraction attention far beyond the borders of France. The most important factor here is his book *God Without Being*, but the breadth of his interests and orientation made him an interesting dialogue partner and lecturer in a variety of contexts. He lectured on Heidegger, Descartes, the history of philosophy, and theological topics. He also formed close bonds to a number of American scholars, and this led in the long term to his appointment to a professorship at the University of Chicago, which he held in addition to his post in France. He is still a professor of the philosophy of religion and theology at the University of Chicago Divinity School, and he is also a member of the department of philosophy and "The Committee on Social Thought" at the same institution (like Paul Ricoeur at an earlier period).

In 1989, Marion became professor and director of the philosophical faculty at the University X in Paris (Nanterre), a position that both Lévinas and Ricoeur had held before him. He was also appointed to a guest professorship at the Institut Catholique in Paris in 1991. He was appointed to a professorship at the Sorbonne (Paris IV) in 1996, and to a number of additional positions that gave him a central place in the philosophical milieu in France, above all because of his Descartes scholarship. It is worth mentioning this, because there were discussions throughout the 1980s about whether Marion was not really a "closet theologian" who employed philosophy in order to promote a specific theological agenda. He himself has always rejected this assertion, and these appointments make it clear that his reputation as a philosopher has not in any way suffered because of his intense involvement in theological questions.

Overview of His Writings

Marion has written a great deal. The following presentation selects some of his works that are most central in terms of their relevance to theology and the philosophy of religion. This means that we leave out works that belong rather to the history of philosophy, such as his studies of Descartes.[2] The list below shows that *God Without Being* is the work that brought his breakthrough and that the reading of this book led to a wider interest in his other books.

The Idol and Distance. Five Studies was originally published in 1977; an English translation came in 2001. This is an attempt to do theology in the wake of the challenges by Nietzsche and Heidegger. It also reveals the breadth and the extent in Marion's orientation, since he casts sidelong glances at contemporary French philosophy, represented by Lévinas and Derrida, and also integrates perspectives from important patristic writers. This book can to some extent be called a form of philosophical theology. It aims to elaborate an understanding of how distance is necessary in order both to understand God's nearness and to avoid idolatry. Marion develops these insights in connection to the relationships within the Trinity, while at the same time insisting that distance or withdrawal is a presupposition of the divine presence – and something that makes it impossible to speak of God as an object. God as distance is something that one can only receive, not something that one can exhaustively understand. This is why another word for the same situation is *grace*. Such "definitions" of God as distant (not far away), incomprehensible, unthinkable, and infinite, are not only an echo of ideas that are found in many of the church fathers in the apophatic tradition; they also point ahead to central themes in Marion's next book, which was his theological breakthrough.

In *God Without Being* (1982; English 1991), Marion attempts *inter alia* to think of God in a way that overcomes certain parts of the Western metaphysical conceptual definition of God. In this way, he tries to follow up Heidegger's concerns in his criticism of onto-theology in Western metaphysics. Marion sees metaphysical definitions of this kind as the expression of a form of idolatry. An idol, in the specific meaning of

---

[2] A virtually complete bibliography of Marion's works will be found in Horner, *Jean-Luc Marion*.

this term (not in the sense in which it is used today in popular culture), is what it is in virtue of how it functions for the person who uses it. This means that the idol is subordinate to the limitations that lie in the perspective of the one who creates it. The problem, therefore, is not so much that the idol serves as the reference for a god, as that the idol expresses the fact that the one who sets it up and uses it thereby makes himself lord over reality. Ultimately, this means that the subject establishes himself as god. This points to a central theme in Marion's thinking, namely, the wish to establish a phenomenologically anchored understanding of how the divine can find expression in the life of the human person without being subjected to the coercion or violence that lies either in idolatry or in the human person's intentions. This is the interest that lies behind his analysis of so-called "saturated phenomena" (see below) – phenomena that we do not grasp if we see them only as phenomena posited by intentionality.

In this context, the *icon* presents itself as an alternative to the idol, because the icon makes the invisible visible, without representing it in the same way as concepts (which often function as idols in Marion's thinking). The icon opens to the door onto the invisible in a way that is expressed not least in *love*. In the icon, the invisible becomes visible as the one who sees me. This makes me something other than happens when I merely make what I myself see an object (see *God Without Being*, 29f.). At the same time, the icon maintains the distance that allows me to become a subject for the icon, or that constitutes me as a subject, while the icon itself can appear to me as a subject, not as an object.

God Without Being can be regarded as Marion's central theological work not only because it deals comprehensively with a long list of themes, but also because it functions as a nodal point, so to speak, in which most of the theologically relevant themes in his writings are set out. This book is a vigorous attempt to anchor the human person's relationship to God in phenomena that appear not to be wholly governed by human intentionality.

The books *Prolegomena to Charity* (1986, English 2002) and *Being Given. Toward a Phenomenology of Givenness* (1997, English 2002) develop in various ways the understanding of gift. *Gift* is another motif that is most central and constant in Marion's writings (see below), and he developed elements of an understanding of this in several other books prior to *Being Given*. At the same time, both *Prolegomena to Charity* and *The Erotic Phenomenon* (2003, English 2007) also take up elements linked to the understanding of love. The latter book especially reveals Marion to be an intense and open-hearted – we might perhaps say: unabashed – phenomenologist who gives thorough descriptions of the most sensual aspects of the love between a man and a woman.

Finally, we should mention *In Excess. Studies of Saturated Phenomena* (2001, English 2002). Its title indicates the phenomena in which Marion is particularly interested. These are exemplified in the gift, the icon, and love – phenomena that are so permeated or laden with content that they cannot be grasped simply or exhaustively. They tend to flow over or transcend that which can be caught or measured as expressions of intentionality (cf. the concept of *excess*). We shall look more closely at the themes of this book in the next section.

Key Themes in His Writings

I have already mentioned the themes in *God Without Being*, which is assuredly one of the most original and creative contributions to the philosophy of religion with its basis in the phenomenological tradition that has been made in recent decades.[3] Marion attempts here to develop an idea of God that avoids, or takes a detour around, a metaphysical idea of God as a being or as Being. This is, of course, not a recipe for a form of atheism, but an attempt to think of God on other premises than those found in the metaphysical tradition. In this way, he also indicates that it is problematic to regard this tradition as the only basis on which one can articulate the philosophical insights that lie behind and in Christian theology. At the same time, he accepts the validity of the criticism of the onto-theological way of thinking that was articulated not least by Heidegger.

What, then, is the constructive element in this way of thinking about God? We see immediately that Marion moves out beyond metaphysics, since the constructive element consists in thinking of God as love – as God's agape reveals itself in Jesus. The love that is revealed in and as Christ is not linked to any specific place or epoch, but is "at once abandoned to and removed from historical destiny." This paradoxical formulation underlines how the very idea of God – formulated by means of the idea of love – both expresses something that is more than we can imagine, and also leaves it mark on thinking itself. But when God is thought of as love in this way, love must be thought of as a gift.[4] The element of gift – which marks that which cannot be controlled or given a place in a system – thus also becomes decisively important for the way in which Marion elaborates the idea of God.

God *gives* himself in a gift that is love. An important point here is that although this gift can be recognized and acknowledged, it is not something that the human person can make fully his or her own. The central point in this inability to make the gift fully one's own is that God cannot be a part of that which the human person possesses and controls. God cannot be something that becomes a part of the human person's own being and is thereby given a place in the human person's world. This is why agape is also something that transcends our knowledge. When this is emphasized, we see the connection between the three concepts in Marion that I wish to bring out here: God without being, the gift, and permeated or saturated phenomena that cannot be reduced to human intentionality or be seen as a result of this intentionality.

There are two reasons why agape eludes us in this way. Philosophically speaking, it eludes us because we operate within a given and fixed horizon of understanding. Theologically speaking, it eludes us because we are finite beings who are also marked by sin. This means that the only way to come into contact with love, and to be marked by it, is by loving. This makes it possible to see the world differently, and to relate to

---

[3] An important Scandinavian study that analyzes Marion in a larger context and also compares him with Derrida is Svenungsson, Jayne: *Guds Återkomst: En Studie Av Gudsbegreppet Inom Postmodern Filosofi* (Göteborg: Glänta produktion, 2004).

[4] Marion, *God Without Being* (Chicago: University of Chicago Press, 1991), xxi f.

it differently, than the way of seeing that is given through cognitive knowledge and the sinful self. It is when God withdraws (so to speak) that the world can appear in our eyes as God's gift, a gift that is marked by who God is – as love.

Let us now indicate briefly some important aspects of Marion's understanding of gift. First of all, God's gift – and God as gift – are accessible only thanks to God's withdrawal. It is through God's withdrawal that the one who receives the gift can receive it *as* a gift. In connection with this withdrawal, the important point is that, precisely in this way, God becomes something we can know something about and relate to, as something that is not made our own, something that we ourselves do not master. At the same time, however, we can affirm that God is the one who has given the gift.

Thanks to the distance that the gift posits or marks between the giver and the receiver, it is possible for the receiver to see the gift as an expression of the giver. This means that the distance, as a gift, posits something that allows God to be recognized, while at the same time preventing us from taking hold of God and mastering him. This, however, is not the positive element in the gift. The positive element is that the gift leads us back to God and allows us to see God as the starting point and source.

I have already pointed out that Marion operates with a concept of so-called "saturated phenomena" – permeated, fully laden, or saturated phenomena. These have a larger and richer content of meaning than we are directly able to give these phenomena when we seek to understand them. At the same time, we can have an intuition that they contain something more, or are richer, than we grasp by means of our understanding. Phenomena of this kind possess *a priori* an infinity of meanings that cannot be captured by us once and for all, but that demand that we relate to them receptively and that we develop our understanding of them in a form of endless hermeneutics.

This way of thinking about such phenomena appears very formal; and theologically speaking, it is not a simple matter to make it one's own. But when, for example, Marion sees the resurrection of Jesus as a phenomenon of this kind, we see more clearly the kind of theological gain he can win from this phenomenology. The resurrection transcends what we are able to comprehend, and we continually need a fresh interpretation of what this means for people who believe in the resurrection: how are they to relate to the world? In this way, Marion opens the door to a postmodern form of theological hermeneutics in which there are no definitive and complete definitions of theologically significant phenomena. His phenomenological alternative to metaphysics is thus also a warning against forms of metaphysics that function as closed and closing systems of thought and faith. But it is also perfectly possible to see his definition of the saturated phenomena, which must be made one's own on the basis of something more than our already-established resources of understanding, as a philosophically anchored development of what the theological category of *revelation* attempts to capture.

We can get an impression of how the various motifs in Marion's writings are brought together in the following passage from *God Without Being* (49), which offers a good illustration and summary. Marion writes:

God can give himself to be thought without idolatry only starting from himself alone: to give himself to be thought as love, hence as gift; to give himself to be thought as a thought of the gift. Or better, as a gift for thought, as a gift that gives itself to be thought. But a gift, which gives itself forever, can be thought only by a thought that gives itself to the gift to be thought. Only a thought that gives itself can devote itself to a gift for thought. But, for thought, what is it to give itself, if not to love?

Marion's Position Today

Marion has not founded any clear "school," but his writings are an indication of the general openness to theological and religious themes that can be felt in much postmodern philosophy. The debate about his philosophy also shows that he seems to lack a clarified relationship between theology and philosophy. Although he insists that he works in philosophy, he seems not to recognize that his own thinking presupposes theological insights that one can no longer assume are generally taken for granted in European philosophy. There is a positive and a negative aspect to the fact that Marion himself does not appear to see the relevance of this criticism. Positively, this means that he can allow himself in a relatively unperturbed and bold manner to work as a philosopher in a way that opens up a front vis-à-vis theological and theologically relevant themes and that thereby brings to light a dimension in Western and phenomenological philosophy that is certainly present, but that some have ignored or neglected to study. Negatively, however, this means that he can be dismissed by those who refuse to be convinced. They can say that what he is really doing is to write philosophy on hidden theological premises – premises that many no longer believe they can share. It is therefore possible that Marion would gain by taking up and elaborating more clearly in future how he sees the relationship between theology and philosophy, both in general and in his own thinking.

Bibliography

Primary Literature

For a much more complete bibliography, which also includes articles etc., see Horner, 2001.

Sur l'ontologie grise de Descartes. Science cartusienne et savoir aristotélicien dans les "Regulae" (Paris: J. Vrin, 1975). English: *Descartes' Grey Ontology. Cartesian Science and Aristotelian Thought in the Regulae* (South Bend, IN: St. Augustine's Press, 2004).
L'idole et la distance: cinq études (Paris: B. Grasset, 1977). English: *The Idol and Distance: Five Studies* [Perspectives in Continental Philosophy, ed. John D. Caputo] (New York: Fordham University Press, 2001).

Dieu sans l'être (Paris: Arthème Fayard, 1982, 1987). English: *God Without Being* (Chicago: University of Chicago Press, 1991).

Prolégomènes à la Charité (Paris: Éditions de la Différence, 1991). English: *Prolegomena to Charity* (New York: Fordham University Press, 2002).

Sur le prisme métaphysique de Descartes. Constitution et limites de l'onto-théo-logie dans la pensée cartésienne (Paris: Presses Universitaires de France, 1986). English: *On Descartes' Metaphysical Prism: The Constitution and the Limits of the Onto-theo-logy of Cartesian Thought* (Chicago: University of Chicago Press, 1999).

Réduction et donation: recherches sur Husserl, Heidegger et la phenomenology (Paris: Presses Universitaires de France, 1989). English: *Reductiion and Givenness: Investigations of Husserl, Heidegger and Phenomenology* (Evanston, IL: Northwestern University Press, 1998).

La croisée du visible. Revised ed. (Paris: Editions de la Différence, 1996). English: *The Crossing of the Visible* (Stanford: Stanford University Press, 2004).

Questions cartésiennes. Méthode et métaphysique (Paris: Presses Universitaires de France, 1991). English: *Cartesian Questions: Method and Metaphysics* (Chicago: University of Chicago Press, 1999).

Etant donné. Essai d'une phénoménologie de la donation (Paris: Presses Universitaires de Paris, 1997). English: *Being Given: Toward a Phenomenology of Givenness* (Stanford: Stanford University Press, 2002).

De surcroît: études sur les phénomènes saturés (Paris: Presses Universitaires de France, 2001). English: *In Excess: Studies of Saturated Phenomena* (New York: Fordham University Press, 2002).

Le phénomène érotique: Six méditations (Paris: Grasset, 2003) English: *The Erotic Phenomenon* (Chicago: Chicago University Press, 2006).

Secondary Literature

Horner, Robyn, *Rethinking God as Gift: Marion, Derrida, and the Limits of Phenomenology*. Perspectives in Continental Philosophy, 19 (New York: Fordham University Press, 2001).

Horner, Robyn, *Jean-Luc Marion: A Theo-Logical Introduction* (Burlington, VT: Ashgate, 2005).

Svenungsson, Jayne, *Guds Återkomst: En Studie Av Gudsbegreppet Inom Postmodern Filosofi*. Logos Pathos, 3 (Göteborg: Glänta produktion, 2004).

Index

Note: **bold** page numbers indicate figures; numbers in brackets preceded by *n* refer to footnotes.

Abolition of Man, The (Lewis) 684
Abraham 166, 650
Act and Being (Bonhoeffer) 114
Acting Person, The (Wojtyła) 295
Acts of the Apostles 422, 631, 638
aesthetics 5, 43, 123, 132, 258–62, 464, 658, 696
Aeterni Patris (encyclical) 38
Afanasiev, Nicolas 12, 59, 371–7, **372**
    biography of 371–3
    and Bulgakov 371–372, 377
    eucharistic ecclesiology of 371, 372, 373–7, 436
    historical approach of 371
    legacy of 376–7
    liturgical theology of 373
    pastoral work of 372
    and Schmemann 371, 374, 377, 405
    and Vatican II/ecumenical work 372–3, 374
Africa 135, 612–13, 614
    Pentecostalism in 634
Against Ethics (Caputo) 736, 738
Against Religion (Yannaras) 728
agape 749–50
aggiornamento 6, 207, 240–41
Ahlin, Lars 154
Alexander, Kimberley 632
Alexandria (Egypt) 416, 417
Alexandrian tradition 249
alienation 105, 106, 107, 109, 110
Allers, Rudolf 251
Alstrup, Nils 189
Althaus, Paul 24, 90, 92
Altizer, J.J. 29, 572, 740
Alves, Ruben 614, 618
Ambrose, St 260
Anabaptists 537
Analogical Imagination, The (Tracy) 530, 532, 533, 534
anamnesis 445, 446
Anderson, Allan 634
angels 84, 344, 345, 587

Anglicanism 5, 135, 142, 356, 437
    in dialogue with Catholicism 479, 480–81
    schism and 480
Ansbacher Ratschlag declaration 90
Anselm 9, 68, 260
anthropology 48, 72, 85, 142, 145, 173, 187, 193, 438, 524–5, 622, 673, 706
    and Christology 231–2, 233
Anthropology in Theoretical Perspective (Pannenberg) 177
anti-Semitism 90, 660
antinomism 56–7, 90, 355
Apo of Győr, Maron Vilmos 43
apophaticism 4, 10, 11, 56–7, 58, 59, 382–3, 386, 553
    Yannaras and 726–7, 728–30, 732–3
aporia 206, 275
apostolicity 441–6, 609
Approches du Christ (Daniélou) 276–8
Aquinas, Thomas 6, 8, 49, 50, 195, 201, 214, 249, 537, 583, 681, 741, 742
    destiny and 203–4
    on grace/nature 204
    Husserl and 675–6
    on limits of philosophy 275
    and modernist crisis 12–14, 38, 659
    Rahner and 225, 227, 231
    Stein and 672
    see also Thomism
Arabic-speaking Christianity 415
ARCIC I/II (Anglican-Roman Catholic International Committee) 475, 477, 479, 480, 481, 482, 483
Aristotle/Aristotelian philosophy 388, 453, 664, 703, 729
Arminius, Jacob 31
art 27, 193, 201, 259, 268, 344, 493, 674, 726
Art et scholastique (Maritain) 268, 662
asceticism 399, 417, 420, 430
Assmann, Hugo 618, 625
Athanasius 180, 182–3, 397, 421, 422, 428, 681

atheism 54, 191–2, 205, 215, 559, 565, 585–6, 625, 682, 683, 684
Athens (Greece) 53
atonement 30–31, 117, 118–19, 139, 142, 422, 424
Augustine 8, 13, 14(n42), 34, 40, 97, 209, 255, 260, 278, 303, 306, 358, 365, 377, 420, 428, 480, 537, 582–3, 664, 681, 698, 738–9
   City of God 306, 582, 588
   doctrine of grace 138
Aulén, Gustaf 139, 147
authenticity 241, 242, 620
authority 475, 479
autonomy 22, 104, 116, 119–20, 138–9, 144, 205, 386, 666, 693
   of apostles 442
   of creation 138–9, 144
   of the secular 204
   of theology 532, 562
   of women 598, 601, 605
Avis, Paul 482
Ayer, A.J. 559, 562

Badiou, Alain 586, 736
baptism 33, 139–40, 160, 375, 396
   New Testament meaning of 638–9
   Spirit 631–2, 633
Baptist Church 31
Barmer Declaration of Jesus Christ 73
   Lutheran rejection of 90–91, 95
Barth, Karl 3, 5, 12, 23, 24–27, 65–74, **66**, 101, 235, 322, 573–4, 636, 681
   and Bonhoeffer 114, 144
   and Catholic theology 66, 67, 69
   Christocentrism of 8, 90, 252
   creation theology of 70–72, 74
   criticisms of 74, 143, 144, 173, 174, 179, 190, 541
   dialectical-theological period 25
   diastasis in 69–70
   and divine otherness 4
   and doctrine of God 190
   and dogmatics 66, 67–8, 69
   and ecumenical movement 17, 65, 67, 355, 608
   ethics and 68, 72–3
   on faith 114, 115
   on God's divinity/humanity 73
   and Grundtvig 135, 136–8
   and hourglass model 25
   influence/legacy of 65, 74
   and Jenson 509, 510
   and Jüngel 187, 188, 189, 190, 194, 195
   and liberal theology 65, 79
   life/work 65–7
   and Moltmann 159, 161, 162, 168
   and Nazism 66–7, 73, 537
   on necessity of theology 28
   and neo-Protestant theology 65
   Orthodox theology and 394, 428, 430
   and Pelikan 487
   on predestination 26–7
   and Prenter 135, 138–9
   Romans commentary 24, 31, 65, 69–70, 78, 80, 471
   Trinitarianism of 11, 25–6, 34, 68, 179, 509, 552
   and Wingren 147, 149
   writings of 67–73
   writings of, key themes in 69–73
Basil the Great 430, 494
Baur, F.C. 22
Behr, John 60
Behr-Sigel, Elizabeth 61
Being as Communion (Zizioulas) 436, 439, 440–41, 443–4, 445
Being Given (Marion) 748
Being and Time (Heidegger) 46, 676
Bekennende Kirche 114
Belgium 41, 214, 281–2
Belloc, Hilaire 647, 651
Benedict XVI *see* Ratzinger, Joseph
Berdyaev, Nicolas 341, 681, 725
Berdyayev, Nikolai 380, 381, 389, 389(n13)
Bergson, Henri 40, 268, 658
Bernard of Clairvaux 202, 380
Bernstein, Richard J. 577
Bethge, Eberhard 114, 115
Beyond God the Father (Daly) 520–21, 594
Bhaskar, Roy 562
Bibawi, George 419, 419(n8)
Biblical Literature, Society of 327, 328–9
biblical scholarship 174, 327
biblical theology 151–3
Billing, Einar 139, 147, 149–50
Billot, Louis Cardinal 38
bioethics 47–8
Bishoy of Damietta 419
Blake, William 691, 692–3, 698, 715
Blessed are the Consumers (McFague) 525, 526
Blessed Rage for Order (Tracy) 530, 534–5
Bloch, Ernst 159, 161, 165, 168
Blondel, Maurice 39, 204, 221, 584
Bloy, Léon 659

Body of God, The (McFague) 517, 522
Boethius 193, 477, 681
Boethius (Chadwick) 477
Boeve, Lieven 45, 46
Boff, Leonardo 45, 143, 553, 618, 625, 626
Bolotov, V.V. 348
Bonaventure, St 256, 260, 303, 664
Bonhoeffer, Dietrich 9, 29, 113–21, 235, 612
  and Barth 114, 117, 118, 144
  Christology lecture (1933) 115–16
  criticisms of 116
  Ethik 115, 116–17, 119, 120
  on faith 115–16, 117–18, 119, 120
  importance of 120–21
  letters from prison 113–14
  Letters and Papers from Prison 115, 119–20
  as liberation theologian 113
  on living "as if God did not exist" 113, 119, 120, 191, 194
  Nachfolge 116, 119
  piety of 113
  and postwar Germany 121
  in resistance to Nazism 113, 114–15, 119, 537
  on secularization 113, 114, 119–20, 121
  on ultimate/penultimate things 116–17
  on uses of law 118, 120
  Widerstand und Ergebung 115, 120
  writings of 114–20
  writings of, key themes in 115–20
Bonino, Serge-Thomas 50
Borgman, Erik 286
Botte, Bernard 374, 409
Bouillard, Henri 8, 251
Bouyer, Louis 213, 270, 404, 406
Braaten, Carl 35, 510, 511
Bread in the Wilderness (Merton) 719
Bréhier, Émile 663–4
Bride of the Lamb, The (Bulgakov) 55(n4), 344, 347
Bring, Ragnar 147
Britain (UK) 240, 435, 595, 715
  see also Cambridge University; Oxford University
Brunner, Emil 23, 24, 25, 412, 681
  and Barth 66, 68, 74
Brunner, Peter 136, 141, 510
Buber, Martin 252, 253, 681
Buckley, James 501, 505
Buddhism 32, 206, 270, 316, 318, 322–3, 525, 595, 648
  Zen 717–18, 719, 720, 723

Bulgakov, Sergei 12, 54–6, 58, 60, 341–9, 362(n17), 380, 381, 382
  and Afanasiev 371–2, 377
  and Catholicism 343, 347
  early life 341–3
  eschatology of 344, 347, 349
  and Florovsky 353, 355, 356, 357, 362, 365
  German idealism and 341, 343, 348
  importance of 349
  kenosis and 349
  liturgy and 345–6
  Marxism and 341, 342
  mature theology of 347–8
  in Paris 341, 343, 344, 347
  sophiology of 343, 344, 346–7, 348–9
  theological method of 348
  writings 344–9
  writings, key themes in 345–9
Bultmann, Rudolf 6, 9, 12, 23, 24, 30, 77–86, 136, 149, 278, 470, 689, 703
  accused of heresy 81
  and Barth 25, 66, 74, 78, 190
  biography 77–81
  demythologization program 74, 80–81, 84–5, 86
  on faith/history 77–8, 80, 81–2, 85–6
  and Gogarten 79
  and Heidegger 79–80, 83–4
  hermeneutics of 79, 83–5, 115
  influence of 86
  and Jüngel 187, 189, 193, 194
  and liberal theology 77, 78
  and Moltmann 159, 165
  in Nazi period 79–80, 85–6
  pre-understanding concept of 83–4
  on synoptic tradition 78, 80
  theology 81–6
  and Tillich 28, 79
Bunyan, John 681, 683, 692
Burning Bush, The (Bulgakov) 344, 345, 347, 348–9
Butler, Joseph 681
Butler, Judith 576
Byzantine theology 8, 353, 393

Caffara, Carlo 48
Cajetan, Thomas 40, 50
Calvin, Jean 165, 561
Calvin, John/Calvinism 21, 30–31, 35, 428
Cambridge University (UK) 477, 478, 548, 581–2
Camus, Albert 282, 719, 720, 722, 723

capitalism 651
Cappadocians 8, 257, 380, 382, 383, 428, 438, 494
Cappuyen, M. 406
Caputo, John D. 5, 12, 576, 577–8, 588, 735–42
   biography of 735–7
   and Derrida/deconstructivism 736
   existentialism and 735
   on hyper-realism 741
   importance of 742
   on khôra 737–8, 739, 742
   on kingdom of God/eschatology 740, 741
   on negative theology/mysticism 737
   radical hermeneutics of 737–8, 739
   on religion-philosophy interrelation 736
   "weak" theology of 47, 735, 737, 739–40, 742
   writings of 737–41
   writings of, key themes in 739–41
Catholic Church/Catholic theology 3–4, 37–51, 85, 206–7
   classical/romantic orthodoxies 49–50
   Communio/Concilium camps 42, 43, 45, 47, 49, 222, 262
   Conciliar debates 41–3, 49–50
   contraception and 42
   correlation/re-contextualization project 45–6
   crisis in (1950s) 225
   and development of doctrine 10–11, 13
   dialogue with Protestant theology 263
   ecumenical 135, 437, 499–500, 608, 610
   Enlightenment/Romantic legacies of 37
   and eucharist 203
   feminist 594, 599, 600–601
   grace-nature controversy 204, 205
   Heidegger and 46–7, 50
   liberal/conservative criticisms of 48
   and liberalism/post-liberalism 31, 32
   and liberation theology 618, 626, 627–8
   Lonergan's transformation of 243–4
   and modernism/postmodernism 5, 7, 12, 38–9, 43–4, 45–7, 50
   as 'mother' 209–10
   neo-scholasticism in 38–9
   as 'open narrative' 46, 51
   as open narrative 46, 51
   opposition to 169
   paradox in 202–3
   patristic revival in 8, 268, 269, 270
   and Pentecostalism 638
   post-Conciliar 43, 44, 45, 49, 222, 270, 271, 279, 285, 288, 307, 312, 2812
   post-*Humanae Vitae* 42–3
   and Protestant theology 35, 43–5, 159, 263, 316
   reform of 213, 215, 216, 217
   ressourcement project 39–41, 49–50
   Second Vatican Council *see* Vatican II
   Strict Observance Thomism 38, 39, 40
   Thomist *see* Aquinas, Thomas; Thomism
   three strands of 41–2
Catholicism (de Lubac) 48, 202–3, 204–5, 251
causal joint 452, 458
causality, instrumental/proper 661
Chadwick, Henry 12, 475–84
   and ARCIC I/II 475, 477, 479, 480, 481, 482, 483
   biography of 475–8
   critical scholarship of 478–9
   ecumenical method of 481–3
   ecumenical theology of 477, 479–81
   ethics of 483–4
   on eucharist 480
   and General Synod 477–8
   on justification 475, 480
   on primacy 479–80
   on Romanticism 483–4
   on theological language 482–3
Chadwick, William Owen 475
Chalcedon, Council of (AD 451) 230, 287, 357, 395, 398, 400
Chan, Simon 637
Character and the Christian Life (Hauerwas) 538–9
Charismatic Movement 607, 637
Chenu, Marie-Dominique 13–14, 40, 213, 214, 216, 282, 374
Chesterton, G.K. 645–53, 681
   biography of 646–8
   Catholicism of 647
   on Christ 650
   on "common mind" 653
   distributism of 651
   on epochs of Christianity 650–51
   Father Brown and 647–8
   influence of 652–3
   literary style of 647
   range/diversity of 646, 652–3
   and theological tradition 652
   theological writings of 648–3
Chicago Declaration (1993) 317, 319, 324

Chicago Divinity School (US) 529, 746
Childs, Brevard 501–2
Chinese religions 316
Chrétiens désunis (Congar) 217
Chrismation 396
Christ
　abandoned by God 165, 167
　and alienation 105, 109, 110
　authority of 176
　as centre/boundary 116
　and church/community 34–5, 78, 114,
　　136–7, 139, 359, 360
　as divine-human union 54, 56, 57, 58, 59,
　　70, 230–32, 259, 422
　and Dying God myth 687–9
　and feminist theology 602–4
　hidden/concrete 119, 120
　historical 80, 81–2, 110, 189, 191, 284–5, 322
　imitation of 294
　Jesus as 81, 82, 105, 109–10
　as Lord of the world 113–14
　and love of neighbor 126, 129
　not a Christian 82, 85, 86
　and Old Testament 276, 277
　and Paul 86, 189
　and the poor/oppressed 145
　resurrection of *see* resurrection of Christ
　revelation of 24, 26, 28, 44, 45, 48, 74, 95
　righteousness of 138, 141
　and salvation 232–3, 234
　and Spirit 144
　suffering/death of 187, 193, 235, 288
　transfiguration of 432–3
　and war 97–8
　and "Word of God" theology 71
Christa (statue) 602
Christian mystical tradition 6
Christian socialism 585, 651
Christian Theology: An Introduction (McGrath)
　561
Christian Tradition, The (Pelikan) 488, 491, 492,
　494
Christianity, Democracy and the Radical Ordinary
　(Hauerwas) 540
Christianity and the World/Chinese religions
　(Küng) 318
christliche Glaub, Der (Elert) 93–5
Christocentrism 8, 14(*n*44), 90, 95
Christolatry 602
Christology 21, 438, 564
　and anthropology 231–2, 233

Catholic 43, 44, 45, 215, 315
Chalcedonian 395, 398, 400
and ecumenism 316, 608
feminist 332–3
and feminist theology 602
from above/below 173, 176–7, 231, 259
historical basis of 189
lecture on (Bonhoeffer) 115–16, 119
and liberation theology 625–6
messianic 164
ontologization of 144
and pneumatology 400–401, 439, 440–41,
　639
Protestant 68, 71–2, 97, 109–10, 139, 141,
　144, 150, 175–7
transcendental 231–2, 234
universal 138
Christosphere 274
Christus praesens 168
Chronicles, 2 464, 467, 469
church 31–2, 65, 78, 142, 206–7
　and eucharist 373–6
　national 137, 139–40
　as people of God 165
　and the poor/oppressed 145
　rediscovery of 371
　sacramentality of 136–7
Church in Ancient Society (Chadwick) 478, 484
Church Dogmatics (Barth) 25, 67–8, 70, 174, 584
　theology of creation in 71, 72, 138–9
Church of England General Synod 477–8
Church Fathers 8, 9–10, 12–13, 97, 174–5, 193,
　228–9, 257, 260, 263, 273, 303, 348, 428
　wisdom of 428
　see also desert fathers; Greek Fathers
Church of the Holy Spirit (Afanasiev) 372, 375–6,
　377
Church in the Power of the Spirit (Moltmann)
　162–3, 165
Church Universal (*Una Sancta*) 364
church-state relations 72, 90, 93, 95, 98, 118,
　542–3, 613, 661–3
　destiny and 96, 97
Church's Ministry (Prenter) 142
Cistercians 210
City of God (Augustine) 306, 582, 588
classicism 49–50
Claudel, Paul 210
Clement of Alexandria 257, 260, 277, 330
Clément, Olivier 379, 420
Clement of Rome 443

Climacus, John 420
Coakley, Sarah 12, 547–5
　biography of 547–9
　on consent/control 551
　on doctrine 550, 552
　importance/influence of 555
　interdisciplinary approach of 548–9, 550, 555
　key themes of 552–4
　on knowledge of God 550–51
　overview of thought 549–51
　on prayer 547, 548, 549, 551, 552–4
　on sacrifice/ascesis 554
　on sexual desire 548, 549, 551, 553–4, 555
　théologie totale of 554, 555
　Trinitatianism of 552–4
Cold War 67, 103, 187, 281, 324, 613, 615
colonialism/postcolonialism 333–4, 570, 614
Comforter, The (Bulgakov) 55(*n*4), 344, 347–8
Coming of God, The (Moltmann) 162, 163, 167
Communio group 42–3, 47, 49, 222, 270
Community of Character, A (Hauerwas) 539
Community of St John 43
Conciliar debates 41–3, 49–50
Concilium (journal) 42, 43, 45, 47, 222, 227, 249
Concord, Formula of (1577) 93, 96, 118
Concordia Theological Seminary (US) 488
Confessing Church (Germany) 79, 80, 114, 116, 159, 161
Confessio Augustana 118, 142, 308, 430–31, 431, 500
confession 433
confessional texts 493
Congar, Yves 12, 14, 39, 40, 41, 136, 142, 179, 213–22, 252, 253, 305, 435
　biography 213–16
　on church reform/tradition 213, 215, 216, 217
　and *Concilium* 222, 316
　and Dominican Order 213, 214
　ecclesiology of 213, 214
　ecumenism of 214, 215, 217–18, 374, 614
　and feminist theology 553
　importance/influence 218, 221–2
　and 'la nouvelle théologié' 215
　laity, theology of 215, 217, 219–20
　and Protestantism 214
　and Schillebeeckx 281, 282
　and Vatican II 215, 218, 220, 623
　writings of 216–17
　writings of, key themes in 217–21

Congregation for the Doctrine of Faith 287, 301, 628
Congregationalism 31
Conrad-Martius, Hedwig 669, 670
consciousness 241–2
Constantinople, fall of (1453) 53
consumer culture 524
contraception 42, 50, 421
contrapuntal reading 9–10
conversion 243, 244–6
Coptic church 415, 417, 418–19
　reform movement in 423–4
Corinthians, 1 605, 632, 638, 700, 739
Corinthians, 2 463
Corpus Areopagiticum 380
Corpus Mysticum (de Lubac) 203
Counter-Reformation 205
Courage to be, The (Tillich) 27, 105
Court, John 466
Cox, Harvey 29, 635
creation
　and environmental crisis 130–31
　and good/evil 707–8
　and Gospel 148–9
　phenomenology of 140–41
　philosophy of 123, 124
　and redemption 182–3
　theology of 54, 55, 70–72, 74, 91, 136, 141, 154–5, 210, 249, 430
　see also natural theology
Creation and Law (Wingren) 149, 150
Creation and Recreation (Frye) 693, 694, 695
Creation and Redemption (Prenter) 139, 140–41
Credo (Wingren) 150, 153
creed, the 148–9, 155
Creeds and Confessions of Faith in the Christian Tradition 3
critical realism 562–3, 564
Croatto, Severino 618, 624
croissance spirituelle de l'infant, La (Timiadis) 432
cross, theology of 27, 85, 144, 145, 154–5, 162–3, 164, 165, 166–7, 469–70
　glory and 465
　liberation theology and 625–6
Crossing the Threshold of Hope (Wojtyła) 292, 294
Crucified God, The (Moltmann) 162, 165, 166
Cullmann, Oscar 17, 374
cultural theology 7, 27–8, 77, 91–2, 94, 103, 104–5, 110–11, 286, 511, 518, 526, 530

cultural-linguistic model 500–501, 504–5
Cupitt, Don 548
Cyprian, Bishop of Carthage 209, 372, 376
Cyril of Alexandria 397, 422, 511

Dalai Lama 517, 525, **716**, 718(*n*8), 723
Daly, Mary 520–21, 572, 594, 598, 599, 602
Daniélou, Jean 6–7, 8, 12, 39, 40, 41, 208(*n*18), 215, 249, 267–79, 404, 745
   biography/career 267–71
   on Christ 376–8
   and *Communio* 270
   and correspondances/symbolism 272, 273
   and de Lubac 269–70
   and Eastern religion 270
   ecumenical work of 270, 374
   and existentialism 269–70, 278–9
   and French Catholic revival 268
   as Jesuit 268–9
   key themes of 274–8
   on knowledge of God/revelation 274–6
   patristic theology of 270, 271
   and *ressourcement* 269, 278
   and science/mathematics 273–4
   theological vision/method 271–4
   and theology of history 269, 271–2, 274, 276–8
   and Thomism 268, 278
   typological method 269, 272–3
   and von Balthasar 249, 251
Danish-Norwegian Reformation church 118
Dante 260, 681, 698, 700
Dawkins, Richard 561
Day, Dorothy 525, 652
Dayton, Donald W. 636
de Beauvoir, Simone 593–4
de Lubac, Henri 5, 8, 9, 12, 14, 40, 41, 47, 201–11, 213, 249, 269–70, 281, 303, 347, 374, 584, 745
   and Aquinas 201, 203–4
   biography 201, 202, 208
   on Buddhism 206, 270
   on Church as 'mother' 209–10
   in clash with Jesuit authorities 206
   and *Communio* 43, 222
   corpus mysticum and 203
   on destiny 203–4
   and fourfold sense of Scripture 269
   and grace-nature controversy 204, 205–6, 258
   on individuals/society and Catholicism 202, 204–5
   and medieval Catholic figures 201–2, 208, 210
   and neo-scholasticism 204, 208, 210–11
   nuptial theology of 208–9
   on Origen 202, 206, 208–9, 210
   on paradox of Catholic dogma 202–3
   and Vatican II 207
   and von Balthasar 251, 252
de Menasce, Jean 268
de Montcheuil, Yves 203
De Petter, Dominic 281
death 191, 192, 233
death of God theology 4, 29, 510–11, 572, 574, 575–6, 586–7, 726
   and weak theology 740
Death (Jüngel) 192
Debate on Sophia, The (Lossky) 381–2
deconstructivism 736
Dei Verbum 14, 207, 221, 226, 270, 304, 305, 311
Deir al-Suryani monestary (Egypt) 417, 418
demythologization debate 74, 80–81, 84–5, 86
Denmark 118, 124, 126, 147, 155, 609
   Prenter's essay on ("Christ – Denmark") 137–8
Derrida, Jacques 5, 47, 60, 570, 571, 572, 584, 586, 588, 736, 745, 749(*n*3)
Descartes, René 745, 746
desert fathers 417, 420
destiny 9, 14, 94, 96–7, 98, 203–4, 205
   and law 96
Deus Caritas Est (encyclical) 301
Deutsche Christen 68, 79, 90, 91, 116
Devil, the 140, 152
Di Noia, Augustine 50
dialectical theology 23–44, 114, 135, 164, 187, 394
   Barth and 66, 68, 70, 71
   Bultmann and 78, 165
   Elert and 89, 95
   Wingren and 147, 151
Dieu et nous (Daniélou) 274–6
Dignitatis humanae 309
DiNoia, James 505, 506
Dionysius the Aeropagite 47, 255, 260, 380, 393, 397, 583, 729
distributism 651
Diversités et Communion (Congar) 218
doctrine, development of 9–11, 13

doctrine of God 177–8, 190, 315, 316, 625
  Sophia and 343
Does God Exist? (Küng) 318
dogma/dogmatics 66, 67–8, 69, 104, 139, 151, 487, 675
  history of 39, 97
Dominican Order 213, 214, 215–16
Dominion of the Word (Prenter) 136–8
Dominum et vivificantem (encyclical) 297–8
Dort, Synod of (1618–19) 30
Dostoyevsky, Fyodor 341, 342
double personal agency 452, 458
doubt 27, 102, 561
doxology 256, 430, 431, 583
dualistic method 106, 107
Dube, Musa W. 333
Duchesne, Louis 270
Dunn, James D.G. 637–8

Early Christian Thought and the Classical Tradition (Chadwick) 476
East and West (Chadwick) 478
Easter 43, 470, 625, 740
Ebeling, Gerhard 29, 114, 188, 711
Ecclesiam Suam (encyclical) 216
ecclesiology 12, 35, 60, 139–40, 142, 150, 203, 303, 475, 626
  Catholic renewal in 213, 315
  and ecumenism 607, 609
  eucharistic 371, 373–4, 436
  Orthodox 404
  and sacrament/ministry 307–8
Eckhart, Meister 6, 380, 384, 720, 741, 742
eco-theology 60, 130–31, 132, 154, 159, 163, 165, 518, 522–3
economics 50, 317, 344
ecumenical movement 8, 17, 65, 67, 135, 148, 164, 168–9, 175, 217–18, 499–501, 607–15
  apostolicity/episcopacy and 609
  criticisms of 610–11, 612
  emergence of 607
  and eschatology 218
  global South and 610–11, 614–15
  language/terminology and 431, 475, 482–3
  and liberation theology 500
  mission in 610–11
  Orthodox 341, 430–31, 437
  and Pentecostalism 637–8, 639, 640
  resources of 608–9
  social ethics of 612–15
  theology/statements of 609, 610–12

Trinity and 509
  see also under specific theologians
Edwards, Jonathan 511
Egypt 415–17, 418, 423
Einar Billing (Wingren) 149–50
EKDV (United Evangelical Lutheran Church) 89
ekklēsia of wo/men 331, 332
El-Meskeen, Matta *see* Matta, Father
Elements of Faith (Yannaras) 728
Elert, Werner 12, 89–98
  anti-Semitism of 90
  and Barmen Declaration 90–91
  and Barth 89, 90, 92, 94
  biography 89–90
  on church-state relations 90, 93, 95, 96, 97
  on culture-Christianity 91–2, 94
  and defeat of Germany 97–8
  dogmatics of 93–7
  on early church/Church Fathers 97
  ethics of 95–7
  on fellowship of blood 92, 95, 96
  and Germany's defeat 97–8
  on law 95–6
  and Lutheran renaissance 89, 91–3
  and Nazism 89, 90–91, 93–7
  on reason/revelation 96–7, 98
Eliade Mircea 165
Eliot, T.S. 691, 692
Ellacuría, Ignacio 618, 623, 626
Emery, Gilles 50
empathy 673–5
Enlightenment 13, 37, 45, 91, 160, 205, 210, 309–10, 512, 571
  'second age of' 243–4
Enotes tes Ekklesias (Zizioulas) 436, 437
Entretiens d'automne (Congar) 213
environment, theology of *see* eco-theology
epistemology 123, 124, 125, 126, 143, 164, 562, 658
Erasmus 31
Erlangen (Germany) 89–90, 92, 97
Erotic Phenomenon, The (Marion) 748
Erring: A Postmodern A/theology (Taylor) 573
eschatology 2, 35, 43, 59, 68, 80, 86, 94, 104, 181, 277, 344, 347
  and church apostolicity 441–6
  liberationist 306
  and mission 442–3
  Moltmann's 162, 163, 164, 167–8
  and trinitarian theology 540–41

essentialism/anti-essentialism 30
Eternal Church, The (Matta) 421
Eternal Life? (Küng) 318
eternity 26, 181, 676–7
    and creation 54
"Eternity in Time" (Kvarme) 411
Ethical Demand, The (Løgstrup) 124, 126–7, 128–9, 140–41
ethics 68, 72–3, 104, 124, 187, 261, 324, 483–4, 658
    common in religions 287
    "double" 328–9
    Elert's 95–7
    Løgstrup's 126–9, 132
    Pauline 79
    social ecumenical 612–15
    Yannaras's 731–2
Ethik (Bonhoeffer) 115, 116–17, 119, 120
eucharist 59, 97, 203, 345, 410, 438
eucharistic ecclesiology 371, 373–6, 446
Eusebius 210
Evagrius of Pontus 420
Evangelical Catholics 514
Evangelical Lutheran church 160, 162
Evangelicalism 30–31, 213, 607
Everlasting Man, The (Chesterton) 649–51, 681
evil, problem of 685–7, 703, 705–6, 710
exegesis 7, 21, 116, 174, 243, 267, 272–3, 706, 712
    Bultmann's 77, 78
    Father Matta's 420, 422, 424
    Küng's 320, 321
    Origen's 206, 208, 362(*n*18)
    Palamas's 386, 387
    Ramsay's 465–7
    Ratzinger's 307, 311
    Ricoeur's 706, 709, 711, 712
    and systematic theology 288
    see also historical-critical method
existential theology 6, 7, 10, 11–12, 24, 60, 70, 83, 225, 269–70
    neo-Palamite 384–5
    and theology of history 159
    Zen as 720–21
Exodus 272, 513, 600, 624
Experiences in Theology (Moltmann) 164
experiential theology 29–30
expressionist painting 27
Ezekiel 464

faith 27, 82–3, 114, 115
    and baptismal covenant 139–40
    and community 78
    confession of 141
    and culture 91–2, 104–5
    and doubt/unbelief 102
    experience of 291, 469
    and glory 469
    and historical Jesus 81–2
    and history 77–78, 80, 81–2, 85–6
    individualization of 173
    and knowledge 71, 74, 676–7
    and philosophy 657–8, 663–6
    and post-liberal theology 32–3
    and reason 37, 50
    and scripture 139
    and secularization 28–9
    social foundations of 2220
    and terror 93, 98
    and war 97–8
Faith and Order Commission 148, 427, 436, 477–8, 609
Faith and Understanding (Bultman) 80
Fall, the 109, 142, 257–8
Farrer, Austin 12, 451–61
    on divine action/history 456
    on divine-human relation 452, 453–5, 456, 457, 459
    on "double personal agency"/"causal joint" 452, 458
    and formalism/volunteerism 453
    as formative theologian 452, 459, 460
    on "images of revelation" 454–5, 456
    importance/influence of 451, 460–61
    metaphysical personalism of 360, 453
    multi-disciplinary/inclusive approach of 453–4, 457, 460
    as process theologian 461
    on science/personhood 459–60
    sermon on hope 451–2
    on Trinity 456–8
Faulkner, William 719, 720, 722, 723
fellowship 9, 22, 32–3, 97, 154, 439
    of blood 92, 95, 96
    of peoples 137–8
Fellowship of St Alban and St Sergius 341, 355, 356, 374, 390
feminist theology 30, 159, 161, 327, 329–31, 438, 472, 547, 593–605
    Afro-American (womanist theology) 576, 596, 602–3
    Catholic 594, 599, 600–601
    characteristics of 596–7, 604
    Christology and 602

critique of 605
defined 595
emergence of 593–5
in Europe 595
feminine God in 520–22, 549, 599, 601
Gospels and 331, 605
as interdisciplinary theology 604
kenosis and 525, 552
Latina/lesbian 576, 595, 596
and liberation theology 594–5, 621
and patriarchal norms 593, 594, 598–9, 602, 603
Paul and 330
picture of God in 598–604
pioneers of 594–5
post-Christian/Wicca 598
postmodern 572, 576, 601
and poststructuralism/essentialism 597
theological language and 520–22, 594(n2)
Trinity and 438, 552–4, 600–601
in US 593, 594, 595
and women's/gender studies 596–7
see also Coakley, Sarah
Fessard, Gaston 269
Feuerbach, Ludwig 191, 321, 513, 586, 601
fideistic theology 565
filioque 57, 144, 379, 390, 439
Finite and Eternal Being (Stein) 673, 676, 677
Finite and Infinite (Farrer) 453, 456
Fiorenza, émigrés from 7, 17, 55, 56
First Vatican Council 239
First World War 23, 24, 39, 65, 89, 91, 102, 201, 281, 613, 670
Florovsky, Georges 8, 11, 56, 57, 58–59, 343–4, 353–66, **354**, 371, 379, 384, **658**
  and Bulgakov/sophiology 353, 355, 356, 357, 362, 365, 381(n2), 382
  on catholicity/*sobornost* 359–61
  on Christian Hellenism 361–2
  Christology of 357–8
  and Church Fathers 355, 360–62, 363
  early life 354–5
  Eastern bias of 363
  ecumenism of 355, 363–5
  and eschatology/living tradition 358–62
  historical theology of 355, 359–60
  importance/influence of 353, 365–6
  and neo-patristic synthesis 353, 355, 357, 365–6
  in Paris 355, 725

Romanticism of 363
in US 356, 390
and World Council of Churches 355, 427, 436
FOAG (Faith and Order Advisory Group) 478
For the Life of the World (Schmemann) 410–11
Ford, David F. 9, 221
form-historical school 151, 153
Foucault, Michel 60
Fouilloux, Étienne 215
foundationalism/post-foundationalism 501, 547, 562–3
Foundations of Dogmatics (Weber) 159
Fox, Patricia A. 435(n3), 438
France 41, 201–2, 203, 658, 660
  church-state relations in 204–5, 661–3
  cultural renaissance in (1920s) 267–8
  Third Republic 203, 204, 214
  see also Paris
Francis of Assisi 380
Frank, F.H.R. 92
free will 31
freedom 91–2, 113–14, 118, 120, 259, 309–10, 620, 732
  of God 181, 468
  and nature 398
Freedom of Morality, The (Yannaras) 727, 730, 731
Freedom of the Will (Farrer) 459
Frei, Hans 5, 9, 74, 499, 502, 505, 512, 571–2, 573, 574
Freire, Paulo 619, 622
Frere, Walter 374
Friedan, Betty 594
Friend of the Bridegroom, The (Bulgakov) 344, 345
Frostin, Per 621
Frye, Northrop 12, 488, 493, 691–700
  Bible course of 694, 695
  on Bible as literature 696, 698–700
  and Blake 691, 692–3
  fundamentalism and 692, 697, 698, 699
  legacy of 695–6
  on myth/metaphor 694, 695–6, 699
  on religious language 696–8
  and St. Mary's, Fairford 691, 693, 696
Fuchs, Ernst 29, 187, 188, 189, 193
fundamentalism 30, 540, 635, 692, 697, 698, 699
Future of Roman Catholic Theology (Lindbeck) 499–500

Gadamer, Hans-Georg 40, 136, 259, 282, 510, 532, 736
Gardeil, Ambroise 214
Garrigou-Lagrange, Reginald 38, 660
Gaudium et spes 48, 207, 226, 255, 271, 295, 296, 297, 298
    Ratzinger's criticism of 305–6
Gayed, Nazir (Pope Shenouda III) 417, 418
Geertz, Clifford 500
Geist in Welt (Rahner) 227, 230, 234
GEM (Generalised Empirical Method) 50
gender issues 47–8, 61, 518
    see also women
Genesis 9–10, 71, 182, 605, 695, 698
Genesis of Doctrine (McGrath) 561
German idealism 54, 55–6, 341, 343, 348, 382
Germany 22, 37, 40, 41, 43, 124, 187, 595
    East 187–8
    Nazi period *see* Nazism
    non-Nazi church in (*Bekennende Kircher*) 114, 116
    see also Confessing Church; Erlangen; Göttingen
Gibbon, Edward 492, 494
Gibson, M.T. 477
Gifford Lectures 476, 494, 529, 530, 541, 549, 560
gift 4, 16, 138, 231, 295, 708, 710–11, 748
    economy of (Ricoeur) 710–11
    Marion on 748, 749, 750
Gilson, Etienne 201, 380, 659, 664
Glass of Vision, The (Farrer) 453–4, 457–8
Global Ethic Foundation 315, 323, 324
Global Responsibility (Küng) 317
globalization 319, 614–15, 627
glory 463–5, 472
    and the cross 465, 468
    and faith 469
    in John's Gospel 464–5
Glory of God and the Transfiguration of Christ (Ramsay) 463–4
gnosticism 80, 361(*n*16)
God
    as abyss 27
    as agency acting/being as becoming (Farrer) 453
    correlative/collaborative relationship with 141
    and creation 54, 55, 57–8, 105
    doctrine of *see* doctrine of God
    essence/energies of 57–8, 60
    and eucharist 59
    faithfulness of 25
    and fear/terror 93, 94, 98
    as feminine 520–22, 549, 599, 601
    glory of 463–5
    as ground of being 27, 106, 109
    hidden 26, 94, 96, 98, 115
    and the human person 82–4, 94, 227, 228
    humanity of 54, 73, 177
    immanence of 15
    inner threeness of *see* Trinitarianism
    judgement of 92, 96
    kingdom of 24, 72, 77, 81, 105
    and love-freedom 58, 59, 60, 85, 244
    mercy of 97, 129, 130, 605, 621, 631, 661, 740
    natural desire for 204
    as one who answers 107
    openness of 31, 231
    otherness of 4, 23, 58, 69–70, 82
    paternal-monarchical model of 520–21
    promise of 166
    and religious symbols 108
    and secularization 29
    self-revelation of 25, 95, 176, 177–8, 180, 275, 275–6, 298, 513, 599
    sovereignty of 178, 180–81, 183, 194, 287–8, 735
    thinking/talking about 194
    unity of 143–4
    weakness of 47, 735, 737, 739–40, 742
God and Man (Stănisloae) 395
God as the Mystery of the World (Jüngel) 191–2
God, Sexuality and the Self (Coakley) 553–4
God without Being (Marion) 46–7, 745, 746, 747–8, 749, 750–51
God-is-dead theology *see* death of God theology
God's Being is in Becoming (Jüngel) 190
G*d 327, 332, 333
Goethe, Johann Wolfgang von 92, 160, 263, 493
Gogarten, Friedrich 23, 66, 74, 79, 124, 136, 174
Golden Rule 324, 710–11
Good Samaritan 33
Gospel and the Catholic Church (Ramsay) 465, 467, 470, 471
Gospel and Church (Wingren) 149, 150
Gospels 71–2, 73, 136, 189
    baptism in 638–9
    eschatology in 442–3, 637–8
    and feminist theology 331, 605
    law and 94, 96, 148–9, 154–5
    literary techniques in 276
    and secularization 121, 173

society/culture and 150, 305
    as treasure 137
    see also John's Gospel; Luke's Gospel; Matthew's Gospel
Göttingen (Germany) 66, 161, 174, 669, 670
grace 31, 44, 57, 72, 73, 85, 92, 137, 138, 141, 235, 259, 284, 383, 469, 538, 666, 747
    baptismal 276
    "cheap"/"costly" 116
    and fellowship 97
    and national church 139–40
    and nature 40–41, 50, 91, 204, 205–6, 252, 258
    and terror 93
Great Awakenings 30
Great Code, The (Frye) 694, 696, 698, 699–700
Greece 427, 725–6, 733
Greek Fathers 202, 267, 344, 361, 438, 495, 725
Greene, Graham 646, 652
Gregorios, Paulos 415
Gregory the Great 483
Gregory Nazianzen 275–6, 377, 399, 494
Gregory of Nyssa 10, 13, 251, 252, 267, 275, 276, 278, 377, 397, 494, 511, 550
Greshake, Gisbert 143
Grillmeier, Alois 251
Grisbrooke, W. Jardine 409
Grundkurs des Glaubens (Rahner) 230
Grundtvigian theology 135–43
Grundtvig's Challenge to Modern Theology (Prenter) 142
Guardini, Romano 40, 225, 227, 251, 253
Gunkel, Herman 77
Gunton, Colin 509
Gutiérrez, Gustavo 45, 618, 619–21, 622

Habermas, Jürgen 308, 309, 574
Hagia Sophia, church of (Constantinople) 343
Halik, Tomas 47
Hamann, Johann Georg 37, 260
Harnack, Adolf von 65, 77, 361(n16), 487, 488, 489, 491, 494, 495
Hart, David Bentley 5
Hart, Kevin 576
Hartford Appeal 405
Hartmann, Nicolai 174
Hartshorne, Charles 461, 559
Harvard Divinity School 329, 334, 356, 548–9
Hauerwas, Stanley 33, 503, 537–44
    biography of 537–8
    on "character"/"virtue" 538–9
    on Christian practices/scripture 539–40
    on church-state/elites 542–3
    ecumenism of 544
    influence/criticisms of 544
    on narrative theology 539
    on political/practical theology 540, 541–3, 544
    Trinitarianism of 540–41
healing 632, 634, 635(n15)
Hedenius, Ingemar 151
Hegel, G.W.F. 22, 26, 175, 179, 269, 318, 382, 572, 703
Heidegger and the Areopagite (Yannaras) 726–7
Heidegger, Martin 5, 6, 14, 15, 149, 193, 225, 227, 233, 261, 282, 510, 669, 672, 676, 677
    and Bultmann 79–80, 83–4
    and Caputo 735, 736, 737, 741
    and Catholic theology 46–7, 50
    and Løgstrup 124, 125
    and Marion 746, 747, 749
    and Tillich 102
    and Yannaras 725, 726–7
Heidelberg 174, 175, 176
Heretica (periodical) 124
Heretics (Chesterton) 645
Hermann, Rudolf 138
hermeneutics 46, 47, 77, 79, 83–5, 115, 136, 143, 177, 194, 282, 288, 529, 706–7, 736
    demythologization debate 74, 80–81, 84–5, 86
    four stages of (Ricoeur) 708–9
    and liberation theology 624
    and postmodern theology 571–2, 750
    pre-understanding and 83–4
    radical 737–8, 739
Herrlichkeit (von Balthasar) 258
Herrmann, Wilhelm 65, 78
Herzen, Alexander 354, 358, 365
hesychasm 379, 394
Hibbs, Thomas 50
Hilary of Poitiers 428
Hinduism 32, 33, 270, 316, 318
Hinkelammert, Franz 618, 625
Hirsch, Emanuel 124
historical-critical method 23, 79, 80, 86, 189, 272, 311, 509, 540
history 12, 38–9, 50, 77, 78, 79, 269, 303, 487
    and creation/redemption 182–3
    and doctrine of God 177–8, 181
    dogma and 39, 97
    and existential theology 159, 165
    and faith 77–8, 80, 81–2, 85–6, 91–2
    and kingdom of God 105

and language 489–90
and revelation 91
Hitler, Adolf 89, 90, 95, 113, 114–15, 118, 291, 292–3
Holiness Movement 631, 633, 636, 637, 639–40
Holland, Scott 470
Hollenweger, Walter J. 634–5, 636
Holy Spirit 33, 35, 55, 57, 59, 105, 138, 163, 244, 274
    and Church 218, 221, 374, 375, 444–6
    and Orthodoxy 347
    and scripture 70
    see also trinitarian theology
Holy Things/Holy People/Holy Ground (Lathrop) 412
Honecker, Martin 226
Honest to God (Robinson) 29, 548
Hooft, Wilem Adolf Visser't 218, 430
hope 140, 160, 162, 164, 165, 166, 451–2, 614, 703, 706
Hörer des Wortes (Rahner) 227, 228, 234
Hoskyns, E.C. 465, 470
human rights 309, 325, 593–4, 613
Humanae Vitae (encyclical) 42–3
Humani Generis (encyclical) 40, 206, 216
humanism 126–7, 205, 235
    integral 659–60, 662
Humanisme intégral (Maritain) 660, 662, 663
humanum 285, 287
Humboldt University (Berlin) 174
Husserl, Edmund 79, 125, 281, 669, 670, 675–6
hyper-realism 741
hypostasis 57, 60, 362(*n*18), 382–3, 387–8, 395, 730, 733

Iaşi (Romania) 53
Idealism 89, 91, 101, 102, 310–11, 362, 675–6
Idol and Distance, The (Marion) 747
idols/idolatry 15–16, 625, 747–8
Ignatius of Antioch 330, 375, 377, 438, 443
Ignatius of Loyola/Ignatian theology 43–4, 229, 234, 244, 257, 258, 278
Ihmel, Ludvig 92
illumination, theory of 34
Immortal Image of God, The (Stăniloae) 395
In Excess (Marion) 748
In the Image and Likeness of God (Lossky) 383
In Memoizry of Her (Schüssler Fiorenza) 328, 329–31
Incarnation of God (Küng) 318, 321
India 460, 518, 718
Infallibility (Lindbeck) 499–500

Infallible? An Enquiry (Küng) 42, 318
Ingarden, Roman 669
Insight: A Study of Human Understanding (Lonergan) 240–41
International Theological Commission 253
Irenaeus 147, 182, 183, 257, 260, 347, 375, 420
Irigaray, Luce 576, 586, 601
Isaac the Syrian 417, 420
Isaiah 209, 464, 696
Islam 32, 33, 213, 287, 316, 318, 323, 416, 422, 424, 595, 664
Iwand, Hans-Joachim 159, 174

Jackelén, Antje 164
Jacob's Ladder (Bulgakov) 344, 345
Jalons pour une théologie du laicat (Congar) 217
Japan 135, 168
Jaspers, Karl 174
Jenson, Robert 9, 11, 26, 34–5, 179, 509–14
    and "death of God" theology 511–12
    ecumenism of 510, 511, 514
    and God in history 513–14
    importance/influence of 514
    theological method of 512
    Trinitarianism of 509, 511, 513, 514
    writings of 510–14
    writings of, key themes in 511–14
Jerusalem, Council of (AD 49) 43
Jesuits 43, 201, 202, 206, 207, 215–16, 225, 240, 251, 267, 269
Jesus: Mirriam's Chil, Sophi's Prophet (Schüssler Fiorenza) 329
Jesus Christ, or the Restoration of Man (Stăniloae) 394
Jesus – God and Man 177–8
Jesus-Sophia 329, 330, 601, 604
Jewish Christianity 268, 272–3
Joachim of Fiore 208, 210, 306
Johannes Community 252
John the Baptist 344, 345, 638
John Chrysostom 260, 377, 428, 445, 607
John of the Cross 260, 291, 291–2, 295, 673, 718
John of Dalyatha 420
John, Gospel of 79, 80, 214, 256, 258, 277, 333, 410, 422, 470, 607
    glory in 464–5
    unity/death linkage in 467
John of Kronstadt 420
John Paul II (Karol Wojtyła) 6, 9, 12, 47–8, 208, 221, 253, 278, 291–8, 292, 430
    assassination attempt on 296
    biography 291–6

and *Communio* theologians/Thomists 47
on experience of faith 291
founds Pontifical Institutes 48
and gender issues 47–8
on gift of self/personhood 295, 296–7
and John of the Cross 291–2, 293, 294, 295
and Kant 296, 297
on loving one's neighbour 297
on marriage/spousal love 294–5, 296, 298
on moral theology 294
in Nazi occupied Poland 291–3, 295
as Pontiff 295–6
in Soviet occupied Poland 293–5
and Stein 677–8
on Trinity 297–8
and Vatican II 295
John XXIII 6, 42, 207, 218, 226, 253, 315, 373
Johnson, Elizabeth A. 143, 600–601, 604
Journal of Theological Studies 476, 479, 480, 482
Judaism 85, 137, 166, 176, 208–9, 287, 322, 323, 333, 361(*n*16), 411, 501, 504, 740
judgement 92, 96
Jülicher, Adolf 77
Jüngel, Eberhard 9, 26, 74, 159, 169, 187–96, 235, 530
anthropology and 187, 190, 193, 195
and atheism/death of God 191–2, 194
and Barth 187, 188, 189, 190, 194, 195
biography of 187–9
character/relationship with students 188, 189
contribution/influence of 187, 190, 191–2, 195–6
on death 191, 192
on death of Jesus 187, 193
doctrine of God 190, 191, 194–5
on justification doctrine 192
linguistic philosophy of 194, 195
and Moltmann 189, 192, 195
on revelation 191, 193
sermons of 192, 196
on thinking about God 194, 195
and Trinitarianism 190, 509
and Tübingen scholars 187, 188, 189
writings of 189–95
writings of, key themes in 193–5
Jungian psychology 47
justification doctrine 27, 164, 189, 308, 317–18, 475, 480, 538, 560, 625
Justification, Doctrine of, Joint Declaration on (1999) 175, 192, 610

Justification. The Heart of the Christian Faith (Jüngel) 192

kabod 464, 466
Kähler, Martin 102
Kampf um das Christenum, Der (Elert) 91
Kant, Immanuel 25, 44, 70, 125, 149, 174, 239, 261, 263, 296, 297, 382, 509, 684, 703
pure reason notion of 37, 50
Kärkkäinen, Veli-Matti 632–3
Käsemann, Ernst 159, 189
Kasper, Walter 159, 187, 222, 310, 608
Katongole, Emmanuel 614
Kavanagh, Aidan 374, 412
Keller, Catherine 577, 740
Kelsey, David 502
kenosis/kenotic theology 55, 261, 349, 471–2, 740
and feminist theology 525, 552
Kern, Cyprian 371, 404
Kerr, Fergus 13, 40–41, 48
kerygma 80, 81, 84, 86, 94, 96, 725
Keshishian, Aram 415
khôra 737–8, 739, 742
Kierkegaard, Søren 7, 23, 25, 124, 126, 269–70, 321, 341, 666, 681, 735
Kiev (Russia/Ukraine) 53
Kilby, Karen 44–5
King, Martin Luther 525, 612, 696
kingdom of God 24, 72, 77, 81, 105, 123, 130–31, 166, 287, 411, 443, 541, 611
Caputo on 741, 742
and liberation theology 624
and Pentecostalism 637
and political theory 663
Kireevsky, Ivan 358, 363
knowledge 571, 675, 737
and asceticism 399
and faith 71, 74, 676–7
of God 57, 58, 68, 70, 726–7
theories of 34
Koch, Hal 126
koinônia see fellowship
Koutroubis, Demetrios 725–6
Kristeva, Julia 60, 576
Küng, Hans 41, 42, 43, 159, 169, 179, 189, 222, 249, 306, 315–25
biography of 315–17
and Chicago Declaration 317, 319, 324
Christology of 318, 321, 322, 325
on church 320–21, 325
and *Concilium* 316, 325

ecclesiastical sanctions against 315, 316, 322
ecumenism of 315–16, 317–18, 320, 322, 325
on faith/knowledge of God 321–2
and global ethic 315, 316–17, 319, 322–5
importance/influence of 325
on justification doctrine 317–18
on papal infallibility 318, 320, 321
paradigm analysis method of 318–19, 323
and Ratzinger 306, 315
and Vatican II 315, 320
writings 317–25
writings, key themes in 320–25
Kurillus VI (Mina al-Mutawahhid) 416, 418, 423
Kvarme, Ole Christian 411
kyriarchy 331, 333

LaCugna, Catherine M. 179
Lamb of God, The (Bulgakov) 55(n4), 344, 347, 362(n18), 381, 381–2
Lambeth Conference (1888) 481
Lancaster University (UK) 548
Land, Steven J. 637
language and theology 327, 331–3, 431, 475, 482–3, 519–21, 534, 561, 696–8
postmodernism and 572, 577
see also cultural-linguistic model; metaphors/analogies
Larsen, Kristoffer Olesen 124, 126
Lash, Nicholas 477, 582, 589
Lathrop, Gordon 412
Latin America 660
see also liberation theology
Lausanne Movement 612
law 98, 684, 686–7
and Gospel 93, 94, 98, 148–9, 154–5
three uses of 95–6, 118, 120
Le Saulchoir (France) 39
Lebendige Orthodoxie (Timiadis) 432
Leo XI 648
Leo XIII 13, 38, 239, 651, 652
Lessing, Gotthold Ephraim 160, 479, 483
Leuenberg Agreement 1973 218, 609, 610
Levering, Matthew 50
Lévinas, Emmanuel 46–7, 132, 585, 745, 746
Leviticus 465
Lewis, C.S. 12, 477, 561, 646, 652, 681–9, **682**
atheism/conversion of 682–3
biography/writings 682–4
on Gospels/myth 687–9
influence of 689
principle ideas of 684–9

theism of 684–7
theological background of 681
liberal theology 29–30, 65, 94, 101, 114, 572, 574, 577
critiques of 48, 77, 78–9, 149
liberation theology 285, 438, 472, 529, 534, 617–28
and Black/feminist theologies 621
Bonhoeffer and 113
characteristics/core points 623–6
Christology/cross and 625–6
criticisms of 173, 622, 626–8
diversity of 618, 624, 627
dualism and 620–21
ecclesiology of 626
economic development and 618–19
and feminist theology 526
Gutiérrez on 45, 618, 619–21, 622
historical Jesus and 620, 621, 624, 628
idolatry and 625
and liberation/salvation 620–21, 623, 625
Lindbeck and 500
method/structure of 621–3
Moltmann and 159, 164, 189
and neoliberalism/market fundamentalism 625, 627
Rahner and 45
renewal of 627–8
and social sciences 622
theological shifts in 617, 621
as threat 622–3
Vatican II and 623–4
World Forum on (2003) 627
Lidman, Sara 154, 155
Life Abundant (McFague) 524
Life and Teaching of St. Gregory Palamas (Stănisloae) 394
Lim, David 632
Lindbeck, George 5, 32–3, 499–506, 512
and Barth 500
on collapse of Christendom 503
and cultural-linguistic model 500–501, 504–5
on doctrine 500
ecumenism of 499–501, 503, 504, 505
on Israel-like church 503–4, 505
postliberal theology of 499, 501–6, 561
and postmodern theology 573–4
and Tracy 506, 559, 563
on truth/scripture 501–3
universalism of 504, 505
and Vatican II 499, 500

linguistic philosophy 123, 194
Lipps, Hans 124, 125, 670
literature 50, 132, 193, 252, 267–8, 483–4, 493, 519, 726
　aesthetics of 717, 719–20, 721–3
Literature and the Christian Life (McFague) 519
liturgical theology 12, 143, 144, 345–6, 374, 396–7, 403, 404–9, 412, 421
　liturgy-theology separation in 407–9
　scholastic approach 407–8
　tradition and 490–92
Liturgical Theology, Introduction to (Schmemann) 405, 409, 412
liturgism 408
Living Tradition (Orthodox anthology) 372
The Living Word, The (*Predikan*, Wingren) 149, 150–51
logical positivism 452
Logos 105, 249, 333, 398–9
Løgstrup, Knud Ejler 6, 24, 28, 30, 74, 123–32, 147, 195
　biography of 124–5
　on Christian faith/ethics 128–9, 132
　on creation/kingdom of God 123, 130–31
　environmental theology of 130–31
　epistemology of 123, 124, 125, 126
　The Ethical Demand 124, 126–7, 128–9, 140–141
　humanist-Christian synthesis of 126–8
　influence of 132
　on love of neighbor/interdependence 126–8
　on mercy 130
　Metafysikk I–IV 124, 140
　Opgør med Kierkegaard 124, 129
　phenomenology of 125–6
　philosophy of senses of 131
　philosophy/theology distinction in 123
　and Prenter 135, 136, 140–41
　resistance to Nazism 124, 126
　on sovereign expressions of life 129–30
　and Tidehverv movement 124, 126, 129
　on trust 127, 129–30
Loisy, Alfred 38
Lonergan, Bernard 50, 239–46
　and anthropology 245
　and Aquinas 239, 241
　on authenticity/inauthenticity 241, 242
　biography of 239–41
　on consciousness 241–2
　contribution/influence of 246
　on conversion 243, 244–6
　on human knowledge 240–41

　phases/functions of theology of 242–3
　philosophy of religion 244, 245
　on sin 242
　and Tracy 529, 530
　on tradition/renewal 239, 245, 246
　on transformation of Catholic theology 243–4
Lord's Supper, The (Afanasiev) 373, 377
Lossky, Nikolai 380, 610
Lossky, Vladimir 4, 8, 9, 12, 15, 17, 56–9, 344, 353, 379–90, **380**, 420, 725
　biography of 380–82
　Catholicism and 380
　concept of person/nature of 385, 386
　importance/influence of 390
　influence of 59, 379
　medieval theology and 380–81
　negative theology of 15, 380, 384
　neo-Palamite synthesis of 379, 381, 383, 384–90
　and *ousia/energeia* distinction 379, 384, 386–7
　personalist mode of thought in 384–90
　on Trinity 382–3, 386–7, 388, 389–90
　writings of 381–4
Lotz, Johannes B. 46
Louth, Andrew 11
Louvain (Belgium) 37, 38, 46, 282
love 34, 47, 48, 140, 195, 374, 541
　and beauty 261
　and economy of gift 710–11
　erotic 725, 726, 727, 731, 748
　and freedom 58, 59, 60, 85
　of God 244
　God as 191, 749
　as Golden Rule 710–11
　of neighbour 33, 44, 126–8, 141, 297, 710
　and Trinity 297–8
Love Almighty and Ills Unlimited (Farrer) 459
Love and Responsibility (Wojtyła) 294–5, 296–7
Lovejoy, Arthur O. 491
Löwith, Karl 175
Loyola, Ignatius 8
Luke's Gospel 33, 180, 296, 333, 442, 468, 638, 696
Lumen Gentium 207, 217, 226, 373, 608
Lund (Sweden) 147–8, 149, 150, 155, 164
Luther, Martin 8, 21, 31, 71, 93, 135, 147, 165, 214, 308, 428, 496, 530, 659–60
　justification doctrine 27, 164
　ubiquity doctrine 141
Lutheran Doctrine, The (Elert) 92

Lutheran theology 35, 73, 74, 80, 85, 169, 308, 509–10
   Bonhoeffer and 114, 116, 117
   Catholic theology and 499–500
   ecumenism and 218, 609, 610
   faith/autonomy in 138
   and Grundtvigian theology 138–40
   and law 95–6, 118
   and Nazism 90, 118
   and Orthodox theology 428, 429, 430–31
   renaissance in 89, 91–3
   two-spheres thinking in 116–17, 120
Lutheran World Federation 89, 135, 148, 218, 607
Lyotard, Jean-François 570–71

McDonnell, Killian 638
McFague, Sallie 5, 517–26, **518**, 574
   anthropology of 524–5
   on Christian tradition 518–19
   criticisms of 523
   and Dalai Lama 517, 525
   eco-theology of 518, 522–3, 524–5
   ethical concerns of 524
   on God as mother 520–22
   on humanity-nature relationship 523–5
   importance of 517, 526
   liberation theology and 526
   religious autobiographies and 519, 525
   on religious language 519–21, 523, 526
   on theology and science 522–3
McGrath, Alister 12, 559–65
   atheism and 559, 565
   biography of 559–60
   and critical realism 562–3, 564
   and Dawkins 561
   and fideistic theology 565
   historical theology of 560–61
   importance/influence of 565
   on justification doctrine 560
   natural theology of 563–4
   post-foundationalism of 562–3
   on revelation 563, 564, 565
   on science and theology 559, 561–2
   on theological doctrine/language 561, 564
   writings of 560–65
   writings of, key themes in 561–5
McIntosh, Mark A. 257
MacIntyre, Alasdair 33, 562
McPartlan, Paul 48, 371, 435, 437, 438
McPherson, Jay 694, 695
Mâle, Emile 692, 693

Man and the Incarnation (Wingren) 148–9, 150, 155
Man and the State (Maritain) 660, 662
Marburg school 79
Marcel, Gabriel 270, 720
Marchal, Joseph A. 334
Maréchal, Joseph 44, 50, 269
Mariology 215, 253, 347
   see also Virgin Mary
Marion, Jean-Luc 5, 12, 46–7, 263, 575, 585, 736, 745–51, **746**
   on agape 749–50
   biography of 745–7
   and Descartes 745, 746, 747
   on excess 748
   on gift 748, 749, 750
   on idolatry 747–8
   importance of 745, 751
   not a theologian 745, 746, 747
   on saturated phenomena 748, 750
   on visuality/images 15–16
   writings of 747–51
   writings of, key themes in 749–51
Maritain, Jacques 6, 12, 268, 657–66, **658**, 681, 717(*n*4), 735
   and Aquinas 659
   biography/writings 658–61
   on Christian humanism 659–60
   on grace 666
   on instrumental/proper causality 661
   "integral humanism" of 659–60, 662
   on original sin 661, 664–5
   on philosophy-faith connection 657–8, 663–6
   on politics/church-state relations 658, 661–3
   on scripture 657, 665
   in Second World War 660
   and Vatican II 660, 661
Marmion, Columba 278
marriage 7, 34, 93, 208–9, 295, 296, 330, 542
Marrou, Henri 270
Marx, Karl 34, 55, 269, 321, 586
Marxism 7, 45, 135, 142, 174, 207, 288, 306, 310, 341, 342, 559, 585, 586, 596, 622
Mary *see* Mariology; Virgin Mary
Mary Through the Centuries (Pelikan) 493
materialism 54, 274, 587, 658, 659, 685
   theological 737, 741, 742
mathematics 50, 273–4
Matta, Father (Matta El-Meskeen) 415–24
   biblical commentaries of 419, 422
   biography of 416–19

in clashes with Coptic church 415–16, 418, 419, 421
criticisms of 424
ecumenism of 421, 422–3
on eucharist 421
importance of 416, 423–4
and Islam 416, 422, 424
on letters of Antony 420, 421
monastic life of 416, 417, 420, 421
obscurity/marginalization of 415–16
in patriarchal election 418–19
on patristic tradition 421–2
on prayer 417, 420, 422
and Shenouda 417, 418–19, 419–20(*n*10), 421, 423
on social issues 421
writings of 415, 418, 420–23
writings of, three themes in 422
Matthew's Gospel 297, 330, 333
Mauriac, François 38, 267
Maurice, F.D. 135, 138, 471–2
Maximus, St 251, 252, 255, 257, 258, 393, 395, 397, 398, 436, 438, 439, 511, 729
medieval theology 38, 40, 175, 201–2, 204, 205, 304, 727
    and philosophy 662–3
    and Radical Orthodoxy 582, 584, 585
    see also Aquinas, Thomas; Thomism
Méditation sur l'Eglise (de Lubac) 206–7
Melanchthon, Philipp 95–6
mercy 97, 129, 130, 605, 621, 631, 661, 740
Mere Christianity (Lewis) 683, 684, 687–9
Merleau-Ponty, Maurice 282
Merton, Thomas 12, 715–23, **716**
    aesthetics of 717, 719–20, 721–3
    biography 715–18
    and Buddhism 717–18, 719, 720–21
    on contemplation/prayer 721–2, 723
    conversion to Catholicism 716
    importance of 715
    legacy of 723
    mysticism of 717
    and political/social issues 717, 719
    as Trappist monk 716–18
    two key themes of 720–23
    two vocations of 716
    writings of 718–20
Metafysikk I-IV (Løgstrup) 124, 140
metanarratives 570–71
Metaphorical Theology (McFague) 520–21, 522, 523

metaphors/analogies 455, 519–20, 564, 639, 694, 706, 708
Metaphysicals, The 452
metaphysics 123, 452, 658, 675, 727, 730, 741
Method in Theology (Lonergan) 241, 244, 245
Methodism 31, 537, 609
Metropolitan Evlogy 343, 381
Metropolitan Sergei 381
Metz, Johann Baptist 45, 159, 226(*n*1), 230, 234–5
Meyendorff, John 8, 17, 57, 353, 357, 379, 384, 405, 427, 436, 726
Milbank, John 5, 33–4, 45, 49, 206, 581, 584, 585, 588–9
Milton, John 21–2, 681, 692
Mina al-Mutawahhid (Kurillus VI) 416, 418, 423
Mina, Father 418
ministry 60, 140, 142, 149, 155, 219–20, 285, 438, 475
miracles 84, 85, 587, 686
Miracles (Lewis) 683, 684
Mirandola, Giovanni Pico della 208(*n*15), 210
Mission Church (Scandinavia) 169
Mission and Grace (Rahner) 229
Mitchell, Basil 461
Models of God (McFague) 521–2
modernist crisis 6–7, 12–14, 38–9, 569–71, 577
modernist theology 4, 9–11, 12–14, 98, 263
    Catholic 5, 7, 12, 38–9, 43–4, 45–7, 50, 281
    dualism in 16
Möhler, Johann Adam 358, 359, 363, 365
Molnar, Paul D. 179
Moltmann, Jürgen 11, 12, 26, 29, 143, 159–69, 175, 235, 258, 511, 626
    biography 160–61
    and Catholic theology 159
    on the cross/resurrection 162–3, 164, 165, 166–7
    epistemology of 164
    eschatology of 162, 163, 164, 167–8, 742
    and existential theology 159
    "family" of 161, 168–9, 179–80
    on history/time 159, 165–6
    on hope 160, 162, 164, 165, 166, 614, 703
    importance of 35, 159, 168–9
    and Jüngel 189, 192, 195
    methodologies 163
    pastoral/confessional works 164
    problems with 168
    Trinitarianism of 163, 165, 166, 167, 179–80, 509

writings, five phases of 162–8
writings, themes in 164–8
Moltmann-Wendel, Elisabeth 159, 161
Moment of Christian Witness, The (von Balthasar) 44
monachisme orthodoxe, Le (Timiadis) 432
monastic revival 415, 416, 418, 432, 726
Mondésert, Claude 8
Montague, George 638
Moore, Lazarus 417
Moore, Stephen D. 334
moral theology 33, 42, 294
Morphologie des Luthertums (Elert) 92–3, 95
Moscow Council (1917–18) 376–7
Moscow Patriarchate 56, 343–4
Moscow (Russia) 53, 341–2, 381
Moses 550, 600
Müller, Max 46
Münster, University of 66, 227, 304, 315, 328, 670
music 50, 250, 583
Muslim Brotherhood 416
My Five Universities (Wingren) 151
Mystical Element in Heidegger's Thought (Caputo) 736, 737
Mystical Theology of the Eastern Church (Lossky) 382–3, 390, 725
Mystici Coproris (encyclical) 203, 608
mysticism 229, 235, 257, 530, 669, 715, 717, 737
myth 84–5, 682, 683, 687–8, 694, 695, 698, 706

Nachfolge (Bonhoeffer) 116, 119
nationalism/national churches 54, 68, 79, 90, 91, 98, 135, 139
natural theology 136–7, 205, 523, 541, 563–4
naturalistic/humanistic method 106
Nature of Doctrine, The (Lindbeck) 32–3, 500–501, 573
Nature of Religion, The 499
Nazism 25, 61, 66–7, 73, 660, 670–71, 673
 Bonhoeffer and 113, 114–17, 118
 Bultmann and 79–80, 85–6
 church-state relations under 90, 93, 95
 defeat of 97–8, 121
 in Denmark 124
 Deutsche Christen movement 68, 79, 90, 91, 116
 Elert and 89, 90–91, 93–7
 Løgstrup and 124, 126
 non-Nazi church in (*Bekennende Kircher*) 114

Prenter and 135
Wojtyła and 291–3
negative theology 15, 344, 380, 384, 737, 741, 742
Nein! (Barth) 25, 68
Neo-Kantism 125, 126
neo-Palamist school 379, 383, 384–90, 393
 and existentialism 384–5
 persons/godhead in 388
 Trinity in 382–3, 386–7, 388, 389–90
neo-patristic school 8, 56–9, 60, 61, 353, 355, 357, 363, 365–6
 essence/energies of God in 56–7, 58, 60
 Lossky and 382
 Stăniloae and 393, 401
 tradition and 57–8
 Trinity in 57
neo-patristic synthesis 344, 436
neo-Protestantism 65, 69, 70, 93, 94, 98
neo-scholasticism 12, 13, 58, 204, 208, 210–11, 251, 270
neoliberal theology 29–30, 31–4
neoliberalism 503, 569, 625, 627
Nestorianism 633–4, 633(n10)
Netherlands 41, 595, 671, 673
New Climate for Theology (McFague) 524–5
New Testament theology 78, 79, 150, 209, 284–5
 demythologization debate 74, 80–81, 84–5, 86
 Hebrew scripture and 466
 see also Gospels; Paul, St
Newman, John Henry 9, 10, 11, 13, 37, 46, 255, 480, 481, 492, 493
Nicene creed 139, 445
Nichols, Aidan 38, 44, 306, 373
Niebuhr, H.R. 24, 32, 537, 681
Nietzsche, Friedrich 34, 40, 47, 160, 174, 191, 194, 269, 321, 530, 572, 666, 747
Niewiadomski, Józef 164
nihilism 510, 511, 512, 584, 586–8
Nikodemus of the Holy Mountain 53, 728
Nissiotis, Nikos 59, 427
Norway 118, 121, 169, 595(n3)
Notra Aetate 255, 270
nouvelle théologie 12–13, 49, 206, 215, 262, 268, 282, 500
 and Radical Orthodoxy 584
nuptial theology 48, 208–9, 275
Nygren, Anders 139, 147, 148, 149, 584, 681

Oakes, Edward 468–9

Offenbarung als Geschichte (Heidelberg circle) 176
oikonomia 58
Old Testament 176, 182, 208–9, 272, 275–6
  see also specific books
Olsson, Herbert 147
O'Meara, Thomas F. 38–9
On Being a Christian (Küng) 318
On Divine Wisdom and Godmanhood (Bulgakov) 347–8
On the Foundation of a Philosophy of Religion (Rahner) 227–8
On Religion (Caputo) 737, 738–9
ontology 34, 43, 50, 105–6, 114, 509, 562, 676, 727, 733
  as bridge between theology and philosophy 106
  and Christology 116
  of creation 278
open narrative, Catholicism as 46, 51
Open Theism 31
Opening the Bible (Merton) 719
Opgør med Kierkegaard (Løgstrup) 124, 129
Origen 10, 13, 27, 202, 206, 208–9, 210, 249, 251, 252, 255, 257, 259, 362(*n*18)
  Contra Celsum 478
  von Balthasar and 257–8, 259, 260–61
Orthodox Church/Orthodox theology 3–4, 53–61, 272, 429–40, 725
  and atheism/materialism 54
  as Church Universal 364, 365
  development of doctrine in 11
  divine-human union in 54, 56, 57, 68
  ecumenical 341, 430–31, 437
  and existentialism 60
  future of 60–61
  and German idealism 54, 55–6, 341, 343, 348
  humanity of God/sophiology in 53–6
  hypostasis in 57, 60
  and liberalism/post-liberalism 31, 32
  liturgical 144
  monastic revival in 415, 416, 418
  and nationalism 54
  neo-patristic school *see* neo-patristic school
  ousia/energeia distinction in 379, 382, 383, 384, 385, 386
  in Paris *see* Russian émigrés *under* Paris
  and postmodernism 5, 60
  and Protestant theology 35
  pseudomorphosis of 355, 355(*n*6)
  reform of 342, 415, 728
  revival of 7–8, 53, 416–17
  Russian school *see* Russian school
  social issues and 60–61
  and Sophia Affair 53, 56, 343–4
  theological academies and 53
  trinitarian 55, 57
  "Western captivity" of 407
  and World Council of Churches 427
  Zizioulas and 59–60
Orthodox Dogmatic Theology (Stăniloae) 395
Orthodox Prayer Life (Matta) 420
Orthodox Slavophiles 54, 358, 359, 365, 380
Orthodox Spirituality (Stăniloae) 396
Orthodox Theology (Lossky) 383
Orthodoxy (Chesterton) 648–9
Orthodoxy and the West (Yannaras) 727–8
otherness 4, 15, 16, 58, 731
Otto, Rudolf 79, 244, 681, 682
Ouellet, Marc 48
Oumançoff, Raïssa 658, 659
ousia 55, 57
  and *energiae* 379, 382, 383, 384, 385, 386–7
Oxford University (UK) 451, 452, 476, 477, 483

paganism 209–10, 595, 649, 687–8
Palamas, St Gregory 8, 53, 344, 379, 381, 383, 393, 726, 729
  see also neo-Palamist school
Pan-Orthodoxy 353, 365
Pannenberg, Wolfhart 9, 11, 12, 26, 34, 35, 74, 144, 159, 168, 173–84, 192, 195, 258, 510, 511
  on anthropology 173, 177
  and Barth/dialectical theology 173, 174, 176
  biography 173–5
  and Bultmann 173
  on creation/redemption 182–3
  and doctrine of God 177–8
  ecumenical work of 175
  importance/influence of 183–4
  and interdisciplinary dialogue 173, 175, 177
  key themes of 179–84
  methodological study 177
  and Nietzsche 174
  on predestination 175
  on revelation 174, 176–8, 183–4
  and Tracy 530, 532–3, 534
  and Trinitarian doctrine 179–81, 182, 509
pantheism 79, 109, 356, 523, 600, 601
papal infallibility 318, 320, 321

paradigm analysis method 318–19, 323
Paris (France) 55, 282, 341, 343, 344, 347, 390, 404, 660, 704, 746–7
  Russian émigrés in 7–8, 17, 354, 365, 372, 379, 381, 725–6
Parliament of World Religions 317, 319, 324
Pascal, Blaise 273, 321
Pasternak, Boris 717, 717(*n*4), 719, 720, 722, 723
pastoral work 227, 229
patriarchy 330, 331, 593, 594, 598, 602, 605
patristic tradition 8, 12–13, 40, 182, 204, 205, 210, 215, 511
  Orthodoxy and 55–6, 57, 59, 202, 348, 421–2, 438, 725
  Radical Orthodoxy and 582, 584, 585
  and truth 255
Paul and Jesus (Jüngel) 189
Paul, St 24, 47, 79, 82, 85, 189, 277, 330, 333, 377, 422, 463, 464, 466, 638, 739–40
Paul VI 42, 216, 221, 271, 295, 373
Péguy, Charles 39, 252, 260, 267–8, 658
Pelikan, Jaroslav 9, 11, 487, 487–96, **487**
  academic career 487–8
  and Barth 487, 489
  conversion to Orthodoxy 488, 494–5
  on development of doctrine 492
  and Harnack 487, 488, 489, 491, 494, 495
  on history of dogma 491, 496
  on history/historians 489–90, 491, 495–6
  on Luther 493, 496
  and Newman 492, 493
  and "polyglot" 489–90, 492
  range of writings of 493
  on tradition/liturgy 490–92
Pentecostal movement 31, 35, 607, 627, 631–40
  apostolic/oneness schism 633–4
  and Catholic theology 638
  diversity of 633–4
  divine gifts in 632, 636–7
  doctrinal grammar of 636–7
  ecclesiology of 632–3
  ecumenism and 637–8, 639, 640
  eschatology of 632, 637, 638–9
  in global South 634
  and Holiness Movement 631, 633, 636, 637
  as missionary fellowship 632, 633
  and pneumatology 631, 639
  practice-philosophy distinction in 636, 638
  Spirit baptism in 631–2, 633, 634, 636, 637–9, 640
  and Trinity 633, 634
  in US 631–2, 633, 635

perichoresis 143, 383, 386, 388, 388–9, 389, 396, 401
Periti 41, 42
Person and Eros (Yannaras) 59, 727
personalist doctrines 379, 384–90, 393, 394, 395, 401
personhood 57, 59–60, 459–60
  God and 82–4, 94, 395–6
Petersen, Douglas 635, 635(*n*15)
phenomenology 10, 12, 16, 47, 83, 94, 281, 283, 575, 669, 671–2, 675–6
  Løgstrup's 123, 125–6, 140–41
  Marion's 745, 746, 748, 750
Philo 267
Philokalia 53, 393, 394, 397–8, 728
philosophie chrétienne, De la (Maritain) 660, 664
Philosophy of Economics (Bulgakov) 344
philosophy of religion 4, 5, 79, 82–4, 115, 123, 547, 548, 704, 745, 748
Pic de la Mirandole (de Lubac) 208
Pickstock, Catherine 5, 581, 583, 584, 585, 588
Pieper, Josef 46
Pietists 147
piety 113, 141, 143
Pinckaers, Servais-Théodore 49
Pinnock, Clark 31, 506
pistis theou 24
Pius XI 648, 651
Pius XII 40, 208, 216, 608, 660
Pixley, Jorge 618, 624
Placher, William 504, 505
Plaskow, Judith 328
Plato/Platonism 9–10, 70, 138, 208(*n*15), 256, 310, 384, 492, 653, 703, 729
  and Radical orthodoxy 583, 584
Plotinus 260, 664
Plurality and Ambiguity (Tracy) 530
pneumatology 35, 138, 139, 142, 164, 395, 396, 438, 439
  and Christology 400–401, 439, 440–41
  and Pentecostalism 631, 639
poetry 272, 454, 681
Poland 291–5
  Nazi occupied 291–3
  Soviet occupied 293–5
political theology 29, 102–3, 132, 159, 164, 191, 267, 269, 285, 315, 344, 541–3
  and ecumenical movement 613
  see also church-state relations; feminist theology
polysemy 700
Porvoo Common Statement 609, 610

positivism 13, 14(n44), 513, 658
　revelational 144
postliberal theology 5, 32–4, 499, 501–6, 512, 574–5, 577
　as research program 505–6
Postmodern Metaphysisc (Yannaras) 5, 727, 730, 731
postmodern theology 4–5, 12–14, 263, 514, 569–78, 712
　Catholic 45–7
　controversy surrounding 569
　and crisis in modernity 569–71, 577
　and deconstructivism 575–6
　dogma and 573–4
　dualism and 570, 571, 572, 577–8, 620–21
　and feminist theology 572, 576, 601
　and God-is-dead theology 572, 574, 575–6
　growth of 571–4
　Jewish 589
　metanarratives and 571
　ongoing developments in 574–7
　and postliberal theology *see* postliberal theology
　and poststructuralism 576–7
　and pre-modern theology 16
　and Radical Orthodoxy 575, 576, 577, 583, 584
　"weak" 47, 735, 737, 739–40
postsecular philosophy 585–6
poststructuralism 597
poverty 610–11, 614, 617, 618, 621–2, 624, 627, 628
　see also liberation theology
Power of the Word (Schüssler Fiorenza) 333–4
praxis 116–17, 120, 227, 613, 621, 622, 623
prayer 150, 269, 346, 372, 396, 417, 420, 547
　and feminist theology 551
　and Trinity 552–4
Prayers and Tears of Jacques Derrida (Caputo) 736, 738
predestination 21, 26–7, 161
Predestination and Perseverance (Moltmann) 162
Predikan (Wingren) 149
Prenter, Regin 24, 74, 135–45, 412
　anthropology of 142–3, 145
　Barthian-Grundtigian period 136–8
　on bodiliness/suffering 142–3, 144–5
　Christology of 141
　Church's Ministry 142
　and contemporary thinkers 135, 136
　Creation and Redemption 139, 140–41
　dogmatic theology of 139

Dominion of the Word 136–8
　ecclesiology of 139–40, 142
　on fellowship of peoples 137–8
　on grace/faith 138
　and Grundtvigian theology 135–43
　liturgical theology of 143, 144
　and Løgstrup 135, 136, 140–41
　Lutheran-Grundtvigian period 138–40
　and Marxism 135, 142
　on real/secondary theology 136
　resistance to Nazism 135
　on sacramentality of the church 136–7
　on sanctification/piety 141
　and *sola scriptura* principle 139, 141
　Spiritus Creator 135, 138, 141, 143
　theological relevance of 143–5
　trinitarianism of 138, 139, 141, 142–4
　on Word/faith 142
Priests for God (Schüssler Fiorenza) 328
primacy doctrine 308, 325, 475, 479–80
Primauté du spirituel (Maritain) 268, 662
Prinzip Hoffnung (Bloch) 165
Priscillian of Avila (Chadwick) 476
Problem of Pain, The (Lewis) 683, 684, 685–7
process theology 461, 514, 526, 559
Projekt Weltethos 323, 324, 325
Prolegomena to Charity (Marion) 748
prophets/prophecy 142, 176, 632, 696
Protestant theology 3–4, 21–35
　American evangelical 30–31
　church/community and 31–2, 33–5
　cultural theology and 27–8
　dialectical theology and 23–4
　dialogue with Catholic theology 35, 263, 316
　formal/material principles in 22
　and historical-critical method 23
　and liberation theology 618
　neo- 21–3
　neoliberal/post-liberal 29–30, 31–4
　and Orthodox theology 428, 429
　and postmodernism 5
　secularization and 28–30, 32, 34
　splits/conflicts in 21, 23, 24, 31, 34, 35
　universalism/Trinitarianism and 25–7
　"Word of God" 24, 28, 33, 34
　see also Anglicanism; Lutheran theology
Prussia 22, 89, 90
Przywara, Erich 40, 43, 251, 261
Psalms 93, 260
Pseudo-Dionysius 550, 673
Pseudo-Macarius 420

pseudomorphosis 355, 355(*n*6)
psychology of religion 29

Quaestiones disputatae (Rahner) 227

racism 518, 603, 717, 719
Radcliffe, Timothy 213
Radical Hermeneutics/More Radical Hermeneutics (Caputo) 736, 737–8
Radical Orthodoxy 33–4, 263, 277, 514, 575, 576, 577, 581–9
　catholicity of 582
　criticisms of 589
　emergence of 581–2
　life-doctrine dichotomy and 583
　nihilism and 584, 586–8
　and *nouvelle théologie* 584
　and orthodoxy/modernity 582–5
　and patristic/medieval theology 582, 584, 585
　and postmodern theology 575, 576, 577, 583, 584
　and postsecular philosophy 585–6
　radicalness of 585, 588–9
　"Theory Group" 581
Radical Orthodoxy: A New Theology 581, 582
Rahner, Hugo 252
Rahner, Karl 3, 11, 12, 30, 41, 42, 43, 50, 222, 225–36, **226**, 252, 281, 305, 742
　and Aquinas 225, 227, 231
　biography of 225–7
　and Christology-anthropology 231–2, 233
　on church fathers 228–9
　Concilium and 227, 249, 262, 316
　critiques of 143, 234–6
　on death 233
　on divine/human Jesus 230–32
　on Heidegger 46
　and Ignatius 229, 234
　importance of 246
　on Jesus and salvation 232–3, 234
　on justification of faith 225, 230
　on knowledge of God 227–8
　and liberation theology 45, 623, 625
　on modernity 43–4, 503
　prose style of 44
　and Ratzinger 230, 235–6
　on spirituality/mysticism 227, 228, 229, 233–4, 235
　theological writings 226, 227–36
　theological writings, key themes in 225, 230–36

　and Trinitarian doctrine 179, 509, 552
　and von Balthasar 43–5, 262–3
Ramsey, Michael 135, 136, 374, 463–72
　and Balthasar 463, 464, 467–9, 470
　and Barth 471
　biography of 463(*n*1)
　on Church-theology 470–71
　'dictionary theology' of 466, 467
　exegesis of 465–7
　on glory of Christ's face 463–5, 470
　on glory and the cross 465, 468
　on Hebrew/Christian scripture 464, 466
　kenotic theology of 471–2
　and liberation/feminist theology 472
　and Maurice 471–2
　on Resurrection 469–70
　theological aesthetics of 464
rationalism *see* reason
Ratzinger, Joseph (Benedict XVI) 12, 14, 40, 41, 46, 159, 187, 279, 301–12, 534
　and *Communio* 42–3, 222, 249, 306
　conservatism of 303–4
　on creed/eschatology 306–7
　distinction between Ratzinger's/Pope's writings 301
　on early church 303, 305, 307
　early life/works 304–5
　ecclesiology of 303, 306, 307–8
　on ecumenism 308
　and Enlightenment/crisis of the West 309–10
　on faith 305, 306–7, 310
　and historical-critical method 311
　importance of 312
　Jesus study of 301
　and Küng 306, 315
　and liberation theology 308, 626, 628
　on Marxism 306, 310
　and modernity 310–11
　philosophy and 310–11
　problems with 301–2
　and Rahner 230, 235–6
　on religions 305
　and *ressourcement* movement 303
　on revelation 303, 304
　on scripture/tradition 305, 311–12
　style/originality of 301–3, 306, 312
　on Trinity 307
　and Vatican II 279, 303, 305–6, 309, 311
reason
　and faith 37, 50
　and revelation 96–7

reciprocal circumincession 167
reconciliation 54, 68, 92, 94
redemption 68, 71–2, 142, 149
    creation and 182–3
Reform und Anerkennung Ämter (Küng) 318
Reformation 21, 92, 210, 493
Reformed Church 160, 161, 162, 218, 609, 639–40
Reformed theology 164
Reinach, Adolf 670
Religion against Itself (Jenson) 511
religions 287, 305, 504–5, 575, 595
    dialogue between 315, 316–17, 322–5, 639
    and nihilism 512–13
    as "schools of wisdom" 287
    theology of 29
religious pluralism 32, 46, 218, 526, 610, 611, 662
religious symbols 15–16, 27, 108
Rerum Novarum (encyclical) 651
Resident Aliens (Hauerwas/Willimon) 544
ressourcement project 39–41, 49–50, 207, 269, 278, 303, 500
resurrection of Christ 84, 85, 154, 162–3, 183, 277–8, 513, 650
    and apocalypticism 176
revelation 10, 13, 14, 23, 24, 44, 46, 70–71, 90, 94–5, 191, 193, 286
    and creation 123
    Dogmatic Constitution on *see Dei Verbum*
    exclusiveness of 26
    and freedom 259
    and history 91, 303, 563
    "images of" 454–5
    Pannenberg on 174, 176–8
    and reason 96–7
    stages of 275–6
    as truth 254–5
revisionism 5, 506, 559, 574, 575
Rhetoric and Ethics (Schüssler Fiorenza) 327, 328
Rhineland mystics 210
Ricoeur, Paul 12, 519–20, 585, 703–12, **704**, 745, 746
    and Barth/Bultmann/Moltmann 703, 711
    biography 703–4
    on economy of gift 710–11
    on ethics 707–8
    on evil/hope 703, 705–6, 707, 710
    on Golden Rule 710–11
    importance of 711–12

    theological hermeneutics of 706–7, 708–10, 711, 712
    writings of 705–11
    writings of, key themes in 708–11
Ritschl, Albrecht 23, 102
Ritschl school 379
Robinson, John A.T. 29, 548
Rockne, Blanche 510
Romania 8, 393
Romanides, John 353
Romans, Letter to 24, 31, 65, 69–70, 78, 80, 471, 552
Romanticism 37, 49–50, 98, 483–4, 691
Römerbrief, Der (Barth) 23, 67, 70
Romero, Archbishop 623, 626
Rosenberg, Alfred 85
Rousselot, Pierre 269
Ruether, Rosemary Radford 594, 599–600, 603, 717(*n*4)
Rupert of Deutz 201, 202
Russell, Letty Mandeville 595, 603
Russia 341, 354, 371, 380
    Communist era 55, 343–4, 381
    émigrés from *see* Russian émigrés *under* Paris
    establishment of Orthodox Church in 53
    sophiology in 53–6
    see also Moscow
Russian Orthodoxy 341
    and Sophia Affair 53, 56, 343–4
Russian school 53–6, 341
    influence of 60–61
    and neo-patristic school 57–8, 353

sacraments/sacramental theology 21, 80, 94, 136–7, 140, 187, 191, 195, 282, 365, 438, 514
Sadat, Anwar 419, 419(*n*9)
St Macarius monestary (Egypt) 418, 419, 423
St. Mark (periodical) 418, 420
St Petersburg (Russia) 53
Saint Samuel's monestary (Egypt) 416–17, 418, 423
St Serge, Institut de (Paris) 341, 343, 345, 356, 390
St Sergius Orthodox Theological Institute (Paris) 55, 56, 341, 355, 356, 371, 372, 374, 436
St Vladimir's Seminary (New York) 56, 60, 353(*n*2), 377, 404–5, 436
Sakharov, Sophrony 353

salvation 96, 97, 150, 178, 232–3, 234, 284, 475, 513–14, 541
Sanders, Fred 179
Sartre, Jean-Paul 269
saturated phenomena 748, 750
Sayers, Dorothy L. 646, 652, 681
Scandinavia 74, 92, 118, 143, 147, 166, 169, 243, 621
    feminist theology in 595, 595(*n*3)
Schaull, Richard 613–14
Scheler, Max 40, 124, 268, 294, 669, 670
Scheler (Wojtyła) 294
Schelling, F.W.J. 27, 54, 55, 382
Schillebeeckx, Edward 6, 12, 41, 42, 45, 222, 227, 249, 279, 281–9, 321, 621
    biography of 281–3
    Christology of 284–5, 325
    on church ministry/laity 285, 288–9
    and *Concilium* 281, 282, 288, 316
    and Congar 281, 282
    critiques of 287
    cultural theology of 286
    on dogmatic theology 284
    and existentialism 281, 283, 286
    and *humanum* 285, 287
    importance/influence of 288–9
    on knowledge of God 285–7
    and Marxism/liberation theology 285, 288
    and *la nouvelle théologie* 282
    on sacramental theology 282
    and secular thinkers 282–3, 286
    and Thomism/neo-Thomism 281, 282, 287–8
    Vatican II 281, 283–4, 285, 288
    writings 283–8
    writings, key themes in 285–8
Schleiermacher, Friedrich 22, 65, 69, 92, 151, 563, 572, 574
Schlier, Heinrich 228
Schlink, Edmund 175, 608
Schmaus, Michael 14, 303, 304
Schmemann, Alexander 7, 11, 12, 17, 59, 345, 353, 356, 390, 403–13, 436
    and Afanasiev 371, 374, 377
    and ecclesiology 404
    ecumenism of 411–12
    influence of 411–13
    and liturgical movement/theology 403, 404–10, 412
    in Paris 404, 725–6
    on scholastic approach 407–8
    on secularism 410–11

    in US 404–5
    and Vatican II 405, 409
    vision/methodology of 409–10
Schneider, Reinhold 253
scholasticism/neo-scholasticism 38–9, 263, 269
Schultze, Bernhard 385
Schüssler Fiorenza, Elisabeth 327–35, 603
    biblical scholarship of 327, 333
    and colonialism/postcolonialism 333–4
    "double ethics" of 328–9, 332
    on early church 329–31
    effect of war on 328
    feminist theology of 327, 328, 329–31
    importance/influence of 333–5
    neologisms/language concerns of 327, 331–3
    on Paul 330, 333
    on Sophia 329, 330, 332–3
science 12, 29, 34, 50, 71, 173, 175, 177, 273–4, 430, 522–3, 549, 550, 727
    and modernist crisis 570, 571
    and process theology 559
    and "realism" 561–2
Science of God, A? (Farrer) 459
science of religion 533
Scientific Theology series (McGrath) 560, 561
Scola, Angelo 48
Scotus, Duns 175, 499
scripture 320
    and doctrine of God 315
    faith and 139
    fourfold sense of 269
    Holy Spirit and 70
    and tradition 358–9
Second Vatican Council *see* Vatican II
Second World War 30, 72, 124, 160, 203, 213, 214–15, 227, 270, 281, 327–8, 355, 613
    see also Nazism
secularization 28–30, 32, 34, 49, 587, 615, 622, 726, 732
    Bonhoeffer and 113, 119–20, 121
    Gospels and 121, 173
    Schmemann on 410–11
Seeds of Contemplation (Merton) 719
Segundo, Juan Luis 45, 618
senses, philosophy of 131
September 11 attacks 324
Seraphim of Sarov 420
Sermon on the Mount 116, 277
Seven Storey Mountain, The (Merton) 716–17, 718–19
Sexism and God-talk (Ruether) 599–600

sexual desire 548, 549, 551, 553–4, 555
sexual morality 42
Seymour, William J. 631, 632
Shaking of the Foundations (Tillich) 105
Shaw, George Bernard 645, 647
She Who Is (Johnson) 600–601
Shenouda III 417, 418–19, 419–20(*n*10), 423, 424, 430
Sheppard, Gerald 635
Siewerth, Gustav 46, 261
signe du Temple, Le (Daniélou) 271–2
sin 96, 118, 138, 142, 242, 631
    original 30, 205, 257, 383, 661, 664–5, 706
Skobtsova, Maria 60–61
Sløk, Johannes 124, 126
Smith, James K. 636
Sobrino, Jon 45, 145, 618, 625, 626, 628
social issues 60–61, 132, 151, 187, 191, 269, 315, 320, 416, 518, 519, 529, 542
    and ecumenical movement 612–15
    and fundamental theology 531–4
    see also feminist theology; liberation theology
socialism 101, 103, 104, 138
Societas Ethica 148
Society of Jesus *see* Jesuits
sociology of religion 103, 115, 117, 207
Söderblom, Nathan 147
Søe, N.H. 74
Sofia (Bulgaria) 53
Söhngen, Gottlieb 303, 304
sola scriptura principle 139, 141, 428
Sölle, Dorothee 29, 169
Solov'ev, Vladimir Sergeevich 54, 260, 342, 343, 348, 357, 382
Song of Songs 202
Sophia Affair (1935) 56, 58, 343–4
Sophia Europe conferences 460
Sophia/sophiology 53–6, 277, 343, 346–9, 522, 657, 665
    and feminist theology 601, 604
    Jesus as 329, 330, 332–3, 601, 603–4
    reaction against 353, 355, 356, 357, 381–2
Sørensen, Arne 135, 136
Soskice, Janet Martin 455
soteriology 44, 96, 139, 142
soul 71, 92
Sourchrisces Chrétiennes 8
South Africa 618
sovereign expressions of life 129–30
Speaking in Parables (McFague) 519–20
speaking in tongues 632

"speech-events" 29
Spengler, Oswald 91
Spirit baptism 631–2, 633, 634, 636, 637–9, 640
spirituality 7, 12, 227, 228–9, 233–4
    and dogmatics 229
    and theology 256–8
Spirituality and Communion in the Orthodox Liturgy (Stănisloae) 396–7
Spiritus Creator (Prenter) 135, 138, 141, 143
Stăniloae, Dumitru 3, 8, 9, 57, 163, 379, 384, 393–401
    on asceticism/knowledge 399
    biography of 393–5
    Christology of 395
    importance/influence of 401
    on *logos/logoi* 398–9, 400
    on Orthodox liturgy/church 396–7
    and Palamite/neo-patristic thought 393, 394, 401
    on person-nature 395–6, 398, 400
    personalist thought and 393, 394, 395, 401
    on spiritual life 396–7
    theology-spirituality synthesis of 400
    translation of *Philokalia* 393, 394, 397–8
    Trinitarianism of 395–6, 400–401
    writings of 395–401
    writings of, key themes in 398–401
Stavenhagen, Rudolfo 619
Stein, Edith 6, 12, 669–78
    becomes Carmelite nun 670–71
    biography 669–71
    on faith/knowledge 676–7
    on human person/empathy 673–5
    and Husserl 669, 670, 675–6
    influence of 677–8
    and Nazis 670–71, 673, 678
    phenomenology of 669, 671–2, 675
    on Realism v. Idealism 675–6
    translations/Aquinas studies of 672–3
    writings of 671–7
    writings of, key themes in 673–7
Suárez, Fransisco 40, 41, 50
subjectivity 16, 239, 242, 245, 291, 293, 583
    inter- 396
suffering 142–3, 144–5, 617, 685–7
    of Christ/God 187, 193, 235, 288
Sunday school movement 423
Sunkel, O. 619
Super, Natural Christians (McFague) 523–4
supernatural method 106
Surnaturel (de Lubac) 203–4, 205, 210, 347
Suzuki, D.T. 717(*n*4), 723

Svenungsson, Jayne 4, 16
Sweden 147, 151, 169
Swedish Reformation church 118
Swiss Reformed church 65
synoptic tradition 78
Synoro (journal) 726
Systematic Theology (Jenson) 511
Systematic Theology (Pannenberg) 178, 181
Systematic Theology (Tillich) 28, 104–5
Systematische Beiträge zur Theologie (Moltmann) 163, 164

Tablet, The 42, 48
Tamez, Elsa 618, 625
Tasting and Seeing (Jüngel) 192, 196
Taylor, Mark C. 4, 573, 574, 575–6, 740
Teilhard de Chardin, Pierre 202, 207, 210, 269, 274
teleology 297, 360, 523, 550, 639, 648–9
Teologia de la liberaciòn (Gutiérrez) 619–20
Teresa of Lisieux 253
Tertullian 260, 375
theocracy 97
Theodramatik (von Balthasar) 258, 259
theological aesthetics *see* aesthetics
Theological Investigations (Rahner) 44, 227
Theologie der Hoffnung (Moltmann) 162, 165
Theologik (von Balthasar) 258
theology
 and the Body 470–71, 472
 contextuality of 30
 and development of doctrine 9–11, 13
 diversity of 5–8
 five types of 9
 God/human-centred 78–9
 kenotic 471–2
 methodologies of 106–7
 and modernity 9–11
 of process 461, 514, 526
 recurring themes in 11–12
 and return to source 7–8
 twentieth century revival of 3
 university departments of 151
Theology of the Body (John Paul II) 291, 295, 296, 298
Theology in Conflict (Wingren) 149
Theology of History in St. Bonaventure (Ratzinger) 303–4
Theology of the New Testament (Bultmann) 80
Theology of Pastoral Action (Rahner) 229
Theology and the Philosophy of Science (Pannenberg) 177

Theology and Social Theory (Milbank) 582–3
theosis 58, 183, 274, 359, 386–7, 420, 424, 432
Thessalonica (Greece) 53
Thich Nhat Hanh 718(*n*8), 720–21, 723
Thomism 46, 48, 206, 268, 281, 297, 530, 652, 675
 destiny in 203–4
 neo-neo 49
 Strict Observance 38, 39, 40, 41
 Transcendental 41, 44, 50
 see also Aquinas, Thomas
Thurneynsena, Eduard 23, 66
Tidehverv movement 124, 126, 129
Tillard, J.M.R. 371, 374, 481, 537
Tillich, Paul 6, 7, 9, 11–12, 23, 24, 27–8, 29, 101–11, **102**, 436, 600, 681
 on alienation 105, 106, 107, 109, 110
 and Barth/liberal tradition 101
 biography of 102–3
 Christology of 109–10
 criticisms of 101, 109
 cultural/political concerns of 103, 104–5, 110–11
 doctrine of God 109
 on dogmatics 104
 on doubt/unbelief 102
 and dualism/borderlands 101, 103
 and Heidegger 102
 importance of 101, 110–11
 key themes of 103–4, 105–10
 method of correlation 10, 101, 103, 104, 106–8
 in Nazi Germany 102
 ontology of 105–6
 and postmodern theology 573, 574
 and Ricoeur 704, 711
 theological writings of 103–5
 theonomy and 104
 theory of symbols 105, 108
 on "ultimate concern" 30, 103, 107, 244–5
 in US 101, 103, 104, 110
time 71, 165–6, 181, 513, 676–7
Timiadis, Emilianos 427–33
 biography of 427
 on church fathers 427–9
 on Confessio Augustana 430–31
 on confession/prayer 433
 criticisms of 428
 ecumenism of 429, 430–32
 science and 430
 on transfiguration of Christ 432–3
Tolken som tiger (Wingren) 151

Tolkien, J.R.R. 2–3, 646, 649, 652, 681
Torrance, Thomas F. 179, 559, 561, 562
Tracy, David 5, 12, 45, 506, 529–35, 574, 577–8
    biography/writings 529–30
    criticism of 535
    ecumenism of 530
    five key themes of 534–5
    fundamental theology of 530, 531–5
    on hermeneutics/methodologies 529, 530, 534–5
    importance/influence of 529, 535
    liberation theology and 529, 534
    and Lindbeck 506, 559, 560, 563
    and Lonergan 529, 530
    mysticism and 530
    and Pannenberg 530, 532–3, 535
    on society/public sphere 531–4
    on theological language 534
Tradition et la vie de l'Église (Congar) 221
traditum 46, 50–51
transcendental philosophy 15, 125, 126, 139
Trent, Councils of (1545–63) 49, 305, 480
trinitarian theology 11, 12, 15, 25–6, 68, 240, 297–8
    and eschatology 540–41
    and feminist/liberation theology 438, 552–4, 600–601
    Greek patristic 382–3
    and "images of revelation" 456–8
    and Lutheranism 97
    Moltmann and 159, 163, 164, 165, 166, 167
    in Orthodoxy 55, 57, 59–60, 347, 359, 382–3
    Pannenberg's 179–81, 182
    and Pentecostal movement 633, 634
    Prenter's 138, 139, 141, 142–4
    renaissance of 509
    revelation and 275–6, 513
    and worship 139
Troeltsch, Ernst 21, 22–3, 24, 27, 548, 553
trust 127, 129–30
truth 533, 535, 738
    and beauty/goodness 254, 261
    biblical concept of 13, 14, 14(*n*44), 15–16
    and postmodern theology 569, 570
    as symphonic/mystical 254–6, 261
Truth is Symphonic (von Balthasar) 255
Truth and Method (Gadamer) 259
Tübingen school 37, 161, 187, 188, 189, 306, 315, 316, 317, 325, 358
TULIP acronym 30–31
Turkey 427
Tutu, Desmond 325, 612

typological method 269, 272–3
Tyranowski, Jan 291, 292
Tyrell, George 38

ubiquity doctrine 141
Una Sancta 364
Unam Sanctam collection 213, 214, 216–17
Understanding the Church (Prenter) 142
Unfading Light, The (Bulgakov) 344, 345
United Nations (UN) 315, 325, 613
United States (US) 32, 48, 135, 155, 166, 175, 184, 316, 328, 334, 487, 529, 722
    Evangelicalism in 30–31
    feminist theology in 593, 594, 595
    liberation theology in 602–3
    Lutheranism in 510
    "neo-orthodoxy"/Yale school in 74
    Orthodoxy in 59, 356, 390, 404, 409, 435
    Pentecostalism in 631–2, 633, 635
    postliberal theology in 501–2, 504, 505–6
    postmodern theology in 573
    Tillich in 101, 103, 104, 110
    see also Chigago Divinity School; Yale University/Divinity School
universalism 25–6, 47, 137–8, 505, 512
    criticism of 48

Vahanian, Gabriel 29, 572
van Ruler, Arnold 161
Variations on the Song of Songs (Yannaras) 728, 729–30, 731
Vatican II (1962–65) 41–2, 48, 69, 203, 207, 213, 215, 218, 239, 246, 270, 430
    Afanasiev and 372–3, 374
    as 'council of the laity' 220
    criticisms of 441
    ecumenism and 608
    feminist theology and 594, 595
    Küng and 315
    and liberation theology 623–4
    liturgical movement and 403
    Ratzinger and 279, 303, 305–6, 309, 311
    Schillebeeckx and 281, 283–4, 285, 288
    tradition and 221
    von Balthasar and 249, 253, 262
Vattimo, Gianni 47, 585, 739
Växling och kontinuitet (Wingren) 153
Vedder, Ben 45
Vergil 260
Veritatis Splendor (John Paul II) 47
Verweyen, Hans-Jürgen 302–3, 304
Vianney, Jean-Marie 278

Vietnam War 717, 719
Viller, Marcel 228
Vindication of Tradition, The (Pelikan) 488
Virgin Mary 202, 493
    Mother of God 344, 345, 346, 348–9, 397
    see also Mariology
Vision of God, The (Lossky) 383
Voltaire 651, 659–60
volunteerism 453
von Balthasar, Hans Urs 3, 4, 6, 8, 9, 47, 235,
    249–63, **251**, 281, 303, 584, 745
    and Barth 252, 255, 256
    biography/training/early writings 250–53
    Christology of 257–8
    on church/laity 253
    and *Communio* 43, 222, 249, 270
    creation theology of 249
    and de Lubac 201, 202, 206, 210, 251
    and development of doctrine 10–11
    existential theology and 12
    and French literature 252
    and holistic theological thinking 249
    influence of 262–3
    magnum opus of 43, 44
    on modernity 43–4
    and *le nouvelle théologe* 249, 262
    and Origen 251, 252, 255, 257–8, 259,
        260–61
    Protestant theologians and 263
    and Rahner 43–5, 262–3
    and Ramsay 463, 467–9, 470
    on revelation/freedom 259–60
    Sensorium of 468, 470
    on theological aesthetics 258–62
    on theology-spirituality 256–8
    Trinitarianism of 11, 179, 253, 257–8
    on truth as symphonic/mystical 254–6, 261,
        263
    writings, early 250, 252
    writings, key themes in 254–62
    writings, overview of 253–4
von Campenhausen, Hans 174
von Rad, Gerhard 159, 165, 174
von Speyr, Adrienne 252, 253
Vorgrimler, Herbert 230
Vrai et fausse réforme dans l'Église (Congar) 217

Wadi Rayan (Egypt) 418, 423
Wakefield, James L. 162
war 614, 615
    see also First World War; Second World War

Ward, Graham 5, 576, 581, 584, 585, 587–8, 589
Ware, Kallistos 353, 374
Waugh, Evelyn 646, 648, 652, 691
Ways of Russian Theology (Florovsky) 355, 357,
    381(*n*2)
WCC *see* World Council of Churches
weak theology 47, 735, 737, 739–40, 742
Weakness of God, The (Caputo) 737, 739
Weber, Otto 159, 161, 162
Weiss, Johannes 77
Wells, H.G. 645, 649, 652
Wendenbourg, Dorothea 384–5
Wesley, John/Wesley, Charles 31
Wesleyan Holiness Movement *see* Holiness
    Movement
Westcott, Bishop 479
What I Believe (Küng) 320, 325
What is Man? (Pannenberg) 177
What the Orthodox Church Owes to the West
    (Timiadis) 429
Whitehead, A.N. 461, 559
Widerstand und Ergebung (Bonhoeffer) 115, 120
William of St.-Thierry 201–2
Williams, A.G. 436
Williams, Rowan 15, 54, 365, 385, 451, 484, 548,
    582
Wingren, Gustav 24, 74, 147–55
    and Barth 147, 149
    on Bible/Christian faith 149, 150, 151–3
    biography 147–8
    on the creed 148–9, 155
    criticism of contemporary theology by 152
    ecumenical work of 148
    on God-human antithesis 152–3
    influences on 147, 154
    poetic writing style of 155
    polemicism of 147
    preachings/sermons of 153, 154
    resignation/divorce of 155
    on role of experience 153–4
    as theologian of creation/the cross 154–5
    on training of clergy 150, 151
    writings of 148–55
    writings of, key themes in 150–55
wisdom, divine *see* Sophia/sophiology
Wisdom of God, The (Bulgakov) 344–5
Wittgenstein, Ludwig 33, 286, 500, 537, 574,
    725
Wojtyła, Karol *see* John Paul II
Wolf, Erik 225
Wolf, Ernst 159

women 285, 327, 421
    Jesus and 333
    ordination of 47–8, 61, 155, 318, 480
    Paul and 330
    see also feminist theology
wo/men 331–2
"Word of God" theology see dialectical theology
Word, the 136, 140, 142, 176, 190, 191, 210, 249, 255, 258, 277, 609
    antagonistic aspect of 149
    and law/Gospel 154–5, 623
Words With Power (Frye) 694, 697, 698
Working Group of Protestant and Catholic Theologians 175
World Alliance of Reformed Churches 607
World Council of Churches (WCC) 67, 135, 148, 174, 355, 374, 427, 430–31, 436, 480–81, 607, 611, 613
    Geneva Conference (1966) 613–14
    and Lausanne Movement 612
    liberation theology and 500
    Lima document 482, 609, 610
    Toronto Declaration 608–9
Wünsch, Georg 79

Yale University/Divinity School (US) 74, 499, 501–2, 504, 517, 537, 573, 575, 712
Yannaras, Christos 12, 59, 379, 725–33
    apophaticism of 726–7, 728–9, 732–3
    biography of 725–6
    criticisms of 725, 733
    ecclesiology of 727–8, 732
    ethics of 731–2
    and Heidegger 725, 726–7, 733
    importance of 732–3
    on love 725, 726, 727, 731
    on personal existance 729–31
    postmodern metaphysics of 5, 727
    on secularism 726, 732
    writings of 726–32
    writings of, key themes in 728–32
Yoder, John Howard 539, 541
Yong, Amos 635, 639
Yusab III 423

Zabala, Santiago 47
Zeitgeist 46, 91, 283
Zen and the Birds of Appetite (Merton) 720
Zen Buddhism 717–18, 719, 720, 723
Zen Catholicism 718, 719
Zhivoe predanie 372
Žižek, Slavoj 586, 736
Zizioulas, Johannes 11, 12, 17, 59–60, 353, 371, 373, 435–46, 742
    biography of 435–7
    on church apostolicity 437, 439, 441–6
    ecclesiology of 438–41
    ecumenism of 435, 436, 437
    on eucharistic ecclesiology 436, 443–4, 446
    on fellowship 439
    on history/tradition 440–41
    importance of 435
    on Maximus the Confessor 438, 439
    on neo-patristic synthesis 436
    on pneumatology-Christology 439–41, 444–5
    Trinitarian theology and 438, 440–41
    writings of 437–46
    writings of, key themes in 438–46
    writings on 438
Zoe Movement 725, 726
Zwinglian Protestant tradition 283
Zwischen den Zeiten (periodical) 24, 66